# Wilbur Smith

# Wilbur Smith

# Hungry as the Sea

# The Sound of Thunder

# The Eye of the Tiger

Heinemann/Octopus

*Hungry as the Sea* first published in Great Britain
in 1978 by William Heinemann Limited
*The Sound of Thunder* first published in Great Britain
in 1966 by William Heinemann Limited
*The Eye of the Tiger* first published in Great Britain
in 1975 by William Heinemann Limited

This edition first published in Great Britain
in 1981 jointly by

William Heinemann Limited
10 Upper Grosvenor Street
London W1

in association with

Octopus Books Limited
59 Grosvenor Street
London W1

ISBN 0 905712 57 9

Printed in the United States of America

# Contents

# Hungry as the Sea

*Hungry as the Sea*

This book is for my wife Danielle

Nicholas Berg stepped out of the taxi on to the floodlit dock and paused to look up at the *Warlock*. At this state of the tide she rode high against the stone quay, so that even though the cranes towered above her, they did not dwarf her.

Despite the exhaustion that fogged his mind and cramped his muscles until they ached. Nicholas felt a stir of the old pride, the old sense of value achieved, as he looked at her. She looked like a warship, sleek and deadly, with the high flared bows and good lines that combined to make her safe in any seaway.

The superstructure was moulded steel and glittering armoured glass, behind which her lights burned in carnival array. The wings of her navigation bridge swept back elegantly and were covered to protect the men who must work her in the cruellest weather and most murderous seas.

Overlooking the wide stern deck was the second navigation bridge, from which a skilled seaman could operate the great winches and drums of cable, could catch and control the hawser on the hydraulically operated rising fairleads, could baby a wallowing oil rig or a mortally wounded liner in a gale or a silky calm.

Against the night sky high above it all, the twin towers replaced the squat single funnel of the old-fashioned salvage tugs – and the illusion of a man-of-war was heightened by the fire cannons on the upper platforms from which the *Warlock* could throw fifteen hundred tons of sea water an hour on to a burning vessel. From the towers themselves could be swung the boarding ladders over which men could be sent aboard a hulk, and between them was painted the small circular target that marked the miniature heliport. The whole of it, hull and upper decks, was fireproofed so she could survive in the inferno of burning petroleum from a holed tanker of the flaming chemical from a bulk carrier.

Nicholas Berg felt a little of the despondency and spiritual exhaustion slough away, although his body still ached and his legs carried him stiffly, like those of an old man, as he started towards the gang-plank.

'The hell with them all,' he thought. 'I built her and she is strong and good.'

Although it was an hour before midnight, the crew of the *Warlock* watched him from every vantage point they could find; even the oilers had come up from the engine room when the word reached them, and now loafed unobtrusively on the stern working deck.

David Allen, the First Officer, had placed a hand at the main harbour gates with a photograph of Nicholas Berg and a five-cent piece for the telephone call box beside the gate, and the whole ship was alerted now.

David Allen stood with the Chief Engineer in the glassed wing of the main navigation bridge and they watched the solitary figure pick his way across the shadowy dock, carrying his own case.

'So that's him,' David's voice was husky with awe and respect. He looked like a schoolboy under his saggy bush of sun-bleached hair.

'He's a bloody film star.' Vinny Baker, the Chief Engineer, hitched up his sagging trousers with both elbows, and his spectacles slid down the long thin nose, as he snorted. 'A bloody film star,' he repeated the term with utmost scorn.

'He was first to Jules Levoisin,' David pointed out, and again the note of awe as he intoned that name, 'and he is a tug man from way back.'

'That was fifteen years ago.' Vinny Baker released his elbow grip on his trousers and pushed his spectacles up on to the bridge of his nose. Immediately his trousers began their slow but inexorable slide deckwards. 'Since then he's become a bloody glamour boy – and an owner.'

'Yes,' David Allen agreed, and his baby face crumpled a little at the thought of those two legendary animals, master and owner, combined in one monster. A monster which was on the point of mounting his gangway to the deck of *Warlock*.

'You'd better go down and kiss him on the soft spot,' Vinny grunted comfortably, and drifted away. Two decks down was the sanctuary of his control room where neither masters nor owners could touch him. He was going there now.

David Allen was breathless and flushed when he reached the entry port. The new Master was halfway up the gangway, and he lifted his head and looked steadily at the mate as he stepped aboard.

Though he was only a little above average, Nicholas Berg gave the impression of towering height, and the shoulders beneath the blue cashmere of his jacket were wide and powerful. He wore no hat and his hair was very dark, very thick and brushed back from a wide unlined forehead. The head was big-nosed and gaunt-boned, with a heavy jaw, blue now with new beard, and the eyes were set deep in the cages of their bony sockets, underlined with dark plum-coloured smears, as though they were bruised.

But what shocked David Allen was the man's pallor. His face was drained, as though he had been bled from the jugular. It was the pallor of mortal illness or of exhaustion close to death itself, and it was emphasized by the dark eye-sockets. This was not what David had expected of the legendary Golden Prince of Christy Marine. It was not the face he had seen so often pictured in newspapers and magazines around the world. Surprise made him mute and the man stopped and looked down at him.

'Allen?' asked Nicholas Berg quietly. His voice was low and level, without accent, but with a surprising timbre and resonance.

'Yes, sir. Welcome aboard, sir.'

When Nicholas Berg smiled, the edges of sickness and exhaustion smoothed away at his brow and at the corners of his mouth. His hand was smooth and cool, but his grip was firm enough to make David blink.

'I'll show you your quarters, sir.' David took the Louis Vuitton suitcase from his grip.

'I know the way,' said Nick Berg. 'I designed her.'

He stood in the centre of the Master's day cabin, and felt the deck tilt under his feet, although the *Warlock* was fast to the stone dock, and the muscles in his thighs trembled.

'The funeral went off all right?' Nick asked.

'He was cremated, sir,' David said. 'That's the way he wanted it. I have made the arrangements for the ashes to be sent home to Mary. Mary is his wife, sir,' he explained quickly.

'Yes,' said Nick Berg. 'I know. I saw her before I left London. Mac and I were ship-mates once.'

'He told me. He used to boast about that.'

'Have you cleared all his gear?' Nick asked, and glanced around the Master's suite.

'Yes sir, we've packed it all up. There is nothing of his left in here.'

'He was a good man.' Nick swayed again on his feet and looked longingly at the day couch, but instead he crossed to the port and looked out on to the dock. 'How did it happen?'

'My report—'

'Tell me!' said Nicholas Berg, and his voice-cracked like a whip.

'The main tow-cable parted, sir. He was on the afterdeck. It took his head off like a bullwhip.'

Nick stood quietly for a moment, thinking about that terse description of tragedy. He had seen a tow part under stress once before. That time it had killed three men.

'All right.' Nick hesitated a moment, the exhaustion had slowed and softened him so that for a moment he was on the point of explaining why he had come to take command of *Warlock* himself, rather than sending another hired man to replace Mac.

It might help to have somebody to talk to now, when he was right down on his knees, beaten and broken and tired to the very depths of his soul. He swayed again, then caught himself and forced aside the temptation. He had never whined for sympathy in his life before.

'All right,' he repeated. 'Please give my apologies to your officers. I have not had much sleep in the last two weeks, and the flight out from Heathrow was murder, as always. I'll meet them in the morning. Ask the cook to send a tray with my dinner.'

The cook was a huge man who moved like a dancer in a snowy apron and a theatrical chef's cap. Nick Berg stared at him as he placed the tray on the table at his elbow. The cook wore his hair in a shiny carefully coiffured bob that fell to his right shoulder, but was drawn back from the left cheek to display a small diamond earring in the pierced lobe of that ear.

He lifted the cloth of the tray with a hand as hairy as that of a bull gorilla, but his voice was a lyrical as a girl's, and his eyelashes curled soft and dark on to his cheek.

'There's a lovely bowl of soup, and a *pot-au-feu*. It's one of my little special things. You will adore it,' he said, and stepped back. He surveyed Nick Berg with those huge hands on his hips. 'But I took one look at you as you came aboard and I just knew what you really needed.' With a magician's flourish, he produced a half-bottle of Pinch Haig from the deep pocket of his apron. 'Take a nip of that with your dinner, and then straight into bed with you, you poor dear.'

No man had ever called Nicholas Berg 'dear' before, but his tongue was too thick and slow for the retort. He stared after the cook as he disappeared with a sweep of his white apron and the twinkle of the diamond, and then he grinned weakly and shook his head, weighing the bottle in his hand.

'Damned if I don't need it,' he muttered, and went to find a glass. He poured it half full, and sipped as he came back to the couch and lifted the lid of the soup pot. The steaming aroma made the little saliva glands under his tongue spurt.

The hot food and whisky in his belly taxed his last reserves and Nicholas Berg kicked off his shoes as he staggered into his night cabin.


He awoke with the anger on him. He had not been angry in two weeks which was a measure of his despondency.

But when he shaved, the mirrored face was that of a stranger still, too pale and gaunt and set. The lines that framed his mouth were too deeply chiselled, and the early sunlight through the port caught the dark hair at his temple and he saw the frosty glitter there and leaned closer to the mirror. It was the first time he had noticed the flash of silver hair – perhaps he had never looked hard enough, or perhaps it was something new.

'Forty,' he thought. 'I'll be forty years old next June.'

He had always believed that if a man never caught the big one before he was forty, he was doomed never to do so. So what were the rules for the man who caught the big wave before he was thirty, and rode it fast and hard and high, then lost it again before he was forty and was washed out into the trough of boiling white water. Was he doomed also? Nick stared at himself in the mirror and felt the anger in him change its form, becoming directed and functional.

He stepped into the shower, and let the needles of hot water sting his chest. Through the tiredness and disillusion, he was aware, for the first time in weeks, of the underlying strength which he had begun to doubt was still there. He felt it rising to the surface in him, and he thought again of what an extraordinary sea creature he was, how it needed only a deck under him and the smell of the sea in his throat.

He stepped from the shower and dried quickly. This was the right place to be now. This was the place to recuperate – and he realized that his decision not to replace Mac with a hired skipper had been a gut decision. He needed to be here himself.

Always he had known that if you wanted to ride the big wave, you must first be at the place where it begins to peak. It's an instinctive thing, a man just knows where that place is. Nick Berg knew deep in his being that this was the place now, and, with his rising strength, he felt the old excitement, the old 'I'll show the bastards who is beaten' excitement, and he dressed swiftly and went up the Master's private companionway to the upper deck.

Immediately, the wind flew at him and flicked his dark wet hair into his face. It was force five from the south-east, and it came boiling over the great flat-topped mountain which crouched above the city and harbour. Nick looked up at it and saw the thick white cloud they called the 'table cloth' spilling off the heights, and swirling along the grey rock cliffs.

'The Cape of Storms,' he murmured. Even the water in the protected dock leaped and peaked into white crests which blew away like wisps of smoke.

The tip of Africa thrust southwards into one of the most treacherous seas on all the globe. Here two oceans swept turbulently together off the rocky cliffs of Cape Point, and then roiled over the shallows of the Agulhas bank.

Here wind opposed current in eternal conflict. This was the breeding ground of the freak wave, the one that mariners called the 'hundred-year wave', because statistically that was how often it should occur.

But off the Agulhas bank, it was always lurking, waiting only for the right combination of wind and current, waiting for the inphase wave sequence to send its crest rearing a hundred feet high and steep as those grey rock cliffs of Table Mountain itself.

Nick had read the accounts of seamen who had survived that wave, and, at a loss for words, they had written only of a great hole in the sea into which a ship fell helplessly. When the hole closed, the force of breaking water would bury her completely. Perhaps the *Waratah Castle* was one which had fallen into that trough. Nobody would ever know – a great ship of 9,000 tons burden, she and her crew of 211 had disappeared without trace in these seas.

Yet here was one of the busiest sea lanes on the globe, as a procession of giant tankers ploughed ponderously around that rocky Cape on their endless shuttle between the Western world and the oil Gulf of Persia. Despite their bulk, those supertankers were perhaps some of the most vulnerable vehicles yet designed by man.

Now Nick turned and looked across the wind-ripped waters of Duncan Dock at one of them. He could read her name on the stern that rose like a five-storied apartment block. She was owned by Shell Oil, 250,000 dead weight tons, and, out of ballast, she showed much of her rust-red bottom. She was in for repairs, while out in the roadstead of Table Bay, two other monsters waited patiently for their turn in the hospital dock.

So big and ponderous and vulnerable – and valuable. Nick licked his lips involuntarily – hull and cargo together, she was thirty million dollars, piled up like a mountain.

That was why he had stationed the *Warlock* here at Cape Town on the southernmost tip of Africa. He felt the strength and excitement surging upwards in him.

All right, so he had lost his wave. He was no longer cresting and racing. He was down and smothered in white water. But he could feel his head breaking the surface, and he was still on the break-line. He knew there was another big wave racing down on him. It was just beginning to peak and he knew he still had the strength to catch her, to get up high and race again.

'I did it once – I'll damned well do it again,' he said aloud, and went down for breakfast.

He stepped into the saloon, and for a long moment nobody realized he was there. There was an excited buzz of comment and speculation that absorbed them all.

The Chief Engineer had an old copy of *Lloyd's List* folded at the front page and held above a plate of eggs as he read aloud. Nicholas wondered where he had found the ancient copy.

His spectacles had slid right to the end of his nose, so he had to tilt his head far backwards to see through them, and his Australian accent twanged like a guitar.

'In a joint statement issued by the new Chairman and incoming members of the Board, a tribute was paid to the fifteen years of loyal service that Mr Nicholas Berg had given to Christy Marine.'

The five officers listened avidly, ignoring their breakfasts, until David Allen glanced up at the figure in the doorway.

'Captain, sir,' he shouted, and leapt to his feet, while with the other hand, he snatched the newspaper out of Vinny Baker's hands and bundled it under the table.

'Sir, may I present the officers of *Warlock*.'

Shuffling, embarrassed, the younger officers shook hands hurriedly and then applied themselves silently to their congealing breakfasts with a total dedication that precluded any conversation, while Nick Berg took the Master's seat at the head of the long table in the heavy silence and David Allen sat down again on the crumpled sheets of newsprint.

The steward offered the menu to the new Captain, and returned almost immediately with a dish of stewed fruit.

'I ordered a boiled egg,' said Nick mildly, and an apparition in snowy white appeared from the galley, with the chef's cap at a jaunty angle.

'The sailor's curse is constipation, Skipper. I look after my officers – that fruit is delicious and good for you. I'm doing you your eggs now, dear, but eat your fruit first.' And the diamond twinkled again as he vanished.

Nick stared after him in the appalled silence.

'Fantastic cook,' blurted David Allen, his fair skin flushed pinkly and the *Lloyd's List* rustled under his backside. 'Could get a job on any passenger line, could Angel.'

'If he ever left the *Warlock*, half the crew would go with him,' growled the Chief Engineer darkly, and hauled at his pants with elbows below the level of the table. 'And I'd be one of them.'

Nick Berg turned his head politely to follow the conversation.

'He's almost a doctor,' David Allen went on, addressing the Chief Engineer.

'Five years at Edinburgh Medical School,' agreed the Chief solemnly.

'Do you remember how he set the Second's leg? Terribly useful to have a doctor aboard.'

Nick picked up his spoon, and tentatively lifted a little of the fruit to his mouth. Every officer watched him intently as he chewed. Nick took another spoonful.

'You should taste his jams, sir,' David Allen addressed Nick directly at last. 'Absolutely Cordon Bleu stuff.'

'Thank you, gentlemen, for the advice,' said Nick. The smile did not touch his mouth, but crinkled his eyes slightly. 'But would somebody convey a private message to Angel that if he ever calls me "dear" again I'll beat that ridiculous cap down about his ears.'

In the relieved laughter that followed, Nick turned to David Allen and sent colour flying to his cheeks again by asking, 'You seem to have finished with that old copy of the *List*, Number One. Do you mind if I glance at it again?'

Reluctantly, David lifted himself and produced the newspaper, and there was another tense silence as Nick Berg rearranged the rumpled sheets and studied the old headlines without any apparent emotion.

### THE GOLDEN PRINCE OF CHRISTY MARINE DEPOSED

Nicholas hated that name, it has been old Arthur Christy's quirk to name all of his vessels with the prefix 'Golden' and twelve years ago, when Nick had rocketed to head of operations at Christy Marine, some wag had stuck that label on him.

### ALEXANDER TO HEAD THE CHRISTY BOARD OF DIRECTORS

Nicholas was surprised by the force of his hatred for the man. They had fought like a pair of bulls for dominance of the herd and the tactics that Duncan Alexander had used had won. Arthur Christy had said once, 'Nobody gives a damn these days whether it is moral or fair, all that counts is, will it work and can you get away with it?' For Duncan it had worked, and he had got away with it in the grandest possible style.

As Managing-Director in charge of operations, Mr Nicholas Berg helped to build Christy Marine from a small coasting and salvage company into one of the five largest owners of cargo shipping operating anywhere in the world.

After the death of Arthur Christy in 1968, Mr Nicholas Berg succeeded him as Chairman, and continued the company's spectacular expansion.

At present, Christy Marine has in commission eleven bulk carriers and tankers in excess of 250,000 dead weight tons, and has building the 1,000,000 ton giant ultra-tanker *Golden Dawn*. It will be the largest vessel ever launched.

There it was, stated in the baldest possible terms, the labour of a man's lifetime. Over a billion dollars of shipping, designed, financed and built almost entirely with the energy and enthusiasm and faith of Nicholas Berg.

Mr Nicholas Berg married Miss Chantelle Christy, the only child of Mr Arthur Christy. However, the marriage ended in divorce in September of last year and the former Mrs Berg has subsequently married Mr Duncan Alexander, the new Chairman of Christy Marine.

He felt the hollow nauseous feeling in his stomach again, and in his head the vivid image of the woman. He did not want to think of her now, but could not thrust the image aside. She was bright and beautiful as a flame

– and, like a flame, you could not hold her. When she went, she took everything with her, everything. He should hate her also, he really should. Everything, he thought again, the company, his life's work, and the child. When he thought of the child, he nearly succeeded in hating her, and the newsprint shook in his hand.

He became aware again that five men were watching him, and without surprise he realized that not a flicker of his emotions had shown on his face. To be a player for fifteen years in one of the world's highest games of chance, inscrutability was a minimum requirement

In a joint statement issued by the new Chairman and incoming members of the Board, a tribute was paid.

Duncan Alexander paid the tribute for one reason, Nick thought grimly. He wanted the 100,000 Christy Marine shares that Nick owned. Those shares were very far from a controlling interest. Chantelle had a million shares in her own name, and there were another million in the Christy Trust, but insignificant as it was, Nick's holding gave him a voice in and an entry to the company's affairs. Nick had bought and paid for every one of those shares. Nobody had given him a thing, not once in his life. He had taken advantage of every stock option in his contract, had bartered bonus and salary for those options, and now those 100,000 shares were worth three million dollars, meagre reward for the labour which had built up a fortune of sixty million dollars for the Christy father and daughter.

It had taken Duncan Alexander almost a year to get those shares. He and Nicholas had bargained with cold loathing. They had hated each other from the first day that Duncan had walked into the Christy building on Leadenhall Street. He had come as old Arthur Christy's latest *Wunderkind*. The financial genius fresh from his triumphs as financial controller of International Electronics, and the hatred had been instant and deep and mutual, a fierce smouldering chemical reaction between them.

In the end Duncan Alexander had won, he had won it all, except the shares, and he had bargained for those from overwhelming strength. He had bargained with patience and skill, wearing his man down over the months. Using all Christy Marine's reserves to block and frustrate Nicholas, forcing him back step by step, taxing even his strength to its limits, driving such a bargain that at the end Nicholas was forced to bow and accept a dangerous price for his shares. He had taken as full payment the subsidiary of Christy Marine, Christy Towage and Salvage, all its assets and all its debts. Nick had felt like a fighter who had been battered for fifteen rounds, and was now hanging desperately to the ropes with his legs gone, blinded by his own sweat and blood and swollen flesh, so he could not see from whence the next punch would come. But he had held on just long enough. He had got Christy Towage and Salvage – he had walked away with something that was completely and entirely his.

Nicholas Berg lowered the newspaper, and immediately his officers attacked their breakfasts ravenously and there was the clatter of cutlery.

'There is an officer missing,' he said.

'It's only the Trog, sir,' Dave Allen explained.

'The Trog?'

'The Radio Officer, sir. Speirs, sir. We call him the Troglodyte.'

'I'd like all the officers present.'

'He never comes out of his cave,' Vinny Baker explained helpfully.

'All right,' Nick nodded. 'I will speak to him later.'

They waited now, five eager young men, even Vin Baker could not completely hide his interest behind the smeared lenses of his spectacles and the tough Aussie veneer.

'I wanted to explain to you the new set-up. The Chief has kindly read to you this article, presumably for the benefit of those who were unable to do so for themselves a year ago.'

Nobody said anything, but Vin Baker fiddled with his porridge spoon.

'So you are aware that I am no longer connected in any way with Christy Marine. I have now acquired Christy Towage and Salvage. It becomes a completely independent company. The name is being changed.' Nicholas had resisted the vanity of calling it Berg Towage and Salvage. 'It will be known as Ocean Towage and Salvage.'

He had paid dearly for it, perhaps too dearly. He had given up his three million dollars' worth of Christy shares for God alone knew what. But he had been tired unto death.

'We own two vessels. The *Golden Warlock* and her sister ship which is almost ready for her sea trials, the *Golden Witch*.'

He knew exactly how much the company owed on those two ships, he had agonized over the figures through long and sleepless nights. On paper the net worth of the company was around four million dollars; he had made a paper profit of a million dollars on his bargain with Duncan Alexander. But it was paper profit only, the company had debts of nearly four million more. If he missed just one month's interest payments on those debts – he dismissed the thought quickly, for on a forced sale his residue in the company would be worth nothing. He would be completely wiped out.

'The names of both ships have been changed also. They will become simply *Warlock* and *Sea Witch*. From now onwards 'Golden' is a dirty word around Ocean Salvage.'

They laughed then, a release of tension, and Nick smiled with them, and lit a thin black cheroot from the crocodile-skin case while they settled down.

'I will be running this ship until *Sea Witch* is commissioned. It won't be long, and there will be promotions then.'

Nick superstitiously tapped the mahogany mess table as he said it. The dockyard strike had been simmering for a long time. *Sea Witch* was still on the ways, but costing interest, and further delay would prove him mortal.

'I have got a long oil-rig tow. Bight of Australia to South America. It will give us all time to shake the ship down. You are all tug men, I don't have to tell you when the big one comes up, there will be no warning.'

They stirred, and the eagerness was on them again. Even the oblique reference to prize money had roused them.

'Chief?' Nick looked across at him, and the Engineer snorted, as though the question was an insult.

'In all respects ready for sea,' he said, and tried simultaneously to adjust his trousers and his spectacles.

'Number One?' Nick looked at David Allen. He had not yet become accustomed to the mate's boyishness. He knew that he had held a master mariner's ticket for ten years, that he was over thirty years of age and that MacDonald had hand-picked him – he had to be good. Yet that fair unlined face and quick high colour under the unruly mop of blond hair made him look like an undergraduate.

'I'm waiting on some stores yet, sir,' David answered quickly. 'The chandlers have promised for today, but none of it is vital. I could sail in an hour, if it is necessary.'

'All right.' Nick stood up. 'I will inspect the ship at 0900 hours. You'd best get the ladies off the ship.' During the meal there had been the faint tinkle of female voices and laughter from the crew's quarters.

Nick stepped out of the saloon and Vin Baker's voice was pitched to reach him. It was a truly dreadful imitation of what the Chief believed to be a Royal Naval accent.

'0900, chaps. Jolly good show, what?'

Nick did not miss a step, and he grinned tightly to himself. It's an old Aussie custom; you needle and needle until something happens. There is no malice in it, it's just a way of getting to know your man. And once the boots and fists have stopped flying, you can be friends or enemies on a permanent basis. It was so long since he had been in elemental contact with tough physical men, straight hard men who shunned all subterfuge and sham, and he found the novelty stimulating. Perhaps that was what he really needed now, the sea and the company of real men. He felt his step quicken and the anticipation of physical confrontation lift his spirits off the bottom.

He went up the companionway to the navigation deck, taking the steps three at a time, and the doorway opposite his suite opened. From it emerged the solid grey stench of cheap Dutch cigars and a head that could have belonged to some prehistoric reptile. It too was pale grey and lined and wrinkled, the head of a sea-turtle or an iguana lizard, with the same small dark glittery eyes.

The door was that of the radio room. It had direct access to the main navigation bridge and was merely two paces from the Master's day cabin.

Despite appearances, the head was human, and Nick recalled clearly how Mac had once described his radio officer. 'He is the most anti-social bastard I've ever sailed with, but he can scan eight different frequencies simulta-neously, in clear and morse, even while he is asleep. He is a mean, joyless, constipated son of a bitch – and probably the best radio man afloat.'

'Captain,' said the Trog, in a reedy petulant voice. Nick did not ponder the fact that the Trog recognized him instantly as the new Master. The air of command on some men is unmistakable. 'Captain, I have an "all ships signify".'

Nick felt the heat at the base of his spine, and the electric prickle on the back of his neck. It is not sufficient merely to be on the break line when the big wave peaks, it is also necessary to recognize your wave from the hundred others that sweep by.

'Co-ordinates?' he snapped, as he strode down the passageway to the radio room.

'72° 16' south 32° 12' west.'

Nick felt the jump in his chest and the heat mount up along his spine. The high latitudes down there in the vast and lonely wastes. There was something sinister and menacing in the mere figures. What ship could be down there?

The longitudinal co-ordinates fitted neatly in the chart that Nick carried in his mind, like a war chart in a military operations room. She was south and west of the Cape of Good Hope – down deep, beyond Gough and Bouvet Island, in the Weddell Sea.

He followed the Trog into the radio room. On this bright, sunny and windy morning, the room was dark and gloomy as a cave, the thick green blinds drawn across the ports; the only source of light was the glowing dials of the banked communication equipment, the most sophisticated equipment that all the wealth of Christy Marine could pack into her, a hundred thousand dollars' worth of electronic magic, but the stink of cheap cigars was overpowering.

Beyond the radio room was the operator's cabin, the bunk unmade, a tray of soiled dishes on the deck beside it.

The Trog hopped up into the swivel seat, and elbowed aside a brass shell-casing that acted as an ashtray and spilled grey flakes of ash and a couple of cold wet chewed cigar butts on to the desk.

Like a wizened gnome, the Trog tended his dials; there was a cacophony of static and electronic trash blurred with the sharp howl of morse.

'The copy?' Nick asked, and the Trog pushed a pad at him. Nick read off quickly.

CTMZ. 0603 GMT. 70° 16'S. 32° 12'W. All ships in a position to render assistance, please signify. CTMZ.

He did not need to consult the R.T. Handbook to recognize that call-sign 'CTMZ'.

With an effort of will he controlled the pressure that caught him in the chest like a giant fist. It was as though he had lived this moment before. It was too neat. He forced himself to distrust his instinct, forced himself to think with his head and not his guts.

Beyond him he heard his officers' voices on the navigation bridge, quiet voices – but charged with tension. They were up from the saloon already.

'Christ!' he thought savagely. 'How do they know? So quickly?' It was as though the ship itself had come awake beneath his feet and trembled with anticipation.

The door from the bridge slid aside and David Allen stood in the opening with a copy of Lloyd's Register in his hands.

'CTMZ, sir, is the call sign of the *Golden Adventurer*. Twenty-two thousand tons, registered Bermuda 1975. Owners Christy Marine.'

'Thank you, Number One,' Nick nodded. Nicholas knew her well; he personally had ordered her construction before the collapse of the great liner traffic. Nick had planned to use her on the Europe-to-Australia run.

Her finished cost had come in at sixty-two million dollars, and she was a beautiful and graceful ship under her tall light alloy superstructure. Her accommodation was luxurious, in the same class as the *France* or the *United States*, but she had been one of Nick's few miscalculations.

When the feasibility of operation on the planned run had shown up prohibitive in the face of rising costs and diminishing trade, Nick had switched her usage. It was this type of flexible and intuitive planning and improvisation that had built Christy Marine into the goliath she was now.

Nick had innovated the idea of adventure cruises – and changed the ship's name to *Golden Adventurer*. Now she carried rich passengers to the wild and exotic corners of the globe, from the Galapagos Islands to the Amazon, from the remote Pacific islands to the Antarctic, in search of the unusual.

She carried guest lecturers with her, experts on the environments and ecology of the areas she was to visit, and she was equipped to take her passengers ashore to study the monoliths of Easter Island or to watch the mating displays of the wandering albatross on the Falkland Islands.

She was probably one of the very few cruise liners that was still profitable, and now she stood in need of assistance.

Nicholas turned back from the Trog. 'Has she been transmitting prior to this signify request?'

She's been sending in company code since midnight. Her traffic was so heavy that I was watching her.'

The green glow of the sets gave the little man a bilious cast, and made his teeth black, so that he looked like an actor from a horror movie.

'You recorded?' Nick demanded, and the Trog switched on the automatic playback of his tape monitors, recapitulating every message the distressed ship had sent or received since the previous midnight. The jumbled blocks of code poured into the room, and the paper strip printed out with the clatter of its keys.

Had Duncan Alexander changed the Christy Marine code? Nick wondered. It would be the natural procedure, completely logical to any operations man. You lose a man who has the code, you change immediately. It was that simple. Duncan had lost Nick Berg, he should change. But Duncan was not an operations man. He was a figures and paper man, he thought in numbers, not in steel and salt water.

If Duncan had changed, they would never break it. Not even with the Decca. Nick had devised the basis of the code. It was a projection that expressed the alphabet as a mathematical function based on a random six-figure master, changing the value of each letter on a progression that was impossible to monitor.

Nick hurried out of the stinking gloom of the radio room with the print-out in his hands.

The navigation bridge of *Warlock* was gleaming chrome and glass, as bright and functional as a modern surgical theatre, or a futuristic kitchen layout.

The primary control console stretched the full width of the bridge, beneath the huge armoured windows. The old-fashioned wheel was replaced by a single steel lever, and the remote control could be carried out on to the wings of the bridge on its long extension cable, like the remote on a television set, so that the helmsman could con the ship from any position he chose.

Illuminated digital displays informed the master instantly of every condition of his ship: speed across the bottom at bows and stern, speed through the water at bows and stern, wind direction and strength, together with all the other technical information of function and malfunction. Nick had built the ship with Christy money, and stinted not at all.

The rear of the bridge was the navigational area, and the chart-table divided it neatly with its overhead racks containing the 106 big blue volumes of the *Global Pilot* and as many other volumes of maritime publications. Below the table were the multiple drawers, wide and flat to contain the spread Admiralty charts that covered every corner of navigable water on the globe.

Against the rear bulkhead stood the battery of electronic navigational aids, like a row of fruit machines in a Vegas gambling hall.

Nick switched the big Decca Satellite Navaid into its computer mode and the display lights flashed and faded and relit in scarlet.

He fed it the six-figure control, numbers governed by the moon phase and date of dispatch. The computer digested this instantaneously, and Nick gave it the last arithmetical proportion known to him. The Decca was ready to decode and Nick gave it the block of garbled transmission – and waited for it to throw back gibberish at him. Duncan *must* have altered the code. He stared at the printout.

Christy Main from Master of *Adventurer*. 2216 GMT. 72° 16′ S. 32° 05′ W. Underwater ice damage sustained midships starboard. Precautionary shutdown mains. Auxiliary generators activated during damage survey. Stand by.

So Duncan had let the code stand then. Nick groped for the crockskin case of cheroots, and his hand was steady and firm as he held the flame to the top of the thin black tube. He felt the intense desire to shout aloud, but instead, he drew the fragrant smoke into his lungs.

'Plotted,' said David Allen from behind him. Already on the spread chart of the Antarctic he had marked in the reported position. The transformation was complete, the First Officer had become a grimly competent professional. There remained no trace of the high-coloured undergraduate.

Nick glanced at the plot, saw the dotted ice line far above the *Adventurer*'s position, saw the outline of the forbidding continent of Antarctica groping for the ship with merciless fingers of ice and rock.

The Decca printed out the reply:

Master of *Adventurer* from Christy Main. 2222 GMT. Standing by.

The next message from the recording tape was flagged nearly two hours later, but was printed out almost continuously from the Trog's recording.

Christy Main from Master of *Adventurer*. 0005 GMT. 72° 18′ S. 32° 05′ W. Water contained. Restarted mains. New course CAPE TOWN direct. Speed 8 knots. Stand by.

Dave Allen worked swiftly with parallel rulers and protractor.

'While she was without power she drifted thirty-four nautical miles, south-south-east – there is a hell of a wind or big current setting down there,' he said, and the other deck officers were silent and strained. Although none of them would dare crowd the Master at the Decca, yet in order of seniority they had taken up vantage points around the bridge best suited to follow the drama of a great ship in distress.

The next message ran straight out from the computer, despite the fact that it had been dispatched many hours later.

Christy Main from Master of *Adventure*. 0546 GMT. 72° 16′ S. 32° 12′ W. Explosion in flooded area. Emergency shutdown all. Water gaining. Request your clearance to issue 'all ships signify'. Standing by.

Master of *Adventurer* from Christy Main. 0547 GMT. You are cleared to issue signify. Break. Break. Break. You are expressly forbidden to contract tow or salvage without reference Christy Main. Acknowledge.

Duncan was not even putting in the old chestnut, 'except in the event of danger to human life'.

The reason was too apparent. Christy Marine underwrote most of its own bottoms through another of its subsidiaries. The London and European Insurance and Finance Company. The self-insurance scheme had been the brain-child of Alexander Duncan himself when first he arrived at Christy Marine. Nick Berg had opposed the scheme bitterly, and now he might live to see his reasoning being justified.

'Are we going to signify?' David Allen asked quietly.

'Radio silence,' snapped Nick irritably, and began to pace the bridge, the crack of his heels muted by the cork coating on the deck.

'Is this my wave?' Nick demanded of himself, applying the old rule he had set for himself long ago, the rule of deliberate thought first, action after.

The *Golden Adventurer* was drifting in the ice-fields two thousand and more miles south of Cape Town, five days and nights of hard running for the *Warlock*. If he made the go decision, by the time he reached her, she might have effected repairs and restarted, she might be under her own command again. Again, even if she was still helpless, *Warlock* might reach her to find another salvage tug had beaten her to the scene. So now it was time to call the roll.

He stopped his pacing at the door to the radio room and spoke quietly to the Trog.

'Open the telex line and send to Bach Wackie in Bermuda quote call the roll unquote.'

As he turned away, Nick was satisfied with his own forethought in installing the satellite telex system which enabled him to communicate with his agent in Bermuda, or with any other selected telex station, without his message being broadcast over the open frequencies and monitored by a competitor or any other interested party. His signals were bounced through the high stratosphere where they could not be intercepted.

While he waited, Nicholas worried. The decision to go would mean abandoning the Esso oil-rig tow. The tow fee had been a vital consideration in his cash flow situation. Two hundred and twenty thousand sterling, without which he could not meet the quarterly interest payment due in sixty days' time – unless, unless ... He juggled figures in his head, but the magnitude of the risk involved was growing momentarily more apparent – and the figures did not add up. He needed the Esso tow. God, how badly he needed it!

'Bach Wackie are replying,' called the Trog above the chatter of the telex receiver, and Nick spun on his heel.

He had appointed Bach Wackie as the agents for Ocean Salvage because of their proven record of quick and aggressive efficiency. He glanced at his Rolex Oyster and calculated that it was about two o'clock in the morning local time in Bermuda, and yet his request for information on the disposition of all his major competitors was now being answered within minutes of receipt.

For Master *Warlock* from Bach Wackie latest reported positions. *John Ross* dry dock Durban. *Woltema Wolteraad* Esso tow Torres Straits to Alaska Shelf—

That took care of the two giant Safmarine tugs; half of the top opposition was out of the race.

*Wittezee* Shell exploration tow Galveston to North Sea. *Grootezze* lying Brest—

That was the two Dutchmen out of it. The names and positions of the other big salvage tugs, each of them a direct and dire threat to *Warlock*, ran swiftly from the telex and Nicholas chewed his cheroot ragged as he watched, his eyes slitted against the spiralling blue smoke, feeling the relief rise in him as each report put another of his competitors in some distant waters, far beyond range of the stricken ship.

'*La Mouette*,' Nick's hands balled into fists as the name sprang on to the white paper sheet, '*La Mouette* discharged Brazgas tow Golfo San Jorge on 14th reported en route Buenos Aires.'

Nick grunted like a boxer taking a low blow, and turned away from the machine. He walked out on to the open wing of the bridge and the wind tore at his hair and clothing.

'*La Mouette*, the seagull, a fanciful name for that black squat hull, the old-fashioned high box of superstructure, the traditional single stack; Nick could see it clearly when he closed his eyes.

There was no doubt in his mind at all. Jules Levoisin was already running hard for the south, running like a hunting dog with the scent hot in its nostrils.

Jules had discharged in the southern Atlantic three days ago. He would certainly have bunkered at Comodoro. Nick knew how Jules' mind worked, he was never happy unless his bunkers were bulging.

Nick flicked the stub of his cigar away, and it was whisked far out into the harbour by the wind.

He knew that *La Mouette* had refitted and installed new engines eighteen months before. With a nostalgic twinge, he had read a snippet in *Lloyd's List*. But even nine thousand horsepower couldn't push that tubby hull at better than eighteen knots, Nick was certain of that. Yet even with *Warlock*'s superior speed, *La Mouette* was better placed by a thousand miles. There was no room for complacency. And what if *La Mouette* had set out to double Cape Horn instead of driving north up the Atlantic? If that had happened, and with Jules Levoisin's luck it might just have happened, then *La Mouette* was a long way inside him already.

Anybody else but Jules Levoisin, he thought, why did it have to be him? And oh God, why now? Why now when I am so vulnerable – emotionally, physically and financially vulnerable? Oh God, why did it come now?

He felt the false sense of cheer and well-being, with which he had buoyed himself that morning, fall away from him like a cloak, leaving him naked and sick and tired again.

I am not ready yet, he thought; and then realized that it was probably the first time in his adult life he had ever said that to himself. He had always been ready, good and ready, for anything. But not now, not this time.

Suddenly Nicholas Berg was afraid, as he had never been before. He was empty, he realized, there was nothing in him, no strength, no confidence, no resolve. The depth of his defeat by Duncan Alexander, the despair of his rejection by the woman he loved, had broken him. He felt his fear turn to terror, knowing that his wave had come, and would sweep by him now, for he did not have the strength to ride it.

Some deep instinct warned him that it would be the last wave, there would be nothing after it. The choice was go now, or never go again. And he knew he could not go, he could not go against Jules Levoisin, he could not challenge the old master. He could not go – he could not reject the certainty of the Esso tow, he did not have the nerve now to risk all that he had left on a single throw. He had just lost a big one, he couldn't go at risk again.

The risk was too great, he was not ready for it, he did not have the strength for it.

He wanted to go to his cabin and throw himself on his bunk and sleep – and sleep. He felt his knees buckling with the great weight of his despair, and he hungered for the oblivion of sleep.

He turned back into the bridge, out of the wind. He was broken, defeated, he had given up. As he went towards the sanctuary of his day cabin, he passed the long command console and stopped involuntarily.

His officers watched him in a tense, electric silence.

His right hand went out and touched the engine telegraph, sliding the pointer from 'off' to 'stand by'.

'Engine Room,' he heard a voice speak in calm and level tones, so it could not be his own. 'Start main engines,' said the voice.

Seemingly from a great distance he watched the faces of his deck officers bloom with unholy joy, like old-time pirates savouring the prospect of a prize.

The strange voice went on, echoing oddly in his ears, 'Number One, ask the Harbour Master for permission to clear harbour immediately – and, Pilot, course to steer for the last reported position of *Golden Adventurer*, please.'

From the corner of his eye, he saw David Allen punch the Third Officer lightly but gleefully on the shoulder before he hurried to the radio telephone.

Nicholas Berg felt suddenly the urge to vomit. So he stood very still and erect at the navigation console and fought back the waves of nausea that swept over him, while his officers bustled to their seagoing stations.

'Bridge. This is the Chief Engineer,' said a disembodied voice from the speaker above Nick's head. 'Main engines running.' A pause and then that word of special Aussie approbation. 'Beauty!' – but the Chief pronounced it in three distinct syllables, 'Be-yew-dy!'

*Warlock's* wide-flared bows were designed to cleave push the waters open ahead of her and in those waters below latitude 40°, she ran like an old bull otter, slick and wet and fast for the south.

Uninterrupted by any land-mass, the cycle of great atmospheric depressions swept endlessly across those cold open seas, and the wave patterns built up into a succession of marching mountain ranges.

'*Warlock* was taking them on her starboard shoulder, bursting through each crest in a white explosion that leapt from her bows like a torpedo strike, the water coming aboard green and clear over her high foredeck, and sweeping her from stem to stern as she twisted and broke out, dropping sheer into the valley that opened ahead of her. Her twin ferro-bronze propellers broke clear of the surface, the slamming vibration instantly controlled by the sophisticated variable-pitch gear, until she swooped forward and the propellers bit deeply again, the thrust of the twin Mirrlees diesels hurtling her towards the slope of the next swell.

Each time it seemed that she could not rise in time to meet the cliff of water that bore down on her. The water was black under the grey sunless sky. Nick had lived through typhoon and Caribbean hurricane, but had never seen water as menacing and cruel as this. It glittered like the molten slag that pours down the dump of an iron foundry and cools to the same iridescent blackness.

In the deep valleys between the crests, the wind was blanketed so they fell into an unnatural stillness, an eerie silence that only enhanced the menace of that towering slope of water.

In the trough, *Warlock* heeled and threw her head up, climbing the slope in a gut-swooping lift, that buckled the knees of the watch. As she went up, so the angle of her bridge tilted back, and that sombre cheerless sky filled the forward bridge windows with a vista of low scudding cloud.

The wind tore at the crest of the wave ahead of her, ripping it away like white cotton from the burst seams of a black mattress, splattering custard-thick spume against the armoured glass. Then *Warlock* put her sharp steel nose deeply into it. Gouging a fat wedge of racing green over her head, twisting violently at the jarring impact, dropping sideways over the crest, and breaking out to fall free and repeat the cycle again.

Nick was wedged into the canvas master's seat in the corner of the bridge. He swayed like a camel-driver to the thrust of the sea and smoked his black cheroots quietly, his head turning every few minutes to the west, as though he expected at any moment to see the black ugly hull of *La Mouette* come up on top of the next swell. But he knew she was a thousand miles away still, racing down the far leg of the triangle which had at its apex the stricken liner.

'If she *is* running,' Nick thought, and knew that there was no doubt. *La Mouette* was running as frantically as was *Warlock* – and as silently. Jules Levoisin had taught Nick the trick of silence. He would not use his radio until he had the liner on his radar scan. Then he would come through in clear, 'I will be in a position to put a line aboard you in two hours. Do you accept "Lloyd's Open Form"?'

The Master of the distressed vessel, having believed himself abandoned without succour, would over-react to the promise of salvation, and when *La Mouette* came bustling up over the horizon, flying all her bunting and with every light blazing in as theatrical a display as Jules could put up, the relieved Master would probably leap at the offer of 'Lloyd's Open Form' – a decision that would surely be regretted by the ship's owners in the cold and unemotional precincts of an Arbitration court.

When Nick had supervised the design of *Warlock*, he had insisted that she look good as well as being able to perform. The master of a disabled ship was usually a man in a highly emotional state. Mere physical appearance might sway him in the choice between two salvage tugs coming up on him. *Warlock* looked magnificent; even in this cold and cheerless ocean, she looked like a warship. The trick would be to show her to the master of *Golden Adventurer* before he struck a bargain with *La Mouette*.

Nick could no longer sit inactive in his canvas seat. He judged the next towering swell and, with half a dozen quick strides, crossed the bridge deck in those fleeting moments as *Warlock* steadied in the trough. He grabbed the chrome handrail above the Decca computer.

On the keyboard he typed the function code that would set the machine in navigational mode, co-ordinating the transmissions she was receiving from the circling satellite stations high above the earth. From these were calculated *Warlock*'s exact position over the earth's surface, accurate to within twenty-five yards.

Nick entered the ship's position and the computer compared this with the plot that Nick had requested four hours previously. It printed out quickly the distance run and the ship's speed made good. Nick frowned angrily and swung round to watch the helmsman.

In this fiercely running cross sea, a good man could hold *Warlock* on course more efficiently than any automatic steering device. He could anticipate each trough and crest and prevent the ship paying off across the direction of the swells, and then kicking back violently as she went over, wasting critical time and distance.

Nick watched the helmsman work, judging each sea as it came aboard, checking the ship's heading on the big repeating compass above the man's head. After ten minutes, Nick realized that there was no wastage; *Warlock* was making as good a course as was possible in these conditions.

The engine telegraph was pulled back to her maximum safe power-setting, the course was good and yet *Warlock* was not delivering those few extra knots of speed that Nick Berg had relied on when he had made the critical decision to race *La Mouette* for the prize.

Nick had relied on twenty-eight knots against the Frenchman's eighteen, and he was not getting it. Involuntarily, he glanced out to the streaming windows, from which the spinning wipers cleared circular areas of clean glass, Nick looked out across a wilderness of black water, forbidding and cold and devoid of other human presence.

Abruptly Nick crossed to the R/T microphone.

'Engine Room confirm we are top of the green.'

'Top of the green, it is, Skipper.'

The Chief's casual tones floated in above the crash of the next sea coming aboard.

'Top of the green' was the maximum safe power-setting recommended by the manufacturers for those gigantic Mirrlees diesels. It was a far higher setting than top economical power, and they were burning fuel at a prodigious rate. Nick was pushing her as high as he could without going into the 'red' danger area above eighty per cent of full power, which at prolonged running might permanently damage her engines.

Nick turned away to his seat, and wedged himself into it. He groped for his cheroot case, and then checked himself, the lighter in his hand. His tongue and mouth felt furred over and dry. He had smoked without a break every waking minute since leaving Cape Town, and God knows he had slept little enough since then. He ran his tongue around his mouth with distaste before he returned the cheroot to his case, and crouched in his seat staring ahead, trying to work out why *Warlock* was running slow.

Suddenly he straightened and considered a possibility that brought a metallic green gleam of anger into Nick's eyes.

He slid out of his seat, nodded to the Third Officer who had the deck and ducked through the doorway in the back of the bridge into his day cabin. It was a ploy. He didn't want his visit below decks announced, and from his own suite he darted into the companionway.

The engine control room was as modern and gleaming as *Warlock*'s navigation bridge. It was completely enclosed with double glass to cut down the thunder of her eingines. The control console was banked below the windows, and all the ship's functions were displayed in green and red digital figures.

The view beyond the windows into the main engine room was impressive, even for Nick who had designed and supervised each foot of the layout.

The two Mirrlees diesel engines filled the white-painted cavern with only walking space between, each as long as four Cadillac Eldorados parked bumper to bumper and as deep as if another four Cadillacs had been piled on top of them.

The thirty-six cylinders of each block were crowned with a moving forest of valve stems and con-rod ends, each enormous powerhouse capable of pouring out eleven thousand usable horsepower.

It was only custom that made it necessary for any visitor, including the Master, to announce his arrival in the engine room to the Chief Engineer. Ignoring custom, Nick slipped quietly through the glass sliding doors, out of the hot burned-oil stench of the engine room into the cooler and sweeter conditioned air of the control room.

Vin Baker was deep in conversation with one of his electricians, both of them kneeling before the open doors of one of the tall grey steel cabinets which housed a teeming mass of coloured cables and transistor switches. Nick had reached the control console before the Chief Engineer uncoiled his lanky body from the floor and spun round to face him.

When Nick was very angry, his lips compressed in a single thin white line, the thick dark eyebrows seemed to meet above the snapping green eyes and large slightly beaked nose.

'You pulled the over-ride on me,' he accused in a flat, passionless voice that did not betray his fury. 'You're governing her out at seventy per cent of power.'

'That's top of the green in my book,' Vin Baker told him. 'I'm not running my engines, at eighty per cent in this sea. She'll shake the guts out of herself.' He paused and the stern was flung up violently as *Warlock* crashed over the top of another sea. The control room shuddered with the vibration of the screws breaking out of the surface, spinning wildly in the air before they could bite again.

'Listen to her, man. You want me to pour on more of it?'

'She's built to take it.'

'Nothing's built to run that hard, and live in this sea.'

'I want to over-ride out,' said Nick flatly, indicating the chrome handle and pointer with which the engineer could cancel the power settings asked for by the bridge. 'I don't care when you do it – just as long as it's any time within the next five seconds.'

'You get out of my engine room – and go play with your toys.'

'All right,' Nick nodded, 'I'll do it myself.' And he reached for the over-ride gear.

'You take your hands off my engines,' howled Vin Baker, and picked up the ironlocking handle off the deck. 'You touch my engines and I'll break your teeth out of your head, you ice-cold Pommy bastard.'

Even in his own anger, Nick blinked at the epithet. When he thought about the blazing passions and emotions that seethed within him, he nearly laughed aloud. *Ice-cold*, he thought, so that's how he sees me.

'You stupid Bundaberg-swilling galah,' he said quietly, as he reached for the over-ride. 'I don't really care if I have to kill you first, but we are going to eighty per cent.'

It was Vin Baker's turn to blink behind his smeared glasses, he had not expected to be insulted in the colloquial. He dropped the heavy steel handle to the deck. It fell with a clang.

'I don't need it,' he announced, and tucked his spectacles into his back pocket and hoisted his trousers with both elbows. 'It will be more fun to take you to pieces by hand.'

It was only then that Nick realized how tall the engineer was. His arms were ridged with the lean wiry taut muscle of hard physical labour. His fists, as he balled them, were lumpy with scar tissue across the knuckles and the size of a pair of nine-pound hammers. He went down into a fighter's crouch, and rode the plunging deck with an easy flexing of the long powerful legs.

As Nicholas touched the chrome over-ride handle, the first punch came from the level of Baker's knees, but it came so fast that Nick only just had time to sway away from it. It whistled up past his jaw and scraped the skin from the outside corner of his eye – but he counter-punched instinctively, swaying back and slamming it in under the armpit, feeling the blow land so solidly that his teeth jarred his own head. The Chief's breath hissed, but he swung left-handed and a bony fist crushed the pad of muscle on the point of Nick's shoulder, bounced off and caught him high on the temple.

Even though it was a glancing blow, it felt as though a door had slammed in Nick's head, and resounding darkness closed behind his eyes. He fell forward into a clinch to ride the darkness, grabbing the lean hard body and smothering it in a bear hug as he tried to clear the singing darkness in his head.

He felt the Chief shift his weight, and was shocked at the power in that wiry frame, it took all his own strength to hold him. Suddenly and clearly he knew what was going to happen next. There were little white ridges of scar tissue half hidden by the widow's peak of flopping sandy hair on the Chief's forehead. Those scars from previous conflicts warned Nick.

Vin Baker reared back, like a cobra flaring for the strike, and then flung his head forward; it was the classic butt aimed for Nick's face and, had it landed squarely, it would have crushed in his nose and broken his teeth off level to the gums – but Nick anticipated, and dropped his own chin, tucking it down hard so that their foreheads met with a crack like a breaking oak branch.

The impact broke Nick's grip, and both of them reeled apart across the heaving deck, Vin Baker howling like a moon-sick dog and clutching his own head.

'Fight fair, you Pommy bastard!' he howled in outrage, and he came up short against the steel cabinets that lined the far side of the control room. The astonished electrician dived for cover under the control console, scattering tools across the deck.

Vin Baker lay for a moment gathering his lanky frame, and then, as *Warlock* swung hard over, rolling viciously in the cross sea, he used her momentum to hurl himself down the steeply tilting deck, dropping his head again like a battering ram to crush in Nick's ribs as he charged.

Nick turned like a cattle man working an unruly steer. He whipped one arm round Vin Baker's neck and ran with him, holding his head down and building up speed across the full length of the control room. They reached the armoured glass wall at the far end, and the top of Vin Baker's head was the point of impact with the weight of both their bodies behind it.

The Chief Engineer came round at the prick of the needle that Angel forced through the thick flap of open flesh on top of his head. He came round fighting drunkenly, but the cook held him down with one huge hairy arm.

'Easy love.' Angel pulled the needle through the torn red weeping scalp and tied the stitch.

'Where is he, where is the bastard?' slurred the Chief.

'It's all over, Chiefie,' Angel told him gently. 'And you are lucky he bashed you on the head – otherwise he might have hurt you.' He took another stitch.

The Chief winced as Angel pulled the thread up tight and knotted it. 'He tried to mess with my engines. I taught the bastard a lesson.'

'You've terrified him,' Angel agreed sweetly. 'Now you take a swig of this and lie still. I want you in this bunk for twelve hours – and I might come and tuck you in.'

'I'm going back to my engines,' announced the Chief, and drained the medicine glass of brown spirit, then whistled at the bite of the fumes.

Angel left him and crossed to the telephone. He spoke quickly into it, and as the Chief lumbered off the bunk, Nick Berg stepped into the cabin, and nodded to the cook.

'Thank you, Angel.'

Angel ducked out of the cabin and left them facing each other. The Chief opened his mouth to snarl at Nick.

'Jules Levoisin in *La Mouette* has probably made five hundred miles on us while you have been playing prima donna,' said Nick quietly, and Vin Baker's mouth stayed open, although no sound came out of it.

'I built this ship to run fast and hard in just this kind of contest, and now you are trying to do all of us out of prize money.'

Nick turned on his heel and went back up the companionway to his navigation deck. He settled into his canvas chair and fingered the bit purple swelling on his forehead tenderly. His head felt as though a rope had been knotted around it and twisted up tight. He wanted to go to his cabin and take something for the pain, but he did not want to miss the call when it came.

He lit another cheroot, and it tasted like burned tarred rope. He dropped it into the sandbox and the telephone at his shoulder rang once.

'Bridge, this is the Engine Room.'

'Go ahead, Chief.'

'We are going to eighty per cent now.'

Nick did not reply, but he felt the change in the engine vibration and the more powerful rush of the hull beneath him.

'Nobody told me *La Mouette* was running against us. No way that frog-eating bastard's going to get a line on her first,' announced Vin Baker grimly, and there was a silence between them. Something more had to be said.

'I bet you a pound to a pinch of kangaroo dung,' challenged the Chief, 'that you don't know what a galah is, and that you've never tasted a Bundaberg rum in your life.'

Nick found himself smiling, even through the blinding pain in his head.

'Be-yew-dy!' Nick said, making three syllable of it and keeping the laughter out of his voice, as he hung up the receiver.


Dave Allen's voice was apologetic. 'Sorry to wake you, sir, but the *Golden Adventurer* is reporting.'

'I'm coming,' mumbled Nick, and swung his legs off the bunk. He had been in that black death-sleep of exhaustion, but it took him only seconds to pull back the dark curtains from his mind. It was his old training as a watch-keeping officer.

He rubbed away the last traces of sleep, feeling the rasping black stubble of his beard under his fingers as he crossed quickly to his bathroom. He spent forty seconds in bathing his face and combing his tousled hair, and regretfully decided there was no time to shave. Another rule of his was to look good in a world which so often judged a man by his appearance.

When he went out on to the navigation bridge, he knew at once that the wind had increased its velocity. He guessed it was rising force six now, and *Warlock*'s motion was more violent and abandoned. Beyond the warm, dimly lit capsule of the bridge, all those elements of cold water and vicious racing winds turned the black night to a howling tumult.

The Trog was crouched over his machines, grey and wizened and sleepless. He hardly turned his head to hand Nick the message flimsy.

'Master of *Golden Adventurer* to Christy Main,' the Decca decoded swiftly, and Nick grunted as he saw the new position report. Something had altered drastically in the liner's circumstances. 'Main engines still unserviceable. Current setting easterly and increasing to eight knots. Wind rising force six from north-west. Critical ice danger to the ship. What assistance can I expect?'

There was a panicky note to that last line, and Nick saw why when he compared the liner's new position on the spread chart.

'She's going down sharply on the lee shore,' David muttered as he worked quickly over the chart. 'The current and wind are working together – they are driving her down on to the land.'

He touched the ugly broken points of Coatsland's shoreline with the tip of one finger.

'She eighty miles offshore now. At the rate she is drifting, it will take her only another ten hours before she goes aground.'

'If she doesn't hit an iceberg first,' said Nick. 'From the Master's last message, it sounds as though they are into big ice.'

'That's a cheerful thought,' agreed David, and straightened up from the chart.

'What's our time to reach her?'

'Another forty hours, sir,' David hesitated and pushed the thick white-gold lock of hair off his forehead, 'if we can make good this speed – but we may have to reduce when we reach the ice.'

Nick turned away to his canvas chair. He felt the need to pace back and forward, to release the pent-up forces within him. However, any movement in this heavy pounding sea was not only difficult but downright dangerous, so he groped his way to the chair and wedged himself in, staring ahead into the clamorous black night.

He thought about the terrible predicament of the liner's Captain. His ship was a deadly risk, and the lives of his crew and passengers with it.

How many lives? Nick cast his mind back and came up with the figures. The *Golden Adventurer*'s full complement of officers and crew was 235, and there was accommodation for 375 passengers, a possible total of over six hundred souls. If the ship was lost, *Warlock* would be hard put to take aboard that huge press of human life.

'Well, sir, they signed on for adventure,' David Allen spoke into his thoughts as though he had heard them, 'and they are getting their money's worth.'

Nick glanced at him, and nodded. 'Most of them will be elderly. A berth on that cruise costs a fortune, and it's usually only the oldsters who have that sort of gold. If she goes aground, we are going to lose life.'

'With respect, Captain,' David hesitated, and blushed again for the first time since leaving port, 'if her Captain knows that assistance is on the way, it may prevent him doing something crazy.'

Nick was silent. The Mate was right, of course. It was cruel to leave them in the despair of believing they were alone down there in those terrible icefields. The *Adventurer*'s Captain could make a panic decision, one that could be averted if he knew how close succour was.

'The air temperature out there is minus five degrees, and if the wind is at thirty miles an hour, that will make it a lethal chill factor. If they take to the boats in that—' David was interrupted by the Trog calling from the radio room.

'The owners are replying.'

It was a long message that Christy Marine were sending to their Captain. It was filled with those same hollow assurances that a surgeon gives to a cancer patient, but one paragraph had relevance for Nick:

'All efforts being made to contact salvage tugs reported operating South Atlantic.'

David Allen looked at him expectantly. It was the right humane thing to do. To tell them he was only eight hundred miles away, and closing swiftly.

Nervous energy fizzed in Nick's blood, making him restless and angry. On an impulse he left his chair and carefully crossed the heaving deck to the starboard wing of the bridge.

He slid open the door and stepped out into the gale. The shock of that icy air took his breath away and he gasped like a drowning man. He felt tears streaming from his eyes across his cheeks and the frozen spray struck into his face like steel darts.

Carefully he filled his lungs, and his nostrils flared as he smelt the ice. It was that unmistakeable dank smell, he remembered so well from the northern Arctic seas. It was like the body smell of some gigantic reptilian sea monster – and it struck the mariner's chill into his soul.

He could endure only a few seconds more of the gale, but when he stepped back into the cosy green-lit warmth of the bridge, his mind was clear, and he was thinking crisply.

'Mr Allen, there is ice ahead.'

'I have a watch on the radar, sir.'

'Very good,' Nick nodded, 'but we'll reduce to fifty per cent of power.' He hesitated, and then went on, 'and maintain radio silence.'

The decision was hard made, and Nick saw the accusation in David Allen's eyes before he turned away to give the orders for the reduction in power. Nick felt a sudden and uncharacteristic urge to explain the decision to him. He did not know why – perhaps he needed the Mate's understanding and sympathy. Instantly Nick saw that as a symptom of his weakness and vulnerability. He had never needed sympathy before, and he steeled himself against it now.

His decision to maintain radio silence was correct. He was dealing with two hard men. He knew he could not afford to give an inch of sea room to

Jules Levoisin. He would force him to open radio contact first. He needed that advantage.

The other man with whom he had to deal was Duncan Alexander, and he was a hating man, dangerous and vindictive. He had tried once to destroy Nick – and perhaps he had already succeeded. Nick had to guard himself now, he must pick with care his moment to open negotiations with Christy Marine and the man who had displaced him at its head. Nick must be in a position of utmost strength when he did so.

Jules Levoisin must be forced to declare himself first, Nick decided. The Captain of the *Golden Adventurer* would have to be left in the agonies of doubt a little longer, and Nick consoled himself with the thought that any further drastic change in the liner's circumstances or a decision by the Master to abandon his ship and commit his company to the lifeboats would be announced on the open radio channels and would give him a chance to intervene.

Nick was about to caution the Trog to keep a particular watch on Channel 16 for *La Mouette*'s first transmission, then he checked himself. That was another thing he never did – issue unnecessary orders. The Trog's grey wrinkled head was wreathed in clouds of reeking cigar smoke but was bowed to his mass of electronic equipment, and he adjusted a dial with careful lover's fingers; his little eyes were bright and sleepless as those of an ancient sea turtle.

Nick went to his chair and settled down to wait out the few remaining hours of the short Antarctic summer night.

The radar screen had shown strange and alien capes and headlands above the sea clutter of the storm, strange islands, anomalies which did not relate to the Admiralty charts. Between these alien masses shone myriad other smaller contacts, bright as fireflies, any one of which could have been the echo of a stricken ocean liner – but which was not.

As *Warlock* nosed cautiously down into this enchanted sea, the dawn that had never been far from the horizon flushed out, timorous as a bride, decked in colours of gold and pink that struck splendorous splinters of light off the icebergs.

The horizon ahead of them was cluttered with ice, some of the fragments were but the size of a billiard table and they bumped and scraped down the *Warlock*'s side, then swung and bobbed in her wake as she passed. There were others the size of a city block, weird and fanciful structures of honeycombed white ice, that stood as tall as *Warlock*'s upperworks as she passed.

'White ice is soft ice,' Nick murmured to David Allen beside him, and then caught himself. It was an unnecessary speech, inviting familiarity, and before the Mate could answer, Nick turned quickly away to the radar-repeater and lowered his face to the eye-piece in the coned hood. For a minute he studied the images of the surrounding ice in the darkened body of the instrument, then went back to his seat and stared ahead impatiently.

*Warlock* was running too fast, Nick knew it; he was relying on the vigilance of his deck officers to carry her through the ice. Yet still this speed was too slow for his seething impatience.

Above their horizon rose another shoreline, a great unbroken sweep of towering cliff which caught the low sun, and glowed in emerald and amethyst, a drifting tableland of solid hard ice, forty miles across and two hundred feet high.

As they closed with that massive translucent island, so the colours that glowed through it became more hauntingly beautiful. The cliffs were rent by deep bays, and split by crevasses whose shadowy depths were dark sapphire, blue and mysterious, paling out to a thousand shades of green.

'My God, it's beautiful,' said David Allen with the reverence of a man kneeling in a cathedral.

The crests of the ice cliffs blazed in clearest ruby; to windward, the big sea piled in and crashed against those cliffs, surging up them in explosive bursts of white spray. Yet the iceberg did not dip nor swing or work, even in that murderous sea.

'Look at the lee she is making,' Dave Allen pointed. 'You could ride out a force twelve behind her.'

On the leeward side, the waters were protected from the wind by that mountain of sheer ice. Green and docile, they lapped those mysterious blue cliffs, and *Warlock* went into the lee, passing in a ship's length from the plunging rearing action of a wild horse into the tranquillity of a mountain lake, calm, windless and unnatural.

In the calm, Angel brought trays piled with crisp brown-baked Cornish pasties and steaming mugs of thick creamy cocoa, and they ate breakfast at three in the morning, marvelling at the fine pale sunlight and the towers of incredible beauty, the younger officers shouting and laughing when a school of five black killer whales passed so close that they could see their white cheek patterns and wide grinning mouths through the icy clear waters.

The great mammals circled the ship, then ducked beneath her hull, surging up on the far side with their huge black triangular fins shearing the surface as they blew through the vents in the top of their heads. The fishy stink of their breath pervaded the bridge, and then they were gone, and *Warlock* motored calmly along in the lee of the ice, like a holiday launch of day-trippers.

Nicholas Berg did not join the spontaneous gaiety. He munched one of Angel's delicious pies full of meat and thick gravy, but he could not finish it. His stomach was too tense. He found himself resenting the high spirits of his officers. The laughter offended him, now when his whole life hung in precarious balance. He felt the temptation to quell them with a few harsh words, conscious of the power he had to plunge them into instant consternation.

Nick listened to their carefree banter and felt old enough to be their father, despite the few years' difference in their ages. He was impatient with them, irritated that they should be able to laugh like this when so much was at stake – six hundred human lives, a great ship, tens of millions of dollars, his whole future. They would probably never themselves know what it felt like to put a lifetime's work at risk on a single flip of the coin – and then suddenly, unaccountably, he envied them.

He could not understand the sensation, could not fathom why suddenly he longed to laugh with them, to share the companionship of the moment, to be free of pressure for just a little while. For fifteen years, he had not known that sort of hiatus, had never wanted it.

He stood up abruptly, and immediately the bridge was silent. Every officer concentrating on his appointed task, not one of them glancing at him as he paced once, slowly, across the wide bridge. It did not need a word to change the mood, and suddenly Nick felt guilty. It was too easy, too cheap.

Carefully Nick steeled himself, shutting out the weakness, building up his resolve and determination, bringing all his concentration to bear on the Herculean task ahead of him, and he paused at the door of the radio room. The Trog looked up from his machines, and they exchanged a single glance of understanding. Two completely dedicated men, with no time for frivolity.

Nick nodded and paced on, the strong handsome face stern and uncompromising, his step firm and measured – but when he stopped again by the side windows of the bridge and looked up at the magnificent cliff of ice, he felt the doubts surging up again within him.

How much had he sacrificed for what he had gained, how much joy and laughter had he spurned to follow the high road of challenge, how much beauty had he passed along the way without seeing it in his haste, how much love and warmth and companionship? He thought with a fierce pang of the woman who had been his wife, and who had gone now with the child who was his son. Why had they gone, and what had they left him with – after all his strivings?

Behind him, the radio crackled and hummed as the carrier beam opened Channel 16, then it pitched higher as a human voice came through in clear.

'Mayday. Mayday. Mayday. This is the *Golden Adventurer.*'

Nick spun and ran to the radio room as the calm masculine voice read out the co-ordinates of the ship's position.

'We are in imminent danger of striking. We are preparing to abandon ship. Can any vessel render assistance? Repeat, can any vessel render assistance?'

'Good God,' David Allen's voice was harsh with anxiety, 'the current's got them, they're going down on Cape Alarm at nine knots – she's only fifty miles offshore and we are still two hundred and twenty miles from that position.'

'Where is *La Mouette*?' growled Nick Berg. 'Where the hell is she?'

'We'll have to open contact now, sir,' David Allen looked up from the chart. 'You cannot let them go down into the boats – not in this weather, sir. It would be murder.'

'Thank you, Number One,' said Nick quietly. 'Your advice is always welcome.' David flushed, but there was anger and not embarrassment beneath the colour. Even in the stress of the moment, Nick noted that, and adjusted his opinion of his First Officer. He had guts as well as brains.

The mate was right, of course. There was only one thing to consider now, the conservation of human life.

Nick looked up at the top of the ice cliff and saw the low cloud tearing off it, rolling and swirling in the wind, pouring down over the edge like boiling milk frothing from the lip of a great pot.

He had to send now. *La Mouette* had won the contest of silence. Nick stared up at the cloud and composed the message he would send. He must reassure the Master, urge him to delay his decision to abandon ship and give *Warlock* the time to close the gap, perhaps even reach her before she struck on Cape Alarm.

The silence on the bridge was deepened by the absence of wind. They were all watching him now, waiting for the decision, and in that silence the carrier beam of Channel 16 hummed and throbbed.

Then suddenly a rich Gallic accent poured into the silent bridge, a full fruity voice that Nick remembered so clearly, even after all the years.

'Master of *Golden Adventurer* this is the master of salvage tug *La Mouette*. I am proceeding at best speed your assistance. Do you accept Lloyd's Open Form "No cure no pay"?'

Nick kept his face from showing any emotion, but his heart barged wildly against his ribs. Jules Levoisin had broken silence.

'Plot his position report,' he said quietly.

'God! She's inside us,' David Allen's face was stricken as he marked *La Mouette*'s reported position on the chart. 'She's a hundred miles ahead of us.'

'No,' Nick shook his head, 'he's lying.'

'Sir?'

'He's lying. He always lies.' Nick lit a cheroot and when it was drawing evenly, he spoke again to his radio officer.

'Did you get a bearing?' and the Trog looked up from his radio direction-finding compass on which he was tracing *La Mouette*'s transmissions.

'I have only one co-ordinate, you won't get a fix—'

But Nick interrupted him, 'We'll use his best course from Golfo San Jorge for a fix.' He turned back to David Allen. 'Plot that.'

'There's a difference of over three hundred nautical miles.'

'Yes,' Nick nodded. 'That old pirate wouldn't broadcast an accurate position to all the world. We are inside him and running five knots better, we'll put a line over *Golden Adventurer* before he's in radar contact.'

'Are you going to open contact with Christy Main now, sir?'

'No, Mr Allen.'

'But they will do a deal with *La Mouette* – unless we bid now.'

'I don't think so,' Nick murmured, and almost went on to say, 'Duncan Alexander won't settle for Lloyd's Open Form while he is the underwriter, and his ship is free and floating. He'll fight for daily hire and bonus, and Jules Levoisin won't buy that package. He'll hold out for the big plum. They won't do a deal until the two ships are in visual contact – and by that time I'll have her in tow and I'll fight the bastard in the awards court for twenty-five per cent of her value—' But he did not say it. 'Steady as she goes, Mr Allen,' was all he said, as he left the bridge.

He closed the door of his day cabin and leaned back against it, shutting his eyes tightly as he gathered himself. It had been so very close, a matter of seconds and he would have declared himself and given the advantage to *La Mouette*.

Through the door behind him, he heard David Allen's voice. 'Did you see him? He didn't feel a thing – not a bloody thing. He was going to let those poor bastards go into the boats. He must piss ice-water.' The voice was muffled, but the outrage in it was tempered by awe.

Nick kept his eyes shut a moment longer, then he straightened up and pushed himself away from the door. He wanted it to begin now. It was the waiting and the uncertainty which was eroding what was left of his strength.

'Please God, let me reach them in time.' And he was not certain whether it was for the lives or for the salvage award that he was praying.

Captain Basil Reilly, the Master of the *Golden Adventurer*, was a tall man, with a lean and wiry frame that promised reserves of strength and endurance. His face was very darkly tanned and splotched with the dark patches of benign sun cancer. His heavy moustache was silvered like the pelt of a snow fox, and though his eyes were set in webs of finely wrinkled and pouchy skin, they were bright and calm and intelligent.

He stood on the windward wing of his navigation bridge and watched the huge black seas tumbling in to batter his helpless ship. He was taking them broadside now, and each time they struck, the hull shuddered and heeled with a sick dead motion, giving reluctantly to the swells that rose up and broke over her rails, sweeping her decks from side to side, and then cascading off her again in a tumble of white that smoked in the wind.

He adjusted the life-jacket he wore, settling the rough canvas more comfortably around his shoulders as he reviewed his position once more.

*Golden Adventurer* had taken the ice in that eight-to-midnight watch traditionally allotted to the most junior of the navigating officers. The impact had hardly been noticeable, yet it had awoken the Master from deep sleep – just a slight check and jar that had touched some deep chord in the mariner's instinct.

The ice had been a growler, one of the most deadly of all hazards. The big bergs standing high and solid to catch the radar beams, or the eye of even the most inattentive deck watch, were easily avoided. However, the low ice lying awash, with its great bulk and weight almost completely hidden by the dark and turbulent waters, was as deadly as a predator in ambush.

The growler showed itself only in the depths of each wave trough, or in the swirl of the current around it, as though a massive seamonster lurked there. At night, these indications would pass unnoticed by even the sharpest eyes, and below the surface, the wave action eroded the body of the growler, turning it into a horizontal blade that lay ten feet or more below the water level and reached out two or three hundred feet from the visible surface indications.

With the Third Officer on watch, and steaming at cautionary speed of a mere twelve knots, the *Golden Adventurer* had brushed against one of these monsters, and although the actual impact had gone almost unnoticed on board, the ice had opened her like the knife stroke which splits a herring for the smoking rack.

It was classic *Titanic* damage, a fourteen-foot rent through her side, twelve feet below the Plimsoll line, shearing two of her watertight compartments, one of which was her main engine room section.

They had held the water easily until the electrical explosion, and since then, the Master had battled to keep her afloat. Slowly, step by step, fighting all the way, he had yielded to the sea. All the bilge pumps were running still, but the water was steadily gaining.

Three days ago he had brought all his passengers up from below the main deck, and he had battened down all the watertight bulkheads. The crew and passengers were accommodated now in the lounges and smoking rooms. The ship's luxury and opulence had been transformed into the crowded, unhygienic and deteriorating conditions of a city under siege.

It reminded him of the catacombs of the London underground converted to air-raid shelters during the blitz. He had been a lieutenant on shore-leave and he had passed one night there that he would remember for the rest of his life.

There was the same atmosphere on board now. The sanitary arrangements were inadequate. Fourteen toilet bowls for six hundred, many of them seasick and suffering from diarrhoea. There were no baths nor showers, and insufficient power for the heating of water in the handbasins. The emergency generators delivered barely sufficient power to work the ship, to run the pumps, to supply minimal lighting, and to keep the communicational and navigational equipment running. There was no heating in the ship and the outside air temperature had fallen to minus twenty degrees now.

The cold in the spacious public lounges was brutal. The passengers huddled in their fur coats and bulky life-jackets under mounds of blankets. There were limited cooking facilities on the gas stoves usually reserved for adventure tours ashore. There was no baking or grilling, and most of the food was eaten cold and congealed from cans; only the soup and beverages steamed in the cold clammy air, like the breaths of the waiting and helpless multitude.

The desalination plants had not been in use since the ice collision and now the supply of fresh water was critical; even hot drinks were rationed.

Of the 368 paying passengers, only forty-eight were below the age of fifty, and yet the morale was extraordinary. Men and women who before the emergency could and did complain bitterly at a dress shirt not ironed to crisp perfection or a wine served a few degrees too cold, now accepted a mug of beef tea as though it were a vintage Château Margaux, and laughed and chatted animatedly in the cold, shaming with their fortitude the few that might have complained. These were an unusual sample of humanity, men and women of achievement and resilience, who had come here to this outlandish corner of the globe in search of new experience. They were mentally prepared for adventure and even danger, and seemed almost to welcome this as part of the entertainment provided by the tour.

Yet, standing on his bridge, the master was under no illusion as to the gravity of their situation. Peering through the streaming glass, he watched a work party, led by his First Officer, toiling heroically in the bows. Four men in glistening yellow plastic suits and hoods, drenched by the icy seas, working with the slow cold-numbed movements of automatons as they struggled to stream a sea-anchor and bring the ship's head up into the sea, so that she might ride more easily, and perhaps slow her precipitous rush down onto the rocky coast. Twice in the preceding days, the anchors they had rigged had been torn away by sea and wind and the ship's dead weight.

Three hours before, he had called his engineering officers up from below, where the risk to their lives had become too great to chance against the remote possibility of restoring power to his main engines. He had conceded the battle to the sea and now he was planning the final moves when he must abandon his command and attempt to remove six hundred human beings from this helpless hulk to the even greater dangers and hardships of Cape Alarm's barren and storm-rent shores.

Cape Alarm was one of those few pinnacles of barren black rock which thrust out from beneath the thick white mantle of the Antarctic cap, pounded free of ice like an anvil beneath the eternal hammering assault of storm and sea and wind.

The long straight ridge protruded almost fifty miles into the eastern extremity of the Weddell Sea, was fifty miles across at its widest point, and terminated in a pair of bull's horns which formed a small protected bay named after the polar explorer Sir Ernest Shackleton.

Shackleton Bay, with its steep purple-black beaches of round polished pebbles, was the nesting ground of a huge colony of chinstrap penguin, and for this reason was one of *Golden Adventurer*'s regular ports of call.

On each tour, the ship would anchor in the deep and calm waters of the bay, while her passengers went ashore to study and photograph the breeding birds and the extraordinary geological formations, sculptured by ice and wind into weird and grotesque shapes.

Only ten days earlier, *Golden Adventurer* had weighed anchor in Shackleton Bay and stood out into the Weddell Sea. The weather had been mild and still, with a slow oily swell and a bright clear sun. Now, before a force seven gale, in temperatures forty-five degrees colder, and borne on the wild dark sweep of the current, she was being carried back to that same black and rocky shore.

There was no doubt in Captain Reilly's mind – they were going to go aground on Cape Alarm, there was no avoiding that fate with this set of sea and wind, unless the French salvage tug reached them first.

*La Mouette* should have been in radar contact already, if the tug's reported position was correct, and Basil Reilly let a little frown of worry crease the brown parchment skin of his forehead and shadows were in his eyes.

'Another message from head office, sir.' His Second Officer was beside him now, a young man with the shape of a teddy bear swathed in thick woollen jerseys and marine blue top coat. Basil Reilly's strict dress regulations had long ago been abandoned and their breaths steamed in the frigid air of the navigation bridge.

'Very well.' Reilly glanced at the flimsy. 'Send that to the tug master.' The contempt was clear in his voice, his disdain for this haggling between owners and salvors, when a great ship and six hundred lives were at risk in the cold sea.

He knew what he would do if the salvage tug made contact before *Golden Adventurer* struck the waiting fangs of rock, he would override his owner's express orders and exercise his rights as Master by immediately accepting the offer of assistance under Lloyd's Open Form.

'But let him come,' he murmured to himself. 'Please God, let him come,' and he raised his binoculars and slowly swept a long jagged horizon where the peaks of the swells seemed black and substantial as rock. He paused with a leap of his pulse when something white blinked in the field of the glasses and then, with a little sick slide, realized that it was only a random ray of sunlight catching a pinnacle of ice from one of the floating bergs.

He lowered the glasses and crossed from the windward wing of the bridge to the lee. He did not need the glasses now, Cape Alarm was black and menacing against the sow's-belly grey of the sky. Its ridges and valleys picked out with gleaming ice and banked snow, and against her steep shore, the sea creamed and leapt high in explosions of purest white.

'Sixteen miles, sir,' said the First Officer, coming to stand beside him. 'And the current seems to be setting a little more northerly now.' They were both silent, as they balanced automatically against the violent pitch and roll of the deck.

Then the mate spoke again with a bitter edge to his voice, 'Where is that bloddy frog?' And they watched the night of Antarctica begin to shroud the cruel lee shore in funereal cloaks of purple and sable, picked out with the ermine collars and cuffs of ice.


She was very young, probably not yet twenty-five years of age, and even the layers of heavy clothing topped by a man's anorak three sizes too big could not disguise the slimness of her body, that almost coltish elegance of long fine limbs and muscle toned by youth and hard exercise.

Her head was set jauntily on the long graceful stem of her neck, like a golden sunflower, and the profuse mane of long hair was sun-bleached, streaked with silver and platinum and copper gold, twisted up carelessly into a rope almost as thick as a man's wrist and piled on top of her head. Yet loose strands floated down on to her forehead and tickled her nose so that she pursed her lips and puffed them away.

Her hands were both occupied with the heavy tray she carried, and she balanced like a skilled horsewoman against the ship's extravagant plunging as she offered it.

'Come on, Mrs Goldberg,' she wheedled. 'It will warm the cockles of your tum.'

'I don't think so, my dear,' the white-haired woman faltered.

'Just for me, then,' the girl wheedled.

'Well,' the woman took one of the mugs and sipped it tentatively. 'It's good,' she said, and then quickly and furtively, 'Samantha, has the tug come yet?'

'It will be here any minute now, and the Captain is a dashing Frenchman, just the right age for you, with a lovely tickly moustache. I'm going to introduce you first thing.'

The woman was a widow in her late fifties, a little overweight and more than a little afraid, but she smiled and sat up a little straighter.

'You naughty thing,' she smiled.

'Just as soon as I've finished with this,' Samantha indicated the tray, 'I'll come and sit with you. We'll play some klabrias, okay?' When Samantha Silver smiled, her teeth were very straight and white against the peach of her tanned cheeks and the freckles that powdered her nose like gold dust. She moved on.

They welcomed her, each of them, men and women, competing for her attention, for she was one of those rare creatures that radiate such warmth, a sort of shining innocence, like a kitten or a beautiful child, and she laughed and chided and teased them in return and left them grinning and heartened, but jealous of her going, so they followed her with their eyes. Most of them felt she belonged to them personally, and they wanted all of her time and presence, making up questions or little stories to detain her for a few extra moments.

'There was an albatross following us a little while ago, Sam.'

'Yes, I saw it through the galley window—'

'It was a wandering albatross, wasn't it, Sam?'

'Oh, come on, Mr Stewart! You know better than that. It was *Diomedea melanophris*, the black-browed albatross, but still it's good luck. All albatrosses are good luck – that's a scientifically proved fact.'

Samantha had a doctorate in biology and was one of the ship's specialist guides. She was on sabbatical leave from the University of Miami where she held a research fellowship in marine ecology.

Passengers thirty years her senior treated her like a favourite daughter most of the time. However, in even the mildest crisis they became childlike in their appeal to her and in their reliance on her natural strength which they recognized and sought instinctively. She was to them a combination of beloved pet and den-mother.

While a ship's steward refilled her tray with mugs, Samantha paused at the entrance to the temporary galley they had set up in the cocktail room and looked back into the densely packed lounge.

The stink of unwashed humanity and tobacco smoke was almost a solid blue thing, but she felt a rush of affection for them. They were behaving so very well, she thought, and she was proud of them.

'Well done, team,' she thought, and grinned. It was not often that she could find affection in herself for a mass of human beings. Often she had pondered how a creature so fine and noble and worthwhile as the human individual could, in its massed state, become so unattractive.

She thought briefly of the human multitudes of the crowded cities. She hated zoos and animals in cages, remembering as a little girl crying for a bear that danced endlessly against its bars, driven mad by its confinement. The concrete cages of the cities drove their captives into similar strange and bizarre behaviour. All creatures should be free to move and live and breathe, she believed, and yet man, the super-predator, who had denied that right to so many other creatures, was now destroying himself with the same single-

mindedness, poisoning and imprisoning himself in an orgy that made the
madness of the lemmings seem logical in comparison. It was only when she
saw human beings like these in circumstances like these that she could be
truly proud of them – and afraid for them.

She felt her own fear deep down, at the very periphery of her awareness,
for she was a sea-creature who loved and understood the sea – and knew its
monumental might. She knew what awaited them out there in the storm,
and she was afraid. With a deliberate effort she lifted the slump of her
shoulders, and set the smile brightly on her lips and picked up the heavy
tray.

At that moment the speakers of the public-address system gave a preliminary squawk, and then filtered the Captain's cultured and measured tones
into the suddenly silent ship.

'Ladies and gentlemen, this is your Captain speaking. I regret to inform
you that we have not yet established radar contact with the salvage tug *La
Mouette*, and that I now deem it necessary to transfer the ship's company
to the lifeboats.'

There was a sigh and stir in the crowded lounges, heard even above the
storm. Samantha saw one of her favourite passengers reach for his wife and
press her silvery-grey head to his shoulder.

'You have all practised the lifeboat drill many times and you know your
teams and stations. I am sure I do not have to impress upon you the necessity
to go to your stations in orderly fashion, and to obey explicitly the orders of
the ship's officers.'

Samantha set down her tray and crossed quickly to Mrs Goldberg. The
woman was weeping, softly and quietly, lost and bewildered, and Samantha
slipped her arm around her shoulder.

'Come now,' she whispered. 'Don't let the others see you cry.'

'Will you stay with me, Samantha?'

'Of course I will.' She lifted the woman to her feet. 'It will be all right
– you'll see. Just think of the story you'll be able to tell your grandchildren
when you get home.'


Captain Reilly reviewed his preparations for leaving the ship, going over
them item by item in his mind. He now knew by heart the considerable list
he had compiled days previously from his own vast experience of Antarctic
conditions and the sea.

The single most important consideration was that no person should be
immersed, or even drenched by sea water during the transfer. Life expectation
in these waters was four minutes. Even if the victim were immediately
pulled from the water, it was still four minutes, unless the sodden clothing
could be removed and heating provided. With this wind blowing, rising eight
of the Beaufort scale at forty miles an hour and an air temperature of minus
twenty degrees, the chill factor was at the extreme of stage seven, which,
translated into physical terms, meant that a few minutes' exposure would
numb and exhaust a man, and that mere survival was a matter of planning
and precaution.

The second most important consideration was the physiological crisis of his passengers, when they left the comparative warmth and comfort and security of the ship for the shrieking cold and the violent discomfort of a life-raft afloat in an Antarctic storm.

They had been briefed, and mentally prepared as much as was possible. An officer had checked each passenger's clothing and survival equipment, they had been fed high-sugar tablets to ward off the cold, and the life-raft allocations had been carefully worked out to provide balanced complements, each with a competent crew member in command. It was as much as he could do for them, and he turned his attention to the logistics of the transfer.

The lifeboats would go first – six of them, slung three on each side of the ship, each crewed by a navigation officer and five seamen. While the great drogue of the sea-anchor held the ship's head into the wind and the sea, they would be swung outboard on their hydraulic derricks and the winches would lower them swiftly to the surface of a sea temporarily smoothed by the oil sprayed from the pumps in the bows.

Although they were decked-in, powered, and equipped with radio, the lifeboats were not the ideal vehicles for survival in these conditions. Within hours, the men aboard them would be exhausted by the cold. For this reason, none of the passengers would be aboard them. Instead, they would go into the big inflatable life-rafts, self-righting even in the worst seas and enclosed with a double skin of insulation. Equipped with emergency rations and battery-powered locator beacons, they would ride the big black seas more easily and each provide shelter for twenty human beings, whose body warmth would keep the interior habitable, at least for the time it took to tow the rafts to land.

The motor lifeboats were merely the shepherds for the rafts. They would herd them together and then tow them in tandem to the sheltering arms of Shackleton Bay.

Even in these blustering conditions, the two should not take more than twelve hours. Each boat would tow five rafts, and thought the crews of the motor boats would have to change, brought into the canopy of the rafts and rested, there should be no insurmountable difficulties; Captain Reilly was hoping for a tow-speed of between three and four knots.

The lifeboats were packed with equipment and fuel and food sufficient to keep the shipwrecked party for a month, perhaps two on reduced rations, and once the calmer shores of the bay had been reached, the rafts would be carried ashore, the canopies reinforced with slabs of packed snow and transformed into igloo-type huts to shelter the survivors. They might be in Shackleton Bay a long time, for even when the French tug reached them, it could not take aboard six hundred persons, some would have to remain and await another rescue ship.

Captain Reilly took one more look at the land. It was very close now, and even in the gloom of the onrushing night, the peaks of ice and snow glittered like the fangs of some terrible and avaricious monster.

'All right,' he nodded to his First Officer, 'we will begin.'

The mate lifted the small two-way radio to his lips. 'Foredeck. Bridge. You may commence laying the oil now.'

From each side of the bows, the hoses threw up silver dragon-fly wings of sprayed diesel oil, pumped directly from the ship's bunkers; its viscous weight resisted the wind's efforts to tear it away, and it fell in a thick coating across the surface of the sea, broken by the floodlights into the colour spectrum of the rainbow.

Immediately, the sea was soothed, the wind-riven surface flattened by the weight of oil, so the swells passed in smooth and weighty majesty beneath the ship's hull.

The two officers on the wing of the bridge could feel the sick, water-logged response of the hull. She was heavy with the water in her, no longer light and quick and alive.

'Send the boats away,' said the Captain, and the mate passed the order over the radio in quiet conversational tones.

The hydraulic arms of the derricks lifted the six boats off their chocks and swung them out over the ship's side, suspended one moment high above the surface; then, as the ship fell through the trough, the oil-streaked crest raced by only feet below their keels. The officer of each lifeboat must judge the sea, and operate the winch so as to drop neatly onto the back slope of a passing swell – then instantly detach the automatic clamps and stand away from the threatening steel cliff of the ship's side.

In the floodlights, the little boats shone wetly with spray, brilliant electric yellow in colour, and decorated with garlands of ice like Christmas toys. In the small armoured-glass windows the officers' faces also glistened whitely with the strain and concentration of these terrifying moments, as each tried to judge the rushing black seas.

Suddenly the heavy nylon rope that held the cone-shaped drogue of the sea-anchor snapped with a report like a cannon shot, and the rope snaked and hissed in the air, a vicious whiplash which could have sliced a man in half.

It was like slipping the head halter from a wild stallion. *Golden Adventurer* threw up her bows, joyous to be freed of restraint. She slewed back across the scend of the sea, and was immediately pinned helplessly broadside, her starboard side into the wind, and the three yellow lifeboats still dangling.

A huge wave reared up out of the darkness. As it rushed down on the ship, one of the lifeboats sheared her cables and fell heavily to the surface, the tiny propeller churning frantically, trying to bring her round to meet the wave – but the wave caught her and dashed her back against the steel side of the ship.

She burst like a ripe melon and the guts spilled out of her; from the bridge they saw the crew swirled helplessly away into the darkness. The little locator lamps on their lifejackets burned feebly as fire-flies in the darkness and then blinked out in the storm.

The forward lifeboat was swung like a door-knocker against the ship, her forward cable jammed so she dangled stern upmost, and as each wave punched into her, she was smashed against the hull. They could hear the men in her screaming, a thin pitiful sound on the wind, that went on for many minutes as the sea slowly beat the boat into a tangle of wreckage.

The third boat was also swung viciously against the hull. The releases on her clamps opened, and she dropped twenty feet into the boil and surge of water, submerging completely and then bobbing free like a yellow fishing float after the strike. Leaking and settling swiftly, she limped away into the clamorous night.

'Oh, my God,' whispered Captain Reilly, and in the harsh lights of the bridge, his face was suddenly old and haggard. In a single stroke he had lost half his boats. As yet he did not mourn the men taken by the sea, that would come later – now it was the loss of the boats that appalled him, for it threatened the lives of nearly six hundred others.

'The other boats' – the First Officer's voice was ragged with shock – 'the others got away safely, sir.'

In the lee of the towering hull, protected from both wind and sea, the other three boats had dropped smoothly to the surface and detached swiftly. Now they circled out in the dark night, with their spotlights probing like long white fingers. One of them staggered over the wildly plunging crests to take off the crew of the stricken lifeboat, and they left the cracked hull to drift away and sink.

'Three boats,' whispered the Captain, 'for thirty rafts.' He knew that there were insufficient shepherds for his flock – and yet he had to send them out, for even above the wind, he thought he could hear the booming artillery barrage of high surf breaking on a rocky shore. Cape Alarm was waiting hungrily for his ship.

'Send the rafts away,' he said quietly, and then again under his breath, 'And God have mercy on us all.'


'Come on, Number 16,' called Samantha. 'Here we are, Number 16.' She gathered them to her, the eighteen passengers who made up the complement of her allotted life-raft. 'Here we are – all together now. No stragglers.'

They were gathered at the heavy mahogany doors that opened on to the open forward deck.

'Be ready,' she told them. 'When we get the word, we have to move fast.'

With the broadsiding seas sweeping the deck and cascading down over the lee, it would be impossible to embark from landing-nets into a raft bobbing alongside.

The rafts were being inflated on the open deck, the passengers hustled across to them and into the canopied interior between waves and then the laden rafts were lifted over the side by the clattering winches and dropped into the quieter waters afforded by the tall bulk of the ship. Immediately, one of the lifeboats picked up the tow and took each raft out to form the pitiful little convoy.

'Right!' the Third Officer burst in through the mahogany doors and held them wide. 'Quickly!' he shouted. 'All together.'

'Let's go, gang!' sang out Samantha, and there was an awkward rush out on to the wet and slippery deck. It was only thirty paces to where the raft crouched like a monstrous yellow bullfrog, gaping its ugly dark mouth, but the wind struck like an axe and Samantha heard them cry out in dismay. Some of them faltered in the sudden merciless cold.

'Come on,' Samantha shouted, pushing those ahead of her, half-supporting Mrs Goldberg's plump body that suddenly felt as heavy and unco-operative as a full sack of wheat. 'Keep going.'

'Let me have her,' shouted the Third Officer, and he grabbed Mrs Goldberg's other arm. Between them they tumbled her through the entrance of the raft.

'Good on you, love,' the officer grinned at Samantha briefly. His smile was attractive and warm, very masculine and likeable, his name was Ken and he was five years her senior. They would probably have become lovers fairly soon, Samantha knew, for he had pursued her furiously since she stepped aboard in New York. Although she knew she did not love him, yet he had succeeded in arousing her and she was slowly succumbing to his obvious charms and her own passionate nature. She had made the decision to have him, and had been merely savouring it up until then. Now, with a pang, she realized that the moment might never come.

'I'll help you with the others.' She raised her voice above the hysterical shriek of the wind.

'Get in,' he shouted back, and swung her brusquely towards the raft. She crept into the crowded interior and looked back at the brightly lit deck that glistened in the arc lamps.

Ken had started back to where one of the women had slipped and fallen. She sprawled helplessly on the wet deck, while her husband stooped over her, trying to lift her back to her feet.

Ken reached them and lifted the woman easily; the three of them were the only ones out on the open deck now, and the two men supported the woman between them, staggering against the heavy sullen roll of the waterlogged hull.

Samantha saw the wave come aboard and she shrieked a warning

'Go back, Ken! For God's sake go back!' But he seemed not to hear her. The wave came aboard; over the windward rail like some huge black slippery sea-monster, it came with a deep silent rush.

'Ken!' she screamed, and he looked over his shoulder an instant before it reached them. Its crest was higher than his head. They could reach neither the raft, nor the shelter of the mahogany doors. She heard the clatter of the donkey-winch and the raft lifted swiftly off the deck, with a swooping tug in her guts. The operator could not let the rushing power of the wave crash into the helpless raft, throwing it against the superstructure or tearing its belly out on the ship's railing, for the frail plastic skin would rupture and it would collapse immediately.

Samantha hurled herself to the entrance and peered down. She saw the sea take the three figures in a black glittering rush. It cut them down, and swept them away. For a moment, she saw Ken clinging to the railing while the waters poured over him, burying his head in a tumbling fall of white and furious water. He disappeared and when the ship rolled sullenly back, shaking herself clear of the water, her decks were empty of any human shape.

With the next roll of the ship, the winch-operator high up in his glassed cabin swung the dangling raft outboard and lowered it swiftly and dexterously to the surface of the sea where one of the life-boats circled anxiously, ready to take them in tow.

Samantha closed and secured the plastic door-cover, then she groped her way through the press of packed and terrified bodies until she found Mrs Golderg.

'Are you crying, dear?' the elderly woman quavered, clinging to her desperately.

'No,' said Samantha, and placed one arm around her shoulders. 'No, I'm not crying.' And with her free hand, she wiped away the icy tears that streamed down her cheeks.


The Trog lifted his headset and looked at Nick through the reeking clouds of cigar smoke.

'Their radio operator has screwed down the key of his set. He's sending a single unbroken homing beam.'

Nick knew what that meant – they had abandoned *Golden Adventurer*. He nodded once but remained silent. He had wedged himself into the doorway from the bridge. The restless impatience that consumed him would not allow him to sit or be still for more than a few moments at a time. He was slowly facing up to the reality of disaster. The dice had fallen against him and his gamble had been with very survival. It was absolutely certain that *Golden Adventurer* would go aground and be beaten into a total wreck by this storm. He could expect a charter from Christy Main to assist *La Mouette* in ferrying the survivors back to Cape Town, but the fee would be a small fraction of the Esso tow fee that he had forsaken for this wild and desperate dash south.

The gamble had failed and he was a broken man. Of course, it would take months still for the effects of his folly to become apparent, but the repayments of his loans and the construction bills for the other tug still building would slowly throttle and bring him down.

'We might still reach her before she goes aground,' said David Allen sturdily, and nobody else on the bridge spoke. 'I mean there could be a backlash of the current close inshore which could hold her off long enough to give us a chance –' His voice trailed off as Nick looked across at him and frowned.

'We are still ten hours away from her, and for Reilly to make the decision to abandon ship, she must have been very close indeed. Reilly is a good man.' Nick had personally selected him to command the *Golden Adventurer*. 'He was a destroyer captain on the North Atlantic run, the youngest in the navy, and then he was ten years with P & O. They pick only the best—' He stopped talking abruptly. He was becoming garrulous. He crossed to the radarscope and adjusted it for maximum range and illumination before looking down into the eye-piece. There was much fuzz and sea clutter, but on the extreme southern edge of the circular screen there showed the solid luminous glow of the cliffs and peaks of Cape Alarm. In good weather they were a mere five hours' steaming away, but now they had left the shelter of that giant iceberg and were staggering and plunging wildly through the angry night. She could have taken more speed, for *Warlock* was built for big seas, but always there was the deadly menace of ice, and Nick had to hold her at this cautionary speed, which meant ten hours more before they were in sight of *Golden Adventurer* – if she was still afloat.

Behind him, the Trog's voice crackled rustily with excitement. 'I'm getting voice – it's only strength one, weak and intermittent. One of the lifeboats is sending on a battery-powered transmitter.' He held his earphones pressed to his head with both hands as he listened.

'They are towing a batch of life-rafts with all survivors aboard to Shackleton Bay. But they've lost a life-raft,' he said. 'It's broken away from their tow-line, and they haven't got enough boats to search for it. They are asking *La Mouette* to keep a watch for it.'

'Is *La Mouette* acknowledging?'

The Trog shook his head. 'She's probably still out of range of this transmission.'

'Very well.' Nick turned back into the bridge. He had still not broken radio silence, and could feel his officers' disapproval, silent but strong. Again he felt the need for human contact, for the warmth and comfort of human conversation and friendly encouragement. He didn't yet have the strength to bear his failure alone.

He stopped beside David Allen and said, 'I have been studying the Admiralty sailing directions for Cape Alarm, David,' and pretended not to notice that the use of his Christian name had brought a startled look and quick colour to the mate's features. He went on evenly, 'the shore is very steep-to and she is exposed to this westerly weather, but there are beaches of pebble and the glass is going up sharply again.'

'Yes, sir,' David nodded enthusiastically. 'I have been watching it.'

'Instead of hoping for a cross-current to hold her off, I suggest you offer a prayer that she goes up on one of those beaches and that the weather moderates before she is beaten to pieces. There is still a chance we can put ground tackle on her before she starts breaking up.'

'I'll say ten Hail Marys, sir,' grinned David. Clearly he was overwhelmed by this sudden friendliness from his silent and forbidding Captain.

'And say another ten that we hold our lead on *La Mouette*,' said Nick, and smiled. It was one of the few times that David Allen had seen him smile, and he was amazed at the change it made to the stern features. They lightened with a charm and warmth and he had not before noticed the clear green of Nick Berg's eyes and how white and even were his teeth.

'Steady as she goes,' said Nick. 'Call me if anything changes,' and he turned away to his cabin.

'Steady as she goes, it is, sir,' said David Allen with a new friendliness in his voice.


The strange and marvellous lights of the *Aurora Australis* quivered and flickered in running streams of red and green fire along the horizon, and formed an incredible backdrop for the death agonies of a great ship.

Captain Reilly looked back through the small portholes of the leading lifeboat and watched her going to her fate. It seemed to him she had never been so tall and beautiful as in these terrible last moments. He had loved many ships, as if each had been a wonderful living creature, but he had loved no other ship more than *Golden Adventurer*, and he felt something of himself dying with her.

He saw her change her action. The sea was feeling the land now, the steep bank of Cape Alarm, and the ship seemed to panic at the new onslaught of wave and wind, as though she knew what fate awaited her there.

She was rolling through thirty degrees, showing the dull red streak of her belly paint as she came up short at the limit of each huge penduluming arc. There was a headland, tall black cliffs dropping sheer into the turbulent waters and it seemed that *Golden Adventurer* must go full on to them, but in the last impossible moments she slipped by, borne on the backlash of the current, avoiding the cliffs and swinging her bows on into the shallow bay beyond where she was hidden from Captain Reilly's view.

He stood for many minutes more, staring back across the leaping wave-tops and in the strange unnatural light of the heavens his face was greenish grey and heavily furrowed with the marks of grief.

Then he sighed once, very deeply, and turned away, devoting all his attention to guiding his pathetic limping little convoy to the safety of Shackleton Bay.

Almost immediately it was apparent that the fates had relented, and given them a favourable inshore current to carry them up on to the coast. The lifeboats were strung out over a distance of three miles, each of them with its string of bloated and clumsy rafts lumbering along in its wake. Captain Reilly had two-way VHF radio contact with each of them, and despite the brutal cold, they were all in good shape and making steady and unexpectedly rapid progress. Three or four hours would be sufficient, he began to hope. They had lost so much life already, and he could not be certain that there would be no further losses until he had the whole party ashore and encamped.

Perhaps the tragic run of bad luck had changed at last, he thought, and he picked up the small VHF radio. perhaps the French tug was in range at last and he began to call her.

'*La Mouette*, do you read me? Come in, *La Mouette* . . .'

The lifeboat was low down on the water and the output of the little set was feeble in the vastness of sea and ice, yet he kept on calling.

They had accustomed themselves to the extravagant action of the disabled liner, her majestic roll and pitch, as regular as a gigantic metronome. They had adjusted to the cold of the unheated interior of the great ship, and the discomfort of her crowded and unsanitary conditions.

They had steeled themselves and tried to prepare themselves mentally for further danger and greater hardship, but not one of the survivors in life-raft Number 16 had imagined anything like this. Even Samantha, the youngest, probably physically the toughest and certainly the one most prepared by her training and her knowledge and love of the sea, had not imagined what it would be like in the raft.

It was utterly dark, not the faintest glimmer of light penetrated the insulated domed canopy, once its entrance was secured against the sea and the wind.

Samantha realized almost immediately how the darkness would crush their morale and, more dangerously, would induce disorientation and vertigo, so she ordered two of them at a time to switch on the tiny locator bulbs on their life-jackets. It gave just a climmering of light, enough to let them see each others' faces and take a little comfort in the proximity of other humans.

Then she arranged their seating, making them form a circle around the sides with all their legs pointing inwards, to give the raft better balance and to ensure that each of them had space to stretch out.

Now that Ken had gone, she had naturally taken command, and, as naturally, the others had turned to her for guidance and comfort. It was Samantha who had gone out through the opening into the brutal exposure of the night to take aboard and secure the tow-rope from the lifeboat. She had come in again half-frozen, shaking in a palsy of cold, with her hands and face numbed. It had taken nearly half an hour of hard massage before feeling returned and she was certain that she had avoided frost-bite.

Then the tow began, and if the movement of the light raft had been wild before, it now became a nightmare of unco-ordinated movement. Each whim of sea and wind was transmitted directly to the huddling circle of survivors, and each time the raft pulled away or sheered off, the tow-rope brought it up with a violent lurch and jerk. The wave crests whipped up by the wind and feeling the press of the land were up to twenty feet high, and the raft swooped over them and dropped heavily into the troughs. She did not have the lateral stability of a keel, so she spun on her axis until the tow-rope jerked her up and she spun the other way. The first of them to start vomiting was Mrs Goldberg and it spurted in a warm jet down the side of Samantha's anorak.

The canopy was almost airtight, except for the small ventilation holes near the apex of the roof, and immediately the sweetish acrid stench of vomit permeated the raft. Within minutes, half a dozen of the other survivors were vomiting also.

It was the cold, however, that frightened Samantha. The cold was the killer. It came up even through the flexible insulated double skin of the deck, and was transferred into their buttocks and legs. It came in through the plastic canopy and frozd the condensation of their breaths, it even froze the vomit on their clothing and on the deck.

'Sing!' Samantha told them. 'Come on, sing! Let's do "Yankee Doodle Dandy", first. You start, Mr Stewart, come on. Clap your hands, clap hands with your neighbour.' She hectored them relentlessly, not allowing any of them to fall into that paralytic state which is not true sleep but the trance caused by rapidly dropping body temperature. She crawled among them, prodding them awake, popping barley sugar from the emergency rations into their mouths.

'Suck and sing!' she commanded them, the sugar would combat the cold and the sea-sickness. 'Clap your hands. Keep moving, we'll be there soon.'

When they could sing no more, she told them stories – and whenever she mentioned the word 'dog' they must all bark and clap their hands, or crow like the rooster, or bray like the donkey.

Samantha's throat was scratchy with singing and talking, and she was dizzy with fatigue and sick with cold, recognizing in herself the first symptoms of disinterest and lethargy, the prelude to giving up. She roused herself, struggling up into the sitting position from where she had slumped.

'I'm going to try and light the stove and get us a hot drink,' she sang out brightly. Around her there was only a mild stir and somebody retched painfully.

'Who's for a mug of beef tea—' she stopped abruptly. Something had changed. It took her a long moment to realize what it was. The sound of the wind had muted and the raft was riding more easily now, it was moving into a more regular rhythm of sweep and fall, without the dreadful jerk of the tow-rope snapping it back.

Frantically she crawled to the entrance of the raft, and with cold crippled fingers she tore at the fastenings.

Outside the dawn had broken into a clear cold sky of palest ethereal pinks and mauves. Although the wind had dropped to a faint whisper, the seas were still big and unruly, and the waters had changed from black to the deep bottle green of molten glass.

The tow-rope had torn away at the connecting shackle, leaving only a dangling flap of plastic. Number 16 had been the last raft in the line being towed by number three, but of the convoy, Samantha could now see no sign – though she crawled out through the entrance and clung precariously to the side of the raft, scanning the wave-caps about her desperately.

There was no sign of a lifeboat, no sight even of the rocky, ice-capped shores of Cape Alarm. They had drifted away, during the night, into the vast and lonely reaches of the Weddell Sea.

Despair cramped her belly muscles, and she wanted to cry out in protest against this further cruelty of fate, but she prevented herself doing so, and stayed out in the clear and frosty air, drawing it in carefully for she knew that it could freeze her lung tissue. She searched and searched until her eyes streamed with the cold and the wind and concentration. Then at last the cold drove her back into the dark and stinking interior of the raft. She fell wearily among the supine and quiescent bodies, and pulled the hood of her anorak more tightly around her head. She knew it would not take long for them to start dying now, and somehow she did not care. Her despair was too intense, she let herself begin sinking into the morass of despondency which gripped all the others, and the cold crept up her legs and arms. She closed her eyes, and then opened them again with a huge effort.

'I'm not going to die,' she told herself firmly. 'I refuse to just lie down and die,' and she struggled up onto her knees. It felt as though she wore a rucksack filled with lead, such was the physical weight of her despair.

She crawled to the central locker that held all their emergency rations and equipment.

The emergency locator transmitter was packed in polyurethane and her fingers were clumsy with cold and the thick mittens, but at last she brought it out. It was the size of a cigar-box, and the instructions were printed on the side of it. She did not need to read them, but switched on the set and replaced it in its slot. Now for forty-eight hours, or until the battery ran out, it would transmit a DF homing-signal on 121,5 Mega Hertz.

It was possible, just possible, that the French tug might pick up that feeble little beam, and track it down to its source. She set it out of her mind, and devoted herself to the Herculean task of trying to heat half a mug of water on the small solid-fuel stove without scalding herself as she held the stove in her lap and balanced it against the raft's motion. While she worked, she searched for the courage and the words to tell the others of their predicament.

The *Golden Adventurer*, deserted of all human beings, her engines dead, but with her deck lights still burning, her wheel locked hard over, and the morse key in the radio room screwed down to transmit a single unbroken pulse, drifted swiftly down on the black rock of Cape Alarm.

The rock was of so hard a type of formation that the cliffs were almost vertical, and even exposed as they were to the eternal onslaught of this mad sea, they had weathered very little. They still retained the sharp vertical edges and the glossy polished planes of cleanly fractured faults.

The sea ran in and hit the cliff without any check. The impact seemed to jar the very air, like the concussion of bursting high explosive, and the sea shot high in a white fury against the unyielding rock of the cliff, before rolling back and forming a reverse swell.

It was these returning echoes from the cliff that held *Golden Adventurer* off the cliff. The shore was so steep-to that it dropped to forty fathoms directly below the cliffs. There was no bottom on which the ship could gut herself.

The wind was blanketed by the cliff and in the eerie stillness of air, she drifted in closer and closer, rolling almost to her limits as the swells took her broadside. Once she actually touched the rock with her superstructure on one of those rolls, but then the echo-wave nudged her away. The next wave pushed her closer, and its smaller weaker offspring pushed back at her. A man could have jumped from a ledge on the cliff on to her deck as she drifted slowly, parallel to the rock.

The cliff ended in an abrupt and vertical headland, where it had calved into three tall pillars of serpentine, as graceful as the sculptured columns of a temple of Olympian Zeus.

Again, *Golden Adventurer* touched one of those pillars, she bumped it lightly with her stern. It scraped paint from her side and crushed in her rail, but then she was past.

The light bump was just sufficient to push her stern round, and she pointed her bows directly into the wide shallow bay beyond the cliffs.

Here a softer, more malleable rock-formation had been eroded by the weather, forming a wide beach of purple-black pebbles, each the size of a man's head and water-worn as round as cannon balls.

Each time the waves rushed up this stony beach, the pebbles struck against each other with a rattling roar, and the brash of rotten and mushy sea ice that filled the bay susurrated and clinked, as it rose and fell with the sea.

Now *Golden Adventurer* was clear of the cliff, she was more fully in the grip of the wind. Although the wind was dying, it still had force enough to move her steadily deeper into the bay, her bows pointed directly at the beach.

Unlike the cliff shore, the bay sloped up gently to the beach and this allowed the big waves to build up into rounded sliding humps. They did not curl and break into white water because the thick layer of brash ice weighted and flattened them, so that these swells joined with the wind to throw the ship at the beach with smoothly gathering impetus.

She took the ground with a great metallic groan of her straining plates and canted over slowly, but the moving pebble beach moulded itself quickly to her hull, giving gradually, as the waves and wind thrust her higher and higher until she was firm aground; then, as the short night ended so the wind fell further, and in sympathy the swells moderated also and the tide drew back, letting the ship settle more heavily.

By noon of that day, *Golden Adventurer* was held firmly by the bows on the curved purple beach, canted over at an angle of 10°. Only her after end was still floating, rising and falling like a see-saw on the swell patterns which still pushed in steadily, but the plummeting air temperature was rapidly freezing the brash ice around her stern into a solid sheet.

The ship stood very tall above the glistening wet beach. Her upperworks were festooned with rime and long rapier-like stalactites of shining translucent ice hung from her scuppers and from the anchor fair-leads.

Her emergency generator was still running, and although there was no human being aboard her, her lights burned gaily and piped music played softly through her deserted public rooms.

Apart from the rent in her side, through which the sea still washed and swirled, there was no external evidence of damage, and beyond her the peaks and valleys of Cape Alarm, so wild and fierce, seemed merely to emphasize her graceful lines and to underline how rich a prize she was, a luscious ripe plum ready for the picking.

Down in her radio room, the transmitting key continued to send out an unbroken beam that could be picked up for five hundred miles around.


Two hours of deathlike sleep – and then Nick Berg woke with a wild start, knowing that something of direct consequence was about to happen. But it took fully ten seconds for him to realize where he was.

He stumbled from his bunk, and he knew he had not slept long enough. His skull was stuffed with the cottonwool of fatigue, and he swayed on his feet as he shaved in the shower, trying to steam himself awake with the scalding water.

When he went out on to the bridge, the Trog was still at his equipment. He looked up at Nick for a moment with his little rheumy pink eyes, and it was clear that he had not slept at all. Nick felt a prick of shame at his own indulgence.

'We are still inside *La Mouette*,' said the Trog, and turned back to his set. 'I reckon we have an edge of almost a hundred miles.'

Angel appeared on the bridge, bearing a huge tray, and the saliva jetted from under Nick's tongue as he smelled it.

'I did a little special for your brekker, Skipper,' said Angel. 'I call it "Eggs on Angel's Wings".'

'I'm buying,' said Nick, and turned back to the Trog with his mouth full and chewing. 'What of the *Adventurer*?'

'She's still sending a DF, but her position has not altered in almost three hours.'

'What do you mean?' Nick demanded, and swallowed heavily.

'No change in position.'

'Then she's aground,' Nick muttered, the food in his hand forgotten, and at that moment David Allen hurried on to the bridge still shrugging on his pea-jacket. His eyes were puffy and his hair was hastily wetted and combed, but spiky at the back from contact with his pillow. It had not taken him long to hear that the Captain was on the bridge. 'And in one piece, if her transmitter is still sending.'

'It looks like those Hail Marys worked, David.' Nick flashed his rare smile and David slapped the polished teak top of the chart table.

'Touch wood, and don't dare the devil.'

Nick felt his early despair slipping away with his fatigue, and he took another big mouthful and savoured it as he strode to the front windows and stared ahead.

The sea had flattened dramatically, but a weak and butter-yellow sun low on the horizon gave no warmth, and Nick glanced up at the thermometer and read the outside air temperature at minus thirty degrees.

Down here below 60° south, the weather was so unstable, caught up on the wheel of endlessly circling atmospheric depressions, that a gale could rise in minutes and drop to a flat calm almost as swiftly. Yet foul weather was the rule. For a hundred days and more each year, the wind was at gale-force or above. The photographs of Antarctica always gave a completely false impression of fine days with the sun sparkling on pristine snow fields and lovely towering icebergs. The truth was that you cannot take photographs in a blizzard or a white-out.

Nick distrusted this calm, and yet found himself praying that it would hold. He wanted to increase speed again, and was on the point of taking that chance, when the officer of the watch called a sharp alteration of course.

Ahead of them, Nick made out the sullen swirl of hidden ice below the surface, like a lurking monster, and as *Warlock* altered course to avoid it, the ice broke the surface. Black ice, striated with bands of glacial mud, ugly and deadly. Nick did not pass the order for the increase in speed.

'We should be raising Cape Alarm within the hour,' David Allen gloated beside him. 'If this visibility holds.'

'It won't,' said Nick. 'We'll have fog pretty soon,' and he indicated the surface of the sea, which was beginning to steam, emitting ghostly tendrils and eddies of seafret, as the difference between sea and air temperature widened.

'We'll be at the *Golden Adventurer* in four hours more.' David was bubbling with renewed excitement, and he slapped the teak table again. 'With your permission, sir, I'll go down and double-check the rocket-lines and tow equipment.'

While the air around them thickened into a ghostly white soup, and blotted out all visibility to a few hundred yards, Nick paced the bridge like a caged lion, his hands clasped behind his back and a black unlit cheroot clamped between his teeth. He broke his pacing every time that the Trog intercepted another transmission from either Christy Main, Jules Levoisin or Captain Reilly on his VHF radio.

At mid-morning, Reilly reported that he and his slow convoy had reached Shackleton Bay without further losses, that they were taking full advantage of the moderating weather to set up an encampment, and he ended by urging

*La Mouette* to keep a watch on 121,5 Mega Hertz to try and locate the missing life-raft that had broken away during the night. *La Mouette* did not acknowledge.

'They aren't reading on the VHF,' grunted the Trog.

Nick thought briefly of the hapless souls adrift in this cold, and decided that they would probably not last out the day unless the temperature rose abruptly. Then he dismissed the thought and concentrated on the exchanges between Christy Main and *La Mouette*.

The two parties had diametrically changed their bargaining standpoints.

While *Golden Adventurer* was adrift on the open sea, and any salvage efforts would mean that the tug should merely put a rocket-line across her, pass a messenger wire to carry the big steel hawser and then take her in tow, Jules Levoisin had pressed for Lloyd's Open Form 'No cure no pay' contract.

Since the 'cure' was almost certain, 'pay' would follow as a matter of course. The amount of payment would be fixed by the arbitration of the committee of Lloyd's in London under the principles of international maritime law, and would be a percentage of the salved value of the vessel. The percentage decided upon by the arbitrator would depend upon the difficulties and dangers that the salvor had overcome. A clever salvor in an arbitration court could paint a picture of such daring and ingenuity that the award would be in millions of dollars.

Christy Main had been desperately trying to avoid a 'No cure no pay' contract. They had been trying to wheedle Levoisin into a daily hire and bonus contract, since this would limit the total cost of the operation, but they had been met by a Gallic acquisitiveness – right up to the moment when it became clear that *Golden Adventurer* had gone aground.

When that happened, the roles were completely reversed. Jules Levoisin, with a note of panic in his transmission, had immediately withdrawn his offer to go Lloyd's Open Form. For now the 'cure' was far from certain, and the *Adventurer* might already be a total wreck, beaten to death on the rocks of Cape Alarm, in which case there would be 'no pay'.

Now Levoisin was desperately eager to strike a daily hire contract, including the run from South America and the ferrying of survivors back to civilization. He was offering his services at $10,000 a day, plus a bonus of 2½% of any salved value of the vessel. They were fair terms, for Jules Levoisin had given up the shining dream of millions and he had returned to reality.

However, Christy Main, who had previously been offering a princely sum for daily hire, had just as rapidly withdrawn that offer.

'We will accept Lloyd's Open Form, including ferrying of survivors,' they declared on Channel 16.

'Conditions on site have changed,' Jules Levoisin sent back, and the Trog got another good fix on him.

'We are head-reaching on him handsomely,' he announced with satisfaction, blinking his pink eyes rapidly while Nick marked the new relative positions on the chart.

The bridge of *Warlock* was once again crowded with every officer who had an excuse to be there. They were all in working rig, thick blue boiler suits and heavy sea boots, bulked up with jerseys and balaclava helmets, and they watched the plot with total fascination, arguing quietly among themselves.

David Allen came in carrying a bundle of clothing. 'I've got working rig for you, sir. I borrowed it from the Chief Engineer. You are about the same size.'

'Does the Chief know?' Nick asked.

'Not exactly, I just borrowed it from his cabin—'

'Well done, David,' Nick chuckled. 'Please put it in my day cabin.' He felt himself warming more and more to the younger man.

'Captain, sir,' the Trog sang out suddenly. 'I'm getting another transmission. It's only strength one, and it's on 121,5 Mega Hertz.'

'Oh, shit?' David Allen paused in the entrance to the Captain's day cabin. 'Oh, shit?' he repeated, and his expression was stricken. 'It's that bloody missing life-raft.'

'Relative bearing?' snapped Nick angrily.

'She bears 280° relative and 045° magnetic,' the Trog answered instantly, and Nick felt his anger flare again.

The life-raft was somewhere out on their port beam, eighty degrees off their direct course to the *Golden Adventurer*.

The consternation on the bridge was carried in a babble of voices, that Nick silenced with a single black glance – and they stared at the plot in dismayed hush.

The position of each of the tugs was flagged with a coloured pin – and there was another, a red flag, for the position of the *Golden Adventurer*. It was so close ahead of them now, and their lead over *La Mouette* so slender, that one of the younger officers could not remain silent.

'If we go to the raft, we'll be handing it to the bloody frog on a plate.'

The words ended the restraint and they began to argue again, but in soft controlled tones. Nick Berg did not look up at them, but remained bowed over the chart, with his fist on the table-top bunched so fiercely that the knuckles were ivory white.

'Christ, they have probably all had it by now. We'd be throwing it all away for a bunch of frozen stiffs.'

'There is no telling how far off course they are, those sets have a range of a hundred miles.'

'*La Mouette* will waltz away with it.'

'We could pick them up later – after we put a line on *Golden Adventurer*.'

Nick straightened slowly and took the cheroot out of his mouth. He looked across at David Allen and spoke levelly, without change of expression.

'Number One, will you please instruct your junior officers in the rule of the sea.'

David Allen was silent for a moment, then he answered softly 'The preservation of human life at sea takes precedent over all other considerations.'

'Very well, Mr Allen,' Nick nodded. 'Alter 80° to port and maintain a homing course on the emergency transmission.'

He turned away to his cabin. He could control his anger until he was alone, and then he turned and crashed his fist into the panel above his desk.

Out on the navigation bridge behind him nobody spoke nor moved for fully thirty seconds, then the Third Officer protested weakly.

'But we are so close!'

David Allen roused himself, and spoke angrily to the helmsman.

'New course 045° magnetic.'

And as *Warlock* heeled to the change, he flung the armful of clothing bitterly onto the chart table and went to stand beside the Trog.

'Corrections for course to intercept?' he asked.

'Bring her on to 050°,' the Trog instructed, and then cackled without mirth. 'First you call him an ice-water pisser – now you squeal like a baby because he answers a Mayday.'

And David Allen was silent as the *Warlock* turned away into the fog, every revolution of her big variable-pitch propellers carrying her directly away from her prize, and *La Mouette*'s triumphant transmissions taunted them as the Frenchman raced across the last of the open water that separated her from Cape Alarm, bargaining furiously with the owners in London.

The fog seemed so thick that it could be chopped into chunks like cheese. From the bridge it was not possible to see *Warlock*'s tall bows. Nick groped his way into it like a blind man in an unfamiliar room, and all around him the ice pressed closely.

They were in the area of huge tabular icebergs again. The echoes of the great ice islands flared green and malevolently on the radar screen and the awful smell and taste of the ice was on every breath they drew.

'Radio Officer?' Nick asked tensely, without taking his eyes from the swirling fog curtains ahead.

'Still no contact,' the Trog answered, and Nick shuffled on his feet. The fog had mesmerized him, and he felt the shift of vertigo in his head. For a moment he had the illusion that his ship was listing heavily to one side, almost as though it were a space vehicle. He forcibly rejected the hallucination and stared fixedly ahead, tensing himself for the first green loom of ice through the fog.

'No contact for nearly an hour now,' David muttered beside him.

'Either the battery on their DF has run down, or they have snagged ice and sunk—' volunteered the Third Officer, raising his voice just enough for Nick to hear.

'—or else their transmitter is blanketed by an iceberg,' Nick finished for him, and there was silence on the bridge for another ten minutes, except for the quietly requested changes of course that kept *Warlock* zigzagging between the unseen but omnipresent icebergs.

'All right,' Nick made the decision at last. 'We'll have to accept that the raft has floundered and break off the search.' And there was a stir of reawakening interest and enthusiasm. 'Pilot, new course to *Golden Adventurer*, please, and we'll increase to fifty per cent power.'

'We could still beat the Frog.' Again speculation and rising hope buoyed the young officers. 'She could run into ice and have to reduce—' They wished misfortune on *La Mouette* and her Captain, and even the ship beneath Nick's feet seemed to regain its lightness and vibrancy as she turned back for a last desperate run for the prize.

'All right, David,' Nick spoke quietly. 'One thing is certain now, we aren't going to reach the prize ahead of Levoisin. So we are going to play our ace now—' he was about to elaborate, when the Trog's voice squeaked with excitement.

'New contact, on 121,5,' he cried, and the dismay on the bridge was a tangible thing.

'Christ!' said the Third Officer. 'Why won't they just lie down and die!'

'The transmission was blanked by that big berg north of us,' the Trog guessed. 'They are close now. It won't take long.'

'Just long enough to make certain we miss the prize.'

The berg was so big that it formed its own weather system about it causing eddies and currents of both air and water, enough to stir the fog.

The fog opened like a theatre curtain, and directly ahead there was a heart-stopping vista of green and blue ice, with darker strata of glacial mud banding cliffs which disappeared into the higher layers of fog above as though reaching to the very heavens. The sea had carved majestic arches of ice and deep caverns from the foot of the cliff.

'There they are!'

Nick snatched the binoculars from the canvas bin and focused on the dark specks that stood out so clearly against the backdrop of glowing ice.

'No,' he grunted. Fifty emperor penguins formed a tight bunch on one of the flat floes, big black birds standing nearly as tall as a man's shoulder; even in the lens, they were deceptively humanoid.

*Warlock* passed them closely, and with sudden fright they dropped on to their bellies and used their stubby wings to skid themselves across the floe, and drop into the still and steaming waters below the cliff. The floe eddied and swung on the disturbance of *Warlock*'s passing.

*Warlock* nosed on through solid standing banks of fog and into abrupt holes of clear air where the mirages and optical illusions of Antarctica's flawed air maddened them with their inconsistencies, transforming flocks of penguins into herds of elephants or bands of waving men, and placing in their path phantom rocks and bergs which disappeared again swiftly as they approached.

The emergency transmissions from the raft faded and silenced, then beeped again loudly into the silence of the bridge, and seconds later were silent again.

'God damn them,' David swore quietly and bitterly, his cheeks pink with frustration. 'Where the hell are they? Why don't they put up a flare or a rocket?' And nobody answered as another white fog monster enveloped the ship, muting all sound aboard her.

'I'd like to try shaking them up with the horn, sir,' he said, as *Warlock* burst once more into sparkling and blinding sunlight. Nick grunted acquiescence without lowering his binoculars.

David reached up for the red-painted foghorn handle above his head, and the deep booming blast of sound, the characteristic voice of an ocean-going salvage tug, reverberated through the fog, seeming to make it quiver with the volume of the sound. The echoes came crashing back off the ice cliffs of the bergs like the thunder of the skies.


Samantha held the solid-fuel stove in her lap using the detachable fibreglass lid of the locker as a tray. She was heating half a pint of water in the aluminium pannikin, balancing carefully against the wallowing motion of the raft.

The blue flame of the stove lit the dim cavern of plastic and radiated a feeble glow of warmth insufficient to sustain life. They were dying already.

Gavin Stewart held his wife's head against his chest, and bowed his own silver head over it. She had been dead for nearly two hours now, and her body had already cooled, the face peaceful and waxen.

Samantha could not bear to look across at them, she crouched over the stove and dropped a cube of beef into the water, stirring it slowly and blinking against the tears of penetrating cold. She felt thin watery mucus run down her nostrils and it required an effort to lift her arm and wipe it away on her sleeve. The beef tea was only a little above blood warmth, but she could not waste time and fuel on heating it further.

The metal pannikin passed slowly from mittened hand to numbed and clumsy hand. They slurped the warm liquid and passed it on reluctantly, though there were some who had neither the strength nor the interest to take it.

'Come on, Mrs Goldberg,' Samantha whispered painfully. The cold seemed to have closed her throat, and the foul air under the canopy made her head ache with grinding, throbbing pain. 'You must drink—' Samantha touched the woman's face, and cut herself off. The flesh had a putty-like texture and was cooling swiftly. It took long lingering minutes for the shock to pass, then carefully Samantha pulled the hood of the old woman's parka down over her face. Nobody else seemed to have noticed. They were all too far sunk into lethargy.

'Here,' whispered Samantha to the man beside her – and she pressed the pannikin into his hands, folding his stiff fingers around the metal to make certain he had hold of it. 'Drink it before it cools.'

The air around her seemed to tremble suddenly with a great burst of sound, like the bellow of a dying bull, or the rumble of cannon balls across the roof of the sky. For long moments, Samantha thought her mind was playing tricks with her, and only when it came again did she raise her head.

'Oh God,' she whispered. 'They've come. It's going to be all right. They've come to save us.'

She crawled to the locker, slowly and stiffly as an old woman.

'They've come. It's all right, gang, it's going to be all right,' she mumbled, and she lit the globe on her life-jacket. In its pale glow, she found the packet of phosphorus flares.

'Come on now, gang. Let's hear it for Number 16.' She tried to rouse them as she struggled with the fastenings of the canopy. 'One more cheer,' she whispered, but they were still unresponsive, and as she fumbled her way out into the freezing fog, the tears that ran down her cheeks were not from the cold.

She looked up uncomprehendingly, it seemed that from the sky around her tumbled gigantic cascades of ice, sheer sheets of translucent menacing green ice. It took her moments to realize that the life-raft had drifted in close beneath the precipitous lee of a tabular berg. She felt tiny and inconsequential beneath that ponderous mountain of brittle glassy ice.

For what seemed an eternity, she stood, with her face lifted, staring upwards – then again the air resonated with the deep gut-shaking bellow of the siren. It filled the swirling fog-banks with solid sound that struck the cliff of ice above her and shattered into booming echoes, that bounded from wall to wall and rang through the icy caverns and crevices that split the surface of the great berg.

Samantha held aloft one of the phosphorus flares, and it required all the strength of her frozen arm to rip the igniter tab. The flare spluttered and streamed acrid white smoke, then burst into the dazzling crimson fire that denotes distress at sea. She stood like a tiny statue of liberty, holding the flare aloft in one hand and peering with streaming eyes into the sullen fog-banks.

Again the animal bellow of the siren boomed through the milky, frosted air; it was so close that it shook Samantha's body the way the wind moves the wheat on the hillside, then it went on to collide solidly with the cliff of ice that hung above her.

The working of sea and wind, and the natural erosion of changing temperatures had set tremendous forces at work within the glittering body of the berg. Those forces had found a weak point, a vertical fault line, that ran like an axe-stroke from the flattened tableland of the summit, five hundred feet down to the moulded bottom of the berg far below the surface.

The booming sound waves of *Warlock*'s horn found a sympathetic resonance within the body of the mountain that set the ice on each side of the fault vibrating in different frequencies.

Then the fault sheared, with a brittle cracking explosion of glass bursting under pressure, and the fault opened. One hundred million tons of ice began to move as it broke away from the mother berg. The block of ice that the berg calved was in itself a mountain, a slab of solid ice twice the size of Saint Paul's cathedral – and as it swung out and twisted free, new pressures and forces came into play within it, finding smaller faults and flaws so that ice burst within ice and tore itself apart, as though dynamited with tons of high explosive.

The air itself was filled with hurtling ice, some pieces the size of a locomotive and others as small and as sharp and as deadly as steel swords; and below this plunging toppling mass, the tiny yellow plastic raft bobbed helplessly.


'There,' called Nick. 'On the starboard beam.' The phosphorus distress flare lit the fog-banks internally with a fiery cherry red and threw grotesque patterns of light against the belly of lurking cloud. David Allen blew one last triumphant blast on the siren.

'New heading 150°,' Nick told the helmsman and *Warlock* came around handily, and almost instantly burst from the enveloping bank of fog into another arena of open air.

Half a mile away, the life-raft bobbed like a fat yellow toad beneath a glassy green wall of ice. The top of the iceberg was lost in the fog high above, and the tiny human figure that stood erect on the raft and held aloft the brilliant crimson flare was an insignificant speck in this vast wilderness of fog and sea and ice.

'Prepare to pick up survivors, David,' said Nick, and the mate hurried away while Nick moved to the wing of the bridge from where he could watch the rescue.

Suddenly Nick stopped and lifted his head in bewilderment. For a moment he thought it was gunfire, then the explosive crackling of sound changed to a rending shriek as of the tearing of living fibre when a giant redwood tree is falling to the axes. The volume of sound mounted into a rumbling roar, the unmistakeable roar of a mountain in avalanche.

'Good Christ!' whispered Nick, as he saw the cliff of ice begin to change shape. Slowly sagging outwards, it seemed to fold down upon itself. Faster and still faster it fell, and the hissing splinters of bursting ice formed a dense swirling cloud, while the cliff leaned further and further beyond its point of equilibrium and at last collapsed and lifted pressure waves from the green waters that raced out one behind the other, flinging *Warlock*'s bows high as she rode them and then nosed down into the troughs between.

Since Nick's oath, nobody had spoken on the bridge. They clutched for balance at the nearest support and stared in awe at that incredible display of careless might, while the water still churned and creamed with the disturbance and pieces of broken jagged ice, some the size of a country house, bobbed to the surface and revolved slowly, finding their balance as they swirled and bumped against each other.

'Closer,' snapped Nick. 'Get as close as you can.'

Of the yellow life-raft there was no longer any sign. Jagged shards of ice had ripped open its fragile skin and the grinding, tumbling lumps had trodden it and its pitiful human cargo deep beneath the surface.

'Closer,' urged Nick. If by a miracle anybody had survived that avalanche, then they had four minutes left of life, and Nick pushed *Warlock* into the still rolling and roiling mass of broken ice – pushing it open with ice-strengthened bows.

Nick flung open the bridge doors beside him and stepped out into the freezing air of the open wing. He ignored the cold, buoyed up by new anger and frustration. He had paid the highest price to make this rescue, he had given up his chance at *Golden Adventurer* for the lives of a handful of strangers, and now, at this last moment, they had been snatched away from him. His sacrifice had been in vain, and the terrible waste of it all appalled him. Because there was no other outlet for his feelings, he let waves of anger sweep over him and he shouted at David Allen's little group on the foredeck.

'Keep your eyes open. I want those people—'

Red caught his eye, a flash of vivid red, seen through the green water, becoming brighter and more hectic as it rose to the surface.

'Both engines half astern' he screamed. And *Warlock* stopped dead as the twin propellers changed pitch and bit into the water, pulling her up in less than her own length.

In a small open area of green water the red object broke out. Nick saw a human head in a red anorak hood, supported by the thick inflated life-jacket. The head was thrown back, exposing a face as white and glistening with wetness as the deadly ice that surrounded it. The face was that of a young boy, smooth and beardless, and quite incredibly beautiful.

'Get him,' Nick yelled, and at the sound of his voice the eyes in that beautiful face opened. Nick saw they were a misty green and unnaturally large in the glistening pale oval framed by the crimson hood.

David Allen was racing back, carrying life-ring and line.

'Hurry, God damn you.' The boy was still alive, and Nick wanted him. He wanted him as fiercely as he had wanted anything in his life, he wanted at least this one young life in return for all he had sacrificed. He saw that the boy was watching him. 'Come on, David,' he shouted again.

'Here!' called David, bracing himself at the ship's rail and he threw the life-ring. He threw it with an expert round arm motion that sent it skimming forty feet to where the hooded head bobbed on the agitated water. He threw it so accurately that it hit the bobbing figure a glancing blow on the shoulder and then plopped into the water alongside, almost nudging the boy.

'Grab it,' yelled Nick. 'Grab hold!'

The face turned slowly, and the boy lifted a gloved hand clear of the surface, but the movement was blunderingly unco-ordinated.

'There. It's right next to you,' David encouraged. 'Grab it, man!'

The boy had been in the water for almost two minutes already, he had lost control of his body and limbs, he made two inconclusive movements with the raised hand, one actually bumped the ring but he could not hold it and slowly the life-ring bobbed away from him.

'You bloody idiot,' stormed Nick. 'Grab it!' And those huge green eyes turned back to him, looking up at him with total resignation of defeat, one stiff arm still raised – almost a farewell salute.

Nick did not realize what he was going to do until he had shrugged off his coat and kicked away his shoes; then he realized that if he stopped to think about it, he would not go.

He jumped feet first, throwing himself far out to miss the rail below him, and as the water closed over his head he experienced a terrified sense of disbelief at the cold.

It seized his chest in a vice that choked the air from his lungs, it drove needles of agony deep into his forehead, and blinded him with the pain as he rose to the surface again. The cold rushed through his light clothing, it crushed his testicles and his stomach was filled with nausea. The marrow in the bones of his legs and arms ached so that he found it difficult to force his limbs to respond, but he struck out for the floating figure.

It was only forty feet, but halfway there he was seized by a panic that he was not going to make it. He clenched his teeth and fought the icy water as though it was a mortal enemy, but it sapped away his strength with the heat of his body.

He struck the floating figure with one outflung arm before he realized he had reached him, and he clung desperately to him, peering up at *Warlock*'s deck.

David Allen had retrieved the ring by its line and he threw it again. The cold had slowed Nick down so that he could not avoid the ring and it struck him on the forehead, but he felt no pain, there was no feeling in his face or feet or hands.

The fleeting seconds counted out the life left to them as he struggled with the inert figure, slowly losing command of his own limbs as he tried to fit the ring over the boy's body. He did not accomplish it. He got the boy's head and one arm through, and he knew he could do no more.

'Pull,' he screamed in rising panic, and his voice was remote and echoed strangely in his own ears.

He took a twist of line around his arm, for his fingers could no longer hold, and he clung with the remains of his strength as they dragged them in.

Jagged ice brushed and snatched at them, but he held the boy with his free arm.

'Pull,' he whispered. 'Oh, for God's sake, pull!' And then they were bumping against *Warlock*'s steel side, were being lifted free of the water, the twist of line smearing the wet skin from his forearm, staining his sleeve with blood that was instantly dissolved to pink by sea water. He felt no pain.

With the other arm, he hung on to the boy, holding him from slipping out of the life-ring. He did not feel the hands that grabbed at him. There was no feeling in his legs and he collapsed face forward, but David caught him before he struck the deck and they hustled him into the steaming warmth of Angel's galley, his legs dragging behind him.

'Are you okay, Skipper?' David kept demanding, and when Nick tried to reply, his jaw was locked in a frozen rictus and great shuddering spasms shook his whole body.

'Get their clothes off,' grated Angel, and, with an easy swing of his heavily muscled shoulders, lifted the boy's body on to the galley table and laid it out face upwards. With a single sweep of a Solingen steel butcher's knife he split the crimson anorak from neck to crutch and stripped it away.

Nick found his voice, it was ragged and broken by the convulsions of frozen muscles.

'What the hell are you doing, David? Get your arse on deck and get this ship on course for *Golden Adventurer*,' he grated, and would have added something a little more forceful, but the next convulsion caught him, and anyway David Allen had already left.

'You'll be all right.' Angel did not even glance up at Nick as he worked with the knife, ripping away layer after layer of the boy's clothing. 'A tough old dog like you – but I think we've got a ripe case of hypothermia here.'

Two of the seamen were helping Nick out of his sodden clothing, the cloth crackled with the thin film of ice that had already formed. Nick winced with the pain of returning circulation to half-frozen hands and feet.

'Okay,' he said, standing naked in the middle of the galley and scrubbing at himself with a rough towel. 'I'll be all right now, return to your stations.' He crossed to the kitchen range, tottering like a drunk, and welcomed the blast of heat from it, rubbing warmth into himself, still shaking and shuddering, his body mottled puce and purple with cold and his genitals shrunken and drawn up into the dense black bush at his crotch.

'Coffee's boiling. Get yourself a hot drink, Skip,' Angel told him, glancing up at Nick from his work. He ran a quick appreciative glance over Nick's body, taking in the wide rangy shoulders, the dark curls of damp hair that covered his chest, and the trim lines of hard muscle that moulded his belly and waist.

'Put lots of sugar in it – it will warm you the best possible way,' Angel instructed him, and returned his attention to the slim young body on the table.

Angel had put aside his camp airs, and worked with the brusque efficiency of a man who had been trained at his task.

Then suddenly he stopped and stood back for a moment. 'Would you believe! No fun gun!' Angel sighed.

Nick turned just as Angel spread a thick woollen blanket over the pale naked body on the table and began to massage it vigorously.

'You better leave us girls alone together, Skipper,' said Angel with a sweet smile and a twinkle of his diamond earrings, and Nick was left with the memory of a single fleeting glimpse of the stunningly lovely body of a young woman below the pale face and the thick sodden head of copper and gold hair.


Nick Berg was swaddled in a grey woollen blanket, over the boiler suit and bulky jerseys. His feet were in thick Norwegian trawlerman's socks and heavy rubber working boots. He held a china mug of almost boiling coffee in both hands, bending over it to savour the aroma of the steam. It was the third cup he had drunk in the last hour – and yet the shivering spasms still shook him every few minutes.

David Allen had moved his canvas chair across the bridge so he could watch the Trog and work the ship at the same time. Nick could see the loom of the black rock cliffs of Cape Alarm close on their port beam.

The morse beam squealed suddenly, a long sequence of code to which every man on the bridge listened with complete attention, but it needed the Trog to say it for them.

'*La Mouette* has reached the prize.' He seemed to take a perverse relish in seeing their expressions. 'She's beaten us to it, lads. 12½% salvage to her crew—'

'I want it word for word,' snapped Nick irritably, and the Trog grinned spitefully at him before bowing over his pad.

'*La Mouette* to Christy Main. *Golden Adventurer* is hard aground, held by ice and receding tides. Stop. Ice damage to plating appears to be below surface. Stop. Hull is flooded and open to sea. Stop. Under no circumstances will Lloyd's Open Form be acceptable. Emphasize importance of beginning salvage work immediately. Stop. Worsening weather and sea conditions. My final hire offer of $8000 *per diem* plus 2½% of salvaged value open until 1435 GMT. Standing by.'

Nick lit one of his cheroots and irrelevantly decided he must conserve them in future. He had opened his last box that morning. He frowned through the blue smoke and pulled the blanket closer around his shoulders.

Jules Levoisin was playing it tough and hard now. He was dictating terms and setting ultimatums. Nick's own policy of silence was paying off. Probably by now, Jules felt completely safe that he was the only salvage tug within two thousand miles, and he was holding a big-calibre gun to Christy Main's head.

Jules had seen the situation of the *Golden Adventurer*'s hull. If he had been certain of effecting salvage – no, even if there had been a fifty-fifty chance of a good salvage, Jules would have gone Open Form.

So Jules was not happy with his chances, and he had the shrewdest and most appraising eye in the salvage business. It was a tough one then. *Golden Adventurer* was probably held fast by the quicksand effect of beach and ice, and *La Mouette* could build up a mere nine thousand horse-power. It would mean throwing out ground-tackle, putting power on *Adventurer*'s pumps – the problems and solutions passed in review through Nick's mind. It was going to be a tough one, but *Warlock* had twenty-two thousand rated horse-power and a dozen other high cards.

He glanced at his gold Rolex Oyster, and he saw that Jules had set a two-hour ultimatum.

'Radio Officer,' he said quietly, and every man on the bridge stiffened and swayed closer, so as not to miss a word.

'Open the telex line direct to Christy Main, London, and send quote "Personal for Duncan Alexander from Nicholas Berg Master of *Warlock*. Stop. I will be alongside *Golden Adventurer* in one hour forty minutes. Stop. I make firm offer Lloyd's Open Form Contract Salvage. Stop. Offer closes 1300 GMT." '

The Trog looked up at him startled, and blinked his pink eyes swiftly.

'Read it back,' snapped Nick, and the Trog did it in a high penetrating voice and when he finished, waited quizzically, as if expecting Nick to cancel.

'Send it,' said Nick, and rose to his feet. 'Mr Allen,' he turned to David, 'I want you and the Chief Engineer in my day cabin right away.'

The buzz of excitement and speculation began before Nick had closed the door behind him.

David knocked and followed him three minutes later, and Nick looked up from the notes he was making.

'What are they saying?' Nick asked. 'That I am crazy?'

'They're just kids,' shrugged David. 'What do they know?'

'They know plenty, and they're right. I am crazy to go Open Form on a site unseen! But it's the craziness of a man with no other option. Sit down, David.

'When I made the decision to leave Cape Town on the chance of this job – that was when I did the crazy thing.' Nick could no longer keep the steely silence. He had to say it, to talk it out. 'I was throwing dice for my whole bundle. When I turned down the Esso tow, that was when I went on the line for the whole company, *Warlock* and her sister, the whole thing depended on the cash from the Esso tow—'

'I see,' muttered David, and his colour was pink and high, embarrassed by this confidence from Nick Berg.

'What I am doing now is risking nothing. If I lose now, if I fail to pull *Golden Adventurer* out of there, I have lost nothing that is not already forfeit.'

'We could have offered daily hire at a better rate than *La Mouette*,' David suggested.

'No. Duncan Alexander is my enemy. The only way I can get the contract is to make it so attractive, that he has no alternative. If he refuses my offer of Open Form, I will take him up before Lloyd's Committee and his own shareholders. I will make a rope of his own guts and hoist it around his neck. He has to go with me – whereas, if I had offered daily hire at a few thousand dollars less than *La Mouette*—' Nick broke off, reached for the box of cheroots on the corner of his desk, then arrested the gesture and swivelled in his chair at the heavy knock on the cabin door.

'Come!'

Vin Baker's overalls were pristine blue, but the bandage around his head was smeared with engine grease, and he had recovered all the bounce and swagger that Nick had banged out of him against the engine-room windows.

'Jesus!' he said. 'I hear you just flipped. I hear you blew your mind and jumped overboard – and when they fished you out, you up and went Open Form on a bomber that's beating herself to death on Cape Alarm.'

'I'd explain it to you,' offered Nick solemnly, 'only I don't know enough words of one syllable.' The Chief Engineer grinned wickedly at that and Nick went on quickly, 'Just believe me when I tell you that I'm playing with someone else's chips. I'm not risking anything I haven't lost already.'

'That's good business,' the Australian agreed handsomely, and helped himself to one of Nick's precious cheroots.

'Your share of 12½% of daily hire is peanuts and apple jelly,' Nick went on.

'Too right,' Vin Baker agreed, and hoisted at his waistline with his elbows.

'But if we snatch *Golden Adventurer* and if we can plug her and pump her out, and if we can keep her afloat for three thousand miles, there will be a couple of big "M's" – and that's beef and potatoes.'

'You know something,' Vin Baker grunted. 'For a Pommy, I'm beginning to like the sound of your voice.' He said it reluctantly and shook his head, as if he didn't really believe it.

'All I want from you now,' Nick told him, 'are your plans for getting power on to *Golden Adventurer*'s pumps and anchor-winch. If she's up on the beach, we will have to kedge her off and we won't have much time.'

Kedging off was the technique of using a ship's own anchor and power winch to assist the pull of the tug in dragging her off a stranding.

Vin Baker waved the cheroot airily. 'Don't worry about that, I'm here.' And at that moment the Trog put his head through the doorway again, this time without knocking.

'I have an urgent and personal for you, skipper.' He brandished the telex flimsy like a royal flush in spades.

Nick glanced through it once, then read it aloud:

'Master of *Warlock* from Christy Main. Your offer Lloyd's Open Form

"No Cure No Pay" accepted. Stop. You are hereby appointed main salvage contractor for wreck of *Golden Adventurer*. ENDS.'

Nick grinned with that rare wide irresistible flash of very white teeth. 'And so, gentlemen, it looks as though we are still in business – but the devil knows for just how much longer.'

*Warlock* rounded the headland, where the three black pillars of serpentine rock stood into a lazy green sea, across which low oily swells marched in orderly ranks to push in gently against the black cliffs.

They came round to the sudden vista of the wide, ice-choked bay. The abandoned hulk of *Golden Adventurer* was so majestic, so tall and beautiful that not even the savage mountains could belittle her. She looked like an illustration from a child's book of fairy tales, a lovely ice ship, glistening and glittering in the yellow sunlight.

'She's a beauty,' whispered the Chief Engineer, and his voice captured the sorrow they all felt for a great ship in mortal distress. To every single man on the bridge of *Warlock*, a ship was a living thing for which at best they could feel love and admiration; even the dirtiest old tramp roused a grudging affection. But *Golden Adventurer* was like a lovely woman. She was something rare and special, and all of them felt it.

For Nick Berg, the bond was much more deeply felt. She was child of his inspiration, he had watched her lines take shape on the naval architect's drawing-board, he had seen her keel laid and her bare skeleton fleshed out with lovingly worked steel, and he had watched the woman who had once been his wife speak the blessing and then smash the bottle against her bows, laughing in the sunlight while the wine spurted and frothed.

She was his ship, and now, as he would never have believed possible, his destiny depended upon her.

He looked away from her at last to where *La Mouette* waited in the mouth of the bay at the edge of the ice. In contrast to the liner, she was small and squat and ugly, like a wrestler with all the weight in his shoulders. Greasy black smoke rose straight into the pale sky from her single stack, and her hull seemed to be painted the same greasy black.

Through his glasses, Nick saw the sudden bustle of activity on her bridge as *Warlock* burst into view. The headland would have blanketed *La Mouette*'s radar and, with Nick's strict radio silence, this would be the first that Jules Levoisin knew of *Warlock*'s presence. Nick could imagine the consternation on her navigation bridge, and he noted wryly that Jules Levoisin had not even gone through the motions of putting a line on to *Golden Adventurer*. He must have been completely sure of himself, of his unopposed presence. In maritime law, a line on to a prize's hull bestowed certain rights, and Jules should have made the gesture.

'Get *La Mouette* in clear,' he instructed, and picked up the hand microphone as the Trog nodded to him.

'*Salut Jules, ça va?* You pot-bellied little pirate, haven't they caught and hung you yet?' Nick asked kindly in French, and there was a long disbelieving silence on Channel 16 before the fruity Gallic tones boomed from the overhead speaker.

'Admiral James Bond, I think?' and Jules chuckled, but unconvincingly. 'Is that a battle-ship or a floating whore-house? You always were a fancy boy, Nicholas, but what kept you so long? I expected to get a better run for my money.'

'Three things you taught me, *mon brave*: the first was to take nothing for granted; the second was to keep your big yap shut tight when running for a prize; and the third was to put a line on it when you got there – you've broken your own rules, Jules.'

'The line is nothing. I am arrived.'

'And I, old friend, am arrived also. But the difference is that I am Christy Main's contractor.'

'*Tu rigoles!* You are joking!' Jules was shocked. 'I heard nothing of this!'

'I am not joking,' Nick told him. 'My James Bond equipment lets me talk in private. But go ahead, call Christy Main and ask them – and while you are doing it, move that dirty old greaser of yours out the way. I've got work to do.' Nick tossed the microphone back to the Trog. 'Tape everything he sends,' he instructed, and then to David Allen, 'We are going to smash up that ice before it grabs too tight a hold on *Golden Adventurer*. Put your best man on the wheel.'

Nick was a man transformed, no longer the brooding, moody recluse, agonizing over each decision, uncertain of himself and reacting to each check with frustrated and undirected anger.

'When he starts moving – he really burns it up,' thought David Allen, as he listened to Nick on the engine-room intercom.

'I want flank power on both, Chief. We are going to break ice. Then I want you in full immersion with helmet, we are going on board her to take a peek at her engine room.' He swung back to David Allen. 'Number One, you can stand by to take command.' The man of action glorying in the end to inactivity, he almost seemed to dance upon his feet, like a fighter at the first bell. 'Tell Angel I want a hot meal for us before we go into the cold, plenty of sugar in it.'

'I'll ask the steward,' said David, 'Angel is no good at the moment. He's playing dolls with the lass you pulled out the water. God, he'll be dressing her up and wheeling her around in a pram—'

'You tell Angel, I want food – and good food,' growled Nick, and turned away to the window to study the ice that blocked the bay, 'or I'll go down personally and kick his backside.'

'He'd probably enjoy that,' muttered David, and Nick rounded on him.

'How many times have you checked out the salvage gear since we left Cape Town?'

'Four times.'

'Make it five. Do it again. I want all the diesel auxiliaries started and run up, then shut down for freezing and rigged to be swung out. I want to have power on *Adventurer* by noon tomorrow.'

'Sir.'

But before he could go, Nick asked, 'What is the barometric reading?'

'I don't know—'

'From now until the end of this salvage, you will know, at any given moment, the exact pressure and you will inform me immediately any variation over one millibar.'

'Reading is 1018,' David checked hastily.

'It's too high,' said Nick. 'And it's too bloody calm. Watch it. We are going to have a pressure bounce. Watch it like an eagle scout.'

'Sir.'

'I thought I asked you to check the gear.'

The Trog called out, 'Christy Main has just called *La Mouette* and confirmed that we are the main contractor – but Levoisin has accepted daily hire to pick up a full load of survivors from Shackleton Bay and ferry them to Cape Town. Now he wants to speak to you again.'

'Tell him I'm busy.' Nick did not take his attention from the ice-packed bay, then he changed his mind. 'No, I'll talk to him.' He took the hand microphone. 'Jules?'

'You don't play fair, Nicholas. You go behind the back of an old friend, a man who loves you like a brother.'

'I'm a busy man. Did you truly call to tell me that?'

'I think you made a mistake, Nicholas. I think you crazy to go Lloyd's Open on this one. That ship is stuck fast – and the weather! Did you read the met from Gough Island? You got yourself a screaming bastard there, Nicholas. You listen to an old man.'

'Jules I've got twenty-two thousand horses running for me—'

'I still think you made a mistake, Nicholas. I think you're going to burn more than just your fingers.'

'*Au revoir*, Jules. Come and watch me in the awards court.'

'I still think that's a whore-house, not a tug, you are sailing. You can send over a couple of blondes and a bottle of wine—'

'Goodbye, Jules.'

'Good luck, *mon vieux*.'

'Hey, Jules – you say "good luck" and it's the worst possible luck. You taught me that.'

'*Oui*, I know.'

'Then good luck to you also, Jules.' For a minute Nick looked after the departing tug. It waddled away over the oily swells, small and fat-bottomed and cheeky, for all the world like its Master – and yet there was something dejected and crestfallen about her going.

He felt a prick of affection for the little Frenchman, he had been a true and good friend as well as a teacher, and Nick felt his triumph softening to regret.

He crushed it down ruthlessly. It had been a straight, hard but fair run, and Jules had been careless. Long ago, Nick had taught himself that anybody in opposition was an enemy, to be hated and beaten, and when you had done so, you despised them. You did not feel compassion, it weakened your own resolve.

He could not quite bring himself to despise Jules Levoisin. The Frenchman would bounce back, probably snatching the next job out from under Nick's nose, and anyway he had the lucrative contract to ferry the survivors from

Shackleton Bay. It would pay the costs of his long run southwards and leave some useful change over.

Nick's own dilemma was not as easily resolved. He put Jules Levoisin out of his mind, turning away before the French tug had rounded the headland and he studied the ice-choked bay before him with narrow eyes and a growing feeling of concern. Jules had been right – this was going to be a screaming bastard of a job.

The high seas that had thrown *Golden Adventurer* ashore had been made even higher by the equinoctial spring tides. Both had now abated and she was fast.

The liner's hull had swung also, so she was not aligned neatly at right angles to the beach. *Warlock* would not be able to throw a straight pull on to her. She would have to drag her sideways. Nick could see that now as he closed.

Still closer, he could see how the heavy steel hull, half filled with water, had burrowed itself into the yielding shingle. She would stick like toffee to a baby's blanket.

Then he looked at the ice, it was not only brash and pancake ice, but there were big chunks, bergie bits, from rotten and weathered icebergs, which the wind had driven into the bay, like a sheepdog with its flock.

The plunging temperatures had welded this mass of ice into a whole; like a monstrous octopus, it was wrapping thick glistening tentacles around *Adventurer*'s stern. The ice had not yet had sufficient time to become impenetrable, and *Warlock*'s bows were ice-strengthened for just such an emergency – yet Nick knew enough not to underestimate the hardness of ice. 'White ice is soft ice' was the old adage, and yet here there were big lumps and hummocks of green and striated glacial ice in the mass, like fat plums in a pudding, any one of which could punch a hole through *Warlock*'s hull.

Nick grimaced at the thought of having to send Jules Levoisin a mayday.

He spoke to the helmsman quietly. 'Starboard five – midships,' lining *Warlock* up for a fracture-line in the ice-pack. It was vital to come in at a right angle, to take the ice fully on the stem; a glancing blow could throw the bows off line and bring the vulnerable hull in contact with razor ice.

'Stand by, engine room,' he alerted them, and *Warlock* bore down on the ice at a full ten knots and Nick judged the moment of impact finely. Half a ship's length clear, he gave a crisp order.

'Both half back.'

*Warlock* checked, going up on to the ice as she decelerated, but still with a horrid rasping roar that echoed through the ship. Her bows rose, riding up over the ice. It gave with a rending crackle, huge slabs of ice up-ending and tumbling together.

'Both full back.'

The huge twin propellers changed their pitch smoothly into reverse thrust, and the wash boiled into the broken ice, sweeping it clear, as *Warlock* drew back into open water and Nick steadied her and lined her up again.

'Both ahead full.'

*Warlock* charged forward, checking at the last moment, and again thick slabs of white ice broke away, and grated along the ship's side. Nick swung her stern first starboard then port, deftly using the twin screws to wash the broken ice free, then he pulled *Warlock* out and lined up again.

Butting and smashing and pivoting, *Warlock* worked her way deeper into the bay, opening a spreading web of cracks across the white sheet of ice.

David Allen was breathless, as he burst on to the bridge.

'All gear checked and ready, sir.'

'Take her,' said Nick. 'She's broken it up now – just keep it stirred up.' He wanted to add a warning that the big variable-pitch propellers were *Warlock*'s most vulnerable parts, but he had a high enough opinion now of his Mate's ability, so he went on instead, 'I'm going down now to kit up.'

Vin Baker was in the aft salvage hold ahead of him, he had already half finished the tray of rich food and Angel hovered over him, but, as Nick came down the steel ladder, he lifted the cover off another steaming tray.

'It's good,' said Nick, although he could hardly force himself to swallow. The nerves in his stomach were bunched up too tightly. Yet food was one of the best defences against the cold.

'Samantha wants to talk to you, skip.'

'Who the hell is Samantha?'

'The girl – she wants to thank you.'

'Use your head, Angel, can't you see I have other things on my mind?'

Nick was already pulling on the rubber immersion suit over a full-length woollen undersuit. He needed the assistance of a seaman to enter the opening in the chest of the suit.

He had already forgotten about the girl as they closed the chest opening of the suit with a double ring seal, and then over the water-tight bootees and mittens went another full suit of polyurethane. Nick and Vin Baker looked like a pair of fat Michelin men, as their dressers helped them into the full helmets, with wrap-around visors, built-in radio microphones and breathing valves.

'Okay, Chief?' Nick asked, and Vin Baker's voice squawked too loudly into his headphones.

'Clear to roll.'

Nick adjusted the volume, and then shrugged into the oxygen rebreathing set. They were not going deeper than thirty feet, so Nick had decided to use oxygen rather than the bulky steel compressed-air cylinders.

'Let's go,' he said, and waddled to the ladder.

The Zodiac sixteen-foot inflatable dinghy swung overboard with the four of them in it, two divers and two picked seamen to handle the boat. Vin pushed one of them aside and primed the outboard himself.

'Come on, beauty,' he told it sternly, and the big Johnson Seahorse fired at the first kick. Gingerly, they began to feel their way through an open lead in the ice, with the two seamen poling away small sharp pieces that would have ripped the fabric of the Zodiac.

In Nick's radio headset, David Allen's voice spoke suddenly.

'Captain, this is the First Officer. Barometric pressure is 1021 – it looks like it's going through the roof.'

The pressure was bouncing, as Nick had predicted. What goes up, must come down – and the higher she goes, the lower she falls.

Jules Levoisin had warned him it was going to be a screamer.

'Did you read the last met from Gough Island?'

'They have 1005 falling, and the wind at 320° and thirty-five knots.'

'Lovely,' said Nick. 'We've got a big blow coming.' And through the visor of his helmet he looked up at the pale and beautiful sun. It was not bright enough to pain the eye, and now it wore a fine golden halo like the head of a saint in a medieval painting.

'Skipper, this is as close as we can get,' Vin Baker told him, and slipped the motor into neutral. The Zodiac coasted gently into a small open pool in the ice-pack, fifty yards from *Golden Adventurer*'s stern.

A solid sheet of compacted ice separated them, and Nick studied it carefully. He had not taken the chance of working *Warlock* in closer until he could get a look at the bottom here. He wanted to know what depth of water he had to manoeuvre in, and if there were hidden snags, jagged rock to rip through the *Warlock*'s hull, or flat shingle on which he could risk a bump.

He wanted to know the slope of the bottom, and if there was good holding for his ground-tackle, but most of all, he wanted to inspect the underwater damage to *Golden Adventurer*'s hull.

'Okay, Chief?' he asked, and Vin Baker grinned at him through the visor.

'Hey, I just remembered – my mommy told me not to get my feet wet. I'm going home.'

Nick knew just how he felt. There was thick sheet ice between them and *Adventurer*, they had to go down and swim below it. God alone knew what currents were running under the ice, and what visibility was like down there. A man in trouble could not surface immediately, but must find his way back to open water. Nick felt a claustrophobic tightening of his belly muscles, and he worked swiftly, checking out his gear, cracking the valve on his oxygen tank to inflate the breathing bag, checking the compass and Rolex Oyster on his wrist and clipping his buddy line on to the Zodiac, a line to return along, like Theseus in the labyrinth of the Minotaur.

'Let's go,' he said, and flipped backwards into the water. The cold struck through the multiple layers of rubber and cloth and polyurethane almost instantly, and Nick waited only for the Chief Engineer to break through the surface beside him in a cloud of swirling silver bubbles.

'God,' Vin Baker's voice was distorted by the earphones, 'it's cold enough to crack the gooseberries off a plaster saint.'

Paying out the line behind him, Nick sank down into the hazy green depths, looking for bottom. It came up dimly, heavy shingle and pebble, and he checked his depth gauge – almost six fathoms – and he moved in towards the beach.

The light from the surface was filtered through thick ice, green and ghostly in the icy depths, and Nick felt unreasonable panic stirring deep in him. He tried to thrust it aside and concentrate on the job, but it flickered there, ready to burst into flame.

There was a current working under the ice, churning the sediment so that the visibility was further reduced, and they had to fin hard to make headway across the bottom, always with the hostile ceiling of sombre green ice above them, cutting them off from the real world.

Suddenly the *Golden Adventurer*'s hull loomed ahead of them, the twin propellers glinting like gigantic bronze wings in the gloom.

They moved in within arm's length of the steel hull and swam slowly along it. It was like flying along the outer wall of a tall apartment block, a sheer cliff of riveted steel plate – but the hull was moving.

The *Golden Adventurer* was hogging on the bottom, the stern dipping and swaying to the pulse of the sea, the heaving ground-swell that came in under the ice; her stern bumped heavily on the pebbly bottom, like a great hammer beating time to the ocean.

Nick knew that she was settling herself in. Every hour now was making his task more difficult and he drove harder with his swim fins, pulling slightly ahead of Vin Baker. He knew exactly where to look for the damage. Reilly had reported it in minute detail to Christy Main, but he came across it without warning.

It looked as though a monstrous axe had been swung horizontally at the hull, a clean slash, the shape of an elongated teardrop. The metal around it had been depressed, and the paint smeared away so that the steel gleamed as though it had been scoured and polished.

At its widest, the lips of the fifteen-foot rent gaped open by three feet or a little more, and it breathed like a living mouth – for the force of the ground-swell pushing into the gap built up pressure within the hull, then as the swell subsided the trapped water was forcibly expelled, sucking in and out with tremendous pressure.

'It's a clean hole,' Vin Baker's voice squawked harshly. 'But it's too long to pump with cement.'

He was right, of course, Nick had seen that at once. Liquid cement would not plug that wicked gash, and anyway, there wasn't time to use cement, not with weather coming. An idea began forming in his mind.

'I'm going to penetrate.' Nick made the decision aloud, and beside him the Chief was silent for long incredulous seconds, then he covered the edge of fear in his voice with,

'Listen, cobber, every time I've ever been into an orifice shaped like that, it's always meant big trouble. Reminds me of my first wife—'

'Cover for me,' Nick interrupted him. 'If I'm not out in five minutes—'

'I'm coming with you,' said the Chief. 'I've got to take a look at her engine room. This is good a time as any.'

Nick did not argue with him.

'I'll go first,' he said and tapped the Chief's shoulder. 'Do what I do.'

Nick hung four feet from the gash, finning to hold himself there against the current.

He watched the swirl of water rushing into the opening, and then gushing out again in a rash of silver bubbles. Then, as she began to breathe again, he darted forward.

The current caught him and he was hurled at the gap, with only time to duck his helmeted head and cover the fragile oxygen bag on his chest with both arms.

Raw steel snagged at his leg; there was no pain, but almost instantly he felt the leak of seawater into his suit. The cold stung like a razor cut, but he was through into the total darkness of the cavernous hull. He was flung into a tangle of steel piping, and he anchored himself with one arm and groped for the underwater lantern on his belt.

'You okay?' The Chief's voice boomed in his headphones.

'Fine.'

Vin Baker's lantern glowed eerily in the dark waters ahead of him.

'Work fast,' instructed Nick. 'I've got a tear in my suit.'

Each of them knew exactly what to do and where to go. Vin Baker swam first to the water-tight bulkheads and checked all the seals. He was working in darkness in a totally unfamiliar engine room, but he went unerringly to the pump system, and checked the valve-settings; then he rose to the surface, feeling his way up the massive blocks of the main engines.

Nick was there ahead of him. The engine room was flooded almost to the deck above and the surface was a thick stinking scum of oil and diesel, in which floated a mass of loose articles, most of them undefinable, but in the beam of his lantern Nick recognized a gumboot and a grease pot floating beside his head. The whole thick stinking soup rose and fell and agitated with the push of the current through the rent.

The lenses of their lanterns were smeared with the oily filth and threw grotesque shadows into the cavernous depths, but Nick could just make out the deck above him, and the dark opening of the vertical ventilation shaft. He wiped the filth from his visor and saw what he wanted to see and the cold was spreading up his leg. He asked brusquely, 'Okay, Chief?'

'Let's get the hell out of here.'

There were sickening moments of panic when Nick thought they had lost the line to the opening. It had snagged and wrapped around a steam pipe. Nick freed it and then sank down to the glimmer of light through the gash.

He judged his moment carefully, the return was more dangerous than the entry, for the raw bright metal had been driven in by the ice, like the petals of a sunflower – or the fangs in a shark's maw. He used the suck of water and shot through without a touch, turning and finning to wait for Vin Baker.

The Australian came through in the next rush of water, but Nick saw him flicked sideways by the current, and he struck the jagged opening a touching blow. There was instantly a roaring rush of escaping oxygen from his breathing bag, as the steel split it wide, and for a moment the Chief was obscured in the silver cloud of gas that was his life's breath.

'Oh God, I'm snagged,' he shouted, clutching helplessly at his empty bag, plummeting sharply into the green depths at the drastic change in his buoyancy. The heavily leaded belt around his waist had been weighted to counter the flotation of the oxygen bag, and he went down like a gannet diving on a shoal of sardine.

Nick saw instantly what was about to happen. The current had him – it was dragging him down under the hull, sucking him under that hammering steel bottom, where he would be crushed against the stony beach by twenty-two thousand tons of pounding steel.

Nick went head down, finning desperately to catch the swirling body which tumbled like a leaf in high wind. He had a fleeting glimpse of Baker's face, contorted with terror and lack of breath, the glass visor of his helmet already swamping with icy water as the pressure spurted through the non-return valve. The Chief's headset microphone squealed once and then went dead as the water shorted it out.

'Drop your belt,' yelled Nick, but Baker did not respond; he had not heard, his headset had gone and instead he fought ineffectually in the swirling current, drawn inexorably down to brutal death.

Nick got a hand to him and threw back with all his strength on his fins to check their downward plunge, but still they went down and Nick's right hand was clumsy with cold and the double thickness of his mittens as he groped for the quick-release on the Chief's belt.

He hit the rounded bottom of the great hull with his shoulder, and felt them dragged under to where clouds of sediment blew like smoke from the working of the keel. Locked together like a couple of waltzing dancers, they swung around and he saw the keel, like the blade of a guillotine, rise up high above them. He could not reach the Chief's release toggle.

There were only micro-seconds in which to go for this one other chance. He hit his own release and the thick belt with thirty-five pounds of lead fell away from Nick's waist; with it went the buddy line that would guide them back to the waiting Zodiac, for it had been clipped into the back of the belt.

The abrupt loss of weight checked their downward plunge, and fighting with all the strength of his legs, Nick was just able to hold them clear of the great keel as it came swinging downwards.

Within ten feet of them, steel struck stone with a force that rang in Nick's eardrum like a bronze gong but he had an armlock on the Chief's struggling body, and now at last his right hand found the release toggle on the other man's belt.

He hit it, and another thirty-five pounds of lead dropped away. They began to rise, up along the hogging steel hull, faster and faster as the oxygen in Nick's bag expanded with the release of pressure. Now their plight was every bit as desperate, for they were racing upwards to a roof of solid ice with enough speed to break bond or crack a skull.

Nick emptied his lungs, exhaling on a single continuous breath, and at the same time opened the valve to vent his bag, blowing away the precious life-giving gas in an attempt to check their rise – yet still they went into the ice with a force that would have stunned them both, had Nick not twisted over and caught it on his shoulder and outflung arm. They were pinned there under the ice by the cork-like buoyancy of their rubber suits and the remaining gas in Nick's bag.

With mild and detached surprise Nick saw that the lower side of the ice pack was not a smooth sheet, but was worked into ridges and pinnacles, into weird flowing shapes like some abstract sculpture in pale green glass. It was only a fleeting moment that he looked at it, for beside him Baker was drowning.

His helmet was flooded with icy water and his face was empurpled and his mouth contorted into a horrible rictus; already his movements were becoming spasmodic and unco-ordinated, as he struggled for breath.

Nick realized that haste would kill them both now. He had to work fast but deliberately – and he held Baker to him as he cracked the valve on his steel oxygen bottle, reinflating his chest bag.

With his right hand, he began to unscrew the breathing pipe connection into the side of Baker's helmet. It was slow, too slow. He needed touch for this delicate work.

He thought, 'This could cost me my right hand,' and he stripped off the thick mitten in a single angry gesture. Now he could feel – for the few seconds until the cold paralysed his fingers. The connection came free and while he worked, Nick was pumping his lungs like a bellows, hyperventilating, washing his blood with pure oxygen until he felt light-headed and dizzy.

One last sweet breath, and then he unscrewed his own hose connection; icy water flooded through the valve but he held his head at an angle to trap oxygen in the top of his helmet, keeping his nose and eyes clear, and he rescrewed his own hose into Baker's helmet with fingers that no longer had feeling.

He held the Chief's body close to his chest, embracing like lovers, and he cracked the last of the oxygen from his bottle. There was just sufficient pressure of gas left to expunge the water from Baker's helmet. It blew out with an explosive hiss through the valve, and Nick watched carefully with his face only inches from Baker's.

The Chief was choking and coughing, gulping and gasping at the rush of cold oxygen, his eyes watery and unseeing, his spectacles blown awry and the lenses obscured by sea water, but then Nick felt his chest begin to swell and subside. Baker was breathing again, 'which is more than I am doing,' Nick thought grimly – and then suddenly he realized for the first time that he had lost the guide line with his weight belt.

He did not know in which direction was the shore, nor which way to swim to reach the Zodiac. He was utterly disorientated, and desperately he peered through his half-flooded visor for sight of the *Golden Adventurer*'s hull to align himself. She was not there, gone in the misty green gloom – and he felt the first heave of his lungs as they demanded air. And as he denied his body the driving need to breathe, he felt the fear that had flickered deep within him flare up into true terror, swiftly becoming cold driving panic.

A suicidal urge to tear at the green ice roof of this watery tomb almost overwhelmed him. He wanted to try and rip his way through it with bare freezing hands to reach the precious air.

Then, just before panic completely obliterated his reason, he remembered the compass on his wrist. Even then his brain was sluggish, beginning to starve for oxygen, and it took precious seconds working out the reciprocal of his original bearing.

As he leaned forward to read the compass, more sea water spurted into his helmet, spiking needles of icy cold agony into the sinuses of his cheeks and forehead, making the teeth ache in his jaws, so he gasped involuntarily and immediately choked.

Still holding Baker to him, linked by the thick black umbilical cord of his oxygen hose, Nick began to swim out on the reciprocal compass heading. Immediately his lungs began to pump, convulsing in involuntary spasms, like those of childbirth, craving air, and he swam on.

With his head thrown back slightly he saw that the sheet of ice moved slowly above him; at times, when the current held them, it moved not at all, and it required all his self-control to keep finning doggedly, then the current relaxed its grip and they moved forward again, but achingly slowly.

He had time then to realize how exquisitely beautiful was the ice roof; translucent, wonderously carved and sculptured – and suddenly he remembered standing hand in hand with Chantelle beneath the arched roof of the Chartres cathedral, staring up in awe. The pain in his chest subsided, the need to breathe passed, but he did not recognize that as the sign of mortal danger, nor the images that formed before his eyes as the fantasy of a brain deprived of oxygen and slowly dying.

Chantelle's face was before him then, glowing hair soft and thick and glossy as a butterfly's wing, huge dark eyes and that wide mouth so full of promise of delight and warmth and love.

'I loved you,' he thought. 'I really loved you.'

And the image changed. He saw again the incredible slippery explosive liquid burst with which his son was born, heard the first querulous cry as he dangled pink and wet and hairless from the rubber-gloved hand, and felt again the soul-consuming wonder and joy.

'A drowning man—' Nick recognized at last what was happening to him. He knew then he was dying, but the panic had passed, as the cold had passed also, and the terror. He swam on, dreamlike, into the green mists. Then he realized that his own legs were no longer moving; he lay relaxed not breathing, not feeling, and it was Baker's body that was thrusting and working against him.

Nick peered into the glass visor still only inches from his eyes, and he saw that Baker's face was set and determined. He was gulping the pure sweet oxygen and gaining strength with each breath, driving on strongly.

'You beauty,' whispered Nick dreamily, and felt the water shoot into his throat, but there was no pain.

Another image formed before him, an Arrowhead-class yacht with spinnaker set, running free across a bright Mediterranean sea, and his son at the tiller, the dense tumble of curls that covered his small neat head fluttering in the wind, and the same velvety dark eyes as his mother's in the suntanned oval of his face as he laughed.

'Don't let her run by the lee, Peter,' Nicholas wanted to shout to his son, but the image faded into blackness. He thought for a moment that he had passed into unconsciousness, but then he realized suddenly that it was the black rubber bottom of the Zodiac only inches from his eyes, and that the rough hands that dragged him upwards, lifting him and tearing loose the fastening of his helmet, were not part of the fantasy.

Propped against the pillowed gunwale of the Zodiac, held by the two boatmen from falling backwards, the first breaths of sub-zero air were too rich for his starved lungs, and Nick coughed and vomited weakly down the front of his suit.

Nick came out of the shower cabinet. The cabin was thick with steam, and his body glowed dull angry red from the almost boiling water. He wrapped the towel around his waist as he stepped through into his night cabin.

Baker slouched in the armchair at the foot of his bunk. He wore fresh overalls, his hair stood up in little damp spikes around the shaven spot where Angel's cat-gut stitches still held the scabbed wound closed. One of the side frames of his spectacles had snapped during those desperate minutes below *Golden Adventurer*'s stern, and Baker had repaired it with black insulating tape.

He held two glasses in his left hand, and a big flat brown bottle of liquor in the other. He poured two heavy slugs into the glasses as Nick paused in the bathroom door, and the sweet, rich aroma smelled like the sugar-cane fields of northern Queensland.

Baker passed a glass to Nick, and then showed him the bottle's yellow label.

'Bundaberg rum,' he announced, 'the dinky die stuff, sport.'

Nick recognized both the offer of liquor and the salutation as probably the highest accolade the Chief would ever give another human being.

Nick sniffed the dark honey-brown liquor and then took it in a single toss, swirled it once around his mouth, swallowed, shuddered like a spaniel shaking off water droplets, exhaled harshly and said: 'It's still the finest rum in the world.' Dutifully he said what was expected of him, and held out his glass.

'The Mate asked me to give you a message,' said Baker as he poured another shot for each of them. 'Glass hit 1035 and now it's diving like a dingo into its hole – back to 1020 already. It's going to blow – is it ever going to blow!'

They regarded each other over the rims of the glasses.

'We've wasted almost two hours, Beauty,' Nick told him, and Baker blinked at the unlikely name, then grinned crookedly as he accepted it.

'How are you going to plug that hull?'

'I've got ten men at work already. We are going to fother a sail into a collision mat.'

Baker blinked again, then shook his head in disbelief. 'That's Hornblower stuff—'

'The *Witch of Endor*,' Nick agreed. 'So you can read?'

'You haven't got pressure to drive it home,' Baker objected. 'The trapped air from the engine room will blow it out.'

'I'm going to run a wire down the ventilation shaft of the engine room and out through the gash. We'll fix the collision mat outside the hull and winch it home with the wire.'

Baker stared at him for five seconds while he examined the proposition. A sail was fothered by threading the thick canvas with thousands of strands of unravelled oakum until it resembled a huge shaggy doormat. When this was placed over an aperture below a ship's waterline, the pressure of water forced it into the hole, and the water swelled the mass of fibre until it formed an almost watertight plug.

However, in *Golden Adventurer*'s case the damage was extensive and as the hull was already flooded, there was no pressure differential to drive home the plug. Nick proposed to beat that by using an internal wire to haul the plug into the gash.

'It might work.' Beauty Baker was noncommittal.

Nick took the second rum at a gulp, dropped the towel and reached for his working gear laid out on the bunk.

'Let's get power on her before the blow hits us,' he suggested mildly, and Baker lumbered to his feet and stuffed the Bundaberg bottle into his back pocket.

'Listen, sport,' he said. 'All that guff about you being a Pommy, don't take it too seriously.'

'I won't,' said Nick. 'Actually I was born and educated in Blighty, but my father's an American. So that makes me one also.'

'Christ.' Beauty hitched disgustedly at his waist with both elbows. 'If there's anything worse than a bloody Pom, it's a goddamned Yank.'


Now that Nick was certain that the bottom of the bay was clean and free of underwater snags, he handled *Warlock* boldly but with a delicately skilful touch which David Allen watched with awe.

Like a fighting cock, the *Warlock* attacked the thicker ice line along the shore, smashing free huge lumps and slabs, then washing them clear with the propellers, giving herself space to work about *Golden Adventurer*'s stern.

The ominous calm of both sea and air made the work easier, although the vicious little current working below *Adventurer*'s stern complicated the transfer of the big alternator.

Nick had two Yokohama fenders slung from *Warlock*'s side, and the bloated plastic balloons cushioned the contact of steel against steel as Nick laid *Warlock* alongside the stranded liner, holding her there with delicate adjustments of power and rudder and screw pitch.

Beauty Baker and his working party, swaddled in heavy Antarctic gear, were already up on the catwalk of *Warlock*'s forward gantry, seventy feet above the bridge and overlooking *Adventurer*'s sharply canted deck.

As Nick nudged *Warlock* in, they dropped the steel boarding-ladder across the gap between the two ships and Beauty led them across in single file, like a troop of monkeys across the limb of a forest tree.

'All across,' the Third Officer confirmed for Nick, and then added, 'Glass has dropped again, sir. Down to 1005.'

'Very well.' Nick drew *Warlock* gently away from the liner's stern, and held her fifty feet off. Only then did he flick his eyes up at the sky. The midnight sun had turned it to a malevolent jaundiced yellow, while the sun itself was a ball of dark satanic red above the peaks of Cape Alarm, and it seemed that the snowfields and glaciers were washed with blood.

'It's beautiful.' Suddenly the girl was beside him. The top of her head was on a level with his shoulder, and in the ruddy light, her thick roped hair glowed like newly minted sovereigns in red gold. Her voice was low and a little husky with shyness, and touched a chord of response in Nick, but when she lifted her face to him he saw how young she was.

'I came to thank you,' she said softly. 'It's the first chance I've had.'

She wore baggy, borrowed men's clothing that made her look like a little girl dressing up, and her face, free of cosmetics, had that waxy plastic glow of youth, like the polished skin of a ripe apple.

Her expression was solemn and there were traces of her recent ordeal beneath her eyes and at the corners of her mouth. Nick sensed the tension and nervousness in her.

'Angel wouldn't let me come before,' she said, and suddenly she smiled. The nervousness vanished and it was the direct warm unselfconscious smile of a beautiful child that has never known rejection. Nick was shocked by the strength of his sudden physical desire for her, his body moved, clenching like a fist in his groin, and he felt his heart pound furiously in the cage of his ribs.

His shock turned to anger, for she looked but fourteen or fifteen years of age; almost she seemed as young as his own son, and he was shamed by the perversity of his attraction. Since the good bright times with Chantelle, he had not experienced such direct and instant involvement with a woman. At the thought of Chantelle, his emotions collapsed in a disordered tangle, from which only his lust and his anger emerged clearly.

He cupped the anger to him, like a match in a high wind, it gave him strength again. Strength to thrust this aside, for he knew how vulnerable he still was and how dangerous a course had opened before him, to be led by this child woman. Suddenly he was aware that he had swayed bodily towards the girl and had been staring into her face for many long seconds, that she was meeting his glaze steadily and that something was beginning to move in her eyes like cloud shadow across the sunlit surface of a green mountain lake. Something was happening which he could not afford, could not chance – and then he realized also that the two young deck officers were watching them with undisguised curiosity, and he turned his anger on her.

'Young lady,' he said. 'You have an absolute genius for being in the wrong place at the wrong time.' And his tone was colder and more remote than even he had intended it.

Before he turned away from her, he saw the moment of her disbelief turn to chagrin, and the green eyes misted slightly. He stood stiffly staring down the foredeck where David Allen's team was opening the forward salvage hold.

Nick's anger evaporated almost at once, to be replaced by dismay. He realized clearly that he had completely alienated the girl and he wanted to turn back to her and say something gracious that might retrieve the situation, but he could think of nothing and instead lifted the hand microphone to his lips and spoke to Baker over the VHF radio.

'How's it going, Chief?'

There were ten seconds of delay, and Nick was very conscious of the girl's presence near him.

'Their emergency generator has burned out, it will need two days' work to get it running again. We'll have to take on the alternator,' Beauty told him.

'We are ready to give it to you,' Nick told him, and then called David Allen on the foredeck.

'Ready, David?'

'All set.'

Nick began edging *Warlock* back towards the liner's towering stern, and now at last he turned back to the girl. Unaccountably, he now wanted her approbation, so his smile was ready – but she had already gone, taking with her that special aura of brightness.

Nick's voice had a jagged edge to it as he told David Allen, 'Let's do this fast and right, Number One.'

*Warlock* nuzzled *Adventurer*'s stern, the big black Yokohama fenders gentling her touch, and on her foredeck the winch whined shrilly, the lines squealing in their blocks and from the open salvage hatch the four-ton alternator swung out. It was mounted on a sledge for easy handling. The diesel tanks were charged and the big motor primed and ready to start.

It rose swiftly, dangling from the tall gantry, and a dozen men synchronized their efforts, in those critical moments when it hung out over *Warlock*'s bows. A nasty freaky little swell lifted the tug and pushed her across, for the dangling burden was already putting a slight list on her, and it would have crashed into the steel side of the liner had not Nick thrown the screws into reverse thrust and given her a burst of power to hold her off.

The instant the swell subsided, he closed down and slid the pitch to fine forward, pressing the cushioned bows lightly back against *Adventurer*'s side.

'He's good!' David Allen watched Nicholas work. 'He's better than old Mac ever was.' Mackintosh, *Warlock*'s previous skipper, had been careful and experienced, but Nicholas Berg handled the ship with the flair and intuitive touch that even Mac's vast experience could never have matched.

David Allen pushed the thought aside and signalled the winchman. The huge dangling machine dropped with the control of a roosting seagull on to the liner's deck. Baker's crew leapt on it immediately, releasing the winch cable and throwing out the tackle, to drag it away on its sledge.

*Warlock* drew off, and then when Baker's crew was ready, she went in to drop another burden, this time one of the high-speed centrifugal pumps which would augment *Golden Adventurer*'s own machinery – if Baker could get that functioning. It went up out of *Warlock*'s forward hold, followed ten minutes later by its twin.

'Both pumps secured.' Baker's voice had a spark of jubilation in it, but at that moment a shadow passed over the ship, as though a vulture wheeled above on wide-spread pinions, and as Nick glanced up he saw the men on the foredeck lift their heads also.

It was a single cloud seeming no bigger than a man's fist, a thousand or fifteen hundred feet above them, but it had momentarily obscured the lowering sun, before scuttling on furtively down the peaks of Cape Alarm.

'There is still so much to do,' Nick thought, and he opened the bridge door and stepped out on to the exposed wing. There was no movement of air, and the cold seemed less intense although a glance at the glass confirmed that there were thirty degrees still of frost. No wind here, but high up it was beginning.

'Number One,' Nick snapped into the microphone. 'What's going on down there – do you think this is your Daddy's yacht?'

And David Allen's team leapt to the task of closing down the forward hatch, and then tramped back to the double salvage holds on the long stern quarter.

'I am transferring command to the stern bridge.' Nick told his deck officers and hurried back through the accommodation area to the second enclosed bridge, where every control and navigational aid was duplicated, a unique feature of salvage-tug construction where so much of the work took place on the afterdeck.

This time from the aft gantries, they lifted the loaded pallets of salvage gear on to the liner's deck, another eight tons of equipment went aboard *Golden Adventurer*. Then they pulled away and David Allen battened down again. When he came on to the bridge stamping and slapping his own shoulders, red-cheeked and gasping from the cold, Nick told him immediately,

'Take command, David, I'm going on board.' Nick could not bring himself to wait out the uncertain period while Beauty Baker put power and pumps into action.

Anything mechanical was Baker's responsibility, as seamanship was strictly Nick's, but it could take many hours yet, and Nick could not remain idle that long.

From high on the forward gantry, Nick looked out across that satiny ominous sea. It was a little after midnight now and the sun was half down behind the mountains, a two-dimensional disc of metal heated to furious crimson. The sea was sombre purple and the icebergs were sparks of brighter cherry red. From this height he could see that the surface of the sea was crenellated, a small regular swell spreading across it like ripples across a pond, from some disturbance far out beyond the horizon.

Nick could feel the fresh movement of *Warlock*'s hull as she rode this swell, and suddenly a puff of wind hit Nick in the face like the flit of a bat's wing, and the metallic sheen of the sea was scoured by a cat's-paw of wind that scratched at the surface as it passed.

He pulled the draw-string of the hood of his anorak up more tightly under his chin and stepped out on to the open boarding-ladder, like a steeplejack, walking upright and balancing lightly seventy feet above *Warlock*'s slowly rolling foredeck.

He jumped down on to *Golden Adventurer*'s steeply canted, ice-glazed deck and saluted *Warlock*'s bridge far below in a gesture of dismissal.

'I tried to warn you, dearie,' said Angel gently, as she entered the steamy galley, for with a single glance he was aware of Samantha's crestfallen air. 'He tore you up, didn't he?'

'What are you talking about?' She lifted her chin, and the smile was too bright and too quick. 'What do you want me to do?'

'You can separate that bowl of eggs,' Angel told her, and stooped again over twenty pounds of red beef, his sleeves rolled to the elbows about his thick and hairy arms, clutching a butcher's knife in a fist like that of Rocky Marciano.

They worked in silence for five minutes, before Samantha spoke again.

'I only tried to thank him—' And again there was a grey mist in her eyes.

'He's a lower-deck pig,' Angel agreed.

'He is not,' Samantha came in hotly. 'He's not a pig.'

'Well, then, he's a selfish, heartless bastard – with jumped-up ideas.'

'How *can* you say that!' Samantha's eyes flashed now. 'He is not selfish
– he went into the water to get me—'

Then she saw the smile on Angel's lips and the mocking quizzical
expression in his eyes, and she stopped in confusion and concentrated on
cracking the egg shells and slopping the contents into the mixing basin.

'He's old enough to be your father,' Angel needled her, and now she was
really angry; a ruddy flush under the smooth gloss of her skin made the
freckles shine like gold dust.

'You talk the most awful crap, Angel.'

'God, dearie, where did you learn that language?'

'Well, you're making me mad.' She broke an egg with such force that it
exploded down the front of her pants. 'Oh, shit!' she said, and stared at him
defiantly. Angel tossed her a dish-cloth, she wiped herself violently and they
went on working again.

'How old is he?' she demanded at last. 'A hundred and fifty?'

'He's thirty-eight,' Angel thought for a moment, 'or thirty-nine.'

'Well, smart arse,' she said tartly, 'the ideal age is half the man's age, plus
seven.'

'You aren't twenty-six, dearie,' Angel said gently.

'I will be in two years' time,' she told him.

'You really want him badly, hey? A fever of lust and desire?'

'That's nonsense, Angel, and you know it. I just happen to owe him a
rather large debt – he saved my life – but as for wanting him, ha!' She
dismissed the idea with a snort of disdain and a toss of her head.

'I'm glad,' Angel nodded. 'He's not a very nice person, you can see by
those little ferrety eyes of his—'

'He has beautiful eyes—' she flared at him, and then stopped abruptly,
saw the cunning in his grin, faltered and then collapsed weakly on to the
bench beside him, with a cracked egg in one hand.

'Oh, Angel, you are a horrible man and I hate you. How can you make
fun of me now?'

He saw how close she was to tears, and became brisk and business-like.

'First of all, you better know something about him—' and he began to tell
her, giving her a waspish biography of Nicholas Berg, embellished by a
vivid imagination and a wicked sense of humour, together with a quasi-
feminine love of gossip, to which Samantha listened avidly, making an
occasional exclamation of surprise.

'His wife ran away with another man, she could be out of her mind, don't
you think?'

'Dearie, a change is like two weeks at the seaside.'

Or asking a question. 'He owns this ship, actually owns it? Not just
Master?'

'He owns this ship, and its sister, and the company. They used to call him
the Golden Prince. He's a high flyer, dearie, didn't you recognize it?'

'I didn't—'

'Of course you did. You're too much woman not to. There is no more
powerful aphrodisiac than success and power, nothing like the clink of gold
to get a girl's hormones revving up, is there?'

'That's unfair, Angel. I didn't know a thing about him. I didn't know he was rich and famous. I don't give a damn for money—'

'Ho! Ho!' Angel shook his curls and the diamond studs flashed in his ears. But he saw her anger flare again. 'All right, dearie, I'm teasing. But what really attracts you is his strength and air of purpose. The way other men obey, and follow and fear him. The air of command, of power and with it, success.'

'I didn't—'

'Oh, be honest with yourself, love. It was not the fact he saved your life, it wasn't his beautiful eyes nor the lump in his jeans—'

'You're crude, Angel.'

'You're bright and beautiful, and you just can't help yourself. You're like a nubile little gazelle, all skittish and ready, and you have just spotted the herd bull. You can't help yourself, dearie, you're just a woman.'

'What am I going to do, Angel?'

'We'll make a plan, love, but one thing is certain. You're not going to trail around behind him, dressed like an escapee from a junk shop, breathing adoration and hero-worship. He's doing a job. He doesn't need to trip over you every time he turns. Play hard to get.'

Samantha thought about it a moment. 'Angel, I don't want to play it that hard that I never get around to being got – if you follow me.'


Beauty Baker had the work in hand, well organized and going ahead as fast as even Nick, in his overwhelming impatience, could expect.

The alternator had been manhandled through the double doors into the superstructure on B deck, and it had been secured against a steel bulkhead and lashed down.

'As soon as I have power, we'll drill the deck and bolt her down,' he explained to Nick.

'Have you got the lines in?'

'I'll by-pass the main junction box on C deck, and I will select from the temporary box—'

'But you've identified the foredeck winch circuit, and the pumps?'

'Jesus, sport, why don't you go sail your little boat and leave me to do my work?'

On the upper deck one of Baker's gangs was already at work with the gas welding equipment. They were opening access to the ventilation shaft of the main engine room. The gas cutter hissed viciously and red sparks showered from the steel plate of the tall dummy smoke stack. The stack was merely to give the *Golden Adventurer* the traditional rakish lines, and now the welder cut the last few inches of steel plating. It fell away into the deep, dark cavern, leaving a roughly square opening six feet by six feet which gave direct access into the half-flooded engine room fifty feet below.

Despite Baker's advice, Nick took command here, directing the rigging of the winch blocks and steel wire cable that would enable a cable to be taken down into the flooded engine room and out again through that long, viciously fanged gash in the ship's side. When he looked at his Rolex Oyster again, almost an hour had passed. The sun had gone and a luminous green sky filled with the marvellous pyrotechnics of the *Aurora Australis* turned the night eerie and mysterious.

'All right, bosun, that's all we can do now. Bring your team up to the bows.'

As they hurried forward along the open foredeck, the wind caught them, a single shrieking gust that had them reeling and staggering and grabbing for support, then it was past and the wind settled down to nag and whine and pry at their clothing as Nick directed the work at the two huge anchor winches; but he heard the rising sea starting to push and stir the pack-ice, making it growl and whisper menacingly.

They catted the twin sea-anchors and with two men working over *Adventurer*'s side they secured collars of heavy chain to the crown of each anchor. *Warlock* would now be able to drag those anchors out, letting them bump along the bottom, but in the opposite direction to that in which they had been designed to drag, so that the pointed flukes would not be able to dig in and hold.

Then, when the anchors were out to the full reach of their own chains, *Warlock* would drop them, the flukes would dig in and hold. This was the ground-tackle which might resist the efforts of even a force twelve wind to throw *Golden Adventurer* further ashore.

When Baker had power on the ship, the anchor winches would be used to kedge *Golden Adventurer* off the bank. Nick placed much reliance on these enormously powerful winches to assist *Warlock*'s own engines, for even as they worked, he could feel through the soles of his feet how heavily grounded the liner was.

It was tense and heavy labour, for they were working with enormous weights of dead-weight steel chain and shackles. The securing shackle which held the chain collar on the anchor crown alone weighed three hundred pounds and had to be manhandled by six men using complicated tackle.

By the time they had the work finished, the wind was rising force six, and wailing in the superstructure. The men were chilled and tired, and tempers were flashing.

Nick led them back to the shelter of the main superstructure. His boots seemed to be made of lead, and his lungs pumped for the solace of cheroot smoke, and he realized irrelevantly that he had not slept now for over fifty hours – since he had fished that disturbing little girl from the water. Quickly he pushed the thought of her aside, for it distracted him from his purpose, and, as he stepped over the doorsill into the liner's cold but wind-protected main accommodation, he reached for his cheroot-case.

Then he arrested the movement and blinked with surprise as suddenly garish light blazed throughout the ship – deck lights and internal lights, so that instantly a festival air enveloped her and from the loudspeakers on the deck above Nicholas' head wafted soft music as the broadcasting equipment switched itself in. It was the voice of Donna Summer, as limpid and ringing clear as fine-leaded crystal. The sound was utterly incongruous in this place and in these circumstances.

'Power is on!'

Nick let out a low whoop and ran through to B deck. Beauty Baker was standing beside his roaring alternator and hugging himself with glee.

'Howzat, sport?' he demanded. Nick punched his shoulder.

'Right on, Beauty.' He wasted a few moments and a cheroot by placing one of the precious black tubes between Baker's lips and flashing his lighter. The two of them smoked for twenty seconds in close and companionable silence.

'Okay,' Nick ended it. 'Pumps and winches.'

'The two emergency portables are ready to start, and I'm on my way to check the ship's main pumps.'

'The only thing left is to get the collision mat into place.'

'That is your trick,' Baker told him flatly. 'You're not getting me into the water again, ever. I've even given up bathing.'

'Yeah, did you notice I'm standing upwind?' Nick told him. 'But somebody has to go down again to pass the wire.'

'Why don't you send Angel?' Baker grinned evilly. 'Excuse me, cobber – I've got work to do.' He inspected the cheroot. 'After we've pulled this dog off the ground, I hope you will be able to afford decent gaspers.' And he was gone into the depths of the liner, leaving Nick with the one task he had been avoiding even thinking about. Somebody had to go down into that engine room. He could call for volunteers, of course, but then it was another of his own rules to never ask another man to do what you are afraid to do yourself.

'I can leave David to lay out the ground-tackle, but I can't let anybody else put the collision mat in.' He faced it now. He would have to go down again, into the cold and darkness and mortal danger of the flooded engine room.

The ground-tackle that David Allen had laid was holding *Golden Adventurer* handsomely, even in the aggravated swell which was by now pouring into the open mouth of the bay, driven on by the rising wind that was inciting it to wilder abandon.

David had justified Nick's confidence in the seamanlike manner in which he had taken the *Golden Adventurer*'s twin anchors out and dropped them a cable's length offshore, at a finely judged angle to give the best purchase and hold.

Beauty Baker had installed and test-run the two big centrifugals and he had even resuscitated two of the liner's own forward pump assemblies which had been protected by the watertight bulkhead from the sea break-in. He was ready now to throw the switch on this considerable arsenal of pumps, and he had calculated that if Nick could close that gaping rent in the hull, he would be able to pump the liner's hull dry and clean in just under four hours.

Nick was in full immersion kit again, but this time he had opted for a single bottle Drager diving-set; he was off oxygen sets for life, he decided wryly.

Before going down, he paused on the open deck with the diving helmet under his arm. The wind must be rising seven now, he decided, for it was kicking off the tops of the waves in bursts of spray and a low scudding sky of dirty grey cloud had blotted out the rising sun and the peaks of Cape Alarm. It was a cold dark dawn, with the promise of a wilder day to follow.

Nick took one glance across at *Warlock*. David Allen was holding her nicely in position, and his own team was ready, grouped around that ugly black freshly burned opening in *Adventurer*'s stack. He lifted the helmet on to his head, and while his helpers closed the fastenings and screwed down the hose connections, he checked the radio.

'*Warlock*, do you read me?'

Allen's voice came back immediately, acknowledging and confirming his readiness, then he went on, 'The glass just went through the floor, skipper, she's 996 and going down. Wind's force six rising seven and backing. It looks like we are fair in the dangerous quadrant of whatever is coming.'

'Thank you, David,' Nick replied. 'You warm my heart.'

He stepped forward, and they helped him into the canvas bosun's chair. Nick checked the tackle and rigging, that 'once-more-for-luck' check, and then he nodded.

The interior of the engine room was no longer dark, for Baker had rigged floodlights high above in the ventilation shaft, but the water was black with engine oil, and as Nick was lowered slowly down, with legs dangling from the bosun's chair, it surged furiously back and across like some panic-stricken monster trying to break out of its steel cage. That wind-driven swell was crashing into *Golden Adventurer*'s side and boiling in through the opening, setting up its own wave action, forming its own currents and eddies which broke and leaped angrily against the steel bulkheads.

'Slower,' Nick spoke into the microphone. 'Stop!'

His downward progress was halted ten feet above the starboard main engine block, but the confined surge of water broke over the engine as though it were a coral reef, covering it entirely at one instant, and then sucking back and exposing it again at the next.

The rush of the water could throw a man against that machinery with force enough to break every bone in his body, and Nick hung above it and studied the purchases for his blocks.

'Send down the main block,' he ordered, and the huge steel block came down out of the shadows and dangled in the floodlights.

'Stop.' Nick began directing the block into position. 'Down two feet. Stop!'

Now waist-deep in the oily, churning water, he struggled to drive the shackle pin and secure the block to one of the main frames of the hull. Every few minutes a stronger surge would hurl the water over his head, forcing him to cling helplessly, until it relinquished its grip, and his visor cleared sufficiently to allow him to continue his task.

He had to pull out and rest after forty minutes of it. He sat as close as he could to the heat-exchangers of the running diesel engine of the alternator, taking warmth from them and drinking Angel's strong sweet Thermos coffee. He felt like a fighter between rounds, his body aching, every muscle strained and chilled by the efforts of fighting that filthy churned emulsion of sea water and oil, his flanks and ribs bruised from harsh contact with the submerged machinery. But after twenty minutes, he stood up again.

'Let's go,' he said and resettled the helmet. The hiatus had given him a chance to replan the operation, thinking his way around the problems he had found down there; now the work seemed to fall more readily into place, though he had lost all sense of time alone in the infernal resounding cavern of steel and he was not sure of the hour, or the phase of the day, when at last he was ready to carry the messenger out through the gap.

'Send it down,' he ordered into his headset, and the reel of light line came down, swinging and circling under the glaring floodlights to the ship's motion and throwing grotesque shadows into the far corners of the engine room.

The line was of finely plaited Dacron, with enormous strength and elasticity in relation to its thinness and lightness. One end was secured on the deck high above, and Nick threaded it into the sheave blocks carefully, so that it was free to run.

Then he clamped the reel of line on to his belt, riding it on his hip where it could be protected from snagging when he made the passage of the gap.

He realized then how close to final exhaustion he was, and he considered breaking off the work to rest again, but the heightened action of the sea into the hull warned him against further delay. An hour from now the task might be impossible, he had to go, and he reached for the reserve of strength and purpose deep inside himself, surprised to find that it was still there – for the icy chill of the water seemed to have penetrated his suit and entered his soul, dulling every sense and turning his very bones brittle and heavy.

It must be day outside, he realized, for light came through the gash of steel, pale light further obscured by the filthy muck of mixed oil and water contained in the hull.

He clung to one of the engine-room stringers, his head seven feet from the opening, breathing in the slow, even rhythm of the experienced scuba diver, feeling the ebb and flow through the hull, and trying to find some pattern in the action of the water. But it seemed entirely random, a hissing, bubbling ingestion followed by three or four irregular and weak inflows, then three vicious exhalations of such power that they would have windmilled a swimming man end over end into those daggers of splayed steel. He had to choose and ride a middling-sized swell, strong enough to take him through smoothly, without the dangerous power and turbulence of those viciously large swells.

'I'm ready to go now, David,' he said into his helmet. 'Confirm that the work boat is standing by for the pick-up outside the hull.'

'We are all ready.' David Allen's voice was tense and sharp.

'Here we go,' said Nick, this was his wave now. There was no point in waiting longer.

He checked the reel on his belt, ensuring that the line was free to run, and watched the gash suck in clean green water, filled with tiny bright bubbles, little diamond chips that flew past his head to warn him of the lethal speed and power of that flood.

The inflow slowed and stopped as the hull filled to capacity, building up great pressures of air and water, and then the flow reversed abruptly as the swell on the far side subsided, and trapped water began to rush out again.

Nick released his grip on the stringer and instantly the water caught him. There was no question of being able to swim in that mill-race, all he could hope for was to keep his arms at his sides and his legs straight together to give himself a smoother profile, and to steer with his fins.

The accelerating speed appalled him as he was flung head first at that murderous steel mouth, he could feel the nylon line streaming out against his leg, the reel on his belt racing as though a giant marlin had struck and hooked upon the other end.

The rush of his progress seemed to leave his guts behind him as though he rode a fairground roller-coaster, and then a flick of the current turned him, he felt himself beginning to roll – and he fought wildly for control just as he hit.

He hit with a numbing shock, so his vision starred in flashing colour and light. The shock was in his shoulders and left arm, and he thought it might have been severed by that razor steel.

Then he was swirling, end over end, completely disorientated so he did not know which direction was up. He did not know if he was still inside *Golden Adventurer*'s hull, and the nylon line was wrapping itself around his throat and chest, around the precious air tubes and cutting off his air supply like a stillborn infant strangled by its own umbilical cord.

Again he hit something, this time with the back of his head, and only the cushioning of his helmet saved his skull from cracking. He flung out his arms and found the rough irregular shape of ice above him.

Terror wrapped him again, and he screamed soundlessly into his mask, but suddenly he broke out into light and air, into the loose scum of slush and rotten ice mixed with bigger, harder chunks, one of which had hit him.

Above him towered the endless steel cliff of the liner's side and beyond that, the low bruised wind-sky, and as he struggled to disentangle himself from the coils of nylon, he realized two things. The first was that both his arms were still attached to his body, and still functioning, and the second was that *Warlock*'s work boat was only twenty feet away and butting itself busily through the brash of rotten, broken ice towards him.


The collision mat looked like a five-ton Airedale terrier curled up to sleep in the bows of the work boat, just as shaggy and shapeless, and of the same wiry, furry brown colour.

Nick had shed his helmet and pulled an Arctic cloak and hood over his bare head and suited torso. He was balanced in the stern of the work boat as she plunged and rolled and porpoised in the big swells; chunks of ice cracked against her hull, knocking loose chips off her paintwork, but she was steel-hulled, wide and sea-kindly. The helmsman knew his job, working her with calm efficiency to Nick's hand-signals, bringing her in close through the brash ice, under the tall sheer of *Golden Adventurer*'s stern.

The thin white nylon line was the only physical contact with the men on the liner's towering stack of decks, the messenger which would carry heavier tackle. However it was vulnerable to any jagged piece of pancake ice, or the fangs of that voracious underwater steel jaw.

Nick paid out the line through his own numbed hands, feeling for the slightest check or jerk which could mean a snag and a break-off.

With hand-signals, he kept the work boat positioned so that the line ran cleanly into the pierced hull, around the sheave blocks he had placed with such heart-breaking labour in the engine room, from there up the tall ventilation shaft, out of the burned square opening in the stack and around the winch, beside which Beauty Baker was supervising the recovery of the messenger.

The gusts tore at Nick's head so that he had to crouch to shield the small two-way radio on his chest, and Baker's voice was tinny and thin in the buffeting boom of wind.

'Line running free.'

'Right, we are running the wire now,' Nick told him. The second line was as thick as a man's index finger, and it was of the finest Scandinavian steel cable. Nick checked the connection between nylon and steel cable himself, the nylon messenger was strong enough to carry the weight of steel, but the connection was the weakest point.

He nodded to the crew, and they let it go over the side; the white nylon disappeared into the cold green water and now the black steel cable ran out slowly from the revolving drum.

Nick felt the check as the connection hit the sheave block in the engine room. He felt his heart jump. If it caught now, they would lose it all; no man could penetrate that hull again, the sea was now too vicious. They would lose the tackle, and they would lose *Golden Adventurer*, she would break up in the seas that were coming.

'Please God, let it run,' Nick whispered in the boom and burst of sea and wind. The drum halted, made a half turn and jammed. Somewhere down there, the cable had snagged and Nick signalled to the helmsman to take the work boat in closer, to change the angle of the line into the hull.

He could almost feel the strain along his nerves as the winch took up the pull, and he could imagine the fibres of the nylon messenger stretching and creaking.

'Let it run! Let it run!' prayed Nick, and then suddenly he saw the drum begin to revolve again, the cable feeding out smoothly, and streaming down into the sea.

Nick felt light-headed, almost dizzy with relief, as he heard Baker's voice over the VHF, strident with triumph.

'Wire secured.'

'Stand by,' Nick told him. 'We are connecting the two-inch wire now.'

Again, the whole laborious, touchy, nerve-scouring process as the massive two-inch steel cable was drawn out by its thinner, weaker forerunner – and it was a further forty vital minutes, with the wind and sea rising every moment, before Baker shouted, 'Main cable secured, we are ready to haul!'

'Negative,' Nick told him urgently. 'Take the strain and hold.' If the collision mat in the bows hooked and held on the work boat's gunwale, Baker would pull the bows under and swamp her.

Nick signalled to his crew and the five of them shambled up into the bows, bulky and clumsy in their electric-yellow oilskins and work boots. With hand-signals, Nick positioned them around the shaggy head-high pile of the collision mat before he signalled to the helmsman to throw the gear in reverse and pull back from *Golden Adventurer*'s side.

The mass of unravelled oakum quivered and shook as the two-inch cable came up taut and they struggled to heave the whole untidy mass overboard.

There was nearly five tons of it and the weight would have been impossible to handle were it not for the reverse pull of the work boat against the cable.

Slowly, they heaved the mat forward and outward, and the work boat took on a dangerous list under the transfer of weight. She was down at the bows and canting at an angle of twenty degrees, the diesel motor screaming angrily and her single propeller threshing frantically, trying to pull her out from under her cumbersome burden.

The mat slid forward another foot, and snagged on the gunwale, sea water slopped inboard, ankle-deep around their rubber boots as they strained and heaved at the reluctant mass of coarse fibre.

Some instinct of danger made Nick look up and out to sea. *Warlock* was lying a quarter of a mile farther out in the bay, at the edge of the ice, and beyond her, Nick saw the rearing shape of a big wave alter the line of the horizon. It was merely a forerunner of the truly big waves that the storm was running before her, like hounds before the hunter, but it was big enough to make *Warlock* throw up her stern sharply, and even then the sea creamed over the tug's bows and streamed from her scuppers.

It would hit the exposed and hampered work boat in twenty-five seconds, it would hit her broadside while her bows were held down and anchored by mat and cable. When she swamped, the five men who made up her crew would die within minutes, pulled down by their bulky clothing, frozen by the icy green waters.

'Beauty,' Nick's voice was a scream in the microphone, 'heave all – pull, damn you, pull.'

Almost instantly the cable began to run, drawn in by the powerful winch on *Golden Adventurer*'s deck; the strain pulled the work boat down sharply and water cascaded over her gunwale.

Nick seized one of the oaken oars and thrust it under the mat at the point where it was snagged, and using it as a lever he threw all his weight upon it.

'Lend a hand,' he yelled at the man beside him, and he strained until he felt his vision darkening and the fibres of his back-muscles creaking and popping.

The work boat was swamping, they were almost knee-deep now and the wave raced down on them. It came with a great silent rush of irresistible power, lifting the mass of broken ice and tossing it carelessly aside without a check.

Suddenly, the snag cleared and the whole lumpy massive weight of oakum slid overboard. The work boat bounded away, relieved of her intolerable burden, and Nick windmilled frantically with both arms to get the helmsman to bring her bows round to the wave.

They went up the wave with a gut-swooping rush that threw them down on to the floorboards of the half-flooded work boat, and then crashed over the crest.

Behind them the wave slogged into *Golden Adventurer*'s stern, and shot up it with an explosion of white and furious water that turned to white driven spray in the wind.

The helmsman already had the work boat pushing heavily through the pack-ice, back towards the waiting *Warlock*.

'Stop,' Nick signalled him. 'Back up.'

Already he was struggling out of his hood and oilskins, as he staggered back to the stern.

He shouted in the helmsman's face, 'I'm going down to check,' and he saw the disbelieving, almost pleading, expression on the man's face. He wanted to get out of there now, back to the safety of *Warlock*, but relentlessly Nick resettled the diving helmet and connected his air hose.

The collision mat was floating hard against *Golden Adventurer*'s side, buoyant with trapped air among the mass of wiry fibre.

Nick positioned himself beneath it, twenty feet from the maelstrom created by the gashed steel.

It took him only a few seconds to ensure that the cable was free, and he blessed Beauty Baker silently for stopping the winch immediately it had pulled the mat free of the work boat. Now he could direct the final task.

'She's looking good,' he told Baker. 'But take her up slowly, fifty feet a minute on the winch.'

'Fifty feet, it is,' Baker confirmed.

And slowly the bobbing mat was drawn down below the surface.

'Good, keep it at that.'

It was like pressing a field-dressing into an open bleeding wound. The outside pressure of water drove it deep into the gash, while from the inside the two-inch cable plugged it deeper into place. The wound was staunched almost instantly and Nick finned down, and swam carefully over it.

The deadly suck and blow of high pressure through the gap was killed now, and he detected only the lightest movement of water around the edges of the mat; but the oakum fibres would swell now they were submerged, and within hours the plug would be watertight.

'It's done,' said Nick into his microphone. 'Hold a twenty-ton pull on the cable – and you can start your pumps and suck the bitch clean.'

It was a measure of his stress and relief and fatigue that Nick called that beautiful ship a bitch, and he regretted the word as it was spoken.


Nick craved sleep, every nerve, every muscle shrieked for surcease, and in his bathroom mirror his eyes were inflamed, angry with salt and wind and cold; the smears of exhaustion that underlined them were as lurid as the fresh bruises and abrasions that covered his shoulders and thighs and ribs.

His hands shook in a mild palsy with the need for rest and his legs could hardly carry him as he forced himself back to *Warlock*'s navigation bridge.

'Congratulations, sir,' said David Allen, and his admiration was transparent.

'How's the glass, David?' Nick asked, trying to keep the weariness from showing.

'994 and dropping, sir.'

Nick looked across at *Golden Adventurer*. Below that dingy low sky, she stood like a pier, unmoved by the big swells that marched on her in endless ranks, and she shrugged aside each burst of spray, hard aground and heavy with the water in her womb. However, that water was being flung from her, in solid white sheets.

Baker's big centrifugals were running at full power, and from both her port and starboard quarters the water poured. It looked as though the flood gates had been opened on a concrete dam, so powerful was the rush of expelled water.

The oil and diesel mixed with that discharge formed a sullen, iridescent slick around her, sullying the ice and the pebble beach on which she lay. The wind caught the jets from the pump outlets and tore them away in glistening plumes, like great ostrich feathers of spray.

'Chief,' Nick called the ship. 'What's your discharge rate?'

'We are moving nigh on five hundred thousand gallons an hour.'

'Call me as soon as she alters her trim,' he said, and then glanced up at the pointer of the anemometer above the control panel. The wind force was riding eight now, but he had to blink his stinging swollen eyes to read the scale.

'David,' he said, and he could hear the hoarseness in his voice, the flat dead tone. 'It will be four hours before she will be light enough to make an attempt to haul her off, but I want you to put the main towing-cable on board her and make fast, so we will be ready when she is.'

'Sir.'

'Use a rocket-line,' said Nick, and then stood dumbly, trying to think of the other orders he must give, but his brain was blank.

'Are you all right, sir?' David asked with quick concern, and immediately Nick felt the prick of annoyance. He had never wanted sympathy in his life, and he found his voice again. But he stopped the sharp words that came so quickly to his lips.

'You know what to do, David. I won't give you any other advice.' He turned like a drunkard towards his quarters. 'Call me when you've done it, or if Baker reports alteration of trim – or if anything else changes, anything, anything at all, you understand.'

He made it to the cabin before his knees buckled and he dropped his terry robe as he toppled backwards on to his bunk.


At 60° south latitude, there runs the only sea-lane that circumnavigates the entire globe, unbroken by any land mass. This wide girdle of open water runs south of Cape Horn and Australasia and the Cape of Good Hope, and it has the fearsome reputation of breeding the wildest weather on earth. It is the meeting-ground of two vast air masses, the cold slumping Antarctic air, and the warmer, more buoyant airs of the sub-tropics. These are flung together by the centrifugal forces generated by the earth as it revolves on its own axis, and their movement is further complicated by the enormous torque of the coriolis force. As they strike each other, the opposing air masses split into smaller fragments that retain their individual characteristics. They begin to revolve upon themselves, gigantic whirlpools of tortured air, and as they advance, so they gain in strength and power and velocity.

The high-pressure system which had brought that ominously calm and silken weather to Cape Alarm, had bounced the pressure right up to 1035 millibars, while the great depression which pursued it so closely and swiftly had a centre pressure as low as 985 millibars. Such sharp contrast meant that the winds along the pressure-gradient were ferocious.

The depression itself was almost fifteen hundred miles across its circumference, and it reached up to the high troposphere, thirty thousand feet above the level of the sea. The mighty winds it contained reached right off the maximum of the Beaufort scale of force twelve, gusting 120 miles an hour and more. They roared unfettered upon a terrible sea, unchecked by the bulwark of any land mass, nothing in their path, but the sudden jagged barrier of Cape Alarm.

While Nicholas Berg slept the deathlike sleep of utter exhaustion, and Beauty Baker tended his machines, driving them to their limits in an effort to pump *Golden Adventurer* free of her burden of salt water, the storm rushed down upon them.


When her knock was unanswered, Samantha stood uncertainly, balancing the heavy tray against *Warlock*'s extravagant action as she rode the rising swells at the entrance to the bay.

Her uncertainty lasted not more than three seconds, for she was a lady given to swift decision. She tried the door-latch and when it turned, she pushed it open slowly enough to warn anybody on the far side, and stepped into the Captain's day cabin.

'He ordered food,' she justified her intrusion, and closed the door behind her, glancing swiftly around the empty cabin. It had been furnished in the high style of the old White Star liners. Real rosewood panelling and the couch and chairs were in rich brown calf hide, polished and buttoned, while the deck was carpeted in thick shaggy wool, the colour of tropical forest leaves.

Samantha placed the tray on the table that ran below the starboard portholes, and she called softly. There was no reply, and she stepped to the open doorway into the night cabin.

A white terry robe lay in a heap in the centre of the deck, and she thought for one disturbing moment that the body on the bed was naked, but then she saw he wore a thin pair of white silk boxer shorts.

'Captain Berg,' she called again, but softly enough not to disturb him, and with a completely feminine gesture picked up the robe from the floor, folded it and dropped it over a chair, moving forward at the same time until she stood beside his bunk.

She felt a quick flare of concern when she saw the bruises which stood out so vividly on the smooth pale skin, and concern turned to dismay when she realized how he lay like a dead man, his legs trailing over the edge of the bunk and his body twisted awkwardly, one arm thrown back over his shoulder and his head lolling from side to side as *Warlock* rolled.

She reached out quickly and touched his cheek, experiencing a lift of real relief as she felt the warmth of his flesh and saw his eyelids quiver at her touch.

Gently she lifted his legs and he rolled easily on to his side, exposing the sickening abrasion that wrapped itself angrily across back and shoulder. She touched it with a light exploring fingertip and knew that it needed attention, but she sensed that rest was what he needed more.

She stood back and for long seconds gave herself over to the pleasure of looking at him. His body was fined down, he carried no fat on his belly or flanks; clearly she could see the rack of his ribs below the skin, and the muscles of his arms and legs were smooth but well-defined, a body that had been cared for and honed by hard exercise. Yet there was a certain denseness to it, that thickening of shoulder and neck, and the distinctive hair patterns of the mature man.

It might not have the grace and delicacy of the boys she had known, yet it was more powerful than that of even the strongest of the young men who had until then filled her world. She thought of one of them whom she had believed she loved. They had spent two months in Tahiti together on the same field expedition. She had surfed with him, danced and drunk wine, worked and slept sixty consecutive days and nights with him; in the same period they had become engaged to marry, and had argued, and parted, with surprisingly little regret on her part – but he had had the most beautiful tanned and sculptured body she had ever known. Now, looking at the sleeping figure on the bunk, she knew that even he would not have been able to match this man in physical determination and strength.

Angel had been right. It was the power that attracted her so strongly. The powerful, rangy body with the dark coarse hair covering his chest and exploding in flak bursts in his armpits – this, together with the power of his presence.

She had never known a man like this, he filled her with a sense of awe. It was not only the legend that surrounded him, nor the formidable list of his accomplishments that Angel had recounted for her, nor yet was it only the physical strength which he had just demonstrated while the entire crew of *Warlock*, she among them, had watched and listened avidly over the VHF relay. She leaned over him again, and she saw that even in repose, his jawline was hard and uncompromising, and the little creases and lines and marks that life had chiselled into his face, around the eyes and at the corners of the mouth, heightened the effect of power and determination, the face of a man who dictated his own terms to life.

She wanted him, Angel was right, oh God, how she wanted him! They said there was no love at first sight – they had to be mad.

She turned away and unfolded the eiderdown from the foot of the bunk, spreading it over him, and then once again she stooped and gently lifted the fall of thick dark hair from his forehead, smoothing it back with a maternally protective gesture.

Although he had slept on while she lifted and covered him, strangely this lightest of touches brought him to the edge of consciousness and he sighed and twisted, then whispered hoarsely, 'Chantelle, is that you?'

Samantha recoiled at the bitter sharp pang of jealousy with which another woman's name stabbed her. She turned away and left him, but in the day cabin she paused again beside his desk.

There were a few small personal items thrown carelessly on the leather-bound blotter – a gold money clip holding a mixed sheath of currency notes, five pounds sterling, fifty US dollars, deutschmarks and francs, a gold Rolex Oyster perpetual watch, a gold Dunhill lighter with a single white diamond set in it, and a billfold of the smoothest finest calf leather. They described clearly the man who owned them and, feeling like a thief, she picked up the billfold and opened it.

There were a dozen cards in their little plastic envelopes, American Express, Diners, Bank American, Carte Blanche, Hertz No. 1, Pan Am VIP and the rest. But opposite them was a colour photograph. Three people: a man, Nicholas in a cable-stitch jersey, his face bronzed, his hair wind-ruffled; a small boy in a yachting jacket with a curly mop of hair and solemn eyes above a smiling mouth – and a woman. She was probably one of the most beautiful women Samantha had ever seen, and she closed the billfold, replaced it carefully, and quietly left the cabin.

David Allen called the Captain's suite for three minutes without an answer, slapping his open palm on the mahogany chart table with impatience and staring through the navigation windows at the spectacle of a world gone mad.

For almost two hours, the wind had blown steadily from the north-west at a little over thirty knots, and although the big lumpy seas still tumbled into the mouth of the bay, *Warlock* had ridden them easily, even connected as she was, to *Golden Adventurer* by the main tow-cable.

David had put a messenger over the liner's stern, firing the nylon line from a rocket gun, and Baker's men had retrieved the line and winched across first the carrier wire and then the main cable itself.

*Warlock* had let the main cable be drawn out of her by *Adventurer*'s winches, slowly revolving off the great winch drums in the compartment under the tug's stern deck, out through the cable ports below the after navigation bridge where David stood controlling each inch of run and play with light touches on the controls.

A good man could work that massive cable like a fly-fisherman playing a big salmon in the turbulent water of a mountain torrent, letting it slip against the clutchplates, or run free, or recover slack, bringing it up hard and fast under a pull of five hundred tons – or, in dire emergency, he could hit the shear button, and snip through the flexible steel fibre, instantaneously relinquishing the tow, possibly saving the tug itself from being pulled under or being rushed by the vessel it was towing.

It had taken an hour of delicate work, but now the tow was in place, a double yoke made fast to *Golden Adventurer*'s main deck bollards, one on her starboard and one on her port stern quarters.

The yoke was Y-shaped, drooping over the high stern to join at the white nylon spring, three times the thickness of a man's thigh and with the elasticity to absorb sudden shock which might have snapped rigid steel cable. From the yoke connection, the single main cable looped back to the tug.

David Allen was lying back a thousand yards from the shore, holding enough strain on the tow-cable to prevent it sagging to touch and possibly snag on the unknown bottom. He was holding his station with gentle play on the pitch and power of the twin screws, and checking his exact position against the electronic dials which gave him his speed across the ground in both directions, accurate to within a foot a minute.

It was all nicely under control, and every time he glanced up at the liner, the discharge of water still boiled from her pump outlets.

Half an hour previously, he had been unable to contain his impatience, for he knew with a seaman's deep instinct what was coming down upon them out of the dangerous quadrant of the wind. He had called Baker to ask how the work on the liner was progressing. It had been a mistake.

'You've got nothing better to do than call me out of the engine room to ask about my piles, and the FA Cup final? I'll tell you when I'm ready, believe me, sonny, I'll call you. If you are bored, go down and give Angel a kiss, but for God's sake, leave me alone.'

Beauty Baker was working with two of his men in that filthy, freezing steel box deep down in the liner's stern that housed the emergency steering-gear. The rudder was right across at full port lock. Unless he could get power on the steering machinery, she would be almost unmanageable, once she was under tow, especially if she was pulled off stern first. It was vital that the big ship was responding to her helm when *Warlock* tried to haul her off.

Baker cursed and cajoled the greasy machinery, knocking loose a flap of thick white skin from his knuckles when a spanner slipped, but working on grimly without even bothering to lift the injury to his mouth to suck away the welling blood. He let it drop on to the spanner and thicken into a sticky jelly, swearing softly but viciously as he concentrated all his skills on the obdurate steel mass of the steering gear. He knew every bit as well as the First Officer what was coming down upon them.

The wind had dropped to a gentle force four, a moderate steady breeze that blew for twenty minutes, just long enough for the crests of the waves to stop breaking over on themselves. Then slowly, it veered north – and without any further warning, it was upon them.

It came roaring like a ravening beast, lifting the surface of the sea away in white sheets of spray that looked as though red-hot steel had been quenched in it. It laid *Warlock* right over, so that her port rail went under and she was flung up so harshly on her main cable that her stern was pulled down sharply, water pouring in through her stern scuppers.

It took David by surprise, so that she paid off dangerously before he could slam open the port throttle and throw the starboard screw into full reverse thrust. As she came up, he hit the call to the Captain's suite, watching with rising disbelief as the mad world dissolved around him.

Nick heard the call from far away, it only just penetrated to his fatigue-drugged brain, and he tried to respond, but it felt as though his body was crushed under an enormous weight and that his brain was slow and sluggish as a hibernating reptile.

The buzzer insisted, a tinny, nagging whine and he tried to force his eyes open, but they would not respond. Then dimly, but deeply, he felt the wild anguished action of his ship and the tumult that he believed at first was in his own ears, but was the violent uproar of the storm about the tug's superstructure.

He forced himself up on one elbow, and his body ached in every joint. He still could not open his eyes but he groped for the handset.

'Captain to the after bridge?' He could hear something in David Allen's voice that forced him to his feet.

When Nick staggered on to the after navigation bridge, the First Officer turned gratefully to him.

'Thank God you've come, sir.'

The wind had taken the surface off the sea, had stripped it away, tearing each wave to a shrieking fog of white spray and mingling it with the sleet and snow that drove horizontally across the bay.

Nick glanced once at the dial of the wind anemometer, and then discounted the reading. The needle was stuck at the top of the scale. It made no sense, a wind-speed of 120 miles an hour was too much to accept, the instrument had been damaged by the initial gusts of this wind, and he refused to believe it; to do so now would be to admit disaster, for nobody could salvage an ocean-going liner in wind velocities right off the Beaufort scale.

*Warlock* stood on her tail, like a performing dolphin begging for a meal, as the cable brought her up short and the bridge deck became a vertical cliff down which Nick was hurled. He crashed into the control panel and clung for purchase to the foul-weather rail.

'We'll have to shear the cable and stand out to sea.' David Allen's voice was pitched too high and too loud, even for the tumult of the wind and the storm.

There were men on board *Golden Adventurer*, Baker and sixteen others, Nick thought swiftly, and even her twin anchors could not be trusted to hold in this.

Nick clung to the rail and peered out into the storm. Frozen spray and sleet and impacted snow drove on the wind, coming in with the force of buckshot fired at point-blank range, cracking into the armoured glass of the bridge and building up in thick clots and lumps that defeated the efforts of the spinning 'clear vision' panels.

He looked across a thousand yards and the hull of the liner was just visible, a denser area in the howling, swirling, white wilderness.

'Baker?' he asked into the hand microphone. 'What is your position?'

'The wind's got her, she's slewing. The starboard anchor is dragging.' And then, while Nick thought swiftly, 'You'll not be able to take us off in this.' It was a flat statement, an acceptance of the fact that the destinies of Baker and his sixteen men were inexorably linked to that of the doomed ship.

'No,' Nick agreed. 'We won't be able to get you off.' To approach the stricken ship was certain disaster for all of them.

'Shear the cable and stand off,' Baker advised. 'We'll try to get ashore as she breaks up.' Then, with a hangman's chuckle, he went on, 'Just don't forget to come and fetch us when the weather moderates – that is if there is anybody to fetch.'

Abruptly Nick's anger came to the surface through the layers of fatigue, anger at the knowledge that all he had risked and suffered was now to be in vain, that he was to lose *Golden Adventurer*, and probably with her sixteen men, one of whom had become a friend.

'Are you ready to heave on the anchor winches?' he asked. 'We are going to pull the bitch off.'

'Jesus!' said Baker. 'She's still half flooded—'

'We will have a lash at it, cobber,' said Nick quietly.

'The steering-gear is locked, you won't be able to control her. You'll lose *Warlock* as well as—' but Nicholas cut Baker short.

'Listen, you stupid Queensland sheep-shagger, get on to those winches.' As he said it, *Golden Adventurer* disappeared, her bulk blotted out completely by the solid, white curtains of the bizzard.

'Engine room,' Nick spoke crisply to the Second Engineer. 'Disengage the override, and give me direct control of both power and pitch.'

'Control transferred to bridge, sir,' the Engineer confirmed, and Nick touched the shining stainless-steel levers with fingers as sensitive as those of a concert pianist. *Warlock*'s response was instantaneous. She pivoted, shrugging aside a green slithering burst of water which came in over her shoulder and thundered down the side of her superstructure.

'Anchor winches manned.' Beauty Baker's tone was almost casual.

'Stand by,' said Nick, and felt his way through that white inferno. It was impossible to maintain visual reference, the entire world was white and swirling, even the surface of the sea was gone in torn streamers of white; the very pull of gravity, that should have defined even a simple up or down, was confused by the violent pitch and roll of the deck.

Nick felt his exhausted brain begin to lurch dizzily in the first attacks of vertigo. Swiftly he switched his attention to the big compass and the heading indicator.

'David,' he said, 'take the wheel.' He wanted somebody swift and bright at the helm now.

*Warlock* plunged suddenly, so viciously that Nick's bruised ribs were brought in brutal contact with the edge of the control console. He grunted involuntarily with the pain. *Warlock* was feeling her cable, she had come up hard.

'Starboard ten,' said Nick to David, bringing her bows up into that hideous wind.

'Chief,' he spoke into the microphone, his voice still ragged with the pain in his chest. 'Haul starboard winch, full power.'

'Full power starboard.'

Nick slid pitch control to fully fine, and then slowly nudged open the throttles, bringing in twenty-two thousand horse-power.

Held by her tail, driven by the great wind, and tortured by the sea, lashed by her own enormous propellers, *Warlock* went berserk. She corkscrewed and porpoised to her very limits, every frame in her hull shook with the vibration of her screws as her propellers burst out of the surface and spun wildly in the air.

Nick had to clench his jaws as the vibration threatened to crack his teeth, and when he glanced across at the forward and lateral speed-indicators, he saw that David Allen's face was icy white and set like that of a corpse.

*Warlock* was slewing down on the wind, describing a slow left-hand circle at the limit of the cable as the engine torque and the wind took her around.

'Starboard twenty,' Nick snapped, correcting the turn, and despite the rigour of his features, David Allen's response was instantaneous.

'Twenty degrees of starboard wheel on, sir.'

Nick saw the lateral drift stop on the ground speed-indicator, and then with a wild lurch of elation he saw the forward speed-indicator flicked into green. Its electronic digital read out, changing swiftly – they were moving forward at 150 feet a minute.

'We are moving her,' Nick cried aloud, and he snatched up the microphone. 'Full power both winches.'

'Both full and holding,' answered Baker immediately.

And Nick glanced back at the forward speed across the ground, 150, 110, 75 feet a minute. *Warlock*'s forward impetus slowed, and Nick realized with a slide of dismay that it was merely the elasticity of the nylon spring that had given them that reading. The spring was stretching out to its limit.

For two or three seconds, the dial recorded a zero rate of speed. *Warlock* was standing still, the cable drawn out to the full limit of her strength, then abruptly the dial flicked into vivid red; they going backwards, as the nylon spring exerted pressures beyond that of the twin diesels and the big bronze screws – *Warlock* was being dragged back towards that dreadful shore.

For another five minutes, Nick kept both clenched fists on the control levers, pressing them with all his strength to the limit of their travel, sending the great engines shrieking, driving the needles up around the dials, deep into the red 'never exceed' sectors.

He felt tears of anger and frustration scalding his swollen eyelids, and the ship shuddered and shook and screamed under him, her torment transmitted through the soles of his feet and the palms of his hands.

*Warlock* was held down by cable and power, so she could not rise to meet the seas that came out of the roaring whiteness. They tumbled aboard her, piling up on each other, so she burrowed deeper and more dangerously.

'For God's sake, sir,' David Allen was no longer able to contain himself. His eyes looked huge in his bone-white face. 'You'll drive her clean under.'

'Baker,' Nick ignored his Mate, 'are you gaining?'

'No recovery either winch,' Beauty told him. 'She is not moving.'

Nick pulled back the stainless steel levers, the needles sank swiftly back around their dials, and *Warlock* reacted gratefully, shaking herself free of the piled waters.

'You'll have to shear the tow.' Baker's disembodied voice was muted by the clamour of the storm. 'We'll take our chances, sport.'

Beside him, David Allen reached for the red-painted steel box that housed the shear button. It was protected by the box from accidental usage; David Allen opened the box and looked expectantly, almost pleadingly at Nick.

'Belay that?' Nick snarled at him, and then to Baker, 'I'm shortening tow. Be ready to haul again, when I am in position.'

David Allen stared at him, his right hand still on the open lid of the red box.

'Close that bloody thing,' Nick said, and turned to the main cable controls. He moved the green lever to reverse, and felt the vibration in the deck as below him in the main cable room the big drums began to revolve, drawing the thick ice-encrusted cable up over *Warlock*'s stern.

Fighting every inch of the way like a wild horse on a head halter, *Warlock* was drawn in cautiously by her own winches, and the officers watched in mounting horror as out of the white terror of the blizzard emerged the mountainous ice-covered bulk of *Golden Adventurer*.

She was so close that the main cable no longer dipped below the surface of the sea, but ran directly from the liner's stern to the tug's massive fairleads on her stern quarter.

'Now we can see what we are doing,' Nick told them grimly. He could see now that much of *Warlock*'s power had been wasted by not exerting a pull on exactly the same plane as *Golden Adventurer*'s keel. He had been disorientated in the white-out of the blizzard, and had allowed *Warlock* to pull at an angle. It would not happen now.

'Chief,' he said. 'Pull, pull all, pull until she bursts her guts!' And again he slid the throttle handles fully home.

*Warlock* flung up against the elastic yoke, and Nick saw the water spurt from the woven fibres and turn instantly to ice crystals as it was whipped away on the shrieking wind.

'She's not moving, sir,' David cried beside him.

'No recovery either winch,' Baker confirmed almost immediately. 'She's solid!'

'Too much water still in her,' said David, and Nick turned on him as though to strike him to the deck.

'Give me the wheel,' he said, his voice cracking with his anger and frustration.

With both engines boiling the sea to white foam, and roaring like dying bulls, Nick swung the wheel to full port lock.

Wildly *Warlock* dug her shoulder in, water pouring on board her as she rolled, instantly Nick spun the wheel to full starboard lock and she lurched against the tow, throwing an extra ton of pressure on to it.

Even above the storm, they heard *Golden Adventurer* groan, the steel of her hull protesting at the weight of water in her and the intolerable pressure of the anchor winches and *Warlock*'s tow cable.

The groan became a crackling hiss as the pebble bottom gave and moved under her.

'Christ, she's coming!' shrieked Baker, and Nick swung her to full port lock again, swinging *Warlock* into a deep trough between waves, then a solid ridge of steaming water buried her, and Nick was not certain she could survive that press of furious sea. It came green and slick over the superstructure and she shuddered wearily, gone slow and unwieldy. Then she lifted her bows and, like a spaniel, shook herself free, becoming again quick and light.

'Pull, my darling, pull,' Nick pleaded with her.

With a slow reluctant rumble, *Golden Adventurer*'s hull began to slide over the holding, clinging bottom.

'Both winches recovering,' Baker howled gleefully, and *Warlock*'s ground speed-indicator flicked into the green, its little angular figures changing in twinkling electronic progression as *Warlock* gathered way.

They all saw *Golden Adventurer*'s stern swinging to meet the next great ridge of water as it burst around her. She was floating, and for moments Nick was paralysed by the wonder of seeing that great and beautiful ship come to life again, become a living, vital sea creature as she took the seas and rose to meet them.

'We've done it, Christ, we've done it!' howled Baker, but it was too soon for self-congratulation. As *Golden Adventurer* came free of the ground and gathered stern-way under *Warlock*'s tow, so her rudder bit and swung her tall stern across the wind.

She swung, exposing the enormous windage of her starboard side to the full force of the storm. It was like setting a main sail, and the wind took her down swiftly on the rocky headland with its sentinel columns that guarded the entrance to the bay.

Nick's first instinct was to try and hold her off, to oppose the force of the wind directly and he flung *Warlock* into the task, relying on her great diesels and the two anchors to keep the liner from going ashore again – but the wind toyed with them, it ripped the anchors out of the pebble bottom and *Warlock* was drawn stern first through the water, straight down on the jagged rock of the headland.

'Chief, get those anchors up,' Nick snapped into the microphone. 'They'll never hold in this.'

Twenty years earlier, bathing off a lonely beach in the Seychelles, Nick had been caught out of his depth by one of those killer currents that flow around the headlands of oceanic islands, and it had sped him out into the open sea so that within minutes the silhouette of the land was low and indistinct on his watery horizon. He had fought that current, swimming directly against it, and it had nearly killed him. Only in the last stages of exhaustion had he begun to think, and instead of battling it, he had ridden the current, angling slowly across it, using its impetus rather than opposing it.

The lesson he had learned that day was well remembered, and as he watched Baker bring *Golden Adventurer's* dripping anchors out of the wild water he was driving *Warlock* hard, bringing her around on her cable so the wind was no longer in her teeth, but over her stern quarter.

Now the wind and *Warlock's* screws were no longer opposed, but *Warlock* was pulling two points off the wind, as fine a course as Nick could judge barely to clear the most seaward of the rocky sentinels; now the liner's locked rudder was holding her steady into the wind – but opposing *Warlock's* attempt to angle her away from the land.

It was a problem of simple vectors of force, that Nick tried to work out in his head and prove in physical terms, as he delicately judged the angle of his tow and the direction of the wind, balancing them against the tremendous leverage of the liner's locked rudder, the rudder which was dragging her suicidally down upon the land.

Grimly, he stared ahead to where the black rock cliffs were still hidden in the white nothingness. They were invisible, but their presence was recorded on the cluttered screen of the radar repeater. With both wind and engines driving them, their speed was too high, and if *Golden Adventurer* went on to the cliffs like this, her hull would shatter like a water melon hurled against a brick wall.

It was another five minutes before Nick was absolutely certain they would not make it. They were only two miles off the cliffs now, he glanced again at the radar screen, and they would have to drag *Golden Adventurer* at least half a mile across the wind to clear the land. They just were not going to make it.

Helplessly, Nick stood and peered into the storm, waiting for the first glimpse of black rock through the swirling eddies of snow and frozen spray, and he had never felt more tired and unmanned in his entire life as he moved to the shear button ready to cut *Golden Adventurer* loose and let her go to her doom.

His officers were silent and tense around him, while under his feet *Warlock* shuddered and buffeted wildly, driven to her mortal limits by the sea and her own engines, but still the land sucked at them.

'Look!' David Allen shouted suddenly, and Nick spun to the urgency in his voice.

For a moment he did not understand what was happening. He knew only that the shape of *Golden Adventurer's* stern was altered subtly.

'The rudder,' shouted David Allen again. And Nick saw it revolving slowly on its stock as the ship lifted on another big sea.

Almost immediately, he felt *Warlock* making offing from under that lee shore, and he swung her up another point into the wind, *Golden Adventurer* answering her tow with a more docile air, and still the rudder revolved slowly.

'I've got power on the emergency steering gear now,' said Baker.

'Rudder amidships,' Nick ordered.

'Amidships it is,' Baker repeated, and now he was pulling her out stern first, almost at right angles across the wind.

Through the white inferno suddenly appeared the dim snow-blurred outline of the rock sentinels, and the sea broke upon them like the thunder of the heavens.

'God, they are close,' whispered David Allen. So close that they could feel the backlash of the gale as it rebounded from the tall rock walls, moderating the tremendous force that was bearing them down – moderating just enough to allow them to slide past the three hungry rocks, and before them lay three thousand miles of wild and tumultuous water, all of it open sea room.

'We made it, This time we really made it,' said Baker, as though he did not believe it was true, and Nick pulled back the throttle controls taking the intolerable strain off her engines before they tore themselves to pieces.

'Anchors and all,' Nick replied. It was a point of honour to retrieve even the anchors. They had taken her off clean and intact – anchors and all.

'Chief,' he said, 'instead of sitting there hugging yourself, how about pumping her full of Tannerax?' The anti-corrosive chemical would save her engines and much of her vital equipment from further seawater damage, adding enormously to her salvaged value.

'You just never let up, do you?' Baker answered accusingly.

'Don't you believe it,' said Nick, he felt stupid and frivolous with exhaustion and triumph. Even the storm that still roared about them seemed to have lost its murderous intensity. 'Right now I'm going down to my bunk to sleep for twelve hours – and I'll kill anybody who tries to wake me.'

He hung the handmike on its bracket and put his hand on David Allen's shoulder. He squeezed once, and said:

'You did well – you all did very well. Now take her, Number One, and look after her.'

Then he stumbled from the bridge.


It was eight days before they saw the land again. They rode out the storm in the open sea, eight days of unrelenting tension and heart-breaking labour.

The first task was to move the tow-cable to *Golden Adventurer's* bows. In that sea, the transfer took almost 24 hours, and three abortive attempts before they had her head-on to the wind. Now she rode more easily, and *Warlock* had merely to hang on like a drogue, using full power only when one of the big icebergs came within dangerous range, and it was necessary to draw her off.

However, the tension was always there and Nick spent most of those days on the bridge, watchful and worried, nagged by the fear that the plug in the gashed hull would not hold. Baker used timbers from the ship's store to shore up the temporary patch, but he could not put steel in place while *Golden Adventurer* plunged and rolled in the heavy seas, and Nick could not go aboard to check and supervise the work.

Slowly, the great wheel of low pressure revolved over them, the winds changed direction, backing steadily into the west, as the epicentre marched on down the sea lane towards Australasia – and at last it had passed.

Now *Warlock* could work up towing speed. Even in those towering glassy swells of black water that the storm had left them as a legacy, she was able to make four knots.

Then one clear and windy morning under a cold yellow sun, she brought *Golden Adventurer* into the sheltered waters of Shackleton Bay. It was like a diminutive guide-dog leading a blinded colossus.

As the two ships came up into the still waters under the sheltering arm of the bay, the survivors came down from their encampment to the water's edge, lining the steep black pebble beach, and their cheers and shouts of welcome and relief carried thinly on the wind to the officers on *Warlock's* bridge.

Even before the liner's twin anchors splashed into the clear green water, Captain Reilly's boat was puttering out to *Warlock*, and when he came aboard, his eyes were haunted by the hardship and difficulties of these last days, by the disaster of a lost command and the lives that had been ended with it. But when he shook hands with Nick, his grasp was firm.

'My thanks and congratulations, sir!'

He had known Nicholas Berg as Chairman of Christy Marine, and, as no other, he was aware of the magnitude of this his most recent accomplishment. His respect was apparent.

'It's good to see you again,' Nick told him. 'Naturally you have access to my ship's communications to report to your owners.'

Immediately he turned back to the task of manoeuvring *Warlock* alongside, so that steel plate could be swung up from her salvage holds to the liner's deck; it was another hour before Captain Reilly emerged from the radio room.

'Can I offer you a drink, Captain?' Nick led him to his day cabin, and began with tact to deal with the hundred details which had to be settled between them. It was a delicate situation, for Reilly was no longer Master of his own ship. Command had passed to Nicholas as salvage master.

'The accommodation aboard *Golden Adventurer* is still quite serviceable, and, I imagine, a great deal warmer and more comfortable than that occupied by your passengers at present –' Nick made it easier for him while never for a moment letting him lose sight of his command position, and Reilly responded gratefully.

Within half an hour, they had made all the necessary arrangements to transfer the survivors aboard the liner. Levosin on *La Mouette* had been able to take only one hundred and twenty supernumeraries on board his little tug. The oldest and weakest of them had gone and Christy Marine was negotiating for a charter from Cape Town to Shackleton Bay to take off the rest of them. Now that charter was unnecessary, but the cost of it would form part of Nick's claim for salvage award.

'I won't take more of your time.' Reilly drained his glass and stood. 'You have much to do.'

There were another four days and nights of hard work. Nick went aboard *Golden Adventurer* and saw the cavernous engine room lit by the eye-scorching blue glare of the electric welding flames, as Baker placed his steel over the wound and welded it into place. Even then, neither he nor Nick was satisifed until the new patches had been shored and stiffened with baulks of heavy timber. There was a hard passage through the roaring forties ahead of them, and until they had *Golden Adventurer* safely moored in Cape Town docks, the salvage was incomplete.

They sat side by side among the greasy machinery and the stink of the anti-corrosives, and drank steaming Thermos coffee laced with Bundaberg rum.

'We get this beauty into Duncan Docks – and you are going to be a rich man,' Nick said.

'I've been rich before. With me it never lasts long – and it's always a relief when I've spent the stuff.' Beauty gargled the rum and coffee appreciatively, before he went on, shrewdly, 'So you don't have to worry about losing the best goddamned engineer afloat.'

Nick laughed with delight. Baker had read him accurately. He did not want to lose this man.

Nick left him and went to see to the trim of the liner, studying her carefully and using the experience of the last days to determine her best points of tow, before giving his orders to David Allen to raise her slightly by the head.

Then there was the transfer from the liner's bunkers of sufficient bunker oil to top up *Warlock's* own tanks against the long tow ahead, and Bach Wackie in Bermuda kept the telex clattering with relays from underwriters and Lloyd's, with the first tentative advances from Christy Marine; already Duncan Alexander was trying out the angles, manoeuvring for a liberal settlement of Nick's claims, without, as he put it, the expense of the arbitration court.

'Tell him I'm going to roast him,' Nick answered with grim relish.

'Remind him that as Chairman of Christy Marine I advised against underwriting our own bottoms – and now I'm going to rub his nose in it.'

The days and nights blurred together, the illusion made complete by the
imbalance of time down here in the high latitudes, so that Nick could often
believe neither his senses nor his watch when he had been working eighteen
hours straight and yet the sun still burned, and his watch told him it was
three o'clock in the morning.

Then again, it did not seem part of reality when his senior officers,
gathered around the mahogany table in his day cabin, reported that the work
was completed – the repairs and preparation, the loading of fuel, the
embarkation of passengers and the hundred other details had all been
attended to, and *Warlock* was ready to drag her massive charge out into that
unpredictable sea, thousands of miles to the southernmost tip of Africa.

Nick passed the cheroot-box around the circle and while the blue smoke
clouded the cabin, he allowed them all a few minutes to luxuriate in the
feeling of work done, and done well.

'We'll rest the ship's company for twenty-four hours,' he announced in
a rush of generosity. 'And take in tow at 0800 hours Monday. I'm hoping
for a tow speed of six knots – twenty-one days to Cape Town, gentlemen.'

When they rose to leave, David Allen lingered self-consciously. 'The
wardroom is arranging a little Christmas celebration tonight, sir, and we
would like you to be our guest.'


The wardroom was the junior officers' club from which, traditionally, the
Master was excluded. He could enter the small panelled cabin only as an
invited guest, but there was no doubt at all about the genuine warmth of the
welcome they gave him. Even the Trog was there. They stood and applauded
him when he entered, and it was clear that most of them had made an early
start on the gin. David Allen made a speech which he read haltingly from
a scrap of paper which he tried to conceal in the palm of one hand. It was
a speech full of hyperbole, clichés and superlatives, and he was clearly
mightily relieved once it was over.

Then Angel brought in a cake he had baked for the occasion. It was iced
in the shape of '*Golden Adventurer*', a minor work of art, with the figures
'12½%' picked out in gold on its hull, and they applauded him. That 12½%
had significance to set them all grinning and exclaiming.

Then they called on Nick to speak, and his style was relaxed and easy.
He had them hooting with glee within minutes – a mere mention of the
prize money that would be due to them once they brought *Golden Adventurer*
into Cape Town had them in ecstasy.

The girl was wedged into a corner, almost swallowed in the knot of young
officers who found it necessary to press as closely around her as was possible
without actually smothering her.

She laughed with a clear unaffected exuberance, her voice ringing high
above the growl of masculine mirth, so that Nick found it difficult not to
keep looking across at her.

She wore a dress of green clinging material, and Nick wondered where
it had come from, until he remembered that *Golden Adventurer's* passenger

accommodation was intact and that earlier that morning, he had noticed the girl standing beside David Allen in the stern of the work boat as it returned from the liner, with a large suitcase at her feet. She had been to fetch her gear and she probably should have stayed aboard the liner. Nick was pleased she had not.

Nick finished his little speech, having mentioned every one of his officers by name and given to each the praise they deserved, and David Allen pressed another large whisky into his one hand and an inelegant wedge of cake into the other, and then left hurriedly to join the tight circle around the girl. It opened reluctantly, yielding to his seniority and Nick found himself almost deserted.

He watched with indulgence the open competition for her attention. She was shorter than any of them, so Nick saw only the top of that magnificent mane of sun-streaked hair, hair the colour of precious metal that shone as she nodded and tilted her head, catching the overhead lights.

Beauty Baker was on one side of her, dressed in a ready-made suit of shiny imitation sharkskin that made a startling contrast to his plaid shirt and acid-yellow tie; the trousers of the suit needed hoisting every few minutes and his spectacles glittered lustfully as he hung over the girl.

David Allen was close on her other side, blushing pinkly every time she turned to speak to him, plying her with cake and liquor – and Nick found his indulgence turning to irritation.

He was irritated by the presence of a tongue-tied fourth officer who had clearly been delegated to entertain him, and was completely awed by the responsibility. He was irritated by the antics of his senior officers. They were behaving like a troupe of performing seals in their competition for the girl's attention.

For a few moments, the tight circle around her opened, and Nick was left with a few vivid impressions. The green of her dress matched exactly the brilliant sparkling green of her eyes. Her teeth were very white, and her tongue as pink as a cat's when she laughed. She was not the child he had imagined from their earlier encounters; with colour touched to her lips and pearls at her throat, he realized she was in her twenties, early twenties perhaps, but a full woman, nevertheless.

She looked across the wardroom and their eyes met. The laughter stilled on her lips, and she returned his gaze. It was a solemn enigmatic gaze, and he found himself once again regretting his previous rudeness to her. He dropped his gaze from hers and saw now that under the clinging green material, her body was slim and beautifully formed, with a lithe athletic grace. He remembered vividly that one nude glimpse he had been given.

Although the green dress was high-necked, he saw that her breasts were large and pointed, and that they were not trussed by any undergarments; the young shapely flesh was as strikingly arresting as if it had been naked.

It made him angry to see her body displayed in this manner. It did not matter that every young girl in the streets of New York or London went so uncorseted, here it made him angry to see her do the same, and he looked back into her eyes. Something charged there, a challenge perhaps, his own anger reflected? He was not sure. She tilted her head slightly, now it was invitation – or was it? He had known and handled easily so many, many women. Yet this one left him with a feeling of uncertainty, perhaps it was merely her youth, or was it some special quality she possessed? Nicholas Berg was uncertain and he did not relish the feeling.

David Allen hurried to her with another offering, and cut off the gaze that passed between them, and Nick found himself staring at the Chief Officer's slim, boyish back, and listening to the girl's laughter again, sweet and high. But somehow it seemed to be directed tauntingly at Nick, and he said to the young officer beside him,

'Please ask Mr Allen for a moment of his time.' Patently relieved the officer went to fetch him.

'Thank you for your hospitality, David,' said Nick, when he came.

'You aren't going yet, sir?' Nick took a small sadistic pleasure in the Mate's obvious dismay.


He sat at the desk in his day cabin and tried to concentrate. It was the first opportunity he had had to consider the paper work that awaited him. The muted sounds of revelry from the deck below distracted him, and he found himself listening for the sounds of her laughter while he should have been composing his submissions to his London attorneys, which would be taken to the arbitrators of Lloyd's, a document and record of vital importance, the whole basis of his claim against *Golden Adventurer's* underwriters. And yet he could not concentrate.

He swung his chair away from the desk and began to pace the thick sound-deadening carpet, stopping once to listen again as he heard the girl's voice calling gaily, the words unintelligible, but the tone unmistakable. They were dancing, or playing some raucous game which consisted of a great deal of bumping and thumping and shrieks of laughter.

He began to pace again, and suddenly Nick realized he was lonely. The thought stopped him dead again. He was lonely, and completely alone. It was a disturbing realization, especially for a man who had travelled much of life's journey as a loner. Before it had never troubled him, but now he felt desperately the need for somebody to share his triumph. Triumph it was, of course. Against the most improbable odds, he had snatched spectacular victory, and he crossed slowly to the cabin portholes and looked across the darkened bay to where *Golden Adventurer* lay at anchor, all her lights burning, a gay and festive air about her.

He had been knocked off his perch at the top of the tree, deprived of a life's work, a wife and a son – yet it had taken him only a few short months to clamber back to the top.

With this simple operation, he had transformed Ocean Salvage from a dangerously insecure venture, a tottering cash-starved, problem-hounded long chance, into something of real value. He was off and running again now, with a place to go and the means of getting there. Then why did it suddenly seem of so little worth? He toyed with the idea of returning to the revelry in the wardroom, and grimaced as he imagined the dismay of his officers at the Master's inhibiting intrusion.

He turned away from the porthole and poured whisky into a glass, lit a cheroot and dropped into the chair. The whisky tasted like toothpaste and the cheroot was bitter. He left the glass on his desk and stubbed the cheroot, before he went through on to the navigation bridge.

The night lights were so dim after his brightly lit cabin that he did not notice Graham, the Third Officer, until his eyes adjusted to the ruby glow.

'Good evening, Mr Graham.' He moved to the chart table and checked the log. Graham was hovering anxiously, and Nick searched for something to say.

'Missing the party?' he asked at last.

'Sir.'

It was not a promising conversational opening, and despite his loneliness of a few minutes previously, Nick suddenly wanted to be alone again.

'I will stand the rest of your watch. Go off and enjoy yourself.'

The Third Officer gawped at him.

'You've got three seconds before I change my mind.'

'That's jolly decent of you, sir,' called Graham over his shoulder as he fled.

The party in the wardroom had by now degenerated into open competition for Samantha's attention and approbation.

David Allen, wearing a lampshade on his head and, for some unaccountable reason, with his right hand thrust into his jacket in a Napoleonic gesture, was standing on the wardroom bar counter and declaiming Henry's speech before Agincourt, glossing over the passages which he had forgotten with a 'dum-de-dum'. However, when Tim Graham entered, he became immediately the First Officer. He removed the lampshade and inquired frostily,

'Mr Graham, am I correct in believing that you are officer of the watch? Your station at this moment is on the bridge—'

'The old man came and offered to stand my watch,' said Tim Graham.

'Good Lord!' David replaced his lampshade, and poured a large gin for his Third Officer. 'The old bastard must have come over all soft suddenly.'

Beauty Baker, who was hanging off the wall like a gibbon ape, dropped to his feet and drew himself up with rather unsteady dignity, hitched his trousers and announced ominously.

'If anybody calls the old bastard a bastard, I will personally kick his teeth down his throat.' He swept the wardroom with an eye that was belligerent and truculent, until it alighted on Samantha. Immediately it softened. 'That one doesn't count, Sammy!' he said.

'Of course not,' Samantha agreed. 'You can start again.'

Beauty returned to the starting point of the obstacle course, fortified himself with a draught of rum, pushed up his spectacles with a thumb and spat on his palms.

'One to get ready, two to get steady – and three to be off,' sang out Samantha, and clicked the stopwatch. Beauty Baker swung dizzily from the roof, clawing his way around the wardroom without touching the deck, cheered on by the entire company.

'Eight point six seconds!' Samantha clicked the watch, as he ended up on the bar counter, the finishing post. 'A new world record.'

'A drink for the new world champion.'

'I'm next, time me, Sammy!'

They were like schoolboys. 'Hey, watch me, Sammy!' But after another ten minutes, she handed the stopwatch to Tim Graham, who as a late arrival was still sober.

'I'll be back,' she lied, picked up a plate with a large untouched hunk of Angel's cake upon it and was gone before any of them realized it was happening.

Nick Berg was working over the chart-table, so intent that he was not aware of her for many seconds. In the dramatic lighting of the single overhead lamp, the strength of his features was emphasized. She saw the hard line of his jawbone, the heavy brow and the alert widely spaced set of his eyes. His nose was large and slightly hooked, like that of a plains Indian or a desert Bedouin, and there were lines at the corners of his mouth and around his eyes that were picked out in dark shadow. In his complete absorption with the charts and *Admiralty Pilot*, he had relaxed his mouth from its usual severe line. She saw now that the lips were full without being fleshy, and there was a certain sensitivity and voluptuousness there that she had not noticed before.

She stood quietly, enchanted with him, until he looked up suddenly, catching the rapt expression upon her face.

She tried not to appear flustered, but even in her own ears her voice was breathless.

'I'm sorry to disturb you. I brought some cake for Timmy Graham.'

'I sent him below to join the party.'

'Oh, I didn't notice him. I thought he was here.'

She made no move to leave, holding the plate in one hand, and they were silent a moment longer.

'I don't suppose I could interest you in a slice? It's going begging.'

'Share it,' he suggested, and she came to the chart-table.

'I owe you an apology,' he said, and was immediately aware of the harshness in his own voice. He hated to apologize, and she sensed it.

'I picked a bad moment,' she said, and broke off a piece of the cake. 'But this seems a better time. Thank you again, and I'm sorry for all the trouble I caused. I understand now that it nearly cost you the *Golden Adventurer.*'

They both turned to look out of the big armoured glass windows to where she lay.

'She is beautiful, isn't she?' said Nick, and his voice had lost its edge.

'Yes, she's beautiful,' Samantha agreed, and suddenly they were very close in the intimate ruddy glow of the night lights.

He began to talk, stiffy and self-consciously at first, but she drew him on, and with secret joy, she sensed him warming and relaxing. Only then did she begin to put her own ideas forward.

Nick was surprised and a little disconcerted at the depth of her view, and at her easy coherent expression of ideas, for he was still very much aware of her youth. He had expected the giddiness and the giggle, the shallowness and uninformed self-interest of immaturity, but it was not there, and suddenly the difference in their ages was of no importance. They were very close in the night, touching only with their minds, but becoming each minute so much more closely involved in their ideas that time had no significance.

They spoke about the sea, for they were both creatures of that element and as they discovered this, so their mutual delight in each other grew.

From below came the faint unmelodious strains of Beauty Baker leading the ship's officers in a chorus of:

> '—*The working class can kiss my arse*
> *I've got my 12½% at last!*'

And at another stage in the evening, a very worried Tim Graham appeared on the bridge and blurted out,

'Captain, sir, Doctor Silver is missing. She's not in her cabin and we have searched—' He saw her then, sitting in the Captain's chair and his worry turned to consternation. 'Oh, I see. We didn't know – I mean we didn't expect – I'm sorry, sir. Excuse me, sir. Goodnight, sir,' And again he fled the bridge.

'Doctor?' Nick asked.

'I'm afraid so,' she smiled, and then went on to talk about the university, explaining her research project, and the other work she had in mind. Nicholas listened silently, for like all highly competitive and successful men, he respected achievement and ambition.

The chasm that he imagined existed between them shrank rapidly, so that it was an intrusion when the eight-to-twelve watch ended, and the relief brought other human presence to the bridge, shattering the fragile mood they had created around themselves, and denying them further excuse for remaining together.

'Goodnight, Captain Berg,' she said.

'Goodnight, Doctor Silver,' he answered reluctantly. Until that night, he had not even known her name, and there was so much more he wanted to know now, but she was gone from the bridge; as he entered his own suite, Nick's earlier loneliness returned, but with even more poignancy.

During the long day of getting *Golden Adventurer* under tow, the hours of trim and accommodation to the sea, until she was following meekly, settling down to the long journey ahead, Nick thought of the girl at unlikely moments; but when he changed his usual routine and dined in the saloon rather than his own cabin, she was surrounded by a solidly attentive phalanx of young men, and, with a small shock of self-honesty, Nick realized that he was actually jealous of them. Twice during the meal, he had to suppress the sharp jibes that came to his lips, and would have plunged the unfortunate recipient into uncomprehending confusion.

Nick ate no dessert and took coffee alone in his day cabin. He might have relished Beauty Baker's company, but the Australian was aboard *Golden Adventurer*, working on her main engines. Then, despite the tensions and endeavours of the day, his bunk had no attractions for him. He glanced at the clock on the panelled bulk-head above his desk and saw that it was a few minutes after eight o'clock.

On impulse he went through to the navigation bridge, and Tim Graham leapt guiltily to his feet. He had been sitting in the master's chair, a liberty which deserved at the least a sharp reprimand, but Nick pretended not to notice and made a slow round of the bridge, checking every detail from the cable tensions of the tow and power settings of *Warlock's* engines, to the riding lights on both ships and the last log entry.

'Mr Graham,' he said, and the young officer stiffened to attention like the victim before a firing squad, 'I will stand this watch – you may go and get some dinner.'

The Third Officer was so thunderstruck that he needed a large gin before he could bring himself to tell the wardroom of his good fortune.

Samantha did not look up from the board but moved a bishop flauntingly across the front of David Allen's queen, and when David pounced on it with a gurgle of glee, she unleashed her rook from the rear file and said, 'Mate in three, David.'

'One more, Sam, give me my revenge,' pleaded David, but she shook her head and slipped out of the wardroom.

Nicholas became aware of the waft of her perfume. It was an inexpensive but exuberant fragrance – 'Babe', that was it, the one advertised by Hemingway's granddaughter. It suited Samantha perfectly. He turned to her, and it was only then that he was honest enough to admit to himself that he had relieved his Third Officer with the express intention of luring the girl up to the bridge.

'There are whales ahead,' he told her, and smiled one of those rare, irresistible smiles that she had come to treasure. 'I hoped you might come up.'

'Where? Where are they?' she asked with unfeigned excitement, and then they both saw the spout, a golden feather of spray in the low night sunlight two miles ahead.

'*Balaenoptera musculus!*' she exclaimed.

'I'll take your word for it, Doctor Silver, but to me it's still a blue whale.' Nick was still smiling, and she looked abashed for a moment.

'Sorry, I wasn't trying to dazzle you with science.' Then she looked back at the humpy, uninviting cold sea as the whale blew again, a far and ethereal column of lonely spray.

'One,' she said, 'only one.' And the excitement in her voice cooled. 'There are so few of them left now – that might be the last one we will ever see.'

'So few that they cannot find each other in the vastness of the ocean to breed.' Nick's smile was gone also, and again they talked of the sea, of their own involvement with it, their mutual concern at what man had done to it, and what he was still doing to it.

'When the Marxist government of Mozambique took over from the Portuguese colonists, it allowed the Soviets to send in dredges – not trawlers, but dredges – and they dredged the weed beds of Delagoa Bay. They actually *dredged* the breeding grounds of the Mozambique prawn. They took out a thousand tons of prawn, and destroyed the grounds for ever – and they drove an entire species into extinction in six short months.' Her outrage was in her voice as she told it.

'Two months ago the Australians arrested a Japanese trawler in their territorial waters. She had in her freezers the meat of 120,000 giant clams that her crew had torn from the barrier reef with crow bars. The clam population of a single coral reef would not exceed 20,000. That means they had denuded six oceanic reefs in one expedition – and they fined the Captain a thousand pounds.'

'It was the Japanese who perfected the "long line",' Nick agreed, 'the endless floating line, armed with specially designed hooks, and laid across the lanes of migration of the big pelagic surface-feeding fish, the tuna and the marlin. They wipe out the shoals as they advance – wipe them out to the last fish.'

'You cannot reduce any animal population beyond a certain point.' Samantha seemed much older as she turned her face up to Nick. 'Look what they did to the whales.'

Together they turned back to the windows gazing out in hope of another glimpse of that gentle monster, doomed now to extinction, one last look at another creature that would disappear from the seas.

'The Japanese and the Russians again,' said Nick. 'They would not sign the whaling treaty until there were not enough blues left in the seas to make their killing an economic proposition. Then they signed it. When there were two or three thousand blue whales left in all the oceans, that is when they signed.'

'Now they will hunt the Fin and the Sei and the Minke to extinction.'

As they stood side by side staring into the bizarre sun-lit night, searching vainly for that spark of life in the watery wilderness, without thinking Nick lifted his arm; he would have placed it around her shoulders, the age-old protective attitude of man to his woman, but he caught himself at the last moment before he actually touched her. She had felt his movement and tensed for it, swaying slightly towards him in anticipation, but he stepped away, letting his arm fall and stopped over the radarscope. She only realized then how much she had wanted him to touch her, but for the rest of that evening he stayed within the physical limits which he seemed to have set for himself.

The next evening she declined the wardroom's importunate invitations, and after dinner waited in her own cabin, the door an inch ajar so she heard Tim Graham leave the bridge, clattering down the companionway with exuberance, relieved once more of his watch. The moment he entered the wardroom, Samantha slipped from her cabin and ran lightly up to the bridge.

She was with him only minutes after he had assumed the watch and Nick was amused by the strength of his pleasure. They grinned at each other like school children in a successful piece of mischief.

Before the light went, they passed close by one of the big tabular bergs, and she pointed out the line of filth that marked the white ice like the ring around a bathtub that had been used by a chimney sweep.

'Paraffin wax,' she said, 'and undissolved hydrocarbons.'

'No,' he said, 'that's only glacial striation.'

'It's crude oil,' she answered him. 'I've sampled it. It was one of the reasons I took the guide job on *Golden Adventurer*, I wanted first-hand knowledge of these seas.'

'But we are two thousand miles south of the tanker lanes.'

'The beach at Shackleton Bay is thick with wax balls and crude droplets.

We found oil-soaked penguins on Cape Alarm, dead and dying. They hit an oil slick within fifty miles of that isolated shore.'

'I can hardly believe—' Nick started, but she cut across him.

'That's just it!' she said. 'Nobody wants to believe it. Just walk on by, as though it's another mugging victim lying on the sidewalk.'

'You're right,' Nick admitted grudgingly. 'Very few people really care.'

'A few dead penguins, a few little black tar balls sticking to your feet on the beach. It doesn't seem much to shout about, but it's what we cannot see that should terrify us. Those millions of tons of poisonous hydrocarbons that dissolve into the sea, that kill slowly and insidiously, but surely. That's what should really terrify us, Nicholas!'

She had used his given name for the first time, and they were both acutely aware of it. They were silent again, staring intently at the big iceberg as it passed slowly. The sun had touched it with ethereal pinks and dreaming amethyst, but that dark line of poisonous filth was still there.

'The world has to use fossil fuels, and we sailors have to transport them,' he said at last.

'But not at such appalling risks, not with an eye only to the profits. Not in the same greedy thoughtless grabbing petty way as man wiped out the whale, not at the cost of turning the sea into a stinking festering cesspool.'

'There are unscrupulous owners –' he agreed, and she cut across him angrily.

'Sailing under flags of convenience, without control, ships built to dangerous standards, equipped with a single boiler –' she reeled out the charges, and he was silent.

'Then they waived the winter load-line for tankers rounding the Cape of Good Hope in the southern winter, to enable them to carry that extra fifty thousand tons of crude. The Agulhas Bank, the most dangerous winter sea in the world, and they send overloaded tankers into it.'

'That was criminal,' he agreed.

'Yet you were Chairman of Christy Marine, you had a representative on the Board of Control.'

She saw that she had made a mistake. His expression was suddenly ferocious. His anger seemed to crackle like electricity in the ruby gloom of the bridge. She felt an unaccountable flutter of real fear. She had forgotten what kind of man he was.

But he turned away and made a slow circuit of the bridge, elaborately checking each of the gauges and instruments, and then he paused at the far wing and lit a cheroot. She ached to offer some token of reconciliation, but instinctively she knew not to do so. He was not the kind of man who respected compromise or retreat.

He came back to her at last, and the glow of the cheroot lit his features so that she could see the anger had passed.

'Christy Marine seems like another existence to me now,' he said softly, and she could sense the deep pain of unhealed wounds. 'Forgive me, your reference to it took me off balance. I did not realize that you knew of my past history.'

'Everybody on board knows.'

'Of course,' he nodded, and drew deeply on the cheroot before he spoke again. 'When I ran Christy Marine, I insisted on the highest standards of safety and seamanship for every one of our vessels. We opposed the Cape winter-line decision, and none of my tankers loaded to their summer-line on the Good Hope passage. None of my tankers made do with only one boiler, the design and engineering of every Christy Marine vessel was of the same standard as that ship there,' he pointed back at *Golden Adventurer*, 'or this one here,' and he stamped once on the deck.

'Even the *Golden Dawn?*' she asked softly, braving his anger again – but he merely nodded.

'*Golden Dawn*,' he repeated softly. 'It sounds such an absurdly presumptuous name, doesn't it? But I really thought of her as that, when I conceived her. The first million-ton tanker, with every refinement and safety feature that man has so far tested and proved. From inert gas scrubbers to independently articulated main tanks, not one boiler but four, just like one of the old White Star liners – she was really to be the golden dawn of crude oil transportation.

'However, I am no longer Chairman of Christy Marine, and I am no longer in control of *Golden Dawn*, neither her design nor her construction.' His voice was hollow, and in the dim light his eyes seemed shrunken into their cavities like those of a skull. 'Nor yet am I in control of her operation.'

It was all turning out so badly; she did not want to argue with him, nor make him unhappy. However, she had stirred memories and regrets within him, and she wished vainly that she had not disturbed him so. Her instinct warned her she should leave him now.

'Goodnight, Doctor Silver,' he nodded noncommittally at her sudden plea of tiredness.

'My name is Sam,' she told him, wishing that she could comfort him in some way, any way, 'or Samantha, if you prefer it.'

'I do prefer it,' he said, without smiling. 'Goodnight, Samantha.'

She was angry with both herself and him, angry that the good feeling between them had been destroyed, so she flashed at him:

'You really are old-fashioned, aren't you?' and hurried from the bridge.

The following evening she almost did not go up to him, for she was ashamed of those parting words, for having pointed up their age difference so offensively. She knew he was sufficiently aware of their differences, without being reminded. She had done herself harm, and she did not want to face him again.

While she was in the shower of the guest cabin, she heard Tim Graham come clattering down the stairs on the other side of the thin bulkhead. She knew that Nicholas had relieved him.

'I'm not going up,' she told herself firmly, and took her time drying and talcuming and brushing out her hair before she clambered naked and still pink from the hot water into her bunk.

She read for half an hour, a western that Beauty Baker had lent her, and it required all her concentration to follow the print, for her mind kept trying to wander. At last she gave an exclamation of self-disgust, threw back the blankets and began dressing.

His relief and pleasure, when she appeared beside him, were transparent, and his smile was a princely welcome for her. She was suddenly very glad she had come, and this night she effortlessly steered past all the pitfalls.

She asked him to explain how the Lloyd's Open Form contract worked, and she followed his explanations swiftly.

'If they take into consideration the danger and difficulties involved in the salvage,' she mused, 'you should be able to claim an enormous award.'

'I'm going to ask for twenty per cent of the hull value—'

'What is the hull value of *Golden Adventurer*?'

And he told her. She was silent a moment as she checked his mental arithmetic.

'That's six million dollars,' she whispered in awe.

'Give or take a few cents,' he agreed.

'But there isn't that much money in the world!' She turned and stared back at the liner.

'Duncan Alexander is going to agree with you.' Nick smiled a little grimly.

'But,' she shook her head, 'what would anybody do with that much money?'

'I'm asking for six – but I won't get it. I'll walk away with three or four millions.'

'Still, that's too much. Nobody could spend that much, not if they tried for a lifetime.'

'It's spent already. It will just about enable me to pay off my loans, launch my other tug, and to keep Ocean Salvage going for another few months.'

'You owe three or four million dollars?' She stared at him now in open wonder. 'I'd never sleep, not one minute would I be able to sleep—'

'Money isn't for spending,' he explained. 'There is a limit to the amount of food you can eat, or clothes you can wear. Money is a game, the biggest most exciting game in town.'

She listened attentively to it all, happy because tonight he was gay and excited with grand designs and future plans, and because he shared them with her.

'What we will do is this, we'll come down here with both tugs and catch an iceberg.'

She laughed. 'Oh, come on!'

'I'm not joking,' he assured her, but laughing also. 'We'll put tow-lines on a big berg. It may take a week to build up tow speed, but once we get it moving nothing will stop it. We will guide it up into the middle forties, catch the roaring forties and, just like the old wool clippers on the Australian passage, we will run our eastings down.' He moved to the chart table, selected a large-scale chart of the Indian. Ocean and beckoned her to join him.

'You're serious.' She stopped laughing, and stared at him again. 'You really are serious, aren't you?'

He nodded, still smiling, and traced it out with his finger. 'Then we'll swing northwards, up into the Western Australian current, letting the flow carry us north in a great circle, until we hit the easterly monsoon and the north equatorial current.' He described the circle, but she watched his face. They stood very close, but still not touching and she felt herself stirred by the timbre of his voice, as though to the touch of fingers. 'We will cross the

Indian Ocean to the east coast of Africa with the current pushing all the way, just in time to catch the south-westerly monsoon drift – right into the Persian Gulf.' He straightened up and smiled again.

'A hundred billion tons of fresh water delivered right into the dryest and richest corner of the globe.'

'But – but—' she shook her head, 'it would melt!'

'From a helicopter we spray it with a reflective polyurethane skin to lessen the effect of the sun, and we moor it in a shallow specially prepared dock where it will cool its own surrounds. Sure, it will melt, but not for a year or two and then we'll just go out and catch another one and bring it in, like roping wild horses.'·

'How would you handle it?' she objected. 'It's too big.'

'My two tugs hustle forty-four thousand horses – we could pull in Everest, if we wanted.'

'Yes, but once you get it to the Persian Gulf?'

'We cut it into manageable hunks with a laser lance, and lift the hunks into a melting dam with an overhead crane.'

She thought about it. 'It could work,' she admitted.

'It will work,' he told her. 'I've sold the idea to the Saudis already. They are already building the dock and the dams. We'll give them water at one hundredth the cost of using nuclear condensers on sea water, and without the risk of radio-active contamination.'

She was absorbed with his vision, and he with hers. As they talked deep into the long watches of the night, they drew closer in spirit only.

Although each of them treasured those shared hours, somehow neither could bridge the narrow chasm between friendliness and real intimacy. She was instinctively aware of his reserves, that he was a man who had considered life and established his code by which to live it. She guessed that he did nothing unless it was deeply felt, and that a casual physical relationship would offer no attraction to him; she knew of the turmoil to which his life had so recently been reduced, and that he was pulling himself out of that by main strength, but that he was now wary of further hurt. There was time, she told herself, plenty of time – but *Warlock* bore steadily north by north-east, dragging her crippled ward up through the roaring forties; those notorious winds treated her kindly and she made good the six knots that Nick had hoped for.

On board *Warlock*, the attitude of the officers towards Samantha Silver changed from fawning adulation to wistful respect. Every one of them knew of the nightly ritual of the eight-to-midnight watch.

'Bloody cradle-snatcher,' groused Tim Graham.

'Mr Graham, it is fortunate I did not hear that remark,' David Allen warned him with glacial coldness – but they all resented Nicholas Berg, it was unfair competition, yet they kept a new respectful distance from the girl, not one of them daring to challenge the herd bull.

The time that Samantha had looked upon as endless was running out now, and she closed her mind to it. Even when David Allen showed her the fuzzy luminescence of the African continent on the extreme range of the radar-screen, she pretended to herself that it would go on like this – if not for ever, at least until something special happened.

During the long voyage up from Shackleton Bay, Samantha had streamed a very fine-meshed net from *Warlock's* stern, collecting an incredible variety of krill and plankton and other microscopic marine life. Angel had grudgingly given her a small corner of his scullery in return for her services as honorary assistant under-chef and unpaid waitress, and she spent many absorbed hours there each day, identifying and preserving her specimens.

She was working there when the helicopter came out to *Warlock*. She looked up at the buffeting of the machine's rotors as they changed into fine pitch for the landing on *Warlock's* heli-deck, and she was tempted to go up like every idle and curious hand on board, but she was in the middle of staining a slide, and somehow she resented the encroachment on this little island of her happiness. She worked on, but now her pleasure was spoiled, and she cocked her head when she heard the roar of the rotors as the helicopter rose from the deck again and she was left with a sense of foreboding.

Angel came in from the deck, wiping his hands on his apron and he paused in the doorway.

'You didn't tell me he was going, dearie.'

'What do you mean?' Samantha looked up at him, startled.

'Your boyfriend, darling. Socks and toothbrush and all.' Angel watched her shrewdly. 'Don't tell me he didn't even kiss you goodbye.'

She dropped the glass slide into the stainless steel sink and it snapped in half. She was panting as she gripped the rail of the upper deck and stared after the cumbersome yellow machine.

It flew low across the green wind-chopped sea, hump-backed and nose low, still close enough to read the operating company's name 'COURT' emblazoned on its fuselage, but it dwindled swiftly towards the far blue line of mountains.

Nick Berg sat in the jump seat between the two pilots of the big S. 58T Sikorsky and looked ahead towards the flat silhouette of Table Mountain. It was overlaid by a thick mattress of snowy cloud, as the south-easterly wind swirled across its summit.

From their altitude of a mere thousand feet, there were still five big tankers in sight, ploughing stolidly through the green sea on their endless odyssey, seeming to be alien to their element, not designed to live in harmony with it, but to oppose every movement of the waters. Even in this low sea, they wore thick garlands of white at their stubby rounded bows, and Nick watched one of them dip suddenly and take spray as high as her foremast. In any sort of blow, she would be like a pier with pylons set on solid ground. The seas would break right over her. It was not the way a ship should be, and now he twisted in his seat and looked back.

Far behind them, *Warlock* was still visible. Even at this distance, and despite the fact that she was dwarfed by her charge, her lines pleased the seaman in him. She looked good, but that backward glance invoked a pang of regret that he had been so stubbornly trying to ignore – and he had a vivid image of green eyes and hair of platinum and gold.

His regret was spiced by the persistent notion that he had been cowardly. He had left *Warlock* without being able to bring himself to say good bye to the girl, and he knew why he had done so. He would not take the chance of making a fool of himself. He grimaced with distaste as he remembered her exact words, 'You really are old-fashioned, aren't you?'

There was something vaguely repulsive in a middle-aged man lusting after your flesh – and he supposed he must now look upon himself as middle-aged. In six months he would be forty years of age, and he did not really expect to live to eighty. So he was in the middle of the road.

He had always scorned those grey, lined, balding, unattractive little men with big cigars, sitting in expensive restaurants with pretty young girls beside them, the young thing pretending to hang on every pearl-like word, while her eyes focused beyond his shoulder – on some younger man.

But still, it had been cowardice. She had become a friend during those weeks, and she could hardly have been aware of the emotions that she had aroused in him during those long dark hours on *Warlock*'s bridge. She was not to blame for his unruly passions, in no way had she encouraged him to believe that he was more than just an older man, not even a father figure, but just someone with whom to pass an otherwise empty hour. She had been as friendly and cheerful to everyone else on board *Warlock*, from the Mate to the cook.

He really had owed her the common courtesy of a handshake and an assurance of the pleasure he had taken from her company, but he had not been certain he could restrict it to that.

He winced again as he imagined her horror as he blurted out some sort of declaration, some proposal to prolong their relationship or alter its structure into something more intimate, her disenchantment when she realized that behind the façade of the mature and cultured man, he was just as grimy an old lecher as the furtive drooling browsers in the porno-shops of Times Square.

'Let it go,' he had decided. No matter that he was probably in better physical shape now than he had been at twenty-five, to Dr Samantha Silver he was an old man – and he had a frightening vision of an episode from his own youth.

A woman, a friend of his mother's, had trapped the nineteen-year-old Nicholas alone one rainy day in the old beach house at Martha's Vineyard. He remembered his own revulsion at the sagging white flesh, the wrinkles, the lines of stria across her belly and breasts, and the *oldness* of her. She would then have been a woman of forty, the same as he was now, and he had done her the service she required out of some obligation of pity, but afterwards he had scrubbed his teeth until the gums bled and he had stood under the shower for almost an hour.

It was one of the cruel deceits of life that a person aged from the outside inwards. He had thought of himself in the fullness of his physical and mental powers, especially now after bringing in *Golden Adventurer*. He was ready for them to lead on the dragons and he would tear out their jugulars with his bare hands – then she had called him an old-fashioned thing, and he had realized that the sexual fantasy which was slowly becoming an obsession must be associated with the male menopause, a sorry symptom of the ageing process of which he had not been conscious until then. He grinned wryly at the thought.

The girl would probably hardly notice that he had left the ship, at the worst might be a little piqued by his lack of manners, but in a week would have forgotten his name. As for himself, there was enough, and more than enough to fill the days ahead, so that the image of a slim young body and that precious mane of silver and gold would fade until it became the fairy tale it really was.

Resolutely he turned in the jump seat and looked ahead. Always look ahead, there are never regrets in that direction.

They clattered in over False Bay, crossing the narrow isthmus of the Cape Peninsula under the bulk of the cloud-capped mountain, from the Indian Ocean to the Atlantic in under ten minutes

He saw the gathering, like vultures at the lion kill, as the Sikorsky lowered to her roost on the heli-pad within the main harbour area of Table Bay.

As Nick jumped down, ducking instinctively under the still-turning rotors, they surged forward, ignoring the efforts of the Courtline dispatcher to keep the pad clear; they were led by a big red-faced man with a scorched-looking bald head and the furry arms of a tame bear.

'Larry Fry, Mr Berg,' he growled. 'You remember me?'

'Hello, Larry.' He was the local manager for Bach Wackie & Co, Nick's agents.

'I thought you might say a few words to the Press.' But the journalists swarmed around Nick now, demanding, importuning, jostling each other, their minions firing flash bulbs.

Nick felt his irritation flare, and he needed a deep breath and a conscious effort to control his anger.

'All right, lads and ladies.' He held up both hands, and grinned that special boyish grin. They were doing a tough job, he reminded himself. It couldn't be easy to be forced daily into the company of rich and successful men, grabbing for tidbits, and being grossly underpaid for your efforts with the long-term expectation of ulcers and cirrhosis of the liver.

'Play the game with me and I'll play it with you,' he promised, and thought for a moment how it would be if they *didn't* want to speak with him, how it would be if they didn't know who he was, and didn't care.

'Where have you booked me?' he asked Larry Fry now, and turned back to them. 'In two hours' time I'll be in my suite at the Mount Nelson Hotel. You're invited, and there'll be whisky.'

They laughed and tried a few more half-hearted questions, but they had accepted the compromise – at least they had got the pictures.

As they went up the palm-lined drive to the gracious old hotel, built in the days when space included five acres of carefully groomed gardens, Nick felt the stir of memory, but he suppressed that and listened intently to the list of appointments and matters of urgency from which Larry Fry read. The change in the big man's attitude was dramatic. When Nick had first arrived to take command of *Warlock*, Larry Fry had given him ten minutes of his time and sent a deputy to complete the business.

Then Nick had been touched by the mark of the beast, a man on his way down, with as much appeal as a leper. Larry Fry had accorded him the minimum courtesy due the master of a small vessel, but now he was treating him like visiting royalty, limousine and fawning attention.

'We have chartered a 707 from South African Airways to fly *Golden Adventurer*'s passengers to London, and they will take scheduled commercial flights to their separate destinations from there.'

'What about berthing for *Golden Adventurer*?'

'The Harbour Master is sending out an inspector to check the hull before he lets her enter harbour.'

'You have made the arrangements?' Nick asked sharply. He had not completed the salvage until the liner was officially handed over to the company commissioned to undertake the repairs.

'Court are flying him out now,' Larry Fry assured him. 'We'll have a decision before nightfall.'

'Have the underwriters appointed a contractor for the repairs?'

'They've called for tenders.'

The hotel manager himself met Nicholas under the entrance portico.

'Good to see you again, Mr Berg.' He waived the registration procedures. 'We can do that when Mr Berg has settled in.' And then he assured Nick, 'We have given you the same suite.'

Nick would have protested, but already they were ushering him into the sitting-room. If it had been a room lacking completely in character or taste, the memories might not have been so poignant. However, unlike one of those soulless plastic and vinyl coops built by the big chains and so often offered to travellers under the misnomer of 'inns', this room was furnished with antique furniture, oil-paintings and flowers. The memories were as fresh as those flowers, but not as pleasing.

The telephone was ringing as they entered, and Larry Fry seized it immediately, while Nick stood in the centre of the room. It had been two years since last he stood here, but it seemed as many days, so clear was the memory.

'The Harbour Master has given permission for *Golden Adventurer* to enter harbour.' Larry Fry grinned triumphantly at Nick, and gave him the thumbs-up signal.

Nick nodded, the news was an anti-climax after the draining endeavours of the last weeks. Nick walked through to the bedroom. The wallpaper was a quietly tasteful floral design with matching curtains.

From the four-poster bed, Nick remembered, you could look out over the lawns. He remembered Chantelle sitting under that canopy, with a gossamer-sheer bed-robe over her creamy shoulders, eating thin strips of marmaladed toast and then delicately and carefully licking each slim tapered finger with a pink pointed tongue.

Nicholas had come out to negotiate the transportation of South African coal from Richards Bay, and iron ore from Saldanha Bay to Japan. He had insisted that Chantelle accompany him. Perhaps he had the premonition of imminent loss, but he had overridden her objections.

'But Africa is such a primitive place, Nicky, they have things that bite.' And she had in the end gone with him. He had been rewarded with four days of rare happiness. The last four days ever, for though he did not then even suspect it, he was already sharing her bed and body with Duncan Alexander. He had never tired in thirteen years of that lovely smooth creamy body; rather, he had delighted in its slow luscious ripening into full womanhood, believing without question that it belonged to him.

Chantelle was one of those unusual women who grew more beautiful with time; it had always been one of his pleasures to watch her enter a room filled with other internationally acclaimed beauties, and see them pale beside his wife. And suddenly, for no good reason, he imagined Samantha Silver beside Chantelle – the girl's coltish grace would be transmuted to gawkiness beside Chantelle's poise, her manner as gauche as a schoolgirl's beside Chantelle's mature control, a warm lovable little bunny beside the sleekly beautiful mink—

'Mr Berg, London.' Larry Fry called from the sitting-room interrupting him, and with relief Nick picked up the telephone. 'Just keep going forward,' he reminded himself, and before he spoke, he thought again of the two women, and wondered suddenly how much that thick rich golden mane of Samantha's hair would pale beside Chantelle's lustrous sable, and just how much of the mother-of-pearl glow would fade from that young, clear skin—

'Berg,' he said abruptly into the telephone.

'Mr Berg, good morning. Will you speak to Mr Duncan Alexander of Christy Marine?'

Nick was silent for five full seconds. He needed that long to adjust to the name, but Duncan Alexander was the natural extension of his previous thoughts. In the silence he heard the banging of doors and rising clamour of voices, as the journalists converged on the liquor-cabinet next door.

'Mr Berg, are you there?'

'Yes,' he said, and his voice was steady and cool. 'Put him on.'

'Nicholas, my dear fellow.' The voice was glossy as satin, slow as honey, Eton and King's College, a hundred thousand pound accent, impossible to imitate, not quite foppish nor indolent, razor steel in a scabbard of velvet encrusted with golden filigree and precious stones – and Nicholas had seen the steel bared. 'It seems that it is impossible to hold a good man down.'

'But you tried, young Duncan,' Nick answered lightly. 'Don't feel bad about it, indeed you tried.'

'Come, Nicholas. Life is too short for recriminations. This is a new deck of cards, we start equal again.' Duncan chuckled softly. 'At least be gracious enough to accept my congratulations.'

'Accepted.' Nicholas agreed. 'Now what do we talk about?'

'Is *Golden Adventurer* in dock yet?'

'She has been cleared to enter. She'll be tied up within twenty-four hours – and you'd better have your cheque book ready.'

'I hoped that we might avoid going up before the Committee. There has been too much bitterness already. Let's try and keep it in the family, Nicholas.'

'The family?'

'Christy Marine is the family – you, Chantelle, old Arthur Christy – and Peter.'

It was the very dirtiest form of fighting, and Nick found suddenly that he was shaking like a man in fever and that his fist around the receiver was white with the force of his grip. It was the mention of his son that had affected him so.

'I'm not in that family any more.'

'In a way you will always be part of it. It is as much your achievement as any man's, and your son—'

Nick cut across him brusquely, his voice gravelly.

'You and Chantelle made me a stranger. Now treat me like one.'

'Nicholas—'

'Ocean Salvage as main contractor for the recovery of *Golden Adventurer* is open to an offer.'

'Nicholas—'

'Make an offer.'

'As bluntly as that?'

'I'm waiting.'

'Well now. My Board has considered the whole operation in depth, and I am empowered to make you an outright settlement of three-quarters of a million dollars.'

Nick's tone did not alter. 'We have been set down for a hearing at Lloyd's on the 27th of next month.'

'Nicholas, the offer is negotiable within reasonable limits—'

'You are speaking a foreign language,' Nick cut him off. 'We are so far apart that we are wasting each other's time.'

'Nicholas, I know how you feel about Christy Marine, you know the company is underwriting its own—'

'Now you are really wasting my time.'

'Nicholas, it's not a third party, it's not some big insurance consortium, it's Christy Marine—'

He used his name again, though it scalded his tongue.

'Duncan, you're breaking my heart. I'll see you on the 27th of next month, at the arbitration court.' He dropped the receiver on to its bracket, and moved across to the mirror, swiftly combing his hair and composing his features, startled to see how hard and bleak his expression was, and how fierce his eyes.

However, when he went through to the lounge of the suite, he was relaxed and urbane and smiling.

'All right, ladies and gentlemen. I'm all yours,' and one of the ladies of the press, blonde, pretty and not yet thirty but with eyes as old as life itself, took another sip of her whisky as she studied him, then murmured huskily, 'I wouldn't mind at all, duckie.'


*Golden Adventurer* stood tall and very beautiful against the wharf of Cape Town harbour, waiting her turn to go into the dry dock.

Globe Engineering, the contractors who had been appointed to repair her, had signed for her and legally taken over responsibility from *Warlock*'s First Officer. But David Allen still felt an immense proprietary pride in her.

From *Warlock*'s navigation bridge, he could look across the main harbour basin and see the tall, snowy superstructure glistening in the bright hot summer sunshine, towering as high as the giraffe-necked steel wharf cranes; and in gloating self-indulgence, David dwelt on a picture of the liner, wreathed in snow, half obscured by driving sleet and sea fume, staggering in the mountainous black seas off Antarctica. It gave him a solid feeling of achievement, and he thrust his hands deeply into his pockets and whistled softly to himself, smiling and watching the liner.

The Trog thrust his wrinkled head from the radio room.

'There's a call for you on the land-line,' he said, and David picked up the handset.

'David?'

'Yessir.' He drew himself to his full height as he recognized Nicholas Berg's voice.

'Are you ready for sea?'

David gulped, then glanced at the bulkhead clock. 'We discharged tow an hour and ten minutes ago.'

'Yes, I know. How soon?'

David was tempted to lie, estimate short, and then fake it for the extra time he needed. Instinct warned him against lying deliberately to Nicholas Berg.

'Twelve hours,' he said.

'It's an oil-rig tow, Rio to the North Sea, a semi-submersible rig.'

'Yessir,' David adjusted quickly, thank God he had not yet let any of his crew ashore. He had arranged for bunkering at 1300 hours. He could make it. 'When are you coming aboard, sir?'

'I'm not,' said Nick. 'You're the new Master. I'm leaving for London on the five o'clock flight. I won't even get down to shout at you. She's all yours, David.'

'Thank you, sir,' David stuttered, feeling himself flush hot scarlet.

'Bach Wackie will telex you full details of the tow at sea, and you and I will work out your own contract later. But I want you running at top economic power for Rio by dawn tomorrow.'

'Yessir.'

'I've watched you carefully, David.' Nick's voice changed, becoming personal, warmer. 'You're a damn good tug-man. Just keep telling yourself that.'

'Thank you, Mr Berg.'


Samantha had spent half the afternoon helping with the arrangements for taking off the remaining passengers from *Golden Adventurer* and embarking them in the waiting fleet of tourist buses which would distribute them to hotels throughout the city while they waited for the London charter flight.

It had been a sad occasion, farewell to many who had become friends, and remembering those who had not come back from Cape Alarm with them – Ken, who might have been her lover, and the crew of raft Number 16 who had been her special charges.

Once the final bus had left, with the occupants waving for the last time to Samantha, 'Take care, honey!' 'You come and visit with us now, hear?' she was as lonely and forlorn as the silent ship. She stood for a long time staring up the liner's high side, examining the damage where sea and ice had battered her – then she turned and picked her way dejectedly along the edge of the basin, ignoring the occasional whistle or ribald invitation from the fishermen and crew members of the freighters on their moorings.

*Warlock* seemed as welcoming as home, rakish and gallant, wearing her new scars with high panache, already thrusting and impatient at the restraint of her mooring lines. And then Samantha remembered that Nicholas Berg was no longer aboard her, and her spirits sagged again.

'God,' Tim Graham met her at the gangplank. 'I'm glad you got back. I didn't know what to do with your gear.'

'What do you mean?' Samantha demanded. 'Are you throwing me off the ship?'

'Unless you want to come with us to Rio.' He thought about that for a moment, and then he grinned, 'Hey, that's not a bad idea, how about it, old girl? Rio in Carnival time, you and me—'

'Don't get carried away, Timothy,' she warned him. 'Why Rio?'

'The Captain—'

'Captain Berg?'

'No, David Allen, he's the new skipper,' and she lost interest.

'When are you sailing?'

'Midnight.'

'I'd best go pack up.' She left him on the quarterdeck, and Angel pounced on her as she passed the galley.

'Where have you been?' He was in a flutter, all wrists and tossing hair, 'I've been beside myself, darling.'

'What is it, Angel?'

'It's probably too late already.'

'What is it?' She caught his urgency. 'Tell me.'

'He's still in town.'

'Who?' But she knew, they spoke of only one person in these emotional terms.

'Don't be dense, luv. Your crumpet.' She hated it when he referred to Nick like that, but now she let him go on. 'But he won't be very much longer. His plane leaves at five o'clock, he is making the local flight to Johannesburg, and connecting there for London.'

She stared at him.

'Well what are you waiting for?' Angel keened. 'It's almost four o'clock now, and it will take you at least half an hour to reach the airport.'

She did not move. 'But, Angel,' she almost wrung her hands in anguish, 'but what do I do when I get there?'

Angel shook his head and twinkled his diamonds in exasperation. 'Sweet merciful heavens, duckie.' Then he sighed. 'When I was a boy I had two guinea pigs, and they also refused to get it on. I think they were retarded, or something. I tried everything, even hormones, but neither of them survived the shots. Alas, their love was never consummated—'

'Be serious, Angel.'

'You could hold him down while I give him a hormone shot—'

'I hate you, Angel.' She had to laugh, even in her anxiety.

'Dearie, every night for the past month you have tried to set him on fire with your dulcet silvery voice – and we haven't even passed "GO" and collected our first $200—'

'I know, Angel. I know.'

'It seems to me, sweetie, that it's time now to cut out the jawing and to ignite him with that magic little tinderbox of yours.'

'You mean right there in the departure lounge of the airport?' She clapped her hands with delight, then struck a lascivious pose. 'I'm Sam – fly me!'

'Hop, poppet, there is a taxi on the wharf – he's been waiting an hour, with his meter running.'


There is no first-class lounge in Cape Town's DF Malan Airport, so Nicholas sat in the snake-pit, amongst the distraught mothers and their whining, sticky offspring, the harassed tourists loaded like camels with souvenirs and the florid-faced commercial travellers, but he was alone in a multitude; with unconscious deference they allowed him a little circle of privacy and he used the Louis Vuitton briefcase on his knee as a desk.

It occurred to him suddenly how dramatically the balance had swung in the last mere forty days, since he had recognized his wave peaking, but had almost not been able to find the strength for it.

A shadow passed across his eyes, and the little creased crowsfoot appeared between them as he remembered the physical and emotional effort that it had taken to make the 'Go' decision on *Golden Adventurer*, and he shivered slightly in fear of what might have happened if he had not gone. He would have missed his wave, and there would never have been another.

With a small firm movement of his head, he pushed that memory of fear behind him. He had caught his wave, and he was riding high and fast. Now it seemed that the fates were intent on smothering him with largesse: the oil-rig tow for *Warlock*, Rio to the Bravo Sierra field off Norway – then a back-to-back tow from the North Sea through Suez to the new South Australian field, would keep *Warlock* fully employed for the next six months. That was not all, the threatening dockyard strike at Construction Navale Atlantique had been smoothed over and the delivery date for the new tug had come forward by two months. At midnight the night before, a telephone call from Bach Wackie had awakened him to let him know Kuwait and Qatar were now also studying the iceberg-to-water project with a view to commissioning similar schemes; he would have to build himself another two vessels if they decided to go.

'All I need now is to hear that I have won the football pools,' he thought, and turned his head, started and caught his breath with a hiss, as though he had been punched in the ribs.

She stood by the automatic doors, and the wind had caught her hair and torn it loose from its thick twisted knot so that fine gold tendrils floated down on to her cheeks – cheeks that were flushed as though she had run fast, and her chest heaved so that she held one hand upon it, fingers spread like a star between those fine pointed breasts. She was poised like a forest animal that has scented the leopard, fearful, tremulous, but not yet certain in which direction to run. Her agitation was so apparent that he thrust aside his briefcase and stood up.

She saw him instantly, and her face lit with an expression of such unutterable joy, that he was halted in his intention of going towards her, while she in contrast wheeled and started to run towards him.

She collided with a portly, sweating tourist, nearly flooring him and shaking loose a rain of carved native curios and anonymous packets which clattered to the floor around him like ripe fruit.

He snarled angrily, then his expression changed as he looked at her. 'Sorry!' She stooped swiftly, picked up a packet, thrust it into his arms, hit him with her smile, and left him beaming bemusedly after her.

However, now she was more restrained, her precipitous rush calmed to that long-legged thrusting hip-swinging walk of hers, and the smile was a little uncertain as she pushed vainly at the loose streamers of golden hair, trying to tuck them up into the twisted rope on top of her head.

'I thought I'd missed you.' She stopped a little in front of him.

'Is something wrong?' he asked quickly, still alarmed by her behaviour.

'Oh no,' she assured him hurriedly. 'Not any more,' and suddenly she was awkward and coltish again. 'I thought,' her voice hushed, 'it was just that I thought I'd missed you.' And her eyes slid away from his. 'You didn't say goodbye—'

'I thought it was better that way.' And now her eyes flew back to his face, sparking with green fire.

'Why?' she demanded, and he had no answer to give her.

'I didn't want to—' How could he say it to her, without making the kind of statement that would embarrass them both?

Above them, the public address system squawked into life.

'South African Airways announces the departure of their Airbus Flight 235 to Johannesburg. Will passengers please board at Gate Number Two.'

She had run out of time. 'I'm Sam – Fly Me! Please!' she thought, and felt the urge to giggle, but instead she said:

'Nicholas, tomorrow you'll be in London – in mid-winter.'

'It's a sobering thought,' he agreed, and for the first time smiled; his smile closed like a fist around her heart and her legs felt suddenly weak.

'Tomorrow, or at least the day after, I'll be riding the long set at Cape St Francis,' she said. They had spoken of that, on those enchanted nights. He had told her how he had first ridden the surf at Waikiki Beach long ago before the sport had become a craze, and it had been part of their shared experience, part of their love of the sea, drawing them closer together.

'I hope the surf's up for you,' he said. Cape St Francis was three hundred and fifty miles north of Cape Town, simply another beach and headland in a shoreline that stretched in unbroken splendour for six thousand miles, and yet it was unique in all the world. The young and the young-at-heart came in almost religious pilgrimage to ride the long set at Cape St Francis. They came from Hawaii and California, from Tahiti and Queensland, for there was no other wave quite like it.

At the departure gate, the shuffling queue was shortening, and Nick stooped to pick up his briefcase, but she reached out and laid her hand on his biceps, and he froze.

It was the first time she had deliberately touched him, and the shock of it spread through his body like ripples on a quiet lake. All the emotions and passions which he had so strenuously denied came tumbling back upon him, and it seemed that their strength had grown a hundredfold while under restraint. He ached for her, with a deep, yearning, wanting ache.

'Come with me, Nicholas,' she whispered, and his own throat closed so he could not answer. He stared at her, and already the ground hostesses at the gate were peering around irritably for their missing passenger.

She had to convince him and she shook his arm urgently, startled at the hardness of the muscle under her fingers.

'Nicholas, I really want,' she began, intending to finish, 'you to,' but her tongue played a Freudian trick on her, and she said, 'I really want you.'

'Oh God,' she thought, as she heard herself say it, 'I sound like a whore,' and in panic she corrected herself.

'I really want you to,' and she flushed, the blood came up from her neck, dark under the peach of her tan so the freckles glowed on her skin like flakes of gold-dust.

'Which one is it?' he asked, and then smiled again.

'There isn't time to argue.' She stamped her foot, feigning impatience, hiding her confusion, then added, 'Damn you!' for no good reason.

'Who is arguing?' he asked quietly, and suddenly, like magic, she was in his arms, trying to burrow herself deeper and deeper into his embrace, trying to draw all the man smell of him into her lungs, amazed at the softness and warmth of his mouth and the hard rasp of new beard on his chin and cheek, making little soft mewing sounds of comfort deep in her throat as she clung to him.

'Passenger Berg. Will passenger Berg please report to the departure gate,' chanted the public address.

'They're calling me,' Nicholas murmured.

'They can go right to the back of the queue,' she mumbled into his lips.


Sunlight was made for Samantha. She wore it like a cloak that had been woven especially for her. She wore it in her hair, sparkling like jewellery, she used it to paint her face and body in lustrous shades of burnt honey and polished amber, she wore it glowing in golden freckles on her cheeks and nose.

She moved in sunlight with wondrous grace, barefooted in the white sand, so that her hips and buttocks roistered brazenly under the thin green stuff of her bikini.

She sprawled in the sunlight like a sleeping cat, offering her face and naked belly to it, so he felt that if he laid his hand against her throat he would feel her purr deep inside her chest.

She ran in the sunlight, light as a gull in flight, along the hard wet sand at the water's edge, and he ran beside her, tirelessly, mile after mile, the two of them alone in a world of green sea and sun and tall pale hot skies. The beach curved away in both directions to the limit of the eye, smooth and white as the snows of Antarctica, devoid of human life or the scars of man's petty endeavours, and she laughed beside him in the sunlight, holding his hand as they ran together.

They found a deep, clear rock pool in a far and secret place. The sunlight off the water dappled her body, exploding silently upon it like the reflections of light from a gigantic diamond, as she cast aside the two green wisps of her bikini, let down the thick rope of her hair and stepped into the pool, turning, knee-deep, to look back at him. Her hair hung almost to her waist, springing and thick and trying to curl in the salt and wind, it cloaked her shoulders and her breasts peeped through the thick curtains of it. Her breasts, untouched by the sun, were rich as cream and tipped in rose, so big and full and exuberant that he wondered that he had ever thought her a child; they bounced and swung as she moved, and she pulled back her shoulders and laughed at him shamelessly when she saw the direction of his eyes.

She turned back to the pool and her buttocks were white with the pinkish sheen of a deep-sea pearl, round and tight and deeply divided, and, as she bent forward to dive, a tiny twist of copper gold curls peeped briefly and coyly from the wedge where the deep cleft split into her tanned smooth thighs.

Through the cool water, her body was warm as bread fresh from the oven, cold and heat together, and when he told her this, she entwined her arms around his neck.

'I'm Sam the baked Alaska, eat me!' she laughed, and the droplets clung to her eyelashes like diamond chips in the sunlight.

Even in the presence of others, they walked alone; for them, nobody else really existed. Among those who had come from all over the world to ride the long set at Cape St Francis were many who knew Samantha, from Florida and California, from Australia and Hawaii, where her field trips and her preoccupation with the sea and the life of the sea had taken her.

'Hey, Sam!' they shouted, dropping their boards in the sand and running to her, tall muscular young men, burned dark as chestnuts in the sun. She smiled at them vaguely, holding Nicholas' hand a little tighter, and replied to their chatter absentmindedly, drifting away at the first opportunity.

'Who was that?'

'It's terrible, but I can't remember – I'm not even sure where I met him or when.' And it was true, she could concentrate on nothing but Nicholas, and the others sensed it swiftly and left them alone.

Nicholas had not been in the sun for over a year, his body was the colour of old ivory, in sharp contrast to the thick dark body hair which covered his chest and belly. At the end of that first day in the sun, the ivory colour had turned to a dull angry red.

'You'll suffer,' she told him, but the next morning his body and limbs had gone the colour of mahogany and she drew back the sheets and marvelled at it, touching him exploringly with the tip of her fingers.

'I'm lucky, I've got a hide like a buffalo,' he told her.

Each day he turned darker, until he was the weathered bronze of an American Indian, and his high cheek-bones heightened the resemblance.

'You must have Indian blood,' she told him, tracing his nose with her finger-tip.

'I only know two generations back,' he smiled at her. 'I've always been terrified to look further than that.'

She sat over him, crosslegged in the big bed and touched him, exploring him with her hands, touching his lips and the lobes of his ears, smoothing the thick dark curve of his eyebrows, the little black mole on his cheek, and exclaiming at each new discovery.

She touched him when they walked, reaching for his hand, pressing her hip against him when they stood, on the beach sitting between his spread knees and leaning back against his chest, her head tucked into his shoulder – it was if she needed constant physical assurance of his presence.

When they sat astride their boards, waiting far out beyond the three-mile reef for the set of the wave, she reached across to touch his shoulder, balancing the board under her like a skilled horsewoman, the two of them close and spiritually isolated from the loose assembly of thirty or forty surf-riders strung out along the line of the long set.

This far out, the shore was a low dark green rind, above the shaded green and limpid blues of the water. In the blue distance, the mountains were blue on the blue of the sky and above them, the thunder-heads piled dazzling silver, tall and arrogant enough to dwarf the very earth.

'This must be the most beautiful land in the world,' she said, moving her board so that her knee lay against his thigh.

'Because you are here,' he told her.

Under them, the green water breathed like a living thing, rising and falling, the swells long and glassy, sliding away towards the land.

Growing impatient, one of the inexperienced riders would move to catch a bad swell, kneeling on the board and paddling with both hands, coming up unsteadily on to his feet and then toppling and falling as the water left him, and the taunts and friendly catcalls of his peers greeted him as he surfaced, grinning sheepishly, and crawled back on to his board.

Then the ripple of excitement, and a voice calling, 'A three set!' the boards quickly rearranging themselves, sculled by cupped bare hands, spacing out for running room, the riders peering back eagerly over their dark burned shoulders, laughing and kidding each other as the wave set bumped up on the horizon, still four miles out at sea, but big enough so that they could count the individual swells that made up the set.

Running at fifty miles an hour, the swells took nearly five minutes, from the moment when first they were sighted, to reach the line, and during that time Samantha had a little ritual of preparation. First, she hoisted the bottom of her bikini which had usually slipped down to expose a pair of dimples and a little of the deep cleft of her buttocks, then she tightened her top hamper, pulling open the brassiere of her costume and cupping each breast in turn, settling it firmly in its sheath of thin green cloth, grinning at Nick as she did it.

'You're not supposed to watch.'

'I know, it's bad for my heart.'

Then she plucked out a pair of hairpins and held them in her mouth as she twisted the wrist-thick plait of hair tighter until it hung down between her shoulder blades and pinned back the wisps over her ears.

'All set?' he called, and she nodded and answered,

'Ride three?'

The third wave in the set was traditionally the big one, and they let the first one swing them high and drop them again into its trough. Half the other riders were up and away, only their heads still visible above the peak of the wave, the land obscured by the moving wall of water.

The second wave came through, bigger, more powerful, but swooping up and over the crest and most of the other riders went on it, two or three tumbling on the steep front of water, losing their boards, dragged under as the ankle lines came up taut.

'Here we go!' exulted Samantha, and three came rustling, green and peaking, and in the transparent wall of water four big bottle-nosed porpoises were framed, in perfect motion, racing in the wave, pumping their flat delta-shaped tails and grinning that fixed porpoise grin of delight.

'Oh look!' sang Samantha. 'Just look at them, Nicholas!'

Then the wave was upon them and they sculled frantically, weight high on the board, the heart-stopping moment when it seemed the water would sweep away and leave them, then suddenly the boards coming alive under them and starting to run, tipping steeply forward, with the hiss of the waxed fibre-glass through the water.

Then they were both up and laughing in the sunlight, dancing the intricate steps that balanced and controlled the boards, lifted high on the crest, so they could see the sweep of the beach three miles ahead, and the ranks of other riders on the twin waves that had gone before them.

One of the porpoises frolicked with them on the racing crest, ducking under the flying boards, turning on its side to grin up at Samantha, so she stopped and stretched out a hand to touch him, lost her balance, and almost fell while the porpoise grinned at her mischievously and flipped away to rise fin up on her far side.

Now, out on their right hand, the wave was feeling the reef and starting to curl over on itself, the crest arching forwards, holding that lovely shape for long moments, then slowly collapsing.

'Go left,' Nick called urgently to her, and they kicked the boards around and danced up on to the stubby prows, bending at the knees to ride the hurtling craft, their speed rocketing as they cut across the green face of the wave, but behind them the arching wave spread rapidly towards them, faster than they could run before it.

Now at their left shoulders, the water formed a steep vertical wall, and, glancing at it, Samantha found the porpoise swimming head-high beside her, his great tail pumping powerfully, and she was afraid, for the majesty and strength of that wave belittled her.

'Nicholas!' she screamed, and the wave fanned out over her head, arcing across the sky, cutting out the sunlight, and now they flew down a long perfectly rounded tunnel of roaring water. The sides were smooth as blown glass, and the light was green and luminous and weird as though they sped through a deep submarine cavern, only ahead of them was the perfect round opening at the mouth of the tunnel – while behind her, close behind her, the tunnel was collapsing in a furious thunder of murderous white water, and she was as terrified and as exulted as she had ever been in her life.

He yelled at her, 'We must beat the curl,' and his voice was far away and almost lost in the roar of water, but obediently she went forward on her board until all her bare toes were curled over the leading edge.

For long moments they held their own, then slowly the began to gain, and at last they shot out through the open mouth of the tunnel into the sunlight again, and she laughed wildly, still high on the exultation of fresh terror.

Then they were past the reef and the wave firmed up, leaving the white water like lace on the surface far behind.

'Let's go right!' Samantha sang out to stay within the good structure of the wave, and they turned and went back, swinging across the steep face. The splatter of flung water sparkled on her belly and thighs, and the plait of her hair stood out behind her head like the tail of an angry lioness, her arms were extended and her hands held open, unconsciously making the delicate finger gestures of a Balinese temple dancer as she balanced; and miraculously the porpoise swam, fin up, beside her, following like a trained dog.

Then at last, the wave felt the beach and ran berserk, tumbling wildly upon itself, booming angrily, and churning the sand like gruel, and they kicked out of the wave, falling back over the crest and dropping into the sea beside the bobbing boards, laughing and panting at each other with the excitement and terror and the joy of it.

Samantha was a sea-creature with a huge appetite for the fruits of the sea, cracking open the crayfish legs in her fingers and sucking the white sticks of flesh into her mouth with a noisy sensuality, while her lips were polished with butter sauce, not taking her eyes from his face as she ate.

Samantha in the candlelight gulping those huge Knysna oysters, and then slurping the juice out of the shells.

'You're talking with your mouth full.'

'It's just that I've still got so much to tell you,' she explained.

Samantha was laughter, laughter in fifty different tones and intensities, from the sleepy morning chortle when she awoke and found him beside her, to the wild laughter yelled from the crest of a racing wave.

Samantha was loving. With a face of thundering innocence and the virginal, guileless green eyes of a child, she combined hands and a mouth whose wiles and wicked cunning left Nick stunned and disbelieving.

'The reason I ran away without a word was that I did not want to have your ravishment and violation on my conscience,' he shook his head at her disbelievingly.

'I wrote my PhD thesis in those subjects,' she told him blithely, using her forefinger to twist spit-curls in his sweat-dampened chest hairs. 'And what's more, buster, that was just the introductory offer – now we sign you up for a full course of treatment.'

Her delight in his body was endless, she must touch and examine every inch of it, exclaiming and revelling in it without a trace of self-consciousness, holding his hand in her lap and bending her head studiously over it, tracing the lines of his palm with her fingernail.

'You are going to meet a beautiful wanton blonde, give her fifteen babies and live to be a hundred and fifty.'

She touched the little chiselled lines around his eyes and at the corners of his mouth with the tip of her tongue, leaving cool damp smears of saliva on his skin.

'I always wanted a real craggy man all for myself.'

Then, when her examination became more intimate and clinical and he demurred, she told him severely, 'Hold still, this is a private thing between me and himself.'

Then a little later.

'Oh wow! He's real poison!'

'Poison?' he demanded, his manhood denigrated.

'Poison,' she sighed. 'Because he just slays me!'

In fairness, she offered herself for his touch and scrutiny, guiding his hands, displaying herself eagerly.

'Look, touch, it's yours – all yours,' wanting his approval, not able to give him sufficient to satisfy her own need to give. 'Do you like it, Nicholas? Is this good for you? Is there anything else you want, Nicholas, anything at all that I can give you?'

And when he told her how beautiful she was, when he told her how much he wanted her, when he touched and marvelled over the gifts she brought to him, she glowed and stretched and purred like a great golden cat so that when he learned that the Zodiacal sign of her birthday was Leo, he was not at all surprised.

Samantha was loving in the early slippery grey-pearl light of dawn, soft sleepy loving, with small gasps and murmurs and chuckles of deep contentment.

Samantha was loving in the sunlight, spread like a beautiful starfish in the fierce reflected sunlight of the sculptured dunes. The sand coated her body like crystals of sugar, and their cries rose together, high and ecstatic as those of the curious seagulls that floated above them on motionless white wings.

Samantha was loving in the green cool water, their two heads bobbing beyond the first line of breakers, his toes only just touching the sandy bottom and she twined about him like sea kelp about a submerged rock, clutching both their swim suits in one hand and gurgling merrily.

'What's good enough for a lady blue whale is good enough for Samantha Silver! Thar blows Moby Dick!'

And Samantha was loving in the night, with her hair brushed out carefully and spread over him, lustrous and fragrant, a canopy of gold in the lamplight, and she kneeling astride him in almost religious awe, like a temple maid making the sacrifice.

But more than anything else, Samantha was vibrant, bursting life – and youth eternal.

Through her, Nicholas recaptured those emotions which he had believed long atrophied by cynicism and the pragmatism of living. He shared her childlike delight in the small wonders of nature, the flight of a gull, the presence of the porpoise, the discovery of the perfect translucent fan of a papery nautilus shell washed up on the white sand with the rare tentacled creature still alive within the convoluted interior.

He shared her outrage when even those remote and lonely beaches were invaded by an oil slick, tank washings from a VLCC out on the Agulhas current, and the filthy clinging globules of spilled crude oil stuck to the soles of their feet, smeared the rocks and smothered the carcasses of the jackass penguins they found at the water's edge.

Samantha was life itself, just to touch the warmth of her and to drink the sound of her laughter was to be rejuvenated. To walk beside her was to feel vital and strong.

Strong enough for the long days in the sea and sun, strong enough to dance to the loud wild music half the night, and then strong enough to lift her when she faltered and carry her down to their bungalow above the beach, she in his arms like a sleepy child, her skin tingling with the memory of the sun, her muscles aching deliciously with fatigue, and her belly crammed with rich food.

'Oh Nicholas, Nicholas – I'm so happy I want to cry.'

Then Larry Fry arrived; he arrived on a cloud of indignation, red-faced and accusing as a cuckolded husband.

'Two weeks,' he blared. 'London and Bermuda and St Nazaire have been driving me mad for two weeks!' And he brandished a sheath of telex flimsies that looked like the galley proofs for the *Encyclopaedia Britannica*.

'Nobody knew what had happened to you. You just disappeared.' He ordered a large gin and tonic from the white-jacketed bar-tender and sank wearily on to the stool beside Nick. 'You nearly cost me my job, Mr Berg, and that's the truth. You'd have thought I'd bumped you off personally and dumped your body in the bay. I had to hire a private detective to check every hotel register in the country.' He took a long, soothing draught of the gin.

At that moment, Samantha drifted into the cocktail lounge. She wore a loose, floating dress the same green as her eyes, and a respectful hush fell on the pre-luncheon drinkers as they watched her cross the room. Larry Fry forgot his indignation and gaped at her, his bald scorched head growing shining under a thin film of perspiration.

'Godstrewth,' he muttered. 'I'd rather feel that, than feel sick.' And then his admiration turned to consternation when she came directly to Nicholas, laid her hand on his shoulder and in full view of the entire room kissed him lingeringly on the mouth.

There was a soft collective sigh from the watchers and Larry Fry knocked over his gin.

'We must go now, today,' Samantha decided. 'We mustn't stay even another hour, Nicholas, or we will spoil it. It was perfect, but now we must go.'

Nicholas understood. Like him she had the compulsion to keep moving forward. Within the hour, he had chartered a twin-engined Beechcraft Baron. It picked them up at the little earth strip near the hotel and put them down at Johannesburg's Jan Smuts Airport an hour before the departure of the UTA flight for Paris.

'I always rode in the back of the bus before,' said Samantha, as she looked around the first-class cabin appraisingly. 'Is it true that up this end you can eat and drink as much as you like, for free?'

'Yes.' Then Nick added hastily, 'But you don't have to take that as a personal challenge.' Nicholas had come to stand in awe of Samantha's appetites.

They stayed overnight at the George V in Paris and caught the mid-morning TAT flight down to Nantes, the nearest airfield to the shipyards at St Nazaire, and Jules Levoisin was there to meet them at the Château Bougon field.

'Nicholas!' he shouted joyfully, and stood on tiptoe to buss both his cheeks, enveloping him in a fragrant cloud of eau de Cologne and pomade. 'You are a pirate, Nicholas, you stole that ship from under my nose. I hate you.' He held Nicholas at arm's length. 'I warned you not to take the job, didn't I?'

'You did, Jules, you did.'

'So why do you make a fool of me?' he demanded, and twirled his moustaches. He was wearing expensive cashmere and an Yves St Laurent necktie; ashore, Jules was always the dandy.

'Jules, I am going to buy lunch for you at La Rotisserie,' Nicholas promised.

'I forgive you,' said Jules, it was one of his favourite eating-places – but at that moment Jules became aware that Nicholas was not travelling alone.

He stood back, took one long look at Samantha and it seemed that tricolors unfurled around him and brass bands burst into the opening bars of 'La Marseillaise'. For if dalliance was the national sport, Jules Levoisin considered himself veteran champion of all France.

He bowed over her hand, and tickled the back of it with his stiff black moustaches. Then he told Nicholas, 'She is too good for you, *mon petit*, I am going to take her away from you.'

'The same way you did *Golden Adventurer?*' Nick asked innocently.

Jules had his ancient Citroën in the car park. It was lovingly waxed and fitted with shiny gew-gaws and dangling mascots. He handed Samantha into the front seat as though it was a Rolls Camargue.

'He's beautiful,' she whispered, as he scampered around to the driver's door.

Jules could not devote attention to both the road ahead and to Samantha, so he concentrated solely upon her, without deviating from the Citroën's top speed, only occasionally turning to shout, '*Cochon!*' at another driver or jerk his fist at them with the second finger pointed stiffly upwards in ribald salutation.

'Jules' great-great-grandfather charged with the Emperor's cavalry at Quatre Bras,' Nick explained. 'He is a man without fear.'

'You will enjoy La Rôtisserie,' Jules told Samantha. 'I can only afford to eat there when I find somebody rich who wishes a favour of me.'

'How do you know I want a favour?' Nick asked from the back seat, clinging to the door-handle.

'Three telegrams, a telephone call from Bermuda – another from Johannesburg,' Jules chuckled fruitily and winked at Samantha. 'You think I believe Nicholas Berg wants to discuss old times? You think I believe he feels so deeply for his old friend, who taught him everything he knows? A man who treated him like a son, and whom he blatantly robbed—' Jules sped across the Loire bridge and plunged into that tangled web of narrow one-way streets and teeming traffic which is Nantes; a way opened for him miraculously.

In the Place Briand, he handed Samantha gallantly from the Citroën, and in the restaurant he puffed out his cheeks and made little anxious clucking and tut-tutting noises, as Nicholas discussed the wine list with the *sommelier* – but he nodded reluctant approval when they settled on a Chablis Moutonne and a Chambertin-Clos-de-Bèze, then he applied himself with equal gusto to the food, the wine and Samantha.

'You can tell a woman who is made for life and love, by the way she eats,' and when Samantha made wide lascivious eyes at him over her trout, Nicholas expected him to crow like a cockerel.

Only when the cognac was in front of them, and both he and Nick had lit cheroots, did he demand abruptly:

'So, now, Nicholas, I am in a good mood. Ask me.'

'I need a Master for my new tug,' said Nick, and Jules veiled his face behind a thick blue curtain of cigar smoke.

They fenced like masters of épée all the way from Nantes to St Nazaire.

'Those ships you build, Nicholas, are not tugs. They are fancy toys, floating bordellos – all those gimmicks and gadgets—'

'Those gimmicks and gadgets enabled me to do a deal with Christy Marine while you still hadn't realized that I was within a thousand miles.' Jules blew out his cheeks and muttered to himself.

'Twenty-two thousand horsepower, *c'est ridicule*! They are over-powered—'

'I needed every single one of those horses when I pulled *Golden Adventurer* off Cape Alarm.'

'Nicholas, do not keep reminding me of that shameful episode.' He turned to Samantha. 'I am hungry, *ma petite*, and in the next village there is a *pâtisserie*,' he sighed and kissed his bunched fingers, 'you will adore the pastry.'

'Try me,' she invited, and Jules had found a soulmate.

'Those fancy propellers – variable pitch – ouf!' Jules spoke through a mouthful of pastry, and there was whipped cream on his moustache.

'I can make twenty-five knots and then slam *Warlock* into reverse thrust and stop her within her own length.'

Jules changed pace, and attacked from a new direction. 'You'll never find full employment for two big expensive ships like that.'

'I'm going to need four, not two,' Nick contradicted him. 'We are going to catch icebergs,' and Jules forgot to chew, as he listened intently for the next ten minutes. 'One of the beauties of the iceberg scheme is that all my ships will be operating right on the tanker lanes, the busiest shipping lanes in all the oceans—'

'Nicholas,' Jules shook his head in admiration, 'you move too fast for me. I am an old man, old-fashioned—'

'You're not old,' Samantha told him firmly. 'You're only just in your prime.' And Jules threw up both hands theatrically.

'Now you have a pretty girl heaping flattery on my bowed grey head,' he looked at Nicholas; 'is no trick too deceitful for you?'

It was snowing the next morning, a slow sparse sprinkling from a grey woollen sky, when they drove into St Nazaire from the little seaside resort of La Baule twenty-five kilometres up the Atlantic coast.

Jules had a small flat in one of the apartment blocks. It was a convenient arrangement, for *La Mouette*, his command, was owned by a Breton company and St Nazaire was her home port. It was a mere twenty-minute drive before they made out the elegant arch of the suspension bridge which crosses the estuarine mouth of the Loire River at St Nazaire.

Jules drove through the narrow streets of that area of the docks just below the bridge which comprises the sprawling ship-building yards of Construction Navale Atlantique, one of the three largest ship-building companies in Europe.

The slipways for the larger vessels, the bulk carriers and naval craft, faced directly on to the wide smooth reach of the river; but the ways for the small vessels backed on to the inner harbour.

So Jules parked the Citroën at the security gates nearest the inner harbour, and they walked through to where Charles Gras was waiting for them in his offices overlooking the inner basin.

'Nicholas, it is good to see you again.' Gras was one of Atlantique's top engineers, a tall stooped man with a pale face and lank black hair that fell to his eyebrows, but he had the sharp foxy Parisian features and quick bright eyes that belied the morose unsmiling manner.

He and Nicholas had known each other many years, and they used the familiar 'tu' form of address.

Charles Gras changed to heavily accented English when he was introduced to Samantha, and back to French when he asked Nicholas,

'If I know you, you will want to go directly to see your ship now, *n'est-ce pas?*'

*Sea Witch* stood high on her ways, and although she was an identical twin to *Warlock*, she seemed almost twice her size with her underwater hull exposed. Despite the fact that the superstructure was incomplete and she was painted in the drab oxide red of marine primer, yet it was impossible to disguise the symmetrically functional beauty of her lines.

Jules puffed, and muttered 'Bordello' and made remarks about 'Admiral Berg and his battleship', but he could not hide the gleam in his eye as he strutted about the uncompleted navigation bridge, or listened intently as Charles Gras explained the electronic equipment and the other refinements that made the ship so fast, efficient and manoeuvrable.

Nick realized that the two experts should be left alone now to convince each other; it was clear that although this was their first meeting the two of them had established immediate rapport.

'Come.' Nick quietly took Samantha's arm and they stepped carefully around the scaffolding and loose equipment, picking their way through groups of workmen to the upper deck.

The snow had stopped, but a razor of a wind snickered in from the Atlantic. They found a sheltered corner, and Samantha pressed close to Nick, snuggling into the circle of his arm.

High on her ways, *Sea Witch* gave them a sweeping view, through the forest of construction cranes, over the roofs of the warehouses and offices to the river slipways where the keels of the truly big hulls were laid down.

'You spoke about *Golden Dawn*,' Nick said. 'There she is.'

It took some moments for Samantha to realize she was looking at a ship. 'My God,' she breathed. 'It's so big.'

'They don't come bigger,' he agreed.

The structure of steel was almost a mile and a half long, three city blocks, and the hull was as tall as a five-storey building, while the navigation tower was another hundred feet higher than that.

Samantha shook her head. 'It's beyond belief. It looks like – like a city! It's terrifying to think of that thing afloat.'

'That is only the main hull, the tank pods have been constructed in Japan. The last I heard is that they are under tow direct to the Persian Gulf.'

Nick stared solemnly across at the ship, blinking his eyes against the stinging wind.

'I must have been out of my mind,' he whispered, 'to dream up a monster like that.' But there was a touch of defiant pride in his tone.

'It's so big – beyond imagination,' she encouraged him to talk about it. 'How big *is* it?'

'It's not a single vessel,' he explained. 'No harbour in the world could take a ship that size, it could not even approach the continental United States, for that matter, there just is not enough water to float it.'

'Yes?' She loved to listen to him expound his vision, she loved to hear the force and power of his convictions.

'What you're seeing is the carrying platform, the accommodation and the main power source.' He held her closer. 'On to that, we attach the four tank pods, each one of them capable of carrying a quarter of a million tons of crude oil, each tank almost as large as the biggest ship afloat.'

He was still explaining the concept while they sat at lunch, and Charles Gras and Jules Levoisin listened as avidly as she did.

'A single rigid hull of those dimensions would crack and break up in heavy seas,' he took the cruet set and used it to demonstrate, 'but the four individual pods have been designed so that they can move independently of each other. This gives them the ability to ride and absorb the movement of heavy seas. It is the most important principle of ship construction, a hull must ride the water – not try to oppose it.'

Across the table, Charles Gras nodded lugubrious agreement.

'The tank pods hive on to the main hull, and are carried upon it like remora on the body of a shark, not using their own propulsion systems, but relying on the multiple boilers and quadruple screws of the main hull to carry them across the oceans.' He pushed the cruet set around the table and they all watched it with fascination. 'Then, when it reaches the continental shelf opposite the shore discharge site, the main hull anchors, forty or fifty, even a hundred miles offshore, detaches one or two or all of its pod tanks, and they make those last few miles under their own propulsion. In protected water and in chosen weather conditions, their propulsion systems will handle them safely. Then the empty pod ballasts itself and returns to hook on to the main hull.'

As he spoke, Nicholas detached the salt cellar from the cruet and docked it against Samantha's plate. The two Frenchmen were silent, staring at the silver salt cellar, but Samantha watched Nick's face. It was burned dark by the sun now, lean and handsome, and he seemed charged and vital, like a thoroughbred horse in peak of training, and she was proud of him, proud of the force of his personality that made other men listen when he spoke, proud of the imagination and the courage it took to conceive and then put into operation a project of this magnitude. Even though it were no longer his – yet his had been the vision.

Now Nicholas was talking again. 'Civilization is addicted to liquid fossil fuels. Without them, it would be forced into withdrawal trauma too horrible to contemplate. If then we have to use crude, let's pipe it out of the earth, transport and ship it with all possible precautions to protect ourselves from its side effects—'

'Nicholas,' Charles Gras interrupted him abruptly. 'When last did you inspect the drawings of *Golden Dawn*?'

Nick paused, taken in full stride and a little off balance. He frowned as he cast back, 'I walked out of Christy Marine just over a year ago.' And the darkness of those days settled upon him, making his eyes bleak.

'A year ago we had not even been awarded the contract for the construction of *Golden Dawn*.' Charles Gras twisted the stem of his wine glass between his fingers, and thrust out his bottom lip. 'The ship you have just described to us is very different from the ship we are building out there.'

'In what way, Charles?' Nick's concern was immediate, a father hearing of radical surgery upon his first-born.

'The concept is the same. The mother vessel and the four tank pods, but—' Charles shrugged, that eloquent Gallic gesture, 'it would be easier to show it to you. Immediately after lunch.'

'*D'accord*,' Jules Levoisin nodded. 'But on the condition that it does not interfere with the further enjoyment of this fine meal.' He nudged Nicholas. 'If you eat with a scowl on your face, *mon vieux*, you will grow yourself ulcers like a bunch of Loire grapes.'

Standing beneath the bulk of *Golden Dawn*, she seemed to reach up into that low grey snow-sky, like a mighty alp of steel. The men working on the giddy heights of her scaffolding were small as insects, and quite unbelievably as Samantha stared up at them a little torn streamer of wet grey cloud, coming up the Loire basin from the sea, blew over the ship, obscuring the top of her navigation bridge for a few moments.

'She reaches up to the clouds,' said Nick beside her, and the pride was in his voice as he turned back to Charles Gras. 'She looks good?' It was a question, not a statement. 'She looks like the ship I planned—'

'Come, Nicholas.'

The little party picked its way through the chaos of the yard. The squeal of power cranes and the rumble of heavy steel transporters, the electric hissing crackle of the huge automatic running welders combined with the roaring gunfire barrage of the rivetters into a cacophony that numbed the senses. The scaffolding and hoist systems formed an almost impenetrable forest about the mountainous hull, and steel and concrete were glistening wet and rimed with thin clear ice.

It was a long walk through the crowded yard, almost twenty minutes merely to round the tanker's stern – and suddenly Nicholas stopped so abruptly that Samantha collided with him and might have fallen on the icy concrete, but he caught her arm and held her as he stared up at the bulbous stern.

It formed a great overhanging roof like that of a medieval cathedral, so that Nick's head was flung back, and the grip on her arm tightened so fiercely that she protested. He seemed not to hear, but went on staring upwards.

'Yes,' Charles Gras nodded, and the lank black hair flopped against his forehead. 'That is one difference from the ship you designed.'

The propeller was in lustrous ferro-bronze, six-bladed, each shaped with the beauty and symmetry of a butterfly's wing, but so enormous as to make the comparison laughable. It was so big that not even the bulk of *Golden Dawn*'s own hull could dwarf it, each separate blade was longer and broader than the full wingspan of a jumbo jet airliner, a gargantuan sculpture in gleaming metal.

'One!' whispered Nick. 'One only.'

'Yes,' Charles Gras agreed. 'Not four – but one propeller only. Also, Nicholas, it is fixed pitch.'

They were all silent as they rode up in the cage of the hoist. The hoist ran up the outside of the hull to the level of the main deck, and though the wind searched for them remorselessly through the open mesh of the cage, it was not the cold that kept them silent.

The engine compartment was an echoing cavern, harshly lit by the overhead floodlights, and they stood high on one of the overhead steel catwalks looking down fifty feet on to the boiler and condensers of the main engine.

Nick stared down for almost five minutes. He asked no questions, made no judgements, but at last he turned to Charles Gras and nodded once curtly.

'All right. I've seen enough,' he said, and the engineer led them to the elevator station. Again they rode upwards. It was like being in a modern office block – the polished chrome and wood panelling of the elevator, the carpeted passageways high in the navigation tower along which Charles Gras led them to the Master's suite and unlocked the carved mahogany doorway with a key from his watch chain.

Jules Levoisin looked slowly about the suite and shook his head wonderingly. 'Ah, this is the way to live,' he breathed. 'Nicholas, I absolutely insist that the Master's quarters of *Sea Witch* be decorated like this.'

Nick did not smile, but crossed to the view windows that looked forward along the tanker's main deck to her round blunt unlovely prow a mile and a quarter away. He stood with his hands clasped behind his back, legs apart, chin thrust out angrily and nobody else spoke while Charles Gras opened the elaborate bar and poured cognac into the crystal brandy balloons. He carried a glass to Nick who turned away from the window.

'Thank you, Charles, I need something to warm the chill in my guts.' Nick sipped the cognac and rolled it on his tongue as he looked slowly around the opulent cabin.

It occupied almost half the width of the navigation bridge, and was large enough to house a diplomatic reception. Duncan Alexander had picked a good decorator to do the job, and without the view from the window it might have been an elegant Fifth Avenue New York apartment, or one of those penthouses high on the cliffs above Monte Carlo, overlooking the harbour.

Slowly Nick crossed the thick green carpet, woven with the house device, the entwined letters C and M for Christy Marine, and he stopped before the Degas in its place of honour above the marble fireplace.

He remembered Chantelle's bubbling joy at the purchase of that painting. It was one of Degas' ballet pieces, soft, almost luminous light on the limbs of the dancers, and, remembering the unfailing delight that Chantelle had taken in it over the years, he was amazed that she had allowed it to be used on board one of the company ships, and that it was left here virtually unguarded and vulnerable. That painting was worth a quarter of a million pounds.

He leaned closer to it, and only then did he realize how clever a copy of the original it was. He shook his head in dismissal.

'The owners were advised that the sea air may damage the original,' Charles Gras shrugged, and spread his hands deprecatingly, 'and not many people would know the difference.'

That was typical of Duncan Alexander, Nicholas thought savagely. It could only be his idea, the sharp accountant's brain. The conviction that it was possible to fool all of the people all of the time.

Everybody knew that Chantelle owned that work, therefore nobody would doubt its authenticity. That's the way Duncan Alexander would reason it. It could not be Chantelle's idea. She had never been one to accept anything that was sham or dross; it was a measure of the power that he exerted over her, for her to go along with this cheap little fraud.

Nicholas indicated the forgery with his glass and spoke directly to Charles Gras.

'This is a cheat,' he spoke quietly, his anger contained and controlled, 'but it is harmless.' Now he turned away from it and, with a wider gesture that embraced the whole ship, went on, 'But this other cheat, this enormous fraud,' he paused to control the metallic edge that had entered his tone, going on quietly again, 'this is a vicious murderous gamble he is taking. He has bastardized the entire concept of the scheme. One propeller instead of four – it cannot manoeuvre a hull of these dimensions with safety in any hazardous situation, it cannot deliver sufficient thrust to avoid collision, to fight her off a lee shore, to handle heavy seas.' Nick stopped, and his voice dropped even lower, yet somehow it was more compelling. 'This ship cannot, by all moral and natural laws, be operated on a single boiler. My design called for eight separate boilers and condensers, the standard set for the old White Star and Cunard Lines. But Duncan Alexander has installed a single boiler system.

There is no back-up, no fail-safe – a few gallons of sea water in the system could disable this monster.'

Nicholas stopped suddenly as a new thought struck him. 'Charles,' his voice sharper still, 'the pod tanks, the design of the pod tanks. He hasn't altered that, has he? He hasn't cut the corners there? Tell me, old friend, they are still self-propelled, are they not?'

Charles Gras brought the Courvoisier bottle to where Nicholas stood, and when Nick would have refused the addition to his glass, Charles told him sorrowfully, 'Come, Nicholas, you will need it for what I have to tell you now.'

As he poured, he said, 'The pod tankers, their design has been altered also.' He drew a breath to tell it with a rush. 'They no longer have their own propulsion units. They are now only dumb barges that must be docked and undocked from the main hull and manoeuvred only by attendant tugs.'

Nicholas stared at him, his lips blanched to thin white lines. 'No. I do not believe it. Not even Duncan—'

'Duncan Alexander has saved forty-two million dollars by redesigning *Golden Dawn* and equipping her with only a single boiler and propeller.' Charles Gras shrugged again. 'And forty-two million dollars is a lot of money.'


There was a pale gleam of wintry sunlight that flickered through the low grey cloud and lit the fields not far from the River Thames with that incredible vivid shade of English green.

Samantha and Nicholas stood in a thin line of miserably cold parents and watched the pile of struggling boys across the field in their coloured jerseys; the light blue and black of Eton, the black and white of St Paul's, were so muddied as to be barely distinguishable.

'What are they doing?' Samantha demanded, holding the collar of her coat around her ears.

'It's called a scrum,' Nick told her. 'That's how they decide which team gets the ball.'

'Wow. There must be an easier way.'

There was a flurry of sudden movement and the slippery egg-shaped ball flew back in a lazy curve that was snapped up by a boy in the Etonian colours. He started to run.

'It's Peter, isn't it?' cried Samantha.

'Go it, Peter boy!' Nick roared, and the child ran with the ball clutched to his chest and his head thrown back. He ran strongly with the reaching co-ordinated stride of an older boy, swerving round a knot of his opponents, leaving them floundering in the churned mud, and angling across the lush thick grass towards the white-painted goal line, trying to reach the corner before a taller more powerfully built lad who was pounding across the field to intercept him.

Samantha began to leap up and down on the same spot, shrieking wildly, completely uncertain of what was happening, but wild with excitement that infected Nicholas.

The two runners converged at an angle which would bring them to the white line at the same moment, at a point directly in front of where Nick and Samantha stood.

Nick saw the contortion of his son's face, and realized that this was a total effort. He felt a physical constriction of his own chest as he watched the boy drive himself to his utmost limits, the sinews standing out in his throat, his lips drawn back in a frozen rictus of endeavour that exposed the teeth clenched in his jaw.

From infancy, Peter Berg had brought to any task that faced him the same complete focus of all his capabilities. Like his grandfather, old Arthur Christy, and his own father, he would be one of life's winners. Nick knew this instinctively, as he watched him run. He had inherited the intelligence, the comeliness and the charisma, but he bolstered all that with this unquenchable desire to succeed in all he did. The single-minded determination to focus all his talents on the immediate project. Nick felt the pressure in his chest swell. The boy was all right, more than all right, and pride threatened to choke him.

Sheer force of will had driven Peter Berg a pace ahead of his bigger, longer-legged adversay, and now he leaned forward with the ball held in both hands, arms fully extended, reaching for the line to make the touchdown.

He was ten feet from where Nick stood, a mere instant from success, but he was unbalanced, and the St Paul's boy dived at him, crashing into the side of his chest, the impact jarring and brutal, hurling Peter out of the field of play with the ball spinning from his hands and bouncing away loosely, while Peter smashed into the earth on both knees, then rolled forward head over heels, and sprawled face down on the soggy turf.

'It's a touch-down!' Samantha was still leaping up and down.

'No,' said Nick. 'No, it isn't.'

Peter Berg dragged himself upright. His cheek was streaked with chocolate mud and both his knees were running blood, the skin smeared open by the coarse grass.

He did not glance down at his injuries, and he shrugged away the St Paul's boy's patronizing hand, holding himself erect against the pain as he limped back on to the field. He did not look at his father, and the moisture that filled his eyes and threatened to flood over the thick dark lashes were not the tears of pain, but of humiliation and failure. With an overwhelming feeling of kinship, Nick knew that for his son those feelings were harder to bear than any physical agony.

When the game ended he came to Nicholas, all bloodied and mud-smeared, and shook hands solemnly.

'I am so glad you came, sir,' he said. 'I wish you could have watched us win.'

Nick wanted to say: 'It doesn't matter, Peter, it's only a game.' But he did not. To Peter Berg, it mattered very deeply, so Nicholas nodded agreement and then he introduced Samantha.

Again Peter shook hands solemnly and startled her by calling her, 'M'am.' But when she told him, 'Hi, Pete. A great game, you deserved to slam them,' he smiled, that sudden dazzling irresistible flash that reminded her so of

Nicholas and she felt her heart squeezed. Then when the boy hurried away to shower and change, she took Nick's arm.

'He's a beautiful boy, but does he always call you "sir"?'

'I haven't seen him in three months. It takes us both a little while to relax.'

'Three months is a long time—'

'It's all tied up by the lawyers. Access and visiting-rights – what's good for the child, not what's good for the parents. Today was a special concession from Chantelle, but I still have to deliver him to her at five o'clock. Not five past five, five o'clock.'

They went to the Cockpit teashop and Peter startled Samantha again by pulling out her chair and seating her formally. While they waited for the best muffins in Britain to be brought to the table, Nicholas and Peter engaged each other in conversation that was stiff with selfconsciousness.

'Your mother sent me a copy of your report, Peter, I cannot tell you how delighted I was.'

'I had hoped to do better, sir. There are still three others ahead of me.'

And Samantha ached for them. Peter Berg was twelve years of age. She wished he could just throw his arms around Nicholas' neck and say, 'Daddy, I love you,' for the love was transparent, even through the veneer of public-school manners. It shone behind the thick dark lashes that fringed the boy's golden brown eyes, and glowed on the cheeks still as creamy and smooth as a girl's.

She wanted desperately to help them both, and on inspiration she launched into an account of *Warlock*'s salvage of *Golden Adventurer*, a tale with emphasis on the derring-do of *Warlock*'s Master, not forgetting his rescue of Samantha Silver from the icy seas of Antarctica.

Peter's eyes grew enormous as he listened, never leaving her face except to demand of Nicholas, 'Is that true, Dad?' And when the story was told, he was silent for a long moment before announcing, 'I'm going to be a tug captain when I'm big.'

Then he showed Samantha how to spread strawberry jam on her muffins the correct way, and chewing together heartily with cream on their lips the two of them became fast friends, and Nicholas joined their chatter more easily, smiling his thanks at Samantha and reaching under the table to squeeze her hand.

He had to end it at last. 'Listen, Peter, if we are to make Lynwood by five—' and the boy sobered instantly.

'Dad, couldn't you telephone Mother? She just might let me spend the weekend in London with you.'

'I already tried that.' Nick shook his head. 'It didn't work,' and Peter stood up, his feelings cloaked by an expression of stoic resignation.

From the back of Nick's Mercedes 450 Coupé the boy leaned forward into the space between the two bucket seats, and the three of them were very close in the snug interior of the speeding car, their laughter that of old friends.

It was almost dark when Nicholas turned in through Lynwood's stone gateway, and he glanced at the luminous dial of his Rolex. 'We'll just make it.'

The drive climbed the hill in a series of broad even curves through the carefully tended woods, and the three-storied Georgian country house on the crest was ablaze with light in every window.

Nick never came here without that strange hollow feeling in the bottom of his stomach. Once this had been his home, every room, every acre of the grounds had its memories, and now, as he parked under the white columned portico, they came crowding back.

'I have finished the model Spitfire you sent me for Christmas, Dad.' Peter was playing desperately for time now. 'Won't you come up and see it?'

'I don't think so—' Nicholas began, and Peter blurted out before he could finish,

'It's all right, Uncle Duncan won't be here. He always comes down late from London on Friday nights, and his Rolls isn't in the garage yet.' Then, in a tone that tore at Nick like thorns, 'Please. . . . I won't see you again until Easter.'

'Go,' said Samantha. 'I'll wait here.' And Peter turned on her, 'You come too, Sam, please.'

Samantha felt herself infected by that fatal curiosity, the desire to see, to know more of Nick's past life; she knew he was going to demur further, but she forestalled him, slipping quickly out of the Mercedes.

'Okay, Pete, let's go.'

Nick must follow them up the broad steps to the double oaken doors, and he felt himself carried along on a tide of events over which he had no control. It was a sensation that he never relished.

In the entrance hall Samantha looked around her quickly, feeling herself overcome by awe. It was so grand, there was no other word to describe the house. The stair well reached up the full height of the three storeys, and the broad staircase was in white marble with a marble balustrade, while on each side of the hall, glass doors opened on to long reception rooms. But she did not have a chance to look further, for Peter seized her hand and raced her up the staircase, while Nick followed them up to Peter's room at a more sedate pace.

The Spitfire had place of honour on the shelf above Peter's bed. He brought it down proudly, and they examined it with suitable expressions of admiration. Peter responded to their praise like a flower to the sun.

When at last they descended the staircase, the sadness and restraint of parting was on them all, but they were stopped in the centre of the hall by the voice from the drawing-room door on the left.

'Peter, darling.' A woman stood in the open doorway, and she was even more beautiful than the photograph that Samantha had seen of her.

'Dutifully Peter crossed to her. 'Good evening, Mother.'

She stooped over him, cupping his face in her hands, and she kissed him tenderly, then she straightened, holding his hand so he was ranged at her side, a subtle drawing of boundaries.

'Nicholas,' she tilted her head, 'you look marvellous – so brown and fit.'

Chantelle Alexander was only a few inches taller than her son, but she seemed to fill and light the huge house with a shimmering presence, the way a single beautiful bird can light a dim forest.

Her hair was dark and soft and glowing, and her skin and the huge dark sloe eyes were a legacy from the beautiful Persian noblewoman that old Arthur Christy had married for her fortune, and come to love with an obsessive passion.

She was dainty. Her tiny, narrow feet peeped from below the long, dark green silk skirt, and the exquisite little hand that held Peter's was emphasized by a single deep throbbing green emerald the size of a ripe acorn.

Now she turned her head on the long graceful neck, and her eyes took the slightly oriental slant of a modern-day Nefertiti as she looked at Samantha.

For seconds only, the two women studied each other, and Samantha's chin came up firmly as she looked into those deep dark gazelle eyes, touched with all the mystery and intrigue of the East. They understood each other instantly. It was an intuitive flash, like a discharge of static electricity, then Chantelle smiled, and when she smiled the impossible happened – she became more beautiful than before.

'May I present Dr Silver?' Nick began, but Peter tugged at his mother's hand.

'I asked Sam to see my model. She's a marine biologist, and she's a professor at Miami University—'

'Not yet, Pete,' Samantha corrected him, 'but give me time.'

'Good evening, Dr Silver. It seems you have made a conquest.' Chantelle let the statement hang ambiguously as she turned back to Nick. 'I was waiting for you, Nicholas, and I'm so glad to have a chance to speak to you.' She glanced again at Samantha. 'I do hope you will excuse us for a few minutes, Dr Silver. It is a matter of some urgency. Peter will be delighted to entertain you. As a biologist, you will find his guinea pigs of interest, I'm sure.'

The commands were given so graciously, by a lady in such control of her situation, that Peter went to take Samantha's hand and lead her away.

It was one of the customs of Lynwood that all serious discussion took place in the study. Chantelle led the way, and went immediately to the false-fronted bookcase that concealed the liquor cabinet, and commenced the ritual of preparing a drink for Nicholas. He wanted to stop her. It was something from long ago, recalling too much that was painful, but instead, he watched the delicate but precise movement of her hands pouring exactly the correct measure of Chivas Royal Salute into the crystal glass, adding the soda and the single cube of ice.

'What a pretty young girl, Nicholas.'

He said nothing. On the ornate Louis Quatorze desk was a silver-framed photograph of Duncan Alexander and Chantelle together, and he looked away and moved to the fireplace, standing with his back to the blaze as he had done on a thousand other evenings.

Chantelle brought the glass to him, and stood close, looking up at him – and her fragrance touched a deep nostalgic chord. He had first bought *Calèche* for her on a spring morning in Paris; with an effort he forced the memory aside.

'What did you want to speak to me about, is it Peter?'

'No. Peter is doing as well as we can hope for, in the circumstances. He still resents Duncan – but—' she shrugged, and moved away. He had almost forgotten how narrow was her waist, he would still be able to span it with both hands.

'It's hard to explain, but it's Christy Marine, Nicholas. I desperately need the advice of someone I can trust.'

'You can trust me?' he asked.

'Isn't it strange? I would still trust you with my life.' She came back to him, standing disconcertingly close, enveloping him with her scent and heady beauty. He sipped at the whisky to distract himself.

'Even though I have no right to ask you, Nicholas, still I know you won't refuse me, will you?'

She wove spells, he could feel the mesh falling like gossamer around him.

'I always was a sucker, wasn't I?'

Now she touched his arm. 'No, Nicholas, please don't be bitter.' She held his gaze directly.

'How can I help you?' Her touch on his arm disturbed him, and sensing this, she increased the pressure of her fingers for a moment, then lifted her hand and glanced at the slim white gold Piaget on her wrist.

'Duncan will be home soon – and what I have to tell you is long and complicated. Can we meet in London early next week?'

'Chantelle,' he began.

'Nicky, please.' *Nicky*, she was the only one who ever called him that. It was too familiar, too intimate.

'When?'

'You are meeting Duncan on Tuesday morning to discuss the arbitration of *Golden Adventurer*.'

'Yes.'

'Will you call me at Eaton Square when you finish? I'll wait by the telephone.'

'Chantelle—'

'Nicky, I have nobody else to turn to.'

He had never been able to refuse her – which was part of the reason he had lost her, he thought wryly.

There was no engine noise, just the low rush of air past the body of the Mercedes.

'Damn these seats, they weren't made for lovers,' Samantha said.

'We'll be home in an hour.'

'I don't know if I can wait that long,' Samantha whispered huskily. 'I want to be closer to you.'

And they were silent again, until they slowed for the weekend traffic through Hammersmith.

'Peter is a knockout. If only I were ten years old, I'd cash in my dolls.'

'My guess is he would swop his Spitfire.'

'How much longer?'

'Another half hour.'

'Nicholas, I feel threatened,' her voice had a sudden panicky edge to it, 'I have this terrible foreboding—'

'That's nonsense.'

'It's been too good – for too long.'


James Teacher was the head of Salmon Peters and Teacher, the lawyers that Nick had retained for Ocean Salvage. He was a man with a formidable reputation in the City, a leading expert on maritime law – and a tough bargainer. He was florid and bald, and so short that his feet did not touch the floorboards of the Bentley when he sat on the back seat.

He and Nick had discussed in detail where this preliminary meeting with Christy Marine should be held, and at last they had agreed to go to the mountain, but James Teacher had insisted on arriving in his chocolate-coloured Bentley, rather than a cab.

'Smoked salmon, Mr Berg, not fish and chips – that's what we are after.'

Christy House was one of those conservative smoke-stained stone buildings fronted on to Leadenhall Street, the centre of Britain's shipping industry. Almost directly opposite was Trafalgar House, and a hundred yards farther was Lloyd's of London. The doorman crossed the pavement to open Nicholas' door.

'Good to see you again, Mr Berg sir.'

'Hello, Alfred. You taking good care of the shop?'

'Indeed, sir.'

The following cab, containing James Teacher's two juniors and their bulky briefcases, pulled in behind the Bentley and they assembled on the pavement like a party of raiding Vikings before the gates of a medieval city. The three lawyers settled their bowler hats firmly and then moved forward determinedly in spearhead formation.

In the lobby, the doorman passed them on to a senior clerk who was waiting by the desk.

'Good morning, Mr Berg. You are looking very well, sir.'

They rode up at a sedate pace in the elevator with its antique steel concertina doors. Nicholas had never brought himself to exchange them for those swift modern boxes. And the clerk ushered them out on to the top-floor landing.

'Will you follow me, please, gentlemen?'

There was an antechamber that opened on to the board room, a large room, panelled and hung with a single portrait of old Arthur Christy on the entrance wall – fighting jaw and sharp black eyes under beetling white eyebrows. A log fire burned in the open grate, and there was sherry and Madeira in crystal decanters on the central table – another one of the old man's little traditions – that both James Teacher and Nick refused curtly.

They waited quietly, standing facing the door into the Chairman's suite. They waited for exactly four minutes before the door was thrown open and Duncan Alexander stepped through it.

His eyes flicked across the room and settled instantly on Nick, locking with his, like the horns of two great bull buffalo, and the room was very still.

The lawyers around Nick seemed to shrink back and the men behind Duncan Alexander waited, not yet following him into the antechamber, but all of them watched and waited avidly; this meeting would be the gossip of the City for weeks to come. It was a classic confrontation, and they wanted to miss not a moment of it.

Duncan Alexander was a strikingly good-looking man, very tall, two inches taller than Nick, but slim as a dancer, and he carried his body with a dancer's control. His face also was narrow, with the long lantern jaw of a young Lincoln, already chiselled by life around the eyes and at the corners of the mouth.

His hair was very dense and a metallic blond; though he wore it fashionably long over the ears, yet it was so carefully groomed that each gleaming wave seemed to have been sculptured.

His skin was smooth and tanned darker than his hair, sunlamp or skiing at Chantelle's lodge at Gstaad perhaps, and now when he smiled his teeth were dazzling white, perfect large teeth in the wide friendly mouth – but the eyes did not smile though they crinkled at the corners. Duncan Alexander watched from behind the handsome face like a sniper in ambush.

'Nicholas,' he said, without moving forward or offering a hand.

'Duncan,' said Nick quietly, not answering the smile, and Duncan Alexander adjusted the hang of his lapel. His clothes were beautifully cut, and the cloth was the finest, softest wool, but there were foppish little touches: the hacking slits in the tails of the jacket, the double-flapped pockets, and the waistcoat in plum-coloured velvet. Now he touched the buttons with his fingertips, another little distracting gesture, the only evidence of any discomfort.

Nicholas stared at him steadily, trying to measure him dispassionately, and now for the first time he began to see how it might have happened. There was a sense of excitement about the man, a wicked air of danger, the fascination of the leopard – or some other powerful predator. Nick could understand the almost irresistible attraction he had for women, especially for a spoiled and bored lady, a matron of thirteen years who believed there was still excitement and adventure in life that she was missing. Duncan had done his cobra dance, and Chantelle had watched like a mesmerized bird of paradise – until she had toppled from the branch – or that's how Nicholas liked to think it had happened. He was wiser now, much wiser and more cynical.

'Before we begin,' Nick knew that anger was seething to his still surface, must soon bubble through unless he could give it release, 'I should like five minutes in private.'

'Of course.' Duncan inclined his head, and there was a hurried scampering as his minions cleared the doorway into the Chairman's suite. 'Come through.'

Duncan stood aside, and Nick walked through. The offices had been completely redecorated, and Nick blinked with surprise, white carpets and furniture in chrome and perspex, stark abstract geometrical art in solid primary colours on the walls; the ceiling had been lowered by an eggcrate design in chrome steel and free-swivelling studio spotlights gave selected light patterns on wall and ceiling. It was no improvement, Nick decided.

'I was in St Nazaire last week.' Nicholas turned in the centre of the wide snowy floor and faced Duncan Alexander as he closed the door.

'Yes, I know.'

'I went over *Golden Dawn*.'

Duncan Alexander snapped open a gold cigarette case and offered it to Nick, then when he shook his head in refusal, selected one himself. They were special blend, custom-made for him by Benson and Hedges.

'Charles Gras exceeded his authority,' Duncan nodded. 'Visitors are not allowed on *Golden Dawn*.'

'I am not surprised you are ashamed of that death-trap you are building.'

'But you do surprise me, Nicholas.' Duncan showed his teeth again. 'It was your design.'

'You know it was not. You took the idea, and bastardized it. Duncan, you cannot send that,' Nick sought the word, 'monster on to the open sea. Not with one propulsion unit, and a single screw. The risk is too appalling.'

'I tell you this for no good reason, except perhaps that this was once your office,' Duncan made a gesture that embraced the room, 'and because it amuses me to point out to you the faults in your original planning. The concept was sound, but you soured the cream by adding those preposterous, shall we call them Bergean, touches. Five separate propulsion units, and a forest of boilers. It wasn't viable, Nicholas.'

'It was good, the figures were right.'

'The whole tanker market has changed since you left Christy Marine. I had to re-work it.'

'You should have dropped the whole concept if the cost-structure changed.'

'Oh no, Nicholas, I restructured. My way, even in these hard times, I will recover capital in a year, and with a five-year life on the hull there is two hundred million collars' profit in it.'

'I was going to build a ship that would live for thirty years,' Nick told him. 'Something of which we could be proud—'

'Pride is an expensive commodity. We aren't building dynasties any more, we are in the game of selling tanker space.' Duncan's tone was patronizing, that impeccable accent drawn out, emphasizing the difference in their backgrounds. 'I'm aiming at a five-year life, two hundred million profit, and then we sell the hull to the Greeks or Japs. It's a one-time thing.'

'You always were a smash-and-grab artist,' Nick agreed. 'But it isn't like dealing in commodities. Ships aren't wheat and bacon, and the oceans aren't the orderly market floors.'

'I disagree, I'm afraid. The principles are the same – one buys, one sells.'

'Ships are living things, the ocean is a battleground of all the elements.'

'Come, Nicholas, you don't really believe that romantic nonsense.' Duncan drew a gold Hunter from his waist pocket, and snapped open the lid to read the dial, another of his affectations which irritated Nicholas. 'Those are very expensive gentlemen waiting next door.'

'You will be risking human life, the men who sail her.'

'Seamen are well paid—'

'You will be taking a monstrous risk with the life of the oceans. Wherever she goes *Golden Dawn* will be a potential—'

'For God's sake, Nicholas, two hundred million dollars is worth some kind of risk.'

'All right,' Nick nodded. 'Let's forget the environment, and the human life, and consider the important aspects – the money.'

Duncan sighed, and wagged that fine head, smiling as at a recalcitrant child.

'I have considered the money – in detail.'

'You will not get an A1 rating at Lloyd's. You will not get insurance on that hull – unless you underwrite yourself, the same way you did with *Golden Adventurer*, and if you think that's wise, just wait until I've finished with my salvage claim.'

Duncan Alexander's smile twisted slowly, and blood darkened his cheeks under the snow-tan. 'I do not need a Lloyd's rating, though I am sure I could get one if I wanted it. I have arranged continental and oriental underwriters. She will be fully insured.'

'Against pollution claims, also? If you burst that bag of crude on the continental shelf of America, or Europe, they'll hit you for half a billion dollars. Nobody would underwrite that.'

'*Golden Dawn* is registered in Venezuela, and she has no sister ships for the authorities to seize, like they did with the *Torrey Canyon*. To whom will they address the pollution bill? A defunct South American Company? No, Nicholas, Christy Marine will not be paying any pollution bills.'

'I cannot believe it, even of you.' Nick stared at him. 'You are cold-bloodedly talking about the possibility – no, the probability – of dumping a million tons of crude oil into the sea.'

'Your moral indignation is touching. It really is. However, Nicholas, may I remind you that this is family and house business – and you are no longer of either family or house.'

'I fought you every time you cut a corner,' Nick reminded him. 'I tried to teach you that cheap is always expensive in the long run.'

'You taught me?' For the first time Duncan taunted him openly. 'What could you ever teach me about ships or money,' and he rolled his tongue gloatingly around the next words, 'or women?'

Nick made the first movement of lunging at him, but he caught himself, and forced himself to unclench his fists at his sides. The blood sang in his ears.

'I'm going to fight you,' he said quietly. 'I'm going to fight you from here to the Maritime Conference, and beyond.' He made the decision in that moment, he hadn't really realized he was going to do it until then.

'A maritime conference has never taken less than five years to reach a decision restricting one of its members. By that time *Golden Dawn* will belong to some Japanese, Hong-Kong-based company – and Christy Marine will have banked two hundred million.'

'I'll have the oil ports closed to you—'

'By whom? Oil-thirsty governments, with lobbies of the big oil companies?' Duncan laughed lightly, he had replaced the urbane mask. 'You really are out of your depth again. We have bumped heads a dozen times before, Nicholas – and I'm still on my feet. I'm not about to fold up at your fine threats now.'


After that, there was no hope that the meeting in the panelled board room would lead to conciliation. The atmosphere crackled and smouldered with the antagonism of the two leading characters, so that they seemed to be the only persons on the stage.

They sat opposite each other, separated by the glossy surface of the rosewood table top, and their gazes seldom disengaged. They leaned forward in their chairs, and when they smiled at each other, it was like the silent snarl of two old dog wolves circling with hackles erect.

It took an enormous effort of self-control for Nicholas to force back his anger far enough to be able to think clearly, and to allow his intuition to pick up the gut-impressions, the subtle hints of the thinking and planning that were taking place across the table behind Duncan Alexander's handsome mask of a face.

It was half an hour before he was convinced that something other than personal rivalry and antagonism was motivating the man before him. His counter offer was too low to have any hope of being accepted, so low that it became clear that he did not want to settle. Duncan Alexander wanted to go to arbitration – and yet there was nothing he could gain by that. It must be obvious to everyone at the table, beyond any doubt whatsoever, that Nicholas' claim was worth four million dollars. Nicholas would have settled for four, even in his anger he would have gone for four – risking that an arbitration board might have awarded six, and knowing the delay and costs of going to litigation might amount to another million. He would have settled.

Duncan Alexander was offering two and a half. It was a frivolous offer. Duncan was going through the motions only. There was no serious attempt at finding a settlement. He didn't want to come to terms, and it seemed to Nicholas that by refusing to settle he was gaining nothing, and risking a great deal. He was a big enough boy to know that you never, but never, go to litigation if there is another way out. It was a rule that Nicholas had graven on his heart in letters of fire. Litigation makes only lawyers fat.

Why was Duncan baulking, what was he to gain by this obstruction? Nicholas crushed down the temptation to stand up and walk out of the room with an exclamation of disgust. Instead, he lit another cheroot and leaned forward again, staring into Duncan Alexander's steely grey eyes, trying to fathom him, needling, probing for the soft rotten spot – and thinking hard.

What had Duncan Alexander to gain from not settling now? Why did he not try with a low, but realistic offer – what was he to gain?

Then quite suddenly he knew what it was. Chantelle's enigmatic appeal for help and advice flashed back to him, and he knew what it was. Duncan Alexander wanted time. It was as simple as that. Duncan Alexander needed time.

'All right.' Satisfied at last, Nicholas leaned back in the deep leather-padded chair, and veiled his eyes. 'We are still a hundred miles apart. There will be only one meeting-ground. That's in the upper room at Lloyd's. It's set down for the 27th. Are we at least agreed on that date?'

'Of course.' Duncan leaned back also and Nicholas saw the shift of his eyes, the little jump of nerves in the point of his clenched jaws, the tightening of the long pianist's fingers that lay before him on the leather-bound blotter. 'Of course,' Duncan repeated, and began to stand up, a gesture of dismissal.

He lied beautifully; had Nicholas not known he would lie, he might have missed the little tell-tale signs.

In the ancient lift, James Teacher was jubilant, rubbing his little fat hands together. 'We'll give him a go!' Nicholas glanced at him sourly. Win, lose or draw, James Teacher would still draw his fee, and Duncan Alexander's refusal to settle had quadrupled that fee. There was something almost obscene about the little lawyer's exultation.

'They are going to duck,' Nick said grimly, and James Teacher sobered slightly.

'Before noon tomorrow, Christy Marine will have lodged for postponement of hearing,' Nick prophesied. 'You'll have to use *Warlock* with full power on both to pull them before the arbitration board.'

'Yes, you're right,' James Teacher nodded. 'They had me puzzled, I sensed something—'

'I'm not paying you to be puzzled,' Nick's voice was low and hard. 'I'm paying you to out-guess and out-jump them. I want them at the hearing on the 27th, get them there, Mr Teacher.' He did not have to voice the threat, and in a moment, the exultation on James Teacher's rotund features had changed to apprehension and deep concern.

The drawing-room in Eaton Square was decorated in cream and pale gold, cleverly designed as a frame for the single exquisite work of art which it contained, the original of the group of Degas ballet-dancers whose copy hung in *Golden Dawn*'s stateroom. It was the room's centre-piece; cunningly lit by a hidden spotlight, it glowed like a precious jewel. Even the flowers on the ivory grand piano were cream and white roses and carnations, whose pale ethereal blossoms put the painting into stronger contrast.

The only other flash of brightness was worn by Chantelle, she had the oriental knack of carrying vivid colour without it seeming gaudy. She wore a flaming Pucci that could not pale her beauty, and as she rose from the huge shaggy white sofa and came to Nicholas, he felt the soft warm melting sensation in this stomach spreading slowly through his body like a draught of some powerful aphrodisiac. He knew he would never be immune to her.

'Dear Nicky. I knew I could rely upon you.' She took his hand and looked up at him, and still holding his hand she led him to the sofa, and then she settled beside him, like a bright, lovely bird alighting. She drew her legs up under her, her calves and ankles flashed like carved and polished ivory before she tucked the brilliant skirt around them, and lifted the Wedgwood porcelain teapot.

'Orangepekoe,' she smiled at him. 'No lemon and no sugar.'

He had to smile back at her, 'You never forget,' and he took the cup.

'I told you that you looked well,' she said, slowly and unselfconsciously studying him. 'And you really do, Nicholas. When you came down to Lynwood for Peter's birthday in June I was so worried about you. You looked terribly ill and tired – but now,' she tilted her head critically, 'you look absolutely marvellous.'

Now he should tell her that she was beautiful as ever, he thought grimly, and then they would start talking about Peter and their old mutual friends.

'What did you want to talk to me about?' he asked quietly, and there was a passing shadow of hurt in her dark eyes.

'Nicholas, you can be so remote, so—' she hesitated, seeking the correct word, 'so detached.'

'Recently someone called me an ice-cold Pommy bastard,' he agreed, but she shook her head.

'No. I know you are not, but if only—'

'The three most dangerous and inflammatory phrases in the English language,' he stopped her. 'They are "you always" and "you never" and "if only". Chantelle, I came here to help you with a problem. Let's discuss that - only.'

She stood up quickly, and he knew her well enough to recognize the fury in the snapping dark eyes and the quick dancing steps that carried her to the mantelpiece, and she stood looking up at the Degas with her small fists clenched at her sides.

'Are you sleeping with that child?' she asked, and now the fury was raw in her voice.

Nicholas stood up from the sofa.

'Goodbye, Chantelle.'

She turned and flew to him, taking his arm.

'Oh, Nicholas, that was unforgivable, I don't know what possessed me. Please don't go.' And when he tried to disengage her hand. 'I beg you, for the first time ever, I beg you, Nicholas. Please don't go.'

He was still stiff with anger when he sank back on the sofa, and they were silent for nearly a minute while she regained her composure.

'This is all going so terribly badly. I didn't want this to happen.'

'All right, let's get on to safer ground.'

'Nicholas,' she started, 'you and Daddy created Christy Marine. If anything, it was more yours than his. The great days were the last ten years when you were Chairman, all the tremendous achievements of those years—'

He made a gesture of denial and impatience, but she went on softly.

'Too much of your life is locked up in Christy Marine, you are still deeply involved, Nicholas.'

'There are only two things I am involved with now,' he told her harshly. 'Ocean Salvage and Nicholas Berg.'

'We both know that is not true,' she whispered. 'You are a special type of man.' She sighed. 'It took me so long to recognize that. I thought all men were like you. I believed strength and nobility of mind were common goods on the market—' she shrugged. 'Some people learn the hard way,' and she smiled, but it was an uncertain, twisted little smile.

He said nothing for a moment, thinking of all that was revealed by those words, then he replied.

'If you believe that, then tell me what is worrying you.'

'Nicholas, something is terribly wrong with Christy Marine. There is something happening there that I don't understand.'

'Tell me.'

She turned her head away for a moment, and then looked back at him. Her eyes seemed to change shape and colour, growing darker and sadder. 'It is so difficult not to be disloyal, so difficult to find expression for vague doubts and fears,' she stopped and bit her lower lip softly. 'Nicholas, I have transferred my shares in Christy Marine to Duncan as my nominee, with voting rights.'

Nicholas felt the shock of it jump down his nerves and string them tight. He shifted restlessly on the sofa and stared at her, and she nodded.

'I know it was madness. The madness of those crazy days a year ago. I would have given him anything he asked for.'

He felt the premonition that she had not yet told him all and he waited while she rose and went to the window, looked out guiltily and then turned back to him.

'May I get you a drink?'

He glanced at his Rolex. 'The sun is over the yard-arm, what about Duncan?'

'These days he is never home before eight or nine.' She went to the decanter on the silver tray and poured the whisky with her back to him, and now her voice was so low that he barely caught the words.

'A year ago I resigned as executrix of the Trust.'

He did not answer, it was what he had been waiting for, he had known there was something else. The Trust that old Arthur Christy had set up was the backbone and sinews of Christy Marine. One million voting shares administered by three executors, a banker, a lawyer and a member of the Christy family.

Chantelle turned and brought the drink to him.

'Did you hear what I said?' she asked, and he nodded and sipped the drink before he asked,

'The other executors? Pickstone of Lloyd's and Rollo still?'

She shook her head and again bit her lip.

'No, it's not Lloyd's anymore, it's Cyril Forbes.'

'Who is he?' Nick demanded.

'He is the head of London and European.'

'But that's Duncan's own bank,' Nick protested.

'It's still a registered bank.'

'And Rollo?'

'Rollo had a heart attack six months ago. He resigned, and Duncan put in another younger man. You don't know him.'

'My God, three men and each of them is Duncan Alexander – he has had a free hand with Christy Marine for over a year, Chantelle, there is no check on him.'

'I know,' she whispered. 'It was a madness. I just cannot explain it.'

'It's the oldest madness in the world.' Nick pitied her then; for the first time, he realized and accepted that she had been under a compulsion, driven by forces over which she had no control, and he pitied her.

'I am so afraid, Nicholas. I'm afraid to find out what I have done. Deep down I know there is something terribly wrong, but I'm afraid of the truth.'

'All right, tell me everything else.'

'There isn't anything else.'

'If you lie to me, I cannot help you,' he pointed out gently.

'I have tried to follow the new structuring of the company, it's all so complicated, Nicholas. London and European is the new holding company, and – and—' her voice trailed off. 'It just goes round and round in circles, and I cannot pry too deep or ask too many questions.'

'Why not?' he demanded.

'You don't know Duncan.'

'I am beginning to,' he answered her grimly. 'But, Chantelle, you have every right to ask and get answers.'

'Let me get you another drink.' She jumped up lightly.

'I haven't finished this one.'

'The ice has melted, I know you don't like that.' She took the glass and emptied the diluted spirit, refilled it and brought it back to him.

'All right,' he said. 'What else?'

Suddenly she was weeping. Smiling at him wistfully and weeping. There was no sobbing or sniffing, the tears merely welled up slowly as oil or blood from the huge dark eyes, broke from the thick, arched lashes and rolled softly down her cheeks. Yet still she smiled.

'The madness is over, Nicholas. It didn't last very long – but it was a holocaust while it did.'

'He comes home at nine o'clock now,' Nicholas said.

'Yes, he comes home at nine o'clock.'

He took the linen handkerchief from his inner pocket and handed it to her.

'Thank you.'

She dabbed away the tears, still smiling softly.

'What must I do, Nicholas?'

'Call in a team of auditors,' he began, but she shook her head and cut him short.

'You don't know Duncan,' she repeated.

'There is nothing he could do.'

'He could do anything,' she contradicted him. 'He is capable of anything. I am afraid, Nicholas, terribly afraid, not only for myself, but for Peter also.'

Nicholas sat erect then.

'Peter. Do you mean you are afraid of something physical?'

'I don't know, Nicholas. I'm so confused and alone. You are the only person in the world I can trust.'

He could no longer remain seated. He stood up and began to pace about the room, frowning heavily, looking down at the glass in his hand and swirling the ice so that it tinkled softly.

'All right,' he said at last. 'I will do what I can. The first thing is to find out just how much substance there is to your fears.'

'How will you do that?'

'It's best you don't know, yet.'

He drained his glass and she stood up, quick with alarm.

'You aren't going, are you?'

'There is nothing else to discuss now. I will contact you when or if I learn anything.'

'I'll see you down.'

In the hall she dismissed the uniformed West Indian maid with a shake of her head, and fetched Nicholas' top coat from the closet herself.

'Shall I send for the car? You'll not get a cab at five o'clock.'

'I'll walk,' he said.

'Nicholas, I cannot tell you how grateful I am. I had forgotten how safe and secure it is to be with you.' Now she was standing very close to him, her head lifted, and her lips were soft and glossy and ripe, her eyes still flooded and bright. He knew he should leave immediately. 'I know it's going to be all right now.'

She placed one of those dainty ivory hands on his lapel, adjusting it unnecessarily with that proprietary feminine gesture, and she moistened her lips.

'We are all fools, Nicholas, every one of us. We all complicate our lives – when it's so easy to be happy.'

'The trick is to recognize happiness when you stumble on it, I suppose.'

'I'm sorry, Nicholas. That's the first time I've ever apologized to you. It's a day of many first times, isn't it? But I am truly sorry for everything I have ever done to hurt you. I wish with all my heart that it were possible to wipe it all out and begin again.'

'Unfortunately, it doesn't work that way.' With a major effort of will he broke the spell, and stepped back. In another moment he would have stooped to those soft red lips.

'I'll call you if I learn anything,' he said, as he buttoned the top of his coat and opened the front door.

Nicholas stepped out furiously with the cold striking colour into his cheeks, but her presence kept pace with him and his blood raced not from physical exertion alone.

He knew then, beyond all doubt, that he was not a man who could switch love on and off at will.

'You old-fashioned thing.' Samantha's words came back to him clearly – and she was right, of course. He was cursed by a constancy of loyalty and emotion that restricted his freedom of action. He was breaking one of his own rules now, he was no longer moving ahead. He was circling back.

He had loved Chantelle Christy to the limits of his soul, and had devoted almost half of his life to Christy Marine. He realized then that those things could never change, not for him, not for Nicholas Berg, prisoner of his own conscience.

Suddenly he found himself opposite the Kensington Natural History Museum in the Cromwell Road, and swiftly he crossed to the main gates – but it was a quarter to six and they were closed already. Samantha would not have been in the public rooms anyway, but in those labyrinthine vaults below the great stone building. In a few short days, she had made half a dozen cronies among the museum staff. He felt a stab of resentment, of jealousy, that she was with other human beings, revelling in their companionship, delighting in the pleasures of the mind – had probably forgotten he existed.

Then suddenly the unfairness of it occurred to him, how his emotions of a minute previously had been stirring and boiling with the memories of another woman. Only then did he realize that it was possible to be in love with two different people, in two entirely different ways, at exactly the same time.

Troubled, torn by conflicting loves, conflicting loyalties, he turned away from the barred iron gates of the museum.

Nicholas' apartment was on the fifth floor of one of those renovated and redecorated buildings in Queen's Gate.

It looked as though a party of gypsies were passing through. He had not hung the paintings, nor had he arranged his books on the shelves. The paintings were stacked against the wall in the hallway, and his books were pyramided at unlikely spots around the lounge floor, the carpet still rolled and pushed aside, two chairs facing the television set, and another two drawn up to the dining-room table.

It was an eating and sleeping place, sustaining the bare minima of existence; in two years he had probably slept here on sixty nights, few of them consecutive. It was impersonal, it contained no memories, no warmth.

He poured a whisky and carried it through into the bedroom, slipping the knot of his tie and shrugging out of his jacket. Here it was different, for evidence of Samantha's presence was everywhere. Though she had remade the bed that morning before leaving, still she had left a pair of shoes abandoned at the foot of it, a booby trap to break the ankles of the unwary; her simple jewellery was strewn on the bedside table, together with a book, Noel Mostert's *Supership*, opened face down and in dire danger of a broken spine; the cupboard door was open and his suits had been bunched up in one corner to give hanging space to her slacks and dresses; two very erotic and transparent pairs of panties hung over the bath to dry; her talcum powder still dusted the tiled floor and her special fragrance pervaded the entire apartment.

He missed her with a physical ache in the chest, so that when the front door banged and she arrived like a high wind, shouting for him, 'Nicholas, it's me!' as though it could possibly have been anyone else, her hair tangled and wild with the wind and high colour under the golden tan of her cheeks, he almost ran to her and seized her with a suppressed violence.

'Wow,' she whispered huskily. 'Who is a hungry baby, then.' And they tumbled on to the bed clinging to each other with a need that was almost desperation.

Afterwards they did not turn the lights on in a room that had gone dark except for the dim light of the street lamps filtered by the curtains and reflected off the ceiling.

'What was that all about?' she asked, then snuggled against his chest, 'not that I'm complaining, mind you.'

'I've had a hell of a day. I needed you, badly.'

'You saw Duncan Alexander?'

'I saw Duncan.'

'Did you settle?'

'No. There was never really any chance.'

'I'm hungry,' she said. 'Your loving always makes me hungry.'

So he put on his pants and went down to the Italian restaurant at the corner for pizzas. They ate them in bed with a white Chianti from whisky tumblers, and when she was finished, she sighed and said:

'Nicholas, I have to go home.'

'You can't go,' he protested instantly.

'I have work to do – also.'

'But,' he felt a physical nausea at the thought of losing her, 'but you can't go before the hearing.'

'Why not?'

'It would be the worst possible luck, you are my fortune.'

'A sort of good-luck charm?' She pulled a face. 'Is that all I'm good for?'

'You are good for many things. May I demonstrate one of them?'

'Oh, yes please.'

An hour later Nick went for more pizzas.

'You have to stay until the 27th,' he said with his mouth full.

'Darling Nicholas, I just don't know—'

'You can ring them, tell them your aunt died, that you are getting married.'

'Even if I were getting married, it wouldn't lessen the importance of my work. I think you know that is something I will never give up.'

'Yes, I do know, but it's only a couple of days more.'

'All right, I'll call Tom Parker tomorrow.' Then she grinned at him. 'Don't look like that. I'll be just across the Atlantic, we'll be virtually next-door neighbours.'

'Call him now. It's lunchtime in Florida.'

She spoke for twenty minutes, wheedling and charming, while the blood-curdling transatlantic rumblings on the receiver slowly muted to reluctant and resigned mutterings.

'You're going to get me into trouble one of these days, Nicholas Berg,' she told him primly as she hung up.

'Now *there* is a happy thought,' Nick agreed, and she hit him with her pillow.


The telephone rang at two minutes past nine the next morning. They were in the bath together and Nicholas swore and went through naked and steaming and dripping suds.

'Mr Berg?' James Teacher's voice was sharp and businesslike. 'You were right, Christy Marine petitioned for postponement of hearing late yesterday afternoon.'

'How long?' Nicholas snapped.

'Ninety days.'

'The bastard,' grunted Nick. 'What grounds?'

'They want time to prepare their submission.'

'Block them,' Nick instructed.

'I have a meeting with the Secretary at eleven. I'm going to ask for an immediate preliminary hearing to set down and confirm the return date.'

'Get him before the arbitrators,' said Nick.

'We'll get him.'

Samantha welcomed him back to the tub by drawing her knees up under her chin. Her hair was piled on top of her head, but damp wisps hung down her neck and on to her cheeks. She looked pink and dewy as a little girl.

'Careful where you put your toes, sir,' she cautioned him, and he felt the tension along his nerves easing. She had that effect on him.

'I'll buy you lunch at "Les A" if you can tear yourself away from your microscope and fishy-smelling specimens for an hour or two.'

'Les Ambassadeurs? I've heard about it! For lunch there I'd walk across London on freshly amputated stumps.'

'That won't be necessary, but you will have to charm a tribe of wild desert Sheikhs. I understand they are very sympathetic towards blondes.'

'Are you going to sell me into a harem – sounds fun, I've always fancied myself in baggy, transparent bloomers.'

'You, I'm not selling – icebergs, I am. I'll pick you up at the front gates of the museum at one o'clock sharp.'

She went with laughter and a great clatter and banging of doors and Nicholas settled at the telephone.

'I'd like to speak to Sir Richard personally, it's Nicholas Berg.' Sir Richard was at Lloyd's, an old and good friend.

Then he called and spoke to Charles Gras.

There were no new delays or threats to *Sea Witch*'s completion date.

'I am sorry for any trouble you had with Alexander.'

'*Ça ne fait rien*, Nicholas. Good luck at the hearing, I will be watching the *Lloyd's List*.' Nicholas felt a sense of relief. Charles Gras had risked his career to show him *Golden Dawn*. It could have been serious.

Then Nick spoke for nearly half an hour to Bernard Wackie of Bach Wackie in Bermuda. *Warlock* had reported on the telex two hours previously; she was making good passage with her oil-rig tow, would drop off at Bravo II on schedule and pick up her next tow as soon as she had anchored.

'David Allen is a good youngster,' Bernard told Nick. 'But have you got Levoisin for *Sea Witch*?'

'Jules is playing the prima donna, he has not said yes, yet but he'll come.'

'You'll have a good team, then. What's the latest date for *Sea Witch*?'

'End March.'

'The sooner the better, I've got contracts to keep both tugs running hard until the iceberg project matures.'

'I'm having lunch with the Sheikhs today.'

'I know. There's a lot of interest. I've got a good feeling. There is something big brewing, but they are a cagey bunch. The inscrutable smile on the face of the sphinx – when do we see you?'

'I'll come across just as soon as I've got Duncan Alexander into the arbitration court – end of the month, hopefully.'

'We've got a lot to talk about, Nicholas.'

Nick hesitated for the time it took to smoke the first cheroot of the day before he called Monte Carlo – for the call would cost him at least fifty thousand dollars, probably closer to seventy-five. The best is always the cheapest, he reminded himself, picked up the receiver and spoke to a secretary in Monte Carlo, giving his name.

While he waited for the connection he thought how his life was complicating itself one more. Very soon Bach Wackie would not be enough, there would have to be a London branch of Ocean Salvage, offices, secretaries, files, accounts, and then a New York branch, a branch in Saudi, the whole cycle again. He thought suddenly of Samantha, uncluttered and simple happiness, life without its wearisome trappings – then the connection was made and he heard the thin, high, almost feminine voice.

'Mr Berg – Claud Lazarus.' No other greeting no expressions of pleasure at the renewal of contact. Nick imagined him sitting at his desk in the suite high above the harbour, like a human foetus – preserved in spirits, bottled on the museum shelf. The huge bald domed head, the soft putty-coloured rudimentary features, the nose hardly large enough to support the thick spectacles. The eyes distorted and startled by the lenses, changing shape like those of a fish in an aquarium as the light moved. The body underdeveloped, as that of a foetus, narrow shoulders seemingly tapering away to the bowed question mark of a body.

'Mr Lazarus. Are you in a position to undertake an indepth study for me?' It was the euphemism for financial and industrial espionage; Claud Lazarus' network was not limited by frontiers or continents, it spanned the globe with delicately probing tentacles.

'Of course,' he piped softly.

'I want the financial structuring, the lines of control and management, the names of the nominees and their principals, the location and inter-relationship of all the elements of the Christy Marine Group and London European Insurance and Banking Co. Group, with particular reference to any changes in structure during the previous fourteen months. Do you have that?'

'This is being recorded, Mr Berg.'

'Of course. Further. I want the country of registration, the insurers and underwriters of all bottoms traceable to their holdings.'

'Please continue.'

'I want an accurate estimate of the reserves of London and European Insurance in relation to their potential liability.'

'Continue.'

'I am particularly interested in the vessel *Golden Dawn* presently building at the yards of Construction Navale Atlantique at St Nazaire. I want to know if she has been chartered or has contracted with any oil company for carriage of crude and, if so, on what routes and at what rates.'

'Yes?' Lazarus squeaked softly.

'Time is of the essence – and, as always, so is discretion.'

'You need not have mentioned that, Mr Berg.'

'My contact, when you are ready to pass information, is Bach Wackie in Bermuda.'

'I will keep you informed of progress.'

'Thank you, Mr Lazarus.'

'Good day, Mr Berg.'

It was refreshing not to have to pretend to be the bosom comrade of somebody who supplied essentials but nonetheless revolted him, Nick thought, and comforting to know he had the best man in the world for the job.

He looked at his watch. It was lunchtime, and he felt the quick lift of his spirts at the thought of being with Samantha.


Lime Street is a narrow alleyway, with tall buildings down each side of it, which opens off Leadenhall Street. A few yards from the junction, on the lefthand side as you leave the street of shipping, is the covered entrance to Lloyd's of London.

Nicholas stepped out of James Teacher's Bentley and took Samantha on his arm. He paused a moment, with a feeling of certain reverence.

As a seaman, the history of this remarkable institution touched him intimately Not that the building itself was particularly old or venerable. Nothing now remained of the original coffee house, except some of the traditions: the caller who intoned the brokers' names like the offertory in the temple of some exotic religion, the stalls in which the underwriters conducted their business and the name and uniform of the institution's servants, the 'waiters' with brass buttons and red collar tabs.

Rather it was the tradition of concern that was enshrined here, the concern for ships and for all men who went down to the sea in those ships and did their business in great waters.

Perhaps later, Nicholas would find time to take Samantha through the Nelson rooms and show her the displays of memorabilia associated with the greatest of Britain's sailors, the plate and letters and awards. Certainly he would have her as lunch guest in the big dining-room, at the table set aside specifically for visiting sea captains.

But now there were more important considerations to demand all his attention. He had come to hear the verdict given on his future – within a few hours he would know just how high and how fast the wave of his fortune had carried him.

'Come,' he said to Samantha, and led her up the short flight of steps into the lobby, where there was a waiter alerted to receive them.

'We will be using the Committee Room today, sir.'

The earlier submissions by both parties had been heard in one of the smaller offices, leading off the high gallery above the vast floor of the exchange with its rows of underwriters' stalls. However, due to the extraordinary nature of this action, the Committee of Lloyd's had made a unique decision – to have their arbitrators give their findings and make their award in surroundings more in keeping with the importance of the occasion.

They rode up in silence, all of them too tense to make the effort of small-talk, and the waiter led them down the wide corridor, past the Chairman's suite of offices and through the double doors into the grandeur of the room designed by Adams for Bowood House, the country home of the Marquess of Lansdowne. It had been taken to pieces, panel by panel, floor, ceiling, fireplace and plaster mouldings, transported to London and re-erected in its entirety with such care and attention that when Lord Lansdowne inspected it, he found that the floorboards squeaked in exactly the same places as they had before.

At the long table, under the massive glittering pyramids of the three chandeliers, the two arbitrators were already seated. Both of them were master mariners, selected for their deep knowledge and experience of the sea, and their faces were toughened and leathery from the effects of sea and salt water. They talked quietly together, without acknowledging in any way the rows of quietly attentive faces in the rows of chairs facing them – until the minute hand of the antique clock on the Adams fireplace touched its zenith. Then the President of the court looked across at the waiter who obediently closed the double doors and stood to attention before them.

'This Arbitration Court has been set up under the Committee of Lloyd's and empowered to receive evidence in the matter between the Christy Marine Steamship Co. Ltd. and the Ocean Salvage and Towage Co. Ltd. This Court finds common ground in the following areas:

'Firstly, a contract of salvage under Lloyd's Open Form "No Cure No Pay" for the recovery of the passenger liner *Golden Adventurer*, a ship of 22,000 tons gross burden and registered at Southampton, exists between the parties.

'Secondly, that the master of the *Golden Adventurer* while steaming on a south-westerly heading during the night of December 16th at or near 72° 16' south and 32° 12' west—'

The President let no dramatics intrude on his assembly of the facts. He recounted it all in the driest possible terms, succeeding in making *Golden Adventurer*'s plight and the desperate endeavours of her rescuers sound boring. Indeed, his colleague seemed to descend into a condition of coma at the telling of it. His eyes slowly closed, and his head sagged gently sideways, his lips vibrating slightly at each breath – a volume not quite sufficient to make it a snore.

It took nearly an hour, with the occasional consultation of the ship's log books and a loose volume of handwritten and typed notes, before the President was satisfied that he had recounted all the facts, and now he rocked back in his chair and hooked his thumbs into his waistcoat. His expression became decisive, and while he surveyed the crowded room, his colleague stirred, opened his eyes, took out a white linen handkerchief and blew into sharp blasts, one for each nostril, like the herald angel sounding the crack of doom.

There was a stir of reawakened·interest, they all recognized the moment of decision, and for the first time Duncan Alexander and Nicholas Berg looked directly at each other over the heads of the lawyers and company men. Neither of them changed expression, no smile nor scowl, but something implacable and clearly understood passed between them. They did not unlock their gaze, until the President began to speak again.

'Taking into consideration the foregoing, this Court is of the firm opinion that a fair and good salvage of the vessel was effected by the salvors, and that therefore they are entitled to salvage awards commensurate with the services rendered to the owners and underwriters.'

Nicholas felt Samantha's fingers groping for his. He took her hand, and it was slim and cold and dry; he interlocked their fingers and laid their hands upon his upper thigh.

'This Court, in arriving at the value of the salvor's services, has taken into consideration, firstly, the situation and conditions existing on the site of operations. We have heard evidence that much of the work was carried out in extreme weather conditions. Temperatures of thirty degrees below freezing, wind forces exceeding twelve of the Beaufort scale, and extreme icing.

'We have also considered that the vessel *Golden Adventurer* was no longer under command. That she had been abandoned by her passengers, her crew and her Master. She was aground on a remote and hostile coast.

'We have further noted that the salvors undertook a voyage of many thousands of miles, without any guarantee of recompense, but merely in order to be in a position to offer assistance, should that have become necessary.'

Nicholas glanced across the aisle at Duncan Alexander. He sat at ease, as though he were in his box at Ascot. His suit was of sombre gunmetal grey, but on him it seemed flamboyant and the I Zingari tie as rakish as any of Cardin's fantasies.

Duncan turned that fine leonine head and looked directly at Nicholas again. This time Nicholas saw the deep angry glow in his eyes as when a vagrant breeze fans the coals of an open fire. Then Duncan turned his face back towards the President, and he balanced his thrusting square chin on the clenched, carefully manicured fingers of his right fist.

'Furthermore, we have taken into consideration the transportation of the survivors from the site of the striking, to the nearest port of succour, Cape Town in the Republic of South Africa.'

The President was summing up strongly in favour of Ocean Salvage. It was a dangerous sign; so often a judge about to deliver an unfavourable decision prefaced it by building a strong case for the loser and then tearing it down again.

Nicholas steeled himself, anything below three million dollars would not be sufficient to keep Ocean Salvage alive. That was the barest minimum he needed to keep *Warlock* afloat, and to put *Sea Witch* on the water for the first time. He felt the spasm of his stomach muscles as he contemplated his commitments – even with three million he would be at the mercy of the Sheikhs, unable to manoeuvre, a slave to any conditions they wished to set. He would not be off his knees even.

Nicholas squeezed Samantha's hand for luck, and she pressed her shoulder against his.

Four million dollars would give him a fighting chance, a slim margin of choice – but he would still be fighting hard, pressed on all sides. Yet he would have settled for four million, if Duncan Alexander had made the offer. Perhaps Duncan had been wise after all, perhaps he might yet see Nicholas broken at a single stroke.

'Three.' Nicholas held the figure in his head. 'Let it be three, at least let it be three.'

'This Court has considered the written reports of the Globe Engineering Co., the contractors charged with the repairing and refurbishing of *Golden Adventurer*, together with those of two independent marine engineering experts commissioned separately by the owners and the salvors to report on the condition of the vessel. We have also had the benefit of a survey carried out by a senior inspector of Lloyd's of London. From all of this, it seems apparent that the vessel sustained remarkably light damage. There was no loss of equipment, the salvors recovering even the main anchors and chains—'

Strange how that impressed a salvage court. 'We took her off, anchors and all,' Nick thought, with a stir of pride.

'Prompt anti-corrosion precautions by the salvors resulted in minimal damage to the main engines and ancillary equipment—'

It went on and on. Why cannot he come to it now? I cannot wait much longer, Nicholas thought.

'This Court has heard expert opinion and readily accepts that the residual value of the *Gold Adventurer*'s hull, as delivered to the contractors in Cape Town can be fairly set at twenty-six million US dollars or fifteen million, three hundred thousand pounds sterling, and in consideration of the foregoing, we are further of the firm opinion that the salvors are entitled to an award of twenty per cent of the residual hull value—'

For long cold seconds Nicholas doubted his hearing, and then he felt the flush of exultation burning on his cheeks.

'In addition, it was necessary to compute the value of the passage provided to the survivors of the vessel—'

It was six – six million dollars! He was clear and running free as a wild albatross sweeping across the oceans on wide pinions.

Nicholas turned his head and looked at Duncan Alexander, and he smiled. He had never felt so strong and vital and alive in his life before. He felt like a giant, immortal, and at his side was the vibrant young body pressing to him, endowing him with eternal youth.

Across the aisle, Duncan Alexander tossed his head, a gesture of dismissal and turned to speak briefly with his counsel who sat beside him. He did not look at Nicholas, however, and there was a waxen cast to his skin now as though it had a fine sheen of perspiration laid upon it, and the blood had drained away beneath the tan.


'Anyway, another few days and you'd probably have started to find me a boring dolly bird, or one of us would have had a heart attack.' Samantha smiled at him, a pathetic, lopsided little grin, nothing like her usual brilliant golden flashing smile. 'I like to quit while I'm still ahead.'

They sat close on the couch in the Pan Am Clipper Lounge at Heathrow.

Nicholas was shocked by the extent of his own desolation. It felt as though he were about to be deprived of the vital forces of life itself, he felt the youth and strength draining away as he looked at her and knew that in a few minutes she would be gone.

'Samantha,' he said. 'Stay here with me.'

'Nicholas,' she whispered huskily, 'I have to go, my darling. It's not for very long but I have to go.'

'Why?' he demanded.

'Because it's my life.'

'Make me your life.'

She touched his cheek, as she countered his offer.

'I have a better idea, give up *Warlock* and *Sea Witch* – forget your icebergs and come with me.'

'You know I cannot do that.'

'No,' she agreed, 'you could not, and I would not want you to. But, Nicholas, my love, no more can I give up my life.'

'All right, then, marry me,' he said.

'Why, Nicholas?'

'So I don't lose my lucky charm, so that you'd damn well have to do what I tell you.'

And she laughed delightedly and snuggled against his chest. 'It doesn't work like that any more, my fine Victorian gentleman. There is only one good reason for marrying, Nicholas, and that's to have babies. Do you want to give me a baby?'

'What a splendid idea.'

'So that I can warm the bottles and wash the nappies while you go off to the ends of the oceans – and we'll have much together once a month?' She shook her head. 'We might have a baby together one day – but not now, there is still too much to do, there is still too much life to live.'

'Damn it.' He shook his head. 'I don't like to let you run around loose. Next thing you'll take off with some twenty-five year-old oaf, bulging with muscles and—'

'You have given me a taste for vintage wine,' she laughed in denial. 'Come as soon as you can, Nicholas. As soon as you have done your work here, come to Florida and I'll show you my life.'

The hostess crossed the lounge towards them, a pretty smiling girl in the neat blue Pan Am uniform.

'Dr Silver? They are calling Flight 432 now.'

They stood and looked at each other, awkward as strangers.

'Come soon,' she said, and then she stood on tiptoe and placed her arms around his shoulders. 'Come as soon as you can.'


Nicholas had protested vigorouly as soon as James Teacher advanced the proposition. 'I don't want to speak to him, Mr Teacher. The only thing I want from Duncan Alexander is his cheque for six million dollars, preferably guaranteed by a reputable bank – and I want it before the 10th of next month.'

The lawyer had wheedled and jollied Nicholas along. 'Think of the pleasure of watching his face – indulge yourself, Mr Berg, gloat on him a little.'

'I will obtain no pleasure by watching his face, off hand I can think of a thousand faces I'd rather watch.' But in the end Nicholas had agreed, stipulating only that this time the meeting should be at a place of Nicholas' choice, an unsubtle reminder of whose hand now held the whip.

James Teacher's rooms were in one of those picturesque, stone buildings in the Inns of Court covered with ivy, surrounded by small velvety lawns, bisected with paved walkways that connected the numerous blocks, the entire complex reeking with history and tradition and totally devoid of modern comforts. Its austerity was calculated to instil confidence in the clients.

Teacher's rooms were on the third floor. There was no elevator and the stairs were narrow, steep and dangerous. Duncan Alexander arrived slightly out of breath and flushed under his tan. Teacher's clerk surveyed him discouragingly from his cubicle.

'Mr who?' he asked, cupping his hand to one ear. The clerk was a man as old, grey and picturesque as the building. He even affected a black alpaca suit, shiny and greenish with age, together with a butterfly collar and a black string tie like that last worn by Neville Chamberlain as he promised peace in our time.

'Mr who?' and Duncan Alexander flushed deeper. He was not accustomed to having to repeat his name.

'Do you have an appointment, Mr Arbuthnot?' the clerk inquired frostily, and laboriously consulted his diary before at last waving Duncan Alexander through into the spartan waiting-room.

Nicholas kept him there exactly eight minutes, twice as long as he himself had waited in the board room of Christy Marine, and he stood by the small electric fire in the fireplace, not answering Duncan's brilliant smile as he entered.

James Teacher sat at his desk under the windows, out of the direct line of confrontation, like the umpire at Wimbledon, and Duncan Alexander barely glanced at him.

'Congratulations, Nicholas.' Duncan shook that magnificent head and the smile faded to a rueful grin. 'You turned one up for the books, you truly did.'

'Thank you, Duncan. However, I must warn you that today I have an impossible schedule to meet, I can give you only ten minutes.' Nicholas glanced at his watch. 'Fortunately I can imagine only one thing that you and I have to discuss. The tenth of next month, either a transfer to the Bermuda account of Ocean Salvage, or a guaranteed draft by registered airmail to Bach Wackie.'

Duncan held up his hand in mock protest. 'Come now, Nicholas – the salvage money will be there, on the due date set by the Court.'

'That's fine,' Nicholas told him, still smiling. 'I have no taste for another brawl in the debtors' court.'

'I wanted to remind you of something that old Arthur Christy once said—'

'Ah, of course, our mutual father-in-law.' Nicholas said softly, and Duncan pretended not to hear; instead he went on, unruffled.

'He said, with Berg and Alexander I have put together one of the finest teams in the world of shipping.'

'The old man was getting senile towards the end.' Nicholas had still not smiled.

'He was right, of course. We just never got into step. My God, Nicholas, can you imagine if we had been working together, instead of against each other. You the best salt and steel man in the business, and I—'

'I'm touched, Duncan, deeply touched by this new and gratifying esteem in which I find myself held.'

'You rubbed my nose in it, Nicholas. Just as you said you would. And I'm the kind of man who learns by his mistakes, turning disaster to triumph is a trick of mine.'

'Play your trick now,' Nicholas invited. 'Let's see you turn six million dollars into a flock of butterflies.'

'Six million dollars and Ocean Salvage would buy you back into Christy Marine. We'd be on equal terms.'

The surprise did not show on Nicholas' face, not a flicker of an eyelid, not even a tightening of the lips, but his mind raced to get ahead of the man.

'Together we would be unstoppable. We would build Christy Marine into a giant that controlled the oceans, we'd diversify out into ocean oil exploration, chemical containers.' The man had immense presence and charm, he was almost – but not quite – irresistible, his enthusiasm brimming and overflowing, his fire flaring and spreading to light the dingy room, and Nicholas studied him carefully, learning more about him every second.

'Good God, Nicholas, you are the type of man who can conceive of a venture like the *Golden Dawn* or salvage a giant liner in a sub-zero gale, and I am the man who can put together a billion dollars on a wink and whistle. Nothing could stand before us, there would be no frontiers we could not cross.' He paused now and returned Nicholas' scrutiny as boldly, studying the effect of his words. Nicholas lit the cheroot he was holding, but his eyes watched shrewdly through the fine blue veil of smoke.

'I understand what you are thinking,' Duncan went on, his voice dropping confidentially. 'I know that you are stretched out, I know that you need those six big M's to keep Ocean Salvage floating. Christy Marine will guarantee Ocean Salvage outstandings, that's a minor detail. The important thing is us together, like old Arthur Christy saw it, Berg and Alexander.'

Nicholas took the cheroot from his mouth and inspected the tip briefly before he looked back at him.

'Tell me, Duncan,' he asked mildly, 'in this great sharing you envisage, do we put our women into the kitty also?'

Duncan's mouth tightened, and the flesh wrinkled at the corners of his eyes.

'Nicholas,' he began, but Nicholas silenced him with a gesture.

'You said that I need that six million badly, and you were right. I need three million of it for Ocean Salvage and the other three to stop you running that monster you have built. Even if I don't get it, I will still use it to stop you. I'll slap a garnishee order on you by ten minutes past nine on the morning of the eleventh. I told you I would fight you and *Golden Dawn*. The warning still stands.'

'You are being petty,' Duncan said. 'I never expected to see you join the lunatic fringe.

'There are many things you do not know about me, Duncan. But, by God, you are going to learn – the hard way.'


Chantelle had chosen San Lorenzo in Beauchamp Place when Nicholas had refused to go again to Eaton Square. He had learned that it was dangerous to be alone with her, but San Lorenzo was also a bad choice of meeting-ground.

It carried too many memories from the golden days. It had been a family ritual, Sunday lunch whenever they were in town. Chantelle, Peter and Nicholas laughing together at the corner table. Mara had given them the corner table again.

'Will you have the *osso bucco*?' Chantelle asked, peeping at him over the top of her menu.

Nicholas always had the *osso bucco*, and Peter always had the *lasagne*, it was part of the ritual.

'I'm going to have a sole.' Nicholas turned to the waiter who was hovering solicitously. 'And we'll drink the house white.' Always the wine had been a Sancerre; Nicholas was deliberately down-grading the occasion by ordering the carafe.

'It's good.' Chantelle sipped it and then set the glass aside. 'I spoke to Peter last night, he is in the san with flu, but he will be up today, and he sent you his love.'

'Thank you,' he spoke stiffly, stilted by the curious glances from some of the other tables where they had been recognized. The scandal would fly around London like the plague.

'I want to take Peter to Bermùda with me for part of the Easter holidays,' Nicholas told her.

'I shall miss him – he's such a delight.'

Nicholas waited for the main course to be served before he asked bluntly, 'What did you want to speak to me about?'

Chantelle leaned towards him, and her perfume was light and subtle and evocative.

'Did you find out anything, Nicholas?'

'No,' he thought to himself. 'That's not what she wants.' It was the Persian in her blood, the love of secrecy, the intrigue. There was something else here.

'I have learned nothing,' he said. 'If I had, I would have called you.' His eyes bored into hers, green and hard and searching. 'That is not what you wanted,' he told her flatly.

She smiled and dropped her eyes from his. 'No,' she admitted, 'it wasn't.'

She had surprising breasts, they seemed small, but really they were too big for her dainty body. It was only their perfect proportions and the springy elasticity of the creamy flesh that created the illusion. She wore a flimsy silk blouse with a low lacey front, which exposed the deep cleft between them. Nicholas knew them so well, and he found himself staring at them now.

She looked up suddenly and caught his eyes, and the huge eyes slanted with a sly heart-stopping sexuality. Her lips pouted softly and she moistened them with the tip of her tongue.

Nick felt himself sway in his seat, it was a tell-tale mannerism of hers. That set of lips and movement of tongue were the heralds of her arousal, and instantly he felt the response of his own body, too powerful to deny, although he tried desperately.

'What was it?' He did not hear the husk in his voice, but she did and recognized it as readily as he had the flicker of her tongue. She reached across the table and took his wrist, and she felt the leap of his pulse under her fingers.

'Duncan wants you to come back into Christy Marine,' she said. 'And so do I.'

'Duncan sent you to me.' And when she nodded, he asked, 'Why does he want me back? God knows what pains the two of you took to get rid of me.' And he gently pulled his wrist from her fingers and dropped both hands into his lap.

'I don't know why Duncan wants it. He says that he needs your expertise.' She shrugged, and her breasts moved under the silk. He felt the tense ache of his groin, it confused his thinking. 'It isn't the true reason, I'm sure of that. But he wants you.'

'Did he ask you to tell me that?'

'Of course not.' She fiddled with the stem of her glass; her fingers were long and perfectly tapered, the painted nails set upon them with the brilliance or butterflies' wings. 'It was to come from me alone.'

'Why do you think he wants me?'

'There are two possibilities that I can imagine.' She surprised him sometimes with her almost masculine appraisal. That was what made her lapse so amazing; as he listened to her now, Nicholas wondered again how she could ever have let control of Christy Marine pass to Duncan Alexander – then he remembered what a wild and passionate creature she could be. 'The first possibility is that Christy Marine owes you six million dollars, and he has thought up some scheme to avoid having to pay you out.'

'Yes,' Nicholas nodded. 'And the other possibility?'

'There are strange and exciting rumours in the City about you and Ocean Salvage – they say that you are on the brink of something big. Something in Saudi Arabia. Perhaps Duncan wants a share of that.'

Nicholas blinked. The iceberg project was something between the Sheikhs and himself, then he remembered that others knew. Bernard Wackie in Bermuda, Samantha Silver, James Teacher – there had been a leak somewhere then.

'And you? What are your reasons?'

'I have two reasons, Nicholas,' she answered. 'I want control back from Duncan. I want the voting rights in my shares, and I want my rightful place on the Trust. I didn't know what I was doing, it was madness when I made Duncan my nominee. I want it back now, and I want you to get it for me.'

Nicholas smiled, a bitter wintry smile. 'You're hiring yourself a gunman, just the way they do in the Western serials. Duncan and I alone on the deserted street, spurs clinking.' The smile turned to a chuckle, but he was thinking hard, watching her – was she lying? It was almost impossible to tell, she was so mysterious and unfathomable. Then he saw tears well in the depths of those huge eyes, and he stopped laughing. Were the tears genuine, or all part of the intrigue?

'You said you had two reasons.' And now his voice was gentler. She did not answer immediately, but he could see her agitation, the rapid rise and fall of those lovely breasts under the silk, then she caught her breath with a little hiss of decision and she spoke so softly that he barely caught the words.

'I want you back. That's the other reason, Nicholas.' And he stared at her while she went on. 'It was all part of the madness. I didn't realize what I was doing. But the madness is over now. Sweet merciful God, you'll never know how much I've missed you. You'll never know how I've suffered.' She stopped and fluttered one small hand. 'I'll make it up to you, Nicholas, I swear it to you. But Peter and I need you, we both need you desperately.'

He could not answer for a moment, she had taken him by surprise and he felt his whole life shaken again and the separate parts of it tumbled like dice from the cup of chance.

'There is no road back, Chantelle. We can only go forward.'

'I always get what I want, Nicholas, you know that,' she warned him.

'Not this time, Chantelle.' He shook his head, but he knew her words would wear away at him.


Duncan Alexander slumped on the luxurious calf-hide seat of the Rolls, and he spoke into the telephone extension that connected him directly with his office in Leadenhall Street.

'Were you able to reach Kurt Streicher?' he asked.

'I'm sorry, Mr Alexander. His office was unable to contact him. He is in Africa on a hunting safari. They do not know when to expect him back in Geneva.'

'Thank you, Myrtle,' Duncan's smile was completely lacking in humour. Streicher was suddenly one of the world's most industrious sportsmen – last week he had been skiing and was out of contact, this week he was in Africa slaughtering elephant, perhaps next week he would be chasing polar bears in the Arctic. And by then, it would be too late, of course.

Streicher was not alone. Since the salvage award on *Golden Adventurer*, so many of his financial contacts had become elusive, veritable will-o'-the-wisps skipping ahead of him with their cheque books firmly bottoned into their pockets.

'I shall not be back at the office again today,' he told his secretary. 'Please have my pending tray sent round to Eaton Square. I will work on it tonight, and do you think you could get in an hour earlier tomorrow morning?'

'Of course, Mr Alexander.'

He replaced the handset and glanced out of the window. The Rolls was passing Regent's Park, heading in the direction of St John's Wood; three times in the last six months he had taken this route, and suddenly Duncan felt that hot scalding lump deep under his ribs. He straightened up in his seat but the pain persisted, and he sighed and opened the rosewood liquor cabinet, spilled a spoonful of the powder into a glass and topped it with sodawater.

He considered the turbid draught with distaste, then drank it at a gulp. It left an after-taste of peppermint on his tongue, but the relief was almost immediate. He felt the acid burn subside, and he belched softly.

He did not need a doctor to tell him that it was a duodenal ulcer, probably a whole bunch of them – or was that the correct collective noun, a tribe of ulcers, a convocation? He smiled again, and carefully combed his brazen waves of hair, watching himself in the mirror.

The strain did not show on his face, he was sure of that. The façade was intact, devoid of cracks. He had always had the strength, the courage to ride with his decisions. This had been a hard ride, however, the hardest of his life.

He closed his eyes briefly, and saw *Golden Dawn* standing on her ways. Like a mountain. The vision gave him strength, he felt it rising deep within him, welling up to fill his soul.

They thought of him only as a money-man, a paper man. There was no salt in his blood nor steel in his guts – that was what they said of him in the City. When he had ousted Berg from Christy Marine, they had shied off, watching him shrewdly, standing aside and waiting for him to show his guts, forcing him to live upon the fat of Christy Marine, devouring himself like a camel in the desert, running him thin.

'The bastards,' he thought, but it was without rancour. They had done merely what he would have done, they had played by the hard rules which Duncan knew and respected, and by those same rules, once he had shown his guts to be of steel, they would ply him with largesse. This was the testing time. It was so close now, two months still to live through – yet those sixty days seemed as daunting as the hard year through which he had lived already.

The stranding of *Golden Adventurer* had been a disaster. Her hull value had formed part of the collateral on which he had borrowed; the cash she generated with her luxury cruises was budgeted carefully to carry him through the dangerous times before *Golden Dawn* was launched. Now all that had altered drastically. The flow of cash had been switched off, and he had to find six million in real hard money – and find it before the 10th of the month. Today was the 6th, and time was running through his fingers like quicksilver.

If only he had been able to stall Berg. He felt a corrosive welling up to hatred again; if only he had been able to stall him. The bogus offer of partnership might have held him just long enough, but Berg had brushed it aside contemptuously. Duncan had been forced to scurry about in undignified haste, trying to pull together the money. Kurt Streicher was not the only one suddenly unavailable, it was strange how they could smell it on a man, he had the same gift of detecting vulnerability or weakness in others so he understood how it worked. It was almost as though the silver blotches showed on his hands and face and he walked the city pavements chanting the old leper's cry, 'Unclean, Beware, Unclean.'

With so much at stake, it was a piddling amount, six million for two months, the insignificance of it was an insult, and he felt the tension in his belly muscles again and the rising hot acid sting of his digestive juices. He forced himself to relax, glancing again from the window to find that the Rolls was turning into the cul-dec-sac of yellow face-brick apartments piled upon each other like hen-coops, angular and unimaginatively lower middle class.

He squared his shoulders and watched himself in the mirror, practising the smile. It was only six million, and for only two months, he reminded himself, as the Rolls slid to a halt before one of the anonymous buildings.

Duncan nodded to his chauffeur as he held the door open and handed Duncan the pigskin briefcase.

'Thank you, Edward. I should not be very long.'

Duncan took the case and he crossed the pavement with the long, confident stride of an athlete, his shoulders thrown back, wearing his top coat like an opera cloak, the sleeves empty and the tails swirling about his legs, and even in the grey overcast of a March afternoon, his head shone like a beacon fire.

The man who opened the door to him seemed only half Duncan's height, despite the tall black Homburg hat that he wore squarely over his ears.

'Mr Alexander, Shalom, shalom. His beard was so dense and bushy black that it covered the starched white collar and white tie, regulation dress of the strict Hasidic Jew. 'Even though you come to me last, you still bring honour on my house,' and his eyes twinkled, a mischievous sparkling black under thick brows.

'That is because you have a heart of stone and blood like iced water,' said Duncan, and the man laughed delightedly, as though he had been paid the highest compliment.

'Come,' he said, taking Duncan's arm. 'Come in, let us drink a little tea together and let us talk.' He led Duncan down the narrow corridor, and halfway they collided with two boys wearing yamulka on their curly heads coming at speed in the opposite direction.

'Ruffians,' cried the man, stooping to embrace them briefly and then send them on their way with a fond slap on their backsides. Still beaming and shaking the ringlets that dangled out from under the black Homburg, he ushered Duncan into a small croweded bedroom that had been converted to an office. A tall old-fashioned pigeon-holed desk filled one wall and against the other stood an overstuffed horse-hair sofa on which were piled ledgers and box files.

The man swept the books aside, making room for Duncan. 'Be seated,' he ordered, and stood aside while a jolly little woman his size brought in the teatray.

'I saw the award court's arbitration on *Golden Adventurer* in *Lloyd's List*,' the Jew said when they were alone. 'Nicholas Berg is an amazing man, a hard act to follow – I think that is the expression.' He pondered, watching the sudden bloom of anger on Duncan's cheeks and the murderous expression in the pale eyes.

Duncan controlled his anger with an effort, but each time that somebody spoke that way of Nicholas Berg, he found it more difficult. There was always the comparison, the snide remarks, and Duncan wanted to stand up and leave this cluttered little room and the veiled taunts, but he knew he could not afford to, nor could he speak just yet for his anger was very close to the surface. They sat in silence for what seemed a long time.

'How much?' The man broke the silence at last, and Duncan could not bring himself to name the figure for it was too closely related to the subject that had just infuriated him.

'It is not a large amount, and for a short period – sixty days only.'

'How much?'

'Six million,' Duncan said. 'Dollars.'

'Six million is not an impossibly large amount of money, when you have it – but it is a great fortune when you do not.' The man tugged at the thick black bush of his beard. 'And sixty days can be an eternity.'

'I have a charter for *Golden Dawn*,' Duncan said softly. 'A ten-year charter.' He slipped the nine-carat gold catches on the slim, finely grained pigskin briefcase and brought out a batch of Xeroxed sheets. 'As you see, it is signed by both parties already.'

'Ten years?' asked the man, watching the papers in Duncan's hand.

'Ten years, at ten cents a hundred ton miles and a guaranteed minimum annual of 75,000 miles.'

The hand on the man's thick black beard stilled. '*Golden Dawn* has a burden of a million tons – that will gross a minimum of seventy-five million dollars a year.' With an effort he managed to disguise his awe, and the hand resumed its gentle tugging at the beard. 'Who is the charterer?' The thick eyebrows formed two thick black question marks.

'Orient Amex,' said Duncan, and handed him the Xeroxed papers.

'The El Barras field.' The man's eyebrows stayed up as he read swiftly. 'You are a brave man, Mr Alexander. But I never once doubted that.' He read on in silence for another minute, shaking his head slowly so that the ringlets danced on his cheeks. 'The El Barras field.' He folded the papers and looked up at Duncan. 'I think Christy Marine may have found a worthy successor to Nicholas Berg – perhaps the shoes are even a little small, maybe they will begin to pinch your toes soon, Mr Alexander.' He squirmed down in his chair thinking furiously, and Duncan watched him, hiding his trepidation behind a remotely amused half-smile.

'What about the environmentalists, Mr Alexander? The new American Administration, this man Carter is very conscious of environmental dangers.'

'The lunatic fringe,' said Duncan. 'There is too much invested already. Orient Amex have nearly a billion in the new cadmium cracking plants at Galveston, and three of the other oil giants are in it. Let them fuss, we'll still carry in the new cad-rich crudes.'

Duncan spoke with the force of complete conviction. 'There is too much at stake, the potential profits are too large and the opposition is too weak. The whole world is sick of the doom-merchants, the woolly-headed sentimentalists,' he dismissed them with a short abrupt gesture, 'man has already adjusted to a little oil on the beaches, a little smoke in the air, a few less fish in the sea or birds in the sky, and he will go on adjusting.'

The man nodded, listening avidly. 'Yes,' he nodded. 'You are a brave man. The world needs men like you.'

'The important thing is a cadmium catalyst cracking system which breaks down the high carbon atoms of crude and gives back a 90% yield in low carbon instead of the 40% we hope for now. 90% yield, double-double profits, double efficiency—'

'—and double danger.' The man smiled behind his beard.

'There is danger in taking a bath. You might slip and crack your skull, and we haven't invested a billion dollars in bathing.'

'Cadmium in concentrations of 100 parts to the million is more poisonous than cyanide or arsenic; the cad-rich crudes of the El Barras field are concentrated 2000 parts to the million.'

'That's what makes them so valuable,' Duncan nodded. 'To enrich crude artificially with cadmium would make the whole cracking process hopelessly uneconomic. We've turned what appeared to be a hopelessly contaminated oilfield into one of the most brilliant advances in oil refining.'

'I hope you have not under-estimated the resistance to the transportation of—'

Duncan cut him short. 'There will be no publicity. The loading and unloading of the crude will be conducted with the utmost discretion, and the world will not know the difference. Just another ultra-tanker moving across the oceans with nothing to suggest that she is carrying cad-rich.'

'But, just suppose the news did leak?'

Duncan shrugged. 'The world is conditioned to accept anything, from DDT to Concorde, nobody really cares any more. Come hell and high water, we'll carry the El Barras oil. Nobody is strong enough to stop us.'

Duncan gathered his papers and went on softly, 'I need six million dollars for sixty days – and I need it by noon tomorrow.'

'You are a brave man,' the man repeated softly. 'But you are finely stretched out. Already my brothers and I have made a considerable investment in your courage. To be blunt, Mr Alexander, Christy Marine has exhausted its collateral. Even *Golden Dawn* is pawned down to her last rivet – and the charter for Orient Amex does not change that.'

Duncan took another sheaf of papers, bound in a brown folder, and the man lifted an eyebrow in question.

'My personal assets,' Duncan explained, and the man skimmed swiftly through the typed lists.

'Paper values, Mr Alexander. Actual values are 50% of those you list, and that is not six million dollars of collateral.' He handed the folder back to Duncan. 'They will do for a start, but we'll need more than that.'

'What more is there?'

'Share options, stock options in Christy Marine. If we are to share risk, then we must have a share of the winnings.'

'Do you want my soul also?' Duncan demanded harshly, and the man laughed.

'We'll take a slice of that as well,' he agreed amiably.


It was two hours later that Duncan sank wearily into the leather-work of the Rolls. The muscles in his thighs trembled as though he had run a long way and there was a nerve in the corner of his eye that jumped as though a cricket was trapped beneath the skin. He had made the gamble, everything – Christy Marine, his personal fortune, his very soul. It was all at risk now.

'Eaton Square, sir?' the chauffeur asked.

'No,' Duncan told him. He knew what he needed now to smooth away the grinding, destroying tension that wracked his body, and he needed it quickly without fuss and, like the peppermint-tasting powder, like a medicine.

'The Senator Club in Frith Street,' he told the chauffeur.

Duncan lay face down on the massage table in the small green-curtained cubicle. He was naked, except for the towel, and his body was smooth and lean. The girl worked up his spine with strong skilled fingers, finding the little knots of tension in the sleek muscle˙and unravelling them.

'Do you want the soft massage, sir?' she asked.

'Yes,' he said and rolled on to his back. She lifted away the towel from around his waist. She was a pretty blonde girl in a short green tunic with the golden laurel leaf club insignia on the pocket, and her manner was brisk and businesslike.

'Do you want any extras, sir?' Her tone was neutral, and she began to unbutton the green tunic automatically.

'No,' Duncan said. 'No extras,' and closed his eyes, surrendering himself completely to the touch of her expert fingers.

He thought of Chantelle, feeling the sneaking guilt of the moment, but it was so seldom these days that he had the energy for her smouldering demanding Persian passions. He did not have the strength for her, he was drained and weary, and all he wanted was the release, swift and simple. In two months' time it would be different, he would have the strength and energy to pick the world up in his bare hands and shake it like a toy.

His mind was separated from his body, and odd disconnected images flitted across the red darkness of his closed eyelids. He thought again how long it had been since last he and Chantelle had made love together, and he wondered what the world would say if they knew of it.

'Nicholas Berg left a big empty place in his bed also,' they would say.

'The hell with them,' Duncan thought, but without the energy for real anger.

'The hell with all of them.' And he gave himself up to the explosion of light that burst against his eyelids and the dark, but too fleeting, peace that followed it.


Nicholas lay back in the rather tatty old brown leather armchair which was one of James Teacher's concessions to creature comfort and he stared at the cheap hunting prints on the faded wallpaper through a thin fug of cheroot smoke. Teacher could have afforded a decent Gaugin or a Turner, but such vulgar display was frowned on in the Inns of Court. It might lead prospective clients to ponder the amount of the fees that they were to be charged.

James Teacher replaced the telephone and stood up behind his desk. It did not make much difference to his height.

'Well, I think we have covered all the entrances to the warren,' he announced cheerfully, and he began to tick off the items on his fingers. 'The sheriff of the South African supreme court will serve notice of attachment on the hull of *Golden Adventurer* at noon local time tomorrow. Our French correspondent will do the same on *Golden Dawn* —' He spoke for three minutes more, and, listening to him, Nicholas reluctantly admitted to himself that he earned the greater proportion of his enormous fees.

'Well, there it is, Mr Berg. If your hunch is correct—'

'It's not a hunch, Mr Teacher. It's certainty. Duncan Alexander has his backside pinched in the doorway. He's been rushing round the City like a demented man looking for money. My God, he even tried to stall me with that incredible offer of a partnership. No Mr Teacher, it's not a hunch. Christy Marine is going to default.'

'I cannot understand that. Six millions is peanuts,' said James Teacher. 'At least it's peanuts to a company like Christy Marine, one of the healthiest shipping owners.'

'It was, a year ago,' Nicholas agreed grimly. 'But since then, Alexander has had a clear run, no checks, it's not a public company, he administers the shares in the Trust.' He drew on his cheroot. 'I'm going to use this to force a full investigation of the company's affairs. I'm going to have Alexander under the microscope and we'll have a close look at all his pimples and warts.'

Teacher chuckled and picked up the telephone at the first ring. 'Teacher,' he chuckled, and then laughed out loud, nodding, 'Yes,' and 'Yes!' again. He hung up and turned to Nicholas, his face bright red with mirth, fat and round as the setting sun.

'I have a disappointment for you, Mr Berg.' He guffawed. 'An hour ago a transfer was made to the credit of Ocean Salvage in Bermuda by Christy Marine.'

'How much?'

'Every penny, Mr Berg. In full and final payment. Six million and some odd dollars in the legal currency of the United States of America.'

Nicholas stared at him, uncertain as to which of his emotions prevailed – relief at having the money, or disappointment at being prevented from tearing Duncan Alexander to shreds.

'He's a high roller and very fast on his feet,' said Teacher. 'It wouldn't pay to underestimate a man like Duncan Alexander.'

'No, it would not,' Nicholas agreed quietly, knowing that he had done so more than once and each time it had cost him dearly.

'I wonder if your clerk could find out from British Airways when the next flight leaves for Bermuda?'

'You are leaving so soon? Will it be in order to mark my brief and send it direct to Bach Wackie in Bermuda?' Teacher asked delicately.


Bernard Wackie in person was waiting for Nicholas beyond the customs barrier. He was tall and lean and alert, burned by the sun dark as a stick of chew tobacco, and dressed in open-neck shirt and cotton trousers.

'Nicholas, it's good to see you.' His handshake was hard and dry and cool. He was under sixty and over forty, it was impossible to get nearer to his age. 'I'm taking you directly to the office, there is too much to discuss. I don't want to waste time.' And he took Nicholas' arm and hurried him through burning sunlight into the shivery cold of the Rolls air-conditioning.

The car was too big for the island's narrow winding roads. Here ownership of automobiles was restricted to one per family unit, but Bernard made the most of his rights.

He was one of those men whose combination of energy and brilliance made it impossible for him to live in England and to subject himself to the punitive taxes of envy.

'It's hard to be a winner, in a society dedicated to the glorification of the losers,' he had told Nicholas, and had moved his whole operation to this taxless haven.

To a lesser man it would have been suicide, but Bernard had taken over the top floor of the Bank of Bermuda building, with a magnificent view across Hamilton Harbour, and had fitted it out with a marine operations room and a communications system the equal of NATO Command.

From it, he offered a service to efficient, so personally involved, so orientated to every single facet of ship ownership and operation, that not only had his old clients followed him, but others had come flocking.

'No taxes, Nicholas,' he smiled. 'And look at the view.' The picturesque buildings of Hamilton town were painted in candy colours, strawberries and

limes, plum and lemon – and across the bay the cedar trees stood tall in the
sunlight, and the yachts from the pink-painted clubhouse spread multi-
coloured sails across green waters. 'It's better than London in winter, isn't
it?'

'The same temperature,' said Nicholas, and glanced up at the air-
conditioning.

'I'm a hot-blooded man,' Bernard explained, and when his tall nubile
secretary entered to his ring, bearing the Ocean Salvage files like a high
priestess carrying the sacrament, Bernard fell into an awed silence, concentrating all his attention on her pneumatic bosoms; they bounced and strained
against the laws of gravity as though filled with helium.

She flashed a dazzling, painted smile at Nicholas as she placed the files
on Bernard's desk, and then she left with her perfectly rounded buttocks
under the tightly tailored skirt, swinging and dancing to a distant music.
'She can type too,' Bernard assured Nick with a sigh, and shook his head
as if to clear it. He opened the top file.

'Right,' he began. 'The deposit from Christy Marine—'

The money had come in, and only just in time. The next instalment on
*Sea Witch* was already forty-eight hours overdue and Atlantique were
becoming highly agitated.

'Son of a gun,' said Bernard. 'You would not think six million was a easy
sum of money to get rid of, would you?'

'You don't even have to try,' Nick agreed. 'It just spends itself.' Then
with a scowl, 'What's this?'

'They've invoked the escalation clause again, another 3½%.' *Sea Witch*'s
builders had included a clause that related the contract price to the index
cost of steel and the Union labour rates. They had avoided the threatened
dockyard strike by capitulating to Union demands, and now the figures come
back to Nicholas. They were big fat ugly figures. The clause was a festering
canker to Nicholas, draining his strength and money.

They worked on through the afternoon, paying, paying and paying.
Bunkers and the other running costs of *Warlock*, interest and capital
repayments on the debts of Ocean Salvage, lawyers' fees, agents' fees, the six
million whittled away. One of the few payments that gave Nicholas any
pleasure was the 12½% salvage money to the crew of *Warlock*. David Allen's
share was almost thirty thousand dollars, Beauty Baker another twenty-five
thousand – Nick included a note with that cheque, 'Have a Bundaberg on
me?'

'Is that all the payments?' Nicholas asked at last.

'Isn't it enough?'

'It's enough.' Nick felt groggy with jet-lag and from juggling with figures.
'What's next?'

'Good news, next.' Bernard picked up the second file. 'I think I've squared
Esso. They hate you, they have threatened never to use your tugs again, but
they are not going to sue.' Nicholas had breached contract when he deserted
the Esso tow and ran south for *Golden Adventurer*; the breach of contract
suit had been hanging since then. It was a relief to have it aside, Bernard
Wackie was worth every penny of his hire.

'Okay. Next?'

It went on for another six unbroken hours, piled on top of the jet-lag that Nicholas had accumulated across the Atlantic.

'You okay?' Bernard asked at last. Nicholas nodded, though his eyes felt like hard-boiled eggs, and his chin was dark and raspy with beard.

'You want something to eat?' Bernard asked, and then Nick shook his head and realized that it was dark outside. 'Drink? You'll need one for what comes next.'

'Scotch,' Nicholas agreed, and the secretary brought the tray through, and poured the drinks in another respectful hush.

'That will be all, Mr Wackie?'

'For now, honey.' Bernard watched her go, and then saluted Nicholas with his glass.

'I give you the Golden Prince!' And when Nicholas scowled, he went on swiftly, 'No, Nicholas, I'm not shafting you. It's for real. You've done it again. The Sheikhs are fixed to make you an offer. They want to buy you out, clean, take over the whole show, liabilities, everything. Of course, they'll want you to run it for them – two years, while you train one of their own men. A hell of a salary,' he went on crisply, and Nicholas stared at him.

'How much?'

'Two hundred grand, plus 2½% profits.'

'Not the salary,' Nicholas told him. 'How much are they offering for the company?'

'They are Arabs, the first offer is just to stir the pot a little.'

'How much?' Nicholas asked impatiently.

'The sum of five was delicately mentioned.'

'What do you think they'll go to?'

'Seven, seven and half – eight, perhaps.'

Through the fuzz of fatigue, far off like a lantern in the window on a winter's night, Nicholas saw the vision of a new life, a life such as Samantha had shown him. A life uncluttered, uncomplicated, shorn of all but joy and purpose.

'Eight million dollars clear?' Nicholas' voice was husky, and he tried to wipe away the fatigue from his stinging eyelids with thumb and forefinger.

'Maybe only seven,' Bernard demurred, 'but I'd try for eight.'

'I'll have another drink,' Nicholas said.

'That's a splendid idea,' Bernard agreed, and rang for his secretary with an anticipatory sparkle in his eyes.

Samantha wore her hair in twin braids down her back, and hacked-off denim pants which left her long brown legs bare and exposed a pale silver of tight round buttock at each step as she walked away. She had sandals on her feet and sun-glasses pushed up on top of her head.

'I thought you were never coming,' she challenged Nick as he stepped through the barrier at Miami International. He dropped his bag and fielded her rush against his chest. She clung to him and he had forgotten the clean, sun-drenched smell of her hair.

She was trembling with a suppressed eagerness like a puppy, and it was

only when a small quivering sob shook her shoulders that he realized she
was weeping.

'Hey now?' He lifted her chin, and her eyes were flooded. She snuffled
once loudly.

'What's the trouble, little one?'

'I'm just so happy,' Samantha told him, and deeply Nicholas envied the
ability to live so near the surface. To be able to cry with joy seemed to him
at that moment to be the supreme human accomplishment. He kissed her
and she tasted salty with tears. With surprise he felt a choke deep in his
own throat.

The jaded airport crowds had to open and trickle around the two of them
like water around a rock, and they were oblivious to it all.

Even when they came out of the building into the Florida sunlight, she
had both arms around his waist, hampering his stride, as she led him to her
vehicle.

'Good God!' exclaimed Nicholas, and he shied when he saw it. It was a
Chevy van, but its paintwork had been restyled. 'What's that?'

'It's a masterpiece,' she laughed. 'Isn't it?' It was rainbowed, in layers of
vibrant colour and panels of fantastic landscapes and seascapes.

'You did that?' Nick asked, and he took his dark glasses from his breast
pocket, and inspected the seagulls and palm trees and flowers through them.

'It's not that bad,' she protested. 'I was bored and depressed without you.
I needed something to brighten my life.'

One of the panels depicted the translucent green of a curling wave, and
on the face of the wave a pair of human figures on Hawaii boards and a
graceful dolphin shape flew in formation together. Nick leaned closer and
barely recognized the male figure as himself; each detail of the features had
been rendered with loving attention, and he came out of it looking something
between Clark Gable and Superman – only a little more glamorous.

'From memory,' she said proudly.

'It's tremendous,' he told her. 'But I've got bigger biceps, and I'm more
beautiful.'

Despite the wild choice of colour and the romantic style, he realized she
had real talent.

'You don't expect me to ride in that – what if one of my creditors saw
me!'

'Get your mind out of its stiff collar and blue suit, mister. You have just
signed on for the voyage to never-never land by way of the moon.'

Before she started the engine she looked at him seriously out of those
great shining green eyes.

'How long, Nicholas?' she asked. 'How long have we got together this
time?'

'Ten days,' he told her. 'Sorry, but I must be back in London by the 25th.
There is a big one coming up, *the* big one. I'll tell you about it.'

'No.' She covered her ears with both hands. 'I don't want to hear about
it, not yet.'

She drove the Chevy with careless unforced skill, very fast and efficiently,
acknowledging the homage of other male drivers with a grin and a shake of
her braids.

When she slipped off highway 95 and parked in the lot of a supermarket, Nicholas raised an eyebrow.

'Food,' she explained, and then with a lascivious roll of her eyes, 'I reckon to get mighty hungry later.'

She chose steaks, a bag full of groceries and a jug of California Riesling, and would not let him pay. 'In this town, you are my guest.'

Then she paid the toll and took the Rickenbacker causeway across the water to Virginia Key.

'That's the marine division of the University of Miami and that's my lab at the top of the jetty, just beyond that white fishing boat – see it?'

The low buildings were crowded into a corner of the island, between the seaquarium and the wharves and jetties of the University's own little harbour.

'We aren't stopping,' Nicholas observed.

'Are you kidding?' she laughed at him. 'I don't need a controlled scientific environment for the experiment I am about to conduct.'

And with no diminution of speed, the Chevy flew across the long bridge between Virginia Key and Key Biscayne, and three miles on, she turned off sharply left on a narrow dirt track that twisted through a lush tropical maritime forest of banyan and palmetta and palm, and ended at a clapboard shack just above the water.

'I live close to the shop,' Samantha explained, as she clattered up on to the screened porch, her arms full of groceries.

'This is yours?' Nicholas asked. He could just make out the tops of big blocks of condominiums on each side; they were incompletely screened by the palms.

'Pa left it to me. He bought it the year I was born,' Samantha explained proudly. 'My ground stretches from there to there.'

A few hundred yards, but Nicholas realized the value of it. Everybody in the world wants to live on the water, and those condominiums were pressing in closely.

'It must be worth a million.'

'There is no price on it,' she said firmly. 'That's what I tell those awful sweaty little men with their big cigars. Pa left it to me and it's not for sale.'

She had the door open now, bumping it with her denim-clad backside.

'Don't just stand there, Nicholas,' she implored him. 'We've only got ten days.'

He followed her into the kitchen as she dumped her load into the sink, and whirled back to him.

'Welcome by my house, Nicholas,' and then as she slid her arms around his waist, jerked his shirt tails out of his belt and slid her hands up his bare back, 'You'll never know just how welcome. Come, let me show you around – this is the living-room.'

It had spartan furniture, with Indian rugs and pottery, and Samantha's chopped-off denims were discarded in the centre of the floor along with Nicholas' shirt.

'And this – surprise! surprise! – is the bedroom.' She dragged him by one hand, and under the short tee-shirt her bottom reminded him of a chipmunk with its cheeks stuffed with nuts, chewing vigorously.

The tiny bedroom overlooked the beach. The sea breeze fluffed out the curtains and the sound of the low surf breathed like a sleeping giant, a deep regular hiss and sigh that filled the air around them.

The bed was too big for the room, all ornate antique brass, with a cloudy soft mattress and an old-fashioned patchwork quilt in a hundred coloured and patterned squares.

'I don't think I could have lived another day without you,' she said, and unwound the thick plaits of her hair. 'You came like the cavalry, in the very nick of time.'

He reached up and took the golden tresses of her hair, winding them thickly around his wrist, twining them in his fingers, and he pulled her gently down beside him.

Suddenly Nick's life was uncluttered and simple again. Suddenly he was young and utterly carefree again. The petty strivings, the subterfuge, the lies and the cheating did not exist in this little universe that encompassed a tiny wooden shack on the edge of the ocean, and a huge brass bed that clanged and rattled and banted and squeaked with the wholesale, the completely abandoned happiness that was the special miracle called Samantha Silver.


Samantha's laboratory was a square room, built on piles over the water, and the soft hum of the electric pumps blended with the slap of the wavelets below and the burble and blurp of the tanks.

'This is my kingdom,' she told him. 'And these are my subjects.'

There were almost a hundred tanks, like the small glass-sided aquaria for goldfish, and suspended over each of them was a complicated arrangement of coils and bottles and electric wiring.

Nick sauntered across to the nearest of the tanks and peered into it. It contained a single large salt-water clam; the animal was feeding with the double shells agape, the pink soft flesh and frilly gills rippling and undulating in the gentle flow of pumped and filtered sea water. To each half of the shell, thin copper wires were attached with blobs of polyurethane cement.

Samantha came to stand beside him, touching, and he asked her, 'What's happening?'

She touched a switch and immediately the cylindrical scroll above the tank began to revolve slowly and a stylus, after a few preliminary jerks and quivers, began to trace out a regular pattern on the paper scroll, a trough and double peak, the second a fraction lower than the first, and then the trough again.

She said, 'He's wired and bugged.'

'You're a member of the CIA,' he accused.

And she laughed. 'His heart-beat. I'm passing an electric impulse through the heart – the heart is only a millimetre across – but each spasm changes the resistance and moves the stylus.' She studied the curve for a moment. 'This fellow is one very healthy cheerful *Spisula solidissima*.'

'Is that his name?' Nick asked. 'I thought he was a clam.'

'One of fifteen thousand bivalves who use that common generic,' she corrected.

'I had to pick an egghead,' said Nicholas ruefully. 'But what's so interesting about his heart?'

'It's the closest and cheapest thing to a pollution metre that we have discovered so far – or rather,' she corrected herself without false modesty, 'that I have discovered.'

She took his hand and led him down the long rows of tanks. 'They are sensitive, incredibly sensitive to any contamination of their environment, and the heart-beat will register almost immediately any foreign element or chemical, organic or otherwise, in such low concentrate that it would take a highly trained specialist with a spectroscope to detect otherwise.'

Nicholas felt his mild attention changing and growing into real interest as Samantha began to prepare samples of common pollutants on the single bench against the forewall of the cluttered little laboratory.

'Here,' she held up one test tube, 'aromatic carbons, the more poisonous elements of crude petroleum – and here,' she indicated the next tube, 'mercury in a concentration of 100 parts to the million. Did you see the photographs of the human vegetables and the Japanese children with the flesh falling off their bones at Kiojo? That was mercury. Lovely stuff.'

She picked up another tube. 'PCB, a by-product of the electrical industry, the Hudson River is thick with it. And these, tetrahydrofurane, cyclohexane, methylbenzene – all industrial by-products but don't let the fancy names throw you. One day they will come back to haunt us, in newspaper headlines as THF or CMB – one day there will be other human cabbages and babies born without arms or legs.' She touched the other tubes. 'Arsenic, old-fashioned Agatha Christie vintage poison. And then here is the real living and breathing bastard daddy of them all – this is cadmium; as a sulphide so it's easily absorbed. In 100 parts to the million it's as lethal as a neutron bomb.'

While he watched, she carried the tray of tubes across to the tanks and set the ECG monitors running. Each began to record the normal double-peaked heart beat of a healthy clam.

'Now,' she said, 'watch this.'

Under controlled conditions, she began to drip the weak poisoned solutions into the reticulated water systems, a different solution to each of the tanks.

'These concentrations are so low that the animals will not even be aware of trauma, they will continue to feed and breed without any but long-term indications of systemic poisoning.'

Samantha was a different person, a cool quick-thinking professional. Even the white dust-coat that she had slipped over her tee-shirt altered her image and she had aged twenty years in poise and authority as she passed back and forth along the row of tanks.

'There,' she said, with grim satisfaction as the stylus on one recording drum made a slightly double beat at its peak and then just detectably flattened the second peak. 'Typical aromatic carbon reaction.'

The distorted heart-beat was repeated endlessly on the slowly turning drum, and she passed on to the next tank.

'See the pulse in the trough, see the fractional speeding up of the heart spasm? That's cadmium in ten parts to the million, at 100 parts it will kill all sea life, at five hundred it will kill man slowly, at seven hundred parts in air or solution it will kill him very quickly indeed.'

Nicholas' interest became total fascination, as he helped Samantha record the experiments and control the flow and concentration in the tanks. Slowly they increased the dosage of each substance and the moving stylus dispassionately recorded the increasing distress and the final convulsions and spasmodic throes that preceded death.

Nicholas voiced the tickle of horror and revulsion he felt at watching the process of degeneration.

'It's macabre.'

'Yes.' She stood back from the tanks. 'Death always is. But these organisms have such rudimentary nervous systems that they don't experience pain as we know it.' She shuddered slightly herself and went on. 'But imagine an entire ocean poisoned like one of these tanks, imagine the incredible agonies of tens of millions of sea birds, of the mammals, seals and porpoises and whales. Then think of what would happen to man himself—' Samantha shrugged off her white dust-coat.

'Now I'm hungry,' she announced, and then looking up at the fibreglass panels in the roof, 'No wonder! It's dark already!'

While they cleaned and tidied the laboratory, and made a last check of the pumps and running equipment, Samantha told him, 'In five hours we have tested over a hundred and fifty samples of contaminated water and got accurate indications of nearly fifty dangerous substances – at a probable cost of fifty cents a sample.' She switched out the lights. 'To do the same with a gas spectroscope would have cost almost ten thousand dollars and taken a highly specialized team two weeks of hard work.'

'It's a hell of a trick,' Nicholas told her. 'You're a clever lady – I'm impressed, I really am.'

At the psychedelic Chevy van she stopped him, and in the light of the street lamp looked up at him guiltily.

'Do you mind if I show you off, Nicholas?'

'What does that mean?' he asked suspiciously.

'The gang are eating shrimps tonight. Then they'll sleep over on the boat and have the first shot at fish tagging tomorrow – but we don't have to go. We could just get some more steaks and another jug of wine.' But he could see she really wanted to go.


She was fifty-five foot, an old purse-seiner with the ungainly wheelhouse forward looking like a sentry box or an old-fashioned pit latrine. Even with her coat of new paint, she had an old-fashioned look.

She was tied up at the end of the University jetty, and as they walked out to her, so they could hear the voices and the laughter coming up from below decks.

'*Tricky Dicky*,' Nicholas read her name on the high ugly rounded stern.

'But we love her,' Samantha and led him across the narrow, rickety gangplank. 'She belongs to the University. She's only one of our four research vessels. The others are all fancy modern ships, one-hundred-footers, but the

*Dicky* is our boat for short field trips to the gulf or down the Keys, and she's also the faculty clubhouse.'

The main cabin was monastically furnished, bare planking and hard benches, a single long table, but it was as crowded as a fashionable disco-theque, packed solid with sunburned young people, girls and boys all in faded jeans and tee shirts, impossible to judge sexes by clothing or by the length of their sun-tortured and wind-tangled hair.

The air was thick with the rich smell of broiling gulf shrimps and molten butter, and there were gallon jugs of California wine on the table.

'Hey!' Samantha shouted above the uproar of voices raised in heated dispute and jovial repartee. 'This is Nicholas.'

A comparative silence descended on the gathering, and they looked him over with the curious veiled group hostility of any tribe for an interloper, an intruder in a closed and carefully guarded group. Nick returned the scrutiny calmly, met each pair of eyes, while realizing that despite the affected informality of their dress and some of the wildly unkempt hairstyles and the impressive profusion of beards, they were an elite group. There was not a face that was not intelligent, not a pair of eyes that was not alert and quick, and there was that special feeling of pride and self-confidence in all of them.

At the head of the table sat a big impressive figure, the oldest man in the cabin, perhaps Nick's age or a little older, for there were silver strands in his beard and his face was lined and beaten by sun and wind and time.

'Hi, Nick,' he boomed. 'I won't pretend we've never heard of you. Sam has given us all cauliflower ears—'

'You cut that out, Tom Parker,' Samantha stopped him sharply, and there was a ripple of laughter, a relaxation of tension and a casual round of greetings.

'Hi, Nick, I'm Sally-Anne.' A pretty girl with china-blue eyes behind wire-framed spectacles put a heavy tumbler of wine into his hand.

'We are short of glasses, guess you and Sam will have to share.'

She slid up along the bench and gave them a few inches of space and Samantha perched in Nicholas' lap. The wine was a rough fighting red, and it galloped, booted and spurred across his palate but Samantha sipped her share with the same relish as if it had been a '53 Château Lafitte, and she nuzzled Nicholas' ear and whispered:

'Tom is prof of the Biology Department, he's a honey. After you – he's my most favourite man in the world.'

A woman came through from the galley, carrying a huge platter piled high with bright pink shrimps and a bowl of molten butter. There was a roar of applause for her as she placed the dishes in the centre of the table, and they fell upon the food with unashamed gusto.

The woman was tall with dark hair in braids and a strong capable face, lean and supple in tight breeches, but she was older than the other women and she paused beside Tom Parker and draped one arm across his shoulders in a comfortable gesture of long-established affection.

'That's Antoinette, his wife.' The woman heard her name and smiled across at them, and with dark gentle eyes she studied Nicholas and then nodded and made the continental 'O' of thumb and fore-finger at Samantha, before slipping back into the galley.

The food did not inhibit the talk, the lively contentious flow of discussion that swung swiftly from banter to deadly seriousness and back again, bright trained informed minds clicking and cannoning off each other with the crispness of ivory billiard balls, while at the same time buttery fingers ripped the whiskered heads off the shrimps, delving for the crescent of sweet white flesh, then leaving greasy fingerprints on the wine tumblers.

As each of them spoke, Samantha whispered their names and credentials. 'Hank Petersen, he's doing a PhD on the Bluefin Funa – spawning and a trace of its migratory routes. He's the one running the tagging tomorrow.

'That's Michelle Rand, she's on loan from UCLA, and she's porpoises and whales.'

Then suddenly they were all discussing indignantly a rogue tanker captain who the week before had scrubbed his tanks in the middle of the Florida straits and left a thirty-mile slick down the Gulf Stream. He had done it under cover of night, and changed course as soon as he was into the Atlantic proper.

'We finger-printed him,' Tom Parker like an angry bear, 'we had him made, dead in the cross hairs.' Nick knew he was talking of the finger-printing of oil residues, the break-down of samples of the slick under gas spectroscopy which could match them exactly to the samples taken by the Coast Guard from the offender's tanks. The identification was good enough to bear up in an international court of law. 'But the trick is getting the son-of-a-bitch into court.' Tom Parker went on. 'He was fifty miles outside our territorial waters by the time the Coast Guard got to him, and he's registered in Liberia.'

'We tried to cover cases like that in the set of proposals I put up to the last maritime conference.'

Nick joined the conversation for the first time. He told them of the difficulties of legislating on an international scale, of policing and bringing to justice the blatant transgressors; then he listed for them what had been done so far, what was in process and finally what he believed still should be done to protect the seas.

He spoke quietly, succinctly, and Samantha noticed again, with a swell of pride, how all men listened when Nicholas Berg talked. The moment he paused, they came at him from every direction, using their bright young minds like scalpels, tearing into him with sharp lancing questions. He answered them in the same fashion, sharp and hard, armed with total knowledge of his subject, and he saw the shift in the group attitude, the blooming of respect, the subtle opening of ranks to admit him, for he had spoken the correct passwords and they recognized him as one of their own number, as one of the élite.

At the head of the table, Tom Parker sat and listened, nodding and frowning, sitting in judgement with his arm around Antoinette's slim waist and she stood beside him and played idly with a curl of thick wiry hair on the top of his head.

Tom Parker found fish forty miles offshore where the Gulf Stream was setting blue and warm and fast into the north. The birds were working, falling on folded wings down the backdrop of cumulonimbus storm clouds that bruised the horizon. The birds were bright, white pinpoints of light as they fell, and they struck the dark blue water with tiny explosions of white spray, and went deep. Seconds later they popped to the surface, stretching their necks to force down another morsel into their distended crops, before launching into flight again, climbing in steep circles against the sky to join the hunt again. There were hundreds of them and they swirled and fell like snowflakes.

'Anchovy,' grunted Tom Parker, and they could see the agitated surface of the water under the bird flock where the frenzied bait-fish churned. 'Could be bonito working under them.'

'No,' said Nick. 'They are blues.'

'You sure?' Tom grinned a challenge.

'The way they are bunching and holding the bait-fish, it's tuna,' Nick repeated.

'Five bucks?' Tom asked, as he swung the wheel over, and *Tricky Dicky*'s big diesel engine boomed as she went on to the top of her speed.

'You're on,' Nick grinned back at him, and at that moment, they both saw a fish jump clear. It was a brilliant shimmering torpedo, as long as a man's arm. It went six feet into the air, turned in flight and hit the water again with a smack they heard clearly above the diesel.

'Blues,' said Nick flatly. 'Shoal blues – they'll go twenty pounds each.'

'Five bucks,' Tom grunted with disgust. 'Son of a gun, I don't think I can afford you, man,' and he delivered a playful punch to the shoulder which rattled Nick's teeth, then he turned to the open window of the wheelhouse and bellowed out on to the deck, 'Okay, kids, they are blues.'

There was a scramble and chatter of excitement as they rushed for lines and tagging poles. It was Hank's show, he was the bluefin tunny expert, he knew as much about their sex habits, their migratory routes and food chains as any man living, but when it came to catching them, Nick observed drily, he could probably do a better job as a blacksmith.

Tom Parker was no fisherman either. He ran down the shoal, charging *Tricky Dicky* through the centre of it, scattering birds and fish in panic – but by sheer chance one of the gang in the stern hooked in, and after a great deal of heaving and huffing and shouted encouragement from his peers, dragged a single luckless baby bluefin tuna over the rail. It skittered and jumped around the deck, its tail hammering against the planking, pursued by a shrieking band of scientists who slid and slipped in the fish slime, knocked each other down and finally cornered the fish against the rail. The first three attempts to affix the plastic tag were unsuccessful, Hank's lunges with the dart pole becoming wilder as his frustration mounted. He almost succeeded in tagging Samantha's raised backside as she knelt on the deck trying to cradle the fish in both arms.

'You do this often?' Nicholas asked mildly.

'First time with this gang,' Tom Parker admitted sheepishly. 'Thought you'd never guess.'

By now the triumphant band was solicitously returning the fish to the sea, the barbed dart of the plastic tag embedded dangerously near its vitals;

and if that didn't eventually kill it, the rough handling probably would. It had pounded its head on the deck so heavily that blood oozed from the gill covers. It floated away, belly up on the stream, oblivious of Samantha's anguished cried of:

'Swim, fish, get in there and swim!'

'Mind if we try it my way?' Nick asked, and Tom relinquished command without a struggle.

Nicholas picked the four strongest and best co-ordinated of the young men, and gave them a quick demonstration and lecture on how to handle the heavy handlines with the Japanese feather lures, showing them how to throw the bait, and the recovery with an under-hand flick that recoiled the line between the feet. Then he gave each a station along the starboard rail, with the second member of each team ready with a tagging pole and Hank Petersen on the roof of the wheelhouse to record the fish taken and the numbers of the tags.

They found another shoal within the hour and Nicholas circled up on it, closing steadly at good trolling speed, helping the feeding tuna bunch the shoal of frenzied anchovy on the surface, until he could lock *Tricky Dicky's* wheel hard down starboard and leave her to describe her own sedate circles around the shoal. Then he hurried out on to the deck.

The trapped and surrounded fish thrashed the surface until it boiled like a porridge of molten, flashing silver; through it drove the fast dark torpedoes of the hungry tuna.

Within minutes Nick had his four fishermen working to the steady rhythm of throwing the lures into the frothing water, almost instantly striking back on the line as a tuna snatched the feathers, and then swinging hand over head, recovering and coiling line fast with minimum effort, swinging the fish out and up with both hands and then catching its streamlined body under the left armpit like a quarter back picking up a long pass, clamping it there firmly, although the cold firm silver bullet shape juddered and quivered and the tail beat in a blur of movement. Then he taught them to slip the hook from the jaw, careful not to damage the vulnerable gills, holding the fish firmly but gently while the assistant pressed the barbed dart into the thick muscle at the back of the dorsal fin. When the fish was dropped back over the side, there were so few after-affects that it almost immediately began feeding again on the packed masses of tiny anchovies.

Each plastic tag was numbered and imprinted with a request in five languages to mail it back to University of Miami with details of date and place of capture, providing a valuable trace on the movements of the shoals in their annual circumnavigation of the globe. From their spawning grounds somewhere in the Caribbean they worked the Gulf Stream north and east across the Atlantic, then south down and around the Cape of Good Hope with an occasional foray down the length of the Mediterranean Sea – although now the dangerous pollution of that landlocked water was changing their habits. From Good Hope east again south of Australia to take a gigantic swing up and around the Pacific, running the gauntlet of the Japanese long-liners and the California tunny men before ducking down under the terrible icy seas of the Horn and back to their spawning grounds in the Caribbean.

They sat up on the wheelhouse as the *Dicky* ran home in the sunset, drinking beer and talking. Nicholas studied them casually and saw that they possessed so many of the qualities he valued in his fellow humans; they were intelligent and motivated, they were dedicated and free of that particular avarice that mars so many others.

Tom Parker crumpled the empty beer can in a huge fist as easily as if it had been a paper packet, fished two more from the pack beside him and tossed one across to Nick. The gesture seemed to have some special significance and Nicholas saluted him with the can before he drank.

Samantha was snuggled down in luxurious weariness against his shoulder, and the sunset was a magnificence of purple and hot molten crimson. Nicholas thought idly how pleasant it would be to spend the rest of his life doing things like this with people like these.


Tom Parker's office had shelves to the ceiling, and they were sagging with hundreds of bottled specimens and rows of scientific papers and publications.

He sat well back in his swivel chair with ankles crossed neatly in the centre of the cluttered desk.

'I ran a check on you, Nicholas. Damned nerve, wasn't it? You have my apology.'

'Was it an interesting exercise?' Nicholas asked mildly.

'It wasn't difficult. You have left a trail behind you like a—' Tom sought for a comparison, 'like a grizzly bear through a honey farm. Son of a gun, Nicholas, that's a hell of a track record you've got yourself.'

'I've kept busy,' Nicholas admitted.

'Beer?' Tom crossed to the refrigerator in the corner that was labelled 'Zoological Specimens. DO NOT OPEN.'

'It's too early for me.'

'Never too early,' said Tom and pulled the tag on a dewy can of Millers and then picked up Nicholas' statement. 'Yes, you have kept busy. Strange, isn't it, that around some men things just happen.'

Nicholas did not reply, and Tom went on. 'We need a man around here who can *do*. It's all right thinking it out, then you need the catalyst to transform thought and intention into action.' Tom sucked at the can and then licked the froth off his moustache. 'I know what you have done. I've heard you speak, I've seen you move, and those things count. But most important of all, I know you care. I've been watching you carefully, Nick, and you really care, down deep in your guts, the way we do.'

'It sounds as though you're offering me a job, Tom'.

'I'm not going to horse around, Nick, I *am* offering you a job.' He waved a huge paw, like a bunch of broiled pork sausages. 'Hell, I know you're a busy man, but I'd like to romance you into an associate professorship. We'd want a little of your time when it came to hassling and negotiating up in Washington, we'd call for you when we needed real muscle to put our case, when we need the right contacts, somebody with a big reputation to open doors, when we need a man who knows the practical side of the oceans and the men that use them and abuse them.

'We need a man who is a hard-headed businessman, who knows the economics of sea trade, who has built and run tankers, who knows that human need is of paramount importance, but who can balance the human need for protein and fossil fuels against the greater danger of turning the oceans into water deserts.' Tom lubricated his throat with beer, watching shrewdly for some reaction from Nicholas, and when he received no encouragement, he went on more persuasively. 'We are specialists, perhaps we have the specialist's narrow view; God knows, they think of us as sentimentalists, the lunatic fringe of doomsayers, long-haired intellectual hippies. What we need is a man with real clout in the establishment – shit, Nicholas, if you walked into a Congressional committee they'd really jerk out of their geriatric trance and switch on their hearing-aids.' Nicholas was silent still and Tom was becoming desperate. 'What can we offer in return?' I know you aren't short of cash, and it would be a lousy twelve thousand a year, but an associate professorship is a nice title. We start out holding hands with that. Then we might start going steady, a full professorship – chair of applied oceanology, or some juicy title like that which we'd think up. I don't know what else we can offer you, Nick, except perhaps the warm good feeling in your guts when you're doing a tough job that has to be done.' He stopped again, running out of words, and he wagged his big shaggy head sadly.

'You aren't interested, are you?' he asked.

Nick stirred himself. 'When do I start?' he asked, and as Tom's face split into a great beaming grin, Nick held out his hand. 'I think I'll take that beer now.'

The water was cool enough to be invigorating. Nick and Samantha swam so far out that the land was almost lost in the lowering gloom of dusk, and then they turned and swam back side by side. The beach was deserted; in their mood, the lights of the nearest condominiums were no more intrusive than the stars, the faint sound of music and laughter no more intrusive than the cry of gulls.

It was the right time to tell her, and he did it in detail beginning with the offer by the Sheikhs to buy out Ocean Salvage and Towage.

'Will you sell?' she asked quietly. 'You won't, will you?'

'For seven million dollars clear?' he asked. 'Do you know how much money that is?'

'I can't count that far,' she admitted. 'But what would you do if you sold? I cannot imagine you playing bowls or golf for the rest of your life.'

'Part of the deal is that I run Ocean Salvage for them for two years, and then I've been offered a part-time assignment which will fill any spare time I've got left over.'

'What is it?'

'Associate Professor at Miami University.'

She stopped dead and dragged him around to face her.

'You're having me on!' she accused.

'That's a start only,' he admitted. 'In two years or so, when I've finished with Ocean Salvage, there may be a full chair of applied oceanology.'

'It's not true!' she said, and took him by the arms, shaking him with surprising strength.

'Tom wants me to ram-rod the applied aspects of the environmental research. I'll trouble-shoot with legislators and the maritime conference, a sort of hired gun for the Green-Peacers—'

'Oh Nicholas, Nicholas!'

'Sweet Christ!' he accused. 'You're crying again.'

'I just can't help it.' She was in his arms still wet and cold and gritty with beach sand. She clung to him, quivering with joy. 'Do you know what this means, Nicholas? You don't, do you? You just don't realize what this means.'

'Tell me,' he invited. 'What does it mean?'

'What it means is that, in future, we can do everything together, not just munch food and go boom in bed – but everything, work and play and, and *live* together like a man and woman should!' She sounded stunned and frightened by the magnitude of the vision.

'The prospect daunts me not at all,' he murmured gently, and lifted her chin.

They washed off the salt and the sand, crowding together into the thick, perfumed steam of the shower cubicle and afterwards they lay together on the patchwork quilt in the darkness with the sound of the sea as background music to the plans and dreams they wove together.

Every time they both descended to the very frontiers of sleep, one of them would think of something vitally important and prod the other awake to say it.

'I've got to be in London on Tuesday.'

'Don't spoil it all, now,' she murmured sleepily.

'And then we're launching *Sea Witch* on the 7th April.'

'I'm not listening,' she whispered. 'I've got my fingers in my ears.'

'Will you launch her – I mean break the bottle of bubbly and bless her?'

'I've just taken my fingers out again.'

'Jules would love it.'

'Nicholas, I cannot spend my life commuting across the Atlantic, not even for you. I've got work to do.'

'Peter will be there, I'll work that as a bribe.'

'That's unfair pressure,' she protested.

'Will you come?'

'You know I will, you sexy bastard. I wouldn't miss it for all the world.' She moved across the quilt and found his ear with her lips. 'I am honoured.'

'Both of you are sea witches,' Nick told her.

'And you are my warlock.'

'Sea witch and warlock,' he chuckled. 'Together we will work miracles.'

'Look, I know it's terribly forward of me, but seeing that we are both wide awake, and it's only two o'clock in the morning, I would be super ultra-grateful if you could work one of your little miracles for me right now.'

'It will be a great pleasure,' Nick told her.

Nicholas was early, he saw as he came out of the American Consulate and glanced at his Rolex, so he moderated his pace across the Place de la Concorde, despite the gentle misty rain that settled in minute droplets on the shoulders of his trench coat.

Lazarus was at the rendezvous ahead of him, standing under one of the statues in the corner of the square closest to the French Naval Headquarters.

He was heavily muffled against the cold, dressed all in sombre blue with a long cashmere scarf wound around his throat and a dark blue hat pulled down so low as to conceal the pale smooth bulge of his forehead.

'Let's find a warm place,' Nick suggested, without greeting the little man.

'No,' said Lazarus, looking up at him through the thick distorting lenses of his spectacles. 'Let us walk.' And he led the way through the underpass on to the promenade above the embankment of the Seine, and set off in the direction of the Petit Palais.

In the middle of such an inclement afternoon they were the only strollers, and they walked in silence three or four hundred yards while Lazarus satisfied himself absolutely of this, and while he adjusted his mincing little steps to Nick's stride. It was like taking Toulouse-Lautrec for a stroll, Nick smiled to himself. Even when Lazarus began speaking, he kept glancing back over his shoulder, and once when two bearded Algerian students in combat jackets overtook them, he let them get well ahead before he went on.

'You know there will be nothing in writing?' he piped.

'I have a recorder in my pocket,' Nick assured him.

'Very well, you are entitled to that.'

'Thank you,' murmured Nick dryly.

Lazarus paused, it was almost as though a new reel was being fitted into the computer, and when he began talking again, his voice had a different timbre, a monotonous almost electronic tone, as though he was indeed an automaton.

First, there was a recital of share movements in the thirty-three companies which made up the Christy Marine complex, every movement in the previous eighteen months.

The little man reeled them off steadily, as though he were actually reading from the share registers of the companies. He must have had access, Nicholas realized, to achieve such accuracy. He had the date, the number of shares, the transferor and transferee, even the transfer of shares in Ocean Salvage and Towage to Nicholas himself, and the reciprocal transfer of Christy Marine stock, was faithfully detailed, confirming the accuracy of Lazarus' other information. It was all an impressive exhibition of total knowledge and total recall, but much too complicated for Nicholas to make any sense of it. He would have to study it carefully. All that he would hazard was that somebody was putting up a smokescreen.

Lazarus stopped on the corner of the Champs Elysées and the rue de la Boetie. Nicholas glanced down at him and saw his shapeless blob of a nose was an unhealthy purplish pink in the cold, and that his breathing had coarsened and laboured with the exertion of walking. Nick realized suddenly that the little man was probably asthmatic, and as if to confirm this, he took a little silver and turquoise pill-box from his pocket and slipped a single pink capsule into his mouth before leading Nicholas into the foyer of a movie house and buying two tickets.

It was a porno movie, a French version of *Deep Throat* entitled *Gorge Profonde*. The print was scratched and the French dubbing was out of synchronization. The cinema was almost empty, so they found two seats in isolation at the rear of the stalls.

Lazarus stared unblinkingly at the screen, as he began the second part of his report. This was a detailed breakdown of cash movements within the Christy Marine Group, and Nick was again amazed at the man's penetration.

He drew a verbal picture of the assemblage of enormous sums of money, marshalled and channelled into orderly flows by a master tactician. The genius of Duncan Alexander was as clearly identifiable as that flourishing signature with the flamboyant 'A' and 'X' which Nicholas had seen him dash off with studied panache. Then suddenly the cash-flow was not so steady and untroubled, there were eddies and breaks, little gaps and inconsistencies that nagged at Nicholas like the false chimes of a broken clock. Lazarus finished this section of his report with a brief summation of the Group's cash and credit position as at a date four days previously and Nicholas realized that the doubts were justified. Duncan had run the Group out along a knife-edge.

Nicholas sat hunched down in the threadbare velvet seat, both hands thrust into the pockets of his trench-coat, watching the incredible feats of Miss Lovelace on the screen, without really seeing them, while beside him Lazarus took an aerosol can from his pocket, screwed a nozzle on to it and noisily sprayed a fine mist down his own throat. It seemed to relieve him almost immediately.

'Insurance and marine underwriting of vessels owned by the Christy Marine Group of companies.' He began again with names and figures and dates, and Nicholas picked up the trend. Duncan was using his own captive company, London and European Insurance and Banking, to lead the risk on all his vessels, and then he was reinsuring in the marketplace, spreading part of the risk, but carrying a whacking deductible himself, the principle of self-insurance that Nicholas had opposed so vigorously, and which had rebounded so seriously upon Duncan's head with the salvage of *Golden Adventurer*.

The last of the vessels in Lazarus' recital was *Golden Dawn*, and Nicholas shifted restlessly in his seat at the mention of the name, and almost immediately he realized that something strange was taking place.

'Christy Marine did not apply for a Lloyd's survey of this vessel.' Nicholas knew that already. 'But she had been rated first class by the continental surveyors.' It was a much easier rating to obtain, and consequently less acceptable than the prestigious 'A1 at Lloyd's'.

Lazarus went on, lowering his voice slightly as another patron entered the almost deserted cinema and took a seat two rows in front of them.

'And insurance has been effected outside Lloyd's.' The risk was led by London and European Insurance. Again, Duncan was self-insuring, Nicholas noted grimly, but not all of it. 'And further lines were written by—' Lazarus listed the other companies which carried a part of the risk, with whom Duncan had re-insured. But it was all too thin, too nebulous. Again, only careful study of the figures would enable Nicholas to analyse what Duncan was doing, how much was real insurance and how much was bluff to convince his financiers that the risk was truly covered, and their investment protected.

Some of the names of the re-insurers were familiar, they had been on the list of transferees who had taken stock positions in Christy Marine.

'Is Duncan buying insurance with capital?' Nicholas pondered. Was he buying at desperate prices. He must have cover, of course. Without insurance the finance houses, the banks and institutions which had loaned money to Christy Marine to build the monstrous tanker would dig in against Duncan. His own shareholders would raise such hell— No, Duncan Alexander had to have cover, even if it was paper only, without substance, a mere incestuous circle, a snake eating itself tail first.

Oh, but the trail was so cleverly confused, so carefully swept and tied up, only Nicholas' intimate knowledge of Christy Marine made him suspicious, and it might take a team of investigators years to unravel the tortured tapestry of deceit. In the first instant, it had occurred to Nicholas that the easiest way to stop Duncan Alexander was to leak his freshly gleaned suspicions to Duncan's major creditors, to those who had financed the building of *Golden Dawn*. But immediately he realized that this was not enough. There were no hard facts, it was all inference and innuendo. By the time the facts could be exhumed and laid out in all their putrefaction for autopsy, *Golden Dawn* would be on the high seas, carrying a million tons of crude. Duncan might have won sufficient time to make his profit and sell out to some completely uncontrollable Greek or Chinaman, as he had boasted he would do. It would not be so simple to stop Duncan Alexander, it was folly to have believed that for one moment. Even if his creditors were made aware of the flimsy insurance cover over *Golden Dawn*, were they too deeply in already? Would they not then accept the risks, spreading them where they could, and simply twist the financial rope a little tighter around Duncan's throat. No, it was not the way to stop him, Duncan had to be forced to remodify the giant tanker's hull, forced to make her an acceptable moral risk, forced to accept the standard Nicholas had originally stipulated for the vessel.

Lazarus had finished the insurance portion of his report, and he stood up abruptly, just as Miss Lovelace was about to attempt the impossible. With relief, Nick followed him down the aisle and into the chill of a Parisian evening, and they breathed the fumes that the teeming city exhaled as Lazarus led him back eastwards through the VIII^c Arrondissement with those little dancing steps, while he recited the details of the charters of all Christy Marine's vessels, the charterer, the rates, the dates of expiry of contract; and Nicholas recognized most of them, contracts that he himself had negotiated, or those that had been renewed on expiry with minor alterations to the terms. He was relying on the recorder in his pocket, listening only with the surface layer of his mind, pondering all he had heard so far from this extraordinary little man – so that when it came he almost did not realize what he was hearing.

'On 10th January Christy Marine entered a contract of carriage with Orient Amex. The tenure is ten years. The vessel to be employed is the *Golden Dawn*. The rate is 10 cents US per hundred ton miles with a minimum annual guaranteed usage of 75,000 nautical miles.'

Nicholas registered the trigger word *Golden Dawn* and then he assimilated it all. The price, ten cents per hundred ton miles, that was wrong, high, much too high, ridiculously high in this depressed market. Then the name, Orient Amex – what was there about it that jarred his memory?

He stopped dead, and a following pedestrian bumped him. Nicholas shouldered him aside thoughtlessly and stood thinking, ransacking his mind for buried items of information. Lazarus had stopped also and was waiting patiently, and now Nicholas laid a hand on the little man's shoulder.

'I need a drink.'

He drew him into a brasserie which was thick with steam from the coffee machine and the smoke of Caporal and Disque Bleu, and sat him at a tiny table by the window overlooking the sidewalk.

Primly, Lazarus asked for a Vittel water and sipped it with an air of virtue, while Nicholas poured soda into his whisky.

'Orient Amex,' Nicholas asked, as soon as the waiter had left. 'Tell me about it.'

'That is outside my original terms of reference,' Lazarus demurred delicately.

'Charge me for it,' Nicholas invited, and Lazarus paused as the computer reels clicked in his mind, then he began to speak.

'Orient Amex is an American-registered company, with an issued capital of twenty-five million shares at a par value of ten dollars—' Lazarus recited the dry statistics. 'The company is presently undertaking substantial dry-land exploration in Western Australia and Ethiopia, and offshore exploration within the territorial waters of Norway and Chile. It has erected a refinery at Galveston in Texas to operate under the new atomic catalyst cracking process, first employed at its pilot plant on the same site. The plant is projected for initial operation in June this year, and full production in five years.'

It was all vaguely familiar to Nicholas, the names, the process of cracking the low-value high-carbon molecules, breaking up the carbon atoms and reassembling them in volatile low-carbon molecules of high value.

'The company operates producing wells in Texas, and in the Santa Barbara offshore field, in Southern Nigeria, and has proven crude reserves in the El Barras field of Kuwait, which will be utilized by the new cracking plant in Galveston.'

'Good God,' Nicholas stared at him. 'The El Barras field – but it's cadmium-contaminated, it's been condemned by—'

'The El Barras field is a high cadmium field, naturally enriched with the catalyst necessary for the new process.'

'What are the cadmium elements?' Nicholas demanded.

'The western area of the El Barras field has sampled at 2,000 parts per million, and the north and eastern anticline have sampled as high as 42,000 parts per million.' Lazarus recited the figures pedantically. 'The American and Nigerian crudes will be blended with the El Barras crudes during the revolutionary cracking process. It is projected that the yield of low-carbon volatiles will be increased from 40% to 85% by this process, making it five to eight times more profitable, and extending the life of the world's known reserves of crude petroleum by between ten and fifteen years.'

As he listened, Nicholas had a vivid mental image of the stylus in Samantha's laboratory recording the death throes of a cadmium-poisoned clam. Lazarus was talking on dispassionately. 'During the cracking process, the cadmium sulphide will be reduced to its pure metallic, non-toxic form, and will be a form, and will be a valuable by-product, reducing the cost of refining.'

Nicholas shook his head in disbelief, and he spoke aloud. 'Duncan is going to do it. Across two oceans, a million tons at a time, in that vulnerable jerry-built monster of his, Duncan is going to do what no other shipowner has ever dared to do – he's going to carry the cad-rich crudes of El Barras!'

From the balcony windows of his suite in the Ritz, Nicholas could look out across the Place Vendôme at the column in the centre of the square with its spiral bas-relief made from the Russian and Austrian guns and commemorating the little Corsican's feats of arms against those two nations. While he studied the column and waited for his connection, he did a quick calculation and realized that it would be three o'clock in the morning on the eastern seaboard of North America. At least he would find her at home. Then he smiled to himself. If she wasn't at home, he'd want to know the reason why.

The telephone rang and he picked it up without turning away from the window.

There was a confused mumbling and Nicholas asked, 'Who is this?'

'It's Sam Silver – what's the time? Who is it? Good God, it's three o'clock. What do you want?'

'Tell that other guy to put his pants on and go home.'

'Nicholas!' There was a joyous squeal, followed immediately by a crash and clatter that made Nicholas wince and lift the receiver well away from his ear.

'Oh damn it to hell, I've knocked the table over. Nicholas, are you there? Speak to me, for God's sake!'

'I love you.'

'Say that again, please. Where are you?'

'Paris. I love you.'

'Oh,' her tone drooped miserably. 'You sound so close. I thought—' Then she rallied gamely, 'I love you too – how's himself?'

'On the dole.'

'Who is she?'

'Dole is unemployment insurance – welfare—' He sought the American equivalent. 'I mean he is temporarily unemployed.'

'Great. Keep him that way. Did I tell you I love you, I forget?'

'Wake up. Shake yourself. I've got something to tell you.'

'I'm awake – well, almost anyway.'

'Samantha, what would happen if somebody dumped a million tons of 40,000 parts concentration of cadmium sulphide in an emulsion of aromatic Arabian crude into the Gulf Stream, say thirty nautical miles off Key West?'

'That's a freaky question, Nicholas. For three in the morning, that's a bomber.'

'What would happen?' he insisted.

'The crude would act as a transporting medium,' she was struggling to project a scenario through her sleepiness, 'it would spread out on the surface to a thickness of quarter of an inch or so, so you'd end up with a slick of a few thousand miles long and four or five hundred wide, and it would keep going.'

'What would be the results?'

'It would wipe out most of the marine life on the Bahamas and on the eastern seaboard of the States, no, correct that – it would wipe out all marine life, that includes the spawning grounds of the tuna, the freshwater eels and the sperm whale, and it would contaminate—' she was coming fully awake now, and a stirring of horror altered her tone. 'You're macabre, Nicholas, what a sick thing to think about, especially at three in the morning.'

'Human life?' he asked.

'Yes, there would be heavy loss,' she said. 'As sulphide, it would be readily absorbed and in that concentration it would be poisonous on contact, fishermen, vacationers, anybody who walked on a contaminated beach.' She was truly beginning to realize the enormity of it. 'A large part of the population of the cities on the east coast – Nicholas, it could amount to hundreds of thousands of human beings, and if it was carried beyond America on the Gulf Stream, the Newfoundland Banks, Iceland, the North Sea, it would poison the cod fisheries, it would kill everything, man, fish, bird and animal. Then the tail of the Gulf Stream twists around the British Isles and the north continent of Europe – but why are you asking me this, what kind of crazy guessing game is this, Nicholas?'

'Christy Marine has signed a ten-year contract to carry one million ton loads of crude from the El Barras field on the South Arabian Gulf to the Orient Amex refinery in Galveston. The El Barras crude has a cadmium sulphide constituent of between 2,000 and 40,000 parts per million.'

Now there was trembling outrage in her voice as she whispered, 'A million tons! That's some sort of genocide, Nicholas, there has probably never been a more deadly cargo in the history of seafaring.'

'In a few weeks' time *Golden Dawn* will run down her ways at St Nazaire – and when she does, the seeds of catastrophe will be sewn upon the oceans.'

'Her route from the Arabian Gulf takes her around Good Hope.'

'One of the most dangerous seas in the world, the home of the hundred-year wave,' Nicholas agreed.

'Then across the southern Atlantic—'

'— and into the bottle-neck of the Gulf Stream between Key West and Cuba, into the Devil's Triangle, the breeding ground of the hurricanes—'

'You can't let them do it, Nicholas,' she said quietly. 'You just have to stop them.'

'It won't be easy, but I'll be working hard on it this side, there are a dozen tricks I am going to try, but you have to take over on your side,' he told her. 'Samantha, you go get Tom Parker. Get him out of bed, if necessary. He has to hit Washington with the news, hit all the media – television, radio and the press. A confrontation with Orient Amex, challenge them to make a statement.'

Samantha picked up the line he was taking. 'We'll get the Green-Peacers to picket the Orient Amex refinery in Galveston, the one which will process the cadmium crudes. We'll have every environmental agency in the country at work – we'll raise a stink like that of a million corpses,' she promised.

'Fine,' he said. 'You do all that, but don't forget to get your chubby little backside across here for the launching of *Sea Witch*.'

'Chubby obese, or chubby nice?' she demanded.

'Chubby beautiful,' he grinned. 'And I'll have room service ready to send up the food, in a front-end loader.'


Nicholas sat over the telephone for the rest of that day, having his meals brought up to the suite, while he worked systematically down the long list of names he had drawn up with the help of the tape-recording of Lazarus' report.

The list began with all those who it seemed had loaned capital to Christy Marine for the construction of *Golden Dawn*, and then went on to those who had written lines of insurance on the hull, and on the pollution cover for the tanker.

Nicholas dared not be too specific in the summation he gave to each of them, he did not want to give Duncan Alexander an opportunity to throw out a smoke-screen of libel actions against him. But in each case, Nicholas spoke to the top men, mostly men he knew well enough to use their christian names, and he said just enough to show that he knew the exact amount of their involvement with Christy Marine, to suggest they re-examine the whole project, especially with regard to *Golden Dawn*'s underwriting and to her contract of carriage with Orient Amex.

In the quiet intervals between each telephone call, or while a name was tracked down by a secretary, Nicholas sat over the Place Vendôme and carefully re-examined himself and his reasons for what he was doing.

It is so very easy for a man to attribute to himself the most noble motives. The sea had given Nicholas a wonderful life, and had rewarded him in wealth, reputation and achievement. Now it was time to repay part of that debt, to use some of that wealth to protect and guard the oceans, the way a prudent farmer cherishes his soil. It was a fine thought, but when he looked below its shining surface, he saw the shape and movement of less savoury creatures, like the shadows of shark and barracuda in the depths.

There was pride. *Golden Dawn* had been his creation, the culmination of a lifetime's work, it was going to be the laurel crown on his career. But it had been taken from him, and bastardized – and when it failed, when the whole marvellous concept collapsed in disaster and misery, Nicholas Berg's name would still be on it. The world would remember then that the whole grandiose design had originated with him.

There was pride, and then there was hatred. Duncan Alexander had taken his woman and child. Duncan Alexander had wrested his very life from him. Duncan Alexander was the enemy, and by Nicholas' rules, he must be fought with the same single-mindedness, with the same ruthlessness, as he did everything in his life.

Nicholas poured himself another cup of coffee and lit a cheroot; brooding alone in the magnificence of his suite, he asked himself the question:

'If it had been another man in another ship who was going to transport the El Barras crudes – would I have opposed him so bitterly?'

The question needed no formal reply. Duncan Alexander was the enemy.

Nicholas picked up the telephone, and placed the call he had been delaying. He did not need to look in the red calf-bound notebook for the number of the house in Eaton Square.

'Mrs Chantelle Alexander, please.'

'I am sorry, sir. Mrs Alexander is at Cap Ferrat.'

'Of course,' he muttered. 'Thank you.'

'Do you want the number?'

'That's all right, I have it.' He had lost track of time. He dialled again, this time down to the Mediterranean coast.

'This is the residence of Mrs Alexander. Her son Peter Berg speaking.'

Nicholas felt the rush of emotion through his blood, so that it burned his cheeks and stung his eyes.

'Hello, my boy.' Even in his own ears his voice sounded stilted, perhaps pompous.

'Father,' undisguised delight. 'Dad, how are you – sir? Did you get my letters?'

'No, I didn't, where did you send them?'

'The flat – in Queens Gate.'

'I haven't been back there for,' Nicholas thought, 'for nearly a month.'

'I got your cards, Dad, the one from Bermuda and the one from Florida. I just wrote to tell you—' and there was a recital of schoolboy triumphs and disasters.

'That's tremendous, Peter. I'm really proud.'

Nicholas imagined the face of his son as he listened, and his heart was squeezed – by guilt, that he could do so little, could give him so little of his time, squeezed by longing for what he had lost. For it was only at times such as these that he could admit how much he missed his son.

'That's great, Peter—' The boy was trying to tell it all at the same time, gabbling out the news he had stored so carefully, flitting from subject to subject, as one thing reminded him of another. Then, of course, the inevitable question:

'When can I come to you, Dad?'

'I'll have to arrange that with your mother, Peter. But it will be soon. I promise you that.' Let's get away from that, Nick thought, desperately. 'How is *Apache*? Have you raced her yet these holidays?'

'Oh yes, Mother let me have a new set of Terylene sails, in red and yellow. I raced her yesterday.' *Apache* had not actually been placed first in the event, but Nicholas gained the impression that the blame lay not on her skipper but rather on the vagaries of the wind, the unsporting behaviour of the other competitors who bumped when they had the weather gauge, and finally the starter who had wanted to disqualify *Apache* for beating the gun.

'But,' Peter went on, 'I'm racing again on Saturday morning—'

'Peter, where is your mother?'

'She's down at the boathouse.'

'Can you put this call through there? I must speak to her, Peter.'

'Of course.' The disappointment in the child's voice was almost completely disguised. 'Hey, Dad. You promised, didn't you. It will be soon?'

'I promised.'

'Cheerio, sir.'

There was a clicking and humming on the line and then suddenly her voice, with its marvellous timbre and serenity.

*'C'est Chantelle Alexander qui parle.'*

*'C'est Nicholas ici.'*

'Oh, my dear. How good to hear your voice. How are you?'

'Are you alone?'

'No, I have friends lunching with me. The Contessa is here with his new boyfriend, a matador no less!'

The 'Contessa' was an outrageously camp and wealthy homosexual who danced at Chantelle's court. Nicholas could imagine the scene on the wide paved terrace, screened from the cliffs above by the sighing pines and the rococo pink boathouse with its turrets and rusty-coloured tiles. There would be gay and brilliant company under the colourful umbrellas.

'Pierre and Mimi sailed across from Cannes for the day.' Pierre was the son of the largest manufacturer of civil and military jet aircraft in Europe. 'And Robert—'

Below the terrace was the private jetty and small beautifully equipped yacht basin. Her visitors would have moored their craft there, the bare masts nodding lazily against the sky and the small Mediterranean-blue wavelets lapping the stone jetty. Nicholas could hear the laughter and the tinkle of glasses in the background, and he cut short the recital of the guest list.

'Is Duncan there?'

'No, he's still in London – he won't be out until next week.'

'I have news. Can you get up to Paris?'

'It's impossible, Nicky.' Strange how the pet name did not jar from her. 'I must be at Monte Carlo tomorrow, I'm helping Grace with the Spring Charity—'

'It's important, Chantelle.'

'Then there's Peter. I don't like to leave him. Can't you come here? There is a direct flight at nine tomorrow. I'll get rid of the house guests so we can talk in private.'

He thought quickly, then, 'All right, will you book me a suite at the Negresco?'

'Don't be silly, Nicky. We've thirteen perfectly good bedrooms here – we are both civilized people and Peter would love to see you, you know that.'


The Côte d'Azur was revelling in a freakish burst of early spring weather when Nicholas came down the boarding ladder at Nice Airport, and Peter was waiting for him at the boundary fence, hopping up and down and waving both hands above his head like a semaphore signaller. But when Nicholas came through the gate he regained his composure and shook hands formally.

'It's jolly good to see you, Dad.'

'I swear you've grown six inches,' said Nicholas, and on impulse stooped and hugged the child. For a moment they clung to each other, and it was Peter who pulled away first. Both of them were embarrassed by that display of affection for a moment, then quite deliberately Nicholas placed his hand on Peter's shoulder and squeezed.

'Where is the car?'

He kept his hand on the child's shoulder as they crossed the airport foyer, and as Peter became more accustomed to this unusual gesture of affection, so he pressed closer to his father, and seemed to swell with pride.

Characteristically, Nicholas wondered what had changed about him that made it easier for him to act naturally towards those he loved. The answer was obvious, it was Samantha Silver who had taught him to let go.

'Let go, Nicholas.' He could almost hear her voice now.

The chauffeur was new, a silent unobtrusive man, and there were only the two of them in the back seat of the Rolls on the drive back through Nice, and along the coast road.

'Mother has gone across to the Palace. She won't be back until dinner time.

'Yes, she told me. We've got the day to ourselves,' Nicholas grinned, as the chauffeur turned in through the electric gates and white columns that guarded the entrance to the estate. 'What are we going to do?'

They swam and they played tennis and took Peter's Arrowhead-class yacht *Apache* on a long reach up the coast as far as Menton and then raced back, gull-winged and spinnaker set on the wind with the spray kicking up over the bows and flicking into their faces. They laughed a lot and they talked even more, and while Nicholas changed for dinner, he found himself caught up in the almost post-coital melancholy of too much happiness – happiness that was transitory and soon must end. He tried to push the sadness aside, but it persisted as he dressed in a white silk roll-neck and double-breasted blazer and went down to the terrace room.

Peter was there before him, early as a child on Christmas morning, his hair still wet and slicked down from the shower and his face glowing pinkly from the sun and happiness.

'Can I pour you a drink, Dad?' he asked eagerly, already hovering over the silver drinks tray.

'Leave a little in the bottle,' Nicholas cautioned him, not wanting to deny him the pleasure of performing this grown-up service, but with a healthy respect for the elephantine tots that Peter dispensed in a sense of misplaced generosity.

He tasted the drink cautiously, gasped, and added more soda. 'That's fine,' he said, Peter looked proud, and at that moment Chantelle came down the wide staircase into the room.

Nicholas found it impossible not to stare. Was it possible she had grown more lovely since their last meeting, or had she merely taken special pains this evening?

She was dressed in ivory silk, woven gossamer fine, so it floated about her body as she moved, and as she crossed the last ruddy glow of the dying day that came in from the french windows of the terrace, the light struck through the sheer material and put the dainty line of her legs into momentary silhouette. Closer to him, he saw the silk was embroidered with the same thread, ivory on ivory, a marvellous understatement of elegance, and under it the shadowy outline of her breasts, those fine shapely breasts that he remembered so well, and the faint dusky rose suggestion of her nipples. He looked away quickly and she smiled.

'Nicky,' she said. 'I'm so sorry to have left you alone.'

'Peter and I have had a high old time,' he said.

She had emphasized the shape and size of her eyes, and the planes of the bone structure of her cheeks and jawline, with a subtlety that made it appear she wore no make-up, and her hair had a springing electrical fire to it, a rich glowing sable cloud about the small head. The honeyed ivory of her skin had tanned to the velvety texture of a cream-coloured rose petal across her bare shoulders and arms.

He had forgotten how relaxed and gracious she could be, and this magnificent building filled with its treasures standing in its pine forest high above the darkening ocean and the fairylights of the coast was her natural setting. She filled the huge room with a special glow and gaiety, and she and Peter shared an impish sense of fun that had them all laughing at the old well-remembered jokes.

Nicholas could not sustain his resentment, could not bring himself to dwell on her betrayal in this environment, so the laughter was easy and the warmth uncontrived. When they went through to the small informal dining-room, they sat at the table as they had done so often before; they seemed to be transported back in time to those happy almost forgotten years.

There were moments which might have jarred, but Chantelle's instinct was so certain that she could skirt delicately around these. She treated Nicholas as an honoured guest, not as the master of the house; instead she made Peter the host. 'Peter darling, will you carve for us?' and the boy's pride and importance was almost overwhelming, although the bird looked as though it had been caught in a combine-harvester by the time he had finished with it. Chantelle served food and wine, a chicken stuffed in Creole style and a petit Chablis, that had no special associations from the past; and the choice of music was Peter's. 'Music to develop ulcers by', as Nicholas remarked, aside, to Chantelle.

Peter fought a valiant rearguard action to delay the passage of time, but finally resigned himself when Nicholas told him, 'I'll come and see you up to bed.'

He waited while Peter cleaned his teeth with an impressive vigour that might have continued beyond midnight if Nicholas had not protested mildly. When at last he was installed between the sheets, Nicholas stooped over him and the boy wrapped both arms around his neck with a quiet desperation.

'I'm so happy,' he whispered against Nicholas' cheek and when they kissed he crushed Nicholas' lips painfully with his mouth – then, 'Wouldn't it be fabulous if we could be like this always?' he asked. 'If you didn't have to go away again, Dad?'


Chantelle had changed the wild music to the muted haunting melodies of Liszt, and as he came back into the room she was pouring cognac into a thin crystal balloon.

'Did he settle down?' she asked, and then answered herself immediately. 'He's exhausted, although he doesn't know it.'

She brought him the cognac and then turned away and went out through the doors on to the terrace. He followed her out, and they stood at the stone balustrade side by side. The air was clear but chill.

'It's beautiful,' she said. The moon paved a wide silver path across the surface of the sea. 'I always thought that the highway to my dreams.'

'Duncan,' he said. 'Let's talk about Duncan Alexander,' and she shivered slightly, folding her arms across her breasts and grasping her own naked shoulders.

'What do you want to know?'

'In what terms did you give him control of your shares?'

'As an agent, my personal agent.'

'With full discretion?'

She nodded, and he asked next, 'Did you have an escape clause? In what circumstances can you reclaim control?'

'The dissolution of marriage,' she said, and then shook her head. 'But I think I knew that no court would uphold the agreement if I wanted to change it. It's too Victorian. Anytime I want to I could simply apply to have the appointment of Duncan as my agent set aside.'

'Yes, I think you're right,' Nicholas agreed. 'But it might take a year or more, unless you could prove malafides, unless you could prove he deliberately betrayed the trust of agency.'

'Can I prove that, Nicky?' She turned to him now, lifting her face to him. 'Has he betrayed that trust?'

'I don't know yet,' Nicholas told her cautiously, and she cut in,

'I've made a terrible fool of myself, haven't I?' He kept silent, and she went on tremulously, 'I know there is no way I can apologize to you for – for what I did. There is no way that I can make it up to you, but believe me, Nicholas – please believe me when I tell you, I have never regretted anything so much in all my life.'

'It's past, Chantelle. It's over. There is no profit in looking back.'

'I don't think there is another man in the world who would do what you are doing now, who would repay deceit and betrayal with help and comfort. I just wanted to say that.'

She was standing very close to him now, and in the cool night he could feel the warmth of her flesh across the inches that separated them, and her perfume had a subtlely altered fragrance on that creamy skin. She always wore perfume so well, the same way she wore her clothes.

'It's getting cold,' he said brusquely, took her elbow and steered her back into the light, out of that dangerous intimacy. 'We still have a great deal to discuss.'

He paced the thick forest-green carpet, quickly establishing a beat as regular as that of a sentry, ten paces from the glass doors, passing in front of where she sat in the centre of the wide velvet couch, turning just before he reached the headless marble statue of a Greek athlete from antiquity that guarded the double oaken doors into the lobby, and then back in front of her again. As he paced, he told her in carefully prepared sequence all that he had learned from Lazarus.

She sat like a bird on the point of flight, turning her head to watch him, those huge dark eyes seeming to swell larger as she listened.

It was not necessary to explain it to her in layman's language, she was Arthur Christy's daughter, she understood when he told her how he suspected that Duncan Alexander had been forced to self-insure the hull of *Golden Dawn* and how he had used Christy stock to buy re-insurance, stock that he had probably already pledged to finance construction of the vessel.

Nicholas reconstructed the whole inverted pyramid of Duncan Alexander's machinations for her to examine, and almost immediately she saw how vulnerable, how unstable it was.

'Are you certain of all this?' she whispered, and her face was drained of all its lustrous rose tints.

He shook his head. 'I've reconstructed the Tyrannosaurus from a jawbone,' he admitted frankly. 'The shape of it might be a little different, but one thing I am certain of is that it's a big and dangerous beast.'

'Duncan could destroy Christy Marine,' she whispered again. 'Completely!' She looked around slowly, at the house – at the room and its treasures, the symbols of her life. 'He has risked everything that is mine, and Peter's.'

Nicholas did not reply, but he stopped in front of her and watched her carefully as she absorbed the enormity of it all.

He saw outrage turn slowly to confusion, to fear and finally to terror. He had never seen her even afraid before – but now, faced with the prospect of being stripped naked of the armour which had always protected her, she was like a lost animal, he could even see that flutter of her heart under the pale swelling flesh of her bosom, and she shivered again.

'Could he lose everything, Nicholas? He couldn't, could he?' She wanted assurance, but he could not give it to her, all he could give her was pity. Pity was the one emotion, probably the only one, she had never aroused in him, not once in all the years he had known her.

'What can I do, Nicholas?' she pleaded. 'Please help me. Oh God, what must I do?'

'You can stop Duncan launching *Golden Dawn* – until the hull and propulsion has been modified, until it has been properly surveyed and underwritten – and until you have taken full control of Christy Marine out of his hands again.' And his voice was gentle, filled with his compassion as he told her.

'That's enough for one day, Chantelle. If we go on now, we will begin chasing our tails. Tonight you know what could happen, tomorrow we will discuss how we can prevent it. Have you a Valium?'

She shook her head. 'I've never used drugs to hide from things.' It was true, he knew, that she had never lacked courage. 'How much longer can you stay?'

'I have a seat on the eleven o'clock plane. I have to be back in London by tomorrow night – we'll have time tomorrow morning.'


The guest suite opened on to the second-floor balcony which ran along the entire front of the building overlooking the sea and the private harbour.

The five main bedrooms all opened on to this balcony, an arrangement from fifty years previously when internal security against kidnapping and forcible entry had been of no importance.

Nicholas determined to speak to Chantelle about that in the morning. Peter was an obvious target for extortion, and he felt the goose bumps of horror rise on his arms as he imagined his son in the hands of those degenerate monsters who were everywhere allowed to strike and destroy with impunity. There was a price to pay these days for being rich and successful. The smell of it attracted the hyenas and vultures. Peter must be better protected, he decided.

In the sitting-room, there was a well-stocked liquor cabinet concealed behind mirrors, nothing so obvious and resoundingly middle-class as a private bar. The daily papers, in English, French and German were set out on the television table, *France Soir*, *The Times*, *Allgemeine Zeitung*, with even an airmail version of the *New York Times*.

Nicholas flipped open *The Times* and glanced quickly at the closing prices. Christy Marine common stock was at £5·32p, up 15p on yesterday's prices. The market had not sniffed corruption – yet.

He pulled off his silk roll-neck, and even though he had bathed three hours previously, the tension had left his skin feeling itchy and unclean. The bathroom had been lavishly redecorated in green onyx panels and the fittings were eighteen-carat gold, in the shape of dolphins. Steaming water gushed from their gaping mouths at a touch. It could have been vulgar, but Chantelle's unerring touch steered it into Persian opulence instead.

He showered, turning the setting high so that the stinging needles of water scalded away his fatigue and the feeling of being unclean. There were half a dozen thick white terry towelling robes in the glass-fronted warming cupboard, and he selected one and went through into the bedroom, belting it around his naked waist. In his briefcase there was a draft of the agreement of sale of Ocean Salvage and Towage to the Sheikhs. James Teacher and his gang of bright young lawyers had read it, and made a thick sheaf of notes. Nicholas must study these before tomorrow evening when he met them in London.

He took the papers from his case and carried them through into the sitting-room, glancing at the top page before dropping them carelessly on to the low coffee table while he went to pour himself a small whisky, heavily diluted. He brought the drink back with him and sprawled into the deep leather armchair, picked up the papers and began to work.

He became aware of her perfume first, and felt his blood quicken uncontrollably at the fragrance, and the papers rustled in his hand.

Slowly he lifted his head. She had come in utter silence on small bare feet. She had removed all her jewellery and had let down her hair brushing it out on to her shoulders.

It made her seem younger, more vulnerable, and the gown she wore was cuffed and collared in fine soft lace. She moved slowly towards his chair, timorous and for once uncertain, the eyes huge and dark and haunted, and when he rose from the armchair, she stopped and one hand went to her throat.

'Nicholas,' she whispered. 'I'm so afraid, and so alone.' She moved a step closer, and saw his eyes shift, his lips harden, and she stopped instantly.

'Please,' she pleaded softly, 'don't send me away, Nicky. Not tonight, not yet. I'm afraid to be alone – please.'

He knew then that this had been going to happen, he had hidden the certainty of it from himself all that evening, but now it was upon him, and he could do nothing to avoid it. It was as though he had lost the will to resist, as though he stood mesmerized, his resolve softening and melting like wax in the candle flame of her beauty, of the passions which she commanded so skilfully, and his thoughts lost coherence, began to tumble and swirl like storm surf breaking on rock.

She recognized the exact instant when it happened to him, and she came forward silently, with small gliding footsteps, not making the mistake of speaking again and pressed her face to his bare chest framed in the collar of his robe. The thick curling hair was springing over hard flat muscle, and she flared her nostrils at the clean virile animal smell of his skin.

He was still resisting, standing stiffly with his hands hanging at his sides. Oh, she knew him so well. The terrible conflict he must suffer before he could be made to act against that iron code of his own. Oh, she knew him, knew that he was a sexual and physical an animal as she was herself, that he was the only man who had ever been able to match her appetites. She knew the defences he had erected about himself, the fortressing of his passions, the controls and repressions, but she knew so well how to subvert these elaborate defences, she knew exactly what to do and what to say, how to move and touch. As she began now, she found the deliberate act of breaking down his resistance excited her so swiftly that it was pain almost, agony almost, and it required all her own control not to advance too swiftly for him, to control the shaking of her legs and the pumping of her lungs, to play still the hurt and bewildered and frightened child, using his kindness, the sense of chivalry which would not allow him to send her away, in such obvious distress.

Oh God, how her body burned, her stomach cramped with the strength of her wanting, her breasts felt swollen and so sensitive that the contact of silk and lace was almost too painfully abrasive to bear.

'Oh Nicky, please – just for a moment. Just once, hold me. Please, I cannot go on alone. Just for a moment, please.'

She felt him lift his hands, felt the fingers on her shoulders, and the terrible pain of wanting was too much to bear, she could not control it – she cried out, it was a soft little whimper, but the force of it shook her body, and immediately she felt his reaction. Her timing had been immaculate, her natural womanly cunning had guided her. His fingers on her shoulders had been gentle and kindly, but now they hooked cruelly into her flesh.

His back arched involuntarily, his breath drummed from his chest under her ear, a single agonized exhalation like that of a boxer taking a heavy body punch. She felt his every muscle come taut, and she knew again the frightening power, the delirious giddy power she could still wield. Then, at last, joyously, almost fearfully, she experienced the great lordly lift and thrust of his loins – as though the whole world had moved and shifted about her.

She cried out again, fiercely, for now she could slip the hounds she had held so short upon the leash, she could let them run and hunt again. They had been too long denied, but now there was no longer need for care and restraint.

She knew exactly how to hunt him beyond the frontiers of reason, to course him like a flying stag, and his fingers tangled frantically in the foaming lace at her throat as he tried to free her tight swollen breasts. She cried out a third time, and with a single movement jerked open the fastening at his waist, exposing the full hard lean length of his body, and her hands were as frantic as his.

'Oh, sweet God, you're so hard and strong – oh sweet God, I've missed you so.'

There was time later for all the refinements and nuances of love, but now her need was too cruel and demanding to be denied another moment. It had to happen this instant before she died of the lack.

Nicholas rose slowly towards the surface of sleep, aware of a brooding sense of regret. Just before he reached consciousness, a dream image formed in his sleep-starved brain, he relived a moment from the distant past. A fragment of time, recaptured so vividly as to seem whole and perfect. Long ago he had picked a deep-sea trumpet shell at five fathoms from the oceanic wall of the coral reef beyond the Anse Baudoin lagoon of Praslin Island. It was the size of a ripe coconut and once again he found himself holding the shell in both cupped hands gazing into the narrow oval opening, around which the weed-furred and barnacle-encrusted exterior changed dramatically, flaring into the pouting lips and exposing the inner mother-of-pearl surfaces that were slippery to the touch, a glossy satin sheen, pale translucent pink, folded and convoluted upon themselves, shading darker into fleshy crimsons and wine purples as the passage narrowed and sank away into the mysterious lustrous depths of the shell.

Then abruptly, the dream image changed in his mind. The protected opening in the trumpet shell expanded, articulating on jaw-hinges and he was gaping into the deep and terrible maw of some great predatory sea-creature, lined with multiple rows of serrated triangular teeth – sharklike, terrifying, so he cried out in half sleep, startling himself awake, and he rolled quickly on to his side and raised himself on one elbow. Her perfume still lingered on his skin, mingled with the smell of his own sweat, but the bed beside him was empty, though warm and redolent with the memory of her body.

Across the room, the early sun struck a long sliver of light through a narrow chink in the curtains. It looked like a blade, a golden blade. It reminded him instantly of Samantha Silver. He saw her again wearing sunlight like a cloak, barefoot in the sand – and it seemed that the blade of sunlight was being driven up slowly under his ribs.

He swung his feet off the wide bed and padded softly across to that gold and onyx bathroom. There was a dull ache of sleeplessness and remorse behind his eyes and as he ran hot water from the dolphins' mouth into the basin, he looked at himself in the mirror although the steam slowly clouded the image of his own face. There were dark smears below his eyes and his features were gaunt, harsh angles of bone beneath drawn skin.

'You bastard,' he whispered at the shadowy face in the mirror. 'You bloody bastard.'

They were waiting breakfast for him, in the sunlight on the terrace under the gaily coloured umbrellas. Peter had preserved the mood of the previous evening, and he ran laughing to meet Nicholas.

'Dad, hey Dad.' He seized Nicholas' hand and led him to the table.

Chantelle wore a long loose housegown, and her hair was down on her shoulders, so soft that it stirred like spun silk in even that whisper of breeze. It was calculated, Chantelle did nothing by chance; the intimately elegant attire and the loose fall of her hair set the mood of domesticity – and Nicholas found himself resisting it fiercely.

Peter sensed his father's change in mood with an intuitive understanding beyond his years, and his dismay was a palpable thing, the hurt and reproach in his eyes as he looked at Nicholas; and then the chatter dried on his lips and he bent his head studiously over his plate and ate in silence.

Nicholas deliberately refused the festival array of food, took only a cup of coffee, and lit a cheroot, without asking Chantelle's permission, knowing how she would resent that. He waited in silence and as soon as Peter had eaten he said:

'I'd like to speak to your mother, Peter.'

The boy stood obediently.

'Will I see you before you leave, sir?'

'Yes.' Nicholas felt his heart wrung again. 'Of course.'

'We could sail again?'

'I'm sorry, my boy. We won't have time. Not today.'

'Very well, sir' Peter walked to the end of the terrace, very erect and dignified, then suddenly he began to run, taking the steps down two at a time, and he fled into the pine forest beyond the boathouse as though pursued, feet flying and arms pumping wildly.

'He needs you, Nicky,' said Chantelle softly.

'You should have thought about that two years ago.'

She poured fresh coffee into his cup. 'Both of us have been stupid – all right, worse than that. We've been wicked. I have had my Duncan, and you have had that American child.'

'Don't make me angry now,' he warned her softly. 'You've done enough for one day.'

'It's as simple as this, Nicholas. I love you, I have always loved you – God, since I was a gawky schoolgirl,' she had never been that, but Nicholas let it pass, 'since I saw you that first day on the bridge of old *Golden Eagle*, the dashing ship's captain—'

'Chantelle. All we have to discuss is *Golden Dawn* and Christy Marine.'

'No, Nicholas. We were born for each other, Daddy saw that immediately, we both knew it at the same time – it was only a madness, a crazy whim that made me doubt it for a moment.'

'Stop it, Chantelle.'

'Duncan was a stupid mistake. But it's unimportant—'

'No, it's not unimportant. It changed everything. It can never be the same again, besides—'

'Besides, what? Nicky, what were you going to say?'

'Besides, I am building myself another life now. With another very different person.'

'Oh God, Nicky, you aren't serious?' She laughed then, genuine amusement, clapping her hands delightedly. 'My dear, she's young enough to be your daughter. It's the forty syndrome, the Lolita complex.' Then she saw his real anger, and she was quick, retrieving the situation neatly, aware that she had carried it too far.

'I'm sorry, Nicky, I should never have said that.' She paused, and then went on. 'I will say she's a pretty little thing, and I'm sure she's sweet – Peter liked her.' She damned Samantha with light condescension, and then dismissed her as though she were merely a childlike prank of Nicholas', a light and passing folly of no real significance.

'I understand, Nicholas, truly I do. However, when you are ready, as you will be soon, then Peter and I and Christy Marine are waiting for you still. This is your world, Nicholas.' She made a gesture which embraced it all. 'This is your world, you will never really leave it.'

'You are wrong, Chantelle.'

'No.' She shook her head. 'I am very seldom wrong, and on this I cannot be wrong. Last night proved that, it is still there – every bit of it. But let's discuss the other thing now, *Golden Dawn* and Christy Marine.'


Chantelle Alexander lifted her face to the sky and watched the big silver bird fly. It climbed nose high, glinting in sunlight, twin trails of dark unconsumed fuel spinning out behind it as the engines howled under full thrust. With the wind in this quarter, the extended centreline of the main Nice runway brought it out over Cap Ferrat.

Beside Chantelle, only an inch or two shorter than she was, Peter stood and watched it also and she took his arm, tucking her small dainty hand into the crook of his elbow.

'He stayed such a short time,' Peter said, and overhead the big airbus turned steeply on to its crosswind leg.

'We will have him with us again soon,' Chantelle promised, and then she went on. 'Where were you, Peter? We hunted all over when it was time for Daddy to go?'

'I was in the forest,' he said evasively. He had heard them calling, but Peter had hidden in the secret place, the smuggler's cleft in the yellow rock of the cliff; he would have killed himself rather than let Nicholas Berg see him weeping.

'Wouldn't it be lovely if it was like the old times again?' Chantelle asked softly, and the boy stirred beside her, but unable to take his gaze from the aircraft, 'Just the three of us again?'

'Without Uncle Duncan?' he asked incredulously, and high above them the aircraft, with a last twinkle of sunlight, dove deeply into the banks of cumulus cloud that buttressed the northern sky. Peter turned at last to face her.

'Without Uncle Duncan,' he demanded again, 'but that's impossible.'

'Not if you help me, darling.' She took his face in her cupped hands. 'You will help me, won't you?' she asked, and he nodded once, a sharply incisive gesture of assent; she leaned forward and kissed him tenderly on the forehead.

'That's my man,' she whispered.

'Mr Alexander is not available. May I take a message?'

'This is Mrs Alexander. Tell my husband that it's urgent.'

'Oh, I'm terribly sorry, Mrs Alexander.' The secretary's voice changed instantly, cool caution becoming effusive servility. 'I didn't recognize your voice. The line is dreadful. Mr Alexander will speak to you directly.'

Chantelle waited, staring impatiently from the study windows. The weather had changed in the middle of the morning with the cold front sweeping down off the mountains, and now icy wind and rain battered at the windows.

'Chantelle, my dear,' the rich glossy voice that had once so dazzled her, 'is this my call to you?'

'It's mine, Duncan. I must speak to you urgently.'

'Good,' he agreed with her. 'I wanted to speak to you also. Things are happening swiftly here. It's necessary for you to come up to St Nazaire next Tuesday, instead of my joining you at Cap Ferrat.'

'Duncan—'

But he went on over her protest, his voice as full of self-confidence, as ebullient as she had not heard it in over a year.

'I have been able to save almost four weeks on *Golden Dawn*.'

'Duncan, listen to me.'

'We will be able to launch on Tuesday. It will be a make-shift ceremony, I'm afraid, at such short notice.' He was inordinately proud of his own achievement. It annoyed her to hear him. 'What I have arranged is that the pod tanks will be delivered direct to the Gulf from the Japanese yards. They are towing them in their ballast with four American tugs. I will launch the hull here, with workmen still aboard her, and they will finish her off at sea during the passage around Good Hope, in time for her to take on her tanks and cargo at El Barras. We'll save nearly seven and a half million—'

'Duncan!' Chantelle tried again, and this time something in her tone stopped him.

'What is it?'

'This can't wait until Tuesday, I want to see you right away.'

'That's impossible,' he laughed, lightly, confidently. 'It's only five days.'

'Five days is too long.'

'Tell me now,' he invited. 'What is it?'

'All right,' she said deliberately, and the vicious streak of Persian cruelty was in her voice. 'I'll tell you. I want a divorce, Duncan, and I want control of my shares in Christy Marine again.'

There was a long, hissing crackling silence on the line, and she waited, the way the cat waits for the first movement of the crippled mouse.

'This is very sudden.' His voice had changed completely, it was bleak and flat, lacking any timbre or resonance.

'We both know it is not,' she contradicted him.

'You have no grounds.' There was a thin edge of fear now. 'Divorce isn't quite as easy as that, Chantelle.'

'How is this for grounds, Duncan?' she asked, and there was a spiteful sting in her voice now. 'If you aren't here by noon tomorrow, then my auditors will be in Leadenhall Street and there will be an urgent order before the courts—'

She did not have to go on, he spoke across her and there was a note of panic in his voice. She had never heard it before. He said, 'You are right. We do have to talk right away.' Then he was silent again, collecting himself, and his voice was once more calm and careful when he went on, 'I can charter a Falcon and be at Nice before midday. Will that do?'

'I'll have the car meet you,' she said, and broke the connection with one finger. She held the bar down for a second, then lifted her finger.

'I want to place an international call,' she said in her fluent rippling French when the operator answered. 'I do not know the number, but it is person to person. Doctor Samantha Silver at the University of Miami.'

'There is a delay of more than two hours, madame.'

'*J'attendrai*,' she said, and replaced the receiver.


The Bank of the East is in Curzon Street, almost opposite the White Elephant Club. It has a narrow frontage of bronze and marble and glass, and Nicholas had been there, with his lawyers, since ten o'clock that morning. He was learning at first hand the leisurely age-old ritual of oriental bargaining.

He was selling Ocean Salvage, plus two years of his future labour – and even for seven million dollars he was beginning to wonder if it was worth it – and it was not a certain seven millions either. The words tripped lightly, the figures seemed to have no substance in this setting. The only constant was the figure of the Prince himself, seated on the low couch, in a Savile Row suit but with the fine white cotton and gold-corded headdress framing his dark handsome features with theatrical dash.

Beyond him moved a shadowy, ever-changing background of unctuous whispering figures. Every time that Nicholas believed that a point had been definitely agreed, another rose-pink or acid-yellow Rolls-Royce with Arabic script number-plates would deposit three or four more dark-featured Arabs at the front doors and they would hurry through to kiss the Prince on his forehead, on the bridge of nose and on the back of his hand, and the hushed discussion would begin all over again with the newcomers picking up at the point they had been an hour previously.

James Teacher showed no impatience, and he smiled and nodded and went through the ritual like an Arab born, sipping the little thimbles of treacly coffee and watching patiently for the interminable whisperings to be translated into English before making a measured counter proposal.

'We are doing fine, Mr Berg,' he assured Nicholas quietly. 'A few more days.'

Nicholas had a headache from the strong coffee and the Turkish tobacco smoke, and he found it difficult to concentrate. He kept worrying about

Samantha. For four days he had tried to contact her. He had to get out for a while and he excused himself to the Prince, and went down to the Enquiries Desk in the Bank's entrance hall and the girl told him,

'I'm sorry, sir, there is no reply to either of those numbers.'

'There must be,' Nicholas told her. One number was Samantha's shack at Key Biscayne and the other was her private number in her laboratory.

She shook her head. 'I've tried every hour.'

'Can you send a cable for me?'

'Of course, sir.'

She gave him a pad of forms and he wrote out the message.

'Please phone me urgently, reverse charge to—' he gave the number of the Queens Gate flat and James Teacher's rooms, then he thought with the pen poised, trying to find the words to express his concern, but there were none.

'I love you,' he wrote. 'I really do.'


Since Nicholas' midnight call to tell her of the carriage of cadrich crude petroleum, Samantha Silver had been caught up in a kaleidoscope whirl of time and events.

After a series of meetings with the leaders of the Green-Peacers, and other conservation bodies in an effort to publicize and oppose this new threat to the oceans, she and Tom Parker had flown to Washington and met with a deputy director of the Environmental Protection Agency and with two young senators who spearheaded the conservation lobby – but their efforts to go further had been frustrated by the granite walls of big oil interest. Even usually cooperative sources had been wary of condemning or speaking out against Orient Amex's new carbon-cracking technology. As one thirty-year-old Democrat senator had pointed out, 'It's tough to try and take a shot at something that's going to increase the fossil fuel yield by fifty per cent.'

'That's not what we are shooting at,' Samantha had flared, bitter with fatigue and frustration. 'It's this irresponsible method of carrying the cadrich through sensitive and highly vulnerable seaways we are trying to prevent.' But when she presented the scenario she had worked out, picturing the effects on the north Atlantic deluged with a million tons of toxic crude, she saw the disbelief in the man's eyes and the condescending smile of the sane for the slightly demented.

'Oh God, why is common sense the hardest thing in the world to sell?' she had lamented.

She and Tom had gone on to meet the leaders of Green-Peace in the north, and in the west, and they had given advice and promises of support. The Californian Chapter counselled physical intervention as a last resort, as some of their members had successfully interposed small craft between the Russian whalers and the breeding Minkes they were hunting in the Californian Gulf.

In Galveston, they met the young Texans who would picket the Orient Amex refinery as soon as they were certain the ultra-tanker had entered the Gulf of Mexico.

However, none of their efforts were successful in provoking confrontation with Orient Amex. The big oil company simply ignored invitations to debate the charges on radio or television, and stone-walled questions from the media. It's hard to stir up interest in a one-sided argument, Samantha found.

They managed one local Texas television show, but without controversy to give it zip, the producer cut Samantha's time down to forty-five seconds, and then tried to date her for dinner.

The energy crisis, oil tankers and oil pollution were joyless subjects. Nobody had ever heard of cadmium pollution, the Cape of Good Hope was half a world away, a million tons was a meaningless figure, impossible to visualize, and it was all rather a bore.

The media let it drop flat on its face.

'We're just going to have to smoke those fat cats at Orient Amex out into the open,' Tom Parker growled angrily, 'and kick their arses blue for them. The only way we are going to do that is through Greenpeace.'

They had landed back at Miami International, exhausted and disappointed, but not yet despondent. 'Like the man said,' Samantha muttered grimly, as she threaded her gaudy van back into the city traffic flow, 'we have only just begun to fight.'

She had only a few hours to clean herself up and stretch out on the patchwork quilt before she had to dress again and race back to the airport. The Australian had already passed through customs and was looking lost and dejected in the terminal lobby.

'Hi, I'm Sam Silver.' She pushed away fatigue, and hoisted that brilliant golden smile like a flag.

His name was Dr Dennis O'Connor and he was top man in his field, doing fascinating and important work on the reef populations of Eastern Australian waters, and he had come a long way to talk to her and see her experiments.

'I didn't expect you to be so young.' She had signed her correspondence 'Doctor Silver' and he gave the standard reaction to her. Samantha was just tired and angry enough not to take it.

'And I'm a woman. You didn't expect that either,' she agreed. 'It's a crying bastard, isn't it? But then, I bet some of your best friends are young females.'

He was a dinky-die Aussie, and he loved it. He burst into an appreciative grin, and as they shook hands, he said, 'You are not going to believe this, but I like you just the way you are.'

He was tall and lean, sunburned and just a little grizzled at the temples, and within minutes they were friends, and the respect with which he viewed her work confirmed that.

The Australian had brought with him, in an oxygenated container, five thousand live specimens of *E. digitalis*, the common Australian sea water snail, for inclusion in Samantha's experimentation. He had selected these animals for their abundance and their importance in the ecology of the Australian inshore waters, and the two of them were soon so absorbed in the application of Samantha's techniques to this new creature that when her assistant stuck her head through and yelled, 'Hey, Sam, there's a call for you,' she shouted back, 'Take a message. If they're lucky I'll call them back.'

'It's international, person to person!' and Samantha's pulse raced; instantly forgotten was the host of spiral-coned sea snails.

'Nicholas!' she shouted happily, spilled half a pint of sea water down the Australian's trouser leg and ran wildly to the small cubicle at the end of the laboratory.

She was breathless with excitement as she snatched up the receiver and she pressed one hand against her heart to stop it thumping.

'Is that Doctor Silver?'

'Yes! It's me.' Then correcting her grammar, 'It is she!'

'Go ahead, please,' said the operator, and there was a click and pulse on the line as it came alive.

'Nicholas!' she exulted. 'Darling Nicholas, is that you?'

'No.' The voice was very clear and serene, as though the speaker stood beside her, and it was familiar, disconcertingly so, and for no good reason Samantha felt her heart shrink with dread.

'This is Chantelle Alexander, Peter's mother. We have met briefly.'

'Yes.' Samantha's voice was now small, and still breathless.

'I thought it would be kind to tell you in person, before you hear from other sources – that Nicholas and I have decided to remarry.'

Samantha sat down jerkily on the office stool.

'Are you there?' Chantelle asked after a moment.

'I don't believe you,' whispered Samantha.

'I'm sorry,' Chantelle told her gently. 'But there is Peter, you see, and we have rediscovered each other – discovered that we had never stopped loving each other.'

'Nicholas wouldn't—' her voice broke, and she could not go on.

'You must understand and forgive him, my dear,' Chantelle explained. 'After our divorce he was hurt and lonely. I'm sure he did not mean to take advantage of you.'

'But, but – we were supposed to, we were going to—'

'I know. Please believe me, this has not been easy for any of us. For all our sakes—'

'We had planned a whole life together.' Samantha shook her head wildly, and a thick skein of golden hair came loose and flopped into her face, she pushed it back with a combing gesture. 'I don't believe it, why didn't Nicholas tell me himself? I won't believe it until he tells me.'

Chantelle's voice was compassionate, gentle. 'I so wanted not to make it ugly for you, my child, but now what can I do but tell you that Nicholas spent last night in my house, in my bed, in my arms, where he truly belongs.'

It was almost miraculous, a physical thing, but sitting hunched on the hard round stool Samantha Silver felt her youth fall away from her, sloughed off like a glittering reptilian skin. She was left with the sensation of timelessness, possessed of all the suffering and sorrow of every woman who had lived before. She felt very old and wise and sad, and she lifted her fingers and touched her own cheek, mildly surprised to feel that the skin was not dried and withered like that of some ancient crone.

'I have already made the arrangements for a divorce from my present husband, and Nicholas will resume his position at the head of Christy Marine.'

It was true, Samantha knew then that it was true. There was no question, no doubt, and slowly she replaced the receiver of the telephone, and sat staring blankly at the bare wall of the cubicle. She did not cry, she felt as though she would never cry, nor laugh, again in her life.

Chantelle Alexander studied her husband carefully, trying to stand outside herself, and to see him dispassionately. She found it easier now that the giddy insanity had burned away.

He was a handsome man, tall and lean, with those carefully groomed metallic waves of coppery hair. Even the wrist that he shot from the crisp white cuff of his sleeve was covered with those fine gleaming hairs. She knew so well that even his lean chest was covered with thick golden curls, crisp and curly, as fresh lettuce leaves. She had never been attracted by smooth hairless men.

'May I smoke?' he asked, and she inclined her head. His voice had also attracted her from the first, deep and resonant, but with those high-bred accents, the gentle softening of the vowel sounds, the lazy drawling of consonants. The voice and the patrician manner were things that she had been trained to appreciate – and yet, under the mannered cultivated exterior was the flash of exciting wickedness, that showed in the wolfish white gleam of smile, and the sharp glittering grey steel of his gaze.

He lit the custom-made cigarette with the gold lighter she had given him – her very first gift, the night they had become lovers. Even now, the memory of it was piquant, and for a moment she felt the soft melting warmth in her lower belly and she stirred restlessly in her chair. There had been reason, and good reason for that madness, and even now it was over, she would never regret it.

It had been a period in her life which she had not been able to deny herself. The grand sweeping illicit passion, the last flush of her youth, the final careless autumn that preceded middle age. Another ordinary woman might have had to content herself with sweaty sordid gropings and grapplings in anonymous hotel bedrooms, but not Chantelle Christy. Her world was shaped by her own whims and desires, and, as she had told Nicholas, whatever she desired was her to take. Long ago, her father had taught her that there were special rules for Chantelle Christy, and the rules were those she made herself.

It had been marvellous, she shivered slightly at the lingering sensuality of those early days, but now it was over. During the past months she had been carefully comparing the two men. Her decision had not been lightly made.

She had watched Nicholas retrieve his life from the gulf of disaster. On his own, stripped naked of all but that invisible indefinable mantle of strength and determination, he had fought his way back out of the gulf. Strength and power had always moved her, but she had over the years grown accustomed to Nicholas. Familiarity had staled their relationship for her. But now her interlude with Duncan had freshened her view of him, and he had for her all the novel appeal of a new lover – yet with the proven values and qualities of long intimate acquaintance. Duncan Alexander was finished, Nicholas Berg was the future.

But, no, she would never regret this interlude in her life. It had been a time of rejuvenation, she would not even regret Nicholas' involvement with the pretty American child. Later, it would add a certain perverse spice to their own sexuality, she thought, and felt the shiver run down her thighs and the soft secret stirring of her flesh, like the opening of a petalled rosebud. Duncan had taught her many things, bizarre little tricks of arousal, made more poignant by being forbidden and wicked. Unfortunately Duncan relied almost entirely on the tricks, and not all of them had worked for her – the corners of her mouth turned down with distaste as she remembered; perhaps it was just that which had begun the curdling process.

No, Duncan Alexander had not been able to match her raw, elemental sexuality and soaring abandon. Only one man had ever been able to do that. Duncan had served a purpose, but now it was over. It might have dragged on a little longer, but Duncan Alexander had endangered Christy Marine. Never had she thought of that possibility; Christy Marine was a fact of her life, as vast and immutable as the heavens, but now the foundations of heaven were being shaken. His sexual attraction had staled, she might have forgiven him that, but not the other.

She became aware of Duncan's discomfort. He twisted sideways in his chair, crossing and uncrossing his long legs, and he rolled the cigarette between his fingers, studying the rising spiral of blue smoke to avoid the level, expressionless gaze of her dark fathomless eyes. She had been staring at him, but seeing the other man. Now, with an effort, she focused her full attention on him.

'Thank you for coming so promptly,' she said.

'It did seem rather urgent.' He smiled for the first time, glossy and urbane – but with fear down there in the cool grey eyes, and his tension was betrayed by the clenched sinew in the point of his jaw.

Looking closely, as she had not done for many months, she saw how he was fined down. The long tapered fingers were bony, and never still. There were new harder lines to his mouth, and a frown to the set of his eyes. The skin at the corners cracked like oil paint into hundreds of fine wrinkles that the deep brown snow-tan hid from a casual glance. Now he returned her scrutiny directly.

'From what you told me yesterday—'

She lifted her hand to stop him. 'That can wait. I merely wanted to impress you with the seriousness of what is happening. What is really of prime importance now is what you have done with control of my shares and those of the Trust.'

His hands went very still. 'What does that mean?'

'I want auditors, my appointed auditors, sent in—'

He shrugged. 'All this will take time, Chantelle, and I'm not certain that I'm ready to relinquish control.' He was very cool, very casual now and the fear was gone.

She felt a stir of relief, perhaps the horror story that Nicholas had told her was untrue, perhaps the danger was imaginary only. Christy Marine was so big, so invulnerable.

'Not just at the moment, anyway. You'd have to prove to me that doing so was in the best interest of the company and of the Trust.'

'I don't have to prove anything, to anyone,' she said flatly.

'This time you do. You have appointed me—'

'No court of law would uphold that agreement.'

'Perhaps not, Chantelle, but do you want to drag all this through the courts – at a time like this?'

'I'm not afraid, Duncan.' She stood up quickly, light on her feet as a dancer, the lovely legs in loose black silk trousers, soft flat shoes making her seem still smaller, a slim gold chain emphasizing the narrowness of the tiny waist. 'You know I'm afraid of nothing.' She stood over him, and pointed the accuser's finger. The nails tipped in scarlet the colour of fresh arterial blood. 'You should be the one to fear.'

'And precisely what is it you are accusing me of?'

And she told him, reeling off swiftly the lists of guarantees made by the Trust, the transfer of shares and the issues of new shares and guarantees within the Christy Marine group of subsidiaries, she listed the known layering of underwriting cover on *Golden Dawn* that Nicholas had unearthed.

'When my auditors have finished, Duncan darling, not only will the courts return control of Christy Marine to me, but they will probably sentence you to five years at hard labour. They take this sort of thing rather seriously, you know.'

He smiled. He actually smiled! She felt her fury seething to the surface and the set of her eyes altered, colour tinted the smooth pale olive of her cheeks.

'You dare to grin at me,' she hissed. 'I will break you for that.'

'No,' he shook his head. 'No, you won't.'

'Are you denying—' she snapped, but he cut her off with a raised hand, and a shake of that handsome arrogant head.

'I am denying nothing, my love. On the contrary, I am going to admit it – and more, much more.' He flicked the cigarette away, and it hissed sharply in the lapping blue wavelets of the yacht basin. While she stared at him, struck speechless, he let the silence play out like a skilled actor as he selected and lit another cigarette from the gold case.

'For some weeks now I have been fully aware that somebody was prying very deeply into my affairs and those of the company.' He blew a long blue feather of cigarette smoke, and cocked one eyebrow at her, a cynical mocking gesture which increased her fury, but left her feeling suddenly afraid and uncertain. 'It didn't take long to establish that the trace was coming from a little man in Monte Carlo who makes a living at financial and industrial espionage. Lazarus is good, excellent, the very best. I have used him myself, in fact it was I who introduced him to Nicholas Berg.' He chuckled then, shaking his head indulgently. 'The silly things we do sometimes. The connection was immediate. Berg and Lazarus. I have run my own check on what they have come up with and I estimate that even Lazarus could not have uncovered more than twenty-five per cent of the answers.' He leaned forward and suddenly his voice snapped with a new authority. 'You see, Chantelle dear, I am probably one of the best in the world myself. They could never have traced it all.'

'You are not denying then—' She heard the faltering tone in her own voice, and hated herself for it. He brushed her aside contemptuously.

'Be quiet, you silly little woman, and listen to me. I am going to tell you just how deeply you are in – I am going to explain to you, in terms that even you can understand, why you will not send in your auditors, why you will not fire me, and why you will do exactly what I tell you to do.'

He paused and stared into her eyes, a direct trial of strength which she could not meet. She was confused and uncertain, for once not in control of her own destiny. She dropped her eyes, and he nodded with satisfaction.

'Very well. Now listen. I have put it all – everything that is Christy Marine – it is all riding on *Golden Dawn*.'

Chantelle felt the earth turn giddily under her feet and the sudden roaring rush of blood in her ears. She stepped back and the stone parapet caught the back of her knees. She sat down heavily.

'What are you talking about?' she whispered. And he told her, in substantial detail, from the beginning, how it had worked out. From the laying of *Golden Dawn*'s keel in the times of vast tanker tonnage demand. 'My calculations were based on demand for tanker space two years ago, and on construction costs of that time.'

The energy crisis and collapse in demand for tankers had come with the vicious rise in inflation, bloating the costs of construction of *Golden Dawn* by more than double. Duncan had countered by altering the design of the gigantic tanker. He had reduced the four propulsion units to one, he had cut down the steel structuring of the hull reinforcement by twenty per cent, he had done away with elaborate safety functions and fail-safe systems designed by Nicholas Berg, and he had cut it too fine. He had forfeited the A1 Lloyd's rating, the mark of approval from the inspectors of that venerable body; without the insurance backing of that huge underwriting market, he had been forced to look elsewhere to find the cover to satisfy his financiers. The premiums had been crippling. He had to pledge Christy Marine stock, the Trust stock. Then the spiralling cost of production had overtaken him again and he needed money and more money. He had taken it where he could find it, at rates of interest that were demanded, and used more Christy stock as collateral.

Then the insurance cover had been insufficient to cover the huge increase in the cost of the ultra-tanker's hull.

'When luck runs out—' Duncan shrugged eloquently, and went on. 'I had to pledge more Christy stock, all of it. It's all at risk, Chantelle, every single piece of paper, even the shares we retrieved from your Nicholas – and even that wasn't enough. I have had to write cover through front companies, cover that is worthless. Then,' Duncan smiled again, relaxed and unruffled, almost as though he was enjoying himself, 'then, there was that awful fiasco when *Golden Adventurer* went up on the ice, and I had to find six million dollars to pay the salvage award. That was the last of it, I went out for everything then, all of it. The Trust, the whole of Christy Marine.'

'I'll break you,' she whispered. 'I'll smash you. I swear before God—'

'You don't understand, do you?' He shook his head sorrowfully, as though at an obtuse child. 'You cannot break me, without breaking Christy Marine and yourself. You are in it, Chantelle, much much deeper than I am. You have everything, every penny, this house, that emerald on your finger, the future of your brat – all of it is riding on *Golden Dawn*.'

'No.' She closed her eyes very tightly, and there was no colour in her cheeks now.

'Yes. I'm afraid it's yes,' he contradicted. 'I didn't plan it that way. I saw a profit of 200 millions in it, but we have been caught up in circumstances, I'm afraid.'

They were both silent, and Chantelle swayed slightly as the full enormity of it overwhelmed her.

'If you whistle up your hounds now, if you call in your axemen, there will be plenty for them to work on,' he laughed again, 'buckets of dung for us all to wallow in. And my backers will line up to cancel out, *Golden Dawn* will never run down her ways – she is not fully covered, as I explained to you. It all hangs on a single thread, Chantelle. If the launching of *Golden Dawn* is delayed now, delayed by a month – no, by a week even, it will all come tumbling down.'

'I'm going to be sick,' she whispered thickly.

'No, you are not.' He stood up and crossed quickly to her. Coldly he slapped her face, two hard open-handed back and forth blows, that snapped her head from side to side, leaving the livid marks of his fingers on her pale cheeks. It was the first time ever that a man had struck her, but she could not find the indignation to protest. She merely stared at him.

'Pull yourself together,' he snarled at her, and gripped her shoulders fiercely, shaking her as he went on. 'Listen to me. I have told you the worst that can happen. Now, I will tell you the best. If we stand together now, if you obey me implicitly, without question, I will pull off one of the greatest financial coups of the century for you. All it needs is one successful voyage by *Golden Dawn* and we are home free – a single voyage, a few short weeks, and I will have doubled your fortune.' She was staring at him, sickened and shaken to the core of her existence. 'I have signed an agreement of charter with Orient Amex, that will pull us out from under with a single voyage, and the day *Golden Dawn* anchors in Galveston roads and sends in her tank pods to discharge, I will have a dozen buyers for her.' He stepped back, and straightened the lapels of his jacket. 'Men are going to remember my name. In future when they talk of tankers, they are going to talk of Duncan Alexander.'

'I hate you,' she said softly. 'I truly hate you.'

'That is not important.' He waved it away. 'When it is over, I can afford to walk away – and you can afford to let me go. But not a moment before.'

'How much will you make from this, if it succeeds?' she asked, and she was recovering, her voice firmer.

'A great deal. A very great deal of money – but my real reward will be in reputation and achievement. After this, I will be a man who can write his own ticket.'

'For once, you will be able to stand comparison with Nicholas Berg. Is that it?' She saw she had scored immediately, and she pressed harder, trying to wound and destroy. 'But you and I both know it is not true. *Golden Dawn* was Nicholas' inspiration and he would not have had to descend to the cheat and sham—'

'My dear Chantelle—'

'You will never be, could never be the man Nicholas is.'

'Damn you.' Suddenly he was shaking with anger, and she was screaming at him.

'You're a cheat and a liar. For all your airs, you're still a cheap little barrow-boy at heart. You're small and shoddy—'

'I've beaten Nicholas Berg every time I've met him.'

'No, you haven't, Duncan. It was I who beat him for you—'

'I took you.'

'For a while,' she sneered. 'Just for a short fling, Duncan dear. But when he wanted me he took me right back again.'

'What do you mean by that?' he demanded.

'The night before last, Nicholas was here, and he loved me in a way you never could. I'm going back to him, and I'll tell the world why.'

'You bitch.'

'He is so strong, Duncan. Strong where you are weak.'

'And you are a whore.' He half turned away, and then paused. 'Just be at St Nazaire on Tuesday.' But she could see he was hurt, at last she had cut through the carapace and touched raw quick nerves.

'He loved me four times in one night. Duncan, magnificent soaring love. Did you ever do that?'

'I want you at St Nazaire, smiling at the creditors on Tuesday.'

'Even if you succeed with *Golden Dawn*, within six months Nicholas will have your job.'

'But until then you'll do exactly what I say.' Duncan braced himself, a visible effort, and began to walk away.

'You are going to be the loser, Duncan Alexander,' she screamed after him, her voice cracking shrilly with frustration and outrage. 'I will see to that – I swear it to you.'

He subdued the urge to run, and crossed the terrace, holding himself carefully erect, and the storm of her hatred and frustration burst around him.

'Go into the streets where you belong, into the gutter where I found you,' she screamed, and he went up the stone staircase and out of her sight. Now he could hurry, but he found his legs. were trembling under him, his breath was ragged and broken, and there was a tight knot of anger and jealousy turning his guts into a ball.

'The bastard,' he spoke aloud. 'That bastard Berg.'


'Tom? Tom Parker?'

'That's right, who is this, please? His voice was so clear and strong, although the Atlantic Ocean separated them.

'It's Nicholas, Nicholas Berg.'

'Nick, how are you?' the big voice boomed with genuine pleasure. 'God, I'm glad you called. I've been trying to reach you. I've got good news. The best.'

Nicholas felt a quick lift of relief.

'Samantha?'

'No, damn it,' Tom laughed. 'It's the job. Your job. It went up before the Board of Governors of the University yesterday. I had to sell it to them hard – I'll tell you that for free – but they okayed it. You're on, Nick, isn't that great?'

'It's terrific, Tom.'

'You're on the Biology faculty as an associate, it's the end of the wedge, Nicholas. We'll have you a chair by the end of next year, you wait and see.'

'I'm delighted.'

'Christ, you don't sound it,' Tom roared. 'What's bugging you, boy?'

'Tom, what the hell has happend to Samantha?'

And Nicholas sensed the mood change, the silence lasted a beat too long, and then Tom's tone was guileless.

'She went off on a field trip – down the Keys, didn't she tell you?'

'Down the Keys?' Nicholas' voice rose with his anger and frustration. 'Damn it, Tom. She was supposed to be here in France. She promised to come over for the launching of my new vessel. I've been trying to get in touch with her for a week now.'

'She left Sunday,' said Tom.

'What is she playing at?'

'That's a question she might want to ask you sometime.'

'What does that mean, Tom?'

'Well, before she took off, she came up here and had a good weep with Antoinette – you know, my wife. She plays den mother for every hysterical female within fifty miles, she does.'

Now it was Nicholas' turn to be silent, while the coldness settled on his chest, the coldness of formless dread.

'What was the trouble?'

'Good God, Nick, you don't expect me to follow the intimate details of the love life—'

'Can I speak to Antoinette?'

'She isn't here, Nick. She went up to Orlando for a meeting. She won't be back until the weekend.'

The silence again.

'All that heavy breathing is costing you a fortune, Nicholas. You're paying for this call.'

'I don't know what got into Sam.' But he did. Nicholas knew – and the guilt was strong upon him.

'Listen, Nick. A word to the wise. Get your ass across here, boy. Just as soon as you can. That girl needs talking to, badly. That is, if you care about it.'

'I care about it,' Nicholas said quickly. 'But hell, I am launching a tug in two days' time. I've got sea trials, and a meeting in London.'

Tom's voice had an air of finality. 'A man's got to do what he's got to do.'

'Tom, I'll be across there as soon as I possibly can.'

'I believe it.'

'If you see her, tell her that for me, will you?'

'I'll tell her.'

'Thanks, Tom.'

'The governors will want to meet you, Nicholas. Come as soon as you can.'

'It's a promise.'

Nicholas cradled the receiver, and stood staring out of the windows of the site office. The view across the inner harbour was completely blocked by the towering hull of his tug. She stood tall on her ways. Her hull already wore its final coat of glistening white and the wide flaring bows bore the name *Sea Witch* and below that the port of registration, 'Bermuda'.

She was beautiful, magnificent, but now Nicholas did not even see her. He was overwhelmed by a sense of imminent loss, the cold premonition of onrushing disaster. Until that moment when he faced the prospect of losing her, he had not truly known how large a part that lovely golden girl had come to play in his existence, and in his plans for the future.

There was no way that Samantha could have learned of that single night of weakness, the betrayal that still left Nicholas sickened with guilt – there must be something else that had come between them. He bunched his right fist and slammed it against the sill of the window. The skin on his knuckles smeared, but he did not feel the pain, only the bitter frustration of being tied down here in St Nazaire, weighed down by his responsibilities when he should have been free to follow the jack-o'-lantern of happiness.

The loudspeaker above his head gave a preliminary squawk, and then crackled out the message, 'Monsieur Berg. Will Monsieur attend upon the bridge?'

It was a welcome distraction, and Nicholas hurried out into the spring sunshine. Looking upwards, he could see Jules Levoisin on the wing of the bridge. His portly figure foreshortened against the open sky, like a small pugnacious rooster, he stood facing the electronics engineer who was responsible for the installation of *Sea Witch*'s communications system, and Jules' cries of 'Sacré bleu' and 'Merde' and 'Imbécile' carried clearly above the cacophony of shipyard noises.

Nicholas started to run as he saw the engineer's arms begin to wave and his strident Gallic cries blended with those of *Sea Witch*'s new Master. It was only the third time that Jules Levoisin had become hysterical that day, however it was not yet noon. As the hour of launching came steadily closer, so the little Frenchman's nerves played him tricks, he was behaving like a prima ballerina awaiting the opening curtain. Unless Nicholas reached the bridge within the next few minutes, he would need either a new Master or a new electronics engineer.

Ten minutes later, Nicholas had a cheroot in each of their mouths. The atmosphere was still tense but no longer explosive, and gently Nick took the engineer by the elbow, placed his other arm around Jules Levoisin's shoulders and led them both back into the wheel-house.

The bridge installation was complete, and Jules Levoisin was accepting delivery of the special equipment from the contractors, a negotiation every bit as traumatic as the Treaty of Versailles.

'I myself authorized the modification of the MK.IV transponder,' Nicholas explained patiently. 'We had trouble with the same unit on *Warlock*. I should have told you, Jules.'

'You should have,' agreed the little Master huffily.

'But you were perceptive to notice the change from the specification,' Nicholas soothed him, and Jules puffed out his chest a little and rolled the cheroot in his mouth.

'I may be an old dog, but I know all the new tricks.' He removed the cheroot and smugly blew a perfect smoke ring.

When Nicholas at last left them chatting amiably over the massed array of sophisticated equipment that lined the navigation area at the back of the bridge, they were paging him from the site office.

'What is it?' he asked, as he came in through the door.

'It's a lady,' the foreman indicated the telephone lying on the littered desk below the window.

'Samantha,' Nick thought, and snatched up the receiver.

'Nicky.' He felt the shock of quick guilt at the voice.

'Chantelle, where are you?'

'In La Baule.' The fashionable resort town just up the Atlantic coast was a better setting for Chantelle Alexander than the grubby port with its sprawling dockyards. 'Staying at the Castille. God, it's too awful. I'd forgotten how awful it was.'

They had stayed there together, once long ago, in a different life it seemed now.

'But the restaurant is still quite cute, Nicholas. Have lunch with me. I must speak to you.'

'I can't leave here.' He would not walk into the trap again.

'It's important. I must see you.' He could hear that husky tone in her voice, imagine clearly the sensuous droop of the eyelids over those bold Persian eyes 'For an hour, only an hour. You can spare that.' Despite himself, he felt the pull of temptation, the dull ache of it at the base of his belly – and he was angry at her for the power she could still exert over him.

'If it's important, then come here,' he said brusquely, and she sighed at his intransigence.

'All right, Nicholas. How will I find you?'

The Rolls was parked opposite the dockyard gates and Nicholas crossed the road and stepped through the door that the chauffeur held open for him.

Chantelle lifted her face to him. Her hair was cloudy dark and shot with light like a bolt of silk, her lips the colour of ripe fruit, moist and slightly parted. He ignored the invitation and touched her cheek with his lips before settling into the corner opposite her.

She made a little moue, and slanted her eyes at him in amusement.

'How chaste we are, Nicky.'

Nicholas touched the button on the control console and the glass soundproof partition slid up noiselessly between them and the chauffeur.

'Did you send in the auditors?' he asked.

'You look tired, darling, and harassed.'

'Have you blown the whistle on Duncan?' he avoided the distraction. 'The work on *Golden Dawn* is still going ahead. The arc lights were burning over her all night and the talk in the yards is that she is being launched at noon tomorrow, almost a month ahead of schedule. What happened, Chantelle?'

'There is a little bistro at Mindin, it's just across the bridge—'

'Damn it, Chantelle. I haven't time to fool around.'

But the Rolls was already gliding swiftly through the narrow streets of the port, between the high warehouse buildings.

'It will take five minutes, and the Lobster Armoricaine is the local speciality – not to be confused with Lobster Américaine. They do it in a cream sauce, it's superb,' she chatted archly, and the Rolls turned out on to the quay. Across the narrow waters of the inner harbour humped the ugly camouflaged mounds of the Nazi submarine pens, armoured concrete so thick as to resist the bombs of the R.A.F. and the efforts of all demolition experts over the years since then.

'Peter asked me to give you his love. He has got his junior team colours. I'm so proud.'

Nicholas thrust his hands deep into his jacket pockets and slumped down resignedly against the soft leather seat.

'I am delighted to hear it,' he said.

And they were silent then until the chauffeur checked the Rolls at the toll barrier to pay before accelerating out on to the ramp of the St Nazaire bridge. The great span of the bridge rose in a regal curve, three hundred feet above the waters of the Loire River. The river was almost three miles wide here, and from the highest point of the bridge there was an aerial view over the dockyards of the town.

There were half a dozen vessels building along the banks of the broad muddy river, a mighty forest of steel scaffolding, tall gantries and half-assembled hulls, but all of it insignificant under the mountainous bulk of *Golden Dawn*. Without her pod tanks, she had an incomplete gutted appearance, as though the Eiffel Tower had toppled over and somebody had built a modernistic apartment block at one end. It seemed impossible that such a structure was capable of floating. God, she was ugly, Nick thought.

'They are still working on her,' he said. One of the gantries was moving ponderously along the length of the ship like an arthritic dinosaur, and at fifty places the brilliant blue electric fires of the welding torches flickered; while upon the grotesquely riven hull crawled human figures reduced to antlike insignificance by the sheer size of the vessel.

'They are still working,' he repeated it as an accusation.

'Nicholas, nothing in this life is simple—'

'Did you spell it out for Duncan?'

'—except for people like you.'

'You didn't confront Duncan, did you?' he accused bitterly.

'It's easy for you to be strong. It's one of the things that first attracted me.'

And Nicholas almost laughed aloud. It was ludicrous to talk of strength, after his many displays of weakness with this very woman.

'Did you call Duncan's cards?' he insisted, but she put him off with a smile.

'Let's wait until we have a glass of wine—'

'Now,' he snapped 'Tell me right now. Chantelle, I haven't time for games.'

'Yes, I spoke to him,' she nodded. 'I called him down to Cap Ferrat, and I accused him – of what you suspected.'

'He denied it? If he denies it, I now have further proof—'

'No, Nicholas. He didn't deny a thing. He told me that I knew only the half of it.' Her voice rose sharply, and suddenly it all spilled out in a torrent of tortured words. Her composure was eroded swiftly away as she relived the enormity of her predicament. 'He's gambled with my fortune, Nicholas. He's risked the family share of Christy Marine, the Trust shares, my shares, it's all at risk. And he gloated as he told me, he truly gloried in his betrayal.'

'We've got him now.' Nicholas had straightened slowly in his seat as he listened. His voice was grimly satisfied and he nodded. 'That's it. We will stop the *Golden Dawn*, like that—' he hammered his bunched fist into the palm of the other hand with a sharp crack. 'We will get an urgent order before the courts.'

Nicholas stopped suddenly and stared at her. Chantelle was shaking her head slowly from side to side. Her eyes slowly filled, making them huge and glistening, a single tear spilled over the lid and clung in the thick dark lashes like a drop of morning dew.

The Rolls had stopped now outside the tiny bistro. It was on the river front, with a view across the water to the dockyards. To the west the river debouched into the open sea and in the east the beautiful arch of the bridge rose across the pale blue spring sky.

The chauffeur held open the door and Chantelle was gone with her swift birdlike grace, leaving Nicholas no choice but to follow her.

The proprietor came through from his kitchen and fussed over Chantelle, seating her at the window and lingering to discuss the menu.

'Oh, let's drink the Muscadet, Nicholas.' She had always had the most amazing powers of recovery, and now the tears were gone and she was brittle and gay and beautiful, smiling at him over the rim of her glass. The sunlight through the leaded window panes danced in the cool golden wine and rippled on the smoky dark fall of her hair.

'Here's to us, Nicholas darling. We are the last of the great.' It was a toast from long ago, from the other life, and it irritated him now but he drank it silently and then set down the glass.

'Chantelle, when and how are you going to stop Duncan?'

'Don't spoil the meal, darling.'

'In about thirty seconds I'm going to start becoming very angry.'

She studied him for a moment, and saw that it was true. 'All right then,' she agreed reluctantly.

'When are you going to stop him?'

'I'm not, darling.'

He stared at her. 'What did you say?' he asked quietly.

'I'm going to do everything in my power to help him launch and sail the *Golden Dawn*.'

'You don't understand, Chantelle. You're talking about risking a million tons of the most deadly poison—'

'Don't be silly, Nicky. Keep that heroic talk for the newspapers. I don't care if Duncan dumps a million tons of cadmium in the water supply of greater London, just as long as he pulls the Trust and me out of the fire.'

'There is still time to make the modifications to *Golden Dawn*.'

'No, there isn't. You don't understand, darling. Duncan has put us so deeply into it that a delay of a few days even would bring us down. He has stripped the cupboard bare, Nicky. There is no money for modifications, no time for anything, except to get *Golden Dawn* under way.'

'There is always a way and a means.'

'Yes, and the way is to fill *Golden Dawn*'s pod tanks with crude.'

'He's frightened you by—'

'Yes,' she agreed. 'I am frightened. I have never been so frightened in my life, Nicky. I could lose everything – I am terrified. I could lose it all.' She shivered with the horror of it. 'I would kill myself if that happened.'

'I am still going to stop Duncan.'

'No, Nicky. Please just leave it, for my sake – for Peter's sake, it's Peter's inheritance that we are taking about. Let *Golden Dawn* make one voyage, just one voyage – and I will be safe.'

'It's the risk to an ocean, to God alone knows how many human lives, we are talking about.'

'Don't shout, Nicky. People are looking.'

'Let them look. I'm going to stop that monster.'

'No, Nicholas. Without me, you cannot do a thing.'

'You best believe it.'

'Darling, I promise you, after her first voyage we will sell *Golden Dawn*. We'll be safe then, and I can rid myself of Duncan. It will be you and I again, Nicky. A few short weeks, that's all.'

It took all his self-control to prevent his anger showing. He clenched his fists on the starched white tablecloth, but his voice was cool and even.

'Just one more question, Chantelle. When did you telephone Samantha Silver?'

She looked puzzled for a moment as though she was trying to put a face to a name. 'Samantha, oh, your little friend. Why should I want to telephone her?' And then her expression changed. 'Oh, Nicky, you don't really believe I'd do that? You don't really believe I would tell anybody about it, about that wonderful—' Now she was stricken, again those huge eyes brimmed and she reached across and stroked the fine black hairs on the back of Nicholas' big square hand. 'You don't think that of me! I'm not that much of a bitch. I don't have to cheat to get the things I want. I don't have to inflict unnecessary hurt on people.'

'No,' Nicholas agreed quietly. 'You'd not murder more than a million or poison more than a single ocean at a time, would you?' He pushed back his chair.

'Sit down, Nicky. Eat your lobster.'

'Suddenly I'm not hungry.' He stripped two one-hundred-franc notes from his money clip and dropped them beside his plate.

'I forbid you to leave,' she hissed angrily. 'You are humiliating me, Nicholas.'

'I'll send your car back,' he said, and walked out into the sunlight. He found with surprise that he was trembling, and that his jaws were clenched so tightly that his teeth ached.

The wind turned during the night, and the morning was cold with drifts of low, grey, fast-flying cloud that threatened rain. Nicholas pulled up his collar against the wind and the tails of his coat flogged about his legs, for he was exposed on the highest point of the arched bridge of St Nazaire.

Thousands of others had braved the wind, and the guard-rail was lined two and three deep, all the way across the curve of the northern span. The traffic had backed up and half a dozen gendarmes were trying to get it moving again; their whistles shrilled plaintively. Faintly the sound of a band floated up to them, rising and falling in volume as the wind caught it, and even with the naked eye Nicholas could make out the wreaths of gaily coloured bunting which fluttered on the high cumbersome stern tower of *Golden Dawn*.

He glanced at his wristwatch, and saw it was a few minutes before noon. A helicopter clattered noisily under the grey belly of cloud, and hovered about the yards of Construction Navale Atlantique on the gleaming silver coin of its rotor.

Nicholas lifted the binoculars and the eyepieces were painfully cold against his skin. Through the lens, he could almost make out individual features among the small gathering on the rostrum under the tanker's stern.

The platform was decorated with a Tricolour and a Union Jack, and as he watched the band fell silent and lowered their instruments.

'Speech time,' Nicholas murmured, and now he could make out Duncan Alexander, his bared head catching one of the fleeting rays of sun, a glimmer of coppery gold as he looked up at the towering stern of *Golden Dawn*.

His bulk almost obscured the tiny feminine figure beside him. Chantelle wore that particular shade of malachite green which she so dearly loved. There was confused activity around Chantelle, half a dozen gentlemen assisting in the ceremony she had performed so very often. Chantelle had broken the champagne on almost all of Christy Marine's fleet; the first time had been when she was Arthur Christy's fourteen-year-old darling – it was another of the company's many traditions.

Nicholas blinked, believing for an instant that his eyes had tricked him, for it seemed that the very earth had changed its shape and was moving.

Then he saw that the great hull of *Golden Dawn* had begun to slide forward. The band burst into the 'Marseillaise', the heroic strains watered down by wind and distance, while *Golden Dawn* gathered momentum.

It was an incredible, even a stirring sight, and despite himself, Nicholas felt the goose-bumps rise upon his forearms and the hair lift on the back of his neck. He was a sailor, and he was watching the birthing of the mightiest vessel ever built.

She was grotesque, monstrous, but she was part of him. No matter that others had bastardized and perverted his grand design – still the original design was his and he found himself gripping the binoculars with hands that shook.

He watched the massive wooden-wedged arresters kick out from under that great sliding mass of steel as they served to control her stern-first rush down the ways. Steel cable whipped and snaked upon itself like the Medusa's hair, and *Golden Dawn*'s stern struck the water.

The brown muddy water of the estuary opened before her, cleaved by the irresistible rush and weight, and the hull drove deep, opening white-capped rollers that spread out across the channel and broke upon the shores with a dull roar that carried clearly to where Nicholas stood.

The crowd that lined the bridge was cheering wildly. Beside him, a mother held her infant up to watch, both of them screaming with glee.

While *Golden Dawn*'s bows were still on the dockyard's ways her stern was thrusting irresistibly a mile out into the river; forced down by the raised bows it must now be almost touching the muddy bottom for the wave was breaking around her stern quarters.

God, she was huge! Nicholas shook his head in wonder. If only he had been able to build her the right way, what a ship she would have been. What a magnificent concept!

Now her bows left the end of the slips, and the waters burst about her, seething and leaping into swirling vortices.

Her stern started to rise, gathering speed as her own buoyancy caught her, and she burst out like a great whale rising to blow. The waters spilled from her, creaming and cascading through the steel-work of her open decks, boiling madly in the cavernous openings that would hold the pod tanks when she was fully loaded.

Now she came up short on the hundreds of retaining cables that prevented her from driving clear across the river and throwing herself ashore on the far bank.

She fought against this restraint, as though having felt the water she was now eager to run. She rolled and dipped and swung with a ponderous majesty that kept the crowds along the bridge cheering wildly. Then slowly she settled and floated quietly, seeming to fill the Loire River from bank to bank and to reach as high as the soaring spans of the bridge itself.

The four attendant harbour tugs moved in quickly to assist the ship to turn its prodigious length and to line up for the roads and the open sea.

They butted and backed, working as a highly skilled team, and slowly they coaxed *Golden Dawn* around. Her sideways motion left a mile-wide sweep of disturbed water across the estuary. Then suddenly there was a tremendous boil under her counter, and Nicholas saw the bronze flash of her single screw sweeping slowly through the brown water. Faster and still faster it turned, and despite himself Nicholas thrilled to see her come alive. A ripple formed under her bows, and almost imperceptibly she began to creep forward, overcoming the vast inertia of her weight, gathering steerage way, under command at last.

The harbour tugs fell back respectfully, and as the mighty bows lined up with the open sea she drove forward determinedly.

Silver spouts of steam from the sirens of the tugs shot high, and moments later, the booming bellow of their salute crashed against the skies.

The crowds had dispersed and Nicholas stood alone in the wind on the high bridge and watched the structured steel towers of *Golden Dawn*'s hull blending with the grey and misted horizon. He watched her turn, coming around on to her great circle course that would carry her six thousand miles southward to Good Hope, and even at this distance he sensed her change in mood as she steadied and her single screw began to push her up to top economic speed.

Nicholas checked his watch and murmured the age-old Master's command that commenced every voyage.

'Full away at 1700 hours,' he said, and turned to trudge back along the bridge to where he had left the hired Renault.

It was after six o'clock and the site office was empty by the time Nicholas got back to *Sea Witch*. He threw himself into a chair and lit a cheroot while he thumbed quickly through his address book. He found what he wanted, dialled the direct London code, and then the number.

'Good afternoon. This is the *Sunday Times*. May I help you?'

'Is Mr Herbstein available?' Nicholas asked.

'Hold on, please.'

While he waited, Nicholas checked his address book for his next most likely contact, should the journalist be climbing the Himalayas or visiting a guerrilla training camp in Central Africa, either of which were highly likely – but within seconds he heard his voice.

'Denis,' he said. 'This is Nicholas Berg, how are you? I've got a hell of a story for you.'

Nicholas tried to bear the indignity of it with stoicism, but the thick coating of pancake make-up seemed to clog the pores of his skin and he moved restlessly in the make-up chair.

'Please keep still, sir,' the make-up girl snapped irritably; there was a line of unfortunates awaiting her ministrations along the bench at the back of the narrow room. One of them was Duncan Alexander and he caught Nicholas' eye in the mirror and raised an eyebrow in a mocking salute.

In the chair beside him, the anchor-man of 'The Today and Tomorrow Show' lolled graciously; he was tall and elegant with dyed and permanently waved hair, a carnation in his button-hole, a high camp manner and an ostentatiously liberal image.

'I've given you the first slot. If it gets interesting, I'll run you four minutes forty seconds, otherwise I'll cut it off at two.'

Denis Herbstein's Sunday article had been done with high professionalism, especially bearing in mind the very short time he had to put it together. It had included interviews with representatives of Lloyd's of London, the oil companies, environmental experts both in America and England, and even with the United States Coast Guard.

'Try to make it tight and hard,' advised the anchorman. 'Let's not pussyfoot around.' He wanted sensation, not too many facts or figures, good gory horror stuff – or a satisfying punch-up. The *Sunday Times* article had flushed them out at Orient Amex and Christy Marine; they had not been able to ignore the challenge, for there was a question tabled for Thursday by a Labour member in the Commons, and ominous stirrings in the ranks of the American Coast Guard service.

There had been enough fuss to excite the interest of 'The Today and Tomorrow Show'. They had invited the parties to meet their accuser, and both Christy Marine and Orient Amex had fielded their first teams. Duncan

Alexander with all his charisma had come to speak for Christy Marine, and Orient Amex had selected one of their directors who looked like Gary Cooper. With his craggy honest face and the silver hairs at his temple he looked like the kind of man you wanted flying your airliner or looking after your money.

The make-up girl dusted Nicholas' face with powder.

'I'm going to invite you to speak first. Tell us about this stuff – what is it, cadmium?' the interviewer checked his script.

Nicholas nodded, he could not speak for he was suffering the ultimate indignity. The girl was painting his lips.

The television studio was the size of an aircraft hangar, the concrete floor strewn with thick black cables and the roof lost in the gloomy heights, but they had created the illusion of intimacy in the small shell of the stage around which the big mobile cameras cluttered like mechanical crabs around the carcass of a dead fish.

The egg-shaped chairs made it impossible either to loll or to sit upright and the merciless white glare of the arc lamps fried the thick layer of greasy make-up on Nicholas' skin. It was small consolation that across the table Duncan looked like a Japanese Kabuki dancer in make-up too white for his coppery hair.

An assistant director in a sweatshirt and jeans clipped the small microphone into Nicholas' lapel and whispered,

'Give them hell, ducky.'

Somebody else in the darkness beyond the lights was intoning solemnly, 'Four, three, two, one – you're on!' and the red light lit on the middle camera.

'Welcome to The Today and Tomorrow Show,' the anchor-man's voice was suddenly warm and intimate and mellifluous. 'Last week in the French ship-building port of St Nazaire, the largest ship in the world was launched—' In a dozen sentences he sketched out the facts, while on the repeating screens beyond the cameras Nicholas saw that they were running newsreel footage of *Golden Dawn*'s launching. He remembered the helicopter hovering over the dockyard, and he was so fascinated by the aerial views of the enormous vessel taking to the water that when the cameras switched suddenly to him, he was taken by surprise and saw himself start on the little screen as the interviewer began introducing him, swiftly running a thumbnail portrait and then going on:

'Mr Berg has some very definite views on this ship.'

'In her present design and construction, she is not safe to carry even regular crude petroleum oil,' Nicholas said. 'However, she will be employed in the carriage of crude oil that has been contaminated by cadmium sulphide in such concentrations as to make it one of the more toxic substances in nature.'

'Your first statement, Mr Berg, does anyone else share your doubts as to the safety of her design?'

'She does not carry the A1 rating by the marine inspectors of Lloyd's of London,' said Nicholas.

'Now can you tell us about the cargo she will carry – the so-called cad-rich crudes?'

Nicholas knew he had perhaps fifteen seconds to draw a verbal picture of the Atlantic Ocean turned into a sterile poisoned desert; it was too short a time, and twice Duncan Alexander interjected, skilfully breaking up the logic of Nicholas' presentation and before he had finished, the anchor-man glanced at his watch and cut him short.

'Thank you, Mr Berg. Now Mr Kemp is a director of the oil company.'

'My company, Orient Amex, last year allocated the sum of two million U.S. dollars as grants to assist in the scientific study of world environmental problems. I can tell you folks, right now, that we at Orient Amex are very conscious of the problems of modern technology –' He was projecting the oil-company image, the benefactors of all humanity.

'Your company's profit last year, after taxation, was four hundred and twenty-five million dollars,' Nicholas cut in clearly. 'That makes point four seven per cent on environmental research – all of it tax deductible. Congratulations, Mr Kemp.'

The oil man looked pained and went on: 'Now we at Orient Amex,' plugging the company name again neatly, 'are working towards a better quality of life for all peoples. But we do realize that it is impossible to put back the clock a hundred years. We cannot allow ourselves to be blinded by the romantic wishful thinking of *amateur* environmentalists, the weekend scientists and the doomcriers who—'

'Cry *Torrey Canyon*,' Nicholas suggested helpfully, and the oil man suppressed a shudder and went on quickly.

'— who would have us discontinue such research as the revolutionary cadmium cracking process, which could extend the world's utilization of fossil fuels by a staggering forty per cent and give the world's oil reserves an extended life of twenty years or more.'

Again the anchor-man glanced at his watch, cut the oil man off in mid-flow and switched his attention to Duncan Alexander.

'Mr Alexander, your so-called ultra-tanker will carry the cad-rich crudes. How would you reply to Mr Berg?'

Duncan smiled, a deep secret smile. 'When Mr Berg had my job as head of Christy Marine, the *Golden Dawn* was the best idea in the world. Since he was fired, it's suddenly the worst.'

They laughed, even one of the cameramen out beyond the lights guffawed uncontrollably, and Nicholas felt the hot red rush of his anger.

'Is the *Golden Dawn* rated A1 at Lloyd's?' asked the anchor-man.

'Christy Marine has not applied for a Lloyd's listing – we arranged our insurance in other markets.'

Even through his anger Nicholas had to concede how good he was, he had a mind like quicksilver.

'How safe is your ship, Mr Alexander?'

Now Duncan turned his head and looked directly across the table at Nicholas.

'I believe she is as safe as the world's leading marine architects and naval engineers can make her.' He paused, and there was a malevolent gleam in his eyes now, 'So safe, that I have decided to end this ridiculous controversy by a display of my personal confidence.'

'What form will this show of faith take, Mr Alexander?' The anchor-man sensed the sensational line for which he had been groping and he leaned forward eagerly.

'On *Golden Dawn*'s maiden voyage, when she returns from the Persian Gulf fully laden with the El Barras crudes, I and my family, my wife and my step-son, will travel aboard her for the final six thousand miles of her voyage – from Cape Town on the Cape of Good Hope to Galveston in the Gulf of Mexico.' As Nicholas gaped at him wordlessly, he went on evenly, 'That's how convinced I am that *Golden Dawn* is capable of performing her task in perfect safety.'

'Thank you.' The anchor-man recognized a good exit line, when he heard one. 'Thank you, Mr Alexander. You've convinced me – and I am sure you have convinced many of our viewers. We are now crossing to Washington via satellite where—'

The moment the red 'in use' light flickered out on the television camera, Nicholas was on his feet and facing Duncan Alexander. His anger was fanned by the realization that Duncan had easily grandstanded him with that adroit display of showmanship, and by the stabbing anxiety at the threat to take Peter aboard *Golden Dawn* on her hazardous maiden voyage.

'You're not taking Peter on that death trap of yours,' he snapped.

'That's his mother's decision,' said Duncan evenly. 'As the daughter of Arthur Christy, she's decided to give the company her full support,' he emphasized the word 'full'.

'I won't let either of you endanger my son's life for a wild public-relations stunt.'

'I'm sure you will try to prevent it,' Duncan nodded and smiled, 'and I'm sure your efforts will be as ineffectual as your attempts to stop *Golden Dawn*.' He deliberately turned his back on Nicholas and spoke to the oil man. 'I do think that went off rather well,' he said, 'don't you?'

James Teacher gave a graphic demonstration of why he could charge the highest fees in London and still have his desk piled high with important briefs. He had Nicholas' urgent application before a Judge-in-Chambers within seventy-two hours, petitioning for a writ to restrain Chantelle Alexander from allowing the son of their former marriage, one Peter Nicholas Berg, aged twelve years, to accompany her on an intended voyage from Cape Town in the Republic of South Africa to Galveston in the state of Texas aboard the bulk crude-carrier *Golden Dawn*, and/or to prevent the said Chantelle Alexander from allowing the child to undertake any other voyage aboard said vessel.

The Judge heard the petition during a recess in the criminal trial of a young post-office worker standing accused of multiple rape. The judge's oak-panelled book-lined chambers were overcrowded by the two parties, their lawyers, the judge's registrar and the considerable bulk of the judge himself.

Still in his wig and robes from the public court, the judge read swiftly through the written submission of both sides, listened attentively to James Teacher's short address and the rebuttal by his opposite number, before turning sternly to Chantelle.

'Mrs Alexander.' The stern expression wavered slightly as he looked upon the devastating beauty which sat demurely before him. 'Do you love your son?'

'More than anything else in this life.' Chantelle looked at him steadily out of those vast dark eyes.

'And you are happy to take him on this journey with you?'

'I am the daughter of a sailor, if there was danger I would understand it. I am happy to go myself and take my son with me.'

The judge nodded, looked down at the papers on his desk for a moment. 'As I understand the circumstances, Mr Teacher, it is common ground that the mother has custody?'

'That is so, my lord. But the father is the child's guardian.'

'I'm fully aware of that, thank you,' he snapped acidly. He paused again before resuming in the measured tones of judgement, 'We are concerned here exclusively with the welfare and safety of the child. It has been shown that the proposed journey will be made during the holidays and that no loss of schooling will result. On the other hand, I do not believe that the petitioner has shown that there exists reasonable doubts about the safety of the vessel on which the voyage will be made. It seems to be a modern and sophisticated ship. To grant the petition would, in my view, be placing unreasonable restraint on the child's mother.' He swivelled in his chair to face Nicholas and James Teacher. 'I regret, therefore, that I see insufficient grounds to accede to your petition.'

In the back seat of James Teacher's Bentley, the little lawyer murmured apologetically. 'He was right, of course, Nicholas. I would have done the same in his place. These domestic squabbles are always—'

Nicholas was not listening. 'What would happen if I picked up Peter and took him to Bermuda or the States?'

'Abduct him!' James Teacher's voice shot up an octave, and he caught Nicholas' arm with genuine alarm. 'I beg of you, dismiss the thought. They would have the police waiting for you – God!' Now he wriggled miserably in his seat. 'I can't bear to think of what might happen. Apart from getting you sent to gaol, your former wife might even get an order restraining you from seeing your boy again, she could get guardianship away from you. If you did that, you could lose the child, Nicholas. Don't do it. Please don't do it!'

Now he patted Nicholas' arm ingratiatingly. 'You'd be playing right into their hands.' And then with relief he switched his attention to the briefcase on his lap.

'Can we read through the latest draft of the agreement of sale again?' he asked. 'We haven't got much time, you know.' Then, without waiting for a reply, he began on the preamble to the agreement which would transfer all the assets and liabilities of Ocean Salvage and Towage to the Directors of the Bank of the East, as nominees for parties unnamed.

Nicholas slumped in the far corner of the seat, and stared thoughtfully out of the window as the Bentley crawled in the traffic stream out of the Strand, around Trafalgar Square with its wheeling clouds of pigeons and milling throngs of tourists, swung into the Mall and accelerated down the long straight towards the Palace.

'I want you to stall them,' Nicholas said suddenly, and Teacher broke off in the middle of a sentence and stared at him distractedly.

'I beg your pardon?'

'I want you to find a way to stall the Sheikhs.'

'Good God, man.' James Teacher was utterly astounded. 'It's taken me nearly a month – four hard weeks to get them ripe to sign,' his voice choked a little at the memory of the long hours of negotiation. 'I've written every line of the agreement in my own blood.'

'I need to have control of my tugs, I need to be free to act—'

'Nicholas, we are talking about seven million dollars.'

'We are taking about my son,' said Nicholas quietly. 'Can you stall them?'

'Yes, of course I can, if that's what you truly want.' Wearily James Teacher closed the file on his lap. 'How long?'

'Six weeks – long enough for *Golden Dawn* to finish her maiden voyage, one way or the other.'

'You realize that this may blow the whole deal, don't you?'

'Yes, I realize that.'

'And you realize also that there isn't another buyer?'

'Yes.'

They were silent then, until the Bentley pulled up before the Bank building in Curzon Street, and they stepped out on to the pavement.

'Are you absolutely certain?' Teacher asked softly.

'Just do it,' Nicholas replied, and the doorman held the bronze and glass doors open for them.


Bermuda asserted its calming influence over Nicholas the moment he stepped out of the aircraft into its comfortable warmth and clean, glittering sunlight. Bernard Wackie's gorgeous burnt-honey-coloured secretary was there to welcome him. She wore a thin cotton dress the colour of freshly cut pineapple and a flashing white smile.

'Mr Wackie's waiting for you at the Bank, sir.'

'Are you out of your mind, Nicholas?' Bernard greeted him. 'Jimmy Teacher tells me you blew the Arabs out of the window. Tell me it's not true, please tell me it's not true.'

'Oh, come on, Bernard,' Nicholas shook his head and patted him consolingly on the shoulder, 'your commission would only have been a lousy point seven million, anyway.'

'Then you did it!' Bernard wailed, and tried to pull his hand out of Nicholas' grip. 'You screwed it all up.'

'The Sheikhs have been screwing us up for over a month, Bernie baby. I just gave them a belt of the same medicine, and do you know what? They loved it. The Prince sat up and showed real interest for the first time. For the first time we were speaking the same language. They'll still be around six weeks from now.'

'But why? I don't understand. Just explain to me why you did it.'

'Let's go into the plot, and I'll explain it to you.'

In the plot Nicholas stood over the perspex map of the oceans of the globe, and studied it carefully for fully five minutes without speaking.

'That's *Sea Witch*'s latest position, she's making good passage?'

The green plastic disc that bore the tug's number was set in mid-Atlantic.

'She reported two hours ago,' Bernie nodded, and then with professional interest, 'How did her sea trials go off?'

'There were the usual wrinkles to iron out, that's what kept me in St Nazaire so long. But we got them straight – and Jules has fallen in love with her.'

'He's still the best skipper in the game.'

But already Nicholas' attention had switched halfway across the world.

'*Warlock*'s still in Mauritius,' his voice snapped like a whip.

'I had to fly out a new armature for the main generator. It was just bad luck that she broke down in that Godforsaken part of the world.'

'When will she be ready for sea?'

'Allen promises noon tomorrow. Do you want to telex him for an update on that?'

'Later.' Nicholas wet the tip of a cheroot carefully, without taking his eyes off the plot, calculating distances and currents and speeds.

'*Golden Dawn*?' he asked, and lit the cheroot while he listened to Bernard's reply.

'Her pod tanks arrived under tow at the new Orient Amex depot on El Barras three weeks ago.' Bernie picked up the pointer and touched the upper bight of the deep Persian Gulf. 'They took on their full cargoes of crude and lay inshore to await *Golden Dawn*'s arrival.'

For a moment, Nicholas contemplated the task of towing those four gigantic pod tanks from Japan to the Gulf, and then he discarded the thought and listened to Bernard.

'*Golden Dawn* arrived last Thursday and, according to my agent at El Barras, she coupled up with her pod tanks and made her turn around within three hours.' Bernard slid the tip of the pointer southwards down the eastern coast of the African continent. 'I have had no report of her since then, but if she makes good her twenty-two knots, then she'll be somewhere off the coast of Mozambique, or Maputo as they call it now, and she should double the Cape within the next few days. I will have a report on her then, she'll be taking on mail as she passes Cape Town.'

'And passengers,' and Nicholas grimly; he knew that Peter and Chantelle were in Cape Town already. He had telephoned the boy the night before and Peter had been wildly elated at the prospect of the voyage on the ultra-tanker.

'It's going to be tremendous fun, Dad,' his voice cracking with the onset of both excitement and puberty. 'We'll be flying out to the ship in a helicopter.'

Bernard Wackie changed the subject, now picking up a sheaf of telex flimsies and thumbing swiftly through them.

'Right, I've confirmed the standby contract for *Sea Witch*.' Nicholas nodded, the contract was for Jules Levoisin and the new tug to stand by three offshore working rigs, standard exploration rigs, that were drilling in the Florida Bay, that elbow of shallow water formed by the sweep of the

Florida Keys and the low swampy morass of the Everglades. 'It's ridiculous to use a twenty-two-thousand-horsepower ocean-going tug as an oil rig standby,' Bernard lowered the file, and could no longer contain his irritation, 'Jules is going to go bananas sitting around playing nursemaid. You are going to have a mutiny on your hands – and you'll be losing money. The daily hire won't cover your direct costs.'

'She will be sitting exactly where I want her,' said Nicholas, and switched his attention back to the tiny dot of an island in the middle of the Indian Ocean. 'Now *Warlock.*'

'Right. *Warlock.*' Bernie picked up another file. 'I have tendered for a deep-sea tow.'

'Cancel it,' said Nicholas. 'Just as soon as Allen has repaired his generator, I want him running top of the green for Cape Town.'

'For Cape Town – top of the green?' Bernard stared at him. 'Christ, Nicholas. What for?'

'He won't be able to catch *Golden Dawn* before she rounds the Cape, but I want him to follow her.'

'Nicholas, you're out of your mind – do you know what that would cost?'

'If *Golden Dawn* gets into trouble he'll be only a day or two behind her. Tell Allen he is to shadow her all the way into Galveston roads.'

'Nicholas, you're letting this whole thing get out of all proportion. It's become an obsession with you, for God's sake!'

'With her superior speed, *Warlock* should be up with her before she enters the—'

'Listen to me, Nicholas. Let's think this all out carefully. What are the chances of *Golden Dawn* suffering structural failure or crippling breakdown or her maiden voyage – a hundred to one against it? It's that high?'

'That's about right.' Nicholas agreed. 'A hundred to one.'

'What is it going to cost to hold one ocean-going salvage tug on standby, at a lousy fifteen hundred dollars a day – and then to send another halfway around the world at top of the green?' Bernard clasped his brow theatrically. 'It's going to cost you a quarter of a million dollars, if you take into consideration the loss of earnings on both vessels – that's the very least it's going to cost you. Don't you have respect for money any longer?'

'Now you understand why I had to stall the Sheikhs,' Nicholas smiled calmly. 'I couldn't shoot their money on a hundred-to-one chance – but it's not their money yet. It's mine. *Sea Witch* and *Warlock* aren't their tugs, they are mine. Peter isn't their son, he's mine.'

'You're serious,' said Bernard incredulously. 'I do believe you are serious.'

'Right,' Nicholas agreed. 'Damned right, I am. Now get a telex off to David Allen and ask him for his estimated time of arrival in Cape Town.'

Samantha Silver had one towel wrapped around her head like a turban. Her hair was still wet from the luxurious shampooing it had just received. She wore the other towel tucked under her armpits, making a short sarong of it. She still glowed all over from the steaming tub and she smelled of soap and talcum powder.

After a long field trip, it took two or three of these soakings and scrubbings to get the salt and the smell of the mangroves out of her pores, and the Everglades mud from under her nails.

She poured the batter into the pan, the oil spitting and crackling with the heat and she sang out, 'How many waffles can you eat?'

He came through from the bathroom, a wet towel wrapped around his waist, and he stood in the doorway and grinned at her. 'How many have you got?' he asked. She had still not accustomed her ear to the Australian twang.

He was burned and brown as she was, and his hair was bleached at the ends, hanging now, wet from the shower, into his face.

They had worked well together, and she had learned much from him. The drift into intimacy had been gradual, but inevitable. In her hurt, she had turned to him for comfort, and also in deliberate spite of Nicholas. But now, if she turned her head away, she would not really be able to remember his features clearly. It took an effort to remember his name – Dennis, of course, Doctor Dennis O'Connor.

She was detached from it all, as though a sheet of armoured glass separated her from the real world. She went through the motions of working and playing, of eating and sleeping, of laughing and loving, but it was all a sham.

Dennis was watching her from the doorway now, with that slightly puzzled expression, the helpless look of a person who watches another drowning and is powerless to give aid.

Samantha turned away quickly. 'Ready in two minutes,' she said, and he turned back into the bedroom to finish dressing.

She flipped the waffles on to a plate and poured a fresh batch of batter.

Beside her, the telephone rang and she sucked her fingers clean and picked it up with her free hand.

'Sam Silver,' she said.

'Thank God. I've been going out of my mind. What happened to you, darling?'

Her knees went rubbery under her, and she had to sit down quickly on one of the stools.

'Samantha, can you hear me?'

She opened her mouth, but no sound came out.

'Tell me what's happening—' She could see his face before her, clearly, each detail of it so vividly remembered, the clear green eyes below the heavy brow, the line of cheek-bone and jaw, and the sound of his voice made her shiver.

'Samantha.'

'How is your wife, Nicholas?' she asked softly – and he broke off. She held the receiver to her ear with both hands, and the silence lasted only a few beats of her heart, but it was long enough. Once or twice, in moments of weakness during the last two weeks, she had tried to convince herself that it was not true. That it had all been the viciousness of a lying woman. Now she knew beyond any question that her instinct had been correct. His silence was the admission, and she waited for the lie that she knew would come next.

'Would it help to tell you I love you?' he asked softly, and she could not answer. Even in her distress, she felt the rush of relief. He had not lied. At that moment it was the most important thing in her life. He had not lied. She felt it begin to tear painfully, deep in her chest. Her shoulders shook spasmodically.

'I'm coming to get you,' he said into the silence.

'I won't be here,' she whispered, but she felt it welling up into her throat, uncontrollably. She had not wept before, she had kept it all safely bottled away – but now, the first sob burst from her, and with both hands she slammed the telephone back on to its cradle.

She stood there still, shaking wildly, and the tears poured down her cheeks and dripped from her chin.

Dennis came into the kitchen behind her, tucking his shirt into the top of his trousers, his hair shiny and wet with the straight lines of the comb through it.

'Who was that?' he asked cheerfully, and then stopped aghast.

'What is it, love?' He started forward again, 'Come on now.'

'Don't touch me, please,' she whispered huskily, and he stopped again uncertainly. 'We are fresh out of milk,' she said without turning. 'Will you take the van down to the shopping centre?'

By the time Dennis returned, she was dressed and she had rinsed her face and tied a scarf around her head like a gypsy. They chewed cold, unappetizing waffles in silence, until she spoke.

'Dennis, we've got to talk—'

'No,' he smiled at her. 'It's all right, Sam. You don't have to say it. I should have moved on days ago, anyway.'

'Thanks,' she said.

'It was Nicholas, wasn't it?'

She regretted having told him now, but at the time it had been vitally necessary to speak to somebody.

She nodded, and his voice had a sting to it as he went on.

'I'd like to bust that bastard in the mouth.'

'We levelled the score, didn't we?' she smiled, but it was an unconvincing smile, and she didn't try to hold it.

'Sam, I want you to know that for me it was not just another quick shack job.'

'I know that.' Impulsively she reached out and squeezed his hand. 'And thanks for understanding – but is it okay if we don't talk about it any more?'

Peter Berg had twisted round in his safety straps, so that he could press his face to the round perspex window in the fuselage of the big Sikorsky helicopter.

The night was completely, utterly black.

Across the cabin, the Flight Engineer stood in the open doorway, the wind ripping at his bright orange overalls, fluttering them around his body, and he turned and grinned across at the boy, then he made a windmilling gesture with his hand and stapped downwards with his thumb. It was impossible to speak in the clattering, rushing roar of wind and engine and rotor.

The helicopter banked gently and Peter gasped with excitement as the ship came into view.

She was burning all her lights; tier upon tier, the brilliantly lit floors of her stern quarters rose above the altitude at which the Sikorsky was hovering, and, seeming to reach ahead to the black horizon, the tank deck was outlined with the rows of hooded lamps, like the street-lamps of a deserted city.

She was so huge that she looked like a city, there seemed to be no end to her, stretched to the horizon and towering into the sky.

The helicopter sank in a controlled sweep towards the white circular target on the heliport, guided down by the engineer in the open doorway. Skilfully the pilot matched his descent to the forward motion of the ultra-tanker, twenty-two knots at top economical – Peter had swotted the figures avidly – and the deck moved with grudging majesty to the scend of the tall Cape rollers pushing in unchecked from across the length of the Atlantic Ocean.

The pilot hovered, judging his approach against the brisk northwesterly cross-wind, and from fifty feet Peter could see that the decks were almost level with the surface of the sea, pressed down deeply by the weight of her cargo. Every few seconds, one of the rollers that raced down her length would flip aboard and spread like spilled milk, white and frothy in the deck lights, before cascading back over the side.

Made arrogant and unyielding by her vast bulk, the *Golden Dawn* did not woo the ocean, as other ships do. Instead, her great blunt bows crushed the swells, churning them under or shouldering them contemptuously aside.

Peter had been around boats since before he could walk, he too was a sea-creature. But though his eye was keen, it was as yet un-schooled, so he did not notice the working of the long wide deck.

Sitting beside Peter on the bench seat, Duncan Alexander knew to look for the movement in the hull. He watched the hull twisting and hogging, but so slightly, so barely perceptibly, that Duncan blinked it away, and looked again. From bows to stern she was a mile and a half long, and in essence she was merely four steel pods held together by an elaborate flexible steel scaffolding and driven forward by the mighty propulsion unit in the stern. There was small independent movement of each of the tank pods, so the deck twisted as she rolled, and flexed like a long-bow as she took the swells under her. The crest of these swells were a quarter of a mile apart. At any one time, there were four separate wave patterns beneath *Golden Dawn*'s hull, with the peaks thrusting up and the troughs allowing the tremendous dead weight of her cargo to push downwards; the elastic steel groaned and gave to meet these shearing forces.

No hull is ever completely rigid, and elasticity had been part of the ultra-tanker's original design, but those designs had been altered. Duncan Alexander had saved almost two thousand tons of steel, by reducing the stiffening of the central pillar that docked the four pods together, and he had dispensed with the double skins of the pods themselves. He had honed *Golden Dawn* down to the limits at which his own architects had baulked; then he had hired Japanese architects to rework the designs. They had expressed themselves satisfied that the hull was safe, but had also respectfully pointed out that nobody had ever carried a million tons of crude petroleum in a single cargo before.

The helicopter sank the last few feet and bumped gently on to the insulated green deck, with its thick coat of plasticized paint which prevented the striking of spark. Even a grain of sand trodden between leather sole and bare steel could ignite an explosive air and petroleum gas mixture.

The ship's party swarmed forward, doubled under the swirling rotor. The luggage in its net beneath the fuselage was dragged away and strong hands swung Peter down on to the deck. He stood blinking in the glare of deck lamps and wrinkling his nose to the characteristic tanker stench. It is a smell that pervades everything aboard one of these ships, the food, the furniture, the crew's clothing – even their hair and skin.

It is the thin acrid chemical stench of under-rich fumes vented off from the tanks. Oxygen and petroleum gas are only explosive in a mixture within narrow limits: too much oxygen makes the blend under-rich and too much petroleum gas makes it over-rich, either of which mixtures are non-explosive, non-combustible.

Chantelle Alexander was handed down next from the cabin of the helicopter, bringing an instant flash of elegance to the starkly lit scene of bleak steel and ugly functional machinery. She wore a catsuit of dark green with a bright Jean Patou scarf on her head. Two ships officers closed in solicitously on each side of her and led her quickly away towards the towering stern quarters, out of the rude and blustering wind and the helicopter engine roar.

Duncan Alexander followed her down to the deck, shook hands quickly with the First Officer.

'Captain Randle's compliments, sir. He is unable to leave the bridge while the ship is in the inshore channel.'

'I understand.' Duncan flashed that marvellous smile. The great ship drew almost twenty fathoms fully laden and she had come in very close, as close as was prudent to the mountainous coastline of Good Hope with its notorious currents and wild winds. However, Chantelle Christy must not be exposed to the ear-numbing discomfort of the helicopter flight for a moment longer than was necessary, and so *Golden Dawn* had come in through the inner channel, perilously close to the guardian rocks of Robben Island that stood in the open mouth of Table Bay.

Even before the helicopter rose and circled away towards the distant glow of Cape Town city under its dark square mountain, the tanker's great blunt bows were swinging away towards the west, and Duncan imagined the relief of Captain Randle as he gave the order to make the offing into the open Atlantic with the oceanic depths under his cumbersome ship.

Duncan smiled again and reached for Peter Berg's hand.

'Come on, my boy.'

'I'm all right, sir.'

Skilfully Peter avoided the hand and the smile, containing his wild excitement so that he walked ahead like a man, without the skipping energy of a little boy. Duncan Alexander felt the customary flare of annoyance. No more, than that – bare anger at this further rejection by Berg's puppy. They went in single file along the steel catwalk with the child leading. He had never been able to get close to the boy and he had tried hard in the beginning. Now Duncan stopped his anger with the satisfying memory of how neatly he had used the child to slap Berg in the face, and draw the fangs of his opposition.

Berg would be worrying too much about his brat to have time for anything else. He followed Chantelle and the child into the gleaming chrome and plastic corridors of the stern quarters. It was difficult to think of decks and bulkheads rather than floors and walls in here. It was too much like a modern apartment block, even the elevator which bore them swiftly and silently five storeys up to the navigation bridge helped to dispel the feeling of being shipborne.

On the bridge itself, they were so high above the sea as to be divorced from it. The deck lights had been extinguished once the helicopter had gone, and the darkness of the night, silenced by the thick double-glazed windows, heightened the peace and isolation. The riding lights in the bows seemed remote as the very stars, and the gentle lulling movement of the immense hull was only just noticeable.

The Master was a man of Duncan Alexander's own choosing. The command of the flagship of Christy Marine should have gone to Basil Reilly, the senior captain of the fleet. However, Reilly was Berg's man, and Duncan had used the foundering of *Golden Adventurer* to force premature retirement on the old sailor.

Randle was young for the responsibility, just a little over thirty years of age, but his training and his credentials were impeccable, and he was an honours graduate of the tanker school in France. Here top men received realistic training in the specialized handling of these freakish giants in cunningly constructed lakes and scale-model harbours, working thirty-foot models of the bulk carriers that had all the handling characteristics of the real ships.

Since Duncan had given him the command, he had been a staunch ally, and he had stoutly defended the design and construction of his ship when the reporters, whipped up by Nicholas Berg, had questioned him. He was loyal, which weighed heavily, tipping the balance for Duncan against his youth and inexperience.

He hurried to meet his important vistors as they stepped out of the elevator into his spacious, gleaming modern bridge, a short stocky figure with a bull neck and the thrusting heavy jaw of great determination or great stubborness. His greeting had just the right mixture of warmth and servility, and Duncan noted approvingly that he treated even the boy with careful respect. Randle was bright enough to realize that one day the child would be head of Christy Marine. Duncan liked a man who could think so clearly and so far ahead, but Randle was not quite prepared for Peter Berg.

'Can I see your engine room, Captain?'

'You mean right now?'

'Yes.' For Peter the question was superfluous. 'If you don't mind, sir,' he added quickly. Today was for doing things and tomorrow was lost in the mists of the future. Right now, would be just fine.

'Well now,' the Captain realized the request was deadly serious, and that this lad could not be put off very easily, 'we go on automatic during the night. There's nobody down there now – and it wouldn't be fair to wake the engineer, would it? It's been a hard day.'

'I suppose not.' Bitterly disappointed, but amenable to convincing argument, Peter nodded.

'But I am certain the Chief would be delighted to have you as his guest directly after breakfast.'

The Chief Engineer was a Scot with three sons of his own in Glasgow, the youngest of them almost exactly Peter's age. He was more than delighted. Within twenty-four hours, Peter was the ship's favourite, with his own blue company-issue overalls altered to fit him and his name embroidered across the back by the lascar steward, 'PETER BERG'. He wore his bright yellow plastic hard hat at the same jaunty angle as the Chief did, and carried a wad of cotton waste in his back pocket to wipe his greasy hands after helping one of the stokers clean the fuel filters – the messiest job on board, and the greatest fun.

Although the engine control room with its rough camaraderie, endless supplies of sandwiches and cocoa and satisfying grease and oil that made a man look like a professional, was Peter's favourite station, yet he stood other watches.

Every morning he joined the First Officer on his inspection. Starting in the bows, they worked their way back, checking each of the pod tanks, every valve, and every one of the heavy hydraulic docking clamps that held the pod tanks attached to the main frames of the hull. Most important of all they checked the gauges on each compartment which gave the precise indication of the gas mixtures contained in the air spaces under the main deck of the crude tanks.

*Golden Dawn* operated on the 'inert' system to keep the trapped fumes in an over-rich and safe condition. The exhaust fumes of the ship's engine were caught, passed through filters and scrubbers to remove the corrosive sulphur elements and then, as almost pure carbon dioxide and carbon monoxide, they were forced into the air spaces of the petroleum tanks. The evaporating fumes of the volatile elements of the crude mingled with the exhaust fumes to form an over-rich, oxygen-poor, and unexplosive gas.

However, a leak through one of the hundreds of valves and connections would allow air into the tanks, and the checks to detect this were elaborate, ranging from an unceasing electronic monitoring of each tank to the daily physical inspection, in which Peter now assisted.

Peter usually left the First Officer's party when it returned to the stern quarters, he might then pass the time of day with the two-man crew in the central pump room.

From here the tanks were monitored and controlled, loaded and offloaded, the flow of inert gas balanced, and the crude petroleum could be pushed through the giant centrifugal pumps and transferred from tank to tank to make alterations to the ship's trim, during partial discharge, or when one or more tanks were detached and taken inshore for discharge.

In the pump room was kept a display that always fascinated Peter. It was the sample cupboard with its rows of screw-topped bottles, each containing samples of the cargo taken during loading. As all four of *Golden Dawn*'s tanks had been filled at the same off-shore loading point and all with crude from the same field, each of the bottles bore the identical label.

EL BARRAS CRUDE
BUNKERS 'C'
HIGH CADMIUM

Peter liked to take one of the bottles and hold it to the light. Somehow he had always expected the crude oil to be treacly and tarlike, but it was thin as human blood and when he shook the bottle, it coated the glass and the light through it was dark red, again like congealing blood.

'Some of the crudes are black, some yellow and the Nigerians are green,' the pump foreman told him. 'This is the first red that I've seen.'

'I suppose it's the cadmium in it,' Peter told him.

'Guess it is,' the foreman agreed seriously; all on board had very soon learned not to talk down to Peter Berg, he expected to be treated on equal terms.

By this time it was mid-morning and Peter had worked up enough appetite to visit the galley, where he was greeted like visiting royalty. Within days, Peter knew his way unerringly through the labyrinthine and usually deserted passageways. It was characteristic of these great crude-carriers that you might wander through them for hours without meeting another human being. With their huge bulk and their tiny crews, the only place where there was always human presence was the navigation bridge on the top floor of the stern quarters.

The bridge was always one of Peter's obligatory stops.

'Good-morning, Tug,' the officer of the watch would greet him. Peter had been christened with his nickname when he had announced at the breakfast table on his first morning:

'Tankers are great, but I'm going to be a tug captain, like my dad.'

On the bridge the ship might be taken out of automatic to allow Peter to spell the helmsman for a while, or he would assist the junior deck officers while they made a sun shot as an exercise to check against the satellite navigational Decca; then, after socializing with Captain Randle for a while, it was time to report to his true station in the engine.

'We were waiting on you, Tug,' growled the Chief. 'Get your overalls on, man, we're going down the propeller shaft tunnel.'

The only unpleasant period of the day was when Peter's mother insisted that he scrub off the top layers of grease and fuel oil, dress in his number ones, and act as an unpaid steward during the cocktail hour in the elaborate lounge of the owner's suite.

It was the only time that Chantelle Alexander fraternized with the ship's officers and it was a painfully stilted hour, with Peter one of the major sufferers – but the rest of the time he was successful in avoiding the clinging restrictive rulings of his mother and the hated, fiercely but silently resented presence of Duncan Alexander, his stepfather.

Still, he was instinctively aware of the new and disturbing tensions between his mother and Duncan Alexander. In the night he heard the raised voices from the master cabin, and he strained to catch the words. Once, when

he had heard the cries of his mother's distress, he had left his bunk and gone
barefooted to knock on the cabin door. Duncan Alexander had opened it to
him. He was in a silk dressing-gown and his handsome features were swollen
and flushed with anger.

'Go back to bed.'

'I want to see my mother,' Peter had told him quietly.

'You need a damned good hiding,' Duncan had flared. 'Now do as you
are told.'

'I want to see my mother.' Peter had stood his ground, standing very
straight in his pyjamas with both his tone and expression neutral, and
Chantelle had come to him in her nightdress and knelt to embrace him.

'It's all right, darling. It's perfectly all right.' But she had been weeping.
After that there had been no more loud voices in the night.

However, except for an hour in the afternoon, when the swimming-pool
was placed out of bounds to officers and crew, while Chantelle swam and
sunbathed, she spent the rest of the time in the owner's suite, eating all her
meals there, withdrawn and silent, sitting at the panoramic windows of her
cabin, coming to life only for an hour in the evenings while she played the
owner's wife to the ship's officers.

Duncan Alexander, on the other hand, was like a caged animal. He paced
the open decks, composing long messages which were sent off regularly over
the telex in company code to Christy Main in Leadenhall Street.

Then he would stand out on the open wing of *Golden Dawn*'s bridge,
staring fixedly ahead at the northern horizon, awaiting the reply to his last
telex, chafing openly at having to conduct the company's business at such
long remove, and goaded by the devils of doubt and impatience and fear.

Often it seemed as though he were trying to forge the mighty hull onwards,
faster and faster into the north, by the sheer power of his will.


In the north-western corner of the Caribbean basin, there is an area of
shallow warm water, hemmed in on one side by the island chain of the great
Antilles, the bulwark of Cuba and Hispaniola, while in the west the sweep
of the Yucatan peninsula runs south through Panama into the great land-
mass of South America – shallow warm trapped water and saturated tropical
air, enclosed by land-masses which can heat very rapidly in the high hot sun
of the tropics. However, all of it is gently cooled and moderated by the
benign influence of the north-easterly trade winds – winds so unvarying in
strength and direction that over the centuries, sea-faring men have placed
their lives and their fortunes at risk upon their balmy wings, gambling on
the constancy of that vast moving body of mild air.

But the wind does fail; for no apparent reason and without previous
warning, it dies away, often merely for an hour or two, but occasionally –
very occasionally – for days or weeks at a time.

Far to the south and east of this devil's spawning ground, the *Golden
Dawn* ploughed massively on through the sweltering air and silken calm of
the doldrums, northwards across the equator, changing course every few
hours to maintain the great circle track that would carry her well clear of

that glittering shield of islands that the Caribbean carries, like an armoured knight, on its shoulder.

The treacherous channels and passages through the islands were not for a vessel of *Golden Dawn*'s immense bulk, deep draught and limited manoeuvrability. She was to go high above the Tropic of Cancer, and just south of the island of Bermuda she would make her westings and enter the wider and safer waters of the Florida Straits above Grand Bahamas. On this course, she would be constricted by narrow and shallow seaways for only a few hundred miles before she was out into the open waters of the Gulf of Mexico again.

But while she ran on northwards, out of the area of equatorial calm, she should have come out at last into the sweet cool airs of the trades, but she did not. Day after day, the calm persisted, and stifling still air pressed down on the ship. It did not in any way slow or affect her passage, but her Master remarked to Duncan Alexander:

'Another corker today, by the looks of it.'

When he received no reply from his brooding, silent Chairman, he retired discreetly, leaving Duncan alone on the open wing of the bridge with only the breeze of the ship's passage ruffling his thick coppery hair.

However, the calm was not merely local. It extended westwards in a wide, hot belt across the thousand islands and the basin of shallow sea they enclosed.

The calm lay heavily on the oily waters, and the sun beat down on the enclosing land-masses. Every hour the air heated and sucked up the evaporating waters; a fat bubble like a swelling blister began to rise, the first movement of air in many days. It was not a big bubble, only a hundred miles across, but as it rose, the rotation of the earth's surface began to twist the rising air, spinning it like a top, so that the satellite cameras, hundreds of miles above, recorded a creamy little spiral wisp like the decorative-icing flower on a wedding cake.

The cameras relayed the picture through many channels, until at last it reached the desk of the senior forecaster of the hurricane watch at the meteorological headquarters at Miami in Southern Florida.

'Looks like a ripe one,' he grunted to his assistant, recognizing that all the favourable conditions for the formation of a revolving tropical storm were present. 'We'll ask Airforce for a fly-through.'

At forty-five thousand feet the pilot of the US Airforce B52 saw the rising dome of the storm from two hundred miles away. It had grown enormously in only six hours.

As the warm saturated air was forced upwards, so the icy cold of the upper troposphere condensed the water vapour into thick puffed-up silver clouds. They boiled upwards, roiling and swirling upon themselves. Already the dome of cloud and ferociously turbulent air was higher than the aircraft.

Under it, a partial vacuum was formed, and the surrounding surface air tried to move in to fill it. But it was compelled into an anti-clockwise track around the centre by the mysterious forces of the earth's rotation. Compelled to travel the long route, the velocity of the air mass accelerated ferociously, and the entire system became more unstable, more dangerous by the hour,

turning faster, perpetuating itself by creating greater wind velocities and
steeper pressure gradients.

The cloud at the top of the enormous rising dome reached an altitude
where the temperature was thirty degrees below freezing and the droplets
of rain turned to crystals of ice and were smeared away by upper-level jet-
streams. Long beautiful patterns of cirrus against the high blue sky were
blown hundreds of miles ahead of the storm to serve as its heralds.

The US Airforce B52 hit the first clear-air turbulence one hundred and
fifty miles from the storm's centre. It was as though an invisible predator
had seized the fuselage and shaken it until the wings were almost torn from
their roots, and, in one surge, the aircraft was flung five thousand feet
straight upwards.

'Very severe turbulence,' the pilot reported. 'We have vertical wind speeds
of three hundred miles an hour plus.'

The senior forecaster in Miami picked up the telephone and called the
computer programmer on the floor above him. 'Ask Charlie for a hurricane
code-name.'

And a minute later the programmer called him back. 'Charlie says to call
the bitch "Lorna".'

Six hundred miles south-west of Miami the storm began to move forward,
slowly at first but every hour gathering power, spiralling upon itself at
unbelievable velocities, its high dome swelling upwards now through fifty
thousand feet and still climbing. The centre of the storm opened like a
flower, the calm eye extended upwards in a vertical tunnel with smooth
walls of solid cloud rising to the very summit of the dome, now sixty thousand
feet above the surface of the wind-tortured sea.

The entire mass began to move faster, back towards the east, in a directly
contrary direction to the usual track of the gentle trade winds. Spinning and
roaring upon itself, devouring everything in its path, the she-devil called
'Lorna' launched itself across the Caribbean Sea.


Nicholas Berg turned his head to look down upon the impressive skyline
of Miami Beach. The rampart of tall elegant hotel buildings followed the
curve of the beach into the north, and behind it lay the ugly sprawled tangle
of urban development and snarled highways.

The Eastern Airlines direct flight from Bermuda turned on to its base leg
and then on to final approach, losing height over the beach and Biscayne
Bay.

Nicholas felt uncomfortable, the nagging of guilt and uncertainty. His
guilt was of two kinds. He felt guilty that he had deserted his post at the
moment when he was likely to be desperately needed.

Ocean Salvage's two vessels were out there somewhere in the Atlantic,
*Warlock* running hard up the length of the Atlantic in a desperate attempt
to catch up with *Golden Dawn*, while Jules Levoisin in *Sea Witch* was now
approaching the eastern seaboard of America where he would refuel before
going on to his assignment as standby tug on the exploration field in the
Gulf of Mexico. At any moment, the Master of either vessel might urgently
need to have his instructions.

Then there was *Golden Dawn*. She had rounded the Cape of Good Hope almost three weeks ago. Since then, even Bernard Wackie had been unable to fix her position. She had not been reported by other craft, and any communications she had made with Christy Main must have been by satellite telex, for she had maintained strict silence on the radio channels. However, she must rapidly be nearing the most critical part of her voyage when she turned west and began her approach to the continental shelf of North America and the passage of the islands into the Gulf. Peter Berg was on board that monster, and Nicholas felt the chill of guilt. His place was at the centre, in the control room of Bach Wackie on the top floor of the Bank of Bermuda building in Hamilton town. His post was there where he could assess changing conditions and issue instant commands to co-ordinate his salvage tugs.

Now he had deserted his post, and even though he had made arrangements to maintain contact with Bernard Wackie, still it would take him hours, perhaps even days, to get back to where he was needed, if there was an emergency.

But then there was Samantha. His instincts warned him that every day, every hour he delayed in going to her would reduce his chances of having her again.

There was more guilt there, the guilt of betrayal. It was no help to tell himself that he had made no marriage vows to Samantha Silver, that his night of weakness with Chantelle had been forced upon him in circumstances almost impossible to resist, that any other man in his position would have done the same, and that in the end the episode had been a catharsis and a release that had left him free for ever of Chantelle.

To Samantha, it had been betrayal, and he knew that much was destroyed by it. He felt terrible aching guilt, not for the act – sexual intercourse without love is fleeting and insignificant – but for the betrayal and for the damage he had wrought.

Now he was uncertain, uncertain as to just how much he had destroyed, how much was left for him to build upon. All that he was certain of was that he needed her, more than he had needed anything in his life. She was still the promise of eternal youth and of the new life towards which he was groping so uncertainly. If love was needing, then he loved Samantha Silver with something close to desperation.

She had told him she would not be there when he came. He had to hope now that she had lied, he felt physically sick at the thought that she meant it.

He had only a single Louis Vuitton overnight valise as cabin luggage so he passed swiftly through customs, and as he went into the telephone booths, he checked his watch. It was after six o'clock, she'd be home by now.

He had dialled the first four digits of her number before he checked himself.

'What the hell am I phoning for?' he asked himself grimly. 'To tell her I'm here, so she can have a flying start when she runs for the bushes?'

There is nothing so doomed as a timid lover. He dropped the receiver back on its cradle, and went for the Hertz desk at the terminal doors.

'What's the smallest you've got?' he asked.

'A Cougar,' the pretty blonde in the yellow uniform told him. In America, 'small' is a relative term. He was just lucky she hadn't offered him a Sherman tank.

The brightly painted Chevy van was in the lean-to shelter under the spread branches of the ficus tree, and he parked the Cougar's nose almost touching its tail-gate. There was no way she could escape now, unless she went out through the far wall of the shed. Knowing her, that was always a possibility, he grinned mirthlessly.

He knocked once on the screen door of the kitchen and went straight on in. There was a coffee pot beside the range, and he touched it as he passed. It was still warm.

He went through into the living room, and called:

'Samantha!'

The bedroom door was ajar. He pushed it open. There was a suit of denims, and some pale transparent wisps of underwear thrown carelessly over the patchwork quilt.

The shack was deserted, he went down the steps of the front stoop and straight on to the beach. The tide had swept the sand smooth, and her prints were the only ones. She had dropped her towel above the high-water mark but he had to shade his eyes against the ruddy glare of the lowering sun before he could make out her bobbing head – five hundred yards out.

He sat down beside her towel in the fluffy dry sand and lit a cheroot.

He waited, while the sun settled in a wild, fiery flood of light, and he lost the shape of her head against the darkening sea. She was half a mile out now, but he felt no urgency, and the darkness was almost complete when she rose suddenly, waist-deep from the edge of the gentle surf, waded ashore and came up the beach, twisting the rope of her hair over one shoulder to wring the water from it.

Nicholas felt his heart flop over and he flicked the cheroot away and stood up. She halted abruptly, like a startled forest animal, and stood completely still, staring uncertainly at the tall, dark figure before her. She was so young and slim and smooth and beautiful.

'What do you want?' she faltered.

'You,' he said.

'Why? Are you starting a harem?' Her voice hardened and she straightened; he could not see the expression of her eyes, but her shoulders took on a stubborn set.

He stepped forward and she was rigid in his arms and her lips hard and tightly unresponsive under his.

'Sam, there are things I'll never be able to explain, I don't even understand them myself, but what I do know very clearly is that I love you, that without you my life is going to be flat and plain goddamned miserable—'

There was no relaxation of the rigid muscles. Her hands were still held stiffly at her sides and her body felt cold and wet and unyielding.

'Samantha, I wish I were perfect – I'm not. But all I am sure of is that I can't make it without you.'

'I couldn't take it again. I couldn't live through this again,' she said tightly.

'I need you. I am certain of that,' he insisted.

'You'd better be, you son of a bitch. You cheat on me one time more and you won't have anything left to cheat with – I'll take it off clean, at the roots.' Then she was clinging to him. 'Oh God, Nicholas, how I hated you, and how I missed you – and how long you took to come back,' and her lips were soft and tasted of the sea.

He picked her up and carried her up through the soft sand. He didn't trust himself to speak, it would be so easy to say the wrong thing now.


'Nicholas, I've been sitting here waiting for your call.' Bernard Wackie's voice was sharp and alert, the tension barely contained. 'How soon can you get yourself back here?'

'What is it?'

'It is starting to pop. I've got to hand it to you, baby, you've got a nose for it. You smelled this coming.'

'Come on, Bernie!' Nicholas snapped.

'This call is going through three open exchanges,' Bernie told him. 'You want chapter and verse, or did nobody ever tell you that it's a tough game you are in? There is a lot of competition cluttering up the scene. The cheese-heads have one lying handy.' Probably *Wittezee* or one of the other big Dutch tugs, Nicholas thought swiftly. 'They could be streaming a towing wire within a couple of days. And the Yanks are pretty hot numbers, McCormick has one stationed in the Hudson River.'

'All right,' Nick cut through the relish with which Bernie was detailing the threat of hovering competition.

'There is a direct flight at seven tomorrow morning – if I can't make that, I'll connect with the British Airways flight from Nassau at noon tomorrow. Meet me,' Nick ordered.

'You shouldn't have gone running off,' said Bernard Wackie, showing amazing hindsight. Before he could deliver any more pearls of wisdom, Nicholas hung up on him.

Samantha was sitting up in the centre of the bed. She was stark naked, but she hugged her knees to her chest with both arms, and under the gorgeous tangle of her hair her face was desolate as that of a lost child and her green eyes haunted.

'You're going again,' she said softly. 'You only just came, and now you're going again. Oh God, Nicholas, loving you is the toughest job I've ever had in my life. I don't think I have got the muscle for it.'

He reached for her quickly and she clung to him, pressing her face into the thick pad of coarse dark hair that covered his chest.

'I have to go – I think it's *Golden Dawn*,' he said, and she listened quietly while he told it to her. Only when he finished speaking did she begin to ask the questions which kept them talking quietly, locked in each other's arms in the old brass bed, until long after midnight.

She insisted on cooking his breakfast for him, even though it was still dark outside and she was more than half asleep, hanging on to the range for support and turning up the early morning radio show so that the music might shake her awake.

'Good morning, early birds, this is W.W.O.K. with another lovely day ahead of you. A predicted 85° at Fort Lauderdale and the coast, and 80° inland with a 10% chance of rain. We've got a report on hurricane "Lorna" for you also. She's dipping away south, towards the lesser Antilles – so we can all relax, folks – relax and listen to Elton John.'

'I love Elton John,' Samantha said sleepily. 'Don't you?'

'Who is he?' Nicholas asked.

'There! I knew right away we had a lot in common.' She blinked at him owlishly. 'Did you kiss me good morning? I forget.'

'Come here,' he instructed. 'You're not going to forget this one.'

Then, a few minutes later, 'Nicholas, you'll miss your plane.'

'Not if I cut breakfast.'

'It would have been a grotty breakfast anyway.' She was coming awake fast now.

She gave him the last kiss through the open window of the Cougar. 'You've got an hour – you'll just about make it.'

He started the engine and still she held on to the sill.

'Nicholas, one day we will be together – I mean all the time, like we planned? You and me doing our own thing, our own way? We will, won't we?'

'It's a promise.'

'Hurry back,' she said, and he gunned the Cougar up the sandy driveway without looking back.


There were eight of them crowded into Tom Parker's office. Although there was only seating for three, the others found perches against the tiered shelves with their rows of biological specimens in bottles of formaldehyde or on the piles of reference books and white papers that were stacked against the walls.

Samantha sat on the corner of Tom's desk, swinging her long denim-clad legs, and answered the questions that were fired at her.

'How do you know she will take the passage of the Florida Straits?'

'It's an educated guess. She's just too big and clumsy to thread the needle of the islands.' Samantha's replies were quick. 'Nicholas is betting on it.'

'I'll go along with that then,' Tom grunted.

'The Straits are a hundred miles wide—'

'I know what you're going to say,' Samantha smiled, and turned to one of the other girls. 'Sally-Anne will answer that one.'

'You all know my brother is in the Coast Guard – all traffic through the Straits reports to Fort Lauderdale,' she explained. 'And the coastguard aircraft patrol out as far as Grand Bahama.'

'We'll have a fix on her immediately she enters the Straits – we've got the whole U.S. Coast Guard rooting for us.'

They argued and discussed for ten minutes more, before Tom Parker slapped an open palm on the desk in front of him and they subsided reluctantly into silence.

'Okay,' he said. 'Do I understand the proposal to be that this chapter of Green-Peace intercepts the tanker carrying cad-rich crudes before it enters American territorial waters and attempts to delay or divert the ship?'

'That's exactly it,' Samantha nodded, and looked about her for support. They were all nodding and murmuring agreement.

'What are we trying to achieve? Do we truly believe that we will be able to hold up the delivery of toxic crudes to the refinery at Galveston? Let's define our objectives,' Tom insisted.

'In order for evil men to triumph it is necessary only that good men do nothing. We are doing something.'

'Bullshit, Sam,' Tom growled. 'Let's cut down on the rhetoric – it's one of the things that does us more harm than good. You talk like a nut and you discredit yourself before you have begun.'

'All right,' Samantha grinned. 'We are publicizing the dangers, and our opposition to them.'

'Okay,' Tom nodded. 'That's better. What are our other objectives?'

They discussed that for twenty minutes more, and then Tom Parker took over again.

'Fine, now how do we get out there in the Straits to confront this vessel – do we put on our water-wings and swim?'

Even Samantha looked sheepish now. She glanced around for support, but the others were studying their fingernails or gazing with sudden fascination out of the windows.

'Well,' Samantha began, and then hesitated. 'We thought—'

'Go on,' Tom encouraged her. 'Of course, you weren't thinking of using University property, were you? There is actually a law in this country against taking other people's ships – it's called piracy.'

'As a matter of fact—' Samantha gave a helpless shrug.

'And as a senior and highly respected member of the faculty, you would not expect me to be party to a criminal act.'

They were all silent, watching Samantha, for she was their leader, but for once she was at a loss.

'On the other hand, if a party of graduate researchers put in a requisition, through the proper channels, I would be quite happy to authorize an extended field expedition across the Straits to Grand Bahama on board the *Dicky.*'

'Tom, you're a darling,' said Samantha.

'That's a hell of a way to speak to your Professor,' said Tom, and scowled happily at her.


'They came in on the British Airways flight from Heathrow yesterday afternoon. Three of them, here is a list of the names,' Bernard Wackie slid a notepad across the desk, and Nicholas glanced at it quickly.

'Charles Gras – I know him, he's Chief Engineer at Construction Navale Atlantique,' Nicholas explained.

'Right,' Bernard nodded. 'He gave his occupation and employer to Immigration.'

'Isn't that privileged information?'

Bernard grinned. 'I keep my ear to the ground,' and then he was deadly serious again. 'All right, so these three engineers have a small suitcase each and a crate in the hold that weighs three hundred and fifty kilos, and it's marked "Industrial Machinery".'

'Don't stop now,' Nicholas encouraged him.

'And there is an S61N Sikorsky helicopter sitting waiting for them on the tarmac. The helicopter has been chartered direct from London by Christy Marine of Leadenhall Street. The three engineers and the case of machinery are shuttled aboard the Sikorsky so fast that it looks like a conjuring trick, and she takes off and egg-beats for the south.'

'Did the Sikorsky pilot file a flight-plan?'

'Sure did. Servicing shipping, course 196° magnetic. ETA to be reported.'

'What's the range of the 61N – 500 nautical miles?'

'Not bad,' Bernard conceded. '533 for the standard, but this model has long-range tanks, she's good for 750. But that's one way, not the return journey. The helicopter hasn't returned to Bermuda yet.'

'She could refuel aboard – or, if they aren't carrying avgas, she could stay on until final destination,' Nicholas said. 'What else have you got?'

'You want more?' Bernard looked aghast. 'Doesn't anything ever satisfy you?'

'Did you monitor the communications between Bermuda Control, the chopper, and the ship she was servicing?'

'Nix,' Bernard shook his head. 'There was box-up.' He looked shamefaced. 'It happens to the best of us.'

'Spare me the details. Can you get information from Bermuda Control of the time the chopper closed her flight-plan?'

'Jesus, Nicholas, you know better than that. It's an offence to listen in on the aviation frequencies, let alone ask them.'

Nicholas jumped up, and crossed swiftly to the perspex plot. He brooded over it, leaning on clenched fists, his expression smouldering as he studied the large-scale map.

'What does all this mean to you, Nicholas?' Bernard came to stand beside him.

'It means that a vessel at sea, belonging to the Christy Marine fleet, has requested its head office to send machinery spares and specialist personnel by the fastest possible means, without regard to expense. Have you figured the air freight on a package of 350 kilos?'

Nicholas straightened up and groped for the crocodile-skin cheroot case.

'It means that the vessel is broken down or in imminent danger of breakdown somewhere in an area south-west of Bermuda, within an arc of four hundred and fifty miles – probably much closer, otherwise she would have requested service from the Bahamas, and it's highly unlikely they would have operated the chopper at extreme range.'

'Right,' Bernard agreed. Nicholas lit his cheroot and they were both silent a moment.

'A hell of a small needle in a bloody big haystack,' said Bernard.

'You let me worry about that,' Nicholas murmured, still without taking his eyes from the plot.

'That's what you are paid for,' Bernard agreed amiably. 'It's *Golden Dawn*, isn't it?'

'Has Christy Marine got any other vessels in the area?'

'Not as far as I know.'

'Then that was a bloody stupid question.'

'Take it easy, Nicholas.'

'I'm sorry.' Nicholas touched his arm. 'My boy's on that pig.' He took a deep draw on the cheroot, held it a moment, and then slowly exhaled. His voice was calm and businesslike, as he went on:

'What's out weather?'

'Wind at 060° and 15 knots. Cloud three eighths stratocumulus at four thousand feet. Long-range projection, no change.'

'Steady trade winds again,' Nicholas nodded. 'Thank God for all small mercies.'

'There is a hurricane warning out, as you know, but on its present position and track, it will blow itself out to sea a thousand miles south of Grand Bahama.'

'Good,' Nicholas nodded again. 'Please ask both *Warlock* and *Sea Witch* to report their positions, course, speed and fuel-conditions.'

Bernard had the two telex flimsies for him within twenty minutes.

'*Warlock* has made a good run of it,' Nicholas murmured, as the position of the tug was marked on the plot.

'She crossed the equator three days ago,' said Bernard.

'And *Sea Witch* will reach Charleston late tomorrow,' Nicholas observed. 'Are any of the opposition inside us?'

Bernard shook his head. 'McCormick has one in New York and *Wittezee* is halfway back to Rotterdam.'

'We are in good shape,' Nicholas decided, as he balanced the triangles of relative speeds and distances between the vessels.

'Is there another chopper available on the island to get me out to *Warlock*?'

'No,' Bernard shook his head. 'The 61N is the only one based on Bermuda.'

'Can you arrange bunkering for *Warlock*, I mean immediate bunkering – here in Hamilton?'

'We can have her tanks filled an hour after she comes in.'

Nicholas paused and then made the decision. 'Please telex David Allen on *Warlock*, TO MASTER WARLOCK FROM BERG IMMEDIATE AND URGENT NEW SPEED TOP OF THE GREEN NEW COURSE HAMILTON HARBOUR BERMUDA ISLAND DIRECT REPORT EXPECTED TIME OF ARRIVAL ENDS.'

'You're going to run, then?' Bernard asked. 'You are going to run with both your ships?'

'Yes,' Nicholas nodded. 'I'm running with everything I've got.'

*Golden Dawn* wallowed with the dead heavy weight of one million tons of crude oil. Her motion was that of a waterlogged hulk. Broadside to the set of the swells, her tank decks were almost awash. The low seas broke against her starboard rail and the occasional crest flopped over and spread like pretty patches of white lace-work over the green plastic-coated decks.

She had been drifting powerlessly for four days now.

The main bearing of the single propeller shaft had begun to run hot forty-eight hours after crossing the equator, and the Chief Engineer had asked for shut-down to inspect the bearing and effect any repairs. Duncan Alexander had forbidden any shut-down, over-riding the good judgement of both his Master and Chief Engineer, and had only grudgingly agreed to a reduction in the ship's speed.

He ordered the Chief Engineer to trace any fault and to effect what repairs he could, while under reduced power.

Within four hours, the Chief had traced the damaged and leaking gland in the pump that force-lubricated the bearing, but even the running under reduced power setting had done significant damage to the main bearing, and now there was noticeable vibration, jarring even *Golden Dawn*'s massive hull.

'I have to get the pump stripped down or we'll burn her clean out,' the Chief faced up to Duncan Alexander at last. 'Then you'll *have* to shut down and not just a couple of hours either. It will take two days to fit new bearing shells at sea.' The Chief was pale and his lips trembled, for he knew of this man's reputation. The engineer knew that he discarded those who crossed him, and he had the reputation of a special vindictiveness to hound a man until he was broken. The Chief was afraid, but his concern for the ship was just strong enough.

Duncan Alexander changed direction. 'What was the cause of the pump failure in the first place? Why wasn't it noticed earlier? It looks like a case of negligence to me.'

Stung at last, the Chief blurted out, 'If there had been a back-up pump on this ship, we would have switched to secondary system and done proper maintenance.'

Duncan Alexander flushed and turned away. The modifications he had personally ordered to *Golden Dawn*'s design had excluded most of the duplicated back-up systems; anything that kept down the cost of construction had been ordered.

'How long do you need?' He stopped in the centre of the owner's stateroom and glared at his engineer.

'Four hours,' the Scot replied promptly.

'You've got exactly four hours,' he said grimly. 'If you haven't finished by then you will live to regret it. I swear that to you.'

While the engineer stopped his engines, stripped, repaired and reassembled the lubrication pump, Duncan was on the bridge with the Master.

'We've lost time, too much time,' he said. 'I want that made up.'

'It will mean pushing over best economic speed,' Captain Randle warned carefully.

'Captain Randle, the value of our cargo is 85 dollars a ton. We have on board one million tons. I want the time made up.' Duncan brushed his objection aside. 'We have a deadline to meet in Galveston roads. This ship, this whole concept of carrying crude is on trial, Captain. I don't have to keep reminding you of that. The hell with the costs, I want to meet the deadline.'

'Yes, Mr Alexander,' Randle nodded. 'We'll make up the time.'

Three and a half hours later, the Chief Engineer came up to the bridge.

'Well?' Duncan turned on him fiercely as he stepped out of the elevator.

'The pump is repaired, but—'

'What is it, man?'

'I've got a feeling. We ran her too long. I've got a nasty feeling about that bearing. It wouldn't be clever to run her over 50% of power, not until it's been taken down and inspected—'

'I'm ordering revolutions for 25 knots,' Randle told him uneasily.

'I wouldn't do that, man,' the Chief shook his head mournfully.

'Your station is in the engine room,' Duncan dismissed him brusquely, nodded to Randle to order resumption of sailing, and went out to his customary place on the open wing of the bridge. He looked back over the high round stern as the white turbulence of the great propeller boiled out from under the counter and then settled in a long slick wake that soon reached back to the horizon. Duncan stood out in the wind until after dark, and when he went below, Chantelle was waiting for him. She stood up from the long couch under the forward windows of the stateroom.

'We are under way again.'

'Yes,' he said. 'It's going to be all right.'


The engine control was switched to automatic at nine o'clock local time that night. The engine room personnel went up to dinner, and to bed, all except the Chief Engineer. He lingered for another two hours shaking his head and mumbling bitterly over the massive bearing assembly in the long narrow shaft tunnel. Every few minutes, he laid his hand on the massive casting, feeling for the heat and vibration that would warn of structural damage.

At eleven o'clock, he spat on the steadily revolving propeller shaft. It was thick as an oak trunk and polished brilliant silver in the stark white lights of the tunnel. He pushed himself up stiffly from his crouch beside the bearing.

In the control room, he checked again that all the ship's systems were on automatic, and that all circuits were functioning and repeating on the big control board, then he stepped into the elevator and went up.

Thirty-five minutes later, one of the tiny transistors in the board blew with a pop like a champagne cork and a puff of grey smoke. There was nobody in the control room to hear or see it. The system was not duplicated, there was no back-up to switch itself in automatically, so that when the temperature of the bearing began to rise again there was no impulse carried to the alarm system, no automatic shut-down of power.

The massive shaft spun on while the over-heated bearing closed its grip upon the area of rough metal, damaged by the previous prolonged running. A fine sliver of metal lifted from the polished surface of the spinning shaft, and curled like a silver hair spring, was caught up and smeared into the bearing. The whole assembly began to glow a sullen cherry red and then the oxide paint that was daubed on the outer surfaces of the bearing began to blister and blacken. Still the tremendous power of the engine forced the shaft around.

What oil was still being fed between the glowing surfaces of the spinning shaft and the shells of the bearing turned instantly thin as water in the heat, then reached its flash point and burst into flame and ran in little fiery rivulets down the heavy casting of the main bearing, flashing the blistered paintwork alight. The shaft tunnel filled with thick billows of stinking chemical-tainted smoke, and only then did the fire sensors come to life and their alarms repeated on the navigation bridge and in the quarters of Master, First Officer and Chief Engineer.

But the great engine was still pounding along at 70% of power, and the shaft still turned in the disintegrating bearing, smearing heat-softened metal, buckling and distorting under unbearable strains.

The Chief Engineer was the first to reach the central console in the engine control room, and without orders from the bridge he began emergency shut-down of all systems.

It was another hour before the team under the direction of the First Officer had the fire in the shaft tunnel under control. They used carbon dioxide gas to smother the burning paint and oil, for cold water on the heated metal would have aggravated the damage done by heat distortion and buckling.

The metal of the main bearing casting was still so hot when the Chief Engineer began opening it up, that it scorched the thick leather and asbestos gloves worn by his team.

The bearing shells had disintegrated, and the shaft itself was brutally scored and pitted. If there was distortion, the Chief knew it would not be detected by eye. However, even a buckling of one ten thousandth of an inch would be critical.

He cursed softly as he worked, making the obscenities sound like a lullaby; he cursed the manufacturers of the lubricating pump, the men who had installed and tested it, the damaged gland and the lack of a back-up system, but mostly he cursed the stubbornness and intractability of the Chairman of Christy Marine whose ill-advised judgement had turned this functionally beautiful machinery into blackened smoking twisted metal.

It was mid-morning by the time the Chief had the spare bearing shells brought up from stores and unpacked from their wood shavings in the wooden cases; but it was only when they came to fit them that they realized that the cases had been incorrectly stencilled. The half-shells that they contained were obsolete non-metric types, and they were five millimetres undersized for *Golden Dawn*'s shaft; that tiny variation in size made them utterly useless.

It was only then that Duncan Alexander's steely urbane control began to crack; he raged about the bridge for twenty minutes, making no effort to think his way out of the predicament, but abusing Randle and his engineer in wild and extravagant terms. His rage had a paralysing affect on all *Golden Dawn*'s officers and they stood white-faced and silently guilty.

Peter Berg had sensed the excitement and slipped up unobtrusively to watch. He was fascinated by his step-father's rage. He had never seen a display like it before, and at one stage he hoped that Duncan Alexander's eyeballs might actually burst like over-ripe grapes; he held his breath in anticipation, and felt cheated when it did not happen.

At last, Duncan stopped and ran both hands through his thick waving hair; two spikes of hair stood up like devil's horns. He was still panting, but he had recovered partial control.

'Now, sir, what do you propose?' he demanded of Randle, and in the silence Peter Berg piped up.

'You could have new shells sent from Bermuda – it's only three hundred miles away. We checked it this morning.'

'How did you get in here?' Duncan swung round. 'Get back to your mother.'

Peter scampered, appalled at his own indiscretion, and only when he left the bridge did the Chief speak.

'We could have spares flown out from London to Bermuda—'

'There must be a boat—' Randle cut in swiftly.

'Or an aircraft to drop it to us—'

'Or a helicopter—'

'Get Christy Main on the telex,' snapped Duncan Alexander.


It was good to have a deck under his feet again, Nicholas exulted. He felt himself coming fully alive again.

'I'm a sea-creature,' he grinned to himself. 'And I keep forgetting it.'

He looked back to the low silhouette of the Bermuda islands, the receding arms of Hamilton Harbour and the flecking of the multi-coloured buildings amongst the cedar trees, and then returned his attention to the spread charts on the navigation table before him.

*Warlock* was still at cautionary speed. Even though the channel was wide and clearly buoyed, yet the coral reef on each hand was sharp and hungry, and David Allen's full attention was on the business of conning *Warlock* out into the open sea. But as they passed the 100-fathom line, he gave the order to his deck officer,

'Full away at 0900 hours, pilot,' and hurried across to join Nicholas.

'I didn't have much of a chance to welcome you on board, sir.'

'Thank you, David. It's good to be back.' Nicholas looked up and smiled at him. 'Will you bring her round on to 240° magnetic and increase to 80% power?'

Quickly David repeated his order to the helm and then shifted from one foot to the other, beginning to flush under the salt-water tan.

'Mr Berg, my officers are driving me mad. They've been plaguing me since we left Cape Town – are we running on a job – or is this a pleasure cruise?'

Nicholas laughed aloud then. He felt the excitement of the hunt, a good hot scent in the nostrils, and the prospect of a fat prize. Now he had *Warlock* under him, his concern for Peter's safety had abated. Whatever happened now, he could get there very fast. No, he felt good, very good.

'We're hunting, David,' he told him. 'Nothing certain yet—' he paused, and then relented, 'Get Beauty Baker up to my cabin, tell Angel to send up a big pot of coffee and a mess of sandwiches – I missed breakfast – and while we are eating, I'll fill both of you in.'

Beauty Baker accepted one of Nicholas' cheroots.

'Still smoking cheap,' he observed, and sniffed at the four-dollar cheroot sourly, but there was a twinkle of pleasure behind the smeared lenses of his spectacles. Then, unable to contain himself, he actually grinned.

'Skipper tells me we are hunting, is that right?'

'This is the picture—' Nicholas began to spell it out to them in detail, and while he talked, he thought with comfortable self-indulgence, 'I must be getting old and soft – I didn't always talk so much.'

Both men listened in silence, and only when he finished did the two of them begin bombarding him with the perceptive penetrating questions he had expected.

'Sounds like a generator armature,' Beauty Baker guessed, as he puzzled the contents of the wooden case that had been flown out to *Golden Dawn*. 'I cannot believe that *Golden Dawn* doesn't carry a full set of mechanical spares.'

While Baker was fully preoccupied with the mechanics of the situation, David Allen concentrated on the problems of seamanship. 'What was the range of the helicopter? Has it returned to base yet? With her draught, she must be heading for the Florida Straits. Our best bet would be to shape a course for Matanilla Reef at the mouth of the Straits.'

There was a peremptory knock on the door of the guest cabin, and the Trog stuck his grey wrinkled tortoise head through. He glanced at Nicholas, but did not greet him. 'Captain, Miami is broadcasting a new hurricane alert. "Lorna" has kicked northwards, they're predicting a track of north north-west and a speed over the ground of twenty knots.'

He closed the door and they stared at each other in silence for a moment. Nicholas spoke at last.

'It is never one single mistake that causes disaster,' he said. 'It is always a series of contributory errors, most of them of small consequence in themselves – but when taken with a little bad luck—' he was silent a moment and then, softly, 'Hurricane "Lorna" could just be that bit of bad luck.'

He stood up and took one turn around the small guest cabin, feeling caged and wishing for the space of the Master's suite which was now David Allen's. He turned back to Beauty Baker and David Allen, and suddenly he realized that they were hoping for disaster. They were like two old sea wolves with the scent of the prey in their nostrils. He felt his anger rising coldly against them, they were wishing disaster on his son.

'Just one thing I didn't tell you,' he said. 'My son is on *Golden Dawn*.'

The immense revolving storm that was code-named 'Lorna' was nearing full development. Her crest was reared high above the freezing levels so she wore a splendid mane of frosted white ice particles that streamed out three hundred miles ahead of her on the jet stream of the upper troposphere.

From one side to the other, she now measured one hundred and fifty miles across, and the power unleashed within her was of unmeasurable savagery.

The winds that blew around her centre tore the surface off the sea and bore it aloft at speeds in excess of one hundred and fifty miles an hour, generating precipitation that was as far beyond rain as death is beyond life. Water filled the dense cloud-banks so that there was no clear line between sea and air.

It seemed now that madness fed upon madness, and like a blinded and berserk monster, she blundered across the confined waters of the Caribbean, ripping the trees and buildings, even the very earth from the tiny islands which stood in her path.

But there were still forces controlling what seemed uncontrollable, dictating what seemed to be random, for, as she spun upon a spinning globe, the storm showed the primary trait of gyroscopic inertia, a rigidity in space that was constant as long as no outside force was applied.

Obeying this natural law, the entire system moved steadily eastwards at constant speed and altitude above the surface of the earth, until her northern edge touched the land-mass of the long ridge of land that forms the greater Antilles.

Immediately another gyroscopic law came into force, the law of precession. When a deflecting force is applied to the rim of a spinning gyro, the gyro moves not away from, but *directly towards* that force.

Hurricane 'Lorna' felt the land, and, like a maddened bull at the flirt of the matador's cape, she turned and charged towards it, crossing the narrow high strips of Haiti in an orgy of destruction and terror until she burst out of the narrow channel of the Windward Passage into the open beyond.

Yet still she kept on spinning and moving. Now, barely three hundred miles ahead of her, across those shallow reefs and banks prophetically named 'Hurricane Flats' after the thousands of other such storms that had followed the same route during the memory of man, lay the deeper waters of the Florida Straits and the mainland of the continental United States of America.

At twenty miles an hour, the whole incredible heaven-high mass of crazed wind and churning clouds trundled northwestwards.

Duncan Alexander stood under the bogus Degas ballet dancers in the owner's stateroom. He balanced easily on the balls of his feet and his hands were clasped lightly behind his back, but his brow was heavily furrowed with worry and his eyes darkly underscored with plum-coloured swollen bags of sleeplessness.

Seated on the long couch and on the imitation Louis Quatorze chairs flanking the fireplace, were the senior officers of *Golden Dawn* – her Captain, Mate and Chief Engineer, and in the leather-studded wing-backed chair across the wide cabin sat Charles Gras, the engineer from Atlantique. It seemed as though he had chosen his seat to keep himself aloof from the owner and officers of the crippled ultra-tanker.

He spoke now in heavily accented English, falling back on the occasional French word which Duncan translated quickly. The four men listened to him with complete attention, never taking their eyes from the sharp pale Parisian features and the foxy bright eyes.

'My men will have completed the re-assembly of the main bearing by noon today. To the best of my ability, I have examined and tested the main shaft. I can find no evidence of structural damage, but I must emphasize that this does not mean that no damage exists. At the very best, the repairs must be considered to be temporary.' He paused and they waited, while he turned deliberately to Captain Randle. 'I must urge you to seek proper repair in the nearest port open to you, and to proceed there at the lowest speed which will enable you efficiently to work the ship.'

Randle twisted uncomfortably in his seat, and glanced across at Duncan. The Frenchman saw the exchange and a little steel came into his voice.

'If there is structural distortion in the main shaft, operation at speeds higher than this may result in permanent and irreversible damage and complete breakdown. I must make this point most forcibly.'

Duncan intervened smoothly. 'We are fully burdened and drawing twenty fathoms of water. There are no safe harbours on the eastern seaboard of America, that is even supposing that we could get permission to enter territorial waters with engine trouble. The Americans aren't likely to welcome us. Our nearest safe anchorage is Galveston roads, on the Texas coast of the Gulf of Mexico – and then only after the tugs have taken off our pod tanks outside the 100-fathom line.'

The tanker's First Officer was a young man, probably not over thirty years of age, but he had so far conducted himself impeccably in the emergencies the ship had encountered. He had a firm jaw and a clear level eye, and he had been the first into the smoke-filled shaft tunnel.

'With respect, sir,' and they all turned their heads towards him, 'Miami has broadcast a revised hurricane alert that includes the Straits and southern Florida. We would be on a reciprocal course to the hurricane track, a directly converging course.'

'Even at fifteen knots, we would be through the Straits and into the Gulf with twenty-four hours to spare,' Duncan stated, and looked to Randle for confirmation.

'At the present speed of the storm's advance – yes,' Randle qualified carefully. 'But conditions may change—'

The Mate persisted. 'Again, with respect, sir. Our nearest safe anchorage is in the lee of Bermuda Island—'

'Do you have any idea of the value of this cargo?' Duncan's voice rasped. 'No, you do not. Well, I will inform you. It is $85,000,000. The interest on that amount is in the region of $25,000 a day.' His voice rose a note, again that wild note to it. 'Bermuda does not have the facilities to effect major repairs—'

The door from the private accommodation opened silently and Chantelle Alexander stepped into the stateroom. She wore no jewellery, a plain pearl silk blouse and a simple dark woollen skirt, but her skin had been gilded by the sun and she had lightly touched her dark eyes with a make-up that emphasized their size and shape. Her beauty silenced them all and she was fully aware of it as she crossed to stand beside Duncan.

'It is necessary that this ship and her cargo proceed directly to Galveston,' she said softly.

'Chantelle—' Duncan began, and she silenced him with a brusque gesture of one hand.

'There is no question about the destination and the route that is to be taken.'

Charles Gras looked to Captain Randle, waiting for him to assert the authority vested in him by law. But when the young Captain remained silent, the Frenchman smiled sardonically and shrugged a world-weary dismissal of further interest. 'Then, I must ask that arrangements be made for my two assistants and myself to leave this ship immediately we have completed the temporary repairs.' Again Gras emphasized the word 'temporary'.

Duncan nodded. 'If we resume our sailing when you anticipate, and even taking into consideration the low fuel condition of the helicopter, we will be within easy range of the east coast of Florida by dawn tomorrow.'

Chantelle had not taken her eyes from the *Golden Dawn*'s officers during this exchange, and now she went on in the same quiet voice.

'I am quite prepared to accept the resignation of any of the officers of this ship who wish to join that flight.'

Duncan opened his mouth to make some protest at her assumption of his authority, but she turned to him with a small lift of the chin, and something in her expression and the set of her head upon her shoulders reminded him forcibly of old Arthur Christy. There was the same toughness and resilience there, the same granite determination; strange that he had not noticed it before.

'Perhaps I have never looked before,' he thought. Chantelle recognized the moment of his capitulation, and calmly she turned back to face *Golden Dawn*'s officers.

One by one, they dropped their eyes from hers; Randle was the first to stand up.

'If you will excuse me, Mrs Alexander, I must make preparations to get under way again.'

Charles Gras paused and looked back at her, and he smiled again, as only a Frenchman smiles at a pretty woman.

'Magnifique!' he murmured, and lifted one hand in a graceful salute of admiration before he stepped out of the stateroom.

When Chantelle and Duncan were alone together, she turned to him slowly, and she let the contempt show in her expression.

'Any time you feel you have not got the guts for it, let me know, will you?'

'Chantelle—'

'You have got us into this, me and Christy Marine. Now you'll get us out of it, even if it kills you.' Her lips compressed into a thinner line and her eyes slitted vindictively. 'And it would be nice if it did,' she said softly.


The pilot of the Beechcraft Baron pulled back the throttles to 22″ of boost on both engines, and slid the propellers into fully fine pitch, simultaneously beginning a gentle descending turn towards the extraordinary-looking vessel that came up swiftly out of the low early morning haze that spilled over from the islands.

The same haze had blotted the low silhouette of the Florida coast from the western horizon, and even the pale green water and shaded reefs of little Bahamas Bank were washed pale by the haze, and partially obscured by the intermittent layer of stratocumulus cloud at four thousand feet.

The Baron pilot selected 20° of flap to give the aircraft a nosedown attitude which would afford a better forward vision, and continued his descent down through the cloud. It burst in a brief grey puff across the windshield before they were out into sunlight again.

'What do you make of her?' he asked his co-pilot.

'She's a big baby,' the co-pilot tried to steady his binoculars. 'Can't read her name.'

The enormously wide low bows were pushing up a fat sparkling pillow of churning water, and the green decks seemed to reach back almost to the limits of visilibility before rising sheer into the stern quarters.

'Son of a gun,' the pilot shook his head. 'She looks like the vehicle-assembly building on Cape Kennedy.'

'She does too,' agreed his co-pilot. The same square unlovely bulk of that enormous structure was repeated in smaller scale by the navigation bridge of the big ship. 'I'll give her a call on 16.' The co-pilot lowered his binoculars and thumbed the microphone as he lifted it to his lips.

'South-bound bulk carrier, this is Coast Guard November Charlie One Fife Niner overhead. Do you read me?'

There was the expected delay; even in confined and heavily trafficked waters, these big bastards kept a sloppy watch and the spotter fumed silently.

'Coast Guard One Fife Niner, this is *Golden Dawn*. Reading you fife by fife. Going up to 22.'

Two hundred miles away the Trog knocked over the shell-casing, spilling damp and stinking cigar butts over the deck, in his haste to change frequency to channel 22 as the operator on board *Golden Dawn* had stipulated, at the same time switching in both the tape recorder and the radio direction-finder equipment.

High up in *Warlock*'s fire-control tower, the big metal ring of the direction-finding aerial turned slowly, lining up on the transmissions that boomed so clearly across the ether, repeating the relative bearing on the dial of the instrument on the Trog's cluttered bench.

'Good morning to you, *Golden Dawn*,' the lilting Southern twang of the coastguard navigator came back. 'I would be mightily obliged for your port of registry and your cargo manifest.'

'This ship is registered Venezuela.' The Trog dexterously made the fine tuning, scribbled the bearing on his pad, ripped off the page and darted into *Warlock*'s navigation bridge.

'*Golden Dawn* is sending in clear,' he squeaked with an expression of malicious glee.

'Call the Captain,' snapped the deck officer, and then as an afterthought, 'and ask Mr Berg to come to the bridge.'

The conversation between coastguard and ultra-tanker was still going on when Nicholas burst into the radio room, belting his dressing-gown.

'Thank you for your courtesy, sir,' the coastguard navigator was using extravagant Southern gallantry, fully aware that *Golden Dawn* was outside United States territorial waters, and officially beyond his government's jurisdiction. 'I would appreciate your port of final destination.'

'We are en route Galveston for full discharge of cargo.'

'Thank you again, sir. And are you apprised of the hurricane alert in force at this time?'

'Affirmative.'

From *Warlock*'s bridge, David Allen appeared in the doorway, his face set and flushed.

'She must be under way again,' he said, his disappointment so plain that it angered Nicholas yet again. 'She is into the channel already.'

'I'd be obliged if you would immediately put this ship on a course to enter the Straits and close with her as soon as is possible,' Nicholas snapped, and David Allen blinked at him once then disappeared on to his bridge, calling for the change in course and increase in speed as he went.

Over the loudspeaker, the coastguard was being politely persistent.

'Are you further apprised, sir, of the up-date on that hurricane alert predicting storm passage of the main navigable channel at 1200 hours local time tomorrow?'

'Affirmative.' *Golden Dawn*'s replies had become curt.

'May I further trouble you, sir, in view of your sensitive cargo and the special weather conditions, for your expected time of arrival abeam of the Dry Tortugas Bank marine beacon and when you anticipate clearing the channel and shaping a northerly course away from the predicted hurricane track?'

'Stand-by.' There was a brief hum of static while the operator consulted the deck officer and then the *Golden Dawn* came back, 'Our ETA Dry Tortugas Bank beacon is 0130 tomorrow.'

There was a long pause now as the coastguard consulted his headquarters ashore on one of the closed frequencies, and then:

'I am requested respectfully, but officially, to bring to your attention that very heavy weather is expected ahead of the storm centre and that your present ETA Dry Tortugas Bank leaves you very fine margins of safety, sir.'

'Thank you, coastguard One Fife Niner. Your transmission will be entered in the ship's log. This is *Golden Dawn* over and out.'

The coastguard's frustration was evident, clearly he would have loved to order the tanker to reverse her course. 'We will be following your progress with interest, *Golden Dawn*. Bon voyage, this is coastguard One Fife Niner over and out.'

Charles Gras held his blue beret on with one hand, while with the other he lugged his suitcase. He ran doubled up, instinctively avoiding the ear-numbing clatter of the helicopter's rotor.

He threw his suitcase through the open fuselage door and then hesitated, turned and scampered back to where the ship's Chief Engineer stood at the edge of the white-painted helipad target on *Golden Dawn*'s tank deck.

Charles grabbed the Engineer's upper arm and leaned close to shout in his ear.

'Remember, my friend, treat her like a baby, like a tender virgin – if you have to increase speed, do so gently – very gently.' The Engineer nodded, his sparse sandy hair fluttering in the down-draught.

'Good luck,' shouted the Frenchman, *'Bonne chance!'* He slapped the man's shoulder. 'I hope you don't need it!'

He darted back and scrambled up into the fuselage of the Sikorsky, and his face appeared in one of the portholes. He waved once, and then the big ungainly machine rose slowly into the air, hovered for a moment and then banked away low over the water, setting off in its characteristic nose-down attitude for the mainland, still hidden by haze and distance.


Dr Samantha Silver, dressed in thigh-high rubber waders and with her sleeves rolled up above the elbows, staggered under the weight of two ten-gallon plastic buckets of clams as she climbed the back steps of the laboratory building.

'Sam!' down the length of the long passageway, Sally-Anne screamed at her. 'We were going to leave without you!'

'What is it?' Sam dumped the buckets with relief, slopping salt water down the steps.

'Johnny called – the anti-pollution patrol bespoke *Golden Dawn* an hour ago. She's in the Straits, she was abeam Matanilla reef when they spotted her and she will be abeam of Biscayne Key before we can get out there, if we don't leave now.'

'I'm coming.' Sam hefted her heavy buckets, and broke into a rubber-kneed trot. 'I'll meet you down on the wharf – did you call the TV studio?'

'There's a camera team on the way,' Sally-Anne yelled back as she ran for the front doors. 'Hurry, Sam – fast as you like!'

Samantha dumped the clams into one of her tanks, switched on the oxygen and as soon as it began to bubble to the surface, she turned and raced from the laboratory and out of the front doors.


*Golden Dawn*'s deck officer stopped beside the radarscope, glanced down at it idly, then stooped with more attention and took a bearing on the little glowing pinpoint of green light that showed up clearly inside the ten-mile circle of the sweep.

He grunted, straightened, and walked quickly to the front of the bridge. Slowly, he scanned the green wind-chopped sea ahead of the tanker's ponderous bows.

'Fishing boat,' he said to the helmsman. 'But they are under way.' He had seen the tiny flash of a bow wave. 'And they are right in the main navigational channel – they must have seen us by now, they are making a turn to pass us to starboard.' He dropped the binoculars and let them dangle against his chest. 'Oh thank you.' He took the cup of cocoa from the steward, and sipped it with relish as he turned away to the chart-table.

One of the tanker's junior officers came out of the radio room at the back of the bridge.

'Still no score,' he said, 'and only injury time left now,' and they fell into a concerned discussion of the World Cup soccer match being played under floodlights at Wembley Stadium on the other side of the Atlantic.

'If it's a draw then it means that France is in the—'

There was an excited shout from the radio room, and the junior officer ran to the door and then turned back with an excited grin. 'England has scored!'

The deck officer chuckled happily. 'That will wrap it up.' Then with a start of guilt he turned back to his duties, and had another start, this time of surprise, when he glanced into the radarscope.

'What the hell are they playing at!' he exclaimed irritably, and hurried forward to scan the sea ahead.

The fishing boat had continued its turn and was now bows on.

'Damn them. We'll give them a buzz.' He reached up for the handle of the foghorn and blew three long blasts, that echoed out mournfully across the shallow greenish water of the Straits. There was a general movement among the officers to get a better view ahead through the forward bridge windows.

'They must be half asleep out there.' The deck officer thought quickly about calling the Captain to the bridge. If it came to manoeuvring the ship in these confined waters, he flinched from the responsibility. Even at this reduced speed, it would take *Golden Dawn* half an hour and seven nautical miles to come to a stop; a turn in either direction would swing through a wide arc of many miles before the ship was able to make a 90° change of course – God, then there was the effect of the wind against the enormously exposed area of the towering stern quarters, and the full bore of the Gulf Stream driving out of the narrows of the Straits. The problems of manoeuvring the vessel struck a chill of panic into the officer – and the fishing boat was on collision course, the range closing swiftly under the combined speeds of both vessels. He reached for the call button of the intercom that connected the bridge directly to the Captain's quarters on the deck below, but at that moment Captain Randle came bounding up the private staircase from his day cabin.

'What is it?' he demanded. 'What was that blast on the horn?'

'Small vessel holding to a collision course, sir.' The officer's relief was evident, and Randle seized the handle of the foghorn and hung on to it.

'God, what's wrong with them?'

'The deck is crowded,' exclaimed one of the officers without lowering his binoculars. 'Looks as though they have a movie camera team on the top deck.'

Randle judged the closing range anxiously; already the small fishing vessel was too close for the *Golden Dawn* to stop in time.

'Thank God,' somebody exclaimed. 'They are turning away.'

'They are streaming some sort of banner. Can anybody read that?'

'They are heaving-to,' the deck officer yelled suddenly. 'They are heaving-to right under our bows.'


Samantha Silver had not expected the tanker to be so big. From directly ahead, her bows seemed to fill the horizon from one side to the other, and the bow wave she threw up ahead of her creamed and curved like the set of the long wave at Cape St Francis when the surf was up.

Beyond the bows, the massive tower of her navigation bridge stood so tall it looked like the skyline of the Miami beach, one of those massive hotel buildings seen from close inshore.

It made her feel distinctly uneasy to be directly under that on-rushing steel avalanche.

'Do you think they have seen us?' Sally-Anne asked beside her, and when Samantha heard her own unease echoed by the pretty girl beside her, it steeled her.

'Of course they have,' she announced stoutly so that everyone in the small wheelhouse could hear her. 'That's why they blew their siren. We'll turn aside at the last minute.'

'They aren't slowing down,' Hank Petersen, the helmsman, pointed out huskily, and Samantha wished that Tom Parker had been on board with them. However, Tom was up in Washington again, and they had taken the *Dicky* to sea with a scratch crew, and without Tom Parker's written authorization. 'What do you want to do, Sam?' And they all looked at her.

'I know a thing that size can't stop, but at least we're going to make them slow down.

'Are the TV boys getting some stuff?' Samantha asked, to delay the moment of decision. 'Go up, Sally-Anne, and check them.' Then to the others, 'You-all get the banner ready, we'll let them get a good look at that.'

'Listen, Sam.' Hank Petersen's tanned intelligent face was strained. He was a tunny expert, and was not accustomed to handling the vessel except in calm and uncluttered waters. 'I don't like this, we're getting much too close. That thing could churn us right under, and not even notice the bump. I want to turn away now.' His voice was almost drowned by the sudden sky-crashing blast of the tanker's foghorns.

'Son of a gun, Sam, I don't like playing chicken-chicken with somebody that size.'

'Don't worry, we'll get out of their way at the last moment. All right!' Samantha decided. 'Turn 90° to port, Hank. Let's show them the signs, I'm going to help them on the deck.'

The wind tore at the thin white canvas banner as they tried to run it out along the side of the deckhouse, and the little vessel was rolling uncomfortably while the TV producer was shouting confused stage directions at them from the top of the wheelhouse.

Bitterly Samantha wished there was somebody to take command, somebody like Nicholas Berg – and the banner tried to wrap itself around her head.

The *Dicky* was coming around fast now, and Samantha shot a glance at the oncoming tanker and felt the shock of it strike in the pit of her stomach like the blow of a fist. It was huge, and very close – much too close, even she realized that.

At last she managed to get a turn of the thin line that secured the banner around the stern rail – but the light canvas had twisted so that only one word of the slogan was readable. 'POISONER', it accused in scarlet, crudely painted letters followed by a grinning skull and crossed bones.

Samantha dived across the deck and struggled with the flapping canvas; above her head the producer was shouting excitedly; two of the others were trying to help her; Sally-Anne was screaming 'Go back! Go back!' and waving both arms at the great tanker. 'You poison our oceans!'

Everything was becoming confused and out of control, the *Dicky* swung head into the wind and pitched steeply, the person next to her lost his footing and knocked painfully into Samantha, and at that moment she felt the change of the engine beat.

*Tricky Dicky's* diesel had been bellowing furiously as Hank opened the throttle to its stop, using full power to bring the little vessel around from under the menace of those steel bows.

The smoking splutter of the exhaust pipe that rose vertically up the side of the deckhouse, and made all speech difficult – but now it died away, and suddenly there was only the sound of the wind.

Even their own raised voices were silenced, and they froze, staring out at *Golden Dawn* as she bore down on them without the slightest check in her majestic approach.

Samantha was the first to recover, then she ran across the plunging deck to the wheelhouse.

Hank Petersen was down on his knees beside the bulkhead, struggling ineffectually with the conduit that housed the controls to the engine room on the deck below.

'Why have you stopped?' Samantha yelled at him, and he looked up at her as though he were mortally wounded.

'It's the throttle linkage,' he said. 'It's snapped again.'

'Can't you fix it? and the question was mockery. A mile away, *Golden Dawn* came down on them – silent, menacing, unstoppable.


For ten seconds Randle stood rigid, both hands gripping the foulweather rail below the sill of the bridge windows.

His face was set, pale and finely drawn, as he watched the stern of the wallowing fishing boat for the renewed churning of its prop.

He knew that he could not turn nor stop his ship in time to avoid collision, unless the small vessel got under way immediately, and took evasive action by going out to starboard under full power.

'Damn them to hell,' he thought bitterly, they were in gross default. He had all the law and the custom of the sea behind him; a collision would cause very little damage to *Golden Dawn*, perhaps she would lose a little paint, at most a slightly buckled plate in the reinforced bows – and they had asked for it.

He had no doubts about the object of this crazy, irresponsible seamanship. There had been enough controversy before *Golden Dawn* sailed. He had read the objections and seen the nut-case environmentalists on television. The scarlet-painted banner with the ridiculously melodramatic Jolly Roger made it clear that this was a boatload of nutters attempting to prevent *Golden Dawn* entering American waters.

He felt his anger boiling up fiercely. These people always made him furious. If they had their way, there would be no tanker trade, and now they were deliberately threatening him, placing him in a position which might prejudice his own career. He already had the task of taking his ship through the Straits ahead of the hurricane. Every moment was vital – and now there was this.

He would be happy to maintain course and speed, and to run them down. They were flaunting themselves, challenging him to do it – and, by God, they deserved it.

However, he was a seaman, with a seaman's deep concern for human life at sea. It would go against all his instincts not to make an effort to avoid collision, no matter how futile that effort would be. Then beside him one of his officers triggered him.

'There are women on board her – look at that! Those are women!'

That was enough. Without waiting for confirmation, Randle snapped at the helmsman beside him.

'Full port rudder!'

And with two swift paces he had reached the engine room telegraph. It rang shrilly as he pulled back the chromed handle to 'Full Astern'.

Almost immediately, the changed beat came up through the soles of his feet, as the great engine seven decks below the bridge thundered suddenly under all emergency power, and the direction of the spinning main propeller shaft was abruptly reversed.

Randle spun back to face ahead. For almost five minutes, the bows held steady on the horizon without making any answer to the full application of the rudder. The inertia of a million tons of crude oil, the immense drag of the hull through water and the press of wind and current held her on course, and although the single ferro-bronze propeller bit deeply into the green waters, there was not the slightest diminution of the tanker's speed.

Randle kept his hand on the engine telegraph, pulling back on the silver handle with all his strength, as though this might arrest the great ship's forward way through the water.

'Turn!' he whispered to the ship, and he stared at the fishing boat that still lay, rolling wildly, directly in *Golden Dawn*'s path. He noticed irrelevantly that the tiny human figures along the rear rail were waving frantically, and that the banner with its scarlet denunciation had torn loose at one end and was now whipping and twisting like a Tibetan prayer flag over the heads of the crew.

'Turn,' Randle whispered, and he saw the first response of the hull; the angle between the bows and the fishing boat altered, it was a noticeable change, but slowly accelerating and a quick glance at the control console showed a small check in the ship's forward speed.

'Turn, damn it, turn.' Randle held the engine telegraph locked at full astern, and felt the sudden influence of the Gulf Stream current on the ship as she began to come across the direction of flow.

Ahead, the fishing boat was almost about to disappear from sight behind *Golden Dawn*'s high blunt bows.

He had been holding the ship at full astern for almost seven minutes now, and suddenly Randle felt a change in *Golden Dawn*, something he had never experienced before.

There was harsh, tearing, pounding vibration coming up through the deck. He realized just how severe that vibration must be, when *Golden Dawn*'s monumental hull began to shake violently – but he could not release his grip on the engine telegraph, not with that helpless vessel lying in his track.

Then suddenly, miraculously, all vibration in the deck under his feet ceased altogether. There was only the calm press of the hull through the water, no longer the feel of the engine's thrust, a sensation much more alarming to a mariner than the vibration which had preceded it, and simultaneously, a fiery rash of red warning lights bloomed on the ship's main control console, and the strident screech of the full emergency audio-alarm deafened them all.

Only then did Captain Randle push the engine telegraph to 'stop'. He stood staring ahead as the tiny fishing boat disappeared from view, hidden by the angle from the navigation bridge which was a mile behind the bows.

One of the officers reached across and hit the cut-out on the audio-alarm. In the sudden silence every officer stood frozen, waiting for the impact of collision.

*Golden Dawn*'s Chief Engineer paced slowly along the engine-room control console, never taking his eyes from the electronic displays which monitored all the ship's mechanical and electrical functions.

When he reached the alarm board, he stopped and frowed at it angrily. The failure of the single transistor, a few dollars' worth of equipment, had been the cause of such brutal damage to his beloved machinery. He leaned across and pressed the 'test' button, checking out each alarm circuit, yet, while he was doing it, recognizing the fact that it was too late. He was nursing the ship along, with God alone knew what undiscovered damage to engine and main shaft only kept in check by this reduced power setting – but there was a hurricane down there below the southern horizon, and the Chief could only guess at what emergency his machinery might have to meet in the next few days.

It made him nervous and edgy to think about it. He searched in his back pocket, found a sticky mint humbug, carefully picked off the little pieces of lint and fluff before tucking it into his cheek like a squirrel with a nut, sucking noisily upon it as he resumed his restless prowling up and down the control console.

His on-duty stokers and oilers watched him surreptitiously. When the old man was in a mood, it was best not to attract attention.

'Dickson!' the Chief said suddenly. 'Get your lid on. We are going down the shaft tunnel again.'

The oiler sighed, exchanged a resigned glance with one of his mates and clapped his hard-hat on his head. He and the Chief had been down the tunnel an hour previously. It was an uncomfortable, noisy and dirty journey.

The oiler closed the watertight doors into the shaft tunnel behind them, screwing down the clamps firmly under the Chief's frosty scrutiny, and then both men stooped in the confined headroom and started off along the brightly lit pale grey painted tunnel.

The spinning shaft in its deep bed generated a high-pitched whine that seemed to resonate in the steel box of the tunnel, as though it was the body of a violin. Surprisingly, the noise was more pronounced at this low speed setting, it seemed to bore into the teeth at the back of the oiler's jaw like a dentist's drill.

The Chief did not seem to be affected. He paused beside the main bearing for almost ten minutes, testing it with the palm of his hand, feeling for heat or vibration. His expression was morose, and he worried the mint humbug in his cheek and shook his head with foreboding before going on up the tunnel.

When he reached the main gland, he squatted down suddenly and peered at it closely. With a deliberate flexing of his jaw he crushed the remains of the humbug between his teeth, and his eyes narrowed thoughtfully.

There was a thin trickle of seawater oozing through the gland and running down into the bilges. The Chief touched it with his finger. Something had shifted, some balance was disturbed, the seal of the gland was no longer watertight – such a small sign, a few gallons of seawater, could be the first warning of major structural damage.

The Chief shuffled around, still hunched down beside the shaft bed, and he lowered his face until it was only inches from the spinning steel main shaft. He closed one eye, and cocked his head, trying once again to decide if the faint blurring of the shaft's outline was real or merely his over-active imagination, whether what he was seeing was distortion or his own fears.

Suddenly, startlingly, the shaft slammed into stillness. The deceleration was so abrupt that the Chief could actually see the torque transferred into the shaft bed, and the metal walls creaked and popped with the strain.

He rocked back on to his heels, and almost instantly the shaft began to spin again, but this time in reverse thrust. The whine built up swiftly into a rising shriek. They were pulling emergency power from the bridge, and it was madness, suicidal madness.

The Chief seized the oiler by the shoulder and shouted into his ear, 'Get back to control – find out what the hell they are doing on the bridge.'

The oiler scrambled away down the tunnel; it would take him ten minutes to negotiate the long narrow passage, open the watertight doors and reach the control room and as long again to return.

The Chief considered going after him, but somehow he could not leave the shaft now. He lowered his head again, and now he could clearly see the flickering of the outline of the shaft. It wasn't imagination at all, there was a little ghost of movement. He clamped his hands over his ears to cut out the painful shriek of the spinning metal, but there was a new note to it, the squeal of bare metal on metal and before his eyes he saw the ghost outline along the edge of the shaft growing, the flutter of machinery out of balance, and the metal deck under his feet began to quiver.

'God! They are going to blow the whole thing!' he shouted, and jumped up from his crouch. Now the deck was juddering and shaking under his feet. He started back along the shaft, but the entire tunnel was agitating so violently that he had to grab at the metal bulkhead to steady himself, and he reeled drunkenly, thrown about like a captive insect in a cruel child's box.

Ahead of him, he saw the huge metal casting of the main bearing twisting and shaking, and the vibration chattered his teeth in his clenched jaw and drove up his spine like a jack hammer.

Disbelievingly he saw the huge silver shaft beginning to rise and buckle in its bed, the bearing tearing loose from its mountings.

'Shut down!' he screamed. 'For God's sake, shut down!' But his voice was lost in the shriek and scream of tortured metal and machinery that was tearing itself to pieces in a suicidal frenzy.

The main bearing exploded, and the shaft slammed it into the bulkhead, tearing steel plate like paper.

The shaft itself began to snake and whip. The Chief cowered back, pressing his back to the bulkhead and covering his ears to protect them from the unbearable volume of noise.

A sliver of heated steel flew from the bearing and struck him in the face, laying open his upper lip to the bone, crushing his nose and snapping off his front teeth at the level of the gums.

He toppled forward, and the whipping, kicking shaft seized him like a mindless predator and tore his body to pieces, pounding him and crushing him in the shaft bed and splattering him against the pale metal walls.

The main shaft snapped like a rotten twig at the point where it had been heated and weakened. The unbalanced weight of the revolving propeller ripped the stump out through the after seal, as though it were a tooth plucked from a rotting jaw.

The sea rushed in through the opening, flooding the tunnel instantly until it slammed into the watertight doors – and the huge glistening bronze propeller, with the stump of the main shaft still attached, the whole unit weighing one hundred and fifty tons, plummeted downwards through four hundred fathoms to embed itself deeply in the soft mud of the sea bottom.

Freed of the intolerable goad of her damaged shaft, *Golden Dawn* was suddenly silent and her decks still and steady as she trundled on, slowly losing way as the water dragged at her hull.


Samantha had one awful moment of sickening guilt. She saw clearly that she was responsible for the deadly danger into which she had led these people, and she stared out over the boat's side at the *Golden Dawn*.

The tanker was coming on without any check in her speed; perhaps she had turned a few degrees, for her bows were no longer pointed directly at them, but her speed was constant.

She was achingly aware of her inexperience, of her helplessness in this alien situation. She tried to think, to force herself out of this frozen despondency.

'Life-jackets!' she thought, and yelled to Sally-Anne out on the deck, 'The life-jackets are in the lockers behind the wheelhouse.'

Their faces turned to her, suddenly stricken. Up to this moment it had all been a glorious romp, the old fun-game of challenging the money-grabbers, prodding the establishment, but now suddenly it was mortal danger.

'Move!' Samantha shrieked at them, and there was a rush back along the deck.

'Think!' Samantha shook her head, as though to clear it. 'Think!' she urged herself fiercely. She could hear the tanker now, the silken rustling sound of the water under its hull, the sough of the bow wave curling upon itself.

The *Dicky*'s throttle linkage had broken before, when they had been off Key West a year ago. It had broken between the bridge and the engine, and Samantha had watched Tom Parker fiddling with the engine, holding the lantern for him to see in the gloomy confines of the smelly little engine room.

She had not been certain how he did it, but she remembered that he had controlled the revolutions of the engine by hand – something on the side of the engine block, below the big bowl of the air filter.

Samantha turned and dived down the vertical ladder into the engine room. The diesel was running, burbling away quietly at idling speed, not generating sufficient power to move the little vessel through the water.

She tripped and sprawled on the greasy deck, and pulled herself up, crying out with pain as her hand touched the red-hot manifold of the engine exhaust.

On the far side of the engine block, she groped desperately under the air filter, pushing and tugging at anything her fingers touched. She found a coil spring, and dropped to her knees to examine it.

She tried not to think of the huge steel hull bearing down on them, of being down in this tiny box that stank of diesel and exhaust fumes and old bilges. She tried not to think of not having a life-jacket, or that the tanker could tramp the little vessel deep down under the surface and crush her like a matchbox.

Instead, she traced the little coil spring to where it was pinned into a flat upright lever. Desperately she pushed the lever against the tension of the spring – and instantly the diesel engine bellowed deafeningly in her ears, startling her so that she flinched and lost the lever. The diesel's beat died away into the bumbling idle and she wasted seconds while she found the lever again and pushed it hard against its stops once more. The engine roared, and she felt the ship picking up speed under her. She began to pray incoherently.

She could not hear the words in the engine noise, and she was not sure she was making sense, but she held the throttle open, and kept on praying.

She did not hear the screams from the deck above her. She did not know how close the *Golden Dawn* was, she did not know if Hank Petersen was still in the wheelhouse conning the little vessel out of the path of the onrushing tanker – but she held the throttle open and prayed.

The impact when it came was shattering, the crash and crackle of timbers breaking, the rending lurch and the roll of the deck giving to the tearing force of it.

Samantha was hurled against the hot steel of the engine, her forehead striking with such force that her vision starred into blinding white light; she dropped backwards, her body loose and relaxed, darkness ringing in her ears, and lay huddled on the deck.

She did not know how long she was unconscious, but it could not have been for more than a few seconds; the spray of icy cold water on her face roused her and she pulled herself up on to her knees.

In the glare of the single bare electric globe in the deck above her, Samantha saw the spurts of water jets through the starting planking of the bulkhead beside her.

Her shirt and denim pants were soaked, salt water half blinded her, and her head felt as though the skull were cracked and someone was forcing the sharp end of a bradawl between her eyes.

Dimly she was aware that the diesel engine was idling noisily, and that the deck was sloshing with water as the boat rolled wildly in some powerful turbulence. She wondered if the whole vessel had been trodden under by the tanker.

Then she realized it must be the wake of the giant hull which was throwing them about so mercilessly, but they were still afloat.

She began to crawl down the plunging deck. She knew where the bilge pump was, that was one thing Tom had taught all of them – and she crawled on grimly towards it.

Hank Petersen ducked out of the wheelhouse, flapping his arms wildly as he struggled into the life-jacket. He was not certain of the best action to take, whether to jump over the side and begin swimming away from the tanker's slightly angled course, or to stay on board and take his chances with the collision which was now only seconds away.

Around him, the others were in the grip of the same indecision; they were huddled silently at the rail staring up at the mountain of smooth rounded steel that seemed to blot out half the sky. Only the TV cameraman on the wheelhouse roof, a true fanatic oblivious of all danger, kept his camera running. His exclamations of delight and the burr of the camera motor blended with the rushing sibilance of *Golden Dawn*'s bow wave. It was fifteen feet high, that wave, and it sounded like wild fire in dry grass.

Suddenly the exhaust of the diesel engine above Hank's head bellowed harshly, and then subsided into a soft burbling idle again. He looked up at it uncomprehendingly, now it roared again, fiercely, and the deck lurched beneath him. From the stern he heard the boil of water driven by the propeller, and the *Dicky* shrugged off her lethargy and lifted her bows to the short steep swell of the Gulf Stream.

A moment longer Hank stood frozen, and then he dived back into the wheelhouse and spun the spokes of the wheel through his fingers, sheering off sharply, but still staring out through the side glass.

The *Golden Dawn*'s bows filled his whole vision now, but the smaller vessel was scooting frantically out to one side, and the tanker's bows were swinging majestically in the opposite direction.

A few seconds more and they would be clear, but the bow wave caught them and Hank was flung across the wheelhouse. He felt something break in his chest, and heard the snap of bone as he hit, then immediately afterwards there was the crackling rending tearing impact as the two hulls came together and he was thrown back the other way, sprawling wildly across the deck.

He tried to claw himself upright, but the little fishing boat was pitching and cavorting with such abandon that he was thrown flat again. There was another tearing impact as the vessel was dragged down the tanker's side, and then flung free to roll her rails under and bob like a cork in the mill race of the huge ship's wake.

Now, at last, he was able to pull himself to his feet, and doubled over, clutching his injured ribs, he peered dazedly through the wheelhouse glass.

Half a mile away, the tanker was lazily turning up into the wind, and there was no propeller wash from under her counter. Hank staggered to the doorway, and looked out. The deck was still awash, but the water they had taken on was pouring out through the scuppers. The railing was smashed, most of it dangling overboard and the planking was splintered and torn, the ripped timber as white as bone in the sunlight.

Behind him, Samantha came crawling up the ladder from the engine room. There was a purple swelling in the centre of her forehead, she was soaking wet and her hands were filthy with black grease. He saw a livid red burn across the back of one hand as she lifted it to brush tumbled blonde hair out of her face.

'Are you all right, Sam?'

'Water's pouring in,' she said. 'I don't know how long the pump can hold it.'

'Did you fix the motor?' he asked.

Samantha nodded. 'I held the throttle open,' she said, and then with feeling, 'but I'll be damned to hell if I'll do it again. Somebody else can go down there, I've had my turn.'

'Show me how,' Hank said, 'and you can take the wheel. The sooner we get back to Key Biscayne, the happier I'll be.'

Samantha peered across at the receding bulk of *Golden Dawn*.

'My God!' She shook her head with wonder. 'My God! We were lucky!'


'*Mackerel skies and mares' tails,*
*Make tall ships carry short sails.*'

Nicholas Berg recited the old sailors' doggerel to himself, shading his eyes with one hand as he looked upwards.

The cloud was beautiful as fine lacework; very high against the tall blue of the heavens it spread swiftly in those long filmy scrolls. Nicholas could see the patterns developing and expanding as he watched, and that was a measure of the speed with which the high winds were blowing. That cloud was at least thirty thousand feet high, and below it the air was clear and crisp – only out on the western horizon the billowing silver and blue thunderheads were rising, generated by the land-mass of Florida whose low silhouette was still below their horizon.

They had been in the main current of the Gulf Stream for six hours now. It was easy to recognize this characteristic scend of the sea, the short steep swells marching close together, the particular brilliance of these waters that had been first warmed in the shallow tropical basin of the Caribbean, the increased bulk flooding through into the Gulf of Mexico and there heated further, swelling in volume until they formed a hillock of water which at last rushed out through this narrow drainhole of the Florida Straits, swinging north and east in a wide benevolent wash, tempering the climate of all countries whose shores it touched and warming the fishing grounds of the North Atlantic.

In the middle of this stream, somewhere directly ahead of *Warlock*'s thrusting bows, the *Golden Dawn* was struggling southwards, directly opposed to the current which would clip eighty miles a day off her speed, and driving directly into the face of one of the most evil and dangerous storms that nature could summon.

Nicholas found himself brooding again on the mentality of anybody who would do that; again he glanced upwards at the harbingers of the storm, those delicate wisps of lacey cloud.

Nicholas had sailed through a hurricane once, twenty years ago, as a junior officer on one of Christy Marine's small grain carriers, and he shuddered now at the memory of it.

Duncan Alexander was a desperate man even to contemplate that risk, a man gambling everything on one fall of the dice. Nicholas could understand the forces that drove him, for he had been driven himself – but he hated him now for the chances which he was taking. Duncan Alexander was risking Nicholas' son, and he was risking the life of an ocean and of the millions of people whose existence was tied to that ocean. Duncan Alexander was gambling with stakes that were not his to place at hazard.

Nicholas wanted one thing only now, and that was to get alongside *Golden Dawn* and take off his son. He would to that, even if it meant boarding her like a buccaneer. In the Master's suite, there was a locked and sealed arms cupboard with two riot guns, automatic 12 gauge shotguns and six Walther PK.38 pistols. *Warlock* had been equipped for every possible emergency in any ocean of the world, and those emergencies could include piracy or mutiny aboard a vessel under salvage. Now Nicholas was fully prepared to take an armed party on board *Golden Dawn*, and to take his chances in any court of law afterwards.

*Warlock* was racing into the chop of the Gulf Stream and scattering the spray like startled white doves, but she was running too slowly for Nicholas and he turned away impatiently and strode into the navigation bridge.

David Allen looked up at him, a small frown of preoccupation marring the smooth boyish features.

'Wind is moderating and veering westerly,' he said, and Nicholas remembered another line of doggerel:

> *'When the wind moves against the sun*
> *Trust her not for back she'll run.'*

He did not recite it, however, he merely nodded and said:

'We are running into the extreme influence of Lorna. The wind will back again as we move closer to the centre.'

Nicholas went on to the radio room and the Trog looked up at him. It was not necessary for Nicholas to ask, the Trog shook his head. Since that long exchange with the coastguard patrol early that morning, *Golden Dawn* had kept her silence.

Nicholas crossed to the radarscope and studied the circular field for a few minutes; this usually busy seaway was peculiarly empty. There were some small craft crossing the main channel, probably fishing boats or pleasure craft scuttling for protection from the coming storm. All across the islands and on the mainland of Florida the elaborate precautions against the hurricane assault would be coming into force. Since the highway had been laid down on the spur of little islands that formed the Florida Keys, more than three hundred thousand people had crowded in there, in the process transforming those wild lovely islands into the Taj Mahal of ticky-tacky. If the hurricane struck there, the loss of life and property would be enormous, it was probably the most vulnerable spot on a long exposed coastline. For a few minutes, Nicholas tried to imagine the chaos that would result if a million tons of toxic crude oil was driven ashore on a littoral already ravaged by hurricane winds. It baulked his imagination, and he left the radar and moved to the front of the bridge. He stood staring down the narrow throat of water at a horizon that concealed all the terrors and desperate alarms that his imagination could conjure up.

The door to the radio shack was open and the bridge was quiet, so that they all heard it clearly; they could even catch the hiss of breath as the speaker paused between each sentence, and the urgency of his tone was not covered by the slight distortion of the VHF carrier beam.

'Mayday! Mayday! Mayday! This is the bulk oil carrier *Golden Dawn*. Our position is 79° 50′ West 25° 43′ North.'

Before Nicholas reached the chart-table, he knew she was still a hundred miles ahead of them, and, as he pored over the table, he saw his estimate confirmed.

'We have lost our propeller with main shaft failure and we are drifting out of control.'

Nicholas' head flinched as though he had been hit in the face. He could imagine no more dangerous condition and position for a ship of that size – and Peter was on board.

'This is *Golden Dawn* calling the United States Coast Guard service or any ship in a position to afford assistance—'

Nicholas reached the radio shack with three long strides, and the Trog handed him the microphone and nodded.

'*Golden Dawn*, this is the salvage tug *Warlock*. I will be in a position to render assistance within four hours—'

Damn the rule of silence, Peter was on board her.

'—Tell Alexander I am offering Lloyd's Open Form and I want immediate acceptance.'

He dropped the microphone and stormed back on to the bridge, his voice clipped and harsh as he caught David Allen's arm.

'Interception course and push her through the gate,' he ordered grimly. 'Tell Beauty Baker to open all the taps.' He dropped David's arm and spun back to the radio room.

'Telex Levoisin on *Sea Witch*. I want him to give me a time to reach *Golden Dawn* at his best possible speed,' and he wondered briefly if even the two tugs would be able to control the crippled and powerless *Golden Dawn* in the winds of a hurricane.


Jules replied almost immediately. He had bunkered at Charleston, and cleared harbour six hours previously. He was running hard now and he gave a time to *Golden Dawn*'s position for noon the next day, which was also the forecast time of passage of the Straits for hurricane Lorna, according to the meteorological up-date they had got from Miami two hours before, Nicholas thought as he read the telex and turned to David Allen.

'David, there is no precedent for this that I know of – but with my son on board *Golden Dawn* I just have to assume command of this ship, on a temporary basis, of course.'

'I'd be honoured to act as your First Officer again, sir,' David told him quietly, and Nicholas could see he meant it.

'If there is a good salvage, the Master's share will still be yours,' Nicholas promised him, and thanked him with a touch on the arm. 'Would you check out the preparations to put a line aboard the tanker?'

David turned to leave the bridge, but Nicholas stopped him. 'By the time we get there, we will have the kind of wind you have only dreamed about in your worst nightmares – just keep that in mind.'

'Telex,' screeched the Trog. '*Golden Dawn* is replying to our offer.'

Nicholas strode across to the radio room, and read the first few lines of message as it printed out.

OFFER CONTRACT OF DAILY HIRE FOR TOWAGE THIS VESSEL FROM PRESENT POSITION TO GALVESTON ROADS

'The bastard,' Nicholas snarled. 'He's playing his fancy games with me, in the teeth of a hurricane and with my boy aboard.' Furiously he punched his fist into the palm of his other hand. 'Right!' he snapped. 'We'll play just as rough! Get me the Director of the U.S. Coast Guard at the Fort Lauderdale Headquarters – get him on the emergency coastguard frequency and I will talk to him in clear.'

The Trog's face lit with malicious glee and he made the contact.

'Colonel Ramsden,' Nicholas said. 'This is the Master of *Warlock*. I'm the only salvage vessel that can reach *Golden Dawn* before passage of Lorna, and I'm probably the only tug on the eastern seaboard of America with 22,000 horsepower. Unless the *Golden Dawn*'s Master accepts Lloyd's Open Form within the next sixty minutes, I shall be obliged to see to the safety of my vessel and crew by running for the nearest anchorage – and you're going to have a million tons of highly toxic crude oil drifting out of control into your territorial waters, in hurricane conditions.'

The Coast Guard Director had a deep measured voice, and the calm tones of a man upon whom the mantle of authority was a familiar garment.

'Stand by, *Warlock*, I am going to contact *Golden Dawn* direct on Channel 16.'

Nicholas signalled the Trog to turn up the volume on Channel 16 and they listened to Ramsden speaking directly to Duncan Alexander.

'In the event your vessel enters United States territorial waters without control or without an attendant tug capable of exerting that control, I shall be obliged under the powers vested in me to seize your vessel and take such steps to prevent pollution of our waters as I see fit. I have to warn you that those steps may include destruction of your cargo.'

Ten minutes later the Trog copied a telex from Duncan Alexander personal to Nicholas Berg accepting Lloyd's Open Form and requesting him to exercise all dispatch in taking *Golden Dawn* in tow.

'I estimate we will be drifting over the 100-fathom line and entering U.S. territorial waters within two hours,' the message ended.

While Nicholas read it, standing out on the protected wing of *Warlock*'s bridge, the wind suddenly fluttered the paper in his hand and flattened his cotton shirt against his chest. He looked up quickly and saw the wind was backing violently into the east, and beginning to claw the tops of the Gulf Stream swells. The setting sun was bleeding copiously across the high veils of cirrus cloud which now covered the sky from horizon to horizon.

There was nothing more that Nicholas could do now. *Warlock* was running as hard as she could, and all her crew were quietly going about their preparations to pass a wire and take on tow. All he could do was wait, but that was always the hardest part.

Darkness came swiftly but with the last of the light, Nicholas could just make out a dark and mountainous shape beginning to hump up above the southern horizon like an impatient monster. He stared at it with awful fascination, until mercifully the night hid Lorna's dreadful face.


The wind chopped the Gulf Stream up into quick confused seas, and it did not blow steadily, but flogged them with squally gusts and rain that crackled against the bridge windows with startling suddenness.

The night was utterly black, there were no stars, no source of light whatsoever, and *Warlock* lurched and heeled to the patternless seas.

'Barometer's rising sharply,' David Allen called suddenly. 'It's jumped three millibars – back to 1005.'

'The trough,' said Nicholas grimly. It was a classic hurricane formation, that narrow girdle of higher pressure that demarcated the outer fringe of the great revolving spiral of tormented air. 'We are going into it now.'

And as he spoke the darkness lifted, the heavens began to burn like a bed of hot coals, and the sea shone with a sullen ruddy luminosity as though the doors of a furnace had been thrown wide.

Nobody spoke on *Warlock*'s bridge, they lifted their faces with the same awed expressions as worshippers in a lofty cathedral and they looked up at the skies.

Low cloud raced above them, cloud that glowed and shone with that terrible ominous flare. Slowly the light faded and changed, turning a paler sickly greenish hue, like the shine on putrid meat. Nicholas spoke first.

'The Devil's Beacon,' he said, and he wanted to rationalize it to break the superstitous mood that gripped them all. It was merely the rays of the sun below the western horizon catching the cloud peaks of the storm and reflected downwards through the weak cloud cover of the trough – but somehow he could not find the right words to denigrate that phenomenon that was part of the mariner's lore, the malignant beacon that leads a doomed ship on to its fate.

The weird light faded slowly away leaving the night even darker and more foreboding than it had been before.

'David,' Nicholas thought quickly of something to distract his officers, 'have we got a radar contact yet?' and the new Mate roused himself with a visible effort and crossed to the radarscope.

'The range is very confused,' he said, his voice still subdued, and Nicholas joined him at the screen.

The sweeping arm lit a swirling mass of sea clutter, and the strange ghost echoes thrown up by electrical discharges within the approaching storm. The outline of the Florida mainland and of the nearest islands of the Grand Bahamas bank were firm and immediately recognizable. They reminded Nicholas yet again of how little searoom there was in which to manoeuvre his tugs and their monstrous prize.

Then, in the trash of false echo and sea clutter, his trained eye picked out a harder echo on the extreme limits of the set's range. He watched it carefully for half a dozen revolutions of the radar's sweep, and each time it was constant and clearer.

'Radar contact,' he said. 'Tell *Golden Dawn* we are in contact, range sixty-five nautical miles. Tell them we will take on tow before midnight.' And then, under his breath, the old sailor's qualifications, 'God willing and weather permitting.'


The lights on *Warlock*'s bridge had been rheostatted down to a dull rose glow to protect the night vision of her officers, and the four of them stared out to where they knew the tanker lay.

Her image on the radar was bright and firm, lying within the two-mile ring of the screen, but from the bridge she was invisible.

In the two hours since first contact, the barometer had gone through its brief peak as the trough passed, and then fallen steeply.

From 1005 it had crashed to 990 and was still plummeting, and the weather coming in from the east was blustering and squalling. The wind mourned about them on a forever rising note, and torrential rain obscured all vision outside an arc of a few hundred yards. Even *Warlock*'s twin searchlights, set seventy feet above the main deck on the summit of the fire-control gantry, could not pierce those solid white curtains of rain.

Nicholas groped like a blind man through the rain fog, using pitch and power to close carefully with *Golden Dawn*, giving his orders to the helm in a cool impersonal tone which belied the pale set of his features and the alert brightness of his eyes as he searched the swirling bank of rain.

Abruptly another squall struck *Warlock*. With a demented shriek, it heeled the big tug sharply and shredded the curtains of rain, ripping them open so that for a moment Nicholas saw *Golden Dawn*.

She was exactly where he had expected her to be, but the wind had caught the tanker's high navigation bridge like the mainsail of a tall ship, and she was going swiftly astern.

All her deck and port lights were burning, and she carried the twin red riding lights at her stubby masthead that identified a vessel drifting out of control. The following sea driven on by the rising wind piled on to her tank decks, smothering them with white foam and spray, so that the ship looked like a submerged coral reef.

'Half ahead both,' Nicholas told the helmsman. 'Steer for her starboard side.'

He closed quickly with the tanker, staying in visual contact now; even when the rain mists closed down again, they could make out the ghostly shape of her and the glow of her riding lights.

David Allen was looking at him expectantly and Nicholas asked, 'What bottom?' without taking his eyes from the stricken ship.

'One hundred sixteen fathoms and shelving fast.' They were being blown quickly out of the main channel, on to the shallow ledge of the Florida littoral.

'I'm going to tow her out stern first,' said Nicholas, and immediately David saw the wisdom of it. Nobody would be able to get up into her bows to secure a tow-line, the seas were breaking over them and sweeping them with ten and fifteen feet of green water.

'I'll go aft—' David began, but Nicholas stopped him.

'No, David. I want you here – because I'm going on board *Golden Dawn*.'

'Sir,' David wanted to tell him that it was dangerous to delay passing the towing cable – with that lee shore waiting.

'This will be our last chance to get passengers off her before the full hurricane hits us,' said Nicholas, and David saw that it was futile to protest. Nicholas Berg was going to fetch his son.

From the height of *Golden Dawn*'s towering navigation bridge, they could look directly down on to the main deck of the tug as she came alongside.

Peter Berg stood beside his mother, almost as tall as she was. He wore a full life-jacket and a corduroy cap pulled down over his ears.

'It will be all right,' he comforted Chantelle. 'Dad is here. It will be just fine now.' And he took her hand protectively.

*Warlock* staggered and reeled in the grip of the wind as she came up into the tanker's lee, rain blew over her like dense white smoke and every few minutes she put her nose down and threw a thick green slice of sea water back along her decks.

In comparison to the tug's wild action, *Golden Dawn* wallowed heavily, held down by the oppressive weight of a million tons of crude oil, and the seas beat upon her with increasing fury, as if affronted by her indifference. *Warlock* edged in closer and still closer.

Duncan Alexander came through from the communications room at the rear of the bridge. He balanced easily against *Golden Dawn*'s ponderous motion but his face was swollen and flushed with anger.

'Berg is coming on board,' he burst out. 'He's wasting valuable time. I warned him that we must get out into deeper water.'

Peter Berg interrupted suddenly and pointed down at *Warlock*.

'Look!' he cried.

Until that moment, the night and the storm had hidden the small huddle of human shapes in the tug's high forward tower. They wore wet, glistening oilskins and their life-jackets gave them a swollen pregnant look. They were lowering the boarding gantry into the horizontal position.

'There is Dad!' Peter shouted. 'That's him in front.'

At the extremity of her roll, *Warlock*'s boarding gantry touched the railing of the tanker's quarter deck, ten feet above the swamped tank deck – and the leading figure on the tug's upperworks ran out lightly along the gantry, balanced for a moment high above the roaring, racing green water and then leapt across five feet of open space, caught a hand hold and then pulled himself over *Golden Dawn*'s rail.

Immediately the tug sheered off and fell in fifty yards off the tanker's starboard side, half hidden in the rain mists, but holding her station steadily, despite all the wind's and the sea's spiteful efforts to separate the two vessels.

The whole manoeuvre had been performed with an expertise which made it seem almost casual.

'Dad's carried a line across,' Peter said proudly, and Chantelle, looking down, saw that a delicate white nylon thread was being hove in by two seamen on the tanker's quarter deck, while from the tug's fire-control tower a canvas bosun's chair was being winched across.

The elevator doors slid open with a whine and Nicholas Berg strode on to the tanker's bridge. His oilskins still ran with rainwater that splattered on to the deck at his feet.

'Dad!' Peter ran to meet him and Nicholas stooped and embraced him fiercely before straightening; with one arm still about his son's shoulders, he confronted Chantelle and Duncan Alexander.

'I hope both of you are satisfied now,' he said quietly, 'but I for one don't rate our chances of saving this ship very highly, so I'm taking off everybody who is not needed on board to handle her.

'Your tug,' burst out Duncan, 'you've got 22,000 horse-power, and can—'

'There is a hurricane on its way,' said Nicholas coldly, and he shot a glance out at the roaring night. 'This is just the overture.' He turned back to Randle. 'How many men do you want to keep on board?'

Randle thought a moment. 'Myself, a helmsman, and five seamen to handle the tow-lines and work the ship.' He paused and then went on, 'And the pump room personnel to control the cargo.'

'You will act as helmsman, I will control the pump room, and I'll need only three seamen. Get me volunteers,' Nicholas decided. 'Send everybody else off.'

'Sir,' Randle began to protest.

'May I remind you, Captain, that I am salvage master, my authority now supersedes yours.' Nicholas did not wait for his reply. 'Chantelle,' he picked her out, 'take Peter down to the quarter deck. 'You'll go across first.'

'Listen here, Berg,' Duncan could no longer contain himself, 'I insist you pass the towing cable, this ships is in danger.'

'Get down there with them,' Nicholas snapped. 'I'll decide the procedures.'

'Do as he says, darling,' Chantelle smiled up at her husband vindictively. 'You've lost. Nicholas is the only winner now.'

'Shut up, damn you,' Duncan hissed at her.

'Get down to the afterdeck,' Nicholas' voice cracked like breaking ice.

'I'm staying on board this ship,' said Duncan abruptly. 'It's my responsibility. I said I'd see it out and by God I will. I am going to be here to make sure you do your job, Berg.'

Nicholas checked himself, studied him for a long moment, and then smiled mirthlessly.

'Nobody ever called you a coward,' he nodded reluctantly. 'Other things – but not a coward. Stay if you will, we might need an extra hand.' Then to Peter, 'Come, my boy.' And he led him towards the elevator.

At the quarterdeck rail, Nicholas hugged the boy, holding him in his arms, their cheeks pressed tightly together, and drawing out the moment while the wind cannoned and thrummed about their heads.

'I love you, Dad.'

'And I love you, Peter, more than I can ever tell you – but you must go now.'

He broke the embrace and lifted the child into the deep canvas bucket of the bosun's chair, stepped back and windmilled his right arm. Immediately, the winch party in *Warlock*'s upperworks swung him swiftly out into the gap between the two ships and the nylon cable seemed as fragile and insubstantial as a spider's thread.

As the two ships rolled and dipped, so the line tightened and sagged, one moment dropping the white canvas bucket almost to the water level where the hungry waves snatched at it with cold green fangs, and the next, pulling the line up so tightly that it hummed with tension, threatening to snap and drop the child back into the sea, but at last it reached the tug and four pairs of strong hands lifted the boy clear. For one moment, he waved back at Nicholas and then he was hustled away, and the empty bosun's chair was coming back.

Only then did Nicholas become aware that Chantelle was clinging to his arm and he looked down into her face. Her eyelashes were dewed and stuck together with the flying raindrops. Her face ran with wetness and she seemed very small and childlike under the bulky oilskins and life-jacket. She was as beautiful as she had ever been but her eyes were huge and darkly troubled.

'Nicholas, I've always needed you,' she husked. 'But never as I need you now.'

Her existence was being blown away on the wind, and she was afraid.

'You and this ship are all I have left.'

'No, only the ship,' he said brusquely, and he was amazed that the spell was broken. That soft area of his soul which she had been able to touch so unerringly was now armoured against her. With a sudden surge of relief, he realized he was free of her, for ever. It was over; here in the storm, he was free at last.

She sensed it – for the fear in her eyes changed to real terror.

'Nicholas, you cannot desert me now. Oh Nicholas, what will become of me without you and Christy Marine?'

'I don't know,' he told her quietly, and caught the bosun's chair as it came in over *Golden Dawn*'s rail. He lifted her as easily as he had lifted his son and placed her in the canvas bucket.

'And to tell you the truth, Chantelle, I don't really care,' he said, and stepping back, he windmilled his right arm. The chair swooped out across the narrow water, swinging like a pendulum in the wind. Chantelle shouted something at him but Nicholas had turned away, and was already going aft in a lurching run to where the three volunteers were waiting.

He saw at a glance that they were big, powerful, competent looking men.

Quickly Nicholas checked their equipment, from the thick leather gauntlets to the bolt cutters and jemmy bars for handling heavy cable.

'You'll do,' he said. 'We will use the bosun's tackle to bring across a messenger from the tug – just as soon as the last man leaves this ship.'

Working with men to whom the task was unfamiliar, and in rapidly deteriorating conditions of sea and weather, it took almost another hour before they had the main cable across from *Warlock* secured by its thick nylon spring to the tanker's stern bollards – yet the time had passed so swiftly for Nicholas that when he stood back and glanced at his watch, he was shocked. Before this wind they must have been going down very fast on the land. He staggered into the tanker's stern quarters, and left a trail of sea water down the passageway to the elevators.

On the bridge, Captain Randle was standing grim-faced at the helm, and Duncan Alexander snapped accusingly at him.

'You've cut it damned fine.' A single glance at the digital print-out of the depth gauge on the tanker's control console bore him out. They had thirty-eight fathoms of water under them now, and the *Golden Dawn*'s swollen belly sagged down twenty fathoms below the surface. They were going down very swiftly before the easterly gale winds. It was damned fine, Nicholas had to agree, but he showed no alarm or agitation as he crossed to Randle's side and unhooked the hand microphone.

'David,' he asked quietly, 'are you ready to haul us off?'

'Ready, sir,' David Allen's voice came from the speaker above his head.

'I'm going to give you full port rudder to help your turn across the wind,' said Nicholas, and then nodded to Randle. 'Full port rudder.'

'Forty degrees of port rudder on,' Randle reported.

They felt the tiny shock as the tow-cable came up taut, and carefully *Warlock* began the delicate task of turning the huge ship across the rising gusting wind and then dragging her out tail first into the deeper water of the channel where she would have her best chance of riding out the hurricane.


It was clear now that *Golden Dawn* lay directly in the track of Lorna, and the storm unleashed its true nature upon them. Out there upon the sane and rational world, the sun was rising, but here there was no dawn, for there was no horizon and no sky. There was only madness and wind and water, and all three elements were so intermingled as to form one substance.

An hour – which seemed like a lifetime – ago, the wind had ripped away the anemometer and the weather-recording equipment on top of the navigation bridge, so Nicholas had no way of judging the wind's strength and direction.

Out beyond the bridge windows, the wind took the top off the sea; it took it off in thick sheets of salt water and lifted them over the navigation bridge in a shrieking white curtain that cut off visiblity at the glass of the windows. The tank deck had disappeared in the racing white emulsion of wind and water, even the railing of the bridge wings six feet from the windows was invisible.

The entire superstructure groaned and popped and whimpered under the assault of the wind, the pressed aluminium bulkheads bulging and distorting, the very deck flexing and juddering at the solid weight of the storm.

Through the saturated, racing, swirling air, a leaden and ominous grey light filtered, and every few minutes the electrical impulses generated within the sixty-thousand-foot-high mountain of racing, spinning air released themselves in shattering cannonades of thunder and sudden brilliance of eye-searing white lightning.

There was no visual contact with *Warlock*. The massive electrical disturbance of the storm and the clutter of high seas and almost solid cloud and turbulence had reduced the radar range to a few miles, and even then it was unreliable. Radio contact with the tug was drowned with buzzing squealing static. It was possible to understand only odd disconnected words from David Allen.

Nicholas was powerless, caged in the groaning, vibrating box of the navigation bridge, blinded and deafened by the unleashed powers of the heavens. There was nothing any of them could do.

Randle had locked the ultra-tanker's helm amidships, and now he stood with Duncan and the three seamen by the chart-table, all of them clinging to it for support, all their faces pale and set as though carved from chalk.

Only Nicholas moved restlessly about the bridge; from the stern windows where he peered down vainly, trying to get a glimpse of either the tow-cable and its spring, or of the tug's looming shape through the racing white storm, then he came forward carefully, using the foul-weather rail to steady himself against the huge ship's wild and unpredictable motion, and he stood before the control console, studying the display of lights that monitored the pod tanks and the ship's navigational and mechanical functions.

None of the petroleum tanks had lost any crude oil and in all of them the nature of the inert gas was constant, there had been no ingress of air to them; they were all still intact then. One of the reasons that Nicholas had taken the tanker in tow stern first was so that the navigation tower might break the worst of wind and sea, and the fragile bloated tanks would receive some protection from it.

Yet desperately he wished for a momentary sight of the tank deck, merely to reassure himself. There could be malfunction in the pump control instruments, the storm could have clawed one of the pod tanks open, and even now *Golden Dawn* could be bleeding her poison into the sea. But there was no view of the tank decks through the storm, and Nick stooped to the radarscope. The screen glowed and danced and flickered with ghost images and trash – he wasn't too certain if even *Warlock*'s image was constant, the range seemed to be opening, as though the tow-line had parted. He straightened up and stood balanced on the balls of his feet, reassuring himself by the feel of the deck that *Golden Dawn* was still under tow. He could feel by the way she resisted the wind and the sea that the tow was still good.

Yet there was no means of telling their position. The satellite navigational system was completely blanketed, the radio waves were distorted and diverted by tens of thousands of feet of electrical storm, and the same forces were blanketing the marine radio beacons on the American mainland.

The only indication was the ship's electronic log which gave Nicholas the speed of the ship's hull through the water and the speed across the sea bottom, and the depth finder which recorded the water under her keel.

For the first two hours of the tow, *Warlock* had been able to pull the ship back towards the main channel at three and a half knots, and slowly the water had become deeper until they had 150 fathoms under them.

Then as the wind velocity increased, the windage of *Golden Dawn*'s superstructure had acted as a vast mainsail and the storm had taken control. Now, despite all the power in *Warlock*'s big twin propellers, both tug and tanker were being pushed once more back towards the 100-fathom line and the American mainland.

'Where is *Sea Witch?*' Nicholas wondered, as he stared helplessly at the gauges. They were going towards the shore at a little over two knots, and the bottom was shelving steeply. *Sea Witch* might be the ace that took the trick, if she could reach them through these murderous seas and savage winds, and if she could find them in this wilderness of mad air and water.

Again, Nicholas groped his way to the communications room, and still clinging to the bulkhead with one hand he thumbed the microphone.

'*Sea Witch. Sea Witch.* This is *Warlock.* Calling *Sea Witch.*'

He listened then, trying to tune out the snarl and crackle of static, crouching over the set. Faintly he thought he heard a human voice, a scratchy whisper through the interference and he called again and listened and called again. There was the voice again, but so indistinct he could not make out a single word.

Above his head, there was a tearing screech of rending metal. Nicholas dropped the microphone and staggered through on to the bridge. There was another deafening banging and hammering and all of them stood staring up at the metal roof of the bridge. It sagged and shook, there was one more crash and then with a scraping, dragging rush, a confused tangle of metal and wire and cable tumbled over the forward edge of the bridge and flapped and swung wildly in the wind.

It took a moment for Nicholas to realize what it was.

'The radar antennae!' he shouted. He recognized the elongated dish of the aerial, dangling on a thick coil of cable, then the wind tore that loose also, and the entire mass of equipment flapped away like a giant bat and was instantly lost in the teeming white curtains of the storm.

With two quick paces, he reached the radarscope, and one glance was enough. The screen was black and dead. They had lost their eyes now, and, unbelievably, the sound of the storm was rising again.

It boomed against the square box of the bridge, and the men within it cowered from its fury.

Then abruptly, Duncan was screaming something at Nicholas, and pointing up at the master display of the control console. Nicholas, still hanging on to the radarscope, roused himself with an effort and looked up at the display. The speed across the ground had changed drastically. It was now almost eight knots, and the depth was ninety-two fathoms.

Nicholas felt icy despair clutch and squeeze his guts. The ship was moving differently under him, he could feel her now in mortal distress; that same gust which had torn away the radar mast had done other damage.

He knew what that damage was, and the thought of it made him want to vomit, but he had to be sure. He had to be absolutely certain, and he began to hand himself along the foul-weather rail towards the elevator doors.

Across the bridge the others were watching him intently, but even from twenty feet it was impossible to make himself heard above the clamorous assault of the storm.

One of the seamen seemed suddenly to guess his intention. He left the chart-table and groped his way along the bulkhead towards Nicholas.

'Good man!' Nicholas grabbed his arm to steady him, and they fell forward into the elevator as *Golden Dawn* began another of those ponderous wallowing rolls and the deck fell out from under their feet.

The ride down in the elevator car slammed them back and forth across the little coffin-like box, and even here in the depths of the ship they had to shout to hear each other.

'The tow cable,' Nicholas yelled in the man's ear. 'Check the tow cable.'

From the elevator they went carefully aft along the central passageway, and when they reached the double storm doors, Nicholas tried to push the inner door open, but the pressure of the wind held it closed.

'Help me,' he shouted at the seaman, and they threw their combined weight against it. The instant that they forced the jamb open a crack, the vacuum of pressure was released and the wind took the three-inch mahogany doors and ripped them effortlessly from their hinges, and whisked them away, as though they were a pair of playing cards – and Nicholas and the seaman were exposed in the open doorway.

The wind flung itself upon them, and hurled them to the deck, smothering them in the icy deluge of water that ripped at their faces as abrasively as ground glass.

Nicholas rolled down the deck and crashed into the stern rail with such jarring force that he thought his lungs had been crushed, and the wind pinned him there, and blinded and smothered him with salt water.

He lay there helpless as a new-born infant, and near him he heard the seaman screaming thinly. The sound steeled him, and Nicholas slowly dragged himself to his knees, desperately clutching at the rail to resist the wind.

Still the man screamed and Nicholas began to creep forward on his hands and knees. It was impossible to stand in that wind and he could move only with support from the rail.

Six feet ahead of him, the extreme limit of his vision, the railing had been torn away, a long section of its dangling over the ship's side, and to this was clinging the seaman. His weight driven by the wind must have hit the rail with sufficient force to tear it loose, and now he was hanging on with one arm hooked through the railing and the other arm twisted from a shattered shoulder and waving a crazy salute as the wind whipped it about. When he looked up at Nicholas his mouth had been smashed in. It looked as though he had half chewed a mouthful of black currants, and the jagged stumps of his broken front teeth were bright red with the juice.

On his belly, Nicholas reached for him, and as he did so, the wind came again, unbelievably it was stronger still, and it took the damaged railing with the man still upon it and tore it bodily away. They disappeared instantly in the blinding white-out of the storm, and Nicholas felt himself hurled forward towards the edge. He clung with all his strength to the remaining section of the rail, and felt it buckle and begin to give.

On his knees still he clawed himself away from that fatal beckoning gap, towards the stern, and the wind struck him full in the face, blinding and choking him. Sightlessly, he dragged himself on until one outstretched arm struck the cold cast iron of the port stern bollard, and he flung both arms about it like a lover, choking and retching from the salt water that the wind had forced through his nose and mouth and down his throat.

Still blind, he felt for the woven steel of *Warlock*'s main tow wire. He found it and he could not span it with his fist – but he felt the quick lift of his hopes.

The cable was still secured. He had catted and prevented it with a dozen nylon strops, and it was still holding. He crawled forward, dragging himself along the tow-cable, and immediately he realized that his relief had been premature. There was no tension in the cable and when he reached the edge of the deck it dangled straight down. It was not stretched out into the whiteness, to where he had hoped *Warlock* was still holding them like a great sea anchor.

He knew then that what he had dreaded had happened. The storm had been too powerful, it had snapped the steel cable like a thread of cotton, and *Golden Dawn* was loose, without control, and this wild and savage wind was blowing her down swiftly on to the land.

Nicholas felt suddenly exhausted to his bones. He lay flat on the deck, closed his eyes and clung weakly to the severed cable. The wind wanted to hurl him over the side, it ballooned his oilskins and ripped at his face. It would be so easy to open his fingers and to let go – and it took all his resolve to resist the impulse.

Slowly, as painfully as a crippled insect, he dragged himself back through the open, shattered doorway into the central passageway of the stern quarters – but still the wind followed him. It roared down the passageway, driving in torrents of rain and salt water that flooded the deck and forced Nicholas to cling for support like a drunkard.

After the open storm, the car of the elevator seemed silent and tranquil as the inner sanctum of a cathedral. He looked at himself in the wall mirror, and saw that his eyes were scoured red and painful-looking by salt and wind, and his cheeks and lips looked raw and bruised, as though the skin had been rasped away. He touched his face and there was no feeling in his nose nor his lips.

The elevator doors slid open and he reeled out on to the navigation bridge. The group of men at the chart-table seemed not to have moved, but their heads turned to him.

Nicholas reached the table and clung to it. They were silent, watching his face.

'I lost a man,' he said, and his voice was hoarse and roughened by salt and weariness. 'He went overboard. The wind got him'

Still none of them moved nor spoke, and Nicholas coughed, his lungs ached from the water he had breathed. When the spasm passed, he went on.

'The tow-cable has parted. We are loose – and *Warlock* will never be able to re-establish tow. Not in this.'

All their heads turned now to the forward bridge windows, to that inpenetrable racing whiteness beyond the glass, that was lit internally with its glowing bursts of lightning.

Nicholas broke the spell that held them all. He reached up to the signal locker above the chart-table and brought down a cardboard packet of distress flares. He broke open the seals and spilled the flares on to the table. They looked like sticks of dynamite, cylinders of heavily varnished waterproof paper. The flares could be lit, and would spurt out crimson flames, even if immersed in water, once the self-igniter tab at one end was pulled.

Nicholas stuffed half a dozen of the flares into the inner pockets of his oilskins.

'Listen,' he had to shout, even though they were only feet away. 'We are going to be aground within two hours. This ship is going to start breaking up immediately we strike.'

He paused and studied their faces; Duncan was the only one who did not seem to understand. He had picked up a handful of the signal flares from the table and he was looking inquiringly at Nicholas.

'I will give you the word; as soon as we reach the twenty-fathom line and she touches bottom, you will go over the side. We will try and get a raft away. There is a chance you could be carried ashore.'

He paused again, and he could see that Randle and his two seamen realized clearly just how remote that chance was.

'I will give you twenty minutes to get clear. By then, the pod tanks will have begun breaking up—' He didn't want this to sound melodramatic and he searched for some way to make it sound less theatrical, but could think of none. 'Once the first tank ruptures, I will ignite the escaping crude with a signal flare.'

'Christ!' Randle mouthed the blasphemy, and the storm censored it on his lips. Then he raised his voice. 'A million of crude. It will fireball, man.'

'Better than a million-ton slick down the Gulf Stream,' Nicholas told him wearily.

'None of us will have a chance. A million tons. It will go up like an atom bomb.' Randle was white-faced and shaking now. 'You can't do it!'

'Think of a better way,' said Nicholas and left the table to stagger across to the radio room. They watched him go, and then Duncan looked down at the signal flares in his hand for a moment before thrusting them into the pocket of his jacket.

In the radio room, Nicholas called quietly into the microphone. 'Come in, *Sea Witch* – *Sea Witch*, this is *Golden Dawn*.' And only the static howled in reply.

'*Warlock*. Come in, *Warlock*. This is *Golden Dawn*.'

Something else went in the wind, they heard it tear loose, and the whole superstructure shook and trembled. The ship was beginning to break up, it had not been designed to withstand winds like this.

Through the open radio room door, Nicholas could see the control console display. There were seventy-one fathoms of water under the ship, and the wind was punching her, flogging her on towards the shore.

'Come in, *Sea Witch*,' Nicholas called with quiet desperation. 'This is *Golden Dawn*. Do you read me?'

The wind charged the ship, crashing into it like a monster, and she groaned and reeled from the blow.

'Come in, *Warlock*.'

Randle lurched across to the forward windows, and clinging to the rail

he bowed over the gauges that monitored the condition of the ship's cargo.
Checking for tank damage.

'At least he is still thinking.' Nicholas watched him, and above the
Captain's head, the sounding showed sixty-eight fathoms.

Randle straightened slowly, began to turn, and the wind struck again.

Nicholas felt the blow in his stomach, it was a solid thing, like a mountain
in avalanche, a deafening boom of sound and the forward bridge window
above the control console broke inwards.

It burst in a glittering explosion of glass shards that engulfed the figure
of Captain Randle standing directly before it. In a fleeting moment of horror,
Nicholas saw his head half severed from his shoulders by a guillotine of
flying glass, then he crumpled to the deck and instantly the bright pulsing
hose of his blood was diluted to spreading pale pink in the torrent of wind
and blown water that poured in through the opening, and smothered the
navigation bridge.

Charts and books were ripped from their shelves and fluttered like trapped
birds as the wind blustered and swirled in the confines of glass and steel.

Nicholas reached the Captain's body, protecting his own face with an arm
crooked across it, but there was nothing he could do for him. He left Randle
lying on the deck and shouted to the others.

'Keep clear of the windows.'

He gathered them in the rear of the bridge, against the bulkhead where
stood the Decca and navigational systems. The four of them kept close
together, as though they gained comfort from the close proximity of other
humans, but the wind did not relent.

It poured in through the shattered window and raged about the bridge,
tearing at their clothing and filling the air with a fine mist of water, flooding
the deck ankle deep so that it sloshed and ran as the tanker rolled almost to
her beam ends.

Randle's limp and sodden body slid back and forth in the wash and roll,
until Nicholas left the dubious security of the after bulk-head, half-lifted the
corpse under the arms, and dragged it into the radio room and wedged it
into the radio operator's bunk. Swift blood stained the crisply ironed sheets,
and Nicholas threw a fold of the blanket over Randle and staggered back
into the bridge.

Still the wind rose, and now Nicholas felt himself numbed by the force
and persistence of it.

Some loose material, perhaps a sheet of aluminium from the superstructure, or a length of piping ripped from the tank deck below, smashed into
the top of the bridge like a cannon ball and then flipped away into the storm,
leaving a jagged rent which the wind exploited, tearing and worrying at it,
enlarging the opening, so that the plating flapped and hammered and a solid
deluge of rain poured in through it.

Nicholas realized that the ship's superstructure was beginning to go; like
a gigantic vulture, soon the wind would begin stripping the carcass down to
its bones.

He knew he should get the survivors down nearer the water line, so that
when they were forced to commit themselves to the sea, they could do so
quickly. But his brain was numbed by the tumult, and he stood stolidly. It

needed all his remaining strength merely to brace himself against the tearing wind and the ship's anguished motion.

In the days of sail, the crew would tie themselves to the main mast, when they reached this stage of despair.

Dully, he registered that the depth of water under the ship was now only fifty-seven fathoms, and the barometer was reading 955 millibars. Nicholas had never heard of a reading that low; surely it could not go lower, they must be almost at the centre of the revolving hurricane.

With an effort, he lifted his arm and read the time. It was still only ten o'clock in the morning, they had been in the hurricane for only two and a half hours.

A great burning light struck through the torn roof, a light that blinded them with its intensity, and Nicholas threw up his hands to protect his eyes. He could not understand what was happening. He thought his hearing had gone, for suddenly the terrible tumult of the wind was muted, fading away.

Then he understood. 'The eye,' he croaked, 'we are into the eye,' and his voice resounded strangely in his own ears. He stumbled to the front of the bridge.

Although the *Golden Dawn* still rolled ponderously, describing an arc of almost forty degrees from side to side, she was free of the unbearable weight of the wind and brilliant shunshine poured down upon her. It beamed down like the dazzling arc lamps of a stage set, out of the throat of a dark funnel of dense racing swirling cloud.

The cloud lay to the very surface of the sea, and encompassed the full sweep of the horizon in an unbroken wall. Only directly overhead was it open, and the sky was an angry unnatural purple, set with the glaring, merciless eye of the sun.

The sea was still wild and confused, leaping into peaks and troughs and covered with a thick frothy mattress of spindrift, whipped into a custard by the wild winds. But already the sea was subsiding in the total calm of the eye and *Golden Dawn* was rolling less viciously.

Nicholas turned his head stiffly to watch the receding wall of racing cloud. How long would it take for the eye to pass over them, he wondered.

Not very long, he was sure of that, half an hour perhaps – an hour at the most – and then the storm would be on them again, with its renewed fury every bit as sudden as its passing. But this time, the wind would come from exactly the opposite direction as they crossed the hub and went into the far side of the revolving wall of cloud.

Nicholas jerked his eyes away from that racing, heaven-high bank of cloud, and looked down on to the tank deck. He saw at a single glance that *Golden Dawn* had already sustained mortal damage. The forward port pod tank was half torn from its hydraulic coupling, holding only by the bows and lying at almost twenty degrees from the line of the other three tanks. The entire tank deck was twisted like the limb of an arthritic giant, it rolled and pitched out of sequence with the rest of the hull.

*Golden Dawn*'s back was broken. It had broken where Duncan had weakened the hull to save steel. Only the buoyancy of the crude petroleum in her four tanks was holding her together now. Nicholas expected to see the dark, glistening ooze of slick leaking from her; he could not believe that not one of the four tanks had ruptured, and he glanced at the electronic cargo monitor. Loads and gas contents of all tanks were still normal. They had been freakishly lucky so far, but when they went into the far side of the hurricane he knew that *Golden Dawn*'s weakened spine would give completely, and when that happened it must pinch and tear the thin skins of the pod tanks.

He made a decision then, forcing his mind to work, not certain how good a decision it was but determined to act on it.

'Duncan,' he called to him across the swamped and battered bridge. 'I'm sending you and the others off on one of the life-rafts. This will be your only chance to launch one. I'll stay on board to fire the cargo when the storm hits again.'

'The storm has passed,' suddenly Duncan was screaming at him like a madman. 'The ship is safe now. You're going to destroy my ship – you're deliberately trying to break me.' He was lunging across the heaving bridge. 'It's deliberate. You know I've won now. You are going to destroy this ship. It's the only way you can stop me now.' He swung a clumsy round arm blow. Nicholas ducked under it and caught Duncan around the chest.

'Listen to me,' he shouted, trying to calm him. 'This is only the eye—'

'You'd do anything to stop me. You swore you would stop me—'

'Help me,' Nicholas called to the two seamen, and they grabbed Duncan's arms. He bucked and fought like a madman, screaming wildly at Nicholas, his face contorted and swollen with rage, sodden hair flopping into his eyes. 'You'd do anything to destroy me, to destroy my ship—'

'Take him down to the raft deck,' Nicholas ordered the two seamen. He knew he could not reason with Duncan now, and he turned away and stiffened suddenly.

'Wait!' he stopped them leaving the bridge.

Nicholas felt the terrible burden of weariness and despair slip from his shoulders, felt new strength rippling through his body, recharging his courage and his resolution – for a mile away, from behind that receding wall of dreadful grey cloud, *Sea Witch* burst abruptly into the sunlight, tearing bravely along with the water bursting over her bows and flying back as high as her bridgework, running without regard to the hazard of sea and storm.

'Jules,' Nicholas whispered.

Jules was driving her like only a tugman can drive a ship, racing to beat the far wall of the storm.

Nicholas felt his throat constricting and suddenly the scalding tears of relief and thankfulness half-blinded him – for a mile out on *Sea Witch*'s port side, and barely a cable-length astern of her, *Warlock* came crashing out of the storm bank, running every bit as hard as her sister ship.

'David,' Nicholas spoke aloud. 'You too, David.'

He realized only then that they must have been in radar contact with him through those wild tempestuous hours of storm passage, hovering there, holding station on *Golden Dawn*'s crippled bulk and waiting for their first opportunity.

Above the wail and crackle of static from the overhead loudspeaker boomed Jules Levoisin's voice. He was close enough and in the clear eye the interference allowed a readable radio contact.

'*Golden Dawn*, this is *Sea Witch*. Come in, *Golden Dawn*.'

Nicholas reached the radio bench and snatched up the microphone.

'Jules.' He did not waste a moment in greeting or congratulations. 'We are going to take the tanks off her, and let the hull go. Do you understand?'

'I understand to take off the tanks,' Jules responded immediately.

Nicholas' brain was crisp and clear again, he could see just how it must be done. '*Warlock* takes off the port tanks first – in tandem.'

In tandem, the two tanks would be strung like beads on a string, they had been designed to tow that way.

'Then you will take off the starboard side—'

'You must save the hull.' Duncan still fought the two seamen who held him. 'Goddamn you, Berg. I'll not let you destroy me.'

Nicholas ignored his ravings until he had finished giving his orders to the two tug masters. Then he dropped the microphone and grabbed Duncan by the shoulders. Nicholas seemed to be possessed suddenly by supernatural strength, and he shook him as though he were a child. He shook him so his head snapped back and forth and his teeth rattled in his head.

'You bloody idiot,' he shouted in Duncan's face. 'Don't you understand the storm will resume again in minutes?'

He jerked Duncan's body out of the grip of the two seamen and dragged him bodily to the windows overlooking the tank deck.

'Can't you see this monster you have built is finished, finished! There is no propeller, her back is broken, the superstructure will go minutes after the wind hits again.'

He dragged Duncan round to face him, their eyes were inches apart.

'It's over, Duncan. We will be lucky to get away with our lives. We'll be luckier still to save the cargo.'

'But don't you understand – we've got to save the hull – without it—' Duncan started to struggle, he was a powerful man, and quickly he was rousing himself, within minutes he would be dangerous – and there was no time, already *Warlock* was swinging up into her position on *Golden Dawn*'s port beam for tank transfer.

'I'll not let you take off—' Duncan wrenched himself out of Nicholas' grip, there was a mad fanatic light in his eyes.

Nicholas swivelled; coming up on to his toes and swinging from the shoulders he aimed for the point of Duncan's jaw, just below the ear and the thick sodden wedge of Duncan's red-gold sideburns. But Duncan rolled his head with the punch, and the blow glanced off his temple, and *Golden Dawn* rolled back the other way as Nicholas was unbalanced.

He fell back against the control console, and Duncan drove at him, two running paces like a quarter-back taking a field goal, and he kicked right-legged for Nicholas' lower body.

'I'll kill you, Berg,' he screamed, and Nicholas had only time to roll sideways and lift his leg, scissoring it to protect his crotch. Duncan's kick caught him in the upper thigh. An explosion of white pain shot up into his belly and numbed his leg to the thigh, but he used the control console and his good leg to launch himself into a counter-punch, hooking with his right again, under the ribs – and the wind went out of Duncan's lungs with a whoosh as he doubled. Nicholas transferred weight smoothly and swung his left fist up into Duncan's face. It sounded like a watermelon dropped on a concrete floor, and Duncan was hurled backwards against the bulkhead, pinned there for a moment by the ship's roll. Nicholas followed him, hobbling painfully on the injured leg, and he hit him twice more. Left and right, short, hard, hissing blows that cracked his skull backwards against the bulkhead, and brought quick bright rosettes of blood from his lips and nostrils.

As his legs buckled, Nicholas caught him by the throat with his left hand and held him upright, searching his eyes for further resistance, ready to hit again, but there was no fight left in him.

Nicholas let him go, and went to the signal locker. He snatched three of the small walkie-talkie radios from the radio shelves and handed one to each of the two seamen.

'You know the pod tank undocking procedures for a tandem tow?' he asked.

'We've practised it,' one of them replied.

'Let's go,' said Nicholas.

It was a job that was scheduled for a dozen men, and there were three of them. Duncan was of no use to them, and Nicholas left him in the pump control room on the lowest deck of *Golden Dawn*'s stern quarter, after he had closed down the inert gas pumps, sealed the gas vents, and armed the hydraulic releases of the pod tanks for undocking.

They worked sometimes neck-deep in the bursts of green, frothing water that poured over the ultra-tanker's foredeck. They took on board and secured *Warlock*'s main cable, unlocked the hydraulic clamps that held the forward pod tank attached to the hull and, as David Allen eased it clear of the crippled hull, they turned and lumbered back along the twisted and wind-torn catwalk, handicapped by the heavy seaboots and oilskins and the confused seas that still swamped the tank-deck every few minutes.

On the after tank, the whole laborious energy-sapping procedure had to be repeated, but here it was complicated by the chain coupling which connected the two half-mile-long pod tanks. Over the walkie-talkie, Nicholas had to co-ordinate the efforts of his seamen to those of David Allen at the helm of *Warlock*.

When at last *Warlock* threw on power to both of her big propellers and sheered away from the wallowing hull, she had both port pod tanks in tow. They floated just level with the surface of the sea, offering no windage for the hurricane winds that would soon be upon them again.

Hanging on to the rail of the raised catwalk Nicholas watched for two precious minutes with an appraising professional eye. It was an incredible sight, two great shiny black whales, their backs showing only in the troughs, and the gallant little ship leading them away. They followed meekly, and Nicholas' anxiety was lessened. He was not confident, not even satisfied, for there was still a hurricane to navigate – but there was hope now.

'*Sea Witch*,' he spoke into the small portable radio. 'Are you ready to take on tow?'

Jules Levoisin fired the rocket-line across personally. Nicholas recognized his portly but nimble figure high in the fire-control tower, and the rocket left a thin trail of snaking white smoke high against the backdrop of racing, grey hurricane clouds. Arching high over the tanker's tank-deck, the thin nylon rocket-line fell over the catwalk ten feet from where Nicholas stood.

They worked with a kind of restrained frenzy, and Jules Levoisin brought the big graceful tug in so close beside them that glancing up Nicholas could see the flash of a gold filling in Jules' white smile of encouragement. It was only a glance that Nicholas allowed himself, and then he raised his face and looked at the storm.

The wall of cloud was slippery and smooth and grey, like the body of a gigantic slug, and at its foot trailed a glistening white slimy line where the winds frothed the surface of the sea. It was very close now, ten miles, no more, and above them the sun had gone, cut out by the spiralling vortex of leaden cloud. Yet still that open narrow funnel of clear calm air reached right up to a dark and ominous sky.

There was no hydraulic pressure on the clamps of the starboard forward pod tank. Somewhere in the twisted damaged hull the hydraulic line must have sheared. Nicholas and one of the seamen had to work the emergency release, pumping it open slowly and laboriously by hand.

Still it would not release, the hull was distorted, the clamp jaws out of alignment.

'Pull,' Nicholas commanded Jules in desperation. 'Pull all together.' The storm front was five miles away, and already he could hear the deadly whisper of the wind, and a cold puff touched Nicholas' uplifted face.

The sea boiled under *Sea Witch*'s counter, spewing out in a swift white wake as Jules brought in both engines. The tow-cable came up hard and straight; for half a minute nothing gave, nothing moved – except the wall of racing grey cloud bearing down upon them.

Then, with a resounding metallic clang, the clamps slipped and the tank slid ponderously out of its dock in *Golden Dawn*'s hull – and as it came free, so the hull, held together until that moment by the tanks' bulk and buoyancy, began to collapse.

The catwalk on which Nicholas stood began to twist and tilt so that he had to grab for a handhold, and he stood frozen in horrified fascination as he watched *Golden Dawn* begin the final break-up.

The whole tank deck, now only a gutted skeleton, began to bend at its weakened centre, began to hinge like an enormous pair of nutcrackers – and caught between the jaws of the nutcracker was the starboard after pod tank. It was a nut the size of Chartres Cathedral, with a soft liquid centre, and a shell as thin as the span of a man's hand.

Nicholas broke into a lurching, blundering run down the twisting, tilting catwalk, calling urgently into the radio as he went.

'Shear!' he shouted to the seamen almost half a mile away across that undulating plane of tortured steel. 'Shear the tandem tow!'

For the two starboard pod tanks were linked by the heavy chain of the tandem, and the forward tank was linked to *Sea Witch* by the main tow-cable. So *Sea Witch* and the doomed *Golden Dawn* were coupled inexorably, unless they could cut the two tanks apart and let *Sea Witch* escape with the forward tank which she had just undocked.

The shear control was in the control box halfway back along the tank deck, and at that moment the nearest seaman was two hundred yards from it.

Nicholas could see him staggering wildly back along the twisting, juddering catwalk. Clearly he realized the danger, but his haste was fatal, for as he jumped from the catwalk, the deck opened under him, gaping open like the jaws of a steel monster and the seaman fell through, waist deep, into the opening between two moving plates, then as he squirmed feebly, the next lurch of the ship's hull closed the plates, sliding them across each other like the blades of a pair of scissors.

The man shrieked once and a wave burst over the deck, smothering his mutilated body in cold, green water. When it poured back over the ship's side there was no sign of the man, the deck was washed glisteningly clean.

Nicholas reached the same point in the deck, judged the gaping and closing movement of the steel plate and the next rush of sea coming on board, before he leapt across the deadly gap.

He reached the control box, and slid back the hatch, pressing himself into the tiny steel cubicle as he unlocked the red lid that housed the shear button. He hit the button with the heel of his hand.

The four heavy chains of the tandem tow lay between the electrodes of the shear mechanism. With a gross surge of power from the ship's generators and a flash of blue electric flame, the thick steel links sheared as cleanly as cheese under the cutting wire – and, half a mile away, *Sea Witch* felt the release and pounded ahead under the full thrust of her propellers, taking with her the forward starboard tank still held on main tow.

Nicholas paused in the opening of the control cubicle, hanging on to the sill for support and he stared down at the single remaining tank, still caught inextricably in the tangled moving forest of *Golden Dawn*'s twisting, contorting hull. It was as though an invisible giant had taken the Eiffel Tower at each end and was bending it across his knee.

Suddenly there was a sharp chemical stink in the air, and Nicholas gagged on it. The stink of crude petroleum oil gushing from the ruptured tank.

'Nicholas! Nicholas!' The radio set slung over his shoulder squawked, and he lifted it to his lips without taking his eyes from the *Golden Dawn*'s terrible death throes.

'Go ahead, Jules.'

'Nicholas, I am turning back to pick you up.'

'You can't turn, not with that tow.'

'I will put my bows against the starboard quarterdeck rail, directly under the forward wing of the bridge. Be ready to jump aboard.'

'Jules, you are out of your head!'

'I have been that way for fifty years,' Jules agreed amiably. 'Be ready.'

'Jules, drop your tow first,' Nicholas pleaded. It would be almost impossible to manoeuvre the *Sea Witch* with that monstrous dead weight hanging on her tail. 'Drop tow. We can pick up again later.'

'You teach your grandfather to break eggs,' Jules blithely mangled the old saying, giving it a sinister twist.

'Listen Jules, the No. 4 tank has ruptured. I want you to shut down for fire. Do you understand? Full fire shut down. Once I am aboard, we will put a rocket into her and burn off cargo.'

'I hear you, Nicholas, but I wish I had not.'

Nicholas left the control cubicle, jumped the gaping, chewing gap in the decking and scrambled up the steel ladder on to the central catwalk.

Glancing over his shoulder, he could see the endlessly slippery grey wall of racing cloud and wind; its menace was overpowering, so that for a moment he faltered before forcing himself into running back along the catwalk towards the tanker's stern tower half a mile ahead.

The single remaining seaman was on the catwalk a hundred yards ahead of him, pounding determinedly back towards the pick-up point. He also had heard Jules Levoisin's last transmission.

A quarter of a mile across the roiling, leaping waters, Jules Levoisin was bringing *Sea Witch* around. At another time Nicholas would have been impressed by the consummate skill with which the little Frenchman was handling his ship and its burdensome tow, but now there was time and energy for one thing only.

The air stank. The heavy fumes of crude oil burned Nicholas' pumping lungs, and constricted his throat. He coughed and gasped as he ran, the taste and reek of it coated his tongue and seared his nostrils.

Below the catwalk, the bloated pod-tank was punctured in a hundred places by the steel lances of the disintegrating hull, pinched and torn by moving steel girders, and the dark red oil spurted and dribbled and oozed from it like the poisonous blood from the carcass of a mortally wounded dragon.

Nicholas reached the stern tower, barged in through the storm doors to the lowest deck and reached the pump control room.

Duncan Alexander turned to him, as he entered, his face swollen and bruised where Nicholas had beaten him.

'We are abandoning now,' said Nicholas. '*Sea Witch* is taking us off.'

'I hated you from that very first day,' Duncan was very calm, very controlled, his voice even, deep and cultured. 'Did you know that?'

'There's no time for that now.' Nicholas grabbed his arm, and Duncan followed him readily into the passageway.

'That's what the game is all about, isn't it, Nicholas, power and wealth and women – that's the game we played.'

Nicholas was barely listening. They were out on the quarter-deck, standing at its starboard rail, below the bridge, the pick-up point that Jules had stipulated. *Sea Witch* was turning in, only five hundred yards out, and Nicholas had time now to watch Jules handle his ship.

He was running out the heavy tow-cable on free spool, deliberately letting a long bight of it form between the tug and its enormous whalelike burden, and he was using the slack in the cable to cut in towards *Golden Dawn*'s battered, sagging hulk. He would be alongside for the pick-up in less than a minute.

'That was the game we played, you and I,' Duncan was still talking calmly. 'Power and wealth and women—'

Below them *Golden Dawn* poured her substance into the sea in a slick, stinking flood. The waves, battering against her side, churned the oil to a thick filthy emulsion, and it was spreading away across the surface, bleeding its deadly poison into the Gulf Stream to broadcast it to the entire ocean.

'I won,' Duncan went on reasonably. 'I won it all, every time—' He was groping in his pockets, but Nicholas hardly heard him, was not watching him. '—until now.'

Duncan took one of the self-igniting signal flares from his pocket and held it against his chest with both hands, slipping his index finger through the metal ring of the igniter tab.

'And yet I win this one also, Nicholas,' he said. 'Game, set and match.' And he pulled the tab on the flare with a sharp jerk, and stepped back, holding it aloft.

It spluttered once and then burst into brilliant sparkling red flame, white phosphorescent smoke billowing from it.

Now at last Nicholas turned to face him, and for a moment he was too appalled to move. Then he lunged for Duncan's raised hand that held the burning flare, but Duncan was too fast for him to reach it.

He whirled and threw the flame in a high spluttering arc, out over the leaking, stinking tank-deck.

It struck the steel tank and bounced once, and then rolled down the canted oil-coated plating.

Nicholas stood paralysed at the rail staring down at it. He expected a violent explosion, but nothing happened, the flare rolled innocently across the deck, burning with its pretty red twinkling light.

'It's not burning,' Duncan cried. 'Why doesn't it burn?'

Of course, the gas was only explosive in a confined space, and it needed spark. Out here in the open air the oil had a very high flashpoint, it must be heated to release its volatiles.

The flare caught in the scuppers, spluttered and fizzled in a black pool of crude, and only then the crude caught. It caught with a red, slow, sulky flame that spread quickly but not explosively over the entire deck, and instantly, thick billows of dark smoke rose in a dense choking cloud.

Below where Nicholas stood, the *Sea Witch* thrust her bows in and touched them against the tanker's side. The seaman beside Nicholas jumped and landed neatly on the tug's bows, then raced back along *Sea Witch*'s deck.

'Nicholas,' Jules' voice thundered over the loudhailer. 'Jump, Nicholas.' Nicholas spun back to the rail, and poised himself to jump.

Duncan caught him from behind, whipping one arm around his throat, and pulling him backwards away from the rail.

'No,' Duncan shouted. 'You're staying, my friend. You are not going anywhere. You are staying here with me.'

A greasy wave of black choking smoke engulfed them, and Jules' magnified voice roared in Nicholas' ears.

'Nicholas, I cannot hold her here. Jump, quickly, jump!'

Duncan had him off-balance, dragging him backwards, away from the ship's side, and suddenly Nicholas knew what he must do.

Instead of resisting Duncan's arm, he hurled himself backwards and they crashed together into the superstructure – but Duncan bore the combined weight of both their bodies.

His armlock around the throat relaxed slightly and Nicholas drove his elbow into Duncan's side below the ribs, then wrenched his body forward from the waist, reached between his own braced legs and caught Duncan's ankles. He straightened up again, dragging Duncan off his feet and the same instant dropped backwards with his full weight on the deck.

Duncan gasped and his arm fell away, as Nicholas bounced to his feet again, choking in the greasy billows of smoke, and he reached the ship's side.

Below him, the gap between *Sea Witch*'s bows and the tanker's side was rapidly widening and the thrust of the sea and the drag of the tug tow pulled them apart.

Nicholas vaulted on to the rail, poised for an instant and then jumped. He struck the deck and his teeth cracked together with the impact; his injured leg gave under him and he rolled once, then he was up on his hands and knees.

He looked up at *Golden Dawn*. She was completely enveloped now in the boiling column of black smoke. As the flames heated the leaking crude, so it burned more readily. The bank of smoke was shot through now with the satanic crimson of high, hot flame.

As *Sea Witch* sheered desperately away, the first rush of the storm hit them, and for a moment it smeared the smoke away, exposing the tanker's high quarterdeck.

Duncan Alexander stood at the rail above the roaring holocaust of the tank-deck. He stood with his arms extended, and he was burning, his clothing burned fiercely and his hair was a bright torch of flame. He stood like a ritual cross, outlined in fire, and then slowly he seemed to shrivel and he toppled forward over the rail into the bubbling, spurting, burning cargo of the monstrous ship that he had built – and the black smoke closed over him like a funeral cloak.

As the crude oil escaping from the pierced pod tank fed the flames, so the heat built up swiftly, still sufficient to consume only the volatile aromatic spirits which constituted less than half the bulk of the cargo.

The heavy carbon elements, not yet hot enough to burn, boiled off in that solid black column of smoke, and as the returning winds of the hurricane raced over the *Golden Dawn* once more, so that filthy pall was mixed with air and lifted into the cloud bank of the storm, rising first a thousand, then ten, then twenty thousand feet above the surface of the ocean.

And still *Golden Dawn* burned, and the temperatures of the gas and oil mixture trapped in her hull rocketed steeply. Steel glowed red, then brilliant white, ran like molten wax, and then like water – and suddenly the flashpoint of heavy carbon smoke in a mixture of air and water vapour was reached in the womb of this mighty furnace.

*Golden Dawn* and her entire cargo turned into a fireball.

The steel and glass and metal of her hull disappeared in an instantaneous explosive combustion that released temperatures like those upon the surface of the sun. Her cargo, a quarter of a million tons of it, burned in an instant, releasing a white blooming rose of pure heat so fierce that it shot up into the upper stratosphere and consumed the billowing pall of its own hydrocarbon gas and smoke.

The very air burst into flame, the surface of the sea flamed in that white fireball of heat and even the clouds of smoke burned as the oxygen and hydrocarbon they contained exploded.

Once an entire city had been subjected to this phenomena of fireball, when stone and earth and air had exploded, and five thousand German citizens of the city of Cologne had been vaporized, and that vapour burned in the heat of its own release.

But this fireball was spawned by a quarter of a million tons of volatile liquids.

'Can't you get us further away?' Nicholas shouted above the thunder of the hurricane. His mouth was only inches from Jules Levoisin's ear.

They were standing side by side, hanging from the overhead railing that gave purchase on this wildly pitching deck.

'If I open the taps I will part the tow wire,' Jules shouted back.

*Sea Witch* was alternately standing on her nose and then her tail. There was no forward view from the bridge, only green washes of sea water and banks of spray.

The full force of the hurricane was on them once more, and a glance at the radarscope showed the glowing image of *Golden Dawn*'s crippled and bleeding hull only half a mile astern.

Suddenly the glass of the windows was obscured by an impenetrable blackness, and the light in *Sea Witch*'s navigation bridge was reduced to only the glow of her fire-lights and the electronic instruments of her control console.

Jules Levoisin turned his face to Nicholas, his plump features haunted by green shadows in the gloom.

'Smoke bank,' Nicholas shouted an explanation. There was no reek of the filthy hydrocarbon in the bridge, for *Sea Witch* was shut down for fire drill, all her ports and ventilators sealed, her internal air-conditioning on a closed circuit, the air being scrubbed and recharged with oxygen by the big Carrier unit above the main engine room. 'We are directly down wind of the *Golden Dawn*.'

A fiercer rush of the hurricane winds laid *Sea Witch* over on her side, the lee rail deep under the racing green sea, and held her there, unable to rise against the careless might of the storm for many minutes. Her crew hung desperately from any hand hold, the irksome burden of her tow helping to drag her down further, the propellers found no grip in the air, and her engines screamed in anguish.

But *Sea Witch* had been built to live in any sea, and the moment the wind hesitated, she fought off the water that had come aboard and began to swing back.

'Where is *Warlock*?' Jules bellowed anxiously. The danger of collision preyed upon his constantly, two ships and their elephantine tows manoeuvring closely in confined hurricane waters was nightmare on top of nightmare.

'Ten miles east of us.' Nicholas picked the other tug's image out of the trash on the radarscope. 'They had a start, ahead of the wind—'

He would have gone on, but the boiling bank of hydrocarbon smoke that surrounded *Sea Witch* turned to fierce white light, a light that blinded every man on the bridge as though a photograph flashlight had been fired in his face.

'Fireball!' Nicholas shouted, and, completely blinded, reached for the remote controls of the water cannons seventy feet above the bridge on *Sea Witch*'s fire-control tower.

Minutes before, he had aligned the four water cannons, training them down at their maximum angle of depression, so now as he locked down the multiple triggers, *Sea Witch* deluged herself in a pounding cascade of sea water.

*Sea Witch* was caught in a furnace of burning air, and despite the torrents of water she spewed over herself, her paintwork was burned away in instantaneous combustion so fierce that it consumed its own smoke, and almost instantly the bare scorched metal of her exposed upperworks began to glow with heat.

The heat was so savage that it struck through the insulated hull, through the double glazing of the two-inch armoured glass of her bridge windows, scorching and frizzling away Nicholas' eyelashes and blistering his lips as he lifted his face to it.

The glass of the bridge windows wavered and swam as they began to melt – and then abruptly there was no more oxygen. The fireball had extinguished itself, consumed everything in its twenty seconds of life, everything from sea level to thirty thousand feet above it, a brief and devastating orgasm of destruction.

It left a vacuum, a weak spot in the earth's thin skin of air, it formed another low pressure system smaller, but much more intense, and more hungry to be filled than the eye of hurricane Lorna itself.

It literally tore the guts out of that great revolving storm, setting up counter winds and a vortex within the established system that ripped it apart.

New gales blew from every point about the fireball's vacuum, swiftly beginning their own dervish spirals and twenty miles short of the mainland. of Florida, hurricane Lorna checked her mindless, blundering charge, fell in upon herself and disintegrated into fifty different willy-nilly squalls and whirlpools of air that collided and split again, slowly degenerating into nothingness.


On a morning in April in Galveston roads, the salvage tug *Sea Witch* dropped off tow to four smaller harbour tugs who would take the *Golden Dawn* No. 3 pod tank up the narrows to the Orient Amex discharge installation below Houston.

Her sister ship *Warlock*, Captain David Allen commanding, had dropped off his tandem tow of No. 1 and No. 2 pod tanks to the same tugs forty-eight hours previously.

Between the two ships, they had made good salvage under Lloyd's Open

Form of three-quarters of a million tons of crude petroleum valued at $85.50 U.S. a ton. To the prize would be added the value of the three tanks themselves – not less than sixty-five million dollars all told, Nicholas calculated, and he owned both ships and the full share of the salvage award. He had not sold to the Sheikhs yet, though for every day of the tow from the Florida Straits to Texas, there had been frantic telex messages from James Teacher in London. The Sheikhs were desperate to sign now, but Nicholas would let them wait a little longer.

Nicholas stood on the open wing of *Sea Witch*'s bridge and watched the four smaller harbour tugs bustling importantly about their ungainly charge.

He lifted the cheroot to his lips carefully, for they were still blistered from the heat of the fireball – and he pondered the question of how much he had achieved, apart from spectacular riches.

He had reduced the spill from a million to a quarter of a million tons of cad-rich crude, and he had burned it in a fireball. Nevertheless, there had been losses, toxins had been lifted high above the fireball. They had spread and settled across Florida as far as Tampa and Tallahassee, poisoning the pastures and killing thousands of head of domestic stock. But the American authorities had been quick to extend the hurricane emergency procedures. There had been no loss of human life. He had achieved that much.

Now he had delivered the salvaged pod tanks to Orient Amex. The new cracking process would benefit all mankind, and nothing that Nicholas could do would prevent men carrying the cad-rich crudes of El Barras across the oceans. But would they do so in the same blindly irresponsible manner that Duncan Alexander had attempted?

He knew then with utter certainty that it was his appointed life's work, from now on, to try and ensure that they did not. He knew how he was to embark upon that work. He had the wealth that was necessary, and Tom Parker had given him the other instruments to do the job.

He knew, with equal certainty, who would be his companion in that life's work – and standing on the fire-scorched deck of the gallant little vessel he had a vivid image of a golden girl who walked forever beside him in sunlight and in laughter.

'Samantha.'

He said her name aloud just once, and suddenly he was very eager to begin.

# The
# Sound
# of
# Thunder

# The Sound of Thunder

This book is for my children–
SHAUN and LAWRENCE and
CHRISTIAN LAURIE

# Chapter One

Four years of travel in the roadless wilderness had battered the wagons. Many of the wheel-spokes and *disselbooms* had been replaced with raw native timber; the canopies were patched until little of the original canvas was visible; the teams were reduced from eighteen to ten oxen each, for there had been predators and sickness to weed them out. But this exhausted little caravan carried the teeth of five hundred elephant; ten tons of ivory; the harvest of Sean Courtney's rifle; ivory that he would convert into nearly fifteen thousand gold sovereigns once he reached Pretoria.

Once more Sean was a rich man. His clothing was stained and baggy, crudely mended; his boots were worn almost through the uppers and clumsily resoled with raw buffalo hide; a great untrimmed beard covered half his chest and a mane of black hair curled down his neck to where it had been hacked away with blunt scissors above the collar of his coat. But despite his appearance he was rich in ivory, also in gold held for him in the vaults of the Volkskaas Bank in Pretoria.

On a rise of ground beside the road he sat his horse and watched the leisurely plodding approach of his wagons. It is time now for the farm, he thought with satisfaction. Thirty-seven years old, no longer a young man, and it was time to buy the farm. He knew the one he wanted and he knew exactly where he would build the homestead – site it close to the lip of the escarpment so that in the evenings he could sit on the wide stoep and look out across the plain to the Tugela River in the blue distance.

'Tomorrow early we will reach Pretoria.' The voice beside him interrupted his dreaming, and Sean moved in the saddle and looked down at the Zulu who squatted beside his horse.

'It has been a good hunt, Mbejane.'

'Nkosi, we have killed many elephant.' Mbejane nodded and Sean noticed for the first time the strands of silver in the woolly cap of his hair. No longer a young man either.

'And made many marches,' Sean went on and Mbejane inclined his head again in grave agreement.

'A man grows weary of the trek,' Sean mused aloud. 'There is a time when he longs to sleep two nights at the same place.'

'And to hear the singing of his wives as they work the fields.' Mbejane carried it further. 'And to watch his cattle come into the kraal at dusk with his sons driving them.'

'That time has come for both of us, my friend. We are going home to Ladyburg.'

The spears rattled against his raw-hide shield as Mbejane stood up, muscles moved beneath the black velvet of his skin and he lifted his head to Sean and smiled. It was a thing of white teeth and radiance, that smile. Sean had to return it and they grinned at each other like two small boys in a successful bit of mischief.

'If we push the oxen hard this last day we can reach Pretoria tonight, Nkosi.'

'Let us make the attempt.' Sean encouraged him and walked his horse down the slope to intercept the caravan.

As it toiled slowly towards them through the flat white glare of the African morning a commotion started at its rear and spread quickly along the line, the dogs clamoured and the servants shouted encouragement to the rider who raced past them towards the head of the caravan. He lay forward in the saddle, driving the pony with elbows and heels, hat hanging from the leather thong about his neck and black hair ruffled with the speed of his run.

'That cub roars louder than the lion that sired him,' grunted Mbejane, but there was a fondness in his expression as he watched the rider reach the leading wagon and drag the pony from full run down on to his haunches.

'Also he spoils the mouth of every horse he rides.' Sean's voice was as harsh as Mbejane's, but there was the same fond expression in his eyes as he watched his son cut loose the brown body of a springbok from the pommel of his saddle and let it drop into the road beside the wagon. Two of the wagon drivers hurried to retrieve it, and Dirk Courtney kicked his pony and galloped down to where Sean and Mbejane waited beside the road.

'Only one?' Sean asked as Dirk checked the pony and circled back to fall in beside him.

'Oh, no. I got three – three with three shots. The gunboys are bringing the others.' Offhanded, taking as natural that at nine years of age he should be providing meat for the whole company, Dirk slouched down comfortably in the saddle, holding the reins in one hand and the other resting negligently on his hip in faithful imitation of his father.

Scowling a little to cover the strength of his pride and his love, Sean examined him surreptitiously. The beauty of this boy's face was almost indecent, the innocence of the eyes and faultless skin should have belonged to a girl. The sun struck ruby sparks from the mass of dark curls, his eyes spaced wide apart were framed with long black lashes and overscored by the delicate lines of the brow. His eyes were emerald and his skin was gold and there were rubies in his hair – a face fashioned by a jewelsmith. Then Sean looked at the mouth and experienced a twinge of uneasiness. The mouth was too big, the lips too wide and soft. The shape of it was wrong – as though it were about to sulk or whine.

'We are making a full day's trek today, Dirk. No *outspan* until we reach Pretoria. Ride back and tell the drivers.'

'Send Mbejane. He's doing nothing.'

'I told *you* to go.'

'Hell, Dad! I've done enough today.'

'Go, damn you!' Sean roared with unnecessary violence.

'I've only just come back, it's not fair that—' Dirk started, but Sean did not let him finish.

'Every time I ask you to do something I get a mouthful of argument. Now do what I tell you.' They held each other's eyes; Sean glaring and Dirk resentful, sulky. Sean recognized that expression with dismay. This was going to be another of those tests of will that were becoming more frequent between them. Would this end as most of the others had? Must he admit defeat and use the *sjambok* again? When was the last time – two weeks ago – when Sean had reprimanded Dirk on some trivial point concerning the care of his pony. Dirk had stood sullenly until Sean was finished, and then he had walked away among the wagons. Dropping the subject from his mind, Sean was chatting with Mbejane when suddenly there was a squeal of pain from the laager and Sean ran towards it.

In the centre of the ring of wagons stood Dirk. His face still darkly flushed with temper, and at his feet the tiny body of one of the unweaned puppies flopped and whimpered with its ribs stoved in from Dirk's kick.

In anger Sean had beaten Dirk, but even in his anger he had used a length of rope and not the viciously tapered *sjambok* of hippo hide. Then he had ordered Dirk to his living-wagon.

At noon he had sent for him and demanded an apology – and Dirk, uncrying, with lips and jaw set grimly, had refused it.

Sean beat him again, with the rope, but this time coldly – not for the sake of retribution. Dirk did not break.

Finally, in desperation Sean took the *sjambok* to him. For ten hissing strokes, each of which ended with a wicked snap across his buttocks, Dirk lay silently under the whip. His body convulsed slightly at each lash but he would not speak, and Sean beat him with a sickness in his own stomach and the sweat of shame and guilt running into his eyes, swinging the *sjambok* mechanically with his fingers clawed around the butt of it, and his mouth full of the slimy saliva of self-hatred.

When at last Dirk screamed, Sean dropped the *sjambok*, reeled back against the side of the wagon and leaned there gasping – fighting down the nausea which flooded acid-tasting up his throat.

Dirk screamed again and again, and Sean caught him up and held him to his chest.

'I'm sorry, Pa! I'm sorry. I'll never do it again, I promise you. I love you, I love you best of all – and I'll never do it again,' screamed Dirk, and they clung to each other.

For days thereafter not one of the servants had smiled at Sean nor spoken to him other than to acknowledge an order. For there was not one of them, including Mbejane, who would not steal and cheat and lie to ensure that Dirk Courtney had whatever he desired at the exact moment he desired it. They could hate anyone, including Sean, who denied it to him.

That was two weeks ago. And now, thought Sean watching that ugly mouth, do we do it all again?

Then suddenly Dirk smiled. It was one of those changes of mood that left Sean slightly bewildered, for when Dirk smiled his mouth came right. It was irresistible.

'I'll go, Dad.' Cheerfully, as though he was volunteering, he prodded the pony and trotted back towards the wagons.

'Cheeky little bugger!' gruffed Sean for Mbejane's benefit, but silently he queried his share of the blame. He had raised the boy with a wagon as his home and the veld as his schoolroom, grown men his companions and authority over them as his undisputed right of birth.

Since his mother had died five years before he had not known the gentling influence of a woman. No wonder he was a wild one.

Sean shied away from the memory of Dirk's mother. There was guilt there also, guilt that had taken him many years to reconcile. She was dead now. There was no profit in torturing himself. He pushed away the gloom that was swamping the happiness of a few minutes before, slapped the loose end of the reins against the horse's neck and urged it out on to the road – south towards the low line of hills upon the horizon, south towards Pretoria.

He's a wild one. But once we reach Ladyburg he'll be all right, Sean assured himself. They'll knock the nonsense out of him at school, and I'll knock manners into him at home. No, he'll be all right.

That evening, the third of December, 1899, Sean led his wagons down the hills and laagered them beside the Apies River. After they had eaten, Sean sent Dirk to his cot in the living wagon. Then he climbed alone to the crest of the hills and looked back across the land to the north. It was silver-grey in the moonlight, stretching away silent and immeasurable. That was the old life and abruptly he turned his back upon it and walked down towards the lights of the city which beckoned to him from the valley below.

# Chapter Two

There had been a little unpleasantness when he had ordered Dirk to stay with the wagons; in consequence Sean was in an evil mood as he crossed the bridge on the Apies and rode into the city the following morning. Beside him Mbejane ran to keep pace with his horse.

Deep in his own thoughts Sean turned into Church Street before he noticed the unusual activity about him. A column of horsemen forced him to rein his horse to the side of the road. As they passed Sean examined them with interest.

Burghers in a motley of homespun and store clothes, riding in a formation which might imaginatively have been called a column of fours. But what excited Sean's curiosity was their numbers – By God! there must be two thousand of them at least, from lads to greybeards each of them was festooned with bandoliers of ammunition and beside each left knee the butt of a bolt-action Mauser rifle stuck up from its scabbard. Blanket-rolls tied to the saddles, canteens and cooking-pots clattering, they filed past. There was no doubting it. This was a war commando.

From the sidewalk women and a few men called comment at them.

'*Geluk boor!* Shoot straight.'

'*Spoedige terugkoms.*'

And the commandos laughed and shouted back. Sean stooped to a pretty girl who stood beside his horse. She was waving a red scarf and suddenly Sean saw that though she smiled her eyelashes were loaded with tears like dew on a blade of grass.

'Where are they going?' Sean raised his voice above the uproar.

She lifted her head and the movement loosed a tear; it dropped down her cheek, slid from her chin and left a tiny damp spot on her blouse.

'To the train, of course.'

'The train? Which train?'

'Look, here come the guns.'

In consternation Sean looked up as the guns rumbled past, two of them. Uniformed gunners in blue, frogged with gold, sitting stiffly to attention on the carriages, the horses leaning forward against the immense weight of the guns. Tall wheels shod with steel, bronze glittering on the breeches in contrast to the sombre grey of the barrels.

'My God!' breathed Sean. Then turning back to the girl he grasped her shoulder and shook it in his agitation. 'Where are they going? Tell me quickly – where?'

'*Menheer!*' She bridled at his touch and wriggled away from it.

'Please. I'm sorry – you must tell me.' Sean called after her as she disappeared into the crowd.

A minute longer Sean sat stupefied, then his brain began to work again. It was war, then. But where and against whom?

Surely no tribal rising would call out this array of strength. Those guns were the most modern weapons Sean could conceive.

No, this was a white man's war.

Against the Orange Republic? Impossible, they were brothers.

Against the British, then? The idea appalled him. And yet – and yet five years ago there had been rumours. It had happened before. He remembered 1895, and the Jameson Raid. Anything could have happened during the years he had been cut off from civilization – and now he had stumbled innocently into the midst of it.

Quickly he considered his own position. He was British. Born in Natal under the Union Jack. He looked like a burgher, spoke like one, rode like one, he was born in Africa and had never left it – but technically he was just as much an Englishman as if he had been born within sound of Bow bells.

Just supposing it was war between the Republic and Britain, and just supposing the Boers caught him – what would they do with him?

Confiscate his wagons and his ivory certainly, throw him into prison perhaps, shoot him as a spy possibly!

'I've got to get to hell out of here,' he mumbled, and then to Mbejane, 'Come on. Back to the wagons, quickly.' Before they reached the bridge he changed his mind. He had to learn with certainty what was happening. There was one person he could go to, and he must take the risk.

'Mbejane, go back to the camp. Find Nkosizana Dirk and keep him there – even if you have to tie him. Speak to no man and, as you value your life, let Dirk speak with no man. It is understood?'

'It is understood, Nkosi.'

And Sean, to all appearances another burgher among thousands of burghers, worked his way slowly through the crowds and the press of wagons towards a general dealer's store at the top end of the town near the railway station.

Since Sean had last seen it the sign above the entrance had been freshly painted in red and gold. 'I. Goldberg. Importer & Exporter, Dealing in Mining Machinery, Merchant & Wholesaler, Purchasing Agent: gold, precious stones, hides and skins, ivory and natural produce.'

Despite this war, or because of it, Mr Goldberg's emporium was doing good business. It was crowded and Sean drifted unnoticed among the customers, searching quietly for the proprietor.

He found him selling a bag of coffee beans to a gentleman who was plainly sceptical of its quality. The discussion of the merits of Mr Goldberg's coffee beans as opposed to those of his competitor across the street was becoming involved and technical.

Sean leaned against a shelf full of merchandise, packed his pipe, lit it and while he waited he watched Mr Goldberg in action. The man should have been a barrister, his argument was strong enough to convince first Sean and finally the customer. The latter paid, slung the bag over his shoulder and grumbled his way out of the shop, leaving Mr Goldberg glowing pink and perspiring in the flush of achievement.

'You haven't lost any weight, Izzy,' Sean greeted him.

Goldberg peered at him uncertainly over his gold-framed spectacles, beginning to smile until suddenly he recognized Sean. He blinked with shock, jerked his head in a gesture of invitation so his jowls wobbled, and disappeared into the back office. Sean followed him.

'Are you mad, Mr Courtney?' Goldberg was waiting for him, quivering with agitation. 'If they catch you . . .'

'Listen, Izzy. I arrived last night. I haven't spoken to a white man in four years. What the hell is going on here?'

'You haven't heard?'

'No, damn it, I haven't.'

'It's war, Mr Courtney.'

'I can see that. But where? Against whom?'

'On all the borders – Natal, the Cape.'

'Against?'

'The British Empire.' Goldberg shook his head as though he did not believe his own statement. 'We've taken on the whole British Empire.'

'We?' Sean asked sharply.

'The Transvaal Republic and the Orange Free State. Already we have won great victories – Ladysmith is besieged, Kimberley, Mafeking—'

'You, personally?'

'I was born here in Pretoria. I am a burgher.'

'Are you going to turn me in?'

'No, of course not. You've been a good customer of mine for years.'

'Thanks, Izzy. Look, I've got to get out of here as fast as I can.'

'It would be wise.'

'What about my money at the Volkskaas – can I get it out?'

Izzy shook his head sadly. 'They've frozen all enemy accounts.'

'Damn it, God damn it!' Sean swore bitterly, and then, 'Izzy, I've got twenty wagons and ten tons of ivory parked out there on the edge of town – are you interested?'

'How much?'

'Ten thousand for the lot; oxen, wagons, ivory – the lot.'

'It would not be patriotic, Mr Courtney,' Goldberg decided reluctantly. 'Trading with the enemy – besides I have only your word that it's ten tons.'

'Hell, Izzy, I'm not the British Army – that lot is worth twenty thousand quid.'

'You want me to buy sight unseen – no questions asked? All right. I'll give you four thousand – gold.'

'Seven.'

'Four and a half,' countered Izzy.

'You bastard.'

'Four and a half.'

'No, damn you. Five!' growled Sean.

'Five?'

'Five!'

'All right, five.'

'Thanks, Izzy.'

'Pleasure, Mr Courtney.'

Sean described the location of his laager hurriedly.

'You can send someone out to pick it up. I am going to run for the Natal border as soon as it's dark.'

'Keep off the roads and well clear of the railway. Joubert has thirty thousand men in Northern Natal, massed around Ladysmith and along the Tugela heights.' Goldberg went to the safe and fetched five small canvas bags from it. 'Do you want to check?'

'I'll trust you as you trusted me. Good-bye, Izzy.' Sean dropped the heavy bags down the front of his shirt and settle them under his belt.

'Good luck, Mr Courtney.'


# Chapter Three


There were two hours of daylight left when Sean finished paying his servants. He pushed the tiny pile of sovereigns across the tailboard of the wagon towards the last man and went with him through the complicated ritual of farewell, the hand-clapping and clasping, the repetition of the formal phrases – then he stood up from his chair and looked around the circle. They squatted patiently, watching him with wooden black faces – but reflected back from them he could sense his own sorrow at this parting. Men with whom he had lived and worked and shared a hundred hardships. It was not easy to leave them now.

'It is finished,' he said.

'*Yebho*, it is finished.' They agreed in chorus and no one moved.

'Go, damn you.'

Slowly one of them stood and gathered the bundle of his possessions, a *kaross* (or skin blanket), two spears, a cast-off shirt that Sean had given him. He balanced the bundle on his head and looked at Sean.

'Nkosi!' he said and lifted a clenched fist in salute.

'Nonga,' Sean replied. The man turned away and trudged out of the laager.

'Nkosi!'

'Hlubi.'

'Nkosi!'

'Zama.'

A roll call of loyalty – Sean spoke their names for the last time, and singly they left the laager. Sean stood and watched them walk away in the dusk. Not one of them looked back and no two men walked together. It was finished.

Wearily Sean turned back to the laager. The horses were ready. Three with saddles, two carrying packs.

'We will eat first, Mbejane.'

'It is ready, Nkosi. Hlubi cooked before he went.'

'Come on, Dirk. Dinner.'

Dirk was the only one who spoke during the meal. He chattered gaily, wrought up with excitement by this new adventure, while Sean and Mbejane shovelled fat Hlubi's stew and hardly tasted it.

Out in the gathering darkness a jackal yelped, a lonely sound on the evening wind, fitting the mood of a man who had lost friends and fortune.

'It is time.' Sean shrugged into his sheepskin jacket and buttoned it as he stood to kick out the fire, but suddenly he froze and stood with his head cocked as he listened. There was a new sound on the wind.

'Horses!' Mbejane confirmed it.

'Quickly, Mbejane, my rifle.' The Zulu leapt up, ran to the horses and slipped Sean's rifle from its scabbard.

'Get out of the light and keep your mouth shut,' Sean ordered as he hustled Dirk into the shadows between the wagons. He grabbed the rifle from Mbejane and levered a cartridge into the breech and the three of them crouched and waited.

The click and roll of pebbles under hooves, the soft sound of a branch brushed aside.

'One only,' whispered Mbejane. A pack-horse whickered softly and was answered immediately from the darkness. Then silence, a long silence broken at last by the jingle of a bridle as the rider dismounted.

Sean saw him then, a slim figure emerging slowly out of the night and he swung the rifle to cover his approach. There was something unusual in the way the stranger moved, gracefully but with a sway from the hips, long-legged like a colt and Sean knew that he was young, very young to judge by his height.

With relief Sean straightened up from his crouch and examined him as he stopped uncertainly beside the fire and peered into the shadows. The lad wore a peaked cloth cap pulled down over his ears and his jacket was an expensive, honey-coloured chamois. His riding breeches were beautifully tailored and hugged his buttocks snugly. Sean decided that his backside was too big and out of proportion to the small feet clad in polished English hunting boots. A regular dandy, and the scorn was in Sean's tone as he called out.

'Stay where you are, friend, and state your business!'

The effect of Sean's challenge was unexpected. The lad jumped, the soles of his glossy boots cleared the ground by at least six inches, and when he landed again he was facing Sean.

'Talk up. I haven't got all night.'

The lad opened his mouth, closed it again, licked his lips and spoke.

'I was told you were going to Natal.' The voice was low and husky.

'Who told you that?' demanded Sean.

'My uncle.'

'Who is your uncle?'

'Isaac Goldberg.'

Sean digested this intelligence and while he did so he examined the face before him. Cleanshaven, pale, big dark eyes and a laughing kind of mouth that was now pursed with fright.

'And if I am?' Sean demanded.

'I want to go with you.'

'Forget it. Get back on your horse and go home.'

'I'll pay you – I'll pay you well.'

Was it the voice or the posture of the lad, Sean pondered, there was something very odd about him. He stood with a flat leather pouch held in both hands across the front of his hips – in an attitude of defence, as though he were protecting – protecting what? And suddenly Sean knew what it was.

'Take off your cap,' he ordered.

'No.'

'Take it off.'

A second longer the lad hesitated, then in a gesture that was almost defiance he jerked off the cap and two thick black braids of hair, shiny in the firelight, dropped and hung down almost to his waist and transformed him instantly from gawky masculinity into stunning womanhood.

Although he had guessed it, Sean was unprepared for the shock of this revelation. It was not so much her beauty, but her attire that caused the shock. Never in his life had Sean seen a woman in breeches, and now he gasped. Breeches, by God, she might as well be naked from the waist down – even that would be less indecent.

'Two hundred pounds—' She was coming towards him now, offering the pouch. At each step the cloth of the breeches tightened across her thighs and Sean dragged his eyes guiltily back to her face.

'Keep your money, lady.' Her eyes were grey, smoky grey.

'Two hundred on account, and as much again when we reach Natal.'

'I'm not interested.' But he was, those soft lips started to quiver.

'How much then? Name your price.'

'Look, lady. I'm not heading a procession. There are three of us already – one a child. There is hard riding ahead, plenty of it, and an army of Boers in between. Our chances are slim enough as it is. Another member to the party, and a woman at that, will make them prohibitive. I don't want your money, all I want is to get my son to safety. Go home and sit this war out – it won't last long.'

'I'm going to Natal.'

'Good. You go then – but not with us.' Sean could not trust himself longer to resist the appeal of those grey eyes and he turned to Mbejane. 'Horses,' he snapped and walked away from her. She stood watching him quietly as they mounted up, making no protest. She semed very small and alone as Sean looked down at her from the saddle.

'I'm sorry,' he growled. 'Go home now like a good girl,' and quickly he wheeled away and trotted out into the night.

All night they rode, east through the open moonlit land. Once they passed a darkened homestead and a dog barked, but they sheered away and then turned east again and held the great crucifix of the Southern Cross at their right-hand. When Dirk fell asleep in the saddle and slipped sideways, Sean caught him before he hit the ground, pulled him across into his lap and held him there for the rest of the night.

Before dawn they found a clump of bush on the bank of a stream, hobbled the horses and made camp. Mbejane had the billy-can boiling over a small well-screened fire and Sean had rolled Dirk unconscious into his blankets when the girl rode into camp and jumped down from her horse.

'I nearly lost you twice.' She laughed and pulled off the cap. 'Gave me a horrible fright.' She shook down the shiny braids. 'Coffee! Oh good, I'm famished.'

Menacingly Sean climbed to his feet and with clenched fists he glared at her, but undismayed she hobbled her horse and turned it loose before acknowledging him again.

'Don't stand on ceremony, please be seated.' And she grinned at him with such devilment in her grey eyes, aping so faithfully his stance with hands on those indecent hips, that Sean suddenly found himself smiling. He tried to stop it for he knew it was an admission of surrender, but his effort was so unsuccessful that she burst into delighted laughter.

'How's your cooking?' he demanded.

'So, so.'

'You'd better brush up on it because from now on you're working your passage.'

Later, when he had sampled it for the first time, he admitted grudgingly:

'Not bad – in the circumstances,' and wiped the plate with a crust of bread.

'You are too kind, sir.' She thanked him and lugged her blanket-roll into the shade, spread it, pulled off her boots, wriggled her toes and lay back with a sigh.

Sean positioned his own bedroll with care so that, when he opened his eyes, without turning his head he could watch her from under the brim of the hat that covered his face.

He woke at midday and saw that she slept with one cheek in her open hand, the lashes of her eyes meshed together and a few loose strands of dark hair across a face that was damp and flushed in the drowsy heat. He watched her for a long time before silently rising and crossing to his saddle-bags. When he went down to the stream he took with him his flat canvas toilet-bag, the remaining pair of breeches that were neither patched nor too badly stained and a clean silk shirt.

Sitting on a rock beside the water, naked and freshly scrubbed, he regarded his face in the polished steel mirror.

'A big job.' He sighed and started snipping at the great bush of beard which had not felt the scissors in three years.

At dusk, self-conscious as a girl in her first party dress, Sean walked back into the camp. They were all awake. Dirk and the girl sat together on her blanket in such earnest conversation that neither of them noticed his arrival. Mbejane was busy at the fire; he rocked back on his heels and examined Sean without change of expression.

'We'd better eat and get going.'

Dirk and the girl looked up. Her eyes narrowed and then widened thoughtfully.

Dirk gaped at him, and then, 'Your beard's all funny—' he announced, and the girl tried desperately to quell her laughter.

'Get your blankets rolled up, boy.'

Sean tried to break Dirk's grip on the subject, but like a bulldog Dirk held on relentlessly.

'—and why are you wearing your best clothes, Dad?'

# Chapter Four

They rode three abreast in the darkness, Dirk between them and Mbejane trailing behind with the pack-horses. The land rose and fell beneath them like the swells of an endless sea and the way in which the grass moved with the night wind heightened the illusion of waves. Islands in the sea were the dark bulks of the kopjes they passed, and the yelp of a jackal was the voice of a seabird.

'Aren't we holding too far east?' The girl broke the silence and her voice blended with the soft sound of the wind.

'Intentionally,' Sean answered. 'I want to cross the tail of the Drakensberg well clear of the Boer concentrations around Ladysmith and the line of rail,' and he looked over Dirk's head at her. She rode with her face lifted to the sky.

'You know the stars?' he asked.

'A little.'

'So do I. I know them all.' Dirk accepted the challenge and swivelled towards the south. 'That's the Cross with the pointers, and that's Orion with his sword on his belt, and that's the Milky Way.'

'Tell me some others,' the girl invited.

'The others are just ordinary ones – they don't count. They haven't even got names.'

'Oh, but they have and most of them have got a story.'

There was a pause. Dirk was now in an invidious position; either he had to admit ignorance, and Dirk's pride was too large to swallow with ease, or else he would forgo what promised to be a choice series of stories. Large as was his pride, his appetite for stories was even larger.

'Tell me some,' he conceded.

'You see that little clump there underneath the big bright one? They are called the Seven Sisters. Well, once upon a time—'

Within minutes Dirk was completely absorbed. These were even better than Mbejane's stories – probably because they were new, while Dirk could recite from memory Mbejane's entire repertoire. He fell upon any weakness in the plot like a prosecuting attorney.

'But why didn't they just shoot the old witch?'

'They didn't have guns in those days.'

'They coulda used a bow and arrow.'

'You can't kill a witch with a bow and arrow. The arrow just goes – psst – straight through her without hurting her.'

'Hangs teeth!' That was really impressive, but before accepting it Dirk found it necessary to corroborate with expert opinion. He checked with Mbejane, translating the problem to the Zulu. When Mbejane supported the girl Dirk was convinced, for Mbejane was a celebrated authority on the supernatural.

That night Dirk did not fall asleep in the saddle and when they camped before dawn the girl's voice was hoarse with overwork, but her conquest of Dirk was complete and that of Sean was well advanced.

All night while he listened to her voice and the husky bursts of laughter that punctuated it Sean had felt the seed that was planted at their first meeting sinking its roots down into his lower belly and loins, spreading its tendrils up through his chest. He wanted this woman so violently that in her presence his wits failed him. Many times during the night he had attempted to join the discussions, but each time Dirk had brushed his efforts aside with contempt and turned avidly back to the girl. By morning he had made the disturbing discovery that he was jealous of his own son – jealous of the attention Dirk was getting, and for which he hungered so strongly.

While they drank coffee after the morning meal lying on their blankets beneath a grove of syringa trees, Sean remarked:

'You haven't told us your name yet.' And of course it was Dirk that answered.

'She told me. Your name's Ruth – isn't it?'

'That's right, Dirk.'

With an effort Sean clamped down on the senseless anger that boiled up through him, but when he spoke his voice carried traces of it.

'We've heard enough from you for one night, my boy. Now get your head down, close your eyes and your mouth and keep them that way.'

'I'm not sleepy, Dad.'

'Do what I tell you.' Sean jumped up and strode out of the camp. He climbed the small kopje above them. By now it was full daylight and he searched the veld to the horizon on all sides. There was no trace of habitation or human. He climbed down again and fussed with the hobbles of the horses before returning to the grove of syringas.

Despite his protestations Dirk was curled like a sleeping puppy and, near the fire from a large bundle of blankets issued the unmistakable snoring of Mbejane. Ruth lay a little apart from them, a blanket thrown over her legs, her eyes closed and the front of her shirt rising and falling in a manner that gave Sean two good reasons for not sleeping. He lay propped on one elbow and fed his eyes and his imagination on her.

These four years past he had not seen a white woman, four years without the sound of a woman's voice or the comfort of her body. In the beginning it had worried him – the restlessness, the undirected fits of depression, and sudden bursts of temper. But gradually in the long days of hunting and riding, in the endless struggle with drought and storm, with beasts and the elements, he had brought his body under control. Women had faded into unreality, vague phantoms that plagued him only in the night so he twisted and sweated and cried out in his sleep until nature gave him release and the phantoms dispersed for a while to gather strength for their next visitation.

But this was no phantom that lay beside him now. By stretching out a hand he could stroke the faint down on her cheek and feel the blood-warm silk of her skin.

She opened her eyes, they were milky grey with sleep, slowly focusing until they levelled with his and returned his scrutiny.

Because of what she read there, she lifted her left hand from the blanket and held it out towards him. Her riding gloves were off. For the first time he noticed the slender gold ring that encircled her third finger.

'I see,' he muttered dully, and then in protest: 'But you are too young – you're too young to be married.'

'I'm twenty-two years old,' she told him softly.

'Your husband – where is he?' Perhaps the bastard was dead, his one last hope.

'I am going to him now. When war seemed inevitable he went to Natal, to Durban, to find a job and a home for us there. I was to follow him – but the war came earlier than we expected. I was stranded.'

'I see.' I am taking you to another man, he thought with bitterness, and put it in different words. 'So he is sitting in Durban waiting for you to make your own way through the lines.'

'He is with the army of Natal. A week ago he got a message through to me. He wanted me to stay on in Johannesburg and wait until the British capture the city. He says that with so great a force they will be in Johannesburg within three months.'

'Why didn't you wait, then?'

She shrugged. 'Patience is not one of my virtues,' and then the devilment was in her eyes again. 'Besides, I thought it would be fun to run away – it was so terribly dull in Johannesburg.'

'Do you love him?' he demanded suddenly. The question startled her and the smile died on her lips.

'He's my husband.'

'That doesn't answer my question.'

'It was a question you had no right to ask.' She was angry now.

'You have to tell me.'

'Do you love your wife?' she snapped at him.

'I did. She's been dead five years.' And her anger flickered out as swiftly as it had blazed.

'Oh, I'm sorry. I didn't know.'

'Forget it. Forget I ever asked.'

'Yes, that's best. We are getting into an awful tangle.' Her hand with the ring upon it was still held out towards him, lying between them on the soft carpet of fallen leaves. He reached out and lifted it. It was a small hand.

'Mr Courtney – Sean, it's best if – we mustn't – I think we'd better sleep now.' And she withdrew the hand and rolled away from him.


The wind woke them in the middle of the afternoon, it roared in from the east, flattening the grass on the hills and thrashing the branches above their heads.

Sean looked up at the sky with the wind fluttering his shirt and ruffling his beard. He leaned forward against it, towering over Ruth so that suddenly she realized how big he was. He looked like a god of the storm, with long powerful legs braced apart and the muscles of his chest and arms standing out proudly beneath the white silk of his shirt.

'Clouds building up,' Sean shouted above the rush of the wind. 'No moon tonight.'

She stood up quickly and a sudden violent gust threw her off balance. She staggered against him and his arms closed about her. For a moment she was pressed to his chest, could feel the lean, rubbery resilience of his body and smell the man smell of it. It was a shock for both of them, this unexpectedly intimate contact and when she broke away her eyes were wide and grey with fear of the thing she had felt stir within her.

'I'm sorry,' she whispered. 'That was an accident.' And the wind caught her hair and streamed it across her face in a dancing, snapping black tangle.

'We'll upsaddle and ride with the daylight that is left,' Sean decided. 'We won't be able to move tonight.'

The clouds rolled in on the wind, spreading upon themselves, changing shape and dropping closer to the earth. Clouds the colour of smoke and bruises, heavy with the rain they carried.

The night came early, but still the wind roared and buffeted them in the gloom.

'It will drop in an hour or so, then we'll get the rain. We'll try and find shelter while there's still light enough to see.'

On the reverse slope of a kopje they found an overhang of rock and offloaded the packs beneath it. While Sean pegged the horses out on their head ropes to prevent them walking away before the storm, Mbejane cut grass and piled it into a mattress on the rock floor beneath the overhang. Huddled in their oilskins they ate biltong and cold mealie bread and afterwards Mbejane withdrew discreetly to the far end of the shelter and disappeared under his blankets. He had that animal knack of being able to sleep instantly and completely even under the most adverse conditions.

'All right, boy. Get into your blankets.'

'Can't I just . . .' Dirk began his nightly protest.

'No, you can't.'

'I'll sing for you,' Ruth offered.

'What for?' Dirk was puzzled.

'A sleepy-time song – haven't you ever had a lullaby?'

'No.' But Dirk was intrigued. 'What you going to sing?'

'Into your blankets first.'

Sitting beside Sean in the darkness, very conscious of his bulk and the touch of his shoulder against hers, the muted roar of the wind as her accompaniment – Ruth sang.

First the old Dutch folksongs, 'Nooi, Nooi' and 'Jannie met die Hoepel been', then other old favourites like 'Frère Jacques'. Her voice meant something to each of them.

Mbejane woke to the sound of it and made him remember the wind on the hills of Zululand and the singing of the young girls in the fields at harvest-time. It made him glad he was going home.

To Dirk it was the voice of the mother he had hardly known. A safe sound – and soon he slept.

'Don't stop,' whispered Sean.

So she sang for him alone. A love-song from two thousand years ago, filled with all the suffering of her people, but with joy in it also. The wind died away while she sang and her voice died away with it into the vast silence of the night.

The storm broke. The first thunder crashed and the lightning forked jagged-blue through the clouds. Dirk whimpered a little but slept on.

In the stark, blue light Sean saw that Ruth's cheeks were wet with tears and when the darkness closed around them again she started to tremble against him. He reached out for her and she clung to him, small and warm against his chest, and he could taste the salt of her tears on his lips.

'Sean, we mustn't.'

But he lifted her and held her across his chest as he walked out into the night. The lightning blazed again and lit the land with startling brilliance so he could see the horses huddling heads down, and the crisp outline of the kopje above them.

The first raindrops splashed against his shoulders and into his face. The rain was warm and he walked on carrying Ruth. Then the air was filled with rain, an encompassing pearly mist of it in the next flash of lightning, and the night was filled with the odour of rain on dry earth – a clean warm smell.

# Chapter Five

In a still morning, washed so clean by the rain that they could see the mountains, blue and sharp on the southern horizon, they stood together on the crest of the kopje.

'That's the tail of the Drakensberg, we've cleared it by twenty miles. There's very little chance of a Boer patrol this far out. We can ride by day now. Soon we'll be able to work in again and meet the railway beyond the battle lines.'

Because of the beauty of the morning, of the land that dripped away into the great, grassy bowl that was Natal, and of the woman that stood beside him, Sean was gay.

Because of the promise of an end to the journey and the promise of a new one with this woman as his companion, he was content.

When he spoke she turned slowly to look up at him, her chin lifting in acknowledgement of his superior height. For the first time Sean realized that his own mood was not reflected in her eyes.

'You are very lovely,' he said, and still she remained silent, but now he could recognize the shadows in her eyes as sorrow or something even stronger.

'Ruth, you'll come with me?'

'No.' She shook her head slowly, regretfully. The fat black python of hair rolled across her shoulder and hung down against the honey chamois leather of her jacket.

'You must.'

'I cannot.'

'But, last night.'

'Last night was madness . . . the storm.'

'It was right. You know that.'

'No. It was the storm.' She looked away from him towards the sky. 'And now the storm is ended.'

'It was more than that. You know it. It was from the first moment of our meeting.'

'It was a madness based upon deceit. Something that I will have to cover with lies – the way we had to cover it with darkness at the time.'

'Ruth. My God, don't talk about it like that.'

'Very well, I won't. I won't talk about it again, ever.'

'We can't leave it now. You know we can't.'

And in answer she held up her left hand so that the gold upon it caught the sun.

'We'll say good-bye here on a mountain in the sunlight. Though we'll ride together a little farther – it's here we'll say good-bye.'

'Ruth . . .' he started, but she placed the hand across his mouth and he felt the metal of the ring on his lips and it seemed to him that the ring was as cold as his dread of the loss she was about to inflict upon him.

'No,' she whispered. 'Kiss me once more and then let me go.'

# Chapter Six

Mbejane saw it first and spoke quietly to Sean, perhaps two miles out on their flank, like a smudge of brown smoke rising beyond the fold of the nearest ridge, so faint that Sean had to search a moment before he found it. Then he swivelled away from it and hunted frantically for cover. The nearest was an outcrop of red stone half a mile away, much too far.

'What is it, Sean?' Ruth noticed his agitation.

'Dust,' he gold her. 'Horsemen. Coming this way.'

'Boers?'

'Probably.'

'What are we to do?'

'Nothing.'

'Nothing?'

'When they show on the ridge I'll ride to meet them. Try to bluff our way through.' He turned to Mbejane and spoke in Zulu. 'I will go to them. Watch me carefully, but keep moving away. If I lift my arm let the pack-horses go and ride. I will hold them as long as I can, but when I lift my arm then it is finished.' Quickly he unbuckled the saddle-bag which held the gold and handed it to the Zulu. 'With a good start you should be able to hold them off until nightfall. Take the Nkosikazi where she wishes to go and then with Dirk return to my mother at Ladyburg.'

He looked again at the ridge just in time to see two horsemen appear upon it. Sean lifted the binoculars from his chest; in the round field of the glasses the two riders stood broadside, their faces turned towards him so he could make out the shape of their helmets. He saw the burnished sparkle of their accoutrements, the size of their mounts and their distinctive saddlery and he yelled with relief.

'Soldiers!'

As if in confirmation a squadron of cavalry in two neat ranks broke over the skyline with the pennants fluttering gaily on the forest of their lances.

Dirk hooting with excitement, Ruth laughing beside him and Mbejane dragging the pack-horses after them, Sean galloped standing in the stirrups and waving his hat above his head to meet them.

Unaffected by the enthusiasm of the welcome the lancers sat stolidly and watched them come and the subaltern at their head greeted Sean suspiciously as he arrived.

'Who are you, sir?' But he seemed less interested in Sean's reply than in Ruth's breeches and what they contained. During the explanations that followed Sean conceived for the man a growing dislike. Although the smooth, sun-reddened skin and the fluffy, yellow moustache aggravated this feeling, the central cause was the pair of pale blue eyes. Perhaps they always popped out that way, but Sean doubted it. They focused steadily on Sean only during the short period when Sean reported that he had made no contact with the Boer, then they swivelled back to Ruth.

'We'll not detain you longer, Lieutenant,' Sean grunted and gathered his reins to turn away.

'You are still ten miles from the Tugela River, Mr Courtney. Theoretically this area is held by the Boers and although we are well out on the flank of their main army it would be much safer if you entered the British lines under our protection.'

'Thank you, no. I want to avoid both armies and reach Pietermaritzburg as soon as possible.' The subaltern shrugged. 'The choice is yours. But if it were my wife and child . . .' He did not finish, but turned in the saddle to signal the column forward.

'Come on, Ruth.' Sean caught her eye, but she did not move.

'I'm not going with you.' There was a flat quality in her voice and she looked away from him.

'Don't be silly.' It shocked him and gave his reply a harshness that lit sparks of anger in her eyes.

'May I travel with you?' she demanded of the subaltern.

'Well, ma'am.' he hesitated, glancing quickly at Sean before he went on. 'If your husband . . .'

'He's not my husband. I hardly know him.' She cut in and ignored the exclamation of protest from Sean. 'My husband is with your army. I want you to take me with you, please.'

'Well, now . . .! That's a horse of another colour,' the officer drawled, but the lazy arrogance of his tone barely concealed his pleasure at the prospect of Ruth's company. 'I'd be delighted to escort you, ma'am.'

With her knees Ruth backed her mount and fell in beside the subaltern. This small manoeuvre placed her directly facing Sean – as though she were on the far side of a barrier.

'Ruth, please. Let me talk to you about this. Just a few minutes.'

'No.' There was no expression in her voice, nor in her face.

'Just to say good-bye,' he pleaded.

'We've said good-bye.' She glanced from Sean to Dirk and then away.

The subaltern raised his clenched fist high and lifted his voice. 'Column! Column, Forward!' and as his big, glossy hunter started he grinned maliciously at Sean and touched the brim of his helmet in ironical salute.

'Ruth!'

But she was no longer looking at Sean. Her eyes were fixed ahead and as she swept away at the head of the column her chin was up, that smiling type of mouth was drawn into two straight lips and the thick braid of hair thumped against her back with each thrust of the horse beneath her.

'Rough luck, matey!' called a trooper from the rear rank and then they were past.

Hunched in the saddle Sean stared after them.

'Is she coming back, Pa?' Dirk inquired.

'No, she's not coming back.'

'Why not?'

Sean did not hear the question. He was watching, waiting for Ruth to look back at him. But he waited in vain, for suddenly she was gone over and beyond the next fold in the land and a few seconds later the column had followed her. Afterwards there was only the vast emptiness of the land and the sky above – as vast as the emptiness within him.

## *Chapter Seven*

Sean rode ahead. Ten yards behind they followed, Mbejane restraining Dirk from a closer approach for he understood that Sean must now be left alone. Many times in the years they had been together Mbejane and Sean had travelled in this formation – Sean riding ahead with his sorrow or his shame and Mbejane trailing him patiently, waiting for Sean's shoulders to straighten and his chin to lift from where it dropped forward on his chest.

There was no coherence in Sean's thoughts, the only pattern was the rise and swoop of alternate anger and despair.

Anger at the woman, anger almost becoming hatred before the plunge of despair as he remembered she was gone. Then anger building up towards madness, this time directed at himself for letting her go. Again the sickening drop as he realized that there was no means by which he could have held her. What could he have offered her? Himself? Two hundred pounds of muscle and bones and scars supporting a face like a granite cliff? Poor value! His wordly goods? A small sack of sovereigns and another woman's child – By God, that was all he had. After thirty-seven years that was all he had to show! Once more his anger flared. A week ago he had been rich – and his anger found a new target. There was at least somewhere he could seek vengeance, there was a tangible enemy to strike, to kill. The Boer. The Boer had robbed him of his wagons and his gold, had sent him scurrying for safety; because of them the woman had come into his life and because of them she had been snatched away from him.

So be it, he thought angrily, this then is the promise of the future. War!

He straightened in his saddle, his shoulders seemed to fill out wide and square. He lifted his head and saw the shiny snake of a river in the valley below. They had reached the Tugela. Without pause Sean pushed his horse over the lip of the escarpment. On its haunches, loose rock rolling and slithering beneath its hooves, they began the descent.

Impatiently Sean followed the river downstream, searching for a drift.

But between the sheer banks it ran smooth and swift and deep, twenty yards wide and still discoloured with mud from the storm.

At the first place where the far bank flattened sufficiently to promise an easy exit from the water, Sean checked his horse and spoke brusquely.

'We'll swim.'

In reply Mbejane glanced significantly at Dirk.

'He's done this before,' Sean answered him as he dismounted and began to shed his clothing, then to the boy, 'Come on, Dirk. Get undressed.'

They drove the pack-horses in first, forcing them to jump from the steep bank and watched anxiously until their heads reappeared above the surface and they struck out for the far bank. Then all three of them naked, their clothing wrapped in oilskins and lashed to the saddles, they remounted.

'You first, Mbejane.'

A splash that rose above the bank.

'Off you go, Dirk. Remember to hang on to the saddle.'

Another high splash, and Sean flogged his mount as it baulked and danced sideways along the bank. A sudden lunge outwards and the long drop before the water closed over them.

Snorting water, they surfaced and with relief Sean saw Dirk's head bobbing beside that of his horse and heard his shouted excitement. Moments later they stood on the far bank, water streaming from their naked bodies, and laughed together at the fun of it.

Abruptly the laughter was strangled to death in Sean's throat. Lining the bank above them, grinning with the infection of merriment but with Mauser rifles held ready, stood a dozen men. Big men, bearded, festooned with bandoliers of ammunition, dressed in rough clothing and a selection of hats that included a brown derby and a tall beaver.

In imitation of Sean, both Mbejane and Dirk stopped laughing and stared up at the frieze of armed men along the bank. A complete silence fell on the gathering.

It was broken at last by the man in the brown derby as he pointed at Sean with the barrel of his Mauser.

'*Magtig!* But you'd need a sharp axe to cut through that branch.'

'Don't anger him,' warned the gentleman in the beaver. 'If he hits you over the head with it, it will crack your skull!' and they all laughed.

It was hard for Sean to decide which was the more discomforting; the intimate discussion of his nudity, or the fact that the discussion was conducted in the Taal (or Cape Dutch). In his impatience he had walked, or rather swum, into the arms of a Boer patrol. There was just a forlorn hope that he might be able to bluff his way through, and he opened his mouth to make the attempt. But Dirk forestalled him.

'Who are they, Pa, and why are they laughing?' he asked in clear piping English, and Sean's hope died as abruptly as did the Boer laughter when they heard that hated language.

'Oh! So!' growled the man in the beaver, and gestured eloquently with his Mauser. 'Hands up please, my friend.'

'Will you allow me to put my trousers on first?' Sean asked politely.

'Where are they taking us?' For once Dirk was subdued and there was a quiver in his voice that touched Beaver, who rode beside him. He answered for Sean.

'Now don't you worry, you're going to see a general. A real live general.' Beaver's English was intelligible and Dirk studied him with interest.

'Will he have medals and things?'

'*Nee*, man. We don't use such rubbish.' And Dirk lost interest. He turned back to Sean.

'Pa, I'm hungry.'

Again Beaver intervened. He pulled a long black stick of biltong, dried meat, from his pocket and offered it to Dirk.

'Sharpen your teeth on that, *Kerel*.'

With his mouth full Dirk was taken care of and Sean could concentrate on the other Boers. They were convinced they had caught a spy, and were discussing the impending execution. In a friendly manner Sean was admitted to the argument, and they listened with respectful attention to his defence. This was interrupted while they forded the Tugela and climbed the escarpment once more, but Sean continued it while they rode in a bunch along the crest. Finally, he convinced them of his innocence – which they accepted with relief, as none of them were really looking forward to shooting him.

Thereafter the talk turned to more pleasant topics. It was a glorious day, sunshine lit the valley in gold and green. Below them the river twisted and sparkled, working its devious way down from the smoky blue wall of the Drakensberg that stood along the far horizon. A few fat clouds dawdled across the sky, and a light breeze took the edge off the heat.

The youngsters in the party listened avidly as Sean spoke of elephant beyond the Limpopo, and of the wide land that waited for men to claim it.

'After the war . . .' they said, and laughed in the sun. Then a change in the wind and a freak lie of the hills brought a faint but ugly sound down to them and the laughter died.

'The guns,' said one of them.

'Ladysmith.'

Now it was Sean's turn to ask the questions. They told him how the commandos had raced down on the town of Ladysmith and rolled up the force that stood to oppose them. Bitterly they remembered how old Joubert had held his horsemen and watched while the broken English army streamed back into the town.

'Almighty! Had he loosed us on them then! We would sweep them into the sea.'

'If Oom Paul had commanded instead of old Joubert, the war would be finished already – but instead we sit and wait.'

Gradually Sean filled in the picture of the war in Natal. Ladysmith was invested. General George White's army was bottled and corked within the town. Half the Boer army had moved forward along the railway and taken up a defensive line straddling the Escarpment, overlooking the river and the tiny village of Colenso.

Below them on the great plain of the Tugela, General Buller was massing his army for the breakthrough to relieve Ladysmith.

'But let him try – Oom Paul is waiting for him.'

'Who is Oom Paul – Surely not Kruger?' Sean was puzzled. Oom Paul was the affectionate nickname of the President of the South African Republic.

'*Nee*, man! This is another Oom Paul. This one is Vecht-General Jan Paulus Leroux of the Wynberg commando.' And Sean caught his breath.

'Is he a big man with red hair and a temper to go with it?'

Laughter, and then. '*Ja!* that's the one. Do you know him?'

'Yes. I know him.'

So my brother-in-law is now a general, Sean grinned to himself, and then asked:

'Is this the general we are going to visit?'

'If we can find him.'

Young Dirk will meet his uncle at last – and Sean found himself anticipating the reunion with a tingle of pleasure.

# Chapter Eight

The canvas of the tent did little to moderate the volume of the voice within. It carried clearly to where Sean waited with his escort.

'Must I drink coffee and shake hands with ever *rooinek* we catch? Have I not already enough work for ten men, but you must bring me more? Send him to one of the Field-Cornets! Send him to Pretoria and let them lock him up! Do whatever you like with him if he is a spy – but, in the name of a merciful providence, don't bring him to me.'

Sean smiled happily. Jan Paulus certainly hadn't lost his voice. There was an interval of comparative quiet while Beaver's voice mumbled within the tent. Then again the muted bellow.

'No! I will not! Take him away.'

Sean filled his lungs, cupped his hands about his mouth and shouted at the tent.

'Hey, you bloody Dutchman! Are you afraid to meet me again? You think I'll knock your teeth out like I did last time.'

A few moments of appalling stillness, then the clattering of an overturned stool and the flap of the tent was thrown open. Into the sunlight, blinking in the glare, but scowling, the red hair that fringed his bald plate burning like a bush-fire, and his shoulders hunched aggressively, came Jan Paulus. His face turned from side to side as he searched for the source of the insult.

'Here,' called Sean, and Jan Paulus stopped dead. Uncertainly he peered at Sean.

'You!' He took a pace forward and then, 'It is you, isn't it. Sean!' And he began to laugh. His right hand that had been clenched into a huge fist unfolded and was thrust forward.

'Sean! Hell, man! Sean!'

They gripped hands and grinned at each other.

'Come into the tent. Come on in, man.'

Once they were inside, Jan Paulus's first question was:

'Where's Katrina? Where is my little sister?' and immediately the smile was gone from Sean's face. He sat down heavily on the *reimpje* stool and took off his hat before he answered.

'She's dead, Paulus. She's been dead these last four years.'

Slowly the expression on Jan Paulus's face changed until it was bleak and hard.

'How?' he asked.

And what can I answer him, thought Sean. Can I tell him she killed herself for some reason that no one will ever know.

'Fever,' he said. 'Blackwater fever.'

'You did not send word to us.'

'I did not know where to find you. Your parents—'

'They too are dead,' Jan Paulus interrupted brusquely and turned away from Sean to stare at the white canvas wall of the tent. There was silence between them then as they remembered the dead in sorrow, made more poingnant by its utter helplessness. At last Sean stood up and went to the entrance of the tent.

'Dirk. Come here.'

Mbejane pushed him forward and he crossed to Sean and took his hand. Sean led him into the tent.

'Katrina's son,' he said and Jan Paulus looked down at him.

'Come here, boy.' Hesitantly Dirk went to him. Suddenly Jan Paulus dropped into a squat so that his eyes were on a level with those of the child. He took Dirk's face between the palms of his hands and studied it carefully.

'Yes,' he said. 'This is the type of son she would breed. The eyes—' His voice stumbled and stopped. A second longer he looked into Dirk's eyes. Then he spoke again.

'Be proud,' he said and stood up. Sean motioned at the flap of the tent, and thankfully Dirk scampered out to where Mbejane waited.

'And now?' Jan Paulus asked.

'I want passage through the lines.'

'You are going over to the English?'

'I am English,' said Sean. Frowning a little, Jan Paulus considered this before he asked:

'You will give me your word not to take up arms with them?'

'No,' answered Sean and Jan Paulus nodded, it was the answer he had expected.

'There is a debt between us,' he decided. 'I have not forgotten the time of the elephant. This is full payment of that debt.' He crossed to the portable desk and dipped a pen. Still standing he wrote rapidly, fanned the paper dry and proffered it to Sean.

'Go,' he said. 'And I hope we do not meet again, for next time I will kill you.'

'Or I you,' Sean answered him.

# Chapter Nine

That afternoon Sean led his party across the steel railway bridge over the Tugela, on through the deserted village of Colenso and out again across the plain. Far ahead, sown on the grass plain like a field of white daisies, were the tents of the great British encampment at Chievely Siding. But long before he reached it Sean came to a guard post manned by a sergeant and four men of an illustrious Yorkshire regiment.

"Ullo, Piet. And where the hell do you think you're off to?'

'I am a British subject,' Sean informed them. The sergeant ran an eye over Sean's beard and patched coat. He glanced at the shaggy pony he rode, and then considered the direction from which Sean had approached.

'Say that again,' he invited.

'I am a British subject,' Sean repeated obligingly in an accent that fell heavily on the Yorkshireman's ear.

'And I'm a ruddy Japanee,' agreed the sergeant cheerfully. 'Let's have your rifle, mate.'

Two days Sean languished in the barbed-wire prison compound while the Intelligence Department cabled the Registrar of Births at Ladyburg and waited for his reply. Two long days during which Sean brooded incessantly, not on the indignities which had been inflicted on him, but on the woman he had found and loved and lost again so quickly. These two days of enforced inactivity came at precisely the worst moment. By repeating over and over in his imagination each word that had passed between them, by feeling again each contact of their hands and bodies, by forming her face in his mind's eye and gloating over every detail of it – Sean burned her memory so deeply into himself that it was there for all time. Although he did not even know her surname, he would never forget her.

By the time he was released with apologies and given back his horses, rifle, moneybag and packs – Sean had driven himself into a mood of such overpowering depression that it could only be alleviated by liquor or physical violence.

The village of Frere, which was the first station south on the line to the coast, promised both of these.

'Take Dirk with you,' instructed Sean, 'beyond the town find a camp beside the road and make a big fire, so I can find you in the dark.'

'What will you do, Nkosi?'

Sean started towards the dingy little canteen that catered for the thirsty of Frere.

'I'm going there,' he answered.

'Come, Nkosizana.' As he and Dirk continued on down the street Mbejane was deciding how long he should give Sean before coming to fetch him. It was many years since the Nkosi had headed for a bar in such a determined fashion, but then there had been much to distress him these last few days. He will need until midnight, Mbejane decided, then he will be in a condition conducive to sleep.

From the door Sean surveyed the interior of the canteen. A single large room with a trestle bar counter along the back wall, and the room was comfortably full of warmth and men and the smell of liquor and cigars. Still standing in the entrance, Sean slipped his hand into the pocket of his trousers and surreptitiously counted his money – ten sovereigns he had allowed himself, more than sufficient for the purchase of the liquor he intended to consume.

As he worked his way through the crowd towards the bar, he looked at the men about him. Soldiers mostly, from a dozen different regiments. Colonials and Imperial troops, other ranks predominating, although a party of junior officers sat at a table against the far wall. Then there were a few civilians whom he judged to be transport drivers, contractors and business men, two women with the officers whose profession was never in doubt, and a dozen black waiters.

'What will it be, ducks?' the large woman behind the counter asked as he reached it and Sean regarded her moustache and her term of address with disfavour.

'Brandy.' He was in no mood for the niceties.

'You want the bottle, ducks?' She had recognized his need.

'That will do for a start,' he agreed.

He drank three large brandies, and with a faint dismay knew that they were having no effect – apart from sharpening his imagination to the point where he could clearly see Ruth's face before his eyes, complete in every detail down to the little black beauty spot high on her cheek and the way the corners of her eyes slanted upwards as she smiled. He would have to make a more active approach to forgetfulness.

Leaning back with both elbows on the counter and the glass clutched in his right hand, he studied the men about him once more. Evaluating each of them as a source of distraction and then discarding and moving his attention on, he was finally left with the small group around the gaming-table.

Seven players, the game draw poker, and from what he could see the stakes were modest. He picked up his bottle, crossed the room to join the circle of spectators and took up his position behind a sergeant of yeomanry who was receiving a battering from the cards. A few hands later the sergeant drew one to fill his flush, missed and pushed the bluff – raising twice until he was called by two pairs across the table. He threw his hand in and blew through his lips in disgust.

'That cleans me out.' He gathered the few coins left on the table in front of him and stoop up.

'Rough luck, Jack. Anyone care to take his place?' The winner looked around the circle of spectators. 'Nice friendly little game, table stakes.'

'Deal me in.' Sean sat down, placed his glass and bottle strategically at his right hand and stacked five gold sovereigns in front of him.

'The man's got gold! Welcome.'

Sean ducked the first hand, lost two pounds to three queens on the next, and won five pounds on the third. The pattern of his luck was set, he played with cold single-mindedness – and when he wanted cards it seemed he had only to wish for them.

What was the old adage? – 'Unlucky in love, and the cards turn hot.' Sean grinned without amusement and filled a small straight with the five of hearts, beat down the three sevens that came against him and drew the pot towards him to swell the pile of his winnings. Up about thirty or forty pounds. He was enjoying himself now.

'A small school, gentlemen.' Three players had dropped out in the last hour leaving four of them at the table. 'How about giving the losers a chance to recoup?'

'You want to raise the stakes?' Sean asked the speaker. He was the only other winner, a big man with a red face and the smell of horses about him. Transport rider, probably.

'Yes, if everyone agrees. Make the minimum bet five pounds.'

'Suits me,' grunted Sean, and there was a murmur of agreement round the table. With heavy money out an air of caution prevailed at first, but slowly the game opened up. Sean's luck cooled a little, but an hour later he had built up his kitty on a series of small wins to a total of seventy-five pounds. Then Sean dealt a strange hand.

The first caller on Sean's left raised before the draw, and was raised in turn by the gentleman with the horsy smell, number three called and Sean fanned his cards open.

With a gentle elation he found the seven, eight, nine and ten of Clubs – with a Diamond six. A pretty little straight dealt pat.

'Call your twenty, and raise it twenty,' he offered, and there was a small stir of excitement among the onlookers.

'Call.' Number one was short of cash.

'Call,' echoed Horse Odour and his gold clinked into the pot.

'I'm dropping.' Number three closed his cards and pushed them away. Sean turned back to number one.

'How many cards?'

'I'll play with these.' Sean felt the first premonition of disaster.

'And you?' he asked Horse Odour.

'I'm also happy with what I have.'

Two pat hands against his small straight; and from the suit distribution, Sean's four Clubs, one of them would certainly be a flush. With a queasy feeling in his stomach Sean knew he was in trouble, knew his hand to be a loser.

Break the straight and go for the other Club, still not a certain winner, but the only thing worth trying.

'I'll draw one.' He tossed the six of Diamonds into the welter of discards, and dealt to himself from the top of the pack.

'My bet.' Number one's face was glowing with confidence. 'I'll raise the maximum – another forty. Cost you eighty pounds to look at me, boys. Let's see the colour of your money.'

'I'd like to push you – but that's the limit. I'll call.' Horse Odour's expression was completely neutral but he was sweating in a light sheen across his forehead.

'Let me go to the books.' Sean picked up his cards and, from behind the other four, pressed out the corner of the card he had drawn. It was black, he opened it a little more – a black six. Slowly he felt the pressure build up within him like a freshly fired boiler. He drew a long breath and opened the card fully.

'I'll call also.' He spoke on a gusty outgoing breath.

'Full house,' shouted number one. 'Queen's full – beat that, you bastards!'

Horse Odour slapped his cards down viciously, his red face crumbling in disappointment. 'Goddam it – of all the filthy luck. I had an ace-high flush.' Number one giggled with excitement and reached for the money.

'Wait for it, friend,' Sean advised him, and spread his cards face up upon the table.

'It's a flush. My full house beats you,' protested number one.

'Count the pips—' Sean touched each card as he named them, 'six, seven, eight, nine and the ten – all Clubs. Straight flush! You come second by a day's march.' He lifted number one's hands off the money, pulled it towards him and began stacking it in columns of twenty.

'Pretty hot run of luck you're having,' Horse Odour gave his opinion, his face still twisted with disappointment.

'Yes,' agreed Sean. Two hundred and sixty-eight pounds. Very pretty.

'Funny how it comes to you on the big hands,' Horse Odour went on. 'And especially when you're dealing. What did you say your profession was?'

Without looking up Sean began transferring the stacks of sovereigns to his pockets. He was smiling a little. The end to a perfect evening, he decided.

Satisfied that the money was secure Sean looked up at Horse Odour and turned that smile full upon him.

'Come along then, laddie,' he said.

'It will be a pleasure.' Horse Odour shoved his chair back and stood up.

'It will indeed,' agreed Sean.

Horse Odour led down the back-stairs into the yard, followed by Sean and the entire clientele of the canteen. At the bottom he paused, judging Sean's footstep on the wooden stairs behind him – then he spun and hit, swinging his body into the punch.

Sean rolled his head, but it caught him on the temple and he went over backwards into the crowd behind him. As he fell he saw Horse Odour jerk back the tail of his jacket and bring out the knife. It shone dull silver in the light from the canteen windows – skinning knife, curved, eight inches of blade.

The crowd scattered leaving Sean lying on the stairs, and Horse Odour came in to kill him, making an ugly sound, bringing the knife arching down from overhead, a clumsy, unprofessional blow.

Only slightly stunned, Sean followed the silver sweep of the knife with ease and the man's wrist slapped loudly into Sean's open left hand.

For a long moment the man lay on top of Sean, his knife-arm helpless in Sean's grip, while Sean assessed his strength – and with regret realized it was no match. Horse Odour was big enough, but the belly pressed against

Sean's was flabby and large, and the wrist in Sean's hands was bony without the hard rubbery give of sinew and muscle.

Horse Odour started to struggle, trying to wrestle his knife-arm free, the sweat dewed on his face and then began to drip – it had an oily, unpleasant smell like rancid butter that blended poorly with the odour of horses.

Sean tightened his grip on the man's wrist, at first using only the strength of his forearm.

'Aah!' Horse Odour stopped struggling. Sean brought in the power of his whole arm, so he could feel his shoulder muscles bunching and writhing.

'Jesus Christ!' Shrieking, as bone cracked in his wrist, Horse Odour's fingers sprang open and the knife thumped on to the wooden stairs.

Still holding him, Sean sat up, then came slowly to his feet.

'Leave us, friend.' Sean flung him backwards into the dust of the yard. He was breathing easily, still feeling cold and detached as he looked down and watched Horse Odour scrabbling to his knees, nursing his broken wrist.

Perhaps it was the man's first movement towards flight that triggered Sean – or perhaps it was the liquor he had drunk that twisted his emotions, aggravated his sense of loss and frustration and channelled it into this insane outburst of hatred.

Suddenly it seemed to Sean that here before him on the ground was the source of all his ills – this was the man who had taken Ruth from him.

'You bastard!' he growled. The man sensed the change in Sean and scrambled to his feet, his face turning desperately from side to side as he sought an avenue of escape.

'You filthy bastard!' Sean's voice rose, shrill with the strength of this new emotion. For the first time in his life Sean craved to kill. He advanced upon the man slowly, his fists opening and closing, his face contorted and the words that spilled from his mouth no longer making sense.

A great stillness had fallen upon the yard. In the shadows the watchers stood, chilled with the dreadful fascination of it. The man was frozen also, only his head moved and no sound came from his open lips – and Sean closed in with the weaving motion of a cobra in erection.

At the last moment the man tried to run, but his legs were slack and heavy with fear – and Sean hit him in the chest with a sound like an axe swung against a tree-trunk.

As he fell Sean went in after him, straddling his chest, roaring incoherently with only a single word recognizable – the name of the woman he loved. In his madness he felt the man's face breaking up under his fists, felt the warm splatter of blood thrown into his own face and on to his arms, and heard the shouts of the crowd.

'He'll kill him!'

'Get him off!'

'For Chrissake give me a hand – he's as strong as a bloody ox.'

Their hands upon him, an arm locked around his throat from behind, the shock as someone hit him with a bottle, the press of their bodies as they swarmed over him.

With men clinging to him, two of them riding his back and a dozen others on his arms and legs, Sean came to his feet.

'Pull his legs out from under him.'

'Get him down, man. Get him down.'

With a convulsive heave Sean swung the men on his arms into violent collision with each other. They released him.

He kicked his right leg free, and those on his other leg let go and scattered. Reaching over his shoulders he plucked the men off his back and stood alone, his chest swelling and subsiding as he breathed, the blood from the bottle gash in his scalp trickling down his face and soaking into his beard.

'Get a gun!' someone shouted.

'There's a shotgun under the bar.' But no one left the circle that ringed him in, and Sean glared around at them his eyes staring wildly from the plain of glistening blood that was his face.

'You've killed him!' a voice accused him. And the words reached Sean through the madness, his body relaxed slightly and he tried to wipe away the blood with the open palm of his hand. They saw the change in him.

'Cool down, mate. Fun's fun but the hell with murder.'

'Easy, now. Let's have a look what you've done to him.'

Sean looked down on the body, and he was confused and then suddenly afraid. The man was dead – he was certain of it.

'Oh, my God!' he whispered, backing away, wiping at his eyes ineffectually and smearing blood.

'He pulled a knife. Don't worry, mate, you've got witnesses.' The temper of the crowd had changed.

'No,' Sean mumbled; they didn't understand. For the first time in his life he had abused his strength, had used it to kill without purpose. To kill for the pleasure of it, to kill in the manner in which a leopard kills.

Then the man moved slightly, he rolled his head and one of his legs flexed and straightened. Sean felt hope leap within him.

'He's alive!'

'Get a doctor.'

Fearfully Sean approached and knelt beside the man, he unknotted the scarf from around his own throat and cleaned the bloody mouth and nostrils.

'He'll be all right – leave him to the Doc.'

The doctor came, a lean and laconic man chewing tobacco. In the yellow light of a hurricane lamp he examined and prodded while they crowded close about him craning to see over his shoulders. At last the doctor stood up.

'All right. He can be moved. Carry him up to my surgery.' Then he looked at Sean. 'Did you do it?'

Sean nodded.

'Remind me not to annoy you.'

'I didn't mean to – it just sort of happened.'

'Is that so?' The doctor shot a stream of yellow tobacco juice into the dust of the yard. 'Let's have a look at your head.' He pulled Sean's head down to his own level and parted the sodden black hair.

'Nicked a vein. Doesn't need a stitch. Wash it and a little iodine.'

'How much, Doc, for the other fellow?' Sean asked.

'You paying?' The doctor looked at him quizzically.

'Yes.'

'Broken jaw, broken collar-bone, about two dozen stitches and a few days in bed for concussion,' he mused, adding it up. 'Say two guineas.'

Sean gave him five. 'Look after him, Doc.'

'That's my job.' And he followed the men who were carrying Horse Odour out of the yard.

'Guess you need a drink, mister. I'll buy you one,' someone offered. The whole world loves a winner.

'Yes,' agreed Sean. 'I need a drink.'

Sean had more than one drink. When Mbejane came to fetch him at midnight he had a deal of difficulty getting Sean up on to the back of the horse. Half-way to the camp Sean slid off and subsided into the road, so Mbejane loaded him sideways – head and arms hanging over to port and legs dangling starboard.

'It is possible that tomorrow you will regret this,' Mbejane told him primly as he unloaded him beside the fire and rolled him still booted and bloody into his blanket.

He was correct.

# Chapter Ten

In the dawn as Sean cleaned his face with a cloth dipped in a mug of hot water, regarding its reflection in the small metal mirror, the only fact that gave him the faintest satisfaction was the two hundred-odd sovereigns he had salvaged from the night's debauch.

'Are you sick, Pa?' Dirk's ghoulish interest in Sean's condition added substantially to his evil temper.

'Eat your breakfast.' Sean's tone was calculated by its sheer malevolence to dry up further questioning.

'There is no food.' Mbejane fell into the familiar role of protector.

'Why not?' Sean focused his bloodshot eyes upon him.

'There is one among us who considers the purchase of strong drink, and other things, more important than food for his son.'

From the pocket of his jacket Sean drew a handful of sovereigns. 'Go!' he ordered. 'Buy food and fresh horses. Go quickly so that in my grave illness I may not be afflicted with the wisdom of your counsel. Take Dirk with you.'

Mbejane examined the money, and grinned.

'The night was not wasted.'

When they had gone back to Frere, Dirk trotting beside the huge half-naked Zulu and his voice only fading at a distance of a hundred yards, Sean poured himself another mug of coffee and cupping it in his hands he sat staring into the ash and pink coals of the fire. He could trust Mbejane to use the money with care, he had the bargaining patience peculiar to his race that could if necessary devote two days to the purchase of a single ox. These things did not concern Sean now. Instead he went over the events of the previous night. Still sickened by his display of murderous rage, he tried to justify it. Taking into account the loss of nearly all he owned, the accumulation of years of hard work that had been stripped from him in a single day; the hardship and uncertainty that had followed. And finally he had reached the flash point when liquor and poker-tensed nerves had snapped the last reserve in him and translated it all into that violent outburst.

But that was not all, he knew he had avoided the main issue. *Ruth.* As he came back to her a wave of hopeless longing overwhelmed him, a tender despair such as he had never experienced before. He groaned aloud, and lifted his eyes to the morning star which was fading on the pink horizon as the sun came up behind.

For a while longer he wallowed in the softness of his love, remembering the way she walked, the dark serenity of her eyes and her mouth when she smiled and her voice when she sang – until it threatened to smother him in its softness.

Then he sprang to his feet and paced restlessly in the grass beside the fire. We must leave this place, ride away from it – go quickly. I must find something to do, some way to keep from thinking of it, something to fill my hands which ache now from the need to hold her.

Along the road, going north to Colenso, a long column of infantry filed past him in the dawn. He stopped his pacing and watched them. Each man leaned forward against his pack and the rifles stood up behind their shoulders.

Yes, he thought, I will go with them. Perhaps at the place to which they march I can find what I could not find last night. We will go home to Ladyburg, riding hard on fresh horses. I will leave Dirk with my mother, then come back to this war.

He began to pace again impatiently. Where the hell was Mbejane?

From the heights above, Sean looked down on Ladyburg. The village spread in a neat circle around the spire of the church. He remembered the spire as beacon-bright in its cladding of new copper, but nineteen years of weather had dulled it to a mellow brown.

Nineteen years. It did not seem that long. There were goods yards around the station now, a new concrete bridge over the Baboon Stroom, the blue gums in the plantation beyond the school were taller, and the flamboyants that had lined the main street were gone.

With a strange reluctance Sean turned his head and looked out to the right, across the Baboon Stroom, close in against the escarpment, to where he had left the sprawling Dutch gabled homestead of Theuniskraal with its roof of combed yellow thatch and the shutters of yellow-wood across the windows.

It was there, but not as he remembered it. Even at this distance he could see the walls were flaking and mottled with patches of dampness; the thatch was shaggy as the coat of an airedale; one of the shutters tilted slightly from a broken hinge; the lawns were brown and ragged where the bare earth showed through. The dairy behind the house had crumbled, its roof gone and the remains of its walls jutted forlornly upwards to the height of a man's shoulder.

'Damn the little bastard!' Sean's anger flared abruptly as he saw the neglect with which his twin brother had treated the lovely old house. 'He's so lazy he wouldn't get out of a bed he'd peed in.'

To Sean it was not just a house. It was the place his father had built, which had sheltered Sean on the day of his birth and through the years of his childhood. When his father died under the Zulu spears at Isandlawana, half the farm and the house had belonged to Sean; he had sat in the study at nights with the logs burning in the stone fireplace and the mounted buffalo head above it throwing distorted, moving shadows up on to the plaster ceiling. Although he had given his share away – yet it was still his home. Garry, his brother, had no right to let it decay and fall apart this way.

'Damn him!' Sean voiced his thoughts out loud – then almost immediately his conscience rebuked him. Garry was a cripple, his lower leg shot away by the blast of a careless shotgun. And Sean had fired that shotgun. Will I never be free of that guilt, how long must my penance continue? He protested at the goad of his conscience.

That is not your only trespass against your brother, his conscience reminded him. Who sired the child he calls his son? Whose loins sowed the seed that became man-child in the belly of Anna, your brother's wife?

'It has been a long time, Nkosi.' Mbejane had seen the expression on his face as Sean looked towards Theuniskraal and remembered those things from the past that were better forgotten.

'Yes.' Sean roused himself, and straightened in the saddle. 'A long road and many years. But now we are home again.'

He looked back towards the village, searching the quarter beyond the main street and the hotel for the roof of that little cottage on Protea Street. As he found it, showing through the tall, fluffy blue gum trees, there was a lift in his mood, a new excitement. Did she live there still? How would she look – a little grey surely; had her fifty years marked her deeply, or had they treated her with the same consideration which she showed all those with whom *she* came in contact? Had she forgiven him for leaving without a farewell? Had she forgiven his long years of silence since then? Did she understand the reasons why he had never written – no word or message, except that anonymous gift of ten thousand pounds he had transferred to her bank account. Ten thousand miserable little pounds, which he had hardly noticed among all the millions he had won and lost in those days long ago when he was one of the lords of the Witwatersrand goldfields.

Again the sense of guilt closed in upon him. As he knew with utter certainty that she *had* understood, that she *had* forgiven. For that was Ada, the woman who was his stepmother – and whom he loved beyond the natural love one owes their own full-blooded mother.

'Let's go down,' he said and kicked his horse to a canter.

'Is this home, Pa?' Dirk shouted as he rode beside him.

'Yes, my boy. This is home.'

'Will Gran'ma be here?'

'I hope so,' Sean answered, and then softly, 'Beyond all other things, I hope that she will.'

Over the bridge above the Baboon Stroom, past the cattle-pens alongside the line of rail, past the old wood and iron station buildings with the sign, white and black faded to grey, 'Ladyburg. Altitude 2,256 ft. above sea level', swinging left into the dusty main street which was wide enough to turn a full span of oxen, and down to Protea Street rode Sean and Dirk, with Mbejane and the pack-mule trailing far behind.

At the corner Sean checked his mount to a walk, drawing out the last few minutes of anticipation until they stopped outside the wicket fence of white that encompassed the cottage. The garden was neat and green, gay with beds of Barberton daisies and blue rhododendrons. The cottage had been enlarged, a new room built on the far side, and it was crisp-looking in a coat of new whitewash. A sign at the gate said in gold letters on a green ground.

'Maison Ada.
High-class Costumier'

Sean grinned. 'The old girl's gone all French, by God.' Then to Dirk, 'Stay here!'

He swung down from his horse, handed the reins to Dirk and went through the gate. At the door he paused self-consciously and adjusted his cravat. He glanced down at the severe dark broadcloth suit and new boots which he had purchased in Pietermaritzburg, slapped the dust from his breeches, stroked his newly trimmed beard into place, gave his moustache a twirl and knocked on the door.

It was opened at last by a young lady. Sean did not recognize her. But the girl reacted immediately, flushing slightly, attempting to pat her hair into place without drawing attention to its disarray, trying to dispose of the sewing in her hands, and exhibiting all the signs of confusion peculiar to the unmarried female who finds herself suddenly and unexpectedly in the presence of a large, well-dressed and attractive male. But Sean felt a twinge of pity as he looked at her scarred face, ugly with the purple cicatrice of acne.

Sean lifted his hat. 'Is Mrs Courtney here?'

'She's in the workroom, sir. Who shall I tell her is calling?'

'Don't tell her anything – it's a surprise,' Sean smiled at her, and she lifted her hands self-consciously in an attempt to mask the ruin of her face.

'Won't you come in, sir?' She turned her head aside, shyly – as though to hide it.

'Who is it, Mary?' Sean started at the voice from the depths of the cottage, it hadn't changed at all – and the years dropped away.

'It's a gentleman, Aunt Ada. He wants to see you.'

'I'm coming. Ask him to sit down, and please bring us coffee, Mary.'

Mary escaped thankfully and left Sean standing alone in the small sitting-room, twisting his hat in big brown hands, staring up at the daguerreotype print of Waite Courtney above the mantel. Although he did not recognize the fact, the face of his father in the picture was almost his own – the same eyes under heavy black brows, the same arrogance about the mouth, even the identical thrust of stubbornness in the jaw beneath the thick spade-shaped beard – and the big, hooked Courtney nose.

The door from the work-room opened and Sean swung quickly to face it. Ada Courtney came through it smiling, until she saw him, then she stopped and the smile died on her lips and she paled. Uncertainly her hand lifted to her throat and she made a small choking sound.

'Dear God,' she whispered.

'Ma.' Sean fidgeted his feet awkwardly. 'Hello, Ma. It's good to see you.'

'Sean.' The colour flooded back into her cheeks. 'For a moment I thought – you're grown so much like your father. Oh, Sean!' And she ran to him. He tossed his hat on to the sofa and caught her around the waist as she came.

'I've waited for you. I knew you'd come.'

Sean scooped her up and kissed her into a confusion of joy and laughter, swinging her while he did it, laughing himself.

'Put me down,' Ada gasped at last, and when he did she clung to him.

'I knew you'd come back. At first there were bits in the newspaper about you, and people told me things – but these last years there has been nothing, nothing at all.'

'I'm sorry.' Sean sobered.

'You're a bad boy.' She was sparkling with excitement, her hair had escaped from its bun and a wisp of it hung down her cheek. 'But it's so good to have you back—' and suddenly she was crying.

'Don't, Ma. Please don't.' He had never seen her cry before.

'It's just that . . . It's the surprise.' She brushed impatiently at her tears. 'It's nothing.'

Desperately Sean sought something to distract her. 'Hey!' he exclaimed with relief, 'I've another surprise for you.'

'Later,' she protested. 'One at a time.'

'This won't wait.' He led her to the door and out on to the front stoep with his arm around her shoulders.

'Dirk,' he shouted. 'Come here.'

He felt her standing very still as they watched Dirk coming up the garden walk.

'This is your Gran'ma.' He introduced them.

'Why is she crying?' Dirk eyed her with frank curiosity.

Later they sat at the table in the kitchen while Ada and Mary plied them with food. Ada Courtney believed that the first thing to do with a man was feed him.

Mary was almost as excited as Ada, she had taken full advantage of the few minutes she had been alone, and now her hair was freshly brushed and she wore a gay new apron, but the powder with which she had tried to cover the terrible disfiguration of the skin served only to call attention to it. In sympathy Sean refrained from looking at her, and Mary noticed. Shyly she devoted herself to winning Dirk's attention. She fussed over him quietly – and Dirk accepted this as the natural order of things.

While they ate Sean filled in the missing years for Ada with a brief outline

of his activities, glossing over the death of Dirk's mother, and other things
of which he had no reason to be proud. He came to the end of it.

'And so here we are.

>     "Home is the sailor, home from the sea,
>     And the hunter home from the hill."

Dirk, don't put so much in your mouth and keep it closed when you chew.'

'How long will you stay? Mary, see if there are any cream-puffs in the
jar – Dirk is still hungry,' said Ada.

'You'll make him sick. I don't know; not long though – there's a war on.'

'You're going to join?'

'Yes.'

'Oh, Sean. Must you?' Knowing that he must. While he selected a cheroot
from his case Sean studied her closely for the first time. There was grey now
as he had known there would be, almost as much grey as black; long streaks
of it across her temples and the texture of her skin had altered, losing the
moisture of youth, drying out so that it creased around the eyes and stretched
tight across her hands to show the knuckles more prominently and the
blueness of veins beneath it. She was plumper also, her bosom was full and
round, each breast having lost its separate identity in the whole.

Yes the other qualities whose memories he had treasured so long ago still
persisted, seemed indeed to have grown stronger; the composure which
showed in the stillness of her hands and body, yet was given the lie by the
humour that hovered around her lips; the eyes whose depths held compassion
and a sure understanding of those things they looked upon. But mostly it
was the indefinable aura of goodness about her – looking at her, he sensed
again that behind those eyes no destructive thought could live for long.

Sean lit the cheroot and spoke while the smoke masked his face.

'Yes, Ma. I must go.'

And Ada, whose husband had ridden to war also, and not ridden home,
could not prevent the sadness showing for an instant in her eyes.

'Yes. I suppose you must. Garry has gone already – and Michael has
been agitating to follow him.'

'Michael?' Sean fired the question.

'Garry's son – he was born a short while after – after you left Ladyburg.
He will be eighteen this winter.'

'What's he like?' Sean's voice was too eager. Michael – so that is what
my son is named. My first-born. By God, my first-born, and I didn't even
know his name until he was almost fully grown. Ada was looking at him
with her own question unasked in her eyes.

'Mary, take Dirk through to the bathroom please. Try and get a little of
that food from around his mouth.' When they had gone she answered Sean's
question.

'He's a tall boy, tall and lean. Dark like his mother, but a serious lad. He
doesn't laugh much. Always top of his class. I like him very much. He comes
here often.' She was silent for a moment, then, 'Sean . . .'

Quickly Sean cut in. 'And how is Garry?' He sensed what she was going
to ask.

'Garry has not changed very much. He has had a run of bad luck . . .

Poor Garry, things have been bad on the farm. The rinder-pest ravaged his herds, he had to borrow money from the bank.' She hesitated an instant. 'And he is drinking a lot these days. I can't be sure of it – he never visits the hotel and I have never seen him take a drink. But it must be that.'

'I'll find out where he is when I go up to Colenso.'

'You'll have no difficulty finding him. Garry is a lieutenant-colonel on the General's staff. He was given promotion from major last week, and he has been awarded the Distinguished Service Order to go with his Victoria Cross. He is in charge of liaison between the Imperial and the Colonial troops.'

'Good God!' Sean was stunned. 'Garry a colonel!'

'General Buller thinks very highly of him. The General is also a holder of the Victoria Cross.'

'But,' Sean protested. 'You know how Garry got that decoration. It was a mistake. If Garry is on the General's staff – then Lord have mercy on the British Army!'

'Sean, you mustn't talk about your brother that way.'

'Colonel Garrick Courtney.' Sean laughed out loud.

'I don't know what there is between you and Garry. But it's something very nasty – and I don't want any of it in this house.' Ada's tone was fierce and Sean stopped laughing.

'I'm sorry.'

'Before we close the subject, I want to warn you. Please be very careful how you handle Garry. Whatever happened between you two – and I don't want to know what it is – Garry still hates you. Once or twice he started talking about you but I stopped him. Yet I know it from Michael – the boy has picked it up from his father. It's almost an obsession with him. Be careful of Garry.'

Ada stood up. 'And now about Dirk. What a lovely child he is, Sean. But I'm afraid you've spoiled him a little.'

'He's a tiger,' Sean admitted.

'What schooling has he been given?'

'Well, he can read a little—'

'You'll leave him here with me. I'll enrol him when the school term begins.'

'I was going to ask. I'll leave money with you.'

'Ten years ago there was a very large and mysterious deposit to my bank account. It wasn't mine – so I placed it out at interest.' She smiled at him and Sean looked guilty. 'We can use that.'

'No,' he said.

'Yes,' she contradicted. 'And now tell me when you are leaving.'

'Soon.'

'How soon?'

'Tomorrow.'

# Chapter Eleven

Since climbing the World's View road out of Pietermaritzburg, Sean and Mbejane had travelled in sunshine and in companionship. The feelings between them were solid, compacted by time and the pressure of trouble and shared laughter into a shield of affection – so that now they were happy as only men can be together. The jokes were old jokes, and the responses almost automatic – but the excitement between them was new, in the same way that each day's sun is new. For they were riding to war, to another meeting with death, so that everything else lost significance. Sean felt free, the thoughts and relationships with other people which had weighed him down over the past months slipped away. Like a ship clear for action he hurried with a new lightness to meet his chance.

At the same time he could stand aside from himself and grin tolerantly at his own immaturity. By God, we're like a couple of kids sneaking out of school. Then, following the thought further – he was suddenly thankful. Thankful that this was so; thankful that there was still this capacity to forget everything else and approach the moment in childlike anticipation. For a while this new habit of self-appraisal asserted itself; I am no longer young and I have learned much, gathered it brick by brick along the way and trimmed each brick and cemented it into the wall. The fortress of my manhood is not yet completed, but what I have built so far is strong. Yet the purpose of a fortress is to protect and hold safely those things that are precious; if, during the building, a man loses and expends those things which he wishes to protect, then the finished fortress is a mockery. I have not lost it all, a little I have used in barter. I have traded a little faith for the knowledge of evil; exchanged a little laughter for the understanding of death; a measure of freedom for two sons (and this was a good trade) – but I know there is still something left.

At his side Mbejane noticed the change of Sean's mood, and he moved in front of it to turn it once more into the sunshine.

'Nkosi, we must hurry if you wish to reach your drinking-place at Frere.'

With an effort Sean thrust his thoughts aside, and laughed. They rode on into the north, and on the third day they reached Chievely.

Sean remembered his innocent amazement when, as a youth, he had joined Lord Chelmsford's column at Rorke's Drift at the beginning of the Zulu War. He had believed then no greater accumulation of men was possible. now he looked across the encampment of the British Army before Colenso and smiled; Chelmsford's little force would have been lost in the artillery and ordnance park, yet beyond that the tents stretched away for two miles. Row upon row of white canvas cones with the horse lines in between – and to the rear the orderly acres of transport vehicles, thousands of them, with the draught animals scattered grazing across the veld almost to the range of the eye.

It was an impressive sight not only in its immensity but also in its neat and businesslike layout; so was the military precision of the blocks of men at drill, the massed glitter of their bayonets as they turned and marched and countermarched.

When Sean wandered into the camp and read the names of the regiments at the head of each row of tents he recognized them as the sound of glory. But the new khaki uniforms and pith helmets had reduced them all to a homogeneous mass. Only the cavalry retained a little of the magic in the pennants that fluttered gaily at their lance-tips. A squadron trotted past him and Sean eyed their mounts with envy. Great shiny beasts, as arrogant as the men upon their backs. Horse and rider given an air of inhuman cruelty by the slender bright-tipped lance they carried.

A dozen times Sean asked his question, 'Where can I find the Guides,' and though the answer was given in the dialects of Manchester and Lancashire, in the barely intelligible accents of Scotland and Ireland, each had a common factor – they were all singularly unhelpful.

Once he stopped to watch a group training with one of the new Maxim machine-guns. Clumsy, he decided, no match against a rifle. Later he would remember this judgement and feel a little foolish.

All morning he trudged through the camp, with Mbejane trailing him, and at noon he was tired and dusty and bad-tempered. The Natal Corps of Guides appeared to be a mythical unit. He stood on the edge of the camp and looked out across the open veld, pondering his next move in the search.

Half a mile out on the grassy plain a thin drift of blue smoke caught his eye. It issued from a line of bush that obviously marked the course of a stream. Whoever had picked that spot to camp certainly knew how to make himself comfortable in the veld. Compared to the bleak surroundings of the main encampment it would be paradise; protected from the wind, close to firewood and water, well away from the attention of senior officers. That was his answer, Sean grinned and set out across the plain.

His guess was proved correct by the swarm of black servants among the trees. These could only be Colonial troops, each with a personal retainer. Also, the wagons were drawn up in the circular formation of the laager. With a feeling of homecoming Sean approached the first white man he saw.

In an enamel hipbath beneath the shade of a mimosa tree this gentleman sat, waist deep, while a servant added hot water from a large black kettle.

'Hello,' Sean greeted him. The man looked up from his book, removed the cheroot from his mouth and returned Sean's greeting.

'I'm looking for the Guides.'

'Your search is ended, my friend. Sit down.' Then to the servant, 'Bring the Nkosi a cup of coffee.'

Thankful, Sean sank into the *reimpje* chair near the bath and stretched his legs out before him. His host laid aside the book and began to lather his hairy chest and armpits while he studied Sean with frank appraisal.

'Who's in charge here?' Sean asked.

'You want to see him?'

'Yes.'

The bather opened his mouth and yelled.

'Hey! Tim!'

'What you want?' The reply came from the nearest wagon.

'Fellow here to see you.'

'What's *he* want?'

'Says he wants to talk to you about his daughter.'

There was a long silence while the man in the wagon digested this, then:

'What's he look like?'

'Big bloke, with a shotgun.'

'You're joking!'

'The hell I am! Says if you don't come out he's coming in to get you.'

The canvas of the wagon canopy was lifted cautiously and an eye showed behind the slit. The ferocious bellow that followed startled Sean to his feet. The canvas was thrown aside and out of the wagon vaulted the Commanding Officer of the Guides. He moved in on Sean with his arms held like a wrestler. For a moment Sean stared at him, then he answered the bellow and dropped into a defensive crouch.

'Yaah!' The man charged and Sean met him chest to chest, locking his arms around him as they closed.

'Tim Curtis, you miserable bastard,' he roared in laughter and in pain as Tim tried to pull his beard out by the roots.

'Sean Courtney, you evil son of a bitch,' breathless as the air was forced from his lungs by Sean's hug.

'Let's have a drink.' Sean punched him.

'Let's have a bottle.' Tim caught his ears and twisted.

At last they broke apart and stood laughing incoherently in the pleasure of meeting again.

The servant returned with Sean's coffee and Tim waved him away disgustedly. 'None of that slop! Get a bottle of brandy out of my chest.'

'You two know each other, I presume.' The man in the bath interrupted them.

'Know each other! Jesus, I worked five years for him!' snorted Tim. 'Digging his dirty gold out of the ground. Worst boss I ever had.'

'Well, now's your chance,' Sean grinned, 'because I've come to work for you.'

'You hear that Saul? The idiot wants to join.'

'*Mazeltov.*' The bather dunked the tip of his cheroot in his bath water, flicked it away and stood up. He offered Sean a soapy hand.

'Welcome to the legion of the lost. My name's Saul Friedman. I gather yours is Sean Courtney. Now where's that bottle and we'll celebrate your arrival.'

The commotion had summoned the others from their wagons and Sean was introduced to each of them. It seemed the uniform of the Guides was a khaki tunic without insignia or badges of rank, slouch hats and riding breeches. There were ten of them. A tough-looking bunch and Sean found their company to his liking.

Naked except for a towel draped round his waist, Saul did duty as barman, then they all settled down in the shade to a bout of drinking. Tim Curtis entertained them for the first twenty minutes with a biographical and biological account of Sean's career, to which Saul contributed comments that were met with roars of laughter. It was obvious that Saul was the Company wit, a function which he performed with distinction. He was the youngest of them all, perhaps twenty-five years old, and physically the smallest. His body was thin and hairy, and in a pleasant sort of way he was extremely ugly. Sean liked him.

An hour later when the brandy had taken them to the stage of seriousness which precedes wild and undirected hilarity, Sean asked,

'Captain Curtis . . .'

'Lieutenant, and don't forget it,' Tim corrected him.

'Lieutenant, then. What is our job, and when do we do it?'

Tim scowled at his empty glass, then looked across at Saul. 'Tell him,' he instructed.

'As mentioned earlier, we are the legion of the lost. People look on us with pity and a mild embarrassment. They pass us by on the far side of the street, making the sign of the Cross and murmuring a spell to avert the evil eye. We live here in our own little leper colony.'

'Why?'

'Well, first of all, we belong to the most miserable little runt in the entire army of Natal. An officer, who, despite a formidable array of medals, would not inspire confidence in a young ladies' choir. He is chief liaison officer for the Colonial troops on the general staff. Lieutenant-Colonel Garrick Courtney, V.C., D.S.O.' Saul paused and his expression changed. 'No relation of yours, I trust?'

'No,' lied Sean without hesitation.

'Thank God,' Saul continued. 'Anyway, this is why people pity us. The embarrassment arises from the fact that nobody recognizes our official existence. Even the drawing of rations must be preceded by a comic opera dialogue between Tim and the Quartermaster. But because we are called "Guides" everybody expects us to get out there and start doing a bit of guiding. So in some weird fashion the failure of General Buller to advance even one hundred yards in three months is laid at our door.' Saul filled his glass. 'Anyway, we haven't run out of brandy yet.'

'You mean we don't do anything?' Sean asked incredulously.

'We eat, we sleep and we drink.'

'Occasionally we go visiting,' Tim added. 'Now is as good a time as any.'

'Who do we visit?'

'There is a most enterprising woman in the area, not five miles distant. She owns a travelling circus – forty wagons and forty girls. They follow along behind the main army to comfort and encourage it. Let's go and get some comfort and encouragement. If we start now we'll get to the head of the line – first come, first served.'

'I'll leave you to it,' Saul stood up and drifted away.

'He's a good kid,' Tim observed as he watched him leave.

'Is it against his religion?'

'No. But he's married and takes it seriously. How about you?'

'I'm not married.'

'Let's go then.'

Much later they rode home together in the moonlight, both pleasantly melancholy with love and liquor. The girl who had taken Sean to her wagon was a friendly lass with a pair of fat maternal bosoms.

'I like you, mister,' she had told him afterwards.

'I like you also,' he replied truthfully.

Although Sean experienced no more shame or guilt than after satisfying any of his other bodily needs, yet he knew that half an hour with a stranger in a wagon bed was a very poor substitute.

He began to hum the tune that Ruth had sung on the night of the storm.

## Chapter Twelve

Lieutenant-Colonel Garrick Courtney removed his uniform jacket and hung it carefully on the dumb-valet beside his desk. The way a houseproud wife straightens a picture on her wall, he touched the purple watered silk on which was suspended the heavy, bronze cross, until it hung to his satisfaction. His lips moving, he read the inscription again. 'For Valour', and smiled.

The champagne he had drunk during lunch made his brain feel like a great brilliant diamond set in his skull, sharp and hard and clear.

He sat down, swivelled the chair sideways to the desk and stretched his legs out in front of him.

'Send him in, Orderly!' he shouted, and dropped his eyes to his boots. You couldn't tell the difference, he decided. No one could tell by looking at them which one was flesh and bone beneath the polished leather – or which leg was carved wood with a cunningly articulated ankle.

'Sir.' The voice startled him and he pulled his legs in guiltily, hiding them beneath his chair.

'Curtis!' He looked up at the man who stood before his desk. Tim stood rigidly to attention, staring stolidly over Garry's head, and Garry let him stand. He felt satisfaction that this hulking bastard must use those two powerful legs to pay respect to Garrick Courtney. Let him stand. He waited, watching him, and at last Tim fidgeted slightly and cleared his throat.

'At ease!' There was no doubt now as to who held the power. Garry picked up the paper-knife from his desk and turned it in his hands as he spoke.

'You're wondering why I sent for you.' He smiled expansively. 'Well, the reason is that I have a job for you at last. I lunched with General Buller today.' He paused to let that absorb. 'We discussed the Offensive. He wanted my views on certain plans he has in mind.' Garry caught himself. 'Anyway, that is beside the point. I want you and your men to reconnoitre the river on both sides of Colenso. See here.' Garry spread a map on the desk in front of him. 'There are fords marked here and here.' He jabbed at the map with the paper-knife. 'Find them and mark them well. Check the bridges – both the railway and the road bridge, make certain they are intact. Do it tonight. I want your full report in the morning. You can go.'

'Yes, sir.'

'Oh, Curtis—' Garry stopped him as he stooped in the entrance of the tent. 'Don't fail. Find those fords.' The canvas flap dropped closed behind the American, and Garry opened the drawer of his desk and took out a silver flask set with carnelians. He unscrewed it and sniffed the contents before he drank.


With the dawn, in bedraggled pairs the Guides dribbled into camp. Sean and Saul were the last to return. They dismounted, turned their horses over to the servants and joined the group around the fire.

'Yes?' Tim looked up from where he squatted with a mug of coffee cupped in his hands. His clothing was soaked and steam lifted off it as it dried in the heat from the flames. 'They've blown the rail bridge – but the road bridge is still intact.'

'You're sure?'

'We walked across.'

'That's something anyway,' grunted Tim, and Sean raised a sceptical eyebrow.

'You think so. Hasn't it occurred to you that they've left the bridge because that is where they *want* us to cross?'

No one replied and Sean went on wearily:

'When we checked the bridges, Saul and I did a bit of exploring on the far side. Just beyond the railway bridge there is a series of little kopjes. We crawled around the bottom of them.'

'And?'

'There are more Boers sitting on those kopjes than there are quills on a porcupine's back. Whoever tries to cross those bridges in daylight is going to get the Bejesus shot out of him.'

'Lovely thought!' growled Tim.

'Charming, isn't it? Further contemplation of it will make me puke. What did you find?'

'We found plenty of water.' Tim glanced down at his sodden clothing. 'Deep water.'

'No ford,' Sean anticipated gloomily.

'None. But we found a ferryboat on the bank with the bottom knocked out of it. That could be the excuse for marking a ford on the map.'

'So now you can go and tell our beloved Colonel the glad tidings.' Saul grinned. 'But one gets you five that it has no effect. My guess is that Buller will attack Colenso within the next two days. He might just be able to get a couple of thousand men across that bridge, then we'd have a chance.'

Tim regarded him balefully. 'And the Guides will be the first across. All very well for you. The Rabbi has reduced your target area considerably – but what about us?'


'But it's marked on the map,' protested Lieutenant-Colonel Garrick

Courtney. His head was bowed so that Tim could see the pink scalp through the furrows the comb had left in his sandy-brown hair.

'I've seen dragons and sea monsters marked on maps, sir,' Tim answered, and Garry looked up at him coldly with pale blue eyes.

'You're not paid to be a comedian, Curtis.'

'I beg your pardon, sir,' and Garry frowned. Curtis could make the 'sir' sound like an insult.

'Who did you send?' he demanded.

'I went myself, sir.'

'You could have missed it in the dark.'

'If there is a ford there, it would have a road or at least a path leading down to it. I wouldn't have missed that, sir.'

'But in the darkness you could have been mistaken,' insisted Garry. 'You might have missed something that would be obvious in daylight.'

'Well, sir . . .'

'Good.' Briskly Garry went on. 'Now, the bridges. You say these are still intact.'

'Only the road bridge, but . . .'

'But what?'

'The men I sent report that the hills beyond the river are heavily defended. Almost as though the bridge has been preserved to bait a trap.'

'Curtis.' Deliberately Garry laid his paper-knife upon the map before him. His nose was too large for the space between his eyes and when he pursed his lips this way he looked, Tim thought, like a bird – a sparrow, a little brown sparrow.

'Curtis,' Garry repeated softly. 'It seems to me you have very little enthusiasm for this business. I send you out to do a job and you come back with a long list of excuses. I don't think you realize how important this is.'

Chirp, chirp – little sparrow. Tim smiled secretly and Garry flushed.

'For instance. Who did you sent to reconnoitre these bridges – reliable men, I hope?'

'They are, sir.'

'Who?'

'Friedman.'

'Oh! The little Jewish lawyer. A wise choice, Curtis, a commendably wise choice.' Garry sniffed and picked up the paper-knife.

*My God!* Curtis marvelled. *He's a Jew-baiter as well, this little sparrow has all the virtues.*

'Who else did you send?'

'A new recruit.'

'A new recruit? A new recruit!' Garry dropped the knife and lifted his hands in appeal.

'I happen to have worked for him before the war. I know him well, sir. He's a first-class man. I'd trust him before anyone else you could name. In fact, I was going to ask you to approve his promotion to sergeant.'

'And what is the name of this paragon?'

'Funnily enough it's the same as yours, sir. Although he tells me you're not related. His name is Courtney. Sean Courtney.'

Slowly, very slowly, the expression of Garry's face altered. It became smooth, neutral. Pale also, the lifeless, translucent paleness of a corpse's face. All life died in his eyes as well – they were looking inwards, back into the secret places of long ago. The dark places. They saw a small boy climbing a hill.

*He was climbing up through thick bush, young legs strong beneath him. Climbing in deep shade, with the smell of leaf-mould and the soft murmur of insects, sweating in the heat of a Natal summer's morning, eyes straining ahead through the dense green foliage for a glimpse of the bush buck they were hunting, the dog leaning eagerly against the leash and the same eagerness pumping in his own chest.*

*The dog barked once, and immediately the brush and stir of a big body moving ahead of them, the click of a hoof against rock, then the rush of its run.*

*The shot, a blunt burst of sound, and the buck bleating wounded as it thrashed through the grass, and Sean's voice high and unbroken: 'I got him. I got him first shot! Garry. Garry! I got him, I got him!'*

*Into the sunlight, the dog dragging him. Sean wild with excitement, running down the slope towards him with the shotgun. Sean falling, the gun flung from his hands, the roar of the second shot and the blow that knocked Garry's leg out from under him.*

*Sitting now in the grass and staring at the leg. The little white splinters of bone in the pulped flesh and the blood pumping dark and strong and thick as custard.*

*'I didn't mean it . . . Oh God, Garry, I didn't mean it. I slipped. Honest, I slipped.'*

Garry shuddered, a violent almost sensual spasm of his whole body, and the leg beneath the desk twitched in sympathy.

'Are you all right, sir?' There was an edge of concern on Tim's voice.

'I am perfectly well, thank you, Curtis.' Garry smoothed back the hair from his temples. There were deep bays of baldness there and his hairline was frayed and irregular. 'Please continue.'

'Well, I was saying – it looks like a trap. They've left those bridges because . . .'

'It is your duty to collect information, Curtis. It is the duty of the general staff to evaluate it. I think that completes your report? Good, then you may leave.'

He must have a drink now, already his hand was on the handle of the drawer.

'Oh, Curtis.' His voice croaked with the terrible dryness in his throat, but he spoke on through it. 'That promotion you spoke of is approved. Make the man a sergeant.'

'Very well, sir.'

'Of course, in the event of a frontal assault on the bridges he will act as guide for the first attack.'

'Sir?'

'You see the need for it, don't you?' Tim had never heard this wheedling tone from him before. It was almost as though he wanted Tim's approval. As though he were trying to justify his decision. 'I mean, he knows the bridges. He's been over them. He's the one who knows them, isn't he?'

'Yes, sir.'

'And after all, he's a sergeant. I mean, we should send someone with rank – we can't just send anybody.'

'I could go, sir.'

'No. No. We'll need you at the ford.'

'As you wish.'

'You won't forget, will you? You *will* send him, won't you?' Almost pleading now.

'I'll send him,' agreed Tim and stooped out of the tent. Garry jerked open the drawer and his fingernails scrabbled on the rough wood in their haste to find the flask.

# Chapter Thirteen

*To General Sir Redvers Buller, V.C.,*
*Officer Commanding,*
*British Expeditionary Army of Natal*

*At Chievely*

*December 19th 1899*

Sir,

I have the honour to report that in accordance with orders received a reconnaissance was carried out by officers and men of the Natal Corps of Guides on the night of December 18th. The results of which are set out below:

*Ford marked 'A' on attached Map:* Although the ford promises passage for a large body of men, it is difficult to locate in darkness and a night crossing is not recommended.

*Bridge marked 'B' on attached Map:* This is a road bridge of metal construction. At present it is undamaged, probably due to its sturdy construction resisting demolition by the enemy.

*Bridge marked 'C' on attached Map:* This is a railway bridge also constructed of metal, but has been demolished by the enemy.

*General:* Limited penetration of the area beyond the Tugela River by elements of the N.C.G. revealed the presence of the enemy on the hills marked 'D' and 'E'. However, no evidence of artillery or excessive force was noted.

*Courtney G., Lieutenant-Colonel*
*Officer Commanding N.C.G.,*
*In the Field.*

EXTRACT FROM THE BATTLE ORDERS OF GENERAL SIR REDVERS BULLER V.C.
MADE AND SIGNED ON THE NIGHT OF DECEMBER 19TH 1899.

. . . The force commanded by Brigadier Lyttelton will advance on and
capture the village of Colenso. Thereafter it will seize and cross the metal
bridge, and drive the enemy from the kopjes on the far bank. (See attached
Map.)'

# *Chapter Fourteen*

They lay in the grass, side by side, and the dew had soaked through the
backs of their tunics. The night was still and silent. No clouds above and the
fat stars were very bright. Ahead of them the silver smear of the Milky Way
threw the silhouette of the Tugela heights into bold relief, gave it an aspect
of brooding menace.

Saul yawned loudly, and immediately Sean was forced to do the same.
Though they had not slept that night, it was not the weariness – but the
symptom of nerves wound tight at the prospect of going in against the Boer
guns . . .

'Another hour and a half until dawn,' Saul whispered, and Sean grunted.
There was no profit in counting the hours. At forty-seven minutes past six
the sun would rise, and from behind them the British Army would move
forward across the brown grass plain.

Once more Sean rose to his knees and swept the ground before them with
his eyes, letting them move slowly along the bank of the Tugela, picking up
the loom of the steel road bridge a hundred paces ahead of them, accounting
for each bush on this bank, that they had not multiplied or moved. Then
satisfied, he sank down again.

'My God, it's cold!' He could feel Saul shivering beside him.

'It will warm up quite soon.' Sean grinned in the darkness as he answered.
The clear night sky had allowed yesterday's warmth to escape, the grass and
their clothing were wet, even the steel of the rifles was painfully cold to
touch – but Sean had long ago learned to ignore physical discomfort. He
could, when necessary, lie completely motionless while tsetse flies settled on
his neck and sank their red-hot needles into the soft skin behind his ears.
Nevertheless, it was a relief when the false dawn showed and it was time
to move.

'I'll go in now,' he whispered.

'Good luck – I'll have breakfast ready when you come back.'

This was a job for one man. A job than Sean did not relish. They had made certain that there were no enemy on this side of the river, now at the last minute when it was too late for the Boers to alter their dispositions – someone had to cross and find out in what strength they were holding the bridge. A couple of Boer Maxims sited to command the bridge at short range, or even demolition charges set ready to blow, would mean that the chances of success instead of being slim would be non-existent.

Sean slung his rifle across his back and began crawling forward through the grass. Twice he stopped to listen briefly, but there was little time – true dawn in an hour. He reached the bridge and lay in its heavy shadow, staring across at the far bank. Nothing moved. In the starlight the kopjes loomed like the backs of dark whales in the grassy sea. He waited five minutes – long enough for a restless sentry to fidget – still nothing.

'Here we go,' he whispered aloud, and suddenly he was afraid. For an instant he did not recognize the sensation, for he had experienced it only three or four times in his life, but never with so little cause. He crouched beside the steel girders of the bridge, with the weakness in his legs and his belly full of the oiliness. It was only when he caught the taste of it at the back of his throat, a taste a little like that of fish oil mixed with the effluence of something long dead, that he knew what it was.

I'm afraid. His first reaction was of surprise, which changed quickly to alarm.

This was how it happened. He knew it happened to other men. He had heard them talk of it around the camp fires, remembered the words and the pity underlying them.

'*Ja, his gunboy led him back to camp. He was shaking like a man with fever, and he was crying. I thought he was hurt. "Daniel," I said, "Daniel, what is wrong?"*

' *"It broke," he said with the tears running into his beard. "It broke there in my head, I heard it break. I threw the gun away and I ran."*

' *"Did he charge, Daniel?" I asked.*

' *"No, man. I didn't even see him, just heard him feeding close by in the catbush. Then it broke in my head and I was running."*

'*He was no coward. I had hunted with him many times, seen him kill an elephant from a charge so that it fell close enough to touch with the gun-barrel. He was good, but he had lived too close to it. Then suddenly it broke in his head. He hasn't hunted again.*'

I have accumulated fear the way an old ship collects barnacles and weed below the water-line, now it is ready to break in me also – Sean knew. Knew also that if he ran now, as the old hunter had run, he would never hunt again.

Crouching in the darkness, sweating in the cold of dawn with the iciness of his fear, Sean wanted to vomit. He was physically sick, breathing heavily through his open mouth, the warm oiliness in his belly coming close to venting itself, so weak with it that his legs began to tremble and he caught at one of the iron girders of the bridge for support.

A minute that seemed like all eternity, he stood like that. Then he began to fight it, bearing down on it, stiffening his legs and forcing them to move forward. Consciously he checked the relaxation of his sphincter muscle – that close he had come to the ultimate degradation.

He knew then that the old joke about cowards was true. And that it applied to him also.

He went up on to the bridge; picking up each foot deliberately, swinging it forward, laying it down and moving the weight of his body over it. His breathing was deliberate, each breadth taken and expelled at the command of his brain. He couldn't trust his body now to perform even the simplest task – not after it had betrayed him so monstrously.

Had they been waiting at the bridge, the Boers would have killed him that morning. Without caution he paced slowly down the centre of it, big and heavily moving in the starlight and his footsteps rang on the metal.

Under his feet the metal gave way to gravel. He was across. He kept walking, down the middle of the road, following the gentle curve towards the dark hills.

He walked on with his terror and the sound of it roared in his head like the sound of the sea. The sling of his rifle slipped from his shoulder and the weapon clattered into the road. He stood for a full minute before he could gather himself to stoop and pick it up. Then he turned and went back. Pacing slowly, counting his footsteps, measuring them out – one each second – timing them carefully to prevent himself from running. Because if he ran he knew it was finished. He too would never hunt again.

'You all right?' Saul was waiting.

'Yes.' Sean sank down beside him.

'See anything?'

'No.'

Saul was staring at him. 'Are you sure you're all right?'

Sean sighed. Once before he had been afraid. Fear had come to him in a caved-in mineshaft, later he had gone back and left his fear in the same mineshaft, and had walked away from it alone. In the same way he had hoped to leave it now beyond the river, but this time it had followed him back. With a certainty he knew that it would never leave him from now onwards. It would always be near.

I will have to tame it, he thought. I will have to break it to the halter and the curb.

'Yes, I'm all right,' he answered Saul. 'What's the time?'

'Half-past five.'

'I'll send Mbejane back now.'

Sean stood up and went to where Mbejane waited with their horses. He handed Mbejane the small square of green cloth which was the prearranged signal that neither the bridge nor the town was defended in force. The red square he replaced in his breast-pocket.

'I will come back,' Mbejane told him.

'No.' Sean shook his head. 'There is nothing for you here.'

Mbejane untied the horses. 'Stay in peace.'

'Go in peace.' Sean was thankful that Mbejane would not be there as witness, should he break under his new-found fear.

But I must not break, he decided grimly. Today will be the test. If I can last out this day, then perhaps I will have tamed it.

He went back to where Saul waited in the darkness, and together they lay and watched the dawn come on.

## Chapter Fifteen

The darkness drew back, each minute enlarging the circle of their vision. Now the upper words of the bridge stood out, a neat geometrical pattern against the dark bulk of the heights. Then he could see the patterns of dark bush against pale grass and rock.

The new light distorted distance, made the high ground seem remote and no longer hostile. A flight of egrets flew in long formation above the course of the river, high enough to catch the sun so that they were birds of bright, glowing gold in a world of shadow. And the dawn brought with it a small cold wind whose voice in the grass blended with the murmur of the river.

Then the sun hit the heights as though to bless the army of the Republic. The mist in the gullies writhed in agony at its warmth, lifted into the wind and smeared away.

The rim of the sun pushed up over the edge of the land, and the day came bright and clean with dew.

Through his glasses Sean studied the crest of the high ground. At a hundred paces there were traces of smoke as the Boer Army brewed coffee.

'You think they'll spot us?' asked Saul.

Sean shook his head without lowering his glasses. Two small bushes and the thin screen of grass they had constructed during the night hid them effectively.

'Are you sure you are all right?' Saul asked once more. From the set of his face Sean seemed to be in pain.

'Stomach gripes,' Sean grunted. Let it start soon, please let it start. The waiting is the worst.

Then the ground trembled under his chest, the faintest vibration, and Sean felt relief flood through him. 'Here come the guns,' he said, and using the cover of one of the bushes, he stood up and looked behind him.

In a single column, following each other at strictly spaced intervals, the guns were moving into action. They were coming in fast, still tiny with distance but growing as the gunners astride the lead horses of each team urged them on. Closer now so that Sean could see the whip arms rising and falling, he heard the rumble and rattle of the carriage and faintly the shouts of the outriders.

Sixteen guns, one hundred and fifty horses to drag them, and a hundred men to serve them. But in the vastness of the great plain before Colenso the column seemed small and insignificant. Sean looked beyond them and saw the foot soldiers following them, line upon line, like the poles of a fence,

thousands of them creeping forward across the plain. Sean felt the old wild
elation begin. He knew the army was centred upon the line of markers
which he and Saul had laid early the previous night, and that the two of
them would be the first across the bridge – the first of all those thousands.

But it was elation of a different quality to anything he had experienced
before. It was sharper and more poignant, seasoned by the red pepper of his
fear. So that for the first time in his life Sean learned that fear can be a
pleasurable sensation.

He watched the patterns of men and guns evolve upon the brown gaming-
table – counters thrown down at chance, to be won or irretrievably lost at
the fall of the dice of war. Knowing also that he was one of the counters,
afraid and strangely jubilant in this knowledge.

The guns were close now. He could make sense of the shooting, see the
features of the men and even recognize his own feelings in their faces.

Close, perhaps too close. Uneasily Sean glanced back at the forbidding
heights beyond the river and gauged the range. Two thousand yards perhaps,
long rifle shot. And still the guns came on.

'Jesus Christ! Are they mad?' Sean asked aloud.

'They must engage now.' Saul also saw the danger. 'They can't come
closer.'

And still the guns came on. The sound of their charge was low thunder;
dust from the dew-damp earth rose reluctantly behind them; horses with
wide mouths throwing froth as they drove against the traces.

'They're in range now. They must stop, they must!' groaned Sean.

Then at last the column splayed open, alternate guns wheeling left and
right still at full gallop. Swinging broadside to the waiting Boer rifles.

'My God! My God!' Sean mouthed the blasphemy in agony as he watched.
'They'll be massacred.'

Gunners rising in the stirrups, leaning back to check the carriages. The
Gun-Captains jumping from their mounts, letting them gallop free as they
ran to begin the unhitching and the pointing.

In this helpless moment while men swarmed over the guns, man-handling
them to train upon the heights; while the horses still reared and whinnied
in hysterical excitement; before the shells could be unloaded and stacked
beside their pieces – in that moment the Boer rifles opened together. It was
a sound that lacked violence, strangely unwarlike, muted by distance to the
popping of a hundred strings of fireworks, and at first there was no effect.
The grass was thick enough to hide the strike of the bullets, the dust too lazy
with dew to jump and mark their fall.

Then a horse was hit and fell kicking, dragging its mate on to its knees
also. Two men ran to cut it loose, but one of them never reached it. He sat
down suddenly in the grass with his head bowed. Two more horses dropped,
another reared and pawed wildly at the air with one front leg flapping
loosely where a bullet had broken the bone above the knee.

'Get out!' roared Sean. 'Pull back while there's still time,' but his voice
did not carry to the gun crews, could not carry above the shouting and the
screaming of wounded horses.

There was a new sound now which Sean could not identify, a sound like
hair on a tin roof, isolated at first then more frequent until it was a hundred

hammers clanging together in broken rhythm – and he knew it was the sound of bullets striking the metal of the guns.

He saw:

A gunner fall foward and jam the breech of the piece until he was dragged clear;

A loader drop the shell he was carrying and stumble on with his legs folding until he subsided and lay still;

One of the horses break loose and gallop away across the plain dragging a tangle of torn traces behind it;

A covey of wild pheasant rise together out of the grass near the batteries and curve away along the river before dropping on stiff wings back into cover;

And behind the guns the infantry in neat lines advancing placidly towards the huddle of deserted cottages that was Colenso.

Then, with a crash that made the earth jump, and with sixteen long spurts of blue smoke, the guns came into action.

Sean focused his glasses on the ridge in time to see the first shells burst along the crest. The evil blossoms of greenish-yellow lyddite fumes bloomed quickly in the sunlight, then drifted oily-thick on the wind.

Again the guns crashed, and again – each salvo more ragged than the last until it became a continuous stuttering, hammering roar. Until the stark outline of the ridge was blurred and indefinite in the dust and lyddite fumes. There was smoke also, a fine greyish mist of it banked along the heights – the smoke of thousands of rifles.

Quickly Sean set the rear sight of his Lee-Metford at a thousand yards, wriggled forward on his elbows, hunched down over his rifle and began shooting blindly into the smoke on the heights. Beside him Saul was firing also.

Twice Sean emptied his magazine before looking back at the guns. The tempo of their fire had slackened. Most of the horses were down in the grass. Dead men were draped across the gun carriages, others badly wounded crouched for cover behind the mountings, and where six men had served each piece before, now four or only three carried shell and loaded and fired.

'The fools, the bloody fools,' Sean whispered, and began to shoot again, concentrating his whole attention on the routine of jerking the bolt back, sliding it forward in the same motion, sighting up into the mist of gun smoke, and firing. He did not count the shots and each time the weapon clicked empty he groped for another clip from his bandolier and re-loaded. He was starting to sweat now, could feel it trickling down his armpits, his ears buzzed from the concussion of the rifle and his shoulder was beginning to throb.

Gradually a sense of unreality induced by the clamour of the guns and the smell of burnt powder came over him. It seemed that all he would ever do was lie and shoot at nothing, shoot at smoke. Then reality faded further so that all of existence was the vee and dot of a rifle sight, standing solid in mist. And the mist had no shape. In his ears was the vast buzzing silence that drowned all the other sounds of battle. He was alone and tranquil, heavy and dulled by the hypnotic drift of smoke and the repetitive act of loading and firing.

Abruptly the mood was broken. Over them passed a rustle like giant
wings, then a crack as though Satan had slammed the door of hell. Startled
he looked up and saw a ball of shimmering white smoke standing in the air
above the guns, spinning and spreading, growing in the sky like a flower.

'What the . . .'

'Shrapnel,' grunted Saul. 'Now they're finished.'

Then crack and crack again as the Boer Nordenfeldts planted their cotton
flowers of smoke above the plain, flailing the guns and the men who still
worked them with a buzzing, hissing storm of steel.

Then there were voices. Confused and dazed by the gunfire, it took Sean
a minute to place them. He had forgotten the infantry.

'Close up there.'

'Close up on the right. Keep the line!'

'Don't run. Steady, men. Don't run.'

Long lines of men, lines that bulged and lagged and straightened again
at the urging of their officers. Evenly spaced, plodding quietly with their
rifles held across their chests, they passed the guns. Behind them they left
khaki bundles lying on the plain, some of the bundles lay still but others
writhed and screamed. As the gaps appeared in the lines they were quickly
filled at the chant of 'Close up. Close up there on the flank.'

'They are heading for the railway bridge.' Sean felt the first premonition
of disaster. 'Don't they know that it's been destroyed?'

'We'll have to stop them.' Saul scrambled to his feet beside Sean.

'Why didn't the fools follow our markers?' Angrily Sean shouted the
question that had no answer. He did it to gain time, to postpone the moment
when he must leave the flimsy cover of the grass shelter and go out into the
open where the shrapnel and the Mausers swept the ground. Sean's fear
came back on him strongly. He didn't want to go out there.

'Come on, Sean. We must stop them.' And Saul started to run. He looked
like a skinny little monkey, capering out towards the advancing waves of
foot soldiers. Sean sucked in his breath and held it a moment before he
followed.

Twenty yards ahead of the leading rank of infantry, carrying a naked
sword in one hand and stepping out briskly on long legs, came an officer.

'Hey, you!' Sean shouted at him, waving his hat to catch his attention. He
succeeded. The officer fixed him with bright blue eyes like a pair of bayonets
and the waxed points of his grey moustache twitched. He strode on towards
Sean and Paul.

'You're heading for the wrong bridge,' Sean yelled at him, his voice high-
pitched with agitation. 'They've blown the rail bridge, you'll never get across
there.'

The officer reached them and checked his stride.

'And who the hell are you, if it's not a rude question?'

'We're the ground scouts . . .' Sean started, then leapt in the air as a
Mauser bullet flicked into the ground between his legs. 'And put that bloody
sword away – you'll have every Boer on the Tugela competing for you.'

The officer, a colonel by the crowns on his shoulders, frowned at Sean.

'The correct form of address, Sergeant . . .'

'The hell with that!' Sean roared at him. 'Swing your advance on to the road bridge.' He pointed with agitation at the metal superstructure of the bridge that showed on the left through the thorn trees. 'If you continue as you're going they'll cut you to pieces.'

A moment longer the Colonel fixed Sean with his bayonet eyes, then he lifted a silver whistle to his lips and blew a piercing blast.

'Take cover,' he shouted. 'Take cover!'

And immediately the first rank dropped into the grass. Behind them the other ranks lost their rigidity, as men hesitated.

'Get into the town,' a voice shouted. 'Take cover in the buildings.' And they broke and ran, a thousand men, jostling each other, racing for the security of the cottages of Colenso. Pouring into the single street, diving into doorways and windows. Within thirty seconds they had all gone to ground.

'Now, what's this all about?' demanded the Colonel, turning back to Sean. Impatiently Sean repeated himself, standing out in the open and uncomfortably aware that for absence of other targets the Boers were beginning to take a very active interest in them.

'Are you sure?'

'Dammit! Of course, I'm sure. The bridge is destroyed and they have torn up all the barbed wire fences and thrown them into the river. You'll never get across there.'

'Come along.' The Colonel set off towards the nearest cottage and Sean walked beside him. Afterwards he was never certain how he had managed to cover that hundred yards without running.

'For God's sake, put that sword away,' he growled at the Colonel as they walked with the flit, spang, flit, spang of bullets around them.

'Nervous, Sergeant?' And for the first time the Colonel grinned.

'You're damn right, I am.'

'So am I. But it would never do to let the men see that, would it?' He steadied the scabbard on his hips and ran the sword back into it. 'What's your name, Sergeant?'

'Sean Courtney, Natal Corps of Guides. What's yours?' Sean ducked instinctively as a bullet cracked past his head, and the Colonel smiled again at the familiarity.

'Acheson. John Acheson. 2nd Battalion, Scots Fusiliers.'

And they reached the cottage. No longer able to restrain himself, Sean dived thankfully through the kitchen door and found Saul already there. He handed Sean a cheroot and held a match for him.

'These crazy Souties!' he observed. 'And you're as bad as he is – strolling around in the middle of a battle.'

'Right, Courtney.' Acheson followed him into the kitchen. 'Let's go over the situation.'

He listened quietly while Sean explained in detail. He had to shout to lift his voice above the whistle and rack of the Boer artillery and the roar of a thousand Lee-Metford rifles as they replied from the windows and doorways of the village. Around them the kitchen was being used as a dressing-station and the moan and whimper of wounded men added to the hubbub of battle.

When Sean had finished Acheson turned away and strode to the window. He looked out across the railway tracks, to where the guns stood. They were drawn up in precise parade-ground formation. But now they were silent.

Dribbling back towards the shelter of a deep donga – or gully – in the rear, the surviving gunners dragged their wounded with them.

'The poor bastards,' Sean whispered, as he saw one of the retreating gunners killed, shot in the head so that his helmet was thrown spinning upwards in a brief pink cloud of blood.

The sight seemed to rouse Acheson also.

'All right,' he said. 'We'll advance on the road bridge. Come on, Courtney.'

Behind him someone cried out, and Sean heard him fall. But he did not look round. He watched the bridge ahead of him. Although his legs moved mechanically under him it seemed to come no nearer. The thorn trees were thicker here beside the river and they gave a little cover from the merciless marksmen on the far bank. Yet men were falling steadily, and the shrapnel raged and cracked above them.

'Let's get across. Get the best seats on the other side,' Saul shouted beside him.

'Come on, then,' agreed Sean and they ran together. They were first on to the bridge, with Acheson just behind them. Bullets left bright scars on the grey painted metal, and then suddenly, miraculously, they were across. They had crossed the Tugela.

A drainage ditch beside the road and they dived into it, both of them panting. Sean looked back. Over the bridge poured a mass of khaki, all semblance of order gone as they crowded into the bottleneck and the fire from the Boers churned into them.

Once across, the leaders fanned out along the river, crouching below the dip of the bank, while behind them the slaughter on the bridge continued. A struggling mass of cursing, running, angry, frightened and dying men.

'It's a bloody abattoir.' Sean was appalled as he watched it. Dead and wounded men were falling over the low guard rail, splashing into the brown waters of the Tugela to sink or strike out clumsily for the banks. But a steady stream of men was coming across and going to ground in the two-deep drainage ditches, and beneath the angle of the river bank.

It was clear to Sean that the attack was losing its impetus. As the men jumped down into the ditches he saw in their faces and in the way they flattened themselves into shelter that they had lost all stomach for the attack. The ordeal of the bridge had destroyed the discipline that had held their steady advance into those neatly controlled ranks; Officers and men were inextricably mixed into a tired and badly frightened rabble. There was no contact between the different groups in the drainage trenches and those lying in the lee of the river banks – and already there was little cover for the men who were still coming across. The fire from the Boer positions never faltered, and now the bridge was blocked with the bodies of the fallen, so that each new wave had to climb over them, stepping on dead and wounded alike, while the storm of Boer rifle-fire lashed them like wind-driven rain.

Rivulets of fresh bright blood dribbled down the supports of the bridge in ghastly contrast to the grey paint, and the surface of the river was stained by a chocolate-brown cloud of it spreading slowly downstream. Here and there a desperate rallying voice was lifted in the hubbub of incoherent shouts and groans.

'Here the 21st. Form on me the 21st.'

'Independent fire. On the heights. Ten rounds rapid.'

'Stretcher-bearer!'

'Bill. Where are you, Bill?'

'Jesus Christ! Jesus sobbing Christ!'

'Up, you men! Get up!'

'Come on the 21st. Fix bayonets.'

Some of them were head and shoulders out of the ditch returning the Boer fire, a few were drinking from their water-bottles already. A sergeant struggled with a jammed rifle and swore softly without looking up, while beside him a man sat with his back against the wall of the ditch, his legs sprawled open, and watched while the blood pumped from the wound in his belly.

Sean stood and felt the wind of a bullet slap against his cheek, while low in his stomach the slimy reptile of fear coiled itself tighter. Then he scrambled up the side of the ditch.

'Come on!' he roared and started running towards the hills. It was open here, like a meadow, and ahead of him an old barbed-wire fence sagged on rotten poles. He reached it, lifted his foot and kicked with his heel. The fence pole snapped level with the ground, the wire collapsed. He jumped over it.

'They're not coming,' Saul shouted beside him, and Sean stopped. The two of them were alone in the middle of the field – and the Boer rifles were seeking them eagerly.

'Run, Saul!' Sean shouted and snatched off his hat. 'Come on, you bastards.' He waved at the men behind him.

A bullet missed him so narrowly that he staggered in the wind of its passage.

'This way! Follow us! Come on!' Saul had not left him. He was dancing with excitement, and flapping his arms.

'Come back.' Acheson's voice floated across to them. He stood in the drainage ditch, showing clear from the waist up. 'Come back, Courtney!'

The attack was finished. Sean knew it in that instant, and saw the wisdom of Acheson's decision. Further advance over the open meadowland below the heights was suicide. The resolve that had carried him this far collapsed, and his terror snapped the leash he had held upon it. He ran back blindly, sobbing, leaning forward, his elbows pumping in time to his fear-driven feet.

Then suddenly Saul was hit beside him. It took him in the head, threw him forward, his rifle spinning from his hands, squawking hoarsely with pain and surprise as he went down skidding on his belly. And Sean ran on.

'Sean!' Saul's voice left behind him.

'Sean!' A cry of dreadful need, and Sean closed his mind against it and ran on towards the safety of the ditch.

'Sean. Please!' and he checked and stood uncertain with the Mausers barking above and the bullets clipping the grass around him.

*Leave him*, shrieked Sean's terror. *Leave him. Run! Run!*

Saul crawled towards him, blood on his face and his eyes fastened on Sean's face.

'Sean!'

*Leave him. Leave him.*

But there was hope in that pitiful blood-smeared face, and the fingers of Saul's hands clawed among the coarse grass roots as he dragged himself forward.

It was beyond all reason. But Sean went back to him.

Beneath the spurs of his terror Sean found the strength to lift him and run with him.

Hating him as he had never hated before, Sean blundered towards the drainage ditch carrying Saul. The acceleration of his brain slowed down the passage of time so that he seemed to run for ever.

'Damn you!' he mouthed at Sean, hating him.

'Damn you to hell!' The words came easily from his mouth, an inarticulate expression of his terror.

Then the ground gave way beneath his feet and he fell. Together they dropped into the drainage ditch and Sean rolled away from him. He lay on his stomach and pressed his face into the earth and shook as a man shakes in high fever.

Slowly he came back from that far place where fear had driven him, and he lifted his head.

Saul sat against the bank of the ditch. His face was streaked with a mixture of blood and dirt.

'How are we doing?' Sean croaked and Saul looked at him dully. It was bright and very hot here in the sun. Sean unscrewed the stopper of his water-bottle and held it to Saul's lips. Saul swallowed painfully and water spilled from the corner of his mouth down his chin and on to his tunic.

Then Sean drank and finished panting with pleasure.

'Let's have a look at your head.'

He lifted Saul's hat from his head, and the blood that had accumulated around the sweat band poured in a fresh flood down Saul's neck. Parting the sodden black hair Sean found the groove in the flesh of his scalp.

'Grazed you,' he grunted and groped for the field dressing in the pocket of Saul's tunic. While he bound an untidy turban round Saul's head he noticed that a strange stillness had fallen on the field, a stillness accentuated rather than broken by the murmur of voices from the men around him and the occasional report of a rifle from the heights above.

The battle was over. At least we got across the river, he thought bitterly. The only problem that now remains is getting back again.

'How's that feel?' He had wet his handkerchief and wiped some of the blood and dust from Saul's face.

'Thank you, Sean.' Suddenly Sean realized that Saul's eyes were full of tears and it embarrassed him. He looked away from them.

'Thank you for . . . for coming back to get me.'

'Forget it.'

'I'll never forget it. Never as long as I live.'

'You'd have done the same.'

'No, I don't think so. I wouldn't have been able to. I was so scared, so afraid, Sean. You'd never know. You'll never know what it's like to be that afraid.'

'Forget it, Saul. Leave it alone.'

'I've got to tell you. I owe it to you – from now on I owe you . . . If you hadn't come back I'd be . . . I'd still be out there. I owe you.'

'Shut up, damn you!' He saw that Saul's eyes were different, the pupils had shrunk to tiny black specks and he was shaking his head in a meaningless idiotic fashion. The bullet had concussed him. But this could not prevent Sean's anger. 'Shut up,' he snarled. 'You think I don't know about fear. I was so scared out there – I hated you. Do you hear that? I hated you!'

And then Sean's voice softened. He had to explain to Saul and himself. He had to tell him about it, to justify it and place it securely in the scheme of things.

Suddenly he felt very old and wise. In his hands he held the key to the whole mystery of life. It was all so clear, for the first time he understood and he could explain it.

They sat close together in the sun, isolated from the men around them, and Sean's voice sank to an urgent whisper as he tried to make Saul understand, tried to pass on to him this knowledge that embraced all truth.

Beside them lay a corporal of the Fusiliers. He lay on his back, dead, and the flies swarmed over his eyes and laid their eggs. They looked like tiny grains of rice clustered in the lashes around his dead open eyes.

Saul leaned heavily against Sean's shoulder, now and then he shook his head in confusion as he listened to Sean. Listened to Sean's voice tripping and stumbling then starting to hurry as his ideas broke up and crumpled, heard the desperation in it as Sean strove to retain just a few grains of all that knowledge which had been his a few moments before. Heard it peter out into silence and sorrow as he found that it was gone.

'I don't know,' Sean admitted at last.

Then Saul spoke, his voice was dull and his eyes would not focus properly as he peered at Sean from beneath the blood-soiled turban of bandages.

'Ruth,' he said, 'You speak like Ruth does. Sometimes in the night when she cannot sleep she tries to tell me. Almost I understand, almost she finds it and then she stops. "I don't know," she says at last. "I just don't know." '

Sean jerked away from him, and stared into his face. 'Ruth?' he asked quietly.

'Ruth – my wife. You'd like her, Sean – she'd like you. So brave – she came to me through the Boer lines. All the way from Pretoria – riding alone. She came to me. I couldn't believe it. All that way. She just walked into camp one day and said, "Hello, Saul. I'm here!" just like that! You'll like her when you meet her, Sean. She's so beautiful, so serene . . .'

In October when the big winds blow they come for the first time on a still day. It has been hot and dry for perhaps a month, then you hear them from far away, roaring softly. The roar mounts quickly, the dust races brown on the wind and the trees lean away from it, threshing and churning their branches. You see it coming but all your preparations are nothing when it hits. The vast roaring and the dust envelope you and you are numbed and blinded by the violence of it.

In the same way Sean saw it coming, he recognized it as the murderous rage which before had nearly killed a man, but still he could not prepare himself. And then it was upon him and the roaring filled his head and narrowed his vision so that all he could see was the face of Saul Friedman. The face was in profile for Saul was staring back across the plain of Colenso towards the English lines.

Sean lifted the dead corporal's rifle and laid it across his lap. With his thumb he slipped off the safety-catch, but Saul did not notice the movement.

'She's in Pietermaritzburg, I had a letter from her last week,' he murmured, and Sean shifted the rifle in his lap so that the muzzle aimed into the side of Saul's chest below the armpit.

'I sent her down to Pietermaritzburg. She's staying with her uncle there.' Saul lifted his hand and touched his head. Sean curled his finger on the trigger. 'I wish you could meet her, Sean. She'd like you.' Now he looked into Sean's face, and there was such pathetic trust in his eyes. 'When I write I am going to tell her about today – about what you did.'

Sean took up the slack in the trigger until he could feel the final resistance.

'We both owe you—' Saul stopped and smiled shyly. 'I just want you to know that I'll never forget it.'

Kill him, roared Sean's head. Kill him now – kill him quickly. Don't let him talk.

It was the first conscious command his instinct had issued.

*Now! Do it now!* But his trigger-finger relaxed.

This is all that stands between you and Ruth. Do it, do it now. The roaring in his head abated. The big wind had passed by and he could hear it receding. He lifted the rifle and slowly pushed the safety-catch across.

In the stillness after the wind he knew suddenly that from now on Saul Friedman was his special charge. Because he had come so close to taking it from him, Saul's life had become a debt of honour.

He laid the rifle aside and closed his eyes wearily.

'We'd better think about getting out of here,' he said quietly. 'Otherwise I might never get around to meeting this beauty of yours.'

# Chapter Sixteen

'Hart has got himself into a mess out there!' General Sir Redvers Buller's voice matched the pompous jut of his belly and he leaned back against the weight of the telescope he held to his eye. 'What do you think, Courtney?'

'Well, he certainly hasn't reached the drift, sir. It looks to me as though he's been pinned down in the loop of the river,' Garry agreed.

'Damn the man! My orders were clear,' growled Buller. 'What can you make of the guns – can you see anything there?'

Every telescope in the party of officers swivelled back to the centre, to where the corrugated iron roofs of Colenso showed above the thorn trees, dimly through the dust and the smoke.

'I can't . . . Garry started, then jumped uncontrollably as the naval 4·7 bellowed from its emplacement beside them. Every time that morning it had fired, Garry had jumped. If only I knew when it was going to, he thought and jumped again as it bellowed.

'They are not being served,' one of the other staff officers interposed and Garry envied him his composure and his calmness of voice. His own hands were trembling so that he must grip hard with both hands to keep his binoculars focused on the town. Each time the naval gun fired the dust of its recoil drifted over them, also the sun was fierce and he was thirsty. He thought of the flask in his saddle-bags and the next bellow of the gun caught him completely off guard. This time both his feet left the ground.

'. . . Do you agree, Courtney?' Buller's voice, he had not heard the beginning of the question.

'I do indeed, sir.'

'Good.' The General turned to his A.D.C. 'Send a rider to Hart. Tell him to pull out of there before he gets badly mauled. Quick as you can, Clery.'

At that moment Garry made a remarkable discovery. Behind the inscrutable mask of his face with its magnificent silver moustache, behind the bulging expressionless eyes – General Sir Redvers Buller was every bit as agitated and uncertain as was Garry Courtney. His continual appeals to Garry for support confirmed this. Of course, Garry did not consider that another reason why Buller addressed his appeals to him, rather than the regular officers of his staff, was because this was the one quarter from which Buller could rely on unquestioning support.

'That takes care of the left flank.' Buller was clearly relieved at his decision as he searched out towards the right, fixing the low round bulk of Hlangwane Kopje in the field of his telescope. 'Dundonald seems to be keeping his end up.' Earlier, there had been desultory rifle and pompom fire from the right flank. Now it was silent.

'But the centre . . .' As though he had been delaying the moment, Buller at last turned his attention on the holocaust of dust and flame and shrapnel that enveloped Colenso.

'Come along.' He snapped his telescope closed. 'We'd better have a closer look at what they've accomplished there.' And he led his staff back to the horses. Careful that no one should usurp his place at the General's right hand, Garry limped along beside him.

At the headquarters of Lyttelton's Brigade, established in a deep donga half a mile before the first scattered buildings of the town, it took Buller half a minute to find out what had been accomplished. It appalled him.

'We hold the town, sir. And three companies have advanced to the road bridge and seized it. But we cannot hope to hold it. I have sent a runner ordering them to withdraw on the town.'

'But why aren't the guns firing? What's happened to Colonel Long?'

'The guns have been silenced. Long is badly wounded.'

While Buller sat his horse, slowly absorbing this, a sergeant of the Transvaal Staats Artillerie jerked the lanyard of his quick-firing Nordenfeldt and fired the shell which changed a British reverse into a resounding defeat that would echo around the world.

From out of the broken and rocky complex of hills on the north bank the shell arched upwards; over the river with its surface churned to brown by shrapnel and short shell and blood; high over the deserted guns manned only by corpses; shrieking over the heads of the surviving gunners as they crouched in the rear with their wounded, forcing them to duck as they had ducked a thousand times before; plunging in its descent over the town of Colenso where weary men waited; down across thorn tree and mimosa and brown grass veld littered with dead men; falling at last in a tall jump of dust and smoke in the midst of General Buller's staff.

Beneath him Garry's horse dropped, killed instantly, pinning his leg so that had it been flesh and bone, not carved oak, it would have been crushed. He felt the blood soaking through his tunic and splattered in his face and mouth.

'I've been hit. Help me, God help me, I'm wounded.' And he writhed and struggled in the grass, wiping the blood on his face.

Rough hands freed his leg and dragged him clear of his horse.

'Not your blood. You're all right. Not your blood, it's his.'

On his hands and knees Garry stared in horror at the Surgeon-Major who had stood beside him and who had shielded him from the blast. Shrapnel had cut his head away, and the blood still spouted from his neck as though it were a severed hose.

Around him men fought their panic-stricken horses as they reared and whinnied. Buller was doubled up in the saddle, clutching the side of his chest.

'Sir, sir, Are you all right?' An A.D.C. had the reins and was bringing Buller's horse under control. Two officers ran to Buller and helped him down. He stood between them, his face contorted with pain, and and his voice when he spoke was shaky, but hoarse.

'Disengage, Lyttelton! Disengage on your whole front!'

'Sir,' protested the Brigadier. 'We hold the town. Let me cover the guns until nightfall when we can retrieve them at our . . .'

'Damn you, Lyttelton. You heard me. Pull your brigade back immediately. The attack has failed.' Buller's breathing wheezed in his throat and he still clutched the side of his chest with both hands.

'To withdraw now will mean accepting heavier losses than we have suffered already. The enemy artillery is accurately ranged . . .'

'Pull them out, do you hear me!' Buller's voice rose to a shout.

'The guns . . .' Lyttelton tried again, but Buller had already turned to his A.D.C.

'Send riders to Lord Dundonald's Brigade. He must retire immediately. I give him no latitude of discretion, he is to disengage his force at once and withdraw. Tell him . . . tell him the attack has failed on left and centre, tell him the guns are lost and he is in danger of being surrounded. Go. Ride fast.'

There was a murmur among them, horrified as they listened to these orders. Miserably every eye turned to Lyttelton, silently they pleaded with him, for he was the senior officer present.

'General Buller.' He spoke softly, but with an urgency that caught even Buller's shell-shocked attention. 'At least, let me try to recover the guns. We cannot abandon them. Let me call for volunteers. . . .'

'I'll go, sir. Please let me try.' A young subaltern elbowed Garry aside in his eagerness. Garry knew who he was, all of them did, for apart from being one of the most promising and popular youngsters in Buller's command – he was also the only son of the legendary Lord Roberts.

Assisted by his A.D.C., Buller moved to the shade of a mimosa tree and sank down heavily with his back against the rough bark of the trunk. He looked up at young Roberts, dully, without apparent interest.

'All right, Bobbie, Lyttelton will give you men. Off you go then.' He pronounced the sentence of death upon him, and Roberts laughed excitedly, gaily, and ran to his horse.

'I think we are all in need of refreshment. Will you join me in a sandwich and a glass of champagne, gentlemen?' Buller nodded to his A.D.C., who hurried to bring food and drink from his saddle-bags. A stray shell burst twenty yards away, scattering clods of earth over them. Stolidly Buller brushed a piece of dry grass from his whiskers and selected a smoked salmon sandwich.

## Chapter Seventeen

Sean crawled down the drainage ditch towards the bank of the river. A shell burst on the edge of the ditch and scattered clods of earth over his back. He paused to brush a tangle of grass roots out of his whiskers and then crawled on to where Colonel Acheson squatted on his haunched in earnest conversation with a captain of the Fusiliers.

'Hey, Colonel Acheson. I doubt you'll need me again, will you?' The Captain looked shocked at Sean's term of address, but Acheson grinned briefly.'

'A runner just got through. We have been ordered to withdraw.'

'What a pity!' Sean grunted sarcastically. 'Just when we were knocking the daylights out of old brother Boer,' and all three of them ducked as a machine-gun hammered lumps of dirt out of the bank above their heads. Then Sean took up from where he had been interrupted. 'Well, in that case – I'll be leaving you.'

'Where are you going?' the Captain demanded suspiciously.

'Not across that bridge.' Sean removed the stub of his cheroot from his mouth and pointed with it at the grey structure with its gruesome streaks of new paint. 'I've got a wounded man with me. He'll never make it. Have you got a match?'

Automatically the Captain produced a box of wax matches from his breast-pocket. 'Thanks. I'm going to swim him downstream and find a better place to cross.' Sean re-lit his cheroot, blew a cloud of smoke and returned the Captain's matches.

'A pleasure meeting you, Colonel Acheson.'

'You have permission to fall out, Courtney.' A second longer they looked into each other's eyes, and Sean experienced a powerful desire to shake this man's hand but instead he started crawling back along the ditch.

'Courtney!' Sean paused and glanced over his shoulder. 'What's the name of the other Guide?'

'Friedman. Saul Friedman.'

Acheson scribbled briefly in his notebook, then returned it to his pocket. 'You'll hear more about today – good luck.'

'And to you, sir.'

From a tree that hung out over the brown water of the Tugela, Sean hacked a bushy green branch with his bayonet.

'Come on,' and Saul slid down the greasy clay of the bank, waist-deep into the river beside Sean.

'Leave your rifle.' Obediently Saul dropped it into the river.

'What's the bush for?'

'To cover our heads.'

'Why are we waiting?'

'For Acheson to create a diversion when he tries to get back across the bridge.'

At that moment a whistle shrilled on the bank above them. Immediately a fierce covering fire blared out and a party of khaki-clad figures stampeded out on to the bridge.

'Now,' grunted Sean. They sank together into the blood-warm water with only their heads, wreathed in leaves, above the surface. Sean pushed out gently and the current caught them. Neither of them looked back at the shrieking carnage on the bridge as they drifted away.

Twenty minutes later and a half-mile downstream, Sean edged across the current towards the remains of the railway bridge that hung like a broken drawbridge into the river. It offered a perfect access to the south and the embankment of the railway would cover them in their retreat across the plain.

Sean's feet touched mud bottom, then they were under the sagging bridge like chickens under the wing of a hen. He let the branch float away and dragged Saul to the bank between the metal girders.

'Five minutes' rest,' he told him and squatted beside him to rewind the bandage that had come down over Saul's ears. Muddy water streamed from sodden uniforms, and Sean mourned the cheroots in his tunic pocket.

There was another drainage ditch running beside the high gravel embankment of the railway. Along it, walking in a crouch, Sean prodded Saul ahead of him, yelling at him every time he attempted to straighten up and relieve his aching back. Once a sniper on the kopjes behind them thumped a bullet into the gravel near Sean's head, and Sean swore wearily and almost touched his knees with his nose. But Saul did not notice it. With his legs sloppy under him he staggered along in front of Sean, until finally he fell and lay in a sprawling, untidy heap in the bottom of the ditch.

Sean kicked him.

'Get up, damn you!'

'No, Ruth. Don't wake me up yet, It's Sunday. I don't have to work today.' Speaking quite clearly in a reasonable persuasive tone Saul looked up at Sean, but his eyes were matt and the pupils shrunken to black points.

'Get up. Get up!' The use of Ruth's name inflamed Sean. He caught Saul's shoulder and shook him. Saul's head jerked crazily and fresh blood seeped through his bandage. Instantly contrite, Sean laid him back gently.

'Saul, please. You must try. Just a little farther.'

'Glossless,' whispered Saul. 'There is no gloss on it. I don't want it.' And he closed his eyes, his lips bulged open and his breath snored through them in tiny bubbles of spittle.

A suffocating despair dropped down over Sean as he studied Saul's face. The eyes had receded into dark plum-coloured cavities, leaving the skin stretched tight across his cheeks and across the gaunt bony nose.

Not because I nearly killed him, not because I owe it to him. But because – but because? How can you define your feelings for another man. All you can say is – because he is my friend. Then, because he is my friend I cannot leave him here.

Sinking down beside him, Sean lifted his slack body into a sitting position, draped one of Saul's arms around his shoulder and stood up. Saul hung beside him, his head lolled forward on his chest, and Sean looked ahead. He could see the survivors from the bridge struggling back through the village, dragging their wounded with them.

Across the whole breadth of the plain, singly and in twos and threes, harried by shrapnel, beaten, broken, Buller's mighty army was in retreat. And there, not a hundred yards from where Sean crouched in the railway ditch, drawn up neatly in the grass, deserted, forlorn, stood the field guns.

Quickly Sean averted his eyes from them and began plodding away from the river. Over his shoulder he held Saul's wrist, his free arm was wrapped around Saul's waist.

Then slowly he was aware that the Boer fire was crescendoing once more. Shell that had fallen haphazard among the retreating men began to concentrate on an area directly ahead of Sean. Behind him the rifle-fire that had popped spasmodically on the heights now swelled into a fierce, sustained crackle like a bushfire in green forest.

Leaning against the side of the ditch Sean peered ahead through the mimosa trees and the storm of dust and bursting shell. He saw horses, two teams in harness, men with them racing in through the thorn trees, lifting pale dust in a cloud to mingle with the dust of the shells. Far ahead of them, brandishing his cane, leading them in towards the abandoned guns, galloped a figure on a big shiny bay.

'He's laughing.' In wonder, Sean watched the leading rider disappear behind a column of dust and high explosive, only to emerge again as he swerved his mount like a polo player. His mouth was open and Sean saw the glint of white teeth. 'The fool is laughing his head off!'

And suddenly Sean was cheering wildly.

'*Ride, man, Ride!*' he shouted and his voice was lost in the shriek and crash of the bombardment.

'They've come to fetch the guns,' howled Sean. 'Saul, they've come for the guns.' Without knowing how he had done it, mad with the excitement of it, Sean found himself out of the ditch, running with new strength, running with Saul's unconscious weight slung over his shoulder, running through the grass towards the guns.

By the time he reached the battery the first team was already there. The men were down struggling to back the horses up to the trail of the Number One gun. Sean slid the inert body from his shoulder and dropped it in the grass. Two of them were trying to lift the trail of the field gun, but this task required four men.

'Get out of the way!' Sean shouted at them and straddled the long wedge-shaped trail of steel. He locked his hands into the grips and heaved upwards, lifting it clear and high.

'Get the carriage.' Quickly they rolled the detachable axle and wheels in under the trail and locked them into position. Sean stepped back panting.

'Well done!' The younger officer leaned forward in his saddle as he shouted at Sean. 'Get up on the carriage.'

But Sean turned and ran to Saul, he picked him up and stumbled with him to the carriage.

'Grab him!' he grunted at the two soldiers who were already aboard. Between them they dragged Saul up on to the carriage seat.

'No room for you, cock. Why don't you take Taffy's place on the right-hand wheeler?' one of them shouted down, and Sean saw he was correct. The drivers were mounting up, but one saddle was empty.

'Look after him,' he told the man who held Saul.

'Don't worry, I've got him,' the gunner assured him, and then urgently, 'You'd best grab a seat – we're pulling out.'

'Look after him,' Sean repeated and started forward.

In that moment the luck which had protected him all that morning ran out. A shell burst beside him. He felt no pain but his right leg gave under him and he went down on his knees.

He tries to stand but his body would not obey.

'Forward!' shouted the subaltern, and the gun carriage trundled away, gathering speed, beginning to jolt and bounce as the drivers lashed the horses. Sean saw the gunner who held Saul staring back at him from the carriage, his face was contorted with helplessness.

'Look after him!' Sean shouted. 'Promise me you'll look after him.'

The gunner opened his mouth to reply, but another shell burst between them, throwing up a curtain of dust that hid the carriage. This time Sean felt the shrapnel tear into his flesh. It stung like the cut of a razor and he sagged sideways. As he went down he saw that the subaltern had been hit as well. Saw him throw up his arms and fall backwards over the rump of his horse, rolling from the saddle, hitting the ground with his shoulder, one foot caught in the stirrup so that he dragged over the rough ground until the stirrup leather snapped and left him lying. His horse galloped away in pursuit of the careering gun carriage.

Sean dragged himself after it. 'Look after him,' he shouted. 'For God's sake, look after Saul.' But nobody heard that shout for they were gone away amongst the trees, gone away in the dust with the shellfire escorting them like a troop of brown demons.

Still Sean crawled after them, using one hand to reach ahead and claw into the earth and inch his whole body belly down through the grass. His other arm dragged at his side, and he could feel his right leg slithering after him, until it caught and tethered him. He struggled against it, but his toe had hooked in a tuft of coarse grass and he could not free it. He wriggled on to his side and doubled up with his broken arm beneath him to look back at his leg.

There was much blood, a wet, slippery drag-mark of it across the flattened grass, and still it welled up out of his body. But there was no pain, only a dizziness and a weariness in his head.

His leg twisted at a ridiculous angle from his trunk, and the spur on his boot stood up jauntily. He wanted to laugh at the leg, but somehow the effort was too great and he closed his eyes against the glare of the sun.

Near him he heard somebody groaning and for a while he thought it must be Saul. Then he remembered that Saul was safe, and it was the young subaltern. With his eyes closed Sean lay and listened to him die. It was an ugly sound.

# Chapter Eighteen

Battle-General Jan Paulus Leroux stood upon the heights above the Tugela and removed his Terai hat. His head was bald with a fringe of ginger hair above the ears and thick around the back. The skin of his pate was smooth and creamy white where the hat had protected it from the sun, but his face had been weathered and sculptured by the elements until it looked like a cliff of red-stone.

'Bring my pony, Hennie.' He spoke to the lad who stood beside him.

'*Ja*, Oom Paul.' And he hurried away down the reverse slope to the pony laager.

From the firing trench at Jan Paulus's feet one of his burghers looked up at him.

'God has heard our prayers, Oom Paul. He has given us a great victory.'

Jan Paulus nodded heavily, and his voice as he replied was low and humble, without any trace of jubilation.

'*Ja*, Fredevik. In God's name, a great victory.'

But not as great as I had planned it, he thought.

Out of cannon shot, almost out of range of the naked eye, the last tattered remnants of the British were dwindling into the brown distance.

If only they could have waited, he thought with bitterness. So clearly I explained it to them, and they did not heed me.

His whole strategy had revolved upon the bridge. If only his burghers on the kopje below the heights had held their fire and let them cross. Then God would have delivered the enemy to them in thousands instead of hundreds. Caught in the amphitheatre of the heights with the river at their backs none of them would have escaped when his artillery destroyed the bridge behind them. Sadly he looked down upon the trap he had laid with such infinite care. From above he could see the trenches, each of them, masked and cunningly overlapped so that an unbearable fire could sweep the grassy bowl into which he had hoped to lure the British centre. The trap that would never be sprung, for he knew they would not come again.

Hennie climbed back to him, leading his pony, and Jan Paulus mounted quickly.

'Come, let us go down.'

At forty-two years of age, Jan Paulus Leroux was very young for the command he held. There had been opposition in Pretoria to his appointment when old Joubert retired, but President Kruger had ridden rough-shod over it and forced the Volkraad to accept. Ten minutes before, Jan Paulus had sent him a telegraphed message which had justified this confidence.

With long stirrup leathers, his massive body loose and relaxed in the saddle, his *sjambok* trailing from his wrist and the wide-brimmed hat shading his face, Jan Paulus went down to gather the harvest of war.

As he reached the kopjes and rode in among them, his burghers rose from their trenches on the slopes and cheered him. Their voices blended in a savage roar that echoed from the heights like the jubilation of lions on a new kill. Impassively Jan Paulus examined their faces as he passed. They were coated with red dust and burned powder, and sweat had run in dark lines through the grime. One man used his rifle as a crutch to balance himself against his wound, and there were harsh lines of pain around his mouth as he cheered. Jan Paulus checked his pony. 'Lie down, don't be a fool, man!' The man grinned painfully and shook his head.

'*Nee*, Oom Paul. I'm going with you to fetch the guns.'

Brusquely Jan Paulus motioned to the men who stood beside the wounded burgher. 'Take him away. Take him to the doctors.' And he trotted on to where Commandant Van Wyk waited for him.

'I told you to hold your men until they crossed,' he greeted him, and Van Wyk's grin faded.

'*Ja*, Oom Paul. I know. But I could not hold them. The young ones started it. When they saw the guns right there under their noses – I could not hold them.' Van Wyk turned and pointed across the river. 'Look how near they were.'

Jan Paulus looked across the river. The guns were standing in the open, so close and so lightly screened by the intervening thorn scrub that he could count the spokes of the wheels and see the sparkle of the brass breech fittings.

'It was too much temptation,' Van Wyk ended lamely.

'So! It is done, and we cannot undo it with words.' Grimly Jan Paulus determined that this man would never command again. 'Come, we will fetch them.'

At the road bridge Jan Paulus halted the long column of horsemen behind him. Although none of it showed on his face, yet his stomach heaved with horror at what he saw.

'Move them,' he ordered, and as the thirty burghers dismounted and went forward to clear the bridge he called out after them. 'Handle them gently, lift them – do not drag them away like mealie sacks. These were men. Brave men.' Beside him the boy, Hennie, was crying openly. The tears falling on to his patched tweed jacket.

'Be still, Jong,' Jan Paulus murmured gently. 'Tears are for women.' And he urged his pony into the narrow passage between the dead. It was the dust and the sun and the lyddite fumes which had irritated his own eyes, he told himself angrily.

Quietly, lacking the triumphant bearing of victors, they came to the guns and spread out among them. Then a single rifle-shot cracked out and a burgher staggered and clutched the wheel of a gun carriage for support.

Whirling his pony, and flattening himself along its neck, Jan Paulus charged the donga beyond the guns from which the shot had come. Another shot hissed past his head, but by then Jan Paulus had reached the donga. Pulling his mount down from full gallop on to its haunches, he jumped from the saddle and kicked the rifle out of the British private's hands before dragging him to his feet.

'We have killed too much already, you fool.' Stumbling over the English words, his tongue clumsy with rage, he roared into the soldier's face. 'It is finished. Give up.' And then turning on the surviving gunners who huddled along the donga. 'Give up, give up, all of you!' None of them moved for a long minute, then slowly one at a time they stood up and shuffled out of the donga.

While a party of Boers led the prisoners away, and the others went about the business of hitching up the guns and the ammunition wagon, the British stretcher-bearers began filtering forward through the mimosa trees. Soon khaki figures were mingled everywhere with the burghers as they searched like bird-dogs for the wounded.

Two of them, dark-skinned Indians of the Medical Corps, had found a man lying out on the left flank. They were having difficulty with him, and Jan Paulus handed the reins of his pony to Hennie and walked across to them.

In semi-delirium the wounded man was cursing horribly and resisting all attempts by the two Indians to fix splints on his leg.

'Leave me alone, you bastards,' and a flying fist knocked one of them sprawling. Jan Paulus, recognizing the voice and the punch, started to run.

'You behave yourself, or I'll klop you one,' he growled as he reached them. Groggily Sean rolled his head and tried to focus on him.

'What's that? Who are you? Get the hell away from me.'

Jan Paulus did not answer. He was looking at the wounds and they made him want to vomit.

'Give to me.' He took the splints from the shaken bearers and squatted down beside Sean.

'Get away!' Sean screamed at him. 'I know what you're going to do. You're going to cut it off!'

'Sean!' Jan Paulus caught his wrist and held it while Sean writhed and swore.

'I'll kill you, you filthy bastard. I'll kill you if you touch it.'

'Sean! It's me. Look at me!'

And slowly Sean relaxed, his eyes steadied.

'It's you? It's really you?' he whispered. 'Don't let them ... don't let them take my leg. Not like they did to Garry.'

'Be still, or I'll break your stupid head,' growled Jan Paulus. Like his face, his hands were beefy and red, big hands with fingers like calloused sausages, but now they worked as gently as those of a mother on her child. At last, holding the ankle, he looked at Sean.

'Hold fast, now. I must straighten it.'

Sean tried to grin, but his face was grey beneath the coating of battle filth, and sweat squeezed from his skin like a rash of tiny blisters.

'Don't talk so much, you bloody Dutchman. Do it!'

Bone grated on broken bone deep in the torn flesh and Sean gasped. Every muscle in his body convulsed and then relaxed again as he fainted.

'*Ja*', grunted Jan Paulus. 'That's better,' and for the first time the set of his features betrayed his compassion. He finished with the bandages, and for a few seconds continued to squat beside Sean's unconscious body. Then he whispered so low that the two bearers could not catch the words.

'Sleep well, my brother. May God spare you your leg.'

And he stood, all trace of pity and sorrow locked away behind the red-stone of his face.

'Take him away,' he ordered, and waited while they lifted the stretcher and staggered away with it.

He went to his pony, and his feet dragged a little through the grass. From the saddle he looked once more towards the south but the two bearers had disappeared with their burden among the mimosa trees. He touched spurs to his pony's flanks and followed the long procession of wagons, prisoners and guns back towards the Tugela. The only sound was the jingle of harness and the melancholy rumble of wheels.


# Chapter Nineteen


Garrick Courtney watched the champagne spilling into the crystal bowl of his glass. The bubbles swirled in golden patterns, catching the lantern light. The mess corporal lifted the bottle, dexterously caught a drop of wine on his napkin and moved behind Garry to fill the glass of Brigadier Lyttelton, who sat beside him.

'No.' Lyttelton placed a hand over his empty glass to prevent him doing so.

'Come, come, Lyttelton.' Sir Redvers Buller leaned forward and looked down the table. 'That's an excellent wine.'

'Thank you, sir, but champagne is for victory – perhaps we should have a case sent across the river.'

Buller flushed slowly and looked down at his own glass. Once more an ugly silence descended on the mess. In an effort to break it Garry spoke up.

'I do think the withdrawal today was made in extremely good order.'

'Oh. I agree most heartily.' From across the table Lord Dundonald's icy sarcasm added to the gaiety. 'But in all fairness, Colonel, we were travelling very light on our return.'

This oblique reference to the guns sent every eye to Buller's face – Dundonald was showing a reckless disregard of that notorious temper. But as a peer of the realm he could take the chance. With a courteous insolence he met Buller's glare, and held it until the pale bulging eyes faded and dropped.

'Gentlemen.' Buller spoke heavily. 'We have had a most trying day, and for all of us there is still work to do.' He glanced at his A.D.C. 'Clery, will you be kind enough to propose the Queen?'

Alone, Garry limped from the huge marquee mess tent. The smaller tents, lit internally, were a vast field of luminous cones, and above them the night was black satin sown with silver stars. The wine that Garry had drunk during dinner hummed in his head so that he did not notice the dejected silence that smothered the encampment as he picked his way through it.

As Garry entered his headquarters a man stood up from the camp chair beside his desk. In the light of the lantern his features were gaunt, and weariness showed in every line of his body.

'Ah! Curtis.'

'Good evening, sir.'

'You've come to make your report?'

'I have, sir. For what it's worth.'

'Tell me, Curtis – how many casualties?' There was an eagerness behind the question which Tim found ghoulish. Speculatively he examined Garry's face before replying.

'We suffered heavily, out of a strength of twenty we had four killed, two missing and five wounded – three of them seriously.'

'Have you made out a list?'

'Not yet.'

'Well, tell me. Who were they?'

'Killed were Booth, Amery . . .'

No longer could Garry hold his impatience, he blurted out suddenly:

'What about that sergeant?'

'You mean Courtney?'

'Yes. *Yes.*' And now with his impatience was mingled a dread that made his stomach feel hollow.

'Wounded, sir.'

And Garry felt a lift of relief so intense that he must close his eyes and suck in his breath to ride it up.

*Sean was still alive! Thank God. Thank God for that.*

'Where is he now?'

'They've got him down at the railhead hospital. He's being sent out with the first batch of badly wounded.'

'Badly?' Garry's relief changed quickly to concern, and he demanded harshly, 'How badly? *How badly?*'

'That's all they told me. I went down to the hospital but they wouldn't allow me to see him.'

Garry sank into his chair and instinctively reached for the drawer before he checked himself.

'Very well, Curtis. You may go.'

'The rest of my report, sir?'

'Tomorrow. Leave it till tomorrow.'

With the liquor glowing hotly in his belly, Garry set off through the night towards the hospital. It did not matter now that he had planned and hoped that Sean would die. He no longer reasoned, but hurried through the sprawling camp, driven by his desperate need. Unrecognized but strong within him was the hope that he might again draw comfort and strength from that fountain as he had done so long ago. He started to run, stiffly, so the toe of his boot scuffed in the dust with each pace.

Desperately he searched through the hospital. He hurried along the rows of stretchers examining the faces of the wounded; he saw pain and mutilation and slow creeping death soaking like spilt red ink through the white bandages. He heard the moan and murmur and delirious laughter, he smelt the taint of agony-induced sweat blended with the heavy sweetness of corruption and disinfectant – and he hardly noticed them. One face, one face only, he wanted. And he did not find it.

'Courtney.' The medical orderly examined his list, tilting it to catch the lamplight. 'Ah! Yes. Here it is – let's see. Yes! He's gone already – left on the first train an hour ago . . . I can't say, sir, probably to Pietermaritzburg. They've established a big new hospital there. I can't tell you that either, I'm afraid, but they've got him listed here as *dangerous* . . . that's better than *critical* anyway.'

Wearing his loneliness like a cloak, Garry stumbled back to his quarters.

'Good evening, sir.' His servant was waiting for him. Garry always made them wait up. A new man this, they changed so fast. Never could keep a batman more than a month.

Garrick pushed past him, and half fell against the camp bed.

'Steady on, sir. Let's get you on to the bed, sir.' The man's voice was insidiously servile, the voice men used towards drunks. The touch of his hands infuriated Garry.

'Leave me.' He lashed out with a clenched fist across the man's face, throwing him back. 'Leave me. Get out and leave me!'

The servant rubbed his bruised cheek uncertainly, backing away.

'Get out!' Garry hissed at him.

'But, sir—'

'Get out, damn you. Get out!'

The man went out and closed the tent flap softly behind him. Garry stumbled across to it and laced it closed. Then he stood back. Alone. They can't see me now. They can't laugh now. They can't. Oh God, Sean!

He turned from the flap. The dummy leg caught on the rough floor and he fell. One of the straps parted and the leg twisted under him. On his hands and knees he crawled towards the commode across the tent, and the leg jerked and twisted grotesquely behind him.

Kneeling beside the commode he lifted the china basin from its recess and reached into the space below it and he found the bottle. His fingers were too clumsy for the cork, he pulled it with his teeth and spat it on to the floor. Then he held the bottle to his lips and his throat jerked rhythmically as he swallowed. A little of the brandy spilled on to his tunic and stained the ribbon of the Victoria Cross.

He lowered the bottle and rested, panting from the sting of the liquor. Then he drank again more slowly. The trembling of his hands stilled. His breathing smoothed out. He reached up and took the tumbler from the top of the commode, filled it, then placed the bottle beside him on the floor and wriggled into a more comfortable position against the commode.

In front of him his artificial leg twisted on its broken straps at an unnatural angle below the knee. He contemplated it, sipping the brandy slowly and feeling it numb the taste-buds of his tongue.

The leg was the centre of his existence. Insensate, unmoving, still as the eye of a great storm upon which the whole turmoil of his life revolved. The leg – always the leg. Always and only the leg.

Now under the lulling spell of the liquor he had drunk, from the stillness at the centre where the leg lay, he looked outward at the gigantic shadows of the past, and found them preserved and perfect, not distorted or blurred by time, whole and complete in each detail.

While they paraded through his mind, the night telescoped in upon itself so that time had no significance. The hours endured for a few minutes and were gone while the level in the bottle fell and he sat against the commode sipping at the tumbler and watching while the night wasted away. In the dawn the final act was played out before him.

*Himself on a horse in the darkness riding in cold soft rain towards Theuniskraal. One window showing a yellow oblong of lantern light, the rest dark in the greater dark mass of the homestead.*

*The unaccountable premonition of coming horror closing cold and soft as the rain around him, the silence spoiled only by the crunch of his horse's hooves in the gravel of the drive. The thump of his pegleg as he climbed the front steps and the chill of the brass doorknob in his hand as he turned it and pushed it in upon the silence.*

*His own voice slurred with drink and dread. 'Hello. Where's everybody? Anna! Anna! I'm back!'*

*The blue flare of his match and the smell of burnt sulphur and paraffin as he lit the lamp, then the urgent echoing thump of his pegleg along the passage.*

*'Anna, Anna, where are you?'*

*Anna, his bride, lay upon the bed in the darkened room, half-naked, turning quickly away from the light, but he had seen the dead-white face with swollen and bruised lips.*

*The lamp from the table threw bloated shadows on the wall as he stooped over and gently drew down the petticoats to cover the whiteness of her lower body, then turned her to face him. 'My darling, oh Anna, my darling. What's*

*happened?' Through the torn blouse her breasts were engorged and darkly*
*nippled with pregnancy. 'Are you hurt? Who? Tell me who did it?' But she*
*covered her face and broken lips with her hands.*

'My darling, my poor darling. Who was it – one of the servants?'

'No.'

'Please tell me, Anna. What happened?'

*Suddenly her arms were about his neck and her lips close against his ear.*
'You know, Garry! You know who did it.'

'No, I swear I don't. Please tell me.'

*Her voice tight and hoarse with hatred, uttering that word, that one*
*unbelievable horrible word.* 'Sean!'

'Sean!' he said aloud in his desolation. 'Sean. Oh God! and then savagely,
'I hate him. I hate him! Let him die – please God, let him die.'

He closed his eyes, losing his grip upon reality, and felt the first dizzy
swing of vertigo as the liquor took firm hold upon him.

Too late now to open his eyes and focus them upon the bed across the
tent, the giddiness had begun – now he would not be able to hold it down.
The warm, acid-sweet taste of brandy welled up into his throat and mouth
and nose.

# Chapter Twenty

When his servant found him it was the middle of the morning. Garry lay
fully dressed but asleep upon the bed with his sparse hair ruffled, his uniform
stained and grubby, and the leg lying derelict in the centre of the floor.

The servant closed the door softly and studied his master, his nostrils
flaring at the sour smell of stale brandy and vomit.

'Had yourself one hell of a bust-out. Hey – Hop, Skip and Jump?' he
murmured without sympathy. Then he picked up the bottle and examined
the inch of liquor remaining in it. 'Your bloody good health, cock,' he saluted
Garry and drained the bottle, patted his lips delicately and spoke again.
'Right! Let's get your sty cleaned up.'

'Leave me alone,' Garry groaned.

'It's eleven o'clock, sir.'

'Leave me. Get out and leave me.'

'Drink this coffee, sir.'

'I don't want it. Leave me.'

'I've got your bath filled, sir, and a clean uniform laid out for you.'

'What time is it?' Garry sat up unsteadily.

'Eleven o'clock,' the man repeated patiently.

'My leg?' Garry felt naked without it.

'One of the harness makers is stiching the straps, sir. It'll be ready by the time you've bathed.'

Even in a position of rest Garry's hands, laid upon the desk in front of him trembled slightly, and the rims of his eyelids prickled. The skin of his face was stretched like that of a drum over the slow pain that throbbed within his skull.

At last he sighed and picked Lieutenant Curtis's report from the top of the slim sheaf of papers that waited for his attention. Garry skimmed through it dully, few of the names upon it meant anything to him. He saw Sean's name headed the list of wounded, and below him was the little Jewish lawyer. At last satisfied that the report contained nothing to the discredit of Colonel Garrick Courtney, he initialled it and laid it aside.

He picked up the next document. A letter addressed to him as Officer Commanding the Natal Corps of Guides, from a Colonel John Acheson of the Scots Fusiliers. Two pages of neat, pointed handwriting. He was about to discard it and leave it to his Orderly's attention when the name in the body of the text caught his eye. He leaned forward attentively and read quickly from the beginning.

'... pleasure in bringing to your attention ... conduct beyond the call of ... under intense enemy fire ... once more, initiated an advance ... although wounded ... disregard of personal danger ... two members of your Guides.

  Sergeant Sean Courtney.

  Pte. Saul Friedman.

... earnestly recommend ... Distinguished Conduct Medal ... great gallantry and powers of leadership.'

Garry dropped the letter and leaned back in his chair, staring at it as though it were his own death warrant. For a long while he did not move, while the pain kept beating in his head. Then he picked it up once more. Now his hands trembled so violently that the paper fluttered like the wing of a wounded bird.

'Everything of mine, everything I've ever owned – he's taken it from me,' and he looked down at the ribbons on his breast. 'I've never had ... Now this, the one thing.'

A drop of moisture fell on to the letter, blurring the ink.

'I hate him,' he whispered and tore the letter across. 'I hope he dies,' and he tore again and again, ripping it to shreds and at last screwing them into a ball in his clenched fist.

'No. You'll not get that from me. It's mine – it's the one thing you'll never have!' He hurled the crumpled ball against the canvas of the tent, and lowered his head on to his arms upon the desk. His shoulders shook as he sobbed:

'Don't die. Please, Sean, don't die.'

# Chapter Twenty-one

Simply by putting his shoulder against her and shoving her aside, Dirk Courtney cleared a small girl from the doorway and was first down the steps and out into the sun. Without looking back at the schoolhouse he headed for the hole in the back hedge, the others would be following.

They caught up with him while he was selecting a *klei-lat* from the hedge.

'Hurry up,' Dirk ordered. 'We got to get to the river first else they'll get the best place.'

They spread out along the hedge, small boys chattering like a troop of excited monkeys.

'Lend me your knife, Dirkie.'

'Hey, look at my lat.' Nick Peterson brandished the short rod of Port Jackson Willow he had cut and peeled. It whipped with a satisfying swish.

'It's not a lat,' Dirk informed him. 'It's a Lee-Metford.' He looked round at the rest of his team. 'You remember now – I'm Lord Kitchener, and you got to call me "My Lord".'

'And I'm General French,' announced Nick. This was fair enough, after all, he was Dirk's chief lieutenant. It had taken Dirk a mere two weeks and five bloody fist-fights to reach his position as unchallenged leader.

'And I'm General Methuen!' one of the lesser members yelped.

'And I'm General Buller!'

'And I'm General Gatacre!'

'You can't all be generals.' Dirk glared around. 'Only Nick and I are generals. You are all just privates and things.'

'Gee, man, Dirkie! Why you always got to spoil things?'

'You shut your mouth, Brian.' Dirk sensed mutiny, and quickly he diverted their attention. 'Come on, let's go and get ammo.'

Dirk took the long route down the sanitary lane. This way he was unlikely to meet adults and have any of his force seconded to serve elsewhere at wood chopping or gardening under parental control.

'Peaches are nearly ripe,' Nick commented as they passed the Pye orchard.

'Another week,' Dirk agreed, and crawled through the hedge into the Van Essen plantation that spread down to the Baboon Stroom.

'There they are!' someone shouted as they emerged from the trees.

'Boers, General!'

Out on the right, busy along the bank of the river was another bunch of small figures – sons of the Dutch families in the district.

'I'll go and talk to them,' Dirk said. 'You go for ammo.' They trotted off towards the river and Dirk called after them: 'Hey, Nick, get me a good dollop of clay.'

'All right, My Lord.'

With all the dignity of a general, officer and a peer of the realm, Dirk approached the enemy and stopped a short distance from them.

'Hey, Piet, are you ready yet?' he asked haughtily. Piet Van Essen was his second cousin twice removed. A chunky lad but not as tall as Dirk.

'*Ja.*'

'The same rules?' Dirk asked.

'*Ja*, the same rules.'

'No clothes,' Dirk warned him.

'And no throwing with stones,' Piet shot back.

'How many you got?' Dirk began counting the enemy suspiciously.

'Fifteen – same as you.'

'All right then,' Dirk nodded.

'All right then!'


Nick was waiting for him below the bank. Dirk jumped down beside him and accepted the large ball of blue clay that Nick handed him.

'It's just right, Dirkie, not too wet.'

'Good – let's get ready.'

Quickly Dirk stripped off his clothing, pulled the belt from the loops of his pants and buckled it around his waist to hold his spare lats.

'Hide the clothes, Brian,' Dirk ordered and surveyed his naked warriors. Nearly all of them still retained the almost womanly shape of youth; undeveloped chests, protruding stomachs and fat white buttocks.

'They'll come down the river like they do every time,' Dirk said. 'This time we're going to ambush them.' As he spoke he kneaded a handful of clay into a ball and spiked it on to the end of the lat. 'Me and Nick'll wait here – the rest of you on top of the bank in those bushes back there.'

He was looking for a target to practise on, and found it in a water tortoise which was laboriously climbing the far bank.

'Watch that old skilpad.' He interrupted himself; stepped forward with his right hand holding the lat thrown back, then whipped it through in an overhead swing. The ball of clay flew from the end of the rod with a vicious hum and smacked on to the shiny black carapace with a force that left a white starshaped crack upon the shell. The tortoise jerked in its head and limbs and toppled backwards into the stream.

'Good shot!'

'There he is, let me have a shot.'

'That's enough! You'll get plenty shots just now.' Dirk stopped them. 'Now listen to me! When they come me and Nick will hold them here for a bit, then we'll run back along the river and they'll chase us. Wait until they are right underneath you – then give it to them.'

Dirk and Nick crouched side by side, close in against the bank with the water up to their noses. A tuft of reeds hid those parts of their heads still above the surface and within easy reach their loaded clay-lats lay on dry land.

Below water Dirk felt Nick's elbow nudge his ribs, and he nodded carefully. He also had heard the whisper of voices around the bend of the river, and the roll and plop of loose earth dislodged by a careless foot. He turned his head and answered Nick's grin with one just as bloodthirsty, then he peered around the reeds.

Twenty paces in front of him a head appeared cautiously around the angle of the bank and the expression of its face was set and nervous – and Dirk moved his own head back behind the bunch of reeds.

A long silence broken suddenly. 'They're not here.' The voice was squeaky with adolescence and tension. Boetie was a delicate child, small for his age, who insisted on joining the rest of them in games beyond his strength.

Another long silence and then the sound of a wholesale but stealthy approach. Dirk reached out and gripped Nick's arm – the enemy were committed, out in the open – he lifted his mouth above the surface.

'Now!' he whispered and they reached for their lats. The surprise was complete and devastating. As Dirk and Nick rose dripping, with throwing arms cocked, the attackers were bunched in such a way that they could neither run nor return the fire unhampered.

The clay pellets flew into them, slapping loudly on bare flesh, producing howls of anguish and milling, colliding confusion.

'Give it to them,' shouted Dirk, and threw again without picking his man, blindly into the mass of legs and arms and pink backsides. Beside him Nick worked in a silent frenzy of load and throw.

The confusion lasted perhaps fifteen seconds, before the howls of pain became shouts of anger.

'It's only Dirk and Nick.'

'Get them – it's only two of them.'

The first pellet flipped Dirk's ear, the second hit him full in the chest.

'Run! he gasped through the pain, and floundered to the bank. Bent forward to climb from the stream he was frighteningly vulnerable, and a pellet thrown at point-blank range took him in that portion of his anatomy which he was offering to the enemy. The sting of it propelled him from the water and clouded his vision with tears.

'Chase them!'

'Hit them!'

The pack bayed after them, pellets hissed about them and slapped at them as they pelted back along the stream. Before they reached the next bend their backs and bottoms were dappled with the angry red spots which tomorrow would be bruises.

Without discretion, hot with the chase, shouting and laughing, the attackers poured into the trap and as they rounded the bend it closed upon them.

Dirk and Nick stood poised to meet them, and suddenly the bank above their heads was lined with squealing, dancing, naked savages, who hurled a steady stream of missiles into them.

For a minute they stood it, then completely broken they scrambled out of the river-bed with pellets flailing them and raced panic-stricken for the shelter of the plantation.

One of them remained below the bank, kneeling in the mud, sobbing softly. But according to the unspoken laws that governed them this one was exempt from further punishment.

'It's only Boetie,' Nickie shouted. 'Leave him. Come on! Chase the others!' And he scrambled up the bank and led them after the flight. Yelling and shrilling with excitement they streamed away through the brown grass to where Piet Van Essen was desperately trying to stay the route on the edge of the plantation, and gather his men to meet the charge.

But another of them remained below the bank – Dirk Courtney.

There were just two of them now. Screened by the bank, completely alone. Boetie looked up and through his tears saw Dirk coming slowly towards him. He saw the lat in Dirk's hand and the expression on his face. He knew he was alone with Dirk.

'Please, Dirk,' he whispered. 'I give up. Please. I give up.'

Dirk grinned. Deliberately he moulded the clay pellet on to his lat.

'I'll give you all my lunch tomorrow,' pleaded Boetie. 'Not just the sweets, I'll give you all of it.'

Dirk hurled the clay. Boetie's shriek thrilled his whole body. He began to tremble with the pleasure of it.

'I'll give you my new pocket-knife.' Boetie's voice was muffled by sobs and his arms which he had crossed over his face.

Dirk loaded the lat, slowly so he could savour this feeling of power.

'Please, Dirkie. Please, man, I'll give you anything you—' and Boetie shrieked again.

'Take your hands off your face, Boetie.' Dirk's voice was strangled, thick with pleasure.

'No, Dirkie. Please no!'

'Take your hands away, and I'll stop.'

'You promise, Dirkie. You promise you'll stop.'

'I promise,' whispered Dirk.

Slowly Boetie lowered his arms, they were thin and very white, for he always wore long sleeves against the sun.

'You promised, didn't you. I did what you—' and the clay hit him across the bridge of his nose, spreading as it struck, jerking his head back. Immediately there was blood from both nostrils.

Boetie clawed at his face, smearing blood on to his cheeks.

'You promised,' he whimpered. 'You *promised*!' But Dirk was already moulding the next pellet.


Dirkie walked home alone. He walked slowly, smiling a little, with soft hair falling forward on to his forehead and a smear of blue clay on one cheek.

Mary was waiting for him in the kitchen of the cottage of Protea Street. She watched from the window while he slipped through the hedge and crossed the yard. As he came towards the door she noticed the smile on his face. There was hardly sufficient room in her chest for what she felt as she looked at the innocent beauty of his face. She opened the door for him.

'Hello, darling.'

'Hello, Mary,' Dirk greeted her, and his little smile became a thing of such radiance that Mary had to reach for him.

'My goodness, you're covered in mud. Let's get you bathed before your gran'ma gets home.'

Dirk extricated himself from her embrace and moved in on the biscuit-tin.

'I'm hungry.'

'Just one,' Mary agreed, and Dirk took a handful. 'Then I've got a surprise for you.'

'What is it?' Dirk was more interested in the biscuits. Mary had a surprise for him every evening and usually it was something silly like a new pair of socks she had knitted.

'I'll tell you when you're in the bath.'

'Oh, all right.' Still munching Dirk set off for the bathroom. He began to disrobe along the passage dropping first his shirt and then his pants for Mary to retrieve as she followed.

'What is the surprise?'

'Oh Dirk, you've been playing that horrible game again.' Mary knelt beside the tub and gently passed the soapy flannel down his bruised back and buttocks. 'Please promise me you'll never play it again.'

'All right.' It was a very simple matter to extract a promise from Dirk, he had made this particular one before. 'Now, what's your surprise?'

'Guess.' Mary was smiling now, a secret knowing smile which immediately caught Dirk's attention. He studied her scarred face, her ugly loving face.

'Sweets?' he hazarded, and she shook her head and caressed his naked body with the flannel.

'Not socks!'

'No.' She dropped the flannel into the soap-scummed water and clasped him to her chest. 'No, not socks,' she whispered.

He knew then.

'Is it . . .? Is it . . .'

'Yes, Dirkie, it's about your father.'

Instantly he began to struggle.

'Where is he, Mary? Where is he?'

'Into your nightshirt first.'

'Is he here? Has he come home?'

'No, Dirk. He isn't here yet. He's in Pietermaritzburg. But you're going to see him soon. Very soon. Gran'ma has gone now to make reservations on the train. You're going to see him tomorrow.'

His hot, wet body began to tremble in her arms, quivering with excitement.

# Chapter Twenty-two

'In some respects, Mrs Courtney, it was possibly all to the good that we were unable to contact you before.' The Surgeon-Major tamped tabacco into his pipe, and began methodically searching all his pockets.

'Your matches are on the desk.' Ada came to his assistance.

'Oh! Thank you.' He got the pipe drawing, and continued, 'You see, your son was attached to an irregular unit – there was no record of next-of-kin, and when he came to us from Colenso six weeks ago he was, shall we say, in no condition to inform us of your address.'

'Can we see Pa now?' Dirk could no longer contain himself, for the past five minutes he had wriggled and fidgeted on the the the couch beside Ada.

'You'll see your father in a few minutes, young man.' And the surgeon turned back to Ada. 'As it so happens, Mrs Courtney, you have been spared a great deal of anxiety. At first there were grave doubts that we would be able to save your son's life, let alone his right leg. Four weeks it hung in the balance, so to speak. But now' – and he beamed at Ada with justifiable pride – 'well, you'll see for yourself.'

'He's well?' Quickly, anxiously she asked.

'What a formidable constitution your son has, all muscle and determination.' He nodded, still smiling. 'Yes, he's well on the road to recovery. There may be a slight limp in the right leg – but when you weigh that against what might have been ...' He spread his hands eloquently. 'Now the sister will take you through to him.'

'When can he come home?' Ada asked from the doorway.

'Soon – another month, perhaps.'


A deep veranda, cool with shade and the breeze that came in across the hospital lawns. A hundred high metal beds along the wall, a hundred men in grey flannel nightshirts propped against white pillows. Some of them slept, a few were reading, others talked quietly or played chess and cards on boards set between the beds. But one lay withdrawn, staring at, but not seeing, the pair of fiscal shrikes which squabbled raucously over a frog on the lawn.

The beard was gone, removed while he was too weak to protest on the orders of the ward sister who considered it unhygienic, and the result was a definite improvement that even Sean secretly admitted. Shielded for so long, the skin on the lower half of his face was smooth and white like that of a boy; fifteen years had been shaved away with that coarse black matt. Now emphasis was placed on the heavy brows which, in turn, directed attention to his eyes, dark blue, like cloud shadow on mountain lakes. Darker blue at this moment as he considered the contents of the letter he held in his right hand.

The letter was three weeks old, and already the cheap paper was splitting along the creases from constant refolding. It was a long letter, much of it devoted to detailed description of the clumsy sparring along the Tugela River in which Buller's army was now engaged. There was one reference to the headaches from which the writer periodically suffered as a result of his wound which was now externally healed, and many more to the deep gratitude that Saul felt for him. These embarrassed Sean to such an extent that when re-reading the letter he scowled and skipped each one as he came to it.

But there was one paragraph to which Sean returned each time, and read slowly, whispering it to himself so that he could savour each word:

I remember telling you about Ruth, my wife. As you know, she escaped from Pretoria and is in Pietermaritzburg staying with relatives of hers. Yesterday I had a letter from her that contained the most wonderful tidings. We have been married four years this coming June, and now at last as a result of our brief meeting when she arrived in Natal – I am to become a father! Ruth tells me she has determined on a daughter (though I am certain it will be a son!) and she has selected a name. It is a most unusual name, to be charitable – I can see that it will require a great deal of diplomacy on my part to make her change her mind. (Among her many virtues is an obstinacy reminiscent of the rock of ages.) She want to name the poor waif '*Storm*' – Storm Friedman – and the prospect appals me!

Although our faiths differ, I have written to Ruth asking her to agree to your election as 'Sandek' – which is the equivalent of godfather. I can foresee no objection from Ruth (especially in view of the debt which we both owe you) and it needs now only your consent. Will you give it?

At the same time I have explained to Ruth your present situation and address (c/o Greys Hospital!) and asked her to visit you there so that she can thank you personally. I warn you in advance that she knows as much about you as I do – I am not one to hide my enthusiasms!

Lying with the letter clutched in his hand, Sean stared out across the lawns into the sunlight. Beneath the bedclothes, swelling up like a pregnant belly, was the wicker basket that cradled his leg. '*Storm!*' he whispered, remembering the lightning playing blue and blinding white upon her body.

'Why doesn't she come?' Three weeks he had waited for her. 'She knows that I am here, why doesn't she come to me?'

'Visitors for you.' The sister paused beside him and straightened the bedclothes.

'Who?' He struggled up on to his good elbow, with the other arm still in its sling across his chest.

'A lady.' And he felt it surge through him. 'And a small boy.' The cold backwash of disappointment, as he realized it was not her. Then immediately guilt – Ada and Dirk, how could he hope it was someone else?

Without the beard Dirk did not recognize him until he was ten paces away. Then he charged, his cap flew from his head and his dark hair, despite the bonds of brilliantine, sprang up into curls as he ran. He was squeaking incoherently as he reached the bed, clambered up on to Sean's chest to lock both arms around his neck.

It was some time before Sean could prise him loose and look at him.

'Well, boy,' he said, and then again, 'well, my boy.' Unable to trust himself not to lay his love for the child bare for all to see – there were a hundred men watching and grinning – Sean sought diversion by turning to Ada.

She waited quietly, as she had spent half her life waiting, but when he looked at her the tenderness showed in her smile.

'Sean.' She stooped to kiss him. 'What happened to your beard? You look so young.'

They stayed for an hour, most of which was taken up by a monologue from Dirk. In the intervals while he regained his breath Ada and Sean were able to exchange all their accumulated news. Finally, Ada stood up from the chair beside Sean's bed.

'The train leaves in half an hour, and Dirk has school tomorrow. We'll come up from Ladyburg each week-end until you are ready to return home.'

Getting Dirk out of the hospital was like evicting an unruly drunk from a bar. Alone Ada could not manage it and she enlisted a male hospital orderly to the cause. Kicking and struggling in tantrum, Dirk was carried down the veranda with his screams ringing back to Sean long after he had disappeared from view.

'I want my Dad. I want to stay with my Dad.'

## Chapter Twenty-three

Benjamin Goldberg was the executor of his brother's estate. This estate consisted of a forty-per-cent shareholding in Goldberg Bros. Ltd., a company which listed among its assets a brewery, four small hotels and a very large one situated on the Marine Parade at Durban, sixteen butcher shops, and a factory devoted to the manufacture of polony, pork sausages, bacon and smoked ham. The last products caused Benjamin some embarrassment, but their manufacture was too profitable to be discontinued. Benjamin was also the Chairman of the Board of Goldberg Bros., and a sixty-per-cent shareholder. The presence of an army of twenty-five thousand hungry and thirsty men in Natal had increased the consumption of beer and bacon in a manner that caused Benjamin further embarrassment, for he was a peaceable man.

The huge profits forced upon him by the hostilities both troubled and delighted him.

These same two emotions were evoked by the presence in his household of his niece. Benjamin had four sons and not a single daughter, his brother Aaron had left one daughter for whom Benjamin would gladly have traded all four of his own sons. Not that the boys weren't doing very well, all of them settled into the business very nicely. One of them running the Port Natal Hotel, the eldest managing the brewery and the two others in the meat section. But – and here Benjamin sighed – but Ruth! There was a girl for a man's old age. He looked at her across the polished stinkwood breakfast table with its encrustation of silver and exquisite bone china, and he sighed again.

'Now, Uncle Ben, don't start again. Please.' Ruth buttered her toast firmly.

'So all I'm saying is that we need him here. Is that so bad?'

'Saul is a lawyer.'

'*Nu?* Is that so bad. He's a lawyer, but we need a lawyer with us. The fees I pay out to those other *schmoks!*'

'He doesn't want to come into the Company.'

'All right. We know he doesn't want charity. We know he doesn't want your money working for him. We know all about his pride – but now he's got responsibilities. Already he should be thinking about you – and the baby – not so much about what he wants.'

At the mention of the baby, Ruth frowned slightly. Benjamin noticed it, there were few things he did not notice. Young people! If only you could tell them. He sighed again.

'All right. We'll leave it until Saul comes back on leave,' he agreed heavily.

Ruth, who had never mentioned her uncle's offers of employment to Saul, had a momentary vision of living in Pietermaritzburg – close enough to be drowned in the tidal waves of affection that emanated from her Uncle Benjamin, caught like a tiny insect in the suffocating web of family ties and duties. She flashed at him in horror.

'You even mention it to Saul and I'll never speak to you again.'

Her cheeks flushed wondrously and fire burned in her eyes. Even the heavy braid of dark hair seemed to come alive like the tail of an angry lioness, flicking as she moved her head.

*Oi Yoi Yoi!* Benjamin hid his delight behind hooded lids. *What a temper! What a woman! She could keep a man young for ever.*

Ruth jumped up from the table. For the first time he noticed that she wore riding habit.

'Where are you going? Ruth, you're not riding again today.'

'Yes I am.'

'The baby!'

'Uncle Ben, why did you never learn to mind your own business?' And she marched out of the room. Her waist was not yet thickened with pregnancy and she moved with a grace that played a wild discord on the old man's heart strings.

'You should not let her treat you that way, Benjamin.' Mildly, the way she did everything, his wife spoke from across the table.

'There's something troubling that girl.' Carefully Benjamin wiped egg from his moustache, laid the napkin on the table, consulted the gold fob watch he drew from his waistcoat, and stood up. 'Something big. You mark my words.'

It was Friday, strange how Friday had become the pivot on which the whole week turned. Ruth urged the chestnut stallion, and he lengthened his stride under her, surging forward with such power that she had to check him a little and bring him down into an easy canter.

She was early and waited ten impatient minutes in the oak-lined lane behind Greys Hospital before, like a conspirator, the little nurse slipped out through the hedge.

'Have you got it?' Ruth demanded. The girl nodded, glanced around quickly and took an envelope out of her grey nursing cloak. Ruth exchanged it for a gold sovereign. Clutching the coin the nurse started back for the hedge.

'Wait.' Ruth stopped her. This was her only physical contact and she was reluctant to break it so soon. 'How is he?'

'It's all there, m'am.'

'I know – but tell me how he looks. What he does and says,' Ruth insisted.

'Oh, he's looking fine now. He's been up and about on his sticks all week, with that big black savage helping him. The first day he fell and you should have heard him swear. Lordy!' They both laughed together.

'He's a real card, that one. He and sister had another tiff yesterday when she wanted to wash him. He called her a shameless strumpet. She gave him what for all right. But you could see she was ever so pleased and she went around telling everybody about it.'

She burbled on and Ruth listened enchanted, until:

'Then yesterday, you know what he did when I was changing his dressing?' She blushed coyly. 'He gave me a pinch behind!'

Ruth felt a hot flood of anger wash over her. Suddenly she realized that the girl was pretty in an insipid fashion.

'And he said . . .'

'Thank you!' Ruth had to restrain the hand that held her riding-crop. 'I have to go now.' Usually the long skirts of her habit hampered her in mounting, but this time she found herself in the saddle without effort.

'Next week, m'am?'

'Yes,' and she hit the stallion across his shoulder. He lunged forward so violently that she had to clutch at the pommel of the saddle. She rode him as she had never ridden a horse befor, driving him with whip and spur until dark patches of sweat showed on his flanks and froth spattered back along his shoulders, so that by the time she reached a secluded spot on the bank of the Umgeni River far out of town her jealousy had abated and she felt ashamed of herself. She loosened the stallion's girth and petted him a little before leaving him tethered to one of the weeping willows, and picking her way down the bank to her favourite log on the water's edge.

There she settled herself and opened the envelope. If only Sean could have known that his temperature chart, progress report, house-doctor's recommendations, and the sucrose content of his urine were being so avidly studied, he would probably have added a ruptured spleen to his other ills.

At last Ruth folded the pages into their envelope and tucked it away in her jacket of her habit. He must look so different without his beard. She stared into the pool below her and it seemed as though his face formed in the green water and looked back at her. She touched the surface with the toe of her riding-boot so that the ripples spread and shattered the image.

She was left with only the feeling of loneliness.

'I must not go to him,' she whispered, steeling the resolve which had kept her from him these past weeks since she had known he was there. So close – so terribly near.

Determinedly she looked down again into the pool and tried to conjure up the face of her husband. All she saw was a yellowfish, gliding quietly across the sandy bottom with the pattern of its scales showing like the teeth of a file along its sides. She dropped a pebble into the water and the fish darted away.

Saul. Merry little Saul with his monkey face, who made her laugh the way a mother laughs at her child. *I love him*, she thought. And it was true, she loved him. But love has many shapes, and some are the shapes of mountains – tall and jagged and big. While others are the shape of clouds – which have no shape, no sharp outline, soft they blow against the mountain and change and stream away but the mountain stands untouched by them. The mountain stands for ever.

'My mountain,' she murmured, and she saw him again so vividly, standing tall above her in the storm.

'Storm,' she whispered and clasped her open hands across her belly that was still flat and hard.

'Storm,' she whispered and felt the warmth within her. It spread outwards from her womb, the heat rising with it until it was a burning madness she could no longer control. With her skirts flying about her legs she ran to the stallion, her hands trembled on the straps of the girth.

'Just once,' she promised herself. 'Just this once more.' Desperately she clawed up into the saddle.

'Just this once, I swear it!' and then brokenly, 'I can't help myself. I've tried – oh God, how I've tried!'


An appreciative stirring and hum of comment from the beds along the wall followed her as she swept down the hospital veranda. There was urgent grace in the way she held her skirts gathered in one hand, in the crisp staccato tap of her pointed boots along the cement floor and the veiled swing of her hips above. There was unrestrained eagerness in the sparkle in her eyes and the forward thrust of her breasts beneath the wine-coloured jacket. The wild ride which brought her here had flushed her cheeks and tumbled her hair glossy black down her temple and on to her forehead.

Those sick and lonely men reached as though a goddess had passed them by, thrilled by her beauty, yet saddened because she was unattainable. She did not notice them, she did not feel their hungry eyes upon her nor hear the aching whisper of their voices – for she had seen Sean.

He came slowly across the lawns towards the veranda, using the stick awkwardly to balance the drag of his leg. His eyes were downcast and he frowned in thought. Her breath caught in her throat as she saw how wasted was his body. She had not remembered him so tall with shoulders gaunt and wide like the cross-tree of a gallows. Never before had she seen the bony thrust of his jawline, nor the pale smoothness of his skin faintly blue with newshaved beard. But she remembered the eyes heavily overscored with black browns, and his great beaky nose above the wide sensuality of his mouth.

On the edge of the lawn he stopped with feet apart, set the point of the cane between them with both hands clasped over the head of it, and he lifted his eyes and looked at her.

For many seconds neither of them moved. He stood balancing on the cane with his shoulders hunched and his chin raised as he stared at her. She in the shadow of the veranda, her skirts still held in one hand – but the other at her throat, fingers trying to still the emotions that fluttered there.

Gradually his shoulders straightened until he stood tall. He hurled the cane aside and reached both hands open towards her.

Suddenly she was running over the smooth, green lawn. Into his arms, trembling in silent intensity, while he held her.

With both arms around his waist and her face pressed against his chest she could smell the man smell of him and feel the hard muscle of his arms as he enfolded her – and she knew she was safe. As long as she stayed like this – nothing, nobody could touch her.

# Chapter Twenty-four

On the slope of the table-topped mountain that crouches over the town of Pietermaritzburg there is a glade among the wattle trees. It is a secret place where even the timid little blue buck come out to graze in daylight. On a still day you can hear very faintly the pop of the wagon whips on the road below, or farther off the steam whistle of a train. But that is all that intrudes in this wild place.

A butterfly crossed the glade in uncertain wobbling flight, it came out of the sunlight into the dappled, moving shade along the edge, and settled.

'That's good luck,' Sean murmured lazily and Ruth lifted her head from the plaid rug on which they lay. As the butterfly moved its wings, fanning them gently, the iridescent green and yellow markings sparkled in the speck of sunlight that pierced the roof of leaves above them and fell upon it like a spotlight.

'It tickles,' she said, and the insect moved like a living jewel across the smooth white field of her belly. It reached her navel and paused. Then the

tiny tendril of its tongue uncurled and dabbed at the fine sheen of moisture
that their loving had left upon her skin.

'He's come to bless the baby.'

The butterfly skirted the deep, delicately chisseled pit and moved on
downwards.

'Don't you think he's being just a little forward – he doesn't have to bless
that as well?' Ruth asked.

'He certainly seems to know his way around,' Sean admitted dubiously.

The butterfly found its road southwards blocked by a forest of dark curls,
so laboriously it turned and retraced its steps towards the north. Once more
it detoured round her navel and then headed uneeringly for the pass between
her breasts.

'Keep right on, friend,' Sean cautioned, but it turned suddenly and climbed
the steep slope until at last it sat triumphant on the peak.

Sean watched it throbbing its wings, blazing in oriental splendour upon
her nipple, and he felt himself stirred once more.

'Ruth.' His voice was husky again. She rolled her head to look into his
eyes.

'Go away, little butterfly,' and she brushed it from her breast.


Later, after they had slept a little, Ruth woke him and they sat facing
each other on the rug with the open hamper between them.

While Sean uncorked the wine she worked over the hamper with the
dedication of a priestess preparing a sacrifice. He watched her split the bread
rolls and fill them with salty, yellow butter, then open the screw-topped jars
of soused beans and pickled onions and beetroot. A heart of young lettuce
rustled crisply as she plucked its leaves into a wooden bowl, and poured
dressing over them.

Her hair, released from its braid, broke like a black wave over the marble
of her shoulders, then rippled and swung with the small movements of her
body. With the back of her hand she brushed it from her forehead, then
looked up at him and smiled.

'Don't stare. It's bad manners.' She took the glass he offered her and
sipped the cool yellow wine, set it aside and went on to dismember the fat-
breasted chicken. Pretending to ignore his eyes upon her body, she began to
sing, softly, the love-song she had sung on the night of the storm and shyly
her breasts peeped at him through the black curtain of her hair.

She wiped her fingers carefully on a linen napkin, took up the wineglass
again and with elbows on her knees leaned forward slightly and returned
his scrutiny with equal frankness.

'Eat,' she said.

'And you?'

'In a little while. I want to watch you.'

Then he was hungry.

'You eat the way you make love – as though tomorrow you die.'

'I'm taking no chances.'

'You're covered with scars, like an old tom-cat who fights too much,' and she leaned forward and touched his chest with one finger. 'What happened there?'

'Leopard.'

'And there?' She touched his arm.

'Knife.'

'And there?' his wrist.

'Burst shotgun.'

She dropped her hand and caressed the fresh purple cicatrice that twined around his leg like some grotesque parasitic vine.

'This one I know,' she whispered and her eyes were sad as she touched it.

Quickly, to change her mood, he spoke.

'Now it's my turn to ask the questions.' He reached across and laid his open hand upon her stomach where the first faint bulge pressed warmly into his palm.

'What happened there?' he demanded, and she giggled before she replied. 'Burst shotgun – or was it a cannon?'

When she had repacked the hamper she knelt beside him. He lay flat on his back with a long black cheroot between his teeth.

'Have you had sufficient?' she asked.

'My God, yes,' and he sighed happily.

'Well, I haven't.' She leaned over him, took the cheroot from his mouth and flicked it into the brambles.

With the first faint flush of evening in the sky a small breeze came down from the mountain and rustled the leaves above them. The fine hairs upon her forearms came erect, each on its tiny pimple of gooseflesh, and her nipples stood out dark and hard.

'You must not be late back to the hospital on the very first day they've let you out.' She rolled away from him and reached for her clothing. 'Matron will have me hung, drawn and quartered.' Sean agreed. They dressed quickly, and she was remote from him. All the laughter gone from her voice and her face cold and expressionless.

He stood behind her to lace the whalebone corset. He hated to cage that lovely body and was about to say so.

'Saul is coming tomorrow. A month's leave.' Her voice was harsh. His hands stilled and they stood without moving. It was the first time either of them had referred to Saul since that morning a month ago when she had come to him at the hospital.

'Why didn't you tell me sooner?' His voice also was harsh.

'I didn't want to spoil today.' She had not turned towards him, but stood staring out across the glade to the far hills beyond the town.

'We must decide what we are going to tell him.'

'There is nothing to tell him,' she answered flatly.

'But what are we going to do?' Now his voice was ugly with mingled dread and guilt.

'Do, Sean?' She turned slowly and her face was still cold and expressionless. 'We are going to do nothing – nothing at all.'

'But you belong to me?' he cried in protest.

'No,' she answered.

'The child – it's mine!'

At his words her eyes narrowed and the sweet line of her lips hardened in anger.

'No, damn you, it isn't! Not yours – although you sired it.' She flamed at him. It was the first time she had unleashed her temper at him. It startled Sean. 'The child belongs to Saul – and I belong to Saul. We owe you nothing.'

He stared at her. 'You don't mean that,' and the flames of her anger faded. Quickly he tried to press his advantage.

'We'll go away together.'

'*Run away* – you mean. *Sneak away* like a pair of thieves. What would we take with us, Sean? The happiness of a man who loves and trusts us both – that, and your own guilt. You'd never forgive me, nor I you. Even now when we talk of it you cannot meet my eyes. Already you are beginning to hate me a little'

'No! No!'

'And I would hate you,' she whispered. 'Call for my horse, please.'

'You don't love him.' The agonized accusal was wrung from him, but it was as though he had not spoken. She went on dressing.

'He'll want to see you. Half of every letter he writes is about you. I've told him that I've visited you at the hospital.'

'I'm going to tell him,' Sean shouted. 'I'll tell him everything.'

'No, you won't.' She answered him calmly. 'You did not save him at Colenso to destroy him now. You would destroy him – and us. Please call for my horse.'

Sean whistled and they stood together, not touching, not talking, not even looking at each other. Until Mbejane emerged from the bush below the glade leading the horses.

Sean lifted her into the saddle.

'When?' he asked quietly.

'Perhaps never,' she answered and swung the horse away. She did not look back so Sean never saw the tears that streamed down her face. The muffled drum of hooves drowned her sobs and she held her back and her shoulders stiff so that he would not know.


# Chapter Twenty-five

The War Council ended long after dark and when his commandants had upsaddled and ridden away to their laagers among the hills, Jan Paulus sat alone beside the fire.

He was tired, as though his brain was the cold, flabby body of an octopus and its tentacles spread out to every extremity of his body. He was lonely.

Now at the head of five thousand men he was alone as he had never been in the vast solitude of the open veld.

Because of the loneliness and because of the companionship she had given him these past twenty years his thoughts turned to Henrietta, and he smiled in the darkness and felt the longing blunt the edge of his determination.

I would like to go back to the farm, for a week only. Just to see that they are all well. I would like to read to them from the Book and watch the faces of the children in the lamplight. I would like to sit with my sons on the stoep and hear the voices of Henrietta and the girls as they work in the kitchen. I would like . . .

Abruptly he stood up from beside the fire. *Ja*, you would like this and you would like that! Go, then! Give yourself leave of absence as you have refused it to so many others. He clenched his jaw, biting into the stem of his pipe. Or else, sit here and dream like an old woman while twenty-five thousand Englishmen pour across the river.

He strode out of the laager, and the earth tilted upwards beneath his feet as he headed for the ridge. Tomorrow, he thought. Tomorrow.

God has been merciful that they did not rush the ridge two days ago when I had three hundred men to hold it. But now I have five thousand to their twenty-five – so let them come!

Suddenly, as he reached the crest, the valley of the Tugela lay below him. Soft with moonlight so that the river was a black gash in the land. He scowled as he saw the field of bivouac fires that straddled the drift at Trichardts farm.

They have crossed. May God forgive me that I had to let them cross, but I could not meet and hold them with three hundred. Two days I have waited in agony for my columns to cover the twenty miles from Colenso. Two days while the cannon bogged down in the mud. Two days while I watched their cavalry and their foot soldiers and their wagons crossing the drift and I could not stop them.

Now they are ready. Tomorrow they will come up to us. This is where they will come, to try at any other place is madness, a stupidity far beyond any they have shown before.

They cannot try the right, for to reach it they must march across our front. With little cover and the river fencing them in they would expose their flank to us at two thousand yards. No, they cannot try the right – not even Buller will try the right.

Slowly he turned his head and looked out to the left where the tall peaks rose sheer out of the heights. The formation of the ground resembled the back of a gigantic fish. Jan Paulus stood upon its head, on the relatively smooth slope of Tabanyama – but on his left rose the dorsal fin of the fish. This was a series of peaks – Vaalkrans, Brakfontein, Twin Peaks, Conical Hill and, the highest and the most imposing of all, Spion Kop.

Once again, he experienced the nagging prickle of doubt. Surely no man, not even Buller, would throw any army against that line of natural fortresses. It would be senseless as the sea hurling its surf at a line of granit cliffs. Yet the doubt remained.

Perhaps Buller, that pedestrian and completely predictable man; Buller who seemed eternally committed to the theory of frontal assault, perhaps this time he would know that the slopes of Tabanyama were *too* logically the only point at which he could break through. Perhaps he would know that the whole of the Boer Army waited for him there with all their guns. Perhaps he would guess that only twenty burghers guarded each of the peaks on the left flank – that Jan Paulus had not dared to spread his line so thin, and had risked everything on Tabanyama.

Jan Paulus sighed. Now it was past the time for doubt. He had made the choice and tomorrow they would know. Tomorrow, *van more*.

Heavily he turned away and started down towards the laager. The moon was setting behind the black massif of Spion Kop, and its shadow hid the path. Loose rock rolled under his feet. Jan Paulus stumbled and almost fell.

'*Wies Daar?*' The challenge from an outcrop of granite beside the path.

'A friend.' Jan Paulus saw the man now, he leaned against the rock with a Mauser held low across his hips.

'Tell me – what commando are you with?'

'The Wynbergers under Leroux.'

'So! Do you know Leroux?' the sentry asked.

'Yes.'

'What colour is his beard?'

'Red – red as the flames of hell.'

The sentry laughed.

'Tell Oom Paul from me I'll tie a knot in it next time I see him.'

'Best you shave before you try – he might do the same for you,' Jan Paulus warned him.

'Are you his friend?'

'And his kinsman too.'

'The hell with you then also.' The sentry laughed again. 'Will you drink coffee with us?'

It was an ideal opportunity for Jan Paulus to mingle with his men and gauge their temper for tomorrow. '*Dankie.*' He accepted the invitation.

'Good.' The sentry straightened up and Jan Paulus saw he was a big man, made taller by the homburg hat he wore. 'Karl, is there any coffee left in the pot?' He yelled into the darkness beyond the rocks and was answered immediately.

'In the name of God, must you bellow? This is a battlefield, not a political meeting.'

'The English are as loud. I've heard them all night.'

'The English are fools. Must you be the same?'

'For you, only for you.' The sentry dropped his voice to a sepulchral whisper, and then roared again suddenly: 'But what about that damned coffee?'

This one is not short of stomach, Jan Paulus grinned to himself, as the man, still chuckling happily, placed an arm about his shoulder and led him to the screened fire among the rocks. Three burghers squatted about it with blankets draped over their shoulders. They were talking among themselves as the sentry and Jan Paulus approached.

'The moon will be down in half an hour,' one of them said. '*Ja*. I will not be happy to see it gone. If the English plan a night attack, then they will come in the dark of the moon.'

'Who is with you?' Karl asked as they came towards the fire.

'A friend,' the sentry replied.

'From what commando?'

'The Wynbergers,' Jan Paulus answered for himself, and Karl nodded and lifted the battered enamel coffee-pot from the fire.

'So, you are with Oom Paul. And what does he think of our chances for tomorrow?'

'That of a man with one bullet left in thick catbush with a lungshot buffalo coming down in full charge.'

'And does it worry him?'

'Only a madman knows no fear. Oom Paul is afraid. But he tries not to show it, for fear spreads among men like the white sore throat diphtheria,' Jan Paulus replied as he accepted the mug of coffee and settled down against a rock out of the firelight so they would not recognize his face nor the colour of his beard.

'Show it or not,' grunted the sentry as he filled his mug. 'But I reckon he'd give one of his eyeballs to be back on his farm at Wynberg with his wife beside him in the double bed.'

Jan Paulus felt the glow of anger in his belly and his voice as he replied was harsh.

'You think him a coward?'

'I think I would rather stand on a hill a mile behind the fighting and send other men in to die,' the sentry chuckled again, but there was a sardonic note in it.

'I've heard him swear that tomorrow he will be in front wherever the fight is fiercest,' growled Jan Paulus.

'Oh, he said so? So that we fight more cheerfully? But when the Lee-Metfords rip your belly open – how will you know where Oom Paul is?'

'I have told you he is my kin. When you insult him you insult me.' Anger had closed Jan Paulus's throat so that his voice was hoarse.

'Good!' The sentry stood up quickly. 'Let us settle it now.'

'Be still, you fools.' Karl spoke irritably. 'Save your anger for the English,' and then more softly, 'all of us are restless, knowing what tomorrow will bring. Let your quarrel stand.'

'He is right,' Jan Paulus agreed, still choked with anger. 'But when I meet you again . . .!'

'How will you know me?' the sentry demanded.

'Here!' Jan Paulus jerked the wide-brimmed Terai hat from his head and flung it at the man's feet. 'Wear that and give me yours in exchange.'

'Why?' The sentry stood puzzled.

'Then if ever a man comes up to me and says, "You're wearing my hat", he will be saying, "Jan Paulus Leroux is a coward!" '

The man grinned so that his teeth glittered in the firelight, then he dropped his own black homburg into Jan Paulus's lap and stooped to pick up the Terai. In that instant, faintly on the wind, soft as the crackle of dried twigs, they heard the rifle-fire.

'Mausers!' shouted Karl and he leapt to his feet sending the coffee-pot flying.

'On the left,' moaned Jan Paulus in anguish. 'Oh, God help us! They've tried the left.'

The chorus of rifle-fire rose, swelling urgently; and now blending with the crisp crackle of the Mausers was the deep belling of the Le-Metfords.

'Spion Kop! They're on Spion Kop,' and Jan Paulus ran, hurling himself down the path towards the laager with the black homburg jammed down over his ears.

## Chapter Twenty-six

The mist lay heavily on the peak of Spion Kop that morning, so that the dawn was a thing of liquid, pearly light. A soft uncertain thing that swirled about them and condensed in tiny drops upon the metal of their rifles.

Colonel John Acheson was breakfasting on ham sandwiches spread thickly with Gentleman's Relish. He sat on a boulder with his uniform cloak draped over his shoulders and chewed morosely.

'No sign of the jolly old Boer yet,' the captain beside him announced cheerfully.

'That trench is not deep enough.' Acheson glowered at the shallow ditch which had been scraped in the stony soil and which was now filled to capacity with men in all the various attitudes of relaxation.

'I know, sir. But there's not much we can do about it. We're down to bedrock and it would need a wagon-load of dynamite to sink another foot.' The captain selected a sandwich and upended the Relish bottle over it. 'Anyway, all the enemy fire will be from below and the parapets will cover that.' Along the front edge of the trench clods of earth and loose rock had been piled to a height of two feet. Pathetic cover for two thousand men.

'Have you ever been on this mountain before?' Acheson asked politely.

'No, sir, Of course not.'

'Well, what makes you so bloody certain how the land lies. You can't see a thing in this mist.'

'Well, sir, we *are* on the crest, and it *is* the highest ...' But Acheson interrupted him irritably. 'Where are those damned scouts? Haven't they come in yet?' He jumped up and with his cloak swirling about him strode along the trench. 'You men. Can't you get that parapet higher there'.

At his feet a few of them stirred and began half-heartedly piling stone. They were exhausted by the long night climb and the skirmish which had driven the Boer garrison from the mountain, and Acheson heard them muttering sullenly behind him as he walked on.

'Acheson!' Out of the mist ahead of him loomed the figure of General Woodgate followed closely by his staff.

'Sir!' Acheson hurried to meet him.

'Are your men entrenched?'

'As best they can.'

'Good. What of the enemy? Have your scouts reported back yet?'

'No. They're still out there in the mist.' And Acheson pointed into the smoky billows that limited the range of their vision to fifty feet.

'Well, we should be able to hold until we are reinforced. Let me know the moment ...' A small commotion in the mist behind them, and Woodgate paused. 'What is it?'

'My scouts, sir.'

Saul Friedman began delivering his report from a range of twenty feet. His face was working with excitement as he scurried out of the mist.

'False crest! We're on the false crest. The true summit is two hundred yards ahead and there's a rise of ground out on our right flank, like a little knoll all covered with aloes, that enfilades our whole position. There are Boers everywhere. The whole bloody mountain is crawling with them.'

'Good God, man! Are you certain?'

'Colonel Acheson,' snapped Woodgate, 'turn your right flank to face the knoll,' and as Acheson strode away he added under his breath, 'if you have time!' and he felt the agitated swirl of the mist as it was swept away before the wind.


# Chapter Twenty-seven


Jan Paulus stood beside his pony. The mist had dewed in his beard and set it a-sparkle in red-gold. Across both shoulders heavy bandoliers of ammunition drooped, and the Mauser rifle seemed like a child's toy in his huge hairy hands. His jaw was thrust forward in thought as he reviewed his dispositions. All night he had flogged his pony from laager to laager, all night he had roared and bullied and driven men up the slopes of Spion Kop. And now around him the mountain rustled and murmured with five thousand waiting burghers, and in an arc of 120 degrees behind it stood his guns. From Green Hill in the north-west to the reverse slopes of the Twin Peaks in the east, his gunners crouched beside their creusots and their Nordenfeldts, ready to range in upon the crest of Spion Kop.

*All things are ready and now I must earn the right to wear this hat.* He grinned and settled the homburg more firmly over his ears.

'Hennie, take my horse back to the laager.'

The boy led it away and he started up the last slope towards the summit. The light strengthened as he climbed and the burghers among the rocks recognized the flaming beacon of his beard.

'*Goeie Jag*, Oom Paul,' and, '*Kom saam om die Rooi Nekke te skiet,*' they called. Then two burghers ran down to meet him.

'Oom Paul. We've just been forward to Aloe Knoll. There are no English on it!'

'Are you sure?' It seemed too generous a gift of fortune.

'*Ja*, man. They are all on the back of the mountain. We heard them digging and talking there.'

'What commando are you?' Jan Paulus demanded of the men massed around him in the mist.

'The Carolina commando,' voices answered.

'Come,' ordered Jan Paulus. 'Come, all of you. We are going to Aloe Knoll.'

They followed. Skirting the summit, with the brush, brush, brush of hundreds of feet through the grass, hurrying so that their breathing steamed in the moist air. Until abruptly ahead of them humped the dark mound of Aloe Knoll and they swarmed over it and disappeared among the rocks and crevices like a column of ants returning to their nest.

Lying on his belly Jan Paulus lit his pipe and tamped down on the glowing tobacco with a fire-calloused thumb, sucked the smoke into his mouth and peered into the solid white curtain of mist. In the eerie silence that had fallen upon the mountain his stomach rumbled loudly and he remembered that he had not eaten since the previous noon. There was a stick of biltong in his coat pocket.

*A lion hunts best on an empty stomach*, he thought and drew again on his pipe.

'Here comes the wind,' a voice whispered near him, and he heard the rising sibilance of it through the aloes above his head. The aloes stood tall as a man, multi-headed, green candelabra tipped in crimson and gold, nodding slightly in the morning wind.

'*Ja.*' Jan Paulus felt it stirring deep in his chest, that blend of fear and exhilaration that drowned his fatigue. 'Here it comes.' He knocked out his pipe, stuffed it still hot into his pocket and lifted his rifle from the rock in front of him.

Dramatically, as though unveiling a monument, the wind stripped the mists away. Beneath a sky of cobalt blue, soft golden brown in the early sunshine, lay the rounded peak of Spion Kop. A long uneven scar of red earth five hundred yards long was slashed across it.

'*Almagtig!*' Jan Paulus gasped. 'Now we have them.'

Above the crude parapet of the trench, like birds on a fence rail, so close that he could see the chinstraps and the button on each crown, the light khaki helmets contrasted clearly with the darker earth and grass. While beyond the trench, completely exposed from boots to helmets, standing in the open or moving leisurely forward with ammunition and water canteens, were hundreds of English soldiers.

For long seconds the silence persisted, as though the burghers who stared over their rifles at this unbelievable target could not bring themselves to press the triggers on which their fingers rested. The English were too close, too vulnerable. A universal reluctance held the Mausers silent.

'Shoot!' roared Jan Paulus. '*Skiet, Kerels, Skiet,*' and his voice carried to the English behind the trenches. He saw all movement among them suddenly paralysed, white faces turn to stare in his direction – and he sighted carefully into the chest of one of them. The rifle jumped against his shoulder, and the man went down into the grass.

That single shot broke the spell. Gunfire crackled in hysterical unison and the frieze of khaki figures along the trench exploded into violent movement as the bullets thudded amongst them. At that range most of Jan Paulus's burghers could be trusted to knock down four running springbok with five shots. In the few seconds that it took the English to dive into the trench, at least fifty of them went down, dead or wounded, and lay sprawled against the red earth.

Now there were only the helmets and heads above the parapet to shoot at and these were never still. They ducked and weaved and bobbed as Woodgate's men fired and reloaded, and seventeen hundred Lee-Metford rifles added their voices to the pandemonium.

Then the first shell, lobbed from a field gun on the reverse slope of Conical Hill, shrieked over the heads of the burghers and burst in a leap of smoke and red dust fifty feet in front of the English trench. A lull while Jan Paulus's heliograph team below the crest signalled the range correction to the battery, then the next shell burst beyond the trench; another lull and the third fell full upon the trench. A human body was thrown high, legs and arms spinning like the spokes of a wagon wheel. When the dust cleared there was a gap in the parapet and half a dozen men frantically trying to plug it with loose rock.

Together all the Boer guns opened. The constant shriek of big shells was punctuated by the vicious whine of the quick-firing pompoms. And once again a mist covered the peak, this time a thin sluggish mist of dust and lyddite fume which diluted the sunlight and clogged the nostrils and eyes and mouths of men for whom a long, long day had begun.

## Chapter Twenty-eight

Lieutenant-Colonel Garrick Courtney was damnably uncomfortable. It was hot in the sun. Sweat trickled down under his tunic and moistened his stump so that already it was chafed. His field-glasses magnified the glare as he looked out across the Tugela River to the great hump of the mountain four miles away. The glare aggravated the ache behind his eyes, which was a memorial to last night's drinking.

'Woodgate seems to be holding very well. His reinforcements should be up to him soon enough.'

Sir Redvers Buller appeared to be satisfied, and none of his staff had any comment to add. Stolidly they stood and stared through their glasses at the peak which was now faintly blurred with the dust and smoke of battle.

Garrick was puzzling once more the devious lines of authority which

Buller had established for the attack on Spion Kop. Commanding the actual assault was General Woodgate, who was now 'holding very well' on the peak, yet Woodgate was responsible not to Buller but to General Charles Warren, who had his headquarters beyond Trichardts Drift where the column had crossed. Warren was in turn responsible to Buller, who was well back behind the river, standing on a pleasant little hill called Mount Alice.

Everyone on the staff was aware that Buller hated Warren. Garrick was certain that Warren had been given command of an operation which Buller considered very risky, so that in the event it failed Warren would be discredited and goaded into resigning. Of course, if he succeeded, Sir Redvers Buller was still supreme Commander and the credit would therefore accrue to him.

It was a line of reasoning Garrick found easy to follow, in fact, had he been in Buller's position he would have done exactly the same thing. This secret knowledge gave Garry a deal of satisfaction, and standing beside Buller on the slope of Mount Alice he felt very much in tune with him. He found himself hoping that Spion Kop would soon be a bloody slaughter-house, and that Warren would retreat across the river in disgrace. He remembered the occasion in the mess when Sir Charles had referred to him as an 'irregular, and a damned *colonial* irregular – at that!' Garry's fingers tightened on his field-glasses and he glared out at the mountain. He was so deep in his resentment that he hardly noticed the signaller who came running from the mule wagon that housed the field telegraph which connected Buller's headquarters with those of Warren beyond the river.

'Sir! Sir! A message from General Warren.' The urgency of the man's tone caught all their attentions. As one man the entire general staff lowered their glasses and turned to him.

'Let's have it then, my man!' Buller snatched the sheet of notepaper and read it slowly. Then he looked up at Garry and there was something in those pale, bulging eyes, a pleasure, a conspiratory gleam that made Garry almost grin.

'What do you make of that, Courtney?' He handed the sheet across and waited while Garry read it.

'Message from Colonel Crofton on the Spion Kop. *Reinforce at once or all is lost. General Woodgate dead. What do you suggest. Warren.*'

'It seems to me, sir,' Garry spoke slowly, trying to mask the fierce jubilation he felt, 'that Sir Charles Warren is on the verge of panic.'

'Yes, that's the way it looks.' Buller was openly gloating now.

'I would suggest sending him a message that will stiffen him, sir.'

'Yes, I agree.' Buller turned to the signaller and began to dictate. 'The mountain must be held at all costs. No withdrawal. I repeat no withdrawal. Reinforce with Middlesex and Dorset regiments.' Then he hesitated and looked around his staff. 'What do you know of this fellow Crofton. Is he the right man to command on the peak?'

There were non-committal sounds of negation from them until A'Court, Buller's A.D.C., spoke up.

'Sir. There is one excellent man up there – Acheson – Colonel John Acheson. You remember his showing at Colenso?'

Buller nodded thoughtfully and turning back to the signaller he went on with his dictation. 'You must put some really good hard fighting man in command on the peak. Suggest you promote Acheson fo Major-General.'

# Chapter Twenty-nine

In front of the trench the grass was flattened by the repeated counter-attacks that had swept across it, stained by the blood of those who had dragged themselves back from the Boer positions along the crest, and littered with the twisted corpses of those who had not. Every few seconds a shell exploded along the British line, so there was a continual moving forest of bursts, and the shrapnel hissed like the flails of threshing giants.

John Acheson forced himself to his feet and climbed on to the parapet and shouted, 'Come on, lads. This time they'll not stop us!' In the trench below him the dead and the wounded lay upon each other two and three deep, all of them coated with a layer of red dust. The same red dust coated the faces that looked up at him as he shouted again.

'Bugler, sound the charge. Come, lads, forward. Take the bayonet to them.'

The bugle started to sing, brassy and urgent. Acheson hopped like a gaunt, old stork from the parapet and flapped his sword. Behind him he heard laughter from a dozen throats, not the laughter of ordinary men, but the chilling discord of insanity.

'Follow me, the Lancs! Follow me!' His voice rose to a shriek and they scrambled from the trench behind him. Dusty spectres with bloodshot eyes, smeared with dust and their own sweat. Their laughter and their curses blended with the babbling of the wounded, outstripped it and climbed into a chorus of wild cheers. Without form, spreading like spilled oil, the charge flowed out towards the crest. Four hundred men staggering through the dust-storm of shell-fire and the tempest of the Mausers.

Acheson stumbled over a corpse and fell. His ankle twisted with a shock of pain that jolted his dulled senses. He recovered his sword, dragged himself up and limped grimly on towards the rampart of boulders that marked the crest. But this time they did not reach it to be thrown back as they had before. This time the charge withered before it had covered half the distance. In vain Acheson waved them forward, yelling until his voice was a hoarse croak. They slowed and wavered, then at last they broke and streamed back down the open bullet-swept slope to the trench. Tears of frustrated anger streaking his dusty cheeks, Acheson hobbled after them. He fell over the parapet and lay face down on the corpses that lined the trench.

A hand shaking his shoulder roused him and he sat up quickly and tried to control the breathing that shuddered up his throat. Dimly he recognized the man who crouched beside him.

'What is it, Friedman?' he gasped. But the reply was drowned in the arrival of another shell, and the delirious shrieks of a man wounded in the belly in the trench beside them.

'Speak up, man!'

'Heliograph message from Sir Charles Warren,' shouted Saul. 'You have been promoted General. You are in command of the peak.' And then with a dusty sweat-streaked grin he added: 'Well done, sir.'

Acheson stared at him aghast. 'What about General Woodgate?'

'He was shot through the head two hours ago.'

'I didn't know.' Since morning Acheson had known nothing that was happening outside his own small section of the line. His whole existence had closed down to a hundred yards of shrapnel-and bullet-swept earth. Now he peered out at the halocaust around him and whispered, 'In command! No man commands here! The devil is directing this battle.'

'Sir Charles is sending up three more battalions to reinforce us,' Saul shouted into his ear.

'We can well use them,' Acheson grunted, and then, 'Friedman, I've sprained my ankle. I want you to lace up my boot as tight as you can – I'm going to need this foot again before the day is done.'

Saul knelt without argument and began working over his foot. One of the riflemen at the parapet beside him was thrown sideways. He fell across Acheson's lap, and from the wound in his temple the contents of his skull splattered them both. With an exclamation of surprise and disgust Saul pulled back and wiped his face, then he reached forward to drag the body from Acheson's legs.

'Leave him.' Acheson prevented him sharply. 'See to that boot.' While Saul obeyed, Acheson unwound the silk scarf from around his own neck and covered the mutilated head. It was a wound he had seen repeated a hundred times that day, all of them shot through the right side of the head.

'Aloe Knoll,' he whispered fiercely. 'If only we'd taken Aloe Knoll.' Then his tone dulled. 'My poor lads.' And gently he eased the shattered head from his lap.

# Chapter Thirty

'They are ripe now, let us pluck them!' With five hundred of his burghers Jan Paulus had left the shelter of Aloe Knoll and worked his way forward, crawling belly down through the jumble of rocks, until now they were crouched in a line along a fold of dead ground below the false crest. Twenty yards ahead of them was the right-hand extremity of the English trench.

They could not see it, but clearly they heard the incoherent cries of the wounded; the shouts of 'Stretcher-bearer! Stretcher-bearer!' and 'Ammunition boys, here!' and above the splutter of musketry, the continuous metallic rattle of breech bolts reloading.

'You must signal to the guns, Oom Paul.' The burgher next to him reminded him.

'*Ja*,' Jan Paulus removed the homburg from his head and waved with it at the fat mound at Aloe Knoll behind them. He saw his signal briefly acknowledged and knew that the order to cease fire was being flashed by heliograph to the batteries.

They waited, tensed to charge, a long line of men. Jan Paulus glanced along them and saw that each man stared ahead fixedly. Most of their faces masked by beards of fifty different hues, but here and there a lad too young for this work, too young to hide his fear. Thank God my eldest is not yet twelve, or he would be here. He stopped that train of thought guiltily, and concentrated his whole attention on the volume of shell-fire that raged just ahead of them. Abruptly it ceased, and in the comparative silence the rifle-fire sounded strangely subdued. Jan Paulus let the slow seconds pass, counting silently to ten, before he filled his lungs and roared:

'*Vrystaat!* Come on the Free Staters!'

Echoing his cry, yelling wildly, his burghers surged forward over the crest on to the English flank. They came from so close in, seeming to appear as a solid wall from under the English parapet, that the momentum of their charge carried them instantly into the depleted line of shell-shocked, thirst-tormented and dazed Lancashires. Hardly a shot was fired, and though a few individual scuffles rippled the smooth onward flow of the charge – most of the English responded immediately to the shouts of 'Hands Op! Hand Op!' by throwing down their rifles and climbing wearily to their feet with hands held high. They were surrounded by jubilant burghers and hustled over the parapet and down the slope towards Aloe Knoll. A great milling throng of burghers and soldiers spread over fifty yards of the trench.

'Quickly!' Jan Paulus shouted above the hubbub. 'Catch them and take them away.' He was well aware that this was only a very localized victory, involving perhaps a tenth of the enemy. Already cries of 'The Lancs are giving in!', 'Where are the officers?', 'Back, you men', were spreading along the English line. He had planted the germ of defeat among them, now he must spread it through them before he could carry the entire position. Frantically he signalled for reinforcements from the Boer positions along the crest, hundreds of his burghers were already running forward from Aloe Knoll. Another five minutes and complete victory would emerge from the confusion.

'Damn you, sir! What do you think you're doing!' The voice behind him was impregnated with authority, unmistakably that of a high-ranking officer. Jan Paulus wheeled to face a tall and enraged old gentleman, whose pointed grey whiskers quivered with fury. The apoplectic crimson of his countenance clashed horribly with its coating of red dust.

'I am taking your men hands-up away.' Jan Paulus struggled gutturally with the foreign words.

'I'll be damned if you are, sir.' Leaning heavily on the shoulder of a skinny little dark-haired man who supported him, the officer reached forward and shook a finger in Jan Paulus's face. 'There will be no surrender on this hill, Kindly remove your rabble from my trench!'

'Rabble, is it!' roared Jan Paulus. Around them the Boers and the British had ceased all activity and were watching with interest. Jan Paulus turned to the nearest burghers: '*Vat hulle weg!* Take them away!' His gesture that accompanied the order was unmistakable.

'We'll have none of that, sir!' Acheson glared at him before issuing his own order. 'You men, fall back and re-form on the Devonshires. Hurry it up, now. Come along. Come along.'

'Hey!' Jan Paulus held up his hand. 'These are my . . .' He groped for the word. 'My captures.'

'Sir.' Acheson released his grip on Saul's shoulder, drew himself up to his full height and glared up into Jan Paulus's face. 'I will give you five minutes to vacate this trench – otherwise you will become my prisoner. Good day to you.' And he hobbled away through the grass. Jan Paulus stared in disbelief when fifty paces away Acheson turned, folded his arms across his chest, and waited grimly for the expiry of the five minutes. About him he had gathered a handful of battle-stained soldiers and it was clearly his intention to implement his threat with this pitiful little band. Jan Paulus wanted to laugh with frustration – the skinny old goat. But he realized with dismay that most of his prisoners were filtering away and hurrying to join Acheson. He must do something, but what? The whole position was deteriorating into a farce.

'Stop them!' he shouted at his burghers. 'Hold those men – they went hands-up. They cannot change their minds now.'

Then abruptly the whole position altered. Over the skyline behind Acheson and his tiny party poured a solid phalanx of fresh khaki-clad figures. The three battalions of reinforcements sent up from the foot of the mountain by Sir Charles Warren had at last arrived. Acheson glanced over his shoulder and saw them swarming forward. The brown parchment of his face tore laterally in a wide and wicked grin.

'Fix bayonets!' he shrieked, and drew his sword. 'Buglers sound the charge. Charge, men! Charge!'

Hopping and stumbling like a stork with a broken leg, he led them. Behind him, the glittering crest of a wave, a line of bayonets raced down on the trench. Jan Paulus's burghers hated naked steel. There were five hundred of them against two thousand. They broke and blew away like smoke on a high wind. Their prisoners ran with them.

Jan Paulus reached the crest and dropped behind a boulder that already sheltered three men.

'Stop them! Here they come!' he panted.

While the British wave slowed and expended itself against the reef of hidden Mausers, while they fell back with the shrapnel scourging them once more – Jan Paulus knew that he would not stand in the British trench again that day.

He could sense the despondency among his burghers. He knew that already the faint-hearted were slipping away to where their ponies waited at the foot of the mountain. He knew with sickened acceptance that he had lost Spion Kop. Oh! The English had paid a heavy price all right, there must be fifteen hundred of their dead and wounded strewn upon the peak, but they had torn a gap in his line. He had lost Spion Kop and through this breach would pour twenty-five thousand men to relieve Ladysmith, and to drive his burghers out of Natal and into the Transvaal. They had lost. It was finished.

John Acheson tried desperately to ignore the agony of his bloated foot, he tried to shut out the shrill chorus of the wounded pleading for water. There was no water on the peak. He turned his gaze away from the trench where men, drugged with exhaustion, oblivious to the thunder of the bombardment that still raged about them, lay in sleep upon the bodies of their dead and dying comrades.

He looked instead at the sun, that great, bloody orb lightly screened with long streamers of cloud. In an hour it would be dark – and he knew he had lost. The message he held in his hands admitted it, the grotesque piles of dead men that clogged the trench proved it. He re-read the message with difficulty for his vision jerked and swam giddily.

'If you cannot hold until tomorrow, retire at your discretion. Buller.'

Tomorrow. What would tomorrow bring, if not a repetition of today's horror? They had lost. They were going down from this mountain. They had lost.

He closed his eyes and leaned back against the rough stone of the parapet. A nerve in his eyelid began to twitch insistently, he could not stop it.

# Chapter Thirty-one

How many are there left? Half, perhaps. I do not know. Half my men gone, all night I heard their ponies galloping away, and the crack and rumble of their wagons, and I could not hold them.

Jan Paulus stared up at the mountain in the dawn.

'Spion Kop.' He mouthed the name with loathing, but its outline was blurred for his eyes could not focus. They were rimmed with angry red and in each corner was a lump of yellow mucus. His body seemed to have shrunk, dried out like that of an ancient mummy. He slumped wearily in the saddle, every muscle and nerve in his body screamed for rest. To sleep a while. Oh God, to sleep.

With a dozen of his loyal commandants he had tried all night to staunch the dribble of deserters that was bleeding his army to death. He had ridden from laager to laager, blustering, pleading, trying to shame them. With many he had succeeded, but with many he had not – and once he had himself been shamed. He remembered the old man with the long white beard straggling from his yellow, wizened face, his eyes glistening with tears in the firelight.

'Three sons I have given you today, Jan Paulus Leroux. My brothers have gone up your accursed mountain to beg for their bodies from the English. Three sons! Three fine sons! What more do you want from me?' From where he sat against the wheel of his wagon the old man struggled to his feet hugging the blanket around his shoulders, 'You call me coward, Leroux. You say I am afraid.' He stopped and struggled with his breathing, and when he went on his voice was a croak. 'I am seventy-eight years old and you are the first man to ever call me that – if God is merciful you'll be the last.' He stopped again. 'Seventy-eight years. Seventy-eight! and you call me that! Look, Leroux. Look well!' He let the blanket fall away and Jan Paulus stiffened in the saddle as he saw the bloody mess of bandages that swathed the old man's chest 'Tomorrow morning I will be with my sons. I wait for them now. Write on our grave, Leroux! Write *"Cowards"* on our grave!' And through the old lips burst a froth of pink bubbles.

Now with red eyes Jan Paulus stared up at the mountain. The lines of fatigue and shame and defeat were etched deep beside his nostrils and around his mouth. When the mists cleared they would see the English on the crest and with half his men he would go back. He touched the pony with his spurs and started him up the slope.

The sun gilded the mountain mist, it swirled golden and began to dissipate.

Faintly on the morning wind he heard the cheering and he frowned. *The English cheer too soon*, he thought. *Do they think we will not come again?* He urged his pony upward, but as it scrambled over loose rock and scree he reeled drunkenly in the saddle and was forced to cling to the pommel.

The volume of cheering mounted, and he peered uncomprehendingly at the crest above him. The skyline was dotted with figures who danced and waved their hats, and suddenly there were voices all around him.

'They've gone.'

'The mountain is ours.'

'We've won! Praise God, we've won. The English have gone.'

Men crowded about his pony, and dragged him from the saddle. He felt his legs buckle under him, but rough hands were there to support him, and half dragging, half carrying, they bore him up towards the peak.

Jan Paulus sat upon a boulder and watched them harvest the rich crop of battle. He could not sleep yet, not until this was done. He had allowed the English stretcher-bearers to come up his mountain and they were at work along the trench while his own burghers gleaned their dead from along the crest.

Four of them approached Jan Paulus, each holding the corner of a grey woollen blanket as though it were a hammock. They staggered under the load, until they reached the neat line of corpses already laid out on the grass.

'Who knows this man?' one of them called, but there was no reply from the group of silent men who waited with Jan Paulus.

They lifted the body out of the blanket and laid it with the others. One of the burghers who had carried him removed from his clutching, dead fingers a wide Terai hat and placed it over his face. Then he straightened and asked:

'Who claims him?' Unless a friend or a kinsman claimed the corpse it would be buried in a communal grave.

Jan Paulus stood up and walked across to stand over the body. He lifted the hat and replaced it with the homburg from his own head.

'*Ja*. I claim him,' he said heavily.

'Is he kin or friend, Oom Paul?'

'He is a friend.'

'What is his name?'

'I do not know his name. He is just a friend.'

## Chapter Thirty-two

Saul Friedman fidgeted impatiently. In his eagerness he had arrived half an hour before visiting-time began and for this he was doing penance in the bleak little waiting-room of Greys Hospital. He sat forward on the straight-backed chair, twisted his helmet between his fingers and stared at the large sign on the opposite wall.

'Gentlemen are requested *Not* to smoke'.

He had asked Ruth to come with him, but she had pleaded a headache. In a sneaking fashion Saul was glad. He knew that her presence would inhibit his reunion with Sean Courtney. He didn't want polite conversation about the weather and how was he feeling now, and he must come round to dinner some evening. It would have been difficult not to be able to swear if they wanted – it would have been even more difficult in view of Ruth's attitude.

Yesterday, the first day of his leave, he had spoken of Sean with enthusiasm. How many times had she visited him? How was he? Did he limp badly? Didn't Ruth think he was a wonderful person? Twice she replied and, well, no not badly, yes he was very nice. Just about then Saul perceived the truth. Ruth did not like Sean. At first he could hardly believe it. He tried to continue the conversation. But each of her monosyllabic replies confirmed his first suspicion. Of course, she had not said so, but it was so obvious. For some reason she had taken a dislike to Sean which was close to loathing.

Now Saul sat and pondered the reason. He discounted the possibility that Sean had offended her. If that were the case Sean would have received as good as he gave and afterwards Ruth would have related the whole tale with glee and relish.

No, Saul decided, it was something else. Like a swimmer about to dive into icy water, Saul drew a metaphorical deep breath and plunged into the uncharted sea of feminine thought processes. Was Sean's masculinity so overpowering as to be offensive? Had his attention to her been below average (Ruth was accustomed to extravagant reactions to her beauty)? Could it be that . . .? Or, on the other hand, did Sean . . .? Saul was floundering heavily when suddenly, as a shipwrecked victim surfacing for the last time finds a tall ship close alongside with lifeboats being lowered from every derrick, the solution came to him.

Ruth was jealous!

Saul leaned back in the chair, astounded at the depth of his own perception.

His lovely, hot-tempered wife was jealous of the friendship between Sean and himself!

Chuckling tenderly, Saul laid plans to appease Ruth. He'd have to be less fulsome in his praises of Sean. He must get them together and in Sean's presence pay special attention to Ruth. He must . . .

Then his thoughts richocheted off in another direction and he began to think about Ruth. As always when he thought too intensely about her, he experienced a feeling of bemusement similar to what a poor man feels on winning a large lottery.

He had met her at the Johannesburg Turf Club during the big Summer Meeting, and he had fallen in love at a range of fifty paces, so that when he was presented to her, his usually nimble tongue lay like a lump of heavy metal in his mouth and he squirmed and was silent. The friendly smile she bestowed upon him licked across his face like a blow torch, heating it until he felt the skin would blister.

That night, alone in his lodging, he planned his campaign. To its conduct he allocated the sum of five hundred guineas, which was exactly half his savings. The following morning he began his intelligence work, and a week later he had collected a massive volume of information.

She was eighteen years old and was on a visit to relations in Johannesburg, a visit scheduled to last a further six weeks. She came from a rich Natal family of brewers and hotel-keepers, but she was an orphan and a ward of her uncle. While in Johannesburg she rode every day, visited the theatre or danced every night with an assortment of escorts, except Fridays when she attended the Old Synagogue in Jeppe Street.

His opening manoeuvre was the hire of a horse and he waylaid her as she rode out with her cousin. She did not remember him and would have ridden on, but at last his tongue, which was sharpened by three years of practice at the Johannesburg Bar, came to life. Within two minutes she was laughing and an hour later she invited him back to tea with her relatives.

The following evening he called for her in a splendid carriage and they dined at Candy's Hotel and went on to the Ballet in company with a party of Saul's friends.

Two nights later she went with him to the Bar Association Ball and found that he was a superb dancer. Resplendent in brand-new evening dress, with an ugly yet mobile and expressive face, an inch taller than her five feet six, with wit and intelligence that had earned him a wide circle of friends – he was the perfect foil for her own beauty. When he returned her home Ruth had a thoughtful but dreamy look in her eye.

The following day she attended Court and listened to him successfully defend a gentleman accused of assault with intent to do grievous bodily harm. She was impressed by his display and decided that in time he would reach the heights of his profession.

A week later Saul again proved his command of the spoken word in an impassioned declaration of love. His suit was judged and found worthy, and after that it was merely a case of informing the families and sending out the invitations.

Now, at last, four years later they were to have their first child. Saul grinned happily as he thought about it. Tomorrow he would begin his attempt to discourage the adoption of the name 'Storm'. It would be a difficult case to win, one worthy of his talents. In the preceding four years Saul had learned that once Ruth set her small white teeth into something she had a bulldog grip. A great deal of finesse was needed to loosen that grip without invoking her wrath. Saul had an awesome respect for his wife's wrath.

'It's four o'clock.' The little blonde nurse poked her head around the waiting-room door and smiled at him. 'You may go in now. You'll find him out on the veranda.'

Saul's eagerness returned in full flood and he had to restrain himself from bouncing too boisterously down the veranda.

He recognized Sean's bulk, clad in uniform khaki, reclining elegantly in a cane-backed chair and chatting to the men in the row of beds in front of him. He came up behind the chair.

'Don't stand up, Sergeant. Just toss me a salute from where you are.'

'Saul!' Lugging himself out of the chair and pivoting easily on his game leg, Sean gripped both Saul's shoulders in the old show of affection. The pleasure that fired Sean's expression was genuine and that was enough for Saul.

'Good to see you, you old bastard.' He returned Sean's grip, grinning happily. He did not notice how swiftly Sean's pleasure faded, and was replaced by a shifty, nervous smile.

'Have a drink.' They were the first words that came into Sean's mind. He must have time to feel his way. Had Ruth said anything to Saul, had he guessed?

'Water?' Saul grimaced.

'Gin,' whispered Sean, guilt making him garrulous and he went on in a clumsy attempt at humour. 'Water carafe is full of gin. For God's sake don't tell Matron. I smuggle it in. Argue with the nurse whenever she tries to change it – she says "Water stale, must change!" I say, "Like stale water, raised on stale water, stale water strongly indicated in all cases of leg injury!" '

'Give me stale water too,' laughed Saul.

While he poured Sean introduced Saul to the gentleman in the next bed, a Scotsman who agreed with them that stale water was a sovereign therapeutic for shrapnel wound in the chest – a complaint from which he was currently suffering. The three of them settled down to a course of intensive treatment.

At Sean's prodding Saul embarked on a long account of the battle of Spion Kop. He made it seem very funny. Then he went on to describe the final break through at Hlangwane, Buller's eventual relief of Ladysmith, and his cautious pursuit of Leroux's army which was now in full retreat into the Transvaal.

They discussed Lord Roberts's offensive that had driven up from the

Cape, relieved Kimberley, swept on to take Bloemfontein and was now poised for the final thrust up through the belly of the Transvaal to Pretoria which was the heart.

'It will all be over in three months.' The Scotsman gave his opinion.

'You think so?' Sean sneered at him a little, and succeeded in provoking an argument whose flames were fed with gin.

As the level in the carafe fell the time for sober and serious discussion passed and they became sentimental. Tenderly Saul inquired after their injuries.

The Scotsman was being shipped home across the sea, and at the thought of parting they became sad.

Sean was returning the following day to Ladyburg for convalescent leave. At the end of which, if the doctors were satisfied that the pieces of shrapnel in his leg were satisfactorily encysted (two words which Sean had difficulty enunciating) he would be returned to duty.

The word '*duty*' aroused their patriotism and Sean and Saul with arms around each other's shoulders swore a mighty oath that together, comrades in arms, brothers in blood, they would see this war out. Never counting the cost in hardship and danger, together they would ride against the foe.

Suitable music was needed for their mood, and the Scotsman gave them 'The Wild Colonial Boy'. His eyes were moist and his voice quavered with emotion.

Deeply touching, but not entirely appropriate to the occasion, Sean and Saul did 'Hearts of Oak' as a duet, then all three launched into a lively rendition of 'Are you awake, Johnny Cope?'

The Matron arrived in the middle of the third chorus, by which time Johnny Cope and anybody else within a hundred yards could not possibly have been sleeping.

'Gentlemen, visiting hour ended at five o'clock.' She was a fearsome woman with a voice like a cavalry charge, but Saul who had pleaded before hanging judges rose undaunted to the defence.

'Madam.' He opened his address with a bow. 'These men – nay, let me speak with truth – these heroes have made great sacrifice in the name of freedom. Their blood has flowed like gin in defence of that glorious ideal – Freedom! All I ask is that a little of that precious stuff be granted unto them. Madam. In the name of honour, of fairness, and of gratitude I appeal to you.' He ended with one fist clenched above his heart and his head tragically bowed.

'Hoots, mon!'

'Oh good! Very good!'

The two heroes burst into spontaneous and heartwarming applause, but over the Matron's features descended a frosty veil of suspicion. She elevated her nose a little and sniffed.

'You're drunk!' she accused grimly.

'Oh, foul libel! Oh, monstrous untruth.' Saul backed hurriedly out of range.

'All right, Sergeant.' She turned grimly on Sean. 'Where is it?'

'What?' Sean was all helpless innocence.

'The bottle!' She lifted the bedclothes and began her search. Saul picked up his helmet, saluted them behind her back and tiptoed down the veranda.

## Chapter Thirty-three

Sean's leave in Ladyburg passed quickly, much too quickly. Mbejane had disappeared on a mysterious errand into Zululand. Sean guessed that it related to the two wives and their offspring that Mbejane had cheerfully sent to the kraals of their parents when he and Sean had left Ladyburg so many years before.

Dirk was incarcerated each morning in the schoolhouse, and so Sean was free to roam alone upon the hills and over the veld that surrounded the town. Most of his time he spent covering the huge derelict ranch called Lion Kop which spread above the escarpment. After a month he knew the course of every stream and each fold and slope of the land. His leg strengthened with the exercise. It no longer pained him and the scar lost its purple shine and dulled down to a closer match with his skin colour.

But as his strength returned and flesh filled out his shoulders and padded the gaunt bones of his face, so restlessness came back to him. His daily pilgrimage to Lion Kop Ranch became an obsession. He wandered through the bare rooms of the old homestead and saw them as they could be with the thatched roof replaced to keep out the rain and the flaking plaster renewed and freshly painted. He stood before the empty, smoke-blackened fireplace and imagined the glow and the warmth it could give. Stamping across the dusty floors he judged the yellow-wood planking as sound as the massive beams that supported the roof. Then he wandered out across the land, stooping now and then to take up a handful of earth and feel its rich loamy texture.

In the May of 1900 he went to the Deeds Registry at the Magistrate's office and surreptitiously inspected the title. He found that the fifteen thousand acres of Lion Kop Ranch had been purchased from the estate of the late Stephanus Johannes Erasmus by the Ladyburg Banking & Trust Co. Ltd. Transfer had been signed by Ronald Pye, Esq., in his capacity as Chairman of the Bank. Sean grinned. Ronny Pye was his most cherished childhood enemy. This could be very amusing.

Sean settled himself in the deep, soft nest of polished leather formed by the arm-chair and glanced curiously around the panelled office.

'A few changes since you were last here. Hey, Sean?' Ronny Pye interpreted his thoughts accurately.

'A few.' The Ladyburg Banking & Trust Co. was doing very prettily, judging by the furnishings. Some of its prosperity showed on the figure of its Chairman. Plenty of flesh under the solid gold watch-chain, dark but expensive jacket to offset the extravagant waistcoat, fifteen-guinea hand-made boots. Very nice until you looked at the face; pale so that the freckles showed like irregular gold coins, greedy eyes, ears like the handles of a shaving-mug – that much hadn't changed. But although Ronny was just two years Sean's senior, there was plenty of grey in his ginger sideburns and little wrinkles of worry around his eyes.

'Been out to Theuniskraal to visit your sister-in-law yet?' There was a sly expression in Ronny's face as he asked.

'No.'

'No, of course you wouldn't,' Ronny nodded understandingly and managed to convey that the scandal, though old, was by no means dead. Sean felt a repugnance that made him shift in his chair. The little ginger moustache heightened Ronny's resemblance to a bush rat. Now Sean wanted to end the business and get out into the fresh air again.

'Listen, Ronny. I've searched title on Lion Kop. You own it,' he began abruptly.

'Lion Kop?' The previous morning the clerk from the Registry had hurried down to Mr Pye with news that earned him a sovereign. There had been many others calling with the news that Sean had visited the ranch every day for a month. But now Ronny had to search his memory to place the name. 'Lion Kop? Ah, yes! The old Erasmus place. Yes, I do believe we picked it up from the estate. Paid too much for it, I'm afraid.' Here he sighed with resignation. 'But we can hold on to it for another ten years or so and get our money back. No hurry to sell.'

'I want it.' Sean cut short the preliminaries and Ronny laughed easily.

'You're in good company. Half the farmers in Natal want it – but not enough to meet our price.'

'How much?'

The established price of grazing land in the Ladyburg area was one shilling and sixpence an acre. Ten minutes before Ronny had set himself to ask two shillings. But now he was looking into Sean's eyes and remembering a fist crushing his nose and the taste of his own blood. He heard again Sean's arrogant laughter rejecting his overtures of friendship. No, he thought with hatred. No, you big cocky bastard, now you pay for those.

'Three shillings,' he said.

Sean nodded thoughtfully. He understood. Then suddenly he grinned. 'My God, Ronny, I heard you were a pretty sharp business man. But I must have heard wrong. If you paid three shillings for Lion Kop they really caught you with your skirts up.' And Ronny flushed. Sean had probed deep into his pride.

'I paid ninepence,' he snapped. 'I'm selling for three shillings.'

'Make out the deed of sale for £2,250. I'll take it.'

*Damn it! Damn it to hell!* Ronny swore silently. *He would have paid five.*

'That's for the land only. An extra £1,000 for the improvements.'

'Anything else?' Sean inquired.

'No.'

Sean calculated quickly, with transfer tax he could meet the price with a few hundred spare.

'I'll still take it.'

Ronny stared at him while his brain wriggled like a snake. *I didn't realize he wanted it that badly – I could have had his soul!*

'Of course, my Board will have to approve the sale. It depends on them really.' Ronny's Board of Directors consisted of himself, his little sister Audrey, and her husband Dennis Petersen. Ronny held eighty per cent of the shares, and Sean knew this. He had examined the Company's Articles that were lodged with the Registrar.

'Listen to me, dear friend of my youth.' Sean leaned forward across the stinkwood desk and picked up a heavy silver cigar-box. 'You made an offer. I accepted it. I'll be here at four o'clock this afternoon with the money. Please have the documents ready.' Sean lifted the cigar-box in one fist and started to squeeze. The muscles in his forearm writhed like mating pythons and the box crumpled and burst open at the seams. Sean placed the distorted lump of metal on the blotter in front of Ronny.

'Don't misunderstand me, Sean.' Ronny grinned nervously and dragged his eyes away from the box. 'I'm certain I'll be able to convince my Board.'

## Chapter Thirty-four

The following day was a Saturday. No school for Dirk and Sean took him along on the daily ride out to the ranch. Almost beside himself with joy at being alone with his god, Dirkie raced his pony ahead and then circled at full gallop to fall in beside Sean once more. Laughing with excitement, chattering ecstatically for a while, then he could no longer contain his high spirits and he galloped ahead. Before Sean reached the cross-roads below the escarpment he met a small caravan of travellers coming in the opposite direction.

Sean greeted the leader solemnly. 'I see you, Mbejane.' Mbejane had the jaded and slightly sheepish look of a tom-cat returning from a busy night out. 'I see you also, Nkosi.'

There was a long, embarrassed silence while Mbejane took a pinch of snuff and stared fixedly at the sky above Sean's head. Sean was studying Mbejane's travelling companions. There were two in their middle age, which is about thirty-five years old for a Zulu woman. Both of them wore the tall head-dress of clay which denotes matronhood. Though they retained the proud, erect carriage, their breasts were pendulous and empty and the skin of their bellies above the brief aprons was wrinkled with the marks of child-bearing. There were also two girls just beyond puberty, moon-faced, skins glowing with youth, straight and well-muscled, buttocks like ripe melons and firm, round breasts. They hung their heads and giggled shyly.

'Perhaps it will rain tonight,' Mbejane remarked.

'Perhaps.'

'It will be good for the grazing,' Mbejane ploughed on doggedly.

'Who the hell are these women?' Sean could contain his curiosity no longer and Mbejane frowned at this breach of etiquette. Observations on the weather and the grazing should have continued another five minutes.

'Nkosi, these two are my wives.' He gestured at the matrons.

'The other two your daughters?'

'No.' Mbejane paused, then went on gravely: 'It is not fitting that a man of my years should have but two women who are old for work and the bearing of children. I have purchased two younger wives.'

'I see,' said Sean, and kept the grin off his face. Mbejane had invested a large percentage of his capital. 'And what do you propose doing with all your wives, you know we must soon return again to fight?'

'When the time comes they will go to the kraals of their fathers and wait for me there.' Mbejane hesitated delicately. 'I bring them with me until I am certain that I have trodden on the moon of each of them.'

Treading on a woman's moon was the Zulu expression for interrupting her menstrual cycle. Mbejane was making sure his investment bore interest.

'There is a farm upon the hills up there.' Sean seemed to be changing the subject.

'Many times, Nkosi, you and I have spoken of it.' But Mbejane understood and there was an anticipatory gleam in his eyes.

'It is a good farm?' Sean held him a little longer in suspense.

'It is truly an excellent and beautiful farm. The water is sweeter then the juice of the sugar-cane, the earth is richer than the flesh of a young ox, the grass upon it as thick and as full of promise as the hair on a woman's pudendum.' Now Mbejane's eyes were shining with happiness. In his book a farm was a place where a man sat in the sun with a pot of millet beer beside him and listened to his wives singing in the fields. It meant cattle, the only true wealth, and many small sons to herd them. It meant the end of a long weary road.

'Take your wives with you and select the place where you wish to build your kraal.'

'Nkosi.' There is no Zulu equivalent of *thank you*. He could say *I praise you*, but that was not what Mbejane felt. At last he found the word. '*Bayete! Nkosi, Bayete!*' The salute to a King.

Dirk's pony was tethered to the hitching-post in front of the homestead. Using a charred stick Dirk was writing his name in big crude capitals on the wall of the front veranda.

Although the entire house would be replastered and painted Sean found himself quivering with anger. He jumped from his horse roaring and brandishing his *sjambok* and Dirk disappeared round the corner of the house. By the time Sean had regained self-control and was sitting on the veranda wall revelling in the pride of ownership, Mbejane arrived. They chatted a while and then Mbejane led his women away. Sean could trust him to build the beehive huts of his kraal on the richest earth of Lion Kop.

The last girl in the line was Mbejane's youngest and prettiest wife. Balancing the large bundle on her head, her back straight, her buttocks bare except for the strip of cloth that covered the cleft, she walked away with such unconsciously regal grace that Sean was instantly and forcibly reminded of Ruth.

His elation subsided. He stood up and walked away from the old building. Without Ruth in it, this house would not be a home.

He sat alone on the slope of the hills. Again he was reminded of Ruth. This place was so much like their secret glade. Except, of course, there were no wattle trees here.

## Chapter Thirty-five

'Wattle!' exclaimed Ronny Pye and glared at his sister and his brother-in-law. 'He's planting wattle.'

'What for?' Dennis Petersen asked.

'For the bark, man. The bark! There's a fortune in it. Twenty pounds a ton!'

'What do they use it for?'

'The extract is used in tanning leather.'

'If it's so good why haven't other people—' Dennis began, but Ronny brushed him aside impatiently.

'I've gone into it thoroughly. Lion Kop is ideal wattle ground, high and misty. The only other really good ground in the district is Mahobo's Kloof Ranch and Theuniskraal. Thank God you own Mahobo's Kloof! Because that's where we're going to plant our own wattle.' He looked at Dennis but without seeing him as he went on. 'I've spoken to Jackson at Natal Wattle Company. He'll sell us the saplings on the same terms as he's supplying that bastard Courtney, and he'll buy our bark – every scrap of it at a guaranteed twenty pounds a ton. I've hired two men to supervise the planting. Labour will be our big problem, Sean has grabbed every native within twenty miles. He's got an army of them up there.' Suddenly Ronny stopped. He had seen the expression on Dennis's face 'What's wrong with you?'

'Mahobo's Kloof!' Dennis moaned. 'Oh God! Oh my God!'

'What do you mean?'

'He came to see me last week. Sean . . . He wanted an option to purchase. A five years' option.'

'You didn't give it to him!' Ronny screamed.

'He offered three shillings an acre – that's six times as much as I paid for it. How could I refuse.'

'You fool! You blithering bloody idiot! In five years that land will be worth . . .' Ronny gulped, 'It will be worth at least ten pounds!'

'But nobody told me!' Dennis wailed the age-old cry of the might-have-been, the lament of those that never quite succeed.

'Nobody told Sean either.' Audrey spoke softly for the first time and there was that in her voice that made Ronny turn savagely on his handsome sister.

'All right – we all know about you and Sean. But he didn't stay around long enough for you to get your hooks into him, did he?' Ronny stopped himself and glanced guiltily at Dennis. It was years before Audrey had abandoned all hope of Sean's return to Ladyburg and succumbed to Dennis's gentle but persistent courtship. Now Dennis coughed awkwardly and looked at his hands on the desk in front of him.

'Well, anyway,' he murmured, 'Sean's got it and there's nothing we can do about it.'

'Isn't there – hell!' Ronny pulled a notebook towards him and opened it. 'This is how I see it. He's borrowed that ten thousand from his mother – you know the money we tried to get her to invest in the Burley deal.' They all remembered the Burley deal and looked a little ashamed. Ronny hurried on. 'And he's borrowed another five thousand from Natal Wattle – Jackson let is slip out.' Ronny went on with his calculations. When he finished he was smiling again. 'Mr Sean Courtney is stretched about as thin as he can get without breaking. Just one slip, one little slip and – Pow!' He made a chopping motion with his open hand. 'We can wait!'

He selected a cigar from the leather box which had replaced the silver one and lit it before he spoke again. 'By the way – did you know he hasn't been discharged from the army yet? The way the war is going they certainly need good fighting men. That leg of his looks all right to me. Perhaps a word in the right ear – a little pressure somewhere.' Ronny was positively grinning now. His cigar tasted delicious.

# *Chapter Thirty-six*

The doctors at Greys Hospital had given Sean his final examination a week before Christmas. They had judged his disability as roughly one per cent, a slight limp when he was physically tired. This disqualified him from a war wound pension and had made him available for immediate return to duty.

A week after New Year's Day of 1901 the first letter from the army arrived. He was to report immediately to the Officer Commanding the Natal Mounted Rifles – the regiment which had now swallowed up the old Natal Corps of Guides.

The war in South Africa had entered a new phase. Throughout the Transvaal and Orange Free State the Boers had begun a campaign of guerilla warfare alarming in its magnitude. The war was far from over and

Sean's presence was urgently required to swell the army of a quarter of a million British troops already in the field.

He had written begging for an extension of his leave, and had received in reply a threat to treat him as a deserter if he wasn't in Johannesburg by February 1st.

The last two weeks had been filled with frantic activity. He had managed to finish the planting of ten thousand acres of wattle begun the previous May. He had arranged a further large loan from Natal Wattle to pay for the tending of his trees. The repairs and renovation of the Homestead on Lion Kop were completed and Ada had moved from the cottage in Protea Street to act as caretaker and manager of the estate during his absence.

Now, as he rode alone over his land in a gesture of farewell, he had an opportunity to think of other things. The main one of these was his daughter. His first and only daughter. She was two months old now. Her name was Storm and he had never seen her. Saul Friedman had written a long, joyous letter from the front where Sean was soon to join him. Sean had sent hearty congratulations and then tried once again to contact Ruth. He had written her without result and, finally, had abandoned his work on Lion Kop and gone up to Pietermaritzburg. Four days he waited, calling morning and afternoon at the Goldberg mansion – and each time Ruth was either out or indisposed. He had left a bitter little note for her and gone home.

Deep in gloom he rode through his plantations. Great blocks of young trees, row upon endless row, covered the hills of Lion Kop. The older wattle planted ten months before had started to come away. Already it was waist high with fluffy green tops. It was an achievement of almost superhuman proportion, ten months of ceaseless gruelling labour by two thousand native labourers. Now it was done. He had retained a gang of fifty Zulus, who would work under Ada's supervision, clearing the undergrowth between the rows and guarding against fire. That was all there was to it; four years of waiting until the trees reached maturity and were ready for stripping.

But now he was so completely absorbed in thought that he passed over the boundary of Lion Kop without noticing, and rode on along the foot of the escarpment. He crossed the road and the railway line. From ahead the murmur of the White Falls blended with the wind whisper in the grass, and he glimpsed the flash of water cascading down from the high rock in the sunshine. The acacia trees were in bloom, covered with the golden mist of their flowers above, gloomy with shadows beneath.

He crossed the river below the pool of the falls. The escarpment rose steeply above him, striped with dark dense bush in the gulleys, a thousand feet high so it blocked out the sunlight. The pool was a place of fern and green moss, and the rocks were black and slippery with the spray. A cold place, out of the sun – and the water roared as it fell in a white, moving veil like smoke.

Sean shivered and rode on, ambling up the slope of the escarpment. Then he knew that instinct had directed him. In his distress he had come back to the first home he had ever known. This was Courtney land beneath his feet, and spreading down and out towards the Tugela. The nostalgia came upon him more strongly as he climbed, until at last he reached the rim and stood looking down upon the whole of Theuniskraal.

He picked out the landmarks below him; the homestead with the stables and the servants' quarters behind it; the paddocks with the horses grazing heads down and tails swinging; the dip-tanks among the trees – and each of them had some special memory attached to it.

Sean dismounted and sat down in the grass. He lit a cheroot, while his mind went back and picked over the scrap-heap of the past. An hour, and then another, passed before he came back to the present, pulled his watch from the front pocket of his waistcoat and checked the time.

'After one!' he exclaimed, and stood to dust the seat of his pants and settle his hat on to his head before beginning the descent of the escarpment. Instead of crossing the river at the pool, he stayed on Theuniskraal and keeping to higher ground aimed to intersect the road on this side of the bridge. Occasionally he found cattle feeding together in herds of less than a dozen; they were all in condition, fat on the new grass, for the land was not carrying nearly its full capacity. As he passed they lifted their heads and watched him with vacant, bovine expressions of unsurprise.

The forest thickened, then abruptly ended and before him lay one of the small swampy depressions that bellied out from the river. From his look-out on the escarpment this area had been screened by trees, so now for the first time Sean noticed the saddled horse tethered on the far edge of the swamp. Quickly Sean searched for its rider, and found him in the swamp – only his head visible above the bright poisonous green field of papyrus grass. The man's head disappeared again and there was a commotion in the grass; a wild thrashing and the sudden panic-ridden bellow of a beast.

Sean worked his way quickly round the edge of the swamp until he reached the horse. The head and shoulders of the man in the swamp reappeared and Sean could see that he was splattered with mud.

'What's the trouble?' Sean shouted, and the head turned towards him.

'There's a beast bogged down here.'

'Hold on, I'll give you a hand.' Sean stripped his jacket, waistcoat and shirt and hung them with his hat on a branch before going in. Ploughing knee-deep through ooze that bubbled and belched gas as he disturbed it, using both arms to part the coarse tangle of reeds and marsh grass, Sean finally reached them.

The beast was an old black cow; her hindquarters completely submerged in a mudhole and her front legs twisted helplessly under her chest.

'She's just about finished,' said the man. Sean looked at him and saw he was not a man but a youth. Tall for his age, but lightly built. Dark hair, cropped short and the big nose to show he was a Courtney.

With an unnatural tightness in his gut and a shortening of his breath, Sean knew that he was looking at his son.

'Don't just stand there,' snapped the boy. He was covered from the chest down in a glistening evil-smelling coat of mud, sweat pouring down his face and dissolving the spots of mud on his forehead and cheeks, breathing heavily through open mouth, crouching over the animal to hold its head above the surface.

'Have to roll her,' said Sean. 'Keep her head up.' He waded to the hindquarters and the mud bubbled greasily up around his waist. He thrust his arms down through it – groping for the trapped legs.

Sean's hands could only just encompass the thick bone and sinew of the hock. He settled his grip and leaned back against it, straining upwards, gradually bringing the full strength of his body into the pull until he knew that something in his belly was on the point of tearing. He held like that, his whole face contorted, mouth wide open so that his breathing rattled hoarsely up his throat, the great muscles of his chest and arms locked in an iron convulsion.

A minute, two minutes, he held the stance while the boy watched him with a mingled expression of alarm and wonder. Then suddenly there was a squelching popping escape of swamp gas around Sean's chest, and the beast began to move. Slowly at first, reluctantly up through the ooze showed the swell of its rump – then faster, as the mud lost its hold, until, with a final belch and sigh, it yielded and Sean came to his feet holding the legs above the surface – the cow lying exhausted on her side.

'Hell's teeth!' breathed the boy in open admiration. For a moment the beast lay quiescent, then realizing that its legs were free, it began to struggle, thrashing wildly to regain them.

'Hold the head,' shouted Sean, and blundered sideways until he could grab its tail and prevent it from attempting to stand. When the animal was quiet again he began to drag it, moving backwards, towards the firm ground. Like a bobsleigh the carcass slid easily over the carpet of mud and flattened reeds until it grounded. Then Sean jumped clear while she struggled up, stood a moment and then lumbered unsteadily away into the trees.

Sean and his son stood together, gasping, covered with filth, still ankle-deep in mud, watching the cow disappear.

'Thanks. I'd never have done it on my own, sir.' The form of address and the boy's tone touched something deep in Sean.

'It needed two of us,' he agreed. 'What's your name?'

'Courtney, sir. Michael Courtney.' He held out his hand towards Sean.

'Nice to meet you, Mike.' Sean took the hand.

'I know you, don't I, sir? I'm sure I've seen you before – it's been worrying me.'

'I don't think so.' With an effort Sean kept his feelings from showing in his voice and face.

'I'd . . . I'd count it an honour to know *your* name.' As Michael spoke a shyness came upon them both.

What can I tell him? thought Sean. For I must not lie – and yet I cannot tell him the truth.

'My God, what a bloody mess,' he laughed instead. 'We stink like we've been dead ten days.'

Michael seemed to notice their condition for the first time. 'Ma will have a hernia when she sees me,' he laughed also, then, 'Come up to the house. It's not far from here. Have lunch with us and you can clean up – the servants will wash your clothes for you.'

'No.' Sean shook his head. 'I must get back to Ladyburg.'

'Please. I'd like you to meet my mother. My father's not here – he's at the war. But, please come home with me.'

He really wants me to. As Sean looked into his son's eyes the warm feeling that he had been struggling to suppress flooded up from his chest and he felt his face flush with the pleasure of it.

'Mike,' he spoke slowly, groping for the right words. 'Things are a bit difficult right now. I can't take you up on the invitation. But I'd like to see you again and I'll be through this way one day. Shall we leave it until then?'

'Oh!' Michael made no attempt to hide his disappointment. 'Anyway, I'll ride with you as far as the bridge.'

'Good.' Sean picked up his shirt and wiped off the surplus mud, while Michael unhitched their horses.

They rode slowly, in silence at first with the shyness still on them. Then they started to talk, and quickly the barriers between them crumbled. With a feeling of pride that was ridiculous in the circumstances, Sean became aware of the quickness of Michael's brain, the ease of expression unusual in one so young, and the maturity of his views.

They spoke of Theuniskraal.

'It's a good farm.' There was pride in Michael's voice. 'My family has owned it since 1867.'

'You're not running much stock,' Sean grunted.

'Pa has had a run of bad luck. The rinderpest hit us but we'll build it up again – you wait and see.' He was silent a moment, then, 'Pa's not really a cattleman, instead of putting money into stock he spends it on horses – like Beauty here.' He patted the neck of his magnificant golden mare. 'I've tried to argue with him, but—' Then he realized that he was steering close to the leeshore of disloyalty, and he checked himself then went on hurriedly: 'Don't misunderstand me, my father is an unusual man. Right now he's on the army staff – a colonel, and one of General Buller's right-hand men. He is a holder of the Victoria Cross for bravery, and he has been awarded the D.S.O. for the job he is doing now.'

Yes, thought Sean, I have defended Garry also; many times, as often as you will by the time you reach my age. In understanding he changed the direction of the conversation.

They spoke of the future:

'So you want to be a farmer, then?'

'I love this place. I was born here. To me it is not just a piece of land and a house. It is part of a tradition to which I belong – built by men of whom I am proud. After Pa, I will be the only one left to continue it. I won't fail that trust. But . . .'

They had reached the rise above the road, and Michael stopped and looked at Sean as though trying to make up his mind how much he should tell this stranger.

'But?' Sean prompted him gently. For a moment longer Michael stared at him, trying to account for his certainty in this man – for the conviction he had that he could trust him beyond all other men on earth. He felt that he had known him all his life, and between them was something so strong – so good and strong as to be almost tangible.

'But,' he jerked himself back to their conversation, 'that is not all. I want something beyond just land and cattle. It's so difficult to explain. My grandfather was a big man; he worked with people as well as animals. He had . . . you do understand me, don't you?'

'I think so,' Sean nodded 'You feel you'd like to make a place for yourself in the scheme of things.'

'Yes, that's it. I'd like to make decisions other than when to cull and when to brand, or where to build a new dip-tank.'

'What are you going to do about it then?'

'Well, I'm at Cape Town University. This is my third year – I'll have my degree by Christmas.'

'Then what?'

'I don't know, but I'll find something.' Then Michael smiled. 'There's a lot to learn first. Sometimes when I realize how much it frightens me a little.'

They walked their horses down towards the road, so completely absorbed in each other that neither of them noticed the buggy coming towards them from the direction of Ladyburg until it was almost on them.

Then Michael glanced up. 'Hey! Here comes my mother. Now you can meet her.'

With a sense of dread numbing him, Sean realized he was trapped. There was no escape – the buggy was less than fifty yards away, and he could see Anna sitting up behind the coloured driver staring at them.

Michael shouted, 'Hello, Ma!'

'Michael! Whatever have you been doing? Look at you!' There was a shrewishness in her voice now. The years had treated Anna in the manner she deserved, had sharpened her features and exaggerated the catlike set of her eyes. She turned those eyes on Sean and she frowned. The frown cut deep grooves in her forehead and showed the heavy lines of flesh beneath her chin.

'Who's that with you?' she asked Michael.

'A friend. He helped me free a bogged animal. You should have seen him, Ma. He lifted it clean out of the mud.'

Sean saw that she was expensively dressed, ostentatiously so for a farmer's wife on a working day. Velvet and ostrich feathers – those pearls must have cost Garry a small fortune. The rig was new, polished black lacquer picked out with scarlet, and brass fittings – another few hundred pounds' worth. Sean ran his eyes over the horses, matched bays, blood stock – Jesus! he thought.

Anna was still frowning at him, recognition and doubt mixed in her expression. She was starting to flush, her lips trembling.

'Hello, Anna.'

'Sean!' She spat the word.

'It's been a long time. How are you?'

Her eyes slanted venomously. She hardly moved her lips as she snapped at Michael, 'Get away from that man!'

'But ...' The bewildered look on Michael's face hurt Sean like a spear thrust.

'Do as your mother says, Michael,' Sean told him.

'Are you ... are *you* my Uncle Sean?'

'Yes.'

'Get away from him,' shrilled Anna. 'Don't you ever speak to him again. Do you hear me, Michael? He's evil – evil! Don't ever let him near you.

He'll destroy you.' Anna was panting, shaking with rage and hatred, babbling like a madwoman. 'Get off our land, Sean Courtney. Get off Theuniskraal and don't come on again.'

'Very well, Anna. I'm going.'

'Michael. Get on your horse!' she screamed at him. 'Hurry. Come away from him.'

Michael swung up into the saddle.

'Drive on. Drive quickly,' she ordered the coloured coachman. At the touch of the whip the big bays jumped forward and Anna was thrown back against the padded seat. 'Come on, Michael. Come home immediately.'

Michael looked across at Sean. He was bewildered, uncertain. 'I don't . . . I don't believe that you . . .'

'We'll talk again some other time, Mike.'

And suddenly Michael's expression changed, the corners of his mouth drooped and his eyes were dark with regret at having found, and lost, so soon.

'No,' he said, lifted his hand in a gesture of farewell, and wheeled his horse. Crouched forward on its neck he drove in savage pursuit of the buggy.

'Michael,' Sean called after him, but he did not seem to hear.


# Chapter Thirty-seven


And so Sean went back to war. The farewell was an ordeal. Ada was so brave about it that Sean wanted to shake her and shout, 'Cry, damn you! Get it over with!' Dirk threw one of his more spectacular fits. He clung to Sean and yelled until he almost suffocated himself. By the time the train pulled out Sean was in a towering rage that lasted until they reached Pietermaritzburg four hours later.

He took his anger into the saloon on the station and sedated it with half a dozen brandies. Then, with Mbejane carrying his luggage, he worked his way through the crowd on the platform, searching for an empty compartment on the northbound express. As all traffic was on military permit only, his fellow-travellers were exclusively clad in khaki. A vast, drab throng speckled with gay spots of colour, women who were sending men to war and not very happy about it. The sound of weeping blended with the roar of loud voices, men's laughter and the occasional squeal of a child. Suddenly, above it all Sean heard his name called. He peered about and saw an arm waving frantically above the heads of the crowd.

'Sean! Hey, Sean!' Saul's head bobbed into view and then disappeared as he hopped up and down. Sean fought his way through to him and they shook hands delightedly.

'What the hell are you doing here?' Saul demanded.

'Heading back to duty – and you?'

'A week's leave just ended. Came down to see the baby. My God, what luck I spotted you!'

'Is Ruth here?' Sean could not contain the question.

'She's waiting in the carriage outside.'

'I'd like to have a look at this infant.'

'Of course. Let's find a couple of seats first and dump our luggage, then we've got twenty minutes before the train leaves.'

Sean saw her as they came out on to the front steps of the station building. She sat in an open carriage while a coloured coachboy held a parasol over her. She was dressed in dove-grey with big leg-o'-mutton sleeves slashed with pink and a huge hat piled with pink roses. Her face was in profile as she leaned forward over the bundle of white lace on her lap. Sean felt the leap in his chest as he looked at the calm lines of her face. He stopped and whispered,

'My God, she's lovely,' and beside him Saul laughed with pleasure.

'Wait until you meet my daughter!'

She did not see them approach the carriage, she was too intent on her child.

'Ruth, I've a surprise for you,' bubbled Saul. She looked up and Sean was watching her. She went rigid with shock, staring at him while all colour drained away from her face.

'Hello, Ruth.'

She did not reply immediately. Sean saw her mask her face with a pale impassivity.

'Hello, Sean. You startled me.'

Saul had missed the interplay of their emotions. He was climbing up into the carriage beside her.

'Come, have a look.' Now he was opening the lace shawl, leaning over the infant, his face alight with pride.

Silently Sean climbed up into the carriage and sat opposite them.

'Let Sean hold her, Ruth.' Saul laughed. 'Let him get a good look at the loveliest girl in the world.' And he did not notice the way in which Ruth froze again and hugged the child to her protectively.

'Take her, Sean. I promise she'll not wet you too badly, though she might sick up a little,' Saul went on happily.

Sean held out his hands for the infant, watching Ruth's face. It was defiant, but afraid.

'Please,' he said. The colour of her eyes seemed to change a darker bluer grey. The hard lines around her mouth dissolved and her lips quivered pink and moist. She leaned forward and placed her daughter in his arms.

# Chapter Thirty-eight

It was a long, slow journey up to Johannesburg – a journey broken by interminable halts. At every siding there was a delay, sometimes of half an hour but usually of three times that length. Occasionally, without apparent reason, they groaned to a stop in the middle of the veld.

'What the hell is the trouble now?'

'Somebody shoot the driver.'

'Not again!'

Protest and comment were shouted by the angry heads that protruded from the windows of every coach. And when the guard trotted up along the gravelled embankment towards the front of the train, he was followed by a chorus of catcalls and hooting.

'Please be patient, gentlemen. We have to check the culverts and bridges.'

'The war's over.'

'What are you worried about?'

'The jolly old Boer is running so hard he hasn't got time to worry about bridges.'

Men climbed down beside the tracks, and stood in small impatient groups until the whistle blew and they scrambled aboard as the train jolted and began crawling forward again.

Sean and Saul sat together in a corner of a crowded compartment and played Klabrias. Because the majority regarded the cold clean highveld air with the same horror as if it had been a deadly cyanide gas, the windows were tightly closed. The compartment was blue with pipe-smoke and fetid with the smell of a dozen unwashed bodies. The conversation was inevitable. Confine a number of men in a small space and they'll get round to it in under ten minutes.

This company had a vast experience in matters pornographic.

A sergeant had served three years in Bangkok, but it took him two hours to convince his companions that what rumour placed horizontally, nature, in fact, had maintained at the vertical. He carried his point only after an expedition down the corridor from which he returned with another old China hand. This expert produced photographic evidence which was studied minutely and deemed conclusive.

It served also to remind a corporal who had done a tour of duty in India of his visit to the Temple of Konarak. A subject which was good for another hour and paved the way for a smooth entry into a discussion of the famous Elephant House in Shanghai.

They kept it up from noon until nightfall.

In the meantime, Saul had lost interest in the cards and taken a book from his bag and started reading. Sean was bored. He cleaned his rifle. Then he picked his teeth with a match and stared out of the window at the small herds of springbok that grazed along the line of rail. He listened to a detailed account of the pleasures provided by the proprietress of the Elephant House, and decided to give it a wide berth if he ever visited Shanghai.

'What are you reading?' he demanded of Saul at last.

'Huh?' Saul looked up vaguely and Sean repeated the question. '*The Westminster System of Government*', Saul held the book so that Sean could see the title.

'Jesus!' grunted Sean. 'What do you read that stuff for?'

'I am interested in politics,' Saul explained defensively and returned to reading.

Sean watched him for a while then, 'Have you got any other books with you?'

Saul opened his bag again. 'Try this.'

'*The Wealth of Nations*'. Sean handled the book dubiously. 'What's it about?' But Saul was reading again.

Sean opened the heavy volume and glanced idly at the first page. He sighed with resignation for it was a long time since he had read anything but a letter or a bank statement – then his eyes started moving back and forth across the page like the shuttle of a loom. Without knowing it, they were weaving the first threads into a fabric that would cover a part of his soul which until now had been naked.

After an hour Saul looked across. 'What do you make of it?' he asked.

Sean grunted without looking up. He was completely absorbed. This was important. The language of Adam Smith had a certain majestic clarity. With some of his conclusions Sean did not agree but the reasoning evoked a train of thought in Sean's own brain, stimulating it to race ahead and anticipate – sometimes correctly, but often reaching a point wide of where the author was aimed.

He read quickly, knowing that he would go back and read it all again for this was only a scouting party into the unknown territory of economics. With his eyes still fixed on the pages, he groped in the pockets of his tunic, found a stub of pencil and underlined a passage to which he wanted to return. Then he left it and went on. Now he used the pencil frequently.

'No!' he wrote in the margin at one place.

'Good,' at another.

Saul looked up again and frowned as he realized Sean was defacing the book. Then he noticed Sean's expression, saw its scowling concentration and his own face relaxed. He watched Sean from under lowered eyelashes. His feeling for this man of muscle and moods and unexpectedly soft places had passed affection and now reached the borders of adulation. He did not know why Sean had placed protecting wings above him, nor did he care. But it was good to sit quietly, no longer reading, and watch the face of this big man who was more than just a friend.

Alone in the midst of a multitude they sat together. The train snaked northwards across the grassland, spreading a long trail of silver-grey smoke behind it and the sun sank exhausted to the earth and bled on to the clouds. After it was gone the darkness came quickly.

They ate canned meat spread on coarse bread with the blade of a bayonet. There was no lighting in the compartment, so after they had eaten they sat together wrapped in their blankets and talked in darkness. Around them all other conversation died and was replaced by the sounds of sleep. Sean opened one of the windows and the cold sweet air cleaned their minds and sharpened them so that they talked in quietly suppressed excitement.

They talked of men and land and the welding of the two into a nation; and how that nation should be governed. They spoke a little of war and much of the peace that would follow it; of the rebuilding of that which had been destroyed into something stronger.

They saw the bitterness ahead that would flourish like an evil weed nourished on blood and the corpses of the dead and they discussed the means by which it should be rooted out before it strangled the tender growth of a land that could be great.

They had never spoken like this before. Saul hugged his blankets about his shoulders and listened to Sean's voice in the darkness. Like most of his race his perception had been sensitized and sharpened so that he could pick up a new quality, a new sense of direction in this man.

I have had a hand in this, he thought, with a stirring of pride. He is a bull, a wild bull, charging anything that moves; charging without purpose, then breaking his run and swinging on to something new; using his strength to destroy because he had never learned to use it in any other way; confused and angry, roaring at the barbs in his shoulders; chasing everything and as a consequence catching nothing. Perhaps I can help him, show him a purpose and a way out of the arena.

And so they talked on into the night. The darkness added another dimension to their existence. Unseen, their physical forms no longer limited them and it seemed that their minds were freed to move out and meet in the darkness, to combine into a cushion of words that carried each idea forward. Until abruptly, the whole delicate pattern was shattered and lost in the concussion of dynamite and the shriek of escaping steam, the roar of breaking timber and glass, and the confusion of equipment and sleeping bodies thrown violently together as the train reared and twisted and plunged from the tracks. Almost immediately a further sound blended into it all – the crackling of musketry at close range and the steady hammering beat of a Maxim machine-gun.

Sean was pinned helplessly in the complete darkness unable to breathe under an immense weight. He struggled wildly, tearing at the men and baggage above him, his legs bound by loose blankets. The weight eased enough for him to drag air into his lungs, but a knee was driven into his face with such force that his lip burst open and the blood oozed saltily into his mouth. He lashed out and felt the stinging rake of broken glass along his arm.

In the darkness men screamed in terror and in pain, leading the hideous chorus of groans and oaths and gunfire.

Sean dragged his body free of the press, felt men thrashing under him as he stood.

Now he could hear the repeated splintering thud of bullets into woodwork much louder than the guns that fired them.

Someone reeled against him and Sean caught him.

'Saul?'

'Leave me, let me go.' A stranger, Sean released him.

'Saul. Saul. Where are you?'

'Sean.'

'Are you hurt?'

'No.'

'Let's get out of here.'

'My rifle.'

'Bugger your rifle.'

'Where's the window?'

'Blocked.'

At last Sean was able to get some idea of their situation. The coach was on its side with the windows against the earth and the whole welter of dead and broken men piled upon them. The door was high above them, probably jammed.

'We'll have to break out through the roof.' He groped blindly, then swore and jerked his hand back as a splinter of wood knifed up under a fingernail, but he felt a draught of cold air on his face.

'There's a hole.' He reached out again eagerly and felt the torn timber. 'One of the planks is sprung.'

Immediately there was a rush of bodies in the darkness, hands clawed at him as half a dozen men fought to find the opening.

'Get back, you bastards.' Sean struck out with both fists and felt them connect. He was panting and he could feel the sweat sliding down his back. The air was heavy with the body warmth and breath of terrified men.

'Get back. I'll work on it.' He forced his hands into the crack and tore the loose plank out. For an instant he struggled with the temptation to press his face to the narrow opening and suck in the clean air. Then he locked his hands on to the next plank, braced his legs against the roof and heaved back with all his strength. It wouldn't budge. He felt the panic mounting in him once more.

'Find me a rifle, somebody,' he shouted above the uproar.

'Here.' Saul's voice, and the rifle was thrust into his hands. He ran the barrel into the opening and using it as a lever flung his weight on to it. He felt wood tearing, moved the barrel and pulled again. It gave and he cleared the plank and started on the next.

'All right. One at a time. Saul, you first.' With his panic just below the surface, Sean shoved each man unceremoniously through the jagged opening. A fat one stuck and Sean put a boot behind him and pushed. The man squeaked and went out like a champagne cork.

'Is there anyone else?' he shouted in the darkness.

'Sean,' Saul's voice from outside. 'Get out of there.'

'You get under cover,' Sean roared back at him.

The Boer fire still flailed the wrecked train. Then he asked again, 'Is there anyone else?' and a man groaned at Sean's feet.

Quickly Sean found him. Hurt badly, his head twisted. Sean cleared the tangle of baggage from above his body and straightened him out. Can't move him, he decided, safer here until the medicos come. He left him and stumbled over another.

'Damn them,' he sobbed in his dreadful anxiety to get out. This one was dead. He could feel the reptilian clamminess of death on his skin, and he left him and scrabbled his way out into the open night.

After the utter blackness of the comparment, the stars lit the land with a pearly light and he saw the fog of steam hanging above the locomotive in a high, hissing bank, and the leading coaches telescoped into each other, and the others jack-knifed and twisted into a weird sculpture of destruction. At intervals along the chain a few rifles winked a feeble reply to the Boer fire that poured down upon them.

'Sean,' Saul called from where he was crouched beside the overturned coach. Sean ran to him and lifted his voice above the clamour.

'Stay here. I'm going back to look for Mbejane.'

'You'll never find him in this lot. He was with the horses – listen to them.'

From the horse-boxes at the rear of the train came such a sound that Sean hoped never to hear again. Two hundred trapped and frenzied animals – it was far worse than the sound of those men still in the wreckage.

'My God!' whispered Sean. Then his anger rose higher than his fear. 'The bastards,' he grated and looked up at the high ground above them.

The Boers had chosen a place where the line curved along the bank of a river. The watercourse cut off escape on that side, and on the other the ground rose steeply in a double fold that commanded the full length of the railway line.

Along the first fold lay their riflemen, two hundred of them at least, judging by the intensity of their fire, while from above them on the summit ridge the muzzle flashes of the Maxim gun faded and flared as it traversed relentlessly back and forth along the train. Sean watched it hungrily for a moment, then he lifted the rifle that he still carried and emptied the magazine, firing at the Maxim. Immediately the flashes grew brighter as it came questing back to find him, and around Sean's head the air was filled with the swishing crack of a hundred whips.

Sean ducked down while he reloaded, then stood up again to shoot.

'You bastards,' he shouted at them, and his voice must have carried for now the riflemen up there were helping the Maxim to search him out. They were getting very close.

Sean crouched down once more, and beside him Saul was firing also.

'Where did you get the rifle?'

'I went back for it.' Saul punctuated his reply with gunfire and Sean grinned as his fingers fumbled with the reload. 'You're going to get hurt one day,' he said.

'You taught me how to go about it,' Saul retorted.

Once more Sean emptied his magazine to no effect, except that the recoil of the rifle invoked the old high madness in him. It needed only Mbejane's voice beside him to trigger it completely.

'Nkosi.'

'Where the hell have you been?' Sean demanded.

'My spears were lost. I spent much time finding them in the darkness.'

Sean was silent for a moment while he peered up at the ridge. Out on the left there was a gap in the line of riflemen where a narrow donga ran through them and down towards the railway. A small party might be able to go up that gully and pass through the rear of the Boer firing-line. From there the solitary Maxim on the ridge would be very vulnerable.

'Bring your spears, Mbejane.'

'Where are you going?' Saul asked.

'I'm going to try for that machine-gun. Stay here and keep these gentlemen's mind on other things.'

Sean started off along the train towards the outlet of the donga. He covered fifty yards before he realized that not only Mbejane but Saul was with him.

'Where do you think you're going?'

'With you.'

'The hell you are!'

'Watch me.' There was that peculiar note of obstinacy in Saul's voice that Sean had come to recognize, and there was no time to argue. He ran on until he was opposite the donga where again he sought shelter in the lee of an overturned coach while he made his final assessment of the position.

The donga looked narrow but deep, and the scrub-bush that filled it would give them cover to the top where there was a definite gap in the Boer Line.

'It'll do,' he decided aloud, and then to the other two, 'I'll go first, then you follow me, Saul, and watch those big feet of yours.'

He was vaguely aware that some show of resistance was being organized among the survivors of the wreck. He could hear the officers rallying them and now a hundred rifles were returning the Boer fire.

'All right. I'm off.' Sean stood up. 'Follow me as soon as I get across.'

At that moment a new voice hailed them. 'What are you men up to?'

'What's it to you?' Sean flashed impatiently.

'I'm an officer,' and then Sean recognized the voice and the lanky figure with a bared sabre in one hand. 'Acheson!'

A second's hesitation before Acheson recognized him. 'Courtney. What are you doing?'

'I'm going up that donga to attack the Maxim.'

'Think you can reach it?'

'I can try.'

'Good fellow – off you go then. We'll be ready to support you if you make it.'

'See you at the top,' said Sean and ran out towards the mouth of the donga.

They moved quietly in single file upwards and the guns and the shouting cloaked the soft sounds of their advance. Sean could hear the voices of the burghers above them growing closer and louder as they approached – very close now – on the side of the donga just above their heads – then behind them, and they were through.

The donga was shallower here, starting to flatten out as it neared the crest. Sean lifted his head above the side and looked out. Below him he could just make out the lumpy shapes of the Boers in the grass but their rifles threw long orange spouts of flames when seen from above – while the British replies were mere pinpricks of light from around the dark tangle of coaches.

Then Sean's attention focused on the Maxim and he could see why the rifle-fire from below had made no effect on it. Sited just below the crest of the ridge on a forward bulge of the slope, it was protected by a scharnz of rock and earth that had been thrown up in front of it. The thick water-jacketed barrel protruded through a narrow opening and the three men that served it crouched low behind the wall.

'Come on,' whispered Sean, and wriggled up out of the donga on to his belly to begin the stalk.

One of the gunners saw him when he was a few yards from the gun. '*Magtig! Pasop, daars 'n –*' and Sean went in with the rifle clubbed in both hands and the man never finished his warning. Mbejane and Saul followed him in, and for a few seconds the emplacement was filled with a struggling mass of bodies. Then it was over and the three of them panted heavily in the stillness.

'Do you know how to work this thing, Saul?'

'No.'

'Nor do I.' Sean squatted behind the gun and settled his hands on to the twin grips, his thumbs automatically resting on the firing-button.

'*Wat makeer julle daar bo? Skiet, man, skiet!*' a Boer shouted from below, and Sean shouted back, '*Wag maar 'n oomblik – dan skiet ek bedonderd.*'

'*Wie's daar?* Who's that?' the Boer demanded and Sean depressed the gun.

It was too dark to use the sights, so he took a vague aim over the barrel and thrust his thumbs down on the button. Immediately his shoulders shook like those of a man using a jack hammer and he was deafened by the harsh beat of the gun, but he swung the barrel in a low, sweeping arc across the ridge below him.

A storm of shouts and cries of protest broke out along the Boer line, and Sean laughed with savage delight. The Boer fire upon the train withered miraculously as men jumped up and scattered beneath the spray of bullets. Most of them streamed back to where their horses waited behind the crest, keeping well out on the flanks of the Maxim, while a line of cheering British infantry followed them up from the train – giving the support that Acheson had promised.

Only a tiny but determined group of Boers came up the slope towards Sean, yelling angrily and shooting as they came. There was dead ground directly below the emplacement where Sean could not reach them with the Maxim.

'Get out of here. Run out to the sides,' Sean shouted back at Saul and Mbejane as he hoisted the heavy gun on to the rock wall in front of him to improve its field of fire. But the movement twisted the belt of ammunition and after the first burst the gun jammed hopelessly. Sean lifted it above his head, stood like that for an instant and then hurled it among the men below him. It knocked two of them down into the grass. Sean snatched up a pumpkin-sized rock from the top of the wall and sent it after the gun – and another, and another. Howling with the laughter of fear and excitement, he rained rocks upon them. And they broke. Most of them veered out to the sides and joined the general rush for the horses.

Only one man kept coming, a big man who climbed quickly and silently.

Sean missed him with three rocks, and suddenly he was too close – not ten feet away. There he paused and lifted his rifle. Even in the dark, at that range, the Boer could hardly miss and Sean sprang from the top of the wall. For an instant he dropped free, and then with a shock that knocked the wind from both of them, he drove into the burgher's chest. They rolled down the slope, kicking and grappling, bouncing over the rocky ground, until a small thorn bush held them.

'Now, you bloody Dutchman!' rasped Sean. He knew there was only one possible outcome to this encounter. With supreme confidence in his own strength Sean reached for the man's throat, and with a sense of disbelief felt his wrist held in a grip that made the bone creak.

'*Kom, ons slaat aan*,' the burgher's mouth was an inch from Sean's ear, and the voice was unmistakable.

'Jan Paulus!'

'Sean!' The shock of recognition eased his grip for an instant, and Sean broke his hand loose.

Only once in his life had Sean met a man whose strength matched his own – and now again they were pitted against each other. He drove the heel of his right hand up under Jan Paulus's chin, forcing his head back against the encircling left arm. It should have broken Jan Paulus's neck. Instead he locked his arms around Sean's chest below the level of his armpits – and squeezed. Within seconds Sean felt his face swelling and congesting with blood, his mouth opened and his tongue came out between his teeth.

Without breath, yet he maintained the pressure on Jan Paulus's neck, felt it give fractionally – and knew that another inch of movement would snap the vertebrae.

The earth seemed to tilt and turn beneath him, he knew he was going for his vision was blotched with moving patches of deeper darkness – the knowledge gave him a little more strength. He flung it all on to Jan Paulus's neck. It moved. Jan Paulus gave a wild muffled cry and his grip on Sean's chest eased a fraction.

Again, Sean told himself, again. And he gathered all of what was left for the final effort.

Before he could make it, Jan Paulus moved quickly under him, changing his grip, lifting Sean clear of his chest. Then his knees came up under Sean's pelvis and with a convulsive heave drove Sean's lower body forward and over – cartwheeling him so that he was forced to release Jan Paulus's neck and use his hands to break his own fall.

A rock caught him in the small of the back and agony flared in him like sheet lightning in a summer sky. Dimly through it he heard the shouts of the British infantry very near, saw Jan Paulus scramble up and glance down the slope at the starlight on the bayonets, and saw him take off up the slope.

Sean dragged himself to his feet and tried to follow him but the pain in his back was an effective hobble and Jan Paulus reached the crest ten paces ahead of him. But as he ran, another dark shape closed on his flank the way a good dog will quarter on a running rybuck. It was Mbejane and Sean could see the long steel in his hand as he lifted it above Jan Paulus's back.

'No!' shouted Sean. 'No, Mbejane! Leave him! Leave him!'

Mbejane hesitated, slowed his run, stopped and looked back at Sean.

Sean stood beside him, his hands clasped to his back and his breathing hissing in his throat. Below them from the dark rear slope of the ridge came the hoof-beats of a single running pony.

The sound of Jan Paulus's flight dwindled, and they were engulfed in the advance of the lines of the bayonet men from the train. Sean turned and limped back through them.

# Chapter Thirty-nine

Two days later, on the relief train, they reached Johannesburg.

'I suppose we should report to somebody,' Saul suggested as the three of them stood together on the station platform beside the small pile of luggage they had been able to salvage from the train wreck.

'You go and report, if that's what you want,' Sean answered him. 'Me, I'm going to look around.'

'We've got no billets,' Saul protested.

'Follow your Uncle Sean.'

Johannesburg is an evil city, sired by Greed out of a dam named Gold. But it has about it an air of gaiety, of brittle excitement and bustle. When you are away from it you can hate it – but when you return you are immediately re-infected. As Sean was now.

He led them through the portals of the railway building into Eloff Street and grinned as he looked up that well-remembered thoroughfare. It was crowded. The carriages jostled for position with the horse-drawn trams. On the sidewalks beneath the tall three- and four-storeyed buildings the uniforms of a dozen different regiments set off the butterfly colours of the women's dresses.

Sean paused on the station steps and lit a cigar. At that moment the sounds of carriage wheels and human voices were drowned by the plaintive wail of a mine hooter and immediately others joined in signalling the noon. Automatically Sean reached for his pocket-watch to check the time, and noticed the same general movement in the crowded street. He grinned again.

Jo'burg hasn't changed much – still the old habits, the same feeling about it. The mine dumps higher than he remembered them, a few new buildings, a little older and a little smarter – but still the same heartless bitch beneath it all.

And there on the corner of Commissioner Street, ornate as a wedding-cake with its fancy ironwork and corniced roof, stood Candy's Hotel.

With rifle and pack slung over each shoulder, Sean pushed his way through the press on the sidewalk with Saul and Mbejane in his wake. He reached the hotel and went in through the revolving glass doors.

'Very grand.' He looked about the lobby as he dumped his pack on the thick pile of the carpet. Crystal chandeliers, velvet curtains roped with silver, palms and bronze urns, marble tables, fat plush chairs.

'What do you think, Saul. Shall we give this flophouse a try?' His voice carried across the lobby and stilled the murmuring of polite conversation.

'Don't talk so loudly,' Saul cautioned.

A general officer in one of the plush chairs hoisted himself and slowly turned his head to train a monocled stare upon them, while his aide-de-camp leaned across and whispered, '*Colonials*'.

Sean winked at him and moved across to the reception desk.

'Good afternoon, sir.' The clerk regarded them frostily.

'You have reservations for my chief of staff and myself.'

'What name, sir?'

'I'm sorry, I can't answer that question. We are travelling incognito,' Sean told him seriously, and a helpless expression appeared on the man's face. Sean dropped his voice to conspiratory level. 'Have you seen a man come in here carrying a bomb?'

'No.' The man's eyes glazed a little. 'No, sir. No, I haven't.'

'Good.' Sean appeared relieved. 'In that case we'll take the Victoria Suite. Have our luggage sent up.'

'General Caithness has the Victoria Suite, sir.' The clerk was becoming desperate.

'What?' Sean roared. 'How dare you!'

'I didn't . . . We had no . . .' Stuttering, the clerk backed away from him.

'Call the owner,' ordered Sean.

'Yes, sir.' And the clerk disappeared through a door marked 'Private'.

'Have you gone mad?' Saul was fidgeting with embarrassment. 'We can't afford to stay at this place. Let's get out of here.' Under the concentrated scrutiny of every guest in the lobby he was very conscious of their grubby travel-stained uniforms.

Before Sean could answer a woman came through the 'Private' doorway, a very lovely but very angry woman with eyes that blazed like the blue sapphires at her throat.

'I am Mrs Rautenbach – the owner. You asked to see me.'

Sean just smiled at her, and her anger withered slowly as she began to recognize him beneath the creased ill-fitting tunic and without the beard.

'Do you still love me, Candy?'

'Sean?' She was still uncertain.

'Who else?'

'Sean!' And she came to him on the run. Half an hour later General Caithness had been evicted and Sean and Saul were settling comfortably into the Victoria Suite.

Freshly bathed, with only a towel round his waist, Sean lay back in his chair while the barber scraped away his three-day growth of beard.

'Some more champagne?' Candy had not taken her eyes off him for the last ten minutes.

'Thanks.'

She filled his glass, replaced it at his right hand and then touched the thick muscles of his upper arm. 'Still hard,' she murmured. 'You've kept ahead of the years.' Her fingers moved on to his chest. 'Just a little grey here and there – but it suits you,' and then to the barber, 'Haven't you finished yet?'

'One moment more, madam.' He again scissored along the line of Sean's temple, stood back and studied his masterpiece – then, with modest pride, held the mirror for Sean's approval.

'Excellent. Thank you.'

'You may go now. See to the gentleman next door.' Candy had waited long enough. As the door closed behind the barber she turned the key. Sean stood up from the chair and they faced each other across the room.

'My God, but you're big.' Her voice was husky, unashamedly hungry.

'My God, but you're beautiful,' Sean answered her, and they moved slowly to meet in the centre of the floor.

Later they lay quietly while the darkness gathered in the room as evening fell. Then Candy moved her mouth across his shoulder and, the way a cat cleans its kittens, she began gently to lick the long red scratches upon his neck.

When the room was truly dark Candy lit one of the shaded gas-lights and sent down for biscuits and a bottle of champagne. They sat together upon the rumpled bed and talked.

At first there was a shyness between them because of what they had done together – but soon it passed – and they sat up far into the night.

Rare it is for a man to have a friend as well as a lover in one woman – but with Candy this was possible. And to her he released all those things that had been bottled and fomenting within him.

He told her of Michael, and the strange bond between them.

He told her of Dirk, and hinted at his misgivings for the boy.

He spoke of the war and of what he would do when it finished.

He told her of Lion Kop and his wattle.

But one thing he could not tell her. He could not speak of Ruth or the man who was her husband.

# Chapter Forty

During the next few days Sean and Saul reported to the headquarters of the Regional Commander and were assigned neither billets nor duties. Now that they had arrived no one seemed very interested in them. They were told to report daily, and turned loose again. They returned to Candy's Hotel and spent most of the days playing billiards or cards and most of the evenings eating and drinking and talking.

A week of this and Sean was getting bored. He began to feel like a stud stallion. Even a solid diet of heavenly mana begins to pall after a while – so when Candy asked him to escort her to a reception and dinner with which

Lord Kitchener was celebrating his promotion to Supreme Command of the Army in South Africa, Sean accepted with relief.

'You look like some sort of god,' Candy told him as he entered her suite through the concealed doorway which connected it with his own bedroom in the Victoria rooms. When she had shown him this discreet little panel and demonstrated how at a touch it slid silently aside, Sean had thrust down the temptation of asking how many others had used it. It was senseless to resent the nameless host who had passed through the panel to teach Candy all those little tricks with which she now delighted him.

'You don't look too bad yourself.' She was dressed in blue silk, the colour of her eyes, and she wore diamonds at her throat.

'How gallant you are!' She came to him and stroked the silk lapels of his newly tailored evening jacket. 'I wish you'd wear your medals.'

'I haven't any medals.'

'Oh Sean! You must have! With all those bullet holes in you, you must have medals.'

'I'm sorry, Candy.' Sean grinned. At times she was so far from being the glittering sophisticated woman of the world. Although she was a year older than he was, time had not destroyed that fragile quality of skin and hair that most women lose so quickly. There was no thickening of her body, no coarsening of her features.

'Never mind – even without medals, you'll be the handsomest man there tonight.'

'And you the loveliest girl.'

As the carriage rolled down Commissioner Street towards the Grand National Hotel, Sean lay back against the yielding support of soft polished leather. His cigar was drawing evenly with an inch of firm grey ash, the single brandy he had drunk before leaving glowed beneath the starched front of his dress-shirt, a faint aura of bay rum clung and hovered around him – and Candy's hand lay lightly upon his leg.

All these things induced in him a mood of deep contentment. He laughed easily at Candy's chatter and let the smoke of his cigar trickle through his lips – tasting it with an almost childlike pleasure. When the carriage stopped before the entrance to the hotel and rocked gently on its superb springing, he climbed down and stood by the big rear-wheel to guard Candy's skirt as she descended.

Then, with her fingers on his forearm, he guided her up the front steps and through the glass doors into the lobby of the hotel. The splendour of the place did not equal Candy's own establishment. But it was impressive enough – and so was the reception line that awaited them. While they took their places among those waiting to meet the Commander-in-Chief, Sean spoke quietly to an aide-de-camp.

'My Lord, may I present Mr Courtney and Mrs Rautenbach.'

Lord Kitchener had a formidable presence. His hand was cold and hard and he stood as tall as Sean. The eyes that stared for an instant into Sean's held a disqueting rigidity of purpose. Then he turned to Candy and his expression softened momentarily as he bowed over her hand.

'Very kind of you to come, madam.'

Then they were past and into the gaudy of uniforms and velvet and silk.

The whole was dominated by dress scarlet of the Guards and Fusiliers, but there was also the gold-frogged blue of the Hussars, the green of the Foresters, kilts of half a dozen Highland reigments, so that Sean's black dress was conspicuously conservative. Among the glitter of orders and decorations shone the jewellery and white skins of the women.

Here assembled were the prize blooms of the huge tree that was the British Empire. A tree grown strong above the rest of the forest. Two centuries of victory in war had nurtured it, two hundred million persons were its roots that sucked in the treasures of half the world and sent them up along the shipping lanes to that grey city astride the Thames that was its heart. And there this rich sap was digested and transmuted into men. These were the men whose lazy speech and careful nonchalance reflected the smugness and arrogance which made them hated and feared by even the trunk of the great tree that gave them flower. While the lesser trees crowded closer and sent their own roots out to divert a little of its sustenance to themselves, the first disease had already eaten into the wood beneath the bark of the giant. America, India, Afghanistan, and South Africa, had started the dry rot that one day would bring it crashing down with a force that would shatter its bulk into so many pieces as to prove it not teak but soft pine.

Watching them now, Sean felt himself apart from them, closer in spirit and purpose to those shaggy men whose Mausers still shouted desperate defiance at them from the vast brown veld.

These thoughts threatened to spoil his mood and he thrust them down, exchanged his empty glass for another filled with bubbling yellow wine and attempted to join the banter of the young officers who surrounded Candy. He succeeded only in conceiving a burning desire to punch one of them between his downy moustaches. He was savouring the idea with increasing relish when a touch on his arm turned him.

'Hello, Courtney. Seem to find you everywhere there is either a fight or a free drink.' Startled, Sean turned to look into the austere face and incongruously twinkling eyes of Major-General John Acheson.

'Hello, General. I notice you frequent the same areas.' Sean grinned at him.

'Bloody awful champagne. Old K. must be economizing.' Then he ran his eyes over Sean's immaculate evening dress. 'A bit difficult to tell whether you have received the awards for which I recommended you.'

Sean shook his head. 'Still a sergeant. I didn't want to embarrass the General Staff by appearing in my chevrons.'

'Ah!' Acheson's eyes narrowed slightly. 'Must be some hold up. I'll look into it.'

'I assure you I'm quite happy this way.'

Acheson nodded and changed the subject. 'You haven't met my wife?' This was patronage on the grand scale. Sean was not to know that Acheson considered him his personal good luck charm. His own rapid promotion dated from their first meeting. Sean blinked in surprise before answering,

'I haven't yet had the honour.'

'Come along then.'

Sean excused himself from Candy, who dismissed him with a tap of her fan and Acheson steered him through the press towards a group at the end of the room. A dozen paces from it Sean stopped abruptly.

'Something wrong?' Acheson asked.

'No. Nothing.' Sean started forward again, but now his eyes were fastened with fascination on one of the men who was a part of the group towards which they were headed.

A slim figure in the dark blue dress uniform of the Natal Mounted Rifles. Sandy brown hair brushed straight back from his high forehead, nose too big for the mouth and the chin beneath it, slightly round-shouldered but with the highest reward for bravery showing purple and bronze beside the striped ribbon of the Distinguished Service Order on his chest, while on his shoulders the silver crowns and lace proclaimed him a colonel.

Slowly, with a new awakening of his guilt, Sean let his eyes move down to this man's legs. With incomprehension he saw them perfectly matched, booted in polished black leather. Only when the man moved slightly, shifting his weight, Sean saw the leadenness in one of them and understood.

'My dear – I would like to present Mr Courtney. I think you have heard me speak of him. He was with me at Colenso, and on the train a few weeks ago.'

'Indeed. Mr Courtney, this is a great pleasure.' She was plump and friendly but Sean was hardly able to murmur the correct response so conscious was he of the other eyes upon his face.

'And this is Major Peterson of my staff.'

Sean nodded.

'Colonel Courtney you will probably know – seeing that you bear the same name, and not to mention the fact that he is your Commanding Officer.'

For the first time in nineteen years Sean looked into the face of the man he had crippled.

'Hello, Garry,' he said and held out his hand. He stood with it out and waited.

Garry Courtney's lips moved. He hunched his shoulders and his head swung slightly from side to side.

*Take it, Garry. Please take my hand.* Sean tried silently to urge him. Realizing the forbidding set of his own countenance, Sean forced his lips into a smile. It was an uncertain thing that smile, it trembled a little at the corners of his mouth.

In response Garry's own lips relaxed and for a moment Sean saw the terrible longing in his brother's eyes.

'It's been a long time. Garry. Much too long.' Sean prodded forward with his open right hand. *Take it. Oh God, please make him take it.*

Then Garry straightened. As he did so the toe of his right boot scraped softly, awkwardly on the marble floor. The naked longing in his eyes was glazed over, the corners of his mouth lifted upwards in something close to a sneer.

'Sergeant,' his voice was too loud, too high. 'Sergeant, you are incorrectly dressed!' Then he turned, pivoting on the dead leg, and limped slowly away through the throng.

Sean stood with his hand still out and the smile frozen on his mouth.

*You shouldn't have done that to us. We both wanted – I know you wanted it as much as I.*

Sean let his hand fall empty to his side and balled it into a fist.

'You know him?' Acheson asked softly.

'My brother.'

'I see,' Acheson murmured. He saw many things – and one of them was the reason why Sean Courtney was still a sergeant.

Major Peterson coughed and lit a cigar. Mrs Acheson touched the General's arm. 'My dear, Daphne Langford arrived yesterday. There she is with John – we must have them to dinner.'

'Of course, my dear. I will ask them this evening.'

They turned their attention on each other, giving Sean the respite he needed to recover from his snubbing.

'Your glass is empty and so is mine, Courtney. I suggest we go on to something more substantial than K's cooking champagne.'

Brandy, fiery Cape brandy, very different from that soapy liquor they make in France. A dangerous spirit to take in his present mood. And only one mood was possible for Sean after what Garry had done to him – cold, murderous rage.

His face was impassive, politely he responded to Mrs Acheson's charm, once he smile at Candy across the room, but always he sent brandy after brandy down to feed the rage that seethed in his belly; his eyes followed the figure in dark blue as it limped from group to group.

The aide-de-camp who arranged the dinner seating could never have known that Sean was a mere sergeant. As Mrs Rautenbach's guest he believed him to be an influential civilian and placed him high at the long table, between Candy and Mrs Acheson, with Major Peterson below him and a brigadier and two colonels opposite. One of the colonels was Garrick Courtney.

Beneath the almost uninterrupted stare which Sean fastened on him, Garry became nervously garrulous. Never once meeting Sean's eyes, he aimed his remarks higher up the table, and that bronze cross suspended on the ribbon of shot purple silk that bumped against his chest each time he leaned forward gave a weight to his opinions that was evident in the attention they received from the officers of general rank.

The food was excellent. Rock lobster that had run the gauntlet of Boer blockade from the Cape, plump young pheasant, venison, four assorted sauces – even the quality of the champagne had improved. But Sean ate little, instead he gave permanent employment to the wine steward who hovered behind his chair.

'And so' said Garrick as he selected a cigar from the cedarwood box that was offered him, 'I cannot see hostilities continuing another three months at the outside.'

'I agree with you sir,' Major Peterson nodded. 'We'll be back in London for the season.'

'Poppycock!' Sean made his first contribution to the discussion. It was a word he had learned only recently – but he liked it. Besides, there were ladies present.

Peterson's face chameleoned to a creditable match with the scarlet of his dress coat, Acheson started to smile then changed his mind, Candy wriggled in anticipation for she had reached the edge of boredom, and a chilly stillness fell over that area of the table.

'I beg your pardon?' Garry looked at him for the first time.

'Poppycock,' Sean repeated, and the wine steward stepped forward to cascade champagne into the crystal bowl of his glass, an operation which he had repeated at least a dozen times during the course of the evening – but this time it commanded the attention of the entire company.

'You don't agree with me?' Garry challenged.

'No.'

'Why not?'

'Because there are still eighteen thousand Boers in the field, because they are still an organized army, because not once have they had a decisive defeat inflicted on them – but mainly because of the character of these eighteen thousand that are left.'

'You don't—' Garry's voice was petulant, but Acheson interrupted smoothly. 'Excuse me, Colonel Courtney.' Then he turned to Sean. 'I believe you know these people—' he hesitated and then went on, 'you are even related through marriage.'

'My brother-in-law leads the Wynberg commando,' Sean affirmed. The old boy knew more of his past than he suspected – must have made a few inquiries. Sean was flattered and the harshness gone from his voice.

'What in your opinion, will be their course of action from now on?' Acheson pursued the subject and Sean tasted his champagne while he considered his reply.

'They will scatter – break up into their traditional fighting units, the commando.' Acheson nodded, from his position on the General Staff he knew this had already happened.

'In so doing they will avoid the necessity of dragging a supply column with them. Once the rainy season begins these small units will find grazing less of a problem for their horses.'

'Yes.' Sean saw they were all listening now. He thought quickly, cursing the wine that had dulled his brain. 'They will avoid battle, run from it and swing round to jab at the flanks, then run again.'

'Supplies?' asked the Brigadier.

'The veld is their storeroom, each farm upon it a haven.'

'Ammunition, weapons, clothing?' persisted the Brigadier.

'Every British soldier they capture or kill will provide a brand-new Lee-Metford rifle and a hundred rounds of ammunition.'

'But how long can they live like that?' Garry spoke indulgently, as though to a child. 'How far can they run?' He glanced around at the others seeking their support, but everyone was watching Sean.

'How wide is the veld – that is how far they can run.' Sean turned on him, stung by the tone of his voice. 'My God, you know them. Hardship is a way of life with them. Pride, the watchword that will carry them on.'

'You paint a pretty picture.' Garry smiled easily. 'It is unusual to find such appreciation of grand strategy among the rank and file.' Then he looked higher up the table once more with an emphasis that excluded Sean from the conversation. 'As I was saying, General Acheson, I believe—'

'One moment please, Colonel.' Acheson in turn excluded him and put his question to Sean. 'If you had the running of it, what plan of action would you adopt?'

Across the table Garrick Courtney coughed in a manner intended to inform the company that his brother was about to make a fool of himself.

It was not lost on Sean. 'The problem revolves around one single fact. The mobility of the enemy,' he stated grimly.

'Your perception does you great credit,' murmured Garry.

'Our first problem is to contain him and then to wear him down,' Sean went on, trying to ignore the taunts of his brother.

'Contain him?' The Brigadier fired the question.

'Hold him into a limited area,' Sean explained.

'How?'

'Say by a series of set fortifications,' Sean suggested.

'Correct me if I'm wrong – but you propose to divide the whole of the highveld into paddocks and farm the enemy as one would dairy cattle?' Garry was still smiling.

'The new blockhouse lines along the line of rail are proving effective. It should be possible to extend them across the open veld – every time the enemy had to pass through them he would be subject to a mauling by the garrisons and his position would immediately be pin-pointed.

'The cost would be enormous,' Acheson pointed out.

'Not as great as supporting an army of a quarter of a million men in the field for another five years,' Sean brushed his objection aside, he was set on his run of ideas. 'Then, within the defined areas small well-mounted bodies of men, unimpeded by supply wagons and artillery, could be used to raid the commandos – hitting them in an unrelenting series of raids and ambushes. Driving them on to the blockhouse lines, wearing down their horses, giving them no chance to rest, employing exactly their tactics of skirmishing. Against the commandos use counter-commandos.'

Acheson nodded thoughtfully. 'Go on,' he said.

'Then, clear out the farms,' Sean went on recklessly. 'Bring in the women and old men whose crops keep the commandos fed. Force them to operate in a vacuum.'

In the years ahead Sean was to regret the impulse that made him say it. Perhaps Kitchener would have scorched the land without Sean's suggestion, perhaps he had no hand in the formation of the concentration camps that bred bitterness Sean would spend the rest of his life trying to sweeten. But he could never be certain. He was drunk and angry – but later this knowledge would not comfort him.

Now suddenly he felt empty as though in a premonition of the monstrous seed he had sown and he sank into brooding silence while the others passed his ideas back and forth, building on them, already beginning to plan.

When the dinner party broke up and they drifted through to drink coffee, Sean made one more attempt to tear down the barrier between his brother and himself. He went to him with his pride in his hands and offered it. 'I was in Ladyburg last month. All's well there. Ada writes to say—'

'I receive a weekly letter not only from my wife but from my stepmother

and my son. I am fully aware of the latest news from home. Thank you.'
Garry stared over Sean's shoulder as he replied.

'Garry . . .'

'Excuse me.' Garry nodded briefly and limped away to speak to a brother
officer. He kept his back towards Sean.

'Let's go home, Candy.'

'But Sean . . .'

'Come on.'

Sean slept very little that night.


# Chapter Forty-one


The Headquarters of the General Officer Commanding the eastern sector
were tastefully situated in the offices of a brewery company in Plein Street.
Major Peterson was waiting for Garry when he arrived.

'I sent for you two hours ago, sir.'

'I was indisposed,' Garry told him.

'Old Ach is not in a very good mood today – we'd better not keep him
waiting any longer. Come along.'

Down the passage, where orderlies bustled, Peterson led him, and to a
door at the far end. He knocked once and then opened it. Acheson looked
up from his paperwork.

'Colonel Courtney is here, sir.'

'Thank you, Peterson. Come in, Courtney.'

Peterson closed the door and left Garry standing alone on the thick Persian
rug in front of Acheson's desk.

'I sent for you two hours ago, Courtney.' Acheson used the same reprimand,
and Garry shifted his leg uncomfortably.

'I wasn't too well this morning, sir. Had to get the doctor in.'

Acheson fingered his white moustache as he examined the dark circles
beneath Garry's eyes, and the chalky colour of his face. 'Sit down,' he
ordered.

Acheson was silent, watching him. But Garry avoided his eyes. He felt
brittle from the previous night's drinking, his skin dry and sensitive, and he
fidgeted in the chair, clasping and unclasping the hand that lay in his lap.

'I want one of your men,' Acheson spoke at last.

'Of course, sir,' Garry nodded.

'That sergeant – Courtney. I want to give him an independent command.'
Garry sat very still.

'You know who I mean?' Acheson persisted.

'Yes, sir.'

'You should,' Acheson murmured dryly. 'I have personally recommended

him to you on two occasions for recognition.' He flicked through the sheaf
of papers in front of him.

'Yes, sir.' Garry's right hand was opening and closing again.

'I notice you took no action on either of my recommendations.'

'No, sir.'

'May I ask why?'

'I didn't have . . . I didn't think the occasions merited further action.'

'You thought that my judgement was in error?' Acheson asked politely.

'No sir. Of course not, sir.' Garry answered quickly.

'Well, then?' Acheson's eyes were pale blue, but cold.

'I spoke to the man. Congratulated him. After Colenso I gave him leave.'

'Very decent of you – in view of the wounds he received there.'

'I didn't want to . . . You see – he's my brother. It was difficult –
favouritism. I couldn't really do much.' Garry wriggled sideways in his
chair, his hands came up pawing the air as though to pluck words from it.

'Your brother?' Acheson demanded.

'Yes. My brother. I know him, I know him – you don't. You can't have
any idea.' Garry could feel the pattern of his thoughts disintegrating, his
voice sounded shrill in his own ear. He had to explain, he had to tell Acheson.
'My leg,' he shrilled, 'my leg. You see it. Look at it! He did that. He took
my leg. You don't know him. He's evil. He's evil, evil. I tell you he's evil.'

Achesons expression had not changed, but his eyes were colder, more
watchful. Garry had to reach him and make him understand.

'Anna.' Garry's lips were wet and blubbery. 'My wife, Anna. He did that
to her. Everything he touches – you can't know how he is. I know. He's evil.
I tried, I hoped at Colenso – but you can't destroy him. He is the destroyer.'

'Colonel Courtney!' Acheson's voice cut into his tirade, and Garry jerked
at the crack of it. He covered his lips with his fingers and slowly he subsided
into the chair.

'I just want to explain. You don't understand.'

'I think I do,' Acheson clipped the words short and harsh. 'I am granting
you indefinite leave on grounds of ill-health.'

'You can't do that – I won't resign my commission.'

'I have not asked you to,' Acheson snapped. 'I will send the papers to
your hotel this afternoon. You can take tomorrow's train south.'

'But – but, sir—'

'That will be all, Courtney. Thank you.'

Acheson turned his attention once more to his papers.

# Chapter Forty-two

That afternoon Sean spent two hours with Acheson, then he returned to Candy's Hotel and found Saul in the billiard room. Sean selected a cue. Saul laid both balls against the far cushion and straightened.

'Well?' he asked, as Sean chalked his stick.

'You'll never believe it.'

'Tell me, and let me be the judge.'

Grinning secretly Sean cannoned twice and then sank the red.

'From sergeant without portfolio, to a full-blown major and an independent command,' he announced.

'*You?*'

'Me.' Sean chuckled and missed a cannon.

'They must be crazy.'

'Crazy or not. From now on you will stand in my presence, adopt a respectful tone of speech – and miss that shot.'

Saul missed.

'If you're an officer and a gentleman why don't you behave like one and keep your mouth shut when I'm making a play.'

'You also have changed your status.'

'How?'

'You're now a lieutenant,' Sean informed him.

'No!'

'With a gong.'

'A gong?'

'A medal, you fool.'

'I'm overcome. I am speechless.' At last Saul broke down and began to laugh. It was a sound which Sean enjoyed. 'What kind of a gong – and what for?'

'Distinguished Conduct Medal – for the night of the train.'

'But Sean, you . . .'

Sean interrupted. 'Yes, they gave me one also. Old Acheson got quite carried away. He started hanging medals and promotions on everything that moved, with the same dedicated fervour as a bill-poster putting up advertisements for Bovril. He damned nearly pinned a medal on the orderly who brought in the coffee.'

'He gave you coffee?'

'And a cigar,' Sean answered. 'He counted not the cost. It was like two lovers on an assignation. Repeatedly he addressed me as *My dear fellow.*'

'And what is this command he gave you?'

Sean racked his cue and stopped laughing.

'You and I are to head one of the first counter-commandos. Small, lightly equipped units to ride in and ginger up the Boer. Harass him, wear him down, chase the guts out of his horses and keep him moving until he runs on to one of the big columns.'


The following morning they rode out with Major Peterson to inspect the band of volunteers he had assembled for them.

'A mixed bag I'm afraid, Courtney. We've scratched together three hundred and fifteen.' Peterson was gloating a little behind the apology. He had not forgotten that *poppycock*.

'It must have been difficult,' Sean agreed. 'You only had a quarter of a million to choose from. What abour officers?'

'Sorry. Only Friedman here. But I have got you an absolute gem. Sergeant-major. Snaffled him from the Dorsets. Fellow by the name of Eccles. First-class, absolutely first-class.'

'And Tim Curtis – the one I asked for?'

'Sorry again. They've reopened the gold mines. All engineers are being pulled out and sent back to work.'

'Damn it, I wanted him. What about machine-guns?'

'Four Maxims. Bloody lucky to get them.'

'Horses?'

'A bit of a struggle – but you can go down to remount and take your pick.'

Sean went on relentlessly with his demands and questions during the ride out towards Randfontein. His excitement for the challenge of this venture rose steadily as they argued and talked. At last he was taking it seriously. He asked the final and crucial question as they trotted past the sentries into the great army camp on the outskirts of Johannesburg.

'Has Acheson decided in which area I will be operating?'

'Yes.' Peterson dropped his voice. 'South-east Transvaal.'

'That's where Leroux is!'

'That's right. The gentleman who met your train the other day.'

Jan Paulus again!

'Here you are, Courtney.'

A little apart from the main camp stood three lines of white canvas tents. A field kitchen smoked at the far end and around it were clustered Sean's warriors.

'My God, Peterson. You said a mixed bag! You've robbed the army of cooks and batmen. And what are those – *sailors*, Bejusus!'

Peterson smiled thinly and shifted in the saddle.

'Press-ganged them,' he admitted. 'Gunnery detail from *Repulse*. Ah, here comes your sergeant-major.'

Eccles approached in column of fours; bull-built black moustache, a few inches over six feet and all of it held stiffly erect. Peterson introduced them and they appraised each other.

'A right scruffy lot we got here, sir.'

'We've got a bit of work to do, Eccles.'

'That we'ave, sir.'

'Let's get started then.' And they glowered at each other in mutual respect and liking.

A week later they were ready to go. Saul had named them 'Courtney's Fighting Scouts'. They were all well mounted, altough there were some interesting styles of horsemanship evident – especially among the delegates from the Royal Navy. By bullying the quartermaster Sean had arrived at a standard uniform similar to that of the Imperial Light Horse; slouch hats, khaki tunics and riding breeches, bandoliers, puttees and issue boots. They had forty fat and healthy pack-mules, four Maxim machine-guns and Eccles had trained teams to serve them.

Acheson had approved Sean's request to use Charlestown as a base. He had arranged rail transport south to this tiny village near the Natal border, promised support from the big flying columns in the area, and informed Sean that he was expecting *big things* from him. He made it sound like a threat.

## Chapter Forty-three

'But, darling, you haven't even been given a real uniform. You look so drab.' Candy, who was watching him dress from the double bed, held very definite views on what constituted a real uniform. It had gold lace and frogging with, say a Star of the Garter on a rich scarlet ground. 'Lock at those buttons – they're not even shiny.'

'Boers like shiny things – makes good shooting in the sun.' Sean glanced over his shoulder at her. Her hair was fluffed into golden disorder and the blue gown was arranged to provoke rather than conceal. Hastily Sean returned his eyes to his own reflection in the full-length mirror and brushed the hair back along his temples. A touch of grey in it now. Quite dignified, he decided. Pity about the nose. He took it between his fingers and straightened it, a hell of a nose, but when he released his grip it returned immediately to a half-cock position.

'Well, I'll be leaving you now,' he said, and she stood up quickly and the laughter was gone from her lips, they trembled a little.

'I'll come down with you.' She rearranged the gown quickly.

'No.'

'Yes, I have a farewell present for you.'

In the hotel yard, hitched behind four fat mules, was a scotch-cart. She led him to it and lifted the tarpaulin cover.

'A few things I thought you might need.'

Against the cold she had provided a sheepskin coat, six fine woollen blankets and a silk eiderdown, two feather pillows and a mattress; a case of Courvoisier brandy and a case of Veuve Clicquot champagne. Against starvation there was potted salmon, strawberry jam, caviar in little glass jars, tinned delicacies all carefully packed in wooden boxes. For his health a medicine chest complete with a set of surgical instruments. Against the Boer there was a Toledo steel sabre in a leather scabbard worked with silver and a matched pair of Colt revolvers in a mahogany presentation case.

'Candy . . .' Sean stumbled. 'I don't know what to say.'

She smiled a little and took his arm, hugging it. 'There's something else also.' She nodded to one of the grooms who disappeared into the stables and led out a full-blooded Arab stallion with an English hunting saddle on its back.

'My God!' exclaimed Sean, and the stallion danced sideways so that the early sun glowed on the sheen of its coat. It flared the great pink pits of its nostrils and rolled its eyes before rearing high and dragging the groom off his feet.

'Candy, my dear,' Sean repeated.

'Good-bye, Sean.' She lifted her lips for his kiss and then broke away and almost ran back to the hotel.

While Saul shouted ribald encouragement, Mbejane and the groom held its head. Sean mounted the stallion, then they turned it loose and Sean fought to quieten it. At last he brought it under a semblance of control and, crabbing and pracing with arched neck and dainty high-stepping gait, persuaded it to head off in the general direction of Johannesburg railway station.

Eccles watched his approach impassively.

'What the hell are you laughing at, Sergeant-Major?'

'I wasn't laughing, sir.'

Sean dismounted and, with relief, gave the stallion into the care of two of his troopers.

'Nice bit of horseflesh, sir.'

'What do you think he'll fetch?'

'You're going to sell him, sir?' Eccles could not hide his relief.

'You're damn right, I am. But it's a gift, so no sale here in Johannesburg.'

'Well, Colonel Jordan at Charlestown is usually in the market for a good nag. I should be able to get you a price sir. We'll see what we can do.'

Colonel Jordan purchased not only the stallion but the pistols and the sabre as well. The secretary of the Charlestown garrison officers' mess frothed at the mouth with excitement when Eccles drew back the tarpaulin cover from the scotchcart.

When Sean's column rode out into the brown open winter grassland towards the jagged line of the Drakensberg, the little scotch-cart trotted behind with the Maxims and a dozen ammunition cases making a full load.

# Chapter Forty-four

There was cold that first night, and the stars were brilliant, clear and very far away. In the morning the land lay white and brittle in the grip of frost; each blade of grass each twig and fallen leaf transformed into a white-jewelled wonder. A thin scum of ice covered the pool beside which the column had camped.

Mbejane and Sean squatted together. Mbejane with his monkey-skin kaross draped over his shoulders and Sean with the sheepskin coat buttoned to the throat.

'Tonight we will camp below that mountain.' Sean pointed away towards the west at the blue cone that stood out against the lighter blue of the dawn sky. 'You will find us there.'

'Nkosi,' Mbejane nodded over his snuffbox.

'These others.' Sean pointed with his chin at the group of four natives who waited quietly with the spears beside the pool. 'Are they men?'

Mbejane shrugged. 'I know little of them. The best of those I spoke with, perhaps. But they work for gold – and of their hearts I do not know.' Before going on, he regarded their clothing; tattered European cast-offs which were everywhere replacing the traditional tribal costume. 'They dress without dignity. But beneath the rags it is possible that they are men.'

'They are all we have so we must use them. Yet I wish we had those others who now grow fat in the company of their women.'

Mbejane smiled. A week before he had put the message into the grapevine and he knew that both Hlubi and Nonga were at that moment dissipating their accumulations of fat as they trotted north from their kraals along the Umfolozi River. They would be here soon.

'This is the way we will hunt,' Sean told him. 'Your men will spread out ahead of us and search for sign. The horses of those we seek will carry no steel on their hooves. If you find it fresh, then follow it until the run and direction of it is clear. Then return to me in haste.'

Mbejane nodded and sniffed a pinch from his snuffbox.

'While you search, stop at the kraals you find along the way. Speak with the people there, clearly, if the Mabune are here these people will know of it.'

'It will be as you say, Nkosi.'

'The sun comes.' Sean looked up at the glow of it upon the high places while the valleys were blue with shadow. 'Go in peace, Mbejane.'

Mbejane folded his kaross and tied it with a strip of leather. He picked up his stabbing spear and slung the great oval war shield on his shoulder. 'Go in peace, Nkosi.'

Sean watched while he talked with the other trackers, listening to the sonorous rise and fall of his voice. Then they scattered, trotting away into the veld, dwindled and were gone.

'Eccles.'

'Sir.'

'Finished breakfast?'

'Yes, sir.'

The men stood to their horses, blanket-rolls and carbines on the saddles, slouch hats pulled well down and the collars of their greatcoats turned up against the cold. Some were still eating with their bayonets from the cans of shredded beef.

'Let's go, then.'

The column closed up, riding four abreast, the pack-mules and the scotchcart in the centre, the outriders fanning out ahead to screen the advance. It was a tiny command, not a hundred and fifty paces long even with the pack animals, and Saul smiled as he remembered the massive fifteen-mile column that had marched from Colenso to Spion Kop.

Yet it was enough to tickle his pride. Courtney's Fighting Scouts. The task now was to justify the second word of their title.

Saul hooked one leg over the saddle, balanced his notebook upon it – and while they rode he and Sean planned a thorough re-organization of the column.

When they halted at midday the planning was put into effect. A patrol of ten men in charge of the mules, for this duty Sean picked those who were fat, old or ungainly in the saddle. These men would also act as horseholders when the unit went in to fight on foot.

From among his sailors, Sean selected the gunners to captain the four Maxim teams. The riflemen were divided into patrols of ten with the most likely men promoted Sergeant Patrol Leaders, and their warrants noted in Saul's little book.

It was well after nightfall when they offsaddled that night below the dark massif of the mountain. Mbejane was waiting with his men beside a small, well-screened fire.

'I see you, Mbejane.'

'I see you, Nkosi.'

In the firelight Mbejane's legs were coated with dust to the knees and his face was grey with fatigue.

'What news?'

'Old sign. Perhaps a week ago, many men camped over there below the river. Twenty fires not in lines as the soldiers make them. They left no little tin pots as the soldiers do when they have emptied them of meat. No tents, but beds of cut grass – many beds.'

'How many?' It was an idle question for Mbejane could not count as a white man counts. He shrugged.

'As many beds as there are men with us?' Sean sought a comparison.

'More.' Mbejane thought carefully before answering.

'As many again?' Sean persisted.

'Perhaps as many again – but no more than that.'

Probably five hundred men, Sean guessed. 'Which way were they moving?'

Mbejane pointed south-west.

Back towards Vryheid and the protection of the Drakensberg mountain. Yes, it was part of the Wynberg commando without doubt.

'What news from the kraals?'

'There is fear among them. They tell little, and that of no importance.' Mbejane made no attempt to hide his disgust, the contempt that the Zulu feels for every other tribe in Africa.

'You have done well, Mbejane. Rest now for we ride before the dawn.'

Four more days they moved south-west, Sean's trackers sweeping the ground ten miles on each side of their path and finding it empty.

The Drakensberg reared up like a serrated back of a prehistoric monster along the south horizon. There was snow on the peaks.

Sean exercised his men in the counters to a surprise attack. Riflemen wheeling out and dismounting in line to cover the Maxims as they galloped wildly for the nearest high ground. Holders gathering the loose horses and pelting away to the cover of the nearest donga or kopje. Again and again they repeated this manoeuvre.

Sean worked them until they leaned forward in their saddles to nurse aching backsides and cursed him as they rode. He worked them to the edge of exhaustion and then on to a new physical fitness. They sprouted beards, their faces reddened and peeled, then darkened with the sun, their uniforms darkened also, but with dirt. Now they no longer cursed him. There was a new feeling among them, they laughed more and sat solid in the saddle, slept soundly at night despite the cold and woke with eagerness.

Sean was moderately satisfied.


On the morning of the tenth day Sean was scouting ahead of the column with two of his troopers. They had just dismounted to rest among an outcrop of boulders when Sean picked up movement out on the plain ahead. With a savage lift of aniticipation he scrambled down from the boulder on which he was sitting and ran to his horse for his binoculars.

'Damn it!' he mouthed his disappointment as he saw the lance blades glitter in the round strangely fore-shortened field of the glasses. 'Cavalry'.

Half an hour later they met the small patrol of lancers from one of the big columns that were driving south from the line of blockhouses. The young subaltern in command gave Sean a cigar, and the latest news of the war.

De la Rey and Smuts were rampaging north of Johannesburg in the Magaliesberg with forty thousand men chasing their three thousand. South in the Free State another of the great De Wet hunts was in full swing. But this time they would catch him, the subaltern assured Sean. Fifty thousand foot and horse had driven his commando into the angle between the block-house line and the flooded Riet River. In the east it was quieter. The commandos there lacked leadership and were lying up in the mountains around Komatipoort.

'So far it's quiet here also, sir. But I don't like the looks of it. This man Leroux is a nasty piece of work, clever man too, So far he's limited his activities to a few raids. Ten days ago about five hundred of his men hit one of our supply columns near Charlestown. Wiped out the guard and collected enough ammunition to fight a full-scale battle, then made off towards the mountains.'

'Yes,' Sean nodded grimly. 'We found one of his camps.'

'No sign of him since then, sir. We've been scouring the ground for him but so far without luck.'

'What's his force?' Sean asked.

'He can muster three thousand, so they say. My guess is that he's getting himself poised for something really big.'


That night Mbejane came into camp well after midnight. He came to where Sean slept under the scotchcart and with him were two other men. 'Nkosi.'

Sean rolled on his side, instantly awake at the touch. 'Mbejane?' He crawled out from under the cart and stood up.

The moon was up, silver and round and bright. By its light he recognized the men with Mbejane and exclaimed with pleasure:

'By God! Hlubi! Nonga!' Then remembering his manners, 'I see you.'

He stepped forward grinning broadly to clasp their shoulder in turn. And each replied gravely as they returned his embrace. 'I see you, Nkosi.'

'Are you well?'

'I am well. Are you well?'

The catechism of Zulu greeting can be carried on for as long as there is time available. More than a year had passed since Sean had discharged them from his service outside Pretoria, and so Sean must ask each of them for news of his father, his brothers, his herds, and the journey they had made, before he could put his own question.

'You came through Ladyburg?'

'We came that way,' agreed Hlubi.

'You saw the Nkosana Dirk?'

Now for the first time they both smiled, white teeth in the moonlight.

'We sat in council with the Nkosizana,' Hlubi chuckled. 'He grows like a bull calf. Already he wears scars of battle, honourable blackening of one of his eyes.'

'He grows in wisdom also,' Nonga boasted. 'Saying aloud to us those things which are written in the book.'

Hlubi went on: 'He sends greetings to the Nkosi, his father, and asks that he be allowed now to leave his school and join with him once more. For now he is skilled in the matter of books and numbers.'

Sean laughed. 'And what of the Nkosikazi, my mother?' he asked.

'She is well, She sends you this book.' Hlubi produced a travel-stained envelope from his loin-cloth. Sean tucked it away inside his coat to be read at leisure.

'Now.' The formula of greeting completed, Sean could come to the present. 'What news of Mabunu? Have you found sign?'

Mbejane squatted on his haunches and laid his spear and shield beside him. The other followed his example. The meeting came to order.

'Speak,' Mbejane ordered Hlubi.

'We came through the mountains, this being the shorter way,' Hlubi explained. 'In the hills below the mountains we found the road made by many horses, and following it we came upon a level place surrounded by rock. The Mabunu are there with cattle and wagons.'

'How far is this place?' Sean asked eagerly.

'A day's long journey.' Thirty miles.

'How many Mabunu?' Sean asked and Mbejane explained, 'As many as camped at the place I told you of.'

It made sense, Sean decided. Jan Paulus would have split his force into smaller units, for reasons of supply and concealment, until such time as he needed them.

'We will go then,' he said and stood up.

Eccles woke quickly.

'Sergeant-Major. The guides have found a small Boer commando in laager below the mountains. Get the men mounted up.'

'Sir!' Eccles's moustache, rumpled with sleep, quivered like the whiskers of a hunting dog.

While around him the commotion of upsaddling began. Sean kicked life into the fire and in its yellow flickering light he tore a page from his notebook and licked the point of a pencil.

*To all British troops in the field:*

I am in contact with a Boer commando of 500. Will attempt to contain them pending your arrival. The bearer will act as a guide.

S. Courtney (Major).

5th August, 1900. Time 00.46 hours.

'Hlubi,' he called.

'Nkosi!'

'Take this book,' he handed him the note. 'There are soldiers out there.' He swept his arm towards the north. 'Give it to them.'

## Chapter Forty-five

Bunched into a compact column with the gallant little scotchcart bouncing and jolting in the rear, Courtney's Fighting Scouts cantered southwards with the brown winter grass brushing their stirrups.

With Saul beside him and the two Zulus ranging ahead like hunting dogs, Sean rode in the van. He slouched easily in the saddle and tried with both hands to steady Ada's letter as it fluttered in the wind of his passage. It was strange to read the gentle reassuring words as he hurried into battle.

All was well at Lion Kop. The wattle grew apace – free from fire, drought or pestilence. She had hired an assistant manager who worked afternoons only; his mornings required attendance at Ladyburg School. Dirk was earning his princely salary of two shillings and sixpence a week and seemed to be enjoying the work. The arrival of his school report for the period ended at Easter was the occasion for some concern. His average high marks for each subject was followed by the notation, 'Could do much better' or 'Lacks concentration'. The whole was summarized by the Headmaster, 'Dirk is a high-spirited and popular boy. But he must learn to control his temper and to apply himself with more diligence to those subjects he finds distasteful.'

Dirk had recently fought an epic bout of fisticuffs with the Petersen boy, who was two years his senior, and had emerged blooded and bruised, but victorious. Here Sean detected a note of pride in Ada's prim censure. There followed half a page of messages dictated by Dirk in which protestations of filial love and duty were liberally punctuated with requests for a pony, a rifle, and permission to terminate his scholastic career.

Ada went on tersely to say that Garry had recently returned to Ladyburg, but had not yet called upon her.

Finally, she instructed him to take pains with his health, invoked the Almight to his protection, anticipated his swift return to Lion Kop – and ended with love.

Sean folded the letter carefully and tucked it away. Then he let his mind drift, lolling in the saddle while the brown miles dropped steadily behind his horse. There were so many loose or ravel threads to follow – Dirk and Ada, Ruth and Saul, Garrick and Michael – and all of them made him sad.

Then suddenly he glanced sideways at Saul and straightened in the saddle. This was not the time to brood. They had entered the mouth of one of the valleys that sloped upwards towards the massive snow-plastered ramparts of the Drakensberg, and were following a stream whose banks dropped ten feet to the water that gurgled and tinkled over the polished round boulders in its bed.

'How much farther, Nonga?' he called.

'Close now, Nkosi.'

In another valley that ran parallel to the one Sean was following, separated from it by two ridges of broken rock, a young Boer asked the same question.

'How much farther, Oom Paul?'

But before answering, Vecht-Generaal Jan Paulus Leroux eased himself around in the saddle and looked back along the commando of one thousand burghers he was leading to a rendezvous at his laager in the mountains. They rode in a solid mass that clogged the floor of the valley, bearded men in a motley of dark homespun clothing, on ponies shaggy in their winter coats – yet Jan Paulus felt pride swell in his chest as he looked at them. These were the bitter-enders, veterans of half a hundred fights, men forged and tempered in the furnace of battle, razor-sharp and resilient as the finest steel. Then he looked at the boy beside him – a boy in years only for his eyes were old and wise.

'Close now, Hennie.'

'Eccles, we'll halt here. Water the horses. Loosen the girths but don't offsaddle. No fires but the men can rest and eat.'

'Very well, sir.'

'I am going forward to have a look at the laager. While I am away I want you to issue an extra hundred rounds of ammunition to each man. Check the Maxims. I should be back in two hours.'

'When will it be, sir?'

'We'll move forward at dusk, I want to be in position to attack as soon as the moon rises. You can tell the men now.'

As Sean and Nonga left the column and moved on foot up the valley, two men watched them from the ridge. They lay on their bellies among the rocks. Both of them were bearded. One of them wore a British officer's Sam Browne belt over his patched leather jacket, but the rifle that rested on the rock in front of him was a Mauser.

'They send spies to the laager,' he whispered, and his companion answered in the Taal.

'*Ja*, they have found it.'

'Go! Ride quickly to Oom Paul and say for him that we have three hundred khaki ripe and ready for the plucking.'

The other Boer grinned and wriggled backwards, working his way off the skyline. Once below it he ran to his pony and led it down into the grass which would muffle its hoof-beats, before he mounted.

An hour later Sean returned from his reconnaissance.

'We've got them, Eccles,' he grinned savagely at Saul and Eccles.

'They're about two miles ahead in a hidden basin of hills.' He squatted down and smoothed a patch of earth with the palm of his hand. 'Now here is the way we'll do it.' With a twig he drew quickly in the dirt. 'This is our valley. Here we are. This is the laager, hills here and here and here. This is the entrance to the basin. Now, we'll place two Maxims here, with a hundred men below and in front of them like this. I want you—'

Abruptly his earthen map exploded, throwing dirt into his eyes and open mouth. 'What the bloody—' he mouthed as he clawed at his face but the rest of it was lost in the blast of the Mausers.

Through streaming eyes Sean looked up at the ridge. 'Oh my God!' A fire haze of gunsmoke drifted across it like sea spray on a windy day, and he sprang to his feet.

'Into the river. Get the horses into the river,' he roared above the murderous crackle, the shrill fluting whine of ricochets and the continuous slapping of bullets into earth and flesh.

'Into the river. Get into the river!' He ran down the column shouting at the men who were struggling to clear their rifles from the scabbards of plunging, rearing horses. The Boer fire flogged into them, dropping men and horses screaming in the grass. Loose horses scattered along the valley, reins trailing and empty stirrups bouncing against their flanks.

'Leave them! Let them go! Get into the river!' Two of the mules were down, kicking, wounded in the traces of the scotchcart. Sean tore the tarpaulin loose and lifted out one of the Maxims. A bullet splintered the woodwork under his hands.

'You!' he shouted at one of his sailors. 'Grab this!' He passed the gun to

him and the man ran with it cradled in his arms and jumped over the river
bank. With a case of ammunition under each arm Sean followed him. It
seemed as though he ran waist-deep in water, each pace dragging with
painful deliberation and his fear came strongly upon him. A bullet flipped
his hat forward over his eyes, the ammunition cases weighted him down,
and he blundered panic-stricken towards the river. The earth was gone
abruptly from under his feet and he fell, dropping free until, with a shock
that jarred his spine, he struck and toppled forward face-down into the icy
water.

Immediately he scrambled up and, still clutching the Maxim ammunition,
floundered to the steep bank. Above him the Boer fire whipped and sang,
but the bed of the river was crowded with his men, and others still fell and
jumped from the bank to add to the congestion.

Panting and streaming water from his clothing Sean leaned against the
bank while he gathered himself. The stream of survivors into the river-bed
dwindled and stopped. The Boer fire also stuttered out and a comparative
quiet fell over the field, spoiled only by the groaning and cursing of the
wounded.

Sean's first coherent thought was for Saul. He found him holding two
pack-mules under the bank with Nonga and Mbejane beside him holding
another pair. He sent Saul to take command at the far end of the line.

'Sergeant-Major!' Sean shouted, and with relief heard Eccles's reply from
close at hand.

'Here, sir.'

'Spread them out along the bank. Get them to cut firing platforms.'

'Very good, sir,' and immediately he began. 'Here you lot, you heard the
Major! Up off your backsides!'

Within ten minutes there were two hundred rifles lining the bank and the
Maxim was sited and manned behind a scharnz of stone and earth. Those
men who had lost their weapons were tending the wounded. This pitiful
little group were gathered in the middle of the line, they were propped
against the bank, sitting waist-deep in slush and their blood stained the
water pinky-brown.

Sean climbed up on to one of the firing platforms beside Eccles and lifted
his head to peer cautiously over the bank. The area in front of him was a
sickening sight. Dead mules and horses with their packs burst open littering
the grass with blankets and provisions. Wounded animals flopping helpless
or standing quietly with their heads hanging.

'Is there anyone out there still alive?' Sean called, but the dead men gave
him no answer. A sniper on the ridge ploughed a bullet into the ground in
front of Sean's face and he ducked down quickly.

'Most of them managed to crawl in, sir. Those that didn't are better out
there than in the mud here.'

'How many did we lose, Eccles?'

'About a dozen dead, sir, and twice as many wounded. We got off very
lightly.'

'Yes,' Sean nodded 'Most of their initial fire went high. It's a mistake
even the best shots make when shooting downhill.'

'They fair caught us with our pants down,' mused Eccles and Sean did not miss the censure in his tone.

'I know. I should have placed look-outs on the ridge,' he agreed. You're no Napoleon, he told himself, and you've got casualties to prove it.

'How many of them lost their weapons?' he asked.

'We've got two hundred and ten rifles and one Maxim, sir, and I issued an extra hundred rounds to each man just before the attack.'

'Should be enough,' Sean decided. 'Now all that remains is to sweat it out until my native guide brings up reinforcements.'

For half an hour nothing happened beyond a little desultory sniping from the ridge. Sean moved along the line talking to the men.

'How's it going, sailor?'

'Me old ma would have a fit, sir. "George," she'd say, "sitting in the mud is not going to do your piles no good," she'd say, sir.' The man was shot through the stomach and Sean had to force his chuckle through his throat.

'I could use a smoke, though. That I could.'

Sean found a damp cigar in his pocket for him and moved on. A youngster, one of the Colonials, was crying silently as he held against his chest the blood-soaked bundle of bandages that was his hand.

'Giving you pain?' Sean asked gently. The boy looked up at him, the tears smearing his cheeks. 'Go away,' he whispered. 'Please go away.'

Sean walked on. I should have put look-outs on the ridge, he thought again. I should have—

'Flag of truce on the ridge, sir,' a man shouted excitedly and Sean clambered up beside him.

Immediately a hum of comment ran along the line.

'They're hanging out their washing.'

'The bastards want to surrender. They know we've got them licked.'

Sean climbed out of the river-bed and waved his hat at the speck of white that fluttered on the ridge, and a horseman trotted down towards him.

'*Middag, Menheer,*' Sean greeted him. He received only a nod in reply and took the note the man proffered:

*Menheer,*
    I expect the arrival of my Hotchkiss gun at any moment. Your position is not safe. I suggest you lay down your guns to prevent further killing.
                    J. P. Leroux, Vecht-Generaal,
                                    Wynberg commando.

It was written on an irregular scrap of brown wrapping paper in High Dutch.

'My greetings to the General, *Menheer*, but we will hold out here a little longer.'

'As you wish,' the Boer acquiesced, 'but first you must see if any of these' – he pointed at the khaki figures that were scattered among the dead mules and horses – 'you must see if any of them are still alive. And you must destroy the wounded animals.'

'It is kind of you, *Menheer.*'

'You will, of course, make no attempt to pick up weapons or ammunition.'

'Of course.'

The Boer stayed with them while Eccles and half a dozen men searched the field, destroying the maimed animals and examining the fallen troopers. They found one man still alive. The air hissed softly from his severed windpipe and a froth of blood bubbles writhed about the hole. On a blanket they carried him down to the river-bed.

'Eleven dead, sir,' Eccles reported to Sean.

'Eccles, as soon as the truce ends we are going to recover another Maxim and the two cases of ammunition.'

They stood beside the scotchcart and Sean inclined his head to indicate the bulky, blue-metalled weapon that showed from beneath the tarpaulin.

'Very good, sir.'

'I want four men ready below the lip of the bank. Make sure each man has a knife to cut the pack ropes.'

'Yes, sir.' Eccles grinned like a playful walrus and drifted back towards the river, and Sean strolled across to the mounted Boer.

'We have finished, *Menheer*.'

'Good. As soon as I cross the skyline up there – then we'll start again.'

'I agree.' Sean walked back to the river, picking his way through the dead. Already the flies were there, swarming green and metallic, rising like a migrating hive of bees as he passed, then settling again.

Sean reached the bank and below him Saul crouched at the head of a bunch of unarmed men. Behind them stood a very disgruntled Eccles, his moustache drooping in disappointment. Instantly Sean saw what had happened – Saul had used his superior rank to take over command of the volunteers. 'What the hell do you think you're doing?' Sean demanded, and Saul answered him with an obstinate stare.

'You'll stay where you are. That's an order!' He turned to Eccles. 'Take over, Sergeant-Major,' and Eccles grinned.

This was no time to argue. Already the Boer horseman was half way up the ridge. Sean raised his voice and shouted at the long line of men below the bank.

'Listen, all of you. No one is to fire until the enemy do. That way we may be able to spin it out a little longer.' Then less loudly as he spoke to Eccles. 'Don't run, just walk out casually.' Sean jumped down the bank and stood between Eccles and Saul. All three of them peered up at the ridge and saw the Boer reach the crest, wave his hat and disappear.

'Go!' Sean said, and all of them went. Eccles, the four volunteers – and Saul. Flabbergasted, Sean stared at the six of them as they strolled out towards the scotchcart. Then his anger flared. *The stupid little bastard*, and he went also.

He caught up with them as they reached the scotchcart, and in the strained silence of the suspended storm he growled at Saul:

'I'll fix you for this!' and Saul grinned triumphantly.

Still there was a puzzled silence from the ridge – but it could not last much longer.

Together Saul and Eccles slashed at the ropes that held the tarpaulin, and Sean pulled it back and reached for the gun.

'Take it.' He passed it to the man behind him. At that moment a warning shot cracked over their heads.

'Grab one each and run!'

From the ridge and the river came gunfire like a long roll of drums, and they ran doubled beneath their loads and dodging, back towards the river.

The man carrying the Maxim fell headlong. Sean threw the ammunition case he carried, it dropped short of the bank, but skidded forward and toppled over the edge. Hardly pausing in his run, he stooped and gathered the fallen Maxim and went on. Ahead of him first Eccles, then Saul jumped into safety and Sean followed them with the three surviving troopers.

It was over, Sean sat waist-deep in the icy water with the machine-gun clutched to his chest, and all he could think of was his anger at Saul. He glared at him, but Saul and Eccles knelt facing each other grinning and laughing.

Sean handed the gun to the nearest trooper and crossed to Saul. His hand fell heavily on his shoulder and he pulled him to his feet.

'You—' He could not find words cutting enough. If Saul had been killed out there, Ruth would never have believed Sean had not ordered it so. 'You fool,' he said and might have hit him, but he was distracted by the cries from the firing platform beside him.

'The poor bastard!'

'He's up.'

'Lie down, for God's sake, lie down.'

Sean released Saul, jumped up on to the platform and stared through the loophole in the scharnz.

Out in the open the trooper who had carried the Maxim was on his feet. He was moving parallel to the bank, shambling with a curious idiot gait, his hands hanging loosely by his sides. They were shooting at him from the ridge.

Held in the paralysis of horror, none of them went to him. He was hit and he lurched but tottered on with the Boer rifles hunting him, staggering in a circle away from the river. Then, suddenly they killed him and he dropped on to his face.

The gunfire stopped and in the silence the men in the river-bed began to move around, and talk of trivial things, avoiding each other's eyes, ashamed to have watched such a naked intimate thing as that man's dying.

Sean's anger was gone, replaced by guilty thankfulness that it had not been Saul out there in the open.

# Chapter Forty-six

In the long period of stagnation that followed, Sean and Saul sat together against the bank. Though they talked little, the old sense of companionship was restored.

With a rush and rattle the first shell ripped the air above their heads, and with everyone else Sean ducked instinctively. The shell burst in a tall brownish-yellow spurt on the far slope. Consternation bushfired along the river.

'Lummy, they've got a gun!'

'Book me on the next train, mate!'

'Nothing to worry about, boys,' Sean shouted reassuringly. 'They can't reach us with that piece.'

And the next shell burst on the lip of the bank, showering them with earth and pebbles. One startled second they stood dazed and coughing in the fumes, and the next they fell on the bank like a band of competitive grave-diggers. Dust from their exertions rose in a pale brown mist over the river to puzzle the Boers on the ridge. Almost before the arrival of the next shell, each man had hacked out a small earthen cupboard into which he could squeeze himself.

The Boer gunners were alarmingly inconsistent. Two or three rounds would fly wildly overhead and burst in the open veld. The next would land squarely in the river spraying mud and water high in the air. When this happened the sound of sustained cheering drifted faintly down from the ridge, followed by a long pause – presumably while the gunners received the congratulations of their fellows. Then the bombardment would recommence with enthusiastic rapidity, which slowly wound down into another long pause while everybody rested.

During one of these intervals Sean peered through his loop-hole. From a dozen points along the ridge rose pale columns of smoke.

'Coffee break up there, Eccles.'

'The way they do things we can expect another white flag and a couple of their lads coming down with coffee for us as well.'

'I doubt it,' Sean grinned. 'But I think we can expect them to come down though.' Sean pulled out his watch. 'Half-past four now. Two hours to sundown. Leroux must try for a decision before dark.'

'If they come, they'll come from behind,' Saul announced cheerfully and pointed to the slope of ground that menaced their rear. 'To meet a charge from there, we would have to line the far bank and expose our backs to sniping from the ridge.'

Sean considered the problem for a minute. 'Smoke! That's it!'

'I beg yours, sir?'

'Eccles, get the men to build fireplaces of stone along the bed and set grass and branches ready to light,' Sean ordered. 'If they do come from behind we'll screen ourselves with smoke.'

Fifteen minutes of furious activity completed the work. At intervals of ten paces along the river-bed they built flat-topped cairns of stone that rose above the level of the water. On each was piled a large heap of grass and wild hemlock branches gathered from where they overhung the bank of the river.

A little before sunset, in that time of shadows and deceptive light, with a haze rising in the still, cold air to mask them, Leroux charged his horsemen at the river.

Sean heard a low drumming of hooves as though a train passed in the distance and started to his feet.

'Here they come!' somebody shouted. 'The bastards are coming from behind.'

With the low sun at their backs throwing big, distorted shadows ahead of them, they swept down in a long line from the west.

'Light the fires!' bellowed Sean. They were lying flat on their horses, five hundred of them coming in at full gallop and shooting as they came.

'Maxims!' Sean shouted. 'Get the Maxims across!' The teams dragged the heavy unwieldy weapons from their emplacements and floundered with them across the stream. From each of the fires blue smoke spread and lifted. Men coughed and swore and splashed to their new positions. From the ridge a furious covering fire raked the river and then the field-piece crashed shell after shell amongst them.

'Fire at will!' Sean shouted. 'Hit the bastards. Hit them. Hit them hard.'

The din was appalling – gunfire and bursting shells, the hammering beat of the Maxims, shouts of defiance and pain, the thunder of charging hooves, crackling of the flames. Over it all a dense fog of smoke and dust.

With elbows on the rough shale of the bank, Sean aimed and fired and a horse went down, throwing rider and rifle high and clear. Without taking the butt from his shoulder he worked the bolt and fired again. Got him! swaying and twisting in the saddle. Drop, you bastard! That's it – slide forward and fall. Shoot again, and agin. Empty the magazine. Hitting with every shot.

Beside him the matelot traversed the Maxim in a deliberate hammering arc. Fumbling, as he reloaded, Sean watched the Maxim scythe its slow circle of destruction, leaving a shambles of downed horses and struggling men, before its beat stopped abruptly and the matelot crouched over it to fit a fresh belt from the wooden case. A bullet from the ridge, fired blindly into the smoke, hit him in the back of the neck and he fell forward, jamming the gun, blood gushing from his open mouth over the jacketed barrel. His limbs twitched and jerked in the epilepsy of death.

Sean dropped his rifle and dragged the matelot off the gun, levered the first round of the belt into the breech and thrust his thumbs down on the buttons.

They were close now. Sean bore down on the firing handles to raise his
fire, aiming at the chests of the horses. The sailor's blood fried and sizzled
on the hot barrel, and the grass in front of the muzzle flattened and quivered
in the continuous blast.

Above him a solid frieze of milling horses was outlined against the
darkening sky, the men upon them pouring their bullets into the crowded
river-bed. Wounded horses plunged down the bank, rolling and kicking into
the mud.

'Dismount! Dismount! Go in after them!' an old burgher with a neat
blond beard yelled.

Sean dragged the gun around to get him. The man saw him in the smoke
but his right leg was out of the stirrup, his rifle held in the left hand, helpless
in the act of dismounting. Sean saw his eyes were grey and without fear as
he looked down into the muzzle of the Maxim. The burst hit him across the
chest, his arm windmilled, his left foot caught in the stirrup as he went
backwards and his pony dragged him away.

The attack broke. The Boer fire slackened, ponies wheeled away, and
raced back for the shelter of the hills. The old burgher Sean had killed went
with them, dragged upon his back with his head bouncing loosely over the
broken ground. leaving a long slide mark of flattened grass.

Around him Sean's men cheered and laughed and chattered with jubilation.
But in the mud there were many who did not cheer and with a guilty shock
Sean realized he had been standing on the corpse of the sailor who had died
over the gun.

'Our round, that one!' Eccles beamed. Callous among the dead as only an
old soldier can be.

'Yes,' Sean agreed.

Out in the open a horse heaved itself up and stood shivering, one leg
hanging broken under it. A wounded burgher started to cough in the grass,
choking and gasping as he drowned in his own blood.

'Yes, our round, Eccles. Put up the flag. They must come down and collect
the wounded.'

They used lanterns in the darkness to find the wounded and kill the
horses.


'Nkosi, at a place where the river turns and the banks are low, they have
placed men,' Mbejane reported, back from the reconnaissance on which Sean
had sent him. 'We cannot escape that way.'

'I thought as much,' Sean nodded, and held out the open can of bully beef
to Mbejane. 'Eat,' he said.

'What's he say, sir?' Eccles asked.

'The river is held in force downstream.' Sean lit one of the cheroots that
he had recovered in the darkness from the saddle-bag of his dead horse.

'Ruddy cold sitting here in the mud,' Eccles hinted.

'Patience, Sergeant-Major,' Sean smiled. 'We'll give them until midnight.
By then most of them will be down the other side of the ridge drinking
coffee around the fires.'

'You are going to rush the ridge, sir?' Eccles obviously approved.

'Yes. Tell the men. Three hours' rest and then we'll take the ridge.'

'Very good, sir.'

Sean lay back and closed his eyes. He was very weary, his eyes felt gritty from the dust and smoke, his lower body was wet and cold his boots heavy with mud. Lyddite fumes had given him a blinding headache.

I should have put a look-out on the ridge, he thought again. My God! What a mess I've made of this. My first command and already I've lost all the horses and damn-nigh half of my men. I should have put a look-out on the ridge.

## *Chapter Forty-seven*

They took the ridge a few minutes after midnight with hardly any opposition. The few Boer sentries made good time down the far slope and Sean looked down upon the Boer laagers. The camp fires glimmered in an irregular line along the valley. Men stood around them staring up at the ridge. Sean scattered them with a dozen lusty volleys, and then yelled. 'Cease firing. Eccles, get the men settled in. We are going to have visitors fairly soon.'

The Boers had built scharnzes along the crest which saved Sean's men much inconvenience and within ten minutes the Maxims were emplaced and Sean's two hundred unwounded men waited behind walls of rough rock for the Boer counter-attack. This took some time to develop for the situation necessitated a hurried War Council in the valley below. But at last they heard the first stealthy approach of the attackers.

'Here they come, Sergeant-Major. Hold your fire, please.'

The burghers worked their way up cautiously and when Sean could hear their voices whispering among the rocks he decided they were close enough and discouraged further intimacy with volleyed rifle-fire and the use of all his Maxims. The Boers replied with heat and at the height of the exchange the Hotchkiss gun joined in from the valley. Its first shell passed but a few feet over Sean's head, then burst in the valley behind him. The second and third shots dropped neatly among the attacking Boer riflemen and raised such a howl of protest that the gunners, their efforts not appreciated, maintained an aloof and offended silence for the rest of the night.

Sean had expected a determined night attack but it soon became clear that Leroux was fully aware of the danger of closely engaging an inferior force in the dark. He contented himself with keeping Sean awake all night, his burghers taking it in turn to come up and keep the short-range rifle duel going – and Sean began to have qualms about the wisdom of his offensive. Dawn would find him on a rocky ridge, facing a numerically superior force, with his line enchored at neither end, and short enough to be easily flanked and enfiladed. He remembered Spion Kop – and there was little comfort in the memory. But the alternative was to fall back on the river, and his hackles rose at the thought. Unless relief came soon, defeat was certain – better here on the high ground than in the mud. We'll stay, he decided.

In the dawn there was a lull but although the gunfire dwindled to an occasional crack and flash on the lower slope yet Sean could sense an increase of activity among the Boers. Ominous rustlings and the muted sounds of movement on his flanks confirmed his misgivings. But now it was too late to retreat on the river, for already the mountains were showing stark silhouettes against the dawn sky. They seemed very close, as close and unfriendly as the unseen multitude of the enemy waiting out there for the light to come.

Sean stood up. 'Take the gun,' he whispered to the man beside him as he relinquished the Maxim.

All night he had fought with that wicked clumsy weapon and now his hands were claws shaped to the firing grips, and his shoulders ached intolerably. He flexed them as he moved down the line, stopping to chat with the men who lay belly-down behind the scharnz, trying to make his words of encouragement sound convincing.

In their replies he sensed the respect they were forming for him as a fighting man. It was more than respect – closer to a tolerant affection. The same feeling old General Buller had evoked amongst his men. He made mistakes, a lot of men died when he led, but they liked him and followed cheerfully. Sean reached the end of the line.

'How's it going?' he asked Saul softly.

'Fair enough.'

'Any sign of the old Boer?'

'They're pretty close – we heard them talking a few minutes ago. My guess is they're as ready as we are.'

'How's your ammunition?'

'We've got enough to finish this business.'

To finish this business! That would be his decision. When the massacre began, how much must he make them endure before he called for quarter, and they stood up with arms raised in the most shameful of all attitudes?

'You'd better get under cover, Sean. Light's coming fast.'

'Who the hell is looking after whom,' Sean grinned at him. 'I want no more heroics from you,' he said, and walked quickly to his station on the other flank.

The night lifted quickly from the land, and morning came as abruptly as it does only in Africa. The Boer laagers were gone. The Hotchkiss gun was gone. Sean knew that the gun and the Boer horses had been moved back behind the new ridge which now faced their position. He knew also that the rocky ground below him was crawling with the enemy, that they were on his flanks and probably in his rear as well.

Slowly, the way a man looks at a place before he begins a long journey, Sean looked around him at the mountains and the sky and the valley. In the soft light it was very beautiful.

He looked down the gut of the valley towards the grass plains of the highveld. His head jerked with surprise. He felt excitement lift the hair on his forearms. The mouth of the valley was blocked by a dark mass. In the uncertain light it could have been a plantation of wattle trees – oblong and regular and black against the pale grass. But this plantation was moving, changing shape, elongating. Birnam Wood to Dunsinane.

The first rays of the sun slanted in across the crest of the ridge and lit the lance-heads into a thousand minute dazzles.

'Cavalry!' roared Sean. 'By Jesus, look at them.'

The cry was taken up and thrown along the line, yelling, cheering wildly they fired down upon the tiny brown figures that were scurrying away to meet the Boer pickets who galloped in across the floor of the valley, each of them dragging a bunch of a dozen horses after him.

Then above the cheering and the gunfire, high above the sounds of hooves and the cries of panic, a bugle began to sing: 'Bonnie Dundee' – sharp and clear and urgently it commanded the charge.

Sean's rifles fell silent. The cheering faltered and stopped. One by one his men stood up to watch as the lines of lancers moved forward. Walk. Trot. Canter. Gallop. The lance heads dropped Belly-high they flitted like fireflies in front of the solid dark ranks, and that terrible thing swept down upon the tangle of men and frenzied, struggling horses.

Some of the Boers were up now, wheeling away, breaking like game before the beaters.

'My God!' breathed Sean, tensing himself for the burst of sound as the charge struck home. But there was only the drum of hooves – no check, no distortion as the dark squadrons drove through the Boers. Precisely they wheeled, and came back. Broken lances thrown aside, sabres unsheathed, bright and long.

Sean watched a burgher dodging desperately as a lancer followed him. Saw him turning at the last moment and crouching with his arms covering his head. The lancer stood in his stirrups and swung he sabre backhanded. The burgher dropped. Like a polo player the trooper pivoted his horse and rode back over the Boer, leaning low out of the saddle to sabre him again as he knelt in the grass.

'Quarter!' growled Sean, then his voice rising shrilly in horror and disgust. 'Give them quarter. For the love of God, give them quarter!'

But cavalry gives no quarter. They butchered with dispassionate parade-ground precision. Hack and cut, turn and trample until the blades blurred redly – until the valley was strewn with the bodies of men wounded a dozen times.

Sean tore his eyes away and saw the remains of Leroux's commando scattered into the broken ground where the big cavalry mounts could not follow.

Sean sat down on a rock and bit the end off a cheroot. The rank smoke helped cleanse his mouth of the taste of victory.

Two days later Sean led his column into Charlestown. The garrison cheered them and Sean grinned as he watched his men react. Half an hour before they had bumped along, hunched unhappily on their borrowed mounts. Now they sat erect and jaunty, eating the applause and liking the taste.

Then the grin faded from Sean's face as he saw how his band was depleted, and he looked back at the fifteen crowded wagons that carried the wounded.

*If only I'd put look-outs on the ridge.*

## *Chapter Forty-eight*

There was an urgent summons from Acheson waiting for Sean. He caught the northbound express twenty minutes after arriving in Charlestown, hating Saul for the hot bath in which he left him, and for the uniform which Mbejane had persuaded a plump Zulu maid to wash and iron, hating him still more venomously for the invitation to be guest of honour at the officers' mess that night – and knowing that Saul would drink deep on Veuve Clicquot and Courvoisier which had once belonged to Sean.

When Sean arrived in Johannesburg the following morning, with soot from the locomotive adding a subtle touch to the fragrance he had gathered from two unwashed weeks in the veld, there was an orderly to meet him and conduct him to Acheson's suite in the Grand National Hotel.

Major Peterson was patently taken aback by Sean's turn-out, he eyed the stains and tears and dried mud with genteel horror at the contrast they afforded to the breakfast table's crisp white linen and splendid silver. The ripeness of Sean's odour impaired Peterson's appetite and he dabbed at his nose with a silk handkerchief. But Acheson seemed not to notice, he was in festive mood.

'Damned fine show, Courtney. Oh, damned fine. Proved your point entirely. We'll not have much trouble from Leroux for some time, I warrant you. Have another egg? Peterson, pass him the bacon.'

Sean finished eating and filled his coffee cup before he made his request. 'I want to be relieved of this command, I made a bloody mess of it.'

Both Acheson and Peterson stared in horror. 'Good God, Courtney. You've achieved a notable success – the most spectacular in months.'

'Luck,' brusquely Sean interrupted. 'Another two hours and we would have been wiped out.'

'Lucky officers are more valuable to me than clever ones. Your request is refused, Colonel Courtney.' So it's Colonel now, a bribe to get me into the dentist's chair. Sean was mildly amused.

A knock at the door prevented Sean continuing his protestation, and an orderly came into the room and handed Acheson a message.

'Urgent dispatch from Charlestown,' he whispered. Acheson took the paper from him and used it like a conductor's baton as he went on talking.

'I have got three junior officers for you, men to replace your losses. You catch them for us and hold them for my cavalry. That's all I want from you. While you're doing your bit the columns are going to start a series of new drives. This time we are going to sweep every inch of the ground between the blockhouse lines. We are going to destroy the crops and the livestock; burn the farms; take every woman, man and child off the land and put them in detainment camps. By the time we're finished there will be nothing but bare veld out there. We will force them to operate in a vacuum, while we wear them down with a relentless series of drives and raids.' Acheson slapped the table so that the crockery jingled. 'Attrition, Courtney. From now on it's a war of attrition!'

Those words had an uncomfortable familiarity for Sean. And suddenly a picture of desolation formed in his mind. He saw the land – his land – blackened with fire, and the roofless homesteads standing in the wastes. The sound of the empty winds across the land was the wailing of orphans, and the protest of a lost people.

'General Acheson—' he began, but Acheson was reading the dispatch.

'Damn!' he snapped. 'Damn and blast! Leroux again. He doubled back and caught the transport column of those same lancers who cut him up. Wiped it out and disappeared into the mountains.' Acheson laid the message on the table in front of him and stared at it. 'Courtney,' he said, 'go back and, this time, catch him!'

# Chapter Forty-nine

'Breakfast is ready, Nkosi.' Michael Courtney looked up from his book at the servant. 'Thank you, Joseph, I'm coming now.'

These two hours of study each morning passed so quickly. He checked the clock on the shelf above his bed – half-past six already – closed the book and stood up.

While he brushed his hair he watched his reflection in the mirror without attention. His mind was fully occupied with events that would fill this new day. There was work to do.

His reflection looked back at him with serious grey eyes from a face whose lean contours were marred by the big Courtney nose. His hair was black and springy beneath the brush.

He dropped the brush and while he shrugged into his leather jacket he flipped open the book to check a passage. He read it through carefully, then turned and went out into the corridor.

Anna and Garrick Courtney were seated at opposite ends of the long dining-table of Theuniskraal and they both looked up expectantly as he entered.

'Good morning, Mother.' She held up her face for his kiss.

'Good morning, Pa.'

'Hello, my boy.' Garry was wearing full dress, complete with crowns and decorations, and Michael felt a flare of irritation. It was so damned ostentatious. Also it reminded him that he was nineteen years old and there was a war going on while he sat at home on the farm.

'Are you going into town today, Pa?'

'No, I'm going to do some work on my memoirs.'

'Oh,' Michael glanced pointedly at the uniform and his father flushed slightly and applied himself to his meal.

'How are your studies, darling?' Anna broke the silence.

'Well enough, thank you, Mother.'

'I'm certain you'll have as little trouble with the final examinations as you had with the others.' Anna smiled at him possessively and stretched out to touch his hand. Michael withdrew it quickly and laid down his fork.

'Mother, I want to talk to you about enlisting.' Anna's smile froze. At the end of the table Garry straightened in his chair.

'No,' he snapped with unusual violence. 'We've been over this before. You're still a minor and you do as you're told.'

'The war is almost over, darling. Please think of your father and me.'

It began then. Another of those long wheedling, pleading arguments that sickened and frustrated Michael until he stood up abruptly and left the room. His horse was waiting saddled for him in the yard. He threw himself on to its back and swung its head at the gate, lifting it over, and scattering chickens as he landed. He galloped furiously away towards the main dip-tank.

From the dining-room they heard the hooves beat away until they had dwindled into silence. Garry stood up.

'Where are you going?' snapped Anna.

'To my study.'

'To the brandy bottle in your study,' she corrected him contemptuously.

'Don't, Anna.'

'*Don't, Anna*,' she mimicked him. '*Please don't, Anna*. Is that all you can say?' Her voice had lost the genteel inflexion she had cultivated so carefully. Now it contained all the accumulated bitterness of twenty years.

'Please, Anna. I'll stop him going. I promise you.'

'You'll stop him!' She laughed. 'How will you stop him? Will you rattle your medals at him? How will you stop him – you, who have never done one useful thing in all your life?' She laughed again, shrilly. 'Why don't you show him your leg and say, "Please don't leave your poor crippled Daddy".'

Garry drew himself up. His face had gone very pale. 'He'll listen to me. He's my son.'

'Your son!'

'Anna, please—'

'Your son! Oh, that's choice! He's not your son. He's Sean's son.'

'Anna.' He tried to stop her.

'How could you have a son?' She was laughing again, and he could not stand it. He started for the door but her voice followed him, cutting into the two most sensitive places in his soul; his deformity and his impotence.

He stumbled into his study, slammed the door and locked it. Then he crossed quickly to the solid cabinet that stood beside his desk.

He poured the tumbler half-full and drank it. Then he sank into his chair and closed his eyes and reached for the bottle behind him. He poured again carefully and screwed the cap back on to the bottle. This one he would sip slowly, making it last perhaps an hour. He had learned how to keep the glow.

He unbuttoned and removed his tunic, stood up and hung it over the back of the chair, seated himself once more, sipped at the tumbler, then drew towards him the pile of handwritten sheets, and read the one on top.

'Colenso: An account of the campaign in Natal under General Buller.' By Colonel Garrick Courtney, V.C., D.S.O.

He lifted it, laid it aside, and began to read what followed. Having read it so many times before, he had come to believe in it. It was good. He knew it was good. So too did Messrs William Heinemann in London, to whom he had sent a draft of the first two chapters. They were anxious to publish as soon as possible.

He worked on quietly and happily all morning. At midday old Joseph brought a meal to the study. Cold chicken and salads on Delft-ware china, with a bottle of white Cape wine wrapped in a snowy napkin. He worked as he ate.

That evening when he had altered the last paragraph on the final page and laid his pen on the inkstand, he was smiling.

'Now, I will go and see my darling.' He spoke aloud and put on his tunic.

The homestead of Theuniskraal sat on the crest of a rise below the escarpment. A big building of whitewashed walls, thatch and Dutch gables. In front of it the terraced lawns sprawled away, contoured by beds of azaleas and blue rhododendrons and bounded on the one side by the horse paddocks: two large paddocks for the brood mares and the yearlings, where Garry paused beside the low fence and watched the foals nuzzling upwards at the udders.

Then he limped on along the fence towards the smaller enclosure with its nine-foot fence of thick, canvas-padded gumpoles that contained his stud stallion.

Gypsy was waiting for him, nodding his almost snakelike head so that his mane flared golden in the late sunlight, flattening his ears, then pricking them forward, dancing a little with impatience.

'Hey, Boy. Hey there, Gypsy,' Garry called and the stallion thrust his head between the poles to nibble with soft lips at Garry's sleeve.

'Sugar, is that what you're after.' Garry chuckled and cupped his hands while the stallion fed delicately from them.

'Sugar, my darling,' Garry whispered in sensual delight at the touch of the soft muzzle on his skin and Gypsy cocked his ears to listen to his voice.

'That's all. All finished.' The stallion nuzzled his chest and Garry wiped his hands on its neck, caressing the warm and silky coat.

'That's all, my darling. Now run for me. Let me watch you run.' He stepped back and clapped his hands loudly. 'Run, my darling, run.'

The stallion pulled his head back between the poles and went up on his hind legs, whinnying as he reared, cutting at the air with his fore-hooves.

The veins stood out along the belly and upon the tight double-swollen bag of its scrotum.

Swift and virile and powerful, it pivoted upon its quarters.

'Run for me!' shouted Garrick. The stallion came down into full gallop along the track worn by its hooves, sweeping around the paddock with loose dirt flying and the light dancing on his coat as the great muscles bulged beneath.

'Run.' Leaning against the poles of the fence, Garrick watched him with an expression of terrible yearning.

When he stopped again with the first dark patches of sweat dulling his shoulders, Garrick straightened up and shouted across the stable yard.

'Zama, bring her now!'

On a long rein two grooms led the brood mare down towards the paddock. Gypsy's nostrils flared into dark pink caverns and he rolled his eyes until the whites showed.

'Wait, my darling,' whispered Garrick in a voice tight with his own excitement.

## Chapter Fifty

Michael Courtney dismounted among the rocks on the highest point of the escarpment. For a week he had denied the impulse to return to this place. Somehow it seemed a treachery – a disloyalty to both his parents.

Far below and behind him in the forest was the tiny speck of Theuniskraal. Between them the railway angled down towards the sprawled irregular pattern of rooftops that was Ladyburg.

But Michael did not look that way. He stood behind his mare and gazed along the line of bare hills to the gigantic quilt of trees that covered them in the north.

The wattle was tall now, so that the roads between the blocks no longer showed. It was a dark smoky green that undulated like the swells of a frozen sea.

This was as close as he had ever been to Lion Kop. It was a forbidden land, like the enchanted forest of the fairy-tale. He took the binoculars from his saddle-bag and scanned it carefully, until he came to the roof of the homestead. The new thatch, golden and unweathered, stood out above the wattle.

Grandma is there. I could ride across to visit, there would be no harm in that. *He* is not there. *He* is away at the war.

Slowly he replaced the binoculars in the saddle-bag, and he knew he would not go to Lion Kop. He was shackled by the promise he had made to his mother. Like so many other promises he had made.

With dull resignation he remembered the argument at breakfast that morning, and new that they had won again. He could not leave them, knowing that without him they would wither. He could not follow *him* to war.

He smiled ironically as he remembered the fantasies he had imagined. Charging into battle with *him*, talking with *him* beside the camp fire in the evenings, throwing himself in front of a bayonet meant for *him*.

From the look-out on the escarpment Michael had spent hours each day of the last Christmas holiday waiting for a glimpse of Sean Courtney. Now with guilt he remembered the pleasure he had experienced whenever he picked up that tall figure in the field of his binoculars and followed it as it moved between the newly planted rows of wattle.

But he's gone now. There would be no disloyalty if I rode across to see Grandma. He mounted the superb golden mare and sat deep in thought. At last he sighed, swung her head back towards Theuniskraal – and rode away from Lion Kop.

I must never come up here again, he thought determinedly, especially after *he* comes home.

## Chapter Fifty-one

They are tired, tired to the marrow of their bones. Jan Paulus Leroux watched the lethargy of his burghers as they off-saddled and hobbled their horses. They are tired with three years of running and fighting, sick-tired in the certain knowledge of defeat, exhausted with grief for the men they have buried, with grief also for the children and the women with them in the camps. They are wearied by the sight of burned homes scattered about with the bones of their flocks.

Perhaps it is finished, he thought and lifted the battered old Terai from his head. Perhaps we should admit that it is finished, and go in to them. He wiped his face with his scarf and the cloth came away discoloured with the grease of his sweat and the dust of the dry land. He folded the scarf into the pocket of his coat and looked at the fire-blackened ruins of the homestead on the bluff above the river. The fire had spread into the gum trees and the leaves were sere and yellow and dead.

'No,' he said aloud. 'It is not finished – not until we try for this last time,' and he moved towards the nearest group of his men.

'*Ja*, Hennie. How goes it?' he asked.

'Not too bad, Oom Paul.' The boy was very thin, but then all of them were thin. He had spread his saddle-blanket in the grass and lay upon it.

'Good.' Jan Paulus nodded and squatted beside him. He took out his pipe and sucked on it. There was still the taste of tobacco from the empty bowl.

'Will you take a fill, Oom Paul?' One of the others sat up and proffered a pouch of springbok skin.

'*Nee, dankie.*' He looked away from the pouch, shutting out the temptation. 'Keep it for a smoke when we cross the Vaal.'

'Or when we ride into Cape Town,' joked Hennie, and Jan Paulus smiled at him. Cape Town was a thousand miles south of them, but that was where they were going.

'*Ja*, keep it for Cape Town,' he agreed and the smile on his face turned bitter. Bullets and disease had left him with six hundred ragged men on horses half-dead with exhaustion to conquer a province the size of France. But it was the last try. He started to speak then.

'Already Jannie Smuts is into the Cape with a big commando. Pretorius also has crossed the Orange, De la Rey and De Wet will follow – and Zietsmann is waiting for us to join him on the Vaal River. This time the Cape burghers must rise with us. This time . . .'

He spoke slowly, leaning forward with his elbows on his knees, a gaunt giant of a man with his unkempt, ginger beard wiry with dust and streaked about the mouth with yellowish grey. The cuffs of his sleeves were stained with the discharge from the veld sores on his wrists. Men came across from the other groups and squatted in a circle about him to listen and take comfort.

'Hennie, bring my Bible from the saddle-bag. We will read a little from the Book.'

The sun was setting when he closed the Book and looked around at them. An hour had gone in prayer that might more profitably have been spent in rest, but when he looked at their faces he knew the time had not been wasted.

'Sleep now, *Kerels*. We will upsaddle early tomorrow.' If they do not come in the night, he qualified himself silently.

But he could not sleep. He sat propped against his saddle and for the hundredth time re-read the letter from Henrietta. It was dated four months earlier, had taken six weeks to reach him along the chain of spies and commandos which carried their mail. Henrietta was sick with dysentery and both the younger children, Stephanus and baby Paulus, were dead from the *witseerkeel*. The concentration camp was ravaged by this disease and she feared for the safety of the older children.

The light had failed so he could not read further. He sat with the letter in his hands. With such a price as we have paid, surely we could have won something.

Perhaps there is still a chance. Perhaps.

'Upsaddle! Upsaddle! Khaki is coming.' The warning was shouted from the ridge across the river where he had placed his pickets. It carried clearly in the still of the evening.

'Upsaddle! Khaki is coming.' The cry was taken up around the camp. Jan Paulus leaned over and shook the boy beside him, who was too deep in exhaustion to have heard.

'Wake up, Hennie. We must run again.'

Five minutes later he led his commando over the ridge and southward into the night.

## Chapter Fifty-two

'Still holding southwards,' Sean observed. 'Three days' riding and they haven't altered course.'

'Looks like Leroux has got his teeth into something,' agreed Saul.

'We'll halt for half an hour to blow the horses.' Sean lifted his hand and behind him the column lost its shape as the men dismounted and led their horses aside. Although the entire unit had been remounted a week before, the horses were already losing condition from the long hours of riding to which they had been subjected. However, the men were in good shape, lean and hard-looking. Sean listened to their banter and watched the way they moved and laughed. He had built them into a tough fighting force that had proved itself a dozen times since that fiasco a year ago when Leroux had caught them in the mountains. Sean grinned. They had earned the name under which they rode. He handed his horse to Mbejane and moved stiffly towards the shade of a small mimosa tree.

'Have you got any ideas about what Leroux is up to?' he asked Saul as he offered him a cheroot.

'He could be making a try at the Cape railway.'

'He could be,' Sean agreed as he lowered himself gratefully on to a flat stone and stretched his legs out in front of him. 'My God, I'm sick of this business. Why the hell can't they admit it's finished – why must they go on and on?'

'Granite cannot bend.' Saul smiled dryly. 'But I think that now it is very near the point where it must break.'

'We thought that six months ago,' Sean answered him, then looked beyond him. 'Yes, Mbejane, what is it?'

Mbejane was going through the ritual which preceded serious speech. He had come and squatted half a dozen paces from where Sean sat, had laid his spears carefully beside him in the grass, and now he was taking snuff.

'Nkosi.'

'Yes?' Sean encouraged him and waited while Mbejane tapped a little of the dark powder on to his fingernail.

'Nkosi, this porridge has an unusual taste.' He sniffed and sneezed.

'Yes?'

'It seems to me that the spoor has changed.' Mbejane wiped the residual snuff from his nostrils with the pink palm of his hand.

'You speak in riddles.'

'These men we follow ride in a different manner from the way they did before.'

Sean thought about that for a few seconds before he saw it. Yes! He was right. Where previously Leroux's commando had spread and trampled the grass in a road fifty feet wide, since this morning they had ridden in two files as though they were regular cavalry.

'They ride as we do, Nkosi, so the hooves of the horses fall in the tracks of those that lead. In this way it is difficult to tell how many men we follow.'

'We know there are about six hundred. . . . Hold on! I think I see what you . . .'

'Nkosi, it comes to me that there are no longer six hundred men ahead of us.'

'My God! You could be right.' Sean jumped up and began to pace restlessly. 'He is splitting his commando again. We've crossed a dozen rocky places where he could have detached small groups of his men. By evening we'll be following less than fifty men – when that happens they'll break up into individuals, lose us in the dark and head separately for a pre-arranged rendezvous.' He punched his fist into the palm of his hand. 'That's it, by God!' He swung round to face Saul.

'You remember that stream we crossed a mile back – that would have been an ideal place.'

'You're taking a big risk,' Saul cautioned him. 'If we go back now and it turns out you're wrong – then you've lost him for good.'

'I'm right,' Sean snapped. 'I know I am. Get them mounted up – we're going back.'


Sean sat his horse on the bank of the stream and looked down into the clear water that sparkled over gravel and small round boulders.

'They will have gone downstream, otherwise the mud they stirred up would have washed down across the ford.' He turned to Saul. 'I'm going to take fifty men with me so as not to raise too much dust. Give me an hour's start and then follow with the rest of the column.'

'*Mazeltov.*' Saul grinned at him.

With a Zulu tracker on each bank Sean and Eccles and fifty men followed the stream towards the north-west. Behind them the mountains of the Drakensberg were an irregular pale blue suggestion against the sky and around them the brown winter-sere veld spread away in the folded complexity of ridges and the shallow valleys. In the rocky ground along the ridges grew the squat little aloe plants, holding up their multiple flowers like crimson candelabra while in the valleys the stunted thorn bushes huddled along the course of the stream. High, cold cloud obscured the sky. There was no warmth in the pale sunlight, and the wind had a knife-edge to it.

Two miles below the ford Sean was showing his anxiety by leaning forward in the saddle and checking the ground that Mbejane had already covered. Once he called, 'Mbejane, are you sure you haven't missed them?'

Mbejane straightened from his crouch and turned slowly to regard Sean with a look of frigid dignity. Then he shifted his war shield to the other shoulder and, not deigning to answer, he returned to his search.

Fifty yards farther on he straightened again and informed Sean.

'No, Nkosi. I have not missed them.' He pointed with his assegai at the deeply scarred bank up which horses had climbed, and the flattened grass which had wiped the mud from their legs.

'Got them!' Sean exulted in his relief; behind him he heard the stir of excitement run through his men.

'Well done, sir.' Eccles's moustache twitched ferociously as he grinned.

'How many, Mbejane?'

'Twenty, not more.'

'When?'

'The mud has dried.' Mbejane considered the question, stooping to touch the earth and determine its texture. 'They were here at half sun this morning.'

The middle of the morning; they had a lead of five hours.

'Is the spoor fat enough to run upon?'

'It is, Nkosi.'

'Then run, Mbejane.'

The spoor bellied towards the west then swung and steadied in the same persistently southward direction, and Sean's column closed up and cantered after Mbejane.

Southward, always southward. Sean pondered the problem – what could he hope to accomplish with a mere six hundred?

Unless! Sean's brain started to harry a vague idea. Unless he intended slipping through the columns of infantry and cavalry that lay before him and trying for a richer prize.

The railway, as Saul had suggested? No, he discounted that quickly. Jan Paulus would not risk his whole command for such low stakes.

What then? The Cape? By God, that was it – the Cape! That rich and lovely country of wheatlands and vineyards. That serene and secure land, lazing in the security of a hundred years of British rule – and yet peopled by men of the same blood as Leroux and De Wet and Jan Smuts.

Smuts had already taken his commando across the Orange River. If Leroux followed him, if De Wet followed him, if the Cape burghers broke their uneasy neutrality and flocked to join the commandos – Sean's mind baulked at the thought. He left the wider aspect of it and came back to the moment.

All right then, Jan Paulus was riding to the Cape with only six hundred men? No, he must have more. He must be riding to a rendezvous with one of the other commandos. Who? De la Rey? No, De la Rey was in the Magaliesberg. De Wet? No, De Wet was far south – twisting and turning away from the columns that harried him. Zietsmann? Ah, Zietsmann! Zietsmann with fifteen hundred men. That was it.

Where would they meet? On a river obviously, for they must have water for two thousand horses. The Orange was too dangerous – so it must be the Vaal, but whereabouts on the Vaal? It must be a place easily recognizable. One of the fords? No, cavalry used the fords. A confluence of one of the tributaries? Yes, that was it.

Eagerly Sean unbuckled his saddle-bag and pulled from it his map-case.

Holding the heavy cloth map folded against his thigh he twisted sideways in the saddle to study it.

'Here we are now,' he muttered and ran his finger south. 'The Padda River!'

'I beg your pardon, sir.'

'The Padda, Eccles, the Padda!'

'Very well, sir,' agreed Eccles with stolid features covering his bewilderment.


In the dark valley below them the single fire flared briefly, then died to a tiny glow.

'All ready, Eccles,' Sean whispered.

'Sir!' Without raising his voice Eccles placed affirmative emphasis on the monosyllable.

'I'll go down now.' Sean resisted the impulse to repeat his previous orders. He wanted to say again how important it was that no one escaped, but he had learned that once was enough with Eccles. Instead he whispered, 'Listen for my signal.'

The Boers had only one sentry. Secure in the knowledge that their stratagem had thrown off all pursuit, they slept around the poorly screened fire. Sean and Mbejane moved down quietly and squatted in the grass twenty paces from the high rock on which the sentry sat. The man was outlined darkly against the stars and Sean watched him intently for a full minute before he decided.

'He sleeps also.'

Mbejane grunted.

'Take him quietly,' Sean whispered. 'Make sure his rifle does not fall.' Mbejane moved and Sean laid a hand on his shoulder to restrain him. 'Do not kill – it is not necessary.' And Mbejane moved silently as a leopard towards the rock.

Sean waited straining his eyes into the darkness. The seconds dragged by – and suddenly the Boer was gone from the rock. A gasp, a soft sliding sound and stillness.

Sean waited, and then Mbejane was back as silently as he had left.

'It is done, Nkosi.'

Sean laid his rifle aside and cupped his hands over his lips, filled his cheeks and blew the long warbling whistle of a nightbird. At the fire one of the sleepers stirred and muttered. Farther off a horse stamped and blew softly through its nostrils. Then Sean heard a pebble click and the cautious swish of feet through grass, small sounds lost in the wind.

'Eccles?' Sean murmured.

'Sir.'

Sean stood up and they closed in on the camp.

'Wake up, gentlemen. Breakfast is ready.' Sean shouted in the Taal, and each burgher woke to find a man standing over him and the muzzle of a Lee-Metford pressing into his chest.

'Build up that fire,' Sean ordered. 'Take their rifles.' It had been too easy, he spoke roughly in the irritation of anti-climax.

'Mbejane, bring the one from the rock – I want to see how gently you dealt with him.'

Mbejane dragged him into the firelight and Sean's lips tightened as he saw the way the man's head lolled and his legs hung.

'He's dead,' Sean accused.

'He sleeps, Nkosi,' Mbejane denied.

Sean knelt beside him and twisted his face to catch the light. Not a man, a lad with a thin bitter face and the fluff of pale, immature beard on his cheeks. In the corner of his eye a stye had burst to matt the closed lashes with yellow pus. He was breathing.

Sean glanced up at the other prisoners. They were being herded away out of earshot.

'Water, Mbejane.' And the Zulu brought a canteen from the fire while Sean explored the hard swelling above the boy's temple.

'He'll do,' Sean grunted, and curled his lips in distaste at what he must do as soon as the lad recovered. He must do it while he was still groggy and bemused by the blow. From his cupped hand he splashed cold water into his face and the boy gasped and rolled his head.

'Wake up,' Sean urged quietly in the Taal. 'Wake up.'

'Oom Paul?' The Boer mumbled.

'Wake up.' The lad struggled to sit.

'Where . . . You're English!' As he saw the uniform.

'Yes,' Sean snapped. 'We're English. You've been caught.'

'Oom Paul?' The boy looked round wildly.

'Don't worry about him. He'll be with you on the boat to St Helena. Leroux and Zietsmann were both caught on the Vaal yesterday. We were waiting for them at the Padda and they walked right into the trap.'

'Oom Paul caught!' The boy's eyes were wide with shock, still dazed and out of focus. 'But how did you know? There must have been a traitor – someone must have told. How did you know about the meeting-place?' He stopped abruptly as his brain caught up with his tongue. 'But how . . . Oom Paul couldn't be on the Vaal yet, we left him only yesterday.' Then sickeningly he realized what he had done 'You tricked me,' he whispered. 'You tricked me.'

'I'm sorry,' Sean said simply. He stood up and walked across to where Eccles was securing his prisoners.

'When Captain Friedman arrives tell him to bring the column in to the garrison at Vereeniging and wait for me there. I am going ahead with my servant,' he said abruptly, then called across to Mbejane.

'Mbejane, bring my horse.' He would trust no one else to carry the news to Acheson.

The following afternoon Sean reached the railway line guarded by its blockhouses and flagged a northbound train. The next morning he de-trained with soot-inflamed eyes, tired and filthy, at Johannesburg station.

## Chapter Fifty-three

Jan Paulus Leroux checked his horse and behind him the tiny fragment of his commando bunched up and all of them peered eagerly ahead.

The Vaal is a wide, brown river, with sandbanks through which it cuts its own channel. The banks are steep and along them are scattered a few of the ugly, indigenous thorn trees, which provide no cover for an army of three thousand men and horses. But Leroux had chosen the rendezvous with care. Here the tiny Padda River looped down through a complex of small kopjes to join the Vaal and among these kopjes an army might escape detection – but only if it exercised care. Which Zietsmann was not doing.

The smoke from a dozen fires hazed out in a long pale smear across the veld, horses were being watered on one of the sandbanks in the middle of the river, and a hundred men were bathing noisily from the bank, while laundry decked the thorn trees.

'The fool,' snarled Leroux and kicked his pony into a run. He stormed into the laager, flung himself off his horse and roared at Zietsmann.

'*Menheer*, I must protest.'

Zietsmann was nearly seventy years old. His beard was pure white and hung to the fifth button of his waistcoat. He was a clergyman, not a general, and his commando had survived this long because it was so ineffectual as to cause the British no serious inconvenience. Only great pressure from Delarey and Leroux had forced him to take part in this wild plan. For the last three days, as he waited for Leroux to join him, he had been harassed by doubts and misgivings. These doubts were shared by his wife – for he was the only Boer general who still had his woman with him in the field.

Now he stood up from his seat by the fire and glared at this red-bearded giant Leroux, whose face was mottled with fury.

'*Menheer*,' he growled. 'Please remember you are speaking not only to your Elder, but also to a Dominie of the Church.'

In this way was set the tone for the long discussions which were to fill the next four days. During this time Leroux saw his bold design bog down in a welter of trivialities. He did not resent the loss of the first day which was spent in prayer, indeed he realized that this was essential. Without God's blessing and active intervention the enterprise must fail, so the sermon he delivered that afternoon lasted a little over two hours and the text he selected was from Judges – 'Shall I yet again go out to battle against the children of Benjamin, my brother, or shall I cease?' and the Lord said, 'Go up; for tomorrow I will deliver them into thine hand.'

Zietsmann bettered his time by forty minutes. But then, as Leroux's men pointed out, Zietsmann was a professional while Oom Paul was only a lay-preacher.

The next and most critical question was the election of the Supreme Commander for the combined enterprise. Zietsmann was the older by thirty years, a factor heavily in his favour. Also, he had brought sixteen hundred men to the Vaal against Leroux's six hundred. Yet Leroux was the victor of Colenso and Spion Kop, and since then he had fought consistently and with not a little success, including the wrecking of eight trains and the annihilation of four British supply columns. Zietsmann had been second in command at Modder River, but since then he had done nothing but keep his commando intact.

For three days the debate continued with Zietsmann dourly refusing to bring the matter to the vote until he sensed that opinion had swung to his side. Leroux wanted command; not only for personal satisfaction, but also because he knew that under this cautious and stubborn old man they would be lucky to reach the Orange River, let alone force an effective entry into the Cape.

The card that won the hand belonged to Zietsmann, and it was ironic that he had it simply because of his inactivity over the last eighteen months.

When Lord Roberts had marched into Pretoria two years before, his entry had been offered only token resistance, for the Government of the South African Republic had withdrawn along the eastern railway line to Koma-tipoort. With them went the entire contents of the Pretoria Treasury, which totalled two million pounds in gold Kruger sovereigns. Later, when old President Kruger left for Europe, a part of this treasure went with him, but the balance had been shared out among the remainder of the commando leaders as their war chests to continue the fight.

Months before most of Leroux's share had been expended on the purchase of supplies from the native tribes, on ammunition from the Portuguese gun runners and on payment to his men. During a desperate night action with one of the raiding British columns he had lost the balance along with his Hotchkiss gun, twenty of his best men and a hundred irreplaceably precious horses.

Zietsmann, however, had come to the meeting with a pack-mule carrying thirty thousand sovereigns. The successful invasion of the Cape would depend largely upon this gold. On the evening of the fourth day he was duly elected Commander by a majority of two hundred, and within twelve hours he had demonstrated how well-equipped he was for the task.


'So we start in the morning, then,' one of the burghers beside Leroux grunted.

'About time,' another commented. They were breakfasting on biltong – sticks of hard dried meat – for Leroux had succeeded in convincing Zietsmann that cooking-fires were dangerous.

'No sign of Van der Bergh's men?' asked Leroux.

'Not yet, Oom Paul.'

'They are finished, or else they would have been here days ago.'

'Yes, they are finished,' agreed Leroux. 'They must have run into one of the columns.' Twenty good men, he sighed softly, and Hennie was with them. He was very fond of the boy, all of them were. He had become the mascot of the commando.

'At least they are out of it now – the lucky thunders.' The man had spoken without thinking, and Leroux turned on him.

'You can go too hands-up for the British, there is no one to stop you.' The softness of his voice did not cover the ferocity in his eyes.

'I didn't mean it that way, Oom Paul.'

'Well, don't say it then,' he growled, and would have continued, but a shout from the sentry on the kopje above them brought them all to their feet.

'One of the scouts coming!'

'Which way?' Leroux bellowed upwards.

'Along the river. He's riding to burst!'

And the sudden stilling of voices and movement was the only outward sign of the dread that settled upon all of them. In these days a galloping rider carried only evil tidings.

They watched him splash through the shallows and slide from the saddle to swim beside his horse across the deep channel. Then pony and rider, both streaming water, came lunging up the near bank and into the camp.

'Khaki,' shouted the man. 'Khaki coming!'

Leroux ran to catch the pony's head and demanded,

'How many?'

'A big column.'

'A thousand?'

'More than that. Many more – six, seven thousand.'

'*Magtig!*' swore Leroux. 'Cavalry?'

'Infantry and guns.'

'How close?'

'They will be here before midday.'

Leroux left him and ran down the slope to Zietsmann's wagon.

'You heard, *Menheer?*'

'*Ja*, I heard.' Zietsmann nodded slowly.

'We must mount up,' Leroux urged.

'Perhaps they will not find us. Perhaps they will pass us by.'

Zietsmann spoke hesitantly, and Leroux stared at him.

'Are you mad?' he whispered, and Zietsmann shook his head – a confused old man.

'We must mount up and break away towards the south.' Leroux grabbed the lapels of Zietsmann's frock coat and shook them in his agitation.

'No, not the south – it is finished. We must go back,' the old man muttered, then suddenly his confusion cleared. 'We must pray. The Lord will deliver us from the Philistine.'

'*Menheer*, I demand ...' Leroux started, but another urgent warning shouted from the kopje interrupted him.

'Riders! To the south! Cavalry!'

Running to one of the horses Leroux vaulted on to its bare back, with a handful of its mane he turned it towards the kopje and flogged it with his heels, driving it up the steep rocky side, scrambling and sliding in the loose rock until he reached the top and jumped down beside the sentry.

'There!' The burgher pointed.

Like a column of safari ants, tiny and insignificant in the immensity of brown grass and open sky, still four or five miles distant, the squadrons were strung out in extended order across the southern hills.

'Not that way. We cannot go that way. We must go back.' He swung round to the north. 'We must go that way.'

Then he saw the dust in the north also and he felt his stomach slide sickly downwards. The dust drifted low, so thin it might have been only heat haze or the passing of a dust devil – but he knew it was not.

'They are there also,' he whispered. Acheson had thrown his column in from four directions. There was no escape.

'Van der Bergh!' whispered Leroux bitterly. 'He has gone hands-up to the English and betrayed us.' A moment longer he stared at the dust, then quickly he adjusted to the problem of defence.

'The river is our one line,' he muttered. 'With the flanks anchored on this kopje and that one there.' He let his eyes run back up the little valley of the Padda River, carefully memorizing the slope and lay of the land, storing in his mind each of its salient features, already siting the captured Maxims, picking the shelter of the hills and river bank for the horses, deciding where the reserves should be held.

'Five hundred men can hold the north kopje, but we will need a thousand on the river.' He vaulted up on to the pony and called down to the sentry, 'Stay here. I will send men up to you. They must build scharnzes along the ridge – there, and there.'

Then he drove the pony down the slope, sliding on its haunches until it reached the level ground.

'Where is Zietsmann?' he demanded.

'In his wagon.'

He galloped across to it and jerked open the canvas at the entrance.

'*Menheer*,' he began and then stopped. Zietsmann sat on the wagon bed with his wife beside him. A Bible was open on his lap.

'*Menheer*, there is little time. The enemy closes from all sides. They will be upon us in two hours.'

Zietsmann looked up at him, and from the soapy glaze of his eyes Leroux knew he had not heard.

'Thou shalt not fear the arrow that flieth by day, nor the terror that walketh by night,' he murmured.

'I am taking command, *Menheer*,' Leroux grunted. Zietsmann turned back to the book and his wife placed an arm round his shoulders.


We can hold them for this day, and perhaps tomorrow, Leroux decided from where he lay on the highest kopje. They cannot charge their cavalry against these hills, so they must come for us with the bayonet.

It is the guns first that we must fear, and then the bayonet.

'Martinus Van der Bergh,' he said aloud. 'When next we meet I will kill you for this.' And he watched the batteries unlimbering out of rifle-shot across the river, forming their precise geometrical patterns on the brown grass plain.

'*Nou skiet hulle*,' muttered a burgher beside him.

'*Ja*,' agreed Leroux. 'Now they will shoot,' and the smoke gushed from the muzzle of one of the guns out on the plain. The shell burst thunderously on the lower slopes and for an instant the lyddite smoke danced like a yellow ghost, swirling and turning upon itself, before the wind drifted it up to them. They coughed in the bitter-tasting fumes.

The next shell burst on the crest, throwing smoke and earth and rock high into the air, and immediately the rest of the batteries opened together.

They lay behind their hastily constructed earthworks while the shellfire battered the ridge. The shrapnel buzzed and hummed and struck sparks from the rocks, the solid jarring concussions made the earth jump beneath their bellies and dulled their ears so they could hardly hear the screaming of the wounded, and slowly a great cloud of dust and fumes climbed into the sky above them. A cloud so tall that Sean Courtney could see it from where he waited fifteen miles north of the Vaal.

'It looks as though Acheson has caught them,' murmured Saul.

'Yes, he's caught them,' Sean agreed, and then softly, 'The poor bastards.'

'The least they could have done was to let us be in at the kill,' growled Sergeant-Major Eccles. The distant rumble of the guns had awakened his blood lust and his great moustache wriggled with frustration. 'Don't seem right to me, seeing as how we been following the old Boer for going on a year and a half – the least they could have done was to let us be there at the end.'

'We are the cover guns, Eccles. General Acheson is trying to drive them south on to his cavalry, but if any of the birds break back through his line of beaters then they're ours,' Sean explained.

'Well, it just don't seem right to me,' Eccles repeated, then suddenly remembering his manners, he added, 'Begging your pardon, sir.'

## Chapter Fifty-four

Exultantly General Acheson traversed his binoculars across the group of hills. Vaguely through the dust and smoke he could pick out their crests.

'A fair cop, sir!' Peterson grinned.

'A fair cop indeed,' Acheson agreed. They had to shout above the thunder of the guns and beneath them their horses fidgeted and trembled. A dispatch-rider galloped up, saluted and handed Peterson a message.

'What is it?' Acheson asked without lowering his glasses.

'Both Nichols and Simpson are in position for the assault. They seem anxious to engage, sir.' Then Peterson looked up at the holocaust of dust and flame upon the hills. 'They'll be lucky if they find anyone left to fight up there.'

'They will,' Acheson assured him. He was not misled by the deceptive fury of the barrage. They had survived worse at Spion Kop.

'Are you going to let them go, sir?' Peterson insisted gently. For another minute Acheson watched the hills, then he lowered his glasses and pulled his watch from his breast pocket. Four o'clock – three hours more of daylight.

'Yes!' he said. 'Send them in.'

And Peterson scribbled the order and handed it to Acheson for his signature.

'*Hier Kom Hulle.*' Leroux heard the shout in the ceaseless roar of the shells, heard it taken up and passed along the line.

'Here they come.'

'*Pasop!* They are coming.'

He stood up and his stomach heaved at the movement. Poisoned by the lyddite fumes, he fought his nausea and when he had controlled it he looked out along the river. For a second the veil of dust opened so he could see the tiny lines of khaki moving in towards the hills. Yes, they were coming.

He ran down his own line towards the river, shouting as he went.

'Wait until they are certain! Don't shoot until they reach the markers!'

From this corner of the kopje he could look out over every quarter of the field.

'*Ja,* I thought so!' he muttered. 'They come from two sides to split us.' Advancing on the frontage of the river were those same lines of tiny figures. The lines bulged and straightened and bulged again, but always they crept slowly nearer. Already the leading rank was moving up on his thousand-yard markers, in another five minutes they would be in range.

'They stand out well,' Leroux muttered as he ran his eyes along the rows of markers. While most of his men were building the earthworks along the kopjes and the river, others had paced out the ranges in front of these defences. Every two hundred and fifty yards they had erected those small cairns of stones, and over each they had smeared whitish grey mud from the river. It was a trick the British never seemed to understand, and as they advanced the Boer rifles had their range almost to the yard.

'The river is safe,' he decided. 'They cannot break through there,' and he allowed himself time to grin. 'They never learn. Every time they come against the worst side.' Then he switched his attention to the assault on his left flank. This one was dangerous, this was where he must command in person, and he ran back to his original position while around him and overhead the storm of shrapnel and lyddite roared on unabated.

He dropped on his belly between two of his burghers, wriggled forward unbuckling the bandolier from around his chest and draped it over the boulder beside him.

'Good luck, Oom Paul,' a burgher called.

'And to you, Hendrik,' he answered as he set the rear sight of his Mauser at a thousand yards, then laid the rifle on the rock in front of him.

'Close now,' the burgher beside him muttered.

'Very close. Good luck and shoot straight!'

Suddenly the storm lifted and there was silence. A vast aching silence, more shocking than the buzzing, howling roar of the guns. The dust and the smoke drifted away from the crests and after its gloom the sunshine burned down brightly on the hills and the golden brown plain, it sparkled with dazzling brilliance on the sweeping waters of the Vaal, and it lit each tiny khaki figure with stark intensity, so their shadows lay dark on the earth beneath them. They reached the line of markers.

Leroux picked up his rifle. There was one man he had been watching, a man who walked a little ahead of his line. Twice Leroux had seen him pause as if to shout an order to those who followed him.

'You first, my friend,' and he took the officer in his sights, holding him carefully in the notch with the bead obscuring his trunk. Gently he took up the slack in the trigger and the recoil slammed back into his shoulder. With the vicious and characteristic crack of the Mauser stinging his eardrums, Leroux watched the man go down into the grass.

'*Ja!*' he said and reloaded.

Not in simultaneous volley, not with the continuous wild crackle which they had used at Colenso – but in a careful, steady stutter which showed that each shot was aimed – the Boer rifles started the hunt.

'They have learned,' Leroux muttered as he worked the bolt of his rifle, and the empty case pinged away among the rocks. 'They have learned well,' and he killed another man. At two places on the ridge the Maxim guns began their frenzied hammering bursts.

Before it reached the second row of markers, the first line of infantry no longer existed, it was scattered back in the grass, completely annihilated by the terrible accuracy of the Boer fire. The second line walked over them and came on steadily.

'Look at them come,' shouted a burgher farther down the line. Though they had seen it a dozen times before, all of these ragged farmers were awed by the passive, impersonal advance of British infantry.

'These men fight not to live but to die!' muttered the man who lay beside Leroux.

'Then let us help them to die,' Leroux shouted. And below him on the plain the slow inexorable ranks moved forward towards the third row of markers.

'Shoot, *Kerels*. Shoot straight,' Leroux roared, for now he could see the bayonets. He pressed a clip full of ammunition down into the magazine, and with the back of his hand brushed the clinging drops of sweat from his eyebrows, pushed the rifle forward and knocked down four men with his next six shots. Then he saw the change. At one place the line bulged as men began to hurry forward, while on the flanks it wavered and disintegrated as others hung back or crouched down behind pitifully inadequate cover.

'They are breaking!' Leroux howled excitedly. 'They won't reach the slopes.'

The forward movement faltered, no longer able to stand the mauling they were receiving, men turned back or went to ground while their officers hurried along the ranks goading them on. In so doing they proclaimed to the Boer riflemen that they were officers and at that range they did not survive long.

'They're finished!' shouted Leroux, and a thin burst of cheering ran along the ridge while the Boer fire increased in volume, flailing into the milling confusion of a broken infantry assault.

'Hit them, *Kerels*. Keep hitting them!' The following ranks overran the leaders, then in turn faltered and failed as the Maxim and Mauser fire churned into them.

Out on the plain a bugle began to lament, and as it mourned, the last spasmodic forward movement of the assault ceased, and back past the dead and the wounded streamed the retreat.

A single shell rushed overhead to burst in the valley beyond and immediately, as if in frustrated fury, the guns lashed the kopje once more. But in the jump and flash of the shells five hundred Boers cheered and laughed and waved their rifles at the retreating infantry.

'What happened on the river?' Leroux called in the tumult, and after a while the answer came back.

'They did not reach the river. They are broken there also.'

Leroux lifted his hat from his head and wiped the sweat and the dust from his face. Then he looked at the sunset.

'Almighty God, we give you thanks for this day. We ask your mercy and guidance in the days that are to come.'

The shellfire lashed the hills like the surf of a storm-driven sea until the night came. Then in the darkness they saw the fires of the British bivouacs spread like a garden of yellow flowers on the plains around them.


## *Chapter Fifty-five*


'We must break out tonight.' Leroux looked across the fire at Zietsmann.

'No.' The old man spoke softly, not looking at him.

'Why?' demanded Leroux.

'We can hold these hills. They cannot drive us from them.'

'*Ja!* We can hold them tomorrow – two days, a week – but then it is finished. We lost fifty men today from the guns.'

'They lost many hundreds. The Lord smote them and they perished.' Zietsmann looked up at him now and his voice gathered strength. 'We will stay here and place our trust in the Lord.' There was a murmur of agreement from those who listened.

'*Menheer*.' Leroux covered his eyes for a moment, pressing fingers into them to still the terrible aching. He was sick from the lyddite, and tired – tired to the depths of his soul. It would be easier to stay. There would be no dishonour in it for they had fought like no men before them. Two more days and then it would be over without dishonour. He removed his hands from his face. '*Menheer*, if we do not break out tonight we never will. By tomorrow we will not have the strength.' He stopped for the words came slowly, slurred a little from a brain dulled by the lyddite and the hammering of big guns. He looked at his hands and saw the suppurating sores on his wrists. There would be no dishonour. They would fight this last time and then it would be finished.

'But it is not a matter of honour,' he mumbled. Then he stood up and they watched him in silence for he was going to speak. He spread his hands out in appeal, and the firelight lit his face from below leaving his eyes in shadow, dark holes like the sockets of a skull. He stood like that for a while and his rags hung loosely on the gaunt wasted body.

'Burghers . . .' he started. But the words were not there. There was nothing except the need to fight on. He dropped his hands to his sides.

'I am going,' he said with simplicity. 'When the moon goes down I ride,' and he walked away from the fire. One by one other men rose and followed him, and all of them were men of his own commando.

Six men squatted in a circle and watched the moon as it touched the hills. Behind them the horses were saddled and the rifles stuck up from their scabbards. By each of the six hundred horses a burgher lay fully clothed, wrapped in his blanket and trying to sleep. Though the horses stamped and moved restlessly there was no jingling of bits for all of them were carefully muffled.

'We will say it again, so that each of us knows his part.' Leroux looked around the circle. 'I will go first with a hundred men and follow the river towards the east. What is your route, Hendrik?'

'South, through the cavalry until the dawn, then round towards the mountains.'

Leroux nodded and asked the next man:

'And yours?'

'West along the river.'

'*Ja*, and yours?'

He asked each in turn and when all had answered – 'The place of meeting is the old laager by the Hill of Inhlozana. Is this agreed?'

And they waited, watching the moon and listening to the jackals squabbling over the British corpses on the plain. Then the moon went down below the hills and Leroux stood up stiffly.

'*Totsiens, Kerels*. Good luck to all of us.' He took the reins of his pony and led it down towards the Vaal, while in silence a hundred men led their horses after him. As they passed the single wagon beside the Padda, old Zietsmann was waiting and he came forward leading a pack-mule.

'You are going?' he asked.

'*Ja, Menheer*. We must.'

'God go with you.' Zietsmann thrust out his hand and they gripped briefly.

'The mule is loaded. Take the money with you. We will not need it here.'

'Thank you, *Menheer*.' Leroux motioned to one of his men to take the mule. 'Good luck.'

'Good luck, General.' For the first time Zietsmann used his title, and Leroux went down to the perimeter of their defences and out into the veld where the British waited.

With the first pale promise of dawn in the sky, they were through and clear. Though twice during the night heavy outbursts of firing in the darkness far behind them showed that not all of the escaping bands had been so fortunate.

## *Chapter Fifty-six*

Sean and Saul stood beside the little scotchcart and Mbejane brought them coffee.

'My God, it's cold enough to freeze the hanger off a brass monkey.' Sean cupped his hands around the mug and sipped noisily.

'At least you've got a hood to keep your tip warm,' Saul retorted. 'We'd better get moving before we all freeze to the ground.'

'Dawn in an hour,' Sean agreed. 'Time to start walking our beat,' and he called across to Mbejane, 'Kill the fire and bring my horse.'

In double file with the scotchcart bumping along in the rear they started on the outward leg of their patrol. In the last four days they had covered the same ground as many times, tacking backwards and forwards across the beat that Acheson had assigned them. The grass was brittle with frost and crunched under the horses' hooves.

While ahead of them the Zulu trackers ranged like gundogs, and behind the troopers huddled miserably in their greatcoats, Sean and Saul picked up their endless discussion from the point at which they had left it the previous evening. Already they had reached so far into the future that they were talking of a federation under responsible government that would encompass all the territories south of the Zambesi.

'That's what Rhodes has proposed for the last ten years,' Saul pointed out.

'I don't want any part of that wily bastard.' Sean spoke emphatically. 'He'll keep us tied for ever to the apron strings of Whitehall – the sooner we get rid of him and Milner the better, say I.'

'You want to get rid of Imperial rule?' Saul asked.

'Of course, let's end this war and send all of them back across the sea. We can run our own affairs.'

'Colonel, it seems to me you are fighting on the wrong side,' Saul remarked, and Sean chuckled.

'But seriously, Saul ...' He never finished. Mbejane came out of the darkness, running with silent purpose so that Sean checked his horse and felt the skin along his arms prickle with nervous excitement.

'Mbejane?'

'Mabuna!'

'Where? How many?'

He listened to Mbejane's hurried explanation, then swung round to face Sergeant-Major Eccles, who was breathing heavily down his neck.

'Your birds, Eccles. A hundred or so of them, only a mile ahead and coming straight towards us.' Sean's voice was tight with the same excitement that made Eccles's moustache wriggle like an agitated caterpillar on the impassive oval of his face. 'Deploy in single line. They'll walk right on top of us in the dark.'

'Dismounted, sir?'

'No,' Sean answered. 'We'll gun charge them as soon as they show. But for God's sake keep it quiet.'

As Sean sat on his horse with Saul beside him, the two files of troopers opened on each side of them. There was no talking; only the clicking of iron-shod hooves on rock, the rustling of men struggling out of their heavy greatcoats, and the soft rattle and snick of breech-bolts opening and closing.

'Once more into the breach, dear friends,' whispered Saul, but Sean did not answer because he was wrestling with his fear. Even in the cold of dawn his hands were damp. He wiped them on the thighs of his breeches and slid his rifle from the scabbard.

'What about the Maxims?' Saul asked.

'No time to set them up.' Sean knew his voice was hoarse and he cleared his throat before he went on. 'We won't need them – it's six to one.'

He looked along the silent line of his men. A dark line against the grass that was paling in the dawn. He could see that each of his troopers leaned forward in the saddle with his rifle held across his lap. The tension was a tangible thing in the half-darkness; even the horses were infected, they moved beneath their riders, shifting their bodies, nodding with impatience. Please God, let none of them whicker now.

And he peered ahead into the darkness. Waiting with his own fear and the fear of his men so strong that the Boers must surely smell it.

A patch of greater darkness in the dawn, ahead and slightly to the left of centre. Sean watched it for a few seconds and saw it move, slowly, like the moonlit shadow of a tree on the open veld.

'Are you sure they're Boers?' Saul whispered, and the doubt startled Sean. While he hesitated the shadow spread towards them and now he could hear the hooves.

Are they Boers? Desperately he searched for some sign that would allow him to loose his charge. Are they Boers? But there was no sign – only the dark advance and the small sounds of it, the click and creak in the dawn.

They were close now, less than a hundred yards, although it was impossible to tell with certainty for the dark, moving mass seemed to float towards them.

'Sean . . .' Saul's whisper was cut off by the shrill nervous whinny of his horse. The sound was so unexpected that Sean heard the man beside him gasp. Almost immediately came the sign for which Sean waited.

'*Wie's daar?*' The challenge from ahead was in the guttural of the Taal.

'Charge!' yelled Sean and hit his horse with his heels. Instantly the whole of his line jumped forward to hurl itself upon the Boers.

Forward in the pounding hooves, forward in the shouting, in the continuous crackle of rifle-fire that sparkled along the line – with his fear left behind him, Sean spurred at them. Steadying the butt of his rifle under hi right armpit, firing blind, blending his voice with the yelling of six hundred others, leading slightly in the centre of the line; he took his commando down upon the Boers.

They broke before the charge. They had to break for they could not hope to stand against it. They swung and drove their exhausted horses back towards the south.

'Bunch up!' roared Sean. 'Bunch on me!' And his line shortened so they charged knee to knee in a solid wall of men and horses and gunfire before which the Boers fled in wild despair.

Directly in Sean's path lay a struggling, badly wounded horse with its rider pinned underneath it. Jammed into the charge he could not swerve.

'Up, Boy!' he shouted and lifted his horse with his knees and his hands, clearing the tangle and stumbling as they landed. Then forward again in the urgent, jostling clamour of the charge.

'We're gaining!' yelled Saul. 'This time we've got them.'

The horse beside him hit a hole and went down with its leg breaking like a pistol-shot. The trooper was thrown from it high and clear, turning in the air as he fell. The line closed to fill the gap, and pounded on over the grassland.

'There's a kopje ahead,' Sean shouted as he saw the ragged loom of it against the dawn sky. 'Don't let them reach it!' And he raked his spurs along his horse's ribs.

'We won't catch them,' warned Saul. 'They'll get into the rocks.'

'Damn it! God damn it!' groaned Sean. In the past few minutes the light had strengthened. Dawn in Africa comes quickly once it starts. Clearly he could see the leading Boers ride into the rocks, throw themselves from their ponies and duck into cover.

'Faster!' shouted Sean in agony. 'Faster!' as he saw the chance of quick success slip from his grasp. Already Mausers were talking back from the lower slopes of the kopje, and the last burghers were down and scurrying into the rocks. Loose ponies turned wildly into his line, empty stirrups flapping, eyes wide with terror – forcing his men to swerve into each other, dissipating the force of the charge. A loose pack-mule with a small leather pack upon its back climbed up through the rocks until a stray bullet killed it and it rolled into a deep crevice. But nobody saw it fall.

Sean felt the horse between his legs jerk and he was thrown with such violence that the stirrup leathers snapped like cotton and he went up and out, hung for a sickening moment and then swooped down to hit the ground with his chest and shoulder and the side of his face.

While he lay in the grass the charge spent itself like a wave on the kopje, then eddied and swirled into confusion. Dimly Sean was aware of the hooves that trampled about his head, of the sound of the Mausers and the shouts of the men who were swept by them.

'Dismount! Get down and follow them.' Saul's voice and the tone of it roused Sean. With his hands under his chest he pushed himself into a sitting position. The side of his face burned where the skin had been smeared away, his nose was bleeding and the blood turned the earth in his mouth to a gritty paste. His left arm was numb to the shoulder and he had lost his rifle.

Dully he tried to spit the filth from his mouth while he peered at the chaos about him, trying to make sense of it. He shook his head, to joggle the apathy from his brain, while all around him men were being cut down at point-blank range by the Mausers.

'Dismount! Dismount!' The urgency of Saul's voice brought Sean unsteadily to his feet.

'Get down, you bastards!' He took up the cry. 'Get down and chase them.' A horse brushed against him and he staggered but kept his balance. The trooper slid down from its back beside Sean.

'Are you all right, Colonel?' He reached out to steady Sean, but a bullet took him in the chest below his raised arm and killed him instantly. Sean stared down at the body and felt his brain click back into focus.

'The bastards,' he snarled and snatched up the man's rifle, then, 'Come on!' he roared. 'Follow me!' and he led them out of the shambles of struggling horses into the rocks.

In the next half-hour, grimly and irresistibly, they used their superior numbers to drive the Boers back up the kopje. Each outcrop of rocks was a strongpoint that had to be assaulted and carried, and paid for in blood. On a front of perhaps two hundred yards, the attack became a series of isolated skirmishes over which Sean could not maintain command. He gathered those men who were near him and boulder by boulder they fought their way towards the top, while the burghers in front of him held each position until the last moment and then fell back on the next.

The top of the kopje was flattened into a saucer with fifty feet of steep open ground falling away on all sides, and finally sixty burghers reached this natural fortress and held it with the determination of men who knew that they fought for the last time. Twice they threw the British from the lip of the saucer and sent them scrambling and sliding back into the shelter of the broken rock below. After the second repulse a heavy unnatural silence settled on the kopje.

Sean sat with his back to a rock and took the water-bottle that a corporal offered him. He rinsed the slime of blood and congealing saliva from his mouth and spat it pink on to the ground beside him. Then he tilted the bottle and swallowed twice with his eyes tightly closed in the intense pleasure of drinking.

'Thanks.' He passed the bottle back.

'More?' the corporal asked.

'No.' Sean shook his head and looked back down the slope. The sun was well up now, throwing long shadows behind the horses that were grazing far out across the veld below. But at the foot of the slope lay the dead animals, most of them on their sides with legs thrust stiffly out. Blanket-rolls had burst open to litter the grass with the pathetic possessions of the dead men around them.

The men in their khaki and brown were as inconspicuous as piles of dead leaves in the grass, mostly British but with here and there a burgher lying amongst them in the fellowship of death.

'Mbejane.' Sean spoke softly to the big Zulu who squatted beside him. 'Find Nkosi Saul and bring him to see me here.'

He watched the Zulu crawl away. Mbejane had been left behind at the start of that wild gallop, but before Sean was half-way up the kopje he had glanced back to find him kneeling two paces behind, ready with a bandolier of ammunition for the moment when Sean needed it. Neither of them had spoken until this moment. Between them words were seldom necessary.

Sean fingered the raw graze on his face and listened to the murmured conversation of the men around him. Twice he heard clearly the voices of Boers from the saucer above them and once he heard a burgher laugh. They were very close, and Sean moved uneasily against the rock.

Within minutes Mbejane was back with Saul crawling behind him. When he saw Sean, Saul's expression changed quickly.

'Your face! Are you all right?'

'Cut myself shaving.' Sean grinned at him. 'Have a seat. Make yourself comfortable.'

Saul crawled the last few yards and settled himself against Sean's rock. 'Now what?' he asked.

'Ten minutes' rest, then we're going up again,' Sean told him. 'But this time with a little more purpose. I want you to work around the back of the kopje with half the men. Take Eccles with you. We'll rush their whole perimeter at the same moment. When you're in position fire three shots in quick succession then count slowly to twenty. I'll back you from this side.'

'Good.' Saul nodded. 'It'll take me a little while to get round – don't be impatient.' And he was smiling as he rose to his knees and leaned forward to touch Sean's shoulder.

Sean would always remember him like that: big mouth creased at the corners, smiling with white teeth through three days' growth of beard, slouch hat pushed to the back of his head, so his hair fell forward on to his forehead, and sunburned skin flaking from the tip of his nose.

The rock behind them was cracked through. If Saul had not leaned forward to make that gesture of affection he would not have exposed himself.

The sniper on the ridge had seen the brim of his hat above the rock and he held his aim into the crack. At the moment that Saul's fingers touched Sean's shoulder his head moved across the gap and the Boer fired.

The bullet hit Saul in the right temple, slanted diagonally back through his head and came out behind his left ear.

Their faces were but eighteen inches apart and Sean was smiling into Saul's eyes as the bullet hit. Saul's whole head was distorted by the impact, swelling and bursting like a balloon. His lips stretched so that for an instant his smile was a hideous rubbery thing and then he was snatched away and thrown sideways down the slope. He slid to a stop with his head and shoulders mercifully covered by a tuft of the coarse grey grass that grew among the rocks, but his trunk shivered and his legs danced and kicked convulsively.

For a slow count of ten Sean did not move nor did his expression alter. It took him that long to believe what he had seen. Then his face seemed to crumple.

'Saul!' His voice was a croak.

'Saul!' It rose higher, sharp with the realization of his loss.

He came slowly to his knees. Now Saul's body was still, very still and relaxed.

Again Sean opened his mouth but this time the sound he uttered was without form. The way an old bull buffalo bellows at the heart shot, that way Sean gave expression to his grief. A low shuddering cry that carried to the men in the rocks around him and to the Boers in the saucer above.

He made no attempt to touch Saul. He stared at him.

'Nkosi.' Mbejane was appalled at what he saw on Sean's face. His tunic was stiff with his own dried blood. The graze across his cheek was swollen and inflamed and it wept pale lymph. But it was the eyes that alarmed Mbejane.

'Nkosi.' Mbejane tried to restrain him, but Sean did not hear. His eyes were glazing over with the madness that had taken the place of his grief. His head hunched down on his shoulders and he growled like an animal.

'Take them! Take the bastards!' And he went up and over the rock in a twisting leap with the bayoneted rifle held against his chest.

'Come on!' he roared and went up the slope so fast that only one bullet hit him. But it did not stop him and he was over the lip, roaring and clubbing and hacking with the bayonet.

From the rocks four hundred of his men swarmed up after him and boiled over the lip of the saucer. But before they reached Sean he was face to face with Jan Paulus Leroux.

This time it was no match. Jan Paulus was wasted and sick. A gaunt skeleton of the man he had been. His rifle was empty and he fumbled with the reload. He looked up and recognized Sean. Saw him tall and splattered with blood. Saw the bayonet in his hands and the madness in his eyes.

'Sean!' he said and lifted the empty rifle to meet the bayonet. But he could not hold it. With Sean's weight behind it the bayonet glanced off the stock and went on. Jan Paulus felt the tingling slide of the steel through his reluctant flesh and he went over backwards with the bayonet in him.

'Sean,' he cried from his back. Sean stood over him and plucked the bayonet out. He lifted it high with both hands, his whole body poised to drive it down again.

They stared at each other. The British charge swept past them and they were alone. One man wounded in the grass and the other wounded above him with the bayoneted rifle and the madness still on him.

The vanquished in the grass, who had fought and suffered and sacrificed the lives of those he loved.

The victor above him, who had fought and suffered and sacrificed the lives of those he loved.

The game was war. The prize was a land. The penalty for defeat was death.

'*Maak dit klaar!* Make it finished!' Leroux told him quietly. The madness went out in Sean like the flame of a candle. He lowered the bayoneted rifle and let it drop. The weakness of his wound caught up with him and he staggered. With surprise he looked down at his belly and clasped his hands over the wound, and then he sank down to sit beside Jan Paulus.

In the saucer the fight was over.

# Chapter Fifty-seven

'We're ready to move, sir.' Eccles stood beside the scotchcart and looked down at Sean. A massive scowl concealed his concern. 'Are you comfortable?'

Sean ignored the question. 'Who is in charge of the burial details, Eccles?'

'Smith, sir.'

'You have told him about Saul – about Captain Friedman?'

'Yes, sir. They will bury him separately.'

Sean lifted himself painfully on to an elbow and for a minute stared at the two gangs working bare to the waist on the communal graves. Beyond them lay the rows of blanket-wrapped bundles. A fine day's work, he thought bitterly.

'Shall we start, sir?' Eccles asked.

'You've given Smith my orders? Burghers to be buried with their comrades – our men with theirs?'

'It's all taken care of, sir.'

Sean lay back on the bedding that covered the floor of the scotchcart.

'Please send my servant to me, Eccles.'

While he waited for Mbejane, Sean tried to avoid contact with the man who lay beside him in the scotchcart. He knew Jan Paulus was watching him.

'Sean – Menheer, who will say the words for my men?'

'We have no Chaplain.' Sean did not look at him.

'I could say them.'

'General Leroux, it will be another two hours before the work is completed. You are wounded, and it is my duty to get this column with the other wounded back to Vereeniging as soon as I can. We are leaving the burial detail and when they're finished they'll catch us up.' Sean spoke lying on his bank staring up at the sky.

'Menheer, I demand—' Jan Paulus began, but Sean turned angrily towards him.

'Listen, Leroux. I've told you what I'm going to do. The graves will be carefully marked, and later the War Graves Commission will send a Chaplain.'

There was very little room in the scotchcart and they were both big men. Now, as they glared at each other their faces were a foot apart. Sean would have said more, but as he opened his mouth the wound in his guts caught him and he gasped. The sweat broke out heavily across his forehead.

'Are you all right?' Jan Paulus's expression altered.

'I'll feel better once we get to Vereeniging.'

'Ja, you're right. We must go,' agreed Leroux.

Eccles came back with Mbejane.

'Nkosi, you sent for me?'

'Mbejane, I want you to stay here and mark the place where they bury Nkosi Saul. Remember it well, for later you must be able to bring me back to it,' Sean mumbled.

'Nkosi.' Mbejane went away.

'Very well, Eccles. You can start.'

It was a long column. Behind the van rode the prisoners, many of them mounted two up. Then followed the wounded, each in a horse litter of poles and blankets, behind them the scotchcart, and finally Eccles and two hundred troopers of the rearguard. Their progress was slow and dismal.

In the scotchcart neither of them spoke again. They lay in pain, bracing themselves against the jolt and lurch, with the sun beating down mercilessly upon them.

In that dreamlike state induced by pain and loss of blood, Sean was thinking of Saul. At times he would convince himself that it had not happened and he would experience a rush of relieve as though he had woken from a nightmare to find it was not reality. Saul was alive after all. Then his mind would focus with clarity and Saul was dead again. Saul was wrapped in a blanket with the earth above him, and all they had planned was down there with him. Then Sean would grapple once more with the unanswerable.

'Ruth!' he cried aloud, so that Jan Paulus beside him stirred uneasily.

'Are you all right, Sean?'

But Sean did not hear him. Now there was Ruth. Now there was Ruth alone. He felt joy then in his loss, joy quickly swamped with guilt. For an instant he had been glad that Saul was dead, and his treachery sickened him and ached like the bullet in his guts. But still there was Ruth, and Saul was dead. I must not think of it like that. I must not think! And he struggled up into a sitting position and clung to the side of the scotchcart.

'Lie down, Sean,' Jan Paulus told him gently. 'You'll bleed again.'

'You!' Sean shouted at him. 'You killed him.'

'*Ja.*' Leroux nodded his red beard into his chest. 'I killed them, but you also – all of us. *Ja*, we killed them.' And he reached up and took Sean's arm and drew him down into the blankets. 'Now, lie still or we'll bury you also.'

'But why, Paul. Why?' Sean asked softly.

'Does it matter why? They are dead.'

'And now what happens?' Sean covered his eyes from the sun.

'We go on living. That is all, we just go on.'

'But what was it about. Why did we fight?'

'I don't know. Once I knew clearly, but now I have lost the reason,' Leroux answered.

They were silent for a long time and then they began to talk again. Groping together for the things that must take the place of that which had filled these last three years.

Twice that afternoon the column halted briefly while they buried men who had died of their wounds. And each of these deaths – one a burgher and the other a trooper – gave poignancy and direction to the talk in the scotchcart.

In the evening they met a patrol that was scouting ahead of the big columns returning from the Padda River. A young lieutenant came to the scotchcart and saluted Sean.

'I have a message for you from General Acheson, sir.'

'Yes?'

'This fellow Leroux got away from us at the Padda. Zietsmann, the other Boer leader, was killed, but Leroux got away.'

'This is General Leroux,' Sean told him.

'Good God!' He stared at Leroux. 'You caught him. I say – well done, sir. Jolly well done.' In the past two years Jan Paulus had become a legend to the British, so that the lieutenant examined him now with frank curiosity.

'What is your message?' Sean snapped.

'Sorry, sir.' The youngster dragged his eyes away from Jan Paulus. 'All the Boer leaders are meeting at Vereeniging. We are to give them safe conduct into the garrison. General Acheson wanted you to try to contact Leroux with the offer – but, that won't be difficult now. Jolly good show, sir.'

'Thank you, Lieutenant. Please tell General Acheson that we'll be in Vereeniging tomorrow.'

They watched the patrol ride away and disappear over a fold in the land.

'So!' growled Leroux. 'It's surrender then.'

'No,' Sean contradicted him. 'It's peace!'

## Chapter Fifty-eight

The primary school at Vereeniging had been converted into an officers' hospital. Sean lay on his field cot and regarded the picture of President Kruger on the wall opposite him. In this way he was putting off the moment when he must continue with the letter he was writing. So far he had written the address, the date and the salutation: 'My dear Ruth'.

It was ten days since the column had returned from the veld. It was also ten days since the surgeons had cut him open and tied together those parts of his alimentary canal that the bullet had disrupted. He wrote:

I am at this moment well on the way to recovering from a small wound received two weeks ago near the Vaal River – so please take no notice of my current address. [He started a new paragraph.]

God knows I wish the circumstances in which I write were less painful to both of us. You will by now have received an official notification of Saul's death, so there is nothing I can add but to say that he died in circumstances of great personal gallantry. While about to lead a bayonet charge he was shot and killed *instantly*.

I know you will want to be alone in your grief. It will be some weeks before the doctors allow me to travel. By the time I reach Pietermaritzburg I hope you will be sufficiently recovered to allow me to call on you in the hope that I may be able to give you some comfort.

I trust that small Storm continues to increase in weight and beauty. I look forward to seeing her again.

A long while he pondered the ending, and finally decided on 'Your true friend'. He signed it, folded it into its envelope and laid it on the locker beside his bed for posting.

Then he lay back on his pillows and surrendered himself to the ache of loss and the dull pain in his belly.

After a while his physical pain dominated, and he glanced surreptitiously around the ward to ensure there were no nurses about. Then he lifted the sheet, pulled up his nightshirt and began picking at the bandage until he had exposed the edge of the wound with the black horsehair stitches standing stiffly out of it like the knots in a strand of barbed wire. An expression of comical disgust curled his lips. Sean hated sickness – but especially he hated it in his own flesh. The disgust gave way slowly to a helpless anger and he glared at the wound.

'Leave it stand, old Sean. Looking won't make it better.' Sean had been so intent on the evil gash in his stomach that he had not heard the speaker approach. Despite the cane and the limp that dragged his right leg, Leroux moved silently for a big man. He stood now beside the bed and smiled shyly down at Sean.

'Paul!' Guiltily Sean covered himself.

'*Ja*, Sean. How goes it?'

'Not too bad, And you?'

Leroux shrugged. 'They tell me I will need this for a long time to come.' He tapped the ferrule of the cane on the floor. 'May I sit down?'

'Of course.' Sean moved to give him the edge of the bed and Leroux lowered himself with his bad leg stretched stiffly in front of him. His clothing was newly washed and the cuffs of his jacket darned; patches on the elbows, and a long tear in the knee of his breeches had been cobbled together with crude, masculine stitches.

His beard had been trimmed and squared. There were iodine-stained bandages covering the open sores on his wrists, but a red mane of hair hung to the collar of his jacket and the bones of his forehead and cheeks made harsh angles beneath skin that was desiccated and browned by the sun.

'So!' said Sean.

'So!' Leroux answered him and looked down at his hands . Both he and Sean were silent then, awkward and inarticulate, for neither of them dealt easily in words.

'Will you smoke, Paul?' Sean reached for the cheroots on his locker.

'Thank you.' They made a show of selecting and lighting, then silence overwhelmed them again and Leroux scowled at the tip of his cheroot.

'This is good tobacco,' he growled.

'Yes,' agreed Sean and regarded his own cheroot with equal ferocity. Leroux coughed and rolled his cane between the fingers of his other hand.

'*Toe maar*, I just thought I'd come and see you,' he said.

'I'm glad of it.'

'So, you're all right then, hey?'

'Yes. I'm all right,' Sean agreed.

'Good.' Leroux nodded sagely. 'Well, then!' He stood up slowly. 'I had better be going. We are meeting again in an hour. Jannie Smuts has come up from the Cape.'

'I heard so.' Even the hospital was penetrated by rumours of what was happening in the big marquee tent pitched on the parade-ground near the station. Under the chairmanship of old President Steyn the Boer leaders were talking out their future. De Wet was there, and Niemand and Leroux. Botha was there and Hertzog and Strauss and others whose names had echoed across the world these last two years. And now the last of them, Jannie Smuts, had arrived. He had left his commando besieging the little town of O'Kiep in the Northern Cape and travelling up the British-held railway. Now they were all assembled. If they had gained nothing else in these last desperate years, they had at least won recognition as the leaders of the Boer people. This tiny bank of tired and warsick men was treating with the representatives of the greatest military power on earth.

'*Ja*, I have heard so,' Sean repeated, and impulsively he thrust out his hand. 'Good luck, Paul.'

Leroux seized his hand and held it hard, his mouth moved with the pressure of his emotion.

'Sean, we must talk. We have to talk!' he blurted.

'Sit down,' Sean told him and Leroux freed his hand and sank on to the bed once again.

'What must I do, Sean?' he asked. 'It's you who must advise me. Not these . . . not these others from over the sea.'

'You have seen Kitchener and Milner.' It was not a question for Sean knew of the meeting. 'What do they ask of you?'

'They ask everything.' Leroux spoke bitterly. 'They ask for surrender without terms.'

'Will you agree to that?'

For a minute Leroux was silent, and then he lifted his head and looked full into Sean's face.

'So far we have fought to live,' he said and what Sean saw in those eyes he would never forget. 'But now we will fight to die.'

'And by this, what will you achieve?' Sean asked softly.

'Death is the lesser evil. We cannot live as slaves.' Leroux's voice rose sharply. 'This is my land,' he cried.

'No,' Sean told him harshly. 'It is also my land, and the land of my son,' and then his voice softened. 'And the blood of my son is your blood.'

'But these others – this Kitchener, this devil Milner.'

'They are a people apart,' Sean said.

'But you fought with them!' Leroux accused.

'I have done many foolish things,' agreed Sean. 'But, from them I have learned.'

'What are you saying?' demanded Leroux, and Sean could see the sparkle of hope in his eyes. I must say this carefully, thought Sean, I must be very careful. He drew a long breath before he spoke.

'As it stands this moment your people are scattered but alive. If you fight on, the British will stay until you have found the annihilation you seek. If you stop now, then soon they will leave.'

'Will you leave?' demanded Leroux savagely.

'No.'

'And you are British! The British will stay – you and those like you.'

Then Sean grinned at him. It was so sudden, so irresistible that grin, that it threw Leroux off balance.

'Do I look and talk like a *rooinek*, Paul?' he asked in the Taal. 'Which half of my son is burgher and which half British?'

Confused by this sneak attack Leroux stared at him for a long time before he dropped his eyes and fiddled with his cane.

'Come on, man,' Sean told him. 'Make an end to this foolishness. You and I have a lot of work to do.'

'You and I?' Leroux asked suspiciously.

'Yes.'

Leroux laughed, a sudden harsh bellow of laughter.

'You are a *slim Kerel*,' he roared.

'I'll have to think about what you have said.' He rose from the bed and seemed to stand taller now. The laughter filled out his gaunt features and wrinkled his nose.

'I'll have to think very carefully about it.' He reached out his hand again and Sean took it. 'I will come and talk with you again. He turned away abruptly and limped down the ward with his cane tapping loudly.

Jan Paulus kept his word. He visited Sean daily, an hour or so at a time, and they talked. Two days after the Boer surrender he brought another man with him.

Jan Paulus stood a good four inches over him, but though he was slimly built the visitor gave the impression of size.

'Sean, this is Jan Christian Niemand.'

'Perhaps I am lucky we did not meet before, Colonel Courtney.' Niemand's voice, high in timbre, was crisp and authoritative. He spoke the perfect English he had learned at Oxford University. 'What do you think, *Oubas?*' He addressed Jan Paulus by the title which was obviously a private joke between them, and Jan Paulus chuckled.

'Very lucky. Otherwise you also might be using a stick.'

Sean examined Niemand with interest. Hard years of war had muscled his shoulders and he walked like a soldier, yet above the pointed blond beard was the face of a scholar. The skin had a youthful clarity which was almost maidenly, but the eyes were a penetrating blue, the merciless blue of a Toledo steel blade.

His mind had the same resilience, and before many minutes Sean was using all his wits to meet and answer questions that Niemand asked him. It was clear that he was being subjected to some sort of test. At the end of an hour he decided he had passed.

'And now, what are your plans?'

'I must go home,' Sean answered, 'I have a farm and a son – soon, perhaps, a wife.'

'I wish you happiness.'

'It is not yet settled.' Sean admitted. 'I still have to ask her.'

Jannie Niemand smiled. 'Well, then, I wish you luck with your suit. And strength to build a new life.' Suddenly he was serious. 'We also must rebuild what has been destroyed.' He stood up from the bed and Jan Paulus stood with him.

'There will be need of good men in the years ahead.' Niemand held out his hand and Sean took it. 'We will meet again. Count on that.'

## Chapter Fifty-nine

As the train ran in past the great, white mine dumps and Sean leaned from the window of the coach to look ahead at the familiar skyline of Johannesburg, he wondered how such an unlovely city still had the power to draw him back each time. It was as though he was connected to it by an elastic umbilical cord which allowed him a wide range. But when he reached its limit it pulled him back.

'Two days,' he promised himself. 'Two days I'll stay here. Just long enough to hand old Acheson my formal resignation and tell Candy Goodbye. Then I'll head south to Ladyburg – and leave this town to stew in its own evil juices.'

Near at hand a midday hooter howled from one of the mines, and immediately its cry was taken up and answered by the other mines. It sounded as though a pack of hungry wolves were hunting across the valley, the wolves of greed and gold. Those mines that had been forced to close during the hostilities were now back in production, and the black smoke from their stacks sullied the sky and drifted in a dirty mist across the crest of the ridge.

The train slowed, and the unexpected clatter and lurch of the points broke the rhythm of its run. Then it was sliding in along the concrete platform of Johannesburg Station. Sean lifted his luggage down from the rack above his head and passed it out of the open window to Mbejane. The exertion of lifting and carrying no longer caught in his guts; except for the irregular scar near his navel he was completely healed. When he strode down the platform towards the exit he held himself erect, no longer stooping to favour his stomach.

A horsedrawn cab deposited them on the pavement outside Acheson's headquarters, and Sean left Mbejane guarding the luggage while he pushed his way across the crowded lobby and climbed the staircase to the first floor.

'Good afternoon, Colonel.' The orderly sergeant recognized him immediately and jumped to attention with such alacrity that he overturned his stool.

'Afternoon, Thompson,' Sean told him. The honours of his rank still embarrassed him. Thompson relaxed and inquired with more than just the formal concern:

'How are you, sir? Sorry to 'ear about your belly, sir.'

'Thank you, Thompson, I am fine now. Is Major Peterson in?'

Peterson was delighted to see him. He made tender inquiries after the movement of Sean's bowels, for irregularity was often one of the unpleasant aftermaths of a stomach wound. Sean reassured him and Peterson went on:

'Have some tea. The old man is busy right now but he'll see you in ten minutes,' and he shouted for Thompson to bring tea before he returned to the subject of Sean's wound. 'Much of a scar, old chap?' he asked.

Sean loosened his Sam Browne belt, unbuttoned his tunic and pulled his shirt out from his trousers. Peterson came round the desk and inspected Sean's hairy stomach at close range.

'Very neat. Damn good job they did on you.' Peterson gave his expert opinion. 'I got one at Omdurman – one of those fuzzy wuzzies pegged me with his dirty great spear.' And he in turn partially disrobed and displayed his pale hairless chest. From common courtesy Sean was forced to cluck and shake his head at the small triangular cicatrice on Peterson's bosom, although secretly he was not impressed. The attention went to Peterson's head.

'Got another one – damn painful it was too!' and he unbuckled his belt and had his trousers half down when the interleading door opened.

'Hope I'm not interrupting anything, gentlemen?' General Acheson inquired politely. There were a few moments of confusion while they both attempted to dress and make the correct military salutations. Peterson had the nicest decision to make, one not covered by the Articles of War. It was one of the few occasions in history where a divisional commander was received by a senior field officer standing at rigid attention with his trousers round his ankles. Major Peterson affected a rather startling line in scarlet flannel underwear. Once Acheson had understood the reason for this irregularity of dress among his officers, he was strongly tempted to join in the exhibition, for he also had some fine scars, but he restrained himself admirably. He led Sean through to the inner office and gave him a cigar.

'Well, Courtney. I hope you haven't come looking for a job.'

'On the contrary – I want to get the hell out of this business, sir.'

'I think we can arrange that. The Paymaster will be relieved.' Acheson nodded. 'I'll get Peterson to draw up your papers.'
papers.'

'I want to leave tomorrow,' Sean insisted, and Acheson smiled.

'You're in a big hurry. All right. Peterson can post them to you for your signature – your unit has already been disbanded so there is no point in kicking your heels around here.'

'Good!' Sean had anticipated resistance, and he laughed with relief.

'There are just three other items,' Acheson went on, and Sean frowned with quick suspicion.

'Oh?'

'Firstly, a parting gift from His Majesty. A Distinguished Service Order for catching Leroux – there will be an investiture next week. Lord K. would like you to attend personally.'

'Hell, no! If I've got to stay in Johannesburg – I don't want it.'

And Acheson chuckled. 'A surprising lack of gratitude! Peterson can post it to you also. Secondly, I've been able to bring a little influence to bear on the War Claims Adjustment Board. Although Parliament hasn't passed the Bill, they've gone ahead and sanctioned your claim.'

'Good God!' Sean was stunned. At Acheson's suggestion he had registered a claim for ten thousand pounds, his deposit in the Volkskaas Bank, which had been seized by the Boers at the outbreak of war. He had expected nothing from it, and had promptly forgotten about it. 'They haven't made a full award, have they?'

'Don't be naïve, Courtney.' Acheson chuckled. 'Only twenty per cent against a possible further adjustment once the Bill is through the House. Still, two thousand is better than a poke in the eye with a blunt stick. Here's their cheque. You'll have to sign for it.'

Sean examined the slip of paper with rising delight. It would go a little way towards paying off his loan from Natal Wattle. He looked up quickly. 'And the third item?' he asked.

Acheson slipped a small square of cardboard across the desk. 'My card – and a standing invitation to visit and stay as long as you like whenever you are in London.' He stood up and extended his hand. 'Good luck, Sean. And I'd like to think it isn't good-bye.'


In a rosy state of elation induced by freedom and the prospect of a loving farewell with Candy Rautenbach, Sean stopped the cab first at the railway station to reserve a seat on the following morning's southbound train, and to cable Ada of his homecoming. Then, on to Commissioner Street and the lobby of Candy's Hotel to ask for the proprietress.

'Mrs Rautenbach is resting, sir, and cannot be disturbed,' the clerk informed him.

'Good man!' Sean passed him half a guinea and ignored his squawks of protest as he climbed the marble staircase.

He let himself silently into Candy's suite and crossed to her bedroom. He wanted to surprise her; and there could be no doubt that he succeeded beyond his wildest expectations. Candy Rautenbach was not resting. In fact she was most strenuously employed in the entertainment of a gentleman whose tunic, hanging over the back of one of the gilt and red velvet chairs, showed him to be a subaltern in one of His Majesty's regiments.

Sean supported his subsequent actions on the hypothesis that Candy was his exclusive property. In the flood of righteous indignation that overwhelmed him, he took no account of the fact that his visit was a farewell gesture, that his relationship with Candy had been at best vague and intermittent, and that he was the following morning leaving to propose matrimony to someone else. All he saw was the cuckoo in the nest.

So that no discredit may reflect on the courage of the subaltern or the honour of his regiment, we must remember that his knowledge of Candy's domestic arrangements, if not those of her anatomy, was incomplete. She had been introduced to him as *Mrs Rautenbach* and now in this terrible moment as he returned to reality he assumed that the large and angry man who bore down on the bed roaring like a wounded bull, was the one and only Mr Rautenbach come home from the wars. He made preparation for departure, which began with a rapid descent from the high four-poster bed on the opposite side to that of Sean's approach. In a condition of stark mental clarity induced by a super-abundance of adrenalin in the blood stream, the subaltern became aware of his own nudity which prevented flight into the public gaze, of the fact that Mr Rautenbach's threatening advance made such flight imperative, and finally that Mr Rautenbach wore the uniform and insignia of a full colonel. This last consideration weighed most heavily with him, for despite his age he came from an old and respected family with an impressive record of military service and he understood the decencies and orders of society of which one of the strictest was that you did not unite with the wife of an officer who outranked you.

'Sir,' he said, and drew himself up with dignity. 'I think I can explain.'

'You little bugger!' Sean answered him in a tone that suggested his explanation would have little consequence. Taking the shortest route, which was over the bed, Sean went for him. Candy, who had in these first few seconds been too preoccupied with pulling the coverlets over herself to take any active part in the proceedings, now shrieked and lifted the silk eiderdown in such a way that it wrapped around Sean's boots as he leaped over her, and became tangled in his spurs. Sean fell with a crash that reverberated through the whole building and startled the guests in the lobby below, and he lay for the moment stunned with his feet on the bed and his head and shoulders on the floor.

'Get out!' Candy shouted at the subaltern, as Sean began to stir ominously. Then she gathered up an armful of bedclothes and spread them over Sean, winding him and smothering him.

'Hurry up. For God's sake, hurry!' she entreated as her friend hopped with one leg in his breeches. 'He'll tear you to pieces.' And she pounced on top of the struggling, cursing mount of sheets and blankets.

'Don't worry about the boots,' and the subaltern tucked them under one arm, slung his tunic over his shoulders and placed his helmet on the back of his head.

'Thank you, ma'am,' he said, and then with gallantry, 'I sincerely regret any inconvenience I have caused you. Please give my apologies to your husband.'

'Get out, you fool,' she pleaded clinging desperately to Sean as he heaved and swore. After he had left she stood up and waited for Sean to emerge.

'Where is he? I'll kill him. I'll murder the little bastard!' Sean threw off the bedclothes, scrambled to his feet and glared wildly around him. But the first thing he saw was Candy, and Candy was shaking with laughter. There was a lot of Candy to shake and most of it was white and round and smooth, and even if the laughter was a little hysterical it was still a very pleasing spectacle.

'Why did you stop me?' Sean demanded, but he was fast transferring his interest from the subaltern to Candy's bosom.

'He thought you were my husband,' she gasped.

'The little bastard,' growled Sean.

'He was sweet.' And abruptly she stopped laughing. 'And who the hell are you to come barging in here, anyway? Do you think you own the world and everything in it?'

'You belong to me.'

'Like hell, I do!' Candy exploded. 'Now get out of here, you big lumbering ox.'

'Put some clothes on.' Things were taking an unforeseen turn. Sean had expected her to be guilty and contrite.

'Get out of here,' she yelled, as her temper started to run. Sean had never seen her like this and he only just managed to field the large vase she hurled at his head. Frustrated in her desire to hear breaking china, Candy grabbed another missile, an ornamental mirror, which crashed with satisfying violence against the wall behind him. Her boudoir was furnished in splendid Victorian taste and provided an almost unlimited supply of ammunition. Despite Sean's nimble footwork, he could not remain unscathed for ever and finally he was hit by a gilt-framed picture of some nameless officer. Candy's taste leaned rather heavily towards martial men.

'You little bitch!' roared Sean in pain, and he launched a counter-attack. Candy fled, naked and squealing, but he caught her at the door, lifted her on to his shoulder and carried her kicking to the bed.

'Now, my girl,' he grunted as he arranged her, pink bottom up, across his lap. 'I'm going to teach you some manners.'

The first slap left a perfect red print of his hand upon her chubby cheeks, and stilled her struggles. The second slap had considerably less force behind it, and the third was an affectionate pat. But Candy was sobbing pitifully.

With his right hand raised, Sean realized with dismay that for the first time in his life *he was striking a woman!* 'Candy!' He spoke uncertainly, and was amazed that she twisted and sat up in his lap, clasped him about the neck and pressed a damp cheek against him.

Words welled up in his throat, words of apology, a plea for forgiveness – but his good sense prevented them from emerging and instead he demanded huskily, 'Are you sorry for your behaviour?'

Candy gulped and nodded shakily. 'Please forgive me, darling. I deserved that.' And her fingers fluttered at his throat and across his lips. 'Please forgive me, Sean. I'm so terribly sorry.'


They ate dinner in bed that evening. In the early morning, while Sean soaked lazily in the sunken bath and the hot water stung the scratches on his back, they talked.

'I'm catching the morning train home, Candy. I want to be home for Christmas.'

'Oh, Sean! Can't you stay – just a few days?'

'No.'

'When will you come back?'

'I don't know.'

There was a long silence before she spoke again.

'I take it then that I am not included in your plans for the future?'

'You are my friend, Candy,' he protested.

'Now, isn't that nice.' And she stood up. 'I'll order your breakfast.'

In the bedroom she paused and regarded herself slowly in the full-length mirror. The blue silk of her gown matched the blue of her eyes, but at this time of the day there were tiny creases in the skin of her throat.

*I am rich*, she thought, *I don't have to be lonely.* She walked on past the mirror.

# Chapter Sixty

Sean walked slowly up the gravel drive towards the Goldberg mansion. He walked between an avenue of 'Pride of India' trees and around him the green lawns climbed in a series of terraces towards the rococo façade of the house. It was a morning of drowsy warmth and the doves in the Pride of Indias cooed sleepily.

Faintly from among the ornamental shrubbery he heard the tinkle of laughter. He stopped and listened to the sound of it. Suddenly he was shy, loth to meet her again – unable to know how she would receive him for she had not replied to his letter.

At last he left the drive and crossed the carpet of lawn until he reached the lip of an amphitheatre. In the bowl below him stood a miniature replica of the Parthenon temple. Clean, white, marble columns in the sunshine, with a circular fish-pond like a moat around it. He could see the shapes of carp gliding slowly through the green water below the lily pads. The lily blossoms were white and gold and purple.

Ruth sat upon the raised marble edge of the pond. She was dressed all in black from her throat to her toes, but her arms were bared and she held them out and cried:

'Walk, Storm. Walk here to me.'

Ten paces away, her solid bottom solidly planted on the lawn, Storm Friedman regarded her mother seriously from under a bang of dark hair.

'Come on, baby,' Ruth urged her, and very deliberately the child leaned forward. Slowly she elevated her plump posterior until it was pointed towards the sky, displaying a laced and be-ribboned pair of pantaloons beneath the short skirt. She remained like that for a few seconds and then, with an effort, came up on to her feet and stood balanced precariously on her fat, pink legs. Ruth clapped her hands in spontaneous delight, and Storm smiled in triumph, displaying four large white teeth.

'Come here to Mummy,' laughed Ruth and Storm completed a dozen unsteady paces before abandoning this form of locomotion as impractical. Dropping to her hands and knees she finished the course at a canter.

'You cheated!' Ruth accused, and jumped up to catch her under the arms and swing her high. Storm squealed ecstatically. 'More!' she commanded. 'More!'

Sean wanted to laugh with them. He wanted to run down to them and gather them both in his arms. For suddenly he knew that here was the whole meaning of life, his excuse for existing. A woman and a child. *His* woman, and *his* child.

Ruth looked up and saw him. She froze with the child held to her chest. Her face was without expression as she watched him come down the steps into the amphitheatre.

'Hello.' He stopped in front of her, twisting his hat awkwardly between his hands.

'Hello, Sean,' she whispered, then the corners of her mouth lifted in a shy, uncertain smile and she flushed. 'You took so long. I thought you weren't coming.'

A great grin split Sean's face and he stepped forward, but at that moment Storm, who had been staring at him with solemn curiosity, began a series of convulsive leaps accompanied by yells of:

'Man! Man!' Her feet were anchored against Ruth's stomach, which gave power to her thrusts. She leaned out towards Sean determined to reach him, and Ruth was taken by surprise. Sean had to drop his hat and catch Storm before she fell.

'More! More!' yelled Storm, continuing to bounce in Sean's arms. One of the few things Sean knew about babies was that they have a soft pulsing spot on the top of their heads which is very vulnerable, so he clung to his daughter in terror that he drop her and in equal terror that he crush her. Until Ruth stopped laughing, relieved him of his burden and said,

'Come up to the house. You're just in time for tea.'


They crossed the lawn slowly, each of them holding one of Storm's hands, so that the child need no longer concentrate on balancing and could devote her whole attention to the fascinating manner in which her feet kept alternately appearing and disappearing under her.

'Sean. There is one thing I have to know before anything else.' Ruth was looking down at her child, not at him. 'Did you . . .' She paused. 'Saul – Could you have prevented what happened to him. I mean, you didn't . . .' Her voice trailed off.

'No, I didn't,' he said harshly.

'Swear it to me, Sean. As you hope for salvation, swear it to me,' she pleaded.

'I swear it to you. I swear on . . .' He sought for an oath, not on his own life, for that was not strong enough. 'I swear on the life of our daughter.'

And she sighed with relief. 'That was why I did not write to you. I had to know first.'

He wanted to tell her than that he was taking her away with him, he wanted to tell her about Lion Kop and the huge empty house that waited for her to make it into a home. But he knew it was not the moment – not immediately after they had spoken of Saul. He would wait.


He waited while he was introduced to the Goldbergs and was left with them when Ruth took the child into the house to deliver her into the care of the nurse. She returned and he made small conversation during tea and tried not to let them see it in his eyes when he looked at Ruth.

He waited until they were alone together on the lawn and then he blurted it out:

'Ruth, you and Storm are coming home with me.'

She stopped over a rosebush and picked a butter-yellow blossom, then with a slight frown on her face she broke each of the tiny red thorns off the stem before she looked at him.

'Am I, Sean?' she asked innocently, but he should have been warned by the chips of diamond brightness in her eyes.

'Yes,' he said. 'We can be married within the next few days. It will take that long to arrange a special licence and for you to pack. Then I'll take you to Lion Kop – I haven't told you about . . .'

'Damn you,' she said softly. 'Damn your conceit. Damn your arrogance.' And he gawked at her.

'You stroll in with your whip in your hand, crack it once and expect me to bark and jump through the hoop.' She was working herself into a fury now. 'I don't know what dealings you've had with women before – but I for one am not a camp-follower, nor do I intend being treated like one. Did it ever occur to you for one single second that I might not be prepared to accept this favour you intend bestowing on me? How long did it take you to forget that I have been a widow for three short months? What supreme lack of perception made you believe I would run from one man's grave and throw myself into your condescending arms?'

'But, Ruth, I love you.' He tried to stop her outburst, but she shouted at him.

'Then prove it, damn you. Prove it by being gentle. Prove it by treating me like a woman and not a chattel – by *understanding*.'

Now his surprise gave way to an anger every bit as intense as hers, and in his turn he shouted at her.

'You weren't so bloody fussy on the night of the storm – or afterwards!'

As though he had struck her, she stepped back a pace and the mutilated rosebud dropped from her hand.

'You swine,' she whispered. 'Get out, and don't come back.'

'Your servant, ma'am.' He clapped his hat on to his head, swung round and strode away across the lawn. When he reached the gravel drive his steps slowed and he stopped and wrestled with his anger and his pride.

Then slowly he turned. The lawn was an empty sweep of smooth green. She was gone.


Ruth ran up the wide marble staircase, but by the time she reached her bedroom window he was half-way down the drive. From the height of the second floor his figure was foreshortened so he appeared massive, and his dark suit stood out clearly against the pale gravel of the drive. He reached the gates and stopped, she leaned forward eagerly across the sill of the window so he could see her more easily when he turned to look back. She saw him deliberately light a long black cheroot, flick away the match, adjust the hat on his head, square his shoulders – and walk away.

In disbelief she stared at the twin columns of the gate, and the dark green hawthorn hedge behind which he had disappeared. Then slowly she left the window and crossed to the bed and sat down.

'Why didn't he understand?' she asked softly.

She knew she would cry later, in the night when the real loneliness began.

## *Chapter Sixty-one*

Sean returned to Ladyburg in the middle of a misty Natal winter's day. As the train huffed over the rim of the escarpment, he stood on the balcony of his coach and looked out at the vast green stain upon the hills of Lion Kop. The sight of it moved him, but his elation was toned with dark colours.

This is the middle of the way. This year I will be forty-one years old. Out of all that striving and folly something must have emerged. Let me total my assets.

In cash I have a little over two thousand pounds (compliments of the War Claims Adjustment Board). In land I have fifteen thousand acres, with an option to purchase as many more. I have ten thousand acres of standing wattle which, in another year, will be ready for cutting. My loans against this are heavy but not oppressive, so I am a wealthy man.

In things of the flesh I have a number of grey hairs, a fine collection of scars and a broken nose. But I can still lift and carry a two-hundred-pound sack of mealies under each arm, I can eat half a young sheep at a sitting; without field-glasses I can count the number of head in a herd of springbok at a distance of two miles, and Candy who knows about these things made no complaint about my stamina. I am not yet old.

Apart from these things I have a son who belongs to me (and a son and a daughter who do not). Although I have lost the best of them, I have friends – perhaps more friends than enemies.

But as important as any of these is the purpose and direction I have at least achieved. I know what I want. My course is plotted and the wind stands fair.

These are my assets. These are mine to use and enjoy.

What are my liabilities? Borrowed money, the hatred of a brother and a son, and Ruth.

Ruth is gone! Ruth is gone! Clattered the crossties under the coach, Ruth is gone! Ruth is gone! They mocked him.

Sean scowled and forcibly changed the words in his mind.

'The wind is fair! The wind is fair!'

Over the months that followed Sean used his whole energy in the development of Lion Kop. He planned the cutting of his standing bark and decided to reap one-third of it a year before maturity, and another third in each of the subsequent two years. To replace it he used his two thousand pounds not to pay off his loans, but to plant the rest of his land to wattle. When this was done he had to keep busy. He bought himself a theodolite and a book of instruction in elementary survey, and mapped his lands, laid out his block of trees, pegged new roads for access to his plantations when the cutting began.

Once again he had nothing to do, so he went to see Dennis Petersen and spent a long day arguing the purchase of Mahobo's Kloof Ranch on which he had bought an option. He had no cash, and Jackson at Natal Wattle baulked at the suggestion of further loans. When Dennis refused to consider extended terms of payment, Sean called on Ronny Pye at the Ladyburg Banking & Trust. It was a forlorn chance and Sean was genuinely surprised when Ronny gave him a cup of coffee and a cigar, then listened politely to his proposition.

'You're putting it all on one horse, Sean,' Ronny warned him.

'There's only one horse in this race. It can't lose.'

'Very well.' Ronny nodded. 'Here's what I will do with you. I will advance you the full purchase price of Mahobo's Kloof, plus a further ten thousand pounds to develop it. In return you will give me a first bond on Mahobo's Kloof, and a second bond on Lion Kop after Natal Wattle Company's loan.'

Sean took it. A week later Ronny Pye called on Jackson in Pietermaritzburg. After the preliminary sparring Ronny asked him:

'Are you quite happy about those Notes you have out to Courtney?'

'The security is good.' Jackson hesitated. 'But he seems to be going a little wild.'

'I might be willing to take them over for you,' Ronny hinted delicately, and Jackson rubbed his nose thoughtfully to mask his relief.


Happily Sean flung his army of Zulus at the virgin grasslands of Mahobo's Kloof. He delighted in the long ranks of sweating, singing blackmen as they opened the rich, red earth and placed the fragile little saplings.

Dirk was Sean's constant companion in these days. His attendance in the schoolhouse became more sporadic. Convinced that Dirk would never become a scholar, Sean tacitly condoned the gastric disturbances that prevented Dirk leaving for school in the mornings, but cleared miraculously a few minutes later and allowed him to follow Sean out into the plantations. Dirk aped Sean's stance, his seat in the saddle, and his long reaching walk. He listened carefully to Sean's words and repeated them later without omitting the oaths. In the late afternoons they hunted quail and pheasant and guinea-fowl along the slopes of the escarpment. On Sunday when Sean rode across to his neighbours for a bush buck shoot, or a poker session, or merely to drink brandy and talk, then Dirk went with him.

Despite Sean's protest, Ada returned with her girls to the cottage on Protea Street. So the homestead of Lion Kop was a vast empty shell. Sean and Dirk used only three of the fifteen rooms, and even these were sparsely furnished. No carpets on the floor, nor pictures on the walls. A few leather-thonged chairs, iron bedstead, plain deal tables, and a cupboard or two. Piled in odd corners were the books and fishing-rods; a pair of shotguns and a rifle on the rack beside the fireplace. The yellow-wood floor was unpolished with dust and bits of fluff beneath the chairs and beds, dark stains left by the litter of pointer puppies; and in Dirk's bedroom, which Sean never visited, there was a welter of old socks and soiled shirts, school exercise books and trophies of the hunt.

Sean had no interest in the house. It was a place to eat and sleep, it had a roof to keep the rain out, a fireplace for warmth, and lamplight so that he could indulge his new appetite for reading. With reading glasses purchased from a travelling salesman on his nose, Sean spent his evenings wading through books on politics and travel, economics and surveying, mathematics and medicine, while Dirk, ostensibly preparing his schoolwork, sat across the fireplace from him and watched him avidly. Some nights when Sean was engaged in correspondence, he would forget that Dirk was there and the boy would sit up until after midnight.

Sean was now corresponding with both Jannie Niemand and Jan Paulus Leroux. These two had become a political team in the Transvaal, and were already bringing gentle pressure to bear on Sean. They wanted him to organize the equivalent of their South Africa Party, and to lead it in Natal. Sean hedged. Not yet, perhaps later he told them.

Once a month he received and answered a long letter from John Acheson. Acheson had returned to England and the gratitude of the nation. He was now Lord Caisterbrook and from his seat in the House of Lords he kept Sean informed of the temper and mood of the English people and the affairs of State.

Sometimes, more often than was healthy, Sean thought about Ruth. Then he became angry and sad and desperately lonely. Slowly it would build up within him until he could not sleep, then he would go down at night to a friendly widow who lived alone in one of the gangers' cottages beside the new railways yards.

Yet he counted himself happy, until that day at the beginning of September 1903, when he received an embossed card. It said simply:

Miss Storm Friedman requests the pleasure of the company of Colonel Sean Courtney, D.S.O., D.C.M., at a party to celebrate her third birthday. 4 p.m., September 26th.

*R.S.V.P.*
The Golds, Chase Valley,
    Pietermaritzburg.

In the bottom right-hand corner was an inky finger-print about the size of a threepenny-piece.

# Chapter Sixty-two

On the 24th, Sean left by train for Pietermaritzburg. Dirk came back from the station with Ada to his old room in the cottage on Protea Street.

That night Mary lay awake and listened to him cry for his father. Only a thin wooden partition separated them. Ada's cottage had not been designed as a workshop and hostel for her girls. She had solved the problem by enclosing the wide, back veranda and dividing it into cubicles each large enough to hold a bed, a cupboard and a washstand. One of these was Mary's and tonight Dirk was in the cubicle next to hers.

For an hour she lay and listened to him weep, praying quietly that he would exhaust himself and fall asleep. Twice she thought he had done so, but each time after a silence of only a few minutes the tear-muffled sobs started again. Each of them drove needles of physical pain deep into her chest, so that she lay rigid in her bed with her fists clenched until they ached.

Dirk had become the central theme of her existence. He was the one bright tower in the desolation. She loved him with obsessive devotion, for he was so beautiful, so young and clean and straight. She loved the feel of his skin and the springy silk of his hair. When she looked at Dirk her own face did not matter. Her own scarred ruin of a face did not matter.

The months she had been separated from him had been an agony and a dark lonely time. But now he was back and once again he needed her comfort. She slipped from her bed and stood taut with her love, her whole attitude portraying her compassion. The moonlight that filtered in through the mosquito-screened window treated her with the same compassion. It toned down the mottled cicatrice that coarsened the planes of her face and it showed them as they might have been. Her twenty-year-old body beneath the thin nightgown was slender but full-breasted, innocent of the marks that marred her face. A young body, a soft body clad in moon-luminous white like that of an angel.

Dirk sobbed again and she went to him.

'Dirk,' she whispered as she knelt beside his bed. 'Dirk, please don't cry, please, my darling.'

Dirk gulped explosively and rolled away from her, folding his arms across his face.

'Shh! my darling. It's all right now.' She began to stroke his hair. Her touch evoked a fresh outburst of grief from him, liquid choking grief that spluttered and throbbed in the darkness.

'Oh Dirk, please. . . .' And she went into his bed. The sheets were warm and moist where he had lain. She gathered him, held his hot body to her bosom and began to rock him in her arms.

Her own loneliness at last overwhelmed her. Her voice took on a husky quality as she whispered to him. She strained to him – her need growing much greater than his.

One last convulsive sob and Dirk was silent. She felt the tension go out of his back and out of his hard round buttocks that were pressed into her stomach. Straining him even closer, her fingers moved down across his cheek to caress his throat.

Dirk turned towards her, turning within the circle of her arms. She felt his chest heave and subside as he sighed, and his voice stifled with misery.

'He doesn't love me. He went away and left me.'

'I love you, Dirk,' she whispered. 'I love you – we all love you, darling.' And she kissed his eyes and his cheeks and his mouth. The taste of his tears was hot salt.

Dirk sighed again and bowed his head until it was on her bosom. She felt his face nuzzling into the softness and her hands went to the back of his head and drew it closer.

'Dirkie. . . .' Her voice dried up in the strange new heat within her.

In the morning Dirk woke slowly, but with a feeling of wonder. He lay a while and thought about it, unable at first to place the formless shimmering sense of well-being that possessed him.

Then he heard Mary moving about behind the partition of her cubicle. The gurgle and splash of water poured from jug to basin, the rustle of cloth. Finally, the sound of her door softly opened and closed, and her steps moving away towards the kitchen.

The events of the previous evening came back to him, crisp and stark in every detail. Not fully understood, but looming large to overshadow all else in his mind.

He threw the sheets aside and lifted himself on both elbows, drew up his nightshirt and contemplated his body as though he had never seen it before.

He heard footsteps approaching. Quickly he covered himself, pulled the bedclothes over and feigned sleep.

Mary came in quietly and placed a cup of coffee, with a rusk in the saucer, on the bedside table.

Dirk opened his eyes and looked at her.

'You're awake,' she said.

'Yes.'

'Dirk . . .' she started, and then she blushed. It mottled the puckered skin of her cheeks. Her voice fell to a whisper, scratchy with her shame. 'You mustn't ever tell anybody. You must forget about . . . what happened.'

Dirk did not reply.

'Promise me, Dirkie, Please promise me.'

He nodded slowly. Not trusting himself to speak, his throat filled with a knowledge of domination over her.

'It was wrong, Dirkie. It was a terrible thing. We mustn't even think about it again.'

She walked to the door.

'Mary.'

'Yes.' She stopped without turning, her whole body poised like a bird on the point of flight.

'I won't tell anyone – if you come again tonight.'

'No,' she hissed violently.

'Then, I'll tell Granny.'

'No. Oh, Dirkie. You wouldn't.' She was beside the bed now, kneeling, reaching for his hand. 'You mustn't – you mustn't. You promised me.'

'Will you come?' he asked softly. She peered into his face, into the serene perfection of warm brown skin and green eyes with the black silk of his hair curling on to the forehead.

'I can't – it's a terrible, terrible thing that we did.'

'Then I'll tell,' he said.

She stood up and walked slowly out of the cubicle, her shoulders slumped forward in the attitude of surrender. He knew she would come.

# Chapter Sixty-three

In a hired carriage Sean arrived punctually at the Goldberg residence. He arrived like a column of wise men from the east. The seats of the carriage were piled with fancy-wrapped packages. However, Sean's limited knowledge of a three-year-old female's tastes were reflected in his choice of gifts. Every single package contained a doll. There were large china dolls that closed their eyes when reclining, small rag dolls with blonde plaits, a doll that passed water, a doll that squawked when its stomach was squeezed, dolls in a dozen national costumes and dolls in swaddling clothes.

Mbejane followed the carriage leading the gift which Sean considered a master stroke of originality. It was a piebald Shetland pony, complete with a hand-fashioned English saddle and a tiny martingale and reins.

The gravel drive was crowded with carriages. Sean was forced to walk the last hundred yards, his arms filled with presents. Under these circumstances navigation was a little difficult. He took a fix on the hideously ornamented roof of the mansion, which he could just see over the top of his load, and set off blind across the lawns. He was aware of the continuous and piercing shrieking which grew louder as he proceeded, and finally of an insistent tugging on his right trouser leg. He stopped.

'Are those *my* presents?' a voice from somewhere above the level of his knee asked. He craned his head out to one side and looked down into the upturned face of a miniature Madonna. Large shining eyes in an oval of innocent purity framed with shiny dark curls. Sean's heart flipped over.

'That depends what your name is,' he hedged.

'My name is *Miss* Storm Friedman of the Golds, Chase Valley, Pietermaritzburg. *Now* are they my presents?'

Sean bent his knees until he squatted with his face almost on a level with that of the Madonna.

'Many happy returns of the day, Miss Friedman,' he said.

'Oh goody!' She fell on the packages, trembling with excitement while from the mass of fifty children who ringed them in the shrieking continued unabated.

Storm demolished the wrappings in very short order, using her teeth when her fingers were inadequate for the task. One of her small guests attempted to assist her, but she flew at him like a panther kitten with a cry of 'They're *my* presents!' He retired hastily.

At last she sat in a litter of wrappings and dolls and pointed at the single remaining package in Sean's hands.

'That one?' she asked.

Sean shook his head. 'No, that one is for your Mummy. But if you look behind you, you might find something else.'

Mbejane, grinning widely, was holding the Shetland. For seconds Storm was too overcome to speak and then with a sound like a steam-whistle she flew to her feet. Deserting her newly adopted children, she ran to the pony. Behind her a flock of small girls descended on the dolls, vultures when a lion leaves the kill.

'Lift me! Lift me!' Storm was hopping with delirious impatience. Sean took her up and the warm, wriggling little body in his hands made his heart flip again. Gently he set her on the saddle, handed her the reins and led the pony towards the house.

A queen riding in state, followed by an army of her attendants, Storm reached the upper terrace.

Ruth was standing beside the delicacy-laden trestle table with the parents of Storm's guests. Sean handed the lead rein to Mbejane. 'Look after her well,' and he crossed the terrace, very conscious of the many adult eyes upon him, thankful for the hour he had spent that morning at the barber's shop, and for the care he had taken with his attire – a brand-new suit of expensive English broadcloth, boots burnished to a gloss, solid gold watch chain across his belly and a white carnation in his buttonhole.

He stopped in front of Ruth and removed his hat. She held out her hand, palm downwards. Sean knew that he was *not* expected to shake that hand.

'Sean, how good of you to come.'

Sean took her hand. It was a measure of his feelings that he bowed to touch it with his lips – a gesture which he considered French, foppish and undignified.

'It was good of you to ask me, Ruth.'

He produced the box from under his arm and held it out to her. She opened it without a word and her cheeks flushed with pleasure when she saw the long-stemmed roses it contained.

'Oh, how sweet of you!' And Sean's heart did its trick again as she smiled full into his eyes, then slipped her hand into the crook of his arm.

'I'd like you to meet some friends of mine.'

That evening when the other guests had left and Storm, prostrated with nervous and physical exhaustion, had been put to bed, Sean stayed on to dinner with the Goldbergs. By now both Ma and Pa Goldberg were fully aware that Sean's interest in Ruth was not on account of his previous friendship with Saul. All afternoon Sean had followed Ruth around the lawns like a huge St Bernard behind a dainty poodle.

During dinner Sean, who was extremely pleased with himself, Ruth, the Goldbergs and life in general, was able to endear himself to Ma Goldberg and also dull Ben Goldberg's suspicions that he was a penniless adventurer. Over brandy and cigars Sean and Ben discussed the ventures on Lion Kop and Mahobo's Kloof. Sean was completely frank about the financial tightrope which he was walking, and Ben was impressed with the magnitude of the gamble and Sean's cold appraisal of the odds. It was just such a *coup* as this that had put Ben Goldberg where he was today. It made him feel nostalgic and vaguely sentimental of *the old days*, so that when they went through to join the ladies he patted Sean's arm and called him 'My boy'.

On the front steps, while he was preparing to leave, Sean asked, 'May I call on you again, Ruth?' and she answered,

'I'd like that very much.

Now began what was for Sean a novel form of courtship. To his surprise he found he rather enjoyed it. Every Friday night he would entrain for Pietermaritzburg and install himself in the White Horse Hotel. From this base he conducted his campaign. There were dinner parties, either at The Golds or with Ruth's friends or at one of the local hostelries where Sean played host. There were balls and dances, days at the races, picnics and rides over the surrounding hills with Storm on her Shetland bouncing along between them. During Sean's absences from Ladyburg, Dirk moved into the cottage on Protea Street and Sean was relieved that he seemed to accept it with better grace.

The time arrived when at last the first blocks of wattle were ready for the axe. Sean determined to use this as an excuse to inveigle Ruth away to Ladyburg. The Goldbergs froze up solid at the suggestion and only thawed when Sean produced a written invitation from Ada for Ruth to be her guest for the week. Sean went on to explain that it was to be a celebration of his first cutting of bark, which would begin at the end of the week, and that thereafter he could not leave Ladyburg for months.

Ma Goldberg, who was secretly delighted at having Storm all to herself for a whole week, exerted a subtle influence on Ben, and very grudgingly he gave his approval.

Sean decided that Ruth would be treated like visiting Royalty – the grand climax to his suit.

# Chapter Sixty-four

As one of the biggest landowners in the district and because of his war honours, Sean ranked high in the complicated social structure of Ladyburg. Therefore, preparations for Ruth's visit produced an epidemic of excitement and curiosity that affected the entire Ladyburg district. The flood of invitations he released sent women to their wardrobes and sewing-baskets, while the outlying farmers begged accommodation from relatives and friends nearer town. Other leading members of the community, jealous of their social status, road out to Lion Kop with offers to provide entertainment on those three days of the week which Sean had left empty. Reluctantly Sean agreed – he had private plans for those three days.

Ada and her girls were inundated with orders for new clothing, but they still made one afternoon free and came up to the Lion Kop homestead armed with brooms and dusters and tins of polish. Sean and Dirk were driven from the house. They spent that afternoon riding over Sean's estate, looking for the best place to hold the big bush-buck shoot which would be the climax of the week.

With a gang of his Zulus, Mbejane hacked down the jungle of undergrowth around the homestead and dug the barbecue pits.

The Village Management Board met in secret conclave, infected by the general excitement and armed with strict instructions from their wives, they voted unanimously for a civic reception of Ruth Friedman at the station and a formal Ball that night. Dennis Petersen, who had Sean's consent to a barbecue on the night of Ruth's arrival, was placated with the promise that he would be allowed to make a short speech of welcome at the station.

Sean called upon Ronny Pye and was again surprised when Ronny agreed cheerfully to a further loan of one thousand pounds. Ronny signed the cheque with the satisfied air of a spider putting the final thread into his web, and Sean left immediately for Pietermaritzburg to visit a jeweller. He returned home five hundred pounds poorer, with a packet in his breast-pocket that contained a huge square-cut diamond set in a band of platinum. Dirk was at the station to meet him. Sean took one look at him and ordered him to the village barber.

The night before Ruth's arrival Sean and Mbejane fell upon Dirk in a surprise attack and dragged him protesting to the bathroom. Sean was astounded by the large quantities of foreign matter that he removed from Dirk's ears, and by the way in which Dirk's suntan dissolved so readily under an application of soap.

The following morning as her railway coach ground to a jerky halt in front of the station building, Ruth looked down on a mass of strangers surrounding the roped-off area in front of her. Only one family was not represented in the crowd, which included the young ladies and gentlemen of Ladyburg High School in their church clothes.

She stood uncertainly on the balcony of the coach and heard the hum of appreciative comment and speculation. Ruth had relieved the plain black mourning with a wide ribbon of pink around the crown of her hat, pink gloves and gauzy pink veil, which shrouded her face in a misty and mysterious fashion. It was very effective.

Convinced that there was some misunderstanding, Ruth was about to withdraw into the coach, when she noticed a deputation approaching along the roped-off passageway. It was headed by Sean and she recognized the thunderous scowl he wore as his expression of acute embarrassment. She felt an inexplicable urge to burst out laughing, but managed to keep it to a smile as Sean climbed up on to the balcony and took her hand.

'Ruth, I'm terribly sorry. I didn't plan all this – things got a little out of control,' he whispered hurriedly, then he muttered an introduction to Dennis Petersen, who had ponderously mounted the steps behind him. Now Dennis turned to face the crowd and spread his arms in the gesture that Moses might have employed on his return from the mountain.

'Ladies and gentlemen, citizens of Ladyburg, friends—' he began, and from the way he said it Sean knew he was good for another half-hour. He glanced sideways at Ruth and saw that she was smiling. It came as a surprise to him when he realized she was enjoying herself. Sean relaxed a little.

'It gives me great pleasure to welcome to our fair town this lovely lady, friend of one of our foremost . . .' Ruth's fingers found their way surreptitiously into Sean's hand, and Sean relaxed a little more. He saw the wide brim of Ada's hat standing out in the crowd and he smiled at her. She replied with a nod of approval towards Ruth.

By some curious twist of oratory, Dennis was now talking about the new water filtration plant and its benefit to the community.

'—But, my friends, this is only the first of a series of projects planned by your Board.' He paused significantly.

'Hear, hear,' Sean interjected loudly and clapped his hands. The applause was taken up by the crowd, and Sean stepped past Dennis to the rail of the balcony.

'On behalf of Mrs Friedman and myself, I thank you for your friendship and your hospitality.' Then, leaving Dennis on the balcony making helpless little movements with his hands, and silently opening and closing his mouth, Sean spirited Ruth away, ran her through a rapid fire series of introductions and handshakes, gathered Ada and Dirk and got them all into the carriage.

While Sean and Mbejane fussed with the luggage, Ruth and Ada settled their skirts and adjusted their hats before meeting each other's eyes again.

'Although Sean warned me, I didn't expect you to be quite so lovely,' Ada said. Flushing with pleasure and relief, Ruth leaned impulsively across to touch her arm.

'I've been longing to meet you, Mrs Courtney.'

'If you promise to call me Ada, then I'll call you Ruth.'

Sean scrambled into the carriage, flustered and perspiring. 'Let's get the hell out of here.'

That week was to be remembered for many years. The usual Christmas festivities paled into insignificance beside it.

Matrons competed fiercely to provide food, mountains of it, prepared from their closely guarded recipe books. In between cooking they conducted old feuds, began new ones and worried about their daughters.

The young bucks competed on the gymkhana and polo field, then again on the dance floor. Dirk Courtney won the junior tent-pegging event. Then against a visiting team from Pietermaritzburg College he captained the school rugby team to an inglorious 30–0 defeat.

The young ladies competed with equal ferocity, covering it with giggles and blushes. The success of their efforts was measured in the outbreak of betrothals and scandals during the week.

The older men smiled indulgently, until, fortified with bottled spirit, they discarded their dignity and capered and panted around the dance floor. There were three bouts of fisticuffs – but these were between old enemies and none of them were really worth watching.

Only one family held aloof from the festivities. There were many of the young ladies who missed Michael Courtney.

During one of the infrequent lulls of the week, Sean managed to separate Ruth from Ada, and take her out to the homestead at Lion Kop. She moved silently through the empty rooms, appraising each with narrowed thoughtful eyes while Sean hovered anxiously behind her, certain that her silence was disapproval. In fact, Ruth was in ecstasy; a shell, a magnificent shell of a house, with no trace of another woman in it, waiting for her to bring it to life. She could imagine exactly the curtains she wanted, her Persian carpets sent down by Uncle Isaac from Pretoria and now in storage, would look just right once she had the yellow-wood floors polished to a gloss. The kitchen, of course, would have to be completely rebuilt – with a new double Agar stove. The bedroom . . .

Unable to contain himself, Sean blurted out:

'Well, do you like it?'

She turned slowly to him, the mists of thought clearing from her eyes.

'Oh, Sean! It's the most beautiful house in all the world.'

In this emotional moment, Sean put forward the proposition he had planned for that evening.

'Ruth, will you marry me?'

And Ruth, who had planned to hesitate and ask for a little time to consider, replied instantly:

'Oh, yes please!'

She was truly impressed with the ring.

# Chapter Sixty-five

The finale to the week was Sean Courtney's bush-buck shoot.

Sean and Dirk arrived at Protea Cottage with the dawn. They were dressed in rough hunting clothes and the leather gun-cases lay on the floor of the mule-wagon under Sean's feet. It took nearly fifteen minutes for Sean to transfer Ruth, Ada and her girls from the cottage to the carriage. In the same way a man might drive a flock of chickens towards the door of a henhouse. He would get them all moving slowly in front of him, down the path towards the carriage, clucking and fussing. Almost there when suddenly one of them would shriek softly and double back towards the cottage for a forgotten parasol or work-basket and the general movement would break down again.

The third time this happened Sean felt something snap inside his head. He bellowed. A vast hush fell over the ladies and two of them looked as though they might cry.

'Now don't get worked up, dear.' Ada tried to soothe him.

'I am not getting worked up.' Sean's voice quivered with the effort of restraint. 'But if everybody is not in the carriage by the count of ten – then I might easily get that way.'

They were all seated by the count of five and he drove out to the stockpens – a very ruffled rooster.

Carriages and mule-wagons carrying the entire population of the Ladyburg district were waiting in a disorderly tangle in the field beside the stockpen. Sean trotted past in a babble of greeting and comment. One at a time the waiting carriages wheeled into line behind him and the long convoy wound out towards Mahobo's Kloof Farm. The big shoot had begun.

In the middle of the line someone was playing a concertina and the singing started. It spread to each carriage in turn and blended with the sound of wheels and hooves and laughter.

Gradually Sean's irritation smoothed out. Ada's girls were singing *Boland Se Nooinentje* in the back seat. Dirk had jumped down from the carriage and with half a dozen of the youngsters from the village ran ahead of the horses. Ruth's hand touched Sean's leg uncertainly and as he turned and grinned at her he saw the relief in her answering smile.

'What a beautiful day, Sean.'

'Sorry I nearly spoiled it—' he answered.

'Oh, nonsense!' She moved closer to him and suddenly he was happy. All the preparation was worth it. Beside him Ruth laughed softly.

'What's the joke?' Sean reached out and took her hand.

'No joke. I just felt like laughing,' she answered. 'Look how green everything is.' She said it to distract him, to make him look away so that she could study his face. The subterfuge worked.

'The land seems so young now.' His eyes, as he looked at it, took on that gentleness she knew so well. By now she knew many of his moods and she was learning how to induce or redirect each of them. He was such a simple man, yet in that simplicity lay his strength. He is like a mountain, she thought. You know how it will be with the sun on it in the early morning. You know that when the wind is in the south there will be mist covering the crest, and in the evening the shadows will fall in certain patterns across the slopes and the gorges will look dark and blue. Yet also you know the shape of the mountain is unchanged, that it will never change.

'I love you, my mountain,' she whispered, and anticipated the startled expression before it flashed across his face.

'Hey?'

'I love you, my man,' she amended.

'Oh! I love you too.'

And now he is vaguely embarrassed. Oh, God, I could eat him! If I were to reach over and kiss him now in front of everybody . . .! Secretly she savoured the idea.

'What devilment are you planning?' he demanded gruffly. He wasn't supposed to read her so accurately. Taken off balance she stared at him. Suddenly the mountain had shown that it understood exactly the way she felt when she looked at it.

'Nothing,' she denied in confusion. 'I wasn't . . .' Before she realized fully what he was about, he had turned half-way in his seat towards her and lifted her bodily into his lap.

'Sean, no!' she gasped and then her protests were muffled. She heard the laughter of Ada's girls, the hoots of encouragement and applause from the other carriages, and she kicked and struggled, pushing with one hand against his chest and trying to keep her hat on with the other.

By the time he replaced her on the seat beside him, her hair had come down behind, her hat was off and her cheeks and ears were flaming red. She had been very thoroughly kissed.

'Nice shot, Sean!'

'Author! Author!'

'Arrest that man!' The cries and the laughter added to her confusion.

'You're terrible!' Ruth used her hat as a screen behind which she tried to control her blushes. 'In front of all those people, too!'

'That should keep you out of mischief for a while, me lass!'

And suddenly she wasn't so sure of the shape of her mountain.

The cavalcade turned off along the rough track from the main road, splashed through the drift, climbed the far bank and spread out among the trees. Servants, who had been waiting since the previous evening, ran to their masters' horses as they halted. Each vehicle disgorged a noisy blast of children and dogs, and then a more dignified trickle of adults. The women moved without hesitation towards the two huge marquees that had been erected among the trees, while the men unloaded the gun-cases and began assembling their weapons.

Still sitting on the front seat of the wagon, Sean opened the leather case at his feet and while his hands automatically fitted the barrels into the breech piece of his shotgun he allowed himself to review his preparations with a certain amount of satisfaction.

He had selected this site not only for the cool grove of syringa trees which provided shade above and a soft carpet of fallen leaves below, nor for the proximity of the tinkling stream where all the animals could be watered, but also because it was situated within fifteen minutes' walk of the first beat.

Days before a gang of Zulus working under Mbejane had cleared out all the undergrowth beneath the trees, had erected the marquee tents and the trestle tables, dug the cooking pits and even built two grass-walled pit latrines discreetly out of view of the main camp.

Huge log fires were burning in the cooking pits now, but by noon they would have burned down to glowing coal beds. The trestle tables about which the women had already begun working were laden with food. There was a great deal of activity going on in that direction at the moment – most of it talking.

From the other wagons men were starting to drift towards him, buckling on their cartridge belts, hefting shotguns, chatting together nonchalantly in an attempt to disguise their excitement. Under instruction from Sean, Dirk had assembled a rabble of those males who were too young to handle shotguns but too old to stay with the women. These were making no effort to hide *their* excitement. Armed with *sikelas* (the Zulu fighting sticks) they were showing every indication of getting out of hand. Already one small boy was weeping loudly and massaging the welt he had received from a playful *sikela*.

'All right – shut up, all of you,' Sean shouted. 'Dirk will take you up to the beaters. But remember! Once the hunt starts, keep in the line and listen to what you're told. If I catch anybody running about or getting ahead of the line – I'll personally wallop the tar out of him. Do you understand?' It was a long speech to shout and Sean ended with his face flushed ferociously. This gave weight to his words and resulted in a respectful chorus of:

'Yes, Mr Courtney.'

'Off you go, then.'

Whooping, racing each other they poured away through the trees and a comparative peace descended on the camp.

'My God, let alone bush buck, that lot would drive elephant, buffalo and lion panic-stricken ahead of them,' observed Dennis Petersen dryly. 'How about our positions, Sean?'

Aware that he had their complete attention, Sean drew the moment out a little.

'We are going to drive the Elands' Kloof first,' he announced. 'Mbejane and two hundred Zulus are waiting at the head of the Kloof for the signal. The guns will take station at the tail of the Kloof.' Sean paused.

'How about our positions?'

'Patience. Patience.' Sean chided them. 'I know I shouldn't have to repeat the safety rules, but . . .' and he immediately went on to do so. 'No rifles – shotguns only. You'll shoot only in an arc of 45 degrees directly ahead of you – no passing shots to either side. Especially you, Reverend!' That gentleman, who was notoriously trigger-happy, looked suitably abashed.

'My whistle will mean the beaters are too close – all guns up and unloaded immediately.'

'It's getting late, Sean.'

'Let's get on with it.'

'Right,' Sean agreed. 'I'll take centre gun.' There was a murmur of agreement. That was fair enough, the plum to the man who provided the hunt, no one could grudge that. 'On my left flank in this order, Reverend Smiley – since the Almighty will obviously send most of the game his way, I might as well profit by it.' A burst of laughter as Smiley wavered between horror at the blasphemy and delight at his own good fortune. 'Then Ronny Pye, Dennis Petersen, Ian Vermaak, Gerald and Tony Erasmus (you two fight it out in a brotherly fashion), Nick . . .' Sean read from the list in his hand. This in strict order of seniority was the social register of Ladyburg, a proper and exact balancing of wealth and influence, ofpopularity and age. Apart from placing himself in the centre of the line, Sean had not taken much part in the preparation of the list – quite correctly Ada had not trusted his sense of social perception.

'That takes care of the left flank.' Sean looked up from the list. He had been so engrossed in reading that he had not sensed the air of tension and expectancy which had fallen over his audience. A single horseman had crossed the drift and walked his magnificent thoroughbred into the camp. He had dismounted quietly and servants had led his horse away. Now, carrying a shotgun, he was walking towards Sean's wagon.

Sean looked up and saw him. He stared in surprise, while slowly elation mounted within him until it reached his face in a wide grin.

'Garry, glad you could make it!' he called out spontaneously, but Garry's face remained without expression. He nodded a curt greeting. At least he's come, exulted Sean. This is the first overture. Now it's up to me.

'You can take the first position on my right, Garry.'

'Thank you.' Now Garry smiled, but it was a curiously cold grimace and he turned away to talk with the nearest man. A small shiver of disappointment moved the crowd. They had expected something spectacular to happen. All of them knew of the feud between the Courtney brothers and the mystery that surrounded it. But now, with a feeling of anti-climax they turned their attention back to Sean's reading. Sean finished and jumped down from the wagon, and immediately the crowd moved away. Sean sought Garrick and saw him far ahead near the head of the long file of men that was strung out along the footpath that led to Elands' Kloof.

The file moved fast as the hunters stepped out eagerly. Unless he ran, Sean knew he would not be able to pass the men ahead of him and catch up with Garry. I'll wait until we reach the beat, he decided. My God, what a wonderful ending to this week. I have Ruth, now if only I can get back my brother and with him Michael!

From the shoulder of the gorge Sean looked down across Elands' Kloof. A deep slot of a valley, two miles long and five hundred yards wide at this end, but it tapered slowly upwards until it lost its identity in the high ground. The full length of it was clogged solid with dark green bush, a seemingly impenetrable mass above which a few tall trees reared up in a desperate attempt to reach the sunlight. Like the tentacles of a giant squid, creepers and vines lifted from the dark bush to overpower them and drag them down. Here on the shoulder the air was dry and wholesome – down there it would stink of damp earth and rotting vegetable matter.

Lingering as though suddenly reluctant to go down into the humid discomfort of the Kloof, the hunters gathered on the shoulder. Shading eyes against the glare, they peered up towards the head of the gorge where the beaters were a line of dark specks against the green spring grass.

'There go the kids,' someone pointed. Dirk was leading his band along the high ground above the Kloof.

Sean moved across to his twin brother.

'Well, Garry, how are things out at Theuniskraal?'

'Not bad.'

'I read your book – I think it's excellent. It certainly deserved the reception it got in London. Lord Caisterbrook wrote to me to say that your concluding chapter is giving the War Office much food for thought. Well done, Garry.'

'Thank you.' But there was an evasive lack of warmth in Garry's reply. He made no attempt to continue the conversation.

'Michael didn't come out with you today?'

'No.'

'Why not, Garry?' And Garry smiled for the first time, a cool, spiteful smile.

'He didn't want to.'

'Oh!' The hurt showed in Sean's face for an instant, then he turned to the men around him. 'Right, gentlemen, let's get down there.'

In position now, a line of men standing quietly in the gloom and stagnant heat. Each man's neighbour visible only as an indefinite shape among the leaves and vines and fallen trees. Few things sharp – the outline of a hat-brim, the glint of a random beam of sun on gun-metal, a human hand framed in a hole of dark green leaves. The silence heavy as the heat – spoiled by the nervous rustle of a branch, a hastily smothered cough, the click of a shotgun breech.

Sean hooked his thumb across both hammers of his gun and pulled them back to full cock, lifted the twin muzzles to the roof of leaves above his head and fired in rapid succession. He heard the deep booming note of the gun bouncing against the sides of the valley, echoing and fragmenting as it was thrown back upon itself. Then swiftly the silence closed in again.

He stood motionless, tuning his hearing as finely as was possible, but his reward was the thin drone of an insect and the harsh startled cry of a bush lourie. He shrugged, two miles of distance and the mass of vegetation would blanket completely the cries of the beaters and the clatter of their sticks as they thrashed the bush. But they were coming now, of this he was certain, they would have heard his signal shots. He could imagine them moving down the line, two hundred black men interspersed with the small white boys, chanting the rhetorical question which was as old as the drive hunt itself.

'*E'yapi?*' Repeated over and over again, the accent on the first half of the word, shrilling it.

'*E'yapi?* Where are you going?'

And between him and the beaters, in that wedge of tangled bush, there would be the first uneasy stirring. Dainty bodies, dappled with grey, rising from the secret beds of fallen leaves. Hooves, pointed and sharp, splayed and driven deep into soft leaf-mould by the weight of tensed muscle. Ears pricked forward, eyes like wet black satin, shiny moist muzzles quivering and snuffling, corkscrew horns laid back. The whole poised on the edge of flight.

With the taint of gunsmoke in his notrils, Sean opened the action of his shotgun and the empty shells ejected crisply, pinging out to leave the eyes of the breech empty. He selected two fresh cartridges from his belt and slid them home, snapped the gun closed and thumbed the hammers on to half-cock.

Now they would be moving. The does first, ginger-brown and dappled like roe-deer, slipping away down the valley with their fawns long-legged beside them. Then the bucks, the Inkonka, black and big and silent as shadows; crouching as they moved, horns flat against their shoulders. Moving away from the faint cries and the commotion, moving their mates and their young away from danger – down towards the waiting guns.

'I heard something then!' The Reverend Smiley's voice sounded as though he were being strangled, probably by the dog collar which showed as a pale spot in the gloom.

'Shut up, you fool!' Sean gambled his chance of salvation on the rebuke, but he need not have worried for the endearment was drowned by the double blast of Smiley's shotgun – so indecently loud and totally unexpected that Sean's feet left the ground.

'Did you get him?' Sean asked, his voice a little shaky from the fright. No reply.

'Reverend, did you get one?' Sean demanded. He had seen nothing, and heard nothing that might by the most generous stretch of imagination lead anyone to suspect the presence of a bush buck.

'My goodness, I could have sworn . . .' Smiley's reply was in the kind of voice you would expect from beyond the grave. 'Oh dear, I think I must have been mistaken.'

Here we go again, thought Sean with resignation.

'If you run out of cartridges let me know,' he called softly and grinned at Smiley's injured silence. The shots would have turned the game back towards the beaters, they would be starting to mill now as they sought an avenue of escape. Perhaps moving out on the flanks. As if in confirmation of Sean's thoughts, a shotgun thudded out on the left, then another, then two more on the right.

The fun had started in earnest.

In the brief silence he heard the beaters now, their excited cries muffled but urgent.

A blur of movement ahead of him through the screen of branches, just a flick of dark grey and he swung the gun and fired, wallop of the butt on to his shoulder, and thud and scuffle and roll and kick in the undergrowth.

'Got him!' exulted Sean. Still kicking, the head and shoulders of a half-grown ram emerged from under a bramble bush. It was down, mouth open, bleeding, crabbing against the earth, leaving a drag mark through the dead leaves. Boom again, the mercy stroke, and it lay still. Head speckled with tiny buckshot woulds, eyelids quivering into death and the swift rush of blood from the nostrils.

The din of gunfire all about, cries of the beaters and the answering shouts of the gunners, the panic-stricken run and crackle in the bush ahead.

Inkonka, big one, black as a hellhound, three twists in the horn, eyes staring, lunging into the clearing to halt with head up and front legs braced wide, hunted, panting, wild with terror.

Lean forward against the gun, hold the pip on his heaving chest and fire. The bounce of the gun and the long blue gush of smoke. Knock him down with the solid charge of short range buckshot. Cleanly, quickly, without kicking.

'Got him!'

Another one, blundering straight into the gun line, blind with panic, bursting out of the undergrowth almost on top of Sean. Doe with fawn at her heels – let her go.

The doe saw him and wheeled left to take the gap between Sean and Garrick. As it dashed through, Sean looked beyond and saw his brother. Garrick had left his position and closed in on Sean. He was crouched slightly, the shotgun held in both hands, hammers fully cocked – and his eyes were fastened on Sean.

Garrick waited quietly during the initial stages of the beat. The tree-trunk on which he sat was soft and rotten, covered with moss and the orange and white tongues of fungus. From the inside pocket of his jacket he took the silver flask inlaid with carnelians. The first mouthful started his tears and numbed his tongue, but he swallowed it painfully and lowered the flask.

*'He has taken from me everything I ever had of value:*

*My leg:* Garry looked down at the way it stuck out stiffly ahead of him with the heel buried in the damp leaf-mould. He drank again quickly, closing his eyes against the sting of brandy.

*My wife:* In the dark redness behind his eyelids he saw her again, as Sean had left her, lying in torn clothing with bruised and swollen lips.

*My manhood: Because of what he did to her that night, Anna has never let me touch her body. Until then there was hope. But now I am forty-two years old and I am virgin. It is too late.*

*My position: That swine Acheson would never have thrown me out – but for Sean.*

*And now he will take Michael from me.*

He remembered again the premonition of disaster that he had experienced when Anna reported to him how she had found Michael and Sean together on Theuniskraal. It had started then, each little incident building up. The day Michael had stared at the faded but bold entries in the leather-bound stock register. 'Is that Uncle Sean's handwriting?'

That battered saddle Michael had found in the loft above the stables; he had polished it lovingly and restitched the seams, fitted new stirrup leathers, and used it for a year. Until Garry had noticed the crude initials cut into the leather of the flap. 'S.C.' That night Garry had taken the saddle and thrown it into the furnace of the hot-water boiler.

Eight months ago, on Michael's twenty-first birthday, Garry had called him into the panelled study of Theuniskraal, and reluctantly told him of Sean's legacy to him. Michael had held the dog-eared sheet and read it through with his lips moving silently. Then at last he looked up and his voice was shaky. 'Uncle Sean gave me a half-share in Theuniskraal even before I was born. Why, Dad? Why did he do that?' And Garry had no answer for him.

This last week had been the climax. It had taken all Anna's and Garrick's combined influence and entreaties to prevent Michael responding to the invitations Sean had sent. Then the Zulu herd-boy, whose duty was to follow Michael and come to Garrick immediately Michael crossed the boundary of Theuniskraal, reported that each evening Michael rode up to the high ground on the escarpment and sat there until after dark staring in the direction of Lion Kop ranch.

*I am going to lose him, He is my son, even if Sean sired him. But he is my son, and unless I prevent it Sean is going to take that away from me also.*

*Unless I prevent it.* He lifted the flask to his lips once more and found with surprise that it was empty. He screwed the stopper down and returned the flask to his pocket.

Around him the gunfire and the shouting began. From the log beside him he picked up the shotgun and loaded it. He stood up and cocked the hammers.

Sean saw him, coming slowly, limping a little, crouching, making no attempt to fend off the branches that dragged across his face.

'Don't bunch up, Garry. Stay in your position, you're leaving a gap in the line.'

Then he noticed Garry's expression. It seemed that the skin had been stretched tight across the cheek-bones and the nose, so the rims of his nostrils were white. His jaws were chewing nervously and there was a fine sheen of sweat across his forehead. He looked sick or deadly afraid.

'Garry, are you all right?' Alarmed, Sean started towards him – then stopped suddenly. Garry had lifted the shotgun.

'I'm sorry, Sean. But I can't let you have him,' he said. The blank double eyes of the muzzles were all Sean saw of the gun, and below them, Garry's knuckles white with pressure, as he gripped the stock. One finger was hooked forward around the triggers.

Sean was afraid then. He stood without moving for his legs were heavy and numb under him.

'I've got to.' Garry's voice was a croak. 'I have to do it – otherwise you'll take him. You'll destroy him also.'

With fear making his legs clumsy and slow, Sean turned deliberately away from him and walked back to his station. The muscles of his back were stiff with anticipation, knotted so tightly that they ached.

The beaters were close now, he could hear them shouting and thrashing the bush just ahead. He lifted the whistle to his lips and blew three shrill blasts. The shouting died away, and in the comparative silence Sean heard a sound behind him, a sound half-way between a sob and a cry of pain.

Slowly, inchingly, Sean turned his head to look back. Garry was gone.

Beneath him Sean's legs began to tremble, and a muscle in his thigh twitched spasmodically. He sank down and sat on the carpet of soft damp leaves. When he lit a cheroot he used both hands to steady the fluttering flame of the match.

'Dad! Dad!' Dirk came pelting out into the tiny clearing. 'Dad, how many did you get?'

'Two,' said Sean.

'Only two?' And Dirk's voice went flat with disappointment and shame. 'Even Reverend Smiley beat you hollow. He got four!'

## Chapter Sixty-six

Ruth returned to Pietermaritzburg the afternoon following the hunt Sean insisted on accompanying her home. Ada, Dirk and a dozen of the friends Ruth had made during the week were at the station to see them leave. Sean was trying to detach Ruth from the earnest discussion into which all women seem to fall on the eve of a major parting. His repeated, 'You'd better get aboard, my dear,' and 'The flag's up, Ruth', were studiously ignored by all of them, until he found it necessary to take Ruth's arm and bundle her up into the coach. Her head reappeared instantly at the window to take up the discussion at the exact point where Sean had interrupted it. Sean was about to follow her when he saw Dirk. With a stab of guilt Sean realized how blatantly he had neglected Dirk during the week.

'Cheerio, Dirkie,' Sean called gruffly and the boy flew to him and wound his arms tightly around Sean's neck.

'Come on, Dirk. I'll be back tomorrow morning.'

'I want to go with you.'

'You have school tomorrow.' Sean tried to loosen Dirk's hold. The women were watching in silence now, and Sean felt himself flushing with embarrassment. *My God, he's not a baby any more – he's nearly fifteen.* He tried to keep his irritation from showing in his voice as he whispered:

'Stop that now. What will people think of you?'

'Take me with you, Dad. Please take me,' and Dirk quivered against him. The whistle blew and with voluble relief the women turned away and began talking all at once.

'Do you think I'm proud of you when you act like this?' Sean hissed at him. 'Now, behave yourself and shake hands properly.'

Dirk clutched his hand, with the tears filling his eyes.

'Stop it this instant!' Sean turned abruptly and swung himself up into the coach as the train jerked forward and started sliding out of the platform.

Dirk took a few indeterminate paces after it and then stopped with his shoulders shaking uncontrollably, his eyes still fastened on Sean's face as it protruded from the window.

'Your father will be back tomorrow, Dirkie.' Ada laid her hand consolingly on Dirk's shoulder.

'He doesn't love me,' whispered Dirk. 'He never even . . .'

'Of course he does,' Ada interrupted quickly. 'It was just that he was so . . .' But Dirk did not wait for her to finish. He shrugged her hand away, spun round and jumped blindly from the platform on to the tracks, ducked through the barbed-wire fence beyond and ran out across the fields to intercept the train as it made its first long turn on to the slope of the escarpment.

He ran with his face contorted, and the harsh grass brushing his legs, he ran with his arms pumping the rhythm of his racing feet – and ahead of him the train whistled mournfully and crawled out from behind the Van Essen plantation.

It was crossing his front, still fifty yards away, slowly gathering speed for its assault on the escarpment. He would not reach it – even though Sean's coach was the last before the guard's van – he would not reach it.

He stopped, panting, searching wildly for a glimpse of his father – but the window of Sean's compartment was blank.

'Pa!' he shrieked, and his voice was lost in the clatter of the crossties and the hoarse panting of steam.

'Pa!' He waved both arms wildly above his head. 'Pa! It's me. Me – Dirk.'

Sean's compartment moved slowly across his line of vision. For a few brief seconds he looked into the interior.

Sean stood sideways to the window, he was leaning forward with his shoulders hunched and Ruth was in his arms. Her head thrown back, the hat gone from her head and her dark hair in abundant disarray. She was laughing, white teeth and eyes asparkle. Sean leaned forward and covered her open mouth with his own. And then they were past.

Dirk stood like that with his arms raised. Then slowly they sank to his sides. The tension in his lips and around he eyes smoothed away. All expression faded from his eyes and he stood and watched the train puff and twist up the slope until with a last triumphant spurt of steam it disappeared over the skyline.

Dirk crossed the railway line and found the footpath that climbed the hills. Once he lifted his hands and with his thumbs wiped the tears from his cheeks. Then he stopped listlessly to watch a scarab beetle at his feet. The size of a man's thumb, glossy black and horned like a demon, it struggled with a ball of cow-dung three times its own size. Standing on its back legs, thrusting with its front, it rolled the perfect sphere of dung before it. Oblivious of everything but the need to spawn, to bury the ball in a secret place and deposit its eggs upon it, it laboured in silent dedication.

With the toe of his book Dirk flicked the ball away into the grass. The beetle stood motionless, deprived of the whole purpose of its existence. Then it began to search. Back and forth, clicking and scraping its shiny body armour across the hard, bare earth of the path.

Watching its frenzied search dispassionately, Dirk's face was calm and lovely. He lifted his foot and brought his heel down gently on the beetle.

He could feel it wriggling under his boot until with a crunch its carapace collapsed and it spurted brown as tobacco juice. Dirk stepped over it and walked on up the hill.


In the night Dirk sat alone. His arms were clasped around his legs and his forehead rested on his knees. The shafts of moonlight through the canopy of wattle branches had a cold white quality, similar to the emotion that held Dirk's body rigid. He lifted his head. Moonlight lit his face from above, accentuating the perfection of his features. The smooth, broad depth of his forehead, the flaring dark lines of his brows set off the large but delicately formed plane of his nose. But now his mouth was a line of pain, of cold white pain.

'I hate him.' His mouth did not lose the shape of pain as he whispered the words, 'and I hate her. He doesn't care about me any more – all he cares about is that woman.'

The vicious hiss of breath through his lips was the sound of despair.

'I always try to show him . . . No one else but him, but he doesn't care. Why doesn't he understand – Why? Why? Why?'

And he shivered feverishly,

'He doesn't want me. He doesn't care.'

The shivering ceased, and the shape of his mouth changed from pain to hatred.

'I'll show him. If he doesn't want me – then I'll show him.' And the next words he spat as though they were filth from his mouth, 'I hate him.' Around him the wattle branches rustled in the wind. He jumped to his feet and ran, following the moonlit road deeper into the plantations of Lion Kop.

A *meerkat* hunting alone along the road saw him and scampered into the trees like a small grey ferret. But Dirk ran on, faster now as his hatred drove him and his breathing sobbed in rhythm with his feet. He ran with the dry west wind into his face – he needed the wind. His revenge would ride on the wind.

'Now, we'll see,' he shouted suddenly as he ran. 'You don't want me – then have this instead!' And the wattle and wind answered him with a sound like many voices far away.

At the second access road he turned right and ran on into the heart of the plantations. He ran for twenty minutes and when he stopped he was panting wildly.

'Damn you – God damn you all.' His voice came catchy from his dried-out mouth.

'Damn you, then.' And he walked off the road and fought his way into the trees. They were two-year growth not yet thinned, and the branches interlaced to dispute his passage – hands trying to hold him, small desperate hands clutching at him, tugging at his clothing like the supplicating hands of a beggar. But he shrugged them away and beat them off until he was deep in amongst them.

'Here!' he said harshly and dropped to his knees in the soft crackling trash of small twigs and dry leaves that carpeted the earth. Hooking his fingers he raked a pyramid of the stuff, and he sobbed as he worked so that his muttering was broken and without coherence.

'Dry, it's dry. I'll show you then – you don't want— Everything I've done you've. ... I hate you ... Oh, Pa! Why? Why don't you – what have I done?'

And the matchbox rattled. Twice he struck and twice the match broke in his fingers. The third flared blue, spitting tiny sparks of sulphur, burning acrid, settling down to a small yellow flame that danced in the cup of his hands.

'Have this instead!' And he thrust the flame into the pile of kindling. It fluttered, almost died and then grew again as a wisp of grass caught it.

Consumed instantly, the grass was gone and the flame died, gone – almost, but then a leaf and it jumped brightly, orange points of flame in the twigs. The first tiny popping and it spread sideways, a burning leaf swirled upwards.

Dirk backed away as the flame leapt jubilantly into his face. He was no longer sobbing.

'Pa,' he whispered and the flame fastened on to the living leaves of a branch that hung over it. A gust of wind hit it and sprayed sparks and golden orange flame against its neighbour.

'Pa.' Dirk's voice was uncertain, he stood up and wiped his hands nervously against his shirt.

'No.' He shook his head in bewilderment, and the sapling bloomed with fire and the fire whispered softly.

'No.' Dirk's voice rose. 'I didn't really mean ...' but it was lost in the pistol-shots of flame and the whisper that was now a drumming roar.

'Stop it,' he shouted. 'Oh God, I didn't mean it. No! No!' And he jumped forward into the heat of it, into the bright orange glare, kicking wildly at the flaming kindling, scattering it so that it fell and caught again in fifty new points of fire.

'No, stop it. Please stop it!' And he clawed at the burning tree until the heat drove him back. He ran to another sapling and tore a leafy branch from it. He rushed at the fire, beating at it, sobbing again in the smoke and the flame.

Riding joyously on the west wind, roaring red and orange and black, the flames spread out among the trees and left him standing alone in the smoke and the swirling ash.

'Oh Pa! I'm sorry, I'm sorry – I didn't mean it.'

# Chapter Sixty-seven

A shutter kept slamming softly in the wind, but this was not the only reason Michael Courtney could not sleep. He felt trapped, chained by loyalties he could not break; he was aware of the dark oppressive bulk of the Theuniskraal homestead around him. A prison, a place of bitterness and hatred.

He moved restlessly on his bed and the shutter banged and banged. He threw back the single sheet and the floorboards creaked as he stood up from the bed.

'Michael!' The voice from the next room was sharp, suspicious.

'Yes, Mother.'

'Where are you going, darling?'

'There's a loose shutter. I'm going to close it.'

'Put something on, darling. Don't catch cold.'

Stifling, beginning to sweat now in physical discomfort, Michael knew he must get out of this house into the cool freedom of the wind and the night. He dressed quickly but silently, then carrying his boots he crept down the long passage and out on the wide front stoep.

He found the shutter and secured it, then he sat upon the front steps and pulled on his boots before standing again and moving out across the lawns. He stood on the bottom terrace of Theuniskraal's gardens and around him the west wind soughed and shook the trees.

The restlessness of the wind increased his own, so he must get out of the valley – get up on to the high ground of the escarpment. He started to walk, hurrying past the paddocks towards the stables. In the stable yard he stopped abruptly, his tall lean body caught in mid-stride. There was a glow, a soft orange glow on the far hills of Lion Kop.

Then Michael ran, shouting as he passed the grooms' quarters. He threw open the half-door of one of the stalls and snatched the bridle from its peg as he ran to his horse. Hands clumsy with haste, he forced the bit between the animal's teeth and buckled the cheek strap. When he led it out into the yard two of the grooms were standing there, bewildered with sleep.

'Fire!' Michael pointed along the hills. 'Call everybody and bring them to help.' He went up on to the bare back of his horse and looked down at them. 'Bring every man from the location, come in the mule-wagon. Come as fast as you can.' Then he hit his heels into the mare's flanks and drove her out of the yard, laying forward across her back.

Twenty minutes later Michael checked her on the crest of the escarpment. She was blowing heavily between his knees. Still five miles ahead, bright even in the bright moonlight, a circle of fire lay on the dark plantations of

Lion Kop. Above it a black cloud, a cloud that climbed and spread on the wind to hide the stars.

'Oh God – Uncle Sean!' The exclamation wrung from Michael was a cry of physical pain, and he urged the mare forward again. Charging her recklessly through the ford of the Baboon Stroom so that the water flew like exploding glass, then lunging up the far bank and on along the hills.

The mare was staggering in her gallop as Michael kneed her through the gates into the yard of the Lion Kop homestead. There were wagons and many blackmen carrying axes. Michael hauled the mare back so violently that she nearly fell.

'Where is the Nkosi?' he shouted at a big Zulu he recognized as Sean's personal servant.

'He has gone to Pietermaritzburg.'

Michael slid down from his horse and turned her loose.

'Send a man to the village to ask for help.'

'It is done,' the Zulu replied.

'We must move all the livestock from the top paddocks, get the horses out of the stables – it may come this way,' Michael went on.

'I have sent all the wives to do these things.'

'You have done well, then. Now let us go.'

The Zulus were swarming up on to the wagons, clutching the long-handled axes. Michael and Mbejane ran to the lead wagon. Michael took the reins. At that moment two horsemen galloped into the yard. He could not see their faces in the night.

'Who's that? Michael shouted.

'Broster and Van Wyk!' The nearest neighbours.

'Thank God! Will you take the other wagons?'

They dismounted and ran past Michael.

Michael stood with his legs braced apart, he threw his shoulders open as he wielded the whip and then sent it snaking forward to crack an inch above the ears of the lead mules. They lunged forward into the traces and the wagon bounced and clattered out of the yard.

As they galloped in frantic convoy along the main acesss road towards the plantations they met the Zulu women with their children from the location streaming down towards the homestead, their soft voices calling greeting and speed to their men as they passed.

But Michael hardly heard them, he stood with his eyes fastened on the pillar of red flame and smoke that rose from the heart of Sean's trees.

'It is in the trees we planted two years ago.' Mbejane spoke beside him. 'But already it will be close upon the next block of older trees. We cannot hope to stop it there.'

'Where then?'

'This side there are more young trees and a wide road. We can try there.'

'What is your name?' Michael asked.

'Mbejane.'

'I am Michael. The Nkosi's nephew.'

'I know.' Mbejane nodded, then went on, 'Turn off where next the roads meet.'

They came to the cross-roads. In the sector ahead were the young trees

– ten feet high, thick as a man's arm, massed dark leaves and interlacing branches. Far out beyond them in the tall mature wattle was the line of flame. Above it a towering wall of sparks and dark smoke, coming down swiftly on the wind. It would be upon them in less than an hour at its present rate of advance.

A fire like this would jump a thirty-foot road without checking – they must cut back into the young wattle and increase the gap to sixty feet at the least.

Michael swung the wagon off the road and hauled the mules to a halt. He jumped down to meet the other wagons as they came up.

'Go on for two hundred yards – then start your boys in chopping out the wattle towards the fire – we've got to widen the road. I'll start my gang here,' he shouted at Van Wyk.

'Right.'

'Mr Broster – go on to the end of the block and start working back this way – cut the timber out another thirty feet.'

Without waiting to hear more, Broster drove on. These two men, twice Michael's age, conceded him the right of command without argument.

Snatching an axe from the nearest Zulu, Michael issued his orders as he ran to the young wattle. The men crowded after him and Michael selected a tree, took his stance and swung the axe in a low arc from the side. The tree quivered and rained loose leaves upon him at the blow. Smoothly he reversed his grip on the shaft of the axe and swung again from the opposite side. The blade sliced through the soft wood, the tree sagged wearily away from him and groaned as it subsided. He stepped past it to the next. Around him the Zulus spread out along the road and the night rang with the beat of their axes.

Four times during the next half-hour fresh wagons galloped in, wagons loaded with men and driven by Sean's neighbours, until almost three hundred men were using the ax on Sean's lovingly planted and tenderly nursed wattle.

Shoulder to shoulder, chopping in wordless frenzy, trampling the fallen sapling as they moved forward.

Once a man yelled in pain and Michael looked up to see two Zulus dragging another back to the road with his leg half severed by the slip of a careless axe. Dark blood in the moonlight.

One of the neighbours hurried to tend the injured man and Michael turned back to the destruction of the wattle.

Swing, change hands and swing again, the solid *thunk!* and the tree swaying. Shove it over and struggle through the fallen tangle of branches to the next. Swing again, and smell the sweet bleeding sap – feel the ache in the shoulders and the sting of sweat in the burst blisters of the palms.

Then suddenly the other smell, acrid on the wind. Smoke. Michael paused and looked up. The men on each side of him stopped work also and the firelight danced on their naked, sweat-greased bodies as they leaned on their axes and watched it come.

On a front four hundred yards wide, ponderously it rolled down towards them. Not with the explosive white heat of a burning pine forest, but in the awful grandeur of orange and dark red, billowing smoke and torrential sparks.

Gradually the sound of axes died along the line as men stopped and watched this appalling thing come down towards them. It lit their faces clearly, revealing the awe that was on all of them. They could feel the heat now, great gusts of it that shrivelled the tender growth ahead of the flames – and suddenly a freak of the wind sent a bank of black smoke billowing down over the motionless line of men and blotted them out from each other. It cleared as swiftly as it came, and left them coughing and gasping.

'Back! Get back to the road!' yelled Michael and the cry was taken up and thrown along the line. They waded back through the morass of waist-high vegetation and assembled in small subdued groups along the road, standing together helplessly with the axes idle in their hands, fearful in the face of that line of flame and smoke.

'Cut branches to beat with!' Michael whipped their apathy. 'String out along the edge.' He hurried along the road, pushing them back into line, bullying them, cursing in his own fear. 'Come on, the flames will drop when they reach the fallen trees. Cover your faces – use your shirts. Hey, you – don't just stand there.'

With renewed determination each man armed himself with a green branch, and they re-formed along the road.

Quietly they stood in the daylight glare of the flames – black faces impassive, white ones flushed with heat and working anxiously.

'Do you think we'll be able to . . .' Michael started as he reached Ken Broster, and then he stopped. The question he had been about to ask had no answer. Instead he said, 'We've lost three thousand acres already – but if it gets away from us here!'

Involuntarily both of them glanced back at the tall mature wattle behind them.

'We'll hold it here,' Broster stated with a certainty he did not feel.

'I hope you're right,' whispered Michael, then suddenly Broster shouted: 'Oh Christ – look!'

For a moment Michael was blinded by the red glare and unsighted by the smoke. The fire burned unevenly. In places it had driven forward in great wedge-shaped salients of flame and left behind bays of standing wattle that were withering and browning in the heat.

From out of one of these bays, into the springy matt of fallen and trampled branches staggered a man.

'Who the hell . . .' started Michael. The man was unrecognizable. His short ripped to shreds by branches that had also scourged his face into a bloody mask. He floundered forward towards the road, two slack exhausted paces before he fell and disappeared under the leaves.

'The Nkosana.' Mbejane's voice boomed above the thunder of the flames.

'Dirk! It's Dirk Courtney!' Michael started forward.

The heat was painful in Michael's face. How much more intense must it be out there where Dirk was lying. As if they knew their prey was helpless the flames raced forward eagerly, triumphantly to consume him. Whoever went in to rob them would meet the full fury of their advance.

Michael plunged into the brush and ploughed his way towards where

Dirk thrashed feebly, almost encircled by the deadly embrace of the flames – and the heat reached out ahead of the flames to welcome him. Mbejane ran beside him.

'Go back,' shouted Mbejane. 'It needs only one of us.' But Michael did not answer him and they crashed side by side through the brush, racing the fire with Dirk as the prize.

Mbejane reached him first and lifting him, turned back for the road. He took one step before he fell and rose again unsteadily from the mass of branches. Even his vast strength was insufficient in this vacuum of heat. His mouth was open, a pink cave in the glistening black oval of his face, wide open and his chest heaved strenuously as he hunted air, but instead sucked the scalding heat into his throat.

Michael threw himself forward against the heat to reach him. It was almost a solid thing, a barrier of red shimmering glare. Michael could feel it swelling and tightening the skin of his face and drying the moisture from his eyeballs.

'I'll take his legs,' he grunted and reached for Dirk. A patch of brown appeared miraculously on the sleeve of his shirt – singed by the flames as though it had been carelessly ironed. Beneath it the heat sunk a barb of agony into his flesh.

Half a dozen paces together with Dirk between them before Michael tripped and fell, dragging Mbejane down with him. They were a long time rising, all movements slowing down – but when they did they were surrounded.

Two prongs of flame had reached the area of fallen saplings on either side of them. This had slowed them and diminished their fury. But a chance gust of the wind and fuel had forced them to curl inwards on each other, spreading horns of fire ahead of Michael and Mbejane and leaving them enclosed by a dancing, leaping palisade of flame.

'Go through!' croaked Michael, his throat scalded and swollen. 'We must break through.'

And they churned their way towards the encircling wall. Through it, vague and unreal, he could see men beating at the flames – distorted phantoms trying desperately to open a path for them. Mbejane wore only a loin cloth, no breeches, coat nor boots to protect him, as Michael had. He was very near the limit of his strength.

Now looking at Michael across the body of the boy they carried, Mbejane saw a curious thing. Michael's hair crinkled slowly and then began to smoke – smouldering like an old sack.

Michael screamed at the agony of it, a hideous sound that shrilled above the roar and crackle of the flames. But agony was the key that unlocked the last storehouse of his strength. As though it were a rag doll he snatched Dirk's body from Mbejane's grasp and lifting it with both hands on to his shoulders he charged into the fire.

The flames reached to his waist, clawing greedily at him as he ran and the smoke eddied and swirled about him – but he was through.

'Help Mbejane!' he shouted at the Zulu beaters and then he was out on the road. He dropped Dirk and beat at his clothing with his bare hands. His boots were charred and his clothing was alight in a dozen places. He fell and rolled wildly in the dusty road to smother it.

Two Zulus went in to help Mbejane. Two nameless blackmen, two labourers – men of no distinction. Neither of them wore boots. Both of them reached Mbejane as he tottered weakly towards them. One on each side they urged him back towards the road.

At this moment Michael rolled to his knees in the road and despite his own agony watched them with a sickened fascination.

Leading Mbejane between them as though he were a blind man, they stumbled barefooted into the flames and stirred up a great cloud of sparks around them. Then the smoke rolled down over them and they were gone.

'Mbejane!' croaked Michael, and pushed himself to his feet to go to him – then:

'Oh God – Oh, thank God.' Mbejane and one of the Zulus stumbled out of the smoke into the arms of the men who waited for them.

No one went back for the other Zulu. No one went back for him until two hours later when the dawn had broken and the fire had been stopped at the road and the mature wattle had been saved. Then Ken Broster led a small party gingerly into the wilderness of still smouldering ash, into the black desert. They found him on his face. Those parts of him that had lain against the earth were still recognizable as belonging to a human being.

## Chapter Sixty-eight

'Ladyburg in twenty minutes, Mr Courtney.' The conductor put his head round the door of the compartment.

'Thanks, Jack.' Sean looked up from his book.

'I see from this morning's paper that you're engaged to be married?'

'That's right.'

'Well, then, break clean, no hitting low – let's have a good clean fight and good luck to both of you.' Sean grinned and the man went down the passage. Sean packed his book into the briefcase, stood up and followed him.

On the balcony of the coach he stopped and lit a cheroot, then he leaned on the railings and looked out across the veld for his first glimpse of Lion Kop. This had become a ritual whenever he returned to Ladyburg.

This morning he was as happily content as he had ever been in his life. Last night, after conferring with Ma and Pa Goldberg, Ruth had set the wedding date for March next year. By then Sean would have completed his first cutting of bark, and they would take a month to honeymoon in the Cape.

Now, at last, I have everything a man could reasonably ask for, he thought,

and smiled and in that moment he saw the smoke. He straightened up and
flicked the cheroot away.

The train snaked up towards the rim of the escarpment, slowing as the
gradient changed beneath it. It reached the crest and the whole vista of the
Ladyburg valley opened below it. Sean saw the great irregular blot upon his
trees, with the thin grey streams of smoke drifting wearily away across the
hills.

He opened the balcony gate and jumped down from the train. He hit and
slid and rolled down the gravel embankment. The skin was scraped from his
knees and the palms of his hands. Then he was on his feet, running.

Along the road where the fire had been stopped men waited. Sitting
quietly or sprawled in exhausted sleep, all of them were coated with ash and
soot. Their eyes were smoke-inflamed and their bodies ached with fatigue.
But they waited while the black acres smouldered and smoked sullenly – for
if the wind came up again it would fan the ashes to life.

Ken Broster lifted his head from his arm, then sat up quickly.

'Sean's here!' he said. The men around him stirred and then stood up
slowly. They watched Sean approaching, he came with the sloppy, blundering
legs of a man who has run five miles.

Sean stopped a little way off and his breathing wheezed and heaved in
this throat.

'How? How did it happen?'

'We don't know, Sean.' In sympathy Ken Broster dropped his eyes from
Sean's face. You do not stare at a man in anguish. Sean leaned against one
of the wagons. He could not bring himself to look again at the vast expanse
of smouldering desert with the skeletons of the tree-trunks standing out of
it like the twisted and blackened fingers of an arthritic hand.

'One of your men was killed,' Ken told him softly. 'One of your Zulus.'
He hesistated – then went on firmly. 'Others were hurt, badly burned.'
Sean made no reply, he did not seem to understand the words.

'Your nephew and your boy – Dirkie.' Still Sean stared at him dully.

'Mbejane also.' This time Sean seemed to cringe away from him.

'I sent them down to the homestead – the doctor's there.'

Still no reply from Sean, but now he wiped the palm of his hand across
his mouth and eyes.

'Mike and Dirk aren't too bad, skin burns – but Mbejane's feet are in a
hell of a mess.' Ken Broster spoke quickly now. 'Young Dirk got trapped
in front of the flames. Mike and Mbejane went to get him . . . surrounded
. . . down . . . picked him up . . . tried to help . . . useless . . . badly burned
. . . meat off his feet . . .'

To Sean the words were disjointed, meaningless. He leaned against the
wagon. There was looseness in him, a lack of will. *It was too much. Let it
go. Let it all go.*

'Sean, are you all right?' Broster's hands on his shoulders. He straightened
up and looked around him again.

'I must go to them. Lend me a horse.'

'You go ahead, Sean. We'll stay on here and watch it for you. Don't worry
about it, we'll make bloody sure she doesn't start again.'

'Thank you, Ken.' Then he looked around the circle of anxious compassionate faces. 'Thank you,' he said again.

Sean rode slowly into the stable yard on Lion Kop. There were many carriages and servants, black women and children, but a hush came upon them when they recognized him. Surrounded by women, a crude litter lay near the far wall of the yard and Sean walked across to it.

'I see you, Mbejane.'

'Nkosi.' Mbejane's eyelashes were burned away giving his face a bland and slightly puzzled expression. His hands and his feet were bound loosely in bundles of crisp white bandages through which ointment had soaked in yellow patches. Sean squatted behind him. He could not speak. He reached out almost hesistantly and touched Mbejane's shoulder.

'Is it bad?' he asked then.

'No, Nkosi. It is not too bad. My wives have come for me. I will return when I am ready.'

They spoke together a little while, and Mbejane told him of Dirk and how Michael had come. Then he murmured, 'This woman is the wife of the one who died.'

Sean noticed her for the first time. She sat alone in the crowded yard, on a blanket against the wall. A child stood beside her; leaning forward, naked, holding one of her fat, black breasts with both hands as he fed from it. She sat impassively with her legs folded under her, a cloak of ochre-dyed leather draped loosely over her shoulders, but open at the front for the child. Sean moved across to her. The child watched him with large dark eyes, but without removing the nipple from his mouth and the corners of his mouth were wet with spilled milk.

'He was a man,' Sean greeted the woman.

She inclined her head gravely. 'He was a man!' she agreed.

'Where will you go?' Sean asked.

'To my father's kraal.' The high headdress of red clay enhanced the quiet dignity of her reply.

'Select twenty head of cattle from my herds to take with you.'

'*Ngi Yabonga* – I praise you, Nkosi.'

'Go in peace.'

'Stay in peace.' She stood, lifted the child on to her hip and walked slowly from the yard without looking back.

'I will go now, Nkosi.' Mbejane spoke from the litter. The colour of his skin was grey with pain. 'And when I return we will plant again. It was only a small fire.'

'It was only a small fire.' Sean nodded. 'Go in peace, my friend. Drink much beer and grow fat. I will visit you.'

Mbejane chuckled softly and signalled his wives to their places around the litter. They lifted him, young women strong from their work in the fields.

'Stay in peace, Nkosi.' Mbejane lay back painfully upon the soft mattress of fur, and they carried him out of the yard. They began to sing as they passed the gates, moving in double file on each side of the litter, stately and tall, their naked backs glistening with oil, rumps swaying together beneath

the brief loin cloths, and their voices joined high and proud in the ancient
song of welcome to the warrior returned from battle.


Gathered on the stoep of Lion Kop were many of his neighbours and
their wives, come with sympathy and offers of assistance.

Ada was waiting for him as Sean climbed the steps.

'Dirk?' he asked.

'He is well, asleep now. Laudanum.'

'Michael?'

'He is waiting for you. He refused the drug. I've put him in your room.'

On his way down the passage Sean stopped at Dirk's room and looked
in. Dirk lay on his back with bandaged hands folded across his chest. His
face was swollen and laced with ugly red lines where the wattle branches
had clawed him. On the chair beside his bed Mary sat in patient vigil. She
looked at Sean and made to rise. Sean shook his head.

'No. I will come back when he is awake.' He went on down the passage
to his own room.

Three of Ada's girls hovered and chirruped about Michael's bed like birds
whose nests are endangered. They saw him and stopped their chatter. All
Ada's girls held Sean in unexplained awe.

'Oh, Mr Courtney. His poor hands . . .' one little lass began, then blushed
crimson, dropped a hurried curtsy and escaped from the room. The others
followed quickly.

Sean moved across to the bed.

'Hello, Mike.' His voice was gruff, as he saw the blister that hung like
a pale grape on Michael's cheek.

'Hello, Uncle Sean.' The raw places of his face and lips were smeared
with yellow ointment. Sean sat down gingerly on the edge of the bed.

'Thank you, Michael,' he said.


## Chapter Sixty-nine


Ronny Pye called early the following morning. With him came Dennis
Petersen and both of them were wearing suits.

'Very fancy turn-out,' Sean greeted them. 'Business or social?'

'Well, you might say a little of each.' Ronny paused at the top of the
veranda steps. 'May we come in?'

Sean led them to the end of the veranda, and they seated themselves before
anyone spoke again.

'I heard about the fire, Sean. Terrible business. I heard there was a native killed and both Dirk and Michael were hurt. Terrible business.' Ronny shook his head in sympathy.

'Did you also hear that I lost four thousand acres of timber?' Sean inquired politely.

'Heard that also.' Ronny nodded solemnly. 'Terrible business.'

Ronny and Dennis glanced at each other furtively, and then looked down at their hands.

'Very nasty,' Ronny repeated and a silence fell upon them.

'Anything else worrying you?' Sean inquired politely.

'Well, now that you've brought it up—' Ronny reached inside his jacket and withdrew a long folded document tied with a red ribbon. 'Mind you, we don't have to discuss it today. Leave it until you feel better?'

'Talk!' Sean grunted.

'Clause eight.' Ronny spread the document between the coffee-cups on the table. 'In the event of the said security, namely, a certain block of wattle known as No. 2 block of Lion Kop Estates in extent approximately . . .' Ronny hesitated. 'Guess there's no sense in me reading it all. You know what it says. That wattle was part of the collateral for the loan.'

'How long will you give me to raise the money?' Sean asked.

'Well, Sean, you understand there is no period of grace allowed in the contract. Seems to me you'll have to put it up right away.'

'I want a month,' Sean told him.

'A month!' Ronny was shocked and hurt by the request. 'See here now, Sean. I don't honestly— I mean, surely you've got the money. I mean why do you need a month. Just let us have your cheque.'

'You know damned well I haven't got it.'

'Seems to me—' Ronny offered delicately. 'Seems to me if you haven't got it now, there's not much chance you'll have it in a month. No offence, Sean, but we have to look at this thing from a business angle. If you follow me.'

'I follow you.' Sean nodded. 'And I want a month.'

'Give it to him,' blurted Dennis Petersen, his first contribution, and Ronny turned on him instantly with his face twisting into a snarl. The struggle he had within himself to smooth out his features and to restore his voice to its level and reasonable tone lasted fully five seconds.

'Well now, Dennis,' he murmured. 'That's an unusual way to look at it. Seems to me—'

'I spoke to Audrey before we came up here. I promised her . . . Anyway, we both agreed.' Dennis was staring out across the valley, unable to meet his partner's eyes.

Suddenly Ronny Pye chuckled. Yes, by God! It would be even better that way – watching this big arrogant bastard crawling round begging, with his hat in his hands. Sean would go to Jackson first and Ronny had telegraphed Jackson the previous afternoon. He had also telegraphed Nichols at the Standard Bank. By now the message would be spreading swiftly along the network of South African banking channels. Sean Courtney would find it difficult to borrow the price of a meal.

'All right then, Sean. As a special concession you can have a month.' Then all the laughter was gone and he leaned forward in his chair. 'You've got exactly thirty days. Then, by Christ, I am going to sell out under you.'

After they were gone Sean sat alone on the wide veranda. The sunlight on the hills was bright and hot, but in the shade it was cool. He heard Ada's girls chattering somewhere in the house, then one of the giggled shrilly. The sound irritated Sean, his frown deepened and he drew a rumpled envelope from his jacket pocket and smoothed it out on the arm of his chair. Awhile he sat in thought nibbling the stub of a pencil.

Then he wrote: 'Jackson. Natal Wattle'. And again, 'Standard Bank'. Then 'Ben Goldberg'. He paused and considered this last name on his list. Then he grunted aloud and scratched it out with two hard strokes of the pencil. Not from the Godbergs. Leave them out of this.

He wrote again quickly, scrawling a single word – 'Candy' and below it 'Tim Curtis'.

That was all. John Acheson was in England. It would take two months to receive a reply from him.

That was all. He sighed softly and folded the envelope into his pocket. Then he lit a cheroot, sank down in the chair and placed his feet on the low veranda wall in front of him. I'll leave on tomorrow morning's train, he thought.

The windows behind him were open. Lying beyond them in the bedroom Michael Courtney had heard every word of their conversation. Now he stood up painfully from the bed and began to dress. He went out the back way and nobody saw him leave. His mare was in the stables, and on a borrowed saddle he rode back to Theuniskraal.

Anna saw him coming and ran out into the yard to meet him. 'Michael! Oh, Michael. Thank God you are safe. We heard . . .' Then she saw his face and the raw, swollen burns on it and she froze. Michael dismounted slowly and one of the grooms led his horse away.

'Michael, darling. Your poor face.' And she embraced him quickly.

'It's nothing, Mother.'

'Nothing!' She pulled away from him, lips drawn into a tight, hard line. 'You run away in the middle of the night to that . . . that . . . Then you come home days later with your face and your hands in a terrible mess – is that nothing!'

'I'm sorry, Mother. Gran'ma looked after me.'

'You knew I'd be half-dead with worry, sitting here imagining all sorts of things. You didn't send word to me you just let me . . .'

'You could have come to Lion Kop,' he said softly.

'To the home of that monster? Never!' And Michael looked away from her.

'Where's Father?'

'In his study, as usual. Oh, darling, you don't know how I've missed you. Tell me you love me, Michael.'

'I love you,' he repeated automatically and the sensation of suffocating was on him again. 'I must see Dad. It's very urgent.'

'You've just arrived. Let me fix something to eat – let me see to your poor face.'

'I have to see Dad now. I'm sorry.' And he went past her towards the house.

Garry was sitting at his desk when Michael walked into the study.

Michael hated this room. He hated the high smoke-stained ceiling, the oppressive darkness of the panelled walls, the massive hunting trophies, he hated even the carpets and the smell of old paper and dust. From this room had issued the decrees and the pronouncements which had restricted and predetermined his life. This room was the symbol of everything from which he wished to escape. Now he glared around it defiantly, as though it were a living thing – I've come back to extract from you what you owe me, he thought, you've had value from me, now pay me back!

'Michael!' Garrick's boot scraped on the wooden floor as he stood to greet him, and Michael winced at the sound.

'Hello, Dad.'

'Your mother and I, we have been so worried. Why didn't you send word to us?' The hurt was there in Garrick's voice. Michael opened his mouth to apologize in automatic guilt, but the words came out differently from the way he had intended.

'I was busy. I didn't have a chance.'

'Sit down, my boy.' Garrick gestured to one of the polished leather armchairs. He removed the metal-framed spectacles from his nose, but he did not look at Michael's injured face again. He would not think about Sean and Michael together.

'I'm glad you've come back. I was just working on the opening chapters of my new book. It's a history of our family from the time of your great-great-grandfather's arrival at the Cape. I'd very much like your opinion. I'd value it immensely. The considered opinion of a graduate from the South African College.'

The trap was closing. It was so obvious that Michael squirmed. He could almost feel the panelled walls moving in on him. He started to protest: 'Dad, I have to speak to you.' But already Garrick was adjusting his spectacles and shuffling through the papers on his desk, talking quickly.

'I think you'll like it. It should interest you.' Garrick glanced up and smiled at Michael with the eagerness of a child that brings a gift. 'Here we are. I'll start at the beginning. You must allow for it being the first rough draft. It's not polished yet.' And he began to read. At the end of each paragraph he searched for Michael's approval, smiling in anticipation of it. Until Michael could bear it no longer, until he shouted suddenly in the middle of a sentence.

'I want you to pay me out my share of Theuniskrraal.'

There was a momentary break in Garrick's reading, just a flutter in his voice to acknowledge Michael's request and then he went on steadily, but his voice had lost its timbre and was now a lifeless monotone. He finished the paragraph, laid the sheet aside, removed his spectacles and placed them in their case. The lid of the case snapped shut against the tension of its spring and Garry lifted his head slowly.

'Why?'

'I need the money.'

'What for?'

'I need it.'

Garry stood up and moved across to the window. He stood before it with his hand clasped behind him. The green lawns flowed down to the fence that bounded the gardens, and upon them the poinsettia bushes were vivid patches of scarlet. Beyond, the land lifted into the first long roll, golden grass and scattered forest with the cattle feeding beneath and the massive silver and blue clouds piled above.

'It will rain tonight,' Garrick murmured, but Michael did not answer. 'We need it. Three weeks of dry, and the pasture is withering.' Still no reply and Garry returned to his desk.

'I hear there was a fire on Lion Kop last night.'

'There was.'

'They say that your uncle is finished. They say the fire finished him.'

'No!' Michael denied it quickly. 'That's not true.'

'Is that why you want the money, Michael?'

'Yes.'

'You want to give it to Sean?'

'I want to buy a share in Lion Kop Wattle. I don't want to give anything – it will be a business offer.'

'And what about Theuniskraal – it's your home. You were born here.'

'Please, Dad. I've made up my mind.'

'Did Sean suggest this?'

'He did not. He knows nothing about it.'

'It's your idea then. You thought it up all on your own. You're going to sell out your own parents for him. My God, what sort of hold has he over you that you would do that for him.'

Flushing a dusty brick colour, Michael kicked back his chair and jumped to his feet.

'You make it sound like treachery.'

'That's exactly what it is!' shouted Garrick. 'It's Judas's work. Your mother and I – we raised you with everything. We scraped to send you to University, we built our whole lives around you. We worked for the day you would return here to Theuniskraal and . . .' He stopped, panting, and wiped from his chin the bubble of saliva that had burst through his lips. 'Instead you ran off to joint that . . . that swine. How do you think we liked that? Don't you think it nearly broke our hearts? Of all people you had to go to him! And now, now you want half of Theuniskraal to take him as a gift – to buy his . . .'

'Stop that!' Michael warned him sharply. 'And before you go on remember where I got my half of Theuniskraal. Remember who made the original gift.' He picked up his hat and riding-crop and strode towards the door.

'Michael.' The terrible appeal in Garry's voice checked him.

'What is it?'

'Your share – it isn't very much. I hadn't told you before, but there was a time – when you were very young. The rinderpest, I had to—' He couldn't go on.

'What are you trying to tell me?'

'Sit down, Michael. Sit down and I'll show you.' Reluctantly, afraid of what he was about to hear, Michael returned and stood beside his chair.

Garry selected a key from the bunch on his watch-chain and opened the top drawer of his desk. He selected a rolled document, slipped it from its retaining ribbon and handed it without speaking to his son.

Michael spread it and read the words upon the cover.

'Deed of Mortgage'.

With a sliding sensation in his stomach, he turned the page. He did not read it all. Words and groups of words stood out in bolder print, and they were sufficient:

'The Ladyburg Trust & Banking Co.' . . . 'A certain piece of land in extent approx. 25,000 morgen situate in the district of Ladyburg, Magisterial Division of Pietermaritzburg, known as the farm Theuniskraal' . . . 'All constructions, erections and improvements thereon . . . Plus interest at eight and one half per cent.'

'I see.' Michael handed the document back to his father and stood up.

'Where are you going?'

'Back to Lion Kop.'

'No!' Garry whispered. 'No, Michael. Please, my son. No – O God – No!' Michael left the room and closed the door softly behind him.

When Anna came into the room Garry was sitting behind the desk, sitting quietly with his shoulders slumped forward.

'You let him go!' she hissed. Garry did not move, he did not seem to hear.

'He's gone. Gone to your brother – and you let him.' Her voice was very low, but now it rose harshly and she shrieked at him. 'You useless drunken animal. Sitting here playing with your little books. You were not man enough to breed him – your brother had to do that for you! And you are not man enough to keep him – again your brother! You let him go. You've taken my son from me.'

Garry sat unmoving. He saw nothing. He heard nothing. In his head was a soft, misty greyness, and the mist blotted out all sight and sound. It was warm in the mist – warm and safe. No one could reach him here for it wrapped and protected him. He was safe.

'This is all you are good for.' Anna snatched a handful of the manuscript sheets from the desk in front of him. 'Your little pieces of paper. Your dreams and stories of other men – real men.'

She ripped the pages through and through again, then flung them at him. The pieces fluttered and swirled, then settled like dead leaves on his shoulders and in his hair. He did not move. Panting in her grief and anger, she took up what remained of the manuscript and shredded that also, scattering the tiny white scraps about the room.

# Chapter Seventy

The two of them stood together on the station platform. They did not speak. Most of the previous day and night had been spent talking and now there was nothing more to say. They stood together in quiet companionship – and a stranger looking at them would have known immediately they were father and son. Though Michael was not as tall, and he was lean beside Sean's bulk – yet the tone of the skin and the colour of the hair were the same. Both had the big Courtney nose and their mouths were wide and full-lipped.

'I'll telegraph as soon as I hit gold.' Sean had explained to Michael in detail the financial structure of Lion Kop. He had told him how he intended to find the money which would keep it from collapsing.

'I'll hold this end up.' Michael was to begin cutting the wattle which had survived the fire. They had ridden the previous afternoon through the plantations and marked the blocks which were ripe for the axe. 'Good luck, Uncle Sean.'

'Since we are working together now, Mike, I suggest you drop the "Uncle". It's too clumsy for everyday use.'

Michael grinned. 'Good luck, Sean.'

'Thanks, Mike.' They clasped hands, gripping hard, then Sean climbed up into the coach.


Jackson was friendly but firm and Nichols at the Standard Bank was very polite and full of sympathy. Sean caught the northbound train for Johannesburg to fire his last two bullets.

'Colonel Courtney. How good to see you.' The reception clerk at Candy's Hotel came round from behind his desk to greet Sean. 'We were only talking about you last week. Welcome back to Johannesburg.'

'Hello, Frank. Putting on a little weight there, aren't you?' Sean prodded his waistcoat and the man chuckled. 'Tell me, Frank, is Candy . . . is Mrs Rautenbach in?'

'Ah! There've been some changes since you left, sir.' The clerk grinned with just a trace of malice. 'It's not Mrs Rautenbach any longer. No, sir. Mrs Heyns – Mrs Jock Heyns now!'

'Good God! She married Jock!'

'That she did. Two weeks ago – biggest wedding in Jo'burg since the war. Two thousand guests.'

'Where is she now?'

'On the water. Off to England and the Continent for six months' honeymoon.'

'I hope she'll be happy,' Sean murmured softly, remembering the loneliness he had seen in her eyes when he left.

'With all Mr Heyns's money? How can she be otherwise?' the clerk asked in genuine surprise.

'Will you be staying, Colonel?'

'If you have a room.'

'We always have a room for our friends. How long, sir?'

'Two days, Frank.'


Tim Curtis was Chief Engineer on the City Deep. When Sean spoke to him about a loan he laughed.

'Christ! Sean, I only work there – I don't own the bloody mine.'

Sean had dinner with him and his bride of two years' standing. At their urging Sean examined their newborn infant and secretly decided that it looked like an unweaned bulldog.

Extending his stay in Johannesburg, Sean visited the banks. He had dealt with most of them long ago, but the personnel had changed, so he was puzzled that the manager of each institution seemed to have heard of him.

'Colonel Courtney. Now would you be Colonel Sean Courtney of Lion Kop Wattle Estates down in Natal?' And when he nodded he saw the shutters come down in their eyes, like windows barred by a prudent householder against burglars.

On the eighth night he ordered liquor to be sent to his suite – two full bottles of brandy. He drank steadily and desperately. The brandy would not quieten the violent struggles of his brain, but seemed to goad it, distorting his problems and deepening his melancholia.

He lay alone until the dawn paled out the yellow gaslight of the lamps. The brandy hummed giddily in his head and he longed for peace – the peace he had found only in the immense silence and space of the veld. Suddenly a picture formed in his mind of a lonely grave below a little hill. He heard the wind moan over it and saw the brown grass sway. That was peace.

He sat up unsteadily.

'Saul,' he said, and the sadness was heavy on him for the pilgrimage he had promised himself and had not made.

'It is finished here. I'll go now,' and he stood up. The giddiness caught him and he clutched at the head-rail of the bed to steady himself.

## Chapter Seventy-one

He recognized the kopje from four miles off. Into his memory its shape was indelibly etched; the symmetrical slope of the sides cobbled with boulders that glinted dully in the sunshine like the scales of a reptile, the flattened summit ringed by a bolder stratum of rock, the high altar on which the sacrifice to greed and stupidity had been made.

Closer he could discern the aloe plants upon the slopes, fleshy leaves spiked like crowns and jewelled with scarlet blooms. On the plain below the kopje, in the short brown grass, stood a long line of white specks. Sean rode towards them and as he approached each speck evolved into a cairn of whitewashed stones and on each stood a metal cross.

Stiff from the long day in the saddle Sean dismounted slowly. He hobbled the horses, dropped saddle and pack from their backs and turned them loose to feed. He stood alone and lit a cheroot, suddenly reluctant to approach the line of graves.

The silence of the empty land settled gently upon him, a silence not broken but somehow heightened by the sound of the wind across the plain. The harsh tearing as his mount cropped at the dry brown grass seemed sacrilegious in this place, but it roused Sean from his thoughts. He walked towards the double line of graves and stood before one of them. Stamped crudely into the metal of the cross the words 'Here lies a brave burgher'.

He moved along the line of crosses and on each he read those same words. On some of them the printing was irregular, on one the 'r' in burgher had been replaced by a 'g'. Sean stopped and glared at it, hating the man who in his haste and unconcern thad made the epitaph an insult.

'I'm sorry.' He spoke aloud, apologizing to the man who lay beneath it. Then he was embarrassed, angry at himself for the weakness. Only a madman speaks aloud to the dead. He strode away towards the second row of crosses.

'Leading Seaman W. Carter, R.N.' The fat one.

'Corporal Henderson C.F.S.' Twice in his chest and another in the belly.

He walked along the line and read their names. Some were just names, others he saw instantly and vividly. He saw them laughing, or frightened, saw the way they rode, remembered the sound of their voices. This one still owed him a guinea, he remembered the bet.

'Keep it.' He spoke and immediately checked himself again.

Slowly he went on to the end of the line, his momentum running down as he approached the grave that stood separate from the others – the way he had ordered it.

He read the inscription. Then he squatted down comfortably on his haunches beside it and stayed there until the sun settled and the wind turned cold and plaintive. Only then he went to his saddle and loosened the blanket-roll. There was no firewood and he slept fitfully in the cold of the night and the icier cold of his throughts.

In the morning he went back to Saul's grave. For the first time he noticed that grass was growing up between the stones of the cairn and that the cross sagged a little to one side. He shrugged off his coat and went down on his knees, working like a gardener over the grave, weeding out the grass with his hunting knife, making certain the roots were removed. Then he went to the head and lifted the rocks away from around the cross. He tore the cross from the ground and re-dug the hole for it, setting it up again carefully, plugging the base with pebbles and earth and at last packing the whitewashed rocks firmly around it once more.

He stood back, brushed earth and flakes of whitewash from his hands and surveyed his handiwork. It still was not right, there was something missing. He thought about it, frowning heavily until he found the answer.

'Flowers,' he grunted and lifted his head towards the aloes on the kopje above him. He set off up the slope, picking his way through the little of boulders towards the summit. His knife slipped easily through the soft thick stems and the juice oozed heavily from the wounds. With an armful he started back down the slope. Out to one side a patch of colour caught his eye, a sprinkling of pink and white amoung the boulders. He detoured towards it. Hottentot Daisies, each one in perfect trumpet with a pink throat and a fragile yellow tongue. Delighted with his find, Sean laid aside his burden of aloe blooms and went in amongst them. Stooping like a reaper he worked through them towards the lip of a narrow ravine. gathering the flowers into posies and binding the stems together with grass. Finally he reached the ravine and straightened up to rest his aching back.

The ravine was narrow, he could have jumped across it with little effort – but it was deep. He peered down into it without much interest. The cleft was floored with rainwashed sand, and his interest quickened as he made out the half-buried bones of a large animal. But what made him climb down into the ravine was not the bones, but the bulky leather object entangled with them.

Sliding on his backside the last few feet of the descent he reached the bottom, and examined his find. A leather mule-pack, double pouches, and the buckles of the harness almost rusted away. He tugged the whole lot loose from the sand and was surprised at the weight of it.

The leather was dry and brittle, faded almost white with exposure and the locks of the pouches were rusted solid. With his knife he slit the flap of one pouch and out of it cascaded a stream of sovereigns. They fell into the sand, clinking upon each other in a heap that glittered with merry golden smiles.

Sean stared at them in disbelief. He dropped the pack and squatted on his haunches over the pile. Timidly he picked up one of the discs and examined the portrait of the old President, before lifting the coin to his mouth and biting down upon it. His teeth sank into the soft metal and he removed it from his mouth.

'Well, damn me sideways,' he invited, and he laughed out loud. Rocking back on his haunches and lifting his face to the sky he roared out his jubilation and his relief. It went on and on until his laughter dried suddenly, and he sobered.

Cupping a double handful of the gold he asked it:

'Now, where the hell did you come from?' And his answer was in the grim face embossed upon each coin. Boer Gold.

'And who do you belong to?'

The answer was the same, and he let the coins trickle through his fingers. Boer Gold.

'The hell it is!' he growled angrily. 'Starting this minute it's Courtney Gold.' And he began to count it.

As his fingers worked so did his brain. He prepared his case against his own conscience. They owed him the balance outstanding on a train of wagons filled with ivory, they owed him his deposits in the Volkskaas Bank, they owed him for a shrapnel wound in the leg and a bullet in the belly, they owed him for three years of hardship and danger, and they owed him for a friend. As he stacked the sovereigns into piles of twenty he considered his case, found it good and proven, justified it and gave judgement in his own favour.

'I find for the appellant,' he announced, and concentrated his whole attention on the counting. An hour and a half later he reached the total.

There was a huge pile of coins upon the flat rock he had used as a desk. He lit a cheroot and the smoke he drew into his lungs made him lightheaded. His conscience had surrendered unconditionally and in its place was a sense of well-being. All the more intense for the period of depression through which he had come.

'Sean Courtney accepts from the Government of the one-time Republic of the Transvaal an amount of twenty-nine thousand, two hundred pounds, in full discharge of all debts and claims.' He chuckled again and began shovelling the gold back into the leather pouches.

With the heavy pack slung over his shoulders and with his arms full of wild flowers, Sean went down the kopje. He saddled his horse and loaded the pack on to his mule before he went to pile the flowers on Saul's grave. They made a brave show of colour against the brown grass.

He lingered another hour, fussing over his floral arrangements and resisting the temptation to thank Saul. For now he had decided the gold was not a gift from the Republican Government – but from Saul Friedman. This made it even easier to accept.

At last he mounted and rode away. As the man and his horses dwindled into insignificance on the great brown plain, a dust devil came dancing up from the south. A tall, spinning column of heated air and dust and fragments of dry grass, it weaved and swayed towards the graveyard below the kopje. For a time it seemed as though it would pass wide of it, but suddenly it changed direction and dashed down upon the double row of crosses. It snatched up the flowers on Saul's grave, lifted them ripped their petals and scattered them widely across the plain.

## Chapter Seventy-two

With Michael beside him lugging the carpet-bag which was the heaviest item of luggage, Sean left the buggy and crossed the sidewalk into the offices of the Ladyburg Banking & Trust Co.

'Oh! Colonel Courtney,' the young lady at the reception desk enthused. 'I'll tell Mr Pye you are here.'

'Please don't bother. I'll carry the glad news myself.'

Ronny Pye looked up in alarm as the door of his office flew open and the two of them walked in.

'Good morning, Ronny,' Sean greeted him cheerfully. 'Have you bled any good stones today, or is it still too early?'

Guardedly Ronny murmured a reply and stood up.

Sean selected a cigar from the leather box on the desk and sniffed it.

'Not a bad line in horse-dung you've got here,' he remarked and bit the end off. 'Match please, Ronny, I'm a customer, where are your manners?'

Reluctantly, suspiciously, Ronny lit the cigar for him. Sean sat down and placed his feet on the desk with ankles neatly crossed.

'How much do I owe you?' he asked. The question heightened Ronny's suspicion and his eyes settled on the carpet-bag in Michael's hands.

'You mean altogether? Capital *and* interest?'

'Capital *and* interest,' Sean affirmed.

'Well, I'd have to work that out.'

'Give it to me in round figures.'

'Well, very roughly, you understand, it would be around – oh, I don't know – say . . .' He paused. That carpet-bag looked confoundedly heavy. Its sides bulged and he could see the tension in Michael's arm muscles as he held it. 'Say, twenty-two thousand, eight hundred and sixteen pounds, fifteen shillings.' As he named the exact figure Ronny dropped his voice in veneration the way a primitive tribesman might invoke the name of his god.

Sean lowered his feet. Then he leant forward and swept the papers that covered the desk to one side.

'Very well. Pay the man, Michael.'

Solemnly Michael placed the bag in the cleared space. But when Sean winked at him his solemnity cracked and he grinned.

Making no attempt to hide his agitation, Ronny plunged both hands into the mouth of the bag and withdrew two pouches of unbleached vancas. He loosened the draw string of one and spilled gold on to his desk.

'Where did you get this?' he demanded angrily.

'At the end of the rainbow.'

'There's a fortune here,' Ronny protested, as he dipped into the carpet-bag again.

'A Goodly amount, I'll admit.'

'But, but . . .' Ronny was scratching in the pile of coins, hunting for the secret of their origin like a hen for a worm. However, Sean had spent a week in Johannesburg and another two days in Pietermaritzburg visiting every bank and exchanging small parcels of Kruger coin for Victorian and Portuguese, and the coin of half a dozen other States. For a minute Sean watched his efforts with a smile of happy contempt. Then he excused himself.

'We'll be getting on home now.' Sean placed an arm around Michael's shoulder and led him to the door.

'Deposit the balance to my account, there's a good fellow.'

Further protest stillborn on his lips, and despair mingled with frustration, Ronny Pye watched through the window as Lion Kop Wattle Estates climbed up into the buggy, settled its hat firmly, waved a whip in a courteous farewell and trotted sedately out of his clutches.

All that summer the hills of Lion Kop echoed to the thud of axes and the singing of hundreds of Zulus. As each tree toppled and fell in a froth of heaving branches, men with cane-knives moved forward to strip the rich bark and tie it in bundles. Every train that left for Pietermaritzburg towed truckloads of it to the extract plant.

Each long day together strengthened the bonds between Sean and Michael. The evolved a language of their own, notable only for its economy of words. Without lengthy discussion each took charge of a separate sphere of Lion Kop activity. Michael made himself responsible for the maintenance of equipment, the loading and dispatch, all the paperwork and the ordering of material. At first Sean surreptitiously checked his work, but when he found no fault in it he no longer bothered. They parted only at the end of each week; Sean to Pietermaritzburg for obvious reasons, and Michael to Theuniskrral in duty. Michael hated those returns home, he hated Anna's endless accusations of disloyalty and her occasional fits of weeping. But even worse was the silent reproach in Garry's face. Early each Monday morning, with the joy of a released convict he set off for Lion Kop and Sean's welcome:

'What about those bloody axe handles, Mike?'

Only in the evenings they talked freely sitting together on the stoep of the homestead. They spoke of money and war and politics and women and wattle – and they talked as equals, without reserve, as men who work together with a common purpose.

Dirk sat quietly in the shadows and listened to them. Fifteen years old, but Dirk had a capacity for hatred out of all proportion to his age, and he used it all on Michael. Sean's handling of Dirk was in no way different; his school attendance was still spasmodic, he trailed Sean about the plantations and received his full share of rough affection and even rougher discipline – yet he sensed in the relationship between Sean and Michael a terrible threat to his security. Merely by reason of age and experience he was excluded from the evening discussions on the stoep. His few contributions were received with indulgent attention, then the talk would be resumed as though he had not spoken. Dirk sat quietly planning in lurid detail his assassination of Michael. On Lion Kop that summer there were small thefts and unexplained acts of vandalism, all of which affected only Michael. His best riding-boots vanished, his single dress shirt was ripped down the back when he came to don it for the monthly dance at the schoolhouse, his pointer bitch whelped a litter of four puppies, which survived only a week before Michael found them dead in the straw of the barn.


Ada and her young ladies began preparing for the Christmas of 1904 in the middle of December. As their guests, Ruth and Storm came down from Pietermaritzburg on the twentieth and Sean's frequent absences from Lion Kop left a heavy burden of work on Michael. There was an air of mystery in the Protea Street cottage. Sean was strictly excluded from the long sessions in Ada's private rooms, where she and Ruth retired to plan the wedding dress, but this was not the only secret. There was something else, which was keeping all the young ladies in fits of suppressed giggles and excitement. With a little eavesdropping Sean gathered it was something to do with his Christmas present from Ruth. However, Sean had other worries, chief of which was maintaining his position in the fierce competition for Miss Storm Friedman's favours. This included a heavy expenditure on sweetmeats, which were delivered to Storm without Ruth's knowledge. The Shetland pony had been left in Pietermaritzburg and Sean was required to substitute at the cost of his dignity and grass stains on the knees of his breeches. As reward he was invited to take tea each afternoon with Storm and her dolls.

Favourite among all Storm's dolls was a female child with human hair and an insipid expression on its large china face. Storm wept with a broken heart when she found that china head shattered into many pieces. With Sean's help she buried it in the back yard and they stripped Ada's garden of flowers for the grave. Sullenly Dirk watched the funeral. Storm was now completely reconciled to her loss and so thoroughly enjoyed the ceremony that she insisted Sean exhume the body and start again. In all the doll was buried four times and Ada's garden looked as though a swarm of locusts had descended upon it.

## Chapter Seventy-three

Christmas Day started early for Sean. He and Michael supervised the slaughter of ten large oxen for the Zulu labour force, then distributed pay and gifts. To each man a khaki shirt and short pants, and for each of their wives a double handful of coloured beads. There was much singing and laughter. Mbejane, risen from his sickbed for the occasion, made a speech of high dramatic content. Unable to prance on his freshly healed legs, yet he shook his spears, postured and roared his questions at them.

'Has he beaten you?'

'*Ai-bho!*' They hurled the negative back at him.

'Has he fed you?'

'*Yhe-bho!*' explosive accent.

'Is there gold in your pockets?'

'*Yhe-bho!*'

'Is he our father?'

'He is our father!'

All to be construed not too literally, Sean grinned. Then he stepped forward to accept the large earthen pot of millet beer that Mbejane's senior wife presented to him. It was a matter of honour that this be emptied without removing it from the lips, a feat which Sean and then Michael both accomplished. Then they climbed up into the waiting buggy. Mbejane took the reins and with Dirk on the seat beside him drove them down to Ladyburg.

After the first flurry of greeting and good wishes, Ruth led Sean into the back yard followed by everyone else. There stood a large object covered by a tarpaulin which was ceremoniously removed and Sean gaped at what Ruth had given him.

Its paintwork burnished to a high gloss, metal parts and polished leather upholstery sparkling in the sun – stood a motor vehicle.

Stamped in the huge metal wheel hubs, and below the mascot on the radiator were the words 'Rolls-Royce'.

Sean had seen these fiendishly beautiful machines in Johannesburg, and now he was overcome by the feeling of unease they had given him then.

'My dear Ruth, I haven't the words to thank you.' He kissed her heartily to delay the moment when he must approach the monster.

'Do you really like it?'

'Like it? It's the most magnificent thing I have ever seen.' Over her shoulder Sean noticed with relief that Michael had taken over. As the only engineer present, he was seated behind the wheel and speaking authoritatively to the crowd about him.

'Get in!' Ruth ordered.

'Let me look at it first.' With Ruth on his arm, Sean circled the Rolls, never approaching closer than half a dozen paces. The great headlights glared at him malevolently and Sean averted his eyes. His unease was slowly becoming genuine fear as he realized that he was expected not only to ride in the thing, but to direct its course and speed.

Unable to delay longer, he approach and patted the bonnet.

'Hey there!' he told it grimly. With an unbroken animal you must establish mastery from the first contact.

'Get in!' Michael was still in charge and Sean obeyed, placing Ruth in the middle of the front seat and himself nearest the door. On Ruth's lap Storm bounded and squealed with excitement. The delay while Michael consulted the handbook at length did nothing for Sean's confidence.

'Ruth, don't you think it wise to leave Storm behind – just this first time?'

'Oh, she isn't any trouble.' Ruth regarded him quizzically, then smiled. 'It's really quite safe, darling.' Despite her assurance, Sean stiffened in terror when the motor finally roared into life; and he held that pose, staring fixedly ahead, during the whole of their triumphal progress through the streets of Ladyburg. Citizens and servants boiled from the houses along their route and lined the road to cheer in wonder and delight.

At last they were back in Protea Street and when Michael stopped outside the cottage Sean escaped from the vehicle like a man waking from a nightmare. He firmly vetoed the suggestion that the family motor to church, on the grounds that it was irreverent and in bad taste. The Reverend Smiley was flattered that Sean remained awake throughout his sermon, and judged by Sean's worried expression that at last he was in fear for his soul.

After church Michael went out to Theuniskraal to eat Christmas dinner with his parents, but returned early in the afternoon to begin Sean's instruction. The entire population of Ladyburg turned out to watch Sean and Michael circling the block at a walking pace. By early evening Michael decided that Sean was ready for a solo circuit and accordingly he disembarked.

Alone at the wheel, sweating nervously, Sean looked at the sea of expectant faces around him and saw Mbejane grinning hugely in the background.

'Mbejane!' he bellowed.

'Nkosi!'

'Come with me,' and Mbejane's grin dissolved. He backed away a little. It was unnatural that a vehicle should move of its own accord – and Mbejane wanted no part of it.

'Nkosi, there is much pain still in my legs.'

Among the crowd were many of the Zulu labourers from Lion Kop, who had come down from the hills when news of the miracle reached them. Now one of these laughed in such a manner as to cast doubt on Mbejane's courage.

Mbejane drew himself to his full height and withered the man with his eyes, then he stalked proudly to the Rolls, sat on the seat beside Sean and folded his arms across his chest.

Sean drew a deep breath and gripped the steering-wheel with both hands, his eyes narrowed and he scowled ahead down the road.

'Clutch in!' he muttered to himself. 'In gear! Brake off! Throttle down! Clutch out!'

The Rolls leapt forward so violently that both he and Mbejane were nearly thrown over the back of the seat. Fifty yards farther on the machine expired from lack of fuel, a stroke of good fortune because it was unlikely that Sean would have been able to remember the procedure for stopping it.

Grey of face and unsteady of limb, Mbejane alighted from the Rolls for the last time. He never rode in it again – and secretly Sean envied him his freedom. He was greatly relieved to hear that it would be weeks before more fuel could be sent up from Cape Town.

## Chapter Seventy-four

Three weeks before Sean's wedding Ada Courtney went into her orchard one morning early to pick fruit for breakfast. She found Mary there, dressed in her white nightgown, and hanging by her neck from the big avocado tree. Ada cut her down and sent one of the servants to call Doctor Fraser.

Between them they carried the dead girl to her cubicle and laid her on her bed. While Doc Fraser made a hasty examination Ada stood staring down at the face that death had made more pitiful.

'What depths of loneliness drove her to this,' she whispered, and Doc Fraser pulled the sheet over the corpse and looked across at Ada.

'That wasn't the reason – in fact, it might have been better if she were a little more lonely.' He pulled out his tobacco pouch and began to load his pipe. 'Who was her boy friend, Aunt Ada?'

'She had none.'

'She must have.'

'Why do you say that?'

'Aunt Ada, this girl was four months pregnant.'

It was a small funeral, just the Courtney family and Ada's girls. Mary was an orphan and she had no other friends.

Two weeks before the wedding, Sean and Michael finished the season's cut of bark and switched the Zulus to planting out the blocks destroyed by the fire. Together they drew up a draft Profit and Loss Account. Combining their rudimentary knowledge of accounting and arguing far into the night, they finally agreed that from fifteen hundred acres of wattle they had cut fourteen hundred and twenty tons of bark, to gross a little over twenty-eight thousand pounds sterling.

But here all agreement ended. Michael insisted that the stocks of material and expenditure on planting of new trees be carried forward, giving a net profit for the year of nine thousand pounds. Sean wanted to write all expenditure off against income and show a profit of one thousand, so they deadlocked and finally sent all the books to a qualified accountant in Pietermaritzburg. This gentleman sided with Michael.

They then considered the prospects for the coming season and were a little awed when they realized that there would be four thousand acres of wattle to reap and an expected gross of eighty thousand pounds sterling – always providing there were no more fires. That evening, without Sean's knowledge, Michael wrote two letters. One to a manufacturer of heavy machinery in Birmingham, whose name and address Michael had furtively copied from one of the huge boilers in the Natal Wattle Estate Company's plant. The other to the firm of Foyle's booksellers in Charing Cross Road, London, requesting the immediate dispatch of all and any literature on processing of wattle bark. Michael Courtney had caught from Sean the habit of dreaming extravagantly. He had also acquired the trick of setting out to make those dreams become reality.

Three days before the wedding Ada and her young ladies set out for Pietermaritzburg by train and Sean, Michael and Dirk followed in the Rolls.

The three of them arrived dusty and bad-tempered outside the White Horse Hotel. It had been a nerve-racking journey. Sean had enlivened it by shouting incessant warnings, instruction and blasphemy at Michael, the driver.

'Slow down, for God's sake, slow down! Do you want to kill us all!'

'Look out! What that cow!'

'Don't drive so close to the verge!'

Dirk had done his share by demanding halts for urination, hanging over the sides, climbing tirelessly between the front and back seats, and urging Michael to exceed the speed-limit set by Sean. Finally, in anger, Sean had Michael stop the car and administered corporal punishment with the birch of a melkbos tree cut from beside the road.

On arrival Dirk was met by Ada, and led away snivelling. Michael took the Rolls and disappeared in the direction of the Natal Wattle Company's plant, where he was to spend most of the following three days snooping and asking questions, and Sean went to find Jan Paulus Leroux, who had come down from Pretoria in response to Sean's wedding invitation. By the day of the wedding Michael Courtney had complied a small volume of notes on wattle processing, and Jan Paulus had given Sean a minute account of the aims and objects of the South African Party. But in response to his urgings Sean had promised only to 'think about it'.

The wedding ceremony had given everybody much cause for thought. Although Sean had no qualms about marrying in a synagogue, yet he steadfastly refused to undergo the painful little operation which would enable him to do so. His half-hearted suggestion that Ruth should convert to Christianity was met with a curt rejection. Finally, a compromise was agreed, and Ben Goldberg persuaded the local Magistrate to perform a civil ceremony in the dining-room of The Golds.

Ben Goldberg gave the bride away and Ma Goldberg wept a little. Ruth was mangificent in Ada's creation of green satin and seed pearls. Storm wore an exact miniature of Ruth's dress and sparked off a minor brawl with the other flower girls during the ceremony. Michael as Best Man conducted himself with aplomb. He quelled the riot among the flower girls, produced the wedding ring on cue and prompted the groom when he muffed his lines.

The reception on the lawns was attended by a huge crowd of the Goldbergs' friends and business associates and by half the population of Ladyburg, including Ronny Pye, Dennis Petersen and their families. Garrick and Anna Courtney were not there, nor had they acknowledged the invitation.

Brilliant sunshine blessed the day and the lawns were smooth and green as expensive carpets. There were long trestle tables laden with the fruits of Ma Goldberg's kitchen and the products of Ben Goldberg's brewery.

Storm Friedman went from group to group of guests, boosting up her skirts to display the pink ribbons in her pantaloons, until Ruth caught her at it.

Having found his first taste of champagne very much to his liking, Dirk went on to drink six glasses of it behind the rose bushes. He was then copiously ill. Fortunately Michael found him before Sean did, and spirited him away to one of the guest bedrooms and left him there to languish.

With Ruth on his arm, Sean inspected the display of wedding gifts and was impressed. He then circulated among the crowds on the lawn until he reached Jan Paulus and fell into an earnest political discussion. Ruth left them to it and went to change into her going-away clothes.

The prettiest and most blonde of Ada's young ladies caught the bouquet. Immediately thereafter she caught Michael's eye and blushed to match the crimson carnations in her hand.

Amid a hum of appreciative comment and a snowstorm of confetti Ruth returned and, a queen ascending the throne, took her seat in the Rolls. Beside her Sean, in dustcoat and goggles, steeled himself, muttered his usual incantations and gave the Rolls its head. Like a wild horse the machine seemed to rear on its hind wheels and then tear down the driveway scattering gravel and guests. Ruth cluthing desperately at a large hatful of ostrich feathers and Sean shouting at the Rolls to 'Whoa! There, girl,' – they headed out along the road that led through the Valley of a Thousand Hills to Durban and the sea, and disappeared in a tall column of dust.

# Chapter Seventy-five

Three months later, having picked up Storm from Ma Goldberg *en passant*, they reappeared at Lion Kop homestead. Sean had put on weight and both of them had that smugly complacent look found only in the faces of couples returning from a successful honeymoon.

On the front stoep and in the outbuildings of Lion Kop were the crates and packing-cases which contained wedding gifts, Ruth's furniture and carpets, and the additional furniture and curtains they had purchased in Durban. Ruth, ably assisted by Ada, threw herself joyously into the task of unpacking and moving in. Meanwhile Sean began a tour of inspection of the estate to determine how much of it had suffered in his absence, and he felt vaguely cheated when he found that Michael had managed very well without him. The plantations were trim and cleared of undergrowth, the vast black scar through their centre was nearly obliterated with freshly planted rows of saplings, the labour force was half as productive again under the new incentive payment scheme which Michael, in consultation with the Accountant, had introduced. Sean gave Michael a lecture on 'not getting too bloody clever' and 'learning to walk before you run' which he ended with a few words of praise.

Thus encouraged, Michael approached Sean one night when he was alone in his study. Sean was in a state of deep contentment induced by a meal from an enormous roast sirloin which he was digesting, by the fact that Ruth had finally agreed to his adoption of Storm and the change of her name from Friedman to Courtney, and by the prospect of joining Ruth in their gartantuan double bed just as soon as he finished his brandy and his hand-rolled Havana cigar.

'Come in, Michael. Sit down. Have a brandy.' Sean greeted him genially, and almost defiantly Michael crossed the Persian carpet and laid a thick sheaf of papers on the desk in front of him.

'What's this all about?' Sean smiled at him.

'Read it and you'll see.' Michael retreated to a chair across the room. Still smiling Sean glanced at the heading on the top sheet.

'Preliminary estimates and ground plan for proposed Tannin Extraction Plant. Lion Kop Estates.'

The smile faded. Sean turned the page and as he read he began to frown and then to scowl. When at last he finished he relit his dead cigar and sat in silence for five minutes while he recovered from the shock.

'Who put you up to this?'

'Nobody.'

'Where would you sell your extract?'

'Page 5. The outlets are listed there – and the ruling prices over the last ten years.'

'This plant needs 20,000 tons of bark a year – if we planted every foot of Lion Kop and Mahobo's Kloof to wattle we could only supply half of that.'

'We'd buy the rest from the new estates along the valley – we could offer a better price than Jackson, because we'd save railage to Pietermaritzburg.'

'Who would run the plant?'

'I'm an engineer.'

'On paper you are,' Sean grunted. 'What about water?'

'We'd dam the Baboon Stroom above the falls.'

For an hour Sean poked and prodded at the scheme, seeking for a soft spot. His agitation mounted as Michael calmly met each of his queries.

'All right.' Sean growled. 'You've done your homework. Now answer me this one. How the hell do you propose finding seventy thousand pounds to finance this little lot?'

Michael closed his eyes as though he were praying, his jaw was a hard, thrusting line. And suddenly Sean wondered why he had never noticed the strength in that face, the stubborn almost fanatical determination. Michael opened his eyes again and spoke softly.

'A loan on Lion Kop and Mahobo's Kloof for twenty-five thousand, a notarial bond on the plant for as much again – and a public share issue on the balance.'

Sean jumped up from his desk and roared.

'No!'

'Why not?' still calmly and reasonably.

'Because I've spent half my life in debt up to here!' Sean grabbed his own throat. 'Because now at last I'm in the clear and I want to stay that way. Because I know what it feels like to have more money than I need, and I don't like the feeling. Because I'm happy just the way things are now – and I don't want to catch another lion by the tail and have him turn round and claw the hell out of me.' He stopped panting and then shouted: 'Because a certain amount of money belongs to you, but more than that you belong to it. Because I don't want to be that wealthy again!'

Lean and fast as an angry leopard, Michael came out of his chair and smashed a balled fist on to the top of the desk. He glared across at Sean, flushed angry red under his tan, quivering like an arrow.

'Well, I do! Your only objection to my plan is that it's sound,' he blazed. Sean blinked in surprise and then rallied.

'If you get it, you won't like it!' he bellowed, and Michael matched his volume.

'Let me be the judge of that!'

At that moment the door of the study opened and Ruth stood on the threshold and stared at them. They looked like a pair of game cocks with their hackles up.

'What on earth is going on?' she demanded. Both Michael and Sean looked up guiltily, then slowly they relaxed. Michael sat down and Sean coughed awkwardly.

'We are just having a discussion, my dear.'

'Well, you've woken Storm and just about torn the roof off.' Then she smiled and crossed to take Sean's arm. 'Why don't you leave it until tomorrow. Then you can continue your discussion at twenty paces with pistols.'

The pygmies of the Ituri Forests hunt elephant with tiny arrows. Once the barb is lodged they follow quietly and doggedly, camping night after night on the spoor until at last the poison works its way to the animal's heart and brings it down. Michael had placed his arrow-head deep in Sean's flesh.

## Chapter Seventy-six

At Lion Kop Ruth found a happiness she had never expected, had not believed existed.

Up to this time her existence had been ordered and determined by an adoring but strict father, and then in the same manner by Ben Goldberg. The few short years with Saul Friedman has been happy, but now they were as unreal as memories of childhood. Always she had been wrapped in a cocoon of wealth, hemmed in by social taboos and the dignity of the family. Even Saul had treated her as a delicate child for whom all decisions must be made. Life had been placid and orderly, but deadly dull. Only twice she had rebelled, once to run away from Pretoria and again when she had gone to Sean in the hospital. Boredom had been her constant companion.

But now suddenly she was mistress of a complex community. The sensation had been a little overpowering at first and from habit she had appealed to Sean for him to make the fifty decisions that each day brought forward.

'I'll make a bargain with you,' he answered. 'You don't tell me how to grow wattle and I'll not tell you how to run the house – put the damn sideboard where it looks best.'

Hesitantly at first, then with growing confidence and at last with sureness and pride she made Lion Kop into a home of beauty and comfort. The coarse grass and scrub around the homestead fell back to make room for lawns and flower-beds, the outer walls of Lion Kop gleamed in a crisp new coat of whitewash. Inside, the yellow-wood floors shone like polished amber setting off the vivid Bokhara carpets and draped velvet curtains.

After a few disastrous experiments the kitchens began to yield a succession of meals that moved Michael to raptures, and even Sean pronounced them edible.

Yet, with a dozen servants, she had time for other things. To read, to play with Storm and to ride. Sean's wedding gift to her was a string of four golden palaminos. There was time also for long visits from and with Ada

Courtney. The two of them established an accord stronger than that of mother and daughter.

There was time for dancing and barbecues, there was time for laughter and for long quiet evenings when she and Sean sat alone on the wide front stoep or in his study and talked of many things.

There was time for love.

Her body, hard from riding and walking, was also healthy and hot. It was a sculpture sheathed in velvet and fashioned for love.

There was only one dark place in her happiness – Dirk Courtney.

When her overtures were met with sullenness and her small specially cooked gifts were rejected, she realized the cause of his antagonism. She sensed the bitter jealousy which was eating like a canker behind those lovely eyes and the passionately beautiful face. For days she prepared what she would say to him. Then she found the opportunity when he came into the kitchens while she was alone. He saw her and turned quickly to leave, but she stopped him.

'Oh, Dirk, please don't go. I want to discuss something with you.' He came back slowly and leaned against the table. She saw how tall he had grown in the last year, his shoulders were thickening into the shape of manhood and his legs were strong and tapered from the narrow hips that he thrust forward in a calculated insolence.

'Dirk . . .' she began and paused. Suddenly she was unsure of herself. This was not a child as she had imagined; there was a sensuality in that beautiful face she found disturbing – he carried his body with awareness, moving like a cat. Suddenly she was afraid, and she swallowed jerkily before she went on:

'I know how difficult it has been for you – since Storm and I came to live here. I know how much you love your father, how much he means to you. But . . .' She spoke slowly, her carefully prepared speech forgotten so that she had to grope for the words to explain. She tried to show him that they were not in competition for Sean's love; that all of them – Ruth, Michael, Storm and Dirk – formed a whole; that their interests did not overlap, but that each of them gave to Sean and received from him a different kind of love. When at last she faltered into silence she knew he had not listened nor tried to understand. 'Dirk, I like you and I want you to like me.'

With a thrust of his buttocks against the table, Dirk straightened up. He smiled then and let his eyes move down over her body, slowly.

'Can I go now?' he asked, and Ruth stiffened. Then she knew there was no compromise, that she would have to fight him.

'Yes, Dirk. You may go,' she answered. She knew with sudden clarity that he was evil, and if she lost this contest he would destroy her and her child. In that moment she was no longer afraid.

Catlike, Dirk seemed to sense the change in her. For a moment she thought she saw a flicker of doubt, of uncertainty in his eyes – then he turned away and sauntered out of the kitchen.

She guessed that it would come soon, but not as soon as it did.

Every afternoon Ruth would ride out into the plantations with Storm's pony on a lead rein beside her. They made a game of finding Sean and Michael, following the labyrinth of roads that criss-crossed through the blocks of trees, guided by the vague directions of the gangs of Zulus until finally they ran them down and delivered the canteens of coffee and the hamper of sandwiches. Then, all four of them would picnic on the soft carpet of dead leaves beneath the trees.

This afternoon, dressed in riding habit and carrying the hamper, Ruth came out into the kitchen yard. The young Zulu nursemaid was sitting in the shade of the kitchen wall flirting with one of the grooms. Storm was nowhere in sight, and Ruth asked sharply:

'Where is Miss Storm?'

'She went with Nkosana Dirk.' And Ruth felt the tingling premonition of danger.

'Where are they?' and the nursemaid pointed vaguely in the direction of the stables and outbuildings that sprawled away down the back slope of the hill.

'Come with me.' Ruth dropped the hamper and ran with her skirts gathered in one hand. She reached the first row of stables and hurried down them, glancing into each stall as she passed. Then into the feed rooms with the big concrete bins and the smell of oats and molasses and chopped lucerne mixing with the sharp tang of dung and dubbined leather, out again into the sunlight, running for the barns.

Storm screamed in terror, just once, but high and achingly clear, so the silence afterwards quivered with the memory of it.

*The harness room.* Ruth swirled in her run. *God, please No! Don't let it happen. Please! Please!*

She reached the open door of the harness room. It was gloomy and cool within the thick stone walls, and for a moment the scene made no sense to Ruth.

Her back wedged into the far corner, Storm stood with hands lifted to shield her face – small fingers rigid, splayed open, spread like the tip feathers of a bird's wing. Her body shook silently with her sobs.

In front of Storm, squatting on his heels, Dirk leaned forward with one hand outstretched as though he offered a gift. He was laughing.

Then Ruth saw the thing in Dirk's hand move and she froze with horror. It uncoiled from around his wrist, and slowly reached out towards Storm, its head cocked back in a half-loop of its body, tiny black tongue vibrating between the grinning pink lips.

Ruth screamed, and Dirk jumped to his feet and spun to face her with his right hand hidden behind his back.

From the corner Storm darted across the room and buried her face in Ruth's skirts, weeping piteously. Ruth picked her up and held her tight against her shoulder, but she never took her eyes off Dirk's face.

'It's only a *rooi-slang*.' Dirk laughed again, but nervously. 'They're harmless – I was only having a joke.' He brought the snake out from behind his back, dropped it on to the stone-flagged floor and crushed its head under the heel of his riding-boot. He kicked it away against the wall, then with an impatient gesture he brushed the black curls from his forehead and made to leave the room. Ruth stepped across to block his path.

'Nannie, take Miss Storm back to the house.' Gently Ruth handed the child to the Zulu nursemaid and closed the door after them and slid the bolt across.

Now it was darker in the room, two square shafts of sunlight filled with moving dust motes fell from the high windows, and the quiet was spoiled only by the sound of Ruth's laboured breathing.

'I was only having a joke,' Dirk repeated, and grinned defiance at her. 'I suppose you'll run and tell my father?'

The walls of the room were studded with wooden pegs from which were suspended the harness and saddlery. Beside the door hung Sean's raw-hide stockwhips, eight foot of braided leather tapering from the butt handle into nothingness. Ruth lifted one down from the rack and flicked the lash out to lie upon the floor between them.

'No, Dirk, I'm not going to tell your father. This thing is between you and me alone.'

'What are you going to do?'

'I'm going to settle it.'

'How?' Still grinning, he placed his hands on his hips. Beneath rolled sleeves his upper arms bulged smooth and brown as though they had been freshly oiled.

'Like this.' Ruth flicked her skirt aside and stepped forward, using the whip underhand she sent the lash snaking out to coil around Dirk's ankle and immediately she jerked back on it. Taken completely off balance, Dirk went over backwards. His head hit the wall as he fell and he lay stunned.

To give herself space in which to wield the whip, Ruth moved into the centre of the room. Her anger was cold as dry ice, it gave strength to arms already finely muscled from riding, and it seared away all mercy. Now she was a female animal fighting for the survival of herself and her child.

She had learned to use a stockwhip in the process of becoming an expert horsewoman, and her first blow split Dirk's shirt from the shoulder to the waist. He shouted with anger and rolled on to his knees. The next blow cut down from the base of his neck along his spine, paralysing him in the act of rising. The next, across the back of both knees, knocked his legs out from under him.

On his belly Dirk reached for the pitchfork against the wall, but braided leather exploded around his wrist. He shouted again and rolled on his side to nurse the hand against his chest.

Ruth hit him and he writhed across the floor towards her like a wounded leopard with its hindquarters shattered by buckshot. Step by step Ruth retreated before him, and the long lash hissed and cracked.

Without mercy she beat him until his shirt hung in tatters from his waist and shoulders, exposing the smooth white skin with the fat crimson welts superimposed upon it.

She beat him until his shouts turned to shrieks and finally to sobbing.

She beat him until he lay shivering, moaning, moving feebly with his blood sprinkled in dark blobs on the stone paving around him.

Then she folded the whip and turned to open the door. In the stable yard, standing in silent curiosity, were gathered all the grooms and the household servants.

Ruth selected four of them.

'Take the Nkosana to his room.'
Then to one of the grooms,
'Ride to the Nkosi. Tell him to come quickly.'


Sean came quickly, he came wild with anxiety and nearly tore the door off Dirk's bedroom in his haste. He stopped dead on the threshold and stared aghast at Dirk's back.

Stripped to the waist, Dirk lay face downwards on his bed and Ruth worked over him with a sponge. On the table beside her stood a steaming basin and the pungent reek of antiseptic filled the room.

'Good God! What happened to him?'

'I beat him with a stockwhip.' Ruth answered him calmly and Sean gaped at her, then dropped his gaze to Dirk.

'You did that?'

'Yes.'

The anger tightened Sean's mouth.

'Jesus God! You've cut him to pieces. You've half killed him.' And he glanced at Ruth. 'Why?'

'It was necessary.' The absolute assurance and lack of remorse in her reply, confused Sean. He was suddenly uncertain in his anger.

'What did he do?'

'I can't tell you that. It is something private between us. You must ask Dirk.'

Sean crossed quickly to the bed and knelt beside it.

'Dirk. Dirkie, my boy, what happened. What did you do?' And Dirk lifted his face from the pillow and looked at his father.

'It was a mistake. It doesn't matter.' Then he buried his face in the pillow once more, and his voice was muffled, so Sean had excuse for not believing that he had heard correctly.

'What did you say?' he demanded, and there was a short delay before Dirk replied quite distinctly,

'I said – it was my fault.'

'That's what I thought you said.' Sean stood up with a puzzled expression on his face. 'Well, I don't know why you sent for me, Ruth. You seem to have the situation fairly well in hand.' He moved to the door, looked back as though he were going to speak, then, changing his mind, he shook his head and went out.

That night in the quiet, exhausted minutes before sleep, Sean murmured against her cheek, 'I think you did today what I should have done years ago.' And then, with a sleepy chuckle, 'At least there's no doubt in anyone's mind as to who is the mistress of Lion Kop.'

# Chapter Seventy-seven

There was a guileless simplicity in Sean's approach to life – in his mind any problem when met with direct action disintegrated.

If you became obsessed with a woman, you tumbled her. If that didn't produce the desired effect, then you married her.

If you wanted a piece of land or a horse or a house or a gold mine, then you paid your money and took it. If you didn't have the money, you went out and found it.

If you liked a man you drank with him, hunted with him, laughed together. If you disliked him, you either punched him in the head or subjected him to a ponderous sarcasm and mockery. Either way you left him in no doubt of your feelings.

When a son got out of hand you whaled the tripe out of him, then gave him an expensive present to demonstrate your affection. Now he admitted he had been tardy in the matter of Dirk; but Ruth had done a most effective job. It only remained for him to call Dirk into the study and shout at him a little. A week later he returned from a trip to Pietermaritzburg and with an embarrased scowl presented to Dirk his peace offerings. The first was a brassbound leather case, which contained a hand-made shotgun by Greener of London; tooled silver inlay, glossy walnut stock and butt, and interchangeable Damascus barrels. The other was a two-year-old filly from the Hugeunot stud at Worcester in the Cape. By Sun Lord out of Harvest Dance, Sun Dancer was an animal of the most distinguished blood in Africa and of surpassing beauty and speed. Sean paid a thousand guineas for her and considered he had got the best of the bargain.

As far as he was concerned there was no longer any problem with Dirk, and Sean could devote all his energy to furthering the three major ventures in which he was engaged.

Firstly, there was the matter of putting Ruth with child. Here he had her wholehearted co-operation. But their efforts, apart from providing a deal of healthy exercise and pleasure, were singularly unproductive. Sean remembered the deadly skill he had shown in their first encounter and was puzzled. Ruth suggested they keep in training until the rainy season began; she had developed a superstitious belief in the power of thunder. On one of his trips to Pietermaritzburg Sean saw a carved wooden statue of Thor in a junk dealer's window. He bought it for her, and from then on the god stood on their bedside table clutching his hammer and overlooking their strivings with such a knowing expression that at last Ruth turned him face to the wall.

Then there was Michael's Tannin Extract Plant. He had resorted to a piece of underhand villainy that shocked Sean and, he professed, killed his

belief in the essential decency of mankind. Michael had visited each of the
new growers along the valley, men who had followed Sean's lead in the
planting of wattle, and after swearing them to secrecy had offered them
shares in the Company. They were enthusiastic and with Michael at the
head they visited Lion Kop in formal deputation. The meeting was conducted
with so much verbal thunder and lightning thrown about that the Great
God Thor might have been in the Chair. At the end Sean, who had teased
the idea all the months since Michael had approached him and who was
now as enthusiastic as any of them, allowed himself to be persuaded. He
spoke for seventy per cent of the shares and the balance was allotted to the
other growers. A Board of Directors, with Sean as Chairman, was elected
and the Accountant was instructed to proceed with the registration of The
Ladyburg Wattle Co-operative Ltd. For the first time Sean exercised his
majority vote to crush the misgivings of the other shareholders and appoint
Michael Courtney as Plant Engineer. Then, with an older director to act
as a steadying influence, Michael was put aboard the next Union Castle
mailship for England, a letter of authority in his pocket and Sean's warnings
and words of wisdom in his head. Remembering himself at the age of twenty-
three, Sean decided it necessary to point out to Michael that he was being
sent to London to buy machinery and increase his knowledge of it, not to
populate the British Isles nor to tour their hostelries and gaming
establishments.

There was swift reaction from Jackson at Natal Wattle, who regretted
that the contracts between the Tugela Valley growers and his company
would not be renewed – and that owing to heavy demands from elsewhere
he could no longer supply seed or saplings. But Sean's seedbeds were now
well enough established to meet the needs of the whole valley – and, with
luck, their plant would be in production by the beginning of the next cutting
season.

Before Michael and his chaperon returned flushed with the success of
their mission, Sean had another visitor. Jan Paulus Leroux, weary of the
three-year argument he and Sean had conducted with the aid of the postal
authority, arrived at Ladyburg and expressed his intention of staying until
Sean agreed to head the Natal branch of the South African Party and to
contest the Ladyburg seat at the next Legislative Assembly elections. Two
weeks later, after he and Sean had hunted and killed a number of guinea-
fowl, pheasant and bush buck; had consumed huge quantities of coffee and
more moderate quantities of brandy; had talked each other hoarse and had
closed the last gap between them, Jan Paulus left on the Johannesburg train
with the parting words:

'*Toe Maar!* It is settled then.'

The South African Party's platform was a Federation of the Cape, the
Transvaal, the Orange Free State and Natal, under government responsible
to Whitehall. It was opposed by extreme English and Dutch opinion – the
jingoes who shouted 'God Save the King', and the Republicans who wanted
the Almighty to treat the King differently.

After meeting with the men on the list Jan Paulus had given him, Sean
began the campaign. His first convert was Ruth Courtney, won over by the
prospect of the excitement associated with an election battle rather than by

Sean's oratory. Now a week or more of every month was spent in travelling about Natal to attend political gatherings. Ruth rehearsed Sean in his speech – he had only one – until he was word perfect. She kissed the babies and played hostess to the wives, tasks in which Sean showed no special aptitude. She sat beside him on the platform and restrained him from going down into the audience to engage in hand-to-hand combat with hecklers. The way she smiled and the way she walked certainly lost no votes for the South African Party. From London Lord Caisterbrook promised his support, and it looked as though Sean could count on twenty-two seats out of the Assembly's thirty.

On the level ground below the escarpment, hard by the Baboon Stroom, the plant of the Ladyburg Wattle Co-operative took shape. It covered ten acres of ground and beyond it the cottages of the employees were laid out in neat blocks.

Despite Michael's vehement protests, Sean bowed to the will of his fellow directors and a consulting engineer was employed until such time as the plant was in production. Without him they would have lost a year's harvest of bark, for although Michael was eager and tireless, yet he was a young man with no practical experience. Even with the older man to help him, the plant was still a long way from ready before the season's cutting began. When at last the tall silver smoke stack began spewing smoke and the furnaces lit the night with a satanic glow, there were thousands of tons of bark piled up in the open-sided warehouses around the factory.

It was a wonderful season. Good rains had filled the bark with rich sap and when the year ended the Co-operative had shown a profit of ten thousand pounds on its first year's operation – Lion Kop Estates a profit four times greater. Sean had been in and out of debt as swiftly as a small boy visits the bathroom when sent to wash his face.

Despite the good rains, there were only three spectacular storms that summer. On each occasion Sean was away from Lion Kop on business. While the lightning leapt across the hills and the hammer strokes of thunder broke over the valley, Ruth stood at the window of their bedroom and lamented another wasted opportunity. Mbejane did much better – all his seed brought forth fruit and he reaped four fat sons that season.

## Chapter Seventy-eight

It was a busy year for Dirk Courtney also. After his resounding defeat at the thin end of the stockwhip, Dirk and Ruth fell into a state of wary neutrality – but he conceded control of Lion Kop to her

Storm Courtney he ignored, unless she was in Sean's lap or riding on his shoulder. Then he watched them covertly until he could find an excuse to interrupt their play or to get away from Lion Kop. His absences became more frequent; there were trips to Pietermaritzburg and the surrounding districts to play rugby and polo; there were mysterious night excursions to Ladyburg, and in the day he rode away at dawn each morning – Sean believed he rode to school until he received a note from the headmaster asking him to call.

After showing him the attendance register and a copy of Dirk's academic record, the headmaster leaned back in his chair and waited for Sean's comments.

'Not so good, hey?'

'I agree, Mr Courtney. Not so good.'

'Couldn't we send him to a boarding establishment somewhere, Mr Besant?'

'Yes, you could do that,' Besant agreed dubiously, 'but would it serve any real purpose – apart from providing him with expert coaching in rugby football?'

'How else will he get his University entrance?' Sean was impressed with what higher education had done for Michael. He looked upon it as a sovereign alchemy for all the ills of youth.

'Mr Courtney . . .' The headmaster hesitated delicately. He had heard of Sean's temper and did not want a personal demonstration of it. 'Some young men are not really suited for University training.'

'I want Dirk to go,' Sean interjected.

'I doubt that either Stellenbosch or Cape Town Universities share your ambitions.' The schoolroom manner re-asserted itself for a moment, and Besant spoke with dry sarcasm.

'You mean he's stupid?' Sean demanded.

'No, no.' Hurriedly Besant soothed him. 'It's just that he's not, shall we say, academically inclined.'

Sean pondered on that awhile. It seemed a very nice distinction, but he let it go and asked:

'Well, what do you suggest?'

Besant's suggestion was that Dirk Courtney get the hell out of his school – but he phrased it gently.

'Although Dirk is only sixteen – he is very mature for his age. Say you were to start him at the Wattle Company . . .?'

'You recommend I take him away from school, then?' Sean asked thoughtfully, and Besant suppressed a sigh of relief.


Dirk Courtney was apprenticed to the foreman boilermaker at the factory. His first action was to inform his journeyman that he'd be running this show one day and what was he going to do about it? That gentleman, forewarned by Dirk's reputation, regarded him dolefully, spat a long squirt of tobacco juice an inch from Dirk's gleaming toecap, and replied at some length. He then pointed to a kettle on the workshop forge and told Dirk to make him a cup of coffee, and while he was about it to remove his thumb from his posterior orifice. Within a week the two of them were cronies and the man, whose name was Archibald Frederick Longworthy, began to instruct Dirk in arts other than the fabrication of steelplate. Archy was thirty-six years old. He had come out to Africa after completing a five-year term in Leavenworth Prison for the intriguing offence of *Crimen Injuria* – and when he explained the meaning Dirk was delighted.

Archy introduced Dirk to one of his friends, Hazel, a plump and friendly girl who worked at the Ladyburg Hotel as a barmaid and dispensed her favours in the same cheerful manner that she did her liquor – but Dirk quickly became her favourite, and he learned some pretty little tricks from her.

Shrewdly, Archibald Longworthy examined the situation and decided that nothing but profit could come from friendship with Sean Courtney's heir. Besides which the boy was a lot of fun. He could tumble a tart and swig gin with the best of them – also he had a seemingly inexhaustible supply of sovereigns.

In exchange Dirk hero-worshipped Archy, diverting much of his feelings from his father to his first real friend. Ignoring the grey wrists and neck which bespoke Archy's disaffection for soap and water, the pale wispy hair through which pink scalp showed, ignoring also the black tooth in the front of his mouth – Dirk invested him with the glamour and excitement of an old-time pirate.

When Dirk found himself to be suffering from a painless but evil-smelling condition, it was Archy who assured him it was only '*whites*' and went with him to a doctor in Pietermaritzburg. On the train coming home they planned their revenge with much laughter, comradely banter – and rising anticipation.

Hazel was surprised to see them in the middle of a Sunday afternoon, she sat up quickly as they came into her room overlooking the backyard of the hotel.

'Dirkie, you shouldn't come here in the daytime – your Pa will find out.' It was warm in the shabby little room, and the smell of cheap scent and a half-filled chamber-pot blended harshly with the odour of female perspiration. Hazel's thin chemise clung damply to her body and outlined the heavy hang of her breasts and the deep lateral fold around the level of her navel. There were dark smudges below her eyes and a curl was sweat-plastered down her cheek where the pillow had left little creases in the skin. The two of them stood in the doorway and grinned at her, from many experiences Hazel recognized the wolfish eagerness those grins masked.

'What do you want?' Suddenly she was afraid and instinctively she covered the deep cleft of her bosom with one hand.

'Dirkie here wants to have a little chat with you.' Carefully Archy closed the door and turned the key in the lock, then he ambled towards the bed. Manual labour had sheathed his arms in hard, knotty muscle and the hands that hung at his sides were disproportionately large and coated with coarse, blond hair.

'You keep away from me, Archy Longworthy.' Hazel swung her legs off the bed, the chemise pulled up to expose fat white thighs. 'I don't want no trouble, you just leave me alone.'

'You give Dirkie here a clap. Now Dirkie here is my friend and he don't like what you give him.'

'I didn't! It couldn't have been me. I'm clean – I tell you.' She stood up, still holding the front of her chemise closed and back away before him. 'You keep away from me.' Then as Archy jumped forward, 'No – don't I'll . . .' And she opened her mouth to scream, but Archy's hand closed over it like a great hairy spider. She struggled desperately, clawing at the hand over her face.

'Come on, Dirk.' Archy chuckled, as he held her easily with one arm around her waist. Uncertainly Dirk hesitated at the door, no longer grinning.

'Come on, man. I'll hold her.' With a sudden swing of his arm Archy hurled the girl face down on the bed, then jumped across to keep her mouth smothered in the pillow. 'Come on, Dirk, use this!' With his free hand Archy unbuckled the wide belt he wore. The leather was studded with blunt metal spikes. 'Double it over!'

'Hell's teeth, Arch – you reckon we should?' Dirk still hesitated, the belt hanging limply from his hands.

'You scared, or something?' And Dirk's mouth hardened at the gibe. He stepped forward and swung the belt in a full overarm stroke across the wriggling body. Hazel froze at the sting of it and she gasped explosively into the pillow.

'That's the stuff – hold on a second.' Archy hooked his thumb into the thin fabric of her chemise and ripped it down from the shoulder-blades to the hem. Her fat woman's buttocks bulged through, dimpled and white. 'Now, give it hell!'

Again Dirk lifted the heavy doubled leather, he stood poised like that while a sensation of giddy power buoyed him upwards to the level of the gods, then he swung his body down into the next stroke.

## *Chapter Seventy-nine*

'He's unopposed,' Ronny Pye murmured, and beside him Garrick Courtney stirred uneasily.

'Have you heard him speak?' Ronny persisted.

'No.'

'He wants to throw in Natal with that bunch of Dutchmen up in the Free State and Transvaal.'

'Yes, I know.'

'Do you agree with him?'

Garry was silent, he seemed to be engrossed with the antics of the small herd of foals in the paddock in front of them as they chased each other on legs that seemed to have too many joints, clumsy in their fluffy baby coats.

'I'm sending twenty yearlings up to the show sales in Pietermaritzburg

– should average about four, five hundred a head because they're all first-class animals. Be able to let you have a sizable payment on the bond.'

'Don't worry about that now, Garry. I didn't come out here looking for money.' Ronny offered his cigar-case, and when Garry refused he selected one himself and began preparing it carefully. 'Do you agree with this idea of a Union?'

'No.'

'Why not?' Ronny did not look up from his cigar, he did not want to show his eagerness prematurely.

'I fought them – Leroux, Niemand, Botha, Smuts. I fought them – and we won. Now they're sitting up there in Pretoria calmly plotting to take over the whole country – not just the Free State and Transvaal, but Natal and the Cape as well. Any Englishman who helps them is a traitor to his King and his country. He should be put against the wall and shot.'

'Quite a few people round here think that way – quite a few. And yet no one is opposing Sean Courteney – he's just going to walk into the Assembly.

Garry turned and began limping slowly along the paddock fence towards the stables, and Ronny fell in beside him.

'Seems to me and the others we need a good man to put against him – someone with a lot of prestige. Good war record, man who has written a book and knows what's going on – knows how to use words. If we could find someone like that, then we'd be happy to put up the expense money.' He struck a match and waited for the sulphur to clear before he lit his cigar and spoke through the smoke. 'Only three months to election time – we got to get organized right away. He's holding a meeting at the schoolhouse next week.'

Sean's political campaign, which had been ambling along mildly without causing much interest, suddenly took on new dramatic quality.

His first meeting in Ladyburg was attended by most of the local population – all of them so starved for entertainment that they were prepared to listen to Sean reel off the little speech that they had already read reported verbatim in most of the Natal newspapers. With hardy optimism they hoped that question time might be more rewarding – and some of them had prepared queries on such mómentous matters as the price of hunting licences, the public library system, and the control of foot and mouth disease. At the very least it was an opportunity to meet friends from the outlying areas.

But apart from Sean's employees, friends and neighbours, others arrived at the schoolhouse and filled the first two rows of desks. All of them were young men Sean had never seen before, and he eyed them with heavy disapproval while they laughed and joked loudly during the preliminaries.

'Where did this bunch come from?' he demanded of the Chairman.

'They came in on the afternoon train – all in one party.'

'Seems as though they're looking for trouble.' Grimly Sean sensed in them the slightly feverish excitement of men steeling themselves to violence. 'Most of them have been on the bottle.'

'Now, Sean.' Ruth leaned across and laid her hand on his knee. 'You must promise not to get worked up. Don't antagonize them.' Sean opened his mouth to reply, then left it like that as Garry Courtney came in through the crowd around the doorway and moved across to sit with Ronny Pye in the back row.

'Close your mouth, darling,' Ruth murmured and Sean obeyed, then smiled and waved a greeting to his brother. Garry replied with a nod, and immediately fell into deep discussion with Ronny Pye.

Amid coughing and feet shuffling the Chairman rose to introduce Sean to men who had been his schoolmates, who had drunk his brandy and hunted with him. He went on to tell them how Sean had won the Anglo-Boer war virtually single-handed, how he had brought prosperity to the district with his factory and his wattle. Then he ended with a few remarks that had Sean squirming in his seat and trying to get two fingers into his collar.

'So, ladies and gentlemen of our fair district – I give you a man of vision and foresight, a man with a heart as big as his fists – your candidate and mine, Colonel Sean Courtney!'

Sean stood up smiling, to be rocked by a blast of jeers and catcalls from the front rows. The smile faded and his fists curled into great bony hammers on the table in front of him. He scowled down on them, beginning to sweat with anger. A light tug on the tail of his coat steadied him and his fists opened a little. He began to speak, bellowing above the shouts of 'Sit down!', 'Speak up!', 'Give him a chance!', 'Stand down!', and the thunder of booted feet stamping in unison on the wooden floor.

Three times in the uproar he lost the run of his speech and had to turn to Ruth for prompting, scarlet in the face with anger and mortification, while waves of derisive laughter broke over him. He ended up reading out the last half from his notebook – it made little difference that he stumbled and lost his place repeatedly for no one more than three feet away could hear a word. He sat down and a sudden silence descended on the hall, an air of expectancy that made Sean realize that this must have been carefully planned – and that the main entertainment was still to follow.

'*Mr* Courtney.' At the back of the hall Garry Courtney was on his feet, and every head was craned around towards him. 'May I ask you a few questions?'

Sean nodded slowly. So that is it! Garry planned this reception.

'My first question, then. Can you tell us what the name is for a man who sells his country to the enemies of his King?'

'Traitor!' howled the hecklers.

'Boer!' They stood up in a mass and roared at him. The pandemonium lasted perhaps five minutes.

'I'm taking you out of here,' Sean whispered to Ruth and reached for her arm, but she pulled away.

'No, I'm staying.'

'Come on, do as I tell you. This is going to get rough.'

'You'll have to carry me out first,' she flared at him, angry and beautiful.

Sean was about to accept the challenge, when suddenly the uproar ceased abruptly. Again, all heads turned towards Garrick Courtney, where he stood ready with his next question. In the silence he grinned maliciously.

'One other thing, do you mind telling us the nationality and faith of your wife?'

Sean's head jerked back. He felt the sickening physical jolt of it in his stomach, and he started to struggle to his feet. But Ruth was already standing, and she laid a hand on his shoulder to prevent him rising.

'I think I will answer that one, Garry.' She spoke clearly with just that trace of huskiness in her voice.

'I am a Jewess.'

That silence persisted. Still with her hand on Sean's shoulder, standing straight and proud beside him, she held Garry's stare across the room. Garry broke first. Flushing up along his neck, he dropped his eyes and shifted clumsily on his bad leg. Among the men in the front rows the same guilty reaction followed her words. They glanced at each other and then away, moving awkwardly in shame. A man stood up, and started down the aisle towards the door. Half-way there he stopped and turned.

'Sorry, Missus. I didn't know there'd be any of that,' and he went on towards the door. As he passed Ronny Pye he tossed a sovereign into his lap. Another man stood up, grinned uneasily at Ruth and hurried out. Then in twos and threes the others followed him. The last of them trooped out in a bunch, and Sean noted with relish that not all of them returned Ronny's sovereigns.

At the end of the schoolroom Garry dithered, uncertain whether to leave or to stay and attempt to brazen his way out of a situation he had so seriously misjudged.

Sean stood up slowly and encircled Ruth's waist with one arm, he cleared his throat for it was choked with his pride of her.

'Not only that,' he called, 'but she's one of the best goddamned cooks in the district also.' In the laughter and cheers that followed Garry stumbled and pushed his way out of the room.

# Chapter Eighty

The following day Garrick Courtney announced his intention of contesting the Ladyburg seat as an Independent, but not even the Loyalist newspapers gave him an outside chance of winning – until six weeks before polling-day.

On that evening, long after dark, Dirk hitched Sun Dancer at the rail outside the hotel. After he had loosened the girth and slipped the bit from her mouth, he left her to drink at the trough and went up on to the sidewalk. As he sauntered past the bar he peered in through the large window with its gold-and-red-lettered slogan, 'Got a thirst, drink a Goldberg Beer!'

Quickly he checked the clientele at the bar for informers. There were none of his father's foremen – they were always dangerous, nor were Messrs

Petersen or Pye or Erasmus present this evening. He recognized two of the factory mechanics, a couple of railway gangers, a bank clerk, a counter-hand from the Co-operative Society among the half-dozen strangers – and he decided that it was safe. None of these ranked high enough in Ladyburg society to carry news to Sean Courtney of his son's drinking habits.

Dirk walked to the end of the block, paused there for a few seconds, and then strolled casually back. But his eyes were restlessly checking the shadows for tale carriers. Tonight the main street was deserted, and as he came level with the swing doors of the bar he stepped sideways through them and into the warm yellow lamplight of the saloon. He loved this atmosphere – he loved the smell of sawdust, liquor, tobacco smoke and men. It was a place of men. A place of rough voices and laughter, of crude humour and companionship.

A few of the men along the bar glanced up as he entered.

'Hey, Dirk!'

'We've missed you – where have you been all week?'

Dirk returned Archy's greeting self-consciously and when he walked to take the stool beside him at the end of the bar counter he held himself erect and swaggered a little – for this was a place of men.

'Good evening, Dirk. What will it be?' The barman hurried across to him.

'Hello, Henry – is it all right tonight?' Dirk dropped his voice to a whisper.

'Should be – we aren't expecting any snoopers.' Henry reassured him. 'But the door behind you isn't locked.'

Dirk's seat in the corner had been selected with care. From it he could survey each newcomer to the room while being screened himself by the drinkers along the counter. Behind him a door led through the washup into the back yard – a necessary precaution when you're seventeen and both the law and your father forbid you liquor.

'Very well, then – give me the usual.' Dirk nodded.

'You're out late tonight.' Henry remarked as he poured gin into a tumbler and filled it with bottled gingerbeer. 'You been out hunting again?' Henry was a small man in his early fifties, with a pale unsunned face and little blue eyes, and now as he asked the question he winked one of them at Archy Longworthy.

'Did you get it tonight?' Archy took over the catechism.

Dirk laid a finger along the side of his nose. 'What do you think?'
He grinned and they all laughed delightedly.

'Who was it? *Madame?*' Archy drew him out, playing for the other listeners, who were leaning forward still chuckling.

'Oh, her!' Dirk shrugged contemptuously. *Madame* was the code name of the wife of one of the railway drivers. Her husband ran the night train to Pietermaritzburg every alternate day. She was not considered much of a conquest.

'Who then?' Henry kidded softly.

'I'll let you know when I'm finished nesting there myself,' Dirk promised.

'A pretty one?' they insisted. 'Young, hey?'

'She's all right – not too bad.' Dirk tasted his gin.

'Man, you get so much you don't hardly 'preciate it any more,' Archy chided him, grinning at his audience, and Dirk bridled with pleasure. 'Come on, Dirk – tell us, man. Is she hot?'

For answer Dirk extended one finger cautiously and touched his glass, hissed sharply as though he had touched red hot steel and jerked his hand back with an exclamation of pain. They roared with appreciation and Dirk laughed with them, flushing, eager for their acceptance.

'Give us the story—' Henry insisted. 'You don't have to give us the name, just give us the details. Where did you take her?'

'Well—' Dirk hesitated.

'Come on, Dirk. Tell us about it.'

And of course he obliged. Telling it in detail so that the indulgent quality of their laughter changed and they leaned closer to him listening hungrily.

'Jesus! Did she say *that*?'

'Then what did you do?' they encouraged him.

And Dirk told them. He was a natural storyteller and he built up the suspense until there was a small island of attentive silence around him. But the rest of the bar-room was louder with laughter and voices than it had been when he entered. One group in particular were feeling their liquor.

'– So I took her hand,' Dirk went on, 'and I said, "Now I've got a little surprise for you." "What is it?" she asked, as though she didn't know. "Close your eyes and I'll show you." I told her . . .' And a voice rang loudly from across the room:

'– You take that big ugly bastard Courtney. What does he do except drive round in a big motor-car and make speeches.'

Dirk stopped in the middle of a sentence and looked up. Suddenly his face was pale. The man who had spoken was one of the group at the far end of the bar. He was dressed in a shabby overall of blue denim. A man no longer young, with the lines of hardship etched deep around his eyes and mouth.

'You know who gives him his money? I tell you – we give it to him. Without these he'd be finished – he wouldn't last a month.' The man held up his hands, they were calloused and the nails were split and ragged, encrusted with dark semi-circles of dirt. 'That's where he gets his money. Colonel Bloody Courtney.'

Dirk was staring across at the speaker; his hands lay clenched on the counter in front of him. Now suddenly the room was very quiet – so that the man's next words seemed even louder.

'You know what he pays – thirty-two pounds a month top journeyman's wages! Thirty-two pounds a month!'

'The minimum rate is twenty-five—' one of his companions observed dryly. 'I reckon you're free to move on to a better job – if you can find it. Me, I'll stay on here.'

'That's not the point. That big idle bastard's making a fortune out of us – I reckon he can afford to pay more. I reckon . . .'

'Do you reckon you're worth that much?' Dirk jumped up from his stool and shouted the question down the length of the counter. There was a stir of interest and every head turned towards him.

'Leave him, Dirk, he's drunk. Don't start anything,' Henry whispered in agitation, and then raising his voice and turning to the other, 'You've had enough, Norman. Time you were on your way. Your old lady will be waiting dinner for you.'

'Good God!' Norman was peering in Dirk's direction, his eyes focusing blearily.

'Good God! It's Courtney's pup.'

And Dirk's face set into nervous rigidity. He began to walk slowly down the room towards the man.

'Leave him, Dirk.' To restrain him Archy caught his arm as he passed. But Dirk shrugged it off.

'You insulted my father. You called him a bastard!'

'That's right.' Norman nodded. 'Your daddy's a bastard all right. Your daddy's a big lucky bastard who's never done a full day's work in his life – a big, lucky, bloodsucking bastard. And he's whelped an equally useless pup, who spends his time . . .'

Dirk hit him in the mouth, and he went over backwards off the stool, flailing his arms as he fell. He hit the floor with his shoulders and rolled up on to his knees spitting blood and a broken tooth from his mouth.

'You little bastard—' he mouthed through the blood. Dirk stepped forward with his left foot and swung his boot with the whole weight of his body behind it. The toe of his boot thudded into the man's chest and flung him on to his back.

'Christ, stop him,' shouted Henry from behind the bar. But they sat paralysed as Dirk stooped for the bar stool, lifted it above his head and then brought it down, swinging his body with it as though he were chopping a log. The heavy wooden seat hit the man in the centre of his forehead, it hit solidly for the back of his head was against the floor and could not give with the blow. It split his skull cleanly and twin spurts of blood shot from his nostrils into the sawdust on the floor.

'You've killed him.' A single voice broke the long silence that followed.

'Yes.' Dirk agreed. *I've killed him. I've killed a man.* It sang within him savagely. It came up and filled his chest so that he could hardly breathe. And he stood over the corpse not wanting to miss a moment of it. He felt his legs trembling under him, the muscles of his cheeks so tight with excitement they felt they must tear.

'Yes, I killed him.' His voice was choked with the violence of the pleasure that gripped him. His vision narrowed down so that the dead man's face filled the whole field of it. The forehead was deeply dented and the eyes bulged from their sockets.

Around him there was a sudden bustle of consternation.

'You'd better send for his father.'

'I'm getting out of here!'

'No, stay where you are. Nobody must leave.'

'My God, call Doc Fraser.'

'Doc's not wanted – get the police.'

'He was so quick – like a bloody leopard—'

'Christ, I'm getting out of here.'

Two of them stooped over the body.

'Leave him!' snapped Dirk. 'Don't touch him.' Jealous as a young lion of its kill. And instinctively they obeyed. They stood up and moved away. With them everyone else drew back, leaving Dirk standing alone.

'Get his father,' repeated Henry. 'Someone ride out and call Sean Courtney.'

An hour later Sean strode into the room. He wore an overcoat over his nightshirt and his boots had been pulled hurriedly over his bare feet. He stopped on the threshold and glared around the room, his hair in wild disorder from sleep – but when he entered, the atmosphere in the room changed. The tense silence relaxed and every face turned eagerly towards him.

'Mr Courtney – thank God you've come,' blurted the young police constable who was standing beside Dr Fraser.

'How bad is it, Doc?' Sean asked.

'He's dead, Sean.'

'Pa, he insulted . . .' Dirk started.

'Shut up!' Sean ordered him grimly. 'Who is he?' he fired at the constable.

'Norman Ven Eek – one of your fitters from the mill.'

'How many witnesses?'

'Fourteen of them, sir. They all saw it.'

'Right,' Sean ordered, 'get the body down to the police station. You'll be able to take statements from them tomorrow morning.'

'What about the accused . . . I mean what about your son, sir?' The constable corrected himself.

'I'll be responsible for him.'

'I'm not sure that I shouldn't . . .' He saw the expression on Sean's face. 'Well, that will be all right, I suppose,' he agreed reluctantly.

'Pa . . .' Dirk started again.

'I told you to keep your mouth shut – you've done enough damage for one night.' Sean spoke without looking at him, then to the barman,

'Fetch a blanket.' Then to the police constable, 'Get some of them to help you,' and he pointed towards the window which was lined four deep with curious faces.

'Very well, Mr Courtney.'

After they had shuffled out with the blanket-wrapped body, Sean glanced significantly at Dr Fraser.

'I'd better get down there – complete my examination.'

'You go ahead,' Sean agreed and the doctor packed his bag and went. Sean closed the door behind him and slammed the shutters across the window. Then he turned to the men who stood anxiously along the bar.

'What happened?' They stirred restlessly and looked everywhere but at him.

'You, George?' Sean selected one of his mechanics.

'Well, Mr Courtney, your Dirk went up to Norman and hit him off the stool. Then he kicked him as he was trying to get up, then he picked up the stool and hit him with it.' The mechanic stumbled hoarsely through his explanation.

'Did this man provoke him?' Sean demanded.

'Well, he called you a – begging your pardon, Mr Courtney – he called you a big, idle, bloodsucking bastard.'

Sean frowned quickly. 'Did he now! What else did he say?'

'He said you were a slave owner – that you starved your men. He said that he was going to get even with you sometime.' Archy Longworthy took over the telling of it with a note of interrogation in his voice as he glanced round at the others for support. After a few seconds there was a guilty nodding of heads and a few murmurs of agreement. Archy took courage from it. 'He sort of hinted that he was going to wait for you one night and get even.'

'Did he say that in so many words?' Sean's presence dominated the room with such an obvious air of authority that when Archy looked again for support he found it in their faces.

'He said: "One night I'm going to wait for that big bastard – then I'll show him a few things." ' Archy gave them the exact words. No one protested.

'Then what happened?'

'Well then he sort of picked on young Dirk. And "Here's Courtney's brat," he said. "Yellow as his old man, I reckon!" '

'What did Dirk do?' Sean asked.

'Well, Mr Courtney, he just laughed – like a gentleman, sort of, nice and friendly. 'Forget it, he said, – you've had too much to drink.'

A sudden thought occurred to Sean. 'What was Dirk going in here, anyway?'

'Well, it's like this, Mr Courtney – a few weeks ago he lent me a couple pounds. I asked him to call round here tonight so I could give it back to him – that's all it was.'

'He wasn't drinking then?' Sean asked suspiciously.

'Good Lord, no!' Archy was so obviously shocked at the suggestion that Sean nodded.

'All right, what happened then?' he pursued.

'Well, Norman went on ribbing him. Called him a coward and all that – I can't remember the exact words. But at last young Dirk lost his temper. He walked across and hit him off the stool. Well, I guess Norman deserved that – what do you think, boys?' Archy looked at them again.

'That's right – fair made my blood boil to hear him picking on Dirk like that.' The mechanic backed him up and the others murmured agreement.

'Well, then,' Archy took up the tale again, 'Norman's lying on the floor and pulls out his knife.' There was a rustle of astonishment from along the bar. One man opened his mouth and lifted his hand in protest, but suddenly embarrassed, he carried the gesture through and massaged his neck.

'Knife. What knife – where's it now?' Sean leaned forward eagerly. Standing beside him Dirk began to smile softly. When he smiled his face was beautiful.

'Here's the knife.' Henry, the barman, reached under the counter and brought out a large bone-handled clasp knife. Everybody in the room stared at it blankly.

'How did it get there?' Sean asked, and now for the first time he was aware of the sickly guilt-ugly faces in front of him. He knew then for certain it was a lie.

'I took it off Norman afterwards. We thought it best you should be the first to know the truth – you being his father, and all.' Archy wriggled his shoulders ingratiatingly and smiled around at his witnesses.

Slowly Sean turned to the man nearest to him, the bank clerk.

'Is this the knife with which Norman Van Eek threatened my son?'

'Yes, Mr Courtney.' The man's voice squeaked unnaturally.

Sean looked at the man beyond him and repeated the question exactly.

'Yes, that's the one, sir.'

'That's it.'

'Yes.'

'No doubt about it – that's it.'

He asked each man in turn and each answered the same.

'Dirk.' Sean came last to him. He asked it slowly and heavily. Looking into the clear innocent eyes of his son. 'As God is your witness – did Norman Van Eek draw thisknife on you?'

*Please, my son, deny it now. Say it so they all can hear you. If you value my love – tell me the truth now. Please, Dirk, please.* All this he tried to say, tried to convey it with the sheer force of his gaze.

'As God is my witness, Pa,' Dirk answered him and was silent again.

'You have not answered,' Sean insisted. *Please, my son.*

'He drew that knife from the hip pocket of his overalls – the blade was closed. He opened it with the thumbnail of his left hand, Pa,' Dirk explained softly. 'I tried to kick it out of his hand, but hit his chest instead. He fell on to his back and I saw him raise the knife as though he were going to throw it. I hit him with the stool. It was the only way I could stop him.'

All the passion went out of Sean's face. It was stony and hard.

'Very well,' he said. 'We'd better get home now.' Then he addressed the rest of the bar-room. 'Thank you, gentlemen.' And he walked out through the door to the Rolls. Dirk followed him meekly.

The next afternoon Dirk Courtney was released by the local magistrate into his father's custody on bail of fifty pounds, pending the visit of the Circuit Court two weeks later, when he was to stand trial on a charge of manslaughter.

His case was set down at the head of the Court list. The whole district attended the trial, packing the tiny Courthouse and clustering at each of its windows.

After a retirement of seven minutes the jury brought back its verdict and Dirk, walking out of the dock, was surrounded by the laughing, congratulating crowd and borne out into the sunlight.

In the almost deserted Courtroom Sean did not rise from his seat in the front row of chairs. Peter Aaronson, the defence lawyer Sean had imported from Pietermaritzburg, shuffled his papers into his briefcase, made a joke with the Registrar, then walked across to Sean.

'In and out again in seven minutes already – that's one for the record book.' When he smiled he looked like a koala bear. 'Have a cigar, Mr Courtney.' Sean shook his head and Peter thrust a disproportionately large cigar into his own mouth and lit it. 'I tell you truly, though, I was worried by the knife business. I expected trouble there. I didn't like that knife.'

'No more did I,' Sean agreed softly, and Peter held his head on one side examining Sean's face with bright, birdlike eyes.

'But I liked those witnesses – a troupe of performing seals. "Bark," you say to them – Woof! Woof! Just like magic. Someone trained them pretty well.'

'I don't think I understand you,' Sean said to him grimly, and Peter shrugged.

'I'll post my account – but I warn you I'm going to hit you with a big one. Say, five hundred guineas?'

Sean lay back in his seat and looked up at the little lawyer.

'Say, five hundred,' he agreed.

'Next time you need representation – I recommend a bright youngster name of Rolfe. Humphrey Rolfe,' Peter went on.

'You think I'll need a lawyer again?'

'With your boy – you'll need a lawyer,' Peter told him with certainty.

'And you don't want the job?' Sean leaned forward with sudden interest. 'At five hundred guineas a throw?'

'Money I can get anywhere.' Peter took the cigar from his mouth and inspected the fluffy grey ash at its tip. 'Remember the name, Mr Courtney – Humphrey Rolfe. He's a bright boy – and not too fussy.'

He walked away down the aisle lugging his heavy briefcase, and Sean stood up and followed him slowly. Pausing on the steps of the Courthouse he looked across the square. The centre of a small knot of men, Dirk stood laughing, with Archy Longworthy's arm around his shoulder. Archy's voice carried to where Sean stood.

'Don't let any of you get the idea you can tangle with Dirkie here – you'll end up with your teeth busted clean out the back of your head.' Archy grinned so that the blackened tooth showed. 'I say it so you can all hear me. Dirkie here is my friend – and I'm proud of him.'

*You alone*, thought Sean. He looked at his son and saw how tall he stood. Shaped like a man – broad in the shoulders with muscle in his arms, no fat on the belly and long legs dropping away clean from hips.

'But he is only sixteen. He's a child – perhaps there is still time to prevent him setting hard. Then with truth he knew he was deceiving himself, and he remembered what a friend had said to him long ago:

*'Some grapes grew in the wrong soil, some were diseased before they went to the press, and others were spoiled by a careless vintner – not all grapes make good wine.'*

And I am the careless vintner, he thought.

Sean walked across the square. 'You're coming home,' he told Dirk harshly, knowing as he looked at the lovely face that he no longer loved his son. The knowledge nauseated him.

'Congratulations, Colonel. I knew we'd win,' Archy Longworthy beamed, and Sean glanced up him.

'I'll be in my office ten o'clock tomorrow morning. I want to talk to you.'

'Yes, sir!' grinned Archy happily, but he was not grinning when he left Ladyburg on the following evening's train with a month's pay in lieu of notice to compensate him.

# Chapter Eighty-one

With the storm of adverse editorial comment raised by Dirk's trial, Garry Courtney's chances in the coming election increased significantly. The jingo press spoke darkly of a 'surprise outcome, which thinking men will welcome as a true assessment of the worth of the two candidates of the Ladyburg constituency'. Only the Liberal papers reported the generous pension which the Ladyburg Wattle Co-operative Co. voted to Norman Van Eek's widow and orphan.

But everyone knew that Sean Courtney was still a long way ahead. He could be certain of the vote of the two hundred men employed at the factory and on his estates, the other wattle producers of the valley and their employees, as well as a good half of the townsfolk and ranchers – that was until the *Pietermaritzburg Farmer & Trader* devoted a full front page to the exclusive story of one Archibald Frederick Longworthy.

Mr Longworthy related how, by the threat of physical violence and loss of employment, he had been forced to perjure himself in court. How, after the case, he had been summarily dismissed from his work. The exact nature of his perjury was not revealed.

Sean cabled his lawyers in Pietermaritzburg to begin immediate proceedings against the *Farmer & Trader* for defamation of character, libel, contempt, treason, and anything else they could think of. Then, reckless of his own safety, he climbed into the Rolls and raced at thirty miles an hour in pursuit of his cable. He arrived in Pietermaritzburg to find that Mr Longworthy, after signing a sworn statement and graciously accepting a payment of fifty guineas, had departed without leaving a forwarding address. Legal advice was against Sean visiting the editor of the *Farmer & Trader* and laying himself open to a counter-suit of assault and battery. It would be two months before the defamation trial was heard in court, and the election was to be held in ten days' time.

All Sean could do was publish a full-page denial in each of the Liberal papers, then return to Ladyburg at a more sedate pace. There a telegram awaited him from Pretoria. Jan Paulus and Jan Niemand suggested that in the circumstances it might be better if Sean withdraw from nomination. Sean's reply went sizzling back over the wires.

Like a pair in harness, Garry and Sean Courtney swept up to the polling-day finishing line.

The actual voting took place in the Ladyburg Village Management offices under the beady eyes of two Government registration officers. Thereafter, the ballot boxes would be removed to Pietermaritzburg, where on the following day in the City Hall the votes would be counted and the official results announced.

On opposite sides of the square the opposing candidates set up the large marquee tents from which free refreshments would be served to the voters. Traditionally the candidate who fed the largest number would be the loser. Nobody wished to put *their* choice to additional expense, so they patronized the other man's stall. This day, however, both candidates served an almost equal amount of food.

It was a day that threatened the approach of the wet season, humid heat lay trapped beneath grey overcast clouds and the occasional bursts of sunlight stung like the blast of an open furnace door. Sean, suited and waistcoated, sweated with anxiety as he greeted each visitor to his stall with a booming, false *camaraderie*. Beside him Ruth looked like a rose petal, and smelled as sweet. Storm, demure for once, stood between them. Dirk was not there – Sean had found work for him on the far side of Lion Kop. Many sly eyes and snide sallies remarked his absence.

Ronny Pye had persuaded Garry not to wear his uniform. Anna was with him, pretty in mauve and artificial flowers. It was only at closer range that the ugly little lines around her mouth and eyes, and the grey hairs that were woven in the shiny black mass of her hair showed up. Neither she nor Garry let their eyes wander across the square.

Michael arrived and spoke first with his father, kissed his mother dutifully, then crossed to resume the argument Sean had broken off the night before. Michael wanted Sean to buy ten thousand acres of the coastal lowlands around Tongaat and plant it to sugar-cane. Within a few minutes he realized that this was not the best time to push his idea; Sean greeted each of his points with hearty laughter and offered him a cigar. Discouraged but not resigned, Michael went into the ballot office and, settling his problem of divided loyalty, deliberately spoiled his paper. Then he returned to his office at the wattle factory to whip his sugar estimates into shape for the next attack on Sean.

Ada Courtney never left the Protea Street cottage all that day. She had steadfastly denied appeals to join either camp, and refused to allow any of her girls to help in the preparations. She had prohibited any political discussion in her house – and ordered Sean to leave when he had disregarded this rule. Only after Ruth had interceded and Sean had made an abject apology, was he allowed to return. She disapproved of the whole business and considered it undignified and common that members of her family should not only be standing for public office but actually competing for it. Her deep distrust of and contempt for officialdom stemmed from the time the Village Board had wanted to place street lamps along Protea Street. She had attended their next meeting armed with an umbrella, and in vain they had tried to convince her that street lights did not attract mosquitoes.

However, Ada was the only person in the district who did not attend. From mid-morning until polling closed at five o'clock the square was jammed solid with humanity, and when the sealed ballot boxes were borne in state to the railway station, many of them climbed on the same train and went up to Pietermaritzburg for the official counting.

It had been a day of unremitting nervous tension, so a very short time after entering their suite in the White Horse Hotel, Ruth and Sean fell into exhausted sleep in each other's arms . When, in the early morning a brilliant electrical storm raged down upon the town, Ruth moved restlessly in her sleep, coming slowly back to consciousness – and to the realization that she and Sean were already engaged in the business that had been delayed so long. Sean woke at the same time and, for the few seconds that it took him to understand what was happening, was as bewildered as she – then both of them went to it with a will. By dawn Ruth knew that she would bear a son, though Sean felt it was a little soon to tell for certain.

After bathing, they ate breakfast in bed together with a renewed sense of intimacy. Ruth in a white silk gown, with her hair loosed into a shiny mass on her shoulders and her skin glowing as though she had been freshly scrubbed, was extreme provocation to Sean. Consequently they arrived late at the City Hall, much to the agitation of Sean's supporters.

The counting was well advanced. In a roped-off section of the hall ballot officers sat in silent industry at the tables piled with the small pink slips of paper. On a placard above each table was printed the name of the district and the candidates, and between the tables scrutineers paced watchfully.

The body of the hall was filled with a milling, humming swarm of men and women. Before it engulfed them Sean caught a glimpse of Garry and Anna moving through the press, then for the next ten minutes he was subjected to an orgy of hand-shaking, back-slapping and well wishes – interrupted by a bell and a complete silence.

'The result for the legislative assembly seat of Newcastle . . .' a high thin voice announced in the hush '. . . Mr Robert Sampson 986 votes. Mr Edward Sutton 423 votes . . .' And the rest was lost in a burst of cheers and groans. Sampson was the South African Party candidate, and Sean fought his way through the pack that surrounded him.

'Well done, you old son of a gun,' shouted Sean and beat him between the shoulder-blades.

'Thanks, Sean. It looks as though we are home and dry – I never expected a majority that size!' and they wrung each other's hands deliriously.

The morning went on with intervals of excited, buzzing tension exploding into applause as each result was announced. Sean's confidence rose as his party captured each seat that had expected, and one that they were resigned to lose – but then the bell rang again and in the same impersonal tone the Chief Registration Officer at last announced:

'The result for the legislative assembly seat of Ladyburg and the lower Tugela—' he felt the cold emptiness of apprehension in his stomach, and his breath burning up the back of his throat. Standing beside him he could sense the rigidity of Ruth's body and he groped for her hand.

'Colonel *Garrick* Courtney 638 votes. Colonel *Sean* Courtney 631 votes.'

Ruth's hand squeezed hard, but Sean did not reply to the pressure. The two of them stood very still, a tiny island of quiet in the surge and roar – in the triumphant cheers and despairing groans – until Sean said softly: 'I think we'll go back to the hotel, my dear.'

'Yes,' she answered as softly, and the sound of her voice was helpless pity. Together they started across the floor and a way opened to them. A passage lined by faces that bore expressions of regret, happiness, curiosity, indifference and triumphant malice.

Out into the sunlight and across the street to the rank of hirecabs they walked together, while behind them the uproar was muted – sounding at this distance like the voices of wild animals.

Sean handed Ruth up into the coach and was about to join her before he remembered what there was still to be done. He spoke to the driver and gave him money before coming back to Ruth.

'Please wait for me at the hotel, my dear.'

'Where are you going?'

'I must offer Garry our congratulations.'

Through the screen of bodies that surrounded him Garry saw Sean approaching and he felt his body tensing involuntarily – racked by that conflict of hatred and love he bore for this man.

Sean stopped in front of him and smiled. 'Well done, Garry!' he said and offered his right hand. 'You beat me in a hard straight fight – and I'd like to shake your hand.'

Garry took the words up with temerity, examined them with growing realization of their meaning and found that they were true. He had fought Sean and beaten him. This was something that could not be destroyed – something that Sean could never take away from him. *I've beaten him.* For the first time – the very first time in all my life!

It was an emotional orgasm so intense that for a long moment Garry could not move or make any reply.

'Sean . . .' His voice choked up. He caught Sean's outstretched hand in both of his and held it with desperate strength.

'Sean, perhaps now . . .' he whispered, 'I'd like to . . . I mean, when we get back to Ladyburg . . .' Then he stopped and blushed scarlet with embarrassment. Quickly he released Sean's hand and stepped back. 'I thought you might like to come out to Theuniskraal,' he mumbled, 'some day when you're not busy. Look around the old place.' Then more eagerly, 'It's been a long time. I've still got Pa's old . . .'

'Never!' Anna Courtney hissed the word. Neither of them had noticed her cross the hall, but now she appeared suddenly at Garry's side. Her eyes were bright gems of hatred set in their patterns of wrinkles, and her face was white as she glared at Sean. 'Never.' She hissed again, and took Garry's arm. 'Come with me,' she commanded, and Garry followed her meekly. But he glanced back at where Sean still stood, and there was a desperate plea in his eyes. A plea for understanding, for forgiveness of this weakness.

# Chapter Eighty-two

Like one who lives in a hurricane belt, and recognizes the shape of clouds and the breathless hush that precedes high wind – Ruth knew she would have to deal with the brooding undirected rage which would be Sean's reaction to this failure of his plans. His moods came at widely spaced intervals and did not last long – but she feared those moods of his, and like the prudent householder forewarned of the hurricane's approach, she took precautions to minimize its wrath.

When she reached the hotel she sent an urgent summons to the Manager.

'In half an hour I want lunch served in the suite – not your ordinary bill of fare. Something really good.' The Manager thought a moment. 'Oyster! We have a barrel just arrived from Umhlanga Rocks.'

'Excellent.' Ruth liked the man's response to the emergency.

'Then I could do a smoked ham, cold venison, cold rock lobster, salads?'

'Excellent again. What about cheese?'

'Gruyère. Danish Blue. Camembert.'

'Wine?'

'Champagne?'

'Yes,' Ruth agreed instantly. She would shamelessly exploit Sean's weakness for it. 'A bottle of Veuve Clicquot – no, on second thoughts, three bottles.'

'I'll send the wine up first?'

'Immediately – with your best glass and a silver bucket,' Ruth told him.

Then she fled to her toilet. Thank the Lord for French perfume and this morning dress of grey silk she had been saving for just such an occasion. She worked quickly, but with skill, upon her face and hair, and when she was finished she sat quietly before the mirror and composed her features into an expression of peace. The effect was very satisfactory, she decided after critical contemplation. Since it was the way he had first seen it, Sean could never resist her hair in braids. It made her look like a little girl.

'Shall I open the wine, Madam?'

'Yes, please.' She called into the sitting-room, then went through to await the onslaught of the hurricane.

Ten minutes later it came wafting in like a gentle zephyr, with a cigar clamped between its teeth, its hands thrust deep into trouser pockets and a bemused expression on its face.

'Hey, now!' Sean stopped when he saw her, and removed the cigar. 'That's nice!'

The fact that he had noticed her appearance was proof that her weather forecast was hopelessly incorrect and she burst out laughing.

'What's so funny?' Sean asked mildly.

'Nothing and everything. You and me. Have a glass of champagne.'

'Mad woman,' Sean said and kissed her. 'I like your hair like this.'

'Aren't you disappointed?'

'About the result, you mean? Yes, I suppose I am.' He went to the central table and poured wine into the crystal glasses, handed one to her and took up the other.

'I give you a toast – the short, exciting political career of Sean Courtney.'

'You wanted to win so badly – but now . . .?'

Sean nodded. 'Yes, I always want to win. But now that the game is lost . . .' He shrugged. 'Shall I tell you something? I was getting a big sick of all the speechifying and hand-shaking. I feel that even in my sleep I have a vacant grin on my face.' He crossed to one of the leather arm-chairs and sank down into it gratefully. 'There is something else also. Come here and let me tell you about it.'

She went to him, sat in his lap and slid her hand into the front of his shirt so that she could feel the soft springy hair of his chest, and the hard rubbery flesh beneath.

'Tell me,' she said, and he told her about Garry. He spoke slowly, telling her everything – about the leg, how it was when they were children, and finally, about Michael. She was quiet for a while, and he could see the hurt in her eyes that Sean had been another woman's lover. At last she asked:

'Does Garry know that Michael is your son?'

'Yes. Anna told him one night. She told him the night I left Ladyburg – he wanted to kill me.'

'Why did you leave?'

'I couldn't stay on. Garry hated me for siring his son – and Anna hated me because I would not go to her.'

'She still wanted you, then?'

'Yes. That night – the night I left, Anna came to me and asked me to . . .' Sean paused. 'You know what I mean.'

'Yes.' Ruth nodded, hurt still and jealous, but making the effort to understand.

'I refused her – and she went to Garry and, in spite, she told him about the child. My God, what a poisonous bitch she is!'

'But if she wanted you, why did she marry Garry?'

'She was with child. She thought I had been killed in the Zulu war – she married him to provide a father for her child.'

'I see,' Ruth murmured. 'But why do you tell me this?'

'I wanted you to understand how I feel about Garry. After what he did to you at that meeting I can't expect you to have much sympathy for him – but he wasn't trying to hurt you, he was aiming at me. I owe him so much, I never seem able to pay him. That's why . . .'

'That's why you are glad he won today?' Ruth finished for him.

'Yes,' Sean answered eagerly. 'You see, don't you, how important this must have been to him. For the first time he was able to . . . able to . . .' Sean fluttered his hands in frustration as he sought the words.

'He was able to compete with you on equal terms,' Ruth supplied them for him.

'Exactly!' Sean struck the arm of his chair with clenched fist. 'When I went to congratulate him, he was ready to meet me. He invited me out to Theuniskraal – just then that evil, bloody woman interfered and took him away. But somehow I know it's going to be all right now.'

A knock on the outer door interrupted him, and Ruth jumped up from his lap.

'That will be the waiter with the lunch,' but before she was half-way across the room, the knock was repeated with such insistence that it threatened to loosen the plaster.

'I'm coming.' Irritated, Ruth raised her voice and swung the door open.

Led by Bob Sampson a flood of men rushed into the room; jabbering and gesticulating they bore down on Sean.

'What the hell's going on?' he demanded.

'You've won!' shouted Bob. 'A recount, you won on a recount – by ten votes!'

'My God!' breathed Sean, and then so softly that only Ruth heard him, 'Garry. Poor Garry!'

'Open that champagne – send for another case. We're in solidly – all of us!' exulted Bob Sampson. 'So let's drink to the Union of South Africa!'

## Chapter Eighty-three

'Not even this once. Out of so many times, so many things – not even this once.' Already Garry Courtney was drunk. He lay deep in his chair with a tumbler held in both hands, stirring the brown liquid with a circular movement so a few drops slopped over the rims and stained the cloth of his trousers.

'No,' agreed Anna. 'Not even this once.' She stood with her back to him, staring out of the window of their suite into the gaslit street below, for she did not want him to see her face. But she could not control the harsh, gloating quality of her voice. 'Now you can go back to writing your little books. You've made your point – you've proved to yourself and the rest of the world how effective you are.'

Moving her hands slowly, she began to massage her own upper arms with sensual pleasure. A tiny shudder thrilled her so she moved restlessly and her skirts rustled like leaves in the wind. God, how close it had been – and she had been afraid.

'You're a loser, Garry Courtney. You *have* always been – and you *will* always be.'

Again she shuddered with the memory of her fear. He had so nearly escaped. She had seen it begin from the moment the first result was announced, every minute it had grown stronger. Even his voice had changed, deeper with the first hint of confidence in it. He had looked at her strangely, without submission, with the beginning of his contempt. Then the flare of rebellion when he had spoken to Sean Courtney. She had been truly afraid then.

'You are a loser,' she repeated, and heard the sound he made – half-gulp, half-sigh. She waited and when she heard the soft gurgle of brandy poured from bottle to glass she hugged herself tighter and now she smiled as she remembered the announcement of the recount. The way he had shrunk, the way he had crumpled and turned to her with all of it gone – the confidence and contempt wiped away. Gone! Gone for ever. Sean Courtney would never have him. She had made that oath – and now it would be kept.

As so many times before, she played over in her mind the details of that night. The night she had made the oath.

*It was raining. She was standing on the wide stoeb of Theuniskraal, and Sean was leading his horse up across the lawns of Theuniskraal. The damp linen of his shirt clung to his shoulders and chest, the rain had made his beard break out in tiny curls so he looked like a mischievous pirate.*

*'Where's Garry?' Her own voice, and his voice answering.*

*'Don't worry. He's gone into town to see Ada. He'll be back by supper-time.'*

*Then he was coming up the steps towards her, standing tall above her, and his hand on her arm was cold from the rain.*

*'You must take better care of yourself now. You can't stand in the cold any more.' And he led her through the french doors. The top of her head was on a level with his shoulders, and his eyes as he looked down at her were gentle with masculine awe of pregnancy.*

*'You're a damn fine woman, Anna. And I'm sure you're going to make a fine baby.'*

*'Sean!' She remembered how his name had come up her throat like an involuntary exclamation of pain. The fierce forward surge that had flattened her body against his, back arching to send her hips forward searching for his manhood. The coarse electric feeling of his hair in her hands as she pulled his face down and the taste of his mouth opened warm and moist.*

*'Are you mad!' As he tried to break away from her, her arms locked around his body and her face pressed to his chest.*

*'I love you. Please, Sean, please. Just let me hold you, that's all. I just want to hold you.'*

*'Get away from me!' And she felt herself thrown roughly on to the couch beside the fireplace.*

*'You're Garry's wife and you'll soon be the mother of his child. Keep your hot little body for him.' And his face thrust forward, close to hers. 'I don't want you. I could no more touch you than I could go with my own mother. You're Garry's wife. If ever again you look at another man I'll kill you. I'll kill you with my bare hands.'*

*Love congealing instantly, transformed to hatred by his words. Her fingernails raking across his cheek so the blood slid down into his beard, and he caught her wrists. Holding her while she struggled and screamed at him.*

*'You swine, you dirty, dirty swine. Garry's wife you say. Garry's baby you*

*say! Now hear the truth. What I have within me you put there. It's yours — not Garry's!'*

*Then he was backing away from her. 'You're lying. It can't be.'*

*Following him now, speaking those cruel words softly. 'You remember how we said good-bye when you went to war? You remember that night in the wagon?'*

*'Leave me, leave me alone. I've got to think. I didn't know.' And he was gone. She heard the door of his study slam, and she stood in the centre of the floor while the storm surf of her anger abated and exposed the black reefs of hatred beneath.*

*Then she was alone in her bedroom, standing before the mirror — making her oath.*

*'I hate him. There's one thing I can take from him. Garry belongs to me now. Mine, not his. I will take that away from him.'*

*The pins pulled from her hair, so it tumbled to her shoulders. Her fingers tangling it into confusion. Teeth closing on her own lips so she could taste the blood.*

*'Oh God, I hate him' she whispered through the pain. Tearing open the blouse of her dress, watching in the mirror the great pink bosses of her nipples already darkening with the promise of fruition.*

*'I hate him.' Pantaloons torn and discarded, bowls of face powder and cosmetics swept from the dressing-table to burst and fill the room with the pungent reek of perfume.*

*Then lying alone in the darkening room. Waiting for Garry to come.*

Now she turned away from the window and looked down at Garry, triumphantly, knowing he could never escape again.

*I have kept my oath*, she thought, and crossed to the chair.

'Poor Garry.' She forced her voice to croon gently, and she stroked the hair back from his forehead. He looked up at her, surprised, but eager for affection. 'Poor Garry. Tomorrow we'll go home to Theuniskraal.'

She moved the bottle on the side table closer to his hand. Then she kissed his cheek lightly, and went on into the bedroom of the suite — smiling again, secure and safe in his weakness.

# Chapter Eighty-four

Four months passed quickly. Sean, distracted by the responsibilities of his office, the mountains of correspondence, the meetings and sessions, the petitioners and the schemers — offered only a token resistance to Michael's sugar plans. Michael went off to the coast, purchased the land, and became deeply involved with the seller's eldest daughter. This young lady had the dubious distinction of being one of the few divorcees in Natal. When the scandal reached his ears, Sean, secretly pleased that Michael's chastity was at last shed, boarded the Rolls and went off on a flying mission of rescue. He returned to Ladyburg with a penitent Michael in tow. Two weeks later the young lady married a travelling salesman and moved from Tongaat to Durban, whereupon Michael was allowed to return to Tongaat and begin the development of the sugar estate.

Ruth no longer accompanied Sean on all of his absences from Ladyburg. Her swiftly increasing girth and a mild malady which assailed her in the mornings kept her at Lion Kop, where she and Ada spent much time in the design and fabrication of babywear. In this Storm rendered assistance. The matinée jacket, which took three months to knit, was certain to fit the infant perfectly – provided it was a hunchback with its one arm twice as long as the other.

Kept busy from early morning to nightfall in the capacity of overseer on Mahobo's Kloof, Dirk found little time for distraction. Ladyburg was now well covered by Sean's espionage system, and Dirk's few visits were reported in detail.

But on the far side of Ladyburg, derelict and shabby from want of love, brooded the great homestead of Theuniskraal. In the night a single window showed a pale yellow square of light as Garry Courtney sat alone at his desk. In front of him lay a pathetically thin sheaf of papers. Hour after hour he stared at it – but no longer seeing it. He was dry inside, deprived of the juice of life and seeking its substitute in the bottle, which was always near him.

The days drifted into weeks, and they in turn became months – and he drifted with them.

Each afternoon he would go down to the paddocks, then, leaning against the heavy wooden paling, he would watch his bloodstock. Hour after hour he stood unmoving and it seemed that, in time, he left his own body and lived within those richly gleaming skins, as though his own hooves drove deep into the turf as he ran, as though his own voice squealed and his muscles bunched and moved in the savage mating of heaving bodies.

Ronny Pye found him there one afternoon; without Garry being aware of his presence, he came up silently and stood beside him, studying the pale intense face with the chisel-marks of pain and doubt and terrible yearning sculptured deep around the mouth and below the pale blue eyes.

'Hello, Garry.' He spoke softly, but recognizing the pity in his own voice he thrust it aside. There was no room for softness now, and ruthlessly he hardened his resolve.

'Ronny.' Vaguely, Garry turned to him, and when he smiled it was shyly. 'Business or social?'

'Business, Garry.'

'The bond?'

'Yes.'

'What do you want me to do?'

'How about coming into town – we can go over things in my office.'

'Now?'

'Yes, please.'

'Very well.' Garry straightened up slowly. 'I'll come with you.'

They rode together over the crest of ground and down towards the concrete bridge over the Baboon Stroom. Both of them silent – Garry because there was nothing in him, nothing to give voice to; Ronny Pye because of his sense of shame for the thing he was about to do. He was going to take a man's home from him and turn him loose upon a world in which he would have no chance of survival.

At the bridge they stopped automatically to rest their horses, and they sat without speaking, an incongruous pair. One man sitting quietly, slim and wasted, his clothing slightly rumpled, his face austere with suffering; the other plump, red-faced below bright ginger hair, dressed in expensive cloth, fidgeting in the saddle.

There was little sign of life across the river. A long, tired smear of smoke from the wattle factory stack rising straight into the still hot air, a black boy moving cattle down to drink at the river, the huff and clatter and clang of a locomotive shunting in the goods-yards – but otherwise the town of Ladyburg lay slumbering in the heat of a summer afternoon.

Then on the open grassy plain below the escarpment, urgent movement caught Ronny's eye, and he focused his attention upon it with relief.

A horseman riding fast, and even at this distance Ronny recognized him.

'Young Dirk,' he grunted, and Garry roused himself and peered out across the river. Horse and rider blended into one unit, seeming to touch the earth so lightly they were bound to it only by a pale feather of dust that drifted low behind them.

'My God, that little bastard can ride.' In reluctant admiration Ronny shook his head solemnly and a drop of perspiration broke from his hairline and slid down his cheek. The horse reached the road and pivoted neatly, flattening into the increased speed of its run. Movement of such rhythmic grace and power that the watchers were stirred.

'Look at him go!' whistled Ronny. 'Don't reckon there's anything to catch that horse in the whole of Natal.'

'You think so?' Garry's voice was suddenly alive, and his lips were pursed in anger.

'I'm damned certain of it.'

'Mine. My colt – Grey Weather. Over a point-to-point course, I'd match him against any of Sean Courtney's stud.'

And those words gave Ronny Pye the idea. He turned it over in his mind while with slightly narrowed eyes he watched Dirk Courtney race Sun Dancer down towards the wattle factory. When horse and rider had disappeared through the tall gates, Ronny spoke softly:

'Would you back your colt with money?'

'I'd back him with my life.' There was savagery in Garry's voice.

Yes, thought Ronny, this way at least I will give him a chance. This way the fates will make the decision – there will be no blame to my account.

'Would you back him with Theuniskraal?' he asked, and the silence drew out.

'How do you mean?' whispered Garry.

'If you win, the bond on Theuniskraal is set aside.'

'And if I lose?'

'You lose the farm.'

'No,' snapped Garry. 'Christ, no! That's too much.'

Ronny shrugged indifferently. 'It was just an idea – you're probably wise. You wouldn't have much of a chance against Sean.'

Garry gasped sharply, that challenge had wounded deep as a lance. Made it a direct competition between Sean and himself; to ignore it would be to admit he could never win.

'I'll take the bet.'

'The whole bet? You'll cover my money with what you have left of Theuniskraal?'

'Yes, damn you. Yes. I'll show you how much chance I have against him.'

'We'd better get it down in writing,' Ronny suggested gently. 'Then I'll see if I can arrange it with Sean.' He touched his mount with his spurs and they moved forward across the bridge. 'By the way, I think it best we tell nobody about our little bet. We'll pretend it's just an honour match.'

Garry nodded his agreement. But that night when he wrote to Michael he told him about it, then went on to plead with Michael to ride Grey Weather in the race.

Two days before the competition Michael confided in his grandmother. Ada went out to Theuniskraal to try and dissuade Garry from this reckless gamble, without success. Garry was almost fanatical in his determination. The stake meant nothing to him – it was the prospect of winning.

And now he had Grey Weather and Michael to run for him. This time he would win. This time!

# Chapter Eighty-five

In the dark Sean walked with Dirk down the lane to the stables. The clouds banked along the escarpment were fired red by the hidden sun and the wind fretted through the plantations, so that the wattle moaned and shook.

'North wind,' grunted Sean. 'It'll rain before nightfall.'

'Sun Dancer loves the rain,' Dirk answered him tensely, and Sean glanced at him.

'Dirk – if you lose today . . .' he started, but Dirk cut him short.

'I won't lose,' and again as though it were a vow, 'I won't lose!'

'If you'd only show as much determination in other things – the more important . . .'

'Important! Pa, this is important. This is the most important thing I've ever done.' Dirk stopped and turned to his father. He caught Sean's sleeve, clinging to him. 'Pa, I'm doing this for you – for you, Pa!'

Sean looked down and what he saw in his son's face, in that beautiful face, silenced the retort that he was about to make. Where did I go wrong with you, he asked himself with love stained by loathing. Where did you get this blood, why are you this way, demanded his pride and his contempt.

'Thank,' he said dryly, freed his arm and walked on towards the stables.

Sightless in his deep preoccupation with Dirk, Sean was into the stable yard before he noticed Mbejane.

'Nkosi. I see you.' Mbejane rose solemnly from the hand-carved stool on which he sat.

'I see you also,' Sean cried with pleasure, and then controlled himself. A display of emotion in front of lesser persons would embarrass Mbejane. 'You are well?' he asked gravely, and restrained the desire to prod the swelling dignity of Mbejane's stomach, reminding himself that Mbejane's abundant flesh and fat had been carefully cultivated as a sign to the rest of the world of his prosperity.

'I am well,' Mbejane assured him.

'That you have come gives me pleasure.'

'Nkosi, on a day of importance it is right that we should be together – as it was before.' And Mbejane allowed himself to smile for the first time, a smile that within seconds became a mischievous grin that Sean gave back to him. He should have guessed that Mbejane would never miss a fight, or a hunt, or a contest.

Then Mbejane turned to Dirk.

'Do us honour today,' he commanded, as though he spoke to one of his own sons. 'Your father and I will be watching you.' He placed a huge black hand upon Dirk's shoulder as though in benediction, then he turned to gesture with his fly-whisk at the stable-boys waiting behind him.

'Bring the horse!'

Two of them led her out, her hooves ringing on the paving of the yard as she danced a little. Head up, moving greyhound-bellied, pricking her ears forward and back, she saw Dirk and wrinkled the soft velvet of her nostrils as she whickered.

'Hey, girl!' Dirk walked towards her. At his approach she rolled her eyes until the whites showed and her small dainty ears flattened wickedly against her neck.

'Stop that nonsense,' Dirk admonished, and she bared yellow teeth menacingly and reached with her slender snakelike neck. He put out his hand to her and she took his fingers between those terrible teeth and nibbled them tenderly. Then, finished with pretence, she snorted, pricked her ears and nuzzled his chest and neck.

'Where is her blanket? Has she eaten? Put the saddle and bridle in the car.' Dirk snapped a chain of questions and instructions at the stable-boys as he caressed Sun Dancer's face with the gentle hands of a lover.

So many contradictions in one person. Sean watched his son with sadness heavy upon him, oppressive as this red dawn. Where did I go wrong?

'Nkosi, I will walk down with the horse.' Mbejane sensed his mood and sought to end it.

'Better that a man of your station should ride with me in the motor-car,' Sean demurred, and took a fiendish pleasure in the shifty glance that Mbejane cast at the great gleaming Rolls parked at the far end of the yard. *It has eyes like a monster*, thought Mbejane and looked quickly away.

'I will walk with the horse and see that it comes to no harm,' he announced.

'As you wish,' Sean agreed. The small procession set off towards Ladyburg. The two grooms leading Sun Dancer in her red tartan blanket, and Mbejane following sedately with his small black sons carrying his carved stool and his spears behind him.

Two hours later Sean drove the Rolls into the field behind the stockyards. Staring straight ahead, both hands gripping the wheel so that the knuckles of his hands gleamed white – Sean did not hear the shouted greetings nor see the gala crowds and the bunting until the Rolls bumped to a halt in the grass and his hands unfroze slowly from the wheel. Then he exhaled gently and the rigid muscles of his face softened into a grin of uncertain triumph.

'Well, we made it!' He spoke as if he were not quite certain.

'You did very well, my dear.' Ruth's voice was also a little scratchy and she relaxed her protective hold on Storm.

'You should let me drive, Pa.' Dirk was lounging against the saddlery on the back seat. Sean turned furiously upon him, but Dirk was too quick. He flung open the door and was absorbed into the crowd that had gathered around the Rolls before Sean could assemble his words. Sean glowered after him.

'Hello, Sean. Nice to see you.' Dennis Petersen had opened the door at his elbow and Sean hastily rearranged his features into a smile.

'Hello, Dennis. Nice turn-out.'

'Everybody in the district,' Dennis assured him, as they shook hands, and then looked with satisfaction around the field. There were at least fifty carriages parked haphazard along the stockyard fence, an open wagon had been arranged as a refreshment stall with silver urns of coffee and piles of cakes laid out upon it. A dog fight was in progress near the gate, while small boys in already wilted church clothes shrieked and whooped and chased each other through the crowd.

'Who's responsible for the decorations?' Sean asked, surveying the flags and bunting that fluttered from the poles that marked the finishing line and from the wide roped-off lane that led up to them.

'The Board – we voted it last week.'

'Very nice.' Sean was looking now at the stockpen where the horses were. A solid barricade of humanity lined the railings, but he saw Dirk climb over and jump down beside Sun Dancer amid a splatter of applause from the onlookers.

'Good-looking lad.' Dennis was watching Dirk also, but there was something in his tone that added, *but I'm glad he's not mine.*

'Thanks.' The defiance in Sean's voice was not lost on Dennis and he smiled ironically.

'We'd better go across and talk to the other judges, Garrick is waiting.' Dennis jerked his head towards the carriage at the end of the line, and although he had been painfully aware of it, Sean looked at it for the first time.

Together with Pye, Erasmus and his father, Michael was standing beside it watching them. Tall and lean in tight black riding-boots, and an open shirt of white silk accentuating the breadth of his shoulders, he leaned against the wheel. Above him Ada and Anna sat together on the rear seat and suddenly Sean felt a twist of anger in his stomach that Ada should be there with *them*.

'Mother.' He greeted her without smiling.

'Hello, Sean.' And he could not fathom the tone of her voice nor her expression. Was it regret, or perhaps a reluctant rejection? For a long minute they held each other's eyes – until at last Sean had to break, because now, instead of anger, he felt guilty. But he did not understand the source of his guilt – it was only the sorrowful accusation in Ada's eyes that had given it to him.

'Anna.' He greeted her and received in exchange a stiff nod.

'Garry.' Sean tried to smile. He made a movement to lift his right hand, but as he did so he knew it would be rejected, for the same accusation that he had seen in Ada's eyes was also in Garry's. He turned with relief to Michael.

'Hello, Mike. You know you're going to get the pants thrashed off you?'

'I'm going to make you eat those words without salt!' And they laughed together easily, laughed with such obvious joy in each other that Anna moved restlessly in her seat and spoke sharply.

'Can't we get this over with, Ronny?'

'Yes,' Ronny Pye agreed hastily. 'Well, then. Where is young Dirk? We'd better go and find him.'

In a group they left the women and moved through the crowd towards the stockpen where Dirk stood laughing with two girls that Sean recognized as daughters of one of the factory foremen. They were both looking up at Dirk and reacting with such unashamed adoration that Sean felt a lift of indulgent pride. Casually Dirk dismissed the girls and came across to meet them.

'All set, Pa.'

'So I see,' Sean gruffed, and waited for Dirk to show courtesy to the men with him, but Dirk ignored them and spoke only to Ronny Pye.

'Let's hear it.'

'Well, then. A contest between Garry Courtney's colt Grey Weather and Sean Courtney's filly Sun Dancer. An honour match with no stake put up by the owners. Agreed?'

'Right,' said Sean.

Garry opened his mouth and then closed it firmly and nodded. He was sweating a little. He unfolded the handkerchief in his hand and wiped his forehead.

'The distance approximately five miles around four points. The points being firstly the posts that have been erected on this field, secondly the north-eastern boundary marker of the farm Theuniskraal.' Ronny pointed at the crest of the escarpment that stood above them, its slope golden with grass in the morning sun and smeared with streaks of dark green bush. 'Thirdly, the No. 3 diptank of Mahobo's Kloof farm, which you can't see from here as it is behind those trees.' Ronny's arm described a long arc along the crest of the escarpment and stopped pointing at the spires of a clump of saligna gums. 'But both of you know it?' 'Sure,' agreed Dirk, and Michael nodded.

'The fourth and finishing-point is the same as the starting-point – here.' He jerked his thumb at the two posts that fluttered gay with flags.

'Stewards have been posted at the Theuniskraal boundary and the dip-tank – make sure you pass on the far side of them. The judges are Messrs Petersen, Erasmus and myself. All and any dispute regarding the running or interpretation of the rules will be decided by us. . . .' Ronny went on talking and Sean felt his excitement mounting from his stomach and beginning to tingle along his forearms. It was taking a hold on all of them now, even Ronny's voice had an edge to it. Though Sean did not understand that the foxlike eagerness of his face came from the knowledge that this was a contest in which he stood to gain more than any of them. But Garrick understood fully, and his eyes watched Ronny's lips hypnotically.

'That's it, then,' Ronny finished and then to the riders, 'Get saddled up, and bring your horses to the start.'

The judges walked away and left the four Courtneys standing together.

'Sean . . .' Garry spoke first, his eyes were stricken. 'I think you should know . . .' but he did not finish.

'What?' Sean asked abruptly, and at the tone of his voice Garrick straightened up. The thing in his eyes changed shape, and became what Sean had never expected to see there – pride.

'It doesn't matter.' Garry turned and walked purposefully towards his horse, and there was a spring in his stride and a set to his shoulders.

'Good luck, Mike.' Sean punched his arm.

'And the same to you.' Michael started after Garrick, then stopped and turned back to Sean. 'Whatever anyone else says, Sean, I know you didn't plan this.' Then he was striding away.

'What the hell did he mean by that?' puzzled Sean, but Dirk cut into his thoughts.

'Why did you have to do that, Pa?' he demanded.

'What?' Sean looked at him uncomprehendingly.

'Give him luck. Why did you have to give him luck? I'm riding for you – not him. I'm your son – not him!'

The two riders moved together towards the start, and buzzing with excitement the crowd went with them.

Sean walked beside Sun Dancer, with Dirk leaning attentively from the saddle to listen to him.

'Take it gently to the swamp, don't push her for she'll need all her steam in the mud. Michael will gain there, that colt is strong in the leg, but heavy. Follow him and let him break a path for you. Out of the swamp you can catch up and pass him on the slope, push hard there. You must lead him to the top and hold your lead along the crest to the dip-tank.'

'All right, Pa.'

'Now, when you start down again keep well out beyond the Van Essen plantation on to hard ground – that way you can cut the edge of the swamp. My guess is that Mike will come straight down and plough through the middle – but you must take the longer route – and use Sun Dancer's speed against Grey Weather's strength.'

They had reached the starting-posts and the crowd scattered and spread away to line the ropes. An open funnel of humanity faced the two horsemen, then the swamp with its deceptively lush papyrus grass concealing the glutinous mudholes. Beyond it the great soar of the escarpment. A long course. A hard course.

'Are both of you ready?' called Ronny Pye from the sidelines. 'Clear the field, please, Sean.'

Sean put his hand on Dirk's knee.

'Let's see what you can do, boy.' Then he ducked under the ropes into the crowd.

Sun Dancer was skittering nervously, coming up on her back legs and throwing her head so that the mane flew red-gold in the sunlight. She was sweating in dark patches on her shoulders. Michael was circling Grey Weather, keeping him moving gently, leaning forward and patting his neck, talking to him so that he switched his ears, cocking them half back to listen.

'Quiet, please, everybody!' Dennis was using a megaphone, and the buzz of voices descended into an expectant rustling.

'You're under starter's orders now,' he shouted at the riders, 'Turn wide, and walk up together.'

They swung away from the posts, and came together. Dirk touched Sun Dancer with the spur and she jumped back thrusting her quarters into Michael's leg.

'Keep your bloody animal under control,' he snarled at Michael. 'Don't crowd me!'

'Are you nervous, Dirkie?' Obediently Michael wheeled his mount aside.

'Damn you! – I'll show you who's nervous,' and Sun Dancer threw her head in protest, as Dirk sawed her with the curb.

'Come round, swing them round.' Dennis's voice through the megaphone boomed distortedly.

They turned in line and started walking up, twenty yards from the start, two horses with the sunlight glowing on their polished skins. Pale gold and dark red. The crowd sighed softly like wind in the grass.

Ten paces and Sun Dancer was pushing forward, lengthening her stride, crabbing a little.

'Hold your line! Keep together,' Dennis cautioned them, and Dirk yanked her back roughly. The rims of his nostrils were flared and white with tension.

Michael moved up beside him, holding his hands low. The big red colt stepping high in the exaggerated action of an animal under restraint.

Quickening together over the last five paces, their riders hunching lower in the saddles, they came to the posts.

'Go!' bellowed Dennis, and 'Go!' roared a hundred voices. Still in line, matching each other's stride, they changed from a walk into an easy, free, swinging canter. Both Dirk and Michael rising slightly in their stirrups to hold them from headlong flight. Half a mile ahead lay the swamp and beyond it five miles of mountain and rough, rocky ground, of donga and thornbush. They cantered down between the yelling lines and out of the funnel into the open.

The crowd broke and scattered to various points of vantage and Sean ran with them, unslinging his binocular-case, chuckling with excitement in the general confusion of shouts and laughter.

Ruth was waiting for him beside the Rolls and he caught her around the waist and lifted her on to the bonnet.

'Sean, you'll scratch the paintwork,' she protested, as she clutched at her hat and teetered dangerously on the high, round bonnet.

'The hell with the paintwork,' he laughed as he climbed up beside her and she clung to him for support. 'There they are!'

Far out across the field the two horses ran down towards the bright green of the swamp. Sean lifted and focused his binoculars, and suddenly they were so close he expected to hear the drumming of the hooves. Grey Weather was pulling ahead, forcing powerfully with his great shoulders lunging into each stride – and Sun Dancer trailed him with her neck arched against the pressure of the bit. On her back Dirk sat upright with his elbows pressed into his flanks as he held her.

'The little bugger is listening to advice,' Sean growled. 'I quite expected him to be using the whip already.'

Across the distance that separated them Sean could feel as a tangible thing Dirk's determination to win, he could see it in the way he held his shoulders, he could see it in the rigid lines of his arms. But what he did not see were the harsh lines of hatred in Dirk's face as he stared at Michael's back ahead of him.

The beat of hooves changed its tone, no longer ringing on hard ground, but dulling as they reached the swamp. Now lumps of damp clay flew from Grey Weather's hooves and a piece hit Dirk's chest and sprayed dirt on the white silk of his shirt. Sun Dancer's gait altered as she felt the soft ground.

'Easy, girl. Hey there, girl,' Dirk whispered and held her firmly with his knees to give her confidence. The grass brushed his stirrups and ahead of him Grey Weather splashed into the first mudhole, plunged through it and into the swamp proper. The tall papyrus engulfed him.

'The old man was right,' Dirk smiled for the first time. Michael was forcing a path through the reeds, flattening them for Dirk to follow with half the effort. Twice Grey Weather sunk to his belly in potholes of black glue, rearing and struggling to free himself while Dirk skirted them.

Both horses were shiny with mud, and their riders were soaked to the waist and splattered above. The swamp stank like an animal cage and marsh gas erupted sullenly as they disturbed it. Clouds of insects rose about them, a sakabula bird fled shrieking as they ploughed through the papyrus. One of the razor leaves lashed Michael's cheek and a thread of blood ran down his jaw washing the blobs of mud with it and dripped on to his shirt.

Then suddenly the ground firmed under them, the solid papyrus broke into clumps, thinned and was left behind and Grey Weather led them out on to the first slope of the escarpment. He was running heavily now, and grunting with each stride, while Sun Dancer moved up beside him.

'You're finished!' Dirk shouted at Michael as they drew level. 'I'll see you at the finish-line,' and he leaned forward in the saddle and gave Sun Dancer the spurs and the whip together.

Without pressing his horse Michael angled him off towards the right, letting him move under slack rein to pick his own way and he began the first leg of a series of zigzags that would take him to the top.

On the steep ground below the crest Dirk used the whip incessantly, and Sun Dancer went up in a series of scrambling leaps with the loose rock rolling under her hooves. The sweat had washed away the mud from her shoulders and she landed with less control at each jump. 'Pull, you bitch. Pull!' Dirk shouted at her, and looked back in agony at Michael's sedate ascent. He was two hundred yards below and coming steadily. Dirk's movement caught Sun Dancer off balance and she landed awkwardly at the next jump, her hooves scrabbled and she started to fall. Dirk kicked his feet from the stirrups and jumped with the reins still in his hands. The instant he landed he leaned back on the reins to hold her, but she was down on her knees now, sliding back and she pulled Dirk down with her on to the level place below.

They struggled together and when at last he got her on her feet she was trembling with terror, dust and pieces of dry grass coated her muddy legs.

'Damn you! Damn you, you clumsy bitch,' whispered Dirk as he ran his hands over her hocks to check for damage. He glanced back at Michael and found him much closer now.

'Oh, God!' he blurted, snatched up Sun Dancer's reins and ran at the slope dragging her after him. Dirk came out on the crest with sweat pouring down his face and soaking through his shirt. Saliva had dried to a thick gummy froth in his mouth and he was panting harshly – but he had held on to his lead and Sun Dancer was over her trembling fit. She had recovered sufficiently to cavort a little as he mounted.

'This way, Dirkie!' The two stewards standing on the pile of stones that marked the Theuniskraal boundary were waving and shouting wild encouragement. Dirk clouted the spurs into her and was off again, galloping along the ridge, sweeping past them and on towards the clump of gums three miles ahead.

'Catch him, Mike. Ride, man, ride!' Faint shouts behind him – and Dirk knew without looking back that Mike had reached the top and was chasing him. He rode on, grimly mourning the time lost on the ascent and hating both Sun Dancer and Michael for it. At this point he should have led by four hundred yards – not fifty.

Directly ahead now was the gorge through which the Baboon Stroom dropped down the escarpment, its side choked with dark green river bush. Dirk found the path and turned away from the skyline aiming upstream at the ford. Without grass to muffle them Sun Dancer's hooves hammered in staccato rhythm on the hard-packed earth of the path, but also he could hear behind him like an echo the beat of other hooves – Michael was on to the path behind him. Dirk looked back under his own arm. Michael was so close that he could see the laughter lines creasing the corners of his mouth, and the mockery inflamed him.

'I'll show him—!' And Dirk started with the whip again, cracking it across Sun Dancer's flanks and shoulders so that she jumped forward with

a new urgency. Down the steep bank of the river and out on to the white
sandbank, he plunged with Grey Weather's nose drawing level with his
boot. Into the dark green water they rode abreast, throwing up a veil of
spray that sparkled in the sunlight, slipping from their saddles to swim
beside the horses through the deep, while the current moved them down
towards the falls. Up into the saddles again the instant the horses found the
bottom and splashed towards the far bank. Out on to the sand, with water
streaming from sodden clothing, shouting with excitement as they raced for
the narrow path that climbed the far bank. First man on to it would hold
the advantage.

'Give way! I'm leading – give me way,' screamed Dirk furiously.

'Make your own way!' Michael laughed back at him.

'You bastard!' Dirk used his knees and reins to thrust Sun Dancer's
shoulder into Michael, trying to force him clear.

'None of that!' Michael warned him.

'You bastard – I'll show you.'

They rode knee to knee now. Dirk sat up quickly and twisted his foot,
placing his booted toe under Michael's instep. With a sudden vicious lift of
his leg he slipped Michael's foot from the stirrup and threw him sideways.
As he felt himself going over Michael clutched desperately at the pommel,
pulling the saddle with him so it slid on to Grey Weather's flank and the
shift of weight forced the horse to disengage and slew away from the path.
Michael went down on his shoulder into the sand and rolled with his knees
drawn up against his stomach.

'That's for you!' Dirk yelled in defiance as he went up the bank and out
into the open veld again. Behind him in the river-bed Michael staggered to
his feet, his wet clothing coated white with sand, and ran after Grey Weather
who was trotting back towards the water with the saddle hanging under his
chest.

'The dirty little swine. My God, if only Sean knew!' Michael caught the
horse before it started to drink, wrestled the saddle on to his back again and
clinched the girth.

'Now, I can't let him win!' He jumped up on to Grey Weather and booted
him towards the bank. 'I can't let him win.'

Two hundred yards ahead Dirk's shirt was a white blob against the
brown grass. As he rounded the dip-tank and pointed Sun Dancer's head
at the ridge for the last leg, one of the stewards shouted:

'What happened to Michael?'

'He fell in the river,' Dirk called back. 'He's finished!' And his voice rang
with triumph.


'He's leading – Dirk's leading!' Sean stood on the Rolls with his glasses
trained on the clump of gum-trees, and now he was the first to spot the tiny
figure of the horseman as it showed on the crest of the escarpment.

'Where's Michael?' Ruth asked.

'He can't be far behind,' Sean muttered and waited anxiously for him to
appear. He had fretted while he watched Dirk's reckless ascent of the slope,
and cursed him loudly for his brutal treatment of Sun Dancer. Then he had

entreated him to *get a bloody move on* during the run along the ridge with Michael gaining steadily on him. When the two horsemen had veered away from the skyline to cross the Baboon Stroom they had disappeared from view and this was the first glimpse the spectators had received of either competitor since that moment.

'The little idiot's riding too wide. I told him to cut the edge of the swamp – not ride round it altogether.'

'Where's Michael?' Ruth repeated. Sean swung the glasses back and scanned the crest with the first twinges of concern.

'Not showing yet – he must have run into trouble.'

'Do you think he's all right? Has he been hurt?'

'How should I know?' Sean's anxiety made him irritable, but immediately he was penitent and encircled Ruth's waist with his arm. 'He can look after himself, that one. No sense fussing about him.'

Dirk was well down the slope now, leaving a thin trail of dust, for Sun Dancer skidded on her haunches most of the way.

'Still no sign of Michael?' Ruth moved restlessly against him.

'No. Not yet,' Sean grunted. 'Dirk can afford to miss the swamp – he's leading by a quarter of a mile.'

Suddenly a sigh of relief moved the crowd like a gust of wind through a field of wheat.

'There he is!'

'He's coming straight down the slope.'

'He can't make it unless he flies!'

Sean swung his glasses from Dirk to Michael and back, estimating their speeds and positions, allowing for Michael's delay in the swamp, but setting against that the additional distance that Dirk had to cover.

'It's going to be close—' he decided aloud. 'Dirk's got the edge, but it's going to be very close.'

Ada did not see it that way. Dirk was leading and Dirk was going to win. She looked across at Garrick. He stood beside the finishing-post a hundred yards away, but even at that distance there was no mistaking the droop of his shoulders and the air of misery that surrounded him like an aura of defeat. Sun Dancer's hooves were slashing his life to threads.

Unable to bear it a moment longer, Ada jumped down from the carriage and ran through the crowd to where Sean stood like a triumphant colossus on the bonnet of the Rolls.

'Sean.' She reached up and touched his leg, but he was so engrossed he did not feel or hear her.

'Sean,' she shouted and tugged at his trouser-leg.

'Mother?' He turned vaguely to look down at her.

'I must talk to you,' Ada shouted above the sound of the crowd that was rising with excitement.

'Not now. They're coming in to the finish – climb up here where you can see it.'

'Now. I must speak to you now. Come down this instant!' Her tone shocked him, for a second he wavered and peered furtively back at the race. Then he shrugged with resignation and jumped down beside her.

'What is it? Please be quick – I don't want to miss—'

'I'll be quick.' Sean had never seen such a cold fury on her before. 'I wanted to say that I never thought I'd see that day when I had nothing left for you but contempt. Thoughtless you've been often – but never downright merciless.'

'Mother, I . . .' He was bewildered.

'Listen to me. You set out to destroy your brother and you've done it. Well, I hope you have the pleasure of it. You've got Theuniskraal now. Enjoy it, Sean. Sleep well at night.'

'Theuniskraal! What do you mean?' He shouted at her now in his confusion. 'I didn't wager for the farm!'

'Ah, no,' Ada scoffed at him. 'Of course you didn't – you let Ronny Pye do that for you.'

'Pye? What's he got to do with it?'

'Everything! He helped you plan it. He helped you provoke Garry into this stupidity. He holds the mortgage on Theuniskraal.'

'But . . .' Slowly the enormity of it all began to shape up in Sean's mind.

'You took his leg – now take Theuniskraal, but pay for it with my love.' She looked steadily into his eyes, but the pain was there clouding her own. 'Good-bye, Sean. we won't speak to each other again.' And she walked slowly away. She walked like an old woman at last, a tired and worn old woman.

Sean understood and began to run towards the finishing-line. He drove through the crowd like a shark through a shoal of sardines. Over their heads he saw the two horsemen galloping in across the field.

Dirk was leading, standing in the stirrups to thrash Sun Dancer with the whip. His black hair fluttered in the wind, and his shirt filthy with thrown mud. Under him the filly danced on flying hooves and the beat of them drummed above the rising roar of the crowd. Her body was black and shiny with sweat, and froth flew from her gaping pink mouth to form white lace on her chest and flanks.

Fifty hopeless yards behind her plunged the colt with Michael flogging his heels into him with despair. Michael's face was twisted in an agony of frustration. Grey Weather was finished, his legs loose with exhaustion and his breath sawing hoarsely with each stride.

Sean tore his way through the press of bodies that lined the guide ropes. He reached the front rank and shouldered two women from his path. Then he stooped and ducked under the rope into the open.

Sun Dancer was almost up to him, hammering down in a crescendo of hooves, her head nodding with each stride.

'Dirk! Stop her!' roared Sean.

'Pa! Pa! Get out of the way . . .' Dirk screamed back at him, but Sean sprang to intercept him.

'Pa!'

Sean was in front of him, crouching with arms extended. Too close to swing Sun Dancer's head away from him, too late to stop her charge.

'Jump, girl, jump,' shouted Dirk and gathered the horse with his knees, feeling her respond with a bunching of her quarters; feeling her lift her forelegs against her chest and drive upwards in a high parabola. But sensing also the sluggishness of her exhausted body and knowing she had not gone high enough to clear Sean's head.

An aching moment as Sun Dancer lifted clear of the ground, the horrified groan of the crowd as her forelegs smashed into Sean and she twisted in the air, falling. Dirk thrown, his stirrup leathers parting like whip cracks. Then all of them down together in the grass. Shrill screams of women in the crowd.

Sun Dancer struggling up again with a foreleg swinging loosely from the knee, whinnying in the pain of broken bone.

Sean on his back, his head twisted to the side and blood from his torn cheek dribbling into his nose and mouth so that his breathing snored hoarsely.

Dirk with the skin smeared from elbows and one cheek, crawling towards Sean, kneeling beside him, raising both hands clenched, hammering down with them so that his fists splattered the blood, beating them into the chest and slack, unconscious face of his father.

'Why did you? Oh, God, I hate you.' Shock and fury and despair. 'For you! You stopped me, you stopped me.'

Michael dragging Grey Weather down on his haunches, flinging from the saddle, running to them, holding Dirk's arms, dragging him off, fighting him.

'Leave him, you little bastard.'

'He didn't want me to. He stopped me, I hate him. I'll kill him.'

The crowd surging forward, flattening the guide ropes, two men helping Michael hold Dirk, the rest of them ringing Sean's body.

The cries and questions:

'Where's Doc Fraser?'

'Jesus, he's badly hurt!'

'Catch that horse. Get a gun.'

'What about the bets?'

'Don't touch him. Wait . . .'

'Got to straighten his arm.'

'Get a gun. For Christ sake, get a gun.'

Then a new silence on them, their ranks opening quietly and Ruth coming through to him running – Mbejane behind her.

'Sean.' She knelt beside him, clumsy in her pregnancy. 'Sean,' she began again, and the men about her could not look at her face.

'Mbejane, bring him to the car,' she whispered.

He slipped the monkey-skin cloak from his shoulder and let it drop, stooped over Sean and lifted him. The great black muscles of his chest and arms swelled, and he stood with his legs braced wide against the weight.

'His arm, Nkosikazi.'

She arranged the hanging arm comfortably across his chest.

'Bring him,' she repeated and together they walked through the crowd. Sean's head lolled against Mbejane's shoulder like that of a sleeping child. Mbejane laid Sean gently on the back seat with his head in Ruth's lap.

'My daddy,' she kept repeating, her face screwed up with horror at the blood and her tiny body trembling like that of a frightened rabbit.

'Will you drive us please, Michael?' Ruth looked up at him as he stood beside the Rolls. 'Take us to Protea Street.'

With Mbejane loping alongside, the big car bumped across the field

through the throng of anxious watchers, then swung on to the main road
and moved away towards Ladyburg.

# Chapter Eighty-six

While about him the crowds scattered slowly and drifted to their carriages,
Dirk Courtney stood alone and watched the Rolls disappear in its own
blown dust.

Waves of reaction shivered up his legs and turned to heavy nausea in his
gut. The open gravel rash on his face burned like acid spilled upon the skin.

'You'd better go in and have Doc Fraser put something on your face.'
Coming from his carriage with a heavy service revolver, Dennis Petersen
paused beside him.

'Yes,' Dirk answered dully, and Dennis walked on to where two native
grooms held Sun Dancer. Unsteadily on three legs, but quiet now, she stood
between them with her head hanging dejectedly.

Dennis touched the muzzle of the revolver to her forehead, and at the shot
she recoiled violently and dropped, shuddering. Her legs stiffened in one last
convulsion, then she lay still.

Watching, Dirk shuddered in sympathy and then leaned forward to vent
his nausea in the grass. It came up sour and scalding hot. He wiped it from
his mouth with the palm of his hand, then he began to walk. Without
direction, blindly, from the field towards the escarpment.

Over in his mind, keeping pace with his legs like the refrain of a marching
song:

*He doesn't want me. He doesn't want me.*

And then savagely:

*I hope he dies. Please let him die.*

'Please let him die.' Anna Courtney said it softly, so that Garry standing
below her seat in the buggy did not hear her. He stood with his shoulders
hunched, and his head thrust forward in thought, hands hanging at his sides
slowly folding and unfolding, then he raised one of them and squeezed the
fingers into his closed eyelids.

'I'm going to him,' he said. 'God help me, but I'm going to him.'

'No! I forbid it. Leave him – let him suffer as I suffered.'

Slowly, bewildered, Garry shook his head.

'I must. It's too long, too much. I must. Pray God it's not too late.'

'Let him die.' Then suddenly it snapped in her head, broke under the
weight of the hatred so long sustained.

She rose screaming in her seat. 'Die! Damn you. Die!' And Garry uncovered his eyes, and looked at her in alarm.

'Compose yourself, my dear.'

'Die! Die!' Her face was blotched with flaming spots of red, and her voice squawked as though she were being strangled. Garry scrambled up beside her and flung his arms around her protectively.

'Get away from me. Don't touch me.' She screamed at him: fighting from his embrace. 'Because of you I lost him. He was so big, so strong. He was mine – and because . . .'

'Anna, Anna, Please don't.' He tried to soothe her raving. 'Please stop it, my dear.'

'You, you crawling, crippled thing. Because of you.' And suddenly it had to come out, like pus from a canker. 'But I paid you back. I took him from you also – and now he's dead. You'll never have him.' She laughed, gloating, demented.

'Anna. Stop it.'

'That night – do you remember that night? Will you or he ever forget it? I wanted him, I wanted him big like a bull on top of me, I wanted him rutting deep like it was before – I begged him. I pleaded – but because of you. Because of his crippled little weakling brother. Christ, I hated him!' She laughed again, a shriek of pain and hatred. 'I tore my clothing and bit into my own lips, as I had wanted him to do. When you came – I wanted you to . . . but you, I had forgotten you were only half a man! I wanted you to kill him – *kill him!*'

Pale, so that the sweat on his face shone like water on white marble, Garry pulled away from her with loathing.

'All this time I thought he – I believed you.' And he half fell from the buggy, leaning against it for a moment to steady himself. '. . . All this time wasted.' Then he launched himself and began to run, his bad leg jerking and catching under him.

'You want a lift, Garry?' Dennis Petersen drew level with him and called down from the carriage.

'Yes. Oh, yes.' Garry caught the handrail and dragged himself up beside Dennis. 'Take me to him, please, as fast as you can.'

## Chapter Eighty-seven

Silent, deserted, the great house crouched over her. Dark with the shutters closed against the sun, brooding and immense, smelling musty as though old passions had died within its walls.

Anna stood alone in the huge central room and screamed its name. 'Theuniskraal!'

And the thick stone walls smothered the sound of her madness.

'He is dead! Do you hear me? I took him away from all of you.'
And she shrieked in triumphant laughter, with the tears greasing her cheeks.
'I won! Do you hear me? I won!' And her grief distorted the laughter.

She picked up the heavy glass lamp and hurled it across the room; it burst and the paraffin sprayed wide, glistening on the walls and soaking into the carpet.

'Theuniskraal! Hear me! I hate you also. I hate him. I hate you all – all of you.'

She raged through the room, tearing down the gilt-framed pictures and smashing them so that the glass sparkled like tiny jewels in the gloom; she used a chair to smash in the front of the display cabinet and wreck the old china and glassware in it; she swept the books from the shelves into fluttering heaps, and threw their torn pages in the air.

'I hate!' she screamed. 'I hate!' And the great house waited silent. Exhausted with worn-out emotions – old and sad and wise.

'I hate you – all of you.' And she ran out into the passage, through the kitchens to the pantries. On the lowest shelf stood a four-gallon drum of methylated spirit and she panted as she struggled with the stopper. The stopper came out, the clear liquid welled and ran down the metal sides, and she picked the drum up across her chest and stumbled back into the kitchen. It spilled down her skirts, soaking in, drenching the heavy cloth, forming a spreading pool on the stone flags.

'I hate!' She laughed and stumbled, staggering off balance, still clutching the drum she fell against the kitchen range. Hot metal scorched her clothing and burned through to the flesh of her hip, but she did not feel it. Her sodden skirts brushed over the fire-box, a tiny point of flame caught and grew. So when she ran on into the house a fiery train swept behind her.

Back in the central room, she poured from the drum over the books and the carpet, laughing as she splashed the long-draped velvet curtains.

Oblivious of the flames that followed, until her petticoats caught and burned against her legs. Then she screamed again at the agony of her tortured flesh and brain. She dropped the metal drum and it exploded, showering her with liquid blue flame, turning her hair and her face and her whole body into a living torch, a torch that fell and writhed and died before the flames reached the thatch of the roof of Theuniskraal.

# Chapter Eighty-eight

They faced each other across the waist of the dhow, and the bright sunlight threw their shadows along the filthy planking of the deck. Two tall young men, both dark-haired and burned rich brown by the sun, both with the big

Courtney nose – both angry. From the poop three of the Arab crew watched with mild curiosity.

'So, you won't come home, then?' Michael asked. 'You're going through with this childishness?'

'Why do you want me to?'

'Me? Good God, if I never see you again it would be too soon. Ladyburg will be a cleaner town without you.'

'Then why did you come?'

'Your father asked me.'

'Why didn't he come himself?' Dirk's bitterness echoed in his voice.

'He's still a sick man – his head. Hurt badly.'

'If he wanted me, he would have come.'

'He sent for you, didn't he?'

'But why did he want you to win – why did he stop me?'

'Listen to me, Dirk. You're young yet. There are many things you don't understand.'

'Don't I!' And Dirk threw back his head and laughed scornfully. 'Oh, I understand all right. You'd better get off this boat, we're just about to sail.'

'Listen, Dirk . . .'

'Get off. Run back to him – you can have my share.'

'Dirk, listen to me. He said if you refused to come – then I was to give you this.' From inside his coat Michael drew an envelope and offered it.

'What is it?'

'I don't know – but I expect that it's money.'

Dirk came slowly across the deck and took the envelope from him.

'Have you a message for him?' Michael asked, and when Dirk shook his head he turned and jumped down on to the wooden jetty. Immediately a bustle began behind him as the Arab crew cast off the lines.

Standing on the edge of the jetty, Michael watched the stubby little craft drift out on the waters of Durban Bay. He could smell the stench of her bilges, her sides were streaked with human filth, and the single sail that rose slowly as the crew hoisted the long teak boom was stained and patched like a quilt.

The wind took her and the pregnant belly of the sail bulged out, she heeled and thrust forward through the chop of dirty green water – headed towards the bar, where a low surf broke in languid lines of white.

The two half-brothers stared at each other across the widening gap. Neither of them lifted an arm or smiled. The dhow bore away. Dirk's face was a tiny brown fleck above the white of his tropical suit, then suddenly his voice.

'Tell him . . .' Small in the distance. 'Tell him . . .' and the rest of it was lost on the wind, in the soft lap and sigh of the wavelets beneath the jetty.

# Chapter Eighty-nine

Below where they sat on the lip of the escarpment, the walls of Theuniskraal stood up like smoke-browned tombstones marking the burial ground of hatred.

'About time you started rebuilding,' Sean grunted, 'you can't stay on at Protea Street for ever.'

'No.' Garry paused before going on: 'I've picked out the new site for the homestead – there, beyond the number two dip.'

Both of them looked away from the roofless ruins, and they were silent again until shyly Garry asked, 'I'd like you to have a look at the plans. It won't be as big as the old house now that there is just Michael and I. Could you . . .?'

'Good,' Sean cut in quickly. 'Why don't you bring them across to Lion Kop tomorrow evening? Ruth will want you to stay for dinner.'

'I'd like that.'

'Come early,' said Sean, and started to stand up from the rock on which he sat. He moved heavily, awkwardly – and Garry jumped up to help him. Hating the weakness of his slowly mending body, Sean would have brushed Garry's eager hands away. But he saw the expression on his brother's face and instead he submitted meekly.

'Give me an arm over the rough ground, please.' He spoke gruffly.

Side by side, with Sean's arm across Garry's shoulder, they moved to where the buggy waited.

Ponderously Sean climbed up and settled himself into the padded leather seat.

'Thanks.' He gathered up the reins and smiled down at Garry, and Garry flushed with pleasure and looked away to the infinite lines of young wattle trees that covered the hills of Theuniskraal.

'Looks good, doesn't it?' he asked.

'You and Michael have done wonders up here,' Sean agreed, still smiling.

'Courtney Brothers and Son.' Softly Garry spoke the name of the new company which had merged the lands of Theuniskraal and Lion Kop into one vast estate. 'Now at last it is the way it should have been long ago.'

'Until tomorrow, Garry.' Sean flipped the reins and the buggy rolled forward, rocking gently over the uneven surface of the new road.

'Until tomorrow, Sean,' Garry called after him, and watched until the buggy was lost to sight among the blocks of dark mature wattle. Then he walked to his horse and mounted. He sat a while watching the distant ranks of Zulu labourers singing as they worked. He saw Michael moving on horseback amongst them, stopping occasionally to lean from the saddle and urge them on.

And Garry began to smile. The smile smoothed away the lines from around his eyes. He touched the horse with his spurs and cantered down to join Michael.

# The Eye of the Tiger

# The Eye of the Tiger

For my wife, Danielle, with love

'Tiger! Tiger! burning bright
In the forests of the night . . .
In what distant deeps or skies
Burnt the fire of thine eyes?'

WILLIAM BLAKE.

It was one of those seasons when the fish came late. I worked my boat and crew hard, running far northwards each day, coming back into grand harbour long after dark each night, but it was November the 6th when we picked up the first of the big ones riding down on the wine purple swells of the Mozambique current.

By this time I was desperate for a fish. My charter was a party of one, an advertising wheel from New York named Chuck McGeorge, one of my regulars who made the annual six-thousand mile pilgrimage to St Mary's Island for the big marlin. He was a short wiry little man, bald as an ostrich egg and grey at the temples, with a wizened brown monkey face but the good hard legs that are necessary to take on the big fish.

When at last we saw the fish, he was riding high in the water, showing the full length of his fin, longer than a man's arm and with the scimitar curve that distinguishes it from shark or porpoise. Angelo spotted him at the instant that I did, and he hung out on the foredeck stay and yelled with excitement, his gipsy curls dangling on his dark cheeks and his teeth flashing in the brilliant tropical sunlight.

The fish crested and wallowed, the water opening about him so that he looked like a forest log, black and heavy and massive, his tail fin echoing the graceful curve of the dorsal, before he slid down into the next trough and the water closed over his broad glistening back.

I turned and glared down into the cockpit. Chubby was already helping Chuck into the big fighting chair, clinching the heavy harness and gloving him up, but he looked up and caught my eye.

Chubby scowled heavily and spat over the side, in complete contrast to the excitement that gripped the rest of us. Chubby is a huge man, as tall as I am but a lot heavier in the shoulder and gut. He is also one of the most staunch and consistent pessimists in the business.

'Shy fish!' grunted Chubby, and spat again. I grinned at him.

'Don't mind him, Chuck,' I called, 'old Harry is going to set you into that fish.'

'I've got a thousand bucks that says you don't,' Chuck shouted back, his face screwed up against the dazzle of the sun-flecked sea, but his eyes twinkling with excitement.

'You're on!' I accepted a bet I couldn't afford and turned my attention to the fish.

Chubby was right, of course. After me, he is the best billfish man in the entire world. The fish was big and shy and scary.

Five times I had the baits to him, working him with all the skill and cunning I could muster. Each time he turned away and sounded as I brought *Wave Dancer* in on a converging course to cross his beak.

'Chubby, there is a fresh dolphin bait in the ice box: haul in the teasers, and we'll run him with a single bait,' I shouted despairingly.

I put the dolphin to him. I had rigged the bait myself and it swam with a fine natural action in the water. I recognized the instant in which the marlin accepted the bait. He seemed to hunch his great shoulders and I caught the flash of his belly, like a mirror below the surface, as he turned.

'Follow!' screamed Angelo. 'He follows!'

I set Chuck into the fish at a little after ten o'clock in the morning, and I fought him close. Superfluous line in the water would place additional strain on the man at the rod. My job required infinitely more skill than gritting the teeth and hanging on to the heavy fibre glass rod. I kept *Wave Dancer* running hard on the fish through the first frenzied charges and frantic flashing leaps until Chuck could settle down in the fighting chair and lean on the marlin, using those fine fighting legs of his.

A few minutes after noon, Chuck had the fish beaten. He was on the surface, in the first of the wide circles which Chuck would narrow with each turn until we had him at the gaff.

'Hey, Harry!' Angelo called suddenly, breaking my concentration. 'We got a visitor, man!'

'What is it, Angelo?'

'Big Johnny coming up current.' He pointed. 'Fish is bleeding, he's smelt it.'

I looked and saw the shark coming. The blunt fin moving up steadily, drawn by the struggle and smell of blood. He was a big hammerhead, and I called to Angelo.

'Bridge, Angelo,' and I gave him the wheel.

'Harry, you let that bastard chew my fish and you can kiss your thousand bucks goodbye,' Chuck grunted sweatily at me from the fighting chair, and I dived into the main cabin.

Dropping to my knees I knocked open the toggles that held down the engine hatch and I slid it open.

Lying on my belly, I reached up under the decking and grasped the stock of the FN carbine hanging in its special concealed slings of inner tubing.

As I came out on to the deck I checked the loading of the rifle, and pushed the selector on to automatic fire.

'Angelo, lay me alongside that old Johnny.'

Hanging over the rail in *Wave Dancer*'s bows, I looked down on to the shark as Angelo ran over him. He was a hammerhead all right, a big one, twelve feet from tip to tail, coppery bronze through the clear water.

I aimed carefully between the monstrous eyestalks which flattened and deformed the shark's head, and I fired a short burst.

The FN roared, the empty brass cases spewed from the weapon and the water erupted in quick stabbing splashes.

The shark shuddered convulsively as the bullets smashed into his head, shattering the gristly bone and bursting his tiny brain. He rolled over and began to sink.

'Thanks, Harry,' Chuck gasped, sweating and red-faced in the chair.

'All part of the service,' I grinned at him, and went to take the wheel from Angelo.

At ten minutes to one, Chuck brought the marlin up to the gaff, punishing him until the great fish came over on his side, the sickle tail beating feebly, and the long beak opening and shutting spasmodically. The glazed single eye was as big as a ripe apple, and the long body pulsed and shone with a thousand flowing shades of silver and gold and royal purple.

'Cleanly now, Chubby,' I shouted, as I got a gloved hand on the steel trace and drew the fish gently towards where Chubby waited with the stainless-steel hook at the gaff held ready.

Chubby withered me with a glance that told me clearly that he had been pulling the steel into billfish when I was still a gutter kid in a London slum.

'Wait for the roll,' I cautioned him again, just to plague him a little, and Chubby's lip curled at the unsolicited advice.

The swell rolled the fish up to us, opening the wide chest that glowed silver between the spread wings of the pectoral fins.

'Now!' I said, and Chubby sank the steel in deep. In a burst of bright crimson heart blood, the fish went into its death frenzy, beating the surface to flashing white and drenching us all under fifty gallons of thrown sea water.

I hung the fish on Admiralty Wharf from the derrick of the crane. Benjamin, the harbour-master, signed a certificate for a total weight of eight hundred and seventeen pounds. Although the vivid fluorescent colours had faded in death to flat sooty black, yet it was impressive for its sheer bulk – fourteen feet six inches from the point of its bill to the tip of its flaring swallow tail.

'Mister Harry done hung a Moses on Admiralty,' the word was carried through the streets by running bare-footed urchins, and the islanders joyously snatched at the excuse to cease work and crowd the wharf in fiesta array.

The word travelled as far as old Government House on the bluff, and the presidential Land-Rover came buzzing down the twisting road with the gay little flag fluttering on the bonnet. It butted its way through the crowd and deposited the great man on the wharf. Before independence, Godfrey Biddle had been St Mary's only solicitor, island-born and London-trained.

'Mister Harry, what a magnificent specimen,' he cried delightedly. A fish like this would give impetus to St Mary's budding tourist trade, and he came to clasp my hand. As State Presidents go in this part of the world, he was top of the class.

'Thank you, Mr President, sir.' Even with the black homburg on his head, he reached to my armpit. He was a symphony in black, black wool suit, and patent leather shoes, skin the colour of polished anthracite and only a fringe of startlingly white fluffy hair curling around his ears.

'You really are to be congratulated.' President Biddle was dancing with excitement, and I knew I'd be eating at Government House on guest nights again this season. It had taken a year or two – but the President had finally accepted me as though I was island-born. I was one of his children, with all the special privilege that this position carried with it.

Fred Coker arrived in his hearse, but armed with his photographic equipment, and while he set up his tripod and disappeared under the black cloth to focus the ancient camera, we posed for him beside the colossal carcass. Chuck in the middle holding the rod, with the rest of us grouped around him, arms folded like a football team. Angelo and I were grinning and Chubby was scowling horrifically into the lens. The picture would look good in my new advertising brochure – loyal crew and intrepid skipper, hair curling out from under his cap and from the vee of his shirt, all muscle and smiles – it would really pack them in next season.

I arranged for the fish to go into the cold room down at the pineapple export sheds. I would consign it out to Rowland Wards of London for mounting on the next refrigerated shipment. Then I left Angelo and Chubby to scrub down *Dancer*'s decks, refuel her across the harbour at the Shell basin and take her out to moorings.

As Chuck and I climbed into the cab of my battered old Ford pick-up, Chubby sidled across like a racecourse tipster, speaking out of the corner of his mouth.

'Harry, about my billfish bonus—' I knew exactly what he was going to ask, we went through this every time.

'Mrs Chubby doesn't have to know about it, right?' I finished for him.

'That's right,' he agreed lugubriously, and pushed his filthy deep-sea cap to the back of his head.

I put Chuck on the plane at nine the next morning and I sang the whole way down from the plateau, honking the horn of my battered old Ford pick-up at the island girls working in the pineapple fields. They straightened up with big flashing smiles under the brims of the wide straw hats and waved.

At Coker's Travel Agency I changed Chuck's American Express traveller's cheques, haggling the rate of exchange with Fred Coker. He was in full fig, tailcoat and black tie. He had a funeral at noon. The camera and tripod laid up for the present, photographer became undertaker.

Coker's Funeral Parlour was in the back of the Travel Agency opening into the alley, and Fred used the hearse to pick up tourists at the airport, first discreetly changing his advertising board on the vehicle and putting the seats in over the rail for the coffins.

I booked all my charters through him, and he clouted his ten per cent off my traveller's cheques. He had the insurance agency as well, and he deducted the annual premium for *Dancer* before carefully counting out the balance. I recounted just as carefully, for although Fred looks like a schoolmaster, tall and thin and prim, with just enough island blood to give him a healthy all-over tan, he knows every trick in the book and a few which have not been written down yet.

He waited patiently while I checked, taking no offence, and when I stuffed the roll into my back pocket, his gold pince-nez sparkled and he told me like a loving father, 'Don't forget you have a charter party coming in tomorrow, Mister Harry.'

'That's all right, Mr Coker – don't you worry, my crew will be just fine.'

'They are down at the Lord Nelson already,' he told me delicately. Fred keeps his finger firmly on the islands's pulse.

'Mr Coker, I'm running a charter boat, not a temperance society. Don't worry,' I repeated, and stood up. 'Nobody ever died of a hangover.'

I crossed Drake Street to Edward's Store and a hero's welcome. Ma Eddy herself came out from behind the counter and folded me into her warm pneumatic bosom.

'Mister Harry,' she cooed and bussed me, 'I went down to the wharf to see the fish you hung yesterday.' Then she turned still holding me and shouted at one of her counter girls, 'Shirley, you get Mister Harry a nice cold beer now, hear?'

I hauled out my roll. The pretty little island girls chittered like sparrows when they saw it, and Ma Eddy rolled her eyes and hugged me closer.

'What do I owe you, Missus Eddy?' From June to November is a long off-season, when the fish do not run, and Ma Eddy carries me through that lean time.

I propped myself against the counter with a can of beer in my hand, picking the goods I needed from the shelves and watching their legs as the girls in their mini-skirts clambered up the ladders to fetch them down – old Harry feeling pretty good and cocky with that hard lump of green stuff in his back pocket.

Then I went down to the Shell Company basin and the manager met me at the door of his office between the big silver fuel storage tanks.

'God, Harry, I've been waiting for you all morning. Head Office has been screaming at me about your bill.'

'Your waiting is over, brother,' I told him. But *Wave Dancer*, like most beautiful women, is an expensive mistress, and when I climbed back into the pick-up, the lump in my pocket was severely depleted.

They were waiting for me in the beer garden of the Lord Nelson. The island is very proud of its associations with the Royal Navy, despite the fact that it is no longer a British possession but revels in an independence of six years' standing; yet for two hundred years previously it had been a station of the British fleet. Old prints by long-dead artists decorated the public bar, depicting the great ships beating up the channel or lying in grand harbour alongside Admiralty Wharf – men-of-war and merchantmen of John Company victualled and refitted here before the long run south to the Cape of Good Hope and the Atlantic.

St Mary's has never forgotten her place in history, nor the admirals and mighty ships that made their landfall here. The Lord Nelson is a parody of its former grandeur, but I enjoy its decayed and seedy elegance and its associations with the past more than the tower of glass and concrete that Hilton has erected on the headland above the harbour.

Chubby and his wife sat side by side on the bench against the far wall, both of them in their Sunday clothes. This was the easiest way to tell them apart, the fact that Chubby wore the three-piece suit which he had bought for his wedding – the buttons straining and gaping, and the deep-sea cap stained with salt crystals and fish blood on his head – while his wife wore a full-length black dress of heavy wool, faded greenish with age, and black button-up boots beneath. Otherwise their dark mahogany faces were almost identical, though Chubby was freshly shaven and she did have a light moustache.

'Hello, Missus Chubby, how are you?' I asked.

'Thank you, Mister Harry.'

'Will you take a little something, then?'

'Perhaps just a little orange gin, Mister Harry, with a small bitter to chase it down.'

While she sipped the sweet liquor, I counted Chubby's wages into her hand, and her lips moved as she counted silently in chorus. Chubby watched anxiously, and I wondered once again how he had managed all these years to fool her on the billfish bonus.

Missus Chubby drained the beer and the froth emphasized her moustache.

'I'll be off then, Mister Harry.' She rose majestically, and sailed from the courtyard. I waited until she turned into Frobisher Street before I slipped Chubby the little sheath of notes under the table and we went into the private bar together.

Angelo had a girl on each side of him and one on his lap. His black silk shirt was open to the belt buckle, exposing gleaming chest muscles. His denim pants fitted skin-tight, leaving no doubt as to his gender, and his boots were hand-tooled and polished westerns. He had greased his hair and sleeked it back in the style of the young Presley. He flashed his grin like a stage lamp across the room and when I paid him he tucked a banknote into the front of each girl's blouse.

'Hey, Eleanor, you go sit on Harry's lap, but careful now. Harry's a virgin – you treat him right, hear?' He roared with delighted laughter and turned to Chubby.

'Hey, Chubby, you quit giggling like that all the time, man! That's stupid – all that giggling and grinning.' Chubby's frown deepened, his whole face crumpling into folds and wrinkles like that of a bulldog. 'Hey, Mister barman, you give old Chubby a drink now. Perhaps that will stop him cutting up stupid, giggling like that.'

At four that afternoon Angelo had driven his girls off, and he sat with his glass on the table top before him. Beside it lay his bait knife honed to a razor edge and glinting evilly in the overhead lights. He muttered darkly to himself, deep in alcoholic melancholy. Every few minutes he would test the edge of the knife with his thumb and scowl around the room. Nobody took any notice of him.

Chubby sat on the other side of me, grinning like a great brown toad – exposing a set of huge startlingly white teeth with pink plastic gums.

'Harry,' he told me expansively, one thick muscled arm around my neck. 'You are a good boy, Harry. You know what, Harry, I'm going to tell you now what I never told you before.' He nodded wisely as he gathered himself for the declaration he made every pay day. 'Harry, I love you, man. I love you better than my own brother.'

I lifted the stained cap and lightly caressed the bald brown dome of his head. 'And you are my favourite eggshell blond,' I told him.

He held me at arm's length for a moment, studying my face, then burst into a lion's roar of laughter. It was completely infectious and we were both still laughing when Fred Coker walked in and sat down at the table. He adjusted his pince-nez and said primly, 'Mister Harry, I have just received a special delivery from London. Your charter cancelled.' I stopped laughing.

'What the hell!' I said. Two weeks without a charter in the middle of high season and only a lousy two-hundred-dollar reservation fee.

'Mr Coker, you have got to get me a party.' I had three hundred dollars left in my pocket from Chuck's charter.

'You got to get me a party,' I repeated, and Angelo picked up his knife and with a crash drove the point deeply into the table top. Nobody took any notice of him, and he scowled angrily around the room.

'I'll try,' said Fred Coker, 'but it's a bit late now.'

'Cable the parties we had to turn down.'

'Who will pay for the cables?' Fred asked delicately.

'The hell with it, I'll pay.' And he nodded and went out. I heard the hearse start up outside.

'Don't worry, Harry,' said Chubby. 'I still love you, man.'

Suddenly beside me Angelo went to sleep. He fell forward and his forehead hit the table top with a resounding crack. I rolled his head so that he would not drown in the puddle of spilled liquor, returned the knife to its sheath, and took charge of his bank roll to protect him from the girls who were hovering close.

Chubby ordered another round and began to sing a rambling, mumbling shanty in island patois, while I sat and worried.

Once again I was stretched out neatly on the financial rack, God how I hate money – or rather the lack of it. Those two weeks would make all the difference as to whether or not *Dancer* and I could survive the off-season, and still keep our good resolutions. I knew we couldn't. I knew we would have to go on the night run again.

The hell with it, if we had to do it, we might as well do it now. I would pass the word that Harry was ready to do a deal. Having made the decision, I felt that pleasurable tightening of the nerves, the gut thing that goes with danger. The two weeks of cancelled time might not be wasted after all.

I joined Chubby in song, not entirely certain that we were singing the same number, for I seemed to reach the end of each chorus a long time before Chubby.

It was probably this musical feast that called up the law. On St Mary's this takes the form of an Inspector and four troopers, which is more than adequate for the island. Apart from a great deal of 'carnal knowledge under the age of consent' and a little wife-beating, there is no crime worthy of the name.

Inspector Peter Daly was a young man with a blond moustache, a high English colour on smooth cheeks and pale blue eyes set close together like those of a sewer rat. He wore the uniform of the British colonial police, the cap with the silver badge and shiny patent leather peak, the khaki drill starched and ironed until it crackled softly as he walked, the polished leather belt and Sam Browne cross-straps. He carried a malacca cane swagger stick which was also covered with polished leather. Except for the green and yellow St Mary's shoulder flashes, he looked like the Empire's pride, but like the Empire the men who wore the uniform had also crumbled.

'Mr Fletcher,' he said, standing over our table and slapping the swagger stick lightly against his palm. 'I hope we are not going to have any trouble tonight.'

'Sir,' I prompted him. Inspector Daly and I were never friends – I don't like bullies, or persons who in positions of trust supplement a perfectly adequate salary with bribes and kick-backs. He had taken a lot of my hard-won gold from me in the past, which was his most unforgivable sin.

His mouth hardened under the blond moustache and his colour came up quickly. 'Sir,' he repeated reluctantly.

Now it is true that once or twice in the remote past Chubby and I had given way to an excess of boyish high spirits when we had just hung a Moses fish – however, this did not give Inspector Daly any excuse for talking like that. He was after all a mere expatriate out on the island for a three-year contract – which I knew from the President himself would not be renewed.

'Inspector, am I correct in my belief that this is a public place – and that neither my friends nor I are committing a trespass?'

'That is so.'

'Am I also correct in thinking that singing of tuneful and decent songs in a public place does not constitute a criminal act?'

'Well, that is true, but—'

'Inspector, piss off,' I told him pleasantly. He hesitated, looking at Chubby and me. Between the two of us we make up a lot of muscle, and he could see the unholy battle gleam in our eyes. Your could see he wished he had his troopers with him.

'I'll be keeping an eye on you,' he said and, clutching at his dignity like a beggar's rags, he left us.

'Chubby, you sing like an angel,' I said and he beamed at me.

'Harry, I'm going to buy you a drink.' And Fred Coker arrived in time to be included in the round. He drank lager and lime juice which turned my stomach a little, but his tidings were an effective antidote.

'Mister Harry, I got you a party.'

'Mister Coker, I love you.'

'I love you too,' said Chubby, but deep down I felt a twinge of disappointment. I had been looking forward to another night run.

'When are they arriving?' I asked.

'They are here already – they were waiting for me at my office when I got back.'

'No kidding.'

'They knew that your first party had cancelled, and they asked for you by name. They must have come in on the same plane as the special delivery.'

My thinking was a little muzzy right then or I might have pondered a moment how neatly one party had withdrawn and another had stepped in.

'They are staying up at the Hilton.'

'Do they want me to pick them up?'

No, they'll meet you at Admiralty Wharf ten o'clock tomorrow morning.'


I was grateful that the party had asked for such a late starting time. That morning *Dancer* was crewed by zombies. Angelo groaned and turned a light chocolate colour every time he bent over to coil a rope or rig the rods and Chubby sweated neat alcohol and his expression was truly terrifying. He had not spoken a word all morning.

I wasn't feeling all that cheerful myself. *Dancer* was snugged up alongside the wharf and I leaned on the rail of the flying bridge with my darkest pair of Polaroids over my eyes and although my scalp itched I was afraid to take off my cap in case the top of my skull came with it.

The island's single taxi, a '62 Citroën, came down Drake Street and stopped at the top end of the wharf to deposit my party. There were two of them, and I had expected three, Coker had definitely said a party of three.

They started down the long stone-paved wharf, walking side by side, and I straightened up slowly as I watched them. I felt my physical distress fade into the realms of the inconsequential, to be replaced by that gut thing again, the slow coiling and clenching within, and the little tickling feeling along the back of my arms and in the nape of the neck.

One was tall and walked with that loose easy gait of a professional athlete. He was bare-headed and his hair was pale gingery and combed carefully across a prematurely balding pate so the pink scalp showed through. However, he was lean around the belly and hips, and he was aware. It was the only word to described the charged sense of readiness that emanated from him.

It takes one to recognize one. This was a man trained to live with and by violence. He was muscle, a *soldier*, in the jargon. It mattered not for which side of the law he exercised his skills – law enforcement or its frustration – he was very bad news. I had hoped never to see this kind of barracuda cruising St Mary's placid waters. It gave me a sick little slide in the guts to know that it had found me out again. Quickly I glanced at the other man, it wasn't so obvious in him, the edge was blunted a little, the outline blurred by time and flesh, but it was there also – more bad news.

'Nice going, Harry,' I told myself bitterly. 'All this, and a hangover thrown in.'

Clearly now I recognized that the older man was the leader. He walked half a pace ahead, the younger taller man paying him that respect. He was a few years my senior also, probably late thirties. There was the beginnings of a paunch over the crocodile skin belt, and pouches of flesh along the line of his jawbone, but his hair had been styled in Bond Street and he wore his Sulka silk shirt and Gucci loafers like badges of rank. As he came on down the wharf he dabbed at this chin and upper lip with a white handkerchief and I guessed the diamond on his little finger at two carats. It was set in a plain gold ring and the wrist watch was gold also, probably by Lanvin or Piaget.

'Fletcher?' he asked, stopping below me on the jetty. His eyes were black and beady, like those of a ferret. A predator's eyes, bright without warmth. I saw he was older than I had guessed, for his hair was certainly tinted to conceal the grey. The skin of his cheeks was unnaturally tight and I could see the scars of plastic surgery in the hair line. He'd had a facelift, a vain man then, and I stored the knowledge.

He was an old soldier, risen from the ranks to a position of command. He was the brain, and the man that followed him was the muscle. Somebody had sent out their first team and, with a clairvoyant flash, I realized why my original party had cancelled.

A phone call followed by a visit from this pair would put the average citizen of marlin-fishing for life. They had probably done themselves a serious injury in their rush to cancel.

'Mr Materson?' Come aboard –' One thing was certain, they had not come for the fishing, and I decided on a low and humble profile until I had figured out the percentages, so I threw in a belated '– sir.'

The muscle man jumped down to the deck, landing soft-footed like a cat and I saw the way that the folded coat over his arm swung heavily, there was something weighty in the pocket. He confronted my crew, thrusting out his jaw and running his eyes over them swiftly.

Angelo flashed a watered-down version of the celebrated smile and touched the brim of his cap. 'Welcome, sir.' And Chubby's scowl lightened momentarily and he muttered something that sounded like a curse, but was probably a warm greeting. The man ignored them and turned to hand Materson down to the deck where he waited while his bodyguard checked out *Dancer*'s main saloon. Then he went in and I followed him.

Our accommodation is luxurious, at a hundred and twenty-five thousand nicker it should be. The air-conditioning had taken the bite out of the morning heat and Materson sighed with relief and dabbed again with his handkerchief as he sank into one of the padded seats.

'This is Mike Guthrie.' He indicated the muscle who was moving about the cabin checking at the ports, opening doors and generally over-playing his hand, coming on very tough and hard.

'My pleasure, Mr Guthrie.' I grinned with all my boyish charm, and he waved airily without glancing at me.

'A drink, gentlemen?' I asked, as I opened the liquor cabinet. They took a Coke each, but I needed something medicinal for the shock and the hangover. The first swallow of cold beer from the can revitalized me.

'Well, gentlemen, I think I shall be able to offer you some sport. Only yesterday I hung a very good fish, and all the signs are for a big run –'

Mike Guthrie stepped in front of me and stared into my face. His eyes were flecked with brown and pale green, like a hand-loomed tweed.

'Don't I know you?' he asked.

'I don't think I've ever had the pleasure.'

'You are a London boy, aren't you?' He had picked up the accent.

'I left Blighty a long time ago, mate,' I grinned, letting it come out broad. He did not smile, and dropped into the seat opposite me, placing his hands on the table top between us, spreading his fingers palm downwards. He continued to stare at me. A very tough baby, very hard.

'I'm afraid that it is too late for today,' I babbled on cheerfully. 'If we are going to fish the Mozambique, we have to clear harbour by six o'clock. However, we can make an early start tomorrow –'

Materson interrupted my chatter. 'Check that list out, Fletcher, and let us know what you are short.' He passed me a folded sheet of foolscap, and I glanced down the handwritten column. It was all scuba diving gear and salvage equipment.

'You gentlemen aren't interested in big game fishing then?' Old Harry showing surprise and amazement at such an unlikely eventuality.

'We have come out to do a little exploring – that's all.'

I shrugged. 'You're paying, we do what you want to do.'

'Have you got all that stuff?'

'Most of it.' In the off-season I run a cut-rate package deal for scuba buffs which helps pay expenses. I had a full range of diving sets and there was an air compressor built in to *Dancer's* engine room for recharging. 'I don't have the air bags or all that rope –'

'Can you get them?'

'Sure.' Ma Eddy had a pretty good selection of ships' stores, and Angelo's old man was a sail-maker. He could run up the air bags in a couple of hours.

'Right then, get it.'

I nodded. 'When do you want to start?'

'Tomorrow morning. There will be one other person with us.'

'Did Mr Coker tell you it's five hundred dollars a day – and I'll have to charge you for this extra equipment?'

Materson inclined his head and made as if to rise.

'Would it be okay to see a little of that out front?' I asked softly, and they froze. I grinned ingratiatingly.

'It's been a long lean winter, Mr Materson, and I've got to buy this stuff and fill my fuel tanks.'

Materson took out his wallet and counted out three hundred pounds in fivers. As he was doing so he said in his soft purry voice, 'We won't need your crew, Fletcher. The three of us will help you handle the boat.'

I was taken aback. I had not expected that. 'They'll have to draw full wages, if you lay them off. I can't reduce my rate.'

Mike Guthrie was still sitting opposite me, and now he leaned forward. 'You heard the man, Fletcher, just get your niggers off the boat,' he said softly.

Carefully I folded the bundle of five pound notes and buttoned them into my breast pocket, then I looked at him. He was very quick, I could see him tense up ready for me and for the first time he showed expression in those cold speckled eyes. It was anticipation. He knew he had reached me, and he thought I was going to try him. He wanted that, he wanted to take me apart. He left his hands on the table, palms downwards, fingers spread. I thought how I might take the little finger of each hand and snap them at the middle joint like a pair of cheese sticks. I knew I could do it before he had a chance to move, and the knowledge gave me a great deal of pleasure, for I was very angry. I haven't many friends, but I value the few I have.

'Did you hear me speak, boy?' Guthrie hissed at me, and I dredged up the boyish grin again and let it hang at a ridiculous angle on my face.

'Yes, sir, Mr Guthrie,' I said. 'You're paying the money, whatever you say.'

I nearly choked on the words. He leaned back in his seat, and I saw that he was disappointed. He was muscle, and he enjoyed his work. I think I knew then that I was going to kill him, and I took enough comfort from the thought to enable me to hold the grin.

Materson was watching us with those bright little eyes. His interest was detached and clinical, like a scientist studying a pair of laboratory specimens. He saw that the confrontation had been resolved for the present, and his voice was soft and purry again.

'Very well, Fletcher.' He moved towards the deck. 'Get that equipment together and be ready for us at eight tomorrow morning.'

I let them go, and I sat and finished the beer. It may have been just my hangover, but I was beginning to have a very ugly feeling about this whole charter and I realized that after all it might be best to leave Chubby and Angelo ashore. I went out to tell them.

'We've got a pair of freaks, I'm sorry but they have got some big secret and they are dealing you out.' I put the aqualung bottles on the compressor to top up, and we left *Dancer* at the wharf while I went up to Ma Eddy's and Angelo and Chubby took my drawing of the air bags across to his father's workshop.

The bags were ready by four o'clock and I picked them up in the Ford and stowed them in the sail locker under the cockpit seats. Then I spent an hour stripping and reassembling the demand valves of the scubas and checking out all the other diving equipment.

At sundown I ran *Dancer* out to her moorings on my own, and was about to leave her and row ashore in the dinghy when I had a good thought. I went back into the cabin and knocked back the toggles on the engine-room hatch.

I took the FN carbine from its hiding-place, pumped a cartridge into the breech, set her for automatic fire and clicked on the safety catch before hanging her in the slings again.

Before it was dark, I took my old cast net and waded out across the lagoon towards the main reef. I saw the swirl and run beneath the surface of the water which the setting sun had burnished to the colour of copper and flame, and I sent the net spinning high with a swing of shoulders and arms. It ballooned like a parachute, and fell in a wide circle over the shoal of striped mullet. When I pulled the drag line and closed the net over them, there were five of the big silvery fish as long as my forearm kicking and thumping in the coarse wet folds.

I grilled two of them and ate them on the veranda of my shack. They tasted better than trout from a mountain stream, and afterwards I poured a second whisky and sat on into the dark.

Usually this is the time of day when the island enfolds me in a great sense of peace, and I seem to understand what the whole business of living is all about. However, that night was not like that. I was angry that these people had come out to the island and brought with them their special brand of poison to contaminate us. Five years ago I had run from that, believing I had found a place that was safe. Yet beneath the anger, when I was honest with myself, I recognized also an excitement, a pleasurable excitement. That gut thing again, knowing that I was at risk once more. I was not sure yet what the stakes were, but I knew they were high and that I was sitting in the game with the big boys once again.

I was on the left-hand path again. The path I had chosen at seventeen, when I had deliberately decided against the university bursary which I had been awarded and instead I bunked from St Stephen's orphanage in north London and lied about my age to join a whaling factory ship bound for the

Antarctic. Down there on the edge of the great ice I lost my last vestige of appetite for the academic life. When the money I had made in the south ran out I enlisted in a special service battalion where I learned how violence and sudden death could be practised as an art. I practised that art in Malaya and Vietnam, then later in the Congo and Biafra – until suddenly one day in a remote jungle village while the thatched huts burned sending columns of tarry black smoke into an empty brazen sky and the flies came to the dead in humming blue clouds, I was sickened to the depths of my soul. I wanted out.

In the South Atlantic I had come to love the sea, and now I wanted a place beside it, with a boat and peace in the long quiet evenings.

First I needed money to buy those things – a great deal of money – so much that the only way I could earn it was in the practice of my art.

One last time, I thought, and I planned it with utmost care. I needed an assistant and I chose a man I had known in the Congo. Between us we lifted the complete collection of gold coins from the British Museum of Numismatology in Belgrave Square. Three thousand rare gold coins that fitted easily into a medium-sized briefcase, coins of the Roman Caesars and the Emperors of Byzantium, coins of the early states of America and of the English Kings – florins and leopards of Edward III, nobles of the Henrys and angels of Edward IV, treble sovereigns and unites, crowns of the rose from the reign of Henry VIII and five-pound pieces of George III and Victoria – three thousand coins, worth, even on a forced sale, not less than two million dollars.

Then I made my first mistake as a professional criminal. I trusted another criminal. When I caught up with my assistant in an Arab hotel in Beirut I reasoned with him in fairly strong terms, and when finally I put the question to him of just what he had done with the briefcase of coins, he snatched a .38 Beretta from under his mattress. In the ensuing scuffle he had his neck broken. It had been a mistake. I didn't mean to kill the man – but even more I didn't mean him to kill me. I hung a 'DON'T DISTURB' sign on his door and I caught the next plane out. Ten days later the police found the briefcase with the coins in the left-luggage department at Paddington Station. It made the front page of all the national newspapers.

I tried again at an exhibition of cut diamonds in Amsterdam, but I had done faulty research on the electronic alarm system and I tripped a beam that I had overlooked.

The plain clothes security guards who had been hired by the organizers of the exhibition rushed headlong into the uniformed police coming in through the main entrance and a spectacular shoot-out ensued, while a completely unarmed Harry Fletcher slunk away into the night to the sound of loud cries and gunfire.

I was half-way to Schipol airport by the time a cease-fire was called between the opposing forces of the law – but not before a sergeant of the Dutch police received a critical chest wound.

I sat anxiously chewing my nails and drinking innumerable beers in my room in the Holiday Inn near Zürich Airport, as I followed the gallant sergeant's fight for life on the TV set. I would have hated like all hell to have another fatality on my conscience, and I made a solemn vow that if the policeman died I would forget for ever about my place in the sun.

However, the Dutch sergeant rallied strongly and I felt an immense proprietary pride in him when he was finally declared out of danger. And when he was promoted to assistant inspector and awarded a bonus of five thousand crowns I persuaded myself that I was his fairy godfather and that the man owed me eternal gratitude.

Still, I had been shaken by two failures and I took a job as an instructor at an Outward Bound School for six months while I considered my future. At the end of six months, I decided for one more try.

This time I laid the ground-work with meticulous care. I emigrated to South Africa, where I was able with my qualifications to obtain a post as an operator with the security firm responsible for bullion shipments from the South African Reserve Bank in Pretoria to overseas destinations. For a year I worked with the transportation of hundreds of millions of dollars worth of gold bars, and I studied the system in every minute detail. The weak spot, when I found it, was at Rome – but again I needed help.

This time I went to the professionals, but I set my price at a level that made it easier for them to pay me out than put me down and I covered myself a hundred times against treachery.

It went as smoothly as I had planned it, and this time there were no victims. Nobody came out with a bullet or a cracked skull. We merely switched part of a cargo and substituted leaded cases. Then we moved two and a half tons of gold bars across the Swiss border in a furniture removals van.

In Basle, sitting in a banker's private rooms furnished with priceless antiques, above the wide, swift waters of the Rhine on which the stately white swans rode in majesty, they paid me out. Manny Resnick signed the transfer into my numbered account of one hundred and fifty thousand pounds sterling and he laughed a fat hungry little laugh.

'You'll be back, Harry – you've tasted blood now and you'll be back. Have a nice holiday, then come to me again when you've thought up another deal like this one.'

He was wrong, I never went back. I rode up to Zürich in a hire car and flew to Paris Orly. In the men's room there, I shaved off the beard and picked up the briefcase from the pay locker that contained the passort in the name of Harold Delville Fletcher. Then I flew out Pan Am for Sydney, Australia.

*Wave Dancer* cost me one hundred and twenty-five thousand pounds sterling and I took her under a deck load of fuel drums across to St Mary's, two thousand miles, a voyage on which we learned to love each other.

On St Mary's I purchased twenty-five acres of peace, and built the shack with my own hands – four rooms, a thatched roof and a wide veranda, set amongst the palms above the white beach. Except for the occasions when a night run had been forced upon me, I had walked the right-hand path since then.

It was late when I had done my reminiscences and the tide was pushing high up the beach in the moonlight before I went into the shack, but then I slept like an innocent.

They were on time the following morning. Charly Materson ran a tight outfit. The taxi deposited them at the head of the wharf while I had *Dancer* singled up at stem and stern and both engines burbling sweetly.

I watched them come, concentrating on the third member of the group. He was not what I had expected. He was tall and lean with a wide friendly face and dark soft hair. Unlike the others, his face and arms were darkly suntanned, and his teeth were large and very white. He wore denim shorts and a white sweatshirt and he had a swimmer's wide rangy shoulders and powerful arms. I knew instantly who was to use the diving equipment.

He carried a big green canvas kit bag over one shoulder. He carried it easily, though I could see that it was weighty, and he chatted gaily with his two companions who answered him in monosyllables. They flanked him like a pair of guards.

He looked up at me as they came level and I saw that he was young and eager. There was an excitement, an anticipation, about him, that reminded me sharply of myself ten years previously.

'Hi,' he grinned at me, an easy friendly grin and I realized that he was an extremely good-looking youngster.

'Greetings,' I replied, liking him from the first and intrigued as to how he had found a place with the wolf pack. Under my direction they took in the mooring lines and, from this brief exercise, I learned that the youngster was the only one of them familiar with small boats.

As we cleared the harbour, he and Materson came up on to the flying bridge. Materson had coloured slightly and his breathing was raggedy from the mild exertion. He introduced the newcomer.

'This is Jimmy,' he told me, when he had caught his breath. We shook hands and I put his age at not much over twenty. Close up I had no cause to revise my first impressions. He had a level and innocent gaze from sea-grey eyes, and his grip was firm and dry.

'She's a darling boat, skipper,' he told me, which was rather like telling a mother that her baby is beautiful.

'She's not a bad old girl.'

'What is she, forty-four, forty-five feet?'

'Forty-five,' I said, liking him a little more.

'Jimmy will give you your directions,' Materson told me. 'You will follow his orders.'

'Fine,' I said, and Jimmy coloured a little under his tan.

'Not orders, Mr Fletcher, I'll just tell you where we want to go.'

'Fine, Jim, I'll take you there.'

'Once we are clear of the island, will you turn due west?'

'Just how far in that direction do you intend going?' I asked.

'We want to cruise along the coast of the African mainland,' Materson cut in.

'Lovely,' I said, 'that's great. Did anybody tell you that they don't hang out the welcome mat for strangers there?'

'We will stay well offshore.'

I thought a moment, hesitating before turning back to Admiralty Wharf and packing the whole bunch ashore.

'Where do you want to go – north or south of the rivermouth?'

'North,' said Jimmy, and that altered the proposition for the good. South of the river they patrolled with helicopters and were very touchy about their territorial waters. I would not go in there during daylight.

In the north there was little coastal activity. There was a single crash boat at Zinballa, but when its engines were in running order, which was a few days a week, then its crew were mostly blown out of their minds with the virulent palm liquor brewed locally along the coast. When crew and engines were functioning simultaneously, they could raise fifteen knots, and *Dancer* could turn on twenty-two any time I asked her.

The final trick in my favour was that I could run *Dancer* through the maze of off-shore reefs and islands on a dark night in a roaring monsoon, while it was my experience that the crash boat commander avoided this sort of extravagance. Even on a bright sunny day and in a flat calm, he preferred the quiet and peace of Zinballa Bay. I had heard that he suffered acutely from sea sickness, and held his present appointment only because it was far away from the capital, where as a minister of the government the commander had been involved in a little unpleasantness regarding the disappearance of large amounts of foreign aid.

From my point of view he was the ideal man for the job.

'All right,' I agreed, turning to Materson. 'But I'm afraid what you're asking is going to cost you another two-fifty dollars a day – danger money.'

'I was afraid it might,' he said softly.

I brought the *Dancer* around, close to the light on Oyster Point.

It was a bright morning with a high clear sky into which the stationary clouds that marked the position of each group of islands towered in great soft columns of blinding white.

The solemn progress of the trade winds across the ocean was interrupted by the bulwark of the African continent on which they broke. We were getting the backlash here in the inshore channel, and random squalls and gusts of it spread darkly across the pale green waters and flecked the surface chop with white. *Dancer* loved it, it gave her an excuse to flounce and swish her bottom.

'You looking for anything speical – or just looking?' I asked casually, and Jimmy turned to tell me all about it. He was itchy with excitement, and the grey eyes sparkled as he opened his mouth.

'Just looking,' Materson interrupted with a ring in his voice and sharp warning in his expression, and Jimmy's mouth closed.

'I know these waters. I know every island, every reef. I might be able to save you a lot of time – and a bit of money.'

'That's very kind of you,' Materson thanked me with heavy irony. 'However, I believe we can manage.'

'You are paying,' I shrugged, and Materson glanced at Jimmy, inclined his head in a command to follow and led him down into the cockpit. They stood together beside the stern rail and Materson spoke to him quietly but earnestly for two minutes. I saw Jimmy flush darkly, his expresson changing from dismay to boyish sulks and I guessed that he was having his ear chewed to ribbons on the subject of secrecy and security.

When he came back on the flying bridge he was seething with anger, and for the first time I noticed the strong hard line of his jaw. He wasn't just a pretty boy, I decided.

Evidently on Materson's orders, Guthrie, the muscle, came out of the cabin and swung the big padded fighting chair to face the bridge. He lounged in it, even in his relaxation charged with the promise of violence like a resting leopard, and he watched us, one leg draped over the arm rest and the linen jacket with the heavy weight in its pocket folded in his lap.

A happy ship, I chuckled, and ran *Dancer* out through the islands, threading a fine course through the clear green waters where the reefs lurked darkly below the surface like malevolent monsters and the islands were fringed with coral sand as dazzling white as a snowdrift, and crowned with dark thick vegetation over which the palm stems curved gracefully, their tops shaking in the feeble remnants of the trade.

It was a long day as we cruised at random and I tried to get some hint of the object of the expedition. However, still smarting from Materson's reprimand, Jmmy was tight mouthed and grim. He asked for changes of course at intervals, after I had pointed out our position on the large scale admiralty chart which he produced from his bag.

Although there were no extraneous markings on his chart, when I examined it surreptitiously I was able to figure that we were interested in an area fifteen to thirty miles north of the multiple mouths of the Rovuma River, and up to sixteen miles offshore. An area containing perhaps three hundred islands varying in size from a few acres to many square miles – a very big haystack in which to find his needle.

I was content enough to perch up on *Dancer*'s bridge and run quietly along the seaways, enjoying the feel of my darling under me and watching the activity of the sea animals, and birds.

In the fighting chair Mike Guthrie's scalp started to show through the thin cover of hair like strips of scarlet neon lighting.

'Cook, you bastard,' I thought happily, and neglected to warn him about the tropical sun until we were running home in the dusk. The next day he was in agony with white goo smeared over his bloated and incarnadined features and a wide cloth hat covering his head, but his face flashed like the port light of an ocean-goer.

By noon on the second day I was bored. Jimmy was poor company for although he had recovered a little of his good humour he was so conscious of security that he even thought for thirty seconds before accepting an offer of coffee.

It was more for something to do than because I wanted fish for my dinner that when I saw a squadron of small kingfish charging a big shoal of sardine ahead of us, I gave the wheel to Jimmy.

'Just keep her on that heading,' I told him and dropped down into the cockpit. Guthrie watched me warily from his swollen crimson face as I glanced into the cabin and saw that Materson had my bar open and was mixing himself a gin and tonic. At seven hundred and fifty a day I didn't grudge it to him. He hadn't emerged from the cabin in two days.

I went back to the small tackle locker and selected a pair of feather jigs and tossed them out. As we crossed the track of the shoal I hit a kingfish and brought him out kicking, flashing golden in the sun.

Then I recoiled the lines and stowed them, wiped the blade of my heavy bait-knife across the oil stone to brighten up the edge and split the kingfish's belly from anal vent to gills and pulled out a handful of bloody gut to throw it into the wake.

Immediately a pair of gulls that had been weaving and hovering over us screeched with greed and plunged for the scraps. Their excitement summoned others and within minutes there was a shrieking, flapping host of them astern of us.

Their din was not so loud that it covered the metallic snicker close behind me, the unmistakable sound of the slide on an automatic pistol being drawn back and released to load and cock. I moved entirely from instinct. Without thought, the big bait-knife spun in my right hand as I changed smoothly to a throwing grip and turned and dropped to the deck in a single movement, breaking fall with heels and left arm as the knife went back over my right shoulder and I began the throw at the instant that I lined up the target.

Mike Guthrie had a big automatic in his right hand. An old-fashioned naval .45, a killer's weapon, one which would blow a hole in a man's chest through which you could drive a London cab.

Two things saved Guthrie from being pinned to the back of the fighting chair by the long heavy blade of the bait-knife. Firstly, the fact that the .45 was not pointed at me and, secondly, the expression of comical amazement on the man's scarlet face.

I prevented myself from throwing the knife, breaking the instinctive action by a major effort of will, and we stared at each other. He knew then how close he had come, and the grin he forced to his swollen sunburned lips was shaky and unconvincing. I stood up and pegged the knife into the bait chopping board.

'Do yourself a favour,' I told him quietly. 'Don't play with that thing behind my back.'

He laughed then, blustering and tough again. He swivelled the seat and aimed out over the stern. He fired twice, the shots crashing out loudly above the run of *Dancer*'s engines and the brief smell of cordite was whipped away on the wind.

Two of the milling gulls exploded into grotesque bursts of blood and feathers blown to shreds by the heavy bullets, and the rest of the flock scattered with shrieks of panic. The manner in which the birds were torn up told me that Guthrie had loaded with explosive bullets, a more savage weapon than a sawn-off shotgun.

He swivelled the chair back to face me and blew into the muzzle of the pistol like John Wayne. It was fancy shooting with that heavy calibre weapon.

'Tough cooky,' I applauded him, and turned to the bridge ladder, but Materson was standing in the doorway of the cabin with the gin in his hand and as I stepped past him he spoke quietly.

'Now I know who you are,' he said, in that soft purry voice. 'It's been worrying us, we thought we knew you.'

I stared at him, and he called past me to Guthrie.

'You know who he is now, don't you?' and Guthrie shook his head. I don't think he could trust his voice. 'He had a beard then, think about it – a mug shot photograph.'

'Jesus,' said Guthrie. 'Harry Bruce!' I felt a little shock at hearing the name spoken out loud again after all these years. I had hoped it was forgotten for ever.

'Rome,' said Materson. 'The gold heist.'

'He set it up.' Guthrie snapped his fingers. 'I was sure I knew him. It was the beard that fooled me.'

'I think you gentlemen have the wrong address,' I said with a desperate attempt at a cool tone, but was thinking quickly, trying to weigh this fresh knowledge. They had seen a mugshot – where? When? Were they law men or from the other side of the fence? I needed time to think – and I clambered up to the bridge.

'Sorry,' muttered Jimmy, as I took the wheel from him. 'I should have told you he had a gun.'

'Yeah,' I said 'It might have helped.' My mind was racing, and the first turning it took was along the left-hand path. They would have to go. They had blown my elaborate cover, they had sniffed me out and there was only one sure way. I looked back into the cockpit but both Materson and Guthrie had gone below.

An accident, take them both out at one stroke, aboard a small boat there were plenty of ways of a greenhorn could get hurt in the worst possible way. They had to go.

Then I looked at Jimmy, and he grinned at me.

'You move fast,' he said. 'Mike nearly wet himself, he thought he was going to get that knife through his gizzard.'

The kid also? I asked myself – if I took out the other two, he would have to go as well. Then suddenly I felt the same physical nausea that I had first known long ago in the Biafran village.

'You okay, skipper?' Jimmy asked quickly, it had shown on my face.

'I'm okay, Jim,' I said. 'Why don't you go fetch us a can of beer.'

While he was below I reached my decision. I would do a deal. I was certain that they didn't want their business shouted in the streets. I'd trade secrecy for secrecy. Probably they were coming to the same conclusion in the cabin below.

I locked the wheel and crossed quietly to the corner of the bridge, making sure my footsteps were not picked up in the cabin below.

The ventilator there funnels fresh air into the inlet above the saloon table. I had found that the ventilator made a reasonably effective voice tube, that sound was carried through it to the bridge.

However, the effectiveness of this listening device depends on a number of factors, chief of these being the direction and strength of the wind and the precise position of the speaker in the cabin below.

The wind was on our beam, gusting into the opening of the ventilator and blotting out patches of the conversation in the cabin. However, Jimmy must have been standing directly below the vent for his voice came through strongly when the wind roar did not smother it.

'Why don't you ask him now?' and the reply was confused, then the wind gusted and when it cleared, Jimmy was speaking again.

'If you do it tonight, where will you –' and the wind roared, '– to get the dawn light then we will have to –' The entire discussion seemed to be on times and places, and as I wondered briefly what they hoped to gain by leaving harbour at dawn, he said it again. 'If the dawn light is where –' I strained for the next words but the wind killed them for ten seconds, then '– I don't see why we can't –' Jimmy was protesting and suddenly Mike Guthrie's voice came through sharp and hard. He must have gone to stand close beside Jimmy, probably in a threatening attitude.

'Listen, Jimmy boy, you let us handle that side of it. Your job is to find the bloody thing, and you aren't doing so good this far.'

They must have moved again for their voices became indistinct and I heard the sliding door into the cockpit opening and I turned quickly to the wheel and freed the retaining handle just as Jimmy's head appeared over the edge of the deck as he came up the ladder.

He handed me the beer and he seemed to be more relaxed now. The reserve was gone from his manner. He smiled at me, friendly and trusting.

'Mr Materson says that's enough for today. We are to head for home.'

I swung *Dancer* across and the current and we came in from the west, past the mouth of Turtle Bay and I could see my shack standing amongst the palms. I felt a sudden chilling premonition of loss. The fates had called for a new deck of cards, and the game was bigger, the stakes were too rich for my blood but there was no way I could pull out now.

However, I suppressed the chill of despair, and turned to Jimmy. I would take advantage of his new attitude of trust and try for what information I could glean.

We chatted lightly on the run down the channel into grand harbour. They had obviously told him that I was off the leper list. Strangely the fact that I had a criminal past made me more acceptable to the wolf-pack. They could reckon the angles now. They had found a lever, so now they could handle me – though I was pretty sure they had not explained the whole proposition to young James.

It was obviously a relief for him to act naturally with me. He was a friendly and open person, completely lacking in guile. An example of this was the way that his surname had been guarded like a military secret from me, and yet around his neck he wore a silver chain and a Medic-alert tag that warned that J. A. NORTH, the wearer, was allergic to penicillin.

Now he forgot all his former reserve, and gently I drew small snippets of information from him that I might have use for in the future. In my experience it's what you don't know that can really hurt you.

I chose the subject that I guessed would open him up completely.

'See that reef across the channel, there where she's breaking now? That's Devil Fish Reef and there is twenty fathoms sheer under the sea side of her. It's a hangout of some real big old bull grouper. I shot one there last year that weighed in at over two hundred kilos.'

'Two hundred –' he exclaimed. 'My God, that's almost four hundred and fifty pounds.'

'Right, you could put you head and shoulders in his mouth.'

The last of his reserves disappeared. He had been reading history and philosophy at Cambridge but spent too much time in the sea, and had to drop out. Now he ran a small diving equipment supply company and underwater salvage outfit, that gave him a living and allowed him to dive most days of the week. He did private work and had contracted to the Government and the Navy on some jobs.

More than once he mentioned the name 'Sherry' and I probed carefully. 'Girl friend or wife?' and he grinned.

'Sister, big sister, but she's a doll – she does the books and minds the shop, all that stuff,' in a tone that left no doubt as to what James thought about book-keeping and counter-jumping. 'She's a red-hot conchologist and she makes two thousand a year out of her sea shells.' But he didn't explain how he had got into the dubious company he was now keeping, nor what he was doing halfway around the world from his sports shop. I left them on Admiralty Wharf, and took *Dancer* over to the Shell Basin for refuelling before dark.

That evening I grilled the kingfish over the coals, roasted a couple of big sweet yams in their jackets and was washing it down with a cold beer sitting on the veranda of the shack and listening to the surf when I saw the headlights coming down through the palm trees.

The taxi parked beside my pick-up, and the driver stayed at the wheel while his passengers came up the steps on to the stoep. They had left James at the Hilton, and there were just the two of them now – Materson and Guthrie.

'Drink?' I indicated the bottles and ice on the side table. Guthrie poured gin for both of them and Materson sat opposite me and watched me finish the last of the fish.

'I made a few phone calls,' he said when I pushed my plate away. 'And they tell me that Harry Bruce disappeared in June five years ago and hasn't been heard of since. I asked around and found out that Harry Fletcher sailed into Grand Harbour here three months' later – inward bound from Sydney, Australia.'

'Is that the truth?' I picked a little fish bone out of my tooth, and lit a long black island cheroot.

'One other thing, someone who knew him well tells me Harry Bruce has a knife scar across his left arm,' he purred, and I involuntarily glanced at the thin line of scar tissue that laced the muscle of my forearm. It had shrunk and flattened with the years, but was still very white against the dark sun-browned skin.

'Now that's a hell of a coincidence,' I said, and drew on the cheroot. It was strong and aromatic, tasting of sea and sun and spices. I wasn't worried now – they were going to make a deal.

'Yeah, isn't it,' Materson agreed, and he looked around him elaborately. 'You got a nice set-up here, Fletcher. Cosy isn't it, really nice and cosy.'

'It beats hell out of working for a living,' I admitted.

'– Or out of breaking rocks, or sewing mail bags.'

'I should imagine it does.'

'The kid is going to ask you some questions tomorrow. Be nice to him,

Fletcher. When we go you can forget you ever saw us, and we'll forget to tell anybody about that funny coincidence.'

'Mr Materson, sir, I've got a terrible memory,' I assured him.

After the conversation I had overheard in *Dancer*'s cabin, I expected them to ask for an early start time the following morning, for the dawn light seemed important to their plans. However, neither of them mentioned it, and when they had gone I knew I wouldn't sleep so I walked out along the sand around the curve of the bay to Mutton Point to watch the moon come up through the palm trees. I sat there until after midnight.


The dinghy was gone from the jetty but Hambone, the ferry man, rowed me out to *Dancer*'s moorings before sun-up the following morning and as we came alongside I saw the familiar shape shambling around the cockpit, and the dinghy tied alongside.

'Hey, Chubby.' I jumped aboard. 'Your Missus kick you out of bed, then?'

*Dancer*'s deck was gleaming white even in the bad light, and all the metal work was brightly burnished. He must have been at it for a couple of hours; Chubby loves *Dancer* almost as much as I do.

'She looked like a public shit-house, Harry,' he grumbled. 'That's a sloppy bunch you got aboard,' and he spat noisily over the side. 'No respect for a boat, that what.'

He had coffee ready for me, as strong and as pungent as only he can make it, and we drank it sitting in the saloon. Chubby frowned heavily into his mug and blew on the steaming black liquid. He wanted to tell me something.

'How's Angelo?'

'Pleasuring the Rawano widows,' he growled. The island does not provide sufficient employment for all its able-bodied young men – so most of them ship out on three-year labour contracts to the American satellite tracking station and airforce base on Rawano island. They leave their young wives behind, the Rawano widows, and the islands girls are justly celebrated for the high temperature of their blood and their friendly dispositions.

'That Angelo going the shag his brain loose, he's been at it night and day since Monday.'

I detected more than a trace of envy in his growl. Missus Chubby kept him on a pretty tight lead – he sipped noisily at the coffee.

'How's your party, Harry?'

'Their money is good.'

'You not fishing, Harry.' He looked at me. 'I watch you from Coolie Peak, man, you don't go near the channel – you are working inshore.'

'That's right, Chubby.' He returned his attention to his coffee.

'Hey, Harry. You watch them. You be good and careful, hear. They bad men, those two. I don't know the young one – but the others they are bad.'

'I'll be careful, Chubby.'

'You know the new girl at the hotel, Marion? The one over for the season?' I nodded, she was a pretty slim little wisp of a girl with lovely long legs, about nineteen with glossy black hair, freckled skin, bold eyes and an impish smile. 'Well, last night she went with the blond one, the one with the red face.' I knew that Marion sometimes combined business with pleasure and provided for selected hotel guests services beyond the call of duty. On the island this sort of activity drew no social stigma.

'Yes,' I encouraged Chubby.

'He hurt her, Harry. Hurt her bad.' Chubby took another mouthful of coffee. 'Then he paid her so much money she couldn't go to the police.'

I liked Mike Guthrie a little less now. Only an animal would take advantage of a girl like Marion. I knew her well. She had an innocence, a child-like acceptance of life that made her promiscuity strangely appealing. I remembered how I had thought I might have to kill Guthrie one day – and tried not to let the thought perish.

'They are bad men, Harry. I thought it best you know that.'

'Thanks, Chubby.'

'And don't you let them dirty up *Dancer* like that,' he added accusingly. 'The saloon and deck – they were like a pigsty, man.'

He helped me run *Dancer* across to Admiralty Wharf and then he set off homewards, grumbling and muttering blackly. He passed Jimmy coming in the opposite direction and shot him a single malevolent glance that should have shrivelled him in his tracks.

Jimmy was on his own, fresh-faced and jaunty.

'Hi, skipper,' he called, as he jumped down on to *Dancer*'s deck, and I went into the saloon with him and poured coffee for us.

'Mr Materson says you have some questions for me, is that right?'

'Look, Mr Fletcher, I want you to know that I didn't mean offence by not talking to you before. It wasn't me – but the others.'

'Sure,' I said. 'That's fine, Jimmy.'

'It would have been the sensible thing to ask your help long ago, instead of blundering around the way we have been. Anyway, now the others have suddenly decided it's okay.'

He had just told me much more than he imagined, and I adjusted my opinion of Master James. It was clear that he possessed information, and he had not shared it with the others. It was his insurance, and he had probably insisted on seeing me alone to keep his insurance policy intact.

'Skipper, we are looking for an island, a specific island. I can't tell you why, I'm sorry.'

'Forget it, Jimmy. That's all right.' What will there be for you, James North, I wondered suddenly. What will the wolf pack have for you once you have led them to this special island of yours? Will it be something a lot less pleasant than penicillin allergy?

I looked at that handsome young face, and felt an unaccustomed flood of affection for him – perhaps it was his youth and innocence, the sense of excitement with which he viewed this tired and wicked old world. I envied and liked him for that, and I did not relish seeing him pulled down and rolled in the dirt.

'Jim, how well do you know your friends?' I asked him quietly, and he was taken by surprise, then almost immediately he was wary.

'Well enough,' he replied carefully. 'Why?'

'You have known them less than a month,' I said as though I knew, and saw the confirmation in his expression. 'And I have known men like that all my life.'

'I don't see what this has to do with it, Mr Fletcher.' He was stiffening up now, I was treating him like a child and he didn't like that.

'Listen, Jim. Forget this business, whatever it is. Drop it, and go back to your shop and your salvage company.'

'That's crazy,' he said. 'You don't understand.'

'I understand, Jim. I really do. I travelled the same road, and I know it well.'

'I can look after myself. Don't worry about me.' He had flushed up under his tan, and the grey eyes snapped with defiance. We stared at each other for a few moments, and I knew I was wasting time and emotion. If anyone had spoken like this to me at the same age I would have thought him senile.

'All right, Jim,' I said. 'I'll drop it, but you know the score. Just play it cool and loose, that's all.'

'Okay, Mr Fletcher.' He relaxed slowly, and then grinned a charming and engaging grin. 'Thanks anyway.'

Let's hear about this island,' I suggested and he glanced about the cabin.

'Let's go up on the bridge,' he suggested, and out in the open air he took a stub of pencil and a scrap pad from the map bin above the chart table.

'I reckon it lies off the African shore about six to ten miles, and ten to thirty miles north of the mouth of the Rovuma River –'

'That covers a hell of a lot of ground, Jim – as you may have noticed during the last few days. What else do you know about it?'

He hesitated a little longer, before grudgingly doling out a few more coins from his hoard. He took the pencil and drew a horizontal line across the pad.

'Sea level –' he said, and then above the line he raised an irregular profile that started low, and then climbed steeply into three distinct peaks before ending abruptly, '– and that's the silhouette that it shows from the sea. The three hills are volcanic basalt, sheer rock with little vegetation.'

'The Old Men –' I recognized it immediately, '– but you are a long way out in your other calculations, it's more like twenty miles offshore –'

'But within sight of the mainland?' he asked quickly. 'It has to be within sight.'

'Sure, you could see a long way from the tops of the hills,' I pointed out as he tore the sheet from the pad and carefully ripped it to shreds, and dropped them into the harbour.

'How far north of the river?' He turned back to face me.

'Offhand I'd say sixty or seventy miles,' and he looked thoughtful.

'Yes, it could be that far north. It could fit, it depends on how long it would take –' He did not finish, he was taking my advice about playing it cool. 'Can you take us there, skip?'

I nodded. 'But it's a long run and best come prepared to sleep on the boat overnight.'

'I'll fetch the others,' he said, eager and excited once more. But on the wharf he looked back at the bridge.

'About the island, what it looks like and all that, don't discuss it with the others, okay?'

'Okay, Jim,' I smiled back at him. 'Off you go.' I went down to have a look at the admiralty chart. The Old Men were the highest point on a ridge of basalt, a long hard reef that ran parallel to the mainland for two hundred miles. It disappeared below the water, but reappeared at intervals, forming a regular feature amongst the haphazard sprinkling of coral and sand islands and shoals.

It was marked as uninhabited and waterless, and the soundings showed a number of deep channels through the reefs around it. Although it was far north of my regular grounds, yet I had visited the area the previous year as host to a marine biology expedition from UCLA who were studying the breeding habits of the green turtles that abounded there.

We had camped for three days on another island across the tide channel from the Old Men, where there was an all-weather anchorage in an enclosed lagoon, and brackish but just drinkable water in a fisherman's well amongst the palms. Looking across from the anchorage, the Old Men showed exactly the outline that Jimmy had sketched for me, that was how I had recognized it so readily.

Half and hour later, the whole party arrived; strapped on the roof of the taxi was a bulky piece of equipment covered with a green canvas dust sheet. They hired a couple of lounging islanders to carry this, and the overnight bags they had with them, down the wharf to where I was waiting.

They stowed the canvas package on the foredeck without unwrapping it and I asked no questions. Guthrie's face was starting to fall off in layers of sun-scorched skin, leaving wet red flesh exposed. He had smeared white cream over it. I thought of him slapping little Marion around his suite at the Hilton, and I smiled at him.

'You look so good, have you ever thought of running for Miss Universe?' and he glowered at me from beneath the brim of his hat as he took his seat in the fighting chair. During the run northwards he drank beer straight from the can and used the empties as targets. Firing the big pistol at them as they tumbled and bobbed in *Dancer*'s wake.

A little before noon, I gave Jimmy the wheel and went down to use the heads below deck. I found that Materson had the bar open and the gin bottle out.

'How much longer?' he asked, sweaty and flushed despite the air-conditioning.

'Another hour or so,' I told him, and thought that Materson was going to find himself with a drinking problem the way he handled spirits at midday. However, the gin had mellowed him a little and – always the opportunist – I loosened another three hundred pounds from his wallet as an advance against my fees before going up to take *Dancer* in on the last leg through the northern tide channel that led to the Old Men.

The triple peaks came up through the heat haze, ghostly grey and ominous, seeming to hang disembodied above the channel.

Jimmy was examining the peaks through his binoculars, and then he lowered them and turned delightedly to me.

'That looks like it, skipper,' and he clambered down into the cockpit. The three of them went up on to the foredeck, passed the canvas-wrapped deck cargo, and stood shoulder to shoulder at the rail staring through the sea fret at the island as I crept cautiously up the channel.

We had a rising tide pushing us up the channel, and I agreed to use it to approach the eastern tip of the Old Men, and make a landing on the beach below the nearest peak. This coast has a tidal fall of seventeen feet at full springs, and it is unwise to go into shallow water on the ebb. It is easy to find yourself stranded high and dry as the water falls away beneath your keel.

Jimmy borrowed my hand-bearing compass and packed it with his chart a Thermos of iced water and a bottle of salt tablets from the medicine chest into his haversack. While I crept cautiously in towards the beach, Jimmy and Materson stripped off their footwear and trousers.

When *Dancer* bumped her keel softly on the hard white sand of the beach I shouted to them.

'Okay – over you go,' and with Jimmy leading, they went down the ladder I had rigged from *Dancer*'s side. The water came to their armpits, and James held the haversack above his head as they waded towards the beach.

'Two hours!' I called after them. 'If you're longer than that you can sleep ashore. I'm not coming in to pick you up on the ebb.'

Jimmy waved and grinned. I put *Dancer* into reverse and backed off cautiously, while the two of them reached the beach and hopped around awkwardly as they donned their trousers and shoes and then set off into the palm groves and disappeared from view.

After circling for ten minutes and peering down through the water that was clear as a trout stream, I picked up the dark shadow across the bottom that I was seeking and dropped a light head anchor.

While Guthrie watched with interest I put on a face-plate and gloves and went over the side with a small oyster net and a heavy tyre lever. There was forty feet of water under us, and I was pleased to find my wind was still sufficient to allow me to go down and prise loose a netful of the big double-shelled sun clams in one dive. I shucked them on the foredeck, and then, mindful of Chubby's admonitions, I threw the empty shells overboard and swabbed the deck carefully before taking a pailful of the sweet flesh down to the galley. They went into a casserole pot with wine and garlic, salt and ground pepper and just a bite of chilli. I set the gas-plate to simmer and put the lid on the pot.

When I went back on deck, Guthrie was still in the fighting chair.

'What's wrong, big shot, are you bored?' I asked solicitously. 'No little girls to kick around?' His eyes narrowed thoughtfully. I could see him checking out my source of information.

'You've got a big mouth, Bruce. Somebody is going to close it for you one day.' We exchanged a few more pleasantries, none of them much above this level, but it served to pass the time until the two distant figures appeared on the beach and waved and halloed. I pulled up the hook, and went in to pick them up.

Immediately they were aboard, they called Guthrie to them and assembled on the foredeck for one of their group sessions. They were all excited, Jimmy the most so, and he gesticulated and pointed out into the channel, talking quietly but vehemently. For once they seemed all to be in agreement, but by the time they had finished talking there was an hour of sunlight left and I refused to agree to Materson's demands that I should continue our explorations that evening. I had no wish to creep around in the darkness on an ebb tide.

Firmly I took *Dancer* across to the safe anchorage in the lagoon across the channel, and by the time the sun went down below a blazing horizon I had *Dancer* riding peacefully on two heavy anchors, and I was sitting upon the bridge enjoying the last of day and the first Scotch of the evening. In the saloon below me there was the interminable murmur of discussion and speculation. I ignored it, not even bothering to use the ventilator, until the first mosquitoes found their way across the lagoon and began whining around my ears. I went below and the conversation dried up at my entry.

I thickened the juice and served my clam casserole with baked yams and pineapple salad and they ate in dedicated silence.

'My God, that is even better than my sister's cooking' Jimmy gasped finally. I grinned at him. I am rather vain about my culinary skills and young James was clearly a gourmet.

I woke after midnight and went up on deck to check *Dancer*'s moorings. She was all secure and I paused to enjoy the moonlight.

A great stillness lay upon the night, disturbed only by the soft chuckle of the tide against *Dancer*'s side – and far off the boom of the surf on the outer reef. It was coming in big and tall from the open ocean, and breaking in thunder and white upon the coral of Gunfire Reef. The name was well chosen, and the deep belly-shaking thump of it sounded exactly like the regular salute of a minute gun.

The moonlight washed the channel with shimmering silver and highlighted the bald domes of the peaks of the Old Men so they shone like ivory. Below them the night mists rising from the lagoon writhed and twisted like tormented souls.

Suddenly I caught the whisper of movement behind me and I whirled to face it. Guthrie had followed me as silently as a hunting leopard. He wore only a pair of jockey shorts and his body was white and muscled and lean in the moonlight. He carried the big black .45, dangling at arm's length by his right thigh. We stared at each other for a moment before I relaxed.

'You know, luv, you've just got to give up now. You really aren't my type at all,' I told him, but there was adrenalin in my blood and my voice rasped.

'When the time comes to rim you, Fletcher, I'll be using this,' he said, and lifted the automatic, 'all the way up, boy,' and he grinned.

We ate breakfast before sun-up and I took my mug of coffee to the bridge to drink as we ran up the channel towards the open sea. Materson was below, and Guthrie lolled in the fighting chair. Jimmy stood beside me and explained his requirements for this day.

He was tense with excitement, seeming to quiver with it like a young gundog with the first scent of the bird in his nostrils.

'I want to get some shots off the peak of the Old Men,' he explained. 'I want to use your hand-bearing compass, and I'll call you in.'

'Give me your bearings, Jim, and I'll plot it and put you on the spot,' I suggested.

'Let's do it my way, skipper,' he replied awkwardly, and I could not prevent a flare of irritation in my reply.

'All right, then, eagle scout.' He flushed and went to the port rail to sight the peaks through the lens of the compass. It was ten minutes or so before he spoke again.

'Can we turn about two points to port now, skipper?'

'Sure we can,' I grinned at him, 'but, of course, that would pile us on to the end of Gunfire Reef – and we'd tear her belly out.'

It took another two hours of groping about through the maze of reefs before I had worked *Dancer* out through the channel into the open sea and circled back to approach Gunfire Reef from the east.

It was like the child's game of hunt the thimble; Jimmy called 'hotter' and 'colder' without supplying me with the two references that would enable me to place *Dancer* on the precise spot he was seeking.

Out here the swells marched in majestic procession towards the land, growing taller and more powerful as they felt the shelving bottom. *Dancer* rolled and swung to them as we edged in towards the outer reef.

Where the swells met the barrier of coral their dignity turned to sudden fury, and they boiled up and burst in leviathan spouts of spray, pouring wildly over the coral with the explosive shock of impact. Then they sucked back, exposing the evil black fangs, white water cascading and creaming from the barrier, while the next swell moved up, humping its great slick back for the next assault.

Jimmy was directing me steadily southwards in a gradual converging course with the reef, and I could tell we were very close to his marks. Through the compass he squinted eagerly, first at one and then the other peak of the Old Men.

'Steady as you go, skipper,' he called. 'Just ease her down on that heading.'

I looked ahead, tearing my eyes away from the menacing coral for a few seconds, and I watched the next swell charge in and break – except at a narrow point five hundred yards ahead. Here the swell kept its shape and ran on uninterrupted towards the land. On each side, the swell broke on coral, but just at that one point it was open.

Suddenly I remembered Chubby's boast.

'I was just nineteen when I pulled my first jewfish out of the hole at Gunfire Break. Weren't no other would fish with me – don't say as I blame them. Wouldn't go into the Break again – got a little more brains now.'

Gunfire Break, suddenly I knew that was where we were heading. I tried to remember exactly what Chubby had told me about it.

'If you come in from the sea about two hours before high water, steer for the centre of the gap until you come up level with a big old head of brain coral on your starboard side, you'll know it when you see it, pass it close as you can and then come round hard to starboard and you'll be sitting in a big hole tucked in neatly behind the main reef. Closer you are on the back of the reef the better, man –' I remembered it clearly then, Chubby in his talkative phase in the public bar of the Lord Nelson, boastful as one of the very few men who had been through the Gunfire Break. 'No anchor going to hold you there, you got to lean on the oars to hold station in the gap – the hole at Gunfire Break is deep, man, deep, but the jewfish in there are

big, man, big. One day I took four fish, and the smallest was three hundred
pounds. Could have took more – but time was up. You can't stay in Gunfire
Break more than an hour after high water – she sucks out through the Break
like they pulled the chain on the whole damned sea. You come out the same
way you went in, only you pray just a little harder on the way out – 'cos you
got a ton of fish on board, and ten feet less water under your keel. There is
another way out through a channel in the back of the reef. But I don't even
like to talk about that one. Only tried it once.'

Now we were bearing down directly on the Break, Jimmy was going to
run us right into the eye of it.

'Okay, Jim,' I called. 'That's as far as we go.' I opened the throttle and
sheered off, making a good offing before turning back to face Jimmy's wrath.

'We were almost there, damn you,' he blustered. 'We could have gone in
a little closer.'

'You having trouble up there, boy?' Guthrie shouted up from the cockpit.

'No, it's all right,' Jimmy called back, and then turned furiously to me.
'You are under contract, Mr Fletcher –'

'I want to show you something, James –' and I took him to the chart
table. The Break was marked on the admiralty chart by a single laconic
sounding of thirty fathoms, there was no name or sailing instruction for it.
Quickly I pencilled in the bearings of the two extreme peaks of the Old
Men from the break, and then used the protractor to measure the angle they
subtended.

'That right?' I asked him, and he stared at my figures.

'It's right, isn't it?' I insisted and then reluctantly he nodded.

'Yes, that's the spot,' he agreed, and I went on to tell him about Gunfire
Break in every detail.

'But we have got to get in there,' he said at the end of my speech, as
though he had not heard a word of it.

'No way,' I told him. 'The only place I'm interested in now is Grand
Harbour, St Mary's Island,' and I laid *Dancer* on that course. As far as I
was concerned the charter was over.

Jimmy disappeared down the ladder, and returned within minutes with
reinforcements – Materson and Guthrie, both of them looking angry and
outraged.

'Say the word, and I'll tear the bastard's arm off and beat him to death
with the wet end,' Mike Guthrie said with relish.

'The kid says you pulling out?' Materson wanted to know. 'Now that's
not right – is it?'

I explained once more about the hazards of Gunfire Break and they
sobered immediately.

'Take me close as you can – I'll swim in the rest of the way,' Jimmy
asked me, but I replied directly to Materson,

'You'd lose him, for certain sure. Do you want to risk that?'

He didn't answer, but I could see that Jimmy was much too valuable for
them to take the chance.

'Let me try,' Jimmy insisted, but Materson shook his head irritably.

'If we can't get into the Break, at least let me take a run along the reef with the sledge,' Jimmy went on, and I knew then what we were carrying under the canavas wrapping on the foredeck.

'Just a couple of passes along the front edge of the reef, past the entrance to the break.' He was pleading now, and Materson looked questioningly at me. You don't often have opportunities like this offered you on a silver tray. I knew I could run *Dancer* within spitting distance of the coral without risk, but I frowned worriedly.

'I'd be taking a hell of a chance – but if we could agree on a bit of old danger money –'

I had Materson over the arm of the chair and I caned him for an extra day's hire – five hundred dollars, payable in advance.

While we did the business, Guthrie helped Jimmy unwrap the sledge and carry it back to the cockpit.

I tucked the sheath of bank notes away and went back to rig the tow lines. The sledge was a beautifully constructed toboggan of stainless steel and plastic. In place of snow runners, it had stubby fin controls, rudder and hydrofoils, operated by a short joystick below the Perspex pilot's shield.

There was a ring bolt in the nose to take the tow line by which I would drag the sledge in *Dancer*'s wake. Jimmy would lie on his belly behind the transparent shield, breathing compressed air from the twin tanks that were built into the chassis of the sledge. On the dashboard were depth and pressure gauges, directional compass and time elapse clock. With the joystick Jimmy could control the depth of the sledge's dive, and yaw left or right across *Dancer*'s stern.

'Lovely piece of work,' I remarked, and he flushed with pleasure.

'Thanks, skipper, built it myself.' He was pulling on the wet suit of thick black Neoprene rubber and while his head was in the clinging hood I stooped and examined the maker's plate that was riveted to the sledge's chassis, memorizing the legend.

> 'Built by North's Underwater World.
>      5, Pavilion Arcade.
>      BRIGHTON. SUSSEX.'

I straightened up as his face appeared in the opening of the hood.

'Five knots is a good tow speed, skipper. If you keep a hundred yards off the reef, I'll be able to deflect outwards and follow the contour of the coral.'

'Fine, Jim.'

'If I put up a yellow marker, ignore it, it's only a find, and we will go back to it later – but if I send up a red, it's trouble, try and get me off the reef and haul me in.'

I nodded. 'You have three hours,' I warned him. 'Then she will begin the ebb up through the break and we'll have to haul off.'

'That should be long enough,' he agreed.

Guthrie and I lifted the sledge over the side, and it wallowed low in the water. Jimmy clambered down to it and settled himself behind the screen, testing the controls, adjusting his face-plate and cramming the mouth-piece of the breathing device into his mouth. He breathed noisily and then gave me the thumbs up.

I climbed quickly to the bridge and opened the throttles. *Dancer* picked up speed and Guthrie paid out the thick nylon rope over the stern as the sledge fell away behind us. One hundred and fifty yards of rope went over, before the sledge jerked up and began to tow.

Jimmy waved, and I pushed *Dancer* up to a steady five knots. I circled wide, then edged in towards the reef, taking the big swells on *Dancer*'s beam so she rolled appallingly.

Again Jimmy waved, and I saw him push the control column of the sledge forwards. There was a turmoil of white water along her control fins and then suddenly she put her nose down and ducked below the surface. The angle of the nylon rope altered rapidly as the sledge went down, and then swung away towards the reef.

The strain on the rope made it quiver like an arrow as it strikes, and the water squirted from the fibres.

Slowly we ran parallel to the reef, closing the break. I watched the coral respectfully, taking no chances, and I imagined Jimmy far below the surface flying silently along the bottom, cutting in to skim the tall wall of underwater coral. It must have been an exhilarating sensation, and I envied him, deciding to hitch a ride on the sledge when I got the opportunity.

We came opposite the Break, passed it and just then I heard Guthrie shout. I glanced quickly over the stern and saw the big yellow balloon bobbing in our wake.

'He found something,' Guthrie shouted.

Jimmy had dropped a light leaded line, and a sparklet bulb had automatically inflated the yellow balloon with carbon dioxide gas to mark the spot.

I kept going steadily along the reef, and a quarter of a mile farther the angle of the tow line flattened and the sledge popped to the surface in a welter of water.

I swung away from the reef to a safe distance, and then went down to help Guthrie recover the sledge.

Jimmy clambered into the cockpit, and when he pulled off his face-plate his lips were trembling and his grey eyes blazed. He took Materson's arm and dragged him into the cabin, splashing sea water all over Chubby's beloved deck.

Guthrie and I coiled the rope then lifted the sledge into the cockpit. I went back to the bridge, and took *Dancer* on a slow return to the entrance of Gunfire Break.

Materson and Jimmy came up on to the bridge before we reached it. Materson was affected by Jimmy's excitement.

'The kid wants to try for a pick up.' I knew better than to ask what it was.

'What size?' I asked instead, and glanced at my wristwatch. We had an hour and half before the rip tide began to run out through the break.

'Not very big —' Jimmy assured me. 'Fifty pounds maximum.'

'You sure, James? Not bigger?' I didn't trust his enthusiasm not to minimize the effort involved.

'I swear it.'

'You want to put an airbag on it?'

'Yes, I'll lift it with an airbag and then tow it away from the reef.'

I reversed *Dancer* in gingerly towards the yellow balloon that played lightly in the angry coral jaws of the Break.

'That's as close as I'll go,' I shouted down into the cockpit, and Jimmy acknowledged with a wave.

He waddled duck-footed to the stern and adjusted his equipment. He had taken two airbags as well as the canvas cover from the sledge, and was roped up to the coil of nylon rope.

I saw him take a bearing on the yellow marker with the compass on his wrist, then once again he glanced up at me on the bridge before he flipped backwards over the stern and disappeared.

His regular breathing burst in a white rash below the stern, then began to move off towards the reef. Guthrie paid out the bodyline after him.

I kept *Dancer* on station by using bursts of forward and reverse, holding her a hundred yards from the southern tip of the Break.

Slowly Jimmy's bubbles approached the yellow marker, and then broke steadily beside it. He was working below it, and I imagined him fixing the empty airbags to the object with the nylon slings. It would be hard work with the suck and drag of the current worrying the bulky bags. Once he had fitted the slings he could begin to fill the bags with compressed air from his scuba bottles.

If Jimmy's estimate of size was correct it would need very little inflation to pull the mysterious object off the bottom, and once it dangled free we could tow it into a safer area before bringing it aboard.

For forty minutes I held *Dancer* steady, then quite suddenly two swollen green shiny mounds broke the surface astern. The airbags were up – Jimmy had lifted his prize.

Immediately his hooded head surfaced beside the filled bags, and he held his right arm straight up. The signal to begin the tow.

'Ready?' I shouted at Guthrie in the cockpit.

'Ready!' He had secured the line, and I crept away from the reef, slowly and carefully to avoid up-ending the bags and spilling out the air that gave them lift.

Five hundred yards off the reef, I kicked *Dancer* into neutral and went to help haul in the swimmer and his fat green airbags.

'Stay where you are,' Materson snarled at me as I approached the ladder and I shrugged and went back to the wheel.

The hell with them all, I thought, and lit a cheroot – but I couldn't prevent the tickle of excitement as they worked the bags alongside, and then walked them forward to the bows.

They helped Jimmy aboard, and he shrugged off the heavy compressed air bottles, dropping them to the deck while he pushed his face-plate on to his forehead.

His voice, ragged and high-pitched, carried clearly to me as I leaned on the bridge rail.

'Jackpot!' he cried. 'It's the —'

'Watch it!' Materson cautioned him, and James cut himself off and they all looked at me, lifting their faces to the bridge.

'Don't mind me, boys,' I grinned and waved the cheroot cheerily. They turned away and huddled. Jimmy whispered, and Guthrie said, 'Jesus Christ!' loudly and slapped Materson's back, and then they were all exclaiming and laughing as they crowded to the rail and began to lift the airbags and their burden aboard. They were clumsy with it, *Dancer* was rolling heavily, and I leaned forward with curiosity eating a hole in my belly.

My disappointment and chagrin were intense when I realized that Jimmy had taken the precaution of wrapping his prize in the canvas sledge cover. It came aboard as a sodden, untidy bundle of canvas, swathed in coils of nylon rope.

It was heavy, I could see by the manner in which they handled it – but it was not bulky, the size of a small suitcase.

They laid it on the deck and stood around it happily. Materson smiled up at me.

'Okay, Fletcher. Come take a look.'

It was beautifully done, he played like a concert pianist on my curiosity. Suddenly I wanted very badly to know what they had pulled from the sea. I clamped the cheroot in my teeth as I swarmed down the ladder, and hurried towards the group in the bows. I was halfway across the foredeck, right out in the open, and Materson was still smiling as he said softly. 'Now!'

Only then did I know it was a set-up, and my mind began to move so fast that it all seemed to go by in extreme slow motion.

I saw the evil black bulk of the .45 in Guthrie's fist, and it came up slowly to aim into my belly. Mike Guthrie was in the marksman's crouch, right arm fully extended, and he was grinning as he screwed up those speckled eyes and sighted along the thick-jacketed barrel.

I saw Jimmy North's handsome young face contort with horror, saw him reach out to grip the pistol arm but Materson, still grinning, shoved him roughly aside and he staggered away with *Dancer*'s next roll.

I was thinking quite clearly and rapidly, it was not a procession of thought but a set of simultaneous images. I thought how neatly they had dropped the boom on me, a really professional hit.

I thought how presumptuous I had been in trying to make a deal with the wolf pack. For them it was easier to hit than to negotiate.

I thought that they would take out Jimmy now that he had watched this. That must have been their intention from the start. I was sorry for that. I had come to like the kid.

I thought about the heavy soft explosive lead slug that the .45 threw, about how it would tear up the target, hitting with shock of two thousand foot pounds.

Guthrie's forefinger curled on the trigger and I began to throw myself at the rail beside me with the cheroot still in my mouth, but I knew it was too late.

The pistol in Guthrie's hand kicked up head high, and I saw the muzzle flash palely in the sunlight. The cannon roar of the blast and the heavy lead bullet hit me together. The din deafened me and snapped my head back and the cheroot flipped up high in the air leaving a trail of sparks. Then the impact of the bullet doubled me over, driving the air from my lungs, and lifted me off my feet, hurling me backwards until the deck rail caught me in the small of the back.

There was no pain, just that huge numbing shock. It was in the chest, I was sure of that, and I knew that it must have blown me open. It was a mortal wound, I was sure of that also and I expected my mind to go now. I expected to fade, going out into blackness.

Instead the rail caught me in the back and I somersaulted, going over the side head-first and the quick cold embrace of the sea covered me. It steadied me, and I opened my eyes to the silver clouds of bubbles and the soft green of sunlight through the surface.

My lungs were empty, the air driven out by the impact of the bullet, and my instinct told me to claw to the surface for air, but surprisingly my mind was still clear and I knew that Mike Guthrie would blow the top of my skull the moment I surfaced. I rolled and dived, kicking clumsily, and went down under *Dancer*'s hull.

On empty lungs it was a long journey, *Dancer*'s smooth white belly passed slowly above me, and I drove on desperately, amazed that there was strength in my legs still.

Suddenly darkness engulfed me, a soft dark red cloud, and I nearly panicked, thinking my vision had gone – until suddenly I realized it was my own blood. Huge billowing clouds of my own blood staining the water. Tiny zebra-striped fish darted wildly through the cloud, gulping greedily at it.

I struck out, but my left arm would not respond. It trailed limply at my side, and blood blew like smoke about me.

There was strength in my right arm and I forged on under *Dancer*, passed under her keel and rose thankfully towards her far waterline.

As I came up I saw the nylon tow rope trailing over her stern, a bight of it hanging down below the surface and I snatched at it thankfully.

I broke the surface under *Dancer*'s stern, and I sucked painfully for air, my lungs felt bruised and numb, the air tasted like old copper in my mouth but I gulped it down.

My mind was still clear. I was under the stern, the wolf pack was in the bows, the carbine was under the engine hatch in the main cabin.

I reached up as high as I could and took a twist of the nylon rope around my right wrist, lifted my knees and got my toes on to the rubbing strake along *Dancer*'s waterline.

I knew I had enough strength for one attempt, no more. It would have to be good. I heard their voices from up in the bows, raised angrily, shouting at each other, but I ignored them and gathered all my reserve.

I heaved upwards, with both legs and the one good arm. My vision starred with the effort, and my chest was a numbed mass, but I came clear of the water and fell half across the stern rail, hanging there like an empty sack on a barbed-wire fence.

For seconds I lay there, while my vision cleared and I felt the slick warm outpouring of blood along my flank and belly. The flow of blood galvanized me. I realized how little time I had before the loss of it sent me plunging into blackness. I kicked wildly and tumbled headlong on to the cockpit floor, striking my head on the edge of the fighting chair, and grunting with the new pain of it.

I lay on my side and glanced down at my body. What I saw terrified me,

I was streaming great gouts of thick blood, it was forming a puddle under me.

I clawed at the deck, dragging myself towards the cabin, and reached the combing beside the entrance. With another wild effort I pulled myself upright, hanging on one arm, supported by legs already weak and rubbery.

I glanced quickly around the angle of the cabin, down along the foredeck to where the three men were still grouped in the bows.

Jimmy North was struggling to strap his compressed air bottles on to his back again, his face was a mask of horror and outrage and his voice was strident as he screamed at Materson.

'You filthy bloody murderers. I'm going down to find him. I'm going to get his body – and, so help Christ, I'll see you both hanged –'

Even in my own distress I felt a sudden flare of admiration for the kid's courage. I don't think it ever occurred to him that he was also on the list.

'It was murder, cold-blooded murder,' he shouted, and turned to the rail, settling the face-plate over his eyes and nose.

Materson looked across at Guthrie, the kid's back was turned to them, and Materson nodded.

I tried to shout a warning, but it croaked hollowly in my throat, and Guthrie stepped up behind Jimmy. This time he made no mistake. He touched the muzzle of the .45 to the base of Jimmy's skull, and the shot was muffled by the neoprene rubber hood of the diving-suit.

Jimmy's skull collapsed, shattered by the passage of the heavy bullet. It came out through the glass plate of the diving mask in a cloud of glass fragments. The force of it clubbed him over the side, and his body splashed alongside. Then there was silence in which the memory of gunfire seemed to echo with the sound of wind and water.

'He'll sink,' said Materson calmly. 'He had on a weight belt –but we had better try and find Fletcher. We don't want him washed up with that bullet hole in his chest'.

'He ducked – the bastard ducked – I didn't hit him squarely –' Guthrie protested, and I heard no more. My legs collapsed and I sprawled on the deck of the cockpit. I was sick with shock and horror and the quick flooding flow of my blood.

I have seen violent death in many guises, but Jimmy's had moved me as never before. Suddenly there was only one thing I wanted to do before my own violent death overwhelmed me.

I began to crawl towards the engine-room hatch. The white deck seemed to stretch before me like the Sahara desert, and I was beginning to feel the leaden hand of great weariness upon my shoulder.

I heard their footsteps on the deck above me, and the murmur of their voices. They were coming back to the cockpit.

'Ten seconds, please God,' I whispered. 'That's all I need,' but I knew it was futile. They would be into the cabin long before I reached the hatch – but I dragged myself desperately towards it.

Then suddenly their footsteps paused, but the voices continued. They had stopped to talk out on the deck, and I felt a lift of relief for I had reached the engine hatch.

Now I struggled with the toggles. They seemed to have jammed immovably, and I realized how weak I was, but I felt the revitalizing stir of anger through the weariness.

I wriggled around and kicked at the toggles and they flew back. I fought my weakness aside and got on to my knees. As I leaned over the hatch a fresh splattering of bright blood fell on the white deck.

'Eat your liver, Chubby,' I thought irrelevantly, and prised up the hatch. It came up achingly slowly, heavy as all the earth, and now I felt the first lances of pain in my chest as bruised tissue tore.

The hatch fell back with a heavy thump, and instantly the voices on deck were silent, and I could imagine them listening.

I fell on my belly and groped desperately under the decking and my right hand closed on the stock of the carbine.

'Come on!' There was a loud exclamation, and I recognized Materson's voice, and immediately the pounding of running footsteps along the deck towards the cockpit.

I tugged wearily at the carbine, but it seemed to be caught in the slings and resisted my efforts.

'Christ! There's blood all over the deck,' Materson shouted.

'It's Fletcher,' Guthrie yelled. 'He came in over the stern.'

Just then the carbine came free and I almost dropped it down into the engine-room, but managed to hold it long enough to roll clear.

I sat up with the carbine in my lap, and pushed the safety catch across with my thumb, sweat and salt water streamed into my eyes blurring my vision as I peered up at the entrance to the cabin.

Materson ran into the cabin three paces before he saw me, then he stopped and gaped at me. His face was red with effort and agitation and he lifted his hands, spreading them in a protective gesture before him as I brought up the carbine. The diamond on his little finger winked merrily at me.

I lifted the carbine one-handed from my lap, and its immense weight appalled me. When the muzzle was pointed at Materson's knees I pressed the trigger.

With a continuous shattering roar the carbine spewed out a solid blast of bullets, and the recoil flung the barrel upwards, riding the stream of fire from Materson's crotch up across his belly and chest. It flung him backwards against the cabin bulkhead, and split him like the knife-stroke that guts a fish while he danced a grotesque and jerky little death jig.

I knew that I should not empty the carbine, there was still Mike Guthrie to deal with, but somehow I seemed unable to release my grip on the trigger and the bullets tore through Materson's body, smashing and splintering the woodwork of the bulkhead.

Then suddenly I lifted my finger. The torrent of bullets ceased and Materson fell heavily forward.

The cabin stank with burned cordite and the sweet heavy smell of blood.

Guthrie ducked into the companionway of the cabin, crouching with right arm outflung and he snapped off a single shot at me as I sat in the centre of the cabin.

He had all the time he needed for a clean shot at me, but he hurried it, panicky and off-balance. The blast slapped against my ear drums, and the heavy bullet disrupted the air against my cheek as it flew wide. The recoil kicked the pistol high, and as it dropped for his next shot I fell sideways and pulled up the carbine.

There must have been a single round left in the breech, but it was a lucky one. I did not aim it, but merely jerked at the trigger as the barrel came up.

It hit Guthrie in the crook of his right elbow, shattering the joint and the pistol flew backwards over his shoulder, skidded across the deck and thudded into the stern scuppers.

Guthrie spun aside, the arm twisting grotesquely and hanging from the broken joint at the same instant the firing pin of the carbine fell on an empty chamber.

We stared at each other, both of us badly hit, but the old antagonism was still there between us. It gave me strength to come up on my knees and start towards him, the empty carbine falling from my hand.

Guthrie grunted and turned away, gripping the shattered arm with his good hand. He staggered towards the .45 lying in the scuppers.

I saw there was no way I could stop him. He was not mortally hit, and I knew he could shoot probably as well with his good left hand. Still I made my last try and dragged myself over Materson's body and out into the cockpit, reaching it just as Guthrie stooped to pick the pistol out of the scuppers.

Then *Dancer* came to my aid, and she reared like a wild horse as a freak swell hit her. She threw Guthrie off balance, and the pistol went skidding away across the deck. He turned to chase it, his feet slipped in the blood which I has splashed across the cockpit and he went down.

He fell heavily, pinning his shattered arm under him. He cried out, and rolled on to his knees and began crawling swiftly after the glistening black pistol.

Against the outer bulkhead of the cockpit the long flying gaffs stood in their rack like a set of billiard cues. Ten feet long, with the great stainless steel hooks uppermost.

Chubby had filed the points as cruelly as stilettos. They were designed to be buried deep into a game fish's body, and the shock of the blow would detach the head from the stock. The fish could then be dragged on board with the length of heavy nylon rope that was spliced on the hook.

Guthrie had almost reached the pistol as I knocked open the clamp on the rack and lifted down one of the gaffs.

Guthrie scooped up the pistol left-handed, juggling it to get a grip on it, concentrating his whole attention on the weapon and while he was busy I came up on my knees again and lifted the gaff with one hand, throwing it up high and reaching out over Guthrie's bowed back. As the hook flashed down over him I hit the steel in hard, driving it full length through his ribs, burying the gleaming steel to the curve. The shock of it pulled him down on to the deck and once again the pistol dropped from his hand and the roll of the boat pushed it away from him.

Now he was screaming, a high-pitched wail of agony with the steel deep in him. I tugged harder, single-handed, trying to work it into heart or lung and the hook broke from the stock. Guthrie rolled across the deck towards the pistol. He groped frantically for it, and I dropped the gaff stock and groped just as frantically for the rope to restrain him.

I have seen two women wrestlers fighting in a bath of black mud, in a nightclub in the St Pauli district of Hamburg – and now Guthrie and I performed the same act, only in place of mud we fought in a bath of our own blood. We slithered and rolled about the deck, thrown about mercilessly by *Dancer*'s action in the swell.

Guthrie was weakening at last, clawing with his good hand at the great hook buried in his body, and with the next roll of the sea I was able to throw a coil of the rope around his neck and get a firm purchase against the base of the fighting chair with one foot. Then I pulled with all the remains of my strength and resolve.

Suddenly, with single explosive expulsion of breath, his tongue fell out of his mouth and he relaxed, his limbs stretched out limply and his head lolled loosely back and forth with *Dancer*'s roll.

I was tired beyond caring now. My hand opened of its own accord and the rope fell from it. I lay back and closed my eyes. Darkness fell over me like a shroud.


When I regained consciousness my face felt as though it had been scalded with acid, my lips were swollen and my thirst raged like a forest fire. I had lain face up under a tropical sun for six hours, and it had burned me mercilessly.

Slowly I rolled on to my side, and cried out weakly at the immensity of pain that was my chest. I lay still for a while to let it subside and then I began to explore the wound.

The bullet had angled in through the bicep of my left arm, missing bone, and come out through the tricep, tearing a big exit hole. Immediately it had ploughed into the side of my chest.

Sobbing with the effort I traced and probed the wound with my finger. It had glanced over a rib, I could feel the exposed bone was cracked and rough ended where the slug had struck and been deflected and left slivers of lead and bone chips in the churned flesh. It had gone through the thick muscle of my back – and torn out below the shoulder blade, leaving a hole the size of a *demi tasse* coffee cup.

I fell back on to the deck, panting and fighting back waves of giddy nausea. My exploration had induced fresh bleeding, but I knew at least that the bullet has not entered the chest cavity. I still had some sort of a chance.

While I rested I looked blearily about me. My hair and clothing were stiff with dried blood, blood was coated over the cockpit, dried black and shiny or congealed.

Guthrie lay on his back with the gaff hook still in him and the rope around his neck. The gases in his belly had already blown, giving him a pregnant swollen look.

I got up on to my knees and began to crawl. Materson's body half-blocked the entrance to the cabin, shredded by gunfire as though he had been mauled by a savage predator.

I crawled over him, and found I was whimpering aloud as I saw the icebox behind the bar.

I drank three cans of Coca Cola, gasping and choking in my eagerness, spilling the icy liquid down my chest, and moaning and snuffling through each mouthful. Then I lay and rested again. I closed my eyes and just wanted to sleep for ever.

'Where the hell are we?' The question hit me with a shock of awareness. *Dancer* was adrift on a treacherous coast, strewn with reefs and shoals.

I dragged myself to my feet and reached the blood-caked cockpit.

Beneath us flowed the deep purple blue of the Mozambique, and a clear horizon circled us, above which the massive cloud ranges climbed to a tall blue sky. The ebb and the wind had pushed us far out to the east, we had plenty of sea room.

My legs collapsed under me, and I may have slept for a while. When I woke my head felt clearer, but the wound had stiffened horribly. Each movement was agony. On my hand and knees I reached the shower room where the medicine chest was kept. I ripped away my shirt and poured undiluted acriflavine solution into the cavernous wounds. Then I plugged them roughly with surgical dressing and strapped the whole as best I could, but the effort was too much.

The dizziness overwhelmed me again and I crashed down on to the linoleum floor unconscious.

I awoke light-headed, and feeble as a new-born infant.

It was a major effort to fashion a sling for the wounded arm, and the journey to the bridge was an endless procession of dizziness and pain and nausea.

*Dancer*'s engines started with the first kick, sweet as ever she was.

'Take me home, me darling,' I whispered, and set the automatic pilot. I gave her an approximate heading. *Dancer* settled on course, and the darkness caught me again. I went down sprawling on the deck, welcoming oblivion as it washed over me.

It may have been the altered action of *Dancer*'s passage that roused me. She no longer swooped and rolled with the big swell of the Mozambique, but ambled quietly along over a sheltered sea. Dusk was falling swiftly.

Stiffly I dragged myself up to the wheel. I was only just in time, for dead ahead lay the loom of land in the fading light. I slammed *Dancer*'s throttle closed, and kicked her into neutral. She came up and rocked gently in a low sea. I recognized the shape of the land – it was Big Gull Island.

We had missed the channel of Grand Harbour, my heading had been a little southerly and we had run into the southern-most straggle of tiny atolls that made up the St Mary's group.

Hanging on to the wheel for support I craned forward. The canvas-wrapped bundle still lay on the foredeck – and suddenly I knew that I must get rid of it. My reasons were not clear then. Dimly I realized that it was a high card in the game into which I had been drawn. I knew I dare not ferry it back into Grand Harbour in broad daylight. Three men had been killed for it already – and I'd had half my chest shot away. There was some strong medicine wrapped up in that sheet of canvas.

It took me fifteen minutes to reach the foredeck, and I blacked out twice on the way. When I crawled to the bundle of canvas I was sobbing aloud with each movement.

For another half-hour I tried feebly to unwrap the stiff canvas and untie the thick nylon knots. With only one hand and my fingers so numb and weak that they could not close properly it was a hopeless task, and the blackness kept filling my head. I was afraid I would go out with the bundle still aboard.

Lying on my side I used the last rays of the setting sun to take a bearing off the point of the island, lining up a clump of palms and the point of the high ground – marking the spot with care.

Then I opened the swinging section of the foredeck railing through which we usually pulled big fish aboard, and I wriggled around the canvas bundle – got both feet on to it and shoved it over the side. It fell with a heavy splash and droplets splattered in my face.

My exertions had re-opened the wounds and fresh blood was soaking my clumsy dressing. I started back across the deck but I did not make it. I went out for the last time as I reached the break of the cockpit.

The morning sun and a raucous barnyard squawking woke me, but when I opened my eyes the sun seemed shaded, darkened as though in eclipse. My vision was fading, and when I tried to move there was no strength for it. I lay crushed beneath the weight of weakness and pain. *Dancer* was canted at an absurd angle, probably stranded high and dry on the beach.

I stared up into the rigging above me. There were three black-backed gulls as big as turkeys sitting in a row on the cross stay. They twisted their heads sideways to look down at me, and their beaks were clear yellow and powerful. The upper part of the beak ended in a curved point that was a bright cherry red. They watched me with glistening black eyes, and fluffed out their feathers impatiently.

I tried to shout at them, to drive them away but my lips would not move. I was completely helpless, and I knew that soon they would begin on my eyes. The always went for the eyes.

One of the gulls above me grew bold and spreading his wings, planed down to the deck near me. He folded his wings and waddled a few steps closer, and we stared at each other. Again I tried to scream, but no sound came and the gull waddled forward again, then stretched out his neck, opened that wicked beak and let out a hoarse screech of menace. I felt the whole of my dreadfully abused body cringing away from the bird.

Suddenly the tone of the screeching gulls altered, and the air was filled with their wing beats. The bird that I was watching screeched again, but this time in disappointment and it launched itself into flight, the draught from its wings striking my face as it rose.

There was a long silence then, as I lay on the heavily listing deck, fighting off the waves of darkness that tried to overwhelm me. Then suddenly there was a scrabbling sound alongside

I rolled my head again to face it, and at that moment a dark chocolate face rose above deck level and stared at me from a range of two feet.

'Lordy!' said a familiar voice. 'Is that you, Mister Harry?'

I learned later that Henry Wallace, one of St Mary's turtle hunters, had been camped out on the atolls and had risen from his bed of straw to find *Wave Dancer* stranded by the ebb on the sand bar of the lagoon with a cloud of gulls squabbling over her. He had waded out across the bar, and climbed the side to peer into the slaughterhouse that was *Dancer*'s cockpit.

I wanted to tell him how thankful I was to see him, I wanted to promise him free beer for the rest of his life – but instead I started to weep, just a slow welling up of tears from deep down. I didn't even have the strength to sob.

'Little scratch like that,' marvelled MacNab. 'What's all the fussing about?' and he probed determinedly.

I gasped as he did something else to my back; if I had had the strength I would have got up off the hospital bed and pushed that probe up the most convenient opening of his body. Instead I moaned weakly.

'Come on, Doc. Didn't they teach you about morphine and that stuff back in the time when you should have failed your degree?'

MacNab came around to look in my face. He was plump and scarlet-faced, fiftyish and greying in hair and moustache. His breath should have anaesthetized me.

'Harry, my boy, that stuff costs money – what are you, anyway, National Health or a private patient?'

'I just changed my status – I'm private.'

'Quite right, too,' MacNab agreed. 'Man of your standing in the community,' and he nodded to the sister. 'Very well then, my dear, give Mister Harry a grain of morphine before we proceed,' and while he waited for her to prepare the shot he went on to cheer me up. 'We put six pints of whole blood into you last night, you were just about dry. Soaked it up like a sponge.'

Well, you wouldn't expect one of the giants of the medical profession to be practising on St Mary's. I could almost believe the island rumour that he was in partnership with Fred Coker's mortician parlour.

'How long you going to keep me in here anyway, Doc?'

'Not more than a month.'

'A month!' I struggled to sit up and two nurses pounced on me to restrain me, which required no great effort. I could still hardly raise my head. 'I can't afford a month. My God, it's right in the middle of the season. I've got a new party coming next week –'

The sister hurried across with the syringe.

'– You trying to break me? I can't afford to miss a single party –'

The sister hit me with the needle.

'Harry old boy, you can forget about this season. You won't be fishing again,' and he began picking bits of bone and flakes of lead out of me while he hummed cheerily to himself. The morphine dulled the pain – but not my despair. If *Dancer* and I missed half a season we just couldn't keep going. Once again they had me stretched out on the financial rack. God, how I hated money.

MacNab strapped me up in clean white bandages, and spread a little more sunshine.

'You going to lose some function in your left arm there, Harry boy. Probably always be a little stiff and weak, and you going to have some pretty scars to show the girls.' He finished winding the bandage and turned to the

sister. 'Change the dressings every six hours, swab out with Eusol and give
him his usual dose of Aureo Mycytin every four hours. Three Mogadon
tonight and I'll see him on my rounds tomorrow.' He turned back to grin
at me with bad teeth under the untidy grey moustache. 'The entire police
force is waiting outside this very room. I'll have to let them in now.' He
started towards the door, then paused to chuckle again. 'You did a hell of
a job on those two guys, spread them over the scenery with a spade. Nice
shooting, Harry boy.'

Inspector Daly was dressed in impeccable khaki drill, starched and
pristine, and his leather belts and straps glowed with a high polish.

'Good afternoon, Mr Fletcher. I have come to take a statement from you.
I hope you feel strong enough.'

'I feel wonderful, Inspector. Nothing like a bullet through the chest to set
you up.'

Daly turned to the constable who followed him and motioned him to take
the chair beside the bed, and as he sat and prepared his shorthand pad the
constable told me softly, 'Sorry you got hurt, Mister Harry.'

'Thanks, Wally, but you should have seen the other guys.'

Wally was one of Chubby's nephews, and his mother did my laundry. He
was a big, strong, darkly good-looking youngster.

'I saw them,' he grinned. 'Wow!'

'If you are ready, Mr Fletcher,' Daly cut in primly, annoyed by the
exchange. 'We can get on.'

'Shoot,' I said, and I had my story well prepared. Like all good stories,
it was the exact and literal truth, with omissions. I made no mention of the
prize that James North had lifted, and which I had dumped again off Big
Gull island – nor did I tell Daly in which area we had conducted our search.
He wanted to know, of course. He kept coming back to that.

'What were they searching for?'

'I have no idea. They were very careful not to let me know.'

'Where did all this happen?' he persisted.

'In the area beyond Herring Bone Reef, south of Rastafa Point.' This
was fifty miles from the break at Gunfire Reef.

'Could you recognize the exact point where they dived?'

'I don't think so, not within a few miles. I was merely following
instructions.'

Daly chewed his silky moustache in frustration.

'All right, you say they attacked you without warning,' and I nodded.
'Why did they do that – why would they try to kill you?'

'We never really discussed it. I didn't have a chance to ask them.' I was
beginning to feel very tired and feeble again, I didn't want to go on talking
in case I made a mistake. 'When Guthrie started shooting at me with that
cannon of his I didn't think he wanted to chat.'

'This isn't a joke, Fletcher,' he told me stiffly, and I rang the bell beside
me. The sister must have been waiting just outside the door.

'Sister, I'm feeling pretty bad.'

'You'll have to go now, Inspector.' She turned on the two policemen like
a mother hen, and drove them from the ward. Then she came back to
rearrange my pillows.

She was a pretty little thing with huge dark eyes, and her tiny waist was belted in firmly to accentuate her big nicely shaped bosom on which she wore her badges and medals. Lustrous chestnut curls peeped from under the saucy little uniform cap.

'What is your name, then?' I whispered hoarsely.

'May.'

'Sister May, how come I haven't seen you around before?' I asked, as she leaned across me to tuck in my sheet.

'Guess you just weren't looking, Mister Harry.'

'Well, I'm looking now.' The front of her crisp white uniform blouse was only a few inches from my nose. She stood up quickly.

'They say here you're a devil man,' she said. 'I know now they didn't tell me lies.' But she was smiling. 'Now you go to sleep. You've got to get strong again.'

'Yeah, we'll talk again then,' I said, and she laughed out loud.

The next three days I had a lot of time to think for I was allowed no visitors until the official inquest had been conducted. Daly had a constable on guard outside my room, and I was left in no doubt that I stood accused of murder most vile.

My room was cool and airy with a good view down across the lawns to the tall dark-leafed banyan trees, and beyond them the massive stone walls of the fort with the cannons upon the battlements. The food was good, plenty of fish and fruit, and Sister May and I were becoming good, if not intimate, friends. She even smuggled in a bottle of Chivas Regal which we kept in the bedpan. From her I heard how the whole island was agog with the cargo that *Wave Dancer* had brought into Grand Harbour. She told me they buried Materson and Guthrie on the second day in the old cemetery. A corpse doesn't keep so well in those latitudes.

In those three days I decided that the bundle I had dropped off Big Gull Island would stay there. I guessed that from now on there would be a lot of eyes watching me, and I was at a complete disadvantage. I didn't know who the watchers were and I didn't know why. I would keep down off the sky-line until I worked out where the next bullet was likely to come from. I didn't like the game. They could deal me out and I would stick to the action I could call and handle.

I thought a lot about Jimmy North also, and every time I felt myself grieving unnecessarily I tried to tell myself that he was a stranger, that he had meant nothing to me, but it didn't work. This is a weakness of mine which I must always guard against. I become too readily emotionally bound up with other people. I try to walk alone, avoiding involvement, and after years of practice I have achieved some success. It is seldom these days that anyone can penetrate my armour the way Jimmy North did.

By the third day I was feeling much stronger. I could lift myself into a sitting position without assistance and with only a moderate degree of pain.

They held the official inquest in my hospital room. It was a closed session, attended only by the heads of the legislative, judicial and executive branches of St Mary's government.

The President himself, dressed as always in black with a crisp white shirt and a halo of snowy wool around his bald pate, chaired the meeting. Judge

Harkness, tall and thin and sunburned to dark brown, assisted him – while Inspector Daly represented the executive.

The President's first concern was for my comfort and well-being. I was one of his boys.

'You be sure you don't tire yourself now, Mister Harry. Anything you want you just ask, hear? We have only come here to hear your version, but I want to tell you now not to worry. There is nothing going to happen to you.'

Inspector Daly looked pained, seeing his prisoner declared innocent before his trial began.

So I told my story again, with the President making helpful or admiring comments whenever I paused for breath, and when I finished he shook his head with wonder.

'All I can say, Mister Harry, is there are not many men would have had the strength and courage to do what you did against those gangsters, is that right, gentlemen?'

Judge Harkness agreed heartily, but Inspector Daly said nothing.

'And they were gangsters too,' he went on. 'We sent their fingerprints to London and we heard today that those men came here under false names, and that both of them have got police records at Scotland Yard. Gangsters, both of them.' The President looked at Judge Harkness. 'Any questions, Judge?'

'I don't think so, Mr President.'

'Good.' The President nodded happily. 'What about you, Inspector?' And Daly produced a typewritten list. The President made no effort to hide his irritation.

'Mister Fletcher is still a very sick man, Inspector. I hope your questions are really important.'

Inspector Daly hesitated and the President went on brusquely, 'Good, well then we are all agreed. The verdict is death by misadventure. Mister Fletcher acted in self-defence, and is hereby discharged from any guilt. No criminal charges will be brought against him.' He turned to the shorthand recorder in the corner. 'Have you got that? Type it out and send a copy to my office for signature.' He stood up and came to my bedside. 'Now you get better soon, Mister Harry. I expect you for dinner at Government House soon as you are well enough. My secretary will send you a formal invitation. I want to hear the whole story again.'

Next time I appear before a judicial body, as I surely shall, I hope for the same consideration. Having been officially declared innocent I was allowed visitors.

Chubby and Mrs Chubby came together dressed in their standard number one rig. Mrs Chubby had baked one of her splendid banana cakes, knowing my weakness for them.

Chubby was torn by relief at seeing me still alive and outrage at what I had done to *Wave Dancer*. He scowled at me fiercely as he started giving me a large slice of his mind.

'Aint never going to get that deck clean again. It soaked right in, man. That damned old carbine of yours really chewed up the cabin bulkhead. Me and Angelo been working three days at it now, and it still needs a few more days.'

'Sorry, Chubby, next time I shoot somebody I'm going to make them stand by the rail first.' I knew that when Chubby had finished repairing the woodwork the damage would not be detectable.

'When you coming out anyway? Plenty of big fish working out there on the stream, Harry.'

'I be out pretty soon, Chubby. One week tops.'

Chubby sniffed. 'Did hear that Fred Coker wired all your parties for rest of the season – told them you were hurt bad and switched their bookings to Mister Coleman.'

I lost my temper then. 'You tell Fred Coker to get his black arse up here soonest,' I shouted.

Dick Coleman had a deal with the Hilton Hotel. They had financed the purchase of two big game fishing boats, which Coleman crewed with a pair of imported skippers. Neither of his boats caught much fish, they didn't have the feel of it. He had a lot of difficulty getting charters, and I guessed Fred Coker had been handsomely compensated to switch my bookings to him. Coker arrived the following morning.

'Mister Harry, Doctor MacNab told me you wouldn't be able to fish again this season. I couldn't let my parties down, they fly six thousand miles to find you in a hospital bed. I couldn't do that – I got my reputation to think of.'

'Mr Coker, your reputation smells like one of those stiffs you got tucked away in the back room.' I told him, and he smiled at me blandly from behind his gold-rimmed spectacles, but he was right of course, it would be a long time still before I could take *Dancer* out after the big billfish.

'Now don't you fuss yourself, Mister Harry. Soon as you better I will arrange a few lucrative charters for you.'

He was talking about the night run again, his commission on a single run could go as high as seven hundred and fifty dollars. I could handle that even in my present beaten-up condition, it involved merely conning *Dancer* in and out again – just as long as we didn't run into trouble.

'Forget it, Mr Coker. I told you from now on I fish, that's all,' and he nodded and smiled and went on as though I had not spoken.

'Had persistent inquiries from one of your old clients.'

'Body? Box?' I demanded. Body was the illegal carrying to or from the African mainland of human beings, fleeing politicians with the goon squad after them – or on the other hand aspiring politicians trying for radical change in the regime. Boxes usually contained lethal hardware and it was a one-way traffic. In the old days they called it gun-running.

Coker shook his head and said, 'Five, six,' – from the old nursery rhyme: 'Five, six. Pick up sticks.' In this context sticks were tusks of ivory. A massive, highly organized poaching operation was systematically wiping out the African elephant from the game reserves and tribal lands of East Africa. The Orient was an insatiable and high-priced market for the ivory. A fast boat and a good skipper were needed to get the valuable cargo out of an estuary mouth, through the dangerous inshore waters, out to where one of the big ocean-going dhows waited on the stream of the Mozambique.

'Mr Coker,' I told him wearily. 'I'm sure your mother never even knew your father's name.'

'It was Edward, Mister Harry,' he smiled carefully. 'I told the client that the going rate was up. What with inflation and the price of diesel fuel.'

'How much?'

'Seven thousand dollars a trip,' which was not as much as it sounds after Coker had clouted fifteen per cent, then Inspector Peter Daly had to be slipped the same again to dim his eyesight and cloud his hearing. On top of that Chubby and Angelo always earned a danger money bonus of five hundred each for a night run.

'Forget it, Mr Coker,' I said unconvincingly. 'You just fix a couple of fishing parties.' But he knew I couldn't fight it.

'Just as soon as you fit enough to fish, we'll fix that. Meantime, when do you want to do the first night run? Shall I tell them ten days from today? That will be high spring tide and a good moon.'

'All right,' I agreed with resignation. 'Ten days' time.'

With a positive decision made, it seemed that my recovery from the wounds was hastened. I had been in peak physical condition which contributed, and the gaping holes in my arm and back began to shrink miraculously.

I reached a milestone in my convalescence on the sixth day. Sister May was giving me a bed bath, with a basin of suds and a face cloth, when there was a monumental demonstration of my physical well-being. Even I, who was no stranger to the phenomenon, was impressed, while Sister May was so overcome that her voice became a husky little whisper.

'Lord!' she said. 'You've sure got your strength back.'

'Sister May, do you think we should waste that?' I asked, and she shook her head vehemently.


From then onwards I began to take a more cheerful view of my circumstances, and not surprisingly the canvas-wrapped secret off Big Gull Island began to nag me. I felt my good resolutions weakening.

'I'll just take a look,' I told myself. 'When I am sure the dust has really settled.'

They were allowing me up for a few hours at a time now, and I felt restless and anxious to get on with it. Not even Sister May's devoted efforts could blunt the edge of my awakening energy. MacNab was impressed.

'You heal well, Harry old chap. Closing up nicely – another week.'

'A week, hell!' I told him determinedly. Seven days from now I was making the night run. Coker had set it up without trouble – and I was just about stony broke. I needed that run pretty badly.

My crew came up to visit me every evening, and to report progress on the repairs to *Dancer*. One evening Angelo arrived earlier than usual, he was dressed in his courting gear –rodeo boots and all – but he was strangely subdued and not alone.

The lass with him was the young nursery grade teacher from the government school down near the fort. I knew her well enough to exchange smiles on the street. Missus Eddy had summed up her character for me once.

'She's a good girl, that Judith. Not all flighty and flirty like some others. Going to make some lucky fellow a good wife.'

She was also good-looking with a tall willowy figure, neatly and conservatively dressed, and she greeted me shyly.

'How do, Mister Harry.'

'Hello, Judith. Good of you to come,' and I looked at Angelo, unable to hide my grin. He couldn't meet my eye, colouring up as he hunted for words.

'Me and Judith planning to marry up,' he blurted at last. 'Wanted you to know that, boss.'

'Think you can keep him under control, Judith?' I laughed delightedly.

'You just watch me,' she said with a flash of dark eyes that made the question superfluous.

'That's great – I'll make a speech at your wedding,' I assured them. 'You going to let Angelo go on crewing for me?'

'Wouldn't ever try to stop him,' she assured me. 'It's good work he's got with you.'

They stayed for another hour and when they left I felt a small prickle of envy. It must be a good feeling to have someone –apart from yourself. I thought some day if I ever found the right person I might try it. Then I dismissed the thought, raising my guard again. There were a hell of a lot of women – and no guarantee you will pick right.

MacNab discharged me with two days to spare. My clothes hung on my bony frame, I had lost nearly two stone in weight and my tan had faded to a dirty yellow brown, there were big blue smears under my eyes and I still felt weak as a baby. The arm was in a sling and the wounds were still open, but I could change the dressing myself.

Angelo brought the pick-up to the hospital and waited while I said goodbye to Sister May on the steps.

'Nice getting to know you, Mister Harry.'

'Come out to the shack some time soon. I'll grill you a mess of crayfish, and we'll drink a little wine.'

'My contract ends next week. I'll be going home to England then.'

'You be happy, hear,' I told her.

Angelo drove me down to Admiralty, and with Chubby we spent an hour going over *Dancer's* repairs.

Her decks were snowy white, and they had replaced all the woodwork in the saloon bulkhead, a beautiful piece of joinery with which even I could find no fault.

We took her down the channel as far as Mutton Point and it was good to feel her riding lightly under my feet and hear the sweet burble of her engines. We came home in the dusk to tie up at moorings and sit out on the bridge in the dark, drinking beer out of the can and talking.

I told them that we had a run set for the following night, and they asked where to and what the cargo was. That was all – it was set, there was no argument.

'Time to go,' Angelo said at last. 'Going to pick Judith up from night school,' and we rowed ashore in the dinghy.

There was a police Land-Rover parked beside my old pick-up at the back of the pineapple sheds and Wally, the young constable, climbed out as we approached. He greeted his uncle. and then turned to me.

'Sorry to worry you, Mister Harry, but Inspector Daly wants to see you up at the fort. He says it's urgent.'

'God,' I growled. 'It can wait until tomorrow.'

'He says it can't, Mister Harry.' Wally was apologetic, and for his sake I went along.

'Okay, I'll follow you in the pick-up – but we got to drop Chubby and Angelo off first.'

I thought it was probably that Daly wanted to haggle about his pay off. Usually Fred Coker fixed that, but I guessed that Daly was raising the price of his honour.

Driving one-handed and holding the steering wheel with a knee while I shifted gear with my good hand, I followed the red tail lights of Wally's Land-Rover rattling over the drawbridge and parked beside it in the courtyard of the fort.

The massive stone walls had been built by slave labour in the mid-eighteenth century and from the wide ramparts the long thirty-six pounder cannon ranged the channel and the entrance to Grand Harbour.

One wing was used as the island police headquarters, jail and armoury – the rest of it was government offices and the Presidential and State apartments.

We climbed the front steps to the charge office and Wally led me through a side door, and along a corridor, down steps, another corridor, more stone steps.

I had never been down here before and I was intrigued. The stone walls here must have been twenty feet thick, the old powder store probably. I half expected the Frankenstein monster to be lurking behind the thick oak door, iron studded and weathered, at the end of the last passage. We went through.

It wasn't Frankenstein, but next best. Inspector Daly waited for us with another of his constables. I noticed immediately they both wore sidearms. The room was empty except for a wooden table and four P.W.D. type chairs. The walls were unpainted stonework and the floor was paved.

At the back of the room an arched doorway led to a row of cells. The lights were bare hundred-watt bulbs hanging on black electrical cable that ran exposed across the beamed roof. They cast hard black shadows in the angles of the irregularly shaped room.

On the table lay my FN carbine. I stared at it uncomprehendingly.

Behind me Wally closed the oak door.

'Mr Fletcher, is this your firearm?'

'You know damn well it is,' I said angrily. 'Just what the hell are you playing at, Daly?'

'Harold Delville Fletcher, I am placing you under arrest for the unlawful possession of Category A firearms. To wit, one unlicensed automatic rifle type Fabrique Nationale Serial No. 4163215.'

'You're off your head,' I said, and laughed. He didn't like that laugh. The weak little lips below his moustache puckered up like those of a sulky child and he nodded at his constables. They had been briefed, and they went out through the oak door.

I heard the bolts shoot home, and Daly and I were alone. He was standing well away from me across the room – and the flap of his holster was unbuttoned.

'Does his excellency know about this, Daly?' I asked, still smiling.

'His excellency left St Mary's at four o'clock this afternoon to attend the conference of Commonwealth heads in London. He won't be back for two weeks.'

I stopped smiling. I knew it was true. 'In the meantime I have reason to believe the security of the State is endangered.'

He smiled now, thinly and with the mouth only. 'Before we go any further I want you to be sure I am serious.'

'I believe you.' I said.

'I have two weeks with you alone, here, Fletcher. These walls are pretty thick, you can make as much noise as you like.'

'You are a monstrous little turd, you really are.'

'There is only one of two ways you are going to leave here. Either you and I come to an arrangement – or I'll get Fred Coker to come and fetch you in a box.'

'Let's hear your deal, little man.'

'I want to know exactly – and I mean exactly – where your charter carried out their diving operations before the shoot out.'

'I told you – somewhere off Rastafa Point. I couldn't give you the exact spot.'

'Fletcher, you know the spot to within inches. I'm willing to stake *your* life on that. You wouldn't miss a chance like that. You know it. I know it – and they knew it. That's why they tried to sign you off.'

'Inspector, go screw,' I said.

'What is more it was nowhere near Rastafa Point. You were working north of here, towards the mainland. I was interested – I had some reports of your movements.'

'It was somewhere off Rastafa Point,' I repeated doggedly.

'Very well,' he nodded. 'I hope you aren't as tough as you put out, Fletcher, otherwise this is going to be a long messy business. Before we start though, don't waste our time with false data. I'm going to keep you here while I check it out – I've got two weeks.'

We stared at each other, and my flesh began to crawl. Peter Daly was going to enjoy this, I realized. There was a gloating expression on those thin lips and a smoky glaze to his eyes.

'I had a great deal of experience in interrogation in Malaya, you know. Fascinating subjects. So many aspects to it. So often it's the tough, strong ones that pop first – and the little runts that hang on for ever –'

This was for kicks, I saw clearly that he was aroused by the prospect of inflicting pain. His breathing had changed, faster and deeper, there was fresh colour in his cheeks.

'– of course, you are at a physical low ebb right now, Fletcher. Probably your threshold of pain is much lowered after your recent misadventures. I don't think it will take long –'

He seemed to regret that. I gathered myself, tightening up for an attempt.

'No,' he snapped. 'Don't do it, Fletcher.' He placed his hand on the butt of the pistol. He was fifteen feet away. I was one-armed, weak, there was a locked door behind me, two armed constables – my shoulders sagged as I relaxed.

'That's better.' He smiled again. 'Now I think we will handcuff you to the bars of a cell, and we can get to work. When you have had enough you have merely to say so. I think you will find my little electrical set up simple but effective. It's merely a twelve-volt car battery – and I clip the terminals on to interesting parts of the body –'

He reached behind him – and for the first time I noticed the button of an electric bell set on the wall. He pressed it and I heard the bell ring faintly beyond the oaken door.

The bolts shot back and the two constables came back in.

'Take him through to the cells,' Daly ordered, and the constables hesitated. I guessed they were strangers to this type of operation.

'Come on,' snapped Daly, and they stepped up on either side of me. Wally laid a hand lightly on my injured arm, and I allowed myself to be led forward towards the cells – and Daly.

I wanted to have a chance at him, just one chance.

'How's your mom, Wally?' I asked casually.

'She's all right, Mister Harry,' he muttered embarrassedly.

'She get the present I sent up for her birthday?'

'Yeah, she got it.' He was distracted as I intended.

We had come level with Daly, he was standing by the doorway to the cells, waiting for us to go through, slapping the malacca swagger stick against his thigh.

The constables were holding me respectfully, loosely, unsure of themselves, and I stepped to one side pushing Wally slightly off balance – then I spun back, breaking free.

Not one of them was ready for it, and I covered the three paces to Daly before they had realized what I was doing – and I put my right knee into him with my full body weight behind it. It thumped into the crotch of his legs, a marvellously solid blow. Whatever the price I was going to have to pay for the pleasure, it was cheap.

Daly was lifted off his feet, a full eighteen inches in the air, and he flew backwards to crash against the bars. Then he doubled up, both hands pressed into his lower body, screaming thinly – a sound like steam from a boiling kettle. As he went over I lined up for another shot at his face, I wanted to take his teeth out with a kick in the mouth – but the constables recovered their wits and leaped forward to drag me away. They were rough now, twisting the arm.

'You didn't ought to do that, Mister Harry,' Wally shouted angrily. His fingers bit into my bicep and I gritted my teeth.

'The President himself cleared me, Wally. You know that,' I shouted back at him, and Daly straightened up, his face twisted witn agony, still holding himself.

'This is a frame up.' I knew I had only a few seconds to talk, Daly was reeling towards me, brandishing the swagger stick, his mouth wide open as he tried to find his voice

'If he gets me in that cell he's going to kill me, Wally –'

'Shut up!' screeched Daly.

'He wouldn't dare try this if the President –'

'Shut up! Shut up!' He swung the swagger stick, a side-arm cut, that hissed like a cobra. He had gone for my wounds deliberately, and the supple cane snapped around me like a pistol shot.

The pain of it was beyond belief, and I convulsed, bucking involuntarily in their grip. They held me.

'Shut up!' Daly was hysterical with pain and rage. He swung again, and the cane cut deeply into half-healed flesh. This time I screamed.

'I'll kill you, you bastard.' Daly staggered back, still hunched with pain, and he fumbled with his holstered pistol.

What I had hoped for now happened. Wally released me and jumped forward.

'No,' he shouted. 'Not that.'

He towered over Daly's slim crouching form and with one massive brown hand he blocked Daly's draw.

'Get out of my way. That's an order,' shouted Daly, but Wally unclipped the lanyard from the pistol's butt and disarmed him. Stepping back with the pistol in his hand.

'I'll break you for this,' snarled Daly. 'It's your duty –'

'I know my duty, Inspector,' Wally spoke with a simple dignity, 'and it's not to murder prisoners.' Then he turned to me. 'Mister Harry, you'd best get out of here.'

'You're freeing a prisoner –' Daly gasped. 'Man, I'm going to break you.'

'Didn't see no warrant,' Wally cut in. 'Soon as the President signs a warrant, we'll fetch Mister Harry right back in again.'

'You black bastard,' Daly panted at him, and Wally turned to me.

'Get!' he said. 'Quickly.'


It was a long ride out to the shack, every bump in the track hit me in the chest. One thing I had learned from the evening's jollifications was that my original thoughts were correct – whatever that bundle off Big Gull Island contained, it could get a peace-loving gentleman like myself into plenty of trouble.

I was not so trusting as to believe that Inspector Daly had made his last attempt at interrogating me. Just as soon as he recovered from the kick in his multiplication machinery which I had given him, he was going to make another attempt to connect me up to the lighting system. I wondered if Daly was acting on his own, or if he had partners – and I guessed he was alone, taking opportunity as it presented itself.

I parked the pick-up in the yard and went through on to the veranda of my shack. Missus Chubby had been out to sweep and tidy while I was away. There were fresh flowers in a jam-jar on the dining-room table – but more important there was eggs and bacon, bread and butter in the icebox.

I stripped off my blood-stained shirt and dressing. There were thick raised welts around my chest that the cane had left, and the wounds were a mess.

I showered and strapped on a fresh dressing, then, standing naked over the stove, I scrambled a pan full of eggs with bacon and while it cooked, I poured a very dark whisky and took it like medicine.

I was too tired to climb between the sheets, and as I fell across the bed I wondered if I would be fit enough to work the night run on schedule. It was my last thought before sun-up.

And after I had showered again and swallowed two Doloxene pain-killers with a glass of cold pineapple juice and eaten another panful of eggs for breakfast I thought the answer was yes. I was stiff and sore, but I could work. At noon I drove into town, stopped of at Missus Eddy's store for supplies and then went on down to Admiralty.

Chubby and Angelo were on board already, and *Dancer* lay against the wharf.

'I filled the auxiliary tanks, Harry,' Chubby told me. 'She's good for a thousand miles.'

'Did you break out the cargo nets?' I asked, and he nodded.

'They are stowed in the main sail locker.' We would use the nets to deck load the bulky ivory cargo.

'Don't forget to bring a coat – it will be cold out on the stream with this wind blowing.'

'Don't worry, Harry. You the one should watch it. Man, you look bad as you were ten days ago. You look real sick.'

'I feel beautiful, Chubby.'

'Yeah,' he grunted, 'like my mother-in-law,' then he changed the subject. 'What happened to your carbine, man?'

'The police are holding it.'

'You mean we going out there without a piece on board?'

'We never needed it yet.'

'There is always a first time,' he grunted. 'I'm going to feel mighty naked without it.'

Chubby's obsession with armaments always amused me.

Despite all the evidence that I presented to the contrary, Chubby could never quite shake off the belief that the velocity and range of a bullet depended upon how hard one pulled the trigger – and Chubby intended that his bullets go very fast and very far indeed.

The savage strength with which he sent them on their way would have buckled a less robust weapon than the FN. He also suffered from a complete inability to keep his eyes open at the moment of firing.

I have seen him miss a fifteen-foot tiger shark at a range of ten feet with a full magazine of twenty rounds. Chubby Andrews was never going to make it to Bisley, but he just naturally loved firearms and things that went bang.

'It will be a milk run, a ruddy pleasure cruise, Chubby, you'll see,' and he crossed his fingers to avert the hex, and shuffled off to work on *Dancer's* already brilliant brasswork, while I went ashore.

The front office of Fred Coker's travel agency was deserted and I rang the bell on the desk. He stuck his head through from the back room.

'Welcome, Mister Harry.' He had removed his coat and tie and had rolled up his shirt sleeves, about his waist he wore a red rubber apron. 'Lock the front door, please, and come through.'

The back room was in contrast to the front office with its gaudy wallpaper and bright travel posters. It was a long, gloomy barn. Along one wall were piled cheap pine coffins. The hearse was parked inside the double doors at the far end. Behind a grimy canvas screen in one corner was a marble slab table with guttering around the edges and a spout to direct fluid from the guttering into a bucket on the floor.

'Come in, sit down. There is a chair. Excuse me if I carry on working while we talk. I have to have this ready for four o'clock this afternoon.'

I took one look at the frail naked corpse on the slab. It was a little girl of about six years of age with long dark hair. One look was enough and I moved the chair behind the screen so I could see only Fred Coker's bald head, and I lit a cheroot. There was a heavy smell of embalming fluid in the room, and it caught in my throat.

'You get used to it, Mister Harry.' Fred Coker had noticed my distaste.

'Did you set it up?' I didn't want to discuss his gruesome trade.

'It's fixed,' he assured me.

'Did you square our friend at the fort?'

'It's all fixed.'

'When did you see him?' I persisted, I wanted to know about Daly. I was very interested in how Daly felt.

'I saw him this morning, Mister Harry.'

'How was he?'

'He seemed all right.' Coker paused in his grisly task and looked at me questioningly.

'Was he standing up, walking around, dancing a jig, singing, tying the dog loose?'

'No. He was sitting down, and he was not in a very good mood.'

'It figures.' I laughed and my own injuries felt better. 'But he took the pay off?'

'Yes, he took it.'

'Good, then we have still got a deal.'

'Like I told you, it's all fixed.'

'Lay it on me, Mr Coker.'

'The pick up is at the mouth of the Salsa stream where it enters the south channel of the main Duza estuary.' I nodded, that was acceptable. There was a good channel and the holding ground off the Salsa was satisfactory.

'The recognition signal will be two lanterns – one over the other, placed on the bank nearest the mouth. You will flash twice, repeated at thirty-second intervals and when the lower lantern is extinguished you can anchor. Got that?'

'Good.' It was all satisfactory.

'They will provide labour to load from the lighters.'

I nodded, then asked. 'They know that slack water is three o'clock – and I must be out of the channel before that?'

'Yes, Mister Harry. I told them they must finish loading before two hundred hours.'

'All right then – what about the drop off?'

'Your drop-off will be twenty-five miles due east of Rastafa Point.'

'Fine.' I could check my bearings off the lighthouse at Rastafa. It was good and simple.

'You will drop-off to a dhow-rigged schooner, a big one. Your recognition signal will be the same. Two lanterns on the mast, you will flash twice at thirty seconds, and the lower lamp will extinguish. You can then offload. They will provide labour and will put down an oil slick for you to ride in. I think that is all.'

'Except for the money.'

'Except for the money, of course.' He produced an envelope from the front pocket of his apron. I took it gingerly between thumb and forefinger and glanced at his calculations scribbled in ballpoint on the envelope.

'Half up front, as usual, the rest on delivery,' he pointed out.

That was thirty-five hundred, less twenty-one hundred for Coker's commission and Daly's pay-off. It left fourteen hundred, out of which I had to find bonus for Chubby and Angelo – a thousand dollars – not much over.

I grimaced. 'I'll be waiting outside your office at nine o'clock tomorrow morning, Mr Coker.'

'I'll have a cup of coffee ready for you, Mister Harry.'

'That had better not be all,' I told him, and he laughed and stooped once more over the marble slab.

We cleared Grand Harbour in the late afternoon, and I made a fake run down the channel towards Mutton Point for the benefit of a possible watcher with binoculars on Coolie Peak. As darkness fell, I came around on to my true heading, and we went in through the inshore channel and the islands towards the wide tidal mouth of the Duva River.

There was no moon but the stars were big and the break of surf flared with phosphorescence, ghostly green in the afterglow of the setting sun.

I ran *Dancer* in fast, picking up my marks successively – the loom of an atoll in the starlight, the break of a reef, the very run and chop of the water guided me through the channels and warned of shoals and shallows.

Angelo and Chubby huddled beside me at the bridge rail. Occasionally one of them would go below to brew more of the powerful black coffee, and we sipped at the steaming mugs, staring out into the night watching for a flash of paleness that was not breaking water but the hull of a patrol boat.

Once Chubby broke the silence. 'Hear from Wally you had some trouble up at the fort last night.'

'Some,' I agreed.

'Wally had to take him up to the hospital afterwards.'

'Wally still got his job?' I asked.

'Only just. The man wanted to lock him up but Wally was too big.'

Angelo joined in. 'Judith was up at the airport at lunch time. Went up to fetch a crate of school books, and she saw him going out on the plane to the mainland.'

'Who?' I asked.

'Inspector Daly, he went across on the noon plane.'

'Why didn't you tell me before?'

'Didn't think it was important, Harry.'

'No,' I agreed. 'Perhaps it isn't.'

There were a dozen reasons why Daly might go out to the mainland, none of them remotely connected with my business. Yet it made me feel uneasy – I didn't like that kind of animal prowling around in the undergrowth when I was taking a risk.

'Wish you'd brought that piece of yours, Harry,' Chubby repeated mournfully, and I said nothing but wished the same.

The flow of the tide had smoothed the usual turmoil at the entrance to the southern channel of the Duza and I groped blindly for it in the dark. The mud banks on each side were latticed with standing fish traps laid by the tribal fishermen, and they helped to define the channel at last.

When I was sure we were in the correct entrance, I killed both engines and we drifted silently on the incoming tide. All of us listened with complete concentration for the engine beat of a patrol boat, but there was only the cry of a night heron and the splash of mullet leaping in the shallows.

Ghost silent, we were swept up the channel; on each side the dark masses of mangrove trees hedged us in and the smell of the mud swamps was rank and fetid on the moisture-laden air.

The starlight danced in spots of light on the dark agitated surface of the channel, and once a long narrow dugout canoe slid past us like a crocodile, the phosphorescence gleaming on the paddles of the two fishermen returning from the mouth. They paused to watch us for a moment and then drove on without calling a greeting, disappearing swiftly into the gloom.

'That was bad,' said Angelo.

'We will be drinking a lager in the Lord Nelson before they could tell anyone who matters.' I knew that most of the fishermen on this coast kept their own secrets, close with words like most of their kind. I was not perturbed by the sighting.

Looking ahead I saw the first bend coming up, and the current began to push *Dancer* out towards the far bank. I hit the starter buttons, the engines murmured into life, and I edged back into the deep water.

We worked our way up the snaking channel, coming out at last into the broad placid reach where the mangrove ended and firm ground rose gently on each side.

A mile ahead I saw the tributary mouth of the Salsa as a dark break in the bank, screened by tall stands of fluffy headed reeds. Beyond it the twin signal lanterns glowed yellow and soft, one upon the other.

'What did I tell you, Chubby, a milk run.'

'We aren't home yet.' Chubby the eternal optimist.

'Okay, Angelo. Get up on the bows. I'll tell you when to drop the hook.'

We crept on down the channel and I found the words of the nursery rhyme running through my mind as I locked the wheel and took the hand spotlight from the locker below the rail.

'Three, Four, knock at the door, Five, Six, pick up sticks.'

I thought briefly of the hundreds of great grey beasts that had died for the sake of their teeth – and I felt a draught of guilt blow coldly along my spine at my complicity in the slaughter. But I turned my mind away from it by lifting the spotlight and aiming the agreed signal upstream at the burning lanterns.

Three times I flashed the recognition code but I was level with the signal lanterns before the bottom one was abruptly extinguished.

'Okay, Angelo. Let her go.' I called softly as I killed the engines. The anchor splashed over and the chain ran noisily in the silence. *Dancer* snubbed up, and swung around at the restraint of the anchor, facing back down the channel.

Chubby went to break out the cargo nets for loading, but I paused by the rail, peering across at the signal lantern. The silence was complete, except for the clink and croak of the swamp frogs in the reed banks of the Salsa.

In that silence I felt more than heard the beat like that of a giant's heart. It came in through the soles of my feet rather than my ears.

There is no mistaking the beat of an Allison marine diesel. I knew that the old Second World War Rolls-Royce marines had been stripped out of the Zinballa crash boats and replaced by Allisons, and right now the sound I was feeling was the idling note of an Allison marine.

'Angelo,' I tried to keep my voice low, but at the same time transmit my urgency. 'Slip the anchor. For Christ's sake! Quick as you can.'

For just such an emergency I had a shackle pin in the chain, and I thanked the Lord for that as I dived for the controls.

As I started the engines, I heard the thump of the four-pound hammer as Angelo drove out the pin. Three times he struck, and then I heard the end of the chain splash overboard.

'She's gone, Harry,' Angelo called, and I threw *Dancer* in to drive and pushed open the throttles. She bellowed angrily and the wash of her propellers spewed whitely from below her counter as she sprang forward.

Although we were facing downstream, *Dancer* had a five-knot current running into her teeth and she did not jump away handily enough.

Even above our own engines I heard the Allisons give tongue, and from out of the reed-screened mouth of the Salsa tore a long deadly shape.

Even by starlight, I recognized her immediately, the widely flared bows, and the lovely thrusting lines, greyhound waisted and the square chopped-off stern – one of the Royal Navy crash boats who had spent her best days in the Channel and now was mouldering into senility on this fever coast.

The darkness was kind to her, covering the rust stains and the streaky paintwork, but she was an old woman now. Stripped of her marvellous Rolls marines – and underpowered with the more economical Allisons. In a fair run *Dancer* would toy with her – but this was no fair run and she had all the speed and power she needed as she charged into the channel to cut us off, and when she switched on her battle lights they hit us like something solid. Two glaring white beams, blinding in their intensity so I had to throw up my hand to protect my eyes.

She was dead ahead now, blocking the channel, and on her foredeck I could see the shadowy figures of the gun crew crouching around the three-pounder on its wide traversing plate. The muzzle seemed to be looking directly into my left nostril – and I felt a wild and desperate despair.

It was a meticulously planned and executed ambush. I thought of ramming her, she had a marine ply wooden hull, probably badly rotted, and *Dancer*'s fibreglass bows might stand the shock – but with the current against her *Dancer* was not making sufficient speed through the water.

Then suddenly a bull-horn bellowed electronically from the dark behind the dazzling battle lights.

'Heave to, Mr Fletcher. Or I shall be forced to fire upon you.'

One shell from the three-pounder would chop us down, and she was a quick firer. At this range they would smash us into a blazing wreck within ten seconds.

I closed down the throttles.

'A wise decision, Mr Fletcher – now kindly anchor where you are,' the bull-horn squawked.

'Okay, Angelo,' I called wearily, and waited while he rigged and dropped the spare anchor. Suddenly my arm was very painful again – for the last few hours I had forgotten about it.

'I said we should have brought that piece,' Chubby muttered beside me.

'Yeah, I'd love to see you shooting it out with that dirty great cannon, Chubby. That would be a lot of laughs.'

The crash boat manoeuvred alongside inexpertly, with gun and lights still trained on us. We stood helplessly in the blinding illumination of the battle lights and waited. I didn't want to think, I tried to feel nothing – but a spiteful inner voice sneered at me.

'Say good-bye to *Dancer*, Harry old sport, this is where the two of you part company.'

There was more than a good chance that I would be facing a firing squad in the near future – but that didn't worry me as much as the thought of losing my boat. With *Dancer* I was Mister Harry, the damnedest fellow on St Mary's and one of the top billfish men in the whole cock-eyed world. Without her, I was just another punk trying to scratch his next meal together. I'd prefer to be dead.

The crash boat careered into our side, bending the rail and scraping off a yard of our paint before they could hook on to us.

'Motherless bastards,' growled Chubby, as half a dozen armed and uniformed figures poured over our side, in a chattering undisciplined rabble. They wore navy blue bell bottoms and bum-freezers with white flaps down the back of the neck, white and blue striped vests, and white berets with red pom-poms on the top – but the cut of the uniform was Chinese and they brandished long AK.47 automatic assault rifles with forward-curved magazines and wooden butts.

Fighting amongst themselves for a chance to get in a kick or a shove with a gun butt, they drove the three of us down into the saloon, and knocked us into the bench seat against the for'ard bulkhead. We sat there shoulder to shoulder while two guards stood over us with machine-guns a few inches from our noses, and fingers curved hopefully around the triggers.

'Now I know why you paid me that five hundred dollars, boss,' Angelo tried to make a joke of it, and a guard screamed at him and hit him in the face with the gun butt. He wiped his mouth, smearing blood across his chin, and none of us joked again.

The other armed seamen began to tear *Dancer* to pieces. I suppose it was meant to be a search, but they raged through her accommodation wantonly smashing open lockers or shattering the panelling.

One of them discovered the liquor cabinet, and although there were only one or two bottles, there was a roar of approval. They squabbled noisily as seagulls over a scrap of offal, then went on to loot the galley stores with appropriate hilarity and abandon. Even when their commanding officer was assisted by four of his crew to make the hazardous journey across the six inches of open space that separated the crash boat from *Dancer,* there was no diminution in the volume of shouting and laughter and the crash of shattering woodwork and braking glass.

The commander wheezed heavily across the cockpit and stooped to enter the saloon. He paused there to regain his breath.

He was one of the biggest men I had ever seen, not less than six foot six tall and enormously gross – a huge swollen body with a belly like a barrage balloon beneath the white uniform jacket. The jacket strained at its brass buttons and sweat had soaked through at the armpits. Across his breast he wore a glittering burst of stars and medals, and amongst them I recognized the American Naval Cross and the 1918 Victory Star.

His head was the shape and colour of a polished black iron pot, the type they traditionally use for cooking missionaries, and a naval cap, thick with gold braid, rode at a jaunty angle upon it. His face ran with rivers of glistening sweat, as he struggled noisily with his breathing and mopped at the sweat, staring at me with bulging eyes.

Slowly his body began to inflate, swelling even larger, like a great bullfrog, until I grew alarmed – expecting him to burst.

The purple-black lips, thick as tractor tyres, parted and an unbelievable volume of sound issued from the pink cavern of his mouth.

'Shut up!' he roared. Instantly his crew of wreckers froze into silence, one of them with his gun butt still raised to attack the panelling behind the bar.

The huge officer trundled forward, seeming to fill the entire saloon with his bulk. Slowly he sank into the padded leather seat. Once more he mopped at his face, then he looked at me again and slowly his whole face lit up into the most wonderfully friendly smile, like an enormous chubby and lovable baby; his teeth were big and flawlessly white and his eyes nearly disappeared in the rolls of smiling black flesh.

'Mr Fletcher, I can't tell you what a great pleasure this is for me.' His voice was deep and soft and friendly, the accent was British upper class – almost certainly acquired at some higher seat of learning. His English was better than mine.

'I have looked forward to meeting you for a number of years.'

'That's very decent of you to say so, Admiral.' With that uniform he could not rank less.

'Admiral,' he repeated with delight, 'I like that,' and he laughed. It began with a vast shaking of belly and ended with a gasping and straining for breath. 'Alas, Mr Fletcher, you are deceived by appearances,' and he preened a little, touching the medals and adjusting the peak of his cap. 'I am only a humble Lieutenant Commander.'

'That's really tough, Commander.'

'No. No, Mr Fletcher – do not waste your sympathy on me. I wield all the authority I could wish for.' He paused for deep breathing exercises and to wipe away the fresh ooze of sweat. 'I hold the powers of life and death, believe me.'

'I believe you, sir,' I told him earnestly. 'Please don't feel you have to prove your point.'

He shouted with laughter again, nearly choked, coughed up something large and yellow, spat it on to the floor and then told me, 'I like you, Mr Fletcher, I really do. I think a sense of humour is very important. I think you and I could become very close friends.' I doubted it, but I smiled encouragingly.

'As a mark of my esteem you may use the familiar form when addressing me – Suleiman Dada.'

'I appreciate that – I really do, Suleiman Dada, and you may call me Harry.'

'Harry,' he said. 'Let's have a dram of whisky together.' At that moment another man entered the saloon. A slim boyish figure, dressed not in his usual colonial police uniform but in a lightweight silk suit and lemon-coloured silk shirt and matching tie, with alligator-skin shoes on his feet.

The light blond hair was carefully combed forward into a cow's lick, and the fluffy moustache was trim as ever, but he walked carefully, seeming to favour an injury. I grinned at him.

'So, how does the old ball-bag feel now, Daly?' I asked kindly, but he did not answer and went to sit across from Lieutenant Commander Suleiman Dada.

Dada reached out a huge black paw and relieved one of his men of the Scotch whisky bottle he carried, part of my previous stock, and he gestured to another to bring glasses from the shattered liquor cabinet.

When we all had half a tumbler of Scotch in our hands, Dada gave us the toast.

'To lasting friendship, and mutual prosperity.' We drank, Daly and I cautiously, Dada deeply and with evident pleasure. While his head was tilted back and his eyes closed, the crew man attempted to retrieve the bottle of Scotch from the table in front of him.

Without lowering the glass Dada hit him a mighty open handed clout across the side of the head, a blow that snapped his head back and hurled him across the saloon to crash into the shattered liquor cabinet. He slid down the bulkhead and sat stunned on the deck, shaking his head dazedly. Suleiman Dada, despite his bulk, was a quick and fearsomely powerful man, I realized.

He emptied the glass, set it down, and refilled it. He looked at me now, and his expression changed. The clown had disappeared, despite the bal-looning rolls of flesh, I was confronting a shrewd, dangerous and utterly ruthless opponent.

'Harry, I understand that you and Inspector Daly were interrupted in the course of a recent discussion,' and I shrugged.

'All of us here are reasonable men, Harry, of that I am certain.' I said nothing, but studied the whisky in my glass with deep attention. 'This is very fortunate – for let us consider what might happen to an unreasonable man in your position.' He paused, gargled a little with a sip of whisky. Sweat had formed like a rash of little white blisters on his nose and chin. He wiped it away. 'First of all, an unreasonable man might watch while his crew were taken out one at a time and executed. We use pickaxe handles here. It is a gruelling business, and Inspector Daly assures me that you have a special relationship with these two men.' Beside me Chubby and Angelo shifted uneasily in their seats. 'Then an unreasonable man would have his boat taken in to Zinballa Bay. Once that happened there would be no way in which it would ever be returned to him. It would be officially confiscated, out of my humble hands.' He paused, and showed me the humble hands, stretching them towards me. They would have fitted a bull gorilla. We both stared at them for a moment. 'Then the unreasonable man might find himself in Zinballa jail – which, as you are probably aware, is a maximum security political prison.'

I had heard of Zinballa prison, as had everyone on the coast. Those who came out of it were either dead or broken in body and spirit. They called it the 'Lion Cage'.

'Suleiman Dada, I want you to know that I am one of nature's original reasonable men,' I assured him, and he laughed again.

'I was certain of it,' he said. 'I can tell one a mile off,' then again he was serious. 'If we leave here immediately, before the turn of the tide we can be out of the inshore channel before midnight.'

'Yes,' I agreed, 'that we could.'

'Then you could lead us to this place of interest, wait while we satisfy ourselves as to your good faith – which I for one do not doubt one moment – you and your crew will then be free to sail away in your magnificent boat and you could sleep tomorrow night in your own bed.'

'Suleiman Dada – you are a generous and cultivated man. I also have no reason to doubt your good faith,' – no more than that of Materson and Guthrie, I silently qualified the statement – 'and I have a peculiarly intense desire to sleep tomorrow night in my own bed.'

Daly spoke for the first time, snarling quietly under his little moustache. 'I think you should know that a turtle fisherman saw your boat anchored in the lagoon across the channel from the Old Men and Gunfire Reef on the night before the shooting incident – we will expect to be taken that way.'

'I have nothing against a man who takes a bribe, Daly – God knows I done so myself – but then where is the honour among thieves that the poet sings of?' I was very disappointed in Daly, but he ignored my recriminations.

'Don't try any more of your tricks,' he warned me.

'You really are a champion turd, Daly. I could win prizes with you.'

'Please, gentlemen.' Dada held up his hands to halt my flow of rhetoric. 'Let us all be friends. Another small glass of whisky – and then Harry will take us all on a tour of interest.' Dada topped up our glasses, and paused before drinking again. 'I think I should warn you, Harry – I do not like rough water. It does not agree with me. If you take me into rough water I shall be very very angry. Do we understand each other?'

'Just for you I shall command the waters to stand still, Suleiman Dada,' I assured him, and he nodded solemnly, as though it was the very least he expected.

The dawn was like a lovely woman rising from the couch of the sea, soft flesh tones and pearly light, the cloud strands like her hair tresses flowing and tousled, gilded blonde by the early sunlight.

We ran northwards, hugging the quieter waters of the inshore channel. Our order of sailing placed *Wave Dancer* in the van, she ambled along like a blood filly mouthing the snaffle, while half a mile astern the crash boat waddled and wallowed, as the Allisons tried to push her up on to the plane. We were headed for the Old Man and Gunfire Reef.

On board *Dancer* I had the con, standing alone at the wheel upon the open bridge. Behind me stood Peter Daly, and an armed seaman from the crash boat.

In the saloon below us, Chubby and Angelo still sat on the bench seat and three more seamen, armed with assault rifles, kept them there.

*Dancer* had been looted of all her galley stores, so none of us had breakfasted, not even a cup of coffee.

The first paralysing despair of capture had passed – and I was now thinking frenetically, trying to plot my way out of the maze in which I was trapped.

I knew that if I showed Daly and Dada the break at Gunfire Reef they would either explore it and find nothing – which was the most likely for whatever had been there was now packaged and deposited at Big Gull Island – or they would find some other evidence at the break. In both cases I was in for unpleasantness – if they found nothing Daly would have the very great pleasure of connecting me up to the electrical system in an attempt to make me talk. If they found something definite my presence would become superfluous – and a dozen eager seamen would vie for job of executioner. I didn't like the sound of pickhandles – it promised to be a messy business.

Yet the chances of escape seemed remote. Although she was half a mile astern the three-pounder on the foredeck of Dada's crash boat kept us on an effective leash, and we had aboard Daly and four members of the goon squad.

I lit my first cheroot of the day and its effect was miraculous, almost immediately I seemed to see a pin-prick of light at the end of the long dark tunnel. I thought about it a little longer, puffing quietly on the black tobacco, and it seemed worth a try – but first I had to talk to Chubby.

'Daly,' I turned to speak over my shoulder. 'You had better get Chubby up here to take the wheel, I have got to go below.'

'Why?' he demanded suspiciously. 'What are you going to do?'

'Let's just say that whatever it is happens every morning at this time, and nobody else can do it for me. If you make me say more, I shall blush.'

'You should have been on the stage, Fletcher. You really slay me.'

'Funny you should mention that. It had crossed my mind.'

He sent the guard to fetch Chubby from the saloon, and I handed the con to him.

'Stick around, I want to talk to you later,' I muttered out of the side of my mouth and clambered down into the cockpit. Angelo brightened a little when I entered the saloon, and flashed a good imitation of the old bright grin, but the three guards, clearly bored, turned their weapons on me enthusiastically and I raised my hands hurriedly.

'Easy, boys, easy,' I soothed them and sidled past them down the companionway. However, two of them followed me. When I reached the heads they would have entered with me and kept me company. 'Gentlemen,' I protested, 'if you continue to point those things at me during the next few critical moments you will probably pioneer the sovereign cure for constipation.' They scowled at me uncertainly and as I closed the door firmly upon then I added, 'But you really don't want a Nobel prize – do you?'

When I opened it again they were waiting in exactly the same attitudes, as though they had not moved. With a conspiratory gesture I beckoned them to follow. Immediately they showed interest, and I led them to the master cabin. Below the big double bunk I had spent many hours building in a concealed locker. It was about the size of a coffin, and was ventilated. It would accommodate a man lying prone. During the time when I was running human cargo it had been a hidey hole in case of a search – but now I used it as a store for valuables and illicit or dangerous cargo. It contained at the present time five hundred rounds of ammunition for the F.N., a wooden crate of hand grenades, and two cases of Chivas Regal Scotch whisky.

With exclamations of delight the two guards slung their machine-guns on their shoulder straps and dragged out the whisky cases. They had forgotten about me and I slipped away and returned to the bridge. I stood next to Chubby, delaying the moment of take-over.

'You took your time,' growled Daly.

'Never rush a good thing,' I explained, and he lost interest and strolled back to stare across our wake at the following gunboat.

'Chubby,' I whispered. 'Gunfire Break. You told me once there was a passage through the reef from the landward side.'

'At high springs, for a whaleboat and a good man with a steady nerve,' he agreed. 'I did it when I was a crazy kid.'

'It's high spring in three hours. Could I run *Dancer* through?' I asked.

Chubby's expression changed. 'Jesus!' he whispered, and turned to stare at me in disbelief.

'Could I do it?' I insisted quietly, and he sucked his teeth noisily, looking away at the sunrise, scratching the bristles of his chin.

Then suddenly he reached an opinion, and spat over the side. 'You might, Harry – but nobody else I know could.'

'Give me the bearings, Chubby, quickly.'

'It was a long time ago, but,' sketchily he described the approach, and the passage of the break, 'there are three turns in the passage, left right then left again, then there is a narrow neck, brain coral on each hand –*Dancer* might just get through but she'll leave some paint behind. Then you are into the big pool at the back of the main reef. There is room to circle there and wait for the right sea before you shoot the gap out into the open water.'

'Thanks, Chubby,' I whispered. 'Now go below. I let the guards have the spare whisky. By the time I start my run for the break they will be blasted right out through the top of their skulls. I will signal three stamps on the deck, then it will be up to you and Angelo to get those pieces away from them and wrap them up tightly.'

The sun was well up, and the triple-peaked silhouette of the Old Men was rising only a few miles dead ahead when I heard the first raucous shout of laughter and crash of breaking furniture below. Daly ignored it and we ran on over the quiet inshore waters towards the reverse side of Gunfire Reef. Already I could see the jagged line of the Reef, like the black teeth of an ancient shark. Beyond it the tall oceanic surf flashed whitely as it burst, and beyond that lay the open sea.

I edged in towards the reef, and eased open the throttles a fraction. *Dancer*'s engine beat changed, but not enough to alert Daly. He lounged against the rail, bored and unshaven and probably missing his breakfast. I could distinctly hear the boom of the surf on coral now, and from below, the sounds of revelry became continuous. Daly noticed at last, frowned and told the other guard to go below and investigate. The guard, also bored, disappeared below with alacrity and never returned.

I glanced astern. My increase in speed was slowly opening the gap between *Dancer* and the crash boat, and steadily we edged in closer to the reef.

I was looking ahead anxiously, trying to pick up the marks and bearings that Chubby had described to me. Gently I touched the throttles. opening them another notch. The crash boat fell a little farther astern.

Suddenly I saw the entrance to Gunfire Break a thousand yards ahead. Two pinnacles of old weathered coral marked it, and I could see the colour difference of clear sea water pouring through the gap in the coral barrier.

Below there was another screech of wild laughter, and one of the guards reeled drunkenly into the cockpit. He reached the rail only just in time and vomited copiously into the wake. Then his legs gave way and he collapsed on to the deck and lay in an abandoned huddle.

Daly let out an angry exclamation and raced down the ladder. I took the opportunity to push the throttles open another two notches.

I stared ahead, gathering myself for the effort. I must try and open the gap between *Dancer* and her escort a little more, every inch would help to confound her gunners.

I planned to come up level with the channel, and then commit *Dancer* to it under full power, risking the submerged coral fangs rather than test the aim of the gunners aboard the crash boat. It was half a mile of narrow, tortuous channel through the coral before we reached the open sea. For most of it, *Dancer* would be partially screened by coral outcrops, and the weaving of the channel would help to confuse the range of the three-pounder. I was hoping also that the surf working through the gap would give *Dancer* plenty of up-and-down movement, so that she would heave and weave unpredictably like one of those little ducks in a shooting gallery.

One thing was certain: that intrepid mariner, Lieutenant Commander Suleiman Dada, would not risk pursuit through the channel, so I could give his gun layer a rapidly increasing range to contend with.

I ignored the alcoholic din from below, and I watched the mouth of the channel approach rapidly. I found myself hoping that the seamanship of the crash boat's crew and commander was a faithful indication of their marksmanship.

Suddenly Peter Daly flew up the ladder to confront me. His face was pink with anger and his moustache tried to bristle its silky hairs. His mouth worked for a moment before he could speak.

'You gave them the liquor, Fletcher. Oh, you crafty bastard.'

'Me?' I asked indignantly. 'I wouldn't do a thing like that.'

'They're drunk as pigs – all of them,' he shouted, then he turned and looked over the stern. The crash boat was a mile behind us, and the distance was increasing.

'You are up to something,' he shrilled at me, and groped in the side pocket of his silk jacket. At that moment we came level with the entrance to the channel.

I hit both throttles wide open, and *Dancer* bellowed and hurled herself forward.

Still groping in his pocket, Daly was thrown off balance. He staggered backwards, still shouting.

I spun the wheel to full right lock, and *Dancer* whirled like a ballet dancer. Daly changed the direction of his stagger, thrown wildly across the deck he came up hard against the side rail as *Dancer* leaned over steeply in her turn. At that moment Daly dragged a small nickelled-silver automatic from his side pocket. It looked like a .25, the type ladies carry in their handbags.

I left *Dancer*'s wheel for an instant. Stooping, I got my hand on Daly's ankles and lifted sharply. 'Leave us now, comrade,' I said as he went backwards over the rail, falling twelve feet, striking the lower deck rail a glancing blow and then splashing untidily into the water alongside.

I darted back to the wheel, catching *Dancer*'s head before she could pay off, and at the same time stamping three times on the deck.

As I lined *Dancer* up for the entrance I heard the shouts of conflict in the saloon below, and winced as a machine-gun fired with a sound like ripping cloth – Barrapp – and bullets exploded out through the deck behind me, leaving a jagged hole edged with white splinters. At least they were fired at the roof, and were unlikely to have hit either Angelo or Chubby.

Just before I entered the coral portals, I glanced back once more. The crash boat still lumbered along a mile behind, while Daly's head bobbed in the churning white wake. I wondered if they would reach him before the sharks did.

Then there was no more time for idle speculation. As *Dancer* dashed headlong into the channel I was appalled by the task I had set her.

I could have leant over and touched coral outcrops on each hand, and I could see the sinister shape of more coral lurking below the shallow turbulent waters ahead. The waters had expended most of their savagery on the long twisting run through the channel, but the farther in we went the wilder they would become, making *Dancer*'s response to the helm just that much more unpredictable.

The first bend in the channel showed ahead, and I put *Dancer* to it. She came around willingly, swishing her bottom, and with only a trifling yaw that pushed her outwards towards the menacing coral.

As I straightened her into the next stretch, Chubby came swarming up the ladder. He was grinning hugely. Only two things put him into that sort of mood – and one of them was a good punch up. He had skinned his right knuckle.

'All quiet below, Harry. Angelo's looking after them.' He glanced around. 'Where's the policeman?'

'He went for a swim.' I did not take my attention from the channel. 'Where is the crash boat? What are they doing?'

Chubby peered across at her. 'No change. It doesn't seem to have sunk in yet – hold on, though –' his voice changed, '– yes, there they go. They are manning the deck gun.'

We drove on swiftly down the channel, and I risked a quick glance backwards. At that instant I saw the long streak of white cordite smoke blow like a feather from the three-pounder, and an instant later there was the sharp crack of shot passing high overhead, followed immediately by the flat report of the shot.

'Ready for it now, Harry. Left-hander coming up.'

We swept into the next turn, and the next round fell short, bursting in a shower of fragment and blue smoke on one of the coral heads fifty yards off our beam.

I coaxed *Dancer* smoothly into the turn, and as we went into it another shell fell in our wake, lifting a tall and graceful column of white water high above the bridge. The following wind blew the spray over us.

We were halfway through now, and the waves that rushed to meet us were six feet high and angry with the restraint enforced upon them by the walls of coral.

The guncrew of the crash boat were making alarmingly erratic practice. A round burst five hundred yards astern, then the next went between Chubby and me, a stunning blaze of passing shot that sent me reeling in the backwash of disrupted air.

'Here's the neck now,' Chubby called anxiously and my spirit quailed as I saw how the channel narrowed and how bridge-high buttresses of coral guarded it.

It seemed impossible that *Dancer* would pass through so narrow an opening.

'Here we go, Chubby, cross your fingers,' and, still under full throttle, I put *Dancer* at the neck. I could see him grasping the rail with both hands, and I expected the stainless steel to bend with the strength of his grip.

We were halfway through when we hit, with a jarring rending crash. *Dancer* lurched and hesitated.

At the same moment another shell burst alongside. It showered the bridge with coral chips and humming steel fragments, but I hardly noticed it as I tried to ease *Dancer* through the gap.

I sheered off the wall, and the tearing scraping sound ran along our starboard side. For a moment we jammed solidly, then another big green wave raced down on us, lifting us free of the coral teeth and we were through the neck. *Dancer* lunged ahead.

'Go below, Chubby,' I shouted. 'Check if we holed the hull.' Blood was dripping from a fragment scratch on his chin, but he dived down the ladder.

With another stretch of open water ahead, I could glance back at the crash boat. She was almost obscured by an intervening block of coral, but she was still firing rapidly and wildly. She seemed to have heaved to at the entrance to the channel, probably to pick up Daly – but I knew she would not attempt to follow us now. It would take her four hours to work her way round to the main channel beyond the Old Men.

The last turn in the channel came up ahead, and again *Dancer*'s hull touched coral; the sound of it seemed to tear into my own soul. Then at last we burst out into the deep pool in the back of the main reef, a circular arena of deep water three hundred yards across, fenced in by coral walls and open only through the Gunfire Break to the wild surf of the Indian Ocean.

Chubby appeared at my shoulder once more. 'Tight as a mouse's ear, Harry. Not taking on a drop.' Silently I applauded my darling.

Now for the first time we were in full view of the gun crew half a mile away across the reef, and my turn into the pool presented *Dancer* to them broadside. As though they sensed that this was their last chance they poured shot after shot at us.

It fell about us in great leaping spouts, too close to allow me any latitude of decision. I swung *Dancer* again, aimed her at the narrow break, and let her race for the gap in Gunfire Reef.

I committed her and when we had passed the point of no return, I felt my belly cramp up with horror as I looked ahead through the gap to the open sea. It seemed as though the whole ocean was rearing up ahead of me, gathering itself to hurl down upon the frail little vessel like some rampaging monster.

'Chubby,' I called hollowly. 'Will you look at that.'

'Harry,' he whispered, 'this a good time to pray.'

And *Dancer* ran out bravely to meet this freak Goliath of the sea.

It came up, humping monstrous shoulders as it charged, higher and higher still it rose, a glassy green wall and I could hear it rustling – like wildfire in dry grass.

Another shot passed close overhead but I hardly noticed it, as *Dancer* threw up her head and began to climb that mountainous wave.

It was turning pale green along the crest high above, beginning to curl, and *Dancer* went up as though she were on an elevator.

The deck canted steeply, and we clung helplessly to the rail.

'She's going over backwards,' Chubby shouted, as she began to stand on her tail. 'She's turtling, man!'

'Go through her,' I called to *Dancer*. 'Cut through the green!' and as though she heard me she lunged with her sharp prow into the curl of the wave an instant before it could fall upon us and crush the hull.

It came aboard us in a roaring green horror, solid sheets of it swept *Dancer* from bow to stern, six feet deep, and she lurched as though to a mortal blow.

Then suddenly we burst out through the back of the wave, and below us was a gaping valley, a yawning abyss into which *Dancer* hurled herself, falling free, a gut-swooping drop down into the trough.

We hit with a sickening crash that seemed to stun her, and which threw Chubby and me to the deck. But as I dragged myself up again, *Dancer* shook herself free of the tons of water that had come aboard, and she ran on to meet the next wave.

It was smaller, and *Dancer* beat the curl and porpoised over her.

'That's my darling,' I shouted to her and she picked up speed, taking the third wave like a steeple-chaser.

Somewhere close another three-pound shell cracked the sky, but then we were out and running for the long horizon of the ocean and I never heard another shot.

The guard who had passed out in the cockpit from an excess of Scotch whisky must have been washed overboard by the giant wave, for we never saw him again. The other three we left on a small island thirty miles north of St Mary's where I knew there was water in a brackish well, and which would certainly be visited by fishermen from the mainland.

They had sobered by that time, and were all inflicted with nasty hangovers. They made three forlorn figures on the beach as we ran southwards into the dusk. It was dark when we crept into Grand Harbour. I picked up moorings, not tying up to the wharf at Admiralty. I did not want *Dancer*'s glaring injuries to become a subject of speculation around the island.

Chubby and Angelo went ashore in the dinghy – but I was too exhausted to make the effort, and dinnerless I collapsed across the double bunk in the master cabin and slept without moving until Judith woke me after nine in the morning. Angelo had sent her down with a dinner pail of fish cakes and bacon.

'Chubby and Angelo gone up to Missus Eddy's to buy some stores they need to repair the boat,' she told me. 'They'll be down soon now.'

I wolfed the breakfast and went to shave and shower. When I returned she was still there, sitting on the edge of the bunk. She clearly had something to discuss.

She brushed away my clumsy efforts at dressing my wound, and had me sit while she worked on it.

'Mister Harry, you aren't going to get my Angelo killed or jailed, are you?' she demanded. 'If you go on like this, I'm going to make him come ashore.'

'That's great, Judith.' I laughed at her concern. 'Why don't you send him across to Rawano for three years, while you sit here.'

'That's not kind, Mister Harry.'

'Life is not very kind, Judith,' I told her more gently. 'Angelo and I are both doing the best we can. Just to keep my boat afloat, I've got to take a few chances. Some with Angelo. He told me that he's saved enough to buy you a nice little house up near the church. He got the money by running with me.'

She was silent while she finished the dressing, and when she would have turned to go I took her hand and drew her back. She would not look at me, until I took her chin and lifted her face. She was a lovely child, with great smoky eyes and a smoothly silken skin.

'Don't fuss yourself, Judith. Angelo is like a kid brother to me. I'll look after him.'

She studied my face a long moment. 'You really mean that, don't you?' she asked.

'I really do.'

'I believe you,' she said at last, and she smiled. Her teeth were very white against the golden amber skin. 'I trust you.'

Women are always saying that to me. 'I trust you.' So much for feminine intuition.

'You name one of your kids for me, hear?'

'The first one, Mister Harry.' Her smile blazed and her dark eyes flashed. 'That's a promise.'


'They do say that when you fall from a horse you should immediately ride him again – so as not to lose your nerve, Mister Harry.' Fred Coker sat at his desk in the travel agency, behind him a poster of a beefeater and Big Ben – 'England Swings', it said. We had just discussed at great length our mutual concern at Inspector Peter Daly's perfidious conduct, though I suspected that Fred Coker's concern was considerably less than mine. He had collected his commission in advance and nobody had put his head in a noose, nor had they almost wrecked his boat. We were now discussing the subject of whether or not our business arrangement should continue.

'They also say, Mr Coker, that a man with his buttocks hanging out of the holes in his trousers should not be too fussy,' I said, and Coker's spectacles glittered with satisfaction. He nodded his head.

'And that, Mister Harry, is probably the wiser of the two sayings,' he agreed.

'I'll take anything, Mr Coker. Body, box or sticks. Just one thing, the cost of dying has gone up to ten thousand dollars a run – all in advance.'

'Even at that price, we'll find work for you,' he promised, and I realized I had been working cheaply before.

'Soon,' I insisted.

'Very soon,' he agreed. 'You are fortunate. I do not think that Inspector Daly will be returning to St Mary's now. You will save the commission usually payable there.'

'He owes me that at least,' I agreed.

I made three night runs in the next six weeks. Two body carries, and a box job – all below the river into Portuguese waters. The bodies were both singles, silent black men dressed in jungle fatigues,and I took them far south, deep penetrations. They waded ashore on remote beaches and I wondered briefly upon what unholy missions they travelled – how much pain and death would arise from those secret landings.

The box job involved eighteen long wooden crates with Chinese markings. We picked up from a submarine out in the channel, and dropped off in a river-mouth, unloading into pairs of dugout canoes lashed together for stability. We spoke to no one and nobody challenged us.

They were milk runs and I cleared eighteen thousand dollars – enough to carry me and my crew through the off-season in the style to which we were accustomed. More important, the intervals of quiet and rest were sufficient to heal my wounds and give me back my strength. At first I lay for hours in the hammock under the palms, reading or sleeping. Then as it came back to me, I swam and fished and sun-baked, went for oysters and crayfish – until I was hard and lean and sunbrowned again.

The wound healed into a thickened and irregular cicatrice, tribute to MacNab's surgical skills, it curled around my chest and on to my back like an angry purple dragon. In one thing he had been correct, the massive damage to my upper left arm left it stiff and weakened. I could not lift my elbow above shoulder-level, and I lost my title in Indian wrestling to Chubby in the bar of the Lord Nelson. However, I hoped that swimming and regular exercise would strengthen it.

As my strength returned so did my curiosity and sense of adventure. I began dreaming about the canvas-wrapped package off Big Gull Island. In one dream I swam down and opened the package – it contained a tiny feminine figure, the size of a Dresden doll, a golden mermaid with Sister May's lovely face and a truly startling bosom, the tail was the graceful sickle shape of a marlin's. The little mermaid smiled shyly and held out her hand to me. On her palm lay a shiny silver shilling.

'Sex, money and billfish—' I thought when I woke, '—good old uncomplicated Harry, real Freud food.' I knew then that pretty soon I would be going for Big Gull Island.

It was very late in the season before I could prevail on Fred Coker to arrange a straight fishing charter for me, and it turned sour as cheap wine. The party consisted of two overweight, flabby German industrialists with fat bejewelled wives. I worked hard for them, and put both men into fish.

The first was a good black marlin, but the party screwed down on his stardrag, freezing the reel while the fish was still green and crazy to run. It lifted the German's huge backside out of the seat, and before I could release the stardrag for him, it had my three hundred dollar rod down on the gunwale. The fibre-glass rod snapped like a matchstick.

The other member of the party, after losing two decent fish, panted and sweated three hours over a baby blue marlin. When he finally brought it to the gaff, I could hardly bring myself to put the steel in, and I was too ashamed to hang it on Admiralty. We took the photographs on board *Dancer* and I smuggled it ashore wrapped in a tarpaulin. Like Fred Coker I also have a reputation to preserve. The German industrialist, however, was so delighted by his prowess that he slipped an extra five hundred dollars into my avaricious little paw. I told him it was a truly magnificent fish, which was a thousand-dollar lie. I always give good value. Then the wind backed into the south, the temperature of the water in the channel dropped four degrees and the fish were gone. For ten days we hunted far north but it was over, another season was past.

We stripped and cleaned all the billfish equipment and laid it away in thick yellow grease. I pulled *Dancer* up on to the slip at the fuelling basin and we went over her hull, cleaning it down, re-working the temporary patches I had put on the injuries she had received at Gunfire Reef.

Then we painted her until she glistened, sleek and lovely, before we refloated her and took her out to moorings. There we worked lackadaisically on her upper works, stripping varnish, sand-papering, re-varnishing, checking out the electrical system, re-soldering a connection here, replacing wiring there.

I was in no hurry. It would be three weeks before my next charter arrived – an expedition of marine biologists from a Canadian university.

In the meantime the days were cooler, and I was feeling the old glow of good health and bodily well-being again. I dined at Government House, sometimes as often as once a week, and each time I had to tell the full story of the shoot-out with Guthrie and Materson. President Biddle knew the story by heart and corrected me if I omitted a single detail. It always ended with the President crying excitedly, 'Show them your scar, Mister Harry,' and I had to open the starched front of my dress shirt at the dinner table.

They were good lazy days. The island life drifted placidly by. Peter Daly never returned to St Mary's – and at the end of six weeks, Wally Andrews was promoted to acting Inspector and commanding officer of the police force. One of his first acts was to return to me my FN carbine.

This quiet time was spiced by the secret tingle of anticipation which I felt. I knew that one day soon I was going back to Big Gull Island and the piece of unfinished business that lay there in the shallow limpid waters – and I teased myself with the knowledge.

Then one Friday evening I was rounding out the week with my crew in the bar of the Lord Nelson. Judith was with us, having replaced the flock that had previously gathered around Angelo on Friday nights. She was good for him, he no longer drank to the morbid stage.

Chubby and I had just begun the first duet of the evening and were keeping within a few beats of each other when Marion slipped into the seat beside me.

I put one arm around her shoulders and held my tankard to her lips while she drank thirstily, but the distraction caused me to forge even further ahead of Chubby in the song.

Marion worked on the switchboard at the Hilton Hotel. She was a pretty little thing with a sexy pugface and long straight black hair. It was she whom Mike Guthrie had used for a punch-bag so long ago.

When Chubby and I straggled to the end of the chorus, Marion told me, 'There is a lady asking for you, Mister Harry.'

'What lady?'

'At the hotel, one of the guests, she came in on this morning's plane. She knew your name and everything. She wants to see you. I told her I would see you tonight and give you the message.'

'What is she like?' I asked Marion with interest.

'She's beautiful, Mister Harry. Such a lady too.'

'Sounds like my type,' I agreed, and ordered a pint for Marion.

'Aren't you going to see her now?'

'With you beside me, Marion, all the beautiful ladies of the world can wait until tomorrow.'

'Oh, Mister Harry, you are a real devil man.' she giggled, and snuggled a little closer.

'Harry,' said Chubby on my other side, 'I'm going to tell you now what I never told you before.' He took a long swallow from his tankard, then went on with sentimental tears swimming in his eyes. 'Harry, I love you, man. I love you better than my own brother.'


I went up to the Hilton a few minutes before midday. Marion came through from her cubicle behind the reception desk. She still had her earphones around her neck.

'She's waiting for you on the terrace.' She pointed across the vast reception area with its *ersatz* Hawaiian décor. 'The blonde lady in the yellow bikini.'

She was reading a magazine, lying on her belly on one of the reclining sun couches, and she had her back to me so my first impression was of masses of blonde hair, thick and shiny, teased up like the mane of a lion, then falling in a slick golden cascade.

She heard my footsteps on the paving. She glanced around, pushed her sunglasses up on top of her head, then she stood up to face me, and I realized that she was tiny, seeming to reach not much higher than my chest. The bikini also was tiny and showed a flat smooth belly with a deep navel, firm shoulders lightly tanned, small breasts, and a trim waist. Her legs had lovely lines and her neat little feet were thrust into open sandals, the nails painted clear red to match her long fingernails. Her hands as she pushed at her hair were small and shapely.

She wore heavy make-up, but wore it with rare skill, so that her skin had a soft pearly lustre and colour glowed subtly on her cheeks and lips. Her eyes had long dark artificial lashes, and the eyelids were touched with colour and line to give them an exotic oriental cast.

'Duck, Harry!' Something deep inside me shouted a warning, and I almost obeyed. I knew this type well, there had been others like her – small and purringly feline – I had scars to prove it, scars both physical and spiritual. However, one thing nobody can say about old Harry is that he runs for cover when the knickers are down.

Courageously I stepped forward, crinkling my eyes and twisting my mouth into the naughty small boy grin that usually dynamites them.

'Hello,' I said, 'I'm Harry Fletcher.'

She looked at me, starting at my feet and going up six feet four to the top where her gaze lingered speculatively and she pouted her lower lip.

'Hello,' she answered, her voice was husky, breathless-sounding – and carefully rehearsed. 'I'm Sherry North, Jimmy North's sister.'


We were on the veranda of the shack in the evening. It was cool and the sunset was a spectacular display of pyrotechnics that flamed and faded above the palms.

She was drinking a Pimms No. 1 filled with fruit and ice – one of my seduction specials – and she wore a kaftan of light floating stuff through which her body showed in shadowy outline as she stood against the rail backlit by the sunset. I could not be certain as to whether or not she wore anything beneath the kaftan – this and the tinkle of ice in her glass distracted me from the letter I was reading. She had showed it to me as part of her credentials. It was a letter from Jimmy North written a few days before his death. I recognized the handwriting and the turn of phrase was typical of that bright and eager lad. As I read on, I forgot the sister's presence in the memory of the past. It was a long bubbling letter, written as though to a loving friend, with veiled references to the mission and its successful outcome, the promise of a future in which there would be wealth and laughter and all good things.

I felt a pang of regret and personal loss for the boy in his lonely sea grave, for the lost dreams that drifted with him like rotting seaweed.

Then suddenly my own name leapt from that page at me, '— you can't help liking him, Sherry. He's big and tough-looking, all scarred and beat up like an old tom cat that's been out alley-fighting every night. But under it, I swear he is really a softy. He seems to have taken a shine to me. Even gives me fatherly advice!—'

There was more in the same vein that embarrassed me so that my throat closed up and I took a swallow of whisky, which made my eyes water and the words swim, while I finished the letter and refolded it.

I handed it to Sherry, and walked away to the end of the veranda. I stood there for a while looking out over the bay. The sun slid below the horizon and suddenly it was dark and chill.

I went back and lit the lamp, setting it up high so the glare did not fall in our eyes. She watched me in silence until I had poured another Scotch and settled in my cane-backed chair.

'Okay,' I said, 'you're Jimmy's sister. You've come to St Mary's to see me. Why?'

'You liked him, didn't you?' she asked, as she left the rail and came to sit beside me.

'I like a lot of people. It's a weakness of mine.'

'Did he die – I mean, was it like they said in the newspapers?'

'Yes,' I said. 'It was like that.'

'Did he ever tell you what they were doing out here?'

I shook my head. 'They were very cagey – and I don't ask questions.'

She was silent then, dipping long tapered fingers into her glass to pick out a slice of pineapple, nibbling at the fruit with small white teeth, dabbing at her lips with a pink pointed tongue like that of a cat.

'Because Jimmy liked and trusted you, and because I think you know more than you've told anyone, also because I need your help, I am going to tell you a story – okay?'

'I love stories,' I said.

'Have you heard of the "pogo stick"?' she asked.

'Sure, it's a child's toy.'

'It's also the code name for an American naval experimental vertical take-off all-weather strike aircraft.'

'Oh yes, I remember, I saw an article in *Time Magazine*. Questions in the Senate. I forget the details.'

'There was opposition to the fifty million development allocation.'

'Yes, I remember.'

'Two years ago, on the 16th August to be precise, a prototype "pogo stick" took off from Rawano airforce base in the Indian Ocean. It was armed with four air-to-surface "killer whale" missiles, each of them equipped with tactical nuclear warheads—'

'That must have been a fairly lethal package.'

She nodded. 'The "killer whale" is designed as an entirely new concept in missiles. It is an anti-submarine device which will seek and track surfaced or submerged naval craft. It can kill an aircraft carrier or it can change its element – air for water – and go down a thousand fathoms to destroy enemy submarines.'

'Wow,' I said, and took a little more whisky. We were talking heady stuff now.

'Do you recall the 16th August that year – were you here?'

'I was here, but that's a long time ago. Refresh my memory.'

'Cyclone Cynthia,' she said.

'God, of course.' It had come roaring across the island, winds of 150 miles an hour, taking away the roof of the shack and almost swamping *Dancer* at her moorings in Grand Harbour. These cyclones were not uncommon in this area.

'The "pogo stick" took off from Rawano a few minutes before the typhoon struck. Twelve minutes later the pilot ejected and the aircraft went into the sea with her four nuclear missiles and her flight recorder still aboard. Rawano radar was blanked out by the typhoon. They were not tracking.'

It was starting to make some sort of sense at last.

'How does Jimmy fit into this?'

She made an impatient gesture. 'Wait,' she said, then went on. 'Do you have any idea what the value of that cargo might be in the open market?'

'I should imagine you could write your own cheque – give or take a couple of million dollars.' And old bad Harry came to attention, he had been getting exercise lately and growing stronger.

Sherry nodded. 'The test pilot of the "pogo stick" was a Commander in the U.S. Navy named William Bryce. The aircraft developed a fault at fifty thousand feet, just before he came out through the top of the weather. He fought her all the way down, he was a conscientious officer, but at five hundred feet he knew he wasn't going to make it. He ejected and watched the aircraft go in.'

She was speaking carefully, and her choice of words was odd, too technical for a woman. She had learned all this, I was certain – from Jimmy? Or from somebody else?

Listen and learn, Harry, I told myself.

'Billy Bryce was three days on a rubber raft on the ocean in a typhoon before the rescue helicopter from Rawano found him. He had time to do some thinking. One of the things he thought about was the value of that cargo – and he compared it to the salary of a Commander. His evidence at the court of inquiry omitted the fact that the "pogo stick" had gone down within sight of land, and that Bryce had been able to take a fix on a recognizable land feature before he was blown out to sea by the typhoon.'

I could not see any weakness in her story – it looked all right – and very interesting.

'The court of inquiry gave a verdict of "pilot error" and Bryce resigned his commission. His career was destroyed by that verdict. He decided to earn his own retirement annuity and also to clear his reputation. He was going to force the U.S. Navy to buy back its "killer whale" missiles and to accept the evidence of the flight recorder.'

I was going to ask a question, but again Sherry stopped me with a gesture. She did not want her recital interrupted.

'Jimmy had done some work for the U.S. Navy – a hull inspection of one of their carriers – and he had met Bryce at that time. They had become friends, and so Billy Bryce naturally came to Jimmy. Between them they had not sufficient capital for the expedition they needed to mount, so they planned to find financial backers. It isn't the kind of thing you can advertise in the *Times*, and they were working on it when Billy Bryce was killed in his Thunderbird on the M4 near the Heathrow turn-off.'

'There seems to be some sort of curse on this thing,' I said.

'Are you superstitious, Harry?' she asked, looking at me through those slanted tiger eyes.

'I don't knock it,' I admitted, and she nodded, seeming to file the information away before she went on.

'After Billy was dead, Jimmy went on with the project. He found backers. He wouldn't tell me who, but I guessed they were unsavoury. He came out here with them – and you know the rest.'

'I know the rest,' I agreed, and instinctively massaged the thickened scar tissue through the silk of my shirt. 'Except of course the site of the crash.'

We stared at each other.

'Did he tell you?' I asked, and she shook her head.

'Well, it was an interesting story.' I grinned at her. 'It's a pity we can't check out the truth of it.'

She stood up abruptly and went to the veranda rail. She hugged her arms and she was so angry that if she'd had a tail she would have switched it like a lioness.

I waited for her to recover, and the moment came when she shrugged her shoulders and turned back to me. Her smile was light.

'Well, that's that! I thought I was entitled to some of the rewards. Jimmy was my brother – and I came a long way to find you because he liked and trusted you. I thought we could work together – but I guess if you want it all, there's not much I can do about it.'

She shook out her hair, and it rippled and shone in the lamplight. I stood up.

'I'll take you home now,' I said, and touched her arm. She reached up with both arms, and her fingers locked in the thick curly hair at the back of my neck.

'It's a long way home,' she whispered, and pulled my head down, standing on her tiptoes.

Her lips were very soft and moist, and her tongue was thrusting and restless. After a while she drew back and smiled up at me, her eyes were unfocused and her breath was short and fast.

'Perhaps it wasn't a wasted journey, after all?'

I picked her up, and she was light as a child, hugging my neck, pressing her cheek to mine as I carried her into the shack. I learned long ago to eat hearty whenever there was food, because you never know when the famine is going to hit.

Even the soft light of dawn was cruel to her as she lay sprawled in sleep beneath the mosquito net on the big double bed. Her make-up had smeared and caked, and she slept with her mouth open. The mane of blonde hair was a tangled bush and it did not match the triangle of thick dark curls at the base of her belly. I felt repelled by her this morning, for I had learned during the night that Miss Sherry was a raving sadist.

I slipped out of the bed and stood over her a few moments, searching her sleeping face in vain for a resemblance to Jimmy North. I left her, and, still naked, walked out of the shack and down to the beach.

The tide was in and I plunged into the cool clear water and swam out to the entrance to the bay. I swam fast, driving hard in an Australian crawl, and the salt water stung the deep scratches in my back.

It was one of my lucky mornings, old friends were waiting for me beyond the reef, a school of big bottle-nosed porpoise, who came flashing to meet me, their tall fins cutting the dark surface as they steeplechased over the swells. They circled me, whistling and snorting, the blowholes in the tops of their heads gulping like tiny mouths and their own huge mouths fixed in idiotic grins of pleasure.

They teased me for ten minutes before one of the big old bulls allowed me to get a grip on his dorsal fin and gave me a tow. It was a thrilling sleigh ride that had the water creaming wildly about my chest and head. He took me half a mile offshore before the force of water tore me from his back.

It was a long swim back, with the bull dolphin circling me and giving me an occasional friendly prod in the backside, inviting me aboard for another ride. At the reef they whistled farewell and slid gracefully away, and I was happy when I waded ashore. The arm ached a little, but it was the healthy ache of healing and growing strength.

The bed was empty, and the bathroom door was locked. She was probably shaving her armpits with my razor, I thought. I felt a flare of annoyance, an old dog like me doesn't like his routine disturbed. I used the guest shower to sluice off the salt and my annoyance receded under the rush of hot water. Then fresh but unshaven and hungry as a python, I went through to the kitchen. I was frying gammon with pineapple and buttering thick cuts of toast when Sherry came into the kitchen.

She was once more immaculate. She must have carried a complete cosmetic counter in the Gucci handbag, and her hair was dressed and lacquered into its mane and fall.

Her smile was brilliant. 'Good morning, lover,' she said and came to kiss me lingeringly. I was now well disposed towards the world and all its creatures. I no longer felt repelled by this glittering woman. The fine mood of the dolphins had returned and my gaiety must have been infectious. We laughed a lot over the meal and afterwards I took the coffee pot out on to the veranda.

'When are we going to find the pogo stick?' she asked suddenly, and I poured another mug of strong black coffee without answering. Sherry North had evidently decided that a night of her company had made me her slave for life. Now I may not be a connoisseur of women, but on the other hand I have had some little experience – I mean I'm not exactly a virgin – and I didn't rate Sherry North's charms as worth four killer whale missiles and the flight recorder of a secret strike aircraft.

'Just as soon as you show me the way,' I answered carefully. It is an old-fashioned feminine conceit that if a man pleasures them with skill and aplomb, then he must be made to pay for it. I have long believed that it should be the other way around.

She reached across and held my wrist, the tiger's eyes were suddenly big and soulful.

'After last night,' she whispered huskily, 'I know that there is a lot ahead of us, Harry. You and I, together.'

I had lain awake for hours during the night and reached my decision. Whatever lay in the package was not an entire aircraft, but probably some small part of it – something that identified it clearly. It was almost certainly not either the flight recorder or one of the missiles. Jimmy North would not have had sufficient time to remove the recorder from the fuselage, even if he had known where it was situated and had the proper tools. On the other hand the package was the wrong shape and size for a missile, it was a squat round object, not aerodynamically designed.

It was almost certainly some fairly innocuous object. If I took Sherry North with me to recover it, I would be playing only a minor card from my hand – although it would look like a major trump.

I would be giving nothing away, not the site of the crash at Gunfire Reef, nor any of the valuable objects associated with it.

On the other hand, I would be beating the tall grass for tigers. It would be very instructive to see exactly how Mademoiselle North reacted, once she thought she knew the site of the crash.

'Harry,' she whispered again. 'Please,' and she leaned closer. 'You must believe me. I have never felt like this before. From the first moment I saw you – I just knew—'

I roused myself from my calculations and leaned towards her, assuming an expression of simple-minded passion and lust.

'Darling—' I began but my voice choked up, and I enfolded her in a bear hug, feeling her stiffen irritably as I smeared her lipstick and ruffled the meticulously dressed hairstyle. I could sense the effort it required for her to respond with equal passion.

'Do you feel the same way?' she asked from the depths of my embrace, smothered against my chest, and for the fun of watching her play the role she had assigned herself, I picked her up again and carried her through to the frowsy rumpled bed.

'I will show you how I feel for you,' I muttered hoarsely.

'Darling,' she protested desperately, 'not now.'

'Why not?'

'We have so much to do. There will be time later – all the time in the world.' With a show of reluctance I set her down, although truthfully I was thankful for I knew that on top of a huge breakfast of gammon and three cups of coffee, it would have given me heartburn.


It was a few minutes after noon when I cleared Grand Harbour, and swung away south and east. I had told my crew to take a day ashore, I would not be fishing.

Chubby looked down at Sherry North, sprawled bikini-clad on the cockpit deck, and scowled noncommittally, but Angelo rolled his eyes expressively and asked, 'Pleasure cruise?' with a certain inflection.

'You've got a filthy mind,' I scolded him and he laughed delightedly, as though I had paid him the nicest compliment, and the two of them walked away up the wharf.

*Dancer* romped down the necklace of atolls and islands until, a little after three o'clock, I ran the deep-water passage between Little Gull Island and

Big Gull Island, and rounded into the shallow open water between the east shore of Big Gull and the blue water of the Mozambique.

There was enough breeze to make the day pleasantly cool, and to kick up a white flecky chop off the surface.

I manoeuvred carefully, squinting over at Big Gull as I put *Dancer* in position. When I hit the marks I pushed a little upwind to allow for *Dancer*'s fall-back. Then I cut the engines and hurried down to the foredeck to drop the hook.

*Dancer* came around and settled down like a well-behaved lady.

'Is this the place?' Sherry had watched everything I did with her disconcerting feline stare.

'This is it,' and I risked overplaying my part as the besotted lover by pointing out the marks to her.

'I lined up those two palms, the ones leaning over, with that single palm right up on the skyline, see it?'

She nodded silently, again I caught that look as though the information was being carefully filed and remembered.

'Now what do we do?' she asked.

'This is where Jimmy dived,' I explained. 'When he came back on board he was very excited. He spoke secretly with the others – Materson and Guthrie – and they seemed to catch his excitement. Jimmy went down again with rope and a tarpaulin. He was down a long time – and when he came up again, it started, the shooting.'

'Yes,' she nodded eagerly, the reference to her brother's death seemed to leave her unmoved. 'We should go now, before someone else sees us here.'

'Go?' I asked, looking at her. 'I thought we were going to have a look?'

She recognized her mistake. 'We should organize it properly, come back when we are prepared, when we have made arrangements to pick up and transport—'

'Lover,' I grinned, 'I didn't come all this way not to take at least one quick look.'

'I don't think you should, Harry,' she called after me, but already I was opening the engine-room hatch.

'Let's come back another time,' she persisted, but I went down the ladder to the rack which held the air bottles and took down a Draeger twin set. I fitted the breathing valve and tested the seal, sucking air out of the rubber mouth-piece.

Glancing quickly up at the hatch to make sure she was not watching me, I reached across and threw the concealed cut-out switch on the electrical system. Now nobody could start *Dancer*'s engines while I was overboard.

I swung the diving ladder over the stern and then dressed in the cockpit – short-sleeved Neoprene wet suit and hood, weight belt and knife, Nemrod wrap-around face-plate and fins.

I slung the scuba set on my back and picked up a coil of light nylon rope and hooked it on to my belt.

'What happens if you don't come back?' Sherry asked, showing apprehension for the first time. 'I mean what happens to me?'

'You'll pine to death,' I told her, and went over the side, not in a showy back flip but a simple use of the steps, more in keeping with my age and dignity.

The water was transparent as mountain air, and as I went head down I could see every detail of the bottom fifty feet below.

It was a coral landscape, lit with dappled light and wondrous colour. I drifted down to it, and the sculptured shapes of the coral were softened and blurred with sea growth and restless with the sparkling jewels of myriad tropical fish. There were deep gullies and standing towers of coral, fields of eel grass between, and open stretches of blinding white coral sand.

My marks had been remarkably accurate, considering the fact that I had been only just conscious from blood loss. I had dropped the anchor almost directly on top of the canvas package. It lay on one of the open spaces of coral sand, looking like some horrible sea monster, green and squat with the loose ropes floating about it like tentacles.

I crouched beside it, and shoals of tiny fish, zebra-striped in gold and black, gathered around me in such numbers that I had to blow bubbles at them and shoo them off, before I could get on with the job.

I unclipped the nylon rope from my belt, and lashed one end securely to the package with a series of half-hitches. Then I rose to the surface slowly paying out the line. I surfaced thirty feet astern of *Dancer*, swam to the ladder, and clambered into the cockpit. I made the end of the line fast to the arm of the fighting chair.

'What did you find?' Sherry demanded anxiously.

'I don't know yet,' I told her. I had resisted the temptation to open the package on the bottom. I hoped it might be worth the sacrifice to watch her expression as I opened the canvas.

I stripped my diving gear and washed it off with fresh water before stowing it all carefully away. I wanted the tension to eat into her a little longer.

'Damn you, Harry. Let's get it up,' she burst out at last.

I remembered the package as being as heavy as all creation, but then my strength had been almost gone. Now I braced myself against the gunwale and began recovering line. It was heavy, but not impossibly so, and I coiled the wet line as it came in with the old tunny fisherman's wrist action.

The green canvas broke the surface alongside, sodden and gushing water. I reached over and got a purchase on the knotted rope, with a single heave I lifted it over the side and it clunked weightily on to the deck of the cockpit – metal against wood.

'Open it,' ordered Sherry impatiently.

'Right away, madam,' I said, and drew the bait-knife from the sheath on my belt. It was razor sharp, and I cut the ropes with a single stroke for each.

Sherry was leaning forward eagerly as I drew the stiff wet folds of canvas aside, and I was watching her face.

The greedy, anticipatory expression flared suddenly into triumph as she recognized the object. She recognized it before I did, and then instantly she dropped a curtain of uncertainty over her eyes and face.

It was nicely done, she was an actress of skill. Had I not been watching carefully for it, I would have missed the quick play of emotion.

I looked down at the humble object for which already so many men had been killed or mutilated, and I was torn with surprise and puzzlement – and disappointment. It was not what I had expected.

Half of it was badly eaten away as though by a sand-blasting machine, the bronze was raw and shiny and deeply etched. The upper half of it was intact, but tarnished heavily with a thick skin of greenish verdigris, but the lug for the shackle was intact and the ornamentation was still clear through the corrosion – a heraldic crest – or part of it – and lettering in a flowery antique style. The lettering was fragmentary, most of it had been etched away in an irregular flowing line, leaving the bright worn metal.

It was a ship's bell, cast in massive bronze, it must have weighed close to a hundred pounds, with a domed and lugged top and a wide flared mouth.

Curiously I rolled it over. The clapper had corroded solidly, and barnacle and other shellfish had encrusted the interior. I was intrigued by the pattern of wear and corrosion on the outside, until suddenly the solution occurred to me. I had seen other metal objects marked like this after long submersion. The bell had been half buried on the sandy bottom, the exposed portion had been subjected to the tidal rush of Gunfire Break, and the fine grains of coral sand had abrased away a quarter of an inch of the outer skin of the metal.

However, the portion that had been buried was protected, and now I examined the remaining lettering more closely.

### 'VV N  L'

There was an extended 'V' or a broken 'W' followed immediately by a perfect 'N' – then a gap and a whole 'L'; beyond that the lettering had been obliterated again.

The coat of arms worked into the metal on the opposite side of the barrel was an intricate design with two rampart beasts – probably lions – supporting a shield and a mailed head. it seemed vaguely familiar, and I wondered where I had seen it before.

I rocked back on my heels and looked at Sherry North. She was unable to meet my gaze.

'Funny thing,' I mused. 'A jet aircraft with a bloody great brass bell hanging on its nose.'

'I don't understand it,' she said.

'No more do I.' I stood up and went to get a cheroot from the saloon. I lit it and sat back in the fighting chair.

'Okay. Let's hear your theory.'

'I don't know, Harry. Truly I don't.'

'Let's try some guesses,' I suggested. 'I'll begin.'

She turned away to the rail.

'The jet aircraft turned into a pumpkin,' I hazarded. 'How about that one?'

She turned back to me. 'Harry, I don't feel well. I think I'm going to be sick.'

'So, what must I do?'

'Let's go back now.'

'I was thinking of another dive – look around a bit more.'

'No,' she said quickly. 'Please, not now. I don't feel up to it. Let's go. We can come back if we have to.'

I studied her face for evidence of her sickness: she looked like an advert for health food.

'All right,' I agreed; there was not really much point in another dive, but only I knew that. 'Let's go home and try and work it out.'

I stood up and began rewrapping the brass bell.

'What are you going to do with that?' she asked anxiously.

'Redeposit it,' I told her. 'I am certainly not going to take it back to St Mary's and display it in the market place. Like you said, we can always come back.'

'Yes,' she agreed immediately. 'You are right, of course.'

I dropped the package over the side once more and went to haul the hook.

On the homeward run I found Sherry North's presence on the bridge irritated me. There was a lot of hard thinking I had to do. I sent her down to make coffee.

'Strong,' I told her, 'and with four spoons of sugar. It will be good for your seasickness.'

She reappeared on the bridge within two minutes.

'The stove won't light,' she complained.

'You have to open the main gas cylinders first.' I explained where to find the taps. 'And don't forget to close them when you finish, or you'll turn the boat into a bomb.'

She made lousy coffee.


It was late evening when I picked up moorings in Grand Harbour, and dark by the time I dropped Sherry at the entrance of the hotel. She didn't even invite me in for a drink, but kissed me on the cheek and said, 'Darling, let me be alone tonight. I am exhausted. I am going to bed now. Let me think about all this, and when I feel better we can plan more clearly.'

'I'll pick you up here – what time?'

'No,' she said. 'I'll meet you at the boat. Early. Eight o'clock. Wait for me there – we can talk in private. Just the two of us, no one else – all right?'

'I'll bring *Dancer* to the wharf at eight,' I promised her.

It had been a thirsty day, and on the way home I stopped off at the Lord Nelson.

Angelo and Judith were with a noisy party of their own age in one of the booths. They called me over and made room for me between two of the girls.

I brought them each a pint, and Angelo leaned over confidentially. 'Hey, skipper, are you using the pick-up tonight?'

'Yes,' I said. 'To get me home.' I knew what was coming, of course. Angelo acted as though he had shares in the vehicle.

'There's a big party down at South Point tonight, boss,' suddenly he was very free with the "boss" and "skipper", 'I thought if I run you out to Turtle Bay, then you'd let us have the truck. I'd pick you up early tomorrow, promise.'

I took a swallow at my tankard and they were all watching me with eager hopeful faces.

'It's a big party, Mister Harry,' said Judith. 'Please.'

'You pick me up seven o'clock sharp, Angelo, hear?' and there was a spontaneous burst of relieved laughter. They clubbed in to buy me another pint.

I had a disturbed night, with restless sleep interspersed with periods of wakefulness. I had the dream again, when I dived to the canvas package. Once more it contained a tiny Dresden mermaid, but this time she had Sherry North's face and she offered me the model of a jet fighter aircraft that changed into a golden pumpkin as I reached for it. The pumpkin was etched with the letters:

'VV N L'

It rained after midnight, solid sheets of water, that poured off the eaves, and the lightning silhouetted the palm fronds against the night sky.

It was still raining when I went down to the beach, and the heavy drops exploded in minute bomb bursts of spray upon my naked body. The sea was black in the bad light, and the rain squalls reached to the horizon. I swam alone, far out beyond the reef, but when I came back to the beach the excursion had not provided the usual lift to my spirits. My body was blue and shivering with the cold, and a vague but pervading sense of trouble and depression pressed heavily upon me.

I had finished breakfast when the pick-up came down the track through the palm plantation, splashing through the puddles, splattered with mud and with headlights still burning.

In the yard Angelo hooted and shouted, 'You ready, Harry?' and I ran out with a sou'-wester held over my head.

Angelo smelled of beer and he was garrulous and slightly bleary of eye.

'I'll drive,' I told him, and as we crossed the island he gave me a blow-by-blow description of the great party – from what he told me it seemed there might be an epidemic of births on St Mary's in nine months' time.

I was only half listening to him, for as we approached the town so my sense of disquiet mounted.

'Hey, Harry, the kids said to thank you for the loan of the pick-up.'

'That's okay, Angelo.'

'I sent Judith out to the boat – she's going to tidy up, Harry, and get the coffee going for you.'

'She shouldn't have worried,' I said.

'She wanted to do that specially – sort of thank you, you know.'

'She's a good girl.'

'Sure is, Harry. I love that girl,' and Angelo burst into song, 'Devil Woman' in the style of Mick Jagger.

When we crossed the ridge and started down into the valley I had a sudden impulse. Instead of continuing straight down Frobisher Street to the harbour, I swung left on to the circular drive above the fort and hospital and went up the avenue of banyan trees to the Hilton Hotel. I parked the pick-up under the canopy and went through to the reception lobby.

There was nobody behind the desk this early in the morning, but I leaned across the counter and peered into Marion's cubicle. She was at her switchboard and when she saw me her face lit up in a wide grin and she lifted off her earphones.

'Hello, Mister Harry.'

'Hello, Marion, love,' I returned the grin. 'Is Miss North in her room?'

Her expression changed. 'Oh no,' she said, 'she left over an hour ago.'

'Left?' I stared at her.

'Yes. She went out to the airport with the hotel bus. She was catching the seven-thirty plane.' Marion glanced at the cheap Japanese watch on her wrist. 'They would have taken off ten minutes ago.'

I was taken completely off-balance, of all things I had least expected this. It didn't make sense for many seconds – and then suddenly and sickeningly it did.

'Oh Jesus Christ,' I said. 'Judith!' and I ran for the pick-up. Angelo saw my face as I came and he sat up straight in the seat and stopped singing.

I jumped into the driver's seat and started the engine, thrusting the pedal down hard and swinging in a roaring two-wheeled turn.

'What is it, Harry?' Angelo demanded.

'Judith?' I asked grimly. 'You sent her down to the boat, when?'

'When I left to fetch you.'

'Did she go right away?'

'No, she'd have to bath and dress first.' He was telling it straight, not hiding the fact they had slept together. He sensed the urgency of the situation. 'Then she'd have to walk down the valley from the farm.' Angelo had lodgings with a peasant family up near the spring, it was a three-mile walk.

'God, let us be in time,' I whispered. The truck was bellowing down the avenue, and I hit the gears in a racing change as we went out through the gates in a screaming broadside, and I slammed down hard again on the accelerator, pulling her out of the skid by main strength.

'What the hell is it, Harry?' he demanded once again.

'We've got to stop her going aboard *Dancer*,' I told him grimly as we roared down the circular drive above the town. Past the fort a vista of Grand Harbour opened beneath us. He did not waste time with inane questions. We had worked together too long for that and if I said so then he accepted it as so.

*Dancer* was still at her moorings amongst the other island craft, and halfway out to her from the wharf Judith was rowing the dinghy. Even at this distance I could make out the tiny feminine figure on the thwart, and recognize the short business-like oar-strokes. She was an island girl, and rowed like a man.

'We aren't going to make it,' said Angelo. 'She'll get there before we reach Admiralty.'

At the top of Frobisher Street I put the heel of my left hand on the horn ring, and blowing a continuous blast I tried to clear the road. But it was a Saturday morning, market day, and already the streets were filling. The country folk had come to town in their bullocks' carts and ancient jalopies. Cursing with a terrible frustration, I hooted and forced my way through them.

It took us three minutes to cover the half mile from the top of the street down to Admiralty Wharf.

'Oh God,' I said, leaning forward in the seat as I shot through the mesh gates, and crossed the railway tracks.

The dinghy was tied up alongside *Wave Dancer,* and Judith was climbing over the side. She wore an emerald green shirt and short denim pants. Her hair was in a long braid down her back.

I skidded the truck to a halt beside the pineapple sheds, and both Angelo and I hit the wharf at a run.

'Judith!' I yelled, but my voice did not carry out across the harbour.

Without looking back, Judith disappeared into the saloon. Angelo and I raced down to the end of the jetty. Both of us were screaming wildly, but the wind was in our faces and *Dancer* was five hundred yards out across the water.

'There's a dinghy!' Angelo caught my arm. It was an ancient clinker-built mackerel boat, but it was chained to a ring in the stone wharf.

We jumped into it, leaping the eight foot drop and falling in a heap together over the thwart. I scrambled to the mooring chain. It had quarter-inch galvanized steel links, and a heavy brass padlock secured it to the ring.

I took two twists of chain around my wrist, braced one foot against the wharf and heaved. The padlock exploded, and I fell backwards into the bottom of the dinghy.

Angelo already had the oars in the rowlocks.

'Row,' I shouted at him. 'Row like a mad bastard.'

I was in the bows cupping my hands to my mouth as I hailed Judith, trying to make my voice carry above the wind.

Angelo was rowing in a dedicated frenzy, swinging the oar blades flat and low on the back reach and then throwing his weight upon them when they bit. His breathing exploded in a harsh grunt at each stroke.

Half-way out to *Dancer* another rain squall enveloped us, shrouding the whole of Grand Harbour in eddying sheets of grey water. It stung my face, so I had to screw up my eyes.

*Dancer*'s outline was blurred by grey rain, but we were coming close now. I was beginning to hope that Judith would sweep and tidy the cabins before she struck a match to the gas ring in the galley. I was also beginning to hope that I was wrong – that Sherry North had not left a farewell present for me.

Yet still I could hear my own voice speaking to Sherry North the previous day. 'You have to open the main gas cylinders first – and don't forget to close them when you finish, or you'll turn the boat into a bomb.'

Closer still we came to *Dancer* and she seemed to hang on tendrils of rain, ghostly white and insubstantial in the swirling mist.

'Judith,' I shouted, she must hear me now – we were that close. There were two fifty-pound cylinders of Butane gas on board, enough to destroy a large brickbuilt house. The gas was heavier than air, once it escaped it would slump down, filling *Dancer*'s hull with a murderously explosive mixture of gas and air. It needed just one spark from battery or match.

I prayed that I was wrong and yelled again. Then suddenly *Dancer* blew.

It was flash explosion, a fearsome blue light that shot through her. It split her hull with a mighty hammer stroke, and blew her superstructure open, lifting it like a lid.

*Dancer* reared to the mortal blow, and the blast hit us like a storm wind. Immediately I smelled the electric stench of the blast, acrid as an air-sizzling strike of lightning against ironstone.

*Dancer* died as I watched, a terrible violent death, and then her torn and lifeless hull fell back and the cold grey waters rushed into her. The heavy

engines pulled her swiftly down, and she was gone into the grey waters of
Grand Harbour.

Angelo and I were frozen with horror, crouching in the violently rocking
dinghy, staring at the agitated water that was strewn with loose wreckage
– all that remained of a beautiful boat and a lovely young girl. I felt a vast
desolation descend upon me, I wanted to cry aloud in my anguish, but I was
paralysed.

Angelo moved first. He leapt upright with a sound in his throat like a
wounded beast. He tried to throw himself over the side, but I caught and
held him.

'Leave me,' he screamed. 'I must go to her.'

'No.' I fought with him in the crazily rocking dinghy. 'It's no good,
Angelo.'

Even if he could get down through the forty feet of water in which
*Dancer*'s torn hull now lay, what he would find might drive him mad. Judith
had stood at the centre of that blast, and she would have been subjected to
all the terrible trauma of massive flash explosion at close range.

'Leave me, damn you.' Angelo got one arm free and hit me in the face,
but I saw it coming and rolled my head. It grazed the skin from my cheek,
and I knew I had to get him quieted down.

The dinghy was on the point of capsizing. Though he was forty pounds
lighter than me, Angelo fought with maniac strength. He was calling her
name now.

'Judith, Judith,' on an hysterical rising inflection. I released my grip on
his shoulder with my right hand, and swung him slightly away from me,
lining him up carefully. I hit him with a right chop, my fist moving not
more than four inches. I hit him cleanly on the point below his left ear, and
he dropped instantly, gone cold. I lowered him to the floorboards and laid
him out comfortably. I rowed back to the wharf without looking back. I felt
completely numbed and drained.

I carried Angelo down the wharf and I hardly felt his weight in my arms.
I drove him up to the hospital and MacNab was on duty.

'Give him something to keep him muzzy and in bed for the next twenty-
four hours,' I told MacNab, and he began to argue.

'Listen, you broken-down old whisky vat,' I told him quietly, 'I'd love an
excuse to beat your head in.'

He paled until the broken veins in his nose and cheeks stood out boldly.

'Now listen – Harry old man,' he began. I took a step towards him, and
he sent the duty sister to the drug cupboard.

I found Chubby at breakfast and it took only a minute to explain what
had happened. We went up to the fort in the pick-up, and Wally Andrews
responded quickly. He waived the filing of statements and other police
procedure and instead we piled the police diving equipment into the truck
and by the time we reached the harbour, half of St Mary's had formed a
silent worried crowd along the wharf. Some had seen it and all of them had
heard the explosion.

An occasional voice called condolences to me as we carried the diving
equipment to the mackerel boat.

'Somebody find Fred Coker,' I told them. 'Tell him to get down here with a bag and basket,' and there was a buzz of comment.

'Hey, Mister Harry, was there somebody aboard?'

'Just get Fred Coker,' I told them, and we rowed out to *Dancer*'s moorings. While Wally kept the dinghy on station above us, Chubby and I went down through the murky harbour water.

*Dancer* lay on her back in forty-five feet, she must have rolled as she sank – but there was no need to worry about access to her interior, for her hull had been torn open along the keel. She was far past any hope of refloating.

Chubby waited at the hole in the hull while I went in.

What remained of the galley was filled with swirling excited shoals of fish. They were in a feeding frenzy and I choked and gagged into the mouthpiece of my scuba when I saw what they were feeding upon.

The only way I knew it was Judith was the tatters of green cloth clinging to the fragments of flesh. We got her out in three main pieces, and placed her in the canvas bag that Fred Coker provided.

I dived again immediately, and worked my way through the shattered hull to the compartment below the galley where the two long iron gas cylinders were still bolted to their beds. Both taps were wide open, and somebody had disconnected the hoses to allow the gas to escape freely.

I have never experienced anger so intense as I felt then. It was that strong for it fed upon my loss. *Dancer* was gone – and *Dancer* had been half my life. I closed the taps and reconnected the gas hose. It was a private thing – I would deal with it personally.

When I walked back along the wharf to the pick-up, all that gave me comfort was the knowledge that *Dancer* had been insured. There would be another boat – not as beautiful or as well beloved as *Dancer* – but a boat nevertheless.

In the crowd I noticed the shiny black face of Hambone Williams – the harbour ferryman. For forty years he had plied his old dinghy back and forth at threepence a hire.

'Hambone,' I called him over. 'Did you take anybody out to *Dancer* last night?'

'No, sir, Mister Harry.'

'Nobody at all?'

'Only your party. She left her watch in the cabin. I took her out to fetch it.'

'The lady?'

'Yes, the lady with the yellow hair.'

'What time, Hambone?'

'About nine o'clock – did I do wrong, Mister Harry?'

'No, it's all right. Just forget it.'

We buried Judith next day before noon. I managed to get the plot beside her mother and father for her. Angelo liked that. He said he did not want her to be lonely up there on the hill. Angelo was still half doped, and he was quiet and dreamy eyed at the graveside.

The next morning the three of us began salvage work on *Dancer*. We worked hard for ten days and we stripped her completely of anything that had a possible value – from the big-game fishing reels and the FN carbine to the twin bronze propellers. The hull and superstructure were so badly broken up as to be of no value.

At the end of that time *Wave Dancer* had become a memory only. I have had many women, and now they are just a pleasant thought when I hear a certain song or smell a particular perfume. Like them, already *Dancer* was beginning to recede into the past.

On the tenth day I went up to see Fred Coker – and the moment I entered his office I knew there was something very wrong. He was shiny with nervous sweat, his eyes moved shiftily behind the glittering spectacles and his hands scampered about like frightened mice – running over his blotter or leaping up to adjust the knot of his necktie or smooth down the thin strands of hair on his polished cranium. He knew I'd come to talk insurance.

'Now don't get excited please, Mister Harry,' he advised me. Whenever people tell me that, I become very excited indeed.

'What is it, Coker? Come on! Come on!' I slammed one fist on the desk top, and he leapt in his chair so the gold-rimmed spectacles slid down his nose.

'Mister Harry, please—'

'Come on! You miserable little grave worm—'

'Mister Harry – it's about the premiums on *Dancer*.' I stared at him.

'You see – you had never made a claim before – it seemed such a waste to—'

I found words. 'You pocketed the premiums,' I whispered, my voice failing me suddenly. 'You didn't pay them over to the company.'

'You understand,' Fred Coker nodded. 'I knew you'd understand.'

I tried to go over the desk to save time, but I tripped and fell. Fred Coker leapt from his chair, slipping through my outstretched groping fingers. He ran through the back door, slamming it behind him.

I ran straight through the door, tearing off the lock, and leaving it hanging on broken hinges.

Fred Coker ran as though all the dark angels pursued him, which would have been better for him. I caught him at the big doors into the alley and lifted him by the throat, holding him with one hand, pressing his back against a pile of cheap pine coffins.

He had lost his spectacles, and he was weeping with fright, big slow tears welling out of the helpless short-sighted eyes.

'You know I'm going to kill you,' I whispered, and he moaned, his feet dancing six inches above the floor.

I pulled back my right fist and braced myself solidly on the balls of my feet. It would have taken his head off. I couldn't do it – but I had to hit something. I drove my fist into the coffin beside his right ear. The panelling shattered, stove in along its full length. Fred Coker shrieked like an hysterical girl at a pop festival, and I let him drop. His legs could not hold him and he sank to the concrete floor.

I left him lying there moaning and blubbering with terror – and I walked out into the street as near to bankrupt as I'd been in the last ten years.

Mister Harry transformed in a single stroke into Fletcher, wharf rat and land-bound bum. It was a classic case of reversion to type – before I reached the Lord Nelson I was thinking the same way I had ten years before. Already I was calculating the percentages, seeking the main chance once more.

Chubby and Angelo were the only customers in the public bar so early in the afternoon. I told them, and they were quiet. There wasn't anything to say.

We drank the first one in silence, then I asked Chubby, "What will you do now? and he shrugged.

'I've still got the old whaleboat—'It was a twenty-footer, admiralty design, open-decked, but sea-kindly. 'I'll go for stump again, I reckon.' Stump were the big reef crayfish. There was good money in the frozen tails. It was how Chubby had earned his bread before *Dancer* and I came to St. Mary's.

'You'll need new engines, those old Sea Gulls of yours are shot.' We drank another pint, while I worked out my finances – what the hell, a couple of thousand dollars was not going to make much difference to me. 'I'll buy two new twenty horse Evinrudes for the boat, Chubby,' I volunteered.

'Won't let you do it, Harry.' He frowned indignantly and shook his head. 'I got enough saved up working for you,' and he was adamant.

'What about you, Angelo? I asked.

'Guess I'll go sell my soul on a Rawano contract.'

'No,' Chubby scowled at the thought. 'I'll need crew for the stump-boat.'

They were all settled then. I was relieved, for I felt responsible for them both. I was particularly glad that Chubby would be there to care for Angelo. The boy had taken Judith's death very badly. He was quiet and withdrawn, no longer the flashing Romeo. I had kept him working hard on the salvage of *Dancer,* that alone seemed to have given him the time he needed to recover from the wound.

Nevertheless he began drinking hard now, chasing tots of cheap brandy with pints of bitter. This is the most destroying way to take in alcohol, short of drinking meths, that I know of.

Chubby and I took it nice and slow, lingering over our tankards, yet under our jocularity was a knowledge that we had reached a crossroads and from tomorrow we would no longer be travelling together. It gave the evening the fine poignancy of impending loss.

There was a South African trawler in harbour that night that had come in for bunkers and repairs. We at last Angelo passed out cold. Chubby and I began our singing. Six of the trawler's beefy crew members voiced their disapproval in the most slanderous terms. Chubby and I could not allow insults of that nature to pass unchallenged. We all went out to discuss it in the backyard.

It was a glorious discussion, and when Wally Andrews arrived with the riot squad he arrested all of us, even those who had fallen in the fray.

'My own flesh and blood—' Chubby kept repeating as he and I staggered arm and arm into the cells. 'He turned on me. My own sister's son—'

Wally was human enough to send one of his constables down to the Lord Nelson for something to make our durance less vile. Chubby and I became very friendly with the trawlermen in the next cell, passing the bottle back and forth between the bars.

When we were released next morning, Wally Andrews declining to press charges, I drove out to Turtle Bay to begin closing up the shack. I made sure the crockery was clean, threw a few handfuls of mothballs in the cupboards and did not bother to lock the doors. There is no such thing as burglary on St Mary's.

For the last time I swam out beyond the reef, and for half an hour hoped that the dolphins might come. They did not and I swam back, showered and changed, picked up my old canvas and leather campaign bag from the bed and went out to where the pick-up was parked in the yard. I didn't look back as I drove up through the palm plantation, but I made myself a promise that I'd be coming this way again.

I parked in the front lot of the hotel and lit a cheroot. When Marion finished her shift at noon she came out the front entrance and set off down the drive with her cheeky little bottom swinging under the mini skirt.

I whistled and she saw me. She slipped into the passenger's seat beside me.

'Mister Harry, I'm so sorry about your boat—' We talked for a few minutes until I could ask the question.

'Miss North, while she was staying at the hotel, did she make any phone calls or send a cable?'

'I don't remember, Mister Harry, but I could check for you.'

'Now?'

'Sure,' she agreed.

'One other thing, could you also check with Dicky if he got a shot of her?' Dicky was the roving hotel photographer, it was a good chance that he had a print of Sherry North in his file.

Marion was gone for nearly three-quarters of an hour, but she returned with a triumphant smile.

'She sent a cable on the night before she left.' Marion handed me a flimsy copy. 'You can keep this copy,' she told me as I read the message.

It was addressed to: 'MANSON FLAT 5 CURZON STREET 97 LONDON W.1.' and the message read: 'CONTRACT SIGNED RETURNING HEATHROW BOAC FLIGHT 316 SATURDAY.' There was no signature.

'Dicky had to go through all his files – but he found one.' She handed me a six-by-four glossy print. It was of Sherry North reclining on a sun couch on the hotel terrace. She wore her bikini and sunglasses, but it was a good likeness.

'Thanks, Marion.' I gave her a five-pound note.

'Gee, Mister Harry,' she grinned at me as she tucked it into the front of her bra. 'For that price you can take what you fancy.

'I've got a plane to catch, love.' I kissed her on the little snub nose, and slapped her bottom as she climbed out of the cab.

Chubby and Angelo came out to the airport. Chubby was to take care of the pick-up for me. We were all subdued, and shook hands awkwardly at the departure gate. There wasn't much to say, we had said it all the night before.

As the piston-engined aircraft took off for the mainland, I glimpsed the two of them standing together at the perimeter fence.

I stopped over three hours at Nairobi before catching the BOAC flight on to London. I did not sleep during the long night flight. It was many years since I had returned to my native land – and I was coming back now on a grim mission of vengeance. I wanted very much to talk to Sherry North.

When you are flat broke, that is the time to buy a new car and a hundred-guinea suit. Look brave and prosperous, and people will believe you are.

I shaved and changed at the airport and instead of a Hillman I hired a Chrysler from the Hertz Depot at Heathrow, slung my bag in the boot and drove to the nearest Courage pub.

I had a double portion of ham and egg pie, washed down with a pint of Courage while I studied the road map. It was all so long ago that I was unsure of my directions.

The lush and cultivated English countryside was too tame and green after Malaya and Africa, and the autumn sunshine was pale gold when I was used to a brighter fiercer sun – but it was a pleasant drive over the downs and into Brighton.

I parked the Chrysler on the promenade opposite the Grand Hotel and dived into the warren of The Lanes. They were filled with tourists even this late in the season.

Pavilion Arcade was the address I had read so long ago on Jimmy North's underwater sledge, and it took me nearly an hour to find it. It was tucked away at the back of a cobbled yard, and most of the windows and doors were shuttered and closed.

'North's Underwater World' had a ten-foot frontage on to the lane. It was also closed, and a blind was drawn across the single window. I tried without success to peer round the edge of the blind, but the interior was darkened, so I hammered on the door. There was no sound from within, and I was about to turn away when I noticed a square piece of cardboard that had once been stuck on to the bottom of the window but had fallen to the floor inside. By twisting my head acrobatically, I could read the handwritten message which had fortunately fallen face up: Enquiries to Seaview, Downers Lane, Falmer, Sussex. I went back to the car and took the road map out of the glove compartment.

It began to rain as I pushed the Chrysler through narrow lanes. The windscreen wipers flogged sullenly at the spattering drops and I peered into the premature gloom of early evening.

Twice I lost my way but finally I pulled up outside a gate in a thick hedge. The sign nailed to the gate read: NORTH SEAVIEW, and I believed that it might be possible to look southwards on a clear day and see the Atlantic.

I drove down between hedges, and came into the paved yard of an old double-storied red-brick farmhouse, with oak beams set into the walls and green moss growing on the wood-shingle roof. There was a light burning downstairs.

I parked the Chrysler and crossed the yard to the kitchen door, turning up my collar against the wind and rain. I beat on the door, and heard somebody moving around inside. The bolts were shot back and the top half of the stable door opened on a chain. A girl looked out at me.

I was not immediately impressed by her for she wore a baggy blue fisherman's jersey and she was a tall girl with a swimmer's shoulders. I thought her plain – in a striking manner.

Her brow was pale and broad, her nose was large but not bony or beaked, and below it her mouth was wide and friendly. She wore no make-up at all, so her lips were pale pink and there was a peppering of fine freckles on her nose and cheeks.

Her hair was drawn back severely from her face into a thick braid behind her neck. Her hair was black, shimmering iridescent black in the lamplight, and her eyebrows were black also, black and boldly arched over eyes that seemed also to be black until the light caught them and I realized they were the same dark haunted blue as the Mozambique current when the noon sun strikes directly into it.

Despite the pallor of her skin, there was an aura of good and glowing health about her. The pale skin had a lustre and plasticity to it, a quality that was somehow luminous so that when you studied her closely – as I was now doing – it seemed that you could see down through the surface to the flush of clean blood rising warmly to her cheeks and neck. She touched the tendril of silky dark hair that escaped the braid and floated lightly on her temple. It was an appealing gesture, that betrayed her nervousness and belied the serene expression in the dark blue eyes.

Suddenly I realized that she was an unusually handsome woman, for, although she was only in her mid-twenties, I knew she was no longer girl – but full woman. There was a strength and maturity about her, a deep sense of calm that I found intriguing.

Usually the women I choose are more obvious, I do not like to tie up too much of my energy in the pursuit. This was something beyond my experience and for the first time in years I felt unsure of myself.

We had been staring at each other for many seconds, neither of us speaking or moving.

'You're Harry Fletcher,' she said at last, and her voice was low and gently modulated, a cultivated and educated voice. I gaped at her.

'How the hell did you know that?' I demanded.

'Come in.' She slipped the chain and opened the bottom of the stable door, and I obeyed. The kitchen was warm and welcoming and filled with the smell of good food cooking.

'How did you know my name?' I asked again.

'Your picture was in the newspaper – with Jimmy's,' she explained. We were silent again, once more studying each other.

She was taller even than I had thought at first, reaching to my shoulder, with long legs clad in dark blue pants and the tops thrust into black leather boots. Now I could see the narrow waist and the promise of good breasts beneath the thick jersey.

At first I had thought her plain, ten seconds later I had reckoned her handsome, now I doubted I had ever seen a more beautiful woman. It took time for the full effect to sink in.

'You have me at a disadvantage,' I said at last. 'I don't know your name.'

'I'm Sherry North,' she answered, and I stared at her for a moment before I recovered from the shock. She was a very different person from the other Sherry North I had known.

'Did you know that there is a whole tribe of you?' I asked at last.

'I don't understand.' She frowned at me. Her eyes were enchantingly blue under the lowered brows.

'It's a long story.'

'I'm sorry.' For the first time she seemed to become aware that we were standing facing each other in the centre of the kitchen. 'Won't you sit down. Can I get you a beer?'

Sherry took a couple of cans of Carlsberg lager from the cupboard and sat opposite me across the kitchen table.

'You were going to tell me a long story.' She popped the tabs on the cans, and slid one across to me, then looked at me expectantly.

I began to tell her the carefully edited version of my experiences since Jimmy North arrived at St Mary's. She was very easy to talk to, like being with an old and interested friend. Suddenly I wanted to tell her everything, the entire unblemished truth. It was important that from the very beginning it should be right, with no reservations.

She was a complete stranger, and yet I was placing trust in her beyond any person I had ever known. I told her everything exactly as it had happened.

She fed me after dark had fallen, a savoury casserole out of an earthenware pot which we ate with homemade bread and farm butter. I was still talking but no longer about the recent events on St Mary's, and she listened quietly. At last I had found another human being with whom I could talk without reserve.

I went back in my life, in a complete catharsis I told her of the early days, even of the dubious manner in which I had earned the money to buy *Wave Dancer*, and how my good resolutions since then had wavered.

It was after midnight when at last she said: 'I can hardly believe all you've told me. You don't look like that – you look so,' she seemed to search for the word, 'wholesome.' But you could see it was not the word she wanted.

'I work hard at being that. But sometimes my halo falls over my eyes. You see, appearances are deceptive,' I said, and she nodded.

'Yes, they are,' and there was a significance in the way she said it, a warning perhaps. 'Why have you told me all this? It is not really very wise, you know.'

'It was just time that somebody knew about me, I suppose. Sorry, you were elected.'

She smiled. 'You can sleep in Jimmy's room tonight,' she said. 'I can't risk you rushing out and telling anybody else.'

I hadn't slept the night before and suddenly I was exhausted. I felt as though I did not have the strength to climb the stairs to the bedroom – but I had one question still to ask.

'Why did Jimmy come to St Mary's? What was he looking for?' I asked. 'Do you know who he was working with, who they were?'

'I don't know.' She shook her head, and I knew it was the truth. She wouldn't lie to me now, not after I had placed such trust in her.

'Will you help me find out? Will you help me find them?'

'Yes, I'll help you,' she said, and stood up from the table. 'We'll talk again in the morning.'

Jimmy's room was under the eaves, the pitch of the roof giving it an irregular shape. The walls were lined with photographs and packed book-shelves, silver sporting trophies and the treasured *bric-à-brac* of boyhood.

The bed was high and the mattress soft.

I went to fetch my bag from the Chrysler while Sherry put clean sheets upon the bed. Then she showed me the bathroom and left me.

I lay and listened to the rain on the roof for only a few minutes before I slept. I woke in the night and heard the soft whisper of her voice somewhere in the quiet house.

Barefooted and in my underpants I opened the bedroom door and crept silently down the passage to the stairs. I looked down into the hall. There was a light burning and Sherry North stood at the wall-hung telephone. She was speaking so quietly into the receiver, cupping her hands to her mouth, that I could not catch the words. The light was behind her. She wore a flimsy nightdress, and her body showed through the thin stuff as though she was naked.

I found myself staring like a peeping Tom. The lamplight glowed on the ivory sheen of her skin, and there were intriguing secret hollows and shadows beneath the transparent cloth.

With an effort I pulled my eyes off her and went back to my bed. I thought about Sherry's telephone call and felt a vague disquiet, but soon sleep overtook me once more.


In the morning the rain had stopped but the ground was slushy and the grass heavy and wet when I went out for a breath of cold morning air.

I expected to feel awkward with Sherry after the previous night's out-pourings of the soul, but it was not so. We talked easily at breakfast, and afterwards she said, 'I promised I'd help you; what can I do?'

'Answer a few questions.'

'All right, ask me.'

Jimmy North had been very secretive, she did not know he was going to St Mary's. He had told her he had a contract to install some electronic underwater equipment at the Cabora-Bassa Dam in Portuguese Mozam-bique. She had taken him up to the airport with all his equipment. As far as she knew he was travelling alone. The police had come to the shop in Brighton to tell her of his murder. She had read the newspaper reports, and that was all.

'No letters from Jimmy?'

'No, nothing,' I nodded, the wolf-pack must have intercepted his mail. The letter I had been shown by Sherry's impostor was certainly genuine.

'I don't understand anything about this. Am I being stupid?'

'No.' I took out a cheroot, and almost lit it before I stopped myself. 'Okay if I smoke one of these?'

'It doesn't bother me,' she said, and I was glad, for it would have been hell giving them up. I lit it and drew in the fragrant smoke.

'It looks as though Jimmy stumbled on something big. He needed backing and he went to the wrong people. As soon as they thought they knew where it was, they killed him and tried to kill me. When that didn't work they sent out someone impersonating you. When she thought she knew the location of this object, she set a trap for me and went home. Their next move will be a return to the area off Big Gull Island, where they are due for another disappointment.'

She refilled the coffee cups, and I noticed that she had applied make-up this morning – but so lightly that the freckles still showed. I reconsidered the previous night's judgement – and confirmed that she was one of the most beautiful women I had ever met, even in the early morning.

She was frowning thoughtfully, staring into her coffee cup and I wanted to touch one of her slim strong-looking hands that lay on the tablecloth near my own.

'What were they after, Harry? And who are these people who killed him?' she asked at last.

'Two excellent questions. I have leads to both – but we will tackle the questions in the order you asked them. Firstly, what was Jimmy after? When we know that we can go after his murderers.'

'I have no idea at all what it could be.' She looked up at me. The blue of her eyes was lighter than it had been last night, it was the colour of a good sapphire. 'What clues have you?'

'The ship's bell. The design upon it.'

'What does it signify?'

'I don't know, but it shouldn't be too hard to find out.' I could no longer resist the temptation. I placed my hand over hers. It felt as firm and strong as it looked and her flesh was warm. 'But first I should like to check the shop in Brighton and Jimmy's room here. There might be something we can use.'

She had not withdrawn her hand. 'All right, shall we go to the shop first? The police have already been through it all, but they might have overlooked something.'

'Fine. I'll buy you lunch.' I squeezed her hand, and she turned it in my grasp and squeezed back.

'I'll take you up on that,' she said, and I was too astonished by my own reaction to her grip to find a light reply. My throat was dry and my pulse beat as though I'd run a mile. Gently she removed her hand and stood up. 'Let's do the breakfast dishes.'

If the girls of St Mary's could only have seen Mister Harry drying dishes, my reputation would have shattered into a thousand pieces.

She let us into the shop the back way, through a tiny enclosed yard which was almost filled with unusual objects, all of them associated with diving and the underwater world – discarded air bottles and a portable compressor, brass portholes and other salvage from wrecked ships, even the jawbone of a killer whale with all its teeth intact.

'I haven't been in for a long time,' Sherry apologized as she unlocked the back door of the shop. 'Without Jimmy—' she shrugged and then went on,

'—I must really get down to selling up all this junk and closing the shop down. I could re-sell the lease, I suppose.'

'I'm going to look round, okay?'

'Fine, I'll get the kettle going.'

I started in the yard, searching quickly but thoroughly through the piles of junk. There was nothing that had significance as far as I could see. I went into the shop and poked around among the seashells and sharks' teeth on the shelves and in the display case. Finally I saw a desk in the corner and began going through the drawers.

Sherry brought me a cup of tea and perched on the corner of the desk while I piled old invoices, rubber bands and paper clips on the top. I read every scrap of paper and even rifled through the ready reckoner.

'Nothing?' Sherry asked.

'Nothing,' I agreed and glaced at my watch. 'Lunchtime,' I told her.

She locked up the shop and by good fortune we stumbled on English's restaurant. They gave us a secluded table in the back room and I ordered a bottle of Pouilly Fuissé to go with the lobster. Once I recovered from the shock of the price, we laughed a lot during the meal, and it wasn't just the wine. The feeling between us was good and growing stronger.

After lunch we drove back to Seaview and we went up to Jimmy's room.

'This is our best bet,' I guessed. 'If he was keeping secrets, this is where they would be.' But I knew I had a long job ahead of me. There were hundreds of books and piles of magazines – mostly *American Argosy, Trident, The Diver* and other diving publications. There was also a complete shelf of springback files at the foot of the bed.

'I'll leave you to it,' Sherry said, and went.

I took down the contents of a shelf, sat at the reading table and began to skim through the publications. Immediately I saw it was an even bigger task than I had thought. Jimmy had been one of those people who read with a pencil in one hand. There were notes pencilled in the margin, comments, queries and exclamation marks, and anything that interested him was underlined.

I read doggedly, looking for something that could remotely be linked to St Mary's.

Around eight o'clock I began on the shelf that held the springback files. The first two were filled with newspaper clippings on shipwrecks or other marine phenomena. The third of them had an unlabelled, black imitation leather cover. It held a thin sheath of papers, and I saw immediately that they were out of the ordinary.

They were a series of letters filed with their envelopes and stamps still attached. There were sixteen of them in all, addressed to Messrs Parker and Wilton in Fenchurch Street.

Every letter was in a different hand, but all were executed in the elegant penmanship of the last century.

The envelopes were sent from different parts of the old Empire – Canada, South Africa, India – and the nineteenth century postage stamps alone must have been of considerable value.

After I had read the first two letters, it was clear that Messrs Parker and Wilton were agents and factors, and they had acted for a number of distinguished clients in the service of Queen Victoria. The letters were instructions to deal with estates, moneys and securities.

All the letters were dated during the period from August 1857 to July 1858 and must have been offered by a dealer or an antique auctioneer as a lot.

I glanced through them quickly, but the contents were really very dull. However, something on the single page of the tenth letter caught my eye and I felt my nerves jump.

Two words had been underlined in pencil and in the margin was a notation in Jimmy North's handwriting.

'B. Mus. E.6914(8).'

However, it was the words themselves that held me.

'Dawn Light.'

I had heard those words before. I wasn't sure when, but they were significant.

Quickly I began at the top of the page. The sender's address was a laconic 'Bombay', and it was dated 16th Sept. 1857.

My Dear Wilton,

I charge you most strictly with the proper care and safe storage of five pieces of luggage consigned in my name to your London address aboard the Hon. Company's ship *Dawn Light*. Due out of this port before the 25th instant and bound for the Company's wharf in the Port of London.

Please acknowledge safe receipt of same with all despatch.

I remain yours faithfully,

Colonel Sir Roger Goodchild.

Officer Commanding 101st Regiment

Queens Own India Rifles.

Delivery by kind favour of Captain commanding Her Majesty's Frigate *Panther*.

The paper rustled and I realized that my hand was shaking with excitement. I knew I was on to it now. This was the key. I laid the letter carefully on the reading table and placed a silver paper knife upon it to weight it down.

I began to read it again slowly, but there was a distraction. I heard the engine noise of an automobile coming down the lane from the gate. Headlights flashed across the window and then rounded the corner of the house.

I sat up straight, listening. The engine noise died, and car doors slammed shut.

There was a long silence then before I heard the murmur and growl of voices – men's voices. I began to stand up from the table.

Then Sherry screamed. It rang clearly through the old house, and cut into my brain like a lance. It aroused in me a protective instinct so fierce that I was down the stairs and into the hall before I realized I had moved.

The door to the kitchen was open and I paused in the doorway. There were two men with Sherry. The heavier and elder of the two wore a beige camelhair topcoat and a tweed cap. He had a greyish, heavy lined face and deep-sunk eyes. His lips were thin and colourless.

He had Sherry's left hand twisted up between her shoulder-blades, and was holding her jammed against the wall beside the gas stove.

The other man was younger, and he was slim and pale, bare-headed with long straw-yellow hair falling to the shoulders of his leather jacket. He was grinning gleefully as he held Sherry's other hand over the blue flames of the gas ring, bringing it down slowly.

She was struggling desperately, but they held her and her hair had come loose as she fought.

'Slowly, lad,' the man in the cap spoke in a thick strangled voice. 'Give her time to think about it.'

Sherry screamed again as her fingers were forced down remorselessly towards the hissing blue flames.

'Go ahead, luv, shout your head off,' laughed the blond. 'There isn't anybody to hear you.'

'Only me,' I said, and they spun to face me, with expressions of comical amazement.

'Who—' asked the blond, releasing Sherry's arm and reaching quickly for his back pocket.

I hit him twice, left in the body and right in the head, and although neither shot pleased me particularly – there was not the right solidness at impact – the man went down, falling heavily over a chair and crashing into the cupboard. I had no more time for him, and I went for the one in the cloth cap.

He was still holding Sherry in front of him, and as I started forward he hurled her at me. It took me off-balance and I was forced to grab her, to save both of us from falling.

The man turned and darted out of the door behind him. It took me a few seconds to disentangle myself from Sherry and cross the kitchen. As I barged out into the yard he was halfway to an elderly Triumph sports car, and he glanced over his shoulder.

I could almost see him make the calculation. He wasn't going to be able to get into the car and turn it to face the lane before I caught him. He swerved to the left and sprinted into the dark mouth of the lane with the skirts of the camelhair coat billowing behind him. I raced after him.

The surface was greasy with wet clay, and he was making heavy going of it. he slid and almost fell, and I was right behind him, coming up swiftly when he turned and I heard the snap of the knife and saw the flash of the blade as it jumped out. He dropped into a crouch with the knife extended and I ran straight in without a check.

He didn't expect that, the glint of steel will stop most men dead. He went for my belly, a low underhand stroke, but he was shaky and breathless and it lacked fire. I blocked on the wrist and at the same time hit the pressure point in his forearm. The knife dropped out of his hand and I threw him over my hip. He fell heavily on his back, and although the mud softened the impact I dropped on one knee into his belly. It had two hundred and ten pounds of body weight behind it and it drove the air out of his lungs in a loud whoosh. He doubled up like a foetus in the womb, wheezing for breath, and I flipped him over on to his face. The cloth cap fell off his head and I found that he had a thick shock of dark hair shot through with strands of silver. I took a good handful of it, sat on his shoulders and pushed his face deep into the yellow mud.

'I don't like little boys who bully girls,' I told him conversationally, and behind me the engine of the Triumph roared into life. The headlights blazed out and then swung in a wide arc until they burned directly up the narrow lane.

I knew I hadn't taken the blond out properly, it had been a hurried botchy job. I left the man in the mud and ran back down the lane. The wheels of the Triumph spun on the paving of the barnyard and, with its headlights blazing dazzlingly into my eyes, it jumped forward, slewing and skidding as it left the paving and entered the muddy lane. The driver met the skid and came straight at me.

I fell flat and rolled into the cold ooze of a narrow open drain that carried run-off water through the tall hedge.

The Triumph hit the side a glancing blow and the hedge pushed it slightly off its line. The nearside wheels spun viciously on the edge of the stone coping of the drain inches from my face, and mud and a shower of twigs fell on me. Then it was past.

It checked as it came level with the man in the muddy camelhair coat. He was kneeling on the verge of the road and now he dragged himself into the passenger seat of the Triumph. Just as I crawled out of the drain and ran up behind the sports car it pulled away again, mud spraying from the spinning rear wheels. In vain I raced after it, but it gathered speed and tore away up the slope.

I gave up, turned and ran back down the lane, groping for the keys of the Chrysler in my sodden trouser pockets, and realized I had left them on the table in Jimmy's room.

Sherry was leaning in the open doorway of the kitchen. She held her burned hand to her chest and her hair was in tangled disarray. The sleeve of her jersey was torn loose from the shoulder.

'I couldn't stop him, Harry,' she gasped. 'I tried.'

'How bad is it?' I asked her, abandoning all thought of chasing the sports car when I saw her distress.

'Slightly singed.'

'I'll take you to a doctor.'

'No. It doesn't need it,' but her smile was lopsided with pain. I went up to Jimmy's room and from my travelling medicine kit I took a Doloxene for the pain and Mogadon to let her sleep.

'I don't need it,' she protested.

'Do I have to hold your nose and force them down? I asked, and she grinned, shook her head and swallowed them.

'You'd better take a bath,' she said, 'you are soaked,' and suddenly I realized I was sodden and cold. When I came back to the kitchen, glowing from the bath, she was already whoozy with the pills, but she had made coffee for us and strengthened it with a tot of whisky. We drank it sitting opposite each other.

'What did they want?' I asked. 'What did they say?'

'They thought I knew why Jimmy had gone to St Mary's. They wanted to know.'

I thought about that. Something didn't make sense, it worried me.

'I think—' Sherry's voice was unsteady and she staggered slightly as she tried to stand. 'Wow! What did you give me?'

I picked her up and she protested weakly, but I carried her up to her room. It was chintzy and girlish, with rose-patterned wallpaper. I laid her on the bed, pulled off her shoes and covered her with the quilt.

She sighed and closed her eyes. 'I think I'll keep you around,' she whispered. 'You're very useful.'

Thus encouraged, I sat on the edge of the bed and gentled her to sleep, smoothing her hair off her temples and stroking the broad forehead: her skin felt like warm velvet. She was asleep within a minute. I switched off the light, and was about to leave when I thought better of it.

I slipped off my own shoes and crept in under the quilt. In her sleep she rolled quite naturally into my arms, and I held her close.

It was a good feeling and soon I slept also. I woke in the dawn. Her face was pressed into my neck, one leg and arm were thrown over me and her hair was soft and tickling against my cheek.

Without waking her, I gently disengaged myself, kissed her forehead, picked up my shoes and went back to my own room. It was the first time I had spent an entire night with a beautiful woman in my arms, and done nothing but sleep. I felt puffed up with virtue.


The letter lay upon the reading table in Jimmy's room where I had left it and I read it through again before I went to the bathroom. The pencilled note in the margin 'B.Mus.E.6914(8)' puzzled me and I fretted over it while I shaved.

The rain had stopped and the clouds were breaking up when I went down into the yard to examine the scene of the previous night's encounter. The knife lay in the mud and I picked it up and tossed it over the hedge. I went into the kitchen, stamping my feet and rubbing my hands in the cold.

Sherry had started breakfast.

'How's the hand?'

'Sore,' she admitted.

'We'll find a doctor on the way up to London.'

'What makes you think I'm going to London?' she asked carefully, as she buttered toast.

'Two things. You can't stay here. The wolf pack will be back.' She looked up at me quickly but was silent. 'The other is that you promised to help me – and the trail leads to London.'

She was unconvinced, so while we ate I showed her the letter I had found in Jimmy' file.

'I don't see the connection,' she said at last, and I admitted frankly, 'It's not clear to me even.' I lit my first cheroot of the day as I spoke, and the effect was almost magical. 'But as soon as I saw the words *Dawn Light* something went click —' I stopped. 'My God!' I breathed. 'That's it. The *Dawn Light*!' I remembered the scraps of conversation carried to the bridge of *Wave Dancer* through the ventilator from the cabin below.

'To get the dawn light then we will have to —' Jimmy's voice, clear and tight with anticipation. 'If the dawn light is where —' Again the words repeated had puzzled me at the time. They had stuck like burrs in my memory.

I began to explain to Sherry, but I was so excited that it came tumbling out in a rush of words. She laughed, catching my excitement but not understanding the explanations.

'Hey!' she protested. 'You are not making sense.'

I began again, but halfway through I stopped and stared at her silently.

'Now what is it?' She was half amused, half exasperated. 'This is driving me crazy, also.'

I snatched up my fork. 'The bell. You remember the bell I told you about. The one Jimmy pulled up at Gunfire Reef?'

'Yes, of course.'

'I told you it had lettering on it, half eaten away by sand.'

'Yes, go on.'

With the fork I scratched on the butter, using it as a slate.

'—VV N L—'

I drew in the lettering that had been chased into the bronze.

'That was it,' I said. 'It didn't mean anything then – but now —' Quickly I completed the letters, 'DAWN LIGHT.'

And she stared at it, nodding slowly as it fitted together.

'We have to find out about this ship, the *Dawn Light*.'

'How?'

'It should be easy. We know she was an East Indiaman – there must be records – Lloyd's – the Board of Trade?'

She took the letter from my hand and read it again. 'The gallant colonel's luggage probably contained dirty socks and old shirts.' She pulled a face and handed it back to me.

'I'm short of socks,' I said.


Sherry packed a case, and I was relieved to see that she had the rare virtue of being able to travel light. She went down to speak to the tenant farmer while I packed the bags into the Chrysler. He would keep an eye on the cottage during her absence, and when she came back she merely locked the kitchen door and climbed into the Chrysler beside me.

'Funny,' she said. 'This feels like the beginning of a long journey.'

'I have my plans,' I warned and leered at her.

'Once I thought you looked wholesome,' she said sorrowfully, 'but when you do that —'

'Sexy, isn't it ?' I agreed, and took the Chrysler up the lane.

I found a doctor in Haywards Heath. Sherry's hand had now blistered badly, fat white bags of fluid hung from her fingers like sickly grapes. He drained them, and rebandaged the hand.

'Feels worse now,' she murmured as we drove on northwards, and she was pale and silent with the pain of it. I respected her silence, until we were into the suburbs of the city.

'We had better find some place to stay,' I suggested. 'Something comfortable and central.'

She looked across at me quizzically.

'It would probably be a lot more comfortable and cheaper if we got a double room somewhere, wouldn't it?'

I felt something turn over in my belly, something warm and exciting. 'Funny you should say that, I was just about to suggest the same.'

'I know you were,' she laughed for the first time in two hours. 'I saved you the trouble.' She shook her head, still laughing. 'I'll stay with my uncle. He's got a spare room in his apartment in Pimlico, and there is a little pub around the corner. It's friendly and clean – you could do worse.'

'I am crazy about your sense of humour,' I muttered.

She phoned the uncle from a call box, while I waited in the car.

'It's fixed up,' she told me, as she climbed into the passenger seat. 'He's at home.'

It was a ground-floor apartment in a quiet street near the river. I carried Sherry's bag for her as she led the way, and rang the doorbell.

The man that opened the door was small and lightly built. He was sixtyish and he wore a grey cardigan, darned at the elbows. His feet were thrust into carpet slippers. The homely attire was somehow incongruous, for his iron-grey hair was neatly cropped as was the short stiff moustache. His skin was clear and ruddy, but it was the fierce predatory glint of the eye and the military set of the shoulders that warned me. This man was aware.

'My uncle, Dan Wheeler.' Sherry stood aside to introduce us. 'Uncle Dan this is Harry Fletcher.'

'The young man you were telling me about,' he nodded abruptly. His hand was bony and dry and his gaze stung like nettles. 'Come in. Come in, both of you.'

'I won't bother you, sir —' it was quite natural to call him that, an echo of my military training from so long ago, 'I want to find digs myself.'

Uncle Dan and Sherry exchanged glances and I thought she shook her head almost imperceptibly, but I was looking beyond them into the apartment. It was monastic, completely masculine in the severity and economy of furniture and ornaments. Somehow that room seemed to confirm my first impressions of the man. I wanted as little to do with him as I could arrange while seeing as much of Sherry as I possibly could.

'I'll pick you up in an hour for lunch, Sherry,' and when she agreed I left them and returned to the Chrysler. The pub that Sherry recommended was the Windsor Arms, and when I mentioned the uncle's name as she suggested, they put me in a quiet back room with a fine view of sky and television aerials. I lay on the bed fully clothed, and considered the North family and its relatives while I waited for the hour to run by. Of one thing only was I certain – that Sherry North the Second was not going to pass me silently in the night. I was going to keep pretty close station upon her, and yet there was much about her that still puzzled me. I suspected that she was a more complicated person than her serene and lovely face suggested. It was going to be interesting finding out. I put the thought aside, sat up and reached for the telephone. I made three phone calls in the next twenty minutes. One to Lloyd's Register of Shipping in Fenchurch Street, another to the National

Maritime Museum at Greenwich and the last to the India Office Library in Blackfriars Road. I left the Chrysler in the private parking lot behind the pub, a car is more trouble than it is worth in London, and I walked back to the uncle's apartment. Sherry answered the door herself, and she was ready to leave. I liked that about her, she was punctual.

'You didn't like Uncle Dan, did you?' she challenged me over the lunch table and I ducked.

'I made some phone calls. The place that we are looking for is in Blackfriars Road. It's in Westminster. The India Office Library. We will go down there after we've eaten.'

'He really is very sweet when you get to know him.'

'Look, darling girl, he's your uncle. You keep him.'

'But why, Harry? It interests me.'

'What does he do for a living – army, navy?'

She stared at me. 'How did you know that?'

'I can pick them out of a crowd.'

'He's army, but retired – why should that make a difference?'

'What are you going to try?' I waved the menu at her. 'If you take the roast beef, I'll go for the duck,' and she accepted the decoy, and concentrated on the food.

The India Office Archives were housed in one of those square modern blocks of greenish glass and airforce-blue steel panels.

Sherry and I armed ourselves with visitor's passes and signed the book. We made our way first to the Catalogue Room and thence to the marine section of the archives. These were presided over by a neatly dressed but stern-faced lady with greying hair and steel-rimmed spectacles.

I handed her a requisition slip for the dossier which would include material on the Honourable Company's ship *Dawn Light* and she disappeared amongst the laden ceiling-high tiers of steel shelving.

It was twenty minutes before she returned and placed a bulky dossier on the counter top before me.

'You'll have to sign here,' she told me, indicating a column on the stiff cardboard folder. 'Funny! she remarked. 'You are the second one who has asked for this file in less than a year.'

I stared at the signature J. A. North in the last space. We were following closely in Jimmy's footsteps, I thought, as I signed 'RICHARD SMITH' below his name.

'You can use one of the desks over there, dear.' She pointed across the room. 'Please try and keep the file tidy, won't you, then.'

Sherry and I sat down at the desk shoulder to shoulder, and I untied the tape that secured the file.

The *Dawn Light* was of the type known as the Blackwall Frigate, characteristically built at the Blackwall yards in the early nineteenth century. The type was very similar to the naval frigates of that period.

She had been built at Sunderland for the Honourable English East India Company, and she was of 1330 net register tons. At the waterline her dimensions were 226 feet with a beam of twenty-six feet. Such a narrow beam would have made her very fast but uncomfortable in a stiff blow.

She had been launched in 1832, just the year before the Company lost its

China monopoly, and this stroke of ill-fortune seemed to have dogged her whole career.

Also in the file were a whole series of reports of the proceedings of various courts of inquiry. Her first master gloried in the name of Hogge and on her maiden voyage he piled the *Dawn Light* on to the bank at Diamond Harbour in Hooghly River. He was found by the court of inquiry to be under the influence of strong drink at the time and stripped of his command.

'Made a pig of himself,' I observed to Sherry, and she groaned softly and rolled her eyes at my wit.

The trail of misfortune continued. In 1840 while making passage in the South Atlantic the elderly mate who had the dog watch let her come up, and away went her masts. Wallowing helpless with her top hamper dragging alongside, she was found by a Dutchman. They cut away the wreckage and she was dragged into Table Bay. The Salvage Court made an award of £12,000.

In 1846 while half her crew were ashore on the wild coast of New Guinea they were set upon by the cannibals and slaughtered to a man. Sixty-three of her crew died.

Then on the 23rd September, 1857, she sailed from Bombay, outward bound for St Mary's, the Cape of Good Hope, St Helena and the Pool of London.

'The date.' I placed my finger on the line. 'This is the voyage that Goodchild talks of in the letter.'

Sherry nodded without reply, I had learned in the last few minutes that she read faster than I did. I had to restrain her from turning each page when I was only three-quarters finished. Now her eyes darted across each line, her colour was up, a soft flush upon her pale cheeks, and she was biting her underlip.

'Come on,' she urged me. 'Hurry up!' and I had to hold her wrist.

The *Dawn Light* never reached St Mary's – she disappeared. Three months later, she was considered lost at sea with all hands and the underwriters were ordered by Lloyd's to make good their assurances to the owners and shippers.

The manifest of her cargo was impressive for such a small ship for she had loaded out of China and India a cargo that consisted of:

| | |
|---|---|
| 364 chests of tea | 72 tons on behalf of |
| 494 half-chests of tea | Messrs Dunbar and Green. |
| 101 chests of tea | 65 tons on behalf of |
| 618 half-chests of tea | Messrs Simpson, Wyllie & Livingstone. |
| 577 bales of silk | 82 tons on behalf of Messrs Elder and Company. |
| 5 cases goods | 4 tons on behalf of Col. Sir Roger Goodchild. |
| 16 cases goods | 6 tons on behalf of Major John Cotton. |
| 10 cases goods | 2 tons on behalf of Lord Elton. |
| 26 boxes various spices | 2 tons on behalf of Messrs Paulson and Company. |

Wordlessly I laid my finger on the fourth item of the manifest, and again Sherry nodded, with her eyes shining like sapphires. The claim had been settled and the matter appeared closed until, four months later in April, 1858, the East Indiaman *Walmer Castle* arrived in England, carrying aboard the survivors from the *Dawn Light*.

There were six of them. The first mate, Andrew Barlow, a boatswain's mate, and three topmast men. There was also a young woman of twenty-two years, a Miss Charlotte Cotton, who had been a passenger making the homeward passage with her father, a Major in the 40th Foot.

The mate, Andrew Barlow, gave his evidence to the Court of Inquiry, and beneath the dry narrative and the ponderous questions and guarded replies lay an exciting and romantic story of the sea, an epic of shipwreck and survival.

As we read I saw the meagre scraps of knowledge I had scraped together fit neatly into the story.

Fourteen days out from Bombay, the *Dawn Light* was set upon by a furious storm out of the south-east. For seven days the savagery of the storm raged unabated, driving the ship before her. I could imagine it clearly, one of those great cyclones that had torn the roof from my own shack at Turtle Bay.

Once again *Dawn Light* was dismasted, no spars were left standing except the fore lower mast, mizzen lower mast, and bowsprit. The rest had carried away on the tempest and there was no opportunity to set up a jury mainmast or send yards aloft in the mountainous seas.

Thus when land was sighted to leeward, there was no chance that the ship might avoid her fate. A conspiracy of wind and current hurled her down into the throat of a funnel-shaped reef upon which the storm surf burst like the thunder of the heavens.

The ship struck and held, and Andrew Barlow was able with the help of twelve members of his crew to launch one of the boats. Four passengers including Miss Charlotte Cotton left the stricken ship with them, and Barlow, with an unlikely combination of good fortune and seamanship, was able to find a passage through the wild sea and murderous reefs into the quieter waters of the inshore channel.

Finally they ran the boat ashore on the spindrift-smothered beach of an island. Here the survivors huddled for four days while the cyclone blew itself out.

Barlow alone climbed to the summit of the southernmost of the treble peaks of the island. The description was completely clear. It was the Old Man and Gunfire Reef. There was no doubt of it. This then was how Jimmy North had known what he was looking for – the island with three peaks and a barrier of coral reef.

Barlow took bearings off the sea-battered hull of the *Dawn Light* as she lay in the jaws of the reef, swept by each successive wave. On the second day the ship's hull began to break up, and while Barlow watched from the peak, the front half of her was carried up over the reef to disappear into a dark gaping hole in the coral. The stern fell back into the sea and was smashed to matchwood.

When at last the skies cleared and the wind dropped, Andrew Barlow discovered that his small party were all that survived from a ship's company of 149 souls. The others had perished in the wild sea.

To the west, low against the horizon, he descried a low land mass which he hoped was the African mainland. He embarked his party in the ship's boat once more and they made the crossing of the inshore channel. His hopes were fulfilled, it was Africa – but as always she was hostile and cruel.

The seventeen lost beings began a long and dangerous journey southwards, and three months later only Barlow, four seamen and Miss Charlotte Cotton reached the island port of Zanzibar. Fever, wild animals, wild men and misfortune had whittled away their numbers – and even those who survived were starved to gaunt living skeletons, yellowed with fever and riddled with dysentery from foul water.

The court of inquiry had highly commended Andrew Barlow, and the Hon. Company had made him an award of £500 for meritorious service.

When I finished reading, I looked up at Sherry. She was watching me.

'Wow!' she said, and I also felt drained by the magnitude of the old drama.

'It all fits, Sherry,' I said. 'It's all there.'

'Yes,' she said.

'We must see if they have the drawings here.'

The Prints and Drawings Room was on the third floor and a quick search by an earnest assistant soon revealed the *Dawn Light* in all her splendour.

She was a graceful three-masted ship with a long low profile. She had no crossjack or mizzen course. Instead she carried a large spanker and a full set of studding sails. The long poop gave space for several passenger cabins, and she carried her boats on top of her deck-house aft.

She was heavily armed, with thirteen black-painted gunports aside, from which she could run out her long eighteen-pounder cannon to defend herself, in those hostile seas east of the Cape of Good Hope across which she plied to China and India.

'I need a drink,' I said, and picked up the drawings of the *Dawn Light*. 'I'll get them to make copies of these for us.'

'What for?' Sherry wanted to know.

The assistant emerged from her lair amongst the piled trays of old prints and sucked in her cheeks at my request for copies.

'I'll have to charge you seventy-five pence,' she tried to discourage me.

'That's reasonable,' I said.

'And we won't have them ready until next week,' she added inexorably.

'Oh dear,' said I, and gave her the smile. 'I did need them tomorrow afternoon.'

The smile crushed her, she lost the air of purpose and tried to tuck her straying wisps of hair into the side frames of her glasses.

'Well, I'll see what I can do then,' she relented.

'That's very sweet of you, really it is,' and we left her looking confused, but pleased.

My sense of direction was returning and I found my way to El Vino's without trouble. The evening flood of journalists from Fleet Street had not yet swamped it and we found a table at the back. I ordered two Vermouths and we saluted each other over the glasses.

'You know, Harry, Jimmy had a hundred schemes. His whole life was one great treasure hunt. Every week he had found, almost found, the location of a treasure ship from the Armada or a sunken Aztec city, a buccaneer wreck —' she shrugged. 'I have a built-in resistance to believing any of it. But this one —' She sipped the wine.

'Let's go over what we have,' I suggested. 'We know that Goodchild was very concerned that his agent receive five cases of luggage and put it into safe keeping. We know that he was going to ship it aboard *Dawn Light* and he sent advance notice, probably through a personal friend, the captain of the naval frigate *Panther*.

'Good,' she agreed.

'We know that those cases were listed on the ship's manifest. That the ship was lost, presumably with them still on board. We know the exact location of the wreck. We have had it confirmed by the ship's bell.'

'Still good.'

'We only do not know what those cases contained.'

'Dirty socks,' she said.

'Four tons of dirty socks?' I asked, and her expression changed. The weight of the cargo had not meant anything to her.

'Ah,' I grinned at her, 'it went over your head. I thought so. You read so fast you only take in half of it.'

She pulled a face at me.

Four tons, my darling girl, is a great deal of something – whatever it is.'

'All right,' she agreed. 'Figures don't mean much to me, I admit. But it sounds a lot.'

'Say the same weight as a new Rolls Royce – to put it in terms you might understand,' and her eyes widened and turned a darker blue.

'That *is* a lot.'

'Jimmy obviously knew what it was, and had proof sufficient to convince some very hard-headed backers. They took it seriously.'

'Seriously enough to —' and she stopped herself. For an instant I saw the old grief for Jimmy's death in her eyes. I was embarrassed by it, and I looked away, making a show of taking the letter out of my inner pocket.

Carefully I spread it on the table top between us. When I looked at her, she had recovered her composure once more.

The pencilled note in the margin engaged my attention again.

'B.Mus.E.6914(8).' I read it aloud. 'Any ideas?'

'Bachelor of Music.'

'Oh, that's great,' I applauded.

'You do better,' she challenged, and I folded the letter away with dignity and ordered two more drinks.

'Well, that was a good run on that scent,' I said when I had paid the waiter. 'We have an idea what it was all about. Now, we can go on my other lead.'

She sat forward and encouraged me silently.

'I told you about your impostor, the blonde Sherry North?' and she nodded. 'On the night before she left the island she sent a cable to London.'

I produced the flimsy from my wallet and handed it to Sherry. While she read it, I went on: 'This was clearly an okay to her principal, Manson. He must be the big man behind this. I am going to start moving in on him now.' I finished my Vermouth. 'I'll drop you back with your martial uncle and contact you again tomorrow.'

Her lips set in a line of stubbornness which I had not seen before and there was a glint in her eyes like the blue of gun-metal.

'Harry Fletcher, if you think you are going to ditch me just when things start livening up, you must be off your tiny head.'

The cab dropped us in Berkeley Square and I led her into Curzon Street.

'Take my arm quickly,' I muttered, glancing over my shoulder in a secretive manner. Instantly she obeyed, and we had gone fifty yards before she whispered, 'Why?'

'Because I like the feel of it,' I grinned at her and spoke in a natural voice.

'Oh, you!' She made as if to pull away, but I held her and she capitulated. We sauntered up the street towards Shepherd Market, stopping now and then to window-shop like a pair of tourists.

No. 97 Curzon Street was one of those astronomically expensive apartment blocks, six storeys of brick facing, and an ornate street door of bronze and glass beyond which was a marbled foyer guarded by a uniformed doorman. We went on past it, up as far as the White Elephant Club and there we crossed the street and wandered back on the opposite pavement.

'I could go and ask the doorman if Mr Manson occupied Flat No. 5,' Sherry volunteered.

'Great,' I said. 'Then he says "yes", what do you do then? Tell him Harry Fletcher says hello?'

'You are really very droll,' she said, and once more she tried to take her hand away.

'There is a restaurant diagonally opposite No. 97.' I prevented her withdrawal. 'Let's get a table in the front window, drink some coffee, and watch for a while.'

It was a little past three o'clock when we settled at the window seat with a good view across the street, and the next hour passed pleasantly. I found it not a difficult task to keep Sherry amused, we shared a similar sense of humour and I liked to hear her laugh.

I was in the middle of a long, complicated story when I was interrupted by the arrival outside No. 97 of a Silver Wraith Rolls Royce. It pulled to the kerb and a chauffeur in a smart dove-grey uniform left the car and entered the foyer. He and the doorman fell into conversation, and I resumed my story.

Ten minutes later, there was sudden activity opposite. The elevator began a series of rapid ascents and descents, each time discharging a load of matching crocodile-skin luggage. This was carried out by the doorman and chauffeur and packed into the Rolls. It seemed endless, and Sherry remarked, 'Somebody is off on a long holiday.' She sighed wistfully.

'How do you fancy a tropical island with blue water and white sands, a thatched shack amongst the palms—'

'Stop it,' she said. 'On an autumn day in old London, I just can't bear the thought.'

I was about to move into a stronger position when the footman and chauffeur stood to attention and once more the glass doors of the lift opened and a man and woman stepped out of it.

The woman wore a full-length honey mink and her blonde hair was piled high on her head in an elaborate lacquered Grecian style. Anger struck me like a fist in the guts as I recognized her.

It was Sherry North, the First. The nice lady who had blown Judith and *Wave Dancer* to the bottom of Grand Harbour.

With her was a man of medium height with soft brown hair fashionably long and curly over his ears. He had a light tan, probably from a sun lamp, and he was dressed too well. Very expensively, but as flamboyantly as an entertainment personality.

He had a heavy jaw and a long fleshy nose with soft gazelle eyes, but his mouth was pinched and hungry. A greedy mouth that I remembered so well. 'Manson!' I said. 'Jesus! Manson Resnick – Manny Resnick.' He would be just the one Jimmy North would find his way to with his outrageous proposition. In exactly the same way that so long ago I had gone to him with my plans for the gold heist at Rome Airport. Manny was an underworld entrepreneur, and he had clearly climbed a long way up the ladder since our last meeting.

He was keeping great style now, I thought, as he crossed the pavement and entered the back seat of the Rolls, settling down next to the mink-clad blonde.

'Wait here,' I told Sherry urgently, as the Rolls pulled away towards Park Lane.

I ran out on to the pavement and searched wildly for a cab to follow them. There were none and I ran after the Rolls praying desperately for the sight of a big black cab with its top light burning, but ahead of me the Rolls swung right into South Audley Street and accelerated smoothly away.

I stopped at the corner and it was already far ahead, infiltrating the traffic towards Grosvenor Square.

I turned and ambled disappointedly back to where Sherry waited. I knew that Sherry had been correct. Manny and the blonde were off on a long journey. There was no point in hanging around No. 97 Curzon Street any longer.

Sherry was waiting for me outside the restaurant.

'What was that all about?' she demanded and I took her arm. As we walked back towards Berkeley Square, I told her.

'That man is probably the one who ordered Jimmy murdered, who was responsible for having half my chest shot away, who had them to roast your lovely pinkies – in short, the big man.'

'You know him?'

'I did business with him a long time ago.'

'Nice friends you have.'

'I'm trying for a better class lately,' I said, and squeezed her arm. She ignored my gallantry.

'And the woman. Is she the one from St Mary's, the one who blew up your boat and the young girl?'

I experienced a violent return of the anger which had gripped me a few minutes earlier when I had seen that sleek, meticulously polished predator dressed in mink.

Beside me Sherry gasped, 'Harry, you are hurting me!'

'Sorry.' I relaxed my grip on her arm.

'I guess that answers my question,' she muttered ruefully, and massaged her upper arm.

The private bar of the Windsor Arms was all dark oak panels and antique mirrors. It was crowded by the time Sherry and I returned. Outside darkness had fallen and there was an icy wind stirring the fallen leaves in the gutters.

The warmth of the pub was welcome. We found seats in a corner, but the crowd pushed us together, forcing me to place an arm around Sherry's shoulders, and our heads were close so we could hold a very private conversation in this public place.

'I can guess where Manny Resnick and his friend are headed,' I said.

'Big Gull Island?' Sherry asked, and when I nodded she went on, 'He'll need a boat and divers.'

'Don't worry, Manny will get them.'

'And what will we do?'

'We?' I asked.

'A form of speech,' she corrected herself primly. 'What will you do?'

'I have a choice. I can forget about it all – or I can go back to Gunfire Reef and try to find out what the hell was in Colonel Goodchild's five cases.'

'You'll need equipment.'

'It might not be as elaborate as Manny Resnick's will be, but I could get enough together.'

'How are you for money, or is that a rude question?'

'The answer is the same. I could get enough together.'

'Blue water and white sand,' she murmured dreamily.

'—and the palm fronds clattering in the trade winds.'

'Stop it, Harry.'

'Fat crayfish grilling on the coals, and me beside you singing in the wilderness,' I went on remorselessly.

'Pig,' she said.

'If you stay here, you'll never know if it was dirty socks,' I pressed her.

'You'd write and tell me,' she pleaded.

'No, I wouldn't.'

'I'll have to come with you,' she said at last.

'Good girl.' I squeezed her shoulder.

'But I insist on paying my own way, I refuse to become a kept woman.' She had guessed how hard pressed I was financially.

'I should hate to erode your principles,' I told her happily, and my wallet sighed with relief. It was going to be a near run thing to mount an expedition to Gunfire Reef on what I had left.

There was much we had to discuss now that the decision had been made. It seemed only minutes later that the landlord was calling, 'Time, gentlemen.'

'The streets are dangerous at night,' I warned Sherry. 'I don't think we should chance it. Upstairs I have a very comfortable room with a fine view—'

'Come on, Fletcher.' Sherry stood up. 'You had better walk me home, or I shall set my uncle on to you.'

As we walked the half block to her uncle's apartment, we agreed to meet for lunch next day. I had a list of errands to perform in the morning including making the airline reservations, while Sherry had to have her passport renewed and pick up the photostat drawings of the *Dawn Light*.

At the door of the apartment we faced each other, suddenly both of us were shy. It was so terribly corny that I almost laughed. We were like a pair of old-fashioned teenagers at the end of our first date – but sometimes corny feels good.

'Good night, Harry,' she said, and with the age-old artistry of womankind she showed me in some indefinable manner that she was ready for kissing.

Her lips were soft and warm, and the kiss went on for a long time.

'My goodness,' she whispered throatily, and drew away at last.

'Are you sure you won't change your mind – it is a beautiful room, hot and cold water, carpets on the floor, T.V.—'

She laughed shakily and pushed me gently backwards. 'Goodnight, dear Harry,' she repeated, and left me.

I went out into the street and strolled back towards my pub. The wind had dropped but I could smell the damp emanating from the river close by. The street was deserted but the kerb was lined with parked vehicles, bumper to bumper they reached to the corner.

I sauntered along the pavement, in no hurry for bed, even toying with the idea of a stroll down the Embankment first. My hands were thrust deep into the pockets of my car coat, and I was feeling relaxed and happy as I thought about this woman.

There was a lot to think about Sherry North, much that was unclear or not yet explained, but mainly I cherished the thought that perhaps here at last was something that might last longer than a night, a week, or a month – something that was already strong and that would not be like the others, diminishing with the passage of time, but instead would grow ever stronger.

Suddenly a voice beside me said, 'Harry!' It was a man's voice, a strange voice, and I turned instinctively towards it. As I did so I knew that it was a mistake.

The speaker was sitting in the back seat of one of the parked cars. It was a black Rover. The window was open and his face was merely a pale blob in the darkness of the interior.

Desperately I tried to pull my hands out of my pockets and turn to face the direction from which I knew the attack would come. As I turned I ducked and twisted, and something whirred past my ear and struck my shoulder a numbing blow.

I struck backwards with both elbows, connecting solidly and hearing the gasp of pain. Then my hands were clear and I was around, moving fast, weaving, for I knew they would use the cosh again.

They were just midnight shapes, menacing and huge, dressed in dark clothing. It seemed there were a legion of them, but there were only four – and one in the car. They were all big men, and the one had the cosh up to strike again. I hit him under the chin with the palm of my hand, snapping his head backwards and I thought I might have broken his neck, for he went down hard on the pavement.

A knee drove for my groin, but I turned and caught it on the thigh, using the impetus of the turn to counter-punch. It was a good one, jolting me to the shoulder, and the man took it in the chest, and was thrown backwards, but immediately one of them was hugging the arm, smothering it and a fist caught me in the cheek under the eye. I felt the skin tear open.

Another one was on my back, an arm around my throat throttling me, but I heaved and pushed. In a tight knot, locked together, we surged around the pavement.

'Hold him still,' another voice called, low and urgent. 'Let me get a shot at him.'

'What the bloody hell you think we are trying to do?' panted another, and we fell against the side of the Rover. I was pinned there, and I saw the one with the cosh was on his feet. He swung again, and I tried to roll my head, but it caught me in the temple. It did not put me out completely, but it knocked all the fight out of me. I was instantly weak as a child, hardly able to support my own weight.

'That's it, get him into the back.' They hustled me into the centre seat in the back of the Rover and one of them crowded in on each side of me. The doors slammed, the engine whirred and caught and we pulled away swiftly.

My brain cleared, but the side of my head was numb and felt like a balloon. There were three of them in the front seat, one on each side of me in the back. All of them were breathing heavily, and the one next to the driver was massaging his neck and jaw tenderly. The one on my right had been eating garlic, and he panted heavily as he searched me for weapons.

'I think you should know that something died in your mouth a long time ago, and it's still there,' I told him, with a thickened tongue and an ache in my head, but the effort was not worth it. He showed no sign of having heard, but continued doggedly with this task. At last he was satisfied and I readjusted my clothing.

We drove in silence for five munutes, following the river towards Hammersmith, before they had all recovered their breath and tended their wounds, then the driver spoke.

'Listen, Manny wants to talk to you, but he said it's no big thing. He was merely curious. He said also that if you gave us a hard time, not to go to no trouble, just to sign you off and toss you in the river.'

'Charming chap, Manny,' I said.

'Shut up!' said the driver. 'So you see, it's up to you. Behave yourself and you get to live a little longer. I heard you used to be a sharp operator, Harry. We been expecting you to show up, ever since Lorna missed you on the island – but sure as hell we didn't expect you to parade up and down Curzon Street like a brass band. Manny couldn't believe it. He said, "That can't be Harry. He must have gone soft." It made him sad. "How are the mighty fallen. Tell it not in the streets of Ashkelon", he said.'

'That's Shakespeare,' said the one with the garlic breath.

'Shut up,' said the driver and then went on. 'Manny was sad but not that sad that he cried or anything, you understand.'

'I understand,' I mumbled.

'Shut up,' said the driver. 'Manny said, "Don't do it here. Just follow him to a nice quiet place and pick him up. If he comes quietly you bring him to talk to me – if he cuts up rough then toss him in the river".'

'That sounds like my boy, Manny. He always was a soft-hearted little devil.'

'Shut up,' said the driver.

'I look forward to seeing him again.'

'You just stay good and quiet and you might get lucky.'

I stayed that way through the night as we picked up the M4 and rushed westwards. It was two in the morning when we entered Bristol, skirting the city centre as we followed the A4 down to Avonmouth.

Amongst the other craft in the yacht basin was a big motor yacht. She was moored to the wharf and she had her gangplank down. Her name painted on the stern and bows was *Mandrake*. She was an ocean-goer, steel-hulled painted blue and white, with pleasing lines. I judged her fast and sea-kindly, probably with sufficient range to take her anywhere in the world. A rich man's toy. There were figures on her bridge, lights burning in most of her portholes, and she seemed ready for sea.

They crowded me as we crossed the narrow space to the gangplank. The Rover backed and turned and drove away as we climbed to the *Mandrake*'s deck.

The saloon was too tastefully fitted out for Manny Resnick's style, it had either been done by the previous owners or a professional decorator. There were forest-green wall-to-wall carpets and matching velvet curtains, the furniture was dark teak and polished leather and the pictures were choice oils toned to the general décor.

This was half a million pounds worth of vessel, and I guessed it was a charter. Manny had probably taken her for six months and put in his own crew – for Manny Resnick had never struck me as a blue-water man.

As we waited in the centre of the wall-to-wall carpeting, a grimly silent group, I heard the unmistakable sounds of the gangplank being taken in, and the moorings cast off. The tremble of her engines became a steady beat, and the harbour lights slid past the saloon portholes as we left the entrance and thrust out into the tidal waters of the River Severn.

I recognized the lighthouses at Portishead Point and Red Cliff Bay as *Mandrake* came around for the run down-river past Weston-super-Mare and Berry for the open sea.

Manny came at last, he wore a blue silk gown and his face was still crumpled from sleep, but his curls were neatly combed and his smile was white and hungry.

'Harry,' he said, 'I told you that you would be back.'

'Hello, Manny. I can't say it's any great pleasure.'

He laughed lightly and turned to the woman as she followed him into the saloon. She was carefully made up and every hair of the elaborate hairstyle was in its place. She wore a long white house-gown with lace at throat and cuffs.

'You have met Lorna, I believe, Lorna Page.'

'Next time you send somebody to hustle me, Manny, try for a little better class. I'm getting fussy in my old age.'

Her eyes slanted wickedly, but she smiled.

'How's your boat, Harry? Your lovely boat?'

'It makes a lousy coffin.' I turned back to Manny. 'What's it going to be, Manny, can we work out a deal?'

He shook his head sorrowfully. 'I don't think so, Harry. I would like to – truly I would, if just for old times' sake. But I can't see it. Firstly, you haven't anything to trade – and that makes for a lousy deal. Secondly, I know you are too sentimental. You'd louse up any deal we did make for purely emotional reasons. I couldn't trust you, Harry, all the time you'd be thinking about Jimmy North and your boat, you'd be thinking about the little island girl that got in the way, and about Jimmy North's sister who we had to get rid of—' I took a mild pleasure in the fact that Manny had obviously not heard what had happened to the goon squad he had sent to take care of Sherry North, and that she was still very much alive. I tried to make my voice sincere and my manner convincing.

'Listen, Manny, I'm a survivor. I can forget anything, if I have to.'

He laughed again. 'If I didn't know you better, I'd believe you, Harry.' He shook his head again. 'Sorry, Harry, no deal.'

'Why did you go to all the trouble to bring me down here, then?'

'I sent others to do the job twice before, Harry. Both times they missed you. This time I want to make sure. We will be cruising over some deep water on the way to Cape Town, and I'm going to hang some really heavy weights on to you.'

'Cape Town?' I asked. 'So you are going after the *Dawn Light* in person. What is so fascinating about that old wreck?'

'Come on, Harry. If you didn't know, you wouldn't be giving me such a hard time.' He laughed, and I thought it best not to let them know my ignorance.

'You think you can find your way back?' I asked the blonde. 'It's a big sea and a lot of islands look the same. I think you should keep me as insurance,' I insisted.

'Sorry, Harry.' Manny crossed to the teak and brass bar. 'Drink?' he asked.

'Scotch,' I said, and he half filled a glass with the liquor and brought it to me.

'To be entirely truthful with you, part of this is for Lorna's benefit. You made the girl bitter, Harry, I don't know why – but she wanted especially to be there when we say goodbye. She enjoys that sort of thing, don't you, darling, it turns her on.'

I drained the glass. 'She needs turning on – as you and I both know, she's a lousy lay without it,' I observed, and Manny hit me in the mouth, crushing my lips and the whisky stung the raw flesh.

'Lock him up,' he said softly. As the hustled me out of the saloon, and along the deck towards the bows, I took pleasure in knowing that Lorna would have painful questions to answer. On either hand the shore lights moved steadily past us in the night, and the river was black and wide.

Forward of the bridge there was a low deckhouse above the forecastle, and a louvred companionway opened on to a deck ladder that descended to a small lobby. This was obviously the crew's quarters, doors opened off the lobby into cabins and a communal mess.

In the bows was a steel door and a stencilled sign upon it read 'FORE-CASTLE STORE'. They shoved me through the doorway and slammed the heavy door. The lock turned and I was alone in a steel cubicle probably six by four. Both bulkheads were lined with storage lockers, and the air was damp and musty.

My first concern was to find some sort of weapon. The cupboards were all of them locked and I saw that the planking was inch-thick oak. I would need an axe to hack them open, nevertheless I tried. I attempted to break in the doors using my shoulder as a ram, but the space was too confined and I could not work up sufficient momentum.

However, the noise attracted attention. The door swung open and one of the crew stood well back with a big ugly .41 Rueger Magnum in his hand.

'Cut it out,' he said. 'There ain't anything in there,' and he gestured to the pile of old life-jackets against the far wall. 'You just sit there nice and quiet or I'll call some of the boys to help me work you over.' He slammed the door and I sank down on to the life-jackets.

There was clearly a guard posted at the door full-time. The others would be within easy call. I hadn't expected him to open the door and I had been off-balance. I had to get him to do it again – but this time I would have a go. It was a poor chance, I realized. All he had to do was point that cannon into the storeroom and pull the trigger. He could hardly miss.

I needed some sort of distraction, some sort of cover to get close enough. I looked longingly at the lockers again, then turned my attention to my own pockets. They had cleaned me out, my lighter and cheroots, car keys, penknife were all gone. But they had left my handkerchief, three five-pound notes folded into my hip pocket they had overlooked and I had my wristwatch.

I looked down at the pile of life-jackets, and stood again to pull them aside. Beneath them was a small wooden fruit box, it contained discarded cleaning materials. A nylon floorbrush, cleaning rags, a tin of Brasso, half a cake of yellow soap, and a brandy bottle half filled with clear fluid. I unscrewed the cap and sniffed it. It was benzine.

I sat down again and reassessed my position, trying to find a percentage in it without much success.

The light switch was outside the doorway and the light overhead was in a thick glass cover. I stood up and climbed halfway up the lockers, wedging myself there while I unscrewed the light cover and examined the bulb. It gave me a little hope.

I climbed down again and selected one of the heavy canvas life-jackets. The clasp of the steel strap on my wristwatch made a blunt blade and I sawed and hacked at the canvas, tearing a hole large enough to get my forefinger in. I ripped the canvas open and pulled out handfuls of the white kapok stuffing. I piled it on the floor, tearing open more life-jackets until I had a considerable heap.

I soaked the cotton waste with benzine from the bottle and took a handful of it with me when I climbed again to the light fitting. I removed the bulb and was plunged instantly into darkness. Working by sense of touch alone, I pressed the benzine-soaked stuffing close to the electricity terminals. I had nothing to use as insulation so I held the steel strap of my wristwatch in my bare hands and used it to dead-short the terminals.

There was a sizzling blue flash, the benzine ignited instantly and 180 volts hit me like a charge of buckshot, knocking me off my perch. I fell in a heap on to the deck with a ball of flaming kapok in my hands.

Outside I heard faint shouts of annoyance and anger. I had succeeded in shorting the entire lighting system of the forecastle. Quickly I tossed the burning kapok on to the prepared pile, and it burned up fiercely. I brushed the sparks from my hands, wrapped the handkerchief around my mouth and nose, snatched up one of the undamaged life-belts and went to stand against the steel door.

In seconds the benzine burned away and the cotton began to smoulder, fiercely pouring out thick black smoke that smelled vile. It filled the store, and my eyes began to stream with tears. I tried to breathe shallowly but the smoke tore my lungs and I coughed violently.

There was another shout beyond the door.

'Something is burning.' And it was answered, 'For Chrissake, get those lights on.'

It was my cue, I began beating on the steel door and screaming at the top of my voice. 'Fire! The ship is on fire!' It was not all acting. The smoke in my prison was thick and solid, and more boiled off the burning cotton kapok. I realized that if nobody opened that door within the next sixty seconds I would suffocate and my screams must have carried conviction. The guard swung the door open, he carried the big Rueger revolver and shone a flashlight into the storeroom.

I had time only to notice those details and to see that the ship's lights were still dead, shadowy figures milled about in the gloom, some with flashlights – then a solid black cloud of smoke boiled out of the storeroom.

I came out with the smoke like a fighting bull from its pen, desperate for clean air and terrified at how close I had come to suffocating. It gave strength to my efforts.

The guard went sprawling under my rush and the Rueger fired as he went down. The muzzle flame was bright as a flashbulb, lighting the whole area and allowing me to get my bearings on the companion ladder to the deck.

The blast of the shot was so deafening in the confined space that it seemed to paralyse the other shadowy figures. I was halfway to the ladder before one of them leaped to intercept me. I drove my shoulder into his chest and heard the wind go out of him like a punctured football.

There were shouts of concern now, and another big dark figure blocked the foot of the ladder. I had gathered speed across the lobby and I put that and all my weight into a kick that slogged into his belly, doubling him over and dropping him to his knees. As he went over a flashlight lit his face and I saw it was my friend with the garlicky breath. It gave me a lift of pleasure to light me on my way, and I put one foot on his shoulder and used it as a springboard to leap halfway up the ladder.

Hands clutched at my ankle but I kicked them away, and dragged myself to the deck level. I had only one foot on the rungs, and I was clinging with one hand to the life-jacket and with the other to the brass handrail. In that helpless moment, the doorway to the deck was blocked by yet another dark figure – and the lights went on. A sudden blinding blaze of light.

The man above me was the lad with the cosh, and I saw his savage delight as he raised it over my helpless head. The only way to avoid it was to let go the handrail and drop back into the forecastle, which was filled with surging angry goons.

I looked back and was actually opening my grip when behind me, the gunman with the Rueger Magnum sat up groggily, lifted the weapon, tried to brace himself against the ship's movement and fired at me. The heavy bullet cracked past my ear, almost splitting my eardrum and it hit the coshman in the centre of his chest. It picked him up and hurled him backwards across the deck. He hung in the rigging of the foremast with his arms spread like those of a derelict scarecrow, and with a desperate lunge I followed him out on to the deck and rolled to my feet still clutching the life-jacket.

Behind me the Rueger roared again and I heard the bullet splinter the coping of the hatch. Three running strides carried me to the rail and I dived over the side in a gut-swooping drop until I hit the black water flat, but I was dragged deep as the boil of the propellers caught me and swirled me under.

The water was shockingly cold, it seemed to drive in the walls of my lungs and probe with icy lances into the marrow of my bones.

The life-jacket helped pull me to the surface at last and I looked wildly about me. The lights of the coast seemed clear and very bright, twinkling whitely across the black water. Out here in the seaway there was a chop and swell to the surface, alternately lifting and dropping me.

*Mandrake* slid steadily onwards towards the black void of the open sea. With all her lights blazing she looked as festive as a cruise ship as she sailed away from me.

Awkwardly I rid myself of my shoes and jacket, then I managed to get my arms into the sleeves of the life-jacket. When I looked again *Mandrake* was a mile away, but suddenly she began to turn and from her bridge the long white beam of a spotlight leaped out and began to probe lightly and dance across the surface of the dark sea.

Quickly I looked again towards the land, seeking and finding the riding lights of the buoy at English Ground and relating it to the lighthouse on Flatholm. Within seconds the relative bearing of the two lights had altered slightly, the tide was ebbing and the current was setting westerly. I turned with it and began to swim.

The *Mandrake* had slowed and was creeping back towards me. The spotlight turned and flared, swept and searched, and steadily it came down towards me.

I pushed with the current, using a long side stroke so as not to break the surface and show white water, restraining myself from going into an overarm stroke as the brightly lit ship crept closer. The beam of the spotlight was searching the open water on the far side of *Mandrake* as she drew level with me.

The current had pushed me out of her track, and the *Mandrake* was as close as she would come on this leg – about one hundred and fifty yards off

- but I could see the men on her bridge. Manny Resnick's blue silk gown glowed like a butterfly's wing in the bridge lights and I could hear his voice raised angrily, but could not make out the words.

The beam reached towards me like the long cold white finger of an accuser. It quartered the sea in a tight search pattern, back and across, back and across, the next pass must catch me. It reached the end of its traverse, swung out and came back. I lay full in the path of the swinging beam, but at the instant it swept over me, a chance push of the sea lifted a swell of dark water and I dropped into the trough. The light washed over me, diffused by the crest of the swell, and it did not check. It swept onwards in the relentless search pattern.

They had missed me. They were going on, back towards the mouth of the Severn. I lay in the harsh embrace of the canvas life-jacket and watched them bear away and I felt sick and nauseated with relief and the reaction from violence. But I was free. All I had to worry about now was how long it would take to freeze to death.

I began swimming again, watching *Mandrake*'s lights dwindle and lose themselves against the spangled backdrop of the shore.

I had left my wristwatch in the forecastle so I did not know how long it was before I lost all sense of feeling in my arms and legs. I tried to keep swimming but I was not sure if my limbs were responding.

I began to feel a wonderful floating sense of release. The lights of the land faded out, and I seemed to be wrapped in warmth and soft white clouds. I thought that if this was dying it wasn't as bad as its propaganda, and I giggled, lying sodden and helpless in the life-jacket.

I wondered with interest why my vision had gone, it wasn't the way I had heard it told. Then suddenly I realized that the sea fog had come down in the dawn, and it was this that had blinded me. However, the morning light was growing in strength, I could see clearly twenty feet into the eddying fog banks.

I closed my eyes and fell asleep; my last thought was that this was probably my last thought. It made me giggle again as darkness swept over me.

Voices woke me, voices very clear and close in the fog, the rich and lovely Welsh accents roused me. I tried to shout, and with a sense of great achievement it came out like the squawk of a gull.

Out of the fog loomed the dark ungainly shape of an ancient lobster boat. It was on the drift, setting pots, and two men hung over the side, intent on their labours.

I squawked again and one of the men looked up. I had an impression of pale blue eyes in a weathered and heavily lined ruddy face, cloth cap and an old briar pipe gripped in broken yellow teeth.

'Good morning,' I croaked.

'Jesus!' said the lobster man around the stem of his pipe.

I sat in the tiny wheelhouse wrapped in a filthy old blanket, and drank steaming unsweetened tea from a chipped enamel mug – shivering so violently that the mug leaped and twitched in my cupped hands.

My whole body was a lovely shade of blue, and returning circulation was excruciating agony in my joints. My two rescuers were taciturn men, with a marvellous sense of other people's privacy, probably bred into them by a long line of buccaneers and smugglers.

By the time they had set their pots and cleared for the homeward run it was after noon and I had thawed out. My clothes had dried over the stove in the miniature galley and I had a belly full of brown bread and smoked mackerel sandwiches.

We went into Port Talbot, and when I tried to pay them with my rumpled fivers for their help, the older of the two lobster men turned a blue and frosty eye upon me.

'Any time I win a man back from the sea, I'm paid in full, mister. Keep your money.'

The journey back to London was a nightmare of country buses and night trains. When I stumbled out of Paddington Station at ten o'clock the next morning I understood why a pair of bobbies paused in their majestic pacing to study my face. I must have looked like an escaped convict.

The cabby ran a world-weary eye over my two days' growth of dark stiff beard, the swollen lip and the bruised eye. 'Did her husband come home early, mate?' he asked, and I groaned weakly.

Sherry North opened the door to her uncle's apartment and stared at me with huge startled blue eyes.

'Oh my God, Harry! What on earth happened to you? You look terrible.'

'Thanks,' I said. 'That really cheers me up.'

She caught my arm and drew me into the apartment. 'I've been going out of my mind. Two days. I've even called the police, the hospitals – everywhere I could think of.'

The uncle was hovering in the background and his presence set my nerves on edge. I refused the offer of a bath and clean clothes – and instead I took Sherry back with me to the Windsor Arms.

I left the door to the bathroom open while I shaved and bathed so that we could talk, and although she kept out of direct line of sight while I was in the tub, I thought it was developing a useful sense of intimacy between us.

I told her in detail of my abduction by Manny Resnick's trained gorillas, and of my escape – making no attempt to play down my own heroic role – and she listened in a silence that I could only believe was fascinated admiration.

I emerged from the bath with a towel wound round my waist and sat on the bed to finish the tale while Sherry doctored my cuts and abrasions.

'You'll have to go to the police now, Harry,' she said at last. 'They tried to murder you.'

'Sherry, my darling girl, please don't keep talking about the police. You make me nervous.'

'But, Harry –'

'Forget about the police, and order some food for us. I haven't eaten since I can remember.'

The hotel kitchen sent up a fine grilling of bacon and tomatoes, fried eggs, toast and tea. While I ate, I tried to relate the recent rapid turn of events to our previous knowledge, and alter our plans to fit in.

'By the way, you were on the list of expendables. They didn't intend merely holding a barbecue with your fingers. Manny Resnick was convinced that his boys had killed you –' and a queasy expression passed over her lovely face. 'They were apparently getting rid of anyone who knew anything at all about the *Dawn Light*.'

I took another mouthful of egg and bacon and chewed in silence.

'At least we have a timetable now. Manny's charter – which is incidentally called *Mandrake* – looks very fast and powerful, but it's still going to take him three or four weeks to get out to the islands. It gives us time.'

She poured tea for me, milk last the way I like it.

'Thanks, Sherry, you are an angel of mercy.' She stuck out her tongue at me, and I went on, 'Whatever it is we are looking for, it just has to be something extraordinary. That motor yacht Manny has hired himself looks like the Royal Yacht. He must be laying out close to a hundred thousand pounds on this little lark. God, I wish we knew what those five cases contain. I tried to sound Manny out – but he laughed at me. Told me I knew or I wouldn't be taking so much trouble –'

'Oh, Harry.' Sherry's face lit up. 'You've given us the bad news – now stand by for the good.'

'I could stand a little.'

'You know Jimmy's note on the letter – B. Mus?'

I nodded. 'Bachelor of Music?'

'No, idiot – British Museum.'

'I'm afraid you just lost me.'

'I was discussing it with Uncle Dan. He recognized it immediately. It's a reference to a work in the library of the British Museum. He holds a reader's card. He's researching a book, and works there often.'

'Could we get in there?'

'We'll give it a college try.'

I waited almost two hours beneath the vast golden and blue dome of the Reading Room at the British Museum, and the craving for a cheroot was like a vice around my chest.

I did not know what to expect – I had simply filled in the withdrawals form with Jimmy North's reference number – so when at last the attendant laid a thick volume before me, I seized it eagerly.

It was a Secker and Warburg edition, first published in 1963. The author was a Doctor P. A. Ready and the title was printed in gold on the spine: LEGENDARY AND LOST TREASURES OF THE WORLD.

I lingered over the closed book, teasing myself a little, and I wondered what chain of coincidence and luck had allowed Jimmy North to follow this paperchase of ancient clues. Had he read this book first in his burning obsession with wrecks and sea treasure and had he then stumbled on the batch of old letters? I would never know.

There were forty-nine chapters, each listing a separate item. I read carefully down the list.

There were Aztec treasures of gold, the plate and bullion of Panama, buccaneer hoards, a lost goldmine in the Rockies of North America, a valley of diamonds in South Africa, treasure ships of the Armada, the *Lutine* bullion ship from which the famous *Lutine* Bell at Lloyd's had been recovered, Alexandra the Great's chariot of gold, more treasure ships – both ancient and modern – from the Second World War to the sack of Troy, treasures of Mussolini, Prester John, Darius, Roman generals, privateers and pirates of Barbary and Coromandel. It was a vast profusion of fact and fancy, history and conjecture. The treasures of lost cities and forgotten civilizations, from Atlantis to the fabulous golden city of the Kalahari Desert – there was so much of it, and I did not know where to look.

With a sigh I turned to the first page, ducking the introduction and preface. I began to read.

By five o'clock I had skimmed through sixteen chapters which could not possibly relate to the *Dawn Light* and had read five others in depth and by this time I understood how Jimmy North could have been bitten by the romance and excitement of the treasure hunter. It was making me itchy also – these stories of great riches, abandoned, waiting merely to be gathered up by someone with the luck and fortitude to ferret them out.

I glanced at the new Japanese watch with which I'd replaced my Omega, and hurried out of the massive stone portals of the museum and crossed Great Russell Street to my rendezvous with Sherry. She was waiting in the crowded saloon bar of the Running Stag.

'Sorry,' I said, 'I forgot the time.'

'Come on.' She grabbed my arm. 'I'm dying of thirst and curiosity.'

I gave her a pint of bitter for her thirst, but could only inflame her curiosity with the title of the book. She wanted to send me back to the library, before I had finished my supper of ham and turkey from the carvery behind the bar, but I held out and managed to smoke half a cheroot before she drove me out into the cold.

I gave her the key to my room at the Windsor Arms, placed her in a cab and told her to wait for me there. Then I hurried back to the Reading Room.

The next chapter of the book was entitled 'THE GREAT MOGUL AND THE TIGER THRONE OF INDIA.'

It began with a brief historical introduction describing how Babur, descendant of Timur and Genghis Khan, the two infamous scourges of the ancient world, crossed the mountains into northern India and established the Mogul Empire. I recognized immediately that this fell within the area of my interest, the *Dawn Light* had been outward bound from that ancient continent.

The history covered the period of Babur's illustrious successors, Muslim rulers who rose to great power and influence, who built mighty cities and left behind such monuments to man's sense of beauty as the Taj Mahal. Finally it described the decline of the dynasty, and its destruction in the first year of the Indian mutiny when the avenging British forces stormed and sacked the ancient citadel and fortress at Delhi – shooting the Mogul princes out of hand and throwing the old emperor Bahadur Shah into captivity.

Then abruptly the author switched his attention from the vast sweep of history.

In 1665 Jean Baptiste Tavernier, a French traveller and jeweller, visited the court of the Mogul Emperor Aurangzeb. Five years later he published in Paris his celebrated *Travels in the Orient.* He seems to have won special favour from the Muslim Emperor, for he was allowed to enter the fabled treasure chambers of the citadel and to catalogue various items of special interest. Amongst these was a diamond which he named the 'Great Mogul'. Tavernier weighed this stone and listed its bulk at 280 carats. He described this paragon as possessing extraordinary fire and a colour as clear and white 'as the great North Star of the heavens'.

Tavernier's host informed him that the stone had been recovered from the famed Golconda Mines in about 1650 and that the rough stone had been a monstrous 787 carats.

The cut of the stone was a distinctive rounded rose, but was not symmetrical – being proud on the one side. The stone has been unrecorded since that time and many believe that Tavernier actually saw the Koh-i-noor or the Orloff. However, it is highly improbable that such a trained observer and craftsman as Tavernier could have erred so widely in his weights and descriptions. The Koh-i-noor before it was recut in London weighed a mere 191 carats, and was certainly not a rose cut. The Orloff, although rose cut, was and is a symmetrical gem stone and weighs 199 carats. The descriptions simply cannot be mated with that of Tavernier, and all the evidence points to the existence of a huge white diamond that has dropped out of the known world.

In 1739 when Nadir Shah of Persia entered India and captured Delhi, he made no attempt to hold his conquest, but contented himself with vast booty, which included the Koh-i-noor diamond and the peacock throne of Shah Jehan. It seems probable that the Great Mogul diamond was overlooked by the rapacious Persian and that after his withdrawal, Mohammed Shah the incumbent Mogul Emperor, deprived of his traditional throne, ordered the construction of a substitute. However, the existence of this new treasure was veiled in secrecy and although there are references to its existence in the native accounts, only one European reference can be cited.

The journal of the English Ambassador to the Court of Delhi during the year of 1747, Sir Thomas Jenning, describes an audience granted by the Mogul Emperor at which he was 'clad in precious silks and bedecked with flowers and jewels, seated upon a great throne of gold. The shape of the throne was as of a fierce tiger, with gaping jaws and a single glittering cyclopean eye. The body of the tiger was amazingly worked with all manner of precious stones. His majesty was gracious enough to allow me to approach the throne closely and to examine the eye of the tiger which he assured me was a great diamond descended from the reign of his ancestor Aurangzeb.'

Was this Tavernier's 'Great Mogul' now incorporated into the 'Tiger Throne of India'? If it was, then credence is given to a strange set of circumstances which must end our study of this lost treasure.

In 1857 on the 16th September, desperate street fighting filled the streets of Delhi with heaps of dead and wounded, and the outcome of the struggle hung in the balance as the British forces and loyal native troops fought to clear the city of the mutinous sepoys and seize the ancient fortress that dominated the city.

While the fighting raged within, a force of loyal native troops from 101st regiment under two European officers was ordered to cross the river and encircle the walls to seize the road to the north. This was in order to prevent members of the Mogul royal family or rebel leaders from escaping the doomed city.

The two European officers were Captain Matthew Long and Colonel Sir Roger Goodchild—

The name leapt out of the page at me not only because someone had underlined it in pencil. In the margin, also in pencil, was one of Jimmy North's characteristic exclamation marks. Master James's disrespect for books included those belonging to such a venerable institution as the British Museum. I found I was shaking again, and my cheeks felt hot with excitement. This was the last fragment missing from the puzzle. It was all here now and my eyes raced on across the page.

No one will ever know now what happened on that night on a lonely road through the Indian jungle – but six months later, Captain Long and the Indian Subahdar, Ram Panat, gave evidence at the court martial of Colonel Goodchild.

They described how they had intercepted a party of Indian nobles fleeing the burning city. The party included three Muslim priests and two princes of the royal blood. In the presence of Captain Long one of the princes attempted to buy their freedom by offering to lead the British officers to a great treasure, a golden throne shaped like a tiger and with a single diamond eye.

The officers agreed, and the princes led them into the forest to a jungle mosque. In the courtyard of the mosque were six bullock carts. The drivers had deserted, and when the British officers dismounted and examined the contents of these vehicles they proved indeed to contain a golden throne statue of a tiger. The throne had been broken down into four separate parts to facilitate transportation – hindquarters, trunk, forequarters and head. In the light of the lanterns these fragments nestled in beds of straw, blazing with gold and encrusted with precious and semi-precious stones.

Colonel Roger Goodchild then ordered that the princes and priests should be executed out of hand. They were lined up against the outer wall of the mosque and despatched with a volley of musketry. The Colonel himself walked amongst the fallen noblemen administering the *coup-de-grâce* with his service revolver. The corpses were afterwards thrown into a well outside the walls of the mosque.

The two officers now separated, Captain Long with most of the native troops returning to the patrol of the city walls, while the Colonel, Subahdar Ram Panat and fifteen sepoys rode off with the bullock carts.

The Indian Subahdar's evidence at the court martial described how they had taken the precious cargo westwards passing through the British lines by the Colonel's authority. They camped three days at a small native village. Here the local carpenter and his two sons laboured under the Colonel's direction to manufacture four sturdy wooden crates to hold the four parts of the throne. The Colonel in the meantime set about removing from the statue the stones and jewels that were set into the metal. The position of each was carefully noted on a diagram prepared by Goodchild and the stones were numbered and packed into an iron chest of the type used by army paymasters for the safekeeping of coin and specie in the field.

Once the throne and the stones had been packed into the four crates and iron chest, they were loaded once more on to the bullock carts and the journey towards the railhead at Allahabad was continued.

The luckless carpenter and his sons were obliged to join the convoy. The Subahdar recalled that when the road entered an area of dense forest, the Colonel dismounted and led the three craftsmen amongst the trees. Six pistol shots rang out and the Colonel returned alone.

I broke off my reading for a few moments to reflect on the character of the gallant Colonel. I should have liked to introduce him to Manny Resmick, they would have had much in common. I grinned at the thought and read on.

The convoy reached Allahabad on the sixth day and the Colonel claimed military priority to place his five crates upon a troop train returning to Bombay. Having done this he and his small command rejoined the regiment at Delhi.

Six months later, Captain Long supported by the Indian Petty Officer, Ram Panat, brought charges against the commanding officer. We can believe that thieves had fallen out, Colonel Goodchild had perhaps decided that one share was better than three. Be that as it may, nothing has since given a clue to the whereabouts of the treasure.

The trial conducted in Bombay was a *cause célèbre* and was widely reported in India and at home. However, the weakness of the prosecution's case was that there was no booty to show, and dead men tell no tales.

The Colonel was found not guilty. However, the pressure of the scandal left him no choice but to resign his commission and return to London. If he managed somehow to take with him the Great Mogul diamond and the golden tiger throne, his subsequent career gave no evidence of his possessing great wealth. In partnership with a notorious lady of the town he opened a gaming house in the Bayswater Road which soon acquired an unsavoury reputation. Colonel Sir Roger Goodchild died in 1871, probably from tertiary syphilis contracted during his remarkable career in India. His death revived stories of the fabulous throne, but these soon subsided for lack of hard facts and the secret passed on with that sporting gentleman.

Perhaps we should have headed this chapter – 'The Treasure That Never Was'.

'Not on, cock,' I thought happily. 'It was – and is.' And I began once more at the beginning of the story, but this time I made careful notes for Sherry's benefit.

She was waiting for me when I returned, sitting wakefully in the armchair by the window, and she flew at me when I entered.

'Where have you been?' she demanded, 'I've been sitting here all evening eating my heart out with curiosity.'

'You are not going to believe it,' I told her, and I thought she might do me a violence.

'Harry Fletcher, you've got ten seconds to cut out the introductory speeches and give me the goodies – after that I scratch your eyes out.'

We talked until long after midnight, and by then we had the floor strewn with papers over which we pored on knees and elbows. There was an Admiralty Chart of the St Mary's Archipelago, the copies of the drawings of the *Dawn Light,* the notes I had made of the mate's description of the wreck, and those I had made in the Reading Room of the British Museum.

I had out my silver travelling flask and we drank Chivas Regal from the plastic tooth mug as we argued and schemed – trying to guess in what section of the *Dawn Light*'s hull the five crates had been stowed, guessing also how she had broken up on the reef, what part of her had been washed into the break and what part had fallen to the seaward side.

I had made sketches of a dozen eventualities, and I had opened a running list of my minimum equipment requirements for an expedition, to which I added, as various items came to mind, or as Sherry made intelligent suggestions.

I had forgotten that she must be a first rate scuba diver, but I was reminded of this as we talked. I was aware now that she would not be a passenger on this expedition, my feelings towards her were becoming tinged with professional respect, and the mood of exhilaration mixed with cama-raderie was building to a crescendo of physical tension.

Sherry's pale smooth cheeks were flushed with excitement, and we were shoulder to shoulder as we knelt on the carpeted floor. She turned to say something, she was chuckling and the blue lights in her eyes were teasing and inviting, only inches from mine.

Suddenly all the golden thrones and legendary diamonds in this world must wait their turn. We both recognized the moment, and we turned to each other with unashamed eagerness. We were in a consuming fever of urgency, and we became lovers without rising from the floor, right on top of the drawings of the *Dawn Light* – which was probably the happiest thing that had ever happened to that ill-starred vessel.

When at last I lifted her to the bed and we twined our bodies together beneath the quilt, I knew that all the brief amorous acrobatics that had preceded my meeting with this woman were meaningless. What I had just experienced transcended the flesh and became a thing of the spirit – and if it was not loving, then it was the nearest thing to it that I would ever know.

My voice was husky and unsteady with wonder as I tried to explain it to her. She lay quietly against my chest, listening to the words I had never spoken to another woman, and she squeezed me when I stopped talking – which was clearly a command to continue. I think I was still talking when we both fell asleep.


From the air, St Mary's has the shape of one of those strange fish from the ocean's abysmal depths, a squat mis-shapen body with stubby body fins and tailfins in unusual places, and a huge mouth many sizes too big for the rest of it.

The mouth was Grand Harbour and the town nestled in the hinge of the jaws. The iron roofs flash like signal mirrors from the dark green cloak of vegetation. The aircraft circled the island, treating the passengers to a vista of snowy white beaches and water so clear that each detail of the reefs and deeps were whorled and smeared below the surface like some vast surrealistic painting.

Sherry pressed her face to the round Perspex window and exclaimed with delight as the Fokker Friendship sank down over the pineapple fields where the women paused in their labours to look up at us. We touched down and taxied to the single tiny airport building on which a billboard announced 'St Mary's Island – Pearl of the Indian Ocean' and below the sign stood two other pearls of great price.

I had cabled Chubby and he had brought Angelo with him to welcome us. Angelo rushed to the barrier to embrace me and grab my bag, and I introduced him to Sherry.

Angelo's whole manner underwent a profound change. On the island there is one mark of beauty that is esteemed above all else. A girl might have buck teeth and a squint, but if she possessed a 'clear' complexion she would have suitors forming squadrons around her. A clear complexion did not mean that she was free of acne, it was rather a gauge of the colour of the skin – and Sherry must have had one of the clearest complexions ever to land on the island.

Angelo stared at her in a semi-catatonic state as she shook his hand. Then he roused himself, handed me back my bag and instead took hers from her hand. He then fell in a few paces behind her, like a faithful hound, staring at her solemnly and only breaking into his flashing smile whenever she glanced in his direction. He was her slave from the first moment.

Chubby trundled forward to meet us with more dignity, as big and timeless as a cliff of dark granite, and his face was contorted in a frown of even greater ferocity than usual as he took my hand in a huge horny fist and muttered something to the effect that it was good to see me back.

He stared at Sherry and she quailed a little beneath the ferocity of his gaze, but then something happened that I had never seen before. Chubby lifted his battered old sea cap from his head, exposing the gleaming polished brown dome of his pate in an unheard-of display of gallantry, and he smiled so widely that we could see the pink plastic gums of his artificial teeth. He pushed Angelo aside when Sherry's bags were brought out of the hold, picked up one in each hand and led her to the pick-up. Angelo followed her devotedly and I struggled along in the rear under the weight of my own luggage. It was fairly obvious that my crew approved of my choice, for once.

We sat in the kitchen of Chubby's house and Mrs Chubby fed us on banana cake and coffee while Chubby and I worked out a business deal. For a hard-bargained fee, he would charter his stump boat with its two spanking new Evinrude motors for an indefinite period. He and Angelo would crew it at the old wages, and there would be a large 'billfish bonus' at the end of the charter, if it were successful. I went into no detail as to the object of the expedition, but merely let them know that we would be camping on the outer islands of the group and that Sherry and I would be working underwater.

By the time we had agreed and slapped hands on the bargain, the traditional island rite of agreement, it was mid-afternoon and the island fever had already started to reassert its hold on my constitution. Island fever prevents the sufferer from doing today what can reasonably be put off until the morrow, so we left Chubby and Angelo to begin their preparations while Sherry and I stopped only briefly at Missus Eddy's for provisions before pushing the pick-up over the ridge and down through the palms to Turtle Bay.

'It's story book,' murmured Sherry, as she stood under the thatch on the wide veranda of the shack. 'It's make-believe.' She shook her head at the sway-boled palm trees and the aching white sands beyond.

I went to stand behind her, placing my arms around her middle and drawing her to me. She leaned back against me, crossing her own arms over mine and squeezing my hands.

'Oh, Harry, I didn't think it would be like this.' There was a change taking place within her, I could sense it clearly. She was like a winter plant, too long denied the sun, but there were reserves in her that I could not fathom and they troubled me. She was not a simple person, nor easily understood. There were barriers, conflicts within her that showed only as dark shadows in the depths of her ocean-blue eyes, shadows like those of killer sharks swimming deep. More than once when she believed herself unobserved I had caught her looking at me in a manner which seemed at once calculating and hostile – as though she hated me.

That had been before we came to the island, and now it seemed that, like the winter plant, she was blooming in the sun; as though here she could cast aside some restraint of the soul which had curbed her spirit before.

She kicked off her shoes, and barefooted turned within my encircling arms to stand upon tiptoe to kiss me.

'Thank you, Harry. Thank you for bringing me here.'

Mrs Chubby had swept the floors and aired the linen, placed flowers in the jars and charged the refrigerator. We walked through the shack hand in hand – and though Sherry murmured admiration for the utilitarian décor and solid masculine furnishings, yet I thought I detected that gleam in her eye which a woman gets just before she starts pushing the furniture around and throwing out the lovingly accumulated but humble treasures of a man's lifetime.

As she paused to rearrange the bowl of flowers that Mrs Chubby had placed upon the broad camphor-wood refectory table, I knew we were going to see some changes at Turtle Bay – but strangely the thought did not perturb me. I realized suddenly that I was sick to death of being my own cook and housekeeper.

We changed into swimsuits in the main bedroom – for I had found in the very few hours since we had become lovers that Sherry had an overdeveloped sense of personal modesty, and I knew it would take time before I could wean her to the standard casual Turtle Bay swimming attire. However, it was some compensation for my temporary overdress to see Sherry North in a bikini.

It was the first time I had really had an opportunity to look at her openly. The most striking single thing about her was the texture and lustre of her skin. She was tall, and if her shoulders were too wide and her hips a little too narrow, her waist was tiny and her belly was flat with a small delicately chiselled navel. I have always thought that the Turks were right in considering the navel as a highly erotic portion of a woman's anatomy – Sherry's would have launched a thousand ships.

She didn't like me staring at it. 'Oh, Grandma – what big eyes you've got,' she said, and wrapped a towel around her waist like a sarong. But she walked barefooted through the sand with an unconscious push and sway of buttock and breast that I watched with uninhibited pleasure.

We left our towels above the high water mark and ran down over the hard wet sand to the edge of the clear warm sea. She swam with a deceptively slow and easy stroke, that drove her through the water so swiftly that I had to reach out myself and drive hard to catch and hold her.

Beyond the reef we trod water and she was puffing a little. 'Out of training,' she panted.

While we rested I looked out to sea and at that moment a line of black fins broke the surface together in line abreast, bearing down on us swiftly and I could not restrain my delight.

'You are an honoured guest,' I told her. 'This is a special welcome.' The dolphins circled us, like a pack of excited puppies, gambolling and squeaking while they looked Sherry over carefully. I have known them sheer away from most strangers, and it was a rarity for them to allow themselves to be touched on a first meeting and then only after assiduous wooing. However, with Sherry it was love at first sight, almost of the calibre that Chubby and Angelo had demonstrated.

Within fifteen minutes they were dragging her on the Nantucket sleigh ride while she squealed with glee. The instant she fell off the back of one, there was another prodding her with his snout, competing fiercely for her attention.

When at last they had exhausted us both and we swam in wearily to the beach, one of the big bull dolphin followed Sherry into water so shallow it reached to her waist. There he rolled on his back while she scratched his belly with handfuls of coarse white sand and he grinned that fixed idiotic dolphin grin.

After dark, while we sat on the veranda and drank whisky together, we could still hear the old bull whistling and slapping the water with his tail, in an attempt to seduce her into the sea again.

The next morning I gamely fought off a fresh onslaught of island fever, and the temptation to linger in bed, especially as Sherry awoke beside me with the pink glossy look of a little girl, and her eyes were clear, her breath sweet and her lips languorous.

We had to check through the equipment we had salvaged from *Wave Dancer,* and we needed an engine to drive the compressor. Chubby was sent off with a fistful of banknotes and returned with a motor that required much loving attention. As that occupied me for the rest of the day, Sherry was sent off to Missus Eddy's for camping equipment and provisions. We had set a three-day deadline for our departure and our schedule was tight.

It was still dark when we took our places in the boat, Chubby and Angelo at the motors in the stern and Sherry and I perched like sparrows on top of the load.

The dawn was a flaming glory of gold and hot red, promise of another fiery day, as Chubby took us northwards on a course possible only for a small boat and a good skipper. We ran close in on island and reef, sometimes with only eighteen inches of water between our keel and the fierce coral fangs.

All of us were in a mood of anticipation. I truly do not believe it was the prospect of vast wealth that excited me then – all I really needed in my life was another good boat like *Wave Dancer* – rather it was the thought of rare and exquisite treasure, and the chance to win it back from the sea. If what we sought had been merely bullion in bars or coin I do do not think it would have intrigued me half as much. The sea was the adversary and once more we were pitted against each other.

The blazing colours of the dawn faded into the hard hot blue of the sky as the sun rose out of the sea, and Sherry North stood up in the bows to strip off her denim jacket and jeans. Under them she wore her bikini and now she folded the clothes away into her canvas duffle bag and produced a tube of sun lotion with which she began to anoint her fine pale body.

Chubby and Angelo reacted with undisguised horror. They held a hurried and scandalized consultation after which Angelo was sent forward with a sheet of canvas to rig a sun shelter for Sherry. There followed a heated exchange between Angelo and Sherry.

'You will damage your skin, Miss Sherry,' Angelo protested, but she drove him in defeat back to the stern.

There the two of them sat like mourners at a wake, Chubby's whole face creased into a huge brown scowl and Angelo openly wringing his hands in anxiety. Finally, they could stand it no longer and after another whispered discussion Angelo was elected as emissary once more and he crawled forward over the cargo to enlist my support.

'You can't let her do it, Mister Harry,' Angelo pleaded. 'She will go *dark.*'

'I think that's the idea, Angelo,' I told him. However, I did warn Sherry to take care of the sun at noon. Obediently she covered herself when we ran ashore on a sandy beach to eat our midday meal.

It was the middle of the afternoon when we raised the triple peaks of the Old Men and Sherry exclaimed, 'Just as the old mate described them.'

We approached the island from the sea side, through the narrow stretch of calm water between the island and the reef. When we passed the entrance to the channel through which I had taken *Wave Dancer* to escape from the Zinballa crash boat, Chubby and I grinned at each other in fond recollection, then I turned to Sherry and pointed it out to her.

'I plan to set up our base camp on the island, and we will use the gap to reach the area of the wreck.'

'It looks a little risky.' She eyed the narrow channel with reserve.

'It will save us a round journey of nearly twenty miles each day – and it isn't as bad as it looks. Once I took my big fifty-foot cruiser through there at full throttle.'

'You must be crazy.' She pushed her dark glasses up on top of her head to look at me.

'By now you should be a good judge of that.' I grinned at her, and she grinned back.

'I am an expert already,' she boasted. The sun had darkened the freckles on her nose and cheeks and given her skin a glow. She had one of those rare skins that do not redden and become angry when exposed to sunlight. Instead, it was the kind that quickly turned a golden honey brown.

It was high tide when we rounded the northern tip of the island into a protected cove and Chubby ran the whaleboat on to the sand only twenty yards from the first line of palm trees.

We off-loaded the cargo, carrying it up amongst the palms well above the high-water mark and once again covered it with tarpaulins to protect it from the ubiquitous sea salt.

It was late by the time we had finished. The heat had gone out of the sun, and the long shadows of the palms barred the earth as we trudged inland, carrying only our personal gear and a five-gallon container of fresh water. In the back of the most northerly peak, generations of visiting fishermen had scratched out a series of shallow caves in the steep slope.

I selected a large cave to act as our equipment store, and a smaller one as living quarters for Sherry and me. Chubby and Angelo chose another for themselves, about a hundred yards along the slope and screened from us by a patch of scrub.

I left Sherry to sweep out our new quarters with a brush improvised from a palm frond, and to lay out our sleeping bags on the inflatable mattress while I took my cast net and went back to the cove.

It was dark when I returned with a string of a dozen big striped mullet. Angelo had the fire burning and the kettle bubbling. We ate in contented silence, and afterwards Sherry and I lay together in our cave and listened to the big fiddler crabs clicking and scratching amongst the palms.

It's primeval,' Sherry whispered, 'as though we are the first man and woman in the world.'

'Me Tarzan, you Jane,' I agreed, and she chuckled and drew closer to me.

In the dawn Chubby set off alone in the whaleboat on the long return journey to St Mary's. He would return next day with a full load of petrol and fresh water in jerry-cans. Sufficient to last us for two weeks or so.

While we waited for him to return, Angelo and I took on the wearying task of carrying all the equipment and stores up to the caves. I set up the compressor, charged the empty air bottles and checked the diving gear, and Sherry arranged hanging space for our clothes and generally made our quarters comfortable.

The next day, she and I roamed the island, climbing the peaks and exploring the valleys and beaches between. I had hoped to find water, a spring or well overlooked by the other visitors – but naturally there was none. Those canny old fishermen overlooked nothing.

The south end of the island, farthest from our camp, was impenetrable with salt marsh between the peak and the sea. We skirted the acres of evil-smelling mud and thick swamp grass. The air was rank and heavy with rotted vegetation and dead fish.

Colonies of red and purple crabs had covered the mudflats with their holes from which they peered stalk-eyed as we passed. In the mangroves, the herons were breeding, perched long-legged upon their huge shaggy nests, and once I heard a splash and saw the swirl of something in one of the swamp pools that could only have been a crocodile. We left the fever swamps and we climbed to the higher ground, then we picked our way through the thickets of shrub growth towards the southernmost peak.

Sherry decided we must climb this one also. I tried to dissuade her for it was the tallest and steepest. My protests went completely unnoticed, and even after we had made our way on to a narrow ledge below the southern cliff of the peak, she pressed on determinedly.

'If the mate of the *Dawn Light* found a way to the top – then I'm going up there too,' she announced.

'You'll get the same view from there as from the other peaks,' I pointed out.

'That's not the point.'

'What is the point, then?' I asked, and she gave me the pitying look usually reserved for small children and half-wits, refused to dignify the question with an answer, and continued her cautious sideways shuffle along the ledge.

There was a drop of at least two hundred feet below us, and if there is one deficiency in my formidable arsenal of talent and courage, it is that I have no head for heights. However, I would rather have balanced on one leg atop St Paul's Cathedral than admit this to Miss North, and so with great reluctance I followed her.

Fortunately it was only a few paces farther that she uttered a cry of triumph and turned off the ledge into a narrow vertical crack that split the cliff-face. The fracturing of the rock had formed a stepped and readily climbable chimney to the summit, into which I followed her with relief. Almost immediately Sherry cried out again.

'Oh dear God, Harry, look!' and she pointed to a protected area of the wall, in the back of the dark recess. Somebody long ago had patiently chipped an inscription into the flat stone surface.

A. BARLOW.
WRECKED ON THIS PLACE
14th OCT. 1858.

As we stared at it, I felt her hand grope for mine and squeeze for comfort. No longer the intrepid mountaineer, her expression was half fearful as she studied the writing.

'It's creepy,' she whispered. 'It looks as though it was written yesterday – not all those years ago.'

Indeed, the letters had been protected from weathering so that they seemed fresh cut and I glanced around almost as though I expected to see the old seaman watching us.

When at last we climbed the steep chimney to the summit we were still subdued by that message from the remote past. We sat there for almost two hours watching the surf break in long white lines upon Gunfire Reef. The gap in the reef and the great dark pool of the Break showed very clearly from our vantage point, while it was just possible to make out the course of the narrow channel through the coral. From here Arthur Barlow had watched the *Dawn Light* in her death throes, watched her broken up by the high surf.

'Time is running against us now, Sherry,' I told her, as the holiday mood of the last few days evaporated. 'It's fourteen days since Manny Resnick sailed in the *Mandrake*. He will not be far from Cape Town by now. We will know when he reaches there.'

'How?'

'I have an old friend who lives there. He is a member of the Yacht Club – and he will watch the traffic and cable me the moment *Mandrake* docks.'

I looked down the back slope of the peak, and for the first time noticed the blue haze of smoke spreading through the tops of the palms from Angelo's cooking fire.

'I have been a little half-arsed on this trip,' I muttered, 'we have been behaving like a group of school kids on a picnic. From now on we will have to tighten up the security – just across the channel there is my old friend Suleiman Dada, and *Mandrake* will be in these waters sooner than I'd like. We will have to keep a nice low silhouette from now on.'

'How long will we need, do you think?' Sherry asked.

'I don't know, my sweeting – but be sure that it will be longer than we think possible. We are shackled by the need to ferry all our water and petrol from St Mary's – we will only be able to work in the pool during a few hours of each tide when the condition and the height of the water will let us. Who knows what we are going to find in there once we start, and finally we may discover that the Colonel's parcels were stowed in the rear hold of the *Dawn Light* – that part of the ship that was carried out into the open water. If it was, then you can kiss it all goodbye.'

'We've been over that part of it before, you dreadful old pessimist,' Sherry rebuked me. 'Think happy thoughts.'

So we thought happy thoughts and did happy things until at last I made out the tiny dark speck, like a water beetle on the brazen surface of the sea, as Chubby returned from St Mary's in the whaleboat.

We climbed down the peak and hurried back through the palm groves to meet him. He was just rounding the point and entering the cove as we came out on the beach. The whaleboat was low in the water under her heavy cargo of fuel and drinking water. And Chubby stood in the stern as big and solid and as eternal as a great rock. When we waved and shouted he inclined his head gravely in acknowledgement.

Mrs Chubby had sent a banana cake for me and for Sherry a large sunhat of woven palm fronds. Chubby had obviously reported Sherry's behaviour, and his expression was more than normally lugubrious when he saw that the damage was already being done. Sherry was toasted to an edible medium rare.

It was after dark by the time we had carried fifty jerry-cans up to the cave. Then we gathered about the fire where Angelo was cooking an island chowder of clams that he had gathered from the lagoon that afternoon. It was time to tell my crew the true reason for our expedition. Chubby I could trust to say nothing, even under torture – but I had waited to get Angelo into the isolation of the island before telling him. He has been known to commit the most monstrous indiscretions – usually in an attempt to impress one of his young ladies.

They listened in silence to my explanation, and remained silent after I had finished. Angelo was waiting for a lead from Chubby – and that gentleman was not one to charge his fences. He sat scowling into the fire, and his face looked like one of those copper masks from an Aztec temple. When he had created the correct atmosphere of theatrical suspense he reached into his back pocket and produced a purse, so old and well handled that the leather was almost worn through.

'When I was a boy and fished the pool at Gunfire Break, I took a big old Daddy grouper fish. When I open his belly pouch I found this in him.' From the purse he took out a round disc. 'I kept it since then, like a good luck charm, even though I was offered ten pounds for it by an officer on one of my ships.'

He handed me the disc and I examined it in the firelight. It was a gold coin, the size of a shilling. The reverse side was covered with oriental characters which I could not read – but the obverse face bore a crest of two rampant lions supporting a shield and an armoured head. The same design as I had last seen on the bronze ship's bell at Big Gull Island. The legend below the shield read: 'AUS: REGIS & SENAT: ANGLIA.' while the rim was struck with the bold title 'ENGLISH EAST INDIA COMPANY'.

'I always promised me that I would go back to Gunfire Break – looks like this is the time,' Chubby went on, as I examined the coin minutely. There was no date on it, but I had no doubt that it was a gold mohur of the company. I had read of the coin but never seen one before.

'You got this out of a fish's gut, Chubby?' I asked, and he nodded.

'Guess that old grouper seen it shine and took a snap at it. Must have stuck in his belly until I pulled him out.'

I handed the coin back to him. 'Well then, Chubby, that goes to show there is some truth in my story.'

'Guess it does, Harry,' he admitted, and I went to the cave to fetch the drawings of the *Dawn Light* and a gas lantern. We pored over the drawings. Chubby's grandfather had sailed as a topmastman in an East Indiaman, which made Chubby something of an expert. He was of the opinion that all passengers' luggage and other small pieces would be stowed in the fore hold beside the forecastle – I wasn't going to argue with him. Never hex yourself, as Chubby had warned me so often.

When I produced my tide tables and began calculating the time differences for our latitude, Chubby actually smiled. Although it was hard to recognize it as such. It looked much more like a sneer, for Chubby had no faith in rows of printed figures in pamphlets. He preferred to judge the tides by the sea clock in his own head. I have known him to call the tides accurately for a week ahead without reference to any other source.

'I reckon we will have a high tide at one-forty tomorrow,' I announced.

'Man, you got it right for once,' Chubby agreed.


Without the enormous loads that had been forced on her recently, the whaleboat seemed to run with a new lightness and eagerness. The twin Evinrudes put her up on the plane, and she flew at the narrow channel through the reef like a ferret into a rabbit-hole.

Angelo stood in the bows, using hand signals to indicate underwater snags to Chubby in the stern. We had picked good water to come in on, and Chubby met the dying surf with confidence. The little whaleboat tossed up her head and kicked her heels over the swells, splattering us with spray.

The passage was more exhilarating than dangerous, and Sherry whooped and laughed with the thrill of it.

Chubby shot us through the narrow neck between the coral cliffs with feet to spare on each side, for the whaleboat had half of *Wave Dancer*'s beam, then we zigzagged through the twisted gut of the channel beyond and at last burst out into the pool.

'No good trying to anchor,' Chubby growled, 'it's deep here. The reef goes down sheer. We got twenty fathoms under us here and the bottom is foul.'

'How you going to hold?' I asked.

'Somebody got to sit at the motor and keep her there with power.'

'That's going to chew fuel, Chubby.'

'Don't I know it,' he growled.

With a tide only half made, the occasional wave was coming in over the reef. Not yet with much force, just a frothing spill that cascaded into the pool, turning the surface to ginger beer with bubbles. However, as the tide mounted so the surf would come over stronger. Soon it would be unsafe in the pool and we would have to run for it. We had about two hours in which to work, depending on the stage of neap and spring tides. It was a cycle of too little or too much. At low tide there was insufficient water to negotiate the entrance channel – and at high tide the surf breaking over the reef might overwhelm the open whaleboat. Each of our moves had to be finely judged.

Now every minute was precious. Sherry and I were already dressed in our wet suits with face-plates on our foreheads, and it was necessary only for Angelo to lift the heavy scuba sets on to our backs and to clinch the webbing harness.

'Ready, Sherry?' I asked, and she nodded, the ungainly mouthpiece already stuffed into her pretty mouth.

'Let's go.'

We dropped over the side, and sank down together beneath the cigar-shaped hull of the whaleboat. The surface was a moving sheet of quicksilver above us, and the spill over the reef charged the upper layer of water with a rash of champagne bubbles.

I checked with Sherry. She was comfortable, and breathing in the slow rhythm of the experienced diver that conserves air and ventilates the body effectively. She grinned at me, her lips distorted by the mouthpiece and her eyes enormously enlarged by the glass face-plate, and she gave me the high sign with both thumbs.

I pointed my head straight for the bottom and began pedalling with my swimming fins, going down fast, reluctant to waste air on a slow descent.

The pool was a dark hole below us. The surrounding walls of coral shut out much of the light, and gave it an ominous appearance. The water was cold and gloomy, I felt a prickle of almost superstitious awe. There was something sinister about this place, as though some evil and malignant force lurked in the sombre depths.

I crossed my fingers at my sides, and went on down, following the sheer coral cliff. The coral was riddled with dark caves and ledges that overhung the lower walls. Coral of a hundred different sorts, outcropped in weird and lovely shapes, tinted with the complete spectrum of colour. Weeds and marine growth waved and tossed in the movement of water, like the hands of supplicating beggars, or the dark manes of wild horses.

I looked back at Sherry. She was close behind me and she smiled again. Clearly she felt nothing of my own sense of awe. We went on down.

From secret ledges protruded the long yellow antennae of giant crayfish, gently they moved, sensing our presence in the disturbed water. Clouds of multi-coloured coral fish floated along the cliff-face; they sparkled like gemstones in the fading blue light that penetrated into the depths of the pool.

Sherry tapped my shoulder and we paused to peer into a deep black cave. Two great owl eyes peered back at us, and as my eyes became accustomed to the light I made out the gargantuan head of a grouper. It was speckled like a plover's egg, splotches of brown and black on a beige-grey ground and the mouth was a wide slash between thick rubbery lips. As we watched, the huge fish assumed a defensive attitude. It blew itself out, increasing its already impressive girth, spread the gill covers, enlarged the head and finally it opened its mouth in a gape that could have swallowed a man whole – a cavernous maw, lined with spiked teeth. Sherry seized my hand. We drew away from the cave, and the fish closed its mouth and subsided. Any time I wanted to claim a world record grouper I knew where to come looking. Even allowing for the magnifying effect of water I judged that he was close to a thousand pounds in weight.

We went on down the coral wall, and all around us was the wondrous marine world seething with life and beauty, death and danger. Lovely little damsel fish nestled in the venomous arms of giant sea anemone, immune to the deadly darts; a moray eel slid like a long black battle pennant along the coral wall, reached its lair and turned to threaten us with dreadful ragged teeth and glittering snakelike eyes.

Down we went, pedalling with our fins, and now at last I saw the bottom. It was a dark jungle of sea growth, dense stands of sea bamboo and petrified coral trees thrust out of the smothering marine foliage, while mounds and hillocks of coral were worked and riven into shapes that teased the imagination and covered I knew not what.

We hung above this impenetrable jungle and I checked my time-elapse wristwatch and depth gauge. I had one hundred and twenty-eight feet, and time elapsed was five minutes forty seconds.

I gave Sherry the hand signal to remain where she was and I sank down to the tops of the marine jungle and gingerly parted the cold slimy foliage. I worked my way down through it and emerged into a relatively open area below. It was a twilight area roofed in by the bamboo and peopled with strange new tribes of fish and marine animals.

I knew at once that it would not be a simple task to search the floor of the pool. Visibility here was ten feet or less, and the total area we must cover was two or three acres in extent.

I decided to bring Sherry down with me and for a start we would make a sweep along the base of the cliff, keeping in line abreast and within sight of each other.

I inflated my lungs and used the buoyancy to rise from the bottom, out through the thick belt of foliage into the clear.

I did not see Sherry at first, and I felt a quick dart of concern stab me. Then I saw the silver stream of her bubbles rising against the black wall of coral. She had moved away, ignoring my instruction, and I was annoyed. I finned towards her and was twenty feet from her when I saw what she was doing. My annoyance gave way instantly to shock and horror.

The long series of accidents and mishaps that were to haunt us in Gunfire Break had begun.

Growing out of the coral cliff was a lovely fernlike structure, graceful sweeps, branching and rebranching, pale pink shading to crimson.

Sherry had broken off a large branch of it. She held it in her bare hands and even as I raced towards her I saw her legs brush lightly against the red arms of the dreaded fire coral.

I seized her wrists and dragged her off the cruel and beautiful plant. I dug my thumbs into her flesh, shaking her hands viciously, forcing her to drop her fearsome burden. I was frantic in the knowledge that from their cells in the coral branches tens of thousands of minute polyps were firing their barbed poison darts into her flesh.

She was staring at me with great stricken eyes, aware that something bad had happened, but not yet sure what it was. I held her and began the ascent immediately. Even in my anxiety I was careful to obey the elementary rules of ascent, never overtaking my own bubbles but rising steadily with them.

I checked my watch – eight minutes thirty seconds elapsed. That was three minutes at one hundred and thirty feet. Quickly I calculated my decompression stops, but I was caught between the devil of diver's bends and the deep blue sea of Sherry's coming agony.

It hit her before we were halfway to the surface, her face contorted and her breathing went into the shallow ragged panting of deep distress until I feared she might beat the mechanical efficiency of her demand valve, jamming it so that it could no longer feed her with air.

She began to writhe in my grip and the palms of her hands blushed angrily, the livid red weals rose like whiplashes across her thighs – and I thanked God for the protection her suit had given to her torso.

When I held her at a decompression stop fifteen feet below the surface she fought me wildly, kicking and twisting in my grip. I cut the stop fine as I dared, and took her to the surface.

The instant our heads broke clear I spat out my mouthpiece and yelled: 'Chubby! Quick!'

The whaleboat was fifty yards away, but the motor was ticking over steadily and Chubby spun her on her own tail. The instant she was pointed at us, he gave the con to Angelo and scrambled up into the bows. Coming down on us like a great brown colossus.

'It's fire coral, Chubby,' I shouted. 'She's hit hard. Get her out!'

Chubby leaned out and took hold of webbing harness at the back of her neck and he lifted her bodily from the water; she dangled from his big brown fists like a drowning kitten.

I ditched my scuba set in the water for Angelo to recover, shrugging out of the harness, and when I scrambled over the side, Chubby had laid her on the floorboards and he was leaning over her, folding her, in his arms to quieten her struggles and still her moans and sobs of agony.

I found my medical kit under a pile of loose equipment in the bows, and my fingers were clumsy with haste as I heard Sherry's sobs behind me. I snapped the head of an ampoule of morphine and filled a disposable syringe with the clear fluid. Now I was angry as well as concerned.

'You stupid broad,' I snarled at her. 'What made you do a crazy, half-witted thing like that?'

She could not answer me, her lips were shaking and blue, flecked with spittle. I took a pinch of skin on her thigh and thrust the needle into it as I expelled the fluid into her flesh. I went on angrily.

'Fire coral – my God, you aren't an effing conchologist's backside. Isn't a kid on the island that stupid.'

'I didn't think, Harry,' she panted wildly.

'Didn't think —' I repeated, her pain was goading me to new excesses of anger. 'I don't think you've got anything in your head to think with, you stupid little bird-brain.'

I withdrew the needle, and ransacked the medicine box for the anti-histamine spray.

'I should put you over my knee, you —'

Chubby looked up at me. 'Harry, you talk to Miss Sherry just one more word like that and, man '– I'm going to have to break your head, hear?'

With only mild surprise I realized that he meant it. I had seen him break heads before, and knew it was something to avoid, so I told him,

'Instead of making speeches – how about you get us the hell out of here and back to the island.'

'You just treat her gentle, man, otherwise I'm going to roast your arse so you wish you'd been the one that sat on a bunch of fire coral instead of her, hear?'

I ignored this mutinous outburst and sprayed the ugly scarlet weals, coating them with a protective and soothing skin, and then I lifted her into my arms and held her like that while the morphine smoothed out the fearful burning agony of the stings and Chubby ran us back to the island.

When I carried Sherry up to the cave she was already half comatose from the drug. All that night I stayed by her side, helping her through the shivering and sweating fever produced by the virulent poison. Once she moaned and whispered half in delirium, 'I'm sorry, Harry. I didn't know. It's the first time I've dived in coral water. I didn't recognize it.'

Chubby and Angelo did not sleep either. I heard the murmur of their voices from the fireside and every hour one of them would cough outside the cave entrance and then inquire anxiously,

'How's she doing, Harry?'

By the morning Sherry had fought off the worst effects of the poisoning, and the stings had subsided into an ugly rash of blisters. However, it was another thirty-six hours before any of us could raise the enthusiasm to tackle the pool again, then the tides were wrong. We had to wait another day.

The precious hours were slipping away. I could imagine the *Mandrake* making fair passage, she had looked a fast and powerful vessel and each day wasted whittled away the lead I had counted upon.

On the third day, we ran out again to the pool. It was mid-afternoon and we took a chance with the water in the channel, scraping through early in the flood with inches to spare over the sharp coral snags.

Sherry was still in mild disgrace and, with her hands wrapped in acriflavine bandages, she was left in the whaleboat to keep Angelo company. Chubby and I dived together, going down fast and pausing above the swaying bamboo tops only long enough to drop the first marker buoy. I had decided it was necessary to search the pool bottom systematically. I was marking off the whole area into squares, anchoring inflatable buoys above the marine forest on thin nylon line.

We worked for an hour and found nothing that was obviously wreckage, although there were masses of coral covered with marine growth that would bear closer investigation. I marked these on the underwater slate attached to my thigh.

At the end of that hour, our air reserves in the double ninety-cubic-foot bottles were uncomfortably low. Chubby used more air than I did, for he was a much bigger man and his technique lacked finesse, so I regularly checked his pressure gauge.

I took him up and was especially careful on the decompression periods, although Chubby showed his usual impatience. He had never seen as I had, a diver come up too fast so the blood in his veins starts fizzing like champagne. The resultant agonies can cripple a man and an air bubble lodged in the brain can do permanent damage.

'Any luck?' Sherry called as soon as we surfaced, and I gave her the thumbs down as we swam to the whaleboat. We drank a cup of coffee from the Thermos and I smoked an island cheroot while we rested and chatted. I think we were all mildly disappointed that success had not been immediate, but I kept their spirits up by anticipating the first find.

Chubby and I changed our demand valves on to freshly charged bottles and down we went again. This time I would only allow forty-five minutes working at 130 feet, for the effects of gas absorption into the blood are cumulative, and repeated deep diving greatly increases the danger.

We worked carefullly through the forests of bamboo stems and over the tumbled coral blocks, exploring the gullies and cracks between them, pausing every few minutes to map the locations of interesting features, then going on, back and forth on the legs of a search pattern between my marker buoys.

Time elapse was forty-three minutes, and I glanced across at Chubby. None of our wet suits would fit him, so he dived naked except for an ancient black woollen bathing costume. He looked like one of my friendly dolphin – only not as graceful – as he forced his way through the thickets. I grinned at the thought and was about to turn away when a chance ray of light pierced the canopy above us and glinted upon something white on the floor below Chubby. I finned in quickly, and examined the white object. At first I thought it was a piece of clam shell, but then I noticed that it was too thick and regular in shape. I sank down closer to it and saw that it was embedded in a decaying sheet of coelentrate coral. I groped for the small jenny bar on my webbing belt, drew it from its sheath and prised off the lump of coral containing the white object. The lump weighed about five pounds and I slipped it into my netting carrybag.

Chubby was watching me and I gave him the signal for the ascent.

'Anything?' Sherry called immediately we surfaced. Her confinement to the whaleboat was obviously playing the devil with her nerves. She was irritable and impatient – but I was not letting her dive until the ugly, suppurating lesions on her hands and thighs had healed. I knew how easily secondary infection could attack those open sores under these conditions, and I was feeding her antibiotics and trying to keep her quiet.

'I don't know,' I answered, as we swam to the boat and I handed the net bag up to her. She took it eagerly, and while we climbed aboard and stripped our equipment she was examining it closely, turning it over in her hands.

Already the surf was breaking heavily on the reef, boiling into the pool and the whaleboat was swinging and bobbing in the disturbance. Angelo was having difficulty holding her on station – and it was time to go. We had spent as much time underwater as I considered safe for one day, and soon now the heavy oceanic surf would begin leaping the coral barrier and sweeping the pool.

'Take us home, Chubby,' I called and he went to the motors. All our attention was focussed on the wild ride back through the channel. With the flood of the tide the swells came up under our stern, surfing us, coming through under our hull so fast that our relative speed was reversed and the whaleboat's steering was inverted so we threatened to broach to and tumble broadside on to the coral walls of the channel. However, Chubby's seamanship never faltered, and at last we shot out into the protected waters behind the reef and turned for the island.

Now I could give my attention to the object I had recovered from the pool. With Sherry giving me a great deal of advice that I did not really need, and cautioning me to exercise care, I placed the lump of dead coral on the thwart and gave it a smart crack with the jenny bar. It split into three pieces and revealed a number of articles that had been ingested and protected by the living coral polyps.

There were three round grey objects the size of marbles and I picked one out of the coral bed and weighed it in my hand. It was heavy. I handed it to Sherry.

'Guesses?' I asked.

'Musket balls,' she said without hesitation.

'Of course,' I agreed. I should have recognized it and I made amends by identifying the next object.

'A small brass key.'

'Genius!' she said with irony, and I ignored her as I worked delicately to free the white object which had first caught my attention. It came away at last and I turned it over to examine the blue design worked on one side.

It was a segment of white glazed porcelain, a chip from the rim of a plate which had been ornamented by a coat of arms. Half of the design was missing but I recognized the rampant lion immediately, and the words 'Senat. ANGLIA.' It was the device of John Company again, part of a set of ship's plate.

I passed it to Sherry and suddenly I saw how it must have been. I told her my vision and she listened quietly, fondling the chip of porcelain. 'When at last the surf broke her back and the coral tore her in half, she would have gone down by the middle, and all her cargo and gear would have shifted – tearing out her inner bulkhead. It would all have poured out of her, cannon and shot, plate and silver, flask and cup, coin and pistol – it would have littered the floor of the pool, a rich sowing of man-made articles and the coral has sucked it up and absorbed it.'

'The treasure crates?' Sherry demanded. 'Would they have fallen out of the hull?'

'I don't know,' I admitted, and Chubby, who had been listening intently, spat over the side and growled.

'The forehold was always double-skinned, three-inch oak planks, to hold the cargo from shifting in a storm. Anything was in there then, is still in there now.'

'And that opinion would have cost you ten guineas in Harley Street,' I told Sherry, and winked at her. She laughed and turned to Chubby.

'I don't know what we would do without you, Chubby dear,' and Chubby scowled murderously and suddenly found something of engrossing interest out on the distant horizon.

It was only later, after Sherry and I had taken our swim on one of the secluded beaches and had changed into fresh clothes and were sitting around the fire drinking Chivas Regal and eating fresh prawns netted in the lagoon, that the elation of our first minor finds wore off – and I began soberly to consider the implications of the *Dawn Light* broken up and scattered across the marine hothouse of the pool.

If Chubby were wrong and the treasure crates, with their enormous weight of gold, had smashed through the sides of the hold and fallen free, then it would be an endless task searching for them. I had seen two hundred blocks and mounds of coral that day – any one of which could have concealed a part of the tiger throne of India.

If he were correct and the hold had retained its cargo, then the coral polyps would have spread over the entire front section of the vessel as it lay on the bottom, covering the woodwork with layer upon layer of calcified stone, until it had become an armoured repository for the treasure, disguised with a growth of marine plants.

We discussed it in detail, all of us beginning to appreciate the magnitude of the task we had set ourselves, and we agreed that it fell into two separate parts.

First we had to locate and identify the treasure cases, and then we had to wrest them from the stubborn embrace of the coral.

'You know what we are going to need, don't you, Chubby?' I asked, and he nodded.

'You still got those two cases?' I felt ashamed to mention the word gelignite in front of Sherry. It reminded me too vividly of the project for which Chubby and I had found it necessary to lay in large stocks of high explosive. That had been three years ago, during a lean season when I had been desperate for ready cash to keep myself and *Wave Dancer* aloft. Not even by stretching the letter of the law could our project have been considered legal, and I would rather have closed that chapter and forgotten it – but we needed the gelignite now.

Chubby shook his head. 'Man, that stuff began sweating like a stevedore in a heatwave. If you belched within fifty feet of it – it would have blown the top off the island.'

'What did you do with it?'

'Angelo and I took it out into the Mozambique Channel and gave it a deep six.'

'We will need at least a couple of cases. It will take a full shot to break up those big chunks down there.'

'I'll speak to Mister Coker again – he should be able to fix it.'

'Do that, Chubby. Next time you go back to St Mary's you tell Fred Coker to get us three cases.'

'What about the pineapples we saved from *Wave Dancer*?' Chubby asked.

'No good,' I told him, I did not want my obituary to read, 'The man who tried to fuse MK VII hand-grenades in 130 feet of water.'


I was wakened the next morning by the unnatural hush, and the static charged heat of the air. I lay awake listening, but even the fiddler crabs were silent and the perpetual rattle of the palm fronds was stilled. The only sound was the low and gentle breathing of the woman beside me. I kissed her lightly on the cheek and managed to withdraw my bad arm from under her head without waking her. Sherry boasted that she never used a pillow, it was bad for the spine she told me with an air of rectitude, but this didn't prevent her from using any convenient portion of my anatomy as a substitute.

I ambled out of the cave trying to restore the circulation to my limb by massage, and while I made a libation to my favourite palm tree I studied the sky.

It was a sickly dawn, smeared with a dark haze that dimmed the stars. the heated air lay heavy and languorous against the earth, with no breeze to stir it, and my skin prickled in the charged atmosphere.

Chubby was feeding twigs to the fire and blowing life into it, when I returned. He looked up at me and confirmed my diagnosis.

'Weather going to break.'

'What is coming, Chubby?' and he shrugged. 'Glass is down to 28.2, but we'll know by noon,' and he went back to huffing and puffing over the fire.

The weather had affected Sherry also. The hair at her temples was damp with perspiration and she snapped at me peevishly as I changed her dressings, but minutes later she came up behind me as I dressed, and laid her cheek against my naked back.

'Sorry, Harry, it's just so sticky and close this morning,' and she ran her lips across my back, touching the thick raised cicatrice of the bullet scar with her tongue.

'Forgive?' she asked.

Chubby and I dived into the pool at eleven o'clock that morning. We had been down thirty-eight minutes without making any further significant discovery when I heard the tinny clink! clink! clink! – transmitted through the water. I paused and listened, noticing that Chubby had stopped also. It came again, thrice repeated.

On the surface, Angelo had immersed half of a three-foot length of iron rail into the water and was beating out the recall signal upon it with a hammer from the tool kit.

I gave Chubby the open-handed 'wash out' sign and we began the ascent at once.

As we climbed into the boat I asked impatiently, 'What is it, Angelo?' and in reply he pointed out to seaward over the jagged and irregular back of the reef.

I pulled off my mask and blinked my eyes, refocusing after the limited horizons of the marine world.

It lay low and black against the sea, a thin dark smear as though some playful god had drawn a charcoal line across the horizon – but even as I watched, it seemed to grow – spreading wider into the paler blue of the sky, darker and still darker it rose out of the sea. Chubby whistled softly and shook his head.

'Here comes the Lady C. and, man, she is in a big hurry.'

The speed of that low dark front was uncanny. It lifted up, drawing a funeral curtain across the sky and as Chubby gunned the motors and ran for the channel the first racing streamers of cloud spread across the sun.

Sherry came to sit beside me on the thwart and help me strip the clinging wet rubber suit.

'What is it, Harry?' she asked.

'Lady C,' I told her. 'It's the cyclone, the same one that killed the *Dawn Light*. She's out hunting again,' and Angelo fetched the lifebelts from the forepeak and handed one to each of us. We tied them on and sat close together and watched it come on in awesome grandeur, overwhelming the sun, changing the sky from a high pure blue dome into a low grey roof of filthy scudding cloud.

We were running hard before her, leaving the channel and flying across the inner waters to the shelter of the cove. All our faces were turned to watch it, all our hearts quailed at the sense of our own frailty before such force and power.

The cloud front passed over our heads as we ran into the bay, and immediately we were plunged into a twilight world, fraught with the fury to come. The cloud dragged a skirt of cold damp air beneath it. It passed over us, and we shivered in the sudden drop in temperature. With a shriek, the wind was upon us, turning the air into a mixture of sand and driven spray.

'The motors,' Chubby bellowed at me, as the whaleboat touched the beach. Those two new Evinrudes represented half the savings of a lifetime and I understood his concern.

'We'll take them with us.'

'And the boat?' Chubby persisted.

'Sink it. There's a firm bottom of sand for it to lie on.'

As Chubby and I freed the motors, Angelo and Sherry lashed the folds of the tarpaulin over the open deck to secure the equipment, and then used the nylon diving lines to tie down the irreplaceable scuba sets and the waterproof cases that contained my medical kit and tools.

Then, while Chubby and I hefted the two heavy Evinrudes, Angelo allowed the wind to push the whaleboat out into the bay where he pulled the drainplugs and she filled immediately with water. The steep wind-maddened sea poured in over the side, and she went down swiftly in twenty feet of water.

Angelo returned to the beach using a dogged sidestroke with the waves breaking over his head. By this time, Sherry and I had almost reached the line of palm trees.

Doubled under my load, I glanced back. Chubby was lumbering after us. He was similarly burdened by the second motor, doubled also under the dead weight of metal and wading through the waist-high torrent of blown white sand. Angelo emerged from the water and followed him.

They were close behind us as we ran into the trees. If I had hoped to find shelter here, then I was a fool, for we found ourselves transferred from an exposed position of acute discomfort into one of real and deadly danger.

The great winds of the cyclone had thrashed the palms into a lunatic frenzy. The sound of it was a deafening clattering roar that was stunning in its intensity. The long graceful stems of the palms whipped about wildly, and the wind clawed loose the fronds and sent them flying off into the haze of sand and spray like huge misshapen birds.

We ran in single file along one of the ill-defined footpaths, Sherry leading us, covering her head with both hands, while I was for the first time grateful for the scanty cover given me by the big white motor on my shoulder for all of us were exposed to the double threat of danger.

The whipping of the tall palms flung from the fifty-foot-high heads their clusters of iron-hard nuts. Big as a cannon-ball and almost as dangerous, these projectiles bombarded us as we ran. One of them struck the motor I carried, a blow that made me stagger, another fell beside the path and on the second bounce hit Sherry on the lower leg. Even though most of its power was spent, still it knocked her down and rolled her in the sand like a running springbok hit by a high-powered rifle. When she regained her feet she was limping heavily – but she ran on through the lethal hail of coconuts.

We had almost reached the saddle of the hills when the wind increased the power of its assault. I heard its shrieking overhead on a higher angrier note, and coming in across the treetops roaring like a wild beast.

It hurled a new curtain of sand at us, and as I glanced ahead I saw the first palm tree begin to go.

I saw it lean out wearily, exhausted by its efforts to resist the wind, the earth around its base heaved upwards as the root system was torn from the sandy soil. As it came down so it gathered speed; swinging in a terrible arc, like the axe of the headsman, it fell towards us. Sherry was fifteen paces ahead of me, just beginning the ascent of the saddle and she had her face turned downwards, watching her own feet, her hands still held to her head.

She was running into the path of the falling tree, and she seemed so small and fragile beneath that solid bole of descending timber. It would crush her with a single gargantuan blow.

I screamed at her, but although she was so close she could not hear me. The roaring of the wind seemed to swamp all our senses. Down swung the long limber stem of the palm tree, and Sherry ran on into its path. I dropped the motor, shrugging it from my shoulder and I ran forward. Even then I saw I could not reach her in time, and I dived belly down, reaching out to the full stretch of my right arm and I hit Sherry's back foot, slapping it across the other as she swung it forward. The ankle tap of the football field, and it tripped her. She fell flat on her face in the sand. As the two of us lay outstretched the palm tree descended. The fury of its stroke rushed through the air even above the sound of the wind and it struck with a blow that was transmitted through the earth into my body, jarring me and rattling the teeth in my skull.

Instantly I was up and dragging Sherry to her feet. The palm tree had missed her by eighteen inches and she was stunned and terrified. I hugged her for a few moments, trying to give her comfort and strength. Then I lifted her over the palm stem that blocked the path, pointed her at the saddle and gave her a shove.

'Run!' I shouted and she staggered onwards. Angelo helped me lift the motor on to my shoulder once more. We clambered over the tree and toiled on up the slope after Sherry's running figure.

All around us in the palm groves I could hear the thud and crash of other trees falling and I tried to run with my face upturned to catch the next threat before it developed, but another flying coconut hit me a glancing blow on the temple, dimming my vision for a moment I staggered on blindly, taking my chances amongst the monstrous guillotines of the falling palms.

I reached the crest of the saddle without realizing it, and I was unprepared for the full unbroken force of the wind in my back. It hurled me forward, the ground fell away from under my feet as I was thrown over the saddle, my knees gave way and the motor and I rolled headlong down the reverse slope. On the way down we caught up with Sherry North, taking her in the back of the legs. She collapsed on top of me and joined the motor and me on our hurried descent.

One moment I was on top and the next Miss North was seated between my shoulder blades, then the motor was on top of both of us.

When we reached the bottom of the steepest pitch and lay together in a battered and weary heap, we were protected by the saddle from the direct fury of the wind so it was possible to hear what Sherry was saying. It was immediately obvious that she bitterly resented what she considered to be an unprovoked assault, and she was loudly casting doubt on my parentage, character and breeding. Even in my own desperate straits her anger was suddenly terribly comical, and I began to laugh. I saw that she was trying to find sufficient strength to hit me so I decided to distract her.

'— Jack and Jill went up the hill
They each had a dollar and a quarter —'
I croaked at her,
'— Jill came down with half a crown
They didn't go up for water.'

She stared at me for a moment as though I had started frothing at the mouth, then she started to laugh also, but the laughter had a wild hysterical note to it.

'Oh you swine!' she sobbed with laughter, tears streaming down her cheeks and her sodden sand-caked hair dangling in thick dark snakes about her face.

Angelo thought she was weeping when he reached us and he drew her tenderly to her feet and helped her down the last few hundred yards to the caves, leaving me to hoist the motor once more to my bruised shoulder and follow them.

Our cave was well placed to weather the cyclone winds, probably chosen by the old fishermen with that in mind. I retrieved the canvas fly leaf from where it was wrapped around the bole of a palm tree and used it to screen the entrance, piling stones upon the trailing end to hold it down and we had a dimly lit haven into which we crept like two wounded animals.

I had left my motor with Chubby in his cave. I felt at that moment that if I never saw it again it would be too soon, but I knew Chubby would treat it with all the loving care of a mother for her sickly infant and that when the cyclone passed on, it would once more be ready for sea.

Once I had rigged the tarpaulin to screen the cave and keep out the wind, Sherry and I could strip and clean ourselves of the salt and sand. We used a basinful of the precious fresh water for this purpose, each of us taking it in turn to stand in the basin and be sponged down by the other.

I was a mass of scratches and bruises from my long battle with the motor, and although my medical kit was still in the boat at the bottom of the bay, I found a large bottle of mercurochrome in my bag. Sherry began a convincing imitation of Florence Nightingale, with the antiseptic and a roll of cotton wool she anointed my wounds, murmuring condolences and sympathetic sounds.

I rather enjoy being fussed over, and I stood there in a semi-hypnotic state lifting an arm or moving a leg as I was bidden. The first hint that I received that Miss North was not treating my crippling injuries with the true gravity they deserved was when she suddenly emitted a hoot of glee and daubed my most delicate extremity with a scarlet splash of mercuochrome.

'Rudolph the red-nosed reindeer,' she chortled, and I roused myself to protest bitterly.

'Hey! That stuff doesn't wash off.'

'Good!' she cried. 'I'll be able to find you now if you ever get lost in a crowd.' I was shocked by such unseeming levity. I gathered about me my dignity and went to find a pair of dry pants.

Sherry reclined on the mattress and watched me scratching in my bag.

'How long is this going to last?' she asked.

'Five days,' I told her, as I paused to listen to the unabated roar of the wind.

'How do you know?'

'It always lasts five days,' I explained, as I stepped into my shorts and hoisted them.

'That's going to give us a little time to get to know each other.'


We were caged by the cyclone, locked together in the confined few square feet of the cave, and it was a strange experience.

Any venture out into the open forced upon us by nature, or to check how Chubby and Angelo were faring, was fraught with discomfort and danger. Although the trees were stripped of most of their fruit during the first twelve hours and the weaker trees fell during that period also – yet there was still the occasional tree that came crashing down, and the loose trash and fronds flew like arrows on the wind with sufficient force to blind a person or inflict other injury.

Chubby and Angelo worked away quietly on the motors, stripping them down and cleaning them of salt water. They had something to keep them busy.

In our cave, once the initial novelty had passed there developed some crisis of will and decision which I did not properly understand, but which I sensed was critical.

I had never pretended to understand Sherry North in any depth, there were too many unanswered questions, too many areas of reserve, barriers of privacy beyond which I was not allowed to pass. She had not to this time made any declaration of her feelings, there was never any discussion of the future. This was strange, for any other woman I had ever known expected – nay demanded – declarations of love and passion. I sensed also that this indecision was causing her as much distress as it was me. She was caught up in something against which she struggled, and in the process her emotions were being badly mauled.

However, with Sherry there was nothing spoken of – for I had accepted the tacit agreement and we did not discuss any of our feelings for each other. I found this restricting, for I am a lover with a florin turn of speech. If I have not yet succeeded in talking a bird down out of a tree – it is probably because I have never seriously made the attempt. I could make this adjustment without too much pain, however, it was the lack of a future that chafed at me.

It seemed that Sherry did not look for our relationship to last longer than the setting of the sun, yet I knew that she could not feel this way, for in the moments of warmth that interspersed those of gloom, there could be no doubts.

Once when I started to speak of my plans for when we had raised the treasure – how I would have another boat built to my design, a boat that incorporated all the best features of the beloved *Wave Dancer* – how I would build a new dwelling at Turtle Bay that would not deserve the title of shack – how I would furnish it and people it – she took no part in the discussion. When I ran out of words, she turned away from me on the mattress and pretended to sleep although I could feel the tension in her body without touching her.

At another time I found her watching me with that hostile hating look. While an hour later she was in a frenzy of physical passion which was in diametric contrast.

She sorted and mended my clothing from the bag, sitting cross-legged on the mattress and working with neat business-like stitches. When I thanked her, she became caustic and derisive, and we ended up in a blazing row until she flung herself out of the cave and ran through the raging wind to Chubby's cave. She did not return until after dark, with Chubby escorting her and holding a lantern to light her way.

Chubby regarded me with an expression that would have melted a lesser man and frostily refused my invitation to drink whisky, which meant that he was either very sick or very disapproving, then he disappeared again into the storm muttering darkly.

By the fourth day my nerves were in a jangling mess, but I had considered the problem of Sherry's strange behaviour from every angle and I reached my conclusions.

Cooped up with me in that tiny cave she was being forced at last to consider her feelings for me. She was falling in love, probably for the first time in her life, and her fiercely independent spirit was hating the experience. I cannot say in truthfulness that I was enjoying it very much either – or rather I enjoyed the short periods of repentance and loving between each new tantrum – but I looked forward fervently to the moment when she accepted the inevitable and succumbed completely.

I was still awaiting that happy moment when I awoke in the dawn of the fifth day. The island was in a grip of a stillness that was almost numbing after the uproar of the cyclone. I lay and listened to the silence without opening my eyes, but when I felt movement beside me I rolled my head and looked into her face.

'The storm is over,' she said softly, and rose from the bed.

We walked out side by side into the early morning sunlight, blinking around us at the devastation which the storm had created. The island looked like the photographs of a World War I battlefield. The palms were stripped of their foliage, the bare masts pointed pathetically at the sky and the earth below was littered thickly with palm fronds and coconuts. The stillness hung over it all, no breath of wind, and the sky was pale milky blue, still filled with a haze of sand and sea.

From their cave Chubby and Angelo emerged. like big bear and little bear, at the end of winter. They too stood and looked about them uncertainly.

Suddenly Angelo let out a Comanche whoop and leaped four feet in the air. After five days of forced confinement his animal spirits could no longer be suppressed. He took off through the palm trees like a greyhound.

'Last one on the water is a fascist,' he shouted, and Sherry was the first to accept the challenge. She was ten paces behind him when they hit the beach but they dived simultaneously into the lagoon, fully clad, and began immediately pelting each other with handfuls of wet sand. Chubby and I followed at a sedate pace more in keeping with our years. Still wearing his vividly striped pyjamas, Chubby lowered his massive hams into the sea.

'I got to tell you, man, that feels good,' he admitted gravely. I drew deeply on my cheroot as I sat beside him waist deep, then I handed him the butt.

'We lost five days, Chubby,' I said, and immediately he scowled.

'Let's get busy,' he growled, sitting in the lagoon in yellow and purple striped pyjamas, cheroot in his mouth, like a big brown bullfrog.


From the peak we looked down into the shallow waters of the lagoon and although they were still a little murky with spindrift and churned sand, yet the whaleboat was clearly visible. She had drifted sideways in the bay and was lying on the bottom in twenty feet of water with the yellow tarpaulin still covering her deck.

We raised the whaleboat with air bags and once her gunwales broke the surface we were able to bale her out and row her into the beach. The rest of that day was needed to unload the waterlogged cargo, clean and dry it, pump the air bottles, get the motors aboard and prepare for the next visit to Gunfire Reef.

I was beginning to become seriously concerned by the delays which had left us sitting on the island, day after day, while Manny Resnick and his merry men cut away the lead we had started with.

That evening we discussed it around the campfire, and agreed that we had made also no progress in ten days other than to confirm that part of the *Dawn Light*'s wreckage had fallen into the pool.

However, the tides were set fair for an early start in the morning and Chubby ran us through the channel with hardly sufficient light to recognize the coral snags, and when we took up our station in the back of the reef the sun was only just showing its blazing upper rim above the horizon.

During the five days we had lain ashore, Sherry's hands had almost entirely healed, and although I suggested tactfully that she should allow Chubby to accompany me for the next few days, my tact and concern were wasted. Sherry North was suited and finned and Chubby sat in the stern beside the motors holding us on station.

Sherry and I went down fast, and entered the forest of sea bamboo, picking up position from the markers that Chubby and I had left on our last dive.

We were working in close to the base of the coral cliff and I placed Sherry on the inside berth where it would be easier to hold position in the search pattern while she orientated herself.

We had hardly begun the first leg and had swum fifty feet from the last marker when Sherry tapped urgently on her bottles to attract my attention and I pushed my way through the bamboo to her.

She was hanging against the side of the coral cliff upside down like a bat, closely examining a fall of coral and debris that had slid down to the floor of the pool. She was in deep shade under the loom of dark coral so I was at her side before I saw what had attracted her.

Propped against the cliff, its bottom end lying in the mound of debris and weed, was a long cylindrical object which itself was heavily infested with marine growth and had already been partially ingested by the living coral.

Yet its size and regular shape indicated that it was man-made – for it was nine feet long and twenty inches thick, perfectly rounded and slightly tapered.

Sherry was studying it with interest and when I came up she turned to meet me and made signs of incomprehension.

I had recognized what it was immediately and the skin of my forearms and at the nape of my neck felt prickly with excitement. I made a pistol of my thumb and forefinger and mimed the act of firing it, but she did not understand and shook her head so I scribbled quickly on the underwater slate and showed it to her.

'Cannon.'

She nodded vigorously, rolled her eyes and blew bubbles to register triumph before turning back to the cannon.

It was about the correct size to be one of the long nine-pounders that had formed part of the *Dawn Light*'s armament but there was no chance that I should be able to read any inscription upon it, for the surface was crocodile-skinned with growth and corrosion. Unlike the bronze bell that Jimmy North had recovered, it had not been buried in the sand to protect it.

I floated down along the massive barrel examining it closely and almost immediately found another cannon in the deeper gloom nearer the cliff. However, three-quarters of this weapon had been incorporated into the cliff, built into it by the living coral polyps.

I swam in closer, ducking under the first barrel and went into the jumble of debris and fallen coral blocks. I was within two feet of this amorphous mass when with a shock which constricted my breathing and flushed warmly through my blood I recognized what I was looking at.

Quickly and excitedly I finned over the mound of debris, finding where it ended and the unbroken coral began, forcing my way up through the sea bamboo to estimate its size, and pausing to examine any opening or irregularity in it.

The total mass of debris was the size of a couple of railway pullman coaches, but it was only when I pushed aside a larger floating clump of weed and peered into the squared opening of a gun port, from which the muzzle of a cannon still protruded and which had not been completely altered in shape by the encroaching coral, that I was certain that what we had discovered was the entire forward section of the frigate *Dawn Light*, broken off just behind the main mast.

I looked around wildly for Sherry and saw her finned feet protruding from another portion of the wreckage. I pulled her out, removed her mouthpiece and kissed her lustily before replacing it. She was laughing with excitement and when I signalled her that we were ascending, she shook her head vehemently and shot away from me to continue her explorations. It was fully fifteen minutes later that I was able to drag her away and take her up to the whaleboat.

We both began talking at once the moment we had the rubber mouthpieces out of the way. My voice is louder than hers, but she is more persistent. It took me some minutes to assert my rights as expedition leader and I could begin to describe it to Chubby.

'It's the *Dawn Light* sure enough. The weight of her armament and cargo must have pulled her down the instant she was clear of the reef. She went down like a stone, and she is lying against the foot of the cliff. Some of her cannons have fallen out of the hull, and they're lying jumbled around it—'

'We didn't recognize it at first,' Sherry chimed in again, just when I had her quietened down. 'It's like a rubbish dump. Just an enormous heap.'

'From what I could judge she must have broken her back abaft the main mast, but she's been smashed up badly for most of her length. The cannon must have torn up her gundeck and it's only the two ports nearest the bows that are intact—'

'How does she lie?' Chubby demanded, coming immediately to the pith of the matter.

'She's bottom up,' I admitted. 'She must have rolled as she went down.'

'That makes it a real problem, unless you can get in at a gun port or under the waist,' Chubby growled.

'I had a good look,' I told him, 'but I couldn't find a point at which we could penetrate the hull. Even the gunports are solid with growth.'

Chubby shook his head mournfully. 'Man, looks like this place is badly hexed,' and immediately all three of us made the cross-fingered sign against it.

Angelo told him primly, 'You talking up a storm. Shouldn't say that, hear?' but Chubby shook his head again, and his face collapsed into pessimistic folds.

I slapped him on the back and asked him, 'Is it true that you pass iced water – even in hot weather?' and my attempt at humour made him look as cheerful as an unemployed undertaker.

'Oh, leave Chubby alone,' Sherry came to his rescue. 'Let's go down again and try and find a break in the hull.'

'We'll take half an hour's rest,' I said, 'a smoke and a mug of coffee – then we'll go take another look.'

We stayed down so long on the second dive that Chubby had to sound the triple recall signal – and when we surfaced the pool was boiling. The cyclone had left a legacy of high surf, and on the rising tide it was coming in heavily across the reef and pounding in through the gap, higher in the channel than we had ever known it.

We clung to the thwarts in silence as Chubby took us home on a wild ride, and it was only when we entered the quieter waters of the lagoon that we could continue the discussion.

'She's as tight as the Chatwood lock on the national safe deposit,' I told them. 'The one gun port is blocked by the cannon, and I got into the other about four feet before I ran into part of the bulkhead which must have collapsed. It's the den of a big old moray eel that looks like a python – he's got teeth on him like a bulldog and he and I aren't friends.'

'What about the waist?' Chubby demanded.

'No,' I said, 'she's settled down heavily, and the coral has closed her up.'

Chubby put on an expression which meant that he had told us so. I could have beaten him over the head with a spanner, he was so smug –but I ignored him and showed them the piece of woodwork that I had prised off the hull with a crowbar.

'The coral has closed everything up solid. It's like those old forests that have been petrified into stone. The *Dawn Light* is a ship of stone, armour-plated with coral. There is only one way we will get into her – and that is to pop her open.'

Chubby nodded, 'That's the way to do it,' and Sherry wanted to know:

'But if you use explosive, won't it just blow everything to bits?'

'We won't use an atomic bomb,' I told her. 'We'll start with half a stick in the forward gunport. Just enough to kick out a chunk of that coral plating,' and I turned back to Chubby. 'We need that gelignite right away, every hour is precious now, Chubby. We've got a good moon. Can you take us back to St Mary's tonight?' and Chubby did not bother to answer such a superfluous question. It was an indirect slur on his seamanship.

There was a horned moon, with a pale halo around it. The atmosphere was still full of dust from the big winds. The stars also were misty and very far away, but the cyclone had blown great masses of oceanic plankton into the channel so that the sea was a glowing phosphorescent mass wherever it was disturbed.

Our wake glowed green and long, spread behind us like a peacock's tail, and the movement of fish beneath the surface shone like meteors. Sherry dipped her hand over the side and brought it out burning with a weird and liquid flame, and she cooed with wonder.

Later when she was sleepy she lay against my chest under the tarpaulin I had spread to keep off the damp and we listened to the booming of the giant manta rays out in the open water as they leaped high and fell to smack the surface of the sea with their flat bellies and tons of dead weight.

It was long after midnight when we raised the lights of St Mary's like a diamond necklace around the throat of the island.

The streets were utterly deserted as we left the whaleboat at her moorings and walked up to Chubby's house. Missus Chubby opened to us in a dressing-gown that made Chubby's pyjamas look conservative. She had her hair in large pink plastic curlers. I had never seen her without a hat before and I was surprised that she was not as bald as her spouse. They looked so alike in every other way.

She gave us coffee before Sherry and I climbed into the pickup and drove to Turtle Bay. The bedclothes were damp and needed airing but neither of us complained.

I stopped at the Post Office in the early morning and my box was half filled, mostly with fishing equipment catalogues and junk mail, but there were a few letters from old clients inquiring for charter – that gave me a pang – and one of the buff cable envelopes which I opened last. Cables have always borne bad news for me. Whenever I see one of those envelopes with my name peering out of the window like a long-term prisoner I have this queasy feeling in my stomach.

The message read: 'MANDRAKE SAILED CAPETOWN OUTWARD BOUND ZANZIBAR 12.00 HOURS FRIDAY 16TH. STEVE.'

My premonitions of evil were confirmed. *Mandrake* had left Cape Town six days ago. She had made a faster passage than I would have believed possible. I felt like rushing to the top of Coolie Peak to search the horizon. Instead I passed the cable to Sherry and drove down to Frobisher Street.

Fred Coker was just opening the street door of his travel agency as I parked outside Missus Eddy's store and sent Sherry in with a shopping list while I walked on down the street to the Agency.

Fred Coker had not seen me since I had dropped him moaning on the floor of his own morgue, and now he was sitting at his desk in a white shark-skin suit and wearing a necktie which depicted a Hula girl on a palm-lined beach and the legend 'Welcome to St Mary's! Pearl of the Indian Ocean.'

He looked up with a smile that went well with the tie, but the moment he recognized me his expression changed to utter dismay. He let out a bleat like an orphan lamb and shot out of his chair, heading for the back room.

I blocked his escape and he backed away before me, his gold-rimmed glasses glittering like the sheen of nervous sweat that covered his face until the chair caught him in the back of his knees and he collapsed into it. Only then did I give him my big friendly grin – and I thought he would faint with relief.

'How are you, Mister Coker?' He tried to answer but his voice failed him. Instead he nodded his head so rapidly that I understood he was very well.

'I want you to do me a favour.'

'Anything,' he gabbled, suddenly recovering the power of speech. 'Anything, Mister Harry, you have only to ask.'

Despite his protestations it took him only a few minutes to recover his courage and wits. He listened to my very reasonable request for three cases of high explosive, and went into a pantomime to impress me with the utter impossibility of compliance. He rolled his eyes, sucked in his cheeks and made clucking noises with his tongue.

'I want it by noon tomorrow – latest,' and he clasped his forehead as if in agony.

'And if it's not here by twelve o'clock precisely, you and I will continue our discussion on the insurance premiums—'

He dropped his hand and sat upright, his expression once more willing and intelligent.

'That's not necessary, Mister Harry. I can get what you ask – but it will cost a great deal of money. Three hundred dollars a case.'

'Put it on the slate,' I told him.

'Mister Harry!' he cried, 'you know I cannot extend credit.'

I was silent, but I slitted my eyes, clenched my jaws and began to breathe deeply.

'Very well,' he said hurriedly, 'Until the end of the month, then.'

'That's very decent of you, Mister Coker.'

'It's a pleasure, Mister Harry,' he assured me. 'A very great pleasure.'

'There is just one other thing, Mr Coker,' and I could see him mentally quail at my next request, but he braced himself like a hero.

'In the near future I expect to be exporting a small consignment to Zürich in Switzerland.' He sat a little forward in his seat. 'I do not wish to be bothered with customs formalities – you understand?'

'I understand, Mister Harry.'

'Do you ever have requests to send the body of one of your customers back to the near and dear?'

'I beg your pardon?' He looked confused.

'If a tourist were to pass away on the island – say of a heart attack – you would be called on to embalm his corpse for posterity and to ship it out in a casket. Am I correct?'

'It has happened before,' he agreed. 'On three occasions.'

'Good, so you are familiar with the procedure?'

'I am, Mister Harry.'

'Mister Coker, lay in a casket and get yourself a pile of the correct forms. I'll be shipping soon.'

'May I ask what you intend to export – in lieu of a cadaver?' He phrased the question delicately.

'You may well ask, Mister Coker.'

I drove down to the fort and spoke to the President's secretary. He was in a meeting, but he would see me at one o'clock if I would care to lunch with him in his office. I accepted the invitation and, to pass the hours until then, I drove up the track to Coolie Peak as far as the pick-up would take me. There I parked it and walked on to the ruins of the old lookout and signal station. I sat on the parapet looking out across a vista of sea and green islands while I smoked a cheroot and did my last bit of careful planning and decision-making, glad of this opportunity to make certain of my plans before committing myself to them.

I thought of what I wanted from life, and decided it was three things – Turtle Bay, *Wave Dancer II* and Sherry North, not necessarily in that order of preference.

To stay on at Turtle Bay, I had to keep a clean pair of hands in St Mary's, to have *Wave Dancer II* I needed cash and plenty of it, and Sherry North – well, that took plenty of hard thought, and at the end of it my cheroot had burned to a stub and I ground it out on the stone parapet. I took a deep breath and squared my shoulders.

'Courage, Harry me lad,' I said and drove down to the fort.

The President was delighted to see me, coming out into the reception room to welcome me and rising on tip-toe to place an arm around my shoulders and lead me into his office.

It was a room like a baronial hall with a beamed ceiling, panelled walls and English landscapes in massive ornate frames and dark smoky looking oils. The diamond-paned window rose from the floor to the ceiling and looked out over the harbour, and the floor was lush with oriental carpets.

Luncheon was spread on the oaken conference table below the windows – smoked fish, cheese and fruit with a bottle of Château Lafite '62 from which the cork had been drawn.

The President poured two crystal glasses of the deep red wine, offered one to me and then plopped two cubes of ice into his own glass. He grinned impishly as he saw my startled expression. 'Sacrilege, isn't it?' He raised the glass of rare wine and ice cubes to me. 'But, Harry, I know what I like. What is suitable on the Rue Royale isn't necessarily suitable on St Mary's.'

'Right on, sir!' I grinned back at him and we drank.

'Now, my boy, what did you want to talk to me about?'

I found a message that Sherry had gone to visit Missus Chubby when I arrived back at the shack, so I went out on to the veranda with a cold beer. I went over my meeting with President Bingle, reviewing it word for word, and found myself satisfied. I thought I had covered all the openings – except the ones I might need to escape through.

Three wooden cases marked 'Canned Fish. Produce of Norway' arrived on the ten o'clock plane from the mainland addressed to Coker's Travel Agency.

'Eat your liver, Alfred Nobel,' I thought when I saw the legend as Fred Coker unloaded them from the hearse at Turtle Bay and I placed them in the rear of the pick-up under the canvas cover.

'Until the end of the month then, Mister Harry,' said Fred Coker, like the leading man from a Shakespearian tragedy.

'Depend upon it, Mister Coker,' I assured him and he drove away through the palms.

Sherry had finished packing away the stores. She looked so different from yesterday's siren, with her hair scraped back, dressed in one of my old shirts, which fitted her like a nightdress, and a pair of faded jeans with raggedy legs cut off below the knees.

I helped her carry the cases out to the pick-up, and we climbed into the cab.

'Next time we come back here we'll be rich,' I said, and started the motor, forgetting to make the sign against the hex.

We ground up through the palm grove, hit the main road below the pineapple fields and climbed up the ridge.

We came out on the crest above the town and the harbour.

'God damn it!' I shouted angrily, and hit the brakes hard, swinging off the road on to the verge so violently that the pineapple truck following us swerved to avoid running into our rear, and the driver hung out of his window to shout abuse as he passed.

'What is it?' Sherry pulled herself off the dashboard where my manoeuvre had thrown her. 'Are you crazy?'

It was a bright and cloudless day, the air so clear that every detail of the lovely white and blue ship stood out like a drawing. She lay at the entrance to Grand Harbour on the moorings usually reserved for visiting cruise ships, or the regular mail ship.

She was flying a festival burst of signal flags and I could see her crew in tropical whites lining the rail and staring at the shore. The harbour tender was running out to her, carrying the harbour master, the customs inspector and Doctor MacNab.

'*Mandrake?*' Sherry asked.

'*Mandrake* and Manny Resnick,' I agreed, and swung the truck into a U-turn across the road.

'What are you going to do?' she asked.

'One thing I'm not going to do is show myself in St Mary's while Manny and his fly lads are ashore. I've met most of them before in circumstances which are likely to have burned my lovely features clearly into even their rudimentary brains.'

Down the hill at the first bus stop beyond the turn off to Turtle Bay was the small general Dealers' Store which supplied me with eggs, milk, butter and other perishables. The proprietor was delighted to see me and he flourished my outstanding bill like a winning lottery ticket. I paid him, and then closed the door of his back office while I used the telephone.

Chubby did not have a phone, but his next-door neighbour called him to speak to me.

'Chubby,' I told him, 'that big white floating brothel at the mail ship mooring is no friend of ours.'

'What you want me to do, Harry?'

'Move fast. Cover the water cans with stump nets and make like you are going fishing. Get out to sea and come around to Turtle Bay. We'll load from the beach and run for Gunfire Reef as soon as it's dark.'

'I'll be in the bay in two hours,' he said and hung up.

He was there in one hour forty-five minutes. One of the reasons I liked working with him is that you can put money on his promises.

As soon as the sun set and visibility was down to a hundred yards we slipped out of Turtle Bay, and we were well clear of the island by the time the moon came up.

Huddled under the tarpaulin, sitting on a case of gelignite, Sherry and I discussed the arrival of *Mandrake* in Grand Harbour.

'First thing Manny will do, he will send his lads out with a pocketful of bread to ask a few questions around the shops and bars. "Anyone seen Harry Fletcher?" and they'll be queueing up to tell him all about it. How Mister Harry chartered Chubby Andrews' stump boat, and how they been diving looking for seashells. If he gets really lucky somebody will point him in the direction of Frederick Coker Esquire – and Fred will fall over himself to tell all, as long as the price is right.'

'Then what will he do?'

'He will have an attack of the vapours when he hears that I didn't drown in the Severn. When he recovers from that, he will send a team out to ransack and search the shack at Turtle Bay. He will draw a dud card there. Then the lovely Miss Lorna Page will lead them all to the alleged site of the wreck off Big Gull. That will keep them happy and busy for two or three days – until they find they have nothing but the ship's bell.'

'Then?'

'Well, then Manny is going to get mad. I think Lorna is in line for some unpleasantness – but after that I don't know what will happen. All we can do is try to keep out of sight and work like a tribe of beavers to get the Colonel's goodies out of the wreck.'

The next day the state of the tides was such that we could not navigate the channel before the late morning. It gave us time to make preparations. I opened one of the cases of gelignite and took out ten of the waxy yellow sticks. I reclosed the case and buried it with the other two in the sandy soil of the palm grove, well away from the camp.

Then Chubby and I assembled and checked the blasting equipment. It was a home-made contraption, but it had proved its efficiency before. It consisted of two nine-volt transistor batteries in a simple switchbox. We had four reels of light insulated copper wire, and a cigar-box of detonators. Each of the lethal silver tubes was carefully wrapped in cotton wool. There was also a selection of time-delayed detonators of the pencil type in the box.

Chubby and I isolated ourselves while we worked with them, clamping the electric detonators to the hand-made terminals that I had soldered for the purpose.

The use of high explosives is simple in theory, and nerve-racking in practice. Even an idiot can wire it up and hit the button, but in its refined form it becomes an art.

I have seen a medium-sized tree survive a blast of half a case, losing only its leaves and some of its bark – but with half a stick I can drop the same tree neatly across a road to block it effectively, without removing a single leaf. I consider myself something of an artist, and I had taught Chubby all I knew. He was a natural, although he could never be termed an artist – his glee in the proceedings was too frankly childlike. Chubby just naturally loved to blow things up. He hummed happily to himself as he worked with the detonators.

We took up position in the pool a few minutes before noon and I went down alone, armed only with a Nemrod captive air spear gun with a barbed crucifix head I had designed and made myself. The point was needle-sharp, and it was multi-barbed for the first six inches. Twenty-four small sharp barbs, like those used by Batonka tribesmen when they spear catfish in the Zambezi River. Behind the barbs was the crucifix, a four-inch cross-piece which would prevent the victim slipping down the shaft close enough to attack me when I held the reverse end. The line was five hundred pound blue nylon and there was a twenty foot loop of it under the barrel of the spear gun.

I finned down on to the overgrown heap of wreckage and I settled myself comfortably beside the gunport and closed my eyes for a few seconds to accustom them to the gloom, then I peered cautiously into the dark square opening, pushing the barrel of the spear gun ahead of me.

The dark slimy coils of the Moray eel slithered and unwound as it sensed my presence, and it reared threateningly, displaying the fearsome irregular yellow fangs. In the gloom the eyes were black and bright, catching the feeble light like those of a cat.

He was a huge old mugger, thick as my calf and longer than the stretch of both my arms. The waving mane of his dorsal fin was angrily erected as he threatened me.

I lined him up carefully, waiting for him to turn his head and offer a better target. It was a scary few moments, I had one shot and if that was badly placed he would fly at me. I had seen a captive Moray chew mouthfuls out of the woodwork of a dinghy. Those fangs would tear easily through rubber suit and flesh, right down to the bone.

He was weaving slowly, like a flaring cobra, watching me and the range was extreme for accurate shooting. I waited for the moment, and at last he went into the second stage of aggression. He blew up his throat and turned slightly to offer me a profile.

'My God,' I thought, 'I once used to do this for fun,' and I took up the slack in the trigger. The gas hissed viciously and the plunger thudded to the end of its travel as it threw the spear. It flew in a long blur with the line whipping out behind it.

I had aimed for the dark earlike marking at the back of the skull, and I was an inch and a half high and two inches right. The Moray exploded into a spinning, whipping ball of coils that seemed to fill the whole gunport. I dropped the gun and with a push of my fins I shot forward and got a grip of the hilt of the spear. It kicked and thumped in my hands as the eel wound its thick dark body around the shaft. I drew him out of his lair, pinned by a thick bite of skin and rubbery muscle to the barbed head.

His mouth was opened in a silent screech of fury, and he unwound his body and let it fly and writhe like a pennant in a high wind.

The tail slapped into my face, dislodging my mask. Water flooded into my nose and eyes and I had to blow it clear before I could begin the ascent.

Now the eel twisted its head back at an impossible angle and closed the dreadfully gaping jaws on the metal shaft of the spear. I could hear the fangs grinding and squeaking in the steel, and there were bright silver scratches where it had bitten.

I came out through the surface holding aloft my prize. I heard Sherry squeal with horror at the writhing snakelike monster, and Chubby grunted, 'Come to papa, you beauty,' and he leaned out to grasp the spear and lift the eel aboard. He was showing his plastic gums in a happy grin for Moray eel was Chubby's favourite food. He held the neck against the gunwale and, with an expert sweep of his bait-knife, lopped the monstrous head cleanly away, letting it fall into the pool.

'Miss Sherry,' he said, 'you going to love the taste of him.'

'Never!' Sherry shuddered, and drew herself farther away from the bleeding, wriggling carcass.

'Okay, my children, let's have the gelly.' Angelo had the underwater carry-net ready to pass to me, and Sherry slid in over the side prepared to dive. She had the reel of insulated wire and she paid it out smoothly as we went down.

Once again I went directly to the now untenanted gunport and crept into it. The breech of the cannon was jammed solidly against the mass of debris beyond.

I chose two sites to place my shots. I wanted to kick the cannon aside, using it like a giant lever to tear out a slab of the petrified planking. The second shot fired simultaneously would blow into the wall of debris that barred entry to the gundeck.

I wired the shots firmly into place. Sherry passed the end of the line in to me and I snipped and bared the copper wire with the side-cutters before connecting it up to the terminals.

I checked the job once it was finished and then backed out of the port. Sherry was sitting cross-legged on the hull with the reel on her lap and I grinned at her around my mouthpiece and gave her the thumbs up before I retrieved my spear gun from where I had dropped it.

When we climbed over the side of the whaleboat Chubby had the battery switchbox beside him on the thwart and it was wired up. He was scowling with anticipation, as he crouched possessively over the blaster. It would have taken physical force to deprive him of the pleasure of hitting the button.

'Ready to shoot, skipper,' he growled.

'Shoot her then, Chubby.' He fussed with the box a little longer, drawing out the pleasure, then he turned the switch.

The surface of the pool bounced and shivered and we felt the bump come up through the bottom of the boat. Many seconds later there was a surge and frothing of bubbles, as though somebody had dropped a ton of Alka Seltzer into the pool. Slowly it cleared.

'I want you to put the trousers of your suit on, my sweeting,' I told Sherry, and predictably she took the order as an invitation to debate its correctness.

'Why, the water is warm?'

'Gloves and bootees also,' I said, as I began to pull on my own rubber full-length pants. 'If the hull is open we may penetrate her on this dive. You'll need protection against snags.'

Convinced at last, she did what she should have done without question. I still had a lot of work to do before she was properly trained. I thought, as I assembled the other equipment I needed for this descent.

I took the sealed unit underwater torch, the jenny bar and a coil of light nylon line and waited while Sherry completed the major task of wiggling her bottom into the tight rubber pants, assisted faithfully by Angelo. Once she had them hoisted and had buttoned the crotch piece, we were set to go.

When we were halfway down, we came upon the first dead fish floating belly up in the misty blue depths. There were hundreds of them that the explosions had killed or maimed, and they ranged in size from fingerlings to big striped snapper and reef bass as long as my arm. I felt a pang of remorse at the massacre I had perpetrated, but consoled myself with the thought I had killed less than a bluefin tunny would in a single day's feeding.

We went down through this killing ground, and the light caught the eddying and drifting carcasses so they blinked and shone like dying stars in a smoky azure sky.

The bottom of the pool was murky with particles of sand and other material stirred up by the shock of the blast. There was a hole torn in the cover of sea bamboo and we went down into it.

I saw at once that I had achieved my purpose. The explosion had kicked the massive cannon out of the hull, tearing it like a rotten tooth from the black and ancient maw of the gunport. It had fallen to the bed of the pool surrounded by the debris that it had brought away with it.

The upper lip of the gunport had been knocked out, enlarging the opening so that a man might stand almost upright in it. When I flashed the torch into the darkness beyond, I saw that it was a turgid fog of suspended dirt and particles which would take time to settle. My impatience would not allow that, however, and as we settled on the hull I checked my time elapse and air reserves. Quickly I calculated our working time, allowing for my two previous descents which would necessitate additional decompression. I reckoned we had seventeen minutes' safe time before beginning the ascent and I set the swivel ring on my wristwatch before preparing for the penetration.

I used the jettisoned cannon as a convenient anchor point on which to fix the end of the nylon line and then rose again to the opening, paying it out behind me as I went.

I had to remove Sherry North from the gunport, in the few seconds while I was busy with the line she had almost disappeared into the hole in the hull. I made angry signs at her to keep clear, and in return she made an unladylike gesture with two fingers which I pretended not to see.

Gingerly I entered the gunport and found that the visibility was down to about three feet in the murky soup.

The shots had only partially moved the blockage beyond the spot where the cannon had lain. There seemed to be a gap beyond but it needed to be enlarged before I could get through. I used the jenny bar to prise a lump of the wreckage away and discovered that it was the heavy gun carriage that was causing most of the blockage.

Working in freshly blasted wreckage is a delicate business, for it is impossible to know how critically balanced the mass may be. Even the slightest disturbance can bring the whole weight of it sliding and crashing down upon the trespasser, pinning and crushing him beneath it.

I worked slowly and deliberately, ignoring the regular thumps on my rump with which Sherry signalled her burning impatience. Once when I emerged with a section of shattered planking, she took my slate and wrote on it 'I am smaller!!' and underlined the 'smaller' twice in case the double exclamation mark was not noticed when she thrust the slate two inches from my nose. I returned her Churchillian salute and went back to my burrowing.

I had now cleared the area sufficiently to see that my only remaining obstacle was the heavy timber bulk of the gun carriage which was hanging at a drunken angle across the entry to the gundeck. The jenny bar was totally ineffective against this mass, and I could abandon the effort and return with another charge of gelignite tomorrow or I could take a chance.

I glanced at my time elapse and saw that I had been busy for twelve minutes. I reckoned that I had probably been using air more wastefully than usual during my recent exertions. Nevertheless, I decided to take a flier.

I passed the torch and jenny bar out to Sherry, and worked my way carefully back into the opening. I got my shoulder under the upper end of the gun carriage, and moved my feet around until I had a firm stance. When I was solidly placed, I took a good breath of air and began to lift.

Slowly I increased the strain until I was thrusting upwards with all the strength of my legs and back. I felt my face and throat swelling with pumping blood and my eyes felt ready to jump out of their sockets. Nothing moved, and I took another lungful of air and tried again, but this time throwing all my weight on the timber beam in a single explosive effort.

It gave way, and I felt like Samson who had pulled the temple down on his own head. I lost my balance and tumbled backwards in a storm of falling debris that groaned and grated as it fell, thudding and bumping around me.

When silence had settled, I found myself in utter darkness, a thick pea soup of swirling filth that blotted out the light. I tried to move, and found my leg pinned. Panic rushed through me in an icy wave and I fought frantically to free my leg. It took only half-a-dozen terrified kicks before I realized that I had escaped with great good luck. The gun carriage had missed my foot by a quarter of an inch, and had fallen across the rubber swimming fin. I pulled my foot out of the shoe, abandoning it, and groped my way out into the open.

Sherry was waiting eagerly for news, and I wiped the slate and wrote 'OPEN!!' underlining the word twice. She pointed into the gunport, demanding permission to enter and I checked my time elapse. We had two minutes, so I nodded and led the way in.

Flashing the beam of the torch ahead I had visibility of eighteen inches, enough to find the opening I had cleared. There was just sufficient clearance to allow me through without fouling my air bottles or breathing hose.

I paid out the nylon line behind me, like Theseus in the labyrinth of the Minotaur so as not to lose my direction in the *Dawn Light*'s warren of decks and companionways.

Sherry followed me along the line. I could feel her hand touch my foot and brush my leg as she groped after me.

Beyond the blockage, the water cleared a little, and we found ourselves in the low wide chamber of the gundeck. It was murky and mysterious, with strange shapes strewn about us in profusion. I saw other gun carriages, cannonballs strewn loosely or in heaps against angles and corners, and other equipment so altered by long immersion as to be unrecognizable.

We moved slowly forward, our fins stirring up fresh whirlpools of dirt and mud. Here also there were dead fish floating about us, although I noticed some of the red reef crayfish scrambling away like monstrous spiders into the depths of the ship. They at least had survived the blast in their armoured carapaces.

I played the beam of the torch on the deck above our heads, looking for the entry point to the lower decks and the holds. With the ship lying upside down, I had to keep trying to relate the existing geography of the wreck to the drawing I had studied.

About fifteen feet from our entry point I found the forecastle ladder, another dark square opening above my head, and I rose into it, my bubbles blowing upwards in a silver shower and running like liquid mercury across the bulkheads and decking. The ladder was rotted so that it fell to pieces at my touch, the pieces hanging suspended in the water around my head as I went on into the lower deck.

This was a narrow and crowded alleyway, probably serving the passenger cabins and officers' mess. The claustrophobic atmosphere reminded me of the appalling conditions in which the crew of the frigate must have lived.

I ventured gingerly along this passage, attracted powerfully to the doorways on either hand which promised all manner of fascinating discoveries. I resisted their temptation and finned on down the long deck until it ended abruptly against a heavy timber bulkhead.

This would be the outer wall of the well of the forward hold, where it pierced the deck and went down into the ship's belly.

Satisfied with what we had achieved, I turned the beam of the torch on to my wrist and realized with a guilty thrill that we had overrun our working time by four minutes. Every second was taking us closer to the dreaded danger of empty air bottles and uncompleted decompression stops.

I grabbed Sherry's wrist and gave her the cut-throat hand signal for danger before tapping my wristwatch. She understood immediately, and followed me meekly on the long slow journey back through the hull along the guiding line. Already I could feel the stiffening of the demand valve, as it gave me air more reluctantly now that the bottles were almost exhausted.

We came out into the open and I made certain that Sherry was by my side before I looked upwards. What I saw above me made my breathing choke in my throat, and the horror I felt turned to a warm oily liquid sensation in my bowels.

The pool of Gunfire Break had been transformed into a bloody arena. Attracted by the tons of dead fish that had been killed by the blast, the deep-water killer sharks had arrived in their scores. The scent of flesh and blood, together with the excited movements of their fellows transmitted to them through the water, had driven them into that mindless savagery known as the feeding frenzy.

Quickly I drew Sherry back into the gunport and we cowered there, looking up at the huge gliding shapes so clearly silhouetted against the light source of the surface.

Amongst the shoals of smaller sharks there were at least two dozen of the ugly beasts that the islanders called Albacore shark. They were barrel-bodied and swing-bellied, big powerful fish with rounded snouts and wide grinning jaws. They swirled about the pool like some grotesque carousel, with their tails waggling and their mouths opening mechanically to gulp down shreds of flesh. I knew them for greedy but stupid animals, easily discouraged by any aggressive display when not in feeding frenzy. Now they were in intense excitation they would be dangerous, yet I would have accepted the risk of a decompression ascent if it had been for them alone.

What truly appalled me were two other long lithe shapes that sped silently about the pool, turning with a single powerful flick of the long swallow tail, so that the pointed nose almost touched the tip of the tail, then gliding away again with all the power and grace of an eagle in flight.

When either one of these terrible fish paused to feed, the sick-moon mouth opened and the multiple rows of teeth came erect like the quills of a porcupine and flared outwards.

They were a matched pair, each about twelve feet in length from nose to tail-tip, with the standing blade of the dorsal fin as long as a man's arm; they were slaty blue across the back and with snowy white bellies and dark tips to tail and fins, they could bite a man in half and swallow the pieces whole.

One of them saw us crouching in the mouth of the gunport, and it turned sharply and came down over us, planing a few feet above us as we cowered back into the gloom so that I could clearly see the long trailing spikes of the male reproductive organs.

These were the dreaded white death sharks, the most vicious fish of all the seas, and I knew that no attempt to ascend in the clear and decompress adequately with limited air and no protection would be certain death.

If I were to get Sherry out alive I would have to take risks that in any other circumstances would be unthinkable.

Quickly I scribbled on the slate: 'STAY!! I am free ascending for air and gun.'

She read the message and immediately shook her head in refusal and made urgent signs to prevent me, but already I had pulled the pin out of the quick release buckle of my harness and I took the last deep, chest-swelling breath before I thrust my scuba set into her hands. I dropped my weight belt to give myself buoyancy and slid down the side of the hull, using the tumble home to cover me as I finned swiftly for the cover of the cliff.

I had left Sherry what remained of my air supplies, perhaps five or six minutes' breathing if she used it sparingly, and now with only the air that I held in my lungs I had to run the gauntlet of the pool and try for the surface.

I reached the cliff and began to go up, close in against the coral, hoping that my dark suit would blend with the shades. I went up with my back to the coral, facing out into the open pool where the great sinister shapes still swirled and milled.

Twenty feet from the bottom and the air in my lungs was expanding rapidly as the pressure of water decreased. I could not hold it in or it would rupture the tissue of my lungs. I let it trickle from my lips, a silver beacon of bubbles that one of the white death sharks noticed immediately.

He rolled and turned, dashing across the pool with slashing strokes of his tail, bearing down upon me.

Desperately I glanced up the cliff and found six feet above me one of the small caves in the rotten coral. I dived into it just as the shark flashed past me, turned and sped back for a second pass as I shrank into my shallow shelter. The shark lost interest and swirled away to pick up the falling-leaf body of a dead snapper, gulping it down convulsively.

My lungs were throbbing and pumping now for the oxygen had been all absorbed from the air I held, and the carbon-dioxide was building up in my blood. Soon I would begin to black out into anoxia.

I left the shelter of the cave, but, still following the cliff, I drove upwards as hard as I could with the single swimming fin, wishing bitterly for the use of the other still trapped under the gun carriage.

Again I had to release expanding air as I rose, and I knew that in my veins nitrogen was also decompressing too rapidly and soon it would turn to gas and bubble like champagne in my blood.

Above me I saw the silvery moving mirror of the surface and the black cigar shape of the whaleboat's hull suspended upon it. I was coming up fast and I glanced down again. Far below me I could see the shark pack still milling and turning. It looked as though I had escaped their notice.

My lungs burned with the craving for air, and the blood pounded in my temples as I decided that the time had arrived when I must forsake the shelter of the cliff and cross the open pool to the whaleboat.

I kicked out and shot towards the whaleboat where it lay a hundred feet from the reef. Halfway across I glanced down and saw one of the white death's had seen me and was chasing. It came up from the blue depths with incredible speed, and terror gave me new strength as I drove for the surface and the boat.

I was looking down, watching the shark come. It seemed to swell up in size as it rushed towards me. Every detail was burned into my mind in those frantic seconds. I saw the hog's snout with the two slitted nostrils, the golden eyes with the black pupils like arrowheads, the broad blue back from which stood the tall executioner's blade of the dorsal fin.

I came out through the surface so fast that I broke clear to my waist, and I turned in the air and got my good arm over the gunwale of the boat. With all my strength I swung my body forward and jack-knifed my legs up under my chin.

In that instant the white death struck, the water exploded about me as he burst through the surface, I felt the harsh gritty skin tear across the legs of my suit as he brushed against me, then there was a shuddering crash as he struck the hull of the whaleboat.

I saw Chubby and Angelo's startled faces as the boat heeled over and rocked wildly. My violent contortions had thrown the shark off his run, and he had missed my legs and collided with the hull.

Now with one more desperate kick and heave I tumbled over the gunwale and fell into the bottom of the whaleboat. Again the shark crashed into the hull as I went over, missing me again by inches.

I lay there pumping air into my aching lungs, great sweet gulps of it that made me light-headed and giddy as on strong wine.

Chubby was yelling at me, 'Where is Miss Sherry? That big Johnny Uptail get Miss Sherry?'

I rolled on to my back, panting and sobbing for the precious air.

'Spare lungs,' I gasped. 'Sherry waiting in the wreck. She needs air.

Chubby leaped into the bows and dragged the canvas sheet off the extra scuba sets stacked there. In a crisis he is the kind of man I like to have covering for me.

'Angelo,' he growled, 'get them Johnny pills.' They were a pack of copper acetate shark repellent pills which I ordered from an American sports goods catalogue and for which Chubby had professed a deep and abiding scorn. 'Let's see if those fancy things are any bloody good.'

I had breathed enough to drag myself off the floorboards and to tell Chubby: 'We've got problems. The pool is full of big Johnnys, and there are two really mean uptails with them. That one that charged me and another.'

Chubby scowled as he fitted the demand valves to the new sets.

'Did you come straight up, Harry?'

I nodded. 'I left my bottles for Sherry. She's waiting down there.'

'You going to bend, Harry?' He looked up at me and I saw the worry in his eyes.

'Yes,' I nodded, as I dragged myself to my tackle box and lifted the lid.

'I've got to get down again fast – got to put pressure on my blood again before she fizzes.'

I picked out the bandolier of explosive heads for my hand spear. There were twelve of them, and I wished for more as I strapped the bandolier around my thigh. Each head was hand-tapped to screw on to the shaft of a ten foot stainless steel spear. It contained explosive charge equivalent to that of a 12-gauge shotgun shell and I could fire the charge with a trigger on the handle. It was an effective shark-killer.

Chubby hoisted one of the scuba sets on to my back and clinched the harness, and Angelo knelt before me to strap the shark repellent tablets in their perforated plastic containers to my ankles.

'I'll need another weight belt,' I said, 'and I lost a fin. There is a spare set in—' I did not finish the sentence. Blinding burning agony struck me in the elbow of my bad arm. Agony so fierce that I cried aloud, and my arm snapped closed like the blade of a clasp knife. It was an involuntary reaction, the joint doubling as the pressure of bubbles in the blood pressed on nerve and tendons.

'He's bending,' snarled Chubby. 'Sweet Mary, he's bending.' He leapt to the motors and gunned them, taking me in close to the reef. 'Work fast, Angelo,' Chubby shouted, 'we got to get him down again.'

The pain struck again, a fiery cramping agony in my right leg. The knee doubled under me and I whimpered like an infant. Angelo strapped the weight belt around my waist, and thrust the swimming fin on to my crippled leg.

Chubby cut the motors and we coasted in under the lee of the reef, while Chubby scrambled back to where I crouched on the thwart. He stooped over me to thrust the mouthpiece between my lips and open the cocks on the air bottle.

'Okay?' he asked, and I sucked from the set and nodded.

Chubby leaned over the side and peered down into the pool. 'Okay,' he grunted, 'Johnny Uptail gone somewhere else.'

He lifted me like a child, for I had lost the use of arm and leg, and he lowered me into the water between boat and reef.

Angelo hooked the harness of the extra scuba set for Sherry on to my belt, then he passed me the ten-foot spear and I prayed that I would not drop it.

'You go get Miss Sherry out of there,' said Chubby, and I rolled over in a clumsy one-legged duck dive and went down.

Even in the cramping agony of the bends my first concern was to search for the sinister gliding shapes of the white deaths. I saw one of them, but he was deep down, amongst the pack of lumbering Albacore sharks. Clinging to the shelter of the reef, I kicked and wriggled downwards like a maimed water beetle. Thirty feet under the surface the pain began to recede. Renewed pressure of water was reducing the size of the bubbles in my bloodstream, my limbs straightened and I had use of them.

I went down faster, and the relief was swift and blessed. I felt new courage and confidence flooding away my earlier despair. I had air and a weapon. I had a fighting chance now.

I was ninety feet down, in clear sight of the bottom. I could see Sherry's bubbles rising from the smoky blue depths, and the sight cheered me. She was still breathing, and I had a fully charged extra scuba set for her. All I had to do was get it to her.

One of the fat ugly Albacore sharks saw me as I slid down the dark cliff face, and he swerved towards me. Already gorged with food, but endlessly hungry, he came in at me grinning horribly and paddling his wide tail.

I backed up and hung in the water against the cliff, facing him. I had the spear with its explosive head extended towards him, and as I finned gently to hold myself ready the streamers of bright blue dye from the shark repellent tablets smoked out in a cloud around me.

The shark came on in, and I lined up to hit him fairly on the snout, but the instant his head and gills encountered clouds of blue dye he spun away, flapping his tail in shock and dismay. The copper acetate had burned his gills and eyes, and he retreated hurriedly.

'Eat your liver, Chubby Andrews,' I thought. 'They work!'

Down again I went, almost to the tops of the bamboo forest, seeing Sherry still crouched in the gunport thirty feet away watching me. She had exhausted her own air bottles and was using mine – but I could tell by the volume and scanty rate of flow of bubbles that she had only seconds of breathing time left to her.

I started towards her, leaving the cliff – and only her frantic hand signals alerted me. I turned and saw the white death coming like a long blue torpedo. He was skimming the tops of the bamboo, and from one corner of his jaws hung a tattered streamer of flesh. He opened that wide maw to gulp down the morsel, and the rows of fangs gleamed whitely, like the petals of some obscene flower.

I faced him as he charged, but at the same time I fell back kicking my fins in his direction and laying a thick smoke-screen of blue dye between us.

With hard slashing strokes of his tail, he arrowed in the last few yards, but then he hit the blue dye and swirled, altering the direction of his charge as he sheered away.

He passed me so close that his tail struck me a heavy blow on the shoulder, sending me tumbling end over end. For seconds I lost my bearings, but as I recovered my balance and looked wildly about me I found the great shark circling.

He swept around me, forty feet away, and in his full length he seemed to my heated eye as long as a battleship and as blue and as vast as a summer sky. It seemed impossible to believe that these fish grew to almost twice this size. This one was still a baby – I was thankful for that.

Suddenly the slim steel spear in which I had placed so much faith seemed futile, and the shark regarded me with a cold yellow eye across which the pale nictitating membrane flicked occasionally in a sardonic wink, and once he opened his jaws in a convulsive gulp, as though in anticipation of the taste of my flesh.

He continued in those wide racing circles, with myself always at the centre, turning with him and paddling frantically with my fins to match his smooth unforced speed.

As I turned, I unhooked the spare lung from my belt and slung it by the harness on my left shoulder like the shield of a Roman legionary, and I tucked the hilt of the spear under my arm and kept the head pointed at the circling monster.

My whole body tingled with the warm flush of adrenaline in the bloodstream, and my senses were enhanced and sharpened by the adrenaline high – the intensely pleasurable sensation of acute fear to which a man can become an addict.

Each detail of the deadly fish was etched indelibly on my memory, from the gentle pulsing of the multiple gill behind the head to the long trailing ribbons of the remora fish holding by their suckers to the smooth snowy expanse of his belly. With a fish of this size, it would only infuriate him further if I went for a hit with the explosive spear on his snout. My only chance was for a hit on the brain.

I recognized the moment when the shark's distaste for the blue mist of repellent was overcome by his hunger and his anger. His tail seemed to stiffen and it gave a series of rapid strokes, driving his speed up sharply.

I braced myself, lifting the spare scuba protectively, and the shark turned hard and fast, breaking the wide circle and coming in directly at me.

I saw the jaws open like a pit, lined with the wedge-shaped fangs, and at the moment of strike I thrust the twin steel bottles of the scuba into it.

The shark closed its jaws on the decoy and it was torn from my grasp, while the impact of the attack tossed me aside like a floating leaf. When I had gathered myself again I looked around frantically and found the white death was twenty feet away, moving only slowly but worrying the steel bottles the way a puppy chews a slipper.

It was shaking its head in the instinctive reaction which tears lumps of flesh from a victim – but which was now inflicting only deep scratches on the painted metal of the scuba.

This was my chance, my one and only chance. Kicking hard, I spurted above the broad blue back, brushing the tall dorsal fin and I sank down over him, coming in on his blind spot like an attacking fighter pilot from high astern.

I reached out with the steel spear and pressed the tip of it firmly on to the curved blue skull, directly between those cold and deadly yellow eyes – and I squeezed the spring-loaded trigger on the hilt of the spear.

The shot fired with a crack that beat in upon my eardrums, and the spear jumped heavily in my grip.

The white death shark reared on its tail like a startled horse, and once again I was tossed lightly aside by his careless bulk, but I recovered to watch him go into a terrible frenzy. The muscles beneath the smooth skin twitched and rippled at random impulse from the damaged brain, and the shark spun and dived, rolling wildly on its back, arrowing downwards to crash snout first into the rocky bottom of the pool, then it stood on its tail and scooted in aimless parabolas through the pale blue waters.

Still watching it, and keeping a respectful distance, I unscrewed the exploded head off the spear and replaced it with a fresh charge.

The white death still had Sherry's air supply clamped in his jaws. I could not leave it. I trailed his violent, unpredictable manoeuvres warily, and when at last he hung stationary for a moment nose down, suspended on the wide flukes of his tail, I shot in again and once more pressed the explosive charge to his skull, holding it firmly against the cartilaginous dome, so that the full shock of the charge would be transmitted directly to the tiny brain.

I fired the shot, cracking painfully in my own ears, and the shark froze rigidly. It never moved again but still in that frozen rigour it rolled over slowly and began to sink towards the floor of the pool. I darted in and wrested the damaged scuba from his jaws.

I saw immediately the air hoses had been torn and shredded by the shark's teeth, but the bottles were only extensively scratched.

Carrying the lung with me I sprinted across the tops of the bamboo towards the wreck. There were no longer air bubbles rising from the gunport, and as I came in sight of her I saw that Sherry had discarded the last empty scuba set. They were empty, and she was dying slowly.

Yet even in the extreme of slow suffocation she had not made the suicidal attempt to rise to the surface. She was waiting for me, dying slowly, but trusting me.

As I came down beside her, I pulled out my own mouthpiece and offered it to her. Her movements were slow and uncoordinated. The mouthpiece slipped from her grasp and floated upwards, spewing out a torrent of air. I grabbed it and forced it into her mouth, holding it there while lowering myself slightly below her level to induce a readier flow of air.

She began to breathe. Her chest rose and fell in long deep draughts of the precious stuff, and almosty immediately I saw her regaining strength and purpose. Satisfied I turned my attention to removing a demand valve from one of the abandoned lungs from which the air supply was exhausted and using it to replace the one damaged by the shark.

I breathed off it for half a minute, before strapping it on to Sherry's back and retrieving my own mouthpiece.

We had air now, enough to take us through the long period of slow decompression ahead of us. I knelt facing Sherry in the gunport and she grinned lopsidedly around the mouthpiece and lifted her thumb in a high sign and I returned it. You okay, me okay, I thought, and unscrewed the expended head from the spear and renewed it from the bandolier on my thigh.

Then once more I peered from the safety of the gunport out into the open waters of the pool.

As the supply of dead fish was depleted so the shark pack seemed to have dispersed. I saw one or two of the ungainly dark shapes still searching and sniffing the tainted waters, but their frenzy was reduced. They moved in a more leisurely fashion, and I felt happier about taking Sherry out now.

I reached for her hand and was surprised at how small and cold it felt in mine, but she answered my gesture with a squeeze of her fingers.

I pointed to the surface and she nodded. I led her out of the gunport and we slid down the hull and under cover of the bamboo crossed quickly to the shelter of the reef.

Side by side, still holding hands and with our backs to the cliff, we rose slowly up out of the pool.

The light strengthened and when I looked up I could see the whaleboat high above. My spirits rose.

At sixty feet I stopped for a minute to begin decompressing. A fat old

Albacore shark swam past us, blotched and piebald like a pig, but he paid us no attention and I lowered the spear as he drifted away into the hazy distance.

Slowly we rose to the next decompression stop at forty feet, where we stayed for two minutes, allowing the nitrogen in our blood to evaporate out through our lungs gradually. Then up to twenty feet for the next stop.

I peered into Sherry's face-mask and she rolled her eyes at me, clearly she was regaining her courage and cheek. It was all going smoothly now. We were as good as home, and drinking whisky – just another twelve minutes.

The whaleboat was so close it seemed that I could touch it with the spear. I could quite clearly see Chubby's and Angelo's brown faces hanging over the side as they waited anxiously for us to emerge.

I looked away from them, making another careful search of the water about us. At the extreme range of my vision, where the haze of water shaded away to solid blue, I saw something move. It was just a suspicion of a shadow that had come and gone before I had really seen it, but I felt the returning prickle of fear and apprehension.

I hung in the water, completely alert once more, searching and waiting while the last few slow minutes dragged by like crippled insects.

The shadow passed again, this time clearly seen, a swift and deadly movement that left me in no doubt that it was not an Albacore shark. It was the difference between the shape of the prowling hyena in the shadows around the campfire to that of the lion when he hunts.

Suddenly, through the misty blue curtains of water, came the second white death shark. He came swiftly and silently, passing fifty feet away, seeming to ignore us and going on almost to the range of our vision and then turning steeply and returning to pass us again, like a caged animal back and forth along the bars.

Sherry cowered close to me and I disengaged my hand from the death grip in which she had it. I needed both hands now.

On the next pass the shark broke the pattern of its movements and went into the great sweeping circles which always precede attack. Around and around it went, with that pale yellow eye fastened hungrily upon us.

Suddenly my attention was distracted by the slow descent from above of a dozen of the blue plastic shark-repellent containers. Seeing our predicament Chubby must have emptied the entire boxful over the side. One of them passed closely enough for me to snatch it up and hand it to Sherry.

It smoked blue dye in her hand, and I transferred my attention back to the shark. I had sheered off a little from the blue dye, but it was still circling swiftly and grinning loathsomely at us.

I glanced at my watch, three minutes more to be safe, but I could risk sending Sherry out ahead of me. Unlike myself she had not already had a nitrogen fizz in her blood, she would probably be safe in another minute.

The shark tightened its circle, boring in relentlessly on us. Close – so very close that I looked deep into the black spearheaded pupil of his eye, and read his intention there.

I glanced at the watch. It was cutting it fine – very fine, but I decided to send Sherry up. I slapped her shoulder and pointed urgently to the surface. She hesitated, but I slapped her again and repeated my instruction.

She began to rise, going up slowly, the right way, but her legs dangled invitingly. The shark left me and rose slowly in time with her, following her.

She saw it and began to rise faster, smoothly the shark closed in on her. Now I was under them both, and I finned out fast to one side just as the shark went into the stiff-tailed attitude which signalled the instant of his attack.

I was directly under him, as he turned to maul Sherry. I reached up and pressed the spear-head into the softly obscene throat, and I hit the trigger.

I saw the shock kick into the bloated white flesh, and the shark reared away with a convulsive beat of its tail. It shot upwards and went out through the surface, leaping out high and clear, and falling back heavily in a creaming froth of bubbles.

Immediately it began to spin and fly in maddened, crazy circles, as though beset by a swarm of bees. Repeatedly its jaws opened and snapped closed.

Torn with terrible anxiety. I watched Sherry maintain her mental discipline and rise leisurely towards the whaleboat. A pair of huge brown paws were thrust down through the surface to welcome her. As I watched, she came within reach of them. The brown fingers closed on her like steel grab-hooks and she was plucked with miraculous strength from the water.

I could now employ all my attention on the problem of staying alive through the next few minutes before I could follow her. The shark seemed to recover from the shock of the charge, and it exchanged its mindless crazy gyrations for the terrible familiar circling.

I began again on the wide circumference, closing in steadily with each circuit. I glanced at my wristwatch and saw that at last I could begin to rise through the final stage.

I drifted upwards slowly. The agony of the bends was fresh in my memory – but the white death shark was pressing closer and closer.

Ten feet below the whaleboat, I paused again and the shark was suspicious, probably remembering the recent violent explosion in its throat. It ceased its circling and hung motionless in the pale water on the wide pointed wings of his pectoral fins. We stared at each other across a distance of fifteen feet, and I could sense that the great blue beast was gathering himself for the final rush.

I extended the spear to the full reach of my arm, and gently, so as not to trigger him, I finned towards him until the explosive charge was an inch from the nostril slits below the snout.

I hit the trigger and he reared back in shock as the explosive cracked. He whirled away in a wide angry turn and I dropped the spear and shot for the surface.

He was angry as a wounded lion, goaded by the hurts he had received, and he charged for me with his humped back large as a blue mountain and his wide jaws gaping open. I knew there was no turning him this time, nothing short of death would stop him.

As I shot for the surface I saw Chubby's hands waiting for me, the fingers like a bunch of brown bananas, and I loved him at that moment. I lifted my right arm above my head, offering it to Chubby and as the shark flashed across the last few feet that separated us I felt Chubby's fingers close on my wrist.

Then the water exploded about me. I felt the enormous drag on my arm and the powerful disruption of the water as the shark's bulk tore it apart. Then I was lying on my back upon the deck of the whaleboat, dragged from the very jaws of that dreadful animal.

'You got some nice pets, Harry,' said Chubby in a disinterested tone that I knew was forced, and I looked about quickly for Sherry.

'You okay?' I called, as I saw her wet and pale-faced in the stern. She nodded; I doubted she could speak.

I jerked out the quick release pin on my harness, freeing myself of the weight of the scuba.

'Chubby, set up a stick of gelly ready to shoot,' I called, as I rid myself of mask and fins and peered over the side of the whaleboat.

The shark was still with us, circling the whaleboat in a fury of hurt and frustration. He came up to show the full length of his dorsal fin above the surface. I knew he could easily attack and stove in the planking of the whaleboat.

'Oh God, Harry, he's horrible.' Sherry found her voice at last, and I knew how she felt. I hated that loathesome fish with the full force of my recent terror – but I had to distract it from direct attack.

'Angelo, give me that Moray and a bait-knife,' I shouted and he handed me the cold slimy body. I hacked off a ten-pound lump of the dead eel and tossed it into the pool.

The shark swirled and raced for the scrap, gulping it down and scraping the hull of the whaleboat as it passed so close. We rocked violently at its passing.

'Hurry up, Chubby,' I shouted, and fed the shark another lump. It took it as readily as a hungry dog, dashing past under the hull and again bumping the boat so that it swayed unpleasantly and Sherry squeaked and grabbed the gunwale.

'Ready,' said Chubby, and I passed him a two-foot section of the eel with its empty belly cavity hanging open like a pouch.

'Put the stick in there, and tie it up,' I instructed him, and he began to grin.

'Hey, Harry,' he chortled, 'I like it.'

While I fed the monster with scraps of eel, Chubby trussed up the stick of gelignite in a neat parcel of eel flesh, with the insulated copper wire protruding from it. He passed it to me.

'Connect her up,' I instructed, as I coiled a dozen loops of the wire into my left hand.

'Ready to shoot,' grinned Chubby, and I threw the bundle of meat and explosive into the path of the circling shark.

It raced for it, and its glistening blue back broke the surface as it swallowed the offering. Immediately the wire began to stream away over the side and I paid out more from the reel.

'Let him eat it down,' I said and Chubby nodded happily.

'Okay, Chubby, blow the bastard to hell,' I snarled as the fish came to the surface, fin up, and swung around us in another circle, with the copper wire trailing from the corner of the sickle-moon mouth.

Chubby hit the switch, and the shark erupted in a tall burst of pink spray, like a bursting water melon, as his pale blood mingled with the paler flesh and purple contents of the belly cavity, spurting fifty feet into the air and splattering the pool and whaleboat. The shattered carcass wallowed like a bleeding log upon the surface, then rolled over and began to sink.

'Goodbye, Johnny Uptail,' hooted Angelo, and Chubby grinned like a cherub.

'Let's go home,' I said, for already the oceanic surf was breaking over the reef, and I thought I was going to throw up.

However, my indisposition responded miraculously to a treatment of Chivas Regal whisky, even though taken from an enamel mug, and much later in the cave Sherry said: 'I suppose you want me to thank you for saving my life, and all that crap?'

I grinned at her and opened my arms. 'No, my sweeting, just show me how grateful you are,' which she did, and afterwards there were no ugly dreams to spoil my sleep for I was exhausted in body and spirit.


I think all of us were coming to regard the pool at Gunfire Break with a superstitious dread. The series of accidents and mishaps to which we had been subject appeared to be the result of some deliberate malevolent scheme.

It seemed as though each time we returned to the pool it had grown more sinister in its aspect and that an aura of menace was growing about it.

'You know what I think,' Sherry said laughingly, but not completely as a joke. 'I think the spirits of the murdered Mogul princes have followed the treasure to act as guardians—' Even in the bright sunshine of a glorious morning I saw the expressions on the faces of Angelo and Chubby. 'I think the spirits were in those two big Johnny Uptails that we killed yesterday.' Chubby looked as though he had breakfasted off a dozen rotten oysters, he blanched to a waxy golden brown and I saw him make the sign with his right hand.

'Miss Sherry,' said Angelo severely, 'you must never talk like that.' I could see gooseflesh on his forearms. Both he and Chubby had an attack of the ghostlies.

'Yes, cut it out,' I agreed.

'I was joking,' protested Sherry.

'Good joke,' I said, 'you really slayed us.' And we were all silent during the passage of the channel and until we had taken station in the shelter of the reef.

I was sitting in the bows, and when all three of them looked at me I saw by the expressions on their faces that I had a crisis of morale on my hands.

'I will go down alone,' I announced, and there was a small stir of relief.

'I'll go with you,' Sherry volunteered half-heartedly.

'Later,' I agreed,' but first I want to check for Johnnies, and recover the equipment we lost yesterday.'

I went down cautiously, hanging just under the boat for five minutes while

I scrutinized the depths of the pool for those evil dark shapes, and then finning down quietly.

It was cold and eerie in the deeper shades, but I saw that the night tide had scoured the pool and sucked out to sea all the carrion and blood that had attracted the shark pack the previous day.

There was no sign of the huge white death carcasses, and the only fish I saw were the multitudinous shoals of brilliant coral dwellers. A glint of silver from below led me to the spear I had abandoned in my rush for the boat, and I found the empty scubas and the damaged demand valve where we had left them in the gunport.

I surfaced with my load, and there were smiles amongst my crew for the first time that day when I reported the pool clear.

'All right,' I capitalized on the rise of their spirits, 'today we are going to open up the hold.'

'You going in through the hull?' Chubby asked.

'I thought about that, Chubby, but I reckoned that it would need a couple of heavy charges to get in that way. I've decided to go in through the passenger deck into the well.' I sketched it on my slate for them as I explained. 'The cargo will have shifted, it will be lying in a jumble just beyond that bulkhead and once we pop her open here, we can drag it out item by item into the companionway.'

'It's a long haul from there to the gunport.' Chubby lifted his cap and massaged his bald dome thoughtfully.

'I'll rig a light block and tackle at the gundeck ladder and another at the gunport.'

'A lot of work,' Chubby looked sad.

'The first time you agree with me – I'm going to begin worrying that I may be wrong.'

'I didn't say you were wrong,' said Chubby stiffly, 'I just said it was a lot of work. You can't let Miss Sherry haul on a block and tackle, can you now?'

'No,' I agreed. 'We need somebody with beef,' and I prodded his bulging rock-hard gut.

'That's what I thought,' said Chubby mournfully. 'You want me to get geared up?'

'No.' I stopped him. 'Sherry can come down with me to set the charges now.' I wanted her to test her nerves after the previous day's horrors. 'We will blast the well open and then go home. We aren't going to work again immediately after blasting. We are going to let the tide clean the pool of dead fish before going down. I don't want an action replay of yesterday.'

We crept in through the gunport and followed the nylon guide line we had placed on our first visit, along the gundeck, up through the companion ladder to the passenger deck, and then along the dark forbidding tunnel to the dead-end bulkhead of the forward well.

While Sherry held the torch for me, I began to drill a hole through the partition with the brace and bit that I had brought from the surface. It was awkward working without a really firm stance on which to anchor myself, but the first inch and a half was easy going. This layer of wood had rotted to a soft corky consistency, but beyond that I encountered iron hard oak planking and I had to abandon my efforts. I would have been a week at the task.

Unable to place my explosive in prepared shot holes, I would now have to use a larger charge than I really wanted and rely on the tunnel effect of the passageway for a secondary shock to drive the panel inwards. I used six half sticks of gelignite, placed on the corners and in the centre of the bulkhead, and I secured them to bolts driven into the woodwork with a slap hammer.

It took almost half an hour to set up the blast, and afterwards it was a relief to leave the claustrophobic confines of the ancient hull and to rise up through clean clear water to the silver surface, trailing the insulated wires behind us.

Chubby fired the shots while we stripped off our equipment. The shock was cushioned by the hull of the wreck so that it was hardly noticeable to us on the surface.

We left the pool immediately afterwards and ran home with rising spirits to the prospect of a lazy day while we waited for the tide to clean the pool of carrion.

In the afternoon Sherry and I went on a picnic down to the south tip of the island. For provisions we took a wicker-covered two-litre bottle of Portuguese *vinos verde*, but to supplement this we dug out a batch of big sand clams which I wrapped in seaweed and reburied in the sand. Over them I built an open fire of driftwood.

By the time we had almost finished the wine, the sun was setting and the clams were ready to eat. The wine and the food and the glorious sunset had a softening effect on Sherry North. She became doe-eyed and melting, and when the sunset faded at last and made way for a fat yellow lovers' moon, we walked home barefooted on the wet sand.


The next morning Chubby and I worked for half an hour bringing down the equipment we needed from the whaleboat and stacking it on the gundeck of the wreck before we were able to penetrate deeper into the hull.

The heavy charges I had set against the well had wrought the sort of havoc I feared. They had torn out the decking and smashed in the bulkheads of the passenger cabins, blocking the passage for a quarter of its length. We found a good anchor point for our block and tackle and while Chubby rigged it, I left him and floated back to the nearest cabin. I played my torch through the shattered panelling. The interior was, like everything else, smothered in a thick furring of marine growth but I could make out the shape of the simple furniture beneath it.

I eased myself through the gap, and moved slowly across the cluttered deck, fascinated by the objects which I found scattered and heaped about the cabin. There were items of porcelain and china, a shattered washbasin and a magnificent chamber pot with a pink floral design showing through the film of accumulated sediment. There were cosmetic pots and scent bottles, smaller indefinable metal objects and mounds of rotted and amorphous material which may have been clothing, curtaining or mattresses and bed-clothing.

I glanced at my watch and saw that it was time to leave and surface for a change of air bottles. As I turned, a small square object caught my attention and I played the torchbeam upon it while I gently brushed it clear of the thick layer of muddy filth. It was a wooden box, the size of a portable transistor radio, but the lid was beautifully inlaid with mother-of-pearl and tortoiseshell. I picked it up and tucked it under my arm. Chubby had finished rigging the block and tackle and he was waiting for me beside the gundeck ladder. When we surfaced beside the whaleboat I passed the box up to Angelo before climbing aboard.

While Sherry poured coffee for us and Angelo charged the demand valves to the fresh scuba bottles, I lit a cheroot and examined the box.

It was in a sorry state of deterioration, I saw at once. The inlay was rotten and falling out of its seating, the rosewood was swollen and distorted and the lock and hinges half eaten away.

Sherry came to sit beside me on the thwart and examined my prize with me. She recognized it immediately.

'It's a ladies' jewel box,' she exclaimed. 'Open it, Harry. Let's see what's inside.'

I slipped the blade of a screw-driver under the lock and at the first pressure the hinges snapped and the lid flew off.

'Oh, Harry!' Sherry was first into it, and she came out with a thick gold chain and a heavy locket of the same material. 'This stuff is so in fashion, you'd never believe it.'

Everyone was dipping into the box now. Angelo ripped off a pair of gold and sapphire earrings which immediately replaces the brass pair he habitually wore, while Chubby picked an enormous necklace of garnets which he hung around his neck and preened like a teenage girl.

'For my missus,' he explained.

It was the personal jewellery of a middle-class wife, probably some minor official or civil servant – none of it of great value, but in its context it was a fascinating collection. Inevitably Miss North acquired the lion's share – but I managed to snatch away a thick plain gold wedding band.

'What do you want with that?' she challenged me, reluctant to yield a single item.

'I'll find a use for it,' I told her, and gave her one of my looks of deep significance, which was completely wasted for she had returned to ransacking the jewel box.

Nevertheless I tucked the ring safely away in the small zip pocket of my canvas gear bag. Chubby by this stage was bedecked with chunky jewellery like a Hindu bride.

'My God, Chubby, you're a dead ringer for Liz Taylor,' I told him and he accepted the compliment with a graceful inclination of his head.

I had a difficult job getting him interested in a return to the wreck, but once we were in the passenger deck again, he worked like a giant amongst the shattered wreckage.

We hauled out the panelling and timber baulks that blocked the passage by use of the block and tackle and our combined strength, and we dragged it down to the gundeck and stacked it out of the way in the recesses of that gloomy gallery.

We had reached the well of the forward hold by the time our air supplies were almost exhausted. The heavy planking had broken up in the explosion and beyond the opening we could make out what appeared to be a solid dark mass of material. I guessed that this was a conglomerate formed by the cargo out of its own weight and pressure.

However, it was afternoon the following day before I found that I was correct. We were at last into the hold, but I had not expected such a Herculean task as awaited us there.

The contents of the hold had been impregnated with sea water for over a century. Ninety per cent of the containers had rotted and collapsed, and the perishable contents had coalesced into a friable dark mass.

Within this solid heap of marine compost, the metal objects, the containers of stronger and impervious material and other imperishable objects, both large and small, were studded like lucky coins in a Christmas pudding. We would have to dig for them.

At this point we encountered our next problem. At the slightest disturbance of this rotted mass the water was immediately filled with a swirling storm of dark particles that blotted out the beams of the torches and plunged us into clouds of blinding darkness.

We were forced to work by sense of touch alone. It was painfully slow progress. When we encountered some solid body in the softness we had to drag it clear, manoeuvre it down the passage, lower it to the gundeck and there try to identify it. Sometimes we were obliged to break open what remained of the container, to get at the contents.

If they were of little value or interest, we tucked them away in the depths of the gundeck to keep our working field clear.

At the end of the first day's work we had salvaged only one item which we decided was worth raising. It was a sturdy case of hard wood, covered with what appeared to be leather and with the corners bound in heavy brass. It was the size of a large cabin trunk.

It was so heavy that Chubby and I could not lift it between us. The weight alone gave me high hopes. I believed it could very readily contain part of the golden throne. Although the container did not look like one that had been manufactured by an Indian village carpenter and his sons in the middle of the nineteenth century, yet there was a chance that the throne had been repacked before it was shipped from Bombay.

If it did contain part of the throne, then our task would be simplified. We would know what type of container to look for in the future. Using the block and tackle Chubby and I dragged the case down the gundeck to the gunport and there we shrouded it in a nylon cargo net to prevent it bursting open or breaking during the ascent. To the eyes spliced into the circumference of the net we attached the canvas flotation bags and inflated them from our air bottles.

We went up with the case, controlling its ascent by either spilling air from the bags, or adding more from our bottles. We came out beside the whaleboat and Angelo passed us half a dozen nylon slings with which we secured the case before climbing aboard.

The weight of the case defeated our efforts to lift it over the side, for the whaleboat heeled dangerously when the three of us made the attempt. We had to step the mast and use it as a derrick, only then did our combined efforts suffice and the case swung on board, spouting water from its seams. The moment that it sank to the deck Chubby scrambled back to the motors and ran for the channel. The tide pressed closely on our heels as we went.

The case was too weighty and our curiosity too strong to allow us to carry it up to the caves. We opened it on the beach, prising the lid open with a pair of jenny bars. The elaborate locking device in the lid was of brass and had withstood the ravages of salt sea water. It resisted our efforts bravely, but at last with a rending of woodwork the lid flew back and creaked against the heavily corroded hinges.

My disappointment was immediate, for it was clear that this was no tiger throne. It was only when Sherry lifted out one of the large gleaming discs and turned it curiously in her hands that I began to suspect that we had been awarded an enormous bonus.

It was an entrée plate she held, and my first thought was that it was of solid gold. However, when I snatched a mate from its slot in the cunningly designed rack and turned it to examine the hallmarks, I realized that it was silver and gold gilt.

The gold plating had protected it from the sea so that it was perfectly preserved, a masterpiece of the silversmith's art with a raised coat of arms in the centre and the rim wondrously chased with scenes of woods and deer, of huntsmen and birds.

The plate I held weighed almost two pounds and as I set it aside and examined the rest of the set I saw the weight of the chest fully accounted for.

There were servings for thirty-six guests in the set; soup bowls, fish plates, entrée plates, desert bowls, side plates and all the cutlery to go with it. There were serving dishes, a magnificent chafing dish, wine coolers, dish covers and a carving dish almost the size of a baby's bath.

Every piece was wrought with the same coat of arms, and the ornamental scenes of wild animals and huntsmen, and the case had been designed to hold this array of plate.

'Ladies and gentlemen,' I said, 'as your chairman, it behoves me to assure you, one and all, that our little venture is now in profit.'

'It's just plates and things,' said Angelo, and I winced theatrically.

'My dear Angelo, this is probably one of the few complete sets of Georgian banquet silverware remaining anywhere in the world – it's priceless.'

'How much?' asked Chubby, doubtfully.

'Good Lord, I don't know. It would depend of course on the maker and the original owner – this coat of arms probably belongs to some noble house. A wealthy nobleman on service in India, an earl, a duke perhaps, even a viceroy.'

Chubby looked at me as though I was trying to sell him a spavined horse.

'How much?' he repeated.

'At Messrs. Sothebys on a good day,' I hesitated, 'I don't know, say, a hundred thousand pounds.'

Chubby spat into the sand and shook his head. You couldn't fool old Chubby.

'This fellow Sotheby, does he run a loony house?'

'It's true, Chubby,' Sherry cut in. 'This stuff is worth a fortune. It could be more than that .'

Chubby was now torn between natural scepticism and chivalry. It would be an ungentlemanly act to call Sherry a liar. He compromised by lifting his hat and rubbing his head, spitting once more and saying nothing.

However, he handled the case with new respect when we dragged it up through the palms to the caves. We stored it behind the stack of jerrycans, and I went to fetch a new bottle of whisky.

'Even if there is no tiger throne in the wreck, we aren't going to do too badly out of this,' I told them.

Chubby sipped at his whisky mug and muttered, 'A hundred thousand – they've got to be crazy.'

'We've got to go through that hold and the cabins more carefully. We are going to leave a fortune down there if we don't.'

'Even the little items, less spectacular than the silver plate, they have enormous antique value,' Sherry agreed.

'Trouble is when you touch anything down there it stirs up such a fog you can't see the tip of your nose,' gloomed Chubby, and I refilled his mug with good cheer.

'Listen, Chubby, you know the centrifugal water pump that Arnie Andrews has got out at Monkey Bay?' I asked, and Chubby nodded.

'Will he lend it to us?' Arnie was Chubby's uncle. He owned a small market garden on the southern side of St Mary's island.

'He might,' Chubby answered warily. 'Why?'

'I want to try and rig a dredge pump,' I explained and sketched it for them in the sand between my feet. 'We set the pump up in the whaleboat, and we use a length of steam hose to reach the wreck –like this.' I roughed it out with my finger. 'Then we use it like a vacuum cleaner in the hold, suck out all that muck and pump it to the surface—'

'Hey, that's right,' Angelo burst out enthusiastically. 'When it spills out of the pump we run it through a sieve, and we will be able to pick up all the small stuff.''That's right. Only muck and small light items will go up the spout – anything large or heavy will be left behind.'

We discussed it for an hour working out details and refinements on the basic idea. During that time Chubby tried manfully to show no signs of enthusiasm, but finally he could contain himself no longer.

'It might work,' he muttered, which from him was a high accolade.

'Well, you better go fetch that pump then, hadn't you?' I asked.

'I think I will have one more drink,' he procrastinated, and I handed him the bottle.

'Take it with you,' I suggested. 'It will save time.'

He grunted, and went to fetch his overcoat.


Sherry and I slept late, gloating on the lazy day ahead and at the feeling of having the island entirely to ourselves. We did not expect Chubby and Angelo to return before noon.

After breakfast we crossed the saddle between the hills and went down to the beach. We were playing in the shallows, and the rumble of the surf on the outer reef and our own splashing and laughter blanketed any other sounds. It was only by chance that I looked up and saw the light aircraft sweeping in from the landward channel.

'Run!' I shouted at Sherry, and she thought I was joking until I pointed urgently at the approaching aircraft.

'Run! Don't let him see us,' and this time she responded quickly. We floundered naked from the water, and went up the beach at the top of our speed.

Now I could hear the buzz of the aircraft engines and I glanced over my shoulder. It was banking low over the southern-most peak of the island and levelling over the long straight beach towards us.

'Faster!' I yelled at Sherry, as she ran long-legged and full-bottomed ahead of me with the wet tresses of her sable hair dangling down her darkly tanned back.

I looked back and the aircraft was headed directly at us, still about a mile distant, but I could see that it was twin-engined. As I watched, it sank lower towards the snowy expanse of coral sands.

We snatched up our discarded clothing at full run, and sprinted the last few yards into the palm grove. There was a mound formed by a fallen palm tree and the fronds torn off the trees by the storm. It was a convenient shelter and I grabbed Sherry's arm and dragged her down.

We rolled under the shelter of the dead fronds and lay side by side, panting wildly from the run up the beach.

I saw now that it was a twin-engined Cessna. It came down the beach and swept past our hideaway only twenty feet above the water's edge.

The fuselage was painted a distinctive daisy yellow and was blazoned with the name 'Africair'. I recognized the aircraft. I had seen it before at St Mary's Airport on half a dozen occasions, usually discharging or picking up groups of wealthy tourists. I knew that Africair was a charter company based on the mainland, and that its aircraft were for hire on a mileage tariff. I wondered who was paying for the hire on this trip.

There were two persons in the forward seats of the aircraft, the pilot and a passenger, and their faces were turned towards us as it roared past. However, they were too far from us to make out the features and I could not be sure if I knew either of them. They were both white men, that was all that was certain.

The Cessna turned steeply out over the lagoon and, one wing pointed directly down into the crystal water, it swept around and then levelled for another run down the beach.

This time it passed so closely that for an instant I looked up into the face of the passenger as he peered down into the palm grove. I thought I recognized him, but I could not be certain.

The Cessna then turned away, rising slowly, and set a new course for the mainland. There was something about her going that was complacent, the air of someone having achieved his purpose, a job well done.

Sherry and I crawled from our hiding-place and stood up to brush the sand from our damp bodies.

'Do you think they saw us?' she asked timidly.

'With that bottom of yours flashing like a mirror in the sunlight, they could hardly miss.'

'They might have mistaken us for a couple of native fishermen.'

I looked at her, not at her face, and I grinned: 'Fisherman? With those great beautiful boobs?'

'Harry Fletcher, you are a disgusting beast,' she said. 'But seriously, Harry, what is going to happen now?'

'I wish I knew, my sweeting, I wish I knew,' I answered, but I was glad that Chubby had taken the case of silverware back to St Mary's with him. By now it was probably buried behind the shack at Turtle Bay. We were still in profit – even if we had to run for it soon.

The visit by the aircraft instilled in us all a new sense of urgency. We knew now that our time was strictly rationed, and Chubby brought news with him when he returned that was equally disturbing.

'The *Mandrake* cruised for five days in the south islands. They saw her nearly every day from Coolie Peak, and she was messing about like she didn't know what she was doing,' he reported. 'Then on Monday she anchored again in Grand Harbour. Wally says that the owner and his wife went up to the hotel for lunch, then afterwards they took a taxi and went down to Frobisher Street. They spent an hour with Fred Coker in his office, then he drove them down to Admiralty Wharf and they went back on board *Mandrake*. She weighed and sailed almost immediately.'

'Is that all?'

'Yes,' Chubby nodded, 'except that Fred Coker went straight up to the bank afterwards and put fifteen hundred dollars into his savings account.'

'How do you know that?'

'My sister's third daughter works at the bank.'

I tried to show a cheerful face, although I felt ugly little insects crawling around in my stomach. 'Well,' I said, 'no use moping around. Let's try and get the pump assembled so we can catch tomorrow's tide.'

Later, after we had carried the water pump up to the caves, Chubby returned alone to the whaleboat and when he came back he carried a long canvas-wrapped bundle.

'What have you got there, Chubby?' I demanded, and shyly he opened the canvas cover. It was my FN carbine and a dozen spare magazines of ammunition packed into a small haversack.

'Thought it might come in useful,' he muttered.

I took the weapon down into the grove and buried it beside the cases of gelignite in a shallow grave. Its proximity gave me a little comfort when I returned to assist in assembling the water pump.

We worked on into the night by the light of the gas lanterns, and it was after midnight when we carried the pump and its engine down to the whaleboat and bolted it to a makeshift mounting of heavy timber which we placed squarely amidship. Angelo and I were still working on the pump when we ran out towards the reef in the morning. We had been on station for half an hour before we had it assembled and ready to test.

Three of us dived on the wreck – Chubby, Sherry and myself – and we manhandled the stiff black snake of the hose through the gunport and up into the breach through the well of the hold.

Once it was in position, I slapped Chubby on the shoulder and pointed to the surface. He replied with a high sign and finned away, leaving Sherry and me in the passenger deck.

We had planned this part of the operation carefully and we waited impatiently while Chubby went up, decompressing on his way, and climbed into the whaleboat to prime the pump and start the motor.

We knew he had done so by the faint hum and vibration that was transmitted to us down the hose.

I braced myself in the ragged entrance to the hold, and grasped the end of the hose with both hands. Sherry trained the torchbeam on to the dark heap of cargo, and I swung the open end of the hose slowly over the rotted cargo.

I saw immediately that it was going to work, small pieces of debris vanished miraculously into the hose, and it caused a small whirlpool as it sucked in water and floating motes of rubbish.

At this depth and with the RPM provided by the petrol engine, the pump was rated to move thirty thousand gallons of water an hour, which was a considerable volume. Within seconds I had cleared the working area and we still had good visibility. I could start probing into the heap with a jenny bar, breaking out larger pieces and pushing them back into the passage behind us.

Once or twice I had to resort to the block and tackle to clear some bulky case or object, but mostly I was able to advance with only the hose and the jenny bar.

We had moved almost fifty cubic foot of cargo before it was time to ascend for a change of air bottle. We left the end of the hose firmly anchored in the passenger deck, and went up to a hero's welcome. Angelo was in transports of delight and even Chubby was smiling.

The water around the whaleboat was clouded and filthy with the thick soup of rubbish we had pumped out of the hold, and Angelo had retrieved almost a bucketful of small items that had come through the outlet of the pump and fallen into the sieve – it was a collection of buttons, nails, small ornaments from women's dresses, brass military insignia, some small copper and silver coins of the period, and odds and ends of metal and glass and bone.

Even I was impatient to return to the task, and Sherry was so insistent that I had to donate my half-smoked cheroot to Chubby and we went down again.

We had been working for fifteen minutes when I came upon the corner of an up-ended crate similar to others that we had already cleared. Although the wood was soft as cork, the seams had been reinforced with strips of hoop iron and iron nails so I struggled with it for some time before I prised out a plank and pushed it back between us. The next plank came free more readily, and the contents seemed to be a mattress of decomposed and matted vegetable fibre.

I pulled out a large hunk of this and it almost jammed the opening of the hose, but eventually disappeared on its way to the surface. I almost lost interest in this box and was about to begin working in another area – but Sherry showed strong signs of disapproval, shaking her head, thumping my shoulder and refusing to direct the beam of the torch anywhere but at the unappetizing mess of fibre.

Afterwards I asked her why she had insisted and she fluttered her eyelashes and looked important.

'Female intuition, my dear. You wouldn't understand.'

At her urging, I once more attacked the opening in the case, but scratching smaller chunks of the fibre loose so as not to block the hose opening.

I had removed above six inches of this material when I saw the gleam of metal in the depths of the excavation. I felt the first deep throb of certainty in my belly then, and I tore out another plank with furious impatience. It enlarged the opening so I could work in it more easily.

Slowly I removed the layers of compacted fibre which I realized must have been straw originally used as packing. Like a face materializing in a dream, it was revealed.

The first tiny gleam opened to a golden glory of intricately worked metal and I felt Sherry's grip on my shoulder as she crowded down close beside me.

There was a snout, and lips below that were drawn up in a savage snarl, revealing great golden fangs and an arched tongue. There was a broad deep forehead as wide as my shoulders, and ears flattened down close upon the burnished skull – and there was a single empty eyesocket set fairly in the centre of the wide brow. The lack of an eye gave the animal a blind and tragic expression, like some maimed god from mythology.

I felt an almost religious awe as I stared at the huge, wonderfully fashioned tiger's head we had exposed. Something cold and frightening slithered up my spine, and involuntarily I glanced about me into the dark and forbidding recesses of the hold, almost as if I expected the spirits of the Mogul prince guardians to be lurking there.

Sherry squeezed my shoulder again and I returned my attention to the golden idol. but the sense of awe was so strong upon me that I had to force myself to return to the task of clearing the packing from around it. I worked very carefully for I was fully aware that the slightest scratch or damage would greatly reduce the value and the beauty of this image.

When our working time was exhausted we drew back and stared at the exposed head and shoulders, and the torch beam was reflected from the brilliant surface in arrows of golden light that lit the hold like some holy shrine. We turned then and left it to the silence and the dark, while we went up into the sunlight.

Chubby was aware immediately that something significant had happened, but he said nothing until we had climbed aboard and in silence shed our equipment. I lit a cheroot and drew deeply upon it, not bothering to mop the droplets of seawater that ran from my sodden hair down my cheeks. Chubby was watching me but Sherry was withdrawn from us, wrapped in secret thoughts, turned inward upon herself.

'You found it?' Chubby asked at last, and I nodded.

'Yes, Chubby, it's there.' I was surprised to hear that my own voice was husky and unsteady.

Angelo who had not sensed the mood looked up quickly from where he was stacking our equipment. He opened his mouth to say something, but then slowly closed it as he became aware of the charged atmosphere.

We were all silent, moved beyond speech. I had not expected it would be like this, and I looked at Sherry. She met my gaze at last and her dark eyes were haunted.

'Let's go home, Harry,' she said and I nodded at Chubby. He buoyed the hose and dropped it overboard to be retrieved on the following day. Then he threw the motors into gear and swung our bows to face the channel.

Sherry moved across the whaleboat and came to sit beside me on the thwart. I placed my arm about her shoulders but neither of us spoke until the whaleboat slid silently up on to the white beach of the island.

In the sunset Sherry and I climbed to the peak above the camp and we sat close together staring out across the reef, and watching the light fade on the sea and plunge the pool at Gunfire Reef into deeper shadow.

'I feel guilty in a way,' Sherry whispered, 'as though I have committed some dreadful sacrilege.'

'Yes,' I agreed, 'I know what you mean.'

'That thing – it seemed to have a life of its own. It was strange that we should have exposed its head, before any other part of it. Just suddenly to have that face glaring out at one,' she shuddered and was silent for a few moments, 'and yet I felt also a deep satisfaction, a good quiet feeling inside myself. I don't know if I can explain it properly – for the two feelings were so opposite, and yet mingled.'

'I understand. I had the same feelings.'

'What are we going to do with it, Harry, what are we going to do with that fantastic animal?'

Somehow I did not want to talk about money and buyers at that moment – which in itself was a measure of how profound was my involvement with the golden idol.

'Let's go down,' I suggested instead. 'Angelo will be waiting dinner for us.'

Sitting in the firelight with a good meal filling and warming the cold empty place in my belly, and with a mug of whisky in one hand and a cheroot in the other, I felt at last able to tell the others about it.

I explained how we had come upon it, and I described the fearsome golden head. They listened in complete and intent silence.

'We have cleared the head down to the shoulder. I think that is where it ends. It is notched there, probably to fit into the next section. Tomorrow we should be able to lift it clear, but it's going to be ticklish work. We can't just haul it out with the block and tackle. It has to be protected from damage before we can move it.'

Chubby made a suggestion, and for a while we discussed in detail how the head should be handled to minimize the risk of damage.

'We can expect that all five cases containing the treasure were loaded together. I hope to find them in the same part of the hold, probably similarly packed in wooden crates and reinforced with hoop iron—'

'Except for the stones,' Sherry interrupted. 'In the court-martial evidence, the Subahdar described how they were packed in a paymaster's chest.'

'Yes, of course,' I agreed.

'What would that look like?' Sherry asked.

'I saw one on display in the arsenal at Copenhagen which would probably be very similar. It's like a small iron safe – the size of a large biscuit bin.' I sketched the size with the spread of my hands like a fisherman boasting of his catch. 'It is ribbed with iron bands and has a locking rod and a pair of head padlocks at each corner.'

'It sounds formidable.'

'After a hundred-odd years in the pool it will probably be soft as chalk – even if it's still in one piece.'

'We'll find out tomorrow,' Sherry announced with confidence.

We tramped down to the beach in the morning with rain drumming on our oilskins and cascading from them in sheets. The cloud was right down on the peaks, oily dark banks that rolled steadily in from the sea to loose their bomb loads of moisture upon the island.

The force of the rain lifted a fine pearly spray from the surface of the sea, and the moving grey curtains reduced visibility to a few hundred yards so that the island disappeared in a grey haze as we ran out to the reef.

Everything in the whaleboat was cold and clammy and running with water. Angelo had to bale regularly and we huddled miserably in our oilskins while Chubby stood in the stern and slitted his eyes against the slanting, driving rain as he negotiated the channel.

The fluorescent orange buoy still bobbed close in beside the reef and we picked it up and dragged in the end of the hose and connected it to the pump head. It served as an anchor cable and Chubby could cut the motors.

It was a relief to leave the boat, escape from the cold needle lances of the rain and go down into the quiet blue mists of the pool.

After withstanding considerable pressure from Chubby and me. Angelo had at last succumbed to veiled threats and open bribes, and relinquished his ticking mattress stuffed with coconut-fibre. Once the mattress was thoroughly soaked with seawater, it sank readily, and I took it down with me in a neat roll, tied with line.

Only when I had manoeuvred it through the gunport, down the gundeck and into the passenger deck did I cut the line and spread the mattress.

Then Sherry and I returned to the hold where the tiger's head still snarled blindly into the torchlight.

Ten minutes' work was all that was necessary to free the head from its nest. As I suspected, this section ended at shoulder level, and the junction area was neatly flanged – clearly it would mate with the trunk section of the throne, and the flange would engage the female slot to form a joint that would be strong and barely perceivable.

When I rolled the head carefully on to its side I made another discovery. Somehow I had taken it for granted that the idol was made from solid gold, but now I saw that in fact it was a hollow casting.

The actual thickness of metal was only about an inch, and the interior was rough and knobbly to the touch. I realized immediately that a solid idol would have weighed hundreds of tons, and that the cost of such construction would have been prohibitive even to an emperor who could support the construction of a temple as vast as the Taj Mahal.

The thinness of the metal skin had naturally weakened the structure, and I saw immediately when I turned it that the head had already suffered damage.

The rim of the neck cavity was flattened and distorted, probably during its secret journey through the Indian forests in an unsprung cart – or possibly during the wild death struggles of the *Dawn Light* during the cyclone.

Bracing myself in the entrance to the hold, I stooped over it to test its weight, and I cradled the head in my arms like the body of a child. Gradually I increased the strength of my lift and was pleased, but not surprised, when it came up in my arms.

It was, of course, tremendously weighty, and it required all of my strength from a carefully selected stance – but I could lift it. It weighed not much more than three hundred pounds, I thought, as I turned awkwardly under the oppressive load of gleaming gold and laid it gently on the coir mattress that Sherry was holding ready to receive it. Then I straightened up to rest and massage those parts where the sharp edges of metal had bitten into my flesh. While I did so I tried a little mental arithmetic. 300 pounds avoirdupois at 16 ounces to the pound was 4800 ounces, at 150 to the ounce was almost three-quarter of a million dollars. That was the intrinsic value of the head alone. There were three other sections to the throne, all were probably heavier and larger – then there was the value of the stones. It was an astronomic total, but could be doubled or even trebled if the artistic and historical value of the hoard were taken into account.

I abandoned my calculations. They were meaningless at this time, and instead I helped Sherry to fold the mattress around the tiger's head and to rope it all into a secure bundle. Then I could use the block and tackle to drag it down to the companion ladder and lower it to the gundeck.

Laboriously we dragged it to the gunport and there we struggled to pass it through the restricted opening, but at last it was accomplished and we could place the nylon cargo net around it and inflate the airbags. Again we had to step the mast to lift it aboard.

But there was no suggestion that the head should remain covered once we had it safely in the whaleboat, and with what ceremony and aplomb I could muster in the streaming tropical rain, I unveiled it for Chubby and Angelo. They were an appreciative audience. Their excitement superseded even the miserable sodden conditions, and they crowded about the head to fondle and examine it amid shouted comment and giddy laughter. It was the festive gaiety which our first discovery of the treasure had lacked. I had taken the precaution of slipping my silver travelling flask into my gearbag, and now I laced the steaming mugs of black coffee with liberal portions of Scotch whisky and we toasted each other and the golden tiger in the steaming liquor, laughing while the rain gushed down upon us and rattled on the fabulous treasure at our feet.

At last I swilled out my mug over the side and checked my watch.

'We'll do another dive,' I decided. 'You can start the pump again, Chubby.'

Now we knew where to continue the search, and after I had broken out the remains of the case that had contained the head, I saw, in the opening beyond, the side of a similar crate and I pressed the hose into the area to clear it of dirt before proceeding.

My excavations must have unbalanced the rotting heap of ancient cargo, and it needed only the further disturbance caused by suction of the hose to dislodge a part of it. With a groaning and rumbling it collapsed around us and instantly the swirling clouds of muck defeated the efforts of the hose to clear them and we were plunged into darkness once more.

I groped quickly for Sherry through the darkness, and she must have been searching for me, for our hands met and held. With a squeeze she reassured me that she had not been hit by the sliding cargo, and I could begin to clear out the fouled water with the suction hose.

Within five minutes I could make out the yellow glow of Sherry's torch through the murk, and then her shape and the vague jumble of freshly revealed cargo.

With Sherry beside me, we moved farther into the hold again.

The slide had covered the wooden crate on which I had been working, but in exchange it had exposed something else that I recognized instantly, despite its sorry condition, for it was almost exactly as I had described it to Sherry the previous evening, even down to the detail of the rod that ran through the locking device and the double padlocks. The paymaster's chest was, however, almost eaten through with rust and when I touched it my hand came away smeared with the chalky red of iron oxide.

In each end of the case were heavy iron carrying rings, which had most likely swivelled at one time but were now solidly rusted into the metal side – but still they enabled me to get a firm grip and gently to work the chest out of the clutching bed of muck. It came free in a minor storm of debris, and I was able to lift it fairly easily. I doubt that the total weight exceeded a hundred and fifty pounds, and I felt certain that most of that was made up by the massive iron construction.

After the enormously heavy head in its soft bulky mattress, it was a minor labour to get the smaller lighter chest out of the wreck, and it needed only a single airbag to lift it dangling out of the gunport.

Once again the tide and surf were pouring alarmingly into the pool, and the whaleboat tossed and kicked impatiently as we lifted the chest inboard and laid it on the canvas covered heap of scuba bottles in the bows.

Then at last Chubby could start the motors and take us out through the channel. We were still all high with excitement, and the silver flask passed from hand to hand.

'What's it feel like to be rich, Chubby?' I called, and he took a swallow from the flask, screwing up his eyes and then coughing at the sting of the liquor before he grinned at me.

'Just like before, man. No change yet.'

'What you going to do with your share?' Sherry insisted.

'It's a little late in the day, Miss Sherry – if only I had it twenty years ago, then I have use for it – and how.' He took another swallow. 'That's the trouble – you never have it when you're young, and when you're old, it's just too damned late.'

'What about you, Angelo?' Sherry turned to him as he perched on the rusted pay-chest, with his gipsy curls heavy with rain dangling on to his cheeks and the droplets clinging in the long dark eyelashes. 'You're still young, what will you do?'

'Miss Sherry, I've been sitting here thinking about it – and already I've got a list from here to St Mary's and back.'

It took two trips from the beach to the camp before we had both the head and the chest out of the rain and into the cave we were using as the store room.

Chubby lit two gas lanterns, for the lowering sky had brought on the evening prematurely, and we gathered around the chest, while the golden head snarled down upon us from a place of honour, an earthen ledge hewn into the back of the cave.

With a hacksaw and jenny bar, Chubby and I began work on the locking device and found immediately that the decrepit appearance of the metal was deceptive, clearly it had been hardened and alloyed. We broke three hacksaw blades in the first half hour and Sherry professed to be severely shocked by my language. I sent her to fetch a bottle of Chivas Regal from our cave to keep the workers in good cheer and Chubby and I took the Scottish equivalent of a tea-break.

With renewed vigour we resumed our assault on the case, but it was another twenty minutes before he had sawn through the rod. By that time it was dark outside the cave. The rain was still hissing down steadily, but the soft clatter of the palm fronds heralded the rising westerly wind that would disperse the storm clouds by morning.

With the locking rod sawn through, we started it from its ringbolts with a two-pound hammer from the toolbox. Each blow loosened a soft patter of rust scales from the surface of the metal, and it required a number of goodly blows to drive the rod from the clutching fist of corrosion.

Even when it was cleared, the lid would not lift. Although we hammered it from a dozen different directions and I treated it with a further laying on of abuse, it would not yield.

I called another whisky break to discuss the problem.

'What about a stick of gelly?' Chubby suggested with a gleam in his eye, but reluctantly I had to restrain him.

'We need a welding torch,' Angelo announced.

'Brilliant,' I applauded him ironically, for I was fast losing my patience. 'The nearest welding set is fifty miles away – and you make a remark like that.'

It was Sherry who discovered the secondary locking device, a secret pinning through the lid that hooked into recesses in the body of the chest. It obviously needed a key to release this, but for lack of it I selected a half-inch punch and drove it into the keyhole and by luck I caught the locking arm and snapped it.

Chubby started on the lid again, and this time it came up stiffly on corroded hinges with some of the rotting evil-smelling contents sticking inside of it and tearing away from the main body of aged brown cloth. It was woven cotton fabric, a wet solid brick of it, and I guessed that it had been cheap native robes or bolts of cloth used as packing.

I was about to explore further, but suddenly found myself in the second row looking over Sherry North's shoulder.

'You'd better let me do this,' she said. 'You might break something.'

'Come on!' I protested.

'Why don't you get yourself another drink?' she suggested placatingly, as she began lifting off layers of sodden fabric. The suggestion had some merit, I thought, so I refilled my mug and watched Sherry expose a layer of cloth-wrapped parcels.

Each was tied with twine that fell apart at the touch, and the first parcel also disintegrated as she tried to lift it out. Sherry cupped her hand around the decaying mass and scooped it on to a folded tarpaulin placed beside the chest. The parcel contained scores of small nutty objects, varying in size from slightly larger than a match-head to a ripe grape and each had been folded in a wisp of paper, which like the cotton, had completely rotted away.

Sherry picked out one of these lumpy objects and rubbed away the remnants of paper between thumb and forefinger to reveal a large shiny blue stone, cut square and polished on one face.

'Sapphire?' she guessed, and I took it from her and examined it quickly in the lantern light. It was opaque and I contradicted her.

'No, I think it's probably lapis lazuli.' The scrap of paper still adhering to it was faintly discoloured with a blue dye. 'Ink, I should say.' I crumpled it between my fingers. 'At least Roger, the Colonel, took the trouble to identify each stone. He probably wrapped each piece in a numbered slip of paper which related to a master sketch of the throne to enable it to be reassembled.'

'There is no hope of that now,' said Sherry.

'I don't know,' I said. 'It would be a hell of a job, but it would still be possible to put it all together again.'

Amongst our stores was a roll of plastic packets, and I sent Angelo to ferret it out. As we opened each parcel of rotted fabric we superficially cleaned the stones it contained and packed each lot in a separate plastic packet.

It was slow work even though we all contributed and after almost two hours of it we had filled dozens of packets with thousands of semi-precious stones – lapis lazuli, beryl, tiger's eye, garnets, verdite, amethyst, and half a dozen others of whose identity I was uncertain. Each stone had clearly been lovingly cut and exactingly polished to fit into its own niche in the golden throne.

It was only when we had unpacked the chest to its last layer that we came upon the stones of greater value. The old Colonel had obviously selected these first and they had gone into the lowest layer of the chest.

I held a transparent plastic packet of emeralds to the lantern light, and they burned like a bursting green star. We all stared at it as if mesmerized while I turned it slowly to catch the fierce white light.

I laid it aside and Sherry dipped once more into the chest and after a moment's hesitation brought out a smaller parcel. She rubbed away the damp crumbling material, that was wound thick about the single stone it contained.

Then she held up the Great Mogul diamond in the cupped palm of her hand. It was the size of a pullet's egg, cut into a faceted cushion shape, just as Jean Baptiste Tavernier had described it so many hundred years ago.

The glittering array of treasure we had handled before in no way dimmed the glory of this stone, as all the stars of the firmament cannot dull the rising of the sun. They paled and faded away before the brilliance and lustre of the great diamond.

Sherry slowly extended her cupped hand towards Angelo, offering it to him to hold and examine, but he snatched his hands away and clasped them behind his back, still staring at the stone in superstitious awe.

Sherry turned and offered it to Chubby, but with gravity he declined also.

'Give it to Mister Harry. Guess he deserves to be the one.'

I took it from her, and was surprised that such unearthly fire could be so cold to touch. I stood up and I carried it to where the golden tiger's head stood snarling angrily in the unwavering light of the lanterns and I pressed the diamond into the empty eye socket.

It fitted perfectly, and I used my bait-knife to close the golden clasps that held it firmly in place, and which the old Colonel had probably opened with a bayonet a century and a quarter ago.

I stood back then, and I heard the small gasps of wonder. With the eye returned to its socket the golden beast had come to life. It seemed now to survey us with an imperial mien, and at any instant we expected the cave to resound to its crackling wicked snarl of anger.

I went back and took my place in the squatting circle around the rusted chest, and we all stared up at the golden tiger head. We seemed like worshippers in some ancient heathen rite, crouched in awe before the fearsome idol.

'Chubby, my old well beloved and trusted buddy, you will earn yourself an entry on the title page of the book of mercy if you pass me that bottle,' I said, and that broke the spell. They all recovered their voices, competing fiercely for a turn to speak – and it wasn't long before I had to send Sherry to fetch another bottle to lubricate dry throats.

We all got more than a little drunk that night, even Sherry North, and she leaned against me for support as we finally made a riotous way through the rain to our own cave.

'You really are corrupting me, Fletcher,' she stumbled into a puddle, and nearly brought me down. 'This is the first time ever I have been stoned.'

'Be of good cheer, my pretty sweeting, your next lesson in corruption follows immediately.'


When I woke it was still dark and I rose from our bed, careful not to disturb Sherry who was breathing lightly and evenly in the darkness. It was cool so I pulled on shorts and a woollen jersey.

Outside the cave the west wind had broken up the cloud banks. It had stopped raining and the stars were showing in the breaks of the heavens, giving me enough light to read the luminous dial of my wristwatch. It was a little after three o'clock.

As I sought my favourite palm tree, I saw that we had left the lantern burning in the storage cave. I finished what I had to do and went up to the lighted entrance.

The open chest stood where we had left it, as did the priceless golden head with its glittering eye – and suddenly I was struck with the consuming terror that the miser must feel for his hoard. It was so vulnerable.

'—where thieves break in—' I thought, and it was not as though there were any shortage of them in the immediate vicinity.

I had to get it all stowed away safely, and tomorrow would be too late. Despite the pain in my head and the taste of stale whisky in the back of my throat, it must be done now – but I needed help.

Chubby roused to my first soft call at the entrance of his cave, and came out into the starlight, resplendent in his striped pyjamas and as wide awake as if he had drank nothing more noxious than mother's milk before retiring.

I explained my fears and misgivings. Chubby grunted in agreement and went with me back to the storage cave. The plastic bags of gem stones we repacked casually into the iron chest and I secured the lid with a length of nylon line. The golden head we shrouded carefully in a length of green canvas tarpaulin and we carried both down into the palm grove, before returning for spades and the gas lantern.

By the flat white glare of the lantern we worked side by side, digging two shallow graves in the sandy soil within a few feet of where the gelignite and the FN rifle with its spare ammunition were already buried.

We laid the chest and the golden head away and covered them. Afterwards I brushed the soil over them with a palm frond to wipe out all trace of our labours.

'You happy now, Harry?' Chubby asked at last.

'Yeah, I'm happier, Chubby. You go and get some sleep, hear.'

He went away amongst the palms carrying the lantern and not looking back. I knew I would not be able to sleep again, for the spadework had cleared my head and roused my blood. It would be senseless to return to the cave and try to lie quietly beside Sherry until dawn.

I wanted to find some quiet and secret place where I could think out my next moves in this intricate game of chance in which I was involved. I chose the path that led to the saddle between the lesser peaks and as I climbed it, the last of the clouds were blown aside and revealed a pale yellow moon still a week from full. Its light was strong enough to show me the way to the nearest peak and I left the path and toiled upwards to the summit.

I found a place protected from the wind and settled into it. I wished that I had a cheroot with me for I think better with one of them in my mouth. I also think better without a hangover – but there was nothing I could do about either.

After half an hour I had decided that we must consolidate what we had gained to this point. The miser's fears, which had assailed me earlier, still persisted and I had been given clear warning that the wolf pack was out hunting. As soon as it was light we would take what we had salvaged so far – the head and the chest – and run down the islands to St Mary's to dispose of them in the manner which I had already so carefully planned.

There would be time later to return to Gunfire Reef and recover what remained in the misty depths of the pool. Once the decision had been made I felt a lift of relief, a new lightness of spirit, and I looked forward to the solution of the other major puzzle that had troubled me for so long.

Very soon I would be in a position to call Sherry North's hand and have a sight of those cards which she concealed so carefully from me. I wanted to know what caused those shadows in the blue depths of her eyes, and the answers to many other mysteries that surrounded her. That time would soon come.

There was a paling of the sky at last, dawn's first pearling light spread across from the east and softened the harsh dark plain of the ocean. I rose stiffly from my seat amongst the rocks, and picked my way around the peak into the wicked eye of the west wind. I stood there on the exposed face above the camp with the wind raising a rash of goose bumps along my arms and ruffling my hair.

I looked down into the sheltering arms of the lagoon, and in the feeble glimmer of dawn, the darkened ship that was creeping stealthily into the open arms of the bay looked like some pale phantom.

Even as I stared I saw the splash at her bows as she let go her anchor, and she rounded up into the wind showing her full silhouette so that I could not doubt that she was the *Mandrake*.

Before I had recovered my wits, she had dropped a boat which sped in swiftly towards the beach.

I started to run.


I fell once on the path, but the force of my headlong descent from the peak carried me on and with a single roll I was on my feet again, still running.

I was panting wildly as I burst into Chubby's cave, and I shouted, 'Move, man, move! They are on the beach already.'

The two of them tumbled from their sleeping bags. Angelo was tousle-haired and blank-eyed from sleep, but Chubby was quick and alert.

'Chubby,' I snapped, 'go get that piece out of the ground. Jump, man, they'll be coming up through the grove in a few minutes.' He had changed while I spoke, pulling on a shirt and belting his denim breeches. He grunted an acknowledgement. 'I'll follow you in a minute,' I called as he ran out into the feeble light of dawn.

'Angelo, snap out of it!' I grabbed his shoulder and shook him. 'I want you to look after Miss Sherry, hear?'

He was dressed now and he nodded owlishly at me.

'Come on.' I half dragged him as we ran across to my cave. I dragged her out of bed and while she dressed I told her.

'Angelo will go with you. I want you to take a can of drinking water and the two of you get the hell down to the south of the island, cross the saddle first though and keep out of sight. Climb the peak and hide out in the chimney where we found the inscription. You know where I mean.'

'Yes, Harry,' she nodded.

'Stay there. Don't go out or show yourself under any circumstances. Understand?'

She nodded as she tucked the tail of her shirt into her breeches.

'Remember, these people are killers. The time for games is over, this is a pack of wolves that we are dealing with.'

'Yes, Harry, I know.'

'Okay then,' I embraced and kissed her quickly. 'Off you go then.' And they went out of the cave, Angelo lugging a five-gallon can of drinking water, and they trotted away into the palm grove.

Quickly I threw a few items into a light haversack, a box of cheroots, matches, binoculars, water bottle and a heavy jersey, a tin of chocolate and of survival rations, a torch – and I buckled my belt around my waist with the heavy bait-knife in the sheath. Slinging the strap of the haversack over my shoulder, I also ran from the cave and followed Chubby down into the palm grove towards the beach.

I had run fifty yards when there was the thud, thudding of small-arms fire, a shout and another burst of firing. It was directly ahead of me and very close.

I paused and slipped behind the bole of the palm tree while I peered into the lightening shades of the grove. I saw movement, a figure running towards me and I loosened the bait-knife in its sheath and waited until I was sure, before I called softly, 'Chubby!'

The running figure swerved towards me. He was carrying the FN rifle and the canvas bandolier with spare magazines of ammunition, and he was breathing quickly but lightly as he saw me.

'They spotted me,' he grunted. 'There are hundreds of the bastards.'

At that moment I saw more movement amongst the trees. 'Here they come,' I said. 'Let's go.'

I wanted to give Sherry a clear run, so I did not take the path across the saddle, but turned directly southwards to lead the pursuit off her scent. We headed for the swamps at the southern end of the island.

They saw us as we ran obliquely across their front. I heard a shout, answered immediately by others, and then there were five scattered shots and I saw the muzzle flashes bloom amongst the dark trees. A bullet struck a palm trunk high above our heads, a woody thunk, but we were going fast and within minutes the shouts of pursuit were fading behind us.

I reached the edge of the saltmarsh, and swung away inland to avoid the stinking mudflats. On the first gentle slope of the hills I halted to listen and to regain our breath. The light was strengthening swiftly now. Within a short while it would be sunrise and I wanted to be under cover before then.

Suddenly there were distant cries of dismay from the direction of the swamps and I guessed that the pursuit had blundered into the glutinous mud. That would discourage them fairly persuasively, I thought, and grinned.

'Okay, Chubby, let's get on,' I whispered, and as we stood there was a new sound from a different direction.

The sound was muted by distance and by the intervening heights of the ridge, for it came from the seaward side of the island, but it was the unmistakable ripping sound of automatic gunfire.

Chubby and I froze into listening attitudes and the sound was repeated, another long tearing burst of machine-gun fire. Then there was silence, though we listened for three of four minutes.

'Come on,' I said quietly, we could delay no longer and we ran on up the slope towards the southernmost peak.

We climbed quickly in the fast-growing morning light, and I was too preoccupied to feel any qualms as we negotiated the narrow ledge and stepped at last into the deep rock crack where I had arranged to meet Sherry.

The shelter was silent and deserted but I called without hope, 'Sherry! Are you there, love?'

There was no reply from the shadows, and I turned back to Chubby.

'They had a good lead on us. They should have been here,' and only then did that burst of machine-gun fire we had heard earlier take on new meaning.

I removed the binoculars from the haversack and then thrust it away into a crack in the rock.  •

'They've run into trouble, Chubby,' I told him. 'Come on. Let's go and find out what happened.'

Once we were off the ledge we struck out through the jumble of broken rock towards the seaward side of the island, but even in my haste and dreadful anxiety for Sherry's safety, I moved with stealth and we were careful not to show ourselves to a watcher in the groves or on the beaches below us.

As we crossed the divide of the ridge a new vista opened before us, the curve of the beach and the jagged black sweep of Gunfire Reef.

I halted instantly and pulled Chubby down beside me, as we crouched into cover.

Anchored in a position to command the mouth of the channel through Gunfire Reef was the armed crash boat from Zinballa Bay, flagship of my old friend Suleiman Dada. Returning to it from the beach was a small motor-boat, crowded with tiny figures.

'God damn it,' I muttered, 'they really had it planned. Manny Resnick has teamed up with Suleiman Dada. That's what took him so long to get here. While Manny hit the beach, Dada was covering the channel, so we couldn't make a bolt for it like we did before.'

'And he had men on the beach – that was the machine-gun fire. Manny Resnick sailed *Mandrake* into the bay to flush us, and Dada had the back door covered.'

'What about Miss Sherry and Angelo? Do you think they got away? Did Dada's men catch them when they crossed the saddle?'

'Oh God!' I groaned, and cursed myself for not having stayed with her. I stood up and focused the binoculars on the motor-boat as it crawled across the clear waters of the outer lagoon to the anchored crash boat.

'I can't see them.' Even with the aid of the binoculars, the occupants of the dinghy were merely a dark mass, for the morning sun was rising beyond them and the glare off the water dazzled me. I could not make out separate figures, let alone recognize individuals.

'They may have them in the boat – but I can't see.' In my agitation I had left the cover of the rocks, and was seeking a better vantage point, moving about on the sky-line. Out in the open I must have been highlit by the same sun rays that were blinding me.

I saw the familiar flash, and the long white feather of gunsmoke blow from the mounted quick-firer on the bows of the crash boat, and I heard the shell coming with a rushing sound like eagles' wings.

'Get down!' I shouted at Chubby, and threw myself flat amongst the rocks.

The shell burst in very close, with the bright hot glare like the brief opening of a furnace door. Shrapnel and rock fragments trilled and whined around us, and I jumped to my feet.

'Run!' I yelled at Chubby, and we jinked back over the skyline just as the next shell passed over us, making us both flinch our heads at the mighty crack of passing shot.

Chubby was wiping a smear of blood from his forearm as we crouched behind the ridge.

'Okay?' I asked.

'A scratch, that's all. Bit of a rock fragment,' he growled.

'Chubby, I'm going down to find out what happened to the others. No point both of us taking a chance. You wait here.'

'You're wasting time, Harry, I'm coming with you. Let's go.' He hefted the rifle and led the way down the peak. I thought of taking the FN away from him. In his hands it was about as lethal as a slingshot when fired with his closed-eyes technique. Then I left it. It made him feel good.

We moved slowly, hugging any cover there was and searching ahead before moving forward. However, the island was silent except for the sough and clatter of the west wind in the tops of the palms and we saw nobody as we moved up the seaward side of the island.

I cut the spoor left by Angelo and Sherry as they crossed the saddle, above the camp. Their running footsteps had bitten deep into the fluffy soil, Sherry's small slim prints were overlapped by Angelo's broad bare feet.

We followed them down the slope, and suddenly they shied off the track. They had dropped the water-can here and, turning abruptly, had separated slightly, as though they had run side by side for sixty yards.

There we found Angelo, and he was never going to enjoy his share of the spoils. He had been hit by three of the soft heavy-calibre slugs. They had torn through the thin fabric of his shirt, and opened huge dark wounds in his back and chest.

He had bled copiously but the sandy soil had absorbed most of it, and already what was left was drying into a thick black crust. The flies were assembled, crawling gleefully into the bullet holes and swarming on the long dark lashes around his wide open and startled eyes.

Following her tracks I saw where Sherry had run on for twenty paces, and then the little idiot had turned back and gone to kneel beside where Angelo lay. I cursed her for that. She might have been able to escape if she had not indulged in that useless and extravagant gesture.

They had caught her as she knelt beside the body and dragged her down through the palms to the beach. I could see the long slide marks in the sand where she had dug her feet in and tried to resist.

Without leaving the shelter of the trees, I looked down the smooth white sand, following their tracks to where the marks of the motor-boat's keel still showed in the sand of the water's edge.

They had taken her out to the crash boat, and I crouched behind a pile of driftwood and dried palm fronds to stare out at the graceful little ship.

Even as I watched she weighed anchor, picked up speed and passed slowly down the length of the island to round the point and enter the inner lagoon where *Mandrake* was still lying at anchor.

I straightened up and slipped back through the grove to where I had left

Chubby. He had laid the carbine aside and he sat with Angelo's body in his arms, cradling the head against his shoulder. Chubby was weeping, fat glistening tears slid wearily down the seamed brown cheeks and fell from his jaw to wet the thick dark curls of the boy in his arms.

I picked up the rifle and stood guard over them while Chubby wept for both of us. I envied him the relief of tears, the outpouring of pain that would bring surcease. My own grief was as fierce as Chubby's, for I had loved Angelo as much, but it was down deep inside where it hurt more.

'All right, Chubby,' I said at last. 'Let's go, man.' He stood up with the boy still in his arms and we moved back along the ridge.

In a gully that was choked with rank vegetation we laid Angelo in a shallow grave that we scraped with our hands, and we covered him with a blanket of branches and leaves that I cut with my bait-knife before filling the grave. I could not bring myself to throw sand into his unprotected face, and the leaves made a gentler shroud.

Chubby wiped away his tears with the open palm of his hand and he stood up.

'They got Sherry,' I told him quietly. 'She is aboard the crash boat.'

'Is she hurt?' he asked.

'I don't think so, not yet.'

'What do you want to do now, Harry?' he asked, and the question was answered for me.

Somewhere far off towards the camp, we heard a whistle shrill, and we moved up the ridge to a point where we could see down into the inner lagoon and landward side of the island.

*Mandrake* lay where I had last seen her and the Zinballa crash boat was anchored a hundred yards closer to the shore. They had seized the whaleboat and were using her to land men on the beach. They were all armed, and uniformed. They set off immediately into the palm trees and the whaleboat ran back to *Mandrake*.

I put the binoculars on to *Mandrake* and saw that there were developments taking place there also. In the field of the glasses I recognized Manny Resnick in a white open-neck shirt and blue slacks as he climbed down into the whale boat. He was followed by Lorna Page. She wore dark glasses, a yellow scarf around her pale blonde hair and an emerald green slack suit. I felt hatred seethe in my guts as I recognized them.

Now something happened that puzzled me. The luggage that I had seen loaded into the Rolls at Curzon Street was brought out on to the deck by two of Manny's thugs and it also was passed down into the whaleboat.

A uniform crew member of *Mandrake* saluted from the deck, and Manny waved at him in a gesture of airy dismissal.

The whaleboat left *Mandrake*'s side and moved in towards the crash boat. As Manny, his lady friend, bodyguards and luggage were disembarked on to the deck of the crash boat, *Mandrake* weighed anchor, turned for the entrance of the bay, and set out in a determined fashion for the deep-water channel.

'She's leaving,' muttered Chubby. 'Why is she doing that?'

'Yes, she's leaving,' I agreed. 'Manny Resnick has finished with her. He's got a new ally now, and he doesn't need his own ship. She's probably costing him a thousand nicker a day – and Manny was always a shy man with a buck.'

I turned my glasses on to the crash boat again and saw Manny and his entourage enter the cabin.

'There is probably another reason,' I muttered.

'What's that, Harry?'

'Manny Resnick and Suleiman Dada will want as few witnesses as possible to what they intend doing now.'

'Yeah, I see what you mean,' grunted Chubby.

'I think, my friend, that we are about to be treated to the kind of nastiness that will make what they did to Angelo seem kind, by comparison.'

'We've got to get Miss Sherry off that boat, Harry.' Chubby was coming out of the daze of grief into which Angelo's killing had thrown him. 'We've got to do something, Harry.'

'It's a nice thought, Chubby, I agree. But we aren't going to help her much by getting ourselves killed. My guess is that she will be safe until they get their hands on the treasure.'

His huge brown face creased up like that of a worried bulldog.

'What we going to do, Harry?'

'Right now we are going to run again.'

'What do you mean?'

'Listen,' I told him, and he cocked his head. There was the shrill of the whistle again and then faintly we heard voices carried up to us on the wind.

'Looks like their first effort will be brute strength. They've landed the entire goon squad, and they are going to drive the island and put us up like a brace of cock pheasant.'

'Let's go down and have a go,' Chubby growled, and cocked the F.N. 'I got a message for them from Angelo.'

'Don't be a fool, Chubby,' I snapped at him angrily. 'Now listen to me. I want to count how many men they have. Then, if we get a good chance, I want to try and get one of them alone and take his piece off him. Watch for an opportunity, Chubby, but don't have a go yet. Play it very cautious, hear?' I didn't want to refer to his marksmanship in derogatory tones.

'Okay,' Chubby nodded.

'You stay this side of the ridge. Count how many of them come down this side of the island. I'll cross over and do the same on the other side.' He nodded. 'I'll meet you at the spot where the crash boat shelled us in two hours.'

'What about you, Harry?' He made a gesture of handing me the FN – but I didn't have the heart to deprive him.

'I'll be okay,' I told him. 'Off you go, man.'

It was a simple task to keep ahead of the line of beaters for they called to each other loudly to keep their spirits up, and they made no pretence at concealment or stealth, but advanced slowly and cautiously in an extended line.

There were nine of them on my side of the ridge, seven of them were blacks in naval uniform, armed with AK47 assault rifles and two of them were Manny Resnick's men. They were dressed in casual tropical gear and carried sidearms. One of them I recognized as the driver of the Rover that night so long ago, and the passenger in the twin-engined Cessna that had spotted Sherry and me on the beach.

Once I had make my head count, I turned my back on them and ran ahead to the curve of the salt marsh. I knew that when the line of beaters ran into this obstacle, it would lose its cohesion and that it was likely that some of its members would become isolated.

I found an advanced neck of swampland with stands of young mangrove and coarse swamp grass in dense shades of fever green. I followed the edge of this thicket and came upon a spot where a fallen palm tree lay across the neck like a bridge – offering escape in two directions. It had collected a dense covering of blown palm fronds and swamp grass which provided a good hide from which to mount an ambush.

I lay in the back of this shaggy mound of dead vegetation and I had the heavy bait-knife in my right hand ready to throw.

The line of the beaters came on steadily, their voices growing louder as they approached the swamp. Soon I could hear the rustle and scrape of branches as one of them came directly down to where I lay.

He paused and called when he was about twenty feet from me, and I pressed my face close to the damp earth and peered under the pile of dead branches. There was an opening there and I saw his feet and his legs below the knees. His trousers were thick blue serge and he wore grubby white sneakers without socks. At each step his naked ankles showed very black African skin.

It was one of the sailors from the crash boat then, and I was pleased. He would be carrying an automatic weapon. I prefered that to a pistol, which was what Manny's boys were armed with.

Slowly I rolled on to my side and cleared my knife arm. The sailor called again so close and so loud that my nerves jumped and I felt the tingling flush of adrenalin in my blood. His call was answered from farther off, and the sailor came on.

I could hear his soft footfalls on the sand, padding towards me.

Suddenly he came into full view, as he rounded the fall of brushwood. He was ten paces from me.

He was in naval uniform, a blue cap on his head with its gay little red pom-pom on the top, but he carried the vicious and brutal-looking machine-gun on his hip. He was a tall lean youngster in his early twenties, smooth faced and sweating nervously so there was a purple black sheen on his skin, against which his eyes were very white.

He saw me and tried to swing the machine-gun on to me, but it was on his right hip and he blocked himself awkwardly in the turn. I aimed for the notch where the two collarbones meet, that was framed by the opening of his uniform at the base of his throat. I threw overhand, snapping my wrist into it at the moment of release so the knife leapt in a silvery blur and thudded precisely into the mark I had chosen. The blade was completely buried and only the dark walnut handle protruded from his throat.

He tried to cry out, but no sound came, for the blade had severed all his vocal chords as I intended. He sank slowly to his knees facing me in a prayerful attitude with his hands dangling at his sides and the machine-gun hanging on its strap.

We stared at each other for a moment that seemed to last for ever. Then he shuddered violently and a thick burst of bubbling blood poured from his mouth and nose, and he pitched face forward to the ground.

Crouched low, I flipped him on to his back and withdrew the knife against the clinging drag of wet flesh, and I cleaned the blade on his sleeve.

Working swiftly I stripped him of his weapon and the spare magazines in the bandolier on his webbing belt, then, still crouching low, I dragged him by his heels into the gluey mud of the creek and knelt on his chest to force him below the surface. The mud flowed over his face as slowly and thickly as molten chocolate, and when he was totally submerged I buckled the webbing belt around my waist, picked up the machine-gun and slipped back quietly through the breach that I had made in the line of beaters.

As I ran doubled over and using all the cover there was, I checked the load on the AK47. I was familiar with the weapon. I had used it in Biafra and I made sure that the magazine was full and that the breech was loaded before I slipped the strap over my right shoulder and held it ready on my hip.

when I had moved back about five hundred yards I paused and took shelter against the trunk of a palm while I listened. Behind me, the line of beaters seemed to have run into trouble against the swamp, and they were trying to sort themselves out. I listened to the shouts and the angry shrill of the whistle. It sounded like a cup final, I thought, and grinned queasily, for the memory of the man I had killed was still nauseatingly fresh.

Now that I had broken through their line I turned and struck directly across the island towards my rendezvous with Chubby on the south peak. Once I was out of the palm groves on to the lower slopes, the vegetation was thicker, and I moved more swiftly through the better cover.

Halfway to the crest I was startled by a fresh burst of gunfire. This time it was the distinctive whipcracking lash of the FN, a sharper slower beat than the storm of AK47 machine-gun fire that answered it immediately.

I judged by the volume and duration of the outburst that all the weapons involved had emptied magazines in a continuous burst. A heavy silence followed.

Chubby was having a go, after all my warnings. Although I was bitterly angry, I was also thoroughly alarmed by what trouble he had gotten himself into. One thing was certain – Chubby had missed whatever he had aimed at.

I broke from a trot into a run, and angled upwards towards the crest, aiming to reach the area from which the gunfire had sounded.

I burst out of a patch of goosebush into a narrow overgrown path that followed the direction I wanted, and I turned into it and went into a full run.

I topped the rise and almost ran into the arms of one of the uniformed seamen coming in the opposite direction, also at a headlong run.

There were six of his comrades with him in Indian file, all making the best possible speed on his heels. Thirty yards farther back was another who had lost his weapon and whose uniform jacket was sodden with fresh blood,.

On all their faces were expressions of abandoned terror, and they ran with the single-minded determination of men pursued closely by all the legions of hell.

I knew instantly that this rabble were the survivors of an encounter with Chubby Andrews, and that it had been too much for their nerves. They were hell-bent and homewardbound – Chubby's shooting must have improved miraculously, and I made him a silent apology.

So much were the seamen involved with the devil behind them that they seemed not to notice me for the fleeting instant which it took for me to slip the safety-catch on the machine-gun on my hip, brace myself with knees bent and feet spread.

I swung the weapon in a short kicking traverse aimed low at their knees. With a rate of fire like that of an AK47, you must go for the legs, and rely on another three of four hits in the body as the man drops through the sheet of fire. It also defeats the efforts of the short barrel to ride up under the thrust of the recoil.

They went down in a sprawling shrieking mass, punched backwards into each other by the savage strike of the soft heavy-calibre slugs.

I held the trigger down for the count of four, and then I turned and plunged off the path into the thick wall of goosebush. It hid me instantly and I doubled over as I jinked and dodged under the branches.

Behind me, a machine-gun was firing, and the bullets tore and snapped through the thick foliage. None came near me and I settled back into a quick trot.

I guessed that my sudden and completely unexpected attack would have permanently accounted for two or three of the seamen, and may have wounded one or two others.

However, the effect on their morale would be disastrous – especially coming so soon after Chubby's onslaught. Once they reached the safety of the crash boat, I guessed that the forces of evil would debate long and hard before setting foot on the island again. We had won the second round decisively, but they still had Sherry North. That was the major trump in their hands. As long as they held her they could dictate the course of the game.

Chubby was waiting for me amongst the rocks on the saddle of the peak. The man was indestructible.

'Jesus, Harry, where the hell you been?' he growled. 'I've been waiting here all morning.'

I saw that he had retrieved my haversack from the cleft in the rocks where I had left it. It lay with two captured AK47 rifles and bandoliers of ammunition at his feet.

He handed me the water bottle, and only then did I realize how thirsty I was. The heavily chlorinated water tasted like Veuve Clicquot, but I rationed myself to three swallows.

'I got to apologize to you, Harry. I had a go. Just couldn't help it, man. They were bunched up and standing out in the open like a Sunday-school picnic. Just couldn't help myself, gave them a good old squirt. Dropped two of them and the others run like hens, shooting their pieces straight up in the air as they go.'

'Yeah,' I nodded. 'I met them as they crossed the ridge.'

'Heard the shooting. Just about to come and look for you.'

I sat down on the rock beside him, and found my cheroots in the haversack. We each lit one and smoked in grateful silence for a moment which Chubby spoiled.

'Well, we lit a fire under their tails – don't reckon they'll come back for more. But they have still got Miss Sherry, man. Long as they got her, they are winning.'

'How many were there, Chubby?'

'Ten.' He spat out a scrap of tobacco and inspected the glowing tip of the cheroot. 'But I took out two – and I think I winged another.'

'Yeah,' I agreed. 'I met seven on the ridge. I had a go at them also. Aren't more than four left now – and there are eight more out of my bunch. Say a dozen, plus those left on board – another six or seven. About twenty guns still against us, Chubby.'

'Pretty odds, Harry.'

'Let's work on it, Chubby.'

'Let's do that, Harry.'

I selected the newest and least abused of the three machine-guns and there were five full magazines of ammunition for it. I cached the discarded weapons under a slab of flat rock and loaded and checked the other.

We each had another short drink from the water bottle and then I led the way cautiously along the ridge, keeping off the sky-line, back towards the deserted camp.

From the spot at which I had first spotted the approach of the *Mandrake* we surveyed the whole northern end of the island.

As we guessed they would, Manny and Suleiman Dada had taken all their men off the island. Both the whaleboat and the smaller motor-boat were moored alongside the crash boat. There was much confused and meaningless activity on board, and as I watched the scurrying figures I imagined the scenes of terrible wrath and retribution which were taking place in the main cabin.

Suleiman Dada and his new protégé were certainly wreaking a fearful vengeance on their already badly beaten and demoralized troops.

'I want to go down to the camp, Chubby. See what they left for us,' I said at last, and handed him the binoculars. 'Keep watch for me. Three quick shots as a warning signal.'

'Okay, Harry,' he agreed, but as I stood up there was a renewed outbreak of feverish activity on board the crash boat. I took the glasses back from Chubby and watched Suleiman Dada emerge from the cabin and make a laborious ascent to the open bridge. In his white uniform, bedecked with medals that glittered in the sunlight and attended by a host of helpers he reminded me of a fat white queen termite being moved from its royal cell by swarming worker ants.

The transfer was effected at last and as I watched through the binoculars I saw an electronic bullhorn handed to Suleiman. He faced the shore, lifted the hailer to his mouth and through the powerful lens I saw his lips moving. Seconds later the sound reached us clearly, magnified by the instrument and carried by the wind.

'Harry Fletcher. I hope you can hear me.' The deep well-modulated voice was given a harsher sound by the amplifier. 'I plan to put on a demonstration this evening which will convince you of the necessity of co-operating with me. Please be in a position where you can watch. You will find it fascinating. Nine o'clock this evening on the afterdeck of this ship. It's a date, Harry. Don't miss it.'

He handed the bullhorn to one of his officers and went below.

'They're going to do something to Sherry,' muttered Chubby and fiddled disconsolately with the rifle in his lap.

'We'll know at nine,' I said, and watched the officer with the bullhorn climb from the deck into the motor-boat. They set off on a slow circuit of the island, stopping every half mile to shout a repetition of Suleiman Dada's invitation to me at the silent tree-lined shore. He was very anxious for me to attend.

'All right, Chubby,' I glanced at my watch. 'We have hours yet. I'm going down to the camp. Watch out for me.'

The camp had been ransacked and plundered of most items of value, equipment and stores had been smashed and scattered about the caves – but still some of it had been overlooked.

I found five cans of fuel and hid them along with much other equipment that might be of value. Then I crept cautiously down into the grove, and learned with relief that the hiding-place of the chest and the golden tiger's head and the other stores was undisturbed.

Carrying a five-gallon can of drinking water and three cans of corned beef and mixed vegetables I climbed again to the ridge where Chubby waited. We ate and drank and I said to Chubby: 'Get some sleep if you can. It's going to be a long hard night.'

He grunted and curled up in the grass like a great brown bear. Soon he was snoring softly and regularly.

I smoked three cheroots slowly and thoughtfully, but it was only as the sun was setting that I had my first real stroke of genius. It was so clear and simple, and so delightfully apt that it was immediately suspect and I re-examined it carefully.

The wind had dropped and it was completely dark by the time I was certain of my idea and I sat smiling and nodding contentedly as I thought about it.

The crash boat was brightly lit, all her ports glowed and a pair of floods glared whitely down upon the afterdeck, so it looked like an empty stage.

I woke Chubby and we ate and drank again.

'Let's go down to the beach,' I said. 'We'll have a better view from there.'

'It might be a trap,' Chubby warned me morosely.

'I don't think so. They are all on board, and they are playing from strength. They've still got Sherry. They don't have to try any fancy tricks.'

'Man, if they do anything to that girl—' he stopped himself, and stood up. 'All right, let's go.'

We moved silently and cautiously down through the grove with our weapons cocked and our fingers on the triggers, but the night was still and the grove deserted.

We halted amongst the trees at the top of the beach. The crash boat was only two hundred yards away and I leaned my shoulder against the trunk of a palm and focused my glasses on her. It was so clear and close that I could read the writing on the lid of a packet from which one of the sentries took and lit a cigarette.

We had a front row seat for whatever entertainment Suleiman Dada was planning, and I felt the stir of apprehension and knowledge of coming horror blow like a cold breeze across my skin.

I lowered the glasses and whispered softly to Chubby, 'Change your piece for mine,' and he passed me the long-barrelled FN and took the AK47.

I wanted the accuracy of the FN to command the deck of the crash boat. Naturally there was nothing I could do to intervene while Sherry was unharmed, but if they did anything to her – I would make sure she didn't suffer alone.

I squatted down beside the palm tree, adjusted the peep sights of the rifle, and drew a careful bead on the head of the deck guard. I knew I could put a bullet through his temple from where I sat and when I was satisfied I laid the rifle across my lap and settled down to wait.

The mosquitoes from the swamp whined around our ears but both Chubby and I ignored them and sat quietly. I longed for a cheroot to soothe the tension of my nerves, but I was forced to forgo that comfort.

Time passed very slowly, and new fears came to plague me and make the waiting seem even longer than it was – but finally, a few minutes before the promised hour, there was a renewed stirring and bustle on board the crash boat and once more Suleiman Dada was helped up the ladder by his men and he took his place at the bridge rail looking down over the after-deck. He was sweating heavily and it had soaked the area around the armpits and across the back of his white uniform jacket. I guessed that he had passed his own period of waiting by frequent recourse to the whisky bottle, probably from my own stock that had been plundered from the cave.

He laughed and joked with the men around him, his vast belly shaking with mirth and his men echoed the laughter slavishly. The sound of it carried across the water to the beach.

Suleiman was followed by Manny Resnick and his blonde lady friend. Manny was well groomed and cool-looking in his expensive casual clothing. He stood slightly apart from the others, his expression aloof and disinterested. He reminded me of an adult at a children's party, seeing out a boring and mildly unpleasant duty.

In contrast, Lorna Page was excited and shiny-eyed as a girl on her first date. She laughed with Suleiman Dada and leaned expectantly over the rail above the deserted deck. Through the powerful glasses I could see the flush on her cheeks which was not rouge.

I was concentrating on her so that it was only when I felt Chubby move suddenly and restlessly, and heard his grunt of alarm that I swung the glasses downwards on to the deck.

Sherry was there, standing between two of the uniformed sailors. They held her arms and she looked small and frail between them.

She still wore the clothes she had thrown on so hurriedly that morning and her hair was dishevelled. Her face was gaunt and her expression strained – but it was only when I studied her carefully that I saw that what looked like sleepless dark rings below her eyes were in fact bruises. With a cold chill of anger, I realized that her lips were swollen and puffed up as though they had been stung by bees. One of her cheeks was also fatly distorted and bruised.

They had beaten her and knocked her about badly. Now that I looked for it I could see dark splotches of dried blood on her blue shirt, and when one of the guards dragged her around roughly to face the shore I saw that one of her hands was bandaged roughly – and that either blood or disinfectant had stained the bandages.

She looked tired and ill, nearly at the end of her strength. My anger threatened to wipe out my reason. I wanted to inflict hurt upon those that had treated Sherry like this, and I had already begun to lift the rifle with hands that shook with the force of my hatred before I could control myself. I closed my eyes tightly and took a long deep breath to steady myself. The time would come – but it was not now.

When I opened my eyes again and refocused the binoculars, Suleiman Dada had the bullhorn to his lips.

'Good evening, Harry, my dear friend. I am sure you recognize this young lady.' He made a wide gesture towards Sherry and she looked up at him wearily. 'After questioning her closely, a procedure which alas caused her a little discomfort, I am at last convinced that she does not know the whereabouts of the property in which my friends and I are interested. She tells me that you have hidden it.' He paused and mopped his streaming face with a towel handed to him by one of his men before he went on.

'She is no longer of any interest to me – except possibly as a medium of exchange.'

He made a gesture, and Sherry was hustled away below. Something cold and slimy moved in my guts at her going. I wondered if I would ever see her again – alive.

On to the deserted deck filed four of Suleiman's men. Each of them had stripped to the waist and the floodlights rippled on their smooth darkly muscled bodies.

Each of them carried the hickory wooden handles of a pickaxe, and silently they formed up at the points of a star about the open deck. Next a man was led into the open centre by two guards. His hands were tied behind his back. They stood on each side of him and slowly forced him to turn in a circle and show himself while Suleiman Dada's voice boomed through the bullhorn.

'I wonder if you recognize him?' I stared at the stooped creature in canvas prison overalls that hung in filthy grey tatters from his gaunt frame. His skin was pale and waxy with deep-set dark eyes, long scraggly blond hair hung in greasy snakes about his face and his half-grown beard was thin and wispy.

He had lost teeth, probably knocked from his mouth with a careless blow.

'Yes, Harry?' Suleiman laughed fruitily over the loud hailer. 'A sojourn in Zinballa prison does wonders for a man, does it not – but the regulation garb is not as smart as that of an Inspector of Police.'

Only then did I recognize ex-Inspector Peter Daly – the man who I had pitched from the deck of *Wave Dancer* into the waters of the outer lagoon just before I had escaped from Suleiman Dada by running the channel at Gunfire Reef.

'Inspector Peter Daly,' Suleiman confirmed with a chuckle, 'a man who let me down badly. I do not like men who let me down, Harry. I really take it very hard. I brought him along for just such an eventuality. It was a wise precaution, for I believe that a graphic demonstration is so much more convincing than mere words.'

Once again he paused to mop his face and to drink deeply from a glass offered him by one of his men. Daly fell to his knees and looked up at the man on the bridge. His expression was of abject terror, and his mouth dribbled saliva as he pleaded for mercy.

'Very well, we can proceed if you are ready, Harry,' he boomed, and one of the guards produced a large black cloth bag which he pulled over Peter Daly's head and secured with a drawn string around his neck. They dragged him roughly to his feet again.

'It's our own variation on the game of blind man's bluff.'

Through the glasses I saw the liquid flood soak through the front of Peter Daly's canvas trousers, as his bladder emptied in anguished terror. Obviously he had seen this game played before during his stay in Zinballa prison.

'Harry, I want you to use your imagination. Do not see this snivelling filthy creature – but in his place imagine your lovely young lady friend.' He breathed heavily, but when the man beside him offered him the towel again Suleiman struck him a passionless back-handed blow that sent him sprawling across the bridge, and he continued evenly, 'Imagine her lovely young body, imagine her delicious fear as she stands in darkness not knowing what to expect.'

The two guards began to spin Daly between them, as they do in the children's game, around and around he went and now I could faintly hear his muffled shrieks and cries of fear.

Suddenly the two guards stepped away from him, and left the circle of half-naked men with their pick handles. One of them placed the butt of his weapon in the small of Daly's back and shoved him, reeling and staggering across the circle and the man opposite was waiting to drive the end of his club into Daly's belly.

Back and forth he staggered, driven by the thrust of the clubs. Slowly his tormentors increased the savagery of their attack, until one of them hefted his club and swung it like an axe at a tree. It smashed into Daly's ribs.

It was the signal to end it, and as Peter Daly fell to the deck they crowded about him, the clubs rising and falling in a fearsome rhythm and the blows sounding clearly across the lagoon to where we watched in disgust and revulsion.

One after the other they tired, and stepped back to rest from their grim work and Peter Daly's crumpled and broken body lay in the centre of the deck.

'Crude, you will say, Harry – but then you will not deny that it is effective.'

I was sickened by the barbaric cruelty of it, and Chubby muttered beside me, 'He's a monster – I've never heard of nothing like that before.'

'You have until noon tomorrow, Harry, to come to me unarmed and reasonable. We will talk, we will agree on certain matters, we will make an exchange of assets and we will part friends.'

He stopped speaking to watch while one of his men secured a line to Peter Daly's ankle, and they hoisted him to the mast-head of the crash boat where he dangled grotesquely, like some obscene pennant. Lorna Page was looking up at him, her head thrown back so the blonde hair hung down her back and her lips were slightly parted.

'If you refuse to be reasonable, Harry, then at noon tomorrow I shall sail around this island with your lady friend hanging like that—' He pointed up to the corpse whose masked head swung slowly back and forth only a few feet above the deck, '—from the mast. Think about it Harry. Take your time. Think about it well.'

Suddenly the floodlights were switched off, and Suleiman Dada began his laborious descent to the cabin. Manny Resnick and Lorna Page followed him. Manny was frowning slightly, as though he was pondering a business deal, but I could see that Lorna was enjoying herself.

'I think I'm going to throw up' muttered Chubby.

'Get it over then,' I said, 'because we have a lot of work to do.'

I stood up and quietly led the way back into the palm grove. We took it in turns to dig while the other stood guard amongst the trees. I would not use a light for fear of attracting attention from the crash boat and we were both exaggeratedly careful to maintain silence and not to let the clank of metal on metal sound through the grove.

We lifted the remaining cases of gelignite and blasting equipment, then we did the same with the rusted pay chest and carried it to a carefully chosen site below the steeply sloping ground of the peak. Fifty yards up the slope was fold in the ground thickly screened with goosebush and salt grass.

We dug another hole for the chest, going deep into the soft soil until we struck water. Then we repacked the pay chest and reburied it. Chubby climbed up to the hidden fold above us and made his arrangements there.

In the meantime I reloaded the machine-gun and wrapped it lightly in one of my old shirts, the five full magazines placed with it, and I buried the lot under an inch of sand, next to the stem of the nearest palm tree where the recent rain waters had cut a shallow dry runnel down from the slope.

The water-torn trench and the tree were forty paces from the spot where the chest was buried, and I hoped it was far enough. The trench was little more than two feet deep and would provide scanty cover.

The moon came out after midnight and it gave us enough light to check our arrangements. Chubby made sure I was in full view from his hideaway up the slope when I stood beside the shallow runnel. Then I climbed up to him and double-checked him. We lit a cheroot each, sheltering the match and screening the glowing tips with cupped hands, while we went over our planning once again.

I was particularly anxious that there should be no misunderstanding in our timing and signals, and I made Chubby repeat them twice. He did so with long-suffering and theatrical patience, but at last I was satisfied. We dumped the cheroot butts and scraped sand over them and when we went down the slope we both carried palm-frond brooms to sweep out all signs of activity.

The first part of my planning was complete, and we returned to where the golden tiger and the rest of the gelignite was cached. We reburied the tiger and then I prepared a full case of gelignite. It was a massive overdose of explosive, sufficient for a tenfold over-kill – but I have never been a man to stint myself when I have the means to indulge.

I would not be able to use the electric blaster and insulated wire, and I must rely on one of the time-pencil detonators. I have a strong distaste for these temperamental little gadgets. They operate on the principle of acid eating through a thin wire which holds the hammer on a powder cap. When the acid cuts the wire the cap explodes, and the delay in the detonation is governed by the strength of the acid and the thickness of the wire.

There can be a large latitude of error in this timing which on one occasion caused me a nearly fatal embarrassment. However, in this case I had no choice in the matter – and I selected a pencil with a six-hour delay and prepared it for use with the gelignite.

Amongst the equipment overlooked by the looters was my old oxygen rebreathing underwater set. This diving set is almost as dangerous to use as the time pencils. Unlike the aqualung which uses compressed air, the rebreather employs pure oxygen which is filtered and cleansed of carbon dioxide after each breath and then cycled back to the user.

Oxygen breathed at pressures in excess of twice atmospheric becomes as poisonous as carbon monoxide. In other words, if you rebreathe pure oxygen below underwater depths of thirty-three feet, it will kill you. You have to have all your wits together to play around with the stuff – but it has one enormous advantage. It does not blow bubbles on the surface to alarm a sentry and give away your position to him.

Chubby carried the prepared case of gelignite and the rifle when we went back to the beach. It was after three o'clock when I had donned and tested the oxygen set, and then I carried the gelignite down to the water and tested that for buoyancy. It needed a few pounds of lead weights to give it a neutral buoyancy and make it easier to handle in the water.

We had reached the water from the beach around the horn of the bay from the anchored crash boat. The point of sand and palm trees covered us as we worked, and at last I was ready.

It was a long tiring swim. I had to round the point and enter the bay – a distance of almost a mile – and I had to tow the case of explosive with me. It dragged heavily through the water and it took me almost an hour before I could see the lights of the crash boat glimmering above me through the clear water.

Hugging the bottom I crept forward slowly, terribly aware that the moonlight would silhouette me clearly against the white sand of the lagoon bed, for the water was clear as gin and only twenty-five feet deep.

It was a relief to move slowly into the dark shadow cast by the crash boat's hull and to know that I was safe from discovery. I rested for a few minutes, then I unrolled the nylon slings that I had on my belt and secured them to the case of gelignite.

Now I checked the time on my wristwatch, and the luminous hands showed ten minutes past four o'clock.

I crushed the glass ampoule of the time pencil, releasing the acid to begin its slow eroding attack on the wire, and I returned it to its prepared slot in the case of explosive. In six hours, more or less, the whole lot would go up with the force of a two hundred pound aerial bomb.

Now I left the floor of the lagoon and rose slowly to the hull of the crash boat. It was foul with a hanging slimy beard of weed and the hull itself was thick with a rough scale of shell-fish and goose-neck mussels.

I moved slowly along the keel, searching for an anchor point – but there was none and at last I was forced to use the shank of the rudder. I bound the case in position with all the nylon rope I had – and when I was finished I was certain that it would resist even the drag of water when the crash boat was travelling at the top of her speed.

Satisfied at last, I sank once more to the bed of the lagoon and moved off quietly on my return. I made much better speed through the water now without the burden of the gelignite case and Chubby was waiting for me on the beach.

'Fixed up?' he asked quietly, as he helped me shed the oxygen set.

'Just as long as that pencil does its job.'

I was so tired now that the walk back through the grove seemed like an eternity and my feet dragged in the loose footing. I had slept little the previous night, and not at all since then.

This time Chubby watched over me while I slept, and when he shook me gently awake it was after seven o'clock and the daylight was growing swiftly.

We ate a breakfast cold from the can, and I finished it with a handful of high-energy glucose tablets from the survival kit and washed them down with a mug of chlorinated water.

I drew the knife from the sheath on my belt and threw it underhand to pin into the trunk of the nearest palm. It stood there shivering with the force of the impact.

'Show off!' muttered Chubby, and I grinned at him, trying to look relaxed and easy.

'Look, just like the man said – no weapons,' and I spread my empty hands.

'You ready?' he asked, and we both stood up and looked at each other awkwardly. Chubby would never wish me good luck – which was the worst of all possible hex to put on someone.

'See you later,' he said.

'Okay, Chubby.' I held out my hand. He took it and squeezed it hard, then he turned away, picked up the FN rifle and plodded off through the grove.

I watched him out of sight, but he never looked back and I turned away myself and walked down unarmed to the beach.

I walked out from amongst the trees and stood at the water's edge, staring across the narrow strip of water at the crash boat. The dangling corpse had been removed from the masthead, I saw with relief.

For many seconds none of the sentries on deck noticed me, so I raised both hands above my head and gave them a loud 'Halloo'. Instantly there was a boil of activity and clamour of shouted orders on board the crash boat. Manny Resnick and Lorna appeared at the rail and stared across at me, while half a dozen armed seamen dropped into the whaleboat and headed for the beach.

As the boat touched, they leaped out on to the sand and surrounded me with the muzzles of the AK47s pressed eagerly into my back and belly. I kept my hands hoisted at half-mast and tried to maintain an expression of disinterest as a petty officer searched me with deliberate thoroughness for any weapon. When he was at last satisfied, he placed his hand between my shoulderblades and gave me a hearty shove towards the whaleboat. One of the more eager of his men took this as a licence and tried to rupture my kidneys with the butt of his AK47 – but the blow landed six inches high.

I made briskly for the whaleboat to forestall any further martial displays and they crowded into the boat around me pressing the muzzles of their fully loaded weapons painfully into various parts of my anatomy.

Manny Resnick watched me come in over the side of the crash boat.

'Hallo again, Harry,' he smiled without mirth.

'The pleasure is all yours, Manny,' I returned the death's head grin, and another blow caught me between the shoulder-blades and drove me across the deck. I ground my teeth together to control my anger, and I thought about Sherry North. That helped.

Commander Suleiman Dada was sprawled on a low couch covered with plain canvas cushions. He had removed his uniform jacket and it hung heavy with all the braid and medals from a hook on the bulkhead beside him. He wore only a sweat-soaked and greyish sleeveless vest, and even this early in the morning he held a glass of pale brown liquid in his right hand.

'Ah, Harry Fletcher – or should it be Harry Bruce?' he grinned at me like an enormous coal-black baby.

'You take your pick, Suleiman,' I invited him, but I didn't feel like playing word games with him now. I had no illusions about how dangerous was the position in which Sherry and I were placed, and my nerves were painfully tight and fear growled like a caged animal in my belly.

'I have learned so much more about you from my good friends,' he indicated Manny and the blonde Lorna who had followed me into the main cabin. 'Fascinating, Harry. I never dreamed you were a man of such vast talent and formidable achievement.'

'Thanks, Suleiman, you really are a brick, but let's not get carried away with compliments. We have important business – don't we?'

'True, Harry, very true.'

'You have raised the tiger throne, Harry, we know that,' Manny cut in, but I shook my head.

'Only part of it. The rest has gone – but we salvaged what there was.'

'All right, I'll buy that,' Manny agreed. 'Just tell us what there is.'

'There is the head of the tiger, about three hundred pounds weight in gold—' Suleiman and Manny glanced at each other.

'Is that all?' Manny asked, and I knew instinctively that Sherry had told them everything she knew during the beating they had given her. I did not hold that against her. I had expected it.

'There is also the jewel chest. The stones removed from the throne were placed in an iron pay chest.'

'The diamond – the Great Mogul?' demanded Manny.

'We've got it,' I said, and they murmured and smiled and nodded at each other. 'But I'm the only one who knows where it is—' I added softly, and immediately they were tense and quiet again.

'This time I've got something to trade, Manny. Are you interested?.

'We are interested, Harry, very interested,' Suleiman Dada spoke for him, and I was aware of the tension growing between my two enemies now that the loot was almost in view.

'I want Sherry North,' I said.

'Sherry North?' Manny stared at me for a moment, and then let out a brief cough of amusement. 'You're a bigger fool than I thought you were, Harry.'

'The girl is of no further interest to us.' Suleiman took a swallow from his glass, and I could smell his sweat in the rising warmth of the cabin. 'You can have her.'

'I want my boat, fuel and water to get me off the island.'

'Reasonable, Harry, very reasonable,' Manny smiled again as if at a secret joke.

'And I want the tiger's head,' and both Manny and Suleiman laughed out loud.

'Harry! Harry!' Suleiman chided me, still laughing.

'Greedy Harry,' Manny stopped laughing.

'You can have the diamond and about fifty pounds weight of other gem stones—' I tried to sell the idea with all the persuasion I could muster. It was the understandable thing to do for a man in my position, '—in comparison the head is nothing. The diamond is worth a million – the head would just cover my expenses.'

'You are a hard man, Harry,' Suleiman chuckled. 'Too hard.'

'What will I get out of it, then?' I demanded.

'Your life, and be grateful for it,' Manny said softly, and I stared at him. I saw the coldness in his eyes, like those of a reptile and I knew beyond all doubt what his intentions were for me, once I had led them to the treasure.

'How can I trust you?' I went through the motions, however, and Manny shrugged indifferently.

'Harry, how can you not trust us?' Suleiman intervened. 'What could we possibly gain by killing you and your young lady?'

'And what could you possibly lose,' I thought, but I nodded and said, 'Okay. I don't have much choice.'

They relaxed again, smiling at each other and Suleiman lifted his glass in a silent salute.

'Drink, Harry?' he asked.

'It's a little early for me, Suleiman,' I declined, 'but I would like to have the girl with me now.'

Suleiman motioned one of his men to fetch her.

'I want the whaleboat loaded with fuel and water and left on the beach,' I went on doggedly, and Suleiman gave the orders.

'The girl goes with me when we go ashore and after I have shown you the chest and the head, you'll take it and go.' I stared from one to the other. 'You'll leave us on the island unharmed, do we agree?'

'Of course, Harry.' Suleiman spread his hands disarmingly. 'We are all

agreed.' I was afraid that they would see the disbelief in my expression –
so I turned with relief to Sherry as she was led into the cabin.

My relief faded swiftly as I stared at her.

'Harry,' she whispered through her swollen purple lips. 'You came – oh
God, you came.' She took a faltering step towards me.

Her cheek was bruised and swollen horribly, and from the extent of the
oedema I thought perhaps the bone was cracked. The bruising under her
eyes made her look sick and consumptive, and blood had dried in a black
crust on the rims of her nostrils. I didn't want to look at her injuries, so I
took her in my arms and held her to my chest.

They were watching the pair of us with amusement and interest, I felt
their eyes upon us, but I did not want to face them and let them see the
murderous hatred that must show in my eyes.

'All right,' I said, 'let's get it over with.' When at last I turned to face
them, I hoped that my expression was under control.

'Unfortunately, I shall not be going with you,' Suleiman made no effort
to rise from the couch. 'Climbing in and out of small boats, walking great
distances in the sun and through the sand are not my particular pleasures.
I shall say farewell to you here, Harry, and my friends—' again he indicated
Manny and Lorna, '—will go with you as my representatives. Of course,
you will also be accompanied by a dozen of my men – all of them armed and
operating under my instructions.' I thought that this warning was not
entirely for my benefit alone.

'Goodbye, Suleiman. Perhaps we'll meet again.'

'I doubt it, Harry,' he chuckled. 'But God speed and my blessings go with
you.' He dismissed me with one great pink-palmed paw and with the other
he raised his glass and drained the last half-inch of liquor.

Sherry sat close beside me in the motor-boat. She leaned against me, and
her body seemed to have shrivelled with the pain of her ordeal. I put my
arm about her shoulders, and she whispered wearily, 'They are going to kill
us, Harry, you know that, don't you.'

I ignored the question and asked softly, 'Your hand,' it was still wrapped
in the rough bandage, 'what happened?'

Sherry looked up at the blonde girl beside Manny Resnick, and I felt her
shiver briefly against me.

'She did it, Harry.' Lorna Page was chatting animatedly to Manny
Resnick. Her carefully lacquered hairstyle resisted the efforts of the breeze
to ruffle it, and her face was meticulously made up with expensive cosmetics.
Her lipstick was moist and glossy and her eyelids were silvery green, with
long mascaraed lashes around the cat's eyes.

'They held me – and she pulled out my fingernails.' She shuddered again,
and Lorna Page laughed lightly. Manny cupped his hands around a gold
Dunhill lighter for her while she lit a cigarette. 'They kept asking me where
the treasure was – and each time I couldn't answer she pulled out a nail
with the pliers. They made a tearing sound as they came out.' Sherry broke
off and held her injured hand protectively against her stomach. I knew how
near she was to breaking completely and I held her close, trying to transmit
strength to her by physical contact.

'Gently, baby, gently now,' I whispered, and she pressed a little closer to me. I stroked her hair, and tried once again to control my anger, bearing down hard upon it before it clouded my wits.

The motor-boat ran in and grounded on the beach. We climbed out and stood on the white sands while the guards ringed us with levelled weapons.

'Okay, Harry,' Manny pointed. 'There's your boat all ready for you.' The whaleboat was drawn up on the beach. 'The tanks are full and when you've shown us the goods – you can take off.'

He spoke easily, but the girl beside him looked at us with hot predatory eyes – the way a mongoose looks at a chicken. I wondered what way she had chosen for us. I guessed that Manny had promised us to her for her pleasure without reservations – just as soon as he was through with us.

'I hope we aren't going to play games, Harry. I hope you're going to be sensible – and not waste our time.'

I had noticed that Manny had surrounded himself with his own men. Four of them, all armed with pistols, one of them my old acquaintance who had driven the Rover on our first meeting. To balance them there were ten black seamen under a petty officer, and already I sensed that the opposition was divided into two increasingly hostile parties. Manny further reduced the number of seamen in the party by detailing two of them to stay with the motor-boat. Then he turned to me, 'If you are ready, Harry, you may lead the way.'

I had to help Sherry, holding her elbow and guiding her up through the grove. She was so weak that she stumbled repeatedly and her breathing was distressed and ragged before we reached the caves.

With the mob of armed men following us closely, we went on along the edge of the slope. Surreptitiously I glanced at my watch. It was nine o'clock. One hour to go before the case of gelignite under the crash boat blew. The timing was still within the limits I had set. I made a small show out of locating the precise spot where the chest was buried, and it was with difficulty that I refrained from glancing up the slope to where the fold of ground was screened by vegetation.

'Tell them to dig here,' I said to Manny, and stepped back. Four seamen handed their weapons to a comrade and assembled the small folding army-type shovels they had brought with them.

The soil was soft and freshly turned so they went down at an alarming speed. They would expose the chest within minutes.

'The girl's hurt,' I said to Manny, 'she must sit down.' He glanced at me, and I saw his mind work swiftly. He knew Sherry could not run far and I think he welcomed the opportunity to distract some of the seamen – for he spoke briefly to the petty officer and I led Sherry to the palm tree and sat her down against the stem.

She sighed with weary relief, and two of the seamen came to stand over us with cocked weapons.

I glanced up the slope, but there was no sign of anything suspicious there, although I knew Chubby must be watching us intently. Apart from the two guards, everyone else was gathered expectantly around the four men who were already knee-deep in the freshly dug hole.

Even our two guards were consumed with curiosity, their attention kept wandering and they glanced repeatedly at the group forty yards away.

I heard quite clearly the clang as a spade struck the metal of the chest – and there was a shout of excitement. They all crowded around the excavation with a babble of rising voices, beginning to pull and elbow each other for the opportunity to look down into it. Our two guards turned their backs on us, and took a step or two in the same direction. It was more than I could have hoped for.

Manny Resnick shoved two seamen aside roughly, and jumped down into the hole beside the diggers. I heard him shouting, 'All right then, bring those ropes and let's lift it out. Carefully, don't damage anything.'

Lorna Page was leaning out over the hole also. It was perfect. I lifted my right hand and wiped my forehead slowly in the signal I had arranged with Chubby, and as I dropped my hand again, I seized Sherry and rolled swiftly backwards into the shallow rain-washed runnel.

It caught Sherry by surprise, and I had handled her roughly in my anxiety to get under cover. She cried out as I hurt her already painful injuries.

The two guards whirled at the cry, lifting their machine-guns and I knew that they were going to fire – and that the shallow trench provided no cover.

'Now, Chubby, now!' I prayed and threw myself on top of Sherry to shield her from the blast of machine-gun fire and I clapped both hands over her ears to protect them.

At that instant Chubby switched the knob on the electric battery blaster, and the impulse ran down the insulated wire that we had concealed so carefully the night before. There was half a case of gelignite crammed into the iron pay chest – as much explosive as I dared use without destroying Sherry and myself in the blast.

I imagined Chubby's fiendish glee as the case blew. It blew upwards, deflected by the sides of the excavation – but I had packed the sticks of gelignite with sand and handfuls of semiprecious stones to serve as a primitive shrapnel and to contain the blast and make it even more vicious.

The group of men around the hole were lifted high in the air, spinning and somersaulting like a troupe of insane acrobats, and a column of sand and dust shot a hundred feet into the air.

The earth jarred under us, slamming into our prone bodies – then the shock wave tore across us. It knocked sprawling the two guards who had been about to fire down on us, ripping their clothing from their bodies.

I thought my eardrums had both burst, I was completely deafened but I knew that I had saved Sherry's ears from damage, Deafened and half blinded by dust, I rolled off Sherry and scratched frantically in the sandy bottom of the trench. My fingers hit the machine-gun buried there and I dragged it out, pulling of the protective rags and coming swiftly to my knees.

Both the guards nearest me were alive, one crawling to his knees and the other sitting up dazedly with blood from a burst eardrum trickling down his cheek.

I killed them with two short bursts that knocked them down in the sand. Then I looked towards the broken heap of humanity around the excavation.

There was small, convulsive movement there and soft moans and whimpering sounds. I stood up shakily from the trench – and I saw Chubby standing up on the slope. He was shouting, but I heard nothing for the ringing buzzing din in my ears.

I stood there, swaying slightly, peering stupidly around me and Sherry rose to her feet beside me. She touched my shoulder, saying something, and with relief I heard her voice as the ringing in my ears subsided slightly.

I looked again towards the area of the explosion and saw a strange and frightening sight. A half-human figure, stripped of clothing and most of its skin, a raw bleeding thing with one arm half torn loose at the shoulder socket and dangling at its side by a shred of flesh rose slowly from beside the excavation like some horrible phantom from the grave.

It stood like that for a long moment which it took me to recognize Manny Resnick. It seemed impossible that he should have survived that holocaust, but more than that he began walking towards me.

He tottered step after step, closer and closer, and I stood frozen, unable to move myself. I saw then that he was blinded, the flying sand had scorched his eyeballs and flayed the skin from his face.

'Oh God! Oh God!' Sherry whispered beside me, and it broke the spell. I lifted the machine-gun and the stream of bullets that tore into Manny Resnick's chest were a mercy.

I was still dazed, staring about me at the shambles we had created when Chubby reached me. He took my arm and I could hear his voice as he shouted, 'Are you okay, Harry?' I nodded and he went on, 'The whaleboat! We have got to make sure of the whaleboat.'

I turned to Sherry. 'Go to the cave. Wait for me there,' and she turned away obediently.

'Make sure of these first,' I mumbled to Chubby, and we went to the heap of bodies about the shattered iron chest. All of them were dead or would soon be so.

Lorna Page lay upon her back. The blast had torn off her outer clothing and the slim pale body was clad only in lacy underwear, with shreds of the green slack suit hanging from her wrists and draped about her torn and still bleeding legs.

Defying even the explosion, her hairstyle retained its lacquered elegance except for the powdering of fine white sand. Death had played a macabre joke upon her – for a lump of blue lapis lazuli from the jewel chest had been driven by the force of the explosion deep into her forehead. It had embedded itself in the bone of her skull like the eye of the tiger from the golden throne.

Her own eyes were closed while the third precious eye of stone glared up at me accusingly.

'They are all dead,' grunted Chubby.

'Yes, they're dead,' I agreed, and tore my eyes away from the mutilated girl. I was surpised that I felt no triumph or satisfaction at her death, nor at the manner of it. Vengeance, far from being sweet, is entirely tasteless, I thought, as I followed Chubby down to the beach.

I was still unsteady from the effects of the explosion, and although my ears had recovered almost entirely, I was hardpressed to keep up with Chubby. He was light on his feet for such a big man.

I was ten paces behind him as we came out of the trees and stopped at the head of the beach.

The whaleboat lay where we had left her, but the two seamen detailed to guard the motor-boat must have heard the explosion and decided to take no chances.

They were halfway back to the crash boat already, and when they saw Chubby and me, one of them fired his machine-gun in our direction. The range was far beyond the accurate limits of the weapon, and we did not bother to take cover. However, the firing attracted the attention of the crew remaining aboard the crash boat – and I saw three of them run forward to man the quick-firer in the bows.

'Here comes trouble,' I murmured.

The first round was high and wide, cracking into the palms behind us and pitting their stems with the burst of shrapnel.

Chubby and I moved quickly back into the grove and lay flat behind the sandy crest of the beach.

'What now?' Chubby asked.

'Stalemate,' I told him, and the next two rounds from the quick-firer burst in futile fury in the trees above and behind us – but then there was a delay of a few seconds and I saw them training the gun around.

The next shot lifted a tall graceful spout of water from the shallows alongside the whaleboat. Chubby let out a roar of anger, like a lioness whose cub is threatened.

'They are trying to take out the whaleboat!' he bellowed, as the next round tore into the beach in a brief spurt of soft sand.

'Give it to me,' I snapped and took the FN from him, thrusting the short-barrelled AK47 at him and lifting the strap of the haversack off Chubby's shoulder. His marksmanship was not equal to the finer work that was now necessary.

'Stay here,' I told him, and I jumped up and doubled away around the curve of the bay. I had almost entirely recovered from the effects of the blast now – and as I reached the horn of the bay nearest the anchored crash boat I fell flat on my belly in the sand and pushed forward the long barrel of the FN.

The gun crew were still blazing away at the whaleboat, and spouts of sand and water rose in rapid succession about it. The plate of frontal armour of the gun was aimed diagonally away from me, and the backs and flanks of the gun crew were exposed.

I pushed the rate of the fire selector of the FN on to single shot, and drew a few long deep breaths to steady my aim after the long run through the soft sand.

The gun-layer was pedalling the traversing and elevating handles of the gun and had his forehead pressed hard against the pad above the eye-piece of the gunsight.

I picked him up in the peepsight and squeezed off a single shot. It knocked him off his seat and flung him sideways across the breech of the gun. The untended aiming handles spiralled idly and the barrel of the gun lifted lazily towards the sky.

The two gun-loaders looked around in amazement and I squeezed off two more snap shots at them.

Their amazement was altered instantly to panic, and they deserted their posts and sprinted back along the deck, diving into an open hatchway.

I swung my aim across and up to the open bridge of the crash boat. Three shots into the assembled officers and seamen produced a gratifying chorus of yells and the bridge cleared miraculously.

. The motor-boat from the beach came alongside, and I hastened the two seamen up the side and into the deckhouse with three more rounds. They neglected to make the boat fast and it drifted away from the side of the crash boat.

I changed the magazine of the FN and then carefully and deliberately I put a single bullet through each porthole on the near side of the boat. I could hear clearly the shattering crack of glass at each shot.

This proved too much provocation for Commander Suleiman Dada. I heard the donkey winch clatter to life and the anchor chain streamed in over the bows, glistening with seawater, and the moment the fluked anchor broke out through the surface, the crash boat's propellers churned a white wash of water under he stern and she swung round towards the opening of the lagoon.

I kept her under fire as she moved slowly past my hiding-place lest she change her mind about leaving. The bridge was screened by a wind shield of dirty white canvas, and I knew the helmsman was lying behind this with his head well down. I fired shot after shot through the canvas, trying to guess his position.

There was no apparent effect so I turned my attention to the portholes again, hoping for a lucky ricochet within the hull.

The crash boat picked up speed rapidly until she was waddling along like an old lady hurrying to catch a bus. She rounded the horn of the bay, and I stood up and brushed off the sand. then I reloaded the rifle and broke into a trot through the palm grove.

By the time I reached the north tip of the island, and climbed high enough up the slope to look out over the deep-water channel, the crash boat was a mile away, heading resolutely for the distant mainland of Africa, a small white shape against the shaded green of the sea, and the higher harsher blue of the sky.

I tucked the FN under my arm and found a seat from where I could watch her further progress. My wristwatch showed seven minutes past ten o'clock, and I began to wonder if the case of gelignite below the crash boat's stern had, after all, been torn loose by the drag of the water and the wash of the propellers.

The crash boat was now passing between the submerged outer reefs before entering the open inshore waters. The reefs blew regularly, breathing white foam at each surge of the sea as though a monster lay beneath the surface.

The small white speck of the crash boat seemed ethereal and insubstantial in that wilderness of sea and sky, soon she would merge with the wind-flecked and current-chopped waters of the open sea.

The explosion when it came was without passion, its violence muted by distance and its sound toned by the wind. There was a sudden soft waterspout that enveloped the tiny white boat. It looked like an ostrich feather, soft and blowing on the wind, bending when it reached its full height and then losing its shape and smearing away across the choppy surface.

The sound reached me many seconds later, a single unwarlike thud against my still-tender eardrums, and I thought I felt the flap of the blast like the puff of the wind against my face.

When the spray had blown into nothingness the channel was empty, no sign remained of the tiny vessel and there was no mark of her going upon the wind-blown waters.

I knew that with the tide the big evil-looking albacore sharks hunted inshore upon the flood. They would be quick to the taint of blood and torn flesh in the water, and I doubted that any of those aboard the crash boat who had survived the blast would long avoid the attentions of those single-minded and voracious killers. Those that found Commander Suleiman Dada would fare well, I thought, unless they recognized a kindred spirit and accorded him professional privilege. It was a grim little joke, and it gave me only fleeting amusement. I stood up and walked down to the caves.


I found my medical kit had been broken open and scattered during the previous day's looting, but I retrieved sufficient material to clean and dress Sherry's mutilated fingers. Three of the nails had been torn out. I feared that the roots had been destroyed, and that they would never grow again – but when Sherry expressed the same fears, I denied them stoutly.

Once her injuries were taken care of I made her swallow a couple of Codeine for the pain and made a bed for her in the darkness of the back of the cave.

'Rest,' I told her, kneeling to kiss her tenderly. 'Try and sleep. I will fetch you when we are ready to leave.'

Chubby was already busy with the necessary tasks. He had checked the whaleboat and, apart from a few shrapnel holes, found her in good condition. We filled the holes with Pratleys putty from the toolchest, and left her on the beach.

The hole in which the chest had been buried served as a communal grave for the dead men and the woman lying about it. We laid them in it like sardines, and covered them with the soft sand.

We exhumed the golden head from its own grave with its glittering eye still in the broad forehead, and staggering under its weight we carried it down to the whaleboat and padded it with the polythene cushions in the bottom of the boat. The plastic packets of sapphires and emeralds I packed into my haversack and laid it beside the head.

Then we returned to the caves and salvaged all the undamaged stores and equipment – the jerrycans of water and petrol, the scuba bottles and the compressor. It was late afternoon before we had packed it all into the whaleboat and I was tired. I laid the FN rifle on top of the load and stood back.

'Okay, Chubby?' I asked, as I lit our cheroots and we took our first break. 'Reckon we can take it off now.'

Chubby drew on the cheroot and blew a long flag of blue smoke before he spat on the sand. 'I just want to go up and fetch Angelo,' he muttered, and when I stared at him he went on, 'I'm not going to leave the kid up there. It's too lonely here, he'll want to be with his own people in a Christian grave.'

So while I went back to the caves to fetch Sherry, Chubby selected a bolt of canvas and went off into the gathering darkness.

I woke Sherry and made sure she was warmly dressed in one of my jerseys, then I gave her two more Codeine and took her down towards the beach. It was dark now, and I held the flashlight in one hand and helped Sherry with the other. We reached the beach and I paused uncertainly. There was something wrong, I knew, and I played the torch over the loaded vessel.

Then I realized what it was, and I felt a sick little jolt in my belly.

The FN rifle was no longer where I had left it in the whaleboat.

'Sherry,' I whispered urgently, 'get down and stay there until I tell you.'

She sank swiftly to the sand beside the beached hull, and I looked around frantically for a weapon. I thought of the speargun, but it was under the jerrycans, my bait-knife was still pegged into a palm tree in the grove – I had forgotten about it until this moment. A spanner from the toolbox, perhaps – the thought was as far as I got.

'All right, Harry, I've got the gun.' The deep throaty voice spoke out of the darkness close behind me. 'Don't turn around or do anything stupid.'

He must have been lying up in the grove after he had taken the rifle, and now he had come up silently behind me. I froze.

'Without turning around – just toss that flashlight back here. Over your shoulder.'

I did as he ordered and I heard the sand crunch under his feet as he stooped to pick it up.

'All right, turn around – slowly.' As I turned, he shone the powerful beam into my eyes, dazzling me. However, I could still vaguely make out the huge hulking shape of the man beyond the beam.

'Have a good swim, Suleiman?' I asked. I could see that he wore only a pair of short white underpants, and his enormous belly and thick shapeless legs gleamed wetly in the reflected torchlight.

'I am beginning to develop an allergy to your jokes, Harry,' he spoke again in that deep beautifully modulated voice, and I remembered too late how a grossly overweight man becomes light and strong in the supporting salt water of the sea. However, even with the turn of the tide to help him, Suleiman Dada had performed a formidable feat in surviving the explosion and swimming back through almost two miles of choppy water. I doubted any of his men had done so well.

'I think it should be in the belly first,' he spoke again, and I saw that he held the stock of the rifle across his left elbow. With the same hand he aimed the torch beam into my face. 'They tell me that is the most painful place to get it.'

We were silent for moments then, Suleiman Dada breathing with his deep asthmatic wheeze and I trying desperately to think of some way to distract him long enough to give me a chance to grab the barrel of the FN.

'I don't suppose you'd like to go down on your knees and plead with me?' he asked.

'Go screw, Suleiman,' I answered.

'No, I didn't really think you would. A pity, I would have enjoyed that.

But what about the girl, Harry, surely it would be worth a little of your pride —'

We both heard Chubby. He had known there was no way he could cross the open beach undetected, even in the dark. He had tried to rush Suleiman Dada, but I am sure he knew that he would not make it. What he was really doing was giving me the distraction I so desperately needed.

He came fast out of the darkness, running in silently with only the squeak of the treacherous sand beneath his feet to betray him. Even when Suleiman Dada turned the rifle on to him, he did not falter in his charge.

There was the crack of the shot and the long lightning flash of the muzzle blast, but even before that, I was halfway across the distance that separated me from the huge black man. From the corner of my eye I saw Chubby fall, and then Suleiman Dada began to swing the rifle back towards me.

I brushed past the barrel of the FN and crashed shoulder first into his chest. It should have staved his ribs in like the victim of a car smash – instead I found the power of my rush absorbed in the thick padding of dark flesh. It was like running into a feather mattress, and although he reeled back a few paces and lost the rifle, Suleiman Dada remained upright on those two thick tree-trunks of his legs, and before I could recover my own balance I was enfolded in a vast bear hug.

He picked me up off my feet, and pulled me to his mountainously soft chest, trapping both my arms and lifting me so that I could not brace my legs to resist his weight and strength. I experienced a chill of disbelief when I felt the strength of the man, not a hard brutal strength – but something so massive and weighty that there seemed no end to it, almost like the irresistible push and surge of the sea.

I tried with my elbows and knees, kicking and striking to break his hold, but the blows found nothing solid and made no impression upon the man. Instead, the enfolding grip of his arms began to tighten with the slow pulsing power of a giant python. I realized instantly that he was quite capable of literally crushing me to death – and I experienced a sense of panic. I twisted and struggled frantically and unavailingly in his arms, but as he brought more of his immense power to bear upon me, so his breathing wheezed more harshly and he leaned forward, hunching his great shoulders over me and forcing my back into an arc that must soon snap my spine.

I bent back my head, reached up with an open mouth and locked my teeth into the broad flattened nose. I bit in hard, with all my desperation, and quite clearly I felt my teeth slice through the flesh and gristle of his nose and instantly my mouth filled with the warm salty metallic flood of his blood. Like a dog at a bull-baiting, I worried and tugged at his nose.

The man bellowed a roar of agony and anger and he released his crushing grip from around my body to try and tear my teeth from his face. The instant my arms were free I twisted convulsively and got a purchase with both feet in the firm wet sand, so I could put my hip into him for the throw. He was so busy attempting to dislodge the grip of my teeth from his nose that he could not resist the throw and as he went over backwards my teeth tore loose, cutting away a lump of his living flesh.

I spat out the horrid mouthful but the warm blood streamed down my chin and I resisted the temptation to pause and wipe it clean.

Suleiman Dada was down on his back, stranded like some massive crippled black frog, but he would not remain helpless much longer, I had to take him out cleanly now and there was only one place where he might be vulnerable.

I jumped up high over him and came down to knee-drop into his throat, to drive my one knee with the full weight and momentum of my body into his larynx and crush it.

He was swift as a cobra, throwing up both arms to shield his throat and to catch me as I descended on to him. Once again, I was enmeshed by those thick black arms, and we rolled down the beach, locked chest to chest into the warm shallow water of the lagoon.

In a direct contrast of weight for weight like this, I was outmatched, and he came up over me with blood streaming from his injured nose, still bellowing with anger, and he pinned me into the shallows forcing my head below the surface and bearing down upon my chest and lungs with all his vast weight.

I began to drown. My lungs caught fire, and the need to breathe laced my vision with sparks and whorls of fire. I could feel the strength going out of me and my consciouness receding into blackness.

The shot when it sounded was muted and dull. I did not recognize it for what it was, until I felt Suleiman Dada jerk and stiffen, felt the strength go out of him and his weight slip and fall from me.

I sat up coughing and gasping for air, with water cascading from my hair and streaming into my eyes. In the light of the fallen torch I saw Sherry North kneeling on the sand at the edge of the water. She had the rifle still clutched in her bandaged hand and her face was pale and frightened.

Beside me, Suleiman Dada floated face down in the shallow water, his half-naked body glistening blackly like a stranded porpoise. I stood up slowly, water pouring from my clothing and she stared at me, horrified with what she had done.

'Oh God,' she whispered, 'I've killed him. Oh God!'

'Baby,' I gasped. 'That was the best day's work you've ever done,' and I staggered past her to where Chubby lay.

He was trying to sit up, struggling feebly.

'Take it easy, Chubby,' I snapped at him, and picked up the torch. There was fresh blood on his shirt and I unbuttoned it and pulled it open around the broad brown chest.

It was low and left, but it was a lung hit. I saw the bubbles frothing from the dark hole at each breath. I have seen enough gunshot wounds to be something of an authority and I knew that this was a bad one.

He watched my face. 'How does it look?' he grunted. 'It's not sore.'

'Lovely,' I answered grimly. 'Every time you drink a beer it will run out of the hole.' He grinned crookedly, and I helped him to sit up. The exit hole was clean and neat, the FN had been loaded with solid ammunition, and it was only slightly larger than the entry hole. The bullet had not mushroomed against bone.

I found a pair of field dressings in the medical chest and bound up the wounds before I helped him into the boat. Sherry had prepared one of the mattresses and we covered him with blankets.

'Don't forget Angelo,' he whispered. I found the long heartbreaking canvas bundle where Chubby had dropped it, and I carried Angelo down and laid him in the bows.

I shoved the whaleboat out until I was waist-deep, then I scrambled over the side and started the engines. My one concern now was to get proper medical attention for Chubby, but it was a long cold run down the islands to St Mary's.

Sherry sat beside Chubby on the floorboards, doing what little she could for his comfort – while I stood in the stern between the motors and negotiated the deep-water channel before turning southwards under a sky full of cold white stars, bearing my cargo of wounded, and dying and dead.

We had been going almost five hours when Sherry stood up from beside the blanketed form in the bottom of the boat and made her way back to me.

'Chubby wants to talk to you,' she said quietly, and then impulsively she leaned forward and touched my cheek with the cold fingers of her uninjured hand. 'I think he is going, Harry.' And I heard the desolation in her voice.

I passed the con to her. 'You see those two bright stars,' I showed her the pointers of the Southern Cross, 'steer straight for them,' and I went forward to where Chubby lay.

For a while he did not seem to know me, and I knelt beside him and listened to the soft liquid sound of his breathing. Then at last he became aware. I saw the starlight catch his eyes and he looked up at me, and I leaned closer so that our faces were only inches apart.

'We took some good fish together, Harry,' he whispered.

'We are going to take a lot more,' I answered. 'With what we've got aboard now we will be able to buy a really good boat. You and I will be going for billfish again next season – that's for sure.'

Then we were silent for a long time, until at last I felt his hand grope for mine and I took it and held it hard. I could feel the callouses and the ancient line burns from handling heavy fish.

'Harry,' his voice was so faint I could just hear it over the sound of the motors when I laid my ear to his lips, 'Harry, I'm going to tell you something I never told you before. I love you, man,' he whispered. 'I love you better than my own brother.'

'I love you too, Chubby,' I said, and for a little longer his grip was strong again, and then it relaxed. I sat on beside him while slowly that big horny paw turned cold in my hands, and dawn began to pale the sky above the dark and brooding sea.

During the next three weeks, Sherry and I seldom left the sanctuary of Turtle Bay. We went together to stand awkwardly in the graveyard while they buried our friends, and once I drove alone to the fort and spent two hours with President Godfrey Biddle and Inspector Wally Andrews – but the rest of that time we were alone while the wounds healed.

Our bodies healed more quickly than did our minds. One morning as I dressed Sherry's hand, I noticed the pearly white seeds in the healing flesh of her fingertips and I realized that they were the nail roots regrowing. She would have fingernails once more to grace those long narrow hands – I was thankful for that.

They were not happy days, the memories were too fresh and the days were dark with mourning for Chubby and Angelo and both of us knew that the crisis of our relationship was at hand. I guessed what agonies of decision she must be facing, and I forgave her the quick flares of temper, the long sullen silences – and her sudden disappearances from the shack when for hours at a time she walked the long deserted beaches or made a remote and lonely figure sitting out on the headland of the bay.

At last I knew that she was strong enough to face what lay ahead for both of us. One evening I raised the subject of the treasure for the first time since our return to St Mary's.

It lay now buried beneath the raised foundations of the shack. Sherry listened quietly as we sat together upon the veranda, drinking whisky and listening to the sound of the night surf upon the beach.

'I want you to go ahead to make the arrangements for the arrival of the coffin. Hire a car in Zürich and drive down to Basle. I have arranged a room for you at the Red Ox Hotel there. I have picked that hotel because they have an underground parking garage and I know the head porter there. His name is Max.' I explained my plans to her. 'He will arrange a hearse to meet the plane. You will play the part of the bereaved widow and bring the coffin down to Basle. We will make the exchange in the garage, and you will arrange for my banker to have an armoured car to take the tiger's head to his own premises from there.'

'You've got it all worked out, haven't you?'

'I hope so.' I poured another whisky. 'My bank is Falle et Fils and the man to ask for is M. Challon. When you meet him you will give him my name and the number of my account – ten sixty-six, the same as the battle of Hastings. You must arrange with M. Challon for a private room to which we can invite dealers to view the head —' I went on explaining in detail the arrangements I had made, and she listened intently. Now and then she asked a question but mostly she was silent, and at last I produced the air ticket and a thin sheaf of traveller's cheques to carry her through.

'You have made the reservations already?' she looked startled, and when I nodded she thumbed open the booklet of the air ticket. 'When do I leave?'

'On the noon plane tomorrow.'

'And when will you follow?'

'On the same plane as the coffin, three days later – on Friday. I will come in on the BOAC flight at 1.30 p.m. That will give you time to make the arrangements and be there to meet me.'

That night was as tender and loving as it had ever been, but even so I sensed a deeper mood of melancholia in Sherry – as at the time of leave-taking and farewell.

In the dawn, the dolphins met us at the entrance of the bay, and we romped with them for half the morning and then swam in slowly to the beach.

I drove her out to the airport in the old pick-up. For most of the ride she was silent and then she tried to tell me something, but she was confused and she did not make sense. She ended lamely, '—if anything ever happens to us, well, I mean nothing lasts for ever, does it—'

'Go on,' I said.

'No, it's nothing. Just that we should try to forgive each other – if anything does happen.' That was all she would say, and at the airport barrier she kissed me briefly and clung for a second with both arms about my neck, then she turned and walked quickly to the waiting aircraft. She did not look back or wave as she climbed the boarding ladder.

I watched the aircraft climb swiftly and head out across the inshore channel for the mainland, then I drove slowly back to Turtle Bay.

It was a lonely place without her, and that night as I lay alone under the mosquito net on the wide bed, I knew that the risk I was about to take was necessary. Highly dangerous, but necessary. I knew I must have her back here. Without her, it would all be tasteless. I must gamble on the pull I would be able to exert over her outweighing the other forces that governed her. I must let her make the choice herself, but I must try to influence it with every play in my power.

In the morning I drove into St Mary's and after Fred Coker and I had argued and consulted and passed money and promises back and forth, he opened the double doors to his warehouse and I drove the pick-up in beside the hearse. We loaded one of his best coffins, teak with silver-gilt handles, and red velvet-lined interior, into the back of the truck. I covered it with a sheet of canvas and drove back to Turtle Bay. When I had packed the coffin and screwed down the lid it weighed almost five hundred pounds.

When it was dark, I drove back into town and it was almost closing time at the Lord Nelson before I had completed my arrangements. I had just time for a quick drink and then I drove back to Turtle Bay to pack my battered old canvas campaign bag.

At the noon of the next day, twenty-four hours earlier than I had arranged with Sherry North, I boarded the aircraft for the mainland and that evening caught the BOAC connection onwards from Nairobi.

There was no one to meet me at Zürich airport, for I was a full day early, and I passed quickly through customs and immigration and went out into the vast arrivals hall.

I checked my luggage before I went about tidying up the final loose threads of my plan. I found a flight outwards leaving at 1.20 the following day which suited my timing admirably. I made a single reservation, then I drifted over to the inquiries desk and waited until the pretty little blonde girl in the Swissair uniform was not busy, before engaging her in a long explanation. At first she was adamant, but I gave her the old crinkled eyes and smiled that way, until at last she became intrigued with it all – and giggled in anticipation.

'You sure you'll be on duty tomorrow?' I asked anxiously.

'Yes, Monsieur, don't worry, I will be here.'

We parted as friends and I retrieved my bag and caught a cab to the Zürich Holiday Inn just down the road. The same hotel where I had sweated out the survival of the Dutch policeman so long ago. I ordered a drink, took a bath and then settled down in front of the television set. It brought back memories.

A little before noon the following day I sat at the airport café pretending to read a copy of the *Frankfurter Allgemeine Zeitung* and watching the arrivals hall over the top of the page. I had already checked my baggage and my ticket. All I had to do was to go through into the final departure lounge.

I was wearing a new suit purchased that morning of such a bizarre cut and mousy shade of grey, that no one who knew him could believe that Harry Fletcher would be seen in public wearing it. It was two sizes too large for me, and I had padded myself with hotel towels to alter my shape entirely. I had also self-barbered by hair into a short and ragged style and dusted it with talcum powder to put fifteen years on my age. When I peered at my image through gold-rimmed spectacles in the mirror of the men's room, I did not even recognize myself.

At seven minutes past one, Sherry North walked in through the main doors of the terminal. She wore a suit of grey checked wool, a full length black leather coat and a small matching leather hat with a narrow businesslike brim. Her eyes were screened by a pair of dark glasses, but her expression was set and determined as she strode through the crowd of tourists.

I felt the sick slide and churn of my guts as I saw all my suspicions and fears confirmed and the newspaper shook in my hands. Following a pace behind and to her side, was the small neatly dressed figure of the man she had introduced to me as Uncle Dan. He wore a tweed cap and carried an overcoat across his arm. More than ever he exuded an air of awareness, the hunter's alert and confident tread as he followed the girl.

He had four of his men with him. They moved quietly after him, quiet, soberly dressed men with closed watchful faces.

'Oh, you litle bitch,' I whispered, but I wondered why I should feel so bitter. I had known for long enough now.

The group of girl and five men stopped in the centre of the hall and I watched dear Uncle Dan issuing his orders. He was a professional, you could see that in the way he staked out the hall for me. He placed his men to cover the arrivals gate and every exit.

Sherry North stood listening quietly, her face neutral and her eyes hidden by the glasses. Once Uncle Dan spoke to her and she nodded abruptly, then when the four strong-arm men had been placed, the two of them stood together facing the arrivals gate.

'Get out now, Harry,' the little warning voice urged me. 'Don't play fancy games. This is the wolf pack all over again. Run, Harry, run.'

Just then the public address system called the outward flight on which I had made a reservation the previous day. I stood up from the table in my cheap baggy suit and shuffled across to the Inquiries Desk. The little blonde Swissair hostess did not recognize me at first, then her mouth dropped open and her eyes flew wide. She covered her mouth with her hand and her eyes sparkled with conspiratory glee.

'The end booth,' she whispered, 'the end nearest the departures gate.' I winked at her and shuffled away. In the telephone booth I lifted the receiver and pretended to be speaking, but I broke the connection with a finger on the bar and I watched the hall through the glass door.

I heard my accomplice paging.

'Miss Sherry North, will Miss North please report to the inquiries desk.'

Through the glass I saw Sherry approach the desk and speak with the hostess. The blonde girl pointed to the booth beside mine and Sherry turned and walked directly towards me. She was screened from Uncle Dan and his merry men by the row of booths.

The leather coat swung gracefully about her long legs, and her hair was glossy black and bouncing on her shoulders at each stride. I saw she wore black leather gloves to hide her injured hand, and I thought she had never looked so beautiful as in this moment of my betrayal.

She entered the booth beside me and lifted the receiver. Swiftly I replaced my own telephone and stepped out of the booth. As I opened her door she looked around with impatient annoyance.

'Okay, you dumb cop – give me a good reason why I shouldn't break your head,' I said.

'You!' Her expression crumpled, and her hand flew to her mouth. We stared at each other.

'What happened to the real Sherry North?' I demanded, and the question seemed to steady her.

'She was killed. We found her body – almost unrecognizable – in a quarry outside Ascot.'

'Manny Resnick told me he had killed her —' I said. 'I didn't believe him. He also laughed at me when I went on board to do a deal with him and Suleiman Dada for your life. I called you Sherry North and he laughed at me and called me a fool.' I grinned at her lopsidedly. 'He was right – wasn't he? I was a fool.'

She was silent then, unable to meet my eyes. I went on talking, confirming what I had guessed.

'So after Sherry North was killed, they decided not to announce her identity – but to stake out the North cottage. Hoping that the killers would return to investigate the new arrival – or that some other patsy would be sucked in and lead them home. They chose you for the stake-out, because you were a trained police diver. That's right, isn't it?'

She nodded, still not looking at me.

'They should have made sure you knew something about conchology as well. Then you wouldn't have grabbed that piece of fire coral – and saved me a lot of trouble.'

She was over the first shock of my appearance. Now was the time to whistle for Uncle Dan and his men, if she was going to. She remained silent, her face half-turned away, her cheek flushed with bright blood beneath the dark golden tan.

'That first night, you telephoned when you thought I was asleep. You were reporting to your superior officer that a sucker had walked in. They told you to play me along. and – oh baby – how you played me.'

She looked at me at last, dark blue eyes snapping with defiance, words seemed to boil behind her closed lips, but she held them back and I went on.

'That's why you used the back entrance to Jimmy's shop, to avoid the neighbours who knew Sherry. That's why those two goons of Manny's arrived to roast your fingers on the gas-ring. They wanted to find out who you were – because you sure as hell weren't Sherry North. They had killed her.'

I wanted her to speak now. Her silence was wearing my nerves.

'What rank is Uncle Dan – Inspector?'

'Chief Inspector,' she said.

'I had him tabbed the moment I laid eyes on him.'

'If you knew all this, then why did you go through with it?' she demanded.

'I was suspicious at first – but by the time I knew for certain I was crazy stupid in love with you.'

She braced herself, as though I had struck her, and I went on remorselessly.

'I thought by some of the things we did together that you felt pretty good about me. In my book when you love someone, you don't sell them down the river.'

'I'm a policewoman,' she flashed at me, 'and you're a killer.'

'I never killed a man who wasn't trying to kill me first,' I flashed back, 'just the way you hit Suleiman Dada.'

That caught her off-balance. She stammered and looked about her as if she were in a trap.

'You're a thief,' she attacked again.

'Yes,' I agreed. 'I was once – but that was a long time ago, and since then I worked hard on it. With a bit of help, I'd have made it.'

'The throne —' she went on, 'you are stealing the throne.'

'No, ma'am,' I grinned at her.

'What is in the coffin then?'

'Three hundred pounds of beach sand from Turtle Bay. When you see it, think of the times we had there.'

'The throne – where is it?'

'With its rightful owner, the representative of the people of St Mary's, President Godfrey Biddle.'

'You gave it up?' she stared at me with disbelief that faded slowly as something else began to dawn in her eyes. 'Why, Harry, why?'

'Like I said, I'm working hard on it.' Again we were staring hard at each other, and suddenly I saw the clear liquid flooding her dark blue eyes.

'And you came here – knowing what I had to do?' she asked, her voice choking.

'I wanted you to make a choice,' I said, and she let the tears cling like dewdrops in the thick dark eyelashes. I went on deliberately, 'I'm going to walk out of this booth and go out through that gate. If nobody blows the whistle I will be on the next flight out of here and the day after tomorrow, I will swim out through the reef to look for the dolphin.'

'They'll come after you, Harry,' she said, and I shook my head.

'President Biddle has just altered his extradition agreements. Nobody will be able to touch me on St Mary's. I have his word for it.'

I turned and opened the door of the booth. 'I'm going to be lonely as all hell out there at Turtle Bay.'

I turned my back on her then and walked slowly and deliberately to the departures gate, just as they called my flight for the second time. It was the longest and scariest walk of my entire life, and my heart thumped in time to my footsteps. Nobody challenged me and I dared not look back.

As I settled into the seat of the Swissair Caravelle and fastened my seat-belt, I wondered how long it would take her to screw up her nerve enough to follow me out to St Mary's, and I reflected that there was much I still had to tell her.

I had to tell her that I had contracted to raise the rest of the golden throne from Gunfire Break for the benefit of the people of St Mary's. In return President Godfrey Biddle had undertaken to buy me a new deep-sea boat from the proceeds – just like *Wave Dancer* – a token of the people's gratitude.

I would be able to keep my lady in the style to which I was accustomed, and of course there was always the case of Georgian silver gilt plate buried behind the shack at Turtle Bay for the lean and hungry off season. I hadn't reformed *that* much. There would be no more night runs, however.

As the Caravelle took off and climbed steeply up over the blue lakes and forested mountains, I realized that I did not even know her real name.

That would be the first thing I would ask her when I met her at the airport of St Mary's Island – Pearl of the Indian Ocean.

# TITLES IN THIS SERIES

**Eric Ambler**
The Mask of Dimitrios
Passage of Arms
The Schirmer Inheritance
Journey into Fear
The Light of Day
Judgement on Deltchev

**John le Carré**
The Spy Who Came in from the Cold
Call for the Dead
A Murder of Quality
The Looking-Glass War
A Small Town in Germany

**Raymond Chandler***
Farewell My Lovely
The Lady in the Lake
Playback
The Long Goodbye
The High Window
The Big Sleep

**Joseph Conrad**
Lord Jim
The Nigger of the 'Narcissus'
Typhoon
Nostromo
The Secret Agent

**Catherine Cookson**
The Round Tower
The Fifteen Streets
Feathers in the Fire
A Grand Man
The Blind Miller

**Catherine Cookson**
The Mallen Streak
The Girl
The Gambling Man
The Cinder Path
The Invisible Cord

**Monica Dickens**
One Pair of Hands
The Happy Prisoner
Mariana
Kate and Emma
One Pair of Feet

**F. Scott Fitzgerald***
The Great Gatsby
Tender is the Night
This Side of Paradise
The Beautiful and Damned
The Last Tycoon

**Ian Fleming**
Dr. No
Thunderball
Goldfinger
On Her Majesty's Secret Service
Moonraker
From Russia, With Love

**C. S. Forester**
The Ship
Mr Midshipman Hornblower
The Captain from Connecticut
The General
The Earthly Paradise
The African Queen

**E. M. Forster**
Where Angels Fear to Tread
The Longest Journey
A Room with a View
Howards End
A Passage to India

**Fourteen Great Plays***

**John Galsworthy**
The Forsyte Saga:
The Man of Property
In Chancery
To Let
A Modern Comedy:
The White Monkey
The Silver Spoon
Swan Song

**Erle Stanley Gardner**
Perry Mason in the Case of
   the Gilded Lily
The Daring Decoy
The Fiery Fingers
The Lucky Loser
The Calendar Girl
The Deadly Toy
The Mischievous Doll
The Amorous Aunt

**Richard Gordon**
Doctor in the House
Doctor at Sea
Doctor at Large
Doctor in Love
Doctor in Clover
The Facemaker
The Medical Witness

**Graham Greene**
The Heart of the Matter
Stamboul Train
A Burnt-out Case
The Third Man
Loser Takes All
The Quiet American
The Power and the Glory

**Graham Greene**
Brighton Rock
The End of the Affair
It's a Battlefield
England Made Me
The Ministry of Fear
Our Man in Havana

**Ernest Hemingway***
For Whom the Bell Tolls
The Snows of Kilimanjaro
Fiesta
The Short Happy Life of Francis
   Macomber
Across the River and into the Trees
The Old Man and the Sea

**Georgette Heyer**
These Old Shades
Sprig Muslin
Sylvester
The Corinthian
The Convenient Marriage

**Franz Kafka***
The Trial
America
In the Penal Settlement
Metamorphosis
The Castle
The Great Wall of China
Investigations of a Dog
Letter to his Father
The Diaries 1910-1923

**Rudyard Kipling**
The Jungle Book
The Second Jungle Book
Just So Stories
Puck of Pook's Hill
Stalky and Co.
Kim

**Norah Lofts**
Jassy
Bless This House
Scent of Cloves
How Far to Bethlehem?

**D. H. Lawrence**
Sons and Lovers
St. Mawr
The Fox
The White Peacock
Love among the Haystacks
The Virgin and the Gipsy
Lady Chatterley's Lover

**D. H. Lawrence**
Women in Love
The Ladybird
The Man Who Died
The Captain's Doll
The Rainbow

**Robert Ludlum***
The Scarlatti Inheritance
The Osterman Weekend
The Matlock Paper
The Gemini Contenders

**Thomas Mann***
Death in Venice
Tristan
Tonio Kröger
Doctor Faustus
Mario and the Magician
A Man and His Dog
The Black Swan
Confessions of Felix Krull,
   Confidence Man

**W. Somerset Maugham**
Cakes and Ale
The Painted Veil
Liza of Lambeth
The Razor's Edge
Theatre
The Moon and Sixpence

**W. Somerset Maugham**
Sixty-five Short Stories

**Ed McBain***
Cop Hater
Give the Boys a Great Big Hand
Doll
Eighty Million Eyes
Hail, Hail, the Gang's All Here!
Sadie When She Died
Let's Hear it for the Deaf Man

**James A. Michener***
The Source
The Bridges at Toko-Ri
Caravans
Sayonara

**George Orwell**
Animal Farm
Burmese Days
A Clergyman's Daughter
Coming up for Air
Keep the Aspidistra Flying
Nineteen Eighty-Four

**George Orwell**
Down and Out in Paris & London
Homage to Catalonia
Selections from Essays and Journalism:
 1931-1949
The Road to Wigan Pier

**Jean Plaidy**
St. Thomas's Eve
Royal Road to Fotheringay
The Goldsmith's Wife
Perdita's Prince

**Nevil Shute**
A Town Like Alice
Pied Piper
The Far Country
The Chequer Board
No Highway

**Georges Simenon**
Ten Maigret Stories

**Wilbur Smith**
When the Lion Feeds
The Diamond Hunters
Eagle in the Sky
Gold Mine
Shout at the Devil

**Wilbur Smith**
Hungry as the Sea
The Sound of Thunder
The Eye of the Tiger

**John Steinbeck***
The Grapes of Wrath
The Moon is Down
Cannery Row
East of Eden
Of Mice and Men

**Mary Stewart**
The Crystal Cave
The Hollow Hills
Wildfire at Midnight
Airs Above the Ground

**Evelyn Waugh**
Decline and Fall
Black Mischief
A Handful of Dust
Scoop
Put Out More Flags
Brideshead Revisited

**H. G. Wells**
The Time Machine
The Island of Dr. Moreau
The Invisible Man
The First Men in the Moon
The Food of the Gods
In the Days of the Comet
The War of the Worlds

**Morris West**
The Devil's Advocate
The Second Victory
Daughter of Silence
The Salamander
The Shoes of the Fisherman

**Dennis Wheatley**
The Devil Rides Out
The Haunting of Toby Jugg
Gateway to Hell
To the Devil—A Daughter

**John Wyndham**
The Day of the Triffids
The Kraken Wakes
The Chrysalids
The Seeds of Time
Trouble With Lichen
The Midwich Cuckoos

**\*Not currently available in
Canada for copyright reasons**